THEY NEEDED NO ONE ELSE

"Libby—this isn't a game. Do you understand what you're doing to me?" Donovan asked.

Her pulse beat a rapid tattoo against her throat and she found it almost impossible to breathe, but Libby didn't hesitate with her answer. "I think," she murmured softly, "that maybe I do."

"This time, be sure to say exactly what you mean. Be very, very sure."

"What if I were to ask for . . . your soul?" she asked in a breathless whisper.

Surprising her, Donovan uttered a short, bitter laugh. "We wouldn't have a problem. I don't have one."

The moment the last word was out, his mouth came down on hers, and Libby felt as if she had everything she'd ever need right there in her arms.

Books by Sharon Ihle

Wild Rose
Wildcat
The Law and Miss Penny
Marrying Miss Shylo
The Bride Wore Spurs
The Marrying Kind
Tempting Miss Prissy[*]

Published by HarperPaperbacks

[*]coming soon

Harper
Monogram

The Marrying Kind

SHARON IHLE

HarperPaperbacks
A Division of HarperCollinsPublishers

HarperPaperbacks   *A Division of* HarperCollins*Publishers*
10 East 53rd Street, New York, N.Y. 10022

Copyright © 1996 by Sharon Ihle
All rights reserved. No part of this book may be used or reproduced in any manner whatsoever without written permission of the publisher, except in the case of brief quotations embodied in critical articles and reviews. For information address HarperCollins*Publishers*,
10 East 53rd Street, New York, N.Y. 10022.

Cover illustration by Gregg Gulbronson

First printing: March 1996

Printed in the United States of America

HarperPaperbacks, HarperMonogram, and colophon are trademarks of HarperCollins*Publishers*

❖ 10 9 8 7 6 5 4 3 2 1

For my editor, Abigail Kamen Holland,
who was lolling about on the sands of Hawaii,
honeymooning, while I sat chained to my chair,
slaving over this manuscript.

and

For my agent, Patricia Teal,
who was seen perusing the shops along the shores
of Maui at around the same time.
What am I doing wrong?

Write women back into history.

The Marrying Kind

1

**Laramie, Wyoming Territory
1883**

Since she'd heard that trouble came in threes, Libby Justice had high hopes that the rest of her day would go a little easier than it had started.

First thing this morning, she'd accidentally destroyed a perfectly good photo of Sara Duncan's granddaughter by leaving it in the developer too long. In her haste to get back to the darkroom to save the picture, she'd fallen over the sawed-off barrel she used as a trash can and smashed face-first against a corner of the developing table. The vivid blue bruise at the edge of her jaw was already the size of a silver dollar, and promised to grow even larger. Shortly after that, Libby had realized she'd misplaced her spectacles, without which she couldn't tell a man from a hitching post if he stood more than forty feet away.

When she looked up to see the "hitching post" out front of the offices of the *Laramie Tribune* begin walking up the steps toward the door, she had the sinking feeling that her bad luck had only begun. Squinting extra hard when the stranger reached the porch, Libby could see that he was dressed in a fancy white shirt with ruffles down the button path set off by a vest of crimson satin beneath his black suit. She also noticed he carried a small satchel and a larger traveling bag. A citified dandy if she'd ever seen one.

"Damnation," she muttered as the door opened, setting off the little bell above the jamb. Was her day of reckoning finally at hand?

The stranger swaggered up to the counter, tipped his black Stetson, and said, "Good afternoon. I'd like a word with the editor of this newspaper. Is he in?"

At the sight of his handsome features—once she could see them up close—Libby couldn't find her voice. He had ink-black brows and a pair of astonishing silver-blue eyes that twinkled with both mischief and mirth. This fella wasn't just good-looking, but dazzling, a lady-killer and very well aware of it, if the cocky tilt of his upper lip and sparkle in those bewitching eyes meant anything. Where had he come from?

Andrew Savage had mentioned in his last letter that he'd be in the area soon, and had warned that he would stop by the *Tribune*'s offices to handle matters himself if the editorials hadn't improved by the time he left San Francisco. Until now, Libby hadn't thought he'd actually make good on the threat. She'd never seen a photo of the youngest Savage brother, but who else could this slicker be?

"Ma'am?" he said, his cocky expression growing with every minute she ogled him. "Is Mr. Jeremiah Justice in?"

"Oh, ummm, I'm afraid he isn't." Libby paused to get hold of herself. It wasn't as if she'd never seen an attractive man before. "Perhaps I can help you."

"I think it'd be best if I talk with the editor. When do you expect him back?"

He smiled broadly, the creases bracketing his mouth showing off his squared and rather aristocratic jaw. Why did rich folks always seem to have the best bones? Galled by the thought, she buried her natural western twang beneath a mock and slightly British accent—the kind of voice her man-chasing friend, Dell, affected when trying to sound city-born. "I suppose I should have explained Mr. Justice's absence a little better. He's out of the country on business and I'm substituting as editor while he's gone. Are you sure I can't help you?"

"And you are . . . ?"

"Liberty Justice. Jeremiah's daughter."

"Oh, well, in that case . . ." He removed his hat, revealing a head of wavy black hair, then swung his satchel up to the counter and unfastened the clasp. After retrieving a few papers from inside the small bag, he looked back at Libby and said, "I'm afraid my business with the *Tribune* is a little sensitive. But, if you don't mind, I suppose there's no harm in taking it up with you."

Calling his business with her "sensitive" was too kind, Libby decided, as she spotted a few of the letters she'd written to Andrew Savage among his papers. Although confirmation of the stranger's identity came as no surprise, her heart sank. She was caught between a rock and a hard place with no way out, that she could see. Libby dropped the British accent.

"There's no cause for you to worry about discussing sensitive matters around me. Here in Wyoming we grow up tough enough to eat off the same plate as a rattler. I'd appreciate it if you'd get right to the point, Mr. Savage. Have you come here to shut the *Tribune* down?"

He cocked one of those perfectly arched eyebrows as if surprised by the question. Then he hooted. "That's a hell of a thing to say. I'm afraid that you've—"

"Why would you be afraid of me, Mr. Savage?"

At the interruption, he looked haughty, yet vaguely amused. "I'm hardly frightened by you, Miss Justice, but I am thinking that maybe you're just a little 'nervous' about me."

Did it show? Libby's father had taught her to face her fears with confident aggression, no matter how scared she might be; so that's what she did. "Think what you will about my nerves, as long as you understand that I won't be giving up my editorial rights without a fight."

"Is that a fact, ma'am?"

"That's a fact . . . *sir*."

"It looks to me like you've already had one fight for the day, Madam Editor." He laughed, then reached across the counter and lightly brushed the backs of his fingers across the bruise on her jaw. "Did you win or lose?"

Her skin tingling where he'd touched her, Libby instinctively reached up to the spot. Savage grinned. Had he employed the intimate gesture just to rattle her? Be aggressive, she reminded herself; confident. "There's only one fight around here that's any concern of yours, Mr. Savage, and that's the one you insist on having with my family over our editorials. It hasn't been easy for me and my brother, what with our father . . . away. But we're doing the best we can to run the *Tribune* the way he wants us to run it. That ought to be good enough for *your* father, even if he is Randolph T. Savage."

"Are you always so . . . quick on the draw, Miss Justice, or only with strangers who happen into your offices?"

Savage winked at her after that audacious remark, but it failed to annoy her. She was too distracted by the contrast between the startling blue of his eyes and the deep ebony color of his hair. Feeling off-balance and less confident by the minute, the best she could offer in return was a slight shrug.

"If I had come here to put you out of business," he went on to say, "your attitude wouldn't do much to change my mind. There's a lot to be said for holding your cards close to your chest until you know a little more about the other players, ma'am. Maybe you ought to give it a try."

Gambling talk from a newspaper man? Libby was stunned by his rather flippant responses, for Savage had never conveyed anything but a deadly serious and businesslike tone in his letters. She didn't know how to respond or if a response was even called for. She'd imagined that Andrew Savage would be a puffed-up buffoon who'd simply padlock the doors to the *Tribune* with little or no discussion about the matter. Now, she wasn't so sure. Was he implying that he might give her another chance?

"Libby?" came her brother's voice from the pressroom in the back. "Can you come here a minute?"

"Be right there!" she called, relieved to have a few minutes to think about how to proceed from here. "Excuse me, will you, Mr. Savage? I've got to help out in the pressroom. I'm sure it won't take but a minute. Have a seat here in the parlor, won't you?"

Then, assuming he'd take her up on the offer, Libby whirled around and darted through the curtains which shielded the relatively private pressroom from visitors. Bearing down on her brother, who was bent over their newest and best piece of equipment, the Campbell County Press, she muttered, "Damnation, if we aren't up to our necks in trouble now, Jeremy!"

Raising his head out of the bowels of the machine, he asked, "In for what?"

"Andrew Savage himself from the San Francisco Savages is here!"

"God in heaven!" Grabbing a rag dampened with turpentine, Jeremy set to cleaning his hands. "What are we gonna do?"

"I only know what we're *not* gonna do, and that's tuck our tails between our legs and go slinking away from all that matters to us." Libby slid her fingers along the press, caressing the Savage-owned piece of equipment. "At least I did have enough sense to tell him that pa is out of the country, instead of where he really is." She paused, her throat closing over the words to shut off the pain the reminder brought with it. She didn't have a second to waste in grieving over her father, not while the newspaper he'd loved so much looked to be in such jeopardy. "The first thing we've got to do is spread the word around town about the story we made up for pa in case this Savage fellow goes poking around asking questions."

At fifteen—a full nine years younger than Libby— Jeremy still spooked easily. "B-but not everyone's gonna toss in with our cause. What if he goes to see Hayford over at the *Sentinel?* Why, he'd turn on us quicker than a cow pony on a stray if he thought it'd get the *Tribune* shut down!"

Libby recognized the panic in his tone. With his bright rust-colored hair, freckles enough to cover two boys his size, and prominent front teeth, Jeremy even looked the part of the nervous pubescent young man he'd become in the months since their partially deaf father had stepped in front of a team of galloping horses. He walked as if his feet were suddenly too big to propel his knobby, rubber-like legs, and his long, thin arms swung awkwardly, as if powered by a pair of swivels.

But even in the throes of this most troublesome time of life, Jeremy favored their father so much, it brought a tear to Libby's eye whenever she looked upon him. Wiping it away, she said, "I can't imagine why Savage would want to go see Hayford about us. I think we're safe enough if we keep a good eye on him and sweeten up his ears with a little chin music."

Jeremy frowned. "How long's he gonna be in town?"

"I don't know, but I think we'd better talk him into staying right here if we want to make sure and keep him ignorant about pa. How's the spare room look? Is it clean or is Hymie sleeping there again?"

"Far as I know, Nona let him back in the house." Their alternate pressman's troubles with his wife were legendary. "He went fishing today, so I can't say for sure."

"We'll just have to assume the room's free then." Her mind working as smoothly as the new press now, she settled on a plan. "Here's what we'll do; you run tell folks around town that we've got a fellow here from San Francisco who'd take the *Tribune* right out of Laramie if he knew we were running the paper alone. Most folks will go along with keeping our little secret. Just don't mention it to those you think won't. While you're doing that, I'll clean up in here a little and make a fresh bed in the spare room."

Jeremy untied his apron and tossed it on the work table. "I'll get done as fast as I can."

"Good. And when you get back, let me do most of the talking around Savage. Pretend you've got a chicken bone stuck in your throat or something."

"Shucks, Libby, I don't see why we got to go to all that trouble." He headed for the back door. "It's not like we don't know why he's here—he's come to stop you from writing those female suffering editorials, hasn't he?"

"*Suffrage*, and yes," she grumbled. "But we both know that I'm not going to stop writing them."

"Maybe you should. Then we could at least keep the paper for a while longer."

It wasn't that Libby hadn't thought of that, or ignored the risk she took with every mention of the fight for equality. For her, it wasn't a matter of choice. That was her rock and hard place—the rock being her father's newspaper, the hard place, the promise she'd made to her mother as she lay dying the morning after Jeremy was born. Harriet Powers, a "Lucy Stoner" who'd kept her own name after marrying Libby's father, had fought long, hard battles in the name of equality, and had instilled that same sense of pride in her daughter. It was that, and the promise that she would carry the suffrage torch in both the Powers and Justice names that made this an impossible situation. As far as Libby was concerned, there was no point in having a newspaper if she couldn't spread the word of the cause.

"You know I can't stop writing my equal rights articles—I just have to figure out a way to make Andrew Savage *think* I'm going to stop."

And to do that, Libby realized with no small amount of anxiety, she would have to work much harder at keeping both her temper *and* her reckless tongue under control.

In the parlor, William Donovan ignored the Justice woman's offer to make himself at home on one of the chairs. Instead, he paced, as amused as he was puzzled by the odd and rather laughable position he found himself tangled up in.

Just yesterday, he'd been on the last leg of a marathon, winner-take-all poker game in a private car coupled to the train from San Francisco to Cheyenne, Wyoming Territory. That car, as far as Donovan knew, was still rolling on toward Cheyenne, and then to who knew where. But its owner, one Andrew Savage of the Nob Hill Savage clan, had been caught cheating, shot by a disgruntled gambler, and then dumped off a high bridge somewhere in the towering Rocky Mountains of Colorado.

Donovan had never met Savage until he bought into the 'game on wheels,' and hadn't gotten to know him well during the relatively short time they were together, but he hadn't liked him well enough to grieve his passing. Savage ran a dirty game. And that, in Donovan's humble opinion, was the same as horse-thieving or murder. The crooked gambler had died owing Donovan several hundred dollars, however. To make matters worse, Savage had bought in on credit, leaving not so much as an IOU behind for Donovan to collect what was due him.

So he had taken the dead man's satchel hoping to find some hidden cash to help recoup at least part of his losses. It amused him roundly to think the sassy editor of the newspaper thought him to be Andrew Savage simply because he'd carried the leather bag into her offices.

Chuckling to himself, Donovan strolled around the small reception area noting the framed photos and newspaper clippings nailed to the walls of the room. Most were articles about the suffrage movement and photos of Lucy Stone and Susan B. Anthony with her cohorts, including the Laramie favorite, Esther Morris. These were scattered among awards, photos of headlines from both the *San Francisco* and *Laramie Tribune*s, and a letter of commendation from R. T. Savage himself, complimenting Mr. Justice on his years of fine reporting and editorials. Donovan paused to check the date on the commendation. It was less than a year old.

Puzzled all over again, he continued his pacing. Once he'd retired to his compartment aboard the train, he'd gone through the satchel only to make the sad discovery that Savage did not keep extra funds in the little bag. During the rest of the train ride to Laramie, Donovan had perused the letters of censure from the publishing company to the *Laramie Tribune* and had noted the company's displeasure with the little paper regarding its editorial content. Why had the *Tribune* gone astray so soon after receiving such a fine compliment from the parent company?

Liberty Justice came to mind in a flash. Donovan guessed that Jeremiah Justice had been out of the country for close to six months, the time frame during which the condemning letters from Savage Publishing had been written. Recalling the fires burning in the young woman's coffee-brown eyes as she spoke of the newspaper and how much it meant to her, Donovan glanced toward the curtains where she'd disappeared. A sassy little gal, that one, and quirky too, he decided, recalling her manner of dress.

Over her plain white blouse, she wore a buckskin vest with a matching skirt which wasn't a skirt at all, but wide-legged trousers. And they barely reached her ankles. She looked more suited to the range than the offices of a newspaper. Even though the lower part of her legs were decently hidden from view by her footgear, he'd noticed as she whisked into the back room that she wore boots fashioned of rough rawhide like an area cowboy might wear. On top of all that, she'd covered her head and a good deal of her face with the most ungodly hat Donovan had ever seen in his life.

Made of straw, the bonnet was plainly decorated with only a butter-colored ribbon circling the crown and a single sunflower at the center. The hat's wide, curving brim, however, had become a storage bin for a tape measure, a magnifying glass, an assortment of pencils, and a pair of spectacles, if memory served. It also sported a couple of scorch-marks—cigarette burns? Whatever, she was an original, one of a kind gal, for sure.

The funniest thing was that, had she let him get a word in edgewise, she would have realized that he was not Andrew Savage, but William Donovan—known, at his own insistence, simply as Donovan.

Instead of worrying about losing her newspaper, as she undoubtedly was doing at this very moment, "Lippy," as he'd begun to think of her, would then also have known that he'd only stopped by the *Tribune* to inform the editor that Andrew Savage had been killed on his way to Laramie. And, although he was none too proud of himself, Donovan had to admit that she probably would have made yet another discovery on the heels of learning his true identity—that he'd taken it upon himself to deliver this news in the hopes of receiving some kind of reward for returning the dead man's personal belongings. Something in the neighborhood of the three hundred dollars he figured the Savage family still owed him.

Since it didn't take a genius to figure out that a reward, if indeed he was entitled to one, wouldn't be coming from this end of Savage Publishing, Donovan decided that he couldn't let the young woman go on thinking he'd come to ruin her. Lifting the pass-through in the counter, he started for the curtains leading to the back room when a triangular block of wood caught his eye, delaying him. He picked up the item, read the name and title burned into the pine, then, chuckling to himself, tucked it into his jacket pocket.

Letting the sassy newspaperwoman off the hook didn't mean he couldn't tweak her nose a time or two.

2

Back in the pressroom, Libby had just finished cleaning up the spare room and was fluttering around the shelves and machinery, slapping at every exposed surface she passed with her feather duster. More likely than not, Andrew Savage would expect a tour of the newspaper offices, and she didn't want even so much as a speck of lint to weaken her cause. All she wanted to do was impress him with the way she ran the paper. She'd just dropped to her knees to check the underside of the press, when his silken voice reached her from behind.

"Why, my dear Miss Justice, I hope you're not going to all this trouble on my account."

On hands and knees, Libby spun around in the direction of his voice and promptly banged the side of her head against the press. Her hat went flying, spilling her pencils and, she noticed as they skipped across the floor lens-side down, her blasted missing spectacles!

Ignoring them and the other scattered items, she scrambled to her feet and turned to him. "Oh, Mr.

Savage—it's you!" She quickly reminded herself to keep her temper under control, as she brushed a few lengths of tousled hair from her eyes. "You startled me."

"Sorry, ma'am." A sense of guilt prodding him, Donovan joined her by the press and studied her as she caught her breath. "I didn't mean to sneak up on you."

She flushed, looking vulnerable for a moment, even attractive. He'd pretty much dismissed the newspaper-woman as a spinsterish, bookish type—a female who dressed in buckskins simply because she didn't have a snowball's chance in hell of catching a man, no matter what she wore. But now that he'd taken a good look at her without that outrageous hat covering up most of her face, Donovan had to admit that she wasn't quite as homely as he'd assumed. Her dark eyes were bigger somehow, doe-like and naive—a direct contrast to her runaway tongue. The hair that he'd mistakenly assumed was brown, turned out to be auburn, the color you might see reflected off the back of a sleek chestnut colt at sundown. Although she was still pretty rough around the edges, the sight of that burnished curl caressing her smooth though freckled cheek was an unexpected display of femininity. And it made Donovan's pulse leap.

"Are you all right?" he asked, clearing his suddenly husky throat. "It sounded like you rapped the side of your head pretty hard."

"It's nothing." Laughing, she touched the bruise he'd noticed earlier. "As you can see, I'm always banging into something around here."

Donovan thought of pointing out the obvious: If she were actually to wear the glasses now lying on the floor a few feet away, she could probably cut her "accidents" down at least by half. But he abandoned the subject, figuring female vanity might have something to do with her not wearing the glasses.

Instead, he gave into the urge to tease her a little.

Reaching for the item in his pocket, he held it up between them, and asked, "Is this you?"

Libby glanced at the nameplate—the one that proclaimed her as the editor of the *Laramie Tribune*. "Oh, yes, it is, but as I mentioned earlier, I'm just substituting for my father."

"I understand that, but your name—is it Liberty Ann Justice?" She nodded, and he laughed out loud. "Does that mean you're Liberty Ann Justice for all, ma'am, or just for a special few?"

Libby's mouth dropped open. "A-a few? Why, Mr. Savage—I don't know what to say!"

"A rarity for you, I'm sure." His smirk as wry as the words, Donovan set the nameplate down on the shiny surface of the press and offered a half-hearted apology. "I guess a cheeky comment like that could be taken a lot of ways, ma'am. Pardon my missing manners. I must have left them back in San Francisco."

"Yes, well, you're excused . . . I guess." She paused to give a little, nervous laugh. "You know, I have to be honest. You sure aren't what I was expecting, not coming from the esteemed Savage family and all."

If not for that remark, and what it implied about his breeding—or lack of it—Donovan might have cleared the air right then and there, told her his real name and occupation, and gotten the hell out of town. If not for that remark, Miss Liberty Ann Justice might have gone on about her business with hardly a dent put into her day. As it was, she'd inadvertently given him a reason to tease her a little longer—and something to occupy his time until the next train to San Francisco came by.

"I'd like to know just what you mean by that, my dear Miss Justice," he began sternly. "Or may I call you Libby?"

"L-Libby is fine. Just fine." She gulped. "And I didn't mean a thing, really I didn't."

"Yes, well . . ." Donovan gripped his hands behind his back, as if deep in thought. "If you've any hope of keeping this paper open, you're going to have to change your rather impudent attitude. I will not tolerate sass from one of my employees."

"Of course not, nor should you," she said quickly, tossing in just the hint of a curtsy. "I don't know what's come over me today. Please forgive me if I've been rude."

Suddenly she seemed so small and fragile standing there that Donovan almost had a change of heart. But then he saw the fires burning in her dark, dark eyes, a fighting spirit—that and a haughty glare she couldn't quite hide. Libby Justice wasn't humbled or even sorry for insulting him. If anything, she was laughing behind his back. Looking forward to the battle, he not only went ahead with the charade, but thought of a way to improve upon the previous plan.

Leaning in close, but not touching any part of her, Donovan captured her in his gaze. "I'm having a hard time believing that was a sincere apology. I'm thinking that maybe you're just teasing me a little, and that you don't really care what happens to the *Tribune*."

"Oh, but I do care, I do! I'll do anything to keep this paper going. I swear I will."

"Anything?" Donovan made a purposefully lazy perusal of her mouth before adding in a deep voice, "Just exactly what do you have in mind?"

Although her eyes widened for just a second, making him wonder if she didn't know exactly what he'd been suggesting, Libby wasted no time showing him what she had in mind. Either she was a most rare creature, indeed—a female impervious to his charms—or she hadn't the first idea what he'd been insinuating. In any case, the moment the words were out of his mouth, she launched an all out effort to see that his needs were met. Most of them, anyway.

All spunk and fire, the sassy newspaperwoman had whisked him through a surprisingly interesting tour of the pressroom, shown him her outdated photography equipment, and then ushered him into the private editor's office, where he now sat with his feet propped up high on the desk. He was smoking a cheroot she'd dug up from God knew where—it tasted old and looked like a piece of dried-up buffalo flop—and sipping from a bottle of cherry brandy Libby had pulled out of the desk drawer. Her father's favorite, she'd said. Any minute now, he expected her to return to the office, drop to her knees and insist on shining his shoes. At which time, Donovan thought, settling into the role of a publishing scion with relative ease, he would probably take her up on the offer.

Being a "member" of the wealthy Savage clan had its rewards beyond the comforts he was already enjoying. Libby had even insisted that he spend the night at her home in the spare room, a gesture which had touched him so, he'd impulsively asked her to join him for supper this evening. Considering that he usually got out of the game while he was still ahead, no matter what the stakes, Donovan wasn't so sure the invitation wasn't more reckless than impulsive, but he shrugged his doubts away.

Hell, it was only an innocent meal with a small town ink-slinger. Other than the fact her tongue was set on swivels at both ends, what possible harm could there be in spending the evening in such a manner? Besides, if

anyone had to be on their toes tonight, it was Liberty
Ann Justice, not him. Pleased with himself for slipping
so easily into the well-heeled shoes of Andrew Savage,
even if it was just for this short time, Donovan snubbed
out the cheroot against the sole of his boot, then poured
himself another brandy.

Libby had never cared what the men of Wyoming
thought of her, or if she never got married. While Lucy
Stone and Libby's own mother had proved nearly thirty
years ago that a woman could be happily wed without
compromising her position on equal rights, many more
suffragists, including the indomitable Susan B.
Anthony, felt that a woman dividing her loyalties
between a marriage and the cause diluted the strength
of both.

Libby tended to agree with the latter theory, at least,
given the choice of the marriageable men in Laramie.
She couldn't think of a suitable bachelor offhand who
would agree that she was entitled to as many rights as
he was. Just because Wyoming Territory was the first to
grant women the vote, didn't mean all of its menfolk
agreed with passage of the bill. And as far as Libby was
concerned, if a man didn't believe as she did in that
respect, he wasn't even worth pinching her cheeks over.

She was sure, however, that a man of the Savage
family, especially a dandy like Andrew Donovan
Savage, would expect any woman he escorted to a
restaurant to do much more by way of grooming herself
than simply pinching her cheeks. From what little she
knew of them, the entire bunch, led by their imperious
father Randolph Thaddeous, was socially correct right
down to their custom-made shoelaces. How was she to
complete the transformation necessary to impress a

snobbish, arrogant man like that, and in less than an hour? There was only one thing to do—and that was enlist the aid of an expert, her friend Adelia "Dell" Hight.

It had proven to be a miserable waste of time, Libby decided an hour later, as she sat across the table from Andrew Savage. She had an idea that if she and Dell had spent the entire night trying to put her together, the result probably wouldn't have been any better. She felt like a sideshow freak, and if the way her escort tried to hide the horror in his expression every time he glanced at her counted for anything, she looked like one, too.

Even though she was taller and bigger around than Dell, Libby was wearing one of Dell's dresses—a gown which didn't have a clearly defined waist, but sported frilly draperies at the back and an abbreviated train. The color of the dress, a pattern of sprigged, red rose-buds, clashed with Libby's auburn hair; so, instead of using the hat which matched the gown, Dell had fashioned a quick bun at the crown of Libby's head and topped it with an engraved silver comb. Hardly the fashion of the day.

Savage cleared his throat, drawing her attention. "Are you feeling all right, Libby?"

"Excuse me?"

He grinned. "I couldn't help but notice that you were walking like a duck all the way over here. Did you hurt your back, or something?"

"Oh . . . ah, not really." God, how embarrassing to think he'd noticed her odd gait. Her feet were, like the rest of her, bigger than Dell's, and since she didn't own a ladylike pair of shoes, Libby had worn her usual boots, and walked slightly bent over to hide them beneath the hem of her too-short dress. "I, er, twisted my ankle a little earlier today. It's nothing."

Instead of commiserating with her, he laughed. "You seem to have a lot of accidents."

"Yes, I suppose that I do." What had she been thinking to have accepted a dinner invitation from a polished society-type like Andrew Savage? Even with all Dell's fussing, Libby was still nothing more than a painted up hoyden. All she wanted to do now was run out of the restaurant as fast as her legs could carry her. Maybe she could come up with some kind of bogus emergency and skip out on the meal before she made matters worse.

Donovan, who'd been watching the panic build in Libby's expression until she looked away, assumed she was still worried about his shutting down the paper. After he ordered a bottle of wine, he decided to set her mind at ease. "Why don't we get our business out of the way first so we can enjoy our meal?"

Libby whipped her head toward him, sending the silver comb that held her hair in place tumbling across the table. It landed in the center of his china dinner plate, making a terrible racket.

Reacting as though such occurrences were commonplace, Donovan simply lifted the comb from his plate and, repeating his previous question, passed it across the table. "As I was saying, shall we proceed with our business discussion?"

"Oh, sure." As she spoke, Libby wrestled with the length of hair that tumbled down her back when the comb fell out. "Where, ah, were we?"

Although Donovan thought he was finally ready to tell Libby that he was not in any way related to the Savage family, he found himself hesitating. She was obviously nervous about this meeting, and had gone to a lot of trouble to fix herself up tonight—if the uneven face powder and cherry-red lips meant anything. Her make-up looked as if it were wearing her, instead of the other way around. And where had she picked up that ill-fitting dress? Not only was the style dated, but it looked very uncomfortable on her, as if it were too small in the few areas where it clung to her body.

Donovan sighed. He couldn't just pull the rug out from under her after she'd gone to so much trouble to impress him. And there was the matter of pride, hers, certainly, but his, too, for having let the charade go on for so long. Besides, what real harm could there be if he were to continue as the newspaper baron until he'd left town? Anyway, he planned to stop by the offices of R. T. Savage the minute he returned to San Francisco, to offer information about Andrew's sudden "accident," return the dead man's belongings, and try to collect a reward. It wouldn't cost him a thing to plead a case for the *Laramie Tribune* while he was there. And Miss "Lippy" Justice might even come out of the ordeal learning a lesson or two about how to behave around her superiors.

Feeling magnanimous now, instead of guilty, Donovan forged ahead with the new plan. He glanced across the table, trying hard not to stare at Libby's hair—her refreshed bun was listing badly to the left, defying gravity—and said, "Let's see. If I remember correctly, all you want is a little more freedom with your editorials, right?"

"Yes. That and some new photographic equipment." She held her head unnaturally still, as if very aware of her precariously perched bun. "I'm not much good at measuring the right amount of powder for the flash bar we have now. I've singed my hair and set fire to my working hat a couple of times of late. But even worse, since the flash occasionally makes quite an explosion, I can't find many folks in town who'll let me get close enough to them to take their photos anymore. It would be a good investment for Savage Publishing, I think, if they were to send me some new equipment."

"Certainly sounds reasonable to me." Donovan couldn't help but chuckle as he remembered the scorched smudges on the brim of her bonnet. "I don't see why I can't get 'dear old dad' to send you a new camera. Anything else you need?"

"Not as far as equipment is concerned. In fact, I'd give up the new camera if I had to, just for permission to write the *Tribune*'s editorials my way—no censorship, even when the subject is equal rights."

"I see." Donovan brought his index finger to his chin, as if in deep contemplation, though he didn't need to do much thinking on the matter. After reading the letters from the home office to the *Tribune*, he knew that R. T. Savage demanded complete and utter acquiescence from the editor of his Laramie affiliate. While he didn't want to dash the glimmer of hope in Libby's dark eyes, he couldn't very well make promises he had no way of keeping. "I'm afraid what you're asking for is not going to be possible. You'll have to follow Savage guidelines for your editorials, at least until your father returns. Maybe he can take it up with R. T. then."

"But there's no point in even having a newspaper if I can't print the truth!" There was panic in her tone, but a fair amount of outrage, too. "Surely you and your father can understand that. What do you people have against women, anyway?"

The wine arrived then, giving Donovan a moment to consider a change of subject. He wanted out of this conversation, and now. He didn't like discussing this fictional "father" of his any more than he liked being reminded that he'd never had a real father to call his own. All he'd wanted out of this evening was a quiet dinner, a few laughs, and maybe later, a friendly little game of poker at one of the many saloons he'd noticed in town.

Raising his glass toward Libby, he said, "If you're wanting to run an editorial regarding voting rights from time to time, I don't think I'll have too much trouble getting R. T. to 'turn his head' about it, but any freedoms other than that, are simply out of the question. Shall we drink to the conclusion of our business and order our suppers now?"

"No, not yet. Please?"

She hadn't so much as touched her glass, and showed no intention of doing so. He wagged an authoritative finger at her. "Sorry, but I'm hungry and this subject is closed."

Still, Libby didn't make a move toward her wine. It was then Donovan noticed the utter and dogged determination in her expression. "Tell you what," he said, looking for a more gentle way to ease out of the discussion. "What if I promise to have a long talk with R. T., when I get back to San Francisco, about giving you a little more freedom? Would that make you feel better?"

"That depends on what you're planning to say to him. Do you have the slightest idea why my editorials are so important to the women's suffrage movement?"

"They'll help gain the vote nationwide, I suppose."

"Gaining the vote is very important, and yes, my work should help in that way. But the vote is just the first step in gaining equal rights in all areas of our lives—rights you and the men in your family enjoy everyday without even appreciating them!" She lightly banged her fist against the table by way of punctuation. Her bun wobbled, but held steady. "You wouldn't sit still for those injustices if they were directed at you— why should I? And why shouldn't I have the right to express these beliefs in my newspaper's editorials?"

Warmed by the wine—or maybe it was Libby's impassioned speech—Donovan reconsidered. Maybe he could help her a little more when he stopped in at Savage Publishing. "All very interesting and valid points. If that's what you want me to mention to R. T., you've got it."

"Oh, well . . . thanks." She finally paused long enough to take a sip of her wine. "To tell you the truth, you've always been so hard-headed in your letters, you've caught me by surprise. I didn't expect that you'd care what I thought or wanted, or that you'd agree so easily to talk to your father about it."

"I said I would, and I will." Done with the discussion for sure this time, he added, "Now, if you don't mind, I'd like to order our meal."

"In a moment. I'm not quite finished. There are a couple more issues I'd like you to explain to your father."

Donovan managed to contain his exasperated sigh, but he drummed the table with his knuckles as he said, "And they are?"

"The vote is the biggest thing, of course, but gathering enough supporters for the cause is going to be difficult enough, even if I printed a feature everyday. To be tied to running an editorial from 'time to time' is simply not good enough. Next year is an election year, and we're desperate for the vote *now*. I must have complete freedom to print what I see fit as often as necessary."

"For heaven's sake." He laughed a little. "Working toward the vote is a noble crusade for you ladies to strive for, but don't you think you're over-dramatizing the urgency just a bit?"

"No, and for very good reasons. For example, I think it's safe to assume you're not aware that, should I happen to come into possession of the house in which I live,"—

which she had actually owned for the last six months—"our government would expect me to pay taxes on it."

"So? Everyone has to pay taxes, even temporary editors like you."

"But I shouldn't have to—not as long as I have no voice in the legislation of those taxes. That would make me a victim, like many of my sisters, of taxation without representation." Libby slammed both palms flat against the table. The bun bounced a few times, then began to slide, comb and all, toward her ear. She no longer seemed to be aware of it. "It seems to me that you men pitched a fit in Boston over that same issue better than a hundred years ago. You wouldn't accept such tyranny then—why should we accept it now?"

Reminded finally that he didn't have the right to debate this issue with her—not as Andrew Savage, anyway—Donovan tried to end Libby's lively, impassioned speech. "Thank you for all the fascinating information. I'll be sure to address your editorial freedom with R. T. the moment I get home. Now, if you don't mind, I've heard just about all I want to concerning women's rights. My backbone met my belly an hour ago, and if I don't eat soon, I'll fall right out of this chair."

As he waved the waitress over to the table, Libby thought of speaking up again, for she really didn't think Savage had a full grasp of what she was after, but she bit her lip. Something in his expression made her keep the rest of her thoughts to herself. He was looking at her in the oddest way, not like a man impressed with her intelligence or knowledge of the situation, but of one who was about to burst out laughing. A moment later, the comb fell out of her hair again, and this time it landed with a horrendous splash—in her glass of wine.

*   *   *

The following day brought warmer weather and, along with it, a sultry breeze unusual for the middle of June. It made Libby feel restless, wanting something she couldn't quite name, but wanting it badly. And her desire wasn't just to forget about last night and her idiotic attempts to impress Andrew Savage with her ladylike aplomb. She'd been struggling with her concentration all morning and bottling her frustrations until she thought she might explode from the pressure. It was the kind of day on which, had she been younger and faced with less responsibility, she'd have said, "the hell with it," grabbed her bamboo pole, and gone fishing. She closed her eyes, imagining herself lying on the grassy banks of the Laramie River, and could almost feel the sun baking the frustrations right out of her body.

Of course, imagining an afternoon like that was as close as Libby had gotten to the real thing in a long, long time. She hadn't had a moment without serious responsibility since the age of nine—the day after Jeremy came into the world, making her an instant mother to him and housekeeper for her widowed father. She gazed out her office window, wondering why she couldn't seem to allow herself to just toss everything aside for one day, and take that little fishing trip in spite of it all. Other people in business took vacations from their daily chores, but not Liberty Ann Justice—not even long enough to make a decent attempt at behaving like a lady.

Supper itself had gone fairly well after she'd pinned her hair up for a second time. It was after the long walk home that things had gone sour. She'd fluttered her perfumed handkerchief around the man's face, laughed at everything he said (the way Dell had instructed), and even swooned against his shoulder when they reached the stairs leading up, above the pressroom, to the apartment she shared with Jeremy. The swooning part had been the easiest since her legs had been ready to give out anyway after walking "like a duck" all the way home.

But nothing she'd done seemed to make any impression on Savage. He'd acted as if he couldn't wait to be rid of her. And since then, she hadn't seen hide nor hair of him.

As she stared forlornly out at the wide, beckoning skies, it finally occurred to Libby that the sun was no longer rising, or even hanging high in the sky, but was on a westward journey toward home. It wasn't morning any longer—it was way past noon. Why hadn't Savage come to see her yet? Not that she was looking forward to the moment, by any means; but surely their business wasn't yet concluded to his satisfaction.

She had a few bones to pick with him, herself. For a newspaperman, he knew precious little about newspaper offices. It rankled her to think this spoiled son of a rich scion had such power over her, when he apparently knew so little about the working end of the business. He hadn't even realized the press was so new until she'd mentioned it.

Libby glanced around her office, noting that he'd left his satchel sitting on the floor near her desk. He was still here, or at least in town. But what if he'd slipped out of the house before she'd awakened this morning, and was now on the loose, poking his nose around and asking questions? Her position with Savage Publishing was too precarious for her to take a chance on him finding out about her father.

Libby leaped out of her chair, grabbed the satchel, and dashed out of her office, toward the back room. On the way, she collided full on with her employer, who was headed in her direction.

"Urrgh!" He staggered backwards, clutching his belly and gasping for breath. "Ye Gads, Libby! Where are you going in such a hurry?"

"Oh! I'm so sorry! Are you all right? I was worried about you since I hadn't seen you all day. Where have you been?"

"Sleeping. I took a tour of your town last night, and had such a good time—I didn't get to bed till dawn. I was looking for you just now to say good-bye." About then, Libby noticed he was carrying his traveling bag. "I also want to thank you again for your very warm hospitality. I hope I haven't been too much trouble for you."

"Oh, but you can't be leaving town already!"

"Oh, but I can." His words were brisk, clipped. "I'm going to catch the train to San Francisco in a couple of hours, and I have to take care of a few business matters in town on my way out." Before she realized what he was doing, he reached down and took his satchel from her. "I was just coming to get this."

"But, but . . ." She had to stop him somehow! "What about my editorials and such? We never did finish our conversation or address some of the other issues that concern both the *Tribune* and Savage Publishing."

He paused, eyes downcast, as if weighing a very difficult decision. Then he looked her in the eye. "I might as well tell you the rest. I know about your father, and, er, that he's not really out of the country. I heard about his accident over at one of the saloons on Front Street."

"Oh . . . my God." What else could she say? There was no way to deny it—all the man had to do was go to the graveyard for confirmation.

"I'm sorry about your father, Libby, but surely you must have known that, sooner or later, Savage Publishing was bound to find out about his accident."

Libby's heart seized up in her chest and, although she'd filled her lungs not a moment ago, the air inside her froze, making it impossible to speak or breathe.

Donovan could hardly stand the injured look in her doe-like eyes, the terrible sense of loss it suggested. Living without a father his entire life had been tough on him—at times, a nightmare. He couldn't even imagine the pain or sense of abandonment that *losing* a father might bring—but he could see that her grief ran deep.

He was just this side of confessing everything, of dropping to his knees and begging her forgiveness. He realized he had to get out of town while he was still ahead—if, indeed, he still was.

"I admire what you're trying to do with the paper, Libby, and even understand why you lied about your father, but you can't go on like this forever. As I promised, I'll do what I can to make Savage Publishing understand what you want. But do yourself a favor—don't get your hopes up too high." He gave her shoulder a gentle squeeze, then turned and walked out the door.

It's over, Libby thought, feeling sick inside as she watched the newspaperman's image blur into the other "hitching posts" outside. It really and truly was over, for she had no doubt that he had merely spared her the final indignity of padlocking the *Tribune* himself. Men as rich and powerful as all that didn't have to deal with the actual closing of the doors—they hired henchmen to do their dirty work for them. He'd simply come to Laramie to check things out. A hired executioner would take over from here.

Libby recalled his final words as he walked out the door, "Don't get your hopes up." She thought bitterly of all the trouble she'd gone through to impress Andrew Savage. He'd been the one ladling out the chin music all this time, not she! And now he would simply shut her down.

Libby's fingers curled into fists as she envisaged the gang of miscreants Savage Publishing would send to box up her precious Campbell County Press, their filthy, money-grubbing hands taking away everything she lived for, including the *Tribune*'s name.

It couldn't be over yet, she thought, frantically searching for a way to keep the man from boarding the train to San Francisco. It just *couldn't* be! Libby didn't know how she could prevent Savage's departure, or even what she would do with him should she manage the task, but she had to try. After all, what did she have to lose at this point?

She'd vowed at her father's graveside, had she not, that she'd hang onto the *Tribune* as long as possible? And hadn't she promised her mother she'd do anything to help fight for equal rights—anything at all?

Then for what, Libby had to ask herself, was she standing around waiting?

3

Several hours later, as the train roared on toward Utah and beyond, to California, Donovan strolled up to a small counter at the south end of the drawing-room car that served as a bar, and ordered himself a tall shot of Irish whiskey. Glancing behind him as he waited for his drink, he briefly studied the few men occupying plush leather chairs and tables that lined the windows on both sides of the car. Most were enjoying an after-dinner cigar and a brandy, he noted, but none looked particularly interesting or well-fixed enough for him to consider approaching for a friendly little game.

Just as well, he thought, turning back to the bar to find his drink sitting there on the glass top. He wasn't really in the mood for poker, or games of any kind, now that he thought about it. Not after the way his little "game" with Liberty Ann Justice had turned out. When he walked out of the *Tribune*'s office, her ashen features and stricken expression had nearly undone him. Since he'd boarded the train, he'd been thinking about her almost constantly.

He felt sorry for her one minute, full of admiration for her the next, and every blasted second of those minutes he also felt guilty as hell for running out on her. Before he'd left town, he even thought of telling the truth—again. He'd strongly considered informing her who he really was, complete with a guarantee that he wouldn't breathe a word of what he'd learned about her father to anyone in San Francisco. But at the last minute, he'd changed his mind. What the hell good would it have done anyway? Gritty or not, Libby couldn't hope to fool Savage Publishing forever, for Christ's sake. His confession would only have delayed the inevitable—and made him look like an idiot.

Hell, she hadn't even been able to fool him, Donovan thought, recalling the way she'd carried on after supper last night. On the walk home, she'd abruptly turned into a fluttering female, acting as if Cupid had suddenly fired an arrow into her conniving little heart. He'd been amused at first by Libby's awkward, hesitant gestures; and damned if he didn't have to admit that he'd been a little inflamed by them, too. But those amateurish efforts to sway him to her side also irritated him. She hadn't been trying to impress William Donovan. Her act had been for another man: rich, powerful—*dead*—Andrew Savage.

Donovan sighed with regret, or something akin to it, then picked up his drink. He was definitely in a rare mood, one he figured would probably require at least a full week's intake of Irish whiskey—all in one night. He tossed down the liquor in one gulp, shuddered from his teeth to his toes, then gripped the edge of the bar.

"Damn, that's good," he muttered. "Fix me up another one, would you?"

The bartender just smiled, then spun a quarter on the counter in front of Donovan. Waiting until the coin had worn itself out and clattered noisily to the glass, he finally said, "I'll bet you that next drink it's a woman."

Puzzled, Donovan glanced up at the man. "A woman?"

"You, sitting there laughing one minute, scowling at your own reflection on the bar the next. Got to be a woman, right?"

With a lusty chuckle, Donovan nodded. "Probably not the way you're thinking, but yes, it's a woman, all right. Isn't it always?" He tossed two coins onto the glass, paying for his drink and the barkeep's. "You an expert on the subject, are you, or just a lucky guesser?"

"An expert, friend." He poured two tall shots and shoved one Donovan's way. "I've known and loved them all, the short, fat, and the tall. There isn't a thing that surprises me about women anymore. To yours," he said, raising his glass, "whoever the little darlin' might be."

"To little darlin's everywhere." Donovan bumped his glass against the barkeep's in salute, and took a sip, even though he didn't have a "little darlin'" to call his own, and never would—if fortune kept smiling on him. He was quite sure, in any case, that his little darlin' wouldn't be coming to him in the guise of one Liberty Ann Justice. Feeling a sudden need to drink to that, too, Donovan slammed down the rest of his whiskey and took a deep, relaxing breath.

"This little gal that's got you all tangled-up—she your wife?" asked the bartender, taking a pull of his drink. "Or just the gal that wants to *be* your wife?"

Donovan laughed again, roaring this time. "Hell no! This gal is . . . let me put it this way: she'd even surprise an expert like you."

The barkeep shook his head, his slicked-down hair reflecting the light from the small chandelier above. "I don't believe the woman's been born could surprise me."

"Would you care to make a little wager on that?"

The barkeep's eyes glittered. "I've been known to take a bet or two. What do you have in mind?"

"Where do you live when you're not on this train?"

"San Francisco."

"Then here's the bet." Donovan reached into his vest pocket and withdrew his lucky ten dollar gold piece. He tapped his foot against the railing, rattling the even luckier penny he kept in a hollowed-out section of his boot heel. Then he held the gold coin before the bartender's eyes. "I'll wager my favorite betting piece that you've never laid eyes on a gal like this one—not in San Francisco for sure—and what's more, I'll bet you never will."

After glancing over Donovan's shoulder, the barkeep smiled, his expression too smug, too knowing, somehow. "Tell me a little about this gal first."

Donovan leaned forward for more privacy, aware that another customer had approached the bar from behind him, and quickly described Libby. "Well, let's see—she dresses like Calamity Jane, has the face of an angel, and she's bolder than hell—you know, talks straightforward, kind of like men do but her voice is breathless and feminine, husky too, if you get what I'm—"

"Excuse me," a woman interrupted from behind him, "but you wouldn't happen to have any cherry brandy back there, would you?"

At the sound of that voice—one suspiciously like the voice he'd just described—Donovan's tongue felt as if it'd swelled in his throat, choking him. It couldn't be her—not here, not riding the damn train to San Francisco!

The bartender, still smiling, whispered, "I'll take that bet." Then he turned to check his stock behind the counter as Donovan frantically pointed to his glass for a refill.

"Sorry, ma'am," said the barkeep. "The only flavored brandy I have is peach."

"Oh, fudge," she said rather impatiently. "Well, I guess that'll have to do. Give me one, and why don't you pour one for Mr. Savage, here, too. I think he's going to be needing it."

It *was* her! Donovan whipped around and practically bumped into Miss Liberty Ann Justice. "Libby! What a surprise!" And God help him if she wasn't wearing her buckskin trousers and that horrible storage-bin of a hat. "What the—ah, what in the world are you doing here?"

She smiled sweetly. A little too sweetly, he thought. "It's a wonder I made it at all. You wouldn't *believe* the trouble I had arranging for Jeremy and Hymie to take care of the paper while I'm gone, not to mention what I had to go through to get a decent pair of shoes. You didn't give me much time to prepare for the trip, you know."

"But, but . . ." Donovan heard liquor splashing into his glass, and blindly groped for it. "But why did you even *make* the trip?"

"Because I'm going to your father's office with you, of course." She actually looked surprised by the question, maybe even, offended. "No one can plead my cause the way I can, and besides, I figured you could use all the help you could get."

"Oh, Christ, Almighty." Not bothering to excuse himself, Donovan brought the glass to his lips and downed the whiskey. He hadn't gotten half of the liquid swallowed before he choked on it, spraying the glass counter, his shirtsleeves, and Libby's startled face. "What the—" He coughed and sputtered again, then cleared his throat of the vile flavor of rancid fruit. "What the hell was that?" he demanded of the barkeep.

"Peach brandy. The lady ordered it, remember?"

"Yes, but I—"

"Sorry if it *surprised* you a little." The barkeep ran his hand across his slick hair, grinning smugly. "'Course, none of this has surprised me in the least."

Donovan shot the man a nasty look before turning back to Libby, who was wiping her face with her bare fingers. "Now, where were we?" he asked.

"I was buying us a drink and you decided to spit yours at me."

"Oh, Christ—I'm sorry." Donovan pulled his handkerchief from his vest pocket. "Here, I'll take care of that for you, but first let me get rid of this." He lifted the battered straw hat from her head, and dropped it on the counter. When he turned back to Libby, she'd raised her chin high toward the light and closed her eyes, giving him access to the splatters on her face. The angle of her head and mouth made her look as if she were waiting for a kiss—something, he realized with a shock, he was awfully tempted to give her. Whipping his head around to the bartender, he growled, "Where's that whiskey I ordered?"

"Coming right up, sir." Now the man was grinning like a cat.

After glaring at the barkeep again, Donovan caught Libby's chin between his fingers, careful to avoid the bruise, and hastily wiped her face. Then he returned to his drink and took a swallow.

Beside him, Libby lifted her glass of peach brandy and raised it high. "Here's hoping that we can get your father to listen to reason."

Donovan grudgingly bumped his glass against hers, but instead of taking another drink, he asked, "Just what are you planning to do when you get to San Francisco? Where will you go, where will you stay?"

Libby sat her drink down on the bar and turned to him with hands on hips. "Well, for goodness sake.

What kind of a question is that? I would think, after all
I did to make you feel welcome at the *Tribune*, the least
the Savage family could do would be to offer to put me
up for a day or two. Even in Wyoming, that would be
the hospitable thing to do, especially since I can't afford
to stay in a hotel."

"Oh, I, er, hadn't thought of that." Catching the barkeep's eye, Donovan slowly shook his head. "I'm sure I
can find a room for you . . . somewhere."

After fingering his lucky ten dollar gold piece as it
lay on the bar, Donovan slid it across the counter
toward the bartender, then rolled his eyes. "You win."

Her first morning in San Francisco, Libby awoke at
dawn, feeling both amazed and pleased with herself.
She'd done the impossible! So far, just about everything
had gone her way. Back home, it hadn't taken her long
to figure out that if she was going to save the paper,
more drastic steps than keeping Savage in Laramie were
needed. Besides, with less than two hours in which to
come up with a plan, she'd figured her odds of finding
the man, then convincing him to stay, weren't too good.

Libby had briefly considered sending Dell after him
since her disastrous attempts to impress Savage herself
had proved that she did not possess the charms
required to turn a man's head, much less turn him into
a man who'd champion the cause. The trouble with a
plan involving Dell was the fact that her passions did
not lie in saving the *Laramie Tribune* or with the cause.
If Dell had known exactly who Savage and his impressive family were, her sole objective would have been to
get the man to marry *her*. So Libby had decided, the
only way she could save the paper was to follow Savage
to San Francisco herself.

There was no doubt in her mind that Hymie and Jeremy could run the *Tribune* alone for a week or so, and she always had extra editorials on file for emergency use. Hymie's wife, Nona, had agreed to keep an eye on Jeremy and cook his meals; so Libby really didn't have a care in the world except keeping R. T. Savage from closing the doors on her. She could resume working on that problem soon. Once Andrew Donovan Savage—and who'd insisted that she call him Donovan from here on out—woke up, he'd escort her to Savage Publishing as he'd promised.

Libby sat up and propped her pillow between her spine and the headboard of her fluffy four-poster bed. The room Donovan had designated as hers was softly feminine, the snow-white dust ruffle, coverlet, fringed curtains, and lace-edged pillow covers all made of the same puffy, crinkly fabric. The bedside cupboard, washstand, and dressing table had been stained dark to resemble walnut, but she thought they might be made of pine, as was the corner piece, a tall wardrobe with added shelving for shoes. What did Donovan need with a frilly bedroom like this? she wondered. She knew he had two brothers, but never had she heard mention of a sister.

In any case, Libby suspected that the sister, if he had one, wouldn't be living here. The fact that he lived alone didn't surprise Libby—after all, the man was near thirty and certainly old enough to be entitled to his own home— still, she'd been hesitant about staying here with him. He'd been a complete gentleman so far, but this arrangement wouldn't look good at all to the rest of the Savage family, and if it ever got back to the folks in Laramie, well . . . Libby didn't want to even think about that.

Instead, she glanced around the cozy little room again. She hadn't seen much of the rest of the house, except for the staircase she'd climbed to the second level last night, but she'd noticed upon arriving that the place was fairly small and sat shoulder to shoulder to the neighboring Victorian-style houses. What was a man of his wealth doing living in such an unimpressive home? The place was nice enough all right, but far from the mansion she'd been expecting.

Pondering that little inconsistency, Libby raised her arms above her head and stretched, closing her eyes and yawning vigorously at the same time. When she dropped her hands into her lap and opened her eyes a few moments later, she was surprised to see that her bedroom door was open, and that a woman had entered, bag in hand.

"Oh!" said the stranger. "I didn't realize someone had already taken over the room." She started to back out the door, but then stopped and cocked her head. "Are you new in town, sugar? I don't recall seeing you around before."

Flabbergasted by both the intruder's words and her scandalous appearance, Libby took a minute to form her reply. The woman's bosoms looked as if they were ready to fall out of her skimpy red satin dress at any minute. And her hair! It was a cottony shade of blonde Libby had never seen before, and puffed up on top of her head like a great hawk's nest. What was she doing in Donovan's home?

"Cat got your tongue, honey?"

"I-I came in on the train from Laramie with Donovan last night," Libby finally managed to say.

"Really?" The strumpet, or whatever she was, strolled over to the foot of the bed. She smiled then, drawing attention to her painted face and to her bottom lip, which was as unnaturally swollen as the puffy eye above it. "Out recruiting was he? I didn't know Donovan took a hand in that part of the business."

"Recruiting?" Had the man been looking for someone to take over the *Tribune* during his visit to the saloons of Laramie? "I really don't know what all he was up to."

She laughed. "Not many of us do. Are you new to the business, sweetheart?

"Oh, gosh, no."

"How long have you been at it?"

She shrugged. "In one way or another, I suppose, since I was a little girl."

The woman's good eye bugged out. "My goodness, dearie, but you're holding up well. Still, my guess is that you need the rest more than I do. I'll just go bunk with Donovan and let you get back to sleep."

"Wait a minute! Are you his . . . his *wife*?"

The woman laughed robustly. "God, no, honey. Our friend Donovan is definitely *not* the marrying kind."

"If you're not his wife, then are you his, well, girlfriend or something like that?" The wench laughed again, this time sounding like a yard full of chickens.

"No, sugar, I am none of those things to Donovan. Why that man just won't let himself get tied down long enough to be anyone's anything. But he's so good to us girls, you know, treats us real kindly and all, that anytime he wants a favor"—she paused to wink—"he gets it. Know what I mean?" With that, she turned and flounced out the door, leaving a cloud of cheap perfume in her wake.

Stunned, Libby sat there for several minutes wondering exactly where the painted-up hussy fit into Donovan's life, and what on earth she'd meant when she'd referred to herself as one of his "girls." Her thoughts, which were rapidly turning dark, were abruptly interrupted yet again as someone else strode into her room—a boxy little woman with gray hair and an aged cherubic face.

"*Um Gottes willen!* Another lost piggy?" she cried in

a thick accent. She shook a pudgy finger toward Libby. "I don't clean up after piggies! *Nein, nein,* never again! Humph!" With that final oath, she backed out of the room and slammed the door.

That was the last straw. Libby tore back her covers, leaped out of bed, and started across the room.

In his bedroom at the end of the hall, Donovan lay flat on his back in his big brass bed trying to ward off an onslaught of the barmaid's welcoming kisses.

"Dammit all, Joy—get off of me! I'm not even awake yet."

"Oh, but I just wanted to welcome you home real good, honey-face," she said in a cooing voice. "We missed you something terrible."

"Well, I'm here now, so you don't have to miss me at all." Donovan gripped her arms, preparing to push her away from him and off the bed, when in through the opened door strode Libby. From over Joy's shoulder, he could see she was in her nightgown, which billowed behind her like a ship's sail. Her shiny auburn hair was loose, too, tousled from sleep, and flowing every which way across her shoulders. But the biggest surprise of all, other than the fact that she'd barreled her way into his room, was the fire burning bright in her sable-brown eyes, a match, he thought with alarm, to even the bloodiest California sunset.

"Oh, er . . . excuse me for interrupting, but . . ."

"Please, do come in." Donovan waved her toward his bed. "It seems my bedroom is opened to the public this morning."

"Well . . ." Libby was clearly uncomfortable approaching his bed, but annoyed, too. "It seems I have the same problem."

"You've had visitors, too?" Donovan glanced at Joy. "Did you stop by Libby's room on your way here?"

She nodded, then grinned like a naughty little girl. "A drunked-up customer beat on me last night, so I thought I ought to come rest up here till the bruises fade a little."

Looking at her more closely, Donovan spotted the evidence. He lightly ran his finger over her bottom lip, feeling the lump there, then examined her eye, which he was sure would sport a shiner by evening. If there was one thing he couldn't abide, it was men who tested their strength on the soft skin and delicate bodies of women. "Who did this to you?"

"Oh, now don't go worrying about it, honey. Besides, you know how Lil hates for you to get involved in the rougher side of the business."

"I don't care what Lil thinks, Joy, I'm not going to—"

"Umm . . . excuse me again?" Libby was bobbing up and down, giving him the impression that beneath her gown, she was tapping a bare foot against his rug. Ah, yes, he remembered, bold, brave little Libby had some complaints.

"Joy is sorry for disturbing you. Is that it?"

"Not exactly. Right after she left, an old woman popped in and called me a pig—a *pig*!"

After rolling Joy to the side, Donovan slapped his forehead. "Chee-rist! Is today Thursday?"

"Yes," said Libby. "What's that got to do with any-thing?"

"Plenty. I think you just met my housekeeper, Gerda, also known as the whip-cracker. She comes a couple of times a week to leave food, and tries to keep the place looking halfway decent. Sorry if she startled you. As for the name she called you . . ."

"Don't mind Gerda," Joy interrupted, giggling. "She calls all us girls 'pigs.' She's just a dried-up old maid with nothing better to do than keep track of our sins. Don't pay her no never mind."

Sins? Settling her hands against her hips, Libby gave the hussy a long look, then shifted her sharp-eyed gaze to Donovan. Nothing around here made sense. Not the man, not his home, and definitely not his "friends."

Donovan swatted Joy's bottom. "You were leaving, weren't you, sweetheart? Why don't you ladies go on downstairs and get yourselves some breakfast or something. Gerda usually brings along some baked goods."

"Oh, all right. I'll see you later at Lil's." After climbing off the bed, Joy sashayed out of the room, turning to study Libby and her oversized Mother Hubbard nightgown before closing the door behind her.

Libby meant to follow her out the door as Donovan had suggested, but curiosity overrode her common sense. "Does Joy have something to do with the newspaper? And who's Lil? Does she work for the *San Francisco Tribune*, too? I'm very confused."

Donovan sat straight up. He hadn't planned to deal with this misunderstanding so early—hell, he'd hoped he wouldn't have to deal with it at all. "Joy, if you must know," he said irritably, "works as an actress, barmaid, and, ah, general all-around entertainer at Lucky Lil's Theatre and Gaming Saloon. Lil runs the place and I'm her partner."

"But, I thought you worked at Savage Publishing."

He decided to duck the issue. "A man can wear more than one hat, can't he? My interests happen to be varied. And what business is my business to you, anyway?"

"I guess I made it my business after Joy barged into my room."

"I see," he said sarcastically. "Waltzing uninvited into a woman's—or a man's—room does seem a little rude, now that I think of it, not to mention, improper."

"Oh, well, of course—oh, excuse me! I only followed her, not realizing, of course, that you'd be, you know . . ."

She waved apologetically toward the bed, but Donovan was tickled by Libby's suddenly anxious gaze as it trailed along his naked chest to where the sheet was draped dangerously low on his hips. With a wry grin, he said, "That's right, Miss Justice. I sleep in the raw."

"B-but, I-I wouldn't normally walk in on you this way. Since I knew that Joy had come in here, and I didn't think . . ."

Libby's voice faded away, along with her excuses, but the flush on her face roared to life, her cheeks turning a brighter shade of red than a barmaid's dress. Careful to keep his amusement to himself, Donovan made a great show of scanning her nightgown, particularly the little peaks jutting out just below the squared yoke.

"Why did you really come to my room, hm?" he asked in a low, suggestive voice. "Looking for a little insurance that I'll be sure to bend R. T.'s ear in your direction, by any chance?"

"Oh, goodness, no, I wouldn't . . ." Libby glanced down at herself as if she'd suddenly remembered that she wasn't properly dressed, then began to back toward the door. "I'll be ready to go to your father's office with you shortly. I'd like to get going as soon as possible, if you don't mind."

"We might as well. I can see that I'm not going to get any more rest around here today. Just one more thing," he added before she crossed the threshold. "You're not planning to wear your buckskins, are you?" Not that he intended to take her inside with him.

"Oh, goodness, of course not." Her laughter was halting, nervous as she folded her arms across her breasts. "Those are my working clothes. They're far more comfortable and serviceable than dresses for most of what I do, reporting and such, but I did bring something suitable for visiting Savage Publishing."

He nodded. "Have it on and be downstairs in thirty minutes. I have a lot more to accomplish today than trying to save the *Laramie Tribune*."

"I'll be there in fifteen minutes!" Then she scurried on down the hallway, leaving Donovan to contemplate ways of getting out of this mess once and for all.

Nearly two hours later, after a fast breakfast, a short cable railway ride, and an even shorter walk, Donovan guided Libby into the small but picturesque courtyard gracing the entrance of the imposing five-story Savage building. The other businesses lining the street were linked by common walls and similar Italianate facades, but the publishing house, elaborately ornamented with bay windows and High Victorian Gothic design, was set back from them, making room for the courtyard.

He escorted Libby to a circular bench which surrounded a lone shade tree and said, "You'll probably be more comfortable if you wait right here. With any luck, I won't be long."

She grumbled a little, but took a seat on the bench. They'd argued over how best to approach the publisher all during breakfast, with him insisting that the best plan would be to see R. T. in private, and then, if need be, to send for her. She hadn't agreed easily, but in the end, had little choice but to comply with his wishes. And thank God for that, he thought, given the way she was turned out.

Libby was dressed all in black, a none-too flattering color for her fair complexion, if you didn't count the bruise. In place of a fashionable little bonnet, she wore a black lace scarf draped over her head. Between the dress, which was devoid of any kind of ornamentation, her curious tottering gait, and the scarf, Donovan thought she looked like the drunken wife of a preacher on her way to a funeral. Even if he'd *wanted* to take her to see R. T. Savage, he'd have left her outside.

Her stomach churning with anxiety, Libby watched Donovan's fuzzy image divide the glass doors and fade from view. Something was wrong. His confidence, usually so flagrant, no matter the subject, seemed tentative at best. And she had the nagging feeling that he was hiding something, or at least, skipping over some not-so-minor detail. She should have simply demanded that he bring her along when he went to see his father, but she'd been distracted by her aching feet.

Damnation! she muttered inwardly, cursing the impulse that made her buy such miserably uncomfortable high-heeled boots. At the time, she'd thought they'd look nice and fashionable with the mourning dress she was wearing, and also with Dell's fancier gown, should she have occasion to don it. Now all she wanted was to be barefoot. Groaning, Libby massaged the ball of her foot through the stiff, new leather. How would she ever manage the trip back?

If all that wasn't enough to make her feel less-than-adequate, now that she was finally in the big, cosmopolitan city of San Francisco, Libby could easily see that even her best clothing was common and hopelessly dated. All the other ladies she'd passed on the streets were gowned in colorful dresses featuring embroidery, flounces, and drawn-up overskirts which spilled gracefully over fashionably large bustles. And the hats these city women wore! Libby had never seen anything quite like the wide assortment of feathered and fussy bonnets, or the matching parasols seemingly every lady she passed was carrying. Not one of them, she noted wryly, had been wearing a scarf on her head. No wonder Donovan hadn't wanted to introduce her to his father.

Glancing toward the doors where she'd last seen him, Libby was surprised to spot a figure which seemed to be dressed in very much the same manner as he'd been. Surely he hadn't gotten his father to agree to her demands so soon! Sneaking her glasses out of her pocket, she briefly held them against the bridge of her nose and studied the man. It *was* him! And his painfully handsome features were drawn and etched with worry. Lord in heaven—now what?

Rising slowly, Libby buried her glasses in her pocket, then swallowed to ease the sudden ache in her throat. As Donovan approached, she asked, "What's wrong?"

"It shows, huh?"

She nodded. "Just tell it straight out. What happened?"

"Not much. R. T. is out of town, and will be for several more days."

"Well, where did he go? Maybe we can meet with him there."

"Give it up Libby." Donovan's expression was deadly serious. "There's nothing else you can do here. I want you to listen carefully to what I have to say from here on out, and do what I suggest."

"All right," she said, even though his ice-blue eyes still told her that something was wrong. "Exactly what do you think I ought to do now?"

"I want you to let me take you back to my place to pick up your things. After that, I'll see you safely aboard the first train to Laramie."

"Oh, no. I'm not—"

"Let me finish."

She clamped her lips shut, but had a list of objections ready to toss at him. Something definitely wasn't right. Savage family member or not, she intended to find out exactly what.

"Thank you." Donovan made a little courtesy bow. "As I was saying, I'll send you a wire the minute R. T. returns and let you know what he has to say about everything—which, by the way, is exactly what I intended to do all along."

"I thank you for your suggestions," she said sharply, "but I didn't come all this way just to go back home without seeing your father. I'm staying. Anything else?"

"Dammit, Libby." Donovan shoved his hands in his pockets, then turned his back to her and began pacing. "Why do you have to be so stubborn about this? I told you that I've got things under control. I even have an appointment with R. T. a week from Monday. I promise to wire you the minute our meeting is concluded. That should be reassurance enough."

"What did you say?"

"I promised to wire you—"

"Not that." Incredulous, Libby circled Donovan until she could look him right in the eye. "Did you just say you made an *appointment* with R. T.?"

His expression wide with horror, or something close to it, he stood rock-still, giving Libby an even better glimpse of the man inside than before. Things were far worse than just "not right."

Her suspicion cresting, she grabbed the lapel of his jacket, and demanded, "Why the *devil* do you have to make an appointment to see your own father?"

4

The last gambler who'd lost a week's pay to Donovan hadn't looked at him with such contempt or hostility—and Libby still didn't know exactly what he'd done or how he'd deceived her! He backed a safe distance away before trying to explain.

"You're probably going to laugh when you hear this," he said, calling on all his boyish charm. "But I'm surprised I even *got* an appointment with old R. T.!"

"I'm not laughing yet."

"That's because I haven't gotten to the really funny part."

Donovan paused, giving Libby a moment to relax a little, but she was like a rock, as she stood there burning holes in him with her accusing brown eyes.

"I could use a good laugh about now," she muttered. "What's so blasted funny?"

"Well, the truth is, R. T. has no reason to want to see me, even *with* an appointment because . . . well," he chuckled lightly. "I'm not his son."

"Not his son—you mean, biologically?"

"That's right." Watching her carefully, catching the gradual shift in her expression from animosity to curiosity, Donovan decided that Libby was only slightly stunned by the information, but not so shaken he couldn't smooth her ruffled feathers. "I am not, nor have I ever been, a part of the Savage family. The closest I've been to any of them was when I sat next to Andrew during a card game on the train to Laramie."

"*Andrew?* A card game?" She frowned, looking very confused. "I don't understand. If you're not Andrew Savage, why did you come to see me at the *Tribune*? Do you work for Savage Publishing?"

"Good Lord, no. I have nothing to do with the newspaper." Christ, but it felt good to have it all out in the open. Good and almost virtuous. "I'm a gambler by trade and, like I told you, a partner in Lucky Lil's. Savage didn't make it to Laramie to see you because, during that card game, one of the other poker players shot him."

Libby gasped. "Shot him? You mean he's *dead*?"

"As in staring up at the sky, but seeing nothing." He paused to give Libby a moment to digest the significance of that before going on. "Savage left his satchel behind, so I took it, intending to return it to his family—which I'm still trying to do. Does that clear everything up for you?"

Save for the twitching of a muscle near the corner of her left eye, Libby didn't respond right away, or even change her stunned expression. But she did begin to move, her gait rigid and determined, and slowly circled him as if he were some kind of prey.

"Libby?" Following her movements, Donovan spun around on one heel. "Aren't you going to say anything?"

But she just kept circling, glaring now, looking like a beady-eyed vulture just hours from starvation.

"I know when you get to thinking about this, you'll see the humor in the situation." He laughed, surprised to hear a nervous chortle in his voice, then cleared his throat and adopted a sterner manner. Hell, it wasn't like he'd cheated her out of anything. "You'd do well to remember where we are," he warned. "Think of the folks peeking out the windows of Savage Publishing. They can see us down here, you know."

This threat seemed to have some impact on her. Libby abruptly stopped pacing, coming to a halt just inches from him, and at last, she began to talk. And talk. And talk.

"I have a few questions," she began, her adorable features contorted with rage. "Let's start with your real name, you low-down, dirty, egg-sucking varmint."

Christ, but she was pissed—glowing with anger. "It's Donovan, like I said."

"Donovan *what*, you chicken-thieving, mangy dog!"

He tugged at his suddenly too-tight collar, wondering how he could have misread her so. Libby had bitten those words off hard enough to break her teeth—which, he couldn't help but notice, were bared as she waited for his answer. "Donovan is my last name. I never use my given name."

"What is it?" she demanded, tracing his steps as he backed away from her. "Judas? Benedict? Or maybe it's Brutus—yes, that's probably it. Brutus, right?"

His full name, something he never told anyone, was as private to him as his deepest thoughts; but, for a crazy moment, Donovan actually thought that, if he were to share that information with Libby, if he were to give her that small piece of himself, maybe it would somehow help to right the wrong she thought he'd done her.

"It's William," he admitted, spitting the name out like a stream of tobacco juice, "but I never—"

"William, huh?"

Donovan had always hated the name, and with damn good reason. Throughout his life, his mother had called all her paramours "William," no matter what their true identities might have been. She'd claimed she'd done so because the name was her favorite, but Donovan had always known she'd done it because her love life was less confusing that way. He hated the name "William," all right, along with the memories of the men in his mother's life. And hearing the word spewing from Libby's snarling lips made it sound worse than it ever had before, almost like a vile oath.

No longer feigning a firm stand or the sudden harshness in his voice, Donovan muttered, "I'd really appreciate it if you wouldn't call me 'William.'"

"That's fine with me!" she snapped, apparently unimpressed by his candor. "You remind me more of a 'Billy-boy' anyway, or maybe even, 'Willy the weasel'!"

"Don't call me 'Billy.'" Those were the nicknames assigned to Donovan whenever his mother had a new "William" around. "And don't ever call me 'Willy.'"

"That's fine with me, too, because you're nothing but a no-good bastard who doesn't deserve to have a name at all!"

She struck pay dirt there, calling him by the only *sobriquet* which truly fit him. "That's correct, Miss Justice." He struck an injured pose and flattened his palm across his heart. "I am, through no fault of my own, of course, a bastard."

"Don't try to play on my sympathies, you lying sack of garbage." There wasn't so much as a pinch of remorse in her voice. "Especially after all the lies you told me and the promises you made as . . . *Mother of*

God! You even slept in my house—in one of my *beds*!"

"Now, Libby . . ." She was on the move again, the circle around him, tighter. Back on the defense, Donovan tracked her movements. "Having me stay at your home was your idea, not mine. I never asked you to put me up."

"You did so, and you did it by lying to me about who you were! Do you *think* for one minute that I, as a lone woman," she bore down on him, her cheeks shiny with bright red splotches, "would have opened my home, much less one of my bedrooms, to a no-good, stinking polecat like you—'Willy'?"

"*Don't* call me 'Willy'!" Donovan shook his finger in her face. "And stop trying to blame me for everything. I tried to tell you that I wasn't Andrew Savage when I first walked into your newspaper office, but you wouldn't let me."

"That's it." Libby snapped her wrists at him as if throwing garbage onto the compost heap. "I've heard all the lies from you I intend to." With that, she turned and started up Sacramento Street.

Donovan watched her stiff-backed retreat, sorely tempted to just let her stumble around the hills of San Francisco until she calmed down enough to listen to reason. But something inside wouldn't let him—culpability, for one thing. Even though he thought she was overreacting in the extreme, he also felt a certain amount of sympathy, or something close to it. A tough little cookie, she reminded him a little of the sister he'd fabricated for himself as a child. Although Libby had been raised under circumstances completely different than he'd had—by a mother, with a real live father and brother, to boot—he sensed that she was a maverick, like he was. A bit of a loner.

With a heavy sigh, Donovan took off after her and continued to plead his case. "I know how this must sound to you now," he said to her still rigid back. "But once you'd gotten the wrong impression about who I was, it just seemed easier to go along with you."

Libby glanced over her shoulder to deliver her remarks, but never slowed her stride. "I'll just bet it did, you greasy-tongued jackass."

"I only meant to help you, all along. I never meant to cheat you out of anything or hurt you. I don't see why you should be so damned mad."

"Really? Then you're the one who needs glasses, not me!"

Donovan threw his hands up in exasperation, but continued to follow her, defending himself and explaining why he'd done what he'd done, all the way back to his house. Surprisingly enough, Libby managed to find Jackson Street without any help from him—and on foot, no less, instead of by taking the cable railway as they had on the way to Savage Publishing. When they reached the walkway which led to his modest home, Libby was still berating him, no longer over her shoulder, but right to his face.

". . . and I don't believe a word you've said, because there's no way a *stupid* plan like that could have worked, much less helped me!"

"It was working just fine," he insisted, opening the door for her. Gesturing dramatically, Donovan waved Libby inside. "And it would have kept right on working if you hadn't done something so *stupid* as getting on that train."

"Even if boarding that train was stupid," she muttered, marching straight through the foyer and into the parlor, where she dropped onto the first available chair, "and I'm not saying that it was, I only did it because I was trying to save my newspaper! What's your excuse for being so stupid?"

"For the last time . . ." He sighed heavily. "I was just trying to help you a little—still am, in fact. There's nothing more sinister than that to anything I've done."

"Even if I believed you," she lifted her foot and tore at the buttons on her shoe, "it wouldn't matter, because I never asked for your help. Not once."

Tired of trying to defend himself—especially where his behavior was largely indefensible—Donovan strolled over to the bay window and propped himself against the scalloped molding near the frame. This is what helping folks got him, he thought sourly: scolded, like he was some kind of irresponsible kid. And by whom? A pretender to Calamity Jane's throne, that's who!

As Libby struggled with her footgear, he couldn't help but notice that she'd hiked her skirt and petticoats up to her knees, revealing a wide expanse of leg between her plain flannel drawers and drab woolen stockings. The woman didn't even know how to behave out of her buckskins, much less realize what the sight of those creamy legs could do to a man—even a man like himself, who would never, under normal circumstances, be drawn to a woman like her.

But drawn he was, Donovan acknowledged, and this situation was about as bizarre as any he'd been in. He wondered if Libby knew she was flashing him glimpses of her very shapely legs, or if she realized the state she'd worked herself into between her anger and the struggle she was having with her footgear. She looked positively untamed. A few tendrils of mahogany hair had escaped her carefully prepared coif, and now clung to her lightly perspiring cheeks and neck. She was also out of breath, her bosom straining against the ribbed bodice of her somber black dress, and her lips were parted, making room for the tip of her tongue at the edge of her mouth. Hell, he thought, a tug of desire working into a steady, pounding ache, even the real Andrew—a dead man— would sit up and take notice of Libby under these conditions.

"I think there's a buttonhook in the kitchen," he said, looking for a way to distract himself. "I'll just go get it for you."

"Don't bother. I don't want anything from you," she snapped. "Damnation! I hate these stupid shoes, and I hate you, too! Nothing's gone right for me since I laid eyes on you. Everything has gone wrong, and it's all because of you—everything!"

Though he was pretty well argued out, Donovan recognized her challenge as the distraction he sought. "I beg to differ with you . . . 'Lippy.' If you could have kept your big mouth shut long enough for a man to get a word in edgewise, none of this would have happened in the first place. I tried to tell you more than once that I was not Andrew Savage, but you wouldn't give me a chance."

"You had plenty of chances to tell the truth—and all of this *is* your fault, including the fact that I rushed out and bought these miserable boots!" The buttons unhooked at last, Libby strained, tugging on the shoe. When it finally popped off of her foot, she reared back and threw it at Donovan, hurling one last accusation along with it. "This is all your fault, '*Willy*'!"

Not a moment too soon, he ducked, leaving the boot to crash against the glass behind him. "Hey—hey! There's no cause to get violent. You damn near broke my window. And stop calling me, 'Willy'!"

"I wanted to break your big fat head, you double-dealing snake in the grass, and I'll call you 'Willy' any time I take a notion to!" She leaped to her feet and

stormed across the room, steam-piston style, one boot
on, one boot off. Raising her fist when she reached him,
she shook it in his face. "As for violence, you lousy flim-
flammer, when I think about the things you said to me
in Laramie and the way you had me groveling at your
feet, doing something violent is the kindest thing I can
think of!"

"Now, Libb—"

"Don't 'now Libby' me. Not while I can still hear
you saying, *'You want a camera, little lady?'"*—she
mimicked his voice, slaughtering it by adding a countri-
fied accent. *"'Shore 'nuff, ma'am—you kin have anything you want. Juss ask, and it's all yours.'* Why I
ought to punch you right in the mouth for leading me
on that way."

He'd been halfway amused until Libby mentioned
his mouth. Now suddenly, all Donovan could think of
was hers—not punching it, but burying it beneath his
own lips. Without thinking or even questioning himself,
he impulsively dragged her into his arms.

"And what," he asked, his throat tight, "would you
suggest I do to your mouth in return?"

He didn't wait for an answer, or expect one. He just
came down on her, a little too hard at first, and took
what he wanted so badly.

As Donovan suspected she would, Libby fought him
in the beginning, smashing her fists to his shoulders and
twisting in his embrace. Although she struggled mightily, it wasn't long before her inviting mouth became soft
and pliant, and moments after that, as eager as his own.
Something exploded between them then, a power or
force so strong and unfamiliar that Donovan couldn't
identify the sensation. But he did recognize that what
they shared here was no mere kiss. This was an assault
on the senses, an awakening of dark and utterly insane

hungers, a need urging him down a path he was quite sure he should never follow.

Shaken, in spirit, body, in every way imaginable, Donovan drew away from Libby's mouth, and caught his breath. He relaxed his grip then, unable to turn her loose the way he should have, but giving her freedom. Rather than try to escape him as he hoped she would, Libby clung to his jacket, her dark eyes and wondrous expression mirroring his own unexpected and tumultuous feelings. They stared into each other a long moment, briefly glimpsing private places and raw desires, and then as if frightened by what she saw in him, Libby finally broke out of his embrace.

"Jesus," slipped out of her mouth before she fully realized the thought.

Embarrassed, trembling, she turned her back to Donovan and, on trembling legs, made her way to the chair she'd been sitting on earlier. Leaning heavily against the soft velvet upholstery, Libby tried to quell the shaking that had taken over her entire body. Her insides felt as if they'd melted into a big pot of jelly, and even though she was free of Donovan, she could still feel his vigorous embrace and the way his wicked mouth had plumbed her. How in God's name, after all she'd found out about the man, could she have responded to him this way? She ought to be lashing him within an inch of his life, not kissing him!

Libby breathed deeply, still trying to get a grip on herself, and caught Donovan's scent still lingering on her skin. There was something more to the aroma than spicy cologne, something infinitely more disturbing— the slightly salty, earthy tang of the man himself. She shook her head to clear it of such thoughts, and again wondered how she could be so attracted to someone who'd made such a fool of her.

"Libby," came his throaty voice from behind her. His tone wasn't particularly apologetic, but she thought she heard something akin to regret in it. Donovan touched her shoulder then, sending a little shudder up her spine, and gently turned her to face him. "I hope you won't make too much of what just happened here . . ." His gaze skimmed her lips. "I don't know what came over me, and maybe it's best that I don't. It might be a good idea if we just forget about it."

"Oh, well, of course. Why not?" She'd tried to sound relieved by the suggestion, but why did she feel so let down? Perhaps, Libby thought, that was the irony of it all. Back in Laramie, she'd all but busted her buttons in an effort to bedevil Donovan, and to no avail. Yet here in San Francisco, where she'd practically taken his head off with her boot, for some reason, he'd found her irresistible. Comforted by the thought, she smiled and added, "In fact, I've already forgotten about it."

She thought she saw Donovan's eyes narrow for a moment, but then he just shrugged and said, "Good. Now why don't we sit down a minute. There's a few things we ought to talk over."

"I'm fine right where I am. Besides, now that you've shown yourself for what you really are—a lying, cheating gambler—I don't see what we have left to talk about."

"You're still mad at me?"

She should have been madder than hell—Lord, if she shouldn't still have been angry enough to pound a few knots on his head—but for some reason, every drop of her outrage had sizzled away to nothing. It was probably that innocent act he was giving her, the charismatic charm-the-bloomers-off-a-nun grin he displayed whenever he thought he might be in trouble. "Of course I'm still mad," she said, unable to force any harshness in her tone. "But it seems I've calmed down considerably."

"Then we do have something to talk about. I really want to help you, now more than ever. Do you believe that?"

She didn't want to, but Libby knew she had to try to trust him a little if she were to stay in San Francisco long enough to confront R. T. Savage. She definitely required help from someone, and since Donovan was the only person she knew in all of California, her choices were narrow. Either she tossed her lot in with his—on her terms, of course—or she went back to Laramie empty-handed.

Determined to hang onto her newspaper and the fight for equal rights at almost any cost, she said truthfully, "I'm not sure what I believe where you're concerned or if there *is* a way you could help me now."

"There are several ways in which I can help. The first is the easiest—I'd make an excellent choice as an escort when you go to the depot to catch the train back to Laramie. Can I help you pack?"

"Absolutely not. I'm not going anywhere yet."

"I didn't think so." He favored Libby with a smile, not his usual smug or mocking expression, but one of admiration, she thought. "I guess that means you're planning to stay in San Francisco until R. T. returns?"

"That's right, even if I have to sleep on the bench in front of the Savage building until then."

He nodded thoughtfully. "You already informed me that you can't afford a hotel room; so I figure, after what I put you through, I owe you at least room and board. You can stay here, if you like, until you get your business at Savage Publishing straightened out."

Libby hesitated, even though she was very tempted to accept. Donovan was right about her lack of funds, but how could she stay here with him after what they'd just shared? "I don't think that, well, after what happened, it would be very wise of me to stay with you."

He arched one ebony brow and flashed that devastating grin. "I thought you'd forgotten about my little . . . indiscretion."

"I have!" Donovan's bluntness startled her, and Libby had to look away as she considered the offer again. How was she to forget what they'd shared, with him standing so close to her, reminding her about it! "It's just that I'm not sure—"

"There's really nothing for you to worry about. You have my word as a gentleman that you'll be quite safe."

Libby gave him a skeptical look. Now that she knew him to be a gambler and saloon-owner, not the respectable son of a publishing scion, her staying here with him—alone, no less—was even more scandalous and improper than ever; but she honestly couldn't think of another viable choice.

"Oh, all right," she said. "I accept your hospitality. It might even go a long way toward making up for some of the dastardly lies you've told me. Just be sure you don't tell anyone that I'm here—certainly none of the Savages—and stay out of my way when it's time for *me*, not you, to keep that appointment with R. T. when he returns."

"Try not to be so blasted independent for once, would you? Whether you like it or not, you can use my help at Savage Publishing."

"Oh, no, I can't; so the matter's closed."

"The satchel, remember? I have to keep the appointment in order to return Andrew's belongings and inform the poor man of his son's death. You surely don't want to be put in a position of explaining that to him, do you?"

Libby realized that if she tried to see the old man before Donovan explained about Andrew, that R. T.

would be full of questions about his son's visit to Laramie—and wondering why the devil his son hadn't returned to San Francisco with her. She surely did not want to be the bearer of those sad tidings.

"All right," she said with a sigh. "You go first, but leave me and my newspaper out of your conversation with Savage."

"If that's the way you want it, I will; but if I should happen to spot an area regarding your newspaper where I can smooth the way for your talk with the man, I don't see why I can't put in a good word for you. Fair enough?"

"Fair enough," she muttered, wishing he weren't such a handsome and silver-tongued devil. "Now, if that's all, I'd like to go to my room."

Donovan bunched his usually jaunty brows. "There is a little something else I think we should discuss, but I'm not sure exactly how to broach the subject."

"If you're afraid what you have to say might upset me," she said, her mood turning surly, "maybe it would be best to skip the subject altogether."

He shrugged. "Whatever you say. But if I were you, I'd be interested in anything that might help me make the best damn impression I could on Randolph T. Savage."

"Oh?"

Donovan nodded solemnly as he looked her up and down. "You didn't happen to bring any *normal* clothes along, did you?"

"Normal? What do you mean by that?"

"Something other than those buckskins that make you look like Calamity Jane, or the dress you're wearing, which makes you look like a Salvation Army sergeant. When you meet Savage, you'll need to play on his sympathies, not make him feel like you're about to parade a group of suffragists through his office."

Libby glanced down at herself. "I thought this dress made me look businesslike, but maybe it is a little severe. I also brought the red and white gown I wore to supper in Laramie. Would that be better?"

"I'm afraid not." Picturing the outfit and the way Libby had carried herself while wearing it, Donovan cringed. "Please don't take offense, dear, but that one makes you look like you're wearing someone else's dress."

So he'd known all along that she'd been wearing a borrowed gown. Her cheeks burned with humiliation, but Libby was determined enough to impress the publishing magnate, to encourage Donovan's suggestions. "I'm afraid those are the only clothes I brought with me. As I said before, most of my work requires comfort, not style, so I have a very limited wardrobe. Is there a way I can fix them up a little?"

He shook his head. "You don't have to apologize about your clothes, and I don't mean to criticize them either, but I do think we need to get you into something else before you go to see Savage."

"I appreciate your advice, but I'm afraid that it's been quite a struggle for Jeremy and me since pa died. We're just now getting some of the bills caught up." Libby glanced over to where her boot had landed, regretting the two dollars she'd wasted on it. "I'm afraid I simply don't have the extra money to go out and buy new clothes."

"I wasn't suggesting that you should. After what I put you through, I feel that I owe you something more than an apology and a place to stay. Why don't you let me make it up to you by taking you shopping? I'll outfit you from head to toe, and by the time you meet Savage, you'll knock him dead."

Still staring at the uncomfortable boot, again she found herself considering one of Donovan's inappropriate offers. It wouldn't be the right or proper thing to do, accepting clothes from a strange man—one who'd tricked her, at that. It wouldn't be right at all. But right wasn't going to do much to help persuade Savage Publishing to see things her way. And if Donovan had a point about the importance of her appearance—and she suspected that he did have—she really couldn't chance wearing anything she owned.

Lifting her gaze to meet his, Libby gave him a wan smile. "I guess a new dress would go a long way toward making me forget what you did to me in Laramie." But to make sure he wouldn't think of her as beholden to him in anyway, she added, "Since you're willing to do all that for me, I'm willing to call it even between us."

"Done," he said magnanimously, sensing that he'd finally gotten the upper hand with the sassy little ink-slinger.

As promised, Donovan had taken Libby shopping for clothes, and had even spent a whole afternoon showing her the sights of San Francisco—most notably, a lovely carriage ride through heavily wooded and thoroughly charming Golden Gate Park. Having lived in Laramie all her life, Libby had never seen anything like it or the San Francisco Bay, with its throngs of sea gulls and fishing boats. He'd even treated her to restaurant suppers twice now: once at Sam's Grill, where she'd tried green turtle soup; then again last night, when he'd taken her down to the wharf, to a place called the Cobweb Palace, for clam chowder and cracked crab. "A prelude," he'd said then, "to the victory supper of lobster we will soon share at Delmonico's."

Libby didn't have a reason in the world or the right to complain about a thing. Donovan went off to the "theatre" each and every night, leaving her to manage on her own. He slept most of the day, and then disappeared into the night again. His long absences did not bother her, as he did have a business to run, no matter how morally questionable this "theatre" of his might be. Besides, what woman in her right mind groused because a man treated her like a lady?

Left alone much of the time, she'd filled her time by writing editorials and letters home to Jeremy, as well as making a few journeys around the city on her own. Her only source of irritation was Gerda, who'd come by the house another four times since Libby's arrival from Laramie, and still treated Libby as if she were one of the painted ladies from Lucky Lil's. The fact that the *Frau* steadfastly refused to set foot in her room didn't bother Libby much since she was unused to having anyone do her chores for her. But she was tired of feeling like an outcast, especially now that Black Monday—as she'd begun to view it—was here.

Her nerves feeling taut as she sat in one of the lavish waiting rooms at Savage Publishing, Libby made a fast study of her appearance—again. She was wearing the smashing new outfit Donovan had bought for her—the tight-fitting jacket made of terra-cotta sateen set off by olive trim, the draped skirt checkered in strawberry red and white. He'd even insisted on buying her a saucy little English straw bonnet trimmed with pink roses and an ecru ostrich plume, a hat she could wear with everything she owned. She'd never possessed anything quite so cosmopolitan as her new outfit, or so comfortable as the soft kid leather shoes beneath it; but still, she couldn't lose the feeling that something wasn't quite right.

Turning to Donovan for reassurance, Libby held her gloved hand out to him and said, "Look at me—I'm shaking so badly, I can't even hold my fingers steady."

He reached for her hand just as an attractive young woman approached. "Mr. Savage will see you now, Mr. Donovan."

Giving Libby's fingers a quick squeeze, he whispered, "Wish me luck!" Then he lifted himself and Andrew's satchel up from the plush leather couch, and disappeared with the secretary through a pair of wide double doors at the end of the hall.

Donovan walked into the publishing scion's office, sniffing the air. As he'd expected, it was permeated with the heady aroma of money and all the trappings such a vast fortune could buy. The scent of fine leather and premium burled walnut drifted past his nose along with a whiff of rich pipe tobacco. Blindfolded, Donovan would have known in an instant that he'd stepped into the domain of an extremely wealthy man.

Not that another's prosperity made him feel humble or inferior in any way. In fact, ostentatious displays had always annoyed his sense of fair play, or something close to it. Answering what he viewed as a challenge, Donovan displayed the only riches he'd ever possessed—grit enough to choke a full-grown horse—and strode right up to the magnate's expansive desk without waiting for a proper introduction.

"It's, ah, Mr. William Donovan to see you, sir," the secretary said, stumbling over the words.

While his sharp-eyed gaze never left Donovan's face, Savage waved the young woman away. "Thanks, Grace." Then he reached out and shook Donovan's hand, scrutinizing him as he waited for the secretary to close the door behind her. Once she was gone, he finally addressed Donovan.

"Please," he said, his voice pleasant but firm, as he lowered himself onto his plush, barrel-shaped chair. "Have a seat."

"Don't mind if I do."

Donovan chose one of the three walnut and black leather chairs across from the man's desk, set the satchel on the floor beside him, then took another really good look at the man. Savage wasn't at all the way he'd pictured him; in fact, he was quite the opposite. Judging from Andrew's age, his father had to be close to fifty, but the publisher didn't look one hell of a lot older than Donovan. What Donovan could see of Savage's physique appeared to be trim and fit, and he still had a full head of coal-black hair, which was merely sprayed at the temples with gray, rather than streaked clear through. Even his eyes, clear blue in color, were as keen as any young sharper's Donovan had come across.

R. T. smiled as Donovan perused him, and said, "I wasn't sure when I saw the name if it'd really be you, but from what I can see, I'd have to say that it is. What made you come looking for me?"

This odd remark startled Donovan, making him feel like he was playing a game of draw poker, blindfolded. Savage almost sounded as if he'd already received information about his dead son. Before Donovan could draw any conclusions, R. T. asked yet another bizarre question, adding to Donovan's general confusion.

"Did your mother have a hand in this, or does she even know you've come to see me?"

What the hell did his mother have to do with this? Was the man baiting him for some reason, trying to make him feel like a kid in need of parental permission? Donovan tried to draw on his anger, but the hairs at his neck grew stiff with foreboding. "My mother doesn't have a damn thing to do with our business. I've come to see you about one of your sons."

"I guessed as much—or haven't you figured that out." Savage sighed as he reached for a solid gold nail file lying beside his thick felt ink pad. "May I call you William, or are you still known as 'Willy'?"

Still known as 'Willy'? Along with that peculiar statement, something in the man's voice tickled Donovan's memory. Had they met before? Fighting the anger along with his confusion now, he muttered, "I *never* go by 'William' or 'Willy.' I'm just plain Donovan."

"I'll remember that." Savage smiled at him again, the expression warmer, more familiar than ever. His eyes twinkling as he drove the file under the already immaculately groomed nail of his left index finger, R. T. went on with his strange conversation. "Why have you come to me after all these years? Do you need money or a job?"

"Why the *hell* would you think a thing like that?"

"I didn't mean to offend you." R. T. made a fast examination of Donovan's suit. "You look as if you're doing all right. If not for money or a job, are you thinking of staking your claim to the Savage family name?"

Donovan leaped out of his chair. "My claim to the . . . *family name*? What the hell are you talking about?"

"I thought . . ." Savage cocked his head, losing just a little of his cool confidence. "Just exactly what is it you want from me . . . Son?"

5

In far less time than she would have expected, Libby heard the wide double doors at the end of the hall crash open against the walls. Reaching into the cute little lace-edged bag Donovan had insisted on buying for her, she grabbed her spectacles and brought them to her nose in time to see him barreling down the hallway toward her. His expression was frozen, so icy she could have skated across it. What had happened in there?

"Come on. We're leaving," he muttered tightly.

"B-but what about me? Don't I get to—"

"This isn't a good time for it." Tugging her to her feet, Donovan half-dragged Libby alongside him. "I know you have a lot of questions right now—and believe me, I'll answer them all—but you'll have to wait a while. I can't deal with your questions until I get a few answers of my own."

Another protest was on the tip of her tongue, but something in Donovan's tone told Libby to keep her comments to herself. *Never*, even in the heat of their name-calling argument, had she seen him without at least a glimmer of amusement in his eyes, or a slight curl at the corner of his mouth. She couldn't begin to fathom what had happened in R. T.'s office, but she was reasonably certain it had nothing to do with her or the *Tribune*—and that it would probably be best if she were to keep quiet for the time being.

Sticking to that plan, Libby allowed Donovan to drag her down the four flights of stairs, then into a hired carriage which took them a few blocks northwest to Stockton Street, an area which seemed to be the less-respectable part of town. Although Donovan assured her they were only at the fringes of the notorious Barbary Coast section of San Francisco, she kept a lookout for criminal types as he escorted her through one of the three high-arched doorways leading into Lucky Lil's Theatre and Gaming Saloon.

Libby, who'd never even peeked inside such an establishment, donned her glasses in full view of Donovan in order to take her first glimpse at the sordid side of life. Though it was not quite noon, the saloon was better than half-full of customers, men from every kind of business, as far as she could tell by their dress. The rest of the crowd seemed to be female dancers—or actresses, depending on their duties of the moment—all of whom dressed in a manner which showed a good bit of leg and even more cleavage.

As Donovan, who was still standing beside her, scanned the room for his partner, Libby turned her gaze toward the stage, which covered the entire wall at the opposite end of the long room. The performing platform, lighted by gas jets, rose some five or six feet above the main floor and was draped with blood-red curtains of velvet which were tied back. On this stage, five half-naked "actresses" were saucily singing, as a short bald man pounded out a tune on the piano nearby. Although she couldn't quite make out the words, after watching and listening to the reactions of the male customers, Libby had an idea the song was rather ribald.

Most of those patrons clustered around the tables peppered throughout this central area, while others sat in balconies above each side of the stage. Under the fancy balconies on the left were several gaming tables in front of a long bar. On the right, more gaming tables lined a wall that also contained a row of doors to what Libby assumed were offices.

Donovan started to lead her deeper into the saloon, still scanning the crowd for his partner. Her passage was noted by several appreciative "hoots" from the customers, and she was almost relieved when he brought her right up to the bar and called to the woman at the other end.

"Goldy! Come here a minute."

The scantily clad blonde who was tending a customer at the other end of the cherry-wood bar whirled around at the sound of Donovan's voice, then quickly made her way down the narrow plank which served as an elongated foot board to accommodate her diminutive size.

"Hiya, honey," she greeted, all sooty lashes and pouty red lips. "What are you doing here at this time of day?"

"I had a little unexpected business come up. Is Lil in her office?"

"She sure is, honey." With a long, heavy-lidded look in Libby's direction, Goldy asked him, "Is this cute little thing the business that came 'up,' darlin'?"

"No, she's not, and watch how you talk around her. I've got to see Lil privately for a while, and I want you to keep an eye on Miss Justice. Understand?"

Again the barmaid glanced at Libby, this time tossing her a little wink. "Got it, honey. Do you want me to give her the good stuff, too?"

Donovan's gaze quickly skimmed Libby, lingering over her eyeglasses a moment longer than she would have liked. "Give her whatever she wants. Just keep a damn good eye on her, and don't let any of the customers bother her."

With that final order, he turned to Libby and said, "I'll try not to be too long. Make yourself comfortable, but don't leave this stool." Without any warning, Donovan then fit his hands to her waist and lifted her up onto the little round tufted seat.

"B-but I don't want you to leave me here alone. Can't I go to the office with you?"

"No. You'll be all right where you are." Donovan pinched her cheek. "Just keep your glasses on so you can see what's coming your way."

Before Libby could make a retort, Goldy said, "If you want to catch Lil, Donovan, you'd best go stop her. Looks to me like she's heading for the bank."

With a quick glance toward the center of the room, Donovan spotted the woman Goldy referred to and took off in her direction, leaving a completely bewildered Libby to fend for herself. So much for gallantry, she thought sourly. But she did strain to see past the gamblers who were standing around a craps table, for a glimpse of this "partner" of his.

Finally getting the right angle, Libby spotted the red-haired woman Donovan had stopped as she walked toward the doors. She was dressed in a striking gown of royal-blue velvet, one which covered her breasts decently enough, though its low dip in the front brought far too much attention to her impressive bosom.

"What's it gonna be, honey?" asked Goldy, interfering with Libby's fierce study of the woman.

"Huh?"

"What can I get you to drink, sugar?" There was unmistakable laughter in the barmaid's voice. "A beer, some whiskey, a little cognac?"

"Oh, ah . . . nothing, thank you."

Alcohol—at just past *noon*? Libby was scandalized by the idea. She wasn't one to indulge in libations very often, unless you counted the sip or two of cherry brandy she once enjoyed with her father at the end of a long day behind the press. Squaring her back and carefully folding her hands in her lap in a more ladylike way, she let Goldy know in no uncertain terms that she was *not* that kind of female. Then she went back to studying Donovan and the flame-haired hussy.

Something bad had happened in the few moments she'd turned her gaze from them. Donovan appeared to be very angry now, his features set and stony, and it was also painfully clear that he and his partner had much more between them than mere business. Her gaze locked intimately with Donovan's, the hussy raised one of her hands to caress his cheek. It wasn't a moment later that, arm in arm, the pair turned toward the bank of doors and disappeared into one of the offices she'd noticed earlier.

Of course, whatever the two were up to in there was no business of Libby's. They could be longtime lovers, for all she cared. Engaged, even. Her only concerns in this town had to do with Savage Publishing and her little newspaper. So why, she had to wonder, did her heart feel as if it were lodged in her throat, while her stomach felt as if it had plummeted to somewhere south of her navel?

Uncomfortable with the wealth of conflicting emotions running amok inside her, Libby turned to Goldy and said, "You wouldn't happen to have any cherry brandy back there, would you?"

*   *   *

"What in bloody blue hell were you doing at Savage Publishing, for Christ's sake?" Lil demanded, with a scowl creasing the fine lines on her face.

The office, small, square, with only a tiny window, didn't give Donovan much room to maneuver, but he tried to diffuse his anger a little by keeping on the move. "Don't try to turn this around for your sake, Lil. I had legitimate business with the man, which, by the way, had nothing to do with you or me."

"But how did all this happen? You looked at him and said, 'By the way, are you my father?'"

"Not exactly." Donovan stopped pacing and fixed her with a malignant gaze. "He practically told me that I was his son. I want it straight out: Is Randolph Thaddeous Savage my natural father?"

"Christ, Almighty." In much the same manner as Donovan had, Lil now strolled back and forth along the well-worn carpet near the door. "How can you even ask me a question like that?"

"Easy. A simple yes or no will be fine by way of an answer. Is he or isn't he?"

"There's nothing simple about this, and I suspect that you know it." With a gesture of defeat, she turned to him. "All right. If you insist on the truth, here it is: Yes, R. T. Savage *is* the son of a bitch who left me to raise you alone. So what?"

"So what?" Donovan, who generally tried to keep a respectful manner around his mother, struggled mightily to keep a civil tongue in his head. "You've hidden the truth about my father from me all these years, and that's all you can say?"

She just stood there looking at him, unblinking, as if numb to his pain.

Enraged by her indifference, Donovan shouted, "Do you have any idea what it was like to walk into that situation? I didn't have a clue in hell what he was talking about—he actually accused me of coming to him for money!"

"From what I understand, he's got a hell of a lot more than he needs. Maybe you should have demanded a small ransom. The bastard owes you that much."

Donovan shook his head with disgust. "Have you no feelings inside you at all?"

"Oh, I have feelings, Donovan. Trust me, I do."

"They're very well hidden." Donovan couldn't keep the sneer off his lips as he added, "Almost as well hidden as the identity of my father. I guess this means that R. T. was one of your Williams, huh?"

Some of Lil's cool veneer cracked over that remark. "It hurt me less that way. In fact, it was after he left me for the last time that I began using that name for my other . . . friends."

His fingers curled tight, again Donovan had to fight for control of his anger. "Which William were you referring to as my father? You must remember him, the one you said died before I was born!"

Lil's steel-gray eyes hardened. "I lied to protect you. Besides, by then R. T. Savage *was* dead to me."

"But what about me?" Donovan bellowed. "Do I matter at all, or don't my thoughts on the subject count for anything?"

Watching her son's expression darken with rage, Lil backed away from him. "Of course, they count, but you're not considering what I had to go through back when you were born. I never wanted you to find out about R. T., and certainly not the way you did." Lil's voice had grown much softer, less defensive. "I was just trying to protect us both the only way I knew how."

Donovan, who was standing in front of his mother's small pine desk, leaned back against the edge of it to collect himself. More rational now, he said, "I can almost understand why you wouldn't tell a small boy the whole truth, but once I was grown . . . Christ, once we'd moved to San Francisco, where the Savage family practically rules, why didn't you tell me then? Why the hell couldn't you have trusted me with that much of my past?"

"Don't judge me, Donovan," Lil warned, hands on hips. "Don't ever think you can judge me. You have no idea what I went through as a ten-year-old girl when my father dragged me to California to chase a pot of gold along with all the other forty-niners. By the time a claim-jumper killed pa some five years later, leaving me to fend for myself, I'd blossomed pretty well."

Donovan's mother had always been secretive about her early life. After hearing those few things, he had an idea he'd prefer it if she continued that way. "I don't want to know about your transformation into womanhood, Lil. I just want a little more information about my father."

"That's what I'm trying to tell you. Look at me, Donovan." She spread her arms, displaying an amazingly curvy figure and youthful appearance for a woman past forty. "Imagine what I must have looked like thirty years ago, especially to a bunch of love-starved miners."

Lil was a very attractive woman, one who must have been blindingly gorgeous in her youth—but again, this was a subject Donovan did not wish to think about or discuss. "You're beautiful now, and I would imagine, were even more beautiful then; but try to tell me about R. T. without the sordid details, if you can."

She shot him a narrow glance, but went on. "I was a fifteen-year-old orphan with nothing to my name except that beauty and the clothes on my back. It didn't take long for several men to come to my aid, and even less time than that for them to begin fighting over who would win the right to 'take care of me' from then on out."

Donovan abruptly stood up from the desk. "I told you to skip past all that."

Bristling, Lil stomped over to her son. "You can't come slamming in here full up with self-righteous anger, demanding the truth, unless you want to hear all of it—understand? All or nothing. What's it to be?"

Meanwhile, Goldy was refilling Libby's glass at the bar. "We don't get much call for cherry brandy. How is it?"

Libby took a sip, although she had a real good idea how it was by now. "Ummm. Delicious. How long do you think Donovan's going to be in there with that, that woman?"

Goldy laughed. "Who knows? Did you see the look on his face? He was plenty steamed."

"Do they fight a lot?"

"Now and again, like any other partners, I guess. Why are you so interested, sugar?" She winked and leaned across the bar. "Are you sweet on Donovan?"

"No! Gosh, no." Libby raised her glass for another fast sip. "I was just wondering about him and Lil, and if they were, you know, engaged or something."

"Oh, I don't think so. Neither one of them is much for getting tied down, if you know what I mean."

Libby shook her head. "I don't think I do know."

"Donovan for sure isn't the marrying kind—Lord knows enough of us gals have tried to rope him in, and Lil . . ." Goldy paused, thinking about her employer. "Oh, she fawns over the customers, a'course, but I haven't seen her try to cozy up to any man for a good long while."

Or maybe, thought Libby, she's just concentrating on one, and behind closed doors, at that. With a glower in the direction of what she assumed was the manager's office, she shoved her suddenly empty glass toward Goldy.

Donovan sat down on the desk again. "Go ahead then, but do spare me the intimate details."

"I'll do what I can. After picking through that motley lot of miners who wanted to take care of me, I chose a fella named William because I thought he looked more prosperous than the others. He treated me nice and took care of me the best he could. That, by the way, is where I got the name, William." She began to pace the carpet again. "It wasn't long after I moved in with Will that R. T. came along, and I knew somehow that he was a cut above the rest, a man who'd be very successful some day."

"So you left poor Will spinning in your wake and took up with R. T.?"

"That's right." She stopped pacing and turned to confront her son's reproachful gaze. "I was all of sixteen by then to his twenty or twenty-one. I'd never met anyone so dashing or worldly, and I was love cracked for him almost the moment I first saw him. When I became in a family way a couple of years later, I wasn't the least bit upset about it at first. In fact, I was happy to be having the child of a man I actually cared for." Her painted mouth twisted into a frown. "That is, I was happy until I told R. T."

Donovan flinched, as if he might shrug off the sudden ache in his chest. "Not quite up to fatherhood yet, was he?"

Laughing bitterly, Lil said, "Oh, to the contrary. He was quite well acquainted with the joys of parenthood.

When I told him about you, he let me in on a little secret of his own—that he was already married, and the father of a young son."

That R. T. had a son older than Andrew caught Donovan by surprise. Trying to recall what little he knew about the Savage family, he thought back to society columns he'd perused and the endless commentaries on R. T. and his vast holdings, but couldn't remember reading much about his children.

"If you think that was a nasty surprise," said Lil, moving forward, "he also admitted that he'd managed to knock his wife up about the same time he got to me. Cute, huh? The very proper Mrs. Savage was expecting their second baby around the same time you were due!"

Had that child been *Andrew*? Donovan wondered with a start. How could fate have been so cruel as to have sat him beside his own half brother, then made him witness the man's death? He felt sick inside at the thought, then recalled the days and nights he'd dreamed of having a real family—only the fictional family included a cute, impish little sister with eyes like his and a mop of coppery curls. Now it sounded as if part of the family he'd fabricated for himself had been living just across town for most of his life.

Unaware of her son's turmoil, Lil continued. "There isn't much more to tell. R. T. had a legal wife with legal children, and I was on the outside, looking in. After our horrid fight the day he told me about his other family, I thought I'd never see him again. But he showed up shortly after you were born, then every six months or so for a few years, filling both our heads with promises and tales of the day we'd all be together."

"R. T. was going to leave his wife and family for us?"

Lil laughed again, more bitterly than before. "That's what he kept saying, and fool that I was, I believed him at first because, I guess . . . because I wanted to so badly. By the time his wife had her baby after you were born, making three legal sons for R. T., it finally occurred to me that he was just keeping me on the side, and that he'd never leave her."

Slowly rising from the desk, Donovan shoved his hands in his pockets and strolled thoughtfully to the tiny window behind his mother's spindle-back chair. He contemplated the dark alleys and shadowed corners beyond the glass, and how different his life might have been had R. T. been free to marry Lil. Then he shrugged the thought off and turned to face his mother again, understanding her a little better, if still disillusioned by all he'd learned in one short afternoon.

In a hollow voice he asked, "How was R. T. around me? Did he claim me as his son?"

She nodded half-heartedly. "He always wanted to play with you, and tried to get me to change your name from William." She gave a little smirk. "By then, I'd taken to calling him 'William,' like the others. He didn't much like it, but he kept coming around until you were a little better than five."

Memories of his fifth year on this earth were strong to him, and suddenly Donovan had an idea as to why. He remembered the kind man, the one he liked best of his mother's friends, teaching him the finer points of pitching pennies, letting him win one just so he'd know the thrill of feeling the spoils of victory against his palm. Donovan tapped the toe of his boot against his mother's chair now, rattling the coin in the heel, and knew somehow without any clear recollection of the incident, that R. T. Savage had been the one who'd given him that penny.

"Donovan?" said Lil. "Are you still listening?"

"Is there more?"

"Not too much. It was about that time that I decided I just couldn't take his lies anymore, or the way he always got you worked up about being a whole family someday." Lil paused, deep in thought, her brow furrowed with far more wrinkles than she ever allowed to show. "After one of his hurried visits, I packed us up and moved us to San Francisco to get away from him."

Donovan nodded thoughtfully, vaguely remembering the rushed move, the sense of urgency, or maybe desperation, in his mother as she made arrangements for their journey. Something else about that impetuous relocation teased the back of his mind, a dark thing he'd buried good and tight, sealed, perhaps forever. Even if he'd had the desire to break the seal and dig the thing up—which at this point, he did not—Donovan wouldn't have had the chance, as Lil went ahead with her story.

"R. T. lived in Sacramento at the time, so you can imagine my surprise when he struck gold and decided to head for San Francisco, too. I thought of running again, but we were just getting settled, and since I figured he wouldn't be anxious to find us anyway, I decided to stay. I guess I figured wrong."

"I guess you did." Feeling too troubled by today's revelations to discuss the past any longer, Donovan headed for the door. "Thanks for being so honest—at last. I have to go now."

Lil placed a hand on his arm. "All right. I can understand your wanting to go off on your own right now, but would you mind if I ask you a couple of questions first?" Donovan glanced over his shoulder and gave her a short nod. "When R. T., ah, when he talked with you today, did he, ah, ask about me?"

"You bet," he said through a heavy sigh. "He wanted to know if you sent me to him. At first, of course, I didn't know what the hell he was talking about."

"You didn't tell him I'm here in the city, did you?"

He shook his head. "By the time I'd figured out what he was trying to say, I was so shaken up, I just got up and ran out of his office."—which reminded Donovan that he'd left Andrew's satchel behind. "I don't know what R. T.'s thinking about either of us right now—but I have an idea, it isn't good."

"If we're lucky, maybe he's not thinking about us at all." Lil gave his arm a little squeeze. "Two more things, Donovan—one, if you do run into him again, promise you won't ever tell him that I'm here. I couldn't bear it if he knew, if he were to descend from his lofty heights to look down his nose at me."

Still running, Lil?, Donovan wanted to ask her. But, since he'd come for information, not to hurt her, he said, "All right. If he asks, your whereabouts are unknown. What else?"

"I want you to swear that you won't try to see R. T. Savage again, that you will never let him become a part of your life and . . . and let him take you away from me."

This from a woman who was so wrapped up in herself and her fading youth that she couldn't bring herself to admit to the world that she even *had* a grown son? Donovan swiveled to face Lil head on. "Since when did you get so motherly?"

She started to speak, but looked away from him instead and hung her head.

Lil's veiled expression wasn't lost on Donovan. He'd seen that shuttered look in her eyes many times before, knew that his mother was a woman of many secrets. Until today, he'd never realized how many she'd kept from him, but he did grasp that she was hiding something more now. He knew in his gut there was more to this story than she'd confessed, but whatever it was, Lil had no intention of discussing it now. Probably, never.

"Donovan?" As he studied her, he could hardly believe that she suddenly looked old and painted, used up like some of the actresses she hired. "You know I'm not the type to grovel, but in this, I'm begging you. Promise me you'll never go to him again."

He opened the door and walked through it, then slammed it behind him—but still he heard his mother's voice: "Donovan?"

At the bar, her spectacles still perched on the bridge of her nose, Libby eyed her glass, which was almost empty—again. She wondered briefly what the devil she was doing, sitting here drinking brandy in the middle of the day, but then shoved the snifter toward Goldy anyway. It was all because of Donovan and his secret meetings, she decided, because of Donovan and his private "discussions" with voluptuous harlots in enticing blue gowns. All his fault. As usual.

Her gloved fingers curling into fists, she considered storming the office and demanding that he escort her back to Savage Publishing so she could conduct her business at last. Before she could decide what to do next or act on the plan, from the corner of her eye, she spotted a figure bulldozing his way through the crowd. And he was headed toward the bar. Adjusting the tilt of her glasses, Libby peered through them to better make out his features. It was Donovan, as she'd suspected, looking angry and much the way he had when he'd come bursting through Savage's doors just hours earlier. What the devil was going on with that man—and when was he going to let her in on the secret?

When he reached her, he spoke in the same monotone as before and used almost the same words. "Come on, Libby. We're leaving."

In defiance, she pounded both fists against the pitted bar top. "Just a blasted minute. I'm tired of you saying,

'Come on, let's go,' then dragging me here and there. I demand to know what's going on, and what you were doing for so long in that woman's office!"

Donovan moved closer to Libby's little stool and narrowed his gaze. "It's a very private matter, and one I don't want to talk about right now. Why don't we talk about you instead. How many drinks have you had?"

Deeply offended, Libby threw back her shoulders and, in so doing, almost flung herself off the stool. Donovan reached out to break her fall, but by then, Libby had managed to collect herself. Peering up at him, wondering why his image was so fuzzy even though she was still wearing her glasses, she asked suspiciously, "Have you been drinking? You're all wobbly."

"Oh, Christ," he muttered. "You're half shot."

"Am not."

Libby indignantly lifted her chin, but Donovan didn't even seem to notice the gesture. He just reached over and adjusted her glasses, which had somehow gone cockeyed on her. Now she could see him much better, enough to notice that he no longer looked as mad as he had crossing the room. In fact, she'd never seen him looking better. His eyes were all sparkly, both gray and blue, and his mouth was curved at the corners, just the way she liked it. A sudden warmth bloomed in Libby's breast, making her think for a moment of leaning forward and kissing him. She parted her lips and sighed instead, feeling dreamy all over and maybe even a little bit in love.

"Do you know," she whispered thickly, "that you have the most beautiful eyes I have *ever* seen?"

"Oh, Libby—Christ . . ." He rolled those gorgeous eyes, then gripped her elbow. "Come on, let's go."

"In a minute. First I have to tell you that I think . . ." Recalling what Dell had said about flirting with a man, she batted her lashes, making herself dizzy, and damn near fell off the stool again. "I think you're wonnerful. Just *wonnerful*, even if you are a lying 'Willy.'"

He barked a laugh, or something close to it, then muttered, "You were right, Libby—you're not half shot. You're stinking drunk."

"Am . . ." She swung her arms wide, deeply and belligerently offended. "Not!"

And then, much to her horror, she did fall off the bar stool.

6

Libby's eyes were closed when a sudden wave of dizziness swept over her, then her stomach churned and rolled, threatening, for a moment, to erupt. Was she on a boat? Again her stomach churned, this time bringing up an acid taste of bile. The sensation reminded Libby that in her excitement this morning, she hadn't been able to eat a bite of breakfast. The cherry brandy she'd gulped, she realized much too late, had been sloshing around in her empty belly with nothing to do but addle her brain. "Food," she said thickly to no one in particular. "I need some food."

"As soon as we get home."

Donovan's voice. Yes, sparkly-eyed Donovan with the handsome face and naughty mouth was taking her home. Feeling as if she existed in spirit only—her body was no longer spinning, but numb, as if it had flown to another planet—she comprehended in the muddied depths of her sluggish brain that he'd carried her out of the saloon and hoisted her into a carriage. And he was taking her home.

Moments later, at least that's the way it seemed to her, Libby opened her eyes and found herself standing in her fluffy bedroom in his house. Donovan had his arms around her, holding her close—or up. Had she fallen asleep in the carriage?

"How are you feeling now?" he asked.

"I . . . I don't know." She no longer felt dreamy, but sluggish all over, and her vision was a little bit hazy. She reached up to adjust her spectacles only to discover them missing. "My glasses!"

"I have them." Donovan reached into his jacket pocket, then leaned over and carefully set her eye wear on the bedside table. "I took them for safekeeping. Can you stand alone now?"

The moment he released her, Libby swayed.

"I guess not." Taking her back in his arms, Donovan walked her to the edge of the bed and gently sat her down.

"Thanks," she muttered, too ashamed of herself to look him in the eye.

"You're more than welcome." Donovan went on as if nothing were out of order, his voice reflecting neither amusement nor disgust. "Gerda was here this morning, and I'm sure she left some food behind. If you'd still like something to eat, I'll go downstairs and fix a sandwich for you before I leave."

She'd been starving earlier, but now, all she wanted to do was lie down. Libby shook her head. "I'm not feeling well enough to eat right now. And what do you mean, leave? You're not going away again, are you?"

"I have to."

At Donovan's grim tone, Libby looked up to see there wasn't so much as a spark of amusement in his eyes—in fact they seemed flat, steel-like. "What's the matter? You're carrying on like the world's come to an end."

"I have some chores to attend to, is all. Nothing for you to worry about. Will you be all right?"

Eventually, she supposed. Libby glanced in his direction and noticed that her new hat was sitting atop the dresser. The pert little straw crown had been mashed flat and the roses and ostrich plume appeared to be crushed.

"My stars!" she cried. "What happened to my new hat?"

Donovan's mouth puckered as if he were trying mightily not to laugh. "You took exception to a carriage which was following ours up the street. I believe its horse was blowing and snorting too loudly to suit you, so you threw your hat at it."

Libby gasped and brought her hand to her mouth. "*No*, I didn't."

"Oh, yes. I'm afraid you did. By the time we got the carriages stopped, the horse and the cab had run over it."

Closing her eyes as much in shame as horror, Libby groaned.

"Why don't you lie down? After you take a nap, you'll be feeling a lot better. Maybe you can even fix the hat." He started for the door and paused as he opened it. "Is there anything else you need before I go?"

There was a hell of a lot more she needed, and had she not been full of cherry brandy, Libby was fairly certain she'd have known exactly how to express those needs. As it was, she could hardly make sense of the fact that, once again, Donovan was leaving her to fend for herself.

"I guess not," she whispered, defeated. It wasn't until after he'd closed the door behind him that Libby remembered she'd failed—once again—in her mission to save the *Laramie Tribune*. Then she thought of her mother and the even more significant promise she'd made to her, and at last, Libby fell back against her pillows. And cried until she fell asleep.

*   *   *

She slept like a great pile of rocks, waking once just long enough to take several desperate gulps of water from the pitcher on the bed stand before collapsing in slumber again. As the night moved steadily toward dawn, Libby woke again, this time refreshed and, at last, herself again. On the heels of this discovery, she realized that she was absolutely ravenous. Remembering that Gerda usually left a bundle of rolls and several nice fat sausages on her cleaning day, she threw back the covers, stumbled out of bed, then made her way out of the bedroom and down the staircase in the dark.

Once in the hallway that led to the kitchen, Libby was surprised to find a dim glow spilling out of the kitchen to light her way. As she stepped inside the room, she discovered the source—a small lamp sitting on the stove. Assuming that Donovan had lit it for her benefit, should she awaken in the dark, she smiled at the thought as she lifted the towel off the basket of rolls. Maybe he did care about her just a little. Humming to herself now, Libby was on her way to the icebox for the sausages, when a deep male voice came at her from the shadows near the back door.

"Where the hell's your clothes?"

"Oh, my Lord!" With a shriek, Libby flung a roll into the air. "Donovan?" she asked, peering into the darkened corner near the door. "Is that you?"

"No, actually, it's not."

The man took a step toward her, the light catching enough of him to illuminate the lower half of his body. All Libby could tell for sure, was that the man looked as if he were in the middle of undressing. His shirttails were out of his trousers and hanging down below his waist. Surely this had to be Donovan home from the saloon. It sounded like him, and yet . . .

"Donovan? Y-you're scaring me." The man took another step toward her then, illuminating the features she knew so well. "Oh, for heaven's sake! Why didn't you just say it was you, instead of trying to frighten me half to death?"

She expected him to burst out laughing over his little joke, but his features remained somber like his voice. "Donovan's gone," he muttered thickly. "I don't know where he went. I'm R. T. Savage's bastard son."

He didn't laugh over this reference to his earlier chicanery, and neither did Libby. She still didn't see much funny about his pretending to be Andrew Savage.

Donovan moved completely out of the shadows then, revealing himself to be in a rather unruly state. He'd stripped down to his trousers and shirt—his jacket, vest, and necktie were flung sloppily over one of two kitchen chairs—and looked as if he was in the midst of discarding even more of his apparel. His shirt was completely unbuttoned, exposing a wide expanse of his chest, down to his waist. Libby couldn't help but notice the slender triangle of dark hair at his breastbone, or keep her inquisitive eyes from following that narrow band of hair to where it disappeared, like the tail of a kite, beneath the waist of his trousers.

"What're you looking at?" he suddenly asked, causing Libby to jerk her gaze away from areas in which it had no business.

"I—I didn't realize you were getting undressed in here."

He started for her, staggering a bit, she thought, and came to a halt just a whisper away. "It's my house. I can run naked here if I want to. What's your excuse?"

The sharp tang of brandy, or something like it, curled under her nostrils, both gagging and amusing her. So the tables had turned, had they? Donovan was staring hard at her, trying his damnedest to look rigid, maybe even angry, as he waited for her answer—but not quite carrying it off. His eyes, though struggling to bore into her, were languid, the silvery accents usually so ice-like, now soft like flakes from an early snow. Libby had seen her father looking this way before, not in the eyes so much, but in his general appearance, especially during the months after the death of her mother. Something dreadful had happened to Donovan during the past twenty-four hours, a crisis of some kind which had left him badly in need of comfort.

Of course Libby couldn't think what to do for him because she didn't know what his troubles were. "I'm sorry to have come downstairs without dressing, but I had no idea you'd be home, and certainly not that you'd be standing here in the kitchen." She touched the lacy collar at her throat, making sure she was properly buttoned up. "If you'd like, I'll go back upstairs. Do you mind if I take along a little snack with me? I never did eat anything yesterday."

"Don' go." Hesitant and unsure at first, Donovan reached out and touched her arm, massaging the upper part of it through her worn cotton nightdress. Light glistened around his head at the movement, reflections from the lamp bouncing off the pearls of moisture in his rumpled, fog-dampened hair. Something stirred in her belly at the sight, then warmed her down low as she stared up at him in the murky darkness. A new kind of hunger gnawed at her insides, and she realized in an instant that the sensation had nothing to do with a need for sustenance. Donovan was what she craved. Only Donovan.

Still looking at her in that odd, stern-but-amused way, he went on talking as if he'd never paused. "I've had a really rotten night. Sorry if I took it out on you."

She instinctively reached up and cupped the edge of his jaw with her palm, as a mother might comfort her child. "What's happened to you, Donovan? Is there some way I can help?"

He laughed, just a dash of hysteria setting the tone. "Ah, that you could, you adorable little ink-slinger. That you could." Moving even closer, almost, but not quite, pressing the length of his body along hers, Donovan inched his fingers up her forearm until his hand covered hers, which was still at the side of his face. "What's done is done, and nobody can make it right. The me you knew is simply not here anymore." Again he laughed, a kind of plaintive sound now. "Isn't that a hoot?"

As a newspaperwoman, Libby had interviewed people from all walks of life, and helped her father in the business since the age of ten. In that time, she had learned to read and understand even the quirkiest of characters. Although Donovan wasn't making that much sense now, Libby realized she'd had a peek under his cool veneer and found that he wasn't nearly so impervious to pain and the world around him as he pretended to be. He'd been wounded tonight, perhaps, badly, even though he'd tried to laugh off his troubles. She'd seen the anguish weaving in and out of his expression as he spoke, here one minute, gone the next. What could have happened to him over the last few hours? Did it have something to do with his partner?

"What're you looking at now?" he asked, head bowed low, his forehead practically touching hers.

She hadn't realized it until he said something, but Libby had been staring at Donovan's mouth, half out of her mind with thoughts of what he and Lil might have been up to in her office all that time. Reacting impulsively to his words and her own thoughts, she leaned up on tiptoe, then favored him with the gentlest kiss imaginable. When she released him and leaned back, he just stood there staring down at her in the semi-darkness, a new look drifting across his rapidly changing expression. This was one of utter confusion.

"Why the hell did you do that?" Donovan asked, feeling as if his mind and even his body were spinning.

She shrugged. "Because you looked like you needed it. Did you mind so awfully much?"

Mind? Hell, yes, he minded. Nobody had ever kissed him like that before—as if he were worthy of anything more than a few moments of lust—nobody. And he sure as hell hadn't been prepared to experience such a gesture from Miss Liberty Justice, of all people. Since their impulsive moment of passion the day she'd learned his true identity, he'd gone out of his way to make sure something like that wouldn't happen again.

In fact, he'd been struggling for the past ten days with that very chore, and had managed to do what he had to in order to live in the same house with Libby. He'd even learned to look at her without really seeing her, which wasn't easy, given the way her cute little freckles kissed every time she laughed and puckered her button of a nose. He'd done a damn fine job of it, too. Until this moment. Now that she'd gone and kissed him, and in such a somehow more intimate way, how was he to continue ignoring his own responses to her—especially tonight, of all nights?

Or, maybe he didn't have to ignore those responses. Now that he'd been stripped of his identity, left raw and exposed, he was a member of the esteemed Savage clan. Good enough for any woman, he supposed, even the virginal Liberty Ann Justice. And she was lush and real, standing before him with her unbound hair spilling down around the shoulders of her white cotton gown. Surely this seductive, but innocent angel would have no objections to losing her halo to someone with the revered Savage credentials.

Convincing himself more thoroughly, no longer caring about the former limits he'd set on himself, Donovan let himself wonder how Libby's lush auburn locks would feel between his fingers, should he plunge his hands into them. Like satin, he thought, or maybe softer, like the petals of a fragrant blood-red rose. For sure, he thought, giving himself freer rein, her hair would smell of rose petals, should he bury his face in it, like flowers and sunshine.

"Donovan?" she whispered softly, breaking into his delicious thoughts. "Are you all right?"

He opened his eyes, unaware until then that he'd even closed them, and gripped her shoulders for balance. "No, I'm not. Is anyone?"

Chuckling, the sound low and husky, she put her arms around his waist and laid her head against his chest. "I was wondering if you'd fallen asleep standing up, is all—not if you were . . . sane."

"I didn't fall asleep," he muttered, folding his arms around her, squeezing her tight. "And I'm for sure not sane. If I were, I wouldn't be doing anything so crazy as this."

She raised her head. "As crazy as what? Giving me a hug?"

"That, and this, too." He brushed his lips across hers. "And this."

His mouth went back to hers, where he nuzzled more than kissed her, then Donovan's fingers found the buttons at the collar of her nightgown. He struggled with them mightily and, when they were finally free, his lips trailed down along her neck to settle at the hollow of her throat. When the pulse there lurched in response, throbbing strongly against his mouth, he raised his head to try and gauge Libby's true reaction. Her brown eyes seemed black in the murky light, alive with passion. Nowhere in her expression could he detect so much as a spark of the censure he'd expected to find. The look which would tell him he'd gone far enough. Who did she think was kissing her? he wondered. William Donovan, or Donovan Savage?

He couldn't remember how much he'd told her, and suddenly, he didn't want to know. Feeling was all that mattered now, touching her, and tasting those sweet lips once again. Before Donovan fully realized what he intended to do next, he had Libby back in his fierce embrace, his lips fused to hers. Then he dragged her to the kitchen table, where he bent her backward over the redwood top. He was vaguely aware of a chair clattering to the floor as he lifted her hips fully up onto the slab of wood, of glass shattering as he cleared a path upon which she could lie; but he no longer cared about a thing, except the way Libby felt beneath him. Nothing mattered except this moment.

She sighed as Donovan deepened the kiss, the sound gruff and needy, and that was all he needed by way of permission to indulge this suddenly urgent, reckless passion. Still kissing her thoroughly, he slid one of his legs firmly between Libby's and fit his thigh against the gentle rise of her womanhood. Then, responding to her guttural moan at the contact, he reached up to the open collar of her nightgown and yanked the remaining buttons free of their embroidered slots.

Libby's breasts, so warm, full, and almost completely exposed, rose up to meet Donovan's fevered gaze, inviting him in. Unable—or unwilling—to ignore the call, he buried his face in the deep, soft valley there, nuzzling her and thinking he could be quite content to lie between those satiny pillows for the rest of his life. Libby apparently had other ideas. With a throaty groan, she pushed against his chest, her slender fingers fiery against his skin, and separated him from her bosom.

"Donovan, please," she gasped, her breathless voice both wispy and harsh. "Please . . ."

Engulfed by now with undeniable need, especially where his body throbbed incessantly against Libby's heaving belly, he didn't stop to question her request. Innocent that she was, he assumed she needed more privacy—and a softer bed.

"You're right," he ground out between shaky breaths. "We'll go upstairs . . . *now*."

7

He was floating, not as if on water, but among the clouds. The soft billowing puffs of his dreams were not white in color, but cinnamon, the lighter tendrils fog-like, catching fire as he drifted beneath the sun. Donovan's clouds were also unusual in that they seemed made of silk, just like Libby's hair. They even smelled like her, of rose petals—no, wait—roses were what he'd expected; but since he'd actually inhaled it, he thought perhaps the scent had been more like lilacs. Yes, lilacs and springtime, he remembered, recalling at the same time her sweet, breathless voice begging him "please" . . .

As his sluggish brain processed the information, Donovan bolted upright in his bed. Christ! What had he done? Where had she gone? *"Libby?"* he called groggily; but there was no answer. Had he dreamed it all?

His headache caught up with him then, slamming against the inside of his forehead. After giving the pain a few moments to quiet itself a little, Donovan climbed out of bed and reached for his trousers.

*   *   *

Still lying on the mattress, beneath the downy quilt that matched everything in her frilly room, Libby listened to the cries of seagulls as they called to one another. Love songs? she wondered idly. Turning her head toward the open window in hopes of catching a glimpse of the birds, she noticed a pair of flies on the glass, one stacked upon the other in what she assumed was a copulatory embrace. She sighed heavily, just as the yowl of a love-starved alley cat rent the air. Everyone and everything seemed to be indulging their passions. Everyone except Liberty Ann Justice.

Her thoughts automatically slid back to the topic she'd dwelled on since coming across him in the kitchen—Donovan. She'd never really given it a lot of deep thought, but Libby had always assumed that she could live the rest of her life quite happily without ever knowing the intimate embrace of a man. But that was before she'd met Donovan; before he'd touched her, stirring up the kind of yearnings she knew would never settle again until he relieved the quaking inside her.

But could she have given herself to him so easily?, Libby wondered for the thousandth time. If she had allowed Donovan to drag her down the hallway to his bedroom and fling her onto his bed, could she actually have gone through with letting him ravish her? Libby's belly quivered as she pondered what all making love might entail; then she restlessly rolled to her side.

She wished fervently that she had a few answers about the subject. Most women's rights leaders, including Libby's hero, Susan B. Anthony, championed the notion of taking a lover without benefit of marriage, noting that men had long enjoyed this freedom without public chastisement. Etiquette, popular opinion, and—

had he lived to see her through this dilemma—Libby's father, all would demand that a woman remain virtuous until the day she wed. Where would her mother have stood on the issue? Libby wondered, suddenly missing her more than she had in a long, long time. Would her mother have embraced even this most radical dictate of the equal rights proponents, or sided with the more temperate suffragists who did not view sexual freedom as one of the "spoils of war"?

If only her mother had lived to see Libby begin to bud as a woman; then, at least, Libby'd have some idea of what to do the next time Donovan put his hands on her—if he ever tried again when he was sober. Libby's thoughts returned to her mother, and a single teardrop rolled down her cheek. The only advice she'd gotten from her mother regarding men, was never to let any of them tell her she wasn't as good or as smart as they were. Upon realizing that she'd lost sight of that goal in her preoccupation with Donovan, Libby almost gave into the urge to bury her face in the pillow and weep until she was cried out, and might have, had the man in question not barged into her room just then, without so much as knocking on the door.

"You—you're still here!" He looked dazed, disoriented.

"Are you disappointed?"

"No, just . . . surprised."

Donovan finished buttoning his shirt, giving Libby the impression that he'd been dressing himself on the way to her room. If its rumpled appearance was any indication, it was the same shirt he'd been wearing the last time she'd seen him.

"After the way I treated you last night, I wasn't sure you'd want to spend another day under the same roof with me." Yet he barged into her room as if she'd invited him to do so.

Amused, but slightly irritated, too, Libby folded her arms across her breasts. "Which treatment are you talking about? Are you trying to apologize for the way you fondled me in the kitchen or the way you tried to drag me into your bedroom after we went upstairs?"

"Hell, don't hold anything back, Libby," he said sarcastically. "Do tell me exactly what's on your mind."

"I just did. If you're not here to apologize, then what do you want?"

Sighing, Donovan rubbed his hands across his face, careful to avoid his eyeballs, which felt as if they might explode. Christ, why had he drunk so much last night, especially with nothing but a couple of sweet rolls in his belly? He should have waited for this little confrontation until he was better equipped to do battle.

"I did come here to apologize, and for both treatments. I don't usually get liquored-up like that. In fact, I rarely take more than one or two drinks. In my line of work, it doesn't pay for a drunk to be looking after the other rum suckers."

In spite of her foul mood, Libby chuckled softly, propped her pillows beneath her, and raised up a little. "I forgive you for that since I have an apology to make along the same lines. I don't usually drink so much cherry brandy either, and certainly not during daylight hours. I'm willing to call it even on that score, if you are."

"It's a deal." Looking weary, he went on to ask, "I realize this may not be the best time for you, but would it be all right if we talked a little now?"

Though, once again, it wouldn't be the right or proper thing to do, Libby had far too many unanswered questions to let anything so ambiguous as propriety get in the way now. She waved him forward. "You're welcome to stay, as long as you promise to give me a few straight answers for a change."

Nodding, Donovan walked over to Libby's dressing table, removed the little wicker chair, and dragged it over to the edge of the bed. Sinking heavily onto the chair, he balanced his weight as the delicate piece of furniture sagged and creaked beneath him. Then he rubbed his forehead again. "Christ," he said, groaning, "but I feel like hell."

"My sympathies, since I know what that feels like, after my turn in purgatory yesterday. My memory's understandably a little hazy about what happened at Lucky Lil's; but, if I recall, you brought me home and left me here to sleep, while you went on some great mission. Did it have something to do with Savage Publishing?"

"Everything, actually."

Donovan finally lifted his head to meet Libby's gaze. "Well? What happened?" she prompted him.

"You'll never believe it."

Libby sat straight up, making sure the quilt still covered her decently. "Let me decide that."

Donovan wished she hadn't made such an inviting statement, or chosen that moment to adjust her position. Now the quilt was draped low enough to show him that the buttons at the throat of her nightdress were opened—which in turn reminded him of exactly who had unbuttoned them, and how the exquisite softness just below that opening had felt against his lips. He hadn't been so drunk as to forget that.

He cleared his throat and glanced away from the tantalizing sight. "This is probably going to sound real funny to you," he began, feeling like an idiot, "and probably familiar as hell. What would you say if I were to tell you that I really am the son of R. T. Savage?"

Libby's spine stiffened, as did her jaw. "I'd say that you'd better get out of my room before I find something to throw at your head!" She punctuated the sentence by reaching for the pitcher at her bedside.

"Now, Libby . . ."

"As I've warned you before, don't 'Now, Libby' me, especially not while all the humiliating memories of yesterday are still so fresh in my mind—'*Willy.*'"

"Goddammit stop calling me that! There isn't one thing funny about that name to me, and if you *ever* use it again, I won't be responsible for my actions—understand?"

Libby shrank back, suddenly looking tiny and wide-eyed in the folds of the big quilt. Donovan paused to get hold of himself, feeling sick to think that he'd scared her so badly. While the sound of that nickname had always irritated him, now that he'd learned the truth of how the *sobriquet* had evolved, the very thought of it filled him with rage.

Calmer, but still angry, Donovan said, "I came here to talk a few things out with you. Do you want to do that, or trade insults? Make up your mind."

Libby pressed her lips together firmly, then parted them enough to say, "Let's talk."

"All right, then, here it is, straight out. When I first went to see R. T. yesterday, he as much as came right out and told me I was his son."

"Oh, please—"

"Patience, Libby, or I won't tell the rest of the story." Her back was up by now, which relieved Donovan's conscience. He hadn't cared in the slightest for the fear he'd seen in her eyes, especially since he'd been the one to put it there. "Savage recognized my name from long ago, saw my face—which, by the way, looks a little like his—and deduced that I was his long-lost son. I, on the other hand, had no inkling that he was my father. So, without much by way of a response, I ran out of the office to check his claims."

"Don't tell me it checked out." Libby's expression still registered doubt, but he could hear just a touch of speculation in her tone. So she hadn't known his true identity last night. Is that why she'd sent him packing to his own room?

Suddenly grumpy, he snapped, "Yes, it checked out. R. T. Savage definitely is my father."

Libby stared hard at him for a long moment. "You swear this isn't another of your lies?"

Donovan crossed his heart, then held up his right hand, for good measure. "May I never fill a straight again as long as I live if I'm not telling the truth."

"Oh, my God." Her eyes were round with surprise, but he could read her well enough to know that she finally believed him.

"Precisely my reaction at first, since I had a little trouble believing it myself. But after I checked with Lil, who had the information I needed, I went back to see him."

"Your business partner knew about Savage?"

He nodded thoughtfully, wondering if he should explain about his mother, but decided that he had enough to untangle already. "Lil is a very . . . enterprising woman. She happened to have the information I needed to confirm that R. T. was my father. Shortly after we finished talking, I found you pie-eyed at the bar."

Libby folded her arms across her breasts and frowned. "I thought we'd called a draw on talk such as that."

"You're right—forgive me?"

"I guess so." Her mouth fell into a pout, but her eyes were amused. "So you brought me home, then took off. Where did you go after you left?"

"I headed right back to Savage Publishing, of course, to finish up a few loose ends." In spite of his mother's plea, he'd been unable—unwilling, he supposed—to make that final promise to her. Not yet, anyway. Not until he'd gotten the chance to know the man at least a little better. "When I ran out of R. T.'s office earlier, I left Andrew's satchel behind, without explaining anything about it, or even mentioning the fact that he'd been murdered."

"Oh, Lord." Libby gasped. "I'd forgotten about him. If you're R. T.'s . . . oh, Lord." She immediately thought of Jeremy and the fact that she'd been away from Laramie for so long. Guilt adding to the emotions rising in her throat, Libby swallowed hard. "I guess that makes—made—Andrew your brother."

"Half brother, yes, it would seem that he was." He thought back to the poker game on the train and sadly shook his head. "I only met him that one time, but the truth is, I didn't much like him." Donovan wondered briefly if knowing that the man was his brother would have made any difference. He thought not. "Once I told R. T. about Andrew, he naturally got quite upset. The last thing I figured he'd want to talk about was freedom of the press, so I didn't mention you or the *Laramie Tribune* at all."

"Oh, well, of course not. I can certainly understand, there was no place in the conversation for my problems."

"There really wasn't a place to discuss anything but Andrew, once that was out in the open. R. T. said he needed a couple of days to collect his thoughts and to make arrangements for Andrew. He promised me that, as soon as he was able, he'd send a messenger here to summon me."

"Summon you?" What an odd way to invite a long-lost son to visit. "That sounds like a subpoena or something."

"That's probably exactly what it is, Libby. He doesn't know a damn thing about me, except that I carry his blood."

"Oh, I hadn't thought of that." She softly sighed. "All this must be terribly difficult for you."

Maybe, Donovan thought to himself, but he had an idea it hadn't been nearly as hard on him as what he had to do next might be. He must convince this stubborn woman to return to her home. Christ, but he couldn't wait to get Libby out of his house, out of his mind. This had been, without a doubt, the longest ten days of his life. Last night alone had seemed interminable, especially after he'd gotten her up the stairs, and she'd fled for the safety of her own room. He'd come so close, so very, very close to breaking down her door and taking her then—his conscience be damned— that he could hardly look her in the eye this morning. Just thinking of how close he'd come to defiling the only decent woman who'd ever passed through his life made him more determined than ever to send her away.

His tone brooking no disagreement, Donovan launched what he hoped would be a convincing argument for her to get the hell out of town. "Given the circumstances, I think you ought to return to Laramie immediately. I can take care of everything from here on out. Even when R. T. sends for me, I won't know what kind of mood he'll be in or if there will be an opening to bring your troubles up. It could be another week or so before we get around to talking about the *Tribune*."

As usual, Libby's first impulse was to disagree, but then she thought of Jeremy, and hesitated. Would it be fair or even plausible to leave him and the newspaper without her guidance for another week? She considered the wire she'd received from Hymie yesterday, insisting all was well, then recalled the note Jeremy had added requesting that she please bring him back some kind of souvenir from one of the famous San Francisco cable cars, even if it were only a splinter of wood. Nowhere had he mentioned missing her, or even made inquiries about her return. There wasn't a reason in the world to think that Jeremy and crew would be anything other than fine if she were to extend her stay a little.

Her mind made up, Libby smiled broadly as she said, "I wouldn't dream of leaving, now that you've found your father. In fact, this could even make one of those great, weepy stories R. T. likes so much. Why, if he'll let me, maybe I'll write it up for both the *San Francisco* and *Laramie Tribune*s!"

"Oh . . . *Christ*, Libby." His hands against his face again, Donovan heaved himself off the wicker chair and went to stand in front of the window. "You don't quite understand, do you? I'm the *bastard* son, the one he wants to hide. He doesn't give a shit—excuse me, he doesn't care about me at all. In fact, R. T. is probably considering ways of paying me off right now, so that I *won't* claim him as a father. I doubt he wants that information splashed across the fronts of his newspapers." His gaze flickering to her, he added, "Why don't you just give up and go on home? I swear to God, I'll do everything I can here on your behalf."

"I'm not going, Donovan."

Looking back out the window to Gerda's herb garden below, he shook his head, wondering what it would take, short of shanghaiing her, to get this mulish female back where she came from. The next thing he knew, though he hadn't heard her get out of bed, Libby was standing behind him, whispering against the back of his ear.

"I can't wait to meet the man fool enough to turn a fine son like you away." She spoke in dulcet tones, a warm spill of honey to sweeten the bitterness in his heart. "And even if he doesn't want to hear about my troubles at the *Tribune* or won't allow me to print a story about your reunion with him, I still want to go."

She gently laid her head against Donovan's back, then slipped her arms around his waist and gave his middle a light squeeze. "I'm in this with you all the way."

At her touch, Donovan lurched forward a little, his knuckles white where he gripped the windowsill for balance. Goddammit, he thought, drawing in a deep breath to ease the frustration building inside him. This was not what he wanted for himself or for Libby, no matter how fast he always responded to her touch. She was *not* the kind of woman he wanted chasing after him; and she for sure was *not* the kind he could easily bed, no matter how hard his body tried to convince him otherwise. What in God's name did he have to do to convince *her* of that—move another woman in here with him?

As he toyed with the idea, sure that Libby wouldn't stay under the same roof should he make such an arrangement, her voice caressed the back of his ear again, this time smoky and seductive. "I'm sorry for, well, hollering at you the way I did after we got upstairs last night. You were a little drunk, and I was . . . a little scared, I guess."

Swearing softly under his breath, Donovan glanced down to where Libby's hands were clasped dangerously, if innocently, close to his waistband. He could feel each of her soft curves pressed against his body, knew from his previous explorations that all he need do was turn around and reach inside the folds of her nightgown to gain access to the woman. And, now that she knew he really was a Savage, he had an idea that she wouldn't discourage him so quickly.

Raw desire ripped through him in spite of his struggles against it, making him hate Libby at that moment almost as much as he wanted her. Using the hate to his advantage, Donovan broke her hands apart, then turned to launch his final argument against her staying in San Francisco.

"You had every right to be afraid of me. Hell, when I'm drunk, there's no telling who I'll chase after or what I'm liable to do." He forced a laugh. "It's a damn good thing Gerda doesn't stay over—for her, that is."

Libby didn't say a thing to that. She didn't have to. Her expression, a mix of hurt, confusion, and maybe even disgust, said it all.

"I'm the same man I've always been," he went on to explain, his voice harsh. "An honest sort most times, but capable of bilking a sharper when the circumstances leave me with no choice. Women don't fare much better around me."

"What are you trying to say, Donovan? You wanted me last night; but now that you've sobered up, you don't?"

"What I'm saying," he replied gruffly, too aware of her nearness, too unsure of his lightning responses to risk touching Libby even long enough to set her away from him, "is that I'm the kind of gambler who can find a pinprick between the eyes of the queen of spades just by sliding my fingertip across it—or put one there, if need be, just as easily. I'll cheat when necessary—on anyone, for any reason. You, on the other hand . . ." He paused, his eyes flickering over her prim and proper nightdress. "You, my dear lady, are the marrying kind. The kind who expects a man to be, well, something I'm not."

Libby heard every word he said, but for some reason, her mind refused to move past the thought of his fingers—and the fact that they were sensitive enough to detect marked cards. It made her wonder what those accomplished hands might do to her, should they caress her entire body.

Donovan exhaled impatiently. "Now do you see the problem with your staying here any longer?"

Libby forced her concentration back to the conversation, and gave him what he seemed to need so badly: reassurances. "There is no problem, really. When you consider my staunch support for equal rights, we should be a perfect match. I'm not the marrying kind, any more than you are."

"For Christ's sake, Libby, what does suffrage have to do with this? I'm talking about real people here, you and me. When I look at you, I see lace curtains, a neat little cottage, and a bunch of carrot-topped kids running amok in the vegetable garden. Me? I'm a bastard—a real one, you know—a gambler who doesn't always stay on the straight and narrow." Adding what he was sure would be the final inducement, he said, "I'm also a man who isn't terribly particular about who shares his bed."

Libby tried to turn away, but Donovan could see how much that statement stung her. He gripped her shoulders, keeping her in place, and made her listen to the rest of his argument. "What I'm not," he maintained, "is the sort who trifles with virginal types like you—in short, the kind of woman who'll want something from me in the morning that I simply can't give."

"Can't?" she asked. "Or won't?"

In this, Donovan refused to be baited. "Can't, which means I'm not even close to what you're looking for, Miss Justice. And I'm sure as hell not what you need."

She stood silent a long moment, her dark eyes impassive. When she finally spoke, her words were equally distant. "Thank you for being so candid. You're absolutely right—you're not the kind of man I'm looking for at all."

Libby tried to say this as if she believed it; but her gut kept insisting that he hadn't been entirely truthful with her—and that Donovan Savage was exactly what she needed.

*   *   *

Donovan's argument—especially the part about not being particular about who shared his bed—stayed with Libby for the next two days, grating like a dull saw on her already ragged nerves. Like it or not, however, she did understand why he might be reluctant to court a woman like her. Other than making sure her clothes were clean and pressed and that she was properly groomed, she'd never bothered too much with her appearance, and certainly not just to impress anyone of the male species. The night in Laramie when she'd borrowed Dell's dress didn't count since she hadn't been thinking of Donovan as a male, but simply as an employer she had to impress.

She thought of him as a male now. One, much to her chagrin, with whom she suspected she'd fallen a little bit in love. Thinking of doing more than impressing him—of attracting him—Libby'd dressed the day he'd "set her straight" in the new suit he'd purchased for her, then struggled to twist her hair into a rather attractive bun at the top of her head. She'd gone to a lot of trouble to present herself as femininely as possible that day, but the effort had turned out to have been a miserable waste of time. Donovan had hardly even glanced at her when he'd come downstairs, and then, instead of dining with her, had tossed off a flimsy excuse for leaving her alone and taken off into the night.

Today, she'd awakened in a foul mood, one that had made her feel so ornery, she'd donned her comfortable buckskins and rawhide boots. There'd been no point in bothering to primp for a man who showed no inclination to acknowledge her efforts. She'd even defiantly plaited her hair into a pair of braids, and let them hang down the front of her blouse—something she hadn't done in years. Then she'd gone to work. She had articles to write, and a plan to work out with regard to R. T. Savage and his rigid editorial rules. Never again would she allow anything, not even love, if that's what she felt for Donovan, to keep her from remembering the vow she'd made to her mother.

Dressed in that manner and sprawled in the middle of the living room rug with her pencils and writing pads, Libby'd spent the better part of the afternoon writing an article about the history of the cable railway for Jeremy and the *Laramie Tribune*. As she worked her way through the second revision of the piece, a knock sounded at the front door. At first, Libby wasn't inclined to answer the summons since it wasn't her house and she didn't know how Donovan would react to being disturbed during his rest. He'd slammed through the door a couple of hours ago, while she was in the kitchen, and dashed upstairs before she could make it down the hallway to stop him.

The knock sounded again, this time loud enough to rattle the glass in the bay window. Against her better judgment, Libby leaped to her feet and went to open the door.

Donovan's partner stood on the stoop, impatiently tapping her foot. For a moment, the woman looked stunned, as if lost. Then she leaned back, read the numbers nailed to the doorjamb, and looked inside the house again.

Eyeing Libby suspiciously, she asked, "Who the hell are you?"

Libby's first impulse was to slam the door in the redhead's face; instead, she responded in kind to the woman for whom she'd taken an instant dislike. "I'm Liberty Justice. Who the hell are you?"

Lil, although she'd yet to introduce herself, seemed taken aback for a moment. Then, with a toss of her vermilion curls and the bright yellow ostrich tips poking up from them, she boldly entered the house, the frilly skirts of her lemon-colored dress swishing against Libby's worn buckskin trousers as she brushed past her.

"Donovan?" she called, ignoring Libby entirely. She glanced inside the living room and then down the hallway. "Donovan, where are you?"

"He's upstairs resting . . . *ma'am*."

Libby addressed Lil by that term, not out of respect, but due to the age difference between them. This was the first time Libby was seeing the woman up close, let alone in the daylight. She clearly had at least fifteen years on Donovan. Why in the hell was he so attracted to this older woman? she wondered. Not that Lil wasn't pretty, in a cheap sort of way, and she supposed, appealing enough to the opposite sex. Then Libby remembered Donovan's remark about not being terribly particular about his lady friends; and the next thing she knew, Libby was boiling inside.

Gesturing to the still open door, she snapped, "I don't think Donovan wants to be disturbed. Why don't you come back later?"

"Humph. Fat chance, dearie." Apparently amused by something, Lil looked up and down the length of Libby's trousers, then noticed her pigtails. "Just exactly what are you doing here?" she asked, her voice sounding even more amused. "Are you filling in for Gerda? The newsboy? Or are you the gardener?"

Having the sudden urge to hit something, Libby turned and punched the door with her palm. Then she whirled back around toward Lil, forced a smile, and said, "No, ma'am, I happen to be the managing editor of the *Laramie Tribune*, a newspaper which is owned by Savage Publishing."

"*Savage?*" In the time it took her to repeat the name, Lil's cheeks flushed, almost matching her hair. "Did R. T. send you here to snoop around?"

As unsettled now by the overbearing woman as she was piqued, Libby started for the foot of the stairs. "I don't have to answer that, nor do I want to hear any more of your questions. I'll go see if Donovan's awake. Maybe he'll feel like talking to you about Savage Publishing—but I rather doubt it."

As she started up the stairs, Libby heard stiff petticoats and silk undergarments rustling like the feathers of a fighting cock. By the time the significance of that sound occurred to her, not to mention its growing loudness, it was too late.

Lil had already grabbed a handful of Libby's vest and blouse at the nape of her neck. Then she dragged her backwards down the stairs.

8

Rudely awakened by a woman's scream, Donovan lurched out of bed, and promptly fell to the floor.

He was just getting his bearings, when a second scream roared down the hallway, and this time, the voice sounded terribly familiar. *Libby?* Christ, who else could it be? She was the only one staying at his place, other than himself. He scrambled for a pair of trousers and hopped into them on the run, too concerned about what might be happening downstairs to worry about modesty. Although he hadn't time to fasten the buttons, he somehow managed to cover himself decently by the time he reached the top of the stairs.

The scene below on the tiled floor of the foyer—his mother on her knees, her right arm twisted and held painfully behind her back by Libby's vicious grasp—surprised and horrified Donovan so, he let go of his waistband.

His trousers slid down his legs at the exact moment that Libby glanced up to find him standing there. She gasped when she saw him gracing the top step in all his glory, but did not look away. Then, her gaze still pinned to him and her mouth opened in a perfect circle, she released her hold on Lil and slowly backed away from her.

Donovan quickly tugged his trousers up over his hips and set to buttoning them as he descended the stairs. "Christ, Almighty, what in hell is going on down here?"

Lil, still on her knees with her back to her son, moaned as she rubbed her shoulder. "Oh, Donovan, thank God you're home. This—this hoodlum here attacked me!"

"I did not." Libby pressed herself flat against the wall-paper, looking as if she were trying to hide among the trellises and grapevines pictured there. "She attacked me as I was coming upstairs to get you, Donovan."

He glanced from her to Lil, then shook his head. He hadn't thought the person existed—man nor woman—who could get the drop on his mother. Resisting the urge to congratulate Libby on her prowess, Donovan went to Lil's aid. Taking both her hands in his, he lifted her up off the floor, then studied her carefully. She was flushed, disheveled, and out of breath, but she looked more angry than injured. "Are you all right?" he asked, just to be sure.

Lil adjusted the bodice and skirts of her gown, then checked her coif, which was in a state of disarray. Frowning she said, "I think my shoulder's sprained, but other than that, I'm just a little shaken up, is all." She turned to glare at Libby. "No thanks to that crazy street urchin."

Libby bristled, not so much over those words, as over Donovan's attentions to the woman. He'd hardly even looked Libby's way since coming downstairs, what with all his sympathy and understanding going out to Lil and her dramatic explanation for their little fray. She didn't like the woman one bit; nor did she care in the least for the sight of a half-naked Donovan standing there with her, patting her shoulder. He should have been checking to see if *she* were all right, too. Jealousy—and Libby did recognize it as just that—reared up in her, making her forget what little training she'd received as a proper lady.

"I realize this woman is your partner, Donovan," she said, stamping her foot to make sure she had his attention, "but you must surely know that this painted-up saloon tart of yours is lying."

Donovan whipped his head toward her, as Lil did hers. "My what?" he asked, an odd, almost amused expression replacing his concern.

"Your sleazy little saloon tart," she repeated, happy to do so. "She's putting on an act! *She* attacked *me* by grabbing the back of my neck as I went upstairs; and then she tried to strangle me! I was only defending myself, by the time you got downstairs. That's the truth."

For the life of her, Libby couldn't see anything funny about the incident, but Donovan looked as if he were suddenly amused. He glanced at his partner and asked, "Now, why would you attack poor Libby, here?"

"Oh, Christ, Donovan . . . don't listen to her. She's full of shit." Lil flipped her fingers toward Libby, as if the gesture might make Libby disappear. "I just stopped her from disturbing you. I don't know who the hell this little hoyden is, and frankly, I don't care, right about now. I just know I've heard and seen about all I want to of her. Do us both a favor, and toss her out on her scrawny little ass."

Libby raised her fists and planted her feet. "Go ahead. Try it."

"All right!" Donovan held his hands up. "That's enough, from the both of you."

Lil looked up at him and grumbled, but said nothing. It did Libby's heart good to see the woman checked that way, made her feel vindicated, even victorious.

"I have a feeling a little of this is my fault," he went on to say. "Maybe if I introduce you two properly, we can get this mess straightened up without any more fisticuffs."

"I'd much prefer," said Lil, "that you introduced Calamity Jane here to your front porch."

"No more of that talk," he said sharply. "This charming young woman is Liberty Justice, a house guest here at my invitation." Cocking one eyebrow in Libby's direction, he added, "At least, I think it was my invitation."

Almost certain he'd taken her side, Libby managed a shy smile.

"I'm sure Lil didn't mean anything by the things she may have said or done to you," he went on, "but as my mother, I guess she figures she has a right to protect my interests—even when they don't need protecting."

Mother? Had Donovan referred to the woman as his *mother*? Horror-stricken, Libby prayed that she hadn't heard him correctly. He couldn't have said that—anything but that! Her voice sounding squeaky, as if it belonged to someone else, she asked for a repeat. "Did you say that this . . . this lovely woman is your mother?"

Donovan nodded grimly. "That's right."

Libby pushed her back and bottom harder against the wallpaper, wishing in earnest now that she could become part of the scenery depicted there. God, oh, God, how could this be happening—especially on the very same day she'd realized that she was falling in love with the man? And what had she called his mother? A sleazy, painted-up saloon tart? She closed her eyes and bit her bottom lip. Oh, God, no. *No!*

"Now that we've got that straightened out, Son"—Lil's voice, sarcastic and unforgiving, settled around Libby's throat like a noose—"do you think we can have a private talk? I don't have much time this morning, but there are a few things I need to go over with you."

"I don't think Libby will mind. Do you?"

The silence following Donovan's question was awful. Libby knew both he and his mother were looking at her, waiting for her to answer. As much as she wished otherwise, there was nothing to do but face them. She opened her eyes and said, "Oh, no, of course not. Please go ahead. And, er, take your time."

Donovan returned her smile, his expression a lot warmer and more understanding than she would have expected; then he glanced down at himself. "Why don't you go into the kitchen, Lil. I think I'd better get back upstairs and get dressed before we talk."

Before he could leave the room, someone knocked on the front door. Libby did everything she could to avoid looking at or speaking with his mother while he went to check on his visitor. By the time he'd shut the door and returned to the area, Libby's nerves were taut to the point of snapping.

"That was a messenger from Savage Publishing," Donovan explained, displaying a crisp white envelope with the crimson letter *S* embossed at its center. "R. T. wants me to come to his office in one hour."

Lil brushed past Libby as if she weren't even there. "What else does he have to say?"

While mother and son discussed the missive, Libby glanced between the two several times, amazed she hadn't noticed the resemblance before, especially around the eyes. While not the same silvery blue hue as

her son's, Lil's eyes were shaped very much like
Donovan's, with gentle upward slopes at the corners
and enviable banks of thick lashes on both upper and
lower lids, though hers were tawny, not black. His
mother. Lord, she still couldn't believe she'd gotten
into such a tussle with the woman, especially one in
which she'd damn near broken the "saloon tart's" arm.

When he finished examining the paper, Donovan
folded it and stuck it into his trouser pocket. "I'll need
at least an hour to get myself presentable and make the
trip, so why don't you go on back to the theatre, Lil. I'll
catch up with you there later."

"Please, don't go." His mother said the words quietly
and without the commanding tone she'd used earlier,
but Libby could hear the desperation in her plea.

Donovan took her shoulders between his hands.
"Sorry, but I have several questions for R. T., and I
think I'm entitled to the answers."

"But I told you everything you need to know! Why
must—" Lil cut herself off, glancing at Libby, as if suddenly remembering she was in the room.

"I'm going," Donovan said. "And nothing you say is
going to stop me, so you might as well save your breath."

There was an almost lethal silence as mother and son
stared at each other, testing, daring, pushing. Libby, who
couldn't even imagine such a battle of wills between
herself and her mother, or her father, couldn't stand the
tension a moment longer. "I'm going with you," she
announced, surprising herself even more than them.

Donovan turned a stern expression on her. "Oh, no,
you're not. This is one trip I'm making alone."

"You've already had your solo trip to see R. T.—
twice now." Libby started for the stairs. "If you'll recall,
one reason you saw him the first time was because *I* had
business with him. This time, I'm going to talk to that

man, if I have to break down his door." She whisked past him and his mother, grabbed the balustrade, and hoisted herself up on the first step.

"I don't have time for this, Libby!" Donovan shouted, as she started up the stairs. "You can't possibly put yourself together in less than thirty minutes, and I'm not going to wait for you."

Halfway up, Libby turned and looked down to where Donovan stood on the landing. His mother stood directly behind him, looking considerably less formidable than she had earlier. For some reason, this gave Libby an extra dose of courage. "I'll be ready before you are," she warned. "Even if you do leave without me, I'll find my way there. Wait, or don't wait. It doesn't make a damn bit of difference to me."

She started to go back up the stairs, but paused, thinking she really owed Donovan's mother some sort of apology. "Sorry if I was a little rough on you before, ma'am. It was . . . a pleasure to meet you."

Lil frowned, but finally said, "Charmed, I'm sure."

Then, feeling at least a little vindicated, Libby turned and bounded up the rest of the stairs, two at a time.

Because she really didn't want to have to make the trip back to Savage Publishing alone, Libby hurriedly threw on the new suit Donovan had purchased for her and struggled to button her boots. Running short of time, she simply wound the braids she'd already plaited into a pair of flat spirals and pinned them just above her ears. Then came the hard part: settling on a suitable excuse for a bonnet. After several trips to the downtown area, she knew better than to go bareheaded. Which was the lesser of two evils—her work bonnet, with its broad, scorch-marked brim, or the adorable straw hat

Donovan had bought for her, now crushed beyond recognition?

Later, as she sat on the plush leather sofa in R. T.'s waiting room again, she had the dreadful feeling she'd made the wrong choice. She'd reshaped the new hat as best she could, removed the ruined roses and ostrich plume, and replaced them with the sunflower from her work bonnet. Then, because she couldn't rub out the tracks left in the straw by the carriage wheels, she'd covered the thing with the black lace scarf. Donovan, who'd been in too much of a rush when they'd left even to glance her way, kept sneaking quick peeks at her now that they were at the publishing house. Every time he did, his beautiful eyes either rolled or popped out in astonishment.

Libby was thinking of asking him if she'd be better off bareheaded, when R. T.'s secretary approached, smiling warmly as she said to him, "Mr. Savage will see you now, Mr. Donovan."

Under his breath, he whispered to Libby, "Wait here."

Then he rose and followed the attractive young woman down the hall toward the impressive double doors. So did Libby. "Don't forget to introduce me to him," she whispered, taking up residence at his side by slipping her hand into the crook of his elbow.

"You'll pay for this," he muttered. By then, the secretary had bowed out and closed the doors.

R. T. rose from his chair. "Donovan, my boy, it's good to see you again." He beckoned him toward the desk, then gestured toward Libby. "And who is this?"

Left with no choice, Donovan presented her to the publishing magnate. "This is Liberty Justice from the *Laramie Tribune*, sir. She's been wanting to meet with you for several days now."

"Is that a fact?" Circling the desk, R. T. shook Donovan's hand, then turned to Libby. "It's a pleasure to meet you, my dear."

Libby opened her mouth to respond in kind, but suddenly, she couldn't move or speak. She'd been planning this visit since making the decision to board the train in Laramie, dreamed even before that about someday meeting this vastly important man; but now that she was finally here, standing before Randolph Thaddeous Savage himself, she was too bowled over to greet him properly!

Donovan must have realized her quandary, for he reached around behind her and poked her in the ribs, jolting her into action. "Oh, th-thank you, Mr. Savage." Libby giggled as she spoke—not laughed, but *giggled* like a little girl, and then, because she couldn't think what else to do, dropped into an awkward curtsy. "It's a pure and special honor to make your acquaintance, ah, sir."

R. T. chuckled deeply, but Donovan took her by the elbow and raised her up, whispering so only she could hear, "He's not the damn king of England. Get hold of yourself."

"Why don't you two have a seat and make yourselves comfortable?"

Once they'd taken up residence in their plush leather seats in front of his desk, the publisher propped his hip against the corner of the desk, gave Libby's hat a long look, then said, "Justice, hum? You wouldn't happen to be related to Jeremiah Justice, would you?"

"Oh, yes, sir. I'm his daughter."

"And you've been wanting to talk with me, have you?"

"Yes, sir. It's about—"

"Let me guess." R. T. brought his thumb and forefinger to his chin, as if contemplating a major dilemma, making it easy for her to see where Donovan got his swarthy good looks and commanding presence. If the son hadn't already robbed her of her ability to think straight, she was quite sure that R. T. would have stolen her breath away. ". . . and I suppose you're naturally concerned over the letters you've received about the content of your newspaper's editorials. Correct?"

Aware she'd lost part of what he'd said while studying him, Libby stumbled with her reply. "Ah, y-yes, sir, I'm concerned about a lot of things, but the editorials are of major importance."

"Well, you don't need to worry your pretty little head about them anymore." Savage paused to glance at her hat again, looking as if he were thinking of amending the part about her pretty little head, but then went on. "When your father returns from his trip abroad, I'm sure he and I can get this straightened out to everyone's satisfaction. In the meantime, how are you enjoying your visit to San Francisco?"

"Oh, ah, fine, sir, but, Mr. Savage . . . my father is dead, sir." Libby could hardly believe she'd come right out with the truth. Even to herself, she hadn't completely admitted that Jeremiah Justice would never return to Laramie again, that he was gone forever. But she couldn't lie to this man.

His gaze jumping to Donovan for a moment, then back to Libby, R. T. said, "I'm terribly sorry to hear that, young lady. Would you like me to send a new editor to Laramie? I believe my son Francis may have a man here who could fill that position nicely."

"Oh, no!" She hadn't meant to speak out so sharply, but she hadn't come all this way just to turn over the helm of the family newspaper so easily. "I-I feel that I'm quite capable of running the *Tribune* by myself, Mr. Savage. In fact, that's exactly what I've been doing for the last six months. I was hoping that you'd see your way clear to give me a little more freedom with my editorials." She decided not to mention the camera or extra funds.

Again R. T. looked to Donovan, this time shaking his head a little. "In that case, I'll have to give the matter some more thought and let you know my decision later. For now, Donovan, I'd like to address the reason I asked you to come here on such short notice."

Libby had been dismissed, she knew that; but she could hardly find fault with the man. He hadn't been aware of her presence in San Francisco, much less of her desire to see him on business. Far from distressed, Libby was fascinated with the scion, awed to think that Donovan was his son—his *son*! She couldn't even begin to imagine having someone like R. T. Savage as a father. What, she wondered, did Donovan think of his new circumstances? Was he as overwhelmed?

R. T. continued, addressing his son, "I won't be coming to the office tomorrow, and I wanted to personally invite you to my home on Saturday."

Donovan, who was sitting stiffly on the edge of his chair, felt the collar of his crisp new shirt tighten around his throat. "I appreciate the invitation, sir. What's the occasion?"

"It's a family gathering of sorts, a wake for your brother Andrew, of course, but also a celebration. I may have lost a son this week, but I also found one. I intend to present you to the others so that you can take your rightful place in the family. Will you join us?"

Stunned beyond words, Donovan couldn't speak or move at first. What he'd give to have known this man some twenty years ago, especially as he recalled the nights he'd lain awake dreaming of a moment such as this. A father, a real father to call his own—and brothers, too. Was there a coppery-haired sister to go with them? he wondered recklessly.

Or was he even sure he still wanted that elusive dream? He'd grown fond of his independence and used to the fact that he never had to answer to anyone, not even to Lil. Having an honest-to-God family would surely change all that.

"To tell you the truth," he said finally, "I don't think I'd be much good at being a member of the Savage family—or of any family, for that matter. It sounds like too much responsibility for a maverick like me. Frankly, sir, in spite of your claims, I can't imagine that the rest of the family is going to be any too thrilled when they find out about me."

R. T. laughed. "They weren't; but they do know about you now, and have decided to accept you as one of their own. You only need to accept us. Will you?"

Donovan was incredulous. "Mrs. Savage, too?"

"If you're referring to the mother of my children—excuse me, my other children, that is—I lost her to pneumonia some years ago. The new Mrs. Savage is looking forward to meeting you, as are your two brothers and your sister, Susan."

He *did* have a sister. Speechless again, Donovan sat there staring up at the man who openly called him, *Son.* To his right, he could feel Libby gently prodding his ribs with her elbow. When he turned and saw her bright-eyed, eager expression that seemed to be urging him to accept, Donovan had a sudden feeling that he'd shown too much of himself, exposed a need he usually kept buried deep inside.

He glanced back up at his father. "What time do you want me to be there?"

R. T. smiled again, more warmly than before. "Four in the afternoon, but be prepared to stay a while. We'll have some drinks, a little supper, a lot of entertainment, and more." His smile became victorious as he favored Libby with another glance. "And please, Miss Justice, do come along with Donovan."

It wasn't until they were safely back at his house that Libby dared to intrude upon Donovan's privacy. When they'd left the publisher's office, he'd been excited, though not as excited as she'd been; but since then, he'd slipped deep into a brooding, detached mood. Maybe, she thought, he just needed a little cheering up.

"It's been quite an afternoon, hasn't it?" she said brightly. "You must be feeling overwhelmed. I know I am. Your father is possibly the most remarkable, intelligent man I've ever met in my life."

He grumbled something she couldn't understand, as he removed his jacket and hung it on the brass hat rack near the front door.

"If I were you, I think I'd be bursting inside by now!" Libby continued the one-sided conversation, sure that Donovan would join in at any moment. "It must be truly wonderful to find your family after all these years, and then discover that they're waiting to meet you with open arms. I remember what you said the other night about being a bastard, and how you thought—"

"You can't possibly understand what it's like to be a bastard," he said, "or to have a family you don't know thrown at you, so stop pretending that you do."

Donovan had removed his hat and added it to the rack along with his jacket, but he remained standing in front of the tall brass tree, his back to her. Recognizing that he was bound to have a certain amount of shock over the events of the day, Libby quietly strode up

behind him and slipped her hands across his shoulders.
She gently rubbed Donovan's back, kneading his rigid
muscles with gently probing fingertips.

"You're right, of course," she murmured dreamily,
happy to be touching him, to feel the hard, angular male
beneath his smooth satin vest, and to think of him as her
own. "I've always had a loving family by my side, so I
don't really know what it's like to wake up one day to find
that I suddenly have a father. I like to think, however,
that I have some idea how you're feeling right now."

Donovan turned on her so quickly and abruptly, that
Libby instinctively ducked. He caught her arms and
hauled her upright again. "I don't want you to know
how I feel about my family, and I don't want you to
know how I feel about anything else, either—can you
possibly understand that?"

"I—no." Libby wasn't sure what to make of his
mood now. She just knew that it wasn't good.

"Then maybe you'll understand this: I don't want
you to be here anymore." In spite of the declaration, for
a moment, Libby thought Donovan was going to kiss
her. He hovered on the brink of indecision, his hungry
gaze fastened to her mouth; but at the last moment, he
gritted his teeth and went on with the ultimatum. "I
want you out of here by morning."

Libby couldn't have been more stunned if he'd
punched her in the gut. "B-but, I don't have to go home
yet. I was invited to the Savage party, remember?"

"Why would you stay on for that?" His eyes were
glittering like molten silver. "You got what you
wanted—R. T. promised to think about easing his
restrictions on your newspaper. What other reason is
there for you to stay?"

Libby could think of a million reasons to stay, all of
them linked in some way to Donovan; but he was so

upset, so irrational, he frightened her a little. Because she couldn't think what else to say, she repeated her former excuse. "Because I want to go to the party."

"No!" he shouted. Then softer. "No, Libby. I've got enough on my mind as it is. It's better all around if you go now."

"Are you telling me I *have* to leave your house? Are you throwing me out?"

For what seemed like an eternity, Donovan just stared at her, his gaze filled with something akin to longing. "Yes, Libby," he finally muttered with a certain sadness. "That's exactly what I'm saying."

"I see." Her heart, which had been racing with excitement only moments ago, skidded to a sudden halt. She felt as if it'd been torn from her chest. Had she not been flooded with sudden, suffocating pain, Libby might even have lashed out at Donovan to make him hurt the way she was hurting. But it was all she could do to look him in the eye and say, "If that's the way you want it, I'll be out of here first thing in the morning."

Donovan spent a horrid, sleepless night after the confrontation with Libby. His dreams, when he did manage to doze off, were filled with images of R. T. cracking a whip over the backs of his sons, their cowed bodies glistening with sweat as they strained against their traces. The load they pulled up the long steep inclines of Nob Hill included a throne that contained Donovan. The scene was reminiscent of the prodigal son returning home. At the top of the hill stood Libby, dressed in her long, flowing nightgown; several lengths of curly auburn hair tumbled across her shoulders. She was shouting, too, warning him about something, he thought. Before he could make out the words, though, she faded into the morning mist, along with the dream.

Feeling sluggish, Donovan finally dragged himself out of bed and headed downstairs. Even before he reached the kitchen, he could smell the mouth-watering aroma of blueberry muffins baking in the oven, and fresh-ground coffee beans percolating on the stove. So Libby hadn't taken him seriously after all, he thought, not nearly as irritated as he figured he should be to find that she'd disregarded his wishes. Still, Donovan rounded the corner preparing to do battle.

"Ah . . . good morning to you, Mr. Donovan." Gerda nodded toward the table. "Sit and I will feed you."

It was not Libby, after all. He blinked the grit from his eyes and yawned his disappointment away. "Isn't this Friday? What are you doing here?"

"I left a note Tuesday, saying I wouldn't be back until Friday of this week. Didn't you read it?"

He vaguely remembered something about a holy day rearranging her schedule. Nodding, he dropped into a chair. "I forgot. Is Miss Justice up yet?"

"Up and gone, to make room for more of your little piggies. She asked me to give you this." She reached into her apron and tossed a slip of paper onto the table. "Humph, and good riddance, if you ask me."

Gerda waddled over to the stove and poured a cup of coffee, giving Donovan a moment to read Libby's note. *Thanks for everything. Sorry to have been such a bother. The next time you're in Laramie, do me a favor and DON'T stop by to say hello.* It was signed, *Liberty Ann Justice, for herself, and no one else.*

Aw, hell! he thought. This isn't what he'd meant when he'd told Libby to leave his house, not for her to run off like this. He'd have taken her to the depot and even bought a ticket for her, if she hadn't purchased a round-trip fare. He sure never wanted her making her way around the city on her own. Even though ridding himself of Libby is what he'd thought he wanted, Donovan buried his face in his hands.

Several blocks northeast of Donovan's home, Libby reached up and tentatively knocked on a door marked "manager." Amazed at the number of gamblers huddled around the faro table so early in the morning, she tugged her working hat even lower, to hide her face, and impatiently rapped on the door again. It opened at that same moment.

"Well, hello," said Lil, clearly surprised to find Libby standing there. She glanced behind her. "Where's Donovan?"

"Good morning, ma'am. . . . I don't know."

Lil looked her up and down, smirked, and said, "Then what the hell are you doing here?"

9

Just before the door slammed shut in her face, Libby impulsively stuck her foot between it and the jamb. Biting back the urge to cry out as the door smashed against the soft kid leather of her new shoes, she grimaced and said between clenched teeth, "Please? Just give me a minute to explain. Donovan threw me out of his house, and I have nowhere else to go."

Lil pulled the door back a little, easing the pressure on Libby's foot. "He threw you out, you say? Donovan threw you out of his home?"

Swallowing her pride along with the ache in her throat, Libby nodded.

"Well, I'll be . . ." Lil stared at her a moment longer, looking puzzled, then pulled Libby inside her office and closed the door. "That doesn't sound like Donovan at all. He takes everyone in, and for as long as they need to stay. Was it because of our little tiff, you think?"

Her shoulders stiff, Libby managed a little shrug. The last thing she wanted was for *that* subject to enter the conversation. "I can't really say for sure, Mrs. Donovan, but—"

"I'm nobody's misses. Never have been; never will be. Call me Lil."

Libby could have kicked herself. She'd known that Donovan was a bastard—how could she have made such a blunder? "As I was saying, I think Donovan is having a little trouble getting used to the idea of having the Savage family in his life. With me underfoot, it may be too much for him. I can't say, for sure."

"The only thing you said that makes sense is him trying to get used to that damnable R. T. Savage. As for you—hell, his place is usually teeming with folks that don't have anywhere else to go. What'd you do to make him toss you out?"

"Nothing, I swear."

Lil studied her a moment, then her gaze fell to Libby's valise, as if noticing it for the first time. She took it from her and stashed it in a corner of her tiny office. Then she gestured toward the chair behind the desk. "Have a seat, dear. Maybe we do have a few things to talk about."

Although she felt ill at ease, especially taking the only seat in the tiny office, Libby quickly circled the desk and sat down. Lil didn't waste any time grilling her.

"How long have you been staying with Donovan now?"

"Almost two weeks, I guess."

"Hmmm." The skirts of her shiny peach gown swishing noisily, she began pacing, tossing off the next question as easily as if asking Libby if she'd like a cup of tea. "May I assume then, that during that time you've been keeping my son's bed warm?"

Libby didn't know whether she was more shocked by the question or the fact that Donovan's mother was asking it. She took an entire minute to gather herself enough to answer. When she was able to speak, her cheeks felt as if they were aflame. "No, ma'am, you may not assume such a thing. I had my own room, and there I stayed. Alone."

"*Really?*" Looking even more puzzled than before, Lil gave the worn carpet and her feet a rest. Then she studied Libby a moment, taking special note of her odd little bonnet. "Except for your taste in hats, and when you're wearing buckskins and pigtails, you ain't a bad-looking gal. Why aren't you sleeping with him?"

For this, Libby had no answer; but she suddenly wanted desperately to talk it out with another woman. Since her father died, there really hadn't been anyone for her to confide in, at least, not an intimate with the wisdom of an adult. Oh, she and Jeremy shared a lot, but he couldn't possibly understand what was going on with her now or make any more sense of the circumstances than Libby could. Even Dell, God love her, wouldn't be much help since the only thing that interested her, where men were concerned, was a fat bank account. Yet, for some reason, and in spite of Lil's cold, apparently selfish ways, Libby felt she could confide in the woman, without reservation.

Deciding to trust that instinct, she admitted, "He, er, did try to get me to come stay in his room the other night." She could feel her cheeks growing hotter by the minute. "But I—well, he was a little drunk, and I got too scared to go with him."

"Scared . . . of what? Whiskey doesn't make Donovan mean—he don't drink too much often, but when he does, it puts him to sleep. Hell, there ain't but one reason I can think of for a woman to turn tail and run from a man like Donovan." Lil chuckled as she added, "And it's been so long since either of us crossed paths with a woman of virtue, I doubt we'd recognize her."

Libby couldn't stop her embarrassed groan or prevent the sudden splash of color on her cheeks. Lil's bright blue eyes grew huge. "Oh, come on," she chided. "You're not trying to tell me that you've never . . . that you're as pure as the driven snow."

"Except for a few of Donovan's shameless kisses, yes, ma'am, that's exactly what I'm saying." Libby held her head high, but avoided meeting his mother's gaze.

Lil, who'd been pacing again, came to an abrupt halt. "In that case, I suggest you run as fast as you can. Go back to Laramie, and never think of him again."

"Oh, no, ma'am. I can't do that."

"And, why not?"

Libby, who wasn't used to baring her heart and soul this way to anyone, much less to a woman such as this, hedged a little as she admitted, "I—I like Donovan a lot, enough that I don't want to go back just yet."

"In other words, you're falling in love with him?"

Libby sighed. "I think that maybe I am."

"Then get out of town before you take the tumble, because you'll only get your heart—and your virtue—destroyed." Lil leaned across the desk. "Donovan's a bit of a cold shake when it comes to personal attachments." She uttered a short, harsh laugh. "Wonder where he gets it."

"I'll keep that in mind." Libby needed a change of subject. "There's another reason I'm here, and it has nothing to do with your son. Will you help me?"

"If you expect to get anything out of me, you'd best get one thing straight right now." Lil flattened both palms against her desk. "I've gone to a lot of trouble around here to hide the fact that Donovan and I are mother and son. It's strictly for business purposes, you understand; I think it's better for both of us if the employees believe that we're simply good friends. If you want to stay around here, you won't refer to him as my son again."

"No, ma'am, I won't."

Lil straightened and gave Libby a little smile. "And quit calling me ma'am. I'm sure as hell not your mother." Libby had to chuckle over that, and at once felt at ease. Laughing with her, Lil said, "Now let's get down to bedrock: Why have you come to me? I've already told you what kind of man Donovan is, and I can't change his mind if he doesn't want you around."

"Oh, no, I wasn't looking for help with him. I need a place to stay and a little help learning how to get along with society-type folks, is all."

"You mean the Savages, don't you?"

It was the first time Lil had looked angry since Libby had twisted her arm. Libby quickly explained about her newspaper, and what she hoped to accomplish with R. T.; and a few moments later, Lil was laughing.

"In that case," she said, pacing again. "I can help you out with a room, I expect. As for the rest, I'll warn you right now, I don't know a whole lot about society or 'respectable' folks."

"You know more than I do, I'll wager." Libby pushed out of the chair. "I want to thank you for talking to me and for the offer of the room. I wasn't sure, after what happened, you know, with us and all—"

"I think we'd best forget that for now. As for the rest," Lil clucked, "I don't do nothing for free, sugar—I learned that little lesson a long time ago. You've seen what kind of a place I run here. If you can't sing, dance, or serve drinks, then I don't see how I can help you. You sure an innocent like you is up to working here?"

Libby gave herself a minute to think it over. She didn't know much about singing, dancing, or serving drinks, but she realized that she did know one thing for sure right then—she loved Donovan at least enough to give it a try. "My pa used to say that I couldn't carry a tune in a corked jug, and I never did learn how to dance, but I think I can serve drinks without much trouble."

Raising her eyebrows with admiration, Lil said, "All right. But, before I hire you, let's talk about what you can do for me."

At around five the following afternoon, Donovan managed to slip off on his own for the first time since he'd stepped through the sumptuous portals of the Savage family estate, high atop Nob Hill. Discreetly concealing himself behind the lush fronds of a potted palm tree in the corner of the ballroom, he sipped a glass of champagne and watched as a parade of beautifully turned-out men and women paid homage to his father.

They were passing in hordes through the ballroom on the main floor of the mansion, the nattily suited gentlemen commiserating with R. T. over the loss of his son, the bejeweled ladies in velvet and satin ball gowns falling all over themselves in an effort to become acquainted with the handsome son R. T. had recently found. Through it all, Donovan remained aloof, neither taken by his new family, their lavish home, and their affluent friends, nor affronted by any of it either. He remained a distant observer, his curious nature the main reason he'd come to the affair in the first place, and even found himself mildly amused by some of the antics he'd witnessed since stepping into the manse—that is, with the exception of his introduction into society.

Despite his new siblings' efforts to make him feel comfortable, Donovan still felt awkward and embarrassed around them. He sensed gazes on himself, curious speculative eyes of strangers wondering, no doubt, about his mother and the circumstances of his birth— wondering, too, he supposed, whether this "newfound" son had blackmailed his way into the Savage family. He even supposed he was providing his father's guests with a little entertainment.

Most of the entertainment for Donovan did not come from those curious guests or the tuxedoed jugglers slowly rotating around the Italian marble fountain gracing the center of the room. Nor did the serving girls, their lithe young bodies barely covered by Grecian drapes, catch his eye for long. He was having far more fun watching his brothers, Thomas and Francis, greet the other millionaires as they arrived, each trying to outdo the other when it came to dazzling their guests with glib rhetoric.

And then there was Susan, the sister Donovan had long wished for, a genteel, polite woman, attractive enough to have captured the heart of an honest-to-God duke with close ties to the Crown, no less. And yet she was not quite the sort of sister his childhood dreams had conjured. She lacked something he craved; but, for the life of him, he couldn't figure what.

Perhaps, Donovan thought, berating himself, he was being too demanding, too critical; wasn't giving this newfound family of his a chance. Maybe if he was to seek them out, to actually engage one of his siblings in a private conversation, he might discover a common ground that had nothing to do with his suddenly enviable bloodlines.

Donovan was just trying to decide whether to start with one of his brothers, or dear sweet Susan, when he noticed another woman being escorted into the room by one of several purple-liveried servants. She looked vaguely familiar at first glance, but Donovan might have thought nothing of it had he not decided to take a second look at the newcomer. That's when he caught her surreptitiously scanning the room with a pair of spectacles perched near the tip of her nose. Christ, Almighty, if Libby hadn't crashed the party!

He didn't have any idea where she'd gotten it, but she was dressed in a flashy gown of bright rose-colored sateen that sported a scandalously low-cut bodice of emerald velvet. At the valley between her breasts, where the gown dipped to its lowest, she wore a large satin rose that matched the skirt of the gown. He'd imagined Libby at this shindig more than once already, and with a good deal of remorse, as he pictured her wide-eyed curiosity and bubbling laughter over some of the excesses he'd witnessed here today. But never had he dreamed that she'd actually show up! And yet, there she was, nervously making her way across the ballroom.

She was glancing this way and that, searching, Donovan supposed, for his father. When she was close enough, he reached out and grabbed her arm. "What the hell are you doing here?" he demanded.

Libby yelped in surprise, then quickly turned to him with fire in her eyes. "I was invited; remember?"

"I also remember that I sent you packing." That's what he told her; but Donovan couldn't stop thinking about how good she looked, how great she smelled, or how badly he wanted to drag her back behind the palm with him and kiss her till the rose between her breasts wilted from the heat. He went on, unaware at first that he was shouting, "Why aren't you back in Laramie, where you belong?"

"You tossed me out of your house," she gently reminded him. "But I don't believe you have the authority to toss me out of the city, too. I've as much right to be here as you do."

Donovan took a fast glance around to see if anyone had heard him shout, but as far as he could tell, the little disagreement between himself and Libby had gone unnoticed. Determined to keep things that way, he roughly pulled her back behind the palm with him. "Where are you staying? I know you can't afford a hotel. And where the *hell* did you get that . . . that dress?"

Removing his hand from her upper arm, Libby made a great show of studying the row of faint dots his fingertips had left on her skin before favoring him with an answer. "If you must know, and I'm not sure you have the right to know anything about me anymore, I met someone who was more than happy to fix me up with a decent gown so I could attend this party."

"Decent? I don't think so." Donovan's gaze automatically dipped into the bodice of her dress. Near as he could figure, the only thing keeping him from a shocking glimpse of her nipples, was a double row of rose-colored lace tucked beneath the lush green velvet. But something else troubled him even more. "Exactly where are you staying?"

After popping her silk fan open, Libby peered over the top edge of it and murmured, "Again, I'm not sure that it's any of your business, but my new friend has taken me in for a few days."

"What?" Donovan's eyes flared with outrage, and the veins in his neck surfaced like a pair of dueling swords. "Dammit all, Libby! You can't go around trusting strange men, especially in a big city like this."

"I didn't have much choice." She paused to fan her flushed cheeks, knowing they must be scarlet with excitement. Dell had always said, the best way to find out whether a man cared or not, was to try to make him jealous. While Libby didn't know that jealousy was the emotion turning his throat red above his starched white collar, she thought it might be close. Pouting, she added, "I had to make a new friend after you banished me from your home, didn't I? I had nowhere to go and practically no money. Naturally, when I was befriended by the nicest, kindest—"

"Befriended, my ass." Champagne splashed along the back of his hand as Donovan waved his arms, but he hardly noticed. "Hell, all you would have had to do was twitch your tail at any man in town, and you'd have had a place to stay for as long as you liked. Hasn't it occurred to you that, before the night is over, your 'friend' will have you on your back with your bloomers down around your ankles before you can even shout 'uncle'?"

Smiling demurely, Libby waved her fan just beneath her nose. "Why Donovan, I thought you knew me well enough to realize that I'm the kind of woman who'd never shout 'uncle' once I'd agreed to be someone's 'friend.'" He made a kind of strangled sound over that, pleasing her immensely. "If you'll excuse me, I see your father over by the punch bowl. I want to thank him for inviting me to such a lovely party."

Before he could respond, Libby snapped her fan shut, swished around to head toward the fountain, then released the palm frond she'd pulled aside as she made her exit—which in turn slapped Donovan full in the face. Behind her, Libby heard him yelp, but she didn't dare turn around to see what kind of damage she'd inflicted on him. Her legs were shaking so badly she was lucky to be still standing, much less making her way across the room. But so far, knock on wood, everything was working out just the way she'd hoped it would—maybe even a little bit better. Libby didn't know much about men, but she could tell that Donovan Savage cared about her at least a little—enough to be jealous, at any rate—or her name wasn't Liberty Ann

Justice. Now if she could just make a good impression on his father, her troubles might finally be over.

Back in his corner nursing his wounds, Donovan stewed for several minutes in the juices of his anger. He absently rubbed at his right cheek, soothing the welt one of the palm spears had made as it snapped back into position, and worked at calming his suddenly explosive temper. He glanced at what was left of his champagne, thought of tossing it back, but dumped it into the base of the plant instead. At this point, alcohol would only make him feel even more deranged than he already felt. Tugging at the stiff collar of his formal dress shirt, feeling choked by it, he watched Libby sashay up to his father, and begin a rather animated conversation. It was then Donovan decided to act as her escort for the rest of the evening. To hell with her new "friend," whoever and wherever he may be. Someone had to protect her from herself.

". . . and, I'm sorry to say," R. T. commented, "I haven't had the time to review your request. Let me think about this a moment." As he considered his options, the man's gaze skimmed Libby's bosom, lingering there long enough for his eyebrows to lift a little in spontaneous homage. "Tell you what we'll do. My son Francis actually handles most of the newspaper business for me—he's managing editor—so I think it'd be best to turn your problem over to him. If you like, I'll introduce you to him a bit later, and maybe the two of you can set up an appointment."

"Oh, well, if that's what you think is best . . ." She was tired of having her business problems put off. Then, aware that Donovan had drifted up beside her, Libby gave him a brief smile of acknowledgment and gracefully accepted R. T.'s decision. "Then that's what we'll do."

"Good. I'm pleased to know that's settled." R. T. beamed at Donovan. "There you are—I was wondering where you went off to. Your friend here was just . . ."

As his father droned on about editorials and such, Donovan sneaked several furtive glances at Libby. He couldn't help wondering all over again how she'd come to be here, and who her new friend might be. Who'd fixed her hair, piling perfect little curls into an artful coif, complete with a spray of satin roses woven throughout? Where had she gotten not just the gown and matching accessories, but the simple strand of pearls draped provocatively around her throat?

Something ugly churned in him at the thought of another man outfitting her so seductively, of that faceless interloper touching her silken skin even long enough to fasten the clasp of the necklace. The next thing Donovan knew, he was picturing himself tossing Libby onto his bed, then mussing those carefully arranged curls until they were strewn across his pillow. Adding to the illusion, he mentally stripped her, until she was wearing nothing but that somehow tantalizing strand of pearls. His entire body quickened at the thought, then grew rigid with sudden desire— along with something else, something just as urgent and explosive: a rush of anger. Who the hell had taken her in, he wondered, enraged again. And what could he do to prevent her from returning to the bastard tonight?

"Donovan?" said R. T. "You look ready to commit murder."

"What?" He had no idea what his father could be talking about.

"Are you all right, Son?"

Jamming his hands in his pockets, angry at himself now for letting his imagination run away, Donovan muttered, "Sure. All this is just a little . . . overwhelming, I guess."

"Ah, yes, I'm feeling that way myself. Tell you what—why don't we slip away from the party for a while. We haven't had a moment to ourselves, given all the well-wishers and nosy chatterboxes. Come, I'll show you parts of the house where guests are forbidden to enter."

Although R. T. hadn't actually included her in the invitation, in fact, hadn't so much as looked her way when he'd issued it, Libby tagged along with the men. Not only was she curious about the way the Savage family lived, but she had a job to do for Lil that required her to keep either R. T. or his newest son by her side at all times.

Trying to keep from looking too awestruck over the place as she moved out of the ballroom and into an inside courtyard filled with aromatic flowers, bubbling fountains, and marble statuary of Grecian design, Libby recalled the way Savage had classified his living quarters as a house. To her way of thinking, she lived in a house in Laramie, and Donovan lived in a nicer house in San Francisco. However, this Italianate villa constructed of cut stone and marble was anything *but* a house. This was a shrine, an art museum, a palatial castle; all rolled into one.

Marveling over the profusion of oil paintings, gilded furniture, Oriental carpets, and bowed windows featuring dramatic views of the city and bay as R. T. guided her and Donovan toward the home's vast foyer, Libby paused to admire the spiral staircase that led to the second and third floors. She expected to be led up the elegant Oriental runner gracing those circular stairs, but the magnate bypassed them and beckoned her to join him at an elaborately scrolled iron gate a few feet beyond the staircase.

"I thought we'd take the elevator," R. T. explained to Donovan, ordering the attendant to open the gate by just crooking his finger. "I usually like to climb the stairs, but Olivina finds it cumbersome and even dangerous to negotiate them in her ball gowns. Since Miss Justice decided to join us, I thought we should show her the same consideration." He swept his arm toward the car. "After you, dear lady."

Libby stepped into the elevator, awed to find that, like everything else in the magnate's home, the car exuded his vast wealth. Three small paintings depicting idyllic mountain streams were hung among several gilt-framed mirrors along the interior walls. The wainscoted redwood had been recently polished, rubbed with linseed oil, Libby thought, recognizing the scent of a compound also found in her favorite aroma, that of printer's ink. After the conveyance lurched to a start, within a matter of seconds she was standing in the hallway of the second floor of the Savage mansion, her stomach feeling as if it had been left behind, somewhere closer to the first floor.

"Come," said R. T. to Donovan, his long strides eating up the long hallway much faster than Libby could. "Let's go into my study, where we can have a little privacy."

Moments later, when Libby stepped through the massive arched doorway leading into the private library, father and son had already taken seats across from one another at a small, intimate table for two by a window overlooking one of several courtyard gardens. R. T. waved to Libby without really looking at her.

"Take a seat anywhere you like, Miss Justice. Or, if you think you'd be more comfortable, you may wish to return to the party. Just pull the rope near the elevator door, and my man will take you back down."

"Oh, goodness, no. I need to sit for a moment to catch my breath." Trying not to look too agog over the ostentatious display of embroidered purple and gold velvet draperies, shelf upon shelf of leather-bound books, and frescoed walls set off by purple satin furnishings, Libby reclined against a gilded *chaise longue* not far from where the men sat, and pretended disinterest in their conversation.

"As I was saying, Son," R. T. continued; "now that you've seen a little more of the house, I imagine it's quite a shock for you to discover how well we've lived all these years, while you most likely, have lived a little differently. Just exactly what business are you in?"

"I'm half-owner of a gambling theatre here in San Francisco. I do all right."

R. T. nodded thoughtfully. "How long have you lived in the city?"

Donovan shrugged, looking uncomfortable with the line of questioning. Maybe, Libby mused, Lil was wrong to worry about what secrets might be traded between the men.

"I've been here a while."

"And your mother?" R. T. asked so quietly, Libby almost couldn't make out the words. "We haven't even had a chance to talk about her. How is she?"

Taking her cue, Libby jumped to her feet. "Shouldn't you two get back downstairs to greet the rest of your guests? We've been gone a spell."

R. T. turned to her, smiling, but somehow, not smiling. "I'm sure they're fine. You may join them, if you wish." Then he returned his attention to Donovan. "Go on and tell me about your mother, Son. How is she?"

"She's doing fine, thank you," he answered noncommittally. "Healthy, and just as beautiful as ever."

"Umm, I rather assumed she would be." R. T. closed his eyes, as if savoring some private memory, then opened them to resume his queries. "Where is Lillian now, still 'mining' the miners in mother lode country? Or, did she come along to San Francisco with you?"

Libby had been squinting at the subject of an oil painting that took up almost the entire wall above the marble fireplace, and trying to make out the blond woman's features without resorting to her spectacles. When she heard R. T.'s question, she quickly asked, "Who's the pretty lady in the picture, Mr. Savage? Your daughter?"

His gaze pointed, R. T. shot her a thin smile. "The lady is my wife, Olivina. She'll be amused that you think she's young enough to be my daughter."

Libby laughed, hoping she didn't sound too nervous. "That makes her Donovan's stepmother, then, doesn't it?"

"Yes, and I'm sure that amuses her, too." R. T. sighed heavily. "I guess this really wasn't the ideal time for our little discussion after all, Son. Perhaps later, when most of the guests have gone home, we can have that private chat."

Feeling that she'd done the job assigned to her, and done it well, Libby forced a cheerful expression as she followed the men back downstairs to the party. This time, and for reasons Libby wasn't clear about, R. T. bade them use the circular staircase—which not only made for a difficult descent for her, but gave her a momentary attack of vertigo in the bargain.

Once they returned to the ballroom, R. T. pointed out to Donovan a small group of gentlemen who were laughing and talking. "Your friend, Miss Justice, has been wanting to talk with Francis. He can be pulled away from his cronies long enough to make her introduction. Do you mind seeing to that? Olivina is signaling me to join her, and if you know women . . ."—he paused to wink. "I think I'd best go see what she wants—now." Then with a short nod in Libby's direction, he turned and started across the freshly waxed floor.

"I'll be right back," Donovan said to her, excusing himself. Returning a moment later, he presented his half brother to Libby. "This is Francis Savage, managing editor of Savage Publishing. And, Francis, I'd like you to meet Miss Liberty Ann Justice from Laramie, Wyoming Territory."

Obviously catching the pun that could be made of her name, Francis repeated it, grinning just a little. "Liberty Ann Justice, is it? How charming. It's very nice to meet you."

"It's a pleasure to meet you, too, Mr. Savage." Libby shook his hand, warming to him immediately. Francis bore only the vaguest resemblance to Donovan, and even so, she thought, the similarities were more in manner than actual looks. But something about him—the same sort of thing that drew her to his brother—made her feel at ease, as if she could trust him. Sure that her troubles would soon be over, Libby decided to get their business out of the way as quickly as possible. "Your father said that I should make an appointment with you so we can get together and discuss my newspaper, the *Laramie Tribune.*"

"I'm very much aware of your newspaper and your recent problems. Please, on behalf of Savage Publishing and myself, accept my condolences on the loss of your father."

"I appreciate that more than you know." She looked beyond the brow furrowed with concern to the man beneath, and knew instantly the sympathy he offered was sincere.

"As for your efforts," Francis continued, "I must personally commend you for the excellent treatment you gave that heart rending story a couple of years back—I believe the article concerned a poor Irish girl who'd gone mad, and murdered her half-breed husband's uncle."

"Oh, yes, I remember it well. Thank you for your kind words. The story was about John and Lacey Winterhawke, but she wasn't really mad, and she didn't murder his uncle. His death was ruled an accident. The Winterhawke family still lives nearby and comes into Laramie fairly often. I think they have three or four children now."

"It's nice to have a story with a happy ending, isn't it?"

"Oh, yes. I just wish all of them did." Relaxing even more, she said, "Speaking of my stories, I have some questions regarding the editorial guidelines I'm expected to follow, and wonder if—"

"Excuse me for interrupting, Miss Justice." The warmth had gone out of his tone, making him sound like Donovan whenever he was trying to talk her out of doing what she wanted to do. "But I'm afraid there's really no point in setting up a meeting."

"Please, call me Libby." She sensed that anything she could use to her advantage—even something so small as inviting him to address her more personally—could help.

"Libby, then." Francis looked distinctly uncomfortable. "I wish I had better news for you, but Savage Publishing has a very strict policy against promoting equal rights for women."

"I'm aware of that, Mr. Savage, but I was hoping you'd see your way clear to letting me—"

"Please." He held up one hand, then glanced at Donovan with a look that positively cried, "Help!". If she hadn't been so worried on her own account, Libby might even have pitied the poor man. "My hands are tied in this matter. There's really nothing I can do to help you in regard to editorial policy. If you have any other concerns, say of a financial nature . . . ?"

Finances were the last things on her mind. The very last. "I don't think you understand how important this is to me, or what a service I can provide to—"

"I really hate to keep interrupting you this way, but I must. There's absolutely no point in going over your request again, Libby."

"But, why not?"

He looked at her as if *he* wanted to cry. "You leave me no choice but to inform you that, should you run even one more article or editorial in favor of women's rights, I'll be forced to close the doors of the *Tribune* faster than your suffragist friends can cry 'foul'."

10

The elder Savage had of course hired San Francisco's finest orchestra to entertain his guests. Throughout the afternoon and early evening, the musicians pretty much kept to the more mellow tunes by such composers as Tchaikovsky and Brahms. At the precise moment Francis finished his statement, however, they happened to strike up a rousing rendition of "I'll Be Ready When the Great Day Comes."

Had he not noticed that Libby's hands were curled into fists, and been concerned that she was thinking of doing unto his brother as she'd done unto his mother, Donovan might have commented on the irony of it all. Instead, he hooked elbows with Libby, and pulled her away from Francis as he said to him, "If you'll excuse us, please? That's the song we've been waiting to dance to."

Donovan managed to whip Libby in an arc that took her out of range, view, and even hearing distance of his brother, before she finally balked at his interference. "Turn me loose!" She yanked free of his grip. "I don't want to dance with you, so leave me alone!"

"Relax, "Lippy," and don't worry—I don't want to dance with you either." Glancing around for an area where their conversation couldn't be overheard, he prodded her toward the gurgling fountain, cautioning her along the way. "If you want to keep so much as a sliver of a chance to change the company policy, I suggest you keep your complaints to yourself, for the time being."

Tears stung the backs of Libby's eyes as Donovan marched her across the room, but she refused to give into them. Heeding his advice, she muttered low and under her breath, "Oh, what's the use of keeping up pretenses? You heard what your brother said. I don't even have that sliver of a chance, and you know it."

There wasn't much Donovan could say to that. He didn't know a thing about the newspaper business, or Francis really, but he sensed the man had done all he could. As for Libby—although he wasn't one who paid much attention to women's politics—he did know how very much equal rights and the crusade to achieve them meant to her. Even now, broken-hearted as she must be, she was tough to the end, her eyes moist, but filled with as much rage as hurt. He thought he'd washed his hands of Miss Liberty Ann Justice, and several times over, too; but Donovan suddenly found himself enlisting in her army of one.

"Maybe all isn't lost. There must be a way for us to get your point across."

"Us?" She blinked back a tear.

"If you don't mind a little help."

Fresh tears glistened in her eyes, so Donovan glanced away to give her enough privacy to put herself together. As he looked over everyone else in the room, his gaze caught on the brilliant display of opulent jewels at the throats of society's most elite women, who were huddled together in conversation. Settling on the most outrageously ostentatious female of them all, Olivina Blair Savage, Donovan decided that Libby's plight suddenly didn't seem quite so futile.

He turned to her with a big grin, relieved to see that she was dry-eyed. "Don't give up the ship just yet, madam editor. There's one angle you haven't thought of—other women." Nudging her to glance over where his "stepmother" was holding court with the other ladies of prominence, he asked, "Do you remember what R. T. said about going to see what his wife wanted, and the way he emphasized the word, *now*?"

Libby frowned. "Yes, but—"

"Didn't that comment give you the impression that her opinion carried a little weight with the man?"

"Sure, it did. But I also remember that Francis is the managing editor of the Savage newspaper empire, while your father just sits in his chair and rakes in all the money. I don't see what difference it makes, whether he values his wife's opinion or not."

"Don't be so sure. I've been watching this family closely all day." *Boy*, had he been studying them—that and trying to imagine himself squeezed into the family portrait. Donovan could hardly believe it was true—not simply to learn that he finally had a family to call his own, but to find that it was *this* one, the prominent Savage clan. The very idea boggled his mind. "Believe me," he went on to say, vaguely smug in his assessment of his father, "nothing happens here *or* at Savage Publishing that R. T. doesn't oversee or approve personally."

"You really think he makes the final decisions about everything?" Libby glanced at him with anticipation. "Including the *Laramie Tribune*?"

This was the look he liked best: the scheming, calculating, alive with intelligence woman who would not back away from her ideals for anyone—man or woman.

Resisting a sudden urge to steal a kiss, Donovan said, "I'd bet my last dollar on it—and coming from me, that's about as fine a recommendation as you can get."

Libby snapped her head around toward the women so fast, one of her artfully arranged curls tumbled down to the center of her back. "Which one is Olivina?"

Admiring her predatory instincts, he laughed as he said, "Christ, Libby—can't you guess by looking at them?"

"I'm trying, you fool." Whispering, she glared at him. "I can't *see*, remember? I'm not about to put my glasses on here, either. Now which one is she? The blur in the middle, or the blur on the left?"

Still laughing, Donovan reclaimed her hand. "Come on. I'll introduce you; but after that, you're on your own."

Thankfully, Donovan took his time with the introductions, giving Libby ample opportunity to study the two women who could be most important to her cause. As Olivina clasped Libby's hand in greeting and offered her a warm welcome, Libby realized why Donovan thought the woman so easy to spot. She stood out like a raging prairie fire at midnight. Not only was Olivina a stunningly beautiful blond, but her slender figure was highlighted by a tightly fitted dress made of cream satin embroidered with beads of every color imaginable. The extra-long train, which was gathered twice to form two bouffant puffs below her waist, was also made of satin. Its deep rose color matched the diamond and ruby *parure* at her throat, as well as her cream satin slippers, which sported buckles studded with diamonds and rubies. With every little movement, no matter how slight, she glittered like a life-sized gemstone. Libby had never seen anything quite like her.

"And this is my sister, Susan," she heard Donovan say. Barely able to tear her gaze from Olivina, Libby turned to R. T.'s youngest child, who, though elabo-

rately gowned, was a far cry from the sparkling display
of her stepmother. She wore a low-cut evening dress of
sea-foam green silk trimmed with white lace and large
clusters of roses in pink, cream, and deep burgundy. Just
the toes of her green satin slippers peeked out from
beneath yards and yards of lace underskirts. But, as far
as Libby could tell, her only jewelry was a single diamond pendant shaped like a teardrop.

"It's a pleasure to meet you, Miss Justice," she murmured. A coil of coffee-brown hair dangled along one
of Susan's creamy shoulders, swinging like a pendulum
every time she moved her head. Between her reticent
manner and her appearance, there wasn't much about
Donovan's half sister to remind Libby of him. But then
Susan offered a warm smile, the familiar expression
around her mouth drawing much more than Libby's
gaze, and asked, "Will you be visiting our city long?
Maybe I could show you around."

"Oh, I wish I could join you, but I'll be leaving soon,
I'm afraid. I'd really like to take you up on the offer, but
I don't see how I can." And she meant it, too.

"Excuse me for interrupting," said Donovan, doing
just that, "but I think I'll leave you ladies and go about
getting a drink." He tried to duck away, but one of the
women, a countess something from a country he couldn't
remember, placed a restraining hand upon his forearm.

"Don't rush off just yet," she said in a perfectly modulated voice. "Please promise first that you'll consider
coming to my party next week. We're hosting the
Young Gentlemen's Ball this year, and you simply must
attend, or the single ladies, my daughter among them,
will be very disappointed."

"In that case, I'll have to make every effort to be
there. I try never to disappoint a young lady." Donovan
thought he heard a groan coming from the left of him

where Libby was standing, but before he could check on her, the countess was patting his arm again.

"Do be sure to look up my husband, the Earl of Dufferin, and give him your card, so we can send you a proper invitation."

Donovan wondered briefly if the matron would be so anxious to include him in her party if she knew his card was the jack of diamonds. Grinning to himself, he promised, "I'll just go see if I can't find your husband now. Maybe I can talk him out of one of his cards, while I'm in the area." With a slight bow, he made a hasty departure.

Libby, who'd been watching Donovan's performance with decidedly less enthusiasm than the countess, glanced back to the other ladies to find Olivina in the midst of studying her—and with a good bit of curiosity apparent in her pale blue eyes.

"Donovan said that you were here visiting San Francisco, but he neglected to mention where you hail from or what connection you have to him." She flipped the jewel-encrusted wrist that held a Louis XV fan. "I can't say I recall knowing a Justice family here in California."

"I'm from Laramie, in Wyoming Territory, ma'am." Libby allowed the pause as Olivina exchanged glances with the other ladies. She managed to smile in spite of their obvious pity. "As for Donovan, my only connection with him is through Savage Publishing. I run the *Tribune* in Laramie."

"Run?" Olivina delicately fanned herself. "I'm not sure I understand."

"I'm the editor of the *Laramie Tribune*, ma'am. That means I'm in charge of getting the newspaper out on a daily basis and writing the editorials."

"Gracious, me. That sounds like quite a large responsibility for a woman, Miss Justice."

"Running an entire newspaper isn't a particularly easy chore for a man or a woman, but I've managed to do it, and even at a distance, as I've had to do for the past two weeks." She smiled sweetly, making up her mind to test and maybe even push the woman a little. "And please, call me Libby. Most of my friends do, and most of them also belong to the National Woman Suffrage Association. What about you and your friends, Mrs. Savage? Are you members?"

Olivina's gaze narrowed slightly, and her fancy fan began fluttering more rapidly. "I'm afraid not, and as for my friends . . . well, I really can't speak for them." Several of the ladies agreed with Olivina immediately, eschewing the very idea of belonging to such an organization.

"That's too bad." Libby persisted, determined to find out exactly what she was up against. "I suppose you must be allied with Lucy Stone and the American Woman Suffrage Association, in that case. Correct?"

"Sorry, again. You're quite wrong on both counts." Olivina lightly tapped Libby's wrist with the fan she'd just folded. "Now if you'll excuse me? I really must go see to my other guests. Welcome to my home, and do enjoy your visit to our lovely city."

"Oh, ah, thanks for having me." That's what she managed to say, but Libby may as well have been muttering the courtesy to the marble statue of Poseidon rising up from the center of the fountain. Olivina and several of her "followers" had already stepped out of earshot by the time she had the first word out.

"Excuse me," came a small voice from behind her, "but could I talk to you a minute?"

Libby turned to find Susan Savage at her elbow. "Oh, I didn't realize you were still here. I thought you went off with your mother."

"My stepmother, ma'am." Susan colored a little, her shy hazel eyes darting around the room as if seeking approval—or disapproval. "I'm supposed to help her with the hostessing chores, which means I'm to keep the guests entertained. You are a guest, aren't you?"

Libby liked her even more now, especially after she dared to give a little wink, by way of punctuation, at the end of her declaration. "I certainly am—invited by your father, no less."

"That's wonderful news." Smiling, albeit timidly, Susan linked arms with Libby and strolled through a high, arched doorway and down terraced steps that led to one of the estate's formal gardens.

Night had fallen, surprising Libby since the profusion of brilliant lighting inside the mansion had lulled her into thinking it was still daylight. Here in the gardens, where small ornate lanterns illuminated the plants and shrubs, the evening had definitely made an appearance, complete with tendrils of the almost nightly fog that made lazy loops around the treetops. The night felt magical, almost mystical.

As they strolled deeper into the courtyard, Susan, whom Libby guessed to be no more than eighteen, spoke fondly of the Oriental garden with authentically reproduced shrines, pagodas, and miniature plants, through which they passed. It wasn't until they reached the wooded, more private gardens that featured an abundance of shrubs, flowering trees, and hedges trimmed to resemble a menagerie of barnyard animals, that the young woman finally got around to saying what was on her mind.

"I was wondering—if you don't mind my asking, that is—if you really are a female suffragist."

"I certainly am, and proud of it. Are you?"

"Oh, gracious, no!" Laughing, Susan sank down on a marble and brass bench. "I have no reason to march for equal rights. I'm betrothed to Henry, duke of Alaim, and will be wed before the year is out."

Libby joined her on the bench. "So? Don't you want to protect what should be legally yours? And what about voting rights? Don't you think your opinion should be counted as to how you want this country to be run?"

Susan looked at her as if she'd just spoken in Chinese. "I'm not sure I follow you. Once I'm wed and titled—I'll be a duchess, you know—I'll be protected and have more authority than I ever dreamed of, surely, more than I ever wanted."

"Over whom, Susan? Over what?"

The young woman frowned as she considered the questions. "Servants, I suppose, I don't know. I only know that Henry will take care of me, and that, as his wife, I won't have to worry about how the country is run. I won't have to worry about a thing."

"I see." Because she already cared a little about this young woman and a lot about her skewed convictions, Libby went on, trying to make a point. "Do you mind if I tell you the story of a rancher I interviewed back in Laramie?"

"Not at all. I'd love to hear about your hometown."

"If you're sure. I don't want to take you away from your other guests for too long."

"Please, don't worry about them. Tell me about Laramie. Is it really as wild and woolly as they say?"

Libby grimaced. "We'll get to that later. First I want to tell you about this rancher and his wife. I went to their home with the sheriff because the man had sent a message to town claiming that his wife had been kidnapped."

"Oh, how dreadful!" Susan leaned in close to whisper the rest. "Was she taken by . . . *Indians*?"

"No, she wasn't." Libby resisted the urge to educate the woman about Indians. "I went to the poor woman's home as a newspaper reporter, so I could write up a factual story about her disappearance, and maybe even help find her. It turned out to be the hardest assignment I'd ever taken on, and in the end, I didn't write the article or try to help find her."

"Gracious! Why on earth not?"

"I'm getting to that." Libby hated the memories, and rarely dredged them up; but if the telling of the story could help this spoiled, yet good-hearted woman understand why all women had to join together to make their lot better, then it would be worth it. "I found the family living in filth, and that didn't count the fact that the house had a dirt floor." Susan recoiled in horror, as Libby suspected she might. "I was only there a short while, but in that time, I saw babies crawling on hands and knees on that floor, a newborn barely old enough to keep her little eyes open, and a pair of twins not out of diapers yet. A young girl and boy, around five and six, I'd guess, were riding herd on them, while several other children were out in the fields."

She gave Susan a moment to digest that information before going on. "Well, after the rancher—Zeke's his name—told me his sad tale of waking up one morning and finding the missus gone, he scratched his crotch and armpits, in that order, then hawked a load on the floor by my boot."

Susan shuddered from head to toe and grimaced.

"Exactly my first reaction," said Libby. "Then I just stared at the old boy, giving him a really long look, and said, 'Zeke, my friend, are you so sure your wife got kidnapped? Isn't it just as likely she ran away from home?'"

Gasping and laughing at the same time, Susan shrieked, "You didn't!"

"Oh, yes, I did." Libby did manage a little chuckle at the memory before finishing her story. "Zeke looked back at me like I'd lost my mind. Then he asked why in tarnation I thought she'd want to go do a thing like that. I pointed out the miserable excuse for a house, the babies, and the older children running round in the yard. You know what he did then?"

Clearly unused to such tales, an open-mouthed Susan slowly shook her head.

"He actually looked surprised I'd ask such a question, and even requested a clarification by saying, 'You mean 'cause of them kids?' When I nodded, he insisted that the little woman would never run off just on account of them." Libby mimicked the man's voice. "'Why would she,' he says; 'we only got thirteen so far, you know.'"

"Oh . . . oh, gracious." Susan looked as if she didn't know whether to laugh or cry. "Oh, gracious, me."

"Gracious, hell. Old Zeke just didn't understand. It seems a lot of men don't."

Susan nodded, as if agreeing. "That's quite a story all right, but I'm not sure I see why you told it to me. I doubt the duke wants thirteen children, and I sure don't."

As much as she liked Susan, Libby couldn't help but think that, like Zeke, she didn't quite understand. But she continued to try. "The reason I told you that story is because, in all things—from the number of children we have to the laws we obey in this country—whatever the men decide is the way things have to be."

Susan mulled this over for a moment, then shrugged. "But once we're married to them, we can make the men listen to us. You should hear Olivina talk to my daddy! I would say, things around here are done the way *she* decides."

Libby could feeling her temperature rising, as it always did when she couldn't quite get the message across. She took a couple of deep breaths. "Susan, the rules around here, no matter who makes them up, don't have the slightest effect on the way this country is run. It costs your father nothing but a fraction of his money to let Olivina set those rules. What I'm trying to tell you, is that more American women are like Zeke's wife—faced with no say at all—than are like you and Olivina. This kind of life is—" She spread her arms toward the sky just as the moon slid out from behind the clouds to silhouette the mansion's turrets. Libby's hands fell to her lap and she sighed. "This, my new friend, is a fantasy."

Staring up at the gothic towers of her home, Susan fell into thoughtful silence. After a while, she said, "So what you're saying is that you joined the suffragists not just so you could go to the polls and vote with the men, but to help all women to have a better life?"

"Oh, Susan, yes, that's it! I could just hug you. In fact, I think I will." Libby embraced the young woman, feeling a kinship with her, then held her at arm's length. "Do you think you might be interested in joining our group? I can show you how."

Susan didn't think about that for too long. "I'd really like to, but I don't know what daddy would have to say about it. He's not in favor of women getting the vote, so I don't suppose he'd be too fond of the other equal rights matters either."

"But maybe you can help to change his mind about it." Her tone a challenge, Libby went on. "You agree, do you not, that it's high time the women of this country started raising fewer babies and more hell?"

"Well . . . yes."

"How do you plan to raise hell if you have to ask for your father's permission first?"

Susan brought her hand to her mouth, looking as if she were about to burst into giggles, but at the last minute she blanched instead. At first, Libby was afraid she'd been too aggressive in her tactics, which she had to admit, sometimes happened when she became impassioned over the cause. But then she realized that Susan was looking beyond, not at her. Before she could figure out who'd approached, a male voice came at them from behind.

"There you are, Susan, dear. I believe Olivina is looking for you. Something about notifying the guests who'll be observing the fireworks from the top floor?"

"Oh, yes, of course." Susan jumped to her feet, muttering a fast apology. "Excuse me, please." Then she scurried away, leaving Libby to deal with the unidentified intruder alone. She swiveled around on the slick marble seat until she was facing the satin-lined jacket of a man she hadn't seen before.

"Oh, hello," she said breezily. "I don't believe we've been introduced."

The man had a gorgeous head of glossy black hair, not so unlike Donovan's, but the prominent brow beneath his delicate widow's peak was stern and harsh. Through eyes the color of a stormy sea, he looked down at her with undisguised contempt. "I don't think introductions are necessary. You're that Justice woman from Laramie, are you not? Here to make trouble?"

Libby rose, wanting to be on higher ground before she answered such animosity. "I'm afraid you have me at a disadvantage . . . *sir*. Who are you?"

"Thomas Savage." He made no attempt to greet her past that, but went at her again, instead. "Who do you think you are, coming to this home and filling my sister's head with your suffragist propaganda?"

Libby was stunned. This man was *nothing* like Donovan or Francis. But he was one of R. T.'s sons, and like him or not, she had to show him a certain amount of respect. "I—well, I am sorry if I've offended you somehow, but Susan—"

"Susan is part of this family. On her behalf and ours, I'm asking you to leave our home this instant. If you don't, I shall be forced to have you bodily thrown out. Is that understood?"

"Ah! There you are!" Donovan popped out from behind a hedge cut in the shape of an enormous fat sow. "I believe you promised me this dance, Miss Justice." He turned to his half brother, barely able to keep a civil tongue in his head, and muttered, "Excuse us, will you, Thomas?"

Then, before his temper could get the better of him, Donovan escorted her out of the garden and back inside the ballroom. As they moved closer to the circle of dancers, Libby pulled on his arm, beckoning him to stop.

"Thanks for getting me away from that jackass, but please don't take me any farther."

"You've as much right to be here as any one. I'll have a little talk with Thomas later, and maybe with R. T., too—"

"That's not the problem right this minute." She glanced up at him with artful eyes. "I don't want to dance with you."

Taking umbrage to the remark, especially in the face of his recent gallantry, Donovan responded in kind. "It's a little late to be so choosy, isn't it? It's not like your dance card is filled with Savage brothers, or anyone else, you charming little thing, you."

"Oh, please don't go on about your wounded feelings." She rolled her eyes dramatically. "My dance card doesn't have a single name on it, and for a very good reason. I . . . well, I don't have any idea how to dance."

"Thank God for that, because I don't know how to either." At her surprised expression, he went on to explain. "I happened across you and my brother, overheard part of the conversation, and figured, if it were to continue that you might behave in, shall we say, a less-than-ladylike fashion. In other words, I was afraid you might just punch him right in the mouth."

She made a growling sound in her throat. "If you'd heard the way that bully you call a brother was talking to me, I think you might have applauded if I'd punched him. He sure had it coming to him!"

"Hush, dammit." Donovan scanned the room. There was no sign of his brothers or father, and Susan and Olivina were huddled conspiratorially at the edge of a large round couch. Keeping his voice low, he went on to say, "As it happens, I did overhear some of what that son of a bitch had to say to you. I dragged you out of there on my account, too—before I lost control and punched him in the mouth myself. Satisfied?"

Libby's expression softened immediately. "You were thinking of poking your own brother—over me?"

"Not *over* you, so don't go getting all sappy on me. The man was being a rude pig. I don't like to hear anyone spoken to in such a manner, much less a woman."

"Oh, Donovan—you do care." The words flowed from her like a melody, as soft and low as a chord from a bass violin. Then before he knew what she was up to, Libby gripped his lapels, raised herself up on tiptoes, and fit her lips to his for a brief, yet somehow deeply intimate kiss. After coming up for air, she repeated, "You really do care about me, don't you?"

"Libby, for Christ's sake." He removed her tenacious fingers from his lapels, distinctly uncomfortable with the turn in the conversation. "I care about a lot of things, but that doesn't mean . . . it doesn't make me . . ."

Donovan was still trying to find a way to explain himself an hour later as they made their way to the roof of the Savage mansion to watch the fireworks display R. T. had planned. By the time they reached the summit, Libby was laughing gaily, as if she enjoyed his discomfort immensely. Once they made their way to the wrought iron viewing rail which fenced the entire roof of the mansion, she turned her back to him, sneaked her glasses out of her bag, and after perching them on her nose, became so swept up by the sights, nothing else mattered.

"Oh, my God," she cried, leaving vanity behind to fully don her spectacles. "I thought the view of the city from the street was something, but this . . . and at night with the lights twinkling from the houses below . . . it's too much to believe!"

Donovan, who'd never been privy to such a sight himself, merely glanced out at the crisp, clear night. Most of the fog still hovering about the city swirled around the lower buildings, leaving only occasional patches or ghostly images of mist to interfere with the stars above or gas lamps below. Libby, no longer gazing at Donovan with puppy dog eyes, but staring out at the night with open adoration, seemed lost in her own little world.

"So what do you think of my fair city?" he asked, wanting, for reasons he couldn't fathom, to be part of that little world. "Did you imagine it would be this big when you left Laramie?"

"Oh, gosh, no." Still staring out at the night, she sighed deeply. "I mean, I knew San Francisco would be a lot bigger than any place I'd ever been, but I never imagined how tall these five-story buildings could be!"

He pointed toward the bay. "See the big one in the distance, the one that looks like a huge shadow covering several blocks? That's the Palace Hotel, which is seven stories tall."

Libby cut loose with a long low whistle, one worthy of a *stevedore* down at the docks. "I saw that when I got here and wondered what the devil it was. Have you ever been inside the hotel?"

He laughed. "Just once, as the guest of a very wealthy lady."

"How wonderful!" Now, of all moments, Libby chose to turn her rapt gaze on him. "Is it as grand inside as it is on the outside?"

"I—I wouldn't know. I didn't really get much of a tour of the place." Actually, the only tour he'd gotten was inside the lady's bedroom, and he sure as hell wasn't going to go into detail about that. Sorry he'd brought the subject of the hotel up in the first place, Donovan was trying to think of a way to extract himself from the uncomfortable conversation, when R. T. saved him the trouble by firing a pistol into the night.

"For my son Andrew!" he shouted, assured that every guest's attention was on him, whether below on the street or privileged enough to be numbered among close friends and family on the roof. A moment later, the first in a series of rockets shot into the sky with a deafening whistle. The projectiles packed with gunpowder and lampblack exploded in bright red sparkles, showering the darkness with crimson stars. Other cylinders, mixed with yellow sand, erupted to spill waterfalls of golden showers above the crowd, mesmerizing everyone.

In the midst of this dazzling display of fireworks, Donovan heard distant chimes ringing out the hour, echoing in between explosions twelve times over. Gripped with a sudden urge to bestow a kiss on Libby—for luck only, he assured himself—he turned to find that, like Cinderella at the stroke of midnight, she'd disappeared. He began an immediate search of the rooftop, and by the time the fireworks display was over, he'd asked all but one person if they'd seen Libby leave the premises. No one had.

Approaching that final spectator, Donovan said, "It seems Miss Justice has disappeared. You wouldn't know anything about that, would you?"

Thomas chuckled with perverse satisfaction. "No, I wouldn't, but I'm pleased to learn the little baggage had enough sense to get out of here before one of us was forced to do something unspeakably boorish—like toss her off the roof."

Had he not been relatively convinced by now that Libby had sneaked off of her own accord, probably to meet the bastard who was caring for her, Donovan might have ignored this latest comment from his half brother. But as it was, he had nothing more to occupy himself than this gasbag, who was beginning to remind him more and more of dear, departed, Andrew.

Donovan clasped his hands behind his back and spread his feet. "I'm going to assume that you somehow missed the fact that Miss Justice is more or less my guest, and give you exactly one minute to apologize for that remark. While you're at it, you may as well apologize for being so rude to her earlier, out in the garden."

Thomas didn't trouble himself with a polite smile. "I'll be honest with you, Donovan. I'm not the least bit interested in being your friend, much less your half brother; but if that's what my father expects, that's what I'm going to try to do—for him. As long as the rest of us are willing to accept you, I think the least you can do is try to adjust your life so that you can fit into this family a little better. Do you see what I mean?"

Scratching his head, Donovan twisted his mouth into a frown. "Well, hell, brother Tom, I'm not so sure that I do. That didn't sound like much of an apology, where I come from. Were you trying to suggest, instead, that perhaps there's something wrong with the company I keep?"

"Precisely." Thomas allowed himself just a shadow of a smile. "I understand you're involved in the saloon business. I think it would be best all around if you were to sell your interest in that enterprise, and leave all the cheap little trollops like this Justice woman behind with it. I don't think I can make myself any plainer than that."

"No, Tom, you can't—but I sure as hell can." Smiling broadly, Donovan drove his fist right into the center of his brother's mouth.

11

One night later at Lucky Lil's, Donovan was still nursing his swollen knuckles—them, and the aching void left in his gut by Libby's sudden departure. It wasn't that he wanted her back. Hell, no. It wasn't that at all. He hoped to God she'd gone home to Laramie, where she belonged, and that this time, she'd stay there. It was the not knowing that bothered him; the wondering where she'd gone at the precise stroke of midnight, how she'd gotten back to wherever she was staying, and . . . well, he didn't dare *think* about who might have taken her in. Oh, no. If he did that, he might just—

"Can you open?" the dealer asked Donovan, jolting him back to the present.

He stared down at his cards and studied them several times over; but for some reason, he couldn't make sense of his hand. His expression as dark as his thoughts, he muttered, "By me."

What the hell was wrong with him tonight? he wondered. Although Donovan oversaw all the gaming tables, he often sat in as "just another player." If he had troubles, gambling usually took his mind off his worries and relaxed him. But not tonight. This evening he couldn't stop worrying or thinking about Libby. Was she aboard the train and on her way to Laramie, or was she still in San Francisco? Would he ever see her again, if indeed she hadn't left the city? And if he did, for what purpose?

Hell, he'd seen the look in her eyes when she'd realized something he hadn't wanted her to know—that he cared, if only a little. Should their paths cross again, he would encounter a woman who would surely want far more from him than he could possibly give. It would be cruel to see her again, cruel and a little dangerous. So why couldn't he stop thinking about her?

Why couldn't he just let thoughts of her roll off his back, the way they had with his half brother? Donovan hadn't even bothered to explain or excuse himself to the family after the incident on the roof. He had simply wiped the blood from his knuckles—using the jacket of brother Tom's fancy imported suit as a towel—then left the mansion. In search of Libby, he recalled, his mind returning to thoughts of her. Again.

"Ah, excuse me, Mr. Donovan?"

The dealer's voice insinuated that he'd missed yet another cue. Cutting his losses—and a good deal of embarrassment, too—Donovan tossed in his cards and pushed back his chair. "Keep 'em honest, Leon. These fellas are too good for me tonight. I think I'll go test my luck at faro."

Libby was having a damn good time for herself, drifting along in dreamy-ville, as she liked to think of it, when the first knock rattled the doorjamb. Preferring the comfort of slumber, not to mention the warmth of Donovan's embrace as he kissed her over and over again in the dream, she ignored the suddenly alert part of her mind—the part insisting that she wake up—and went right on with her fantasy.

The second knock was louder, sounding as if it had loosened the floorboards. Reluctantly setting her fabricated Donovan aside—he was beginning to fade anyway—she tried to get her bearings. Where was she, and what was all the noise? Who could be knocking on her door so rudely, and in the middle of the night, no less? Her throat felt scratchy and dry, as if lined in wool, and when she inhaled, she thought she smelled smoke. Lord, was the house ablaze?

Libby's door flew open on the third knock and, reluctant or not, so did her eyes. The noise, not just knocking, but raucous piano music as well, blew into the room as if on the tails of a storm. The hallway was lit, silhouetting the shadow of the man who stood in her doorway. A very *large* man. With an involuntary gasp of terror, Libby bolted upright in bed.

"Time to get up," said the hulk in the doorway. "Lil sent me to get you."

It was the little Irish trill in his voice, along with the mention of Lil's name, that brought Libby's memory back. She was at the theatre, lying on a cot in the spare room. Yes, of course. And the hulk, a kindly Irish pugilist who'd had at least one too many fights, was named Seamus. His imposing presence did much to keep unruly gamblers and drinkers under control, even though, if the truth were known, these days the poor man had been known to burst into tears every time he had to use force to remove a customer. Lil had sent the gentle beast the evening before to escort Libby back to the theatre.

"Thank you for waking me. Tell her I'll be down soon." He smiled and nodded, but as he started to back away, Libby detained him a moment longer. "Oh, wait

a minute, Seamus." Although Lil had been expecting
him, Donovan hadn't come to the theatre after the
Savage party last night. Lil hadn't done a very good job
of hiding her concern for her son from Libby. Because
of that, Libby was worried about him on her own
accord. "Did Donovan show up tonight?"

"He's down at the faro table," he said with an almost
toothless grin. "Lil says he looks like he's 'bout ready to
bite himself."

Knowing the look, for Donovan was usually wearing
it when he was around her, Libby chuckled to herself.
"Thanks, Seamus, and by the way, don't mention to
Donovan that I asked about him or that I'm here."

"I willna be speaking of it. Is there anything else,
lass?"

Libby adored the way he called her lass. "Yes, there
is. Would you please ask Joy to come help me?"

"Sure thing."

After Seamus had backed into the hallway and closed
the door to her spartan room, Libby lit the lamp at her
bedside and swung her legs over the edge of the cot. She
rubbed the sleep from her eyes, wondering what
Donovan's mood would be like once he realized she was
here. If he already looked as if he might bite himself, she
supposed she could have a rabid dog on her hands after
he found out that her new "friend" was his mother!

She was in the midst of having a quiet chuckle over
that image when Joy burst into the room without
knocking, as was her wont. "Did you send for me?"

Turning in the barmaid's direction, Libby smiled
warmly and said, "Yes. I was wondering if you'd help
me dress tonight; you know, fix me up kind of special."

Joy closed the door behind her and cocked her head.
"Why doncha wear that buckskin outfit of yours? It
seems to me if you was to strap on a gun with that get-up,

you know, maybe get a big ole hog-leg of a pistol, put it right about here," she jabbed a fingertip at her navel, "then aim the barrel straight down at your fun house, the fellas would probably go crazy."

Looking away to keep her mortified expression from showing, Libby shook her head. "I don't want to look like Calamity Jane, and I sure don't want to be making any men crazy." With the exception of one, she silently amended, but even then, she didn't want to get him *that* crazy. "I was thinking I should wear something completely different for a change." She eyed Joy's scanty costume, then broke into a grin. "Here's what I'd like you to do for me . . ."

Downstairs at the faro table, Donovan had just about decided to call it a night. He'd been making stupid, irrational bets since he sat down—playing to lose is what he'd have called it had he been observing such behavior in any other gambler. And yet, self-punishment wasn't his way at all—at least it hadn't been before. He sat pondering that very disturbing realization, when a lush, slightly impertinent, and very familiar voice slid over his shoulder from behind.

"Would any of you gentlemen care for a drink?"

Sure he'd imagined the voice was Libby's after thinking about her the way he'd been all night, Donovan didn't even glance her way as the barmaid took drink orders from the other gamblers. But when she leaned up close and whispered against the back of his ear so that no one else could hear, and that springtime scent of hers hit him right between the eyes, he damn near fell out of his chair in shock.

"And what about you, Mr. Savage? Anything you need?"

Choking on something—surprise, rage, horror, maybe all three—he spun around on his chair. "W-what the hell are you doing here?" he demanded.

"Earning my keep." Libby straightened, pleased by his reaction, but cautiously placed her little serving tray between herself and Donovan for safety. "What'll it be? A beer? Or should I get you something a little stronger?"

"I'll get it myself," he muttered, jaw tight, as he looked her up and down. "In fact, I'll just go help you with the rest of the drinks." Nodding to the faro dealer without looking at him, he slowly rose from his chair and unnecessarily added, "I'm out of the game."

Libby could practically feel Donovan's gaze burning holes in her back as he followed her to the bar, but it wasn't until after she'd relayed the order to the bartender that he even acknowledged her presence. He did that by gripping her nude shoulders and setting her aside. Then, acting as if he'd merely rearranged a piece of furniture instead of a full-grown woman, he addressed the barkeep.

"Have Suzie or one of the other girls take those drinks to the faro table. This little lady is finished for the night."

"Oh, no, I'm not." Libby straightened and dug in for the fight. "This *little lady* has only begun. If you'll get out of my way, I'll just—"

Donovan jerked the words right out of her mouth as he roughly took her by the hand and hauled her away from the bar. Libby reluctantly allowed him this, only because she didn't want to cause him further embarrassment in his own establishment. Once they'd passed through the doorway and into the relative privacy of the San Francisco night, however, she balked.

"Turn me loose!" She dug at his fingers with her free hand, but he was too strong, and much too determined. "Donovan—let go, you're hurting me!"

Only then did he ease up, but not enough to release her. The full moon and soft glow from a gas lamp directly above them lit his rigid features, bathing him with a pale, buttery sheen. Yet Donovan's face was ashen, his eyes glittering like a pair of cold, hard diamonds. "If you don't want me to hurt you, princess," he hissed, "then stop fighting me."

"But why shouldn't I fight? I haven't done anything wrong."

"No?" His angry, silvery gaze raked the bodice of her scanty costume, becoming almost vicious as he noticed the way the bulk of her breasts seemed ready to plummet over the low scooping neckline of peacock-blue velvet. Joy had strapped her into a corset she called the squash-the-sides-push-'em-up-and-flop-'em-out special, a contraption guaranteed to "pop" the eyeballs of any man, even a eunuch. Libby thought perhaps the garment was working a little too well on Donovan. "You don't think there's anything wrong with running around half-naked in a room full of drunken men?"

Libby tried to hide her grin, but felt the corner of her mouth lift as she softly said, "No, I don't—and if I don't, I can't see why you should. Unless, of course . . . you're jealous."

"*Jealous?* Me?" At that, he finally released her hand, but remained hovered over her, hawk-like in his possessiveness, trapping her there as surely as his grip had. "Jealous, hah! What a hoot."

Still grinning, but no longer trying to hide it, Libby shook off a sudden chill. The barmaid costume may have been unfair competition for Donovan, but it was no match for the damp night air. "If you're not jealous, then what difference does it make to you if I earn my keep at the theatre?"

"What difference?" He thrust his hands above his head. "What difference? I own the place, remember? I didn't hire you, and . . . and I don't want you working for me. Isn't that reason enough?"

"It would be, if not for one little thing." Too cold now to pretend she wasn't, Libby folded her arms beneath her breasts, which increased the length and breadth of her cleavage, and briskly rubbed her hands up and down her chilled skin.

Donovan's gaze raked her bodice and he scowled as he asked, "And that little thing would be?"

"Your partner hired me. I expect she'll want to be the one to fire me."

"My part— Lil hired you? My *mother* is your new friend?"

Libby nodded, so cold now, she was barely able to speak. "A-and, if you don't mind, I'm going b-back inside to work for her now before I f-freeze to death."

"Oh, no—no, no." After practically ripping off his own jacket, Donovan quickly draped it over Libby's shoulders. "You've got a lot of explaining to do." Distracted by a few ribald remarks being bandied about by passers-by, Donovan raised his fists at them. "What are you looking at, huh? Go on, get out of here!"

Several of the strangers snickered and muttered a few more remarks, but they all gave him a wide berth. Donovan's anger seemed to have multiplied after hearing that his mother had taken part in Libby's extended visit. "Come on," he said, taking her by the hand again. "We'll have to finish this little discussion back at my house; but finish it, we will!"

This was exactly what Libby had hoped for, and was the reason she allowed him, again, to drag her away with him. Still, it wasn't until after they'd finally reached his house, out of breath but warmer now, between the jacket and brisk walk, that she was sure she'd made the right decision.

Muttering to himself by then, Donovan pulled her into the foyer, paused just long enough to light a small lamp on the hallway table, then continued on into the living room with Libby still in tow. Once inside the small but cozily furnished room, he didn't bother to offer her a seat or even illuminate the area beyond the steady glow from the foyer and generous swatch of moonlight streaming in through the bay window. He got right down to business.

"When I asked you to leave my house a few days ago, I didn't expect you to go running to my mother, for Christ's sake, or to dress up like, like . . ." He waved at her costume, this time concentrating on the hem of the slender skirt, which ended about two inches short of her knees. Of course, he might have been pointing at her black French stockings or even the red satin garter wrapped around her thigh just above her right knee. "Like . . . like *that*!"

Though it was totally unnecessary, she glanced down at herself. "Like what?" Libby asked innocently. "This is the way the rest of the barmaids dress at your place."

"Yes, well . . . you're not like the rest of my help."

Now that he had her inside his own home, Donovan couldn't seem to get enough distance between himself and Libby. It was she who closed the space a little as she moved toward him, arms spread wide, and said, "What do you mean, I'm different from the rest of the women who work for you? Don't I fill out this dress as well as any of them?"

"Hell, yes, you do, and that's just the problem." He'd looked as if he were about to sit down on the window seat, but as she drew near, he locked his knees and edged in the opposite direction. "You don't belong in a dress like that, and you know it. In fact, I demand that you go upstairs and take it off this instant."

Smiling to herself, feeling more certain than ever that Donovan cared for her, Libby followed him as he moved about the room. "You like me, and you *are* jealous."

"I feel responsible for you, and that's a whole other thing." He shoved his fingers through the hank of dark hair that had fallen over his eye, but it soon tumbled back down his forehead again. "Now get upstairs."

Her smile grew broader. "You walked out on your own business and went to the trouble of bringing me back to your house. It seems to me that a fella would have to be feeling awfully *responsible* to do that." She caught up with him by a corner cupboard filled with volumes and miniatures in silver frames. "Why don't you just admit it and get it over with? You like me—a lot."

Donovan reached out to her then, looking as if he was going to drag her into his arms, but then at the last second, he jammed his hands into his trouser pockets instead. His shirtsleeves were a brilliant, ghostly white in the moonlight, and the satin brocade of his red vest caught sparks of light with each rapid breath he took. "What I do or don't like doesn't have a damn thing to do with this conversation. We're talking about you here, and the fact that you don't belong in a place like Lucky Lil's. Now, are you going to take that goddamned dress off, or do I have to rip it off of you?"

His words and the deliberately harsh way he'd said them were meant to scare her, to bully her into following his orders. Libby knew this without a doubt since she was, if only a little bit, frightened by his dark expression and the threats she saw glittering in his eyes. Instead of turning her away or giving her second thoughts, however, the sensation excited her, sending tiny shivers along her spine that had nothing to do with the cold.

She moved a little closer to Donovan and gave him a long, slow smile. "Actually, I think I'd prefer it if you took the dress off—but try not to rip the material. It isn't mine, you know."

With that remark, he did reach out and drag her into his arms, crushing the breath from her lungs in his fierce embrace. "Goddammit, Libby—this isn't a game. Do you understand what you're asking for, looking the way you do in that dress, saying the things you're saying? Do you understand what you're doing to me at all?"

Her pulse beat a rapid tattoo against her throat and she found it almost impossible to breathe, but Libby didn't hesitate with her answer. "I think," she murmured softly, "that maybe I do."

"Christ, Almighty! You don't give a man much of a chance to behave himself, do you." It wasn't a question. Donovan raised her up higher and tighter in his embrace, leaving just the tips of her toes beneath her for support. His arms rigid ropes of steel, his thighs and other parts of him, hot and hard where he pressed against her legs and belly, he caught her chin in one hand and forced her to look directly into his eyes.

"Just exactly what is it you want from me?" Donovan asked, his voice no longer harsh, but thick and husky. "And this time, be sure you say exactly what you mean. Be very, very sure."

All of your love, all of you, is what she caught herself thinking, but Libby still had barely enough control left to keep from vocalizing the thought. She almost said, "Nothing," because she knew he would never be hers, not even for one night, if she were to ask for more than a few moments in his arms. But she couldn't keep from testing him just a little. Speaking in a breathless whisper, she asked, "What if I were to ask for . . . your soul?"

Surprising her, Donovan uttered a short bitter laugh. "We wouldn't have a problem. I don't have one."

The moment the last word was out, his mouth came down on hers, and in that moment, Libby felt as if she had everything she'd ever need right here in her arms.

12

Libby's next lucid thought came when she realized she and Donovan were lying on the braided rug on the living room floor—and that she was wearing nothing but a pair of frilly drawers, black stockings, and the complicated corset Joy had talked her into donning. Given the way Donovan's fingers were tearing at the laces, she wouldn't be wearing it long. And then what? she wondered, gripped by a sudden attack of nerves.

Aware that she'd tensed, Donovan stilled his hands. Then he looked up at her, his silvery blue eyes glittering wickedly in the pale moonlight, and whispered breathlessly, "I can still let you go, if you've changed your mind, but I have to warn you—this might be your last chance to get away. If you know what's good for you, you'll take it."

Libby met his gaze with determination, hoping with all her heart that the room was dark enough to keep him from seeing the fear lurking there too. "I think I'm a better judge than you are of what's good for me. I happen to believe that staying right here might just be very, *very* good for me."

"Libby . . . sweet Jesus." Her name and the way he said it was like an oath muttered in church, reverent blasphemy. He made a low rumbling noise in his throat, a sound akin to anguish, before giving her one final excuse to escape him. "I only hope you understand what's happening then, and that this is all I can give you. There won't be any promises of tomorrow or a future. Are you still so sure this is what you want?"

Libby forced herself to take plenty of time before answering. What Donovan offered wasn't all she'd hoped for, not by a long shot, and yet she wanted him with a near desperation, needed him too much not to allow a few sacrifices. Besides, wasn't what he proposed the exact kind of relationship so many of her sisters in the cause recommended? "Free love," they shouted to any who'd listen; be free to love and free to leave. It was, supposedly, the only way for a woman even to admit that she cared for a man, if she wanted to make any kind of a mark for herself in this society created for and by men.

Shrugging off the last of her doubts, Libby looked Donovan right in the eye. "I understand what you mean completely. Now are you going to spend the rest of the night talking about what might happen, or do you think we could get to it?"

With a short, guttural laugh, Donovan crushed his mouth down on hers, the tender violence of the kiss touching her soul even as it rocked her body with its impact. Nudging her teeth apart with his tongue, he drove her wild with his explorations, teasing, tasting, tormenting every erotic sensation she held within her grasp. In the midst of his ever-deepening, head-spinning kiss, Libby felt Donovan's hands slide along her shoulders and return to her corset. His fingers busy at the laces again, moments later they were busy at her breasts, sending her deeper into chaos. Libby whimpered a little as his hands touched her nipples, caressing and worshipping them as if he'd never held such glorious treasures in his palm before. When his mouth followed suit, his sinful tongue exploring and laving her breasts even more thoroughly than her mouth, the sensations set off skyrockets within her, rivaling the display at the Savage mansion. Instinctively arching her back, she all but begged him to take her then and there.

"Donovan, my God . . . do something."

"Easy," he whispered, now feathering kisses across the tips of her rigid nipples. "This is something we don't want to rush."

Oh, but she did want to rush, to hurry along to each new delight the way she used to on Christmas morning. Libby could never sit still and wait to patiently open her gifts one package at a time, the way her brother did. She tore into them in a frenzy of eager anticipation, flitting from one treasure to the next until at last, her curiosity was satisfied. She felt that way now, wanting to taste, feel, and experience all there was to know of Donovan, of what his caresses could do to her, of what she could do to him. And, she wanted it all this instant.

Libby tugged at his tie, freeing the bow, then went after the buttons at his starched collar. Frustrated when her fingers couldn't quite manage to loosen the snug buttonhole, she cried, "Help me get your shirt off. I have to feel your chest against me."

Chuckling deeply, Donovan propped himself up on one elbow and gazed down at her. "I had an idea you'd be a handful, sweetheart, but this . . ." he practically growled the rest of the sentence, "Christ, Libby—you're really something."

"The buttons, Donovan."

The shirt was made in France of the finest linen available, interwoven down the frilly button path with silk threads of sparkling gold. It was his favorite shirt, too, but Donovan tore it up the middle as if it were merely a cheap muslin pattern, not the finished product. His gaze still pinned to Libby's expectant features, he quickly shrugged off the shirt, vest and all, then slipped out of his trousers.

Libby couldn't hide a gasp of surprise—or maybe it was sudden uncertainty. She'd had a really good look at every part of Donovan when he'd lost his trousers at the top of the stairs the other day. While the sight had been fascinating, to say the least, at the time, she hadn't concerned herself with the technicalities of the way his body would fit with hers. But now she had to wonder—could she accommodate a man such as this?

Donovan returned to her then, and before she could even figure a way to raise the question, he gathered her in his embrace, the coarse hairs fanned across his upper chest feeling rough against her erect nipples, and Libby promptly forgot her reservations. Her breath caught at the sudden intensity of sensation, then left her panting, starving for air. When Donovan slipped his hand beneath the waistband of her drawers, caressing the sensitive spot just below her navel as he tugged the garment lower and lower, her breathing stopped altogether.

"Relax," he said, tossing her drawers aside. "There's no hurry—remember?"

But there was for Libby. She had a terrible need to hurry, especially now that he'd nudged her legs apart with his knee. She could feel herself radiating heat, craving his touch in the most private of places. And when he did touch her there at last, Libby thought she might die from the pleasure. Reacting with an almost primitive spontaneity, she clenched Donovan's upper arms, her fingers digging into the hard muscles there, then raised her hips to press herself against his fingers as hard as she could. It was an instinctual move, a way to make sure he continued to caress her until there were no more surprises. She sensed that something, the final discovery, lay just around the corner, a heartbeat away.

"Donovan, don't stop . . . I feel so . . . so, oh . . ." The words, coming between gasps, sounded odd to her, husky, and almost foreign. "What do I do now? Tell me what you want me to do."

"I do," he whispered, sounding vaguely amused. "You enjoy."

He abruptly shifted his hips after that, and in the next instant, pushed something hot and hard gently against her maidenhead. Donovan hovered there for what seemed like forever, slowly gaining entrance to her body, then gathered her tightly in his arms. With a muttered oath she couldn't understand, at last he drove home with one final thrust.

Pain lanced through her, swift and sword-like, and Libby had to bite her lip to keep from crying out. She couldn't turn into a blubbering baby now, not after all the coaxing she'd done to urge him to bring her this far so fast. Hadn't he warned her to slow down? Donovan shifted his body again, and preparing herself, she quickly braced for another wave of pain. It didn't happen. Instead of withdrawing and thrusting into her again, he only moved back far enough to see if she was all right. Far enough, in fact, to see the tear pooled at the corner of her eye, a betrayal of the promise she'd made to herself.

"I hurt you," he murmured, his voice hoarse with emotion. "I'm sorry."

"No, you didn't. Not really."

But he didn't believe her. If he had, he wouldn't have cupped her face between his hands the way he did, or gently kissed the teardrop away. Funny, how that little show of affection touched her, tough and independent as Liberty Ann Justice considered herself to be; for that innocent gesture prompted more tears, sent them spilling over both eyelids in a flood of embarrassment.

"Oh, my God, I'm sorry. I-I don't know what's come over me." Libby hiccuped, feeling like an idiot. "I don't mean to be so—"

"Eager?" he said, making it easy for her.

At his bemused tone, the gentle, non-accusing way he spoke, Libby dared a glance into Donovan's eyes. They were smiling warmly, as was his mouth—a mouth, she suddenly realized, she couldn't wait to feel against her own again. Still feeling slightly silly, Libby nodded, teeth tugging at the spot she'd bitten on her bottom lip, and whispered, "Maybe a little too eager, I guess."

He laughed deeply. "In that case, I guess I ought to see if I can't get you going again."

Before she could question or even encourage him, Donovan was kissing her, plumbing her more deeply and thoroughly than before. When she began to stir restlessly beneath him, he slipped his hand between their bodies and quickly brought her back to the edge of that final surprise. Then he started moving within her, hard pulsating male driving in and out of velvety soft female, filling and stretching her until she thought she'd go mad from the delicious frustration of it all. A moment later, with a sudden and surprising intensity, she climaxed in a hard, molten rush, an explosion so fiery, Libby was sure she must have melted at her very core.

Right on the heels of her own release, before she'd gathered an ounce of her wits again, Donovan collapsed against her breasts, his body jerking and thrusting in the final throes of his own passion. Then at once, he stilled and, bodies locked together as one, they rested.

Libby stirred in her own bed the next morning, satisfied, but vaguely disappointed. She felt almost robbed. As she slowly awakened and regained a few of her senses, the night and Donovan's fiercely gratifying lovemaking came back to her. That's when she realized what was missing.

Donovan.

Opening her eyes, Libby turned her head from side to side, even though she knew in advance what she'd find. She was alone, and had been since he'd gallantly escorted her upstairs to her room. He'd left quickly after that, muttering something about taking care of business, and urging her to get a good night's sleep. But she hadn't slept all that well, she recalled, still feeling bereft and unfulfilled.

Oh, she was physically satisfied all right, and in ways she'd never imagined the body could be satisfied; in fact, had she not personally met Zeke, the rancher, she might almost have understood how his wife could have stayed with him long enough to bear at least the first child, if not all thirteen. Almost.

Physical satisfaction obviously hadn't been enough for the poor rancher's woman—and it sure as hell wasn't enough for Libby. She knew now that she wanted more, much, much more, and to hell with Victoria Woodhull and those who claimed that "free love" was the only way for an intelligent, independent woman to live. If she hadn't guessed it about herself before, Libby now knew for certain that she didn't want to be "free" to love other men. She wanted Donovan, and only Donovan, for as long as she lived. And, impossible a dream as it might be, she wanted him to want only her.

In the hallway outside Libby's room, Donovan leaned against her door, fingers splayed around the doorjamb. He'd been standing there for ten minutes dreading what he was sure would turn out to be the kind of confrontation he'd avoided all his life—mainly because he'd had enough sense to avoid virgins. But then, along had come Libby. Absently caressing the mound of wood beneath his palm the way he'd caressed her satiny skin the night before, he considered the fact that women like Libby probably didn't give up their virginity easily—and that when they did, such a gift most surely came with strings. Ties he was not interested in making.

So he continued to stand there, terrified of the strings she might have in mind for him, thinking that by now she'd had time to weave them into a piece of hemp thick enough to hang him. How could he have let himself get into this situation? Had he completely lost his mind? Donovan had wondered that same thing last night after taking Libby up to her room. Hell, he'd run out of his own house like his ass was on fire, *run* like a frightened rabbit—him, frightened, and of a woman, for Christ's sake!

Rationalizing what he'd done, what he had to do now, Donovan decided that not much of what had happened last night had been his fault. Hell, he was almost certain that Libby would never have bedded him, had he not turned out to be a Savage. She'd gotten what she'd wanted—just not for as long as she'd hoped. So why should he feel guilty?

Relaxing a little at the thought, he finally worked up enough courage to tap on her door. He heard what he thought was a muffled yes, so he opened the door a crack and peeked in. "Libby? May I come in?"

"Oh, ah . . . of course."

He heard the rustle of the bed coverings and of Libby adjusting her position. Giving her enough privacy to put herself together, Donovan kept his gaze averted until he'd reach the foot of the bed. When he finally did chance a look at her, he was surprised by what he saw.

There were no recriminating glances or signs of regret in her expression, no pouts or remorseful sighs. In fact, after the wild night they'd spent together, he could hardly believe how bright and innocent she looked this morning. She was wrapped up to her neck in a virginal white nightgown, her loose auburn hair mussed, but tamed enough to tumble over her shoulders in seductive waves. He managed to shake off the urge to plunge his hands back into that silken hair, and might have been able to resist the impulse to get close enough to inhale another whiff of her springtime scent—but then she turned those big calf eyes on him, eyes that demanded no promises and told no lies.

Donovan inched his way to the edge of the bed. "Mind if I sit down?"

"Of course not." She patted the mattress next to her hip. As he sat down beside her, she went on in a much softer voice. "I missed you last night. I wish you could have stayed in here with me."

"I, er," he cleared his throat, not quite as prepared for the confrontation as he'd thought. "I had to go back to the saloon. I work there, you know." Something had changed in her eyes. They were no longer calf-like, but predatory, with the kind of look that said she'd staked her claim on him—on a Savage. That thought made it easy for Donovan to explain the way things were while he still could. "Libby, I . . . let me make this clear. Even if I hadn't gone back to Lil's last night, I wouldn't have stayed in here with you. I make it a habit not to sleep with . . . well, I like to sleep in my own bed, alone."

"Oh," she said breezily, "I guess that does make sense, now that I think of it. No complications that way, right? No getting used to a person snuggled beside you during the night, waking you up, and all."

"Ah, that'd be about it, all right."

He narrowed his gaze, studying her deeply, the way he studied a new player in a poker game. Something was amiss. She was too cheerful, too understanding; but her expression was impossible to read well enough to figure out what she was up to. If she'd been playing poker, she probably could have bluffed him out of a boxed flush with that expression. It occurred to him then that she might not be bluffing, that she didn't care any more than he did, and his "no strings attached" terms really were just fine with her.

Oddly disappointed by the thought, he snapped, "I might as well get right to the point of why I stopped to talk to you before I went to my own room."

"Please do." Beneath the quilt, she drew her legs up and hugged them to her chest. Then she dropped her chin to her knees and glanced up at him like a mournful little puppy.

Donovan had to look elsewhere before he could go on. He settled his gaze on the little bit of lace at her wrists. "I'm trying to be as delicate as I can about this, without causing you any, er, embarrassment."

"Why should I be embarrassed?"

Oddly disconcerted himself, he shrugged. Libby gave him a tight smile, gesturing for him to go on. Feeling as if he'd just been invited to dig his own grave—with his tongue—he explained himself. "I just wanted to make sure you remembered what I told you last night, and that you're not expecting too much from me today."

Libby laughed, surprising him all over again. "Apparently you think I've given you some sort of gift, but I assure you, I don't look at it that way at all. As far as I'm concerned, I finally got the chance to find out what this lovemaking fuss is all about."

So flip was she in her remarks, Donovan thought she might as well have added, "and you were handy." Suddenly irritated, he snapped, "I'm glad to hear that. I do appreciate your position, but I still feel like I owe you a little something. I thought, if I were to have a good long talk with R. T. today about your newspaper, that it might, you know, go a long way toward making things right between us."

So that was it. Libby had been sitting there in a tug-of-war with her heart, trying desperately to listen to Donovan with only her mind so that she might understand exactly what the underlying purpose for his visit might be. Now she knew. He needed to offer something, had to find a way to make things *even* between them—not right. Clearly, he couldn't bear the idea of being beholden to her. Or maybe he felt trapped. As much as she wanted him, all of him, Libby wasn't about to accept anything he offered under either of those terms. Gaining editorial freedom for the *Tribune* was the only thing she was supposed to care about.

Swallowing her pride and a few unshed tears, she toughened her heart and her voice as she said, "Now that you mention it, that does sound like a rather nice compromise. You'll do it, then? You'll talk R. T. into letting me run the *Tribune* my way?"

His gaze flickered with speculation for just a moment, then turned playful. "You got it. In fact, I'll go have that talk with him first thing this morning."

Libby offered her hand, hoping that he wouldn't notice how badly it was trembling. "It's a deal."

He slid his palm across hers in a very provocative manner, then gripped her hand tightly. Taking her by surprise, Donovan pulled Libby out from under the quilt and across his lap. Nuzzling her behind the ear, he whispered, "I can think of a much better way to seal our deal than shaking on it. What do you think?"

Robbing her of the opportunity to think at all, Donovan slid the fingers of his free hand into her hair, then turned her head around until her lips met his. He kissed her deeply, fiercely, stealing her breath, and as she'd feared, a good part of her mind. His lips blistered a trail along the side of her neck, then settled against the hollow at her throat where he began to murmur to her, the sound slightly muffled.

"I've heard it said that the first time isn't usually so good for a woman." He raised up and caught her in his impassioned gaze. "I don't know if that's true, but I figure, as long as we're striking a bargain, you might as well get your money's worth. Besides, I can promise you this—slower *is* better."

Unable to prevent an automatic reaction to both his words and his touch, Libby sucked in her breath. She shouldn't be allowing him this. Somewhere in the back of her mind, she knew that melting every time he touched her could only hurt her in the long run. But where was she to find the strength to turn him away now? How could she, while Donovan was doing such marvelously wicked things to her?

He was kissing her everywhere, her throat, her mouth, the lobes of her ears, sliding his erotically charged hands under her nightgown, along her inner thighs, and at last, reaching and caressing the most wanton part of her. She inhaled sharply at the first onslaught of sensation, and his scent flooded her like mulled wine, hot, heady, filling her senses to overflowing.

She knew she should stop him all right, that she ought to demand he at least hear *her* terms before things went any further. But he hadn't played fair. He'd bribed her by offering another little gift, a surprise package she simply couldn't refuse.

Libby had never, in her entire life that she could recall, done *anything* slowly.

True to his word, three hours later Donovan sat in his father's office, listening to him from across the huge slab of polished burled walnut that served as his desk.

"So you see," R. T. concluded, "there's really nothing I can do to change that policy and help your friend out. Maybe you ought to remind her how lucky she is to have been given the reins of the *Laramie Tribune* at all, and ask her to stop all this nonsense about equal rights. It'll wind up costing her dearly, if she doesn't."

Deeply disappointed, not just for Libby, but with his father somehow, Donovan couldn't quite let it go at that. Hell, what would it hurt the man to give just a little? "Maybe I wasn't clear enough. I'm not asking you to turn your entire publishing empire into a forum for equal rights. Libby runs the *Tribune* in Laramie, for Christ's sake, not San Francisco. I don't see how it'd hurt you to compromise a little by letting her write something about the women's vote, say once a month or so."

R. T. folded his hands together and propped them in the middle of his ink pad. Speaking in a deceptively soft voice, he said, "Perhaps I didn't make myself clear earlier. Thomas—you remember him—the brother you attacked the other night? It may interest you to know, by the way, that you did some damage to his front teeth. Considerable damage, I believe."

Donovan shrugged. "The son of a bitch had it coming. If you're thinking I ought to apologize for punching him, you'll have a long wait."

R. T. waved him off. "No, I don't expect that from you. Thomas can be a bit of a hothead, but my point is that he runs S and S Enterprises for me, which owns Savage Publishing. As general manager, he's instituted a strict policy against any of those businesses promoting equal rights in any way, shape, or form."

"I understand that, I guess." Donovan leaned forward in his chair, leveling a sharp-eyed gaze on his father. "I also understand that you're the man who approves—or breaks—those policies for each of your vast holdings."

R. T. smiled as if really enjoying himself. "Now, why would you think a thing like that?"

Returning his father's smile, feeling like he'd just walked into a game of showdown, winner take all, Donovan felt his pulse quicken as he said, "Good training, I guess. It started a long time ago when I was just a kid. A kindly stranger taught me a few things about gambling."

His unflappable exterior seemed to ruffle just a bit; R. T.'s voice softened. "A stranger, you say?"

Pleased to see that he had his father's rapt attention, Donovan rattled the coin in his heel for good luck before realizing the significance of what he'd done. His own manner less gruff, he went on to say, "A stranger who drove several damn fine points into my thick skull. The first was a little adage: A fool and his money are soon parted." R. T. glanced across the desk and nodded conspiratorially. Feeling he somehow owed it to the man, Donovan added, "I'm sorry to say, those words were the first things to cross my mind the minute I met Andrew."

Leaning back in his chair, R. T. let out a weary sigh. "I suppose I can understand that. Andrew was, well, he never quite grew up, in many ways." He frowned down at his hands for the longest time, but then brightened considerably and asked, "And the next point . . . Son?"

Donovan was more than happy to comply. "To always remember that, no matter how many games of chance I learned, or how well I thought I knew them, the knowledge would be useless unless I learned at least as much about the fellas I was playing against. I have, thanks to that kindly stranger, learned a helluva lot more about people over the years, than about the games they play."

R. T. laughed robustly, something Donovan had never heard him do before. "I guess you remember a little something about your father after all."

"Yes, I guess I do. And that's how I can tell who calls the shots around here. Now what do you say? Will you give the lady just a little more freedom with her paper?"

R. T. didn't even pause to consider the request. "We haven't known each other for long, Son, and I really don't want to get into a situation where we could find ourselves exchanging harsh words; so let me say this just one more time. Savage Pub—" then he corrected himself—"or rather, *I* have a very strict policy against such nonsense, and I am not in the least inclined to let up on it. Now that's enough of this business talk—unless, of course, you want to discuss coming to work for Savage Publishing."

At that moment, Donovan did not want to discuss the position his father had offered him during the party the other night. While he'd been mildly interested at the time, he really hadn't given it much thought since. "I appreciate your making the offer, but frankly, I haven't had much time to think it over."

"Take all the time you need."

There was a rather magnanimous tone in his father's voice, something intangible that irked Donovan. Maybe he was just tired, given the fact that he should have been in bed hours ago, or maybe he was simply worried about how Libby was going to take more bad news. He'd been so sure that he could gain her just a little ground. How was he to tell her nothing had changed?

His thoughts turning darker by the minute, Donovan decided it would be better all around if he were to take his leave while he and R. T. were still on reasonably good terms. Gripping the arms of the plush leather chair, he pushed himself to his feet.

"You're not leaving already are you, Son?"

"I'm afraid I have to." He rubbed his brow. "In my line of work, daylight's for sleeping."

"Oh, I hadn't thought of that." Rising from his chair, R. T. circled the desk and came to within two feet of his son. Speaking now in a softer, more tentative voice, he said, "Before you go, I wonder . . . you haven't told me much about your mother yet. You look like her, you know."

Donovan nodded. "I'd rather not talk about her right now, if you don't mind."

R. T. glanced down at his manicured nails, then abruptly returned his gaze to his son. "As a matter of fact, I do mind; but if that's what you prefer, I can wait a while for news of Lillian. What about your sister? Is she a forbidden subject as well?"

"My sister?" Donovan frowned in confusion, then burst out laughing. "You see what I mean? I must be overly tired to forget that I have a sister these days. Then again, I'm not used to having a family at all. I really haven't had much chance to talk with Susan, but I would like to get to know her better."

The faint lines above R. T.'s brow deepened into furrows. "I'm not talking about Susan. I was asking about your full sister, Lillibeth. What ever became of her?"

13

Instead of heading right to the theatre as his impulses urged, Donovan forced himself to take a long walk along the waterfront area so he could collect his thoughts before confronting his mother. He hated to believe the story R. T. had told him, and yet, as he lost himself in the crowd of restaurateurs, poor folk, and buyers seeking bargains from Sicilian fishermen, his gut said that it was all true. Pausing at a wharf-side stall, the stench of rotting fish heads matching his mood somehow, he became aware of something tugging on the hem of his jacket.

Donovan glanced down to see a small boy looking up at him. "Hey, you come with me," said the youngster in broken English. "Come, my mama has fresh salmon. The best."

The boy reminded Donovan of how he used to hawk his own mother's many talents as an entertainer. He slipped a coin into the kid's palm. "Go back home," he said, ruffling the boy's mop of dirty brown curls. "Tell your mama to feed you some of that salmon."

"You come, too. She got more, oysters and shrimp!"

"Go on now, get going."

Donovan gave the kid a gentle shove, then walked away from the wharf and started toward the theatre. He searched his memory as he sauntered along the waterfront, trying to pick out what was real and what was fantasy. The sister he'd dreamed up for himself so long ago was still easy to picture, a tiny pink bundle of coppery baby curls and bright blue eyes, but had she been real? And if indeed she had been, why couldn't he remember her as that—a living, breathing baby?

As he started up Pacific Avenue, Donovan's thoughts turned to his mother. He'd long ago accepted her for the kind of woman she was, lukewarm running toward cold, both inside and out. That was her nature, the way she'd been shaped and formed by her father and, to a lesser extent, her mother. Because of that and the years of struggling when all they'd had was each other, he'd managed to forgive Lil for hiding the truth about his own father for so long. But this . . . if it was true that his mother had borne a daughter after him, and then . . .

Donovan couldn't allow himself to imagine what had happened to this sister of his beyond that. Even if he could, he had an idea his assumptions might be not nearly as ugly as the truth.

Egged on by something other than anger—a deep sense of loss or something uncomfortably close to it—he increased his pace.

Patience had never been one of Libby's strong points—although earlier in the day, Donovan had made a very good argument against being in a rush to do *some* things.

As a child, she'd been so anxious for nature to fill in the gaping hole where her front teeth had been, that she'd carved a pair of uppers from a cake of her mother's best soap, and worn them until she couldn't bear the taste any longer. A few years later, when she'd been overly eager to see her very first article for the *Tribune* printed in black and white, Libby had jammed her father's press in her haste to get the edition out quickly, and wound up delaying the issue by two hours.

Now that she'd finished writing Jeremy another long letter, one in which she promised again to be back home soon, she could hardly keep herself from flying out the door and racing to Savage Publishing to find out what had happened. Why was Donovan taking so long? He'd promised to come back to the house immediately after his meeting with R. T.

She gravitated over to the bay window as she'd done every five minutes for the past couple of hours, and quickly scanned the street. There was still no sign of him. Idly running her hand up and down the edge of the window casing as she pondered what to do next, Libby caught her fingernail on a loose pocket of wallpaper, tearing a hole in it.

"Damnation!" she muttered, absently working the tear back into the pattern, in hopes of patching it. As she smoothed the crinkled paper, a new thought occurred to Libby, one that filled her with horror. What if Donovan had never even made it to Savage Publishing? What if he'd been in an accident of some kind? No matter how anyone tried to convince her of their safety, Libby didn't trust San Francisco's cable railways. As far as she could tell, all that stood between a passenger and disaster was the brakeman's fragile hold on the brake. If he were to slip, just once . . .

As she imagined the car crashing to the foot of one of the city's steep hills, Libby cringed—and dug her nails into the wallpaper. The hole, which she'd almost masked from view, was now a long, ragged tear. After examining the new damage and deciding it was beyond repair, she concluded there was only one thing to do. Since the tear was near the window frame and wasn't terribly wide, she figured, if she were to neatly remove the offending strip from ceiling to floor, Donovan would never be the wiser.

Libby was about halfway through the task when she heard a key in the lock. As relief replaced her anxiety, she put the chair on which she'd been standing back in its corner position, wadded up the small bit of wallpaper she'd torn away, tucked it into her pocket, then dashed into the foyer.

A short, squat figure met her at the door in place of the handsome man she'd been expecting. "Oh," she grumbled, not bothering to hide her disappointment. "It's you."

"*Ja.*" Carrying two bags of groceries in her arms, Gerda nudged the door shut with her knee. "You are still here?"

"I think you can see that I am." Libby started back toward the living room.

Still toting the groceries, Gerda trailed after her. "How long did Mr. Donovan ask you to stay?"

"Actually," Libby snapped, in no mood to spar with the housekeeper, "he hasn't exactly asked me to stay, not yet anyway."

"*Nein?*"

"*Nein.*" Taking out her frustrations with Donovan and his father on the unsuspecting woman, Libby recklessly admitted, "In fact, he's tried to throw me out of this house—twice now—but I haven't had the good sense to stay away. Does that make you happy?"

Gerda smiled—at least Libby *thought* she was smiling. "You came back anyway and he let you in, *ja?*"

"*Ja.*"

Gerda nodded thoughtfully, then lumbered off toward the kitchen, leaving Libby to finish removing the strip of wallpaper. She was on her second pass—from the bottom up this time, since she'd removed a wider piece at the top—when Gerda lumbered back into the room.

"You must eat," the housekeeper said, holding a supper plate out toward Libby as if it were a gift. Two plump sausages, a thick slab of dark bread slathered with butter, and a cup of milk graced the plate.

"For me?" she asked, whirling around to stand in front of the damaged wall.

"*Ja.*" The housekeeper set the offering on the window seat, then folded her hands across her round belly, and smiled. This time, Libby recognized the expression as just that, a smile. "I clean your room now," Gerda announced; and then she waddled out to the foyer and disappeared.

By the time Donovan stepped through the theatre doorway, reasonably certain he could face his mother without exploding, the place was packed. It seemed every table in the center of the room was filled, as were several of the overhead boxes; and even the gaming area was doing a brisk business as usual. The roulette wheel was spinning almost continually, the steel ball bouncing into place time after time, and at the faro table, the shoe clacked incessantly as the dealer distributed cards. No fewer than three full poker tables were in action, with each of the seven player's seats taken, and the bar was well-populated with onlookers and losers.

As Donovan waded through the theatergoers on his way to Lil's office, his gaze flickered to the entertainers on the stage. Five of Lil's best actresses were warbling out the words to "Oh, Dem Golden Slippers" in unnaturally high voices. By turns, each of them bowed seductively to best show off her bosom, then turned to wriggle her cute little backside. But the routine wasn't the thing which caught his eye. To a woman, they were all wearing the same dress, hosiery, and garter that Libby had dared to parade around in last night before he'd dragged her back to his house.

His temperature on the rise as he recalled that his mother had been the party responsible for Libby's introduction into the saloon business, he glanced up at the seat with the best view in the house—the box dubbed the President's Suite—and saw that Lil was sitting at the rail waving a baton at the dancers like an orchestra conductor. He stared hard at her, willing her to look his way, and when she finally did, Donovan jabbed a finger in the air toward her office then headed that way.

Moments later when she burst into the room, he was staring out through the cracks in her painted window, his hands behind his back.

"Donovan?" Lil said breathlessly as she closed the door behind her. "I wasn't expecting you so soon. What is it? I have the girls working on a new routine, and I don't want them to get into any bad habits."

Feeling a chill settle over the room not so unlike the damp bone-chilling cold of San Francisco fog, he slowly turned to face her. "I'm sure they'll do just fine without you. I'm here about another . . . girl."

"Oh, that." She laughed, then turned toward the door as if the conversation were practically over. "I didn't do anything but make sure Libby had a place to stay for the night. You didn't expect me to turn her out on these streets, did you?"

"No, but thanks for reminding me that I do have a little score to settle with you on her account. We'll have to get to Libby some other time, though."

Her hand inches from the doorknob, Lil tilted her head toward her son. "If you're not here about Libby, what girl are you talking about?"

"Lillibeth."

Lil seemed to sag from head to toe, then might even have fallen had she not stumbled forward to lean against the edge of her desk. Donovan instinctively lunged toward her, even though, from the opposite side of the desk, there wasn't much he could do to help. When he saw that she'd managed to keep her legs under her, he backed away.

"I see her name is familiar to you," he remarked, pinning her with an accusing gaze. "Is there anything else you recall, maybe something insignificant, like the fact that she's your daughter?"

Still hanging onto the desk for support, Lil closed her eyes and took several deep breaths, looking as if she might faint at any moment. Although concerned about her, Donovan just wanted the truth, no matter how painful it might be or what he had to do in order to get at it. Trying to make her more comfortable and less likely to collapse, he carried his mother's chair from it's spot behind the desk, and positioned it right behind her.

"Have a seat, Lil." It wasn't so much an invitation as an order. After she complied, Donovan circled her, clasped his hands to the wooden arms of the chair, and leaned close. "Let's talk about Lillibeth a while. When was she born?"

Her bottom lip quivering, Lil didn't look up at Donovan as she quietly admitted, "Shortly after your fourth birthday. On August twelfth."

"So it's really true?" His fingers tightened on the chair and he thought he might even have rattled it a little. "All this time, I've had a sister and you never thought to mention it to me?"

"I never wanted you to know about her at all!" At last, Lil raised her head, but it was only to glare at him. "Now back away from me."

He didn't budge.

"Damn you, I said to back away! Now do it."

It cost him a lot, something Donovan didn't want to give until he had all the answers, but he reluctantly released his hold on the chair and stepped back a couple of feet. His voice hollow, almost devoid of emotion, he said, "This sister—she had a lot of curly red hair and big blue eyes, didn't she?"

Lil gasped. "Y-yes. Did R. T. remember that about her?"

"No. In fact, he didn't tell me a whole lot about her except her name. The rest came from my own memories. I used to pretend a lot about having a real and complete family—you know, a mother, father, *sister*, and even a couple of brothers. Did you know that?"

Looking miserable, Lil shook her head.

"Well, I did; and I thought of this make-believe family often." He trained one eye on her. "Especially, all the times I was alone at night."

Lil flinched as if he'd struck her, but Donovan wasn't going to let up. Not until he had his answers. "I have kept that fantasy with me for a long, long time, and now I'm wondering if that baby sister with the curls—" A sudden memory froze the words. "Christ! You called her Beth, didn't you?"

"Oh . . . oh, Donovan." Lil's hands flew to her face and then her head fell to her knees. The words, muffled but intelligible, she cried, "I swear I never dreamed you'd remember her. Never for a moment, did I think that. My God, what have I done?"

"I don't know. Why don't you tell me all about it?" Donovan was back at her chair again, and this time, when he hunkered down in front of it, Lil didn't try to send him away. "She was real, then, my fantasy sister wasn't something I made up?"

"No, no." Lil raised her head, looking haggard and worn. "She was with us almost a year, but I didn't know you remembered her, I swear it. I've never forgotten her for a minute."

Donovan raised a skeptical brow.

"Think what you will," Lil said, sounding defensive. "You probably haven't noticed that the dates are the same year after year. Every August around the time of her birthday, I have to take myself away for a couple of days to make peace with myself all over again."

Tears rolled over his mother's eyelids then and began to fall freely down her cheeks. Donovan couldn't ever remember seeing her cry. Not in his entire life. But the sight didn't keep him from asking the next question. "Why do you need that forgiveness so badly? What happened to Beth? Where is she now?"

Lil twisted in the chair, trying to turn away from him, but Donovan took her by the shoulders and held her in place. Beneath his hands, he felt her shrug as she said, "I honestly don't know where she is. Can't we just leave it at that?"

"I don't think so . . . *Mother*." He abruptly stood up. "I don't plan to leave any stones unturned, now that I know how much you've deceived me all these years—first with my father, now with Beth. I want to know what happened to her, and I'm not going to let you out of here until you tell me." Her head hung low, Lil didn't even look up at him. Almost afraid to hear the answer, he asked the question anyway: "Is she dead?"

"I don't know!" A new round of tears dampening her cheeks, Lil raised up. "I-I gave her to a nice family passing through the gold country on their way to southern California. I like to think she's still alive."

"*Gave?*" Donovan's fingers went rigid. For a moment, he wasn't completely sure what he meant to do with them, so he bunched his hands into fists and jammed them into his pockets. Trying hard, so very hard, to understand, he repeated, "Gave. You gave my sister away, like she was a stray puppy?"

Nodding miserably, Lil dabbed at her nose with the back of her hand.

"How could you have done such a thing?"

"I had to, don't you see?" Lil's eyes were bright with something close to fear. "I was barely managing when it was just me and you. I tried for so long as I dared, but couldn't make a go of it after Beth was born. I decided she'd be better off with folks who really wanted her and could care for her."

Suddenly, Donovan couldn't look at his mother any more. He stalked over to the file cabinet, careful to keep his back to her. "Am I supposed to get on my knees now and thank you for being generous enough to keep me?"

"It wasn't the same thing when you were born!"

His mother's tone told Donovan that he'd overstepped the bounds, but in this, he felt he had a right to set the limits. "Tell me how it was different, while I can still stand to be in the same room with you." He heard a little cry from behind him, like that of a wounded animal. Ashamed of himself, Donovan relented a little. "Sorry. I didn't mean that, but I've got to know everything. Tell me, please, and don't leave anything out."

"I'll try." She sniffed a few times, gathering herself, then blew her nose. "As I believe I've already mentioned, I honestly thought R. T. would do right by me after you were born. Shortly after I figured out that he never meant a thing he'd said, I discovered Beth was on the way. I had no one to help me, and by the time she was born, I was desperate."

"That's bull!" Donovan wheeled around to confront her again. "I saw the look on R. T.'s face when he asked about Lillibeth. Surely he'd have done something to help, and maybe even taken her in himself. Did you even ask him if he wanted her?"

Lil lowered her head and stared down at the wrinkled mess her tears had made of her black velvet gown. "No," she said in a hoarse whisper. "I never asked him."

"Why not? He opened his home and his family to me without reservation. He cares about me, Lil, and I think he cares about Beth. Couldn't you at least have given him the option?"

"No." She sounded hard, emotionless. "Even if R. T. had offered to take her, which I doubt his wife would have appreciated, I couldn't have given Beth to him."

"Too much pride, Lil?" Donovan couldn't keep the sarcasm out of his tone. "So much pride, you thought strangers could do better by your own daughter?"

"Pride didn't have a damn thing to do with it." Lil looked as if she were weighing a very difficult decision. When she finally met Donovan's gaze again, she was her usual defiant self. "I won't pretend that I'm proud of everything I've done in my life, especially some of the mistakes I made when your father betrayed me with his wife. But I'll be damned if I'll sit here and answer any more questions, if you're going to condemn me."

"I haven't condemned you." He bit back the urge to add, 'yet.'

"I suspect you might want to when I tell you the reason I didn't give Beth to R. T."

Their eyes still locked, Donovan knew, if he was ever to learn the whole truth, this was one time he'd have to hold his tongue. Nodding slightly, he accepted her terms. "I'm not here to pass judgment on you, Mother. I just want the truth."

"And so, you shall have it." She picked nervously at her fingernails, looking, oddly enough, a little like a schoolgirl. "I fell in love with R. T. almost the moment I met him. He's the only man I've ever loved."

Donovan had never heard his mother use the term "love" on any occasion, and certainly never in conjunction with a feeling she'd experienced. It was a shock to hear her talk this way, and to look into the face he thought he'd known so well, to discover human frailty and a distinct vulnerability. This, from a woman he'd always thought of as a rock. It humbled him a little, made him wonder for a moment about some of the more rigid rules he'd set for his own personal life.

"Back then," Lil went on to say, her voice stronger, "I was young and foolish. Foolish enough to believe in love and forever. When R. T. broke my heart, I thought I would die." She laughed bitterly. "Then, as I thought about it longer, I thought he should be the one to die; but, since I'm incapable of murder, I punished him the only way I knew how. I, ah, went a little wild when I found out he never planned to marry me, and of course, only wound up punishing myself." She sighed, then brushed a teardrop from the corner of her eye. "R. T. isn't Beth's father. I'm not real sure who is."

Donovan was stunned. Even though he'd always known his mother was a little "loose," he had a sudden need to get outside, to fill his entire body with some fresh air. "I think you've managed to give me more information than I actually wanted." He started for the door. "But thanks for being so honest. At least now I know everything."

Lil leaped out of her chair and beat him to the door, positioning herself between him and the way out. "You can't leave yet—not until you understand why I did what I did."

"I think I understand perfectly."

"But you haven't heard *why* I gave Beth away. At least let me explain that."

Donovan did not want to hear any more. He did not. But he could no more walk out on his mother now than he could rid himself of the sick feeling in his gut. "All right. But make it quick, if you don't mind. I need some air."

Pain, or something like it, rolled across Lil's tired features, ironically making her look as if she really were old enough to be his mother. When she spoke, her voice cracked, and even made her sound more like how he imagined a mother would sound. "Even if I'd have known who Beth's father was for sure, I wouldn't have tied myself down with another prospector. That's no kind of life for a woman or a girl. I'd grown strong enough to protect myself by then, but a youngster would never have had a chance. I found a new home for Beth because I couldn't bear the idea of her growing up in the gold fields the way I did."

"You raised me there," he reminded her.

"That wasn't the same as raising a little girl under those conditions." Hatred shadowed her eyes, but Donovan knew it wasn't directed at him. "You were different," she went on to explain, "not only because you were a male, but because you were as independent as hell, almost from the day you were born. The girl . . . Beth," a sudden tremor jerked Lil's shoulders, and she paused to collect herself, "I couldn't bear the idea of what might happen to her if we never got out of the gold country. I never wanted her to learn about men the way I did. You wouldn't have wanted that for her either."

Donovan couldn't argue with that. Though he was just past five when they left the mother lode country for good, he still remembered the way grown men would leer at his mother, some of them pawing her as if she were public domain, others making ribald remarks even though her young son stood at her side. He could understand her motives for sending Beth away, if not condone them; but for that reason, he couldn't quite bring himself to offer what she obviously needed so badly: unconditional forgiveness.

"Have you ever thought about going to look for her?"

"Lots of times," she said, hanging her head again. "But it wouldn't have served any good purpose. That family is all she's ever known, and I doubt they've told her about me. What good would it do to show up now? It would only break her heart and ruin everyone's life. And for what? So I could see how my project turned out? I may not be the best mother ever to hit the earth, but I'm not quite that selfish."

Donovan considered her words, but just couldn't agree. "Is believing that the reason you can sleep at night?"

"If I didn't believe that, I couldn't even live with myself." She raised her chin and looked straight up at him. "I still think I did the best I could by her."

The best Donovan could do by his mother then, was to give her shoulder a squeeze. "Thanks for your candor. I do appreciate it, and promise to give everything I've learned some good hard thought." Thinking he might not be seeing her for a while, Donovan impulsively leaned forward and kissed Lil's forehead.

"Oh, Donovan . . ." Choking back her tears, she reached up and touched his cheek. "If I'd a thought you and R. T. would actually meet up the way you did, if I'd known you'd find out about him and Beth, I never would have kept all these secrets from you. Never. Please believe that much of me."

But he couldn't. Not yet. "It doesn't matter now. What's happened, has happened, and we'll both have to find a way to live with it." He managed a short smile before informing her of the decision he'd just reached. "I intend to keep my interest in the saloon for the time being, but I need a break. You're going to have to get yourself another manager for the gaming end of things. Jack Thibbins ought to be a good man for the job."

"You're walking out on me? Just like that?"

"Not walking . . . just taking a little time for myself. I don't know what I mean to do right now. I only know that I'm not going to be coming back here for a while. Try not to take it too personally."

As he set her aside and reached for the doorknob, she stooped to begging, another rarity in this stone-woman mother of his. "Don't—please don't go this way. What do I have to do to make it right again? Just tell me, I'll do anything."

"It's not you, it's me. I just need to get away for a while." Then, because he could feel himself wavering, Donovan yanked open the door and blindly stormed out of the room, nearly colliding with the man who was standing on the other side—a man who had obviously been eavesdropping.

"Hello, Lil. It's been a long time." R. T.'s gaze traveled from her tear-stained face to her saloon-girl gown. "You're looking downright . . ." He didn't finish the sentence. The disillusionment in his expression said everything.

Having fresh first-hand knowledge of how badly Lil's little secrets could hurt, Donovan slapped his father on the back and said, "You look like you could use a drink. Why don't we go somewhere and have a couple of belts?"

14

By the time Donovan had returned to his house that night, Libby was beside herself with worry. She'd imagined him crushed in a cable railway accident a thousand times, shot by Thomas Savage during a jealous rage, and even swept off his feet by R. T.'s attractive secretary. When that last image had come to her, Libby unfortunately had been standing on a chair, putting the finishing touches on the wallpaper, which, by then, had shrunk away from the windowsill by close to two inches. After picturing Donovan with another woman, she'd manhandled the paper so badly, there was nothing left to do but leave it alone and hope that he never noticed.

When he finally had come through the door, Donovan had been grumpy and uncommunicative. He'd pleaded exhaustion, promising to have a long talk with her first thing in the morning, insisted that his stomach was too upset for him to eat, then gone straight upstairs to his room, leaving Libby alone as she'd been all day.

She hadn't taken his neglect well at first. And not just because he'd left her to dine alone—again. She'd gone upstairs after him, demanding information about his trip to Savage Publishing; and at last, he'd grudgingly admitted that he hadn't gained her any concessions for the *Tribune*, even though that was the major reason he'd gone to see R. T. in the first place. Libby had tried to question him further after that, but Donovan declared that he would not discuss R. T., the publishing company, or even his mother, and had stomped off to his room.

It took a while, but after she'd fixed herself a snack, then retired to her own room for the night, she finally put her anger aside and started worrying about Donovan all over again. Libby lay in the darkness for at least an hour, her eyes squeezed shut, but she couldn't drift off to sleep. She kept hearing something sad in Donovan's voice when he'd spoken to her, recalled seeing something in his remarkable eyes, a glimpse, she thought, of the soul he claimed he did not possess. If that's what she'd seen, it was a lost soul, for sure. The thought made her too restless to sleep, too worried about Donovan not to make sure he was all right. She impulsively threw her covers aside and started for his room.

When Libby reached the end of the hallway, she quietly opened the door and slipped inside the dark room. She could hear Donovan's deep, regular breathing signaling heavy slumber, and almost crept back into the hall without checking him further. But something bade her come closer, to see for herself. Moving stealthily, Libby made her way to the heavy satin drapes, parted them just enough to emit a slender beam of light from what was left of the full moon, then tiptoed over to the side of his mattress. Donovan had made a wreck of his bed coverings. The quilt was hanging off the edge of the mattress, the sheets were tangled around his legs and body, and both of his pillows had fallen or been thrown to the floor. He may have been asleep, but from what she could tell of his rumpled features and the deep furrows along his brow, Donovan wasn't getting much rest.

Libby stood staring down at the troubled man, wondering what she could do to help relax him without awakening him, when suddenly, he stirred. Muttering angry oaths she couldn't quite understand, Donovan rolled from his side to his belly, then exhaled in a loud mournful sigh that sounded almost like a sob. Libby couldn't bear to stand there watching any longer, without doing something to ease his suffering.

In spite of what he'd told her about his penchant for sleeping alone, in spite of the fact that should he awaken, Donovan might be angry enough to throw her out of his house for good, Libby knew what she had to do. After rearranging the sheets and quilt, she lifted the discarded pillows off the floor and carefully tucked one of them under Donovan's head. Then she climbed beneath the covers, fit herself against his backside spoon-style, and gathered him in her arms. Comforting him, she told herself, and not so incidentally, comforting the woman in love, while she was at it.

Still tucked away in her office, hiding from everyone and everything but her past, Lil stood by the window and stared vacantly into the night. Somebody was knocking on her door. She'd given orders not to be disturbed unless there was some kind of an emergency, so she supposed something of that nature was afoot—but she'd yet to move. She couldn't seem to care, not even if the theatre happened to be ablaze. The knocking came again, louder and more insistent.

More irritated than concerned, Lil finally tore herself away from the window and stalked over to the door. "What the hell is it?" The words were already out of her mouth before she'd gotten the door halfway opened, well before she caught a glimpse of her visitor.

"*Rand!* Wha—" Lil quickly scanned the area surrounding R. T.'s imposing figure. "Is Donovan with you?"

"He went on home, Lillian. Our son doesn't know I've come back here." He spoke softly and without rancor, looking so very much like the man she'd first fallen in love with, she couldn't stop staring at him. He took his hat in his hand, smiling as if aware of her discomfort. "May I come in for a moment?"

The logical person inside her screamed *NO!*, encouraged her to slam the door in his face and to never look back, but the broken-hearted female, the crushed spirit she'd buried so long ago, rose up from the dead and forced her to say, "I suppose so, but just for a moment. I'm very busy."

With no further preamble, R. T. marched into the office, closed the door behind him, and dropped his hat onto her desk. Then he turned to her, flashing an even broader smile, the one that once had the power to make her weak in the knees, and said, "I imagine, when I showed up here earlier, it was quite a shock to you."

"To say the least." She was able to talk—Lil was pleased about that—but she hadn't moved away from the door yet. Her knees were too weak to support her. "How'd you find me earlier? Did Donovan tell you I was here?"

"Indirectly. He was quite upset this afternoon after I asked about Lillibeth so I figured he might come to you for some reason. I had my driver follow him here."

Armed with a reason to turn away from him at last—

shame—Lil stared at the expensive fur hat crowning her cheap pine desk, and found in it a symbolic reason to regain her usual strength. The mink hat proved that she and Rand were no longer on common ground, no longer two people struggling to strike it rich, or at least to survive. They were separated by something much more formidable than years, physical absence, or even wealth—something Lil would never have no matter how well her theatre did: social status. Yet the thought of R. T.'s prominence did not humble Lil in the slightest. In fact, it served to bring out the fighting side of her instead.

One fist snug against her hip, she said, "I gather you listened in on my conversation with Donovan long enough to know everything about Lillibeth?"

"What I didn't know, Donovan told me over drinks." He hadn't lost that devastating smile. "At least he told me everything of interest to me, anyway—that she wasn't my daughter."

"In that case, I can't imagine why you stopped by, unless you wanted to try to humiliate me a little more. Sorry to disappoint you, Mr. Savage, but I'm fresh out of secrets."

"Lillian—sweetheart." He spread his arms. "Forgive me if I seemed cold or unfriendly earlier, but it was such a surprise to see you after all these years, and I must admit, a bit of a shock to learn you had . . . others in your life while we were seeing one another."

Bitterness spread throughout Lil, poisoning her tongue and her tone. "Oh, that's right. I forgot the rules—only *you* were allowed to have 'others' in your life. I was supposed to sit chastely, waiting for you to show up between your wife's pregnancies, then get down on my knees and beg for a few moments alone with you, right?"

"Oh, Lillian, you haven't changed a bit." He chuckled deeply, appreciatively. "Let's not argue about the hurts of the past. There's nothing we can do to change a thing either of us has done. If we must talk about those days, I'd much rather we concentrated on the good times we shared."

Finding a fair measure of strength in her anger, Lil strutted past R. T. and circled her desk, placing herself in the position that carried the most authority in her tiny office.

"The only thing we ever shared that I would even think of discussing with you is Donovan. Now that it looks like you've managed to take him away from me, I can't imagine there's a thing left which could be of interest to either of us."

He chuckled again, reminding Lil how much she'd once loved to hear him laugh. Then, collecting himself, he murmured, "Oh, my darling Lillian. I doubt you've lost Donovan—and don't try to tell me that you've forgotten the things which once interested us so much." Arching his eyebrows suggestively, R. T. slipped out of his topcoat and casually draped it over her chair. Then he made his way around to the back of the desk. "I can look in your eyes right now and see that you haven't forgotten a thing about me or what we once had."

Lil stood frozen to the spot, even though R. T.—her Rand—had moved so close, she could see little spikes of gray marching through the forest of black hairs on his head. So close, she could have reached out and touched him with very little effort. Fighting the impulse to do just that, wanting desperately to hold her ground, she demanded, "What do you want?"

"I realize it's been a long time since we've been together, Lillian." His eyes glittering lustily in the semi-darkness, R. T. slipped his hand along her neck. "But, do you really have to ask?"

She'd tried all these years to forget what those hands

could do to her, and in fact, had convinced herself that she had. She thought she'd managed to seal off her feelings as a woman, by turning her back on that part of herself so long ago. How could Rand have walked through her door and stirred her blood so quickly—and by his mere touch alone? What evil lurked in her soul that she could allow this man such power over her?

Even though she felt herself slipping past the point of no return, Lil stuck a defiant chin in his face. "Oh, I think I know what you want, all right, but what I don't know is why you're looking for it here. Don't tell me, that perfect little angel you married doesn't know how to keep your cock from crowing all over town."

Faster than Lil would have imagined, R. T. jerked her off her feet and pinned her to his chest. "That's one of the things I've missed most about you, Lillian." His voice was harsh, guttural. "You have such a wonderfully wicked way with words."

That's what he said, but Rand didn't give her a chance to utter even one more of the words which roused him so. His mouth came down on hers, hard and possessive, just the way she liked it, and Lil was lost to the man she'd never stopped loving.

The following morning, Donovan woke up sensing something was amiss. He opened his eyes, halfway expecting to find Libby lying beside him, but he was alone—as usual. He yawned, breathing deeply, and knew immediately that he hadn't been alone all night. Libby's springtime scent was all around him, on his pillows, saturating the sheets, and most disturbing of all, seeping through the hairs on his chest and into his heart. He closed his eyes, trying to recall when and why she'd come to him; but all he could remember was a feeling of contentment during the night, of being cradled, warmed not only by body heat, but from the inside out, for the first time in his life.

Confused, aching all over as he recalled the confrontation with his mother, yet assuaged somehow as he thought of Libby and the night, Donovan climbed out of bed and dressed himself. On his way downstairs, he checked the guest room, but it was empty. Alarmed as he recalled how angry she'd been over his failure to gain more editorial freedom for her, Donovan hurried downstairs. A fast glance in the living room produced no sign of her, but when he stepped into the kitchen, he found Libby bent over the stove.

Her back to him, wearing Gerda's apron to protect her buckskins from splatters, she was maneuvering sausages around in the frying pan. "Good morning," he said, tossing his white handkerchief onto the floor. "Is it safe to come in here?"

Glancing over her shoulder, Libby favored him with a smile. A *big* smile. "Of course. Come on in and sit down. I figured you'd be starving when you finally got up, so I fixed you some breakfast."

Not sure what he'd done to deserve such royal treatment, especially as uncommunicative as he'd been last night, Donovan picked up his handkerchief and took her up on the offer. He wasn't just starved, but *famished*!

The moment he sat down, Libby produced a mug of coffee for him, then she returned to the stove. He was in the midst of blowing a cool spot on the surface of the steaming brew, when she came back again, this time presenting him with a piping hot casserole dish.

After driving a spoon through the thick brown crust, she said, "There you go. Help yourself. The rest will be ready in a minute."

Donovan slid a suspicious gaze over the edge of the

casserole. The contents looked vaguely familiar, a little like scalloped potatoes, but like nothing he'd ever seen at the breakfast table. "What the hell is that?"

"Macaroni and cheese. And if you don't mind my saying so," she added proudly, "I make the best there is."

The warm, comforting aroma had reached his nose by then, but Donovan couldn't hide his grimace over the thought of forcing such fare down his throat, especially so early in the morning. He didn't bother to lie. "Thanks, Libby. I really do appreciate all the trouble you went through, but . . . well, I don't much care for macaroni and cheese; and even if I did, this isn't exactly my idea of breakfast. I'd rather have some sausage, and maybe a couple of eggs, if you don't mind."

Gerda would have snapped at him, or at least stomped off in a huff, had he dared make such a remark about her cooking, but Libby surprised him with a bright smile.

"The sausages are already cooking, and I'll have your eggs ready in just a few minutes. You could at least taste my macaroni and cheese, while I see to the rest."

Because he was starving and didn't want to irritate the cook—and only because of that, he assured himself—Donovan ladled a sticky spoonful of Libby's 'specialty' onto his plate as she went back to work at the stove. "You're looking nice and perky this morning," he commented, waiting for the macaroni to cool. "Did you get a good night's rest?"

"Oh, gosh, yes. I slept like a baby."

"Is that so?" He grinned. "Woke up hungry every two hours or so, did you?"

She laughed. "No, silly. I meant to say that I slept hard, like a log."

"Oh, then I guess you just woke up the one time and couldn't find your way back to your own bed."

Libby turned toward him, a grease-splattered spatula dangling from her fingers. "I got . . . cold last night. I just came in long enough to warm myself a little. Is that a crime?"

"Not that I know of."

Looking a little sheepish, she came back to the table long enough to shove a dish of sausages and bread under his nose. Donovan reached out and caught her wrist. "Thanks, Libby," he whispered, feeling awkward. "I appreciate the thought."

She shrugged. "It was no trouble. I was already cooking sausages."

"Not that." His fingers slid down to her palm and he squeezed her hand. "For last night. Thanks."

For a moment, he thought she was going to say something deep, maybe dangerously personal, but she just smiled instead and muttered a quick, "You're welcome." Then she flounced back to the stove and finished cooking his eggs.

Later, after Libby had returned to the table for the last time, she sat down with Donovan and picked at a sausage while he ate. After he'd filled his belly enough to relieve the sharpest and most urgent hunger pangs, he decided a bit of an apology was in order.

"I'm sorry I wasn't up to talking last night," he began, wondering how to broach the subject of the saloon without going into detail about his mother. "You deserved an explanation, especially about that damned editorial policy my father insists on having, but I was just too tired to talk about it anymore when I came in."

"You looked tired, too. What about now? Can we talk about me and my concerns with Savage Publishing yet? I can't stay in San Francisco forever, you know. Poor Jeremy and Hymie must be running themselves ragged by now."

Her leaving was another subject Donovan wasn't up to discussing. So he tackled the easier topic. "There really won't be much to talk about until I've had a chance to meet with R. T. and think things over a little more. All I know for sure is that I'm quitting the saloon business, at least for a few months, and may be in a position to help you a great deal, before long."

"*Quitting?*"

Libby's eyes were bigger, browner, and more luminescent than he'd ever seen them. Or had they looked like that all the while, and he'd never allowed himself to get quite so lost in them before? "That's right. Quitting."

"I don't understand," she complained. "And what does Lil think of all this?"

"She and I had a little disagreement. We've parted company, for the time being."

"How on earth can you 'part company' with your own mother?" Those big, beautiful eyes went narrow and judgmental, and for a moment, Donovan considered evading the entire subject of Lillibeth. But something, a need to talk it out perhaps, or maybe even his growing trust in and value for Libby's opinion, coaxed him to tell her all about his secret sister. When he'd finished, he added, "Lil actually wants me to believe that Beth is better off not knowing about us. Can you beat that?"

Libby looked thoughtful, and her eyes were moist. "I think she might be right. Odds are, the people who adopted her never told her about her true mother. Think how many lives could be ruined over this."

"I know all that, but it's eating me up inside, not knowing where she is or if she's happy. Wouldn't you feel the same way if we were talking about Jeremy?"

"Of course I would, and I understand completely what you're saying; but is your curiosity worth all the pain you might cause? That's what I think you ought to consider before you do something rash like hunt her down."

Like it or not, Donovan knew that Libby had raised several very good points. He sighed heavily. "All right. I'll think about it a little longer. In the meantime, I'm thinking about taking my father up on his offer of a job at the newspaper office."

"You, work for Savage Publishing? Are you kidding?"

Donovan shoved another huge forkful of macaroni and cheese into his mouth, and chewed slowly as he came to a final decision. "No, I'm not kidding. In fact, as soon as I'm finished with breakfast, I'm going right over to R. T.'s office."

"Oh, Donovan—this is wonderful!" Her eyes were positively glowing. "What department will you start in? Surely not circulation for the son of the publisher. Oh, I know! You'd probably make a great advertising solicitor!"

"Slow down a minute." Slightly put off by her enthusiasm, although he wasn't exactly sure why, he said, "I haven't even told R. T. that I've decided to join him. I don't know what kind of position he's got in mind for me."

"Sorry, but the way you said it, I thought you'd been with him last night and discussed all this."

Donovan had been with R. T. last night all right, but the only topic of conversation had been Lil and the missing Lillibeth, in whom R. T. had developed a decided lack of interest once he'd confirmed that she was not his daughter. As for the meeting with Lil, it had been brief, awkward, and very uncomfortable for all three "family" members. With nothing more than a good-bye to Lil, Donovan and R. T. had gone to a more respectable saloon for a drink, then continued on their separate ways.

He kept eating, avoiding Libby's questioning gaze, until he couldn't fit another bite into his stomach. Then, doing his damnedest to hide a playful grin, he pushed away from the table, patted his belly, and groaned. "Thanks again for the meal. I guess I'd better get over to Savage Publishing now, to see what kind of job R. T. has lined up for me."

Donovan started for the door, expecting Libby, any minute now, to stop him and beg him to bring her along. "Who knows?" he added, baiting her a little. "Maybe he'll make me the editor for the *San Francisco Tribune*. Wouldn't that be a hoot?"

"That would be pretty funny, all right."

Donovan turned to see that she was clearing the table, not even glancing his way. "Libby? Are you all right?"

"Me?" She slid his plate into a bowl full of soapy water. "I couldn't be better. Why do you ask?"

"I thought . . . well, I figured by now you'd be thinking of ways to get me to take you with me to the office."

Making another pass at the table, this time collecting the leftover sausages and bread, Libby shrugged. "I figured, if you wanted me to go, you'd ask. If you didn't ask, I was planning to make the trip on my own anyway." Setting the dish on the counter, she turned to face him. "I'm tired of begging for your scraps, Mr. Donovan Savage. One way or another, before this day is through, I'm going to have a good, clear idea about what's going on at that publishing company, and why your father is so dead set against my equal rights editorials. You can help me. Or not."

As she started back for the table, looking a lot like a rooster protecting its territory, Donovan burst out laughing. "You're a real beauty when you get fired up, you know that? An honest-to-God beauty."

Libby didn't even favor him with a glance, much less a smile.

"May I have the pleasure, Miss Justice, of escorting you to Savage Publishing?"

She finally looked his way at this, eyes keen and alive, but wary, too. He went on. "I was thinking that, once I'm part of the operation, I might have to hire you to look into our editorial restrictions and make a few changes." She was halfway across the room by then, closing in on him fast. "Do you think you could—" Libby threw herself into his arms, chopping his sentence in half, "make the time this morning?"

"Oh, yes, yes!" She showered him with kisses, his cheeks, his mouth, and even his eyes.

"Christ, Libby." Donovan took her head between his hands, stilling her. "If I'd known you were going to be so damned appreciative, I'd have asked you sooner." Then he helped himself to a kiss, a real kiss that left him wanting ever so much more. "Maybe we ought to make a little extra time right now," he suggested huskily, "so I can find out exactly how grateful you are."

"I can tell you, without wasting a second: Very grateful." She extricated herself from his embrace and headed for the table. "But first things first. We're going to Savage Publishing, just as soon as I clean up a little in here. Oh, and I'll need a minute to change into something more appropriate."

He still thought a better idea would be to drag Libby upstairs and ravish her; but he kept it to himself. "In that case, I'll give you ten minutes to get ready."

"Ten minutes! But it will take me almost that long to finish in here."

"Leave the kitchen. As for fixing up, you only need to do something with your hair." She'd twisted it into a knot at the top of her head, where already it listed so badly, he didn't know what was keeping it in place. "As for your clothes, you look fine, just the way you are."

Libby glanced down at herself, making sure that she did indeed have her buckskins on, then looked back at Donovan in surprise. "B-but I thought I was supposed to be impressing R. T. by wearing fashionable dresses."

"Impress him with your sharp mind and bright ideas instead. Those buckskins represent you as the editor of the *Laramie Tribune*." He paused to give her a wink. "I've noticed that you're a lot more relaxed and confident when you wear your reporter clothes, and that kind of attitude ought to go a long way in your favor today. Oh, and speaking of impressing him, I gave him the impression that you were staying at a boarding house, not here."

She blushed. "Thank you. I was wondering what he thought of me, you know, in that regard."

"Personally, I'm sure he thinks you're wonderful." Then he added impulsively, "So do I."

"Oh, Donovan . . . I-I don't know what to say to that."

Feeling one of those awkward, sappy moments coming over them, he quickly turned it around. "Say you'll leave that big disgusting reporter hat of yours at home. And while we're on the subject of hats, I think you'd better forget about the one I bought you, too. Even with that scarf draped over it, the thing looks like a whole *team* of horses ran over it."

"But I can't go to the city bareheaded."

"You'll think of something." Donovan started for the hall. "Ten minutes, Miss Justice. Don't make me wait."

Feeling as if her heart were turning somersaults, Libby reached for the casserole dish to at least cover the leftovers before heading upstairs. Smiling to herself, she realized that Donovan hadn't touched the bread or eggs and had eaten only part of the one sausage he'd taken. But better than half of her macaroni and cheese casserole was gone.

It was well after noon by the time Donovan met privately with R. T. During that meeting, Francis took Libby on a tour of the vast newspaper offices that made up Savage Publishing. The first stop had been in the pressroom, where she was treated to a demonstration of the huge Hoe rotary press, which was capable of printing up to twenty thousand sheets an hour, a far cry from the couple thousand her Campbell press could produce. Then they'd passed through the distribution section, where the newspapers were separated and bundled, and on through a pair of double doors that led to the reporting and editing section of the building, a large room cluttered with a maze of partitions. Libby had imagined that a publishing house like this would have impressive offices, but—as with the city of San Francisco itself— never had she expected anything of this scale!

"As you can see," Francis explained, "this is where we do most of our news gathering and editing. We naturally have our own wire and gather quite a bit of information through The Western Associated Press, but R. T. is very fond of the sensational kind of stories one can only get by sending reporters out on the streets."

Understanding exactly the kind of story Savage Publishing was known for, she impulsively asked, "You mean they go out looking for train wrecks, fire tragedies, and even stories like your father's? You know, how he lost one son, but gained the son of a forgotten mistress almost on the same day?"

Francis gave her a withering look, but it was accompanied by a wry grin, making her feel comfortable, as if they were old friends. When he led her into yet another hallway, he admitted, "Yes, Miss Justice. Our reporters are constantly on the lookout for stories precisely like the turn of events which brought Donovan into the family. Had this happened to Hearst over at the *Examiner*, father wouldn't even have waited until after the man's son was buried before splashing the sordid details all over the headlines."

"Really? Then why hasn't Hearst responded in kind?"

Francis shrugged, nodding to a group of reporters as they rushed past him on the way to an assignment. "He probably doesn't know about it yet. Father has many influential and powerful allies in this city. I doubt Donovan and his situation, with regard to our family, is openly discussed—whispered about, perhaps, but only among those who trust one another. Now then, what else would you like to see?"

It was easy to guess, by his tone and the abrupt change of subject, that Francis had said all he intended to regarding that aspect of his family. Libby moved onto the Savage business connections. "Donovan told me that your other brother, Thomas, presides over a business called S and S Enterprises. Is it true, that company also owns Savage Publishing?"

"Yes, it is, although, of course, Thomas has nothing to do with the daily business here at the newspaper."

"Then what other companies does S and S own to warrant the name, 'Enterprises'?"

Francis scratched his head in deep thought as they strolled out of the editorial offices. The gesture, along with the guileless, daydreaming expression on his face, reminded Libby of someone, but she couldn't figure who. It certainly wasn't Donovan.

"Actually," Francis said, finally answering as they crossed the wide lobby tiled in marble, "S and S owns a

piece of several small business, but the largest enterprise
and the biggest moneymaker is *Eldorado* Distilleries.
We like to think of it as the Savage family flagship. After
that, I would have to say our oyster beds in the Bay keep
Thomas pretty busy, especially now that Eastern competition is so fierce and the beds are subject to . . ."

Francis droned on about oysters and silt, or something like that, as they climbed the stairs up to R. T.'s
office on the fifth floor; but Libby wasn't really paying
attention to him. She was still reeling over the fact that
the Savage family owned what sounded like a rather
large San Francisco-based distillery. She couldn't recall
how or why, but she did know that the liquor industry
had long been a burr under the saddle of the equal
rights movement. Was there a connection between
Eldorado Distilleries and R. T.'s rigid editorial guidelines?

After Francis approached R. T.'s secretary, spoke
quietly with her a few moments, then returned to
Libby, standing where he'd left her, he gently squeezed
her shoulder. "Grace will make sure we're welcomed in
R. T.'s office. He may not wish to be disturbed just yet.
Are there any other questions I can answer for you
while we wait?"

Libby couldn't have asked for a better opening.
"Well, now that you ask, I am a little curious about
Eldorado Distilleries. You mentioned, it was your family's biggest moneymaker—you surely didn't mean to
say that it produces a bigger income than this newspaper and its affiliates."

"Yes, that's exactly what I meant. The distilleries
bought this publishing house as a sort of wedding present for the future Mrs. Randolph T. Savage." Francis
laughed, but then lowered his voice almost to a whisper. "I probably shouldn't have said that, but I suppose

Donovan will learn about father's rise to San Francisco prominence soon enough. R. T. was well-off when he arrived in this town, but after he purchased the distillery, he became quite wealthy. Trouble was, a man who ran a distillery wasn't much of a catch for a society-bound woman like Olivina—and she's the woman he wanted after my mother died. R. T. bought himself a more respectable business, and as Thomas would say, a well-bred wife."

Libby feigned surprise. "You mean to tell me that R. T. Savage isn't in the newspaper business for the same reason as you and I—the love of a really good story?"

Laughing richly, Francis took Libby's hands in his. "Oh, my dear lady. You are the only person I know—including the members of my family—who understands us journalists and why I love this business so much." He looked directly into her eyes, smiled shyly, and added, "I really do enjoy your company, Libby. I hope you'll be staying with us a while."

Sincerity poured out of Francis along with every other quality he seemed incapable of hiding—warmth, vulnerability, and an almost childlike sense of delight. That was when Libby finally figured out who he reminded her of—her very own father, Jeremiah Justice. No wonder she felt so comfortable in his presence, so safe. She only hoped that Francis wasn't as good a judge of character as her late father was. If he were to guess what she was really thinking about S&S Enterprises, she had an idea that, new friends or not, the apparent heir to Savage Publishing would escort her out of the building faster than his father's fancy shoes could kick her down to the lobby.

The thought gave Libby a start, making her wonder if she should even chance crossing paths with R. T.

today. If she were to blurt out a single word of what she suspected, no doubt he'd get her out of the building even faster than Francis would—perhaps through the nearest window. It would be better for all concerned, especially Donovan, if she were to gather up all the facts she could, and then make an appointment with R. T. Alone.

Her mind made up, Libby grasped Francis's hand, intending to thank him for the tour and make a fast departure; but before she could get a word out, the double doors at the end of the hallway parted.

Then it was too late to run.

15

Inside R. T.'s massive office, Donovan lounged, across the desk from his father. It felt good to be here this time, even right, regardless of the fact that he hadn't exactly been "to the manor born." As an added bonus, he'd discovered, now that he'd gotten to know the man better, that he actually *liked* him. A lot.

Donovan felt pretty much the same way about Francis, the brother he'd once dreamed of having. In fact, he not only accepted the hardworking newspaperman as family, but found in him a great deal to respect, too. Following instincts he'd honed through years of gambling with just about every kind of crook on the face of the earth—including a female sharper dressed as a nun, who kept a spring-loaded card holdout up her voluminous sleeve—Donovan had no doubt that Francis was, above all else, an honest, decent man.

Brother Thomas, of course, was another matter entirely. Maybe later, as he became more integrated into the family, Donovan would stand to be near the foul-tempered oaf long enough to find something about him he liked. Next time they met, he vowed, he'd at least give it a try. As for Susan . . . Donovan couldn't even think about her without also thinking of his lost sister, a reality so fresh and painful he simply wasn't up to facing it yet.

"Enough business for a while," said R. T., breaking into Donovan's thoughts. "Tell me a little more about this Liberty Justice you brought home with you from Wyoming. I have the definite impression she's more than just a cute little reporter to you. Is there something serious going on there?"

"Aw, hell, R. T. I don't think so—at least, I hope not." Sinking back against the plush leather chair, he rolled his eyes. If the truth were known, Donovan would have to admit that, even though he'd never known the meaning of "serious" where a woman was concerned, Libby had managed to shake him up a little. Enough so, that he continually caught himself thinking of ways to keep her around a little longer. He doubted such thoughts qualified as "serious" feelings for her; but even if it were true, he was not about to discuss such unnerving emotions with his father, in spite of his new, rather comfortable relationship with him.

Thinking the better move would be to brush the subject off entirely, he laughed and said, "Libby's bright, she's good-looking, and she needed a little help; so I helped her. That's really all there is between us. Hell, R. T., I'm nothing but a rounder who happens to be a sucker for a damsel in distress."

R. T. laughed along with him, making light of the situation, as Donovan hoped he would. "I'm glad to hear you're not seriously involved with a woman like that."

Donovan didn't care for what that remark suggested. "Don't let Libby's buckskins and men's boots fool you. As far as I can tell, she doesn't pack a gun or a knife."

"Not even strapped to her thigh?"

Donovan shook his head before he realized he'd inadvertently admitted something he normally would have kept to himself.

Looking more thoughtful now, concerned perhaps, R. T. adopted a surprisingly breezy tone, considering his grim expression. "Physical damage isn't what concerns me. If you're not careful, her kind can do much worse than leave a few scars. Believe me when I say that she and all her spinster friends usually have ulterior motives for just about everything they do. As the publisher of this newspaper, I know more about suffragists than I ever cared to know."

Donovan's fingers tightened around the arms of his chair. He did *not* want to discuss his feelings for Libby, and yet he could hardly sit here and allow his father to go on about her as if she were beneath contempt. Just as he was thinking of speaking up, someone knocked on one of the doors and slipped inside the room.

"Excuse me, Mr. Savage," R. T.'s secretary said, pushing the doors shut behind her, "but Francis and Miss Justice have finished their tour. Shall I send them in?"

After exchanging a fast glance with Donovan, R. T. sighed. "I guess you might as well. And Grace—bring us all some refreshments, too. The best."

After his secretary left, R. T. leaned across the desk and spoke in low, rapid tones. "Just remember what I was saying about your little playmate. Go ahead and have some fun with her, but watch your back, Son. In fact, watch your front and every little piece of your business right along with it. Mark my words on this— that girl's nothing but trouble, the kind of trouble that can make things very uncomfortable not just for you, but for our entire family."

Those remarks so shocked Donovan that he could hardly make sense of them. He had no chance to figure out how to respond to such a statement before Libby and Francis waltzed into the office with R. T.'s secretary trailing behind them.

"Ah, there you two are," said R. T., his glib tongue so smooth, Donovan wasn't even sure he'd heard right when listening to R. T. just a moment ago. "Take a seat. Donovan and I were just going over the type of position he might be best suited to here at the newspaper. What do you think he'd be good at, Francis?"

"I really wouldn't know without interviewing him, Father." Francis helped Libby into the chair beside Donovan, then sat down on the seat to her left. "I suppose a lot depends on the positions you've opened up for him. One of them wouldn't be managing editor, by any chance?"

The Savage men laughed together over that remark, but Donovan had an idea that, to Francis, it really wasn't a laughing matter. This was the one area concerning R. T. with which he was a little ill-at-ease. The old man seemed to take great delight in teasing others, especially his sons, making Donovan wonder if he didn't possess a usually concealed streak of cruelty.

All but confirming that theory, R. T. waited an uncomfortably long moment before saying, "No, Francis. I'm not looking to replace you. We're all in agreement that you've done a fine job as managing editor of this newspaper."

Grace returned and immediately approached the desk to serve each of the men a snifter of brandy. Only then did she turn to Libby. "May I get you a cup of tea, Miss Justice? Or perhaps you'd prefer something cool."

"Oh, no thanks. I'm fine."

Donovan caught R. T. studying Libby, and noted his frown. Although their recent conversation was still fresh in his mind, he thought his father's expression may have been prompted more by Libby's "hat" than Libby herself. She'd taken her work bonnet apart, removing all the little odds and ends adorning it, cut the brim down, and then covered the whole thing with her black lace scarf. It looked better than before, and was a definite improvement over the mangled hat he'd bought, but still . . . it looked a little odd.

"A toast to my boys?" said R. T.

While the men "cheered" one another, Libby slipped on her glasses and took the opportunity to glance around the office. The entire interior—the displays of fine leather, expensive furnishings, and dramatic bay view windows—positively reeked with the scent of power. Each carefully selected item pointed to Savage as a person of great power, from his fancy desk to the gilt-framed photograph of himself with President Garfield. Beside that hung another equally impressive photo of him with then newly appointed President Arthur. Again, Libby had to marvel over what heaven it must be to claim an important man such as this as a father.

Turning back to R. T., Libby listened in as the Savage men bantered about what positions Donovan would and would not be qualified to handle. At last, R. T. made a suggestion which made the most sense to her.

"What would you say to joining the staff as an advertising solicitor, Son?"

Libby exchanged a fast glance with Donovan, who was already looking her way with an approving and rather conspiratorial expression. With a triumphant smile, she said, "That's exactly what I suggested for him this morning. It takes an inordinate amount of charm, something Donovan is not lacking, in order to sling the kind of bull necessary to attract new advertisers."

Beside her, Francis dissolved into muffled laughter. To her right, Donovan just sat there grinning at her, looking like his usual amused self. But R. T., she couldn't help but notice, did not seem to be as tickled by her blunt, if accurate, account of what a job in advertising entailed. She blushed, cursing her impulsive tongue, and hoped that she hadn't put herself in too bad a light.

Raising one eyebrow, R. T. continued the conversation with his son. "As your friend so candidly and succinctly put it, I think you could do an excellent job of "slinging the bull." Would you like to start in the advertising department tomorrow?"

He shrugged. "I suppose selling advertising space is as good a way as any to learn this business. I'll be here first thing in the morning."

"Good, then. It's done." R. T. settled back against his chair and eyed Libby. "I imagine your business in San Francisco must be about concluded by now. Do you expect to return to Laramie soon?"

Libby made sure she gave herself plenty of time to formulate her answer without making a fool of herself or jeopardizing Donovan's newfound happiness. Until sitting here watching him interact with his father and brother, she hadn't realized how much becoming a part of this family actually meant to him. Still, she wasn't planning to be so considerate of his feelings as to concede the fight for editorial rights without at least launching one more plea for the cause.

"Actually, sir," she began, her voice carefully modulated to show respect, "most of my business here in San Francisco is concluded, but I simply can't leave without a little more discussion about my editorials. Since both you and Francis have expressed rigid opinions about my so much as mentioning women's rights, I was hoping you might at least tell me why. Maybe we have nothing more than a small misunderstanding."

R. T. didn't answer her at first, but silently studied her from across his elaborate desk instead. She tried not to flinch under his scrutiny; and yet she thought she detected a certain malignancy in his gaze she'd never seen before. Stealing a fast glance at Donovan to determine if he'd noticed the rancor in his father's expression, she realized that he was watching her too, apparently unaware anything was amiss. Libby immediately turned to Francis, hoping to find some confirmation from him, but he was tossing back the rest of his brandy, as oblivious as his brother to the tension radiating across the vast desk.

At last, R. T. broke the strained silence. "All right, Miss Justice, if whys are what you want, then you shall have them. Before you hear what I have to say, I'll apologize in advance, should I inadvertently offend you in any way. That is certainly not my purpose."

"Oh, don't worry, sir." At least he was willing to talk. "I promise not to take offense at your remarks."

"Hey, wait a minute here." Donovan leaned forward in his chair. "You two sound like you're choosing weapons. Can't this editorial problem be settled without what sounds like the beginnings of a big argument?"

R. T. laughed pleasantly. "Now, Son, I don't plan to lynch your friend. She gave me the impression that she wanted the cold, hard facts."

"And I do." Libby turned to Donovan, placing her hand on his forearm. "I appreciate what you're trying to do, but I cannot leave this town without knowing why the newspaper my family has worked for all these years refuses to give me so much as an inch of the freedom

I'm begging for. My mother wouldn't have backed away from this situation, and for that matter, neither would've my father. I can do no less."

Her eyes met his and held for what seemed like several minutes, then Donovan finally shook his head and turned away. "Hell, if this is what you feel you have to do, then have at it."

"Thanks." Libby met R. T.'s hard-eyed stare. "You were saying?"

"That I really have no intention of offending you, and I sincerely hope that I won't. And by the way—Donovan—I'd like for you to pay close attention to what I'm about to say, as well. This is an area of the newspaper business we haven't discussed yet, but you should understand our position a little better."

Pulling his chair as far forward as it would go, R. T. propped his elbows on the desk and favored Libby with a warm smile. "A friend of mine likens the woman's movement to his cable railway business, so I think I'll explain our position in those terms. The drive for equal rights, especially in regard to the vote, is kind of like asking the men of this nation to board a cable car with a new brakeman at the controls—a female. She doesn't know the stops, hasn't the foggiest notion of how steep the hills in these parts can be, and her tiny little hands are too small to fit around the brake. If all that isn't dangerous enough, she's not even physically strong enough to wrestle the car's brake to a stop in the event of trouble. Are you following me here?"

Libby was appalled. Didn't the man hear his own words? "Oh, but Mr. Savage, I don't see what your cable railway system has to do with—"

"Allow me to finish my story, then let me know if you fail to see my point. But please, dear, do keep in mind that there's absolutely nothing personal in anything I'm saying here. All right?"

The things he was saying and the way he was saying them were very personal, indeed, but as far as Libby could tell, she was the only one who noticed. Left with no choice, she settled back in her chair. "Please," she muttered, "do go on."

"Thank you. Most female suffragists would have us change the way this country is run from management to maintenance, even though we've managed to do a very nice job of running it so far." He looked to his sons now, avoiding Libby's gaze entirely. "Now I ask you two—do you see any reason to support a movement which threatens to derail our nation by putting female superintendents in charge and a posse of giddy girls at the brakes?"

Staring down at her own hands, her cheeks aflame, Libby waited for Donovan to reply. He didn't utter a word. To her right, Francis fidgeted in his chair, but like his brother, kept his thoughts to himself. And from across the desk, she could swear she almost heard snickering.

"I thought not," R. T. said, obviously pleased that no one had challenged his stand. "If we at Savage Publishing were to condone this silliness for even one editorial, we'd be opening the door to more of this tripe being splashed across our country's newspapers, until finally, all our fine cable cars were destroyed or driven into the Bay."

At the moment, Libby couldn't think of a better place for R. T. than at the bottom of the Bay. But, as before, she avoided speaking to or looking at him, even though she suspected he was waiting for some kind of comment from her.

After a few more silent moments went by, he asked rather brusquely, "Have I finally made the stand Savage Publishing must take on this issue clear to you, young lady?"

Libby stood up as proudly and determinedly as possible, under the conditions. She was shaking from head to toe, both hot and cold, and so mad that she was sorely tempted to find out if she had the strength to *throw* R. T. Savage into San Francisco Bay from his own impressive window. But she kept her dignity intact as she smiled at him and said, "Yes, sir. I would say that now I know precisely where you stand on the issue." She removed her spectacles and poked them inside her bag. "If you gentlemen will excuse me, I think I'll be on my way."

Donovan, so politely quiet up to this point, leaped out of his chair and claimed her elbow. "I suppose it is time we were on our way."

Libby backed away from him, still maintaining her decorum, but gravely in doubt as to how long she could hold onto it. She favored Donovan with the sweetest smile she could manage and said, "Please don't trouble yourself with me. Stay and visit with your father. I have some personal errands to attend to on the way home, and as you already know, I'm quite capable of finding my way around town on my own."

Reclaiming her arm, she turned to head for the door, but bumped into Francis, who was standing on the other side of her. Libby hadn't even heard him get out of his chair. "Oh, excuse me," she said. "I didn't see you there." She shook his hand. "Thanks again for the lovely tour of the newspaper offices. Next time you're anywhere near Laramie, do stop by and pay us a visit."

"Oh, but must you leave so soon?" He shot a furtive glance in his father's direction. "I-I was hoping we might get together a little later. Over supper, perhaps?"

This was rich. Francis Savage apparently flirting with her, as his thick-skulled father looked on, scowling. If she hadn't been so damned mad, Libby might have burst out laughing. She didn't; but she wasn't so enraged as to miss what she saw as an opportunity to rattle the old goat a little. "That sounds perfectly lovely, Francis. May I let you know a little later?"

"There's no need to bother," said Donovan, reclaiming her elbow. "I've planned a kind of surprise supper for us tonight. Maybe she can join you some other time, Francis."

Able to smile at the thought of both Savage sons fighting over her in the presence of their scornful father, Libby fluttered her eyelashes at Donovan. "That's the first I've heard that I was having supper with you tonight."

"Of course it is. That's why I called it a *surprise* supper."

"Oh, I see."

She supposed she could have kept the little game up for several more minutes, but all Libby wanted at that point was out of the suddenly suffocating office. Peeling Donovan's fingers off her arm, she said, "I'll have to get back to you later, too. I'm not sure I'm up to any more surprises today, and I have a lot to accomplish yet. Now I really do have to go."

Looking beyond Donovan to where R. T. sat, Libby had hoped to see that smug grin wiped off the man's face, but he still wore a rather satisfied smile. Forcing herself to be polite, she murmured, "Good day, Mr. Savage. Thanks for the tour of your offices."

Rising from his chair in the fashion of a gentleman, but not, Libby was sure, as one who felt she deserved the courtesy, R. T. said, "The pleasure was all mine, Miss Justice, all mine."

And that, as far as Libby could remember, was the first statement the man had made all day with which she could agree.

*   *   *

To Libby's amazement, Donovan's biggest surprise was not this supposed supper he'd planned for them, but the dogged determination he'd shown in following after her. She'd stormed out of R. T.'s office, wanting nothing more than a little time and privacy in which to plan her next move. Sticking close by like a hired bodyguard, he'd accompanied her all over town, from the railroad station, where she'd collected a new schedule for eastbound trains and wired her brother to expect her home soon, and on to Market Street, where she'd bought a little wooden replica of a cable car for Jeremy. Donovan had done this in spite of the fact that, throughout the waning afternoon, Libby had refused to talk with him except over the most trivial of matters, insisting that she needed time to think, to plan a new life for herself—a distinct possibility, considering the enormity of what R. T. had told her at Savage Publishing.

Of course, her reasons for ignoring Donovan weren't quite that simple. For one thing, she was still too angry with the father to have a decent, lucid conversation with the son. How could she, when Donovan was so obviously happy with this newfound family of his? Although she wasn't terribly pleased that he hadn't at least tried to back her up in R. T.'s office, she could hardly blame him for keeping quiet. He was trying to become a Savage, not alienate them.

Still, Libby suspected that he felt a little guilty about abandoning her, as it were. He'd insisted on taking her over to O'Farrell Street for a luscious and leisurely supper of succulent lobster at Delmonico's—the very meal he'd promised her the day she'd arrived in San Francisco. Although she appreciated the gesture, and even understood the awkward position he was in regarding his father, by the time they blew in through the front door of Donovan's house that night, Libby was still in a mood, questioning her blind devotion to the cause, her feelings for Donovan, and even the principles for which her own mother and father had stood. She was not in any way prepared for his sudden defense of himself.

"I'm sure you expected me to help you a little more today," he muttered, kicking the door shut behind him, "but Savage Publishing belongs to my father, not me. It's his business to run as he sees fit. I don't know the first thing about how a newspaper should be operated."

"I'm not questioning the way he runs the *Tribune*, or you for taking his side," she snapped. "Now if you don't mind, I'd rather not talk about this."

Libby wandered into the living room, leaving Donovan to light the lamp in the foyer. Inside the house, it was nearly dark—a perfect match for her mood. Strolling over to the bay window, she stared out at the dusky, fog-shrouded landscape and wrapped her arms firmly around her middle, fighting off the chill from the damp night air. She heard Donovan walk into the room and approach her, but Libby didn't turn to face him. God, don't let him start that topic again, she thought, eyes glancing up at the ceiling. She didn't know why she no longer wanted to fight "the good fight." She just knew that she didn't.

"Look," Donovan murmured, sounding close behind and very apologetic, "I'll admit that I didn't like some of the things R. T. said today either. But how can any of us be sure what's best for this country? For all we know, my father could be right about his stand on equal rights."

And that's when it all came together for Libby, when things began to make sense to her again. Before she'd fallen in love with Donovan, those words would have been fighting words. She'd have turned on him like a wildcat, scratching and clawing for equal rights, making damn good and sure he knew how terribly, terribly wrong both he and his father were. But now she had a pretty good idea that the equal rights movement and her love for Donovan were mutually exclusive. Would she have to give up one for the other? How? One choice would tear out her heart, the other, her soul. She was depressed just thinking about it.

Turning to Donovan, she smiled and said what she thought he wanted to hear. "You may have a point about your father. I didn't mean to suggest that he was not a fair man."

His relief was immediately visible. "I'm glad to hear you say that, Libby. I've gotten to know R. T. pretty well lately, and he really is an intelligent, thoughtful man. I'm sure he appreciates that about you, too."

"Thank you for saying so, but it really doesn't matter how he feels about me now. The way I see it, my business with him is concluded." That much, as heartbreaking as it may be, seemed to be true.

"Just like that?" He looked positively flabbergasted.

"Just like that." Libby touched the edge of his jaw, then turned back toward the window so he couldn't see the despair behind those words.

"You're really something," Donovan whispered against the back of her ear. "Do you know that?"

The relief in his voice went a long way in assuaging Libby's sudden feelings of guilt—or maybe it was shame. For the first time in her life, she was happy that her mother wasn't around to see what her daughter was up to. This way she would never have to know that instead of accepting the challenge as a woman and a reporter, she'd bowed to Savage's superior male power, and kept her mouth shut when she should have climbed up on that fancy leather chair and demanded her rights as an editor. What would she do next in the name of love? Completely turn her back on her mother and the promise she'd made to her as she lay dying?

"Libby, are you all right?" Donovan's lips were still nuzzling the back of her neck, making it easier and easier to forget all else. "You're trembling."

"What do you expect from the way you're fondling me?"

His hands circled her waist, then slid along the rough buckskin hugging her soft little tummy as he whispered, "So what you have is a physical problem?"

"Ummm, yes, I would say that it is." His hands moved even lower along her abdomen, whisking away all thoughts of self-recrimination. Soon Libby was smoldering inside as Donovan stroked her, caressing her through layers of fabric both rough and silky, until Libby thought she would go mad with need.

Her head fell back against his chest and she drew in a ragged, gasp of a breath before she could say, "Oh, God, Donovan. Whatever you do, don't stop."

But he did. He had to, in order to indulge himself with a real taste of her, to make certain he'd been mistaken about the hopelessness he'd thought he heard in her voice. Turning Libby in his arms, Donovan glanced into her velvety brown eyes, pleased to see they'd taken on the same lusty glow he felt raging throughout his entire body. Nowhere in her expression could he detect despair or regret. He held her close, so close she could have no doubts about his dire physical condition, then brushed her mouth with his as he whispered, "Give me Liberty . . . or give me death. And you'd better give me one of them pretty damn soon."

Her response was a deep and throaty laugh, which had him needing her all the more. Capturing that beautiful mouth with his, swallowing her laughter and taking it deep inside as if he thought he might preserve it there, Donovan kissed her again. He plumbed her roughly, deeply enough for Libby to gain full knowledge of his exact intentions. By the time he finally ended the kiss, her hands were grasping his buttocks beneath his jacket and one of her legs was hooked around his knee. She was his once again, and still on his terms.

"S-so . . ." He sucked in a euphoric breath. "So tell me, woman, what's it to be? You're not going to stand there and let me die, are you?"

She laughed again, the sound even throatier than before, and said, "I'll do my best to keep you alive, but I can't guarantee that I won't hurt you a little in the process."

A surge of hot desire tore through Donovan at those words, and he had to steal another kiss before raising his head to reply. "Don't sound so pleased with yourself. The way I feel right now, I'm afraid you're the one who could get hurt a little."

Again came that throaty laughter, and suddenly, Donovan couldn't wait another moment. He glanced around the room, figuring, since the rug had been good enough before, it would be good enough now. Before he could even start nudging Libby down to the floor, his gaze snagged on something, momentarily distracting him.

Narrowing his vision to be sure of exactly what he'd spotted among the shadows by the wall, Donovan stared at the area a moment. When he realized what he must be looking at, the thought of even standing in this room, much less dropping his trousers in it, filled him with icy terror.

He went cold inside, and in the very next second, Donovan couldn't have hurt a fly.

16

Libby noticed the change in Donovan immediately. Before she could comment on his sudden "transformation," he grabbed her hand and began dragging her out of the room. "Hey, wait a minute," she cried, wondering what she could have done to dampen his ardor so thoroughly. "Where are you taking me?"

"I, er, thought we ought to go upstairs. More comfortable, you know."

Donovan's gaze swept the floor as he pulled her toward the foyer. What was he looking for? she wondered, or was he hiding something? Libby scanned the rug behind and in front of her, but couldn't find a thing out of place.

When they reached the landing, Donovan abruptly released her. "You go on up," he insisted, waving toward the second floor. "That'll give you a little privacy to, you know, get ready for bed. I'll join you in a minute."

Libby resolved not to budge until she had some idea what was going on. "What happened out there? One minute you couldn't keep your hands off me, and in the next, you can't get rid of me fast enough. What did I do wrong?"

"Hell, nothing, sweetheart." Donovan laughed—actually, it was more of a nervous chortle, kind of like a giggle. Then he flashed the phoniest grin she'd ever seen. "Get going to your room. Everything's fine."

For a crazy moment, Libby wondered if maybe he didn't have another woman stashed in the living room, but she was too worn out both mentally and physically to give the thought much credence. With a weary sigh, she said, "All right. If that's what you want, goodnight."

"This isn't goodnight!" he called after her. "Once I secure the house, I'll be up to join you."

Libby didn't trouble herself by commenting on his odd behavior. She went directly to her room and slammed the door good and loud. But she had no intention of staying there. After grabbing her glasses, which gave Donovan a few seconds in which to embark on his clandestine activities, she quietly opened her door again and crept out into the hallway. She listened intently, but the only sound she could hear from below was the rapid tattoo of Donovan's boots as he took off running down the hallway. Moments later came the clatter of pots and pans, a few muffled curses, then the thunder of his boots as he ran back up the hallway.

Hiding in the shadows, Libby flattened herself against the wall, but the gesture wasn't necessary. Donovan hadn't even looked up as he ran past the landing and ducked back into the living room.

What could be more interesting down there than what she had to offer upstairs? Had she been too forward, too willing? She remembered some schoolgirl chant about free milk and the cow's in the barn, but couldn't recall exactly what point the fable tried to get across. She'd done something wrong, but what?

*   *   *

Aware of the cold sweat trickling down from his brow, Donovan approached the bay window in the living room carrying the mousetraps he'd baited with bits of Libby's casserole. After positioning each of them behind the curtains, he ran out of the room as if the devil was on his trail. He took the stairs two and three at a time, and by the time he burst into Libby's room and slammed the door behind him, he was puffing like a steam engine chugging over the Rockies.

"There . . . we . . . are," he said between gasps. "How come it's so dark in here?"

"Because I'm asleep." Her voice sounded distant and muffled. "Go away."

"Now, Libby," he chided, feeling his way to the foot of the bed. "That's no way to talk. You don't sound like the same seductive woman I held in my arms downstairs."

"I'm not. I've . . . changed my mind."

"In that case," he said, slipping out of his clothes and hanging them from the one of the four posts. "I guess I'll have to convince you all over again." Concerned more about the uninvited guests in his house than Libby's feeble attempt to convince him she'd had second thoughts, Donovan tore back the covers and jumped into bed beside her. She held him at arm's length.

"Hey, what's this?"

"I told you. I've changed my mind. Why don't you go back downstairs and keep chasing after the shadows in the living room."

"Ah, so that's it. You were listening in on me."

She muttered something unintelligible, then tried to roll away and turn her back to him. Chuckling to himself, Donovan pinned Libby's wrists to the pillow on either side of her head, keeping her immobile. "You might be interested to know that the shadows I was chasing were shaped like *mice.*"

"Mice?"

He nodded, fighting a shudder. Through the years, Donovan had faced guns, knives, drunken gamblers, and hands the size of hams clamped firmly around his throat, but never, ever was he more terrified than when confronted by a member of the rodent family. His fears came from long, long ago, but they ran deep, too deep apparently, to fade away as he'd hoped they would have by now.

He tried hard to keep that fear out of his voice as he explained. "That's why I hustled you out of the living room so fast. I didn't want to alarm you by saying that I thought mice or rats had gotten into the house, so I just sent you upstairs while I went to get traps and set them."

"I didn't see any mice in the living room."

"If you need proof, go down and have a look for yourself. I didn't actually see a mouse, but I found where they've eaten away almost an entire strip of wallpaper by the bay window."

"The wall—" For a minute, Donovan thought she was going to apologize for doubting him, but then she burst out laughing.

"You think mice are funny, do you? Fine! You check the traps in the morning, and you take the disgusting creatures outside and bury them. I'd just as soon not have to fool with them anyway, thank you."

Still chuckling softly, Libby said, "I'd be happy to check your traps tomorrow." Then, surprising him, she wrapped her arms around his neck and turned serious. "I'm wondering if maybe you won't be setting traps for me next. Aren't you getting a little tired of me being underfoot?"

"What does that have to do with mice?"

"Nothing, except that I can't stay here forever. Even if I could, there's no point in it. Not now that my business with your father is finished. There's a train to Laramie tomorrow afternoon. If I had any sense, I'd be on it."

"You're not going anywhere tomorrow." He didn't know a hell of a lot about emotions, relationships, or exactly what he was feeling for Libby, but Donovan did know one intractable thing: He was not ready to let her go just yet. "I don't know why you had to bring this up at all dammit, but you've said yourself that it won't matter if you stay in San Francisco another few days or weeks. Your brother and his helper are doing just fine without you."

"It isn't just the paper I'm worried about. I have to think of—"

But Donovan didn't want to hear any more of her excuses for leaving. He hushed her with a well-placed finger. "If you don't stay at least through Saturday, you'll be putting me in a very bad situation with the countess of Timbuktu, or wherever the hell she's from."

"The countess? I'm afraid I don't know what you're talking about."

"She's the society woman giving the Young Gentlemen's Ball Saturday, remember? If you're not here, I'll have to attend the damn thing. There's no telling what all those debutantes will do to try and lasso a fine specimen like myself." He undid the buttons at the throat of her nightgown. "They'll be wanting to put their hands all over me, and kissing me," he showed her exactly what he meant, "and all manner of things just to win me over."

"I see," she murmured, sounding a little breathless. "And that would be so terrible?"

"Oh, yes. Why the next thing you know, one of those society-bound darlings could have me trussed up like a hog at a barbecue. You wouldn't want that kind of life for me, would you?" Moving up to Libby's mouth, he kissed her thoroughly. "What do you say? Stay a few more days and give me life, Liberty, and the pursuit of a little more happiness."

Libby burst out laughing, then caught Donovan's face between her hands and scattered a few kisses across his lips. "All right, you've convinced me to stay until Sunday. After that—"

Donovan silenced her with a kiss. He didn't want to think about "after that." In fact, didn't want to think about anything except how good Libby felt beneath him, how soft and smooth her skin felt against his palms, and how very, very much he wanted her at that moment. He wallowed in sensations like never before, savoring the sweet taste of Libby's mouth and the sunshine bouquet aroma of her hair, and reveled in the intoxicating sound of her cries as he brought her to climax again, and again. His control hanging by a ragged edge, with every nerve ending in his body crying out for release, at last he let himself go, and spun mindlessly into an intense, but bittersweet finish.

Stunned, Donovan lay still atop Libby for several moments, wondering if perhaps he'd died, but far too exhausted to test himself to see if he were still alive. When she moaned beneath him, pointing out that indeed, he'd survived the encounter, he rolled to her side and lay flat on his back.

Something had gone wrong with him. After what they'd just shared—an experience unlike anything he'd ever known—he should have felt hollowed out, empty in both mind and body. But he didn't. Instead, Donovan found himself wanting something more, needing a certain comfort. Remembering the night Libby had come to him and slipped into his bed, and needing to feel that sense of contentment again, he rolled to where she lay, gathered her into his arms, and tucked her head beneath his chin. It wouldn't hurt a thing to stay with her for just a little while. To rest, not sleep, for two hours, tops. It wouldn't hurt a damn thing.

The next morning, Donovan woke up to the sound of birds singing right outside his window—an oddity, considering he never slept with his window open. He yawned, breathing deeply, and picked up the scent of lilacs mingled with the unmistakably earthy aroma of lovemaking. Then something soft and warm—Libby— stirred in his arms, and he knew in an instant he was still in her bed with his head resting not three feet from her open window.

"Oh, Donovan?" her sweet voice called. "Wake up and take a look around—you spent the night in my room."

He cracked one eyelid, even though he knew exactly where he was. "Oh, hell. I must have been more tired than I thought last night. Hope I didn't keep you awake."

"Not at all. In fact, I kind of liked snuggling with you." The minute the words were out, Libby regretted them. She'd agreed to follow Donovan's rules, no strings, no expectations, and had even gone so far as to proclaim herself as a believer in free love. It didn't matter that she'd discovered—too late—those rules weren't for her; but she sure couldn't explain her feelings to him without making herself out a liar. He would realize in a minute that she was just another woman who had her own plans for "trussing him up like a pig at a barbecue"—even if she didn't have a clear idea how to go about it. And then he'd toss her on the first train to Laramie, without looking back.

Donovan tapped the tip of Libby's nose, snapping her out of her musings. "Hey, you—wake up," he said. "Don't expect this snuggling every night you're here. I think last night I probably didn't wake up because down deep I didn't want to have to run bare-assed naked to my room in the dark. Not while there's still mice roaming around the house."

Reminded of her accident with the wallpaper, Libby stuffed the corner of her pillow into her mouth to keep from laughing out loud. Donovan would find out soon enough that he didn't have mice. Surely by daylight, he would see that some*one*, not something, had ruined his wallpaper. After that, it wouldn't take him long to figure out who'd made such a mess of his lovely home.

"What are you laughing at?" he asked, rising up on one elbow.

Donovan loomed above her, his dark hair mussed and falling over one eye. His grin was so wicked and tempting, Libby couldn't remember why she'd been laughing. "Was I?"

"Yes, and if you think it's funny that I'm a little afraid of mice, don't. Everyone's afraid of mice," he insisted. "Aren't you?"

"Not really," she admitted, fighting off a new attack of the giggles—and losing the battle. "E-especially the ones in this house."

"You wouldn't think any of this were funny if some little furry creatures were running up your legs—like this." He dove beneath the covers before she realized what he was up to, and began tickling the bottom of her feet.

Libby shrieked and tried to kick him off the end of the bed at first, but when Donovan slid his hands up her legs, not like a mouse, but like a hungry wolf preparing to devour her, she stilled. He spread hot kisses up her thighs, then feathered them across her belly, his tongue occasionally flicking her navel, turning her moans to something feral and guttural. She was crazy with wanting him, her pulse pounding in her ears, and wondering what he would do next—when Libby realized someone was knocking on the door. Then it abruptly opened.

"Excuse me, Miss Justice," said Gerda. "I thought I heard you awake in here. There's a Miss Susan Savage downstairs to see Mr. Donovan, but he did not come home yet."

Her pulse in her throat now instead of her ears, Libby quickly raised her knees, making a tent out of the puffy quilt, and hoped she'd managed to hide the bulk of Donovan's body.

"Oh, ah . . ." She cleared her throat. "Someone to, er . . . see Donovan?"

"*Ja*—vell, actually, I thought you might receive Miss Savage in Mr. Donovan's place. *Ja?*"

Donovan's head was flat against Libby's belly, his tongue, buried in her navel. She could tell he was trying hard not to move, as she was, too, but oh, the mouth-watering sensations that tongue was rousing in her. Libby squirmed as she caught her breath and said, "Uh, yes. Tell her I'll be down in a few minutes."

Gerda started to back out the door, but stopped. "I baked some special blueberry muffins. Vant me to serve them with some nice, hot tea?"

Donovan suddenly clutched Libby's hips, the only suggestion he gave that he was fighting a catastrophic event, but then sneezed against her belly in spite of the effort. To cover the sound, Libby quickly fell into a coughing fit. At the same time, instinct drove her to clamp her knees shut. When she heard Donovan's response, a low agonized groan, the outrageously embarrassing situation struck her funny bone. She gave into a fit of hysterical laughter.

Gerda, who'd watched Libby's ever-changing expressions with increasing bewilderment, cocked her head and furrowed her brow. "Is everything all right?"

"S-sure," she managed to say between gasps. "I think I got a feather up my nose. Oh, and muffins sound like a great idea."

This time, Gerda finally did step out into the hallway, but she didn't close the door until she'd taken one final long look inside the room.

When Libby felt they were safe, she raised the quilt and screamed in a whisper. "Get out from under there! Do you have any idea what you just put me through?"

"What *I* put *you* through?" Donovan exploded up from between the sheets. "I damn near suffocated under there! And why'd you try to cut me in half with your knees? I think you broke some of my ribs."

"That was an accident." Libby burst out laughing. "I didn't mean to hurt you. I guess it was just an automatic reaction I couldn't control."

"Oh, I see . . ." Donovan took her hand and pulled it beneath the covers. Uttering a low moan when he had her fingers where he wanted them, he muttered, "So is this."

Libby jerked away from him as if she'd touched fire. Maybe, she had. "What are you suggesting?" she whispered harshly. "Your sister's downstairs, and she's waiting not just for me, but for you, too!"

"So what? She can wait a few minutes while we—"

"Don't be ridiculous. I can't . . . you know, with her waiting downstairs." Libby rolled to the edge of the bed, but Donovan caught her from behind.

Fitting her bottom against the part of him that would not be denied, he took her breast into one hand and lightly massaged the nipple as he whispered thickly, "You can . . . and you will. And just to make sure we don't keep *anyone* waiting too long, we'll do it your way—as fast as you want to go." His hand slid lower, parting her legs, and then he began to move, sliding back and forth along the slick curves of her body. By then, Libby couldn't even remember his sister's name.

Twenty minutes later, Libby waltzed into the living room to find Susan sipping a cup of tea. "Sorry to have kept you waiting, but I'm afraid I was overly indulgent with myself today, and slept in."

"Oh, please, don't apologize. I had no idea you were staying here."

"Oh, well, I'm not exactly. Last night it was late, and er, I was only . . ."

"Goodness," Susan blushed and looked away. "You don't have to explain yourself to me. I'm just happy you agreed to come down and talk to me."

Embarrassed, but tingling from head to toe as she recalled the frantic, thrilling lovemaking she and Donovan had just shared, Libby settled on the sofa across from where the young woman sat.

Her composure back in place, Susan remarked, "That's really an unusual outfit. Do all the women in Wyoming dress this way?"

Laughing softly, Libby admitted, "No, I'm kind of an oddity at home, too. I generally explain that I wear these buckskins because of all the traveling I do on horseback as a reporter, but between you and I, they're also a heck of a lot more comfortable than any dress I've ever owned."

Susan was still laughing, making Libby feel completely at ease, when Donovan stepped into the room. He was wearing a trim dark suit without the brocade vest, and in place of his usual string tie, he wore a smoke-gray tie fashioned into a large bow at his throat. Donovan the businessman supplanting Donovan the gambler, she supposed, but Libby missed the charm of his satiny vest.

Smiling warmly at his sister, Donovan glanced repeatedly at the floor near the bay window as he greeted her. "Hello, Susan. What a nice surprise."

"Good morning, Donovan," she replied. "I probably should have sent advance notice of my visit, but I was just too eager to talk with you to wait. I hope you don't mind."

"Not at all." He glanced at Libby, favoring her with a smile which would have gotten him arrested had he flashed it in front of her father when he was alive. "Morning, Libby. You're looking bright-eyed and rosy-cheeked today. Sleep well, did you?"

She willed herself not to blush and tried to think of something sassy to say in return, but the best she could do was, "Thanks. You're looking pretty good yourself."

"I can't remember when I ever felt better."

At least then he had the decency to turn away, giving Libby a chance to regain her composure. After checking all three mousetraps and finding them empty except for bait, Donovan made his way across the room and joined her at the sofa.

"So," he said, addressing his sister. "What are you so eager to talk about?"

Shyly dropping her gaze to her lap, Susan's voice was surprisingly strong as she said, "I've been thinking over some of the things Libby talked to me about the night of our welcome party for you. I'm proud to say that I've decided to join the National Woman Suffrage Association."

Mortified to realize how much influence she'd had on the young woman, Libby beat Donovan to the obvious question. "Oh, but Susan—what about your father? He'll be furious if you join the cause. Are you aware of that?"

Still keeping her eyes downcast, Susan shrugged. "I'm to be married soon, and won't have to answer to him much longer."

"That might be true," said Donovan, "but then you'll have a husband. What if he objects?"

At last, Susan looked up and regarded them both. "I plan to tell Henry about this decision later, but I can't imagine that he'd be terribly interested in our country's political problems, at least regarding suffrage. We'll be living abroad within the year, anyway, and I did so want to do something to help the cause before I go. Surely there must be some way for me to be useful."

Libby and Donovan exchanged glances. She nodded, giving him the floor—Susan was, after all, his sister.

He propped his elbows on his knees and leaned forward. "It sounds to me like you've already made up your mind, even though you know our father won't be happy about it. What are you looking for from me? Advice?"

"Not really." She glanced at Libby, suddenly looking uneasy, then back to her brother. "I just wanted you to know about my decision. I thought, with Libby being so active in women's rights and all, that you'd be . . . happy for me, I guess."

"Of course I am, Susan." He rose and crossed over to her chair. "If you want to champion the women's vote, I think you should. The idea doesn't bother me the way it does R. T. Just be sure to leave the *San Francisco Tribune* and its affiliates out of whatever you do." He laughed heartily, then reached down and took her hand in his. "Speaking of the newspaper, this is my first day on the job at Savage Publishing, and I'm already late. I have to go."

He brought Susan's fingers to his lips, bestowing a kiss to them, and Libby could see the unspoken love, or at least, a deep family affection, reflected in his stormy blue eyes. If Donovan had been planning a sentimental good-bye to Libby, it was interrupted as Gerda lumbered into the living room carrying a serving tray.

"Mr. Donovan!" Her heavily-lidded eyes went round for a moment. "But you are not home."

"Ah, but yes, I am. I . . . just came in."

"I did not hear you arrive." Looking puzzled, she asked, "Do you vant tea and muffins with the ladies, or me to cook you a nice big breakfast?"

"Neither, actually. I have to leave now."

"You just came in and now you must leave?"

"That's right."

Shaking her head and muttering to herself in German, Gerda set the tray on the coffee table and then waddled out of the room. Donovan was one step behind her.

"I really do have to be on my way," he said over his shoulder. "Glad you stopped by, Susan, and good luck with your enterprise. Libby . . . I'll see you later this afternoon."

"Good day, Donovan," said Susan. "Oh, and Henry and I would like to take you and Libby to the Cliff House this coming Saturday. Can you make it?"

At the arched doorway, he turned and shrugged. "Whatever Libby decides is fine with me." And then he was gone.

Looking much more relaxed, Susan settled back against the chair, yet strangely enough, her spine never quite met the fabric. Libby saw the gesture as an opposite to her own social status and upbringing—her idea of relaxing would have been to throw her leg over the arm of the sofa. How long before Donovan would be employing this same stiff-backed formality? No longer looking into her lap, but directly at Libby, Susan said, "I had the feeling you were a little surprised by my decision. I hope the fact that I mentioned you as a major reason for joining the cause didn't upset or embarrass you."

In some ways, it did, but Libby could hardly explain any of them to her. She smiled. "No, of course not. I'm just concerned that I didn't also mention some of the difficulties you'll be facing as a suffragist. Most men don't think much of our activities, and here in San Francisco, I've noticed that many women feel that way, too."

"You don't need to worry about me. I'm stronger than I look." This surprised Libby, as she hadn't noticed a wealth of insight in the young woman before. Susan went on, indeed sounding stronger. "Those few things you said to me the other night got me to thinking about my life and what I hope to accomplish with it, especially the part about my living in a fantasy world, compared to most women. I do want to help others, in particular those who cannot help themselves. I also think it's about time I started raising more . . . hell."

Libby almost laughed out loud. Susan had eked out the word 'hell' with so much effort, she was sure this was the first time the young woman had ever sworn. Something sharp, a feeling close to envy, slashed through Libby's breast as she studied the enthusiasm radiating from Susan's expression. The neophyte suffragist was really excited by the idea that she could make a mark in this male-dominated world, no matter if her contributions made only a barely discernible scratch.

Seeing this in her, watching the embers of pride catch fire in Susan the way they'd once caught fire in her own heart, a lump of regret swelled in Libby's throat. She felt like a traitor to the cause, a turncoat. How could she be dispensing advice on equal rights to anyone?

"How do I sign on?" asked Susan.

"You're absolutely sure you want to do this?"

"One hundred percent, completely."

"If that's the way you feel . . ."

To test her a little, Libby considered the possibility of asking Susan to gather some information she'd been wanting since she'd found out R. T. Savage owned a distillery. She hadn't done a thing about it herself yet because, frankly, she was more than just a little nervous over the idea of rattling the cage of such a powerful man. Especially since the man in question already regarded her with a jaundiced eye. However, if his own daughter were to do a little checking up on his holdings, Libby doubted he'd even notice, much less connect Susan to the NWSA.

Feeling good about the plan, Libby said, "I need some information on a company called *Eldorado* Distilleries. I understand it belongs to your family. Are you aware of that?"

"Of course." She laughed as if Libby had made some grand joke. "We've only been in the newspaper business a few years now. The distillery is our backbone."

"Then perhaps I shouldn't even consider you for this job."

"But why not? You've got to give me a chance."

Careful with her wording, Libby lowered her voice and said, "This job involves the investigation of your family's business. I feel awkward asking you to do such a thing, especially knowing that it won't be easy for you."

Susan contemplated this for a minute. "I can't say I'll enjoy checking up on my family, but easy is all I've ever known. I really want to do something useful, even if part of what I do gets to be a little unpleasant." The excitement was back in her expression, more flagrant than ever. "What is it you want me to do?"

"All right then." Sure she'd given the young woman every chance to back out, Libby said in hushed tones, "I need for you to send a couple of wires regarding *Eldorado* and the liquor industry in general. You may not like the answers you get, and in fact, may choose not to bring them back to me once you study their content. If that's the case, I'll understand and nothing more will be mentioned about it. Either way, you and I will remain friends. Understood?"

"That's it?"

"Yes, that's all there is to it."

Susan leaped out of her chair. "Then I'd better get going. Whom do I wire and what do I say?"

"I'll give you written instructions." Although the tea had gone cold and the muffins were untouched, Libby rose from the sofa and bid Susan follow her as she headed for the credenza in the foyer. After removing paper and pencil from a drawer in the small hutch, Libby jotted down a couple of names and queries. Before she handed the paper to Susan, she asked, "I want this information gathered as quietly as possible. Can you send these wires without your father knowing?"

"Of course. I've got a driver out front who'll be with me all day. Should I wait for the answers or go back to the telegraph office and check on them from time to time?"

Libby shrugged, not certain how long it would take to make the contacts necessary. "Do whatever you feel is safest for you—and while you're at it," she muttered, thinking of more complications, "be sure to use an assumed name, not your own or mine. Make one up, but be sure to mention that you're representing a small group of women from the NWSA here in California."

Her blood heating the way it used to whenever she began an assignment for the cause, Libby handed the note to Susan and issued one final warning. "Get back to me as soon as you have answers, but make sure it's me you come to—and only me."

"I understand." Susan grinned as she stuffed the paper into her velvet bag. "In regard to the cause, I suppose Donovan is the enemy, being a male."

"I wouldn't go so far as to say that," Libby said as she opened the door, "but he is—"

The rest of the sentence died on her tongue when she realized someone was standing on the other side of the threshold.

17

"*Oh . . . hello.*"

There stood almost the last person Libby expected to see today, Donovan's mother, wearing a buttoned up day dress of pale pink calico that screamed respectability.

Lil glanced from Libby to her guest, her expectant expression demanding an introduction. "Hello back, I guess."

"Oh, excuse me, Lil. This is Susan Savage."

Susan extended her hand. "I'm Donovan's half sister."

"Are you now?" Frowning, Lil ignored the young woman's attempt to shake her hand. "You don't look much like him."

Obviously sensing some hostility, Susan recoiled a little. "I've always been told that I favored my mother strongly."

Lil doubled up her fist and planted it on her hip. "So you're what she looked like, huh?"

Susan turned to Libby, her expression begging for a little help getting out of the awkward situation. The best Libby could do was finish the introduction. "Susan, this is Lil . . . well, just Lil, I guess. She's Donovan's—"

"Partner," Lil supplied, laying down her own rules. "Is he in?"

"No, sorry. You just missed him."

Looking thoughtful and disappointed, Lil exhaled heavily. "Are you two coming or going?"

"I was going," said Susan. "It was a pleasure to meet you, Lil, but I have a lot of important errands to run now." She turned to Libby and gave her arm a squeeze. "Thank you for trusting me. I'll come back as quickly as I can." And with that, she stepped around Lil and hurried down the walkway.

"Please come in. I've got fresh blueberry muffins waiting in the living room, and Gerda can have some hot tea ready for us in a minute."

After stepping into the foyer, Lil tugged off her white gloves and glanced around the house. "Where did Donovan get off to so early?"

"Today is his first day working at the publishing company." Until that moment, Libby hadn't realized that Donovan's mother did not know about his new position. Her lovely face blanched with surprise, then crumpled in pain. "He's an advertising solicitor," Libby added lamely.

"Is that a fact?" Looking beaten and a little lost, Lil wandered into the living room. "I guess I will have that tea if you've got the time. See if you can't talk Gerda into shaking a little whiskey into mine."

"I'll see what I can do. Make yourself comfortable." Libby dashed into the kitchen, gave Gerda her instructions, then hurried back into the living room. She found Lil standing near the corner cupboard fingering a pewter vase on one of the shelves.

"I decorated this place for him, you know." Her tone was solemn. She even didn't bother to turn and confirm that it was Libby who'd entered the room. "I chose the paint colors, the wallpaper, and even the matching chintz curtains."

"And you did a lovely job of it." Libby purposefully made the comment short and brusque. She did not want to discuss the wallpaper. Gesturing to the chair Susan had just vacated, the one which faced the west wall, not the bay window, she said, "Why don't you have a seat? Gerda will be in with the tea any time now."

Finally moving away from the cupboard, Lil failed to notice Libby's "directions." She crossed the room instead, and sagged down on the sofa, which would give her a perfect view of the missing wallpaper strip, should she choose to look there.

Taking the chair she'd offered the woman, Libby slid onto it as she tried to think of ways to lighten Lil's obviously dark mood and, not incidentally, keep her distracted. "You're looking lovely today. Is that a new dress?"

Lil smirked, looking at Libby as if she'd grown two heads. "I came here to talk to Donovan about his father, not exchange mindless pleasantries."

Deflated more than offended—she did recall that bluntness, among other things, was a hallmark of Lil's personality—Libby lifted the plate of muffins and offered them as she said, "You seem to be a little sad today. I was just trying to cheer you up. Why don't you at least have a muffin?"

"Thanks, I'll take you up on that, but I don't think anything's going to make me feel better—not even if Donovan walked through that door about now." Lil studied the muffins a moment, then snatched the one most weighed down with berries. Settling it onto the napkin in her lap, she sighed heavily. "I probably couldn't have gotten through to him, even if he were here. He'd never believe the things I'd like to tell him about that father of his, especially since they've obviously gotten so close, he's working for the no-good son of a bitch."

Deeply interested in what Lil had to say about R. T., even if most of it stemmed from hurts of the past, Libby waited until after Gerda served two piping hot cups of tea to ask, "What kind of things were you thinking of telling Donovan?"

After dipping the corner of muffin she'd torn from the whole, Lil scooped it between her lips, and studied Libby closely as she chewed. She took a sip of tea, shuddering slightly, but looking pleased by the addition to her beverage. Then she took another sip, and asked, "What interest is R. T. to you?"

Picking at her own muffin, Libby popped a fat blueberry into her mouth, savored the juicy morsel a moment, then decided to trust Lil with the truth as she knew it. "We're not exactly what you'd call friends. In fact, if I were to choose one word to describe his feelings for me, I think 'hatred' would do it."

The bite of muffin Lil had just raised to her lips fell back down to her lap. "Explain. Tell me why you think R. T. hates you."

Normally, anyone who'd ordered Libby around this way would have gotten a good dose of nothing out of her. But in this case, she felt a certain bond forming, a sense that what they had to say to one another might just be woven with the same thread. "I had a meeting with R. T., his son Francis, and Donovan yesterday. We talked about my equal rights editorials, which they're all very opposed to, and a few other things. It wasn't exactly the words he used or even the way he said them, but I had the feeling the whole time he spoke to me that R. T. almost wished me dead."

"Humph." Lil shook her head in open contempt. "I think he's spent a minute or two wishing the same of me. Believe me, I know the look."

Encouraged by Lil's admission, Libby continued. "I also had the feeling that R. T. is very good at keeping his hatred inside, and that even when he lets it out, it seems to touch only the object of his hatred."

One sienna-brown eyebrow raised high, Lil encouraged, "Go on."

"I'm trying, but this is really hard to explain." She paused, picturing the moment when she'd first felt that malignant gaze burning into her—*through* her. "I would say that R. T. has eyes like a pair of dueling pistols—harmless enough when sheathed, even easy to ignore, until they're pointed at your head. Donovan sat right next to me in R. T.'s office yesterday, and never realized that his father had fired both guns at me. This may sound too crazy to you, but that's the best I can do to explain the way that man struck me."

"You make a hell of a lot of sense to me." Lil laughed, but it was a bitter, gravelly sound. "I don't know what took me so long to recognize those tendencies in Rand, but I do know exactly what you're saying about him."

"You do?" Libby perched on the edge of her chair. "Should I tell Donovan how I feel? After we left the office, he seemed really happy and, frankly, fond of his father. I was afraid to say anything for fear he'd—" Libby cut off her own words, realizing she was getting in a little deeper than she wanted to be, where her feelings about Donovan were concerned. "Well, anyway, I didn't say much. I didn't want to upset him."

The look the woman shot her gave Libby the impression that her thoughts had been transparent. But Lil didn't make any comment about her observations. She just smiled and said, "Let me tell you what I know about Rand and men in general; and then we'll decide what we should tell Donovan, and what we should keep to ourselves. Deal?"

Libby nodded and sank back against her chair, not merely skimming the velvet fabric as Susan would have, but crushing it with her buckskin vest. "Deal."

"Rand—R. T.—stopped by to see me a couple of nights ago. He got the idea that we ought to pick up where we'd left off so long ago." Lil paused to pick at a few muffin crumbs on her napkin. "If he'd'a just asked me outright, I like to think I'd'a said no, but, well, dear, it's been a long time since I've been with any man, much less the one I never could turn away, and ah . . ." She looked up, staring Libby right in the eye. "I realize you haven't been around much, and probably have pretty virginal ears to go with the rest of you. I'll try not to offend you, but let me warn you now—I'm not much good in the tact department."

Libby had to glance away from the woman—after all, this was Donovan's mother—but she did manage to admit, "My *ears* aren't quite as virginal these days as they once were."

"Oh? Just your ears?"

Libby willed, prayed, and threatened her insides in no uncertain terms, but when she heard Lil's lusty chuckle, she knew her cheeks had turned a traitorous shade of crimson anyway.

"*Really?* You mean you and Donovan are sweating up the sheets?"

"Oh, God." Rolling her eyes, Libby tried to think of an amusing or carefree response—never mind striving for glib—but her mind was a complete blank.

Her amusement still ringing in her tone, Lil commented, "And you're still here. Imagine that." She paused, giving Libby hope that she planned to move on to another topic, but the woman did not let go of the subject. "Has he tried to throw you out lately, or at least since you two—"

"No." At last, words formed on Libby's tongue. "In fact, he keeps thinking of crazy excuses to make me stay, but—"

"*Really?* Hmmm." Lil tapped the tip of her chin with her fingernail. "How very interesting."

"Excuse me, ma'am—Lil, but we weren't talking about me and Donovan. I thought we were discussing him and his father. What happened after R. T. came to see you."

A knowing smile continued to ripple across Lil's lips, but she went ahead with the former conversation as if she'd never deviated from it. "Rand sweet-talked me a little at first, then he came round the desk and put his hands on me. Let me tell you sugar, I melted like a snowflake in hell." She cut loose with a bawdy chuckle. "I do hope you have some idea how that feels."

Blushing again, Libby had to look away, but not for long. Lil's tone changed abruptly and her voice became tinny, with a good bit of anger, as she went on with her story.

"But I was a fool that night, a complete imbecile, to have let Rand back in my life for even those few moments of pleasure. I had nothing afterwards, certainly nothing of him. Other than getting screwed, I got exactly the same thing I'd gotten from him before—a big fat zero."

Touched deeply by those last words, and imagining herself in the same situation, Libby went numb inside. "Does Donovan know about R. T.'s visit with you?"

"No, of course not—at least, not as far as I know."
Lil went on spinning her tale, apparently unaware that
Libby's interest had turned morbid. "That's not what I
came to tell Donovan. I wanted him to know that R. T.
came back again last night, and that this time, I was
strong. The moment I set eyes on him, I remembered
how he'd used me all those years ago, and that no good
would come of this now."

Her hand shaking, Lil paused to reach for her tea.
After finishing the contents of the cup, she went on. "I
realized there was no way in hell that arrogant asshole
was ever going to leave his gold-plated, frigid-assed
society wife for me. He didn't do it when he was married to the ugly bitch who bore his legitimate children,
and he wasn't about to do it now."

Her ears burning in spite of her "altered" state,
Libby asked, "What did he say when you told him to
go? I'll bet he didn't like it much."

"An understatement, dearie, because no one tells
R. T. Savage what to do. But since I'd made up my
mind not to be used by him a second time, I told him to
get the hell out of my life once and for all, and never to
darken my door again." She paused dramatically, narrowed one eye, and unbuttoned the bodice of her dress.
"As you guessed, he wasn't interested in taking no for
an answer. You might say we got into it a little." She
pulled the material apart, baring the tops of her breasts.
"R. T. just hates the word 'no'."

When Libby saw that the skin there and around Lil's
throat was mottled with bright blue bruises and long
red welts, she couldn't stifle a gasp of horror. "Oh, my
God, Lil. He didn't . . . force himself on you, did he?"

"No, but rape was definitely on his mind."

R. T. Savage was as big as his son. Just from some of
the horseplay she and Donovan had shared, Libby knew

she could never match such strength, should he ever turn on her. How had Lil fought his father off? "Did you have a gun or something? How on earth did you stop him?"

"I have a gun all right, but it didn't do me much good with Rand. It was in a drawer and I was pinned against the wall." This time, when Lil laughed, the sound was almost jolly. "I did the only thing I could do—I relied on the same protection I use every night. Whenever I have a visitor, especially a male, Seamus's main job is to station himself right outside my door until I come out or call for him. Last night is only the second time I've ever had to 'wake the sleeping giant.' But I can tell you, I was sure happy to find him at his post."

"Then I imagine it didn't take too much for Seamus to convince R. T. to leave."

Again Lil laughed, the deep worry lines around her eyes, softening. "If you recall the size and strength of my bouncer, I would say that he convinced him in spades. I doubt I'll have to sic Seamus on Randolph Savage again."

Muttering more to herself than Lil, Libby mused, "My God. I'm no better off than you are."

"What's that supposed to mean?"

In a bit of a daze, only half listening to Lil, tears filled Libby's eyes as she muttered, "Donovan. Last night. I tried to send him away. I did try, but he, he . . ."

"I hope you don't expect me to believe my son tried to rape you!" Lil sat forward on the edge of her seat, her spine rigid. "Donovan's not like that at all. He would never do such a terrible thing."

"Hum?" Libby blinked, shaking herself out of the trance. "No—oh, no! I didn't mean to say that at all."

"I knew it couldn't be true." Lil tossed her chin high. "My Donovan is a long ways from perfect, but he'd never hurt a woman. At least, not physically."

"No, I don't believe he would either." Libby ran her fingers across her eyelids, staving off tears, but refreshing herself, too. "What I'm trying to say is that it seems my being here with him, you know, in that . . . way, has turned out to be a whole lot more complicated than I ever dreamed it could be." There was a wealth of understanding in Lil's sympathetic expression, making it easy for Libby to sort her feelings. "I honestly thought I could just enjoy whatever time we had together, then walk away. I think I finally understand that, for me to be happy, I need much more than I thought I did from Donovan. I hope you don't mind my saying these things about your son."

"Say what you want about him, but tell me a little more about you first. Didn't you pay attention when your ma explained about men and their ways, or was she as green as you?"

In spite of a brief jab of sorrow, Libby give Lil a warm smile. "My mother never got a chance to explain any of that to me. She died when I was still a girl. Before you ask about my father, I have to say, he wasn't any help either. He wasn't much on personal talk of any kind, but certainly not about women's problems. From the day I started getting noticeable breasts, he turned beet red and stayed that way until he died."

"Oh, honey, I'm sorry. I never meant to bring up bad memories." Lil looked as if she wanted to get off the sofa and offer a hug. She didn't, but Libby couldn't help but be touched just the same.

"My memories are good. I just told you about my folks so you could understand why I've never had a chance to talk about these things."

"I never had that chance either, now that you mention it." Lil's eyes glazed over as she thought back to the past. "My mother died when I was a babe, and as for my father . . . well, no little girl should have to learn about things the way I did."

"Oh, Lil—I didn't know . . ."

"Don't go getting all sappy on me, dearie." Her eyes clear again, she squared her shoulders, matching the hard edge of her jaw. "I don't go in for tears over long ago, or tears caused by worries of the future. Today is about all I let myself think about, and the way I figure it, there isn't enough hours in one day to waste any of them blubbering all over hell. That said, and mind you, I don't want the details of my son's personal life, I don't mind talking with you about your troubles with him if that's what you'd like."

"Oh, Lil, are you sure?" Libby had listened well enough to know what the woman thought of tears spilled for any reason, but in spite of that, she could feel them burning their way through her eyelids.

"Don't make it sound like you're getting such a bargain." Laughing at herself, Lil chortled over the idea. "I never was much of a mother, but if someone like me will do as a kind of ringer for a few minutes, I'll be glad to help you if I can."

"Thanks for offering. I think my troubles are with me, not Donovan. Other women involved in the cause talk and write about the joys of free love and taking lovers with no thought to getting married. They make it sound like that's all a woman needs from a man. I assumed I'd feel that way, too, or maybe I just convinced myself I would because I wanted Donovan so much; but it doesn't work that way for me. Now that I've . . . been with him, I just want him all to myself. He's all I'll ever want, and I don't know what to do about it, or how to go about making him feel that way over me."

Lil nodded solemnly. "Is it safe to assume that you think you've fallen in love with Donovan?"

Risking the woman's wrath, Libby raised her head and displayed what were by now, tear-stained cheeks. "I don't think that I love him, I *know* that I do."

Lil didn't seem to notice the tears, but she came down hard on Libby on the other point. "Then you're a damn fool. My son is many fine things, but he is not the kind of man an intelligent woman falls in love with. I can't see where you can hope for a future with him."

"Don't say it—I know, he's not the marrying kind. He as much as told me that himself, but I don't believe it. I think Donovan hides behind that statement because he doesn't know what a good man he is. If he'll give me a chance, I'm sure I can help him see that he's wrong about that, and therefore, wrong about—"

Lil burst into raucous laughter, interrupting Libby's impassioned speech. When she quieted, she said, "Pardon me, dear, but the next time it crosses your mind to change or 'fix' a man, any man, just forget it and remember me and Rand. I noticed the cruelty in him shortly after we met, but I was young and foolish enough to believe that my love would turn him into a cuddly little puppy. After all, most times, he was so smooth, so very nice, so stinking *loving*, I let myself believe I could scrub away the rough spots and live with him happily ever after. By now you know how that silly little fairy tale ends."

Disheartened, Libby sighed. "Are you saying that I might as well go back to Laramie as fast as I can because Donovan will never be mine?"

Lil methodically brushed the crumbs off her skirt. "I hate to say that, and I won't; but then, I don't want to fill your head up with false hope either. Just understand that Donovan is the kind of man who most times won't let himself *be* the good man he is. I suppose he's lacking the things you need because he's never been around a decent, loving relationship. I like to think he has it inside him to love you, or someone, but that he simply doesn't know how." Lil struggled to her feet. "That's my fault, I expect, since I'm the one who raised him; but there isn't much I can do about it now. If you want the cold, hard facts, I guess, maybe I raised him that way cause I'm not so sure there is such a thing as love."

Libby thought of objecting, of making an impassioned plea in the name of love, but if she hadn't learned another thing from Lil during this discussion, she knew when to keep her thoughts to herself. The woman was done answering questions about life and her son, and she wanted to be on her way. Although she longed to give Lil a hug to show her gratitude, Libby knew instinctively that such a gesture would only make her uncomfortable. Instead of embarrassing her, she showed her gratitude with a few simple words.

"Thank you for listening and advising me, Lil. I really do appreciate everything you had to say, even if I didn't like what I heard here and there."

"No thanks are necessary." Looking a little flustered, Lil buttoned her dress. "You know, I learned a little something here, too. Now that we've talked and I've had a chance to think about the kind of man my son is, I believe it would be a very bad idea for me or you to tell Donovan about his father—especially the part about what he did to me last night."

"But you can't just let R. T. get away with that! It isn't fair."

"R. T. didn't get away with much, dear, and never forget this—life isn't fair." She tapped her finger against her own chin. "It won't do a damn bit of good to try to explain to Donovan how R. T. made you feel in his office, either. If anything, it'll probably make things worse. When you're dealing with a slippery snake like

Rand, I have a feeling, a person simply has to learn about him for themselves. Know what I mean?"

Libby considered the thought, especially in relation to the way the man had mentally assaulted her right in front of his two sons. "You're absolutely right. There is no way to explain that kind of evil unless you've glimpsed it personally."

Lil crossed the short distance between them and shook Libby's hand. "Then we're agreed. It might be best if you don't even mention I stopped by today."

"All right." Libby was thinking of inviting Donovan's mother back again, maybe for a meal, when she noticed Lil had become distracted by something.

Her expression flickering between horror and surprise, Lil said, "Great Caesar's ghost! What happened to the wallpaper?"

Libby's heart lodged in her throat. How could she have forgotten about that damned wallpaper? She practically led the woman who'd put it up to the scene of the crime! "Oh, ah . . ." Libby stumbled around with her answer, hating to lie, afraid to tell the truth. "I think there are some mice in the house."

"Good God, does Donovan know about them?"

Libby didn't like her tone, the underlying suggestion, but she continued digging a verbal hole for herself. "Y-yes, he even set a few traps."

"Did he really?" Lil pulled the curtain aside and stared down at the hard brown little lumps of macaroni and cheese. "How awful for poor Donovan. He's terrified of mice, you know."

"He is?" Libby had noticed he was none too fond of them, but then, who was? "More than most folks, you think?"

"Oh, definitely." As she surveyed the area, Lil briefly explained why. "He and I didn't have a pot to piss in during our early days, and we moved around a lot. We took over an abandoned miner's cabin in Jackson down in Mother Lode country one summer and found the place overrun with damn mice." She slid her fingers along the edge of the paper near the window, her brow bunched in contemplation. "The poor kid was only about five at the time. I had to leave him alone at night while I was dancing and singing to earn enough money to put food in our mouths. I didn't find out until later that every time he went to lie down on his ratty little cot, those mice would run all over him."

A shudder of revulsion ripped through Libby. "Good, Lord. I had no idea."

"Donovan didn't get much sleep that summer in Jackson, but I don't think he has to worry about mice crawling through his hair here. Now that I've studied the damage a little better, I don't think he's got mice a'tall. It looks to me like someone ripped the damn paper right off the wall." Lil turned and headed for the door. "I think I'll go have a little talk with Gerda. She's too damned independent for her own good. Maybe it's time Donovan found himself another housekeeper."

"No, wait!" Libby caught up to her in the foyer. "I can't let you do that. I-I'm the one who did this."

"*You* tore the frigging paper off the wall? What, if I may ask, possessed you to do a thing like that?"

Reminding herself that brashness was Lil's way, Libby stood her ground. "I was waiting for Donovan the other night, worrying about him too, I guess, and I accidentally worked up a little tear with my fingernail. I tried to fix it, but I was so worried about Donovan, that, well, I don't know exactly how it happened, but it just got bigger and bigger. I did everything I could think of to cover it up best I could, but—"

"All right, enough. I believe it was an accident. Save

the story for him." Chuckling to herself, Lil sashayed over to the door and turned the knob. Before letting herself out, she glanced at Libby, raised one eyebrow and said, "You really do care about Donovan, don't you?"

She gulped, but proudly admitted, "As I said before, I love him. In fact, I'm thinking of telling him so tonight, right after I explain about the wallpaper."

Lil wagged her index finger. "Tell him there are no mice, dearie, please do, but take my advice on the rest—don't tell him you love him. Not unless you're fixing to run him off for good."

Late that afternoon at Savage Publishing, Donovan whistled as he strolled into his brother's office and dropped on the desk the names of the new accounts he'd solicited. "There you have it, Francis. Ten new advertisers for the *Tribune*—count 'em—ten."

Whistling his appreciation, Francis looked over the new accounts. "It looks like most of them are located around the Barbary Coast."

"That's right, an area which, until now, has been a relatively untapped source of working capital, I might add."

Francis laughed. "R. T. will be very pleased, I'm sure."

Thinking of paying his father a visit, and not incidentally, gathering a little of his praise in the bargain, Donovan asked, "Did he ever come in today? I thought I'd stop by and say hello before I go on home."

"No, I'm afraid he didn't make it in at all." Francis ran his hand across his high forehead. "He sent a messenger instead, to inform us that he'd been beaten and robbed last night while he was out shopping for Olivina's anniversary gift."

"Beaten? My God—is he badly hurt?"

"He's at home and, according to the message, only damaged cosmetically. There's a black eye, a swollen, bloodied nose, and some sore ribs, but nothing broken, as far as the doctor could tell."

"Christ." Donovan kicked the edge of the desk. "What's this town coming to, when a decent man like R. T. can't walk the streets without getting attacked by hoodlums? Did they catch them yet?"

"I don't have any more details than what I told you. Maybe you ought to stop by the house tonight and at least say hello. We might have more details by then."

Nodding thoughtfully, Donovan said, "I have a few more things to do around here, and I need to stop by my own place first. If you see R. T. before I get there, be sure to tell him that I . . ."—he paused, not exactly sure how to express the sentiment—". . . hope he feels better real soon."

"I will." Francis shook his hand, adding, "If I miss you tonight, I'll see you again first thing tomorrow morning, fireball."

Although that statement coming from the brother he respected so much had gone a long way in lifting Donovan's spirits, he was still concerned and about half-mad as he strolled in through the door of his home that evening. Finding the house as dark as his mood, he called, "Libby? Where are you?"

"In here."

Her voice sounded flat and emotionless coming out of the darkened living room, and her tone raised the hairs at the back of his neck; but Donovan was not about to step foot into that particular room unless it was well lit. "It's too dark in there. Either light the lamps or come out here."

He could hear her heavy sigh, but also the squeak of

her chair as she rose from it, and assumed she was headed to the foyer where the lamp atop the credenza illuminated the surroundings. A moment later, almost like an apparition, Libby suddenly appeared in the doorway.

Her sad brown eyes looking much too large for her drawn face, she said, "Your sister went to work for the cause today by sending some inquiries about Savage operations." Libby waved some papers toward him—telegrams, he thought. "I think we'd better have a little talk."

18

As *he settled down* at the kitchen table with a cup of warmed-over coffee, Donovan chuckled over the information Libby had just given him. "And you're sure *Eldorado* Distilleries is owned by my father?"

"It's owned by S and S Enterprises, which also owns Savage Publishing."

"I wonder what Lil will think of that. We've been buying our whiskey from *Eldorado* for years now."

"My guess," Libby said carefully, "is that she'll change liquor companies; but this isn't about Lucky Lil's. This is about the equal rights movement and the part your father plays in keeping the suffrage amendment off the ballot."

"Aw, come on, Libby." Donovan sounded weary. "I thought we had all that female suffragist talk behind us. R. T. is dead set against women voting, and there isn't a damn thing either one of us can do to change his mind about it. I thought you'd decided to accept that, and just let it be."

She made a point of looking him right in the eye, primarily to make sure he understood how serious she was, but also to gauge his reaction. "I've quit trying to change his mind, but now that I know he isn't just against the idea of the women's vote, but *fighting* it, I can never accept what he's doing."

With one swift and completely unexpected movement, Donovan swept his cup and saucer off the table. Amid the racket of shattering china, he banged his fist down on the hardwood top and declared, "Dammit— I've had enough of this! I'm beginning to think you're trying to turn me against my family. Why? Are you so jealous of them?"

Afraid of what she saw in his expression—a hint of R. T. Savage—Libby couldn't help but recoil a little. But she would not back down from her ideals ever again. "I'm happy you found your family, really I am, and I actually like most of them. But I can't accept your father's position when it means I have to turn my back on what I believe in—especially not now that I have a few more facts."

Donovan muttered something she didn't understand and then said, "Other than the fact you found out we own a distillery, what's so damning about your new 'facts'?"

"Plenty." Libby thought she saw him flinch, a gesture she likened to donning armor. Nor had she missed the way he'd referred to the Savage family as "we." The last thing she wanted to do was hurt Donovan or cast stones at the family he so obviously embraced as his own, but she could not ignore her own principles any longer.

Trying to be as diplomatic as possible, she explained her position. "I thought your father was just being bull-headed by choosing to ignore the movement—and he might have continued to fool me into believing that for a good long while, if I hadn't found out how deeply he's involved himself *against* the cause. I could almost turn my back on his indifference or dislike, but I cannot walk away from the information Susan gathered today. Not when the man in question has the means to do such serious damage to the cause."

Donovan waved impatiently. "Forget the dramatics, Libby, and get on with it. And speaking of Susan, I'm none too pleased about you dragging her into this women's rights business, or with the fact that you seem to be trying to turn your cause into some kind of family war. Just what is this damning evidence Susan turned up about R. T.?"

Her own anger simmering, Libby had to will herself to calm down in order to offer a lucid explanation of R. T.'s activities. If she didn't, Donovan wouldn't even listen, much less believe her. "There are many and varied reasons as to why women are having difficulty gaining the vote, but highly visible among them, are the liquor and textile industries."

"Textiles? You're out to hang harmless old dressmakers, too?"

Hating his sarcasm, the side of him which most closely resembled his father, Libby rose to the challenge and fired a salvo of her own. "Those harmless dressmakers, as you call them, oppose passage of the suffragist act because the minute women get the vote, they'll be slapping restrictions on the horrid way the textile industry abuses child labor in this country. Am I to assume that you're *for* an industry that works eight-year-old children to the bone, fifteen hours a day, and doesn't even bother to feed them?"

Donovan plowed his fingers through the thick bank of hair at his forehead, looking almost apologetic. "For

Christ's sake, Libby, of course not. I didn't mean to sound like I'm making fun of you and what you believe in, but when it comes to my family, you seem to be trying to force something down my throat, I just can't swallow."

"I'm sorry it comes across to you that way, because I'm only trying to provide you with a clear picture of what we're up against, not forcing you to believe anything. With that in mind, please accept the fact that the liquor industry, which is probably even more powerful than clothing manufacturers, fears something worse than a loss of revenues—complete closure. If the suffrage act were to pass, it's entirely possible the female vote would bring about prohibition. While I don't personally believe in the temperance movement, and I would never vote for it, I understand it's gaining quite a lot of support."

Looking thoughtful, Donovan drummed his knuckles against the tabletop. "If that was your best argument for swaying me away from my family, it didn't work. In fact, I believe I finally see why R. T. gets so upset about all this suffragist talk. I doubt he wants his distillery closed any more than I want to see Lucky Lil's shut down. Or haven't you thought of that?"

Overwhelmed by the magnitude of what she was facing, Libby hadn't even considered the impact the temperance movement could make on Donovan's and Lil's business. Troubled as she was by the idea, she couldn't let even that concern stop her. "No, I'm sorry to say, I didn't think of that. Even if I had, it wouldn't change what your father's doing—or what I have to do to fight him."

"And just what is my father doing, other than trying to save his business?"

Libby forgave him his arrogant tone and flippant reply, but only because the stakes for him were twofold—business and personal. "The way the liquor and textile industries have fought against suffragists is through lobbying our legislators and administrative officers in Washington and across the nation. The major contributor of funds used to 'persuade' these legislators into defeating pending bills regarding suffrage is S and S Enterprises, which includes *Eldorado* Distilleries. That's high-powered bribery, pure and simple."

Donovan's jaw tightened as the information filtered in, and his fingers curled with frustration, but he did not look up to meet Libby's gaze. His voice quiet, dejected, he simply said, "What do you expect me to do about it?"

If he'd just said that he understood, or that he even recognized the burden on her shoulders, it would have gone a long way in helping Libby to keep her composure. But this indifference, if that's what it was, splintered her. Anger, disappointment, and even a few tears leaked out through those cracks as she pushed away from the table and said, "I don't want you to do a damn thing, Donovan Savage. I just wanted to make sure you understood what drove me away. Thanks for your lovely hospitality." With that, she rose and started for the door.

Libby heard the ear-splitting screech of Donovan's chair just seconds before he caught her from behind. His arms linked firmly around her waist, he held her tight against his body and muttered, "You're not going anywhere. Not like this."

"There's no point in my staying here any longer. We'll just make each other miserable." It occurred to her then that this really was good-bye. Libby knew it without question. To stay would mean one of them had to back down. Tears falling freely, she turned in his arms and said, "I don't want to leave, but I don't know what else to do. I only know that I'm down to two choices, neither of them acceptable. One, I continue to write my editorials the way your father dictates they should be written and turn my back on his lobbying activities; or two, I refuse to bow to his vast wealth, stand up for what I believe in, and turn what I've learned about R. T. into headlines. If I do that, I'll lose the *Tribune* for sure, and probably have my home taken away from me, too." She uttered a short, bitter laugh. "Which would you choose, Donovan, if you were in my shoes? The first, the coward's way to destruction? Or the second, the harder, more painful way, which would also destroy your baby brother?"

With what felt like near desperation to Libby, Donovan took her face between his hands. "There has to be another choice, one neither of us has thought of yet. There *has* to be, dammit."

Looking more distressed than angry, he came down hard on her mouth, grinding his lips against hers more than kissing them. Branding them, she thought. In return, Libby threw her arms around Donovan's neck, hugging him tightly, wanting to never let him go, then relaxed and rested her head against his shoulder. Tears distorting her already blurred vision, she glanced around the room. Until now she'd thought of the kitchen as warm and cozy, it's walls painted in soft buttery tones, the papered areas festooned with vines and trellises highlighted by little bouquets of buttercups. But not this evening. Now this room seemed cold and dreary, hostile, even though the cute little enameled stove glowed with a still-smoldering fire. Tonight she and Donovan had finally run out of time.

His face buried in her hair, Donovan whispered, "Let me think about this some more. I know there's a solution in here somewhere, but I just can't think straight enough to figure out what it is right now. Besides, you promised you'd stay through Saturday so I don't have to go to the Young Gentlemen's Ball. Remember?"

Busy wiping her tears away, both laughing and crying, Libby could only nod against Donovan's jacket in answer.

"Thank you, sweetheart. I'll make sure you don't regret it." Then he kissed her temple, nuzzling her there a moment before murmuring, "I want you with me tonight, too. Say you'll come with me to see R. T., and that you won't say a word about anything we've discussed here."

The first thought to pop into Libby's mind was that, although Donovan had been unable to find a solution to their insurmountable problems, he'd definitely discovered the way to dry a girl's tears. Incredulous to the point of amused surprise, she broke out of his embrace and held him at arm's length. "I cannot *believe*, after everything I've just explained, that you want to drag me to that man's home."

"This has nothing to do with who's right or who's wrong, Libby. I want you to go there for me, not him." Donovan shuffled his feet, looking very uncomfortable. "I have to go see him, I promised Francis I would, and . . . well, I find this sort of thing difficult. I want you to be there with me."

New tears, but from an entirely different kind of well, sprung into Libby's eyes. "You mean you need me."

"I didn't exactly say that." Those clear blue eyes hid nothing of his discomfort, embarrassment, or feelings that ran deeper than he was willing to admit. "I only know that I don't want to go there alone, and that I want you to come with me. Don't try to make any more out of it than that."

But she'd seen. She'd seen. Smiling through her tears, Libby said, "If you really need me that much, then I'll go."

"Promise, first." Donovan looked both relieved and worried. "Promise you won't bring any of this distillery or lobbying business up, not tonight—and, especially, don't mention the part about Susan. I don't think my father is going to be up to much of anything except hello, after what he's been through."

"What do you mean, 'what he's been through'?"

"Didn't I mention he was injured?"

Libby shook her head, aware already, on a subconscious level, that the man was hurt, but unable to grasp the fleeting thought long enough to know the reason why.

Sounding terribly distressed, Donovan went on. "My father was attacked last night and badly beaten. He could have been killed."

In that same instant, of course, Libby remembered exactly what had happened to the man—and who had tried to kill him. Fighting to keep from blurting out what she knew about the incident, she managed to casually say, "How perfectly awful. Do you know what happened to him?"

"Not the details, but I imagine we'll find out more about this once we arrive at the mansion." He was impatient now, hands in his pockets one minute, fiddling with his watch fob the next. "So, what do you say? Will you go with me, and on my terms?"

Looking him solemnly in the eye, Libby was somehow able to keep a straight face as she said, "I wouldn't want to miss this visit for anything. I promise not to bring up the distillery or women's suffrage, and I won't even breathe your sister's name. Good enough?"

Donovan's silvery blue eyes crackled with sudden insight, or maybe it was suspicion. In any case, Libby could see that he knew she was either giddy with excitement over something, or perhaps realized that she knew something he didn't. But as he usually did when it came to matters concerning this newfound father of his, he just shrugged off his doubts. Then, taking her hand, Donovan didn't even stop to collect topcoats for them as he led her out of the house and into the night.

They were kept waiting a full thirty minutes in R. T.'s expansive study on the first floor of the mansion. A beverage cart containing everything from liqueur to tea, including a cut-glass bowl filled with ice, was at their disposal. Donovan poured himself a stiff brandy, and paced the entire time he waited for his father to appear. Libby donned her glasses, then circled the room like a cat on the prowl, marveling over the excesses, and questioning the morality of one person laying claim to so much. Everywhere she looked, she found fine crystal, gilt-edged furnishings, and beveled mirrors.

Trophies of the animals R. T. had hunted punctuated the redwood walls of the masculine study—a moose head with enormous antlers, the full mount of a bull elk down to its breastbone, a bear of some kind—grizzly she thought—and an animal from the antelope family with long twisted antlers pointed straight up at the ceiling. Glancing quickly around the oval-shaped room, Libby halfway expected to find a few human heads among the trophies, but only a couple of exotic-looking creatures and a fiercely snarling boar stared back at her.

She'd made her way to the elaborately carved walnut and redwood fireplace inset with turquoise tiles, when R. T. finally came into the room. He was limping noticeably, and although he'd yet to face her full on, she could see that his aristocratic nose was swollen and that at least one of his eyes was puffed shut.

"R. T.," said Donovan, crossing the room to greet him. "Christ, but you look like hell. Are you feeling any better?"

"Than what?" said the man, trying to make light of the situation. "Do I feel better than I did last night? No, but I guess I've come around a little since this morning. I was so stiff when I woke up, I could hardly get out of bed."

The men exchanged a warm handshake, then suddenly, R. T. whirled, as if finally aware Libby was in the room. She instinctively reached up to remove her spectacles, but then defiantly left them sitting atop her nose.

"Oh . . . hello, Miss Justice. I'd forgotten that James said Donovan brought a guest with him."

"Hello, Mr. Savage. I'm sorry to hear about your . . . 'accident.'"

Did R. T. narrow his gaze just a little as she spoke, Libby wondered, or was she merely imagining that he knew she was on to him? The man was so slick, she found it impossible to tell which. Whatever he thought he'd heard in her tone didn't stop him from smiling warmly and asking, "Did you two find everything you need? Can I get you something else to drink, or a bite to eat?"

Libby shook her head, her smile twice as sweet and every bit as bogus as R. T.'s. "I'm fine, thank you. So what really happened to you?"

"Christ, Libby," said Donovan, his tone suggesting that she might be overstepping her boundaries. "Let the man sit down and relax."

"That's all right, Son." R. T. chuckled as he sank onto the oversized chair in front of the fireplace. "I suppose this mutilated face of mine is a bit of a curiosity.

Poor dear Olivina burst into tears when she saw me, and hasn't come out of her room since." Again he laughed, but the amusement didn't reach his eyes. They were cold, unflinching, and staring at Libby as if measuring her for a coffin.

Staring right back at him, she asked, "Aren't you going to tell your son who beat you up?" Feeling bold, Libby indulged the silly urge to grin. "If you'd rather, I suppose that I could—"

"Why don't you be a good girl," said R. T., cutting her off, "and go pour me a nice glass of scotch. Two pieces of ice."

"I'd be delighted." Under both men's watchful gazes—and this time, Donovan's was the more malignant—Libby strolled away from the fireplace and headed for the beverage cart. As she fixed the man's drink, R. T. groaned and addressed Donovan. "I was under the impression that Francis told you what happened to me."

Donovan took the chair across from his father. "He only mentioned that you'd been robbed and beaten. Have the police found the men who did this to you yet?"

"Robbed?" Libby interrupted, unable to keep the surprise out of her tone. "You told everyone you were beaten and robbed?"

R. T. turned in his chair, the intensity of his gaze leaving no doubt that he'd drawn both dueling pistols and now had them pointed between her eyes. There was no fear of discovery in his expression, or even concern over what she might know of the truth. Just hatred. Pure, unstrained, unadulterated hatred. Oh, how Libby wanted to blurt out the truth, to burn him here and now and send him to hell in flames. But that gift was not hers to give. She fought the impulse a few moments, her own gaze holding steady under the intensity of R. T.'s glare, until she was quite sure she would not break the promise she'd made to Donovan's mother. At least, not while he was in the room. Resigned to the idea that she would have to keep her silence about what she knew—at least for now—Libby dropped three ice cubes into the man's drink and carried it to him.

"Thank you, my dear," he said, brushing her fingers with his as he took the drink, singeing them with malice. "Now why don't you have a seat and make yourself comfortable." Libby could almost hear the unspoken words, "and shut up!"

Turning away from her, R. T. faced Donovan and spoke as if he were the only other person in the room. "As I was saying, while I was out shopping last evening for a gift for Olivina, I was set upon by young hoodlums, beaten, then robbed of my cash, which I might add, was not an inconsiderable amount."

After flashing a warning glance at Libby, reminding her exactly how he expected her to conduct herself, Donovan said, "Francis told me that much, but not whether the men responsible were caught by the police."

"Not yet, I'm afraid." R. T. looked into his glass just before he took the first sip, and frowned upon finding three pieces of ice, not two as he'd ordered. Libby was ready, waiting for him to turn to her with those accusing blue eyes, but he surprised her by taking a long pull of the drink, then going on with his fabricated story. He complained roundly about the wild youths of San Francisco and how decent folks hid in fear from them, going on and on until Libby thought she would scream from sheer frustration.

She was saved from the fate moments later as Susan joined them in the study. After that, R. T., magnanimous as ever, bade Donovan and Libby to join him and his daughter for supper. The very idea of breaking bread with the man appalled Libby to no end; but left with no choice in the matter, she consoled herself with Susan's company, and allowed herself to at least enjoy the meal, which consisted of a perfect little medallion of beef and huge lobster tails. Miracle of all miracles, she even managed to keep a civil tongue in her head the rest of the evening.

By the time they arrived back at Donovan's house later that night, Libby had convinced herself that he'd either forgotten the brashness of her tongue earlier in the evening, or forgiven her for being what he'd surely considered insolent to his father. But he'd sent her upstairs alone, while he remained on the first floor. It hadn't occurred to Libby until later that he'd probably been checking his mousetraps; but when he finally joined her, long after she'd tucked herself in for the night, the traps had slipped her mind again.

As he'd done the evening before, Donovan disrobed at the foot of the bed, used a post as his closet, then climbed beneath the covers and took her into his arms. It was then she sensed that something intangible had entered the room with him, something heavy with foreboding.

And then he spoke, whispering in the darkness, and in his voice, that ominous visitor finally manifested itself. "I suppose you thought you were being polite to my father this evening, but you didn't do a very good job of hiding your true feelings. Is there nothing I can do to keep you from hating him so? Nothing?"

He hadn't forgotten, and from his tone, Libby knew he hadn't forgiven her rash tongue, either. His question

surprised her, but she responded with the same bluntness and honesty. "No, I'm afraid not. I wish I could
learn to think of him in a more friendly way, but whenever I look at R. T. Savage, all I can see is evil."

Donovan didn't comment on her answer. He didn't
have to. His thoughts were all around her, invading her.
She could reach out and touch them, taste the poison.
He was disappointed, to be sure, but also accusing, as if
convinced she had it within her to change her opinion
of his father, but refused to do him the honor. There
was no way for her to respond to his unspoken charges
without breaking her vow to his mother, or painting his
father as the kind of beast children lived in terror of
finding under their beds.

So Libby remained silent as Donovan pulled her
deeper into his arms and made unhurried love to her.
His touch was sure and gentle, more sensual than ever,
yet their lovemaking was bittersweet, where before it
had been sinfully delicious. His mouth, his hands, all
the pleasures he could bestow belonged to Libby for
these few minutes. He gave everything to her, holding
back only two things—his heart and soul. The words "I
love you" ran circles in her mind, but never dared to
cross her lips. Instead, she gave herself the freedom to
love him with her body—and loved him as she'd never
loved him before.

Determined to commit to memory the way his skin,
so smooth and slick with perspiration, felt beneath her
palms, to forever carry with her the subtle change in his
scent as he became more and more aroused, she
became the aggressor for a few short moments, and
unleashed in him a savage of a different kind.
Donovan's lips both bruised and soothed her everywhere they touched, and then he began to moan from
deep in his throat, a feral kind of sound akin to a growl.

Libby savored it all, the sounds, his scent, his touch, until at last, they reached the highest peak together. It wasn't until they tumbled down the other side of the mountain, miles and miles apart, that she understood nothing had changed.

Everything went quiet then, as if sound didn't exist at all. In that vacuous moment, Libby realized that what they'd shared here tonight had been their last time together. That thought, as the others, went unspoken between them. But even as they lay holding one another in the dim afterglow of their lovemaking, she suspected it was a thought Donovan shared.

As a child, Libby had frequently dreamed of becoming a horse when she grew up. It hadn't occurred to her at the time, but she supposed the fantasy was her way of escaping in this male dominated society, a way of finding freedom. To gallop, wild and free, across the prairie, the wind rippling through her mane, kicking up her heels and tossing her head, answering to no one. She awoke just this side of dawn, that time of night when the morning sun is finally beginning to shove the midnight sky into the oceans of the west, and realized she'd had that same dream again during the night. An unspoken wish to be free.

Beside her, Donovan stirred and began inching his way toward the edge of the mattress. After he quietly slid out of bed, she heard the rustle of his clothing as he removed it from the bed post, but Libby didn't make a sound or move a muscle. If he wanted her to believe that he'd been in his own room for most of the night, so be it. She would go back to sleep and dream again of being a horse. And of being free.

19

The next morning, Donovan leaned over the drafting table in his father's office and studied the sketch R. T. had commissioned of the hoodlums who'd attacked him. "There were three of them?" he asked.

"Around that, I think, the little sons of bitches." R. T. wiped a drop of spittle off his chin. "You know, it's just as likely those boys were the sons of millionaires, as beggars. I think we ought to get the police to round up a special detail to go after all these thieving little bastards. The city's overrun with them!"

Donovan didn't disagree on the point. San Francisco's growing hoodlum population didn't stop at robbery, as they had with R. T., but also set buildings on fire, paraded the streets at night singing obscene songs, and most repulsive of all, took grand sport in stoning Chinese men. But Donovan hadn't come to see his father about ridding San Francisco's streets of its bored youth. He wanted to know a little more about the distillery business and how it tied in with government officials.

Turning his back to the table, he propped his hips against it, shoved his hands in his pockets and said, "I just found out that *Eldorado* Distilleries is yours. Are you aware that I've been doing my whiskey business with you for years?"

R. T. laughed. "No, it never occurred to me. I suppose it should have, since you're partners in a saloon." There was a slight narrowing of his eyes before he went on. "Why are you asking now, Son? Everything all right at the saloon? My men haven't been cheating you out of your profits or anything, have they?"

"Not that I know of." He smiled at his father, enjoying the easy banter they shared. "Maybe I ought to pay a little closer attention next time they deliver."

"Maybe you should." Again R. T. laughed, but it sounded a little strained. "I thought you pretty much stayed away from the saloon since coming to work for me. Don't tell me you're trying to work both jobs!"

"No, nothing like that. In fact, I haven't been back to the theatre for a few days. I was asking about the distillery for another reason. I was wondering if it's true that you're a big contributor toward the campaign against the equal rights movement, you know, where lobbyists are concerned."

R. T. sighed and rolled his eyes as if disgusted, but oddly enough, Donovan thought he saw a fair amount of relief in the man's expression, too. "Libby again, right?"

Hedging slightly, Donovan replied, "A friend of hers, actually; but yes, she told me that, through the distillery, you're one of the biggest contributors in those efforts."

"And so?" Smiling, R. T. strolled across his expansive office toward the desk. "I'm not sure I understand what it is you want to know, Son. I've never kept my objections to this women's suffrage thing secret. Are you asking me how much money I spend lobbying against women's rights? If so, I can't imagine why that should concern you."

Now Donovan wasn't even sure why he'd brought the subject up. It was as if the feeling of warmth he thought he'd just shared with his father had been blown away by an icy wind. "I don't care what you spend your money on, or how much it costs you. I was just wondering, on Libby's behalf, if you could find another cause to back. The women's movement is very, very important to her."

R. T. had reached his chair, but instead of taking it, he gripped the back, his fingers digging deep furrows in the soft leather. "Do you think for one minute that I'd spend even a penny of my money on something that wasn't terribly important to me?"

Donovan had never been the object of his father's wrath, and while he couldn't exactly say he occupied that position now, he felt uncomfortably close to the target. "Of course not, but as I said before—I'm asking on behalf of Libby and her—"

"Libby." Coming from between R. T.'s lips, her name sounded like evil incarnate. "I thought she meant nothing to you, and that, by now, she'd have run back to Wyoming, where she belongs. Why is she still here?"

Silence swelled between them like a great stinking cloud, growing ever larger as the minutes ticked, while Donovan tried to come up with an answer. To extract himself from the awkward position, especially since he couldn't think of a logical answer—logical to him, anyway—he said, "I'm sorry I even brought the subject up. Consider it closed."

"No. I don't think I can close it that easily, Son. I didn't get where I am by dodging disagreeable tasks. I faced them head on. I think I see a distinctly unpleasant task in this Libby woman, and in fact, saw it the first time I met her." His usually composed features, though badly bruised, began to mottle and change shape. "Those suffragists are all alike, picking and hounding a man until they break either his back or his spirit!"

"I'm not going to get into a discussion about Libby or suffragists." And if he had to walk out the door to do it, Donovan knew he would. "Maybe it'd be best if I go."

"No, wait." R. T.'s voice left little doubt that he'd issued a command. "We won't talk about Libby or her blind devotion to the 'cause.' We'll talk about my distillery and another woman, the former Olivina Blair. Come, sit down."

But suddenly, all Donovan wanted was out of the conversation. And out of the room. "I think it would be much better if I leave."

"Perhaps, but before you go, at least let me tell you why I protect my interests so heartily."

"All right." He agreed, but Donovan stayed right where he was at the drafting table.

Apparently unperturbed that his son hadn't done everything he'd been told, R. T. went on. "Are you aware that *Eldorado* Distilleries is how I made my fortune—and how I still collect my fortune?"

Donovan shrugged. "Just from the bills I've run up with the company, I can imagine that it's a real moneymaker, but I thought you struck it rich in the gold fields."

"Oh, I did, son, but not as rich as the distillery made me." He spoke of the company with reverence. "The other businesses compromising S and S are largely toys to keep Thomas and Francis busy. They even kept Andrew out of trouble for a while."

Donovan did not want to talk or think about Andrew. "But Savage Publishing must surely make a profit."

"A little," R. T. conceded, "but nothing of the magnitude I make at the distillery. If not for Olivina, I wouldn't have bought a damn newspaper business in the first place."

Curious now, Donovan crossed the room and stood facing his father from the other side of his desk. "What does she have to do with the *Tribune*?"

Offering his son a smug grin, R. T. evaded the direct question. "I've always considered myself to be a damn fine-looking man, as you are, and by the time I built the distillery into what it is today, I was a damn rich man, too. In all honesty, those attributes weren't nearly enough to capture a woman like Olivina, at least not as my wife."

"She's a very beautiful woman," Donovan said, able to offer the compliment sincerely.

"Oh, Olivina is much more than simply the most beautiful creature in all of California. Along with the Blair family, she's also a leader of society and representative of all things fine and regal. I wanted that for myself. I wanted her Donovan—wanted her on any terms. Surely you can understand that."

Donovan understood better than he thought R. T. could know. Nowhere had there been any mention of love. "I'm with you so far."

"Then you'll certainly understand what I did when I discovered she would never marry me as the owner of a distillery, no matter how well I could feed her expensive tastes. Producing whiskey is not exactly the proper kind of business which would allow her to keep her social standing. Ah, but as a newspaper magnate, I was quite acceptable as husband material." The smug grin wider, he elaborated. "Olivina engineered the Savage family's move into San Francisco's elite, not I. If the women of this country ever get to take part in elections, they'll vote in temperance. Given my circumstances now, I'd practically be out on the street, should that day ever come; so I'm not about to let it happen." His expression darkened. "I think you can guess how long Olivina would stay by my side should my fortunes slide. The women's vote would cost me far, far more than mere money. Now do you see my point?"

Whether he liked it or not, Donovan had to admit that R. T. definitely had one. "Sure, and I can't say that I blame you for taking such a hard stand against equal rights. I just wish there were some other way."

"You let me know if you think of one. In the meantime, I rather like being a respectable businessman of major prominence." He circled the desk, still limping slightly, and patted Donovan's shoulder. "I've noticed that you've become used to your elevated status since joining the family business. It looks good on you, Son. Don't throw it all away over a woman, especially an unfinished hellion like Liberty Justice."

Now R. T. was treading on Donovan's toes. Donovan shook hands with his father and said, "I appreciate your taking the time to explain all this to me. Now, I really have to go. Advertising accounts are waiting, you know."

"That's my boy. And you wait until tomorrow night at the Young Gentlemen's Ball. You'll meet so many beautiful women of quality, not to mention, wealth, you'll wonder why you ever turned your head to take a second look at that rowdy little female reporter. Mark my words."

*　　　*　　　*

Back at Donovan's house, Libby had washed, dressed, and just finished tidying up her room, when she heard someone banging on the door downstairs. She hurried to answer it, and was surprised to find Lil standing there. An unusually bright sun had broken through the thick fog early that morning, burning off all but a few misty tendrils of haze. Yet most of Lil's face and her entire body were wrapped in a cloak. Practically knocking Libby to the ground, she didn't wait for an invitation, but pushed her way inside the house and quickly slammed the door behind her.

"Is Donovan here?" Lil asked, her blue eyes round in panic.

"No, he's not. What's wrong?"

"Nothing or everything. I don't know for sure." Unwrapping her body like a butterfly sheds its cocoon, Lil draped the cloak on the credenza, then staggered breathlessly into the living room. "I've got to sit a minute."

Libby followed Donovan's mother, but didn't join her on the couch. "You're making me very nervous. What happened?"

"It's Seamus. He was gunned down as he left the theatre this morning."

"Oh, no!" Libby clutched her throat. "How bad is he? Will he be all right?"

"Never again, dear. Poor Seamus is dead."

Feeling sick inside, Libby finally did sink down beside Lil on the sofa. "My God. Why would anyone shoot a dear, sweet man like Seamus? Do you know who did it?"

Lil smirked. "That's open to all sorts of speculation, but if you want my opinion, I think our dear Randolph Savage had something to do with it."

While she thought very little of the man, Libby couldn't fathom the idea he'd commit murder. "How can you say that? Did someone see him?"

"No, of course not, and I'm not swearing that it was Rand who had this done; but think about it girl— Seamus had only one enemy in the entire world that I know of: R. T. Savage, from the minute he smashed his fist into the man's face." She sighed heavily and let her head fall back against the sofa. "No one saw exactly what happened, but Seamus had no more than walked out the door, and he was shot. One of the fellas standing around outside said he heard a buggy drive off in the fog, but no one saw the rig or the driver clearly. I don't know. Maybe I'm overreacting 'cause of all the grief that man's put me through."

Libby didn't know what to think; but if there was any chance that Savage had taken part in the death of Lil's bouncer, she suddenly had another concern. "What about you? Do you think your life is in danger, too?"

"I kinda doubt R. T. would come after me that way, although, just to be on the safe side, I wrapped up real good before I came here, so no one would notice me."

"But if he had Seamus killed—"

"Rand's a cold-hearted, conniving bastard, but I think the fact I'm Donovan's mother carries some weight with him. If he did have something to do with the murder, I also think he'd figure I'd take Seamus's death as some kind of warning to keep my nose out of his business from now on. I just come here to let you know what happened, on the outside chance that R. T. done it. There's just no way to know for sure."

"But what do I have to do with any of this?"

Relaxing at last, Lil chuckled. "Sugar, you're the one told me he gave you a look wishing you was dead. I just figured I ought to warn you against pushing him any further than you already have—or who knows what the man will do."

Libby went cold inside as she recalled the look R. T. had given her last night when she'd hinted that she knew more about his injuries than what he'd admitted. She remembered having thought that he looked as if he were measuring her for a coffin. "My God," automatically slipped out as she exhaled. "Oh, my God."

"Libby." Lil sat upright, her spine rigid. "What is it? Have you done more than you told me about?"

"I think . . ." She drew in a breath, still trying to remember and analyze the conversation from the evening before. "I think that maybe I have. Last night when Donovan and I went to see him, I kind of hinted that I knew his accident was no accident."

"You *didn't*!"

"Oh, yes, I did. Not only that, I've enlisted his daughter Susan to work for the cause. She's been digging up a lot of 'unfriendly' information about some of his business dealings."

"That's it." Lil jumped up from the couch. "Even if R. T. had nothing to do with Seamus's death, we've got to get you out of here now, before there's more trouble than you or Donovan can handle."

"Donovan!" Libby looked up at Lil, tears misting her eyes. "What will I tell him?"

"I'll tell him, when the time's right. If you've got your hooks into my boy even a little bit, I'm sure he'd want you to be safe. Besides . . ." She reached down, touching Libby's tear-stained cheek. "You knew you had to go back home soon anyway, didn't you?"

Libby bit her lip, nodding miserably.

"Then, even if I'm completely wrong about R. T., this just saves you the trouble of prolonging the agony."

In that, Lil was right. There was a good bit of confusion here over Seamus and R. T.'s possible involvement in his murder, but Libby did know that her faith in the things she believed in had been restored. She'd been wavering, thinking of giving up the cause for Donovan, as if the fight for equal rights had anything to do, one way or another, regarding the relationship between a man and a woman. She could no more give up the cause than stop breathing. And Donovan had asked her to do neither.

Rising slowly from the couch, Libby impulsively put her arms around Lil and gave her a hug. "Thanks for caring about me. Thanks for . . . everything."

Lil sniffed. "Now, don't go blubbering all over me. I'm not much for this mothering business, you know."

Libby released her, but only stepped back a little. "When you see him again, please tell Donovan that I . . . that I wish him well in his new life. Oh, and don't forget to thank him for everything he tried to do for me."

"I will." She smiled at Libby, looking so serene and motherly, it was hard to think of her as the queen of a dance hall. "If it's any consolation, I've never seen my boy so addle-brained over a female before. You got to him as good as anyone ever will." When the tears started rolling down Libby's cheeks, Lil's tone hardened. "Now you run upstairs and pack. I've got to get back to the theatre and get some sleep. I've been up all night. I'll let myself out."

Libby didn't waste any time after that. Tears falling continually as she worked, she had all her things gathered and stuffed into her small valise within fifteen minutes. The only extra time she took was to double-check the schedule to make certain there was an afternoon train heading toward Laramie—there was—and then make a decision about what to do with the lovely dress Donovan had bought for her. Take it, or leave it. She'd just about settled on taking it—after all, what use would he have for the dress—when she heard the front door slam.

Libby's heart caught in her throat. It probably wasn't Lil—she'd left close to thirty minutes ago. Either she'd come back for some reason or, it suddenly occurred to Libby, maybe R. T. had sent someone here to kill *her*! She stood frozen next to the edge of her bed, afraid to move, afraid not to, when she heard someone shout her name from down in the foyer.

"Libby are you here? Answer me!"

Donovan! Relief flooding her the way her teardrops had just moments ago, she ran down the stairs, wiping her eyes as she went, and caught up to him in the kitchen.

"Oh, it is you," she said breathlessly. "You gave me quite a fright. I wasn't expecting you back so soon."

He'd been heading for the back door, and when he turned, Libby could see that he was in a fret over something. But he wasn't in pain. Not the way she was.

"I'm supposed to be working now," he complained, looking frustrated and charmingly boyish. "*Working*, dammit, understand?"

Libby nodded and managed to smile, wanting to keep with her this picture of him. Donovan had looked very much this way the night they'd first made love. The night he'd tried, not so hard, to convince her it would be a bad idea.

"But I can't work," he went on, "because I keep thinking about you and your damnable equal rights crusade." He waved his arms and hands as he spoke, portraying an anger she didn't hear in his voice. "I want to stand behind you on this issue, but then I think about what it has done to my family, and what more it could

do to the business end of things, and then, hell—"
Ripping off his hat, he dragged his fingers through his
hair, then stared at her apologetically. "I figured I'd better come here and get this over with once and for all."

Lord, was he trying to find a way to say good-bye,
too? "Get what over with?"

"I had a long talk this morning with R. T. about his
investment in blocking the suffrage amendment."

"Oh, God, no." Libby's pulse thrummed in her
throat as she imagined the discussion—and R. T.'s reaction to it. Was he hiring someone to shoot her even
now? "What did he say?"

"He wasn't at all happy, but that can't be much surprise to you, can it?" Donovan didn't wait for or expect
an answer. He went on to defend his father's position.
"If you and your suffragist friends have your way, are
you aware that you could put him out of business—and
I mean all his businesses, not just the distillery?"

"No," she answered honestly. "I only knew that he
would probably lose his distillery, should the women of
this country get the vote and enact temperance laws."

"He stands to lose much more than that." Donovan
was looking at her as if he expected an apology.

"And what do you suggest I do with *my* losses?" As
much as she hated to end things this way, Libby was
dogged in her determination to never back down from
her ideals again. "What about the indignities I'll continue to suffer, right along with the rest of this nation's
women, because of evil men like your father?"

"*Evil*, Libby?" He laughed, no doubt thinking she'd
intentionally overstated her case, then slammed his hat
back down on his head. "Because a man tries to protect
what's his, that makes him evil?"

There was no way she could explain herself. "Sorry if
I sounded a little dramatic, but if you thought I'd back

down after hearing that your father might lose his title as the richest man on the face of the earth, you've got another think coming. My fight against men like R. T. Savage has only begun."

"That's just great." He threw his hands up, as if completely exasperated, but then spread them wide. "I've tried, you know, really tried to see your side of this equal rights thing, and I've even tried to make my father see it, too. After talking with the both of you, it's painfully obvious to me that there isn't a damn thing I can say or do for either of you, and be right. I don't know what you expect me to do now, but whatever it is, I have a feeling I can't do it."

She wanted to feel for him, wanted to sympathize with his unenviable position, but sudden righteous anger ripped through her, forcing Libby to blurt out how *she* felt instead. "In order to do anything I might want, you'd have to get off that comfortable high-priced fence you've been straddling since you met your father, and I don't think you want to."

"Christ, Libby, what was that? An ultimatum?" Donovan's eyes narrowed accusingly. "Are you seriously asking me to choose between you and my family—a family I've never even known that I had?"

"No, of course not," she countered, although she wasn't completely sure she hadn't done just that. "I'd never ask you to give up your family for any reason; but if you think you have to choose between me and them, that's your problem. Mine is, fighting against men like your father. That's my *life*. Can't you see that if I give up the cause, I give up myself?"

"But how in God's name can you equate voting rights with a man's family? If we do things your way, you'll have me turning on my family and maybe even destroying them. I've *dreamed* of having a real family like this for my entire life—is taking that dream away from me what you want?"

"You have no idea what I want. None."

This time, Libby had to turn away from him. She could no longer look at those beautifully sculpted hands without remembering what they could do to her; couldn't bear to let her gaze fall on his full, sensual lips, or even risk a glance into his eyes. Not now; not when she could see them so well in her mind: silvery-blue, crackling with passion, but withholding the love she so desperately wanted to see in them.

"You're right," Donovan said quietly, surprising her by taking her in his arms. "I'm not sure I do understand what it is you want. It was a mistake, my coming here and demanding that we straighten this out once and for all. There is no easy answer, is there."

Easy being the key word, thought Libby, but she didn't express the sentiment. Feeling inexplicably weary, she rested her head against Donovan's chest and quietly murmured, "No, but then my father used to say nothing is worth having if it comes to you too easy— something like that, anyway."

Swaying her in his arms, the movement slight, like waltzing in place, Donovan whispered against Libby's hair. "I don't want us to fight about this any more. Can we call a truce of some kind, at least for now?"

He'd given her the perfect out. And it was way past time to go. Swallowing her tears, Libby forced a grin as she pledged, "I promise, you'll never hear me say another word against your father."

"See? Now that wasn't so hard." Donovan lifted her up on tiptoes, crushing her to his chest, then rewarded her with a blinding smile. "I vow never to belittle, make fun of, or otherwise thwart your attempts to continue your work for the suffrage movement."

"And I now pronounce you man and wife." Impulse made her spout those words, but at the sound of them, Libby suddenly wanted to cry so badly, that she burst into nearly hysterical giggles instead. "Maybe we should say 'I do' or something, just to make the truce sound more official."

Donovan shook his head firmly. "Oh, no. That would be way *too* much like taking wedding vows. But I do think it might be a good idea to seal our vows with a kiss." He didn't give her a chance to do anything but accept as he lifted her chin and fit his mouth to hers for a long, satisfying moment of tenderness. When he ended the kiss, Donovan continued to hold Libby's chin in place as he said, "I meant those vows. I hope you did too."

"I did," she murmured. "But as long as we're making promises, would you mind making another one for me?"

"As long as it fits the boundaries of our truce, I don't see why not. What do you want?"

"I want you to please go see your mother. Today if possible. She loves you very much, you know."

"My mother?" Libby felt his arms grow rigid just before Donovan loosened his hold on her. Leaning back enough to look into her eyes, he asked, "What does Lil have to do with any of this?"

"Just go see her." She blinked, hoping he hadn't noticed the tears welling in the corners of her eyes. "Promise me you'll go to her and make things right between you two again. You never know when you might lose her."

The unspoken reminder of how early and unexpectedly she'd lost her own mother wasn't lost on Donovan. He agreed quickly and easily, as if suddenly made uncomfortable by the subject. "All right. If it's that important to you, I promise to see her as soon as possible. Anything else?"

Sliding her arms around his chest, squeezing him tightly, she whispered, "Just remember who loves you, and everything will be fine."

"Well . . . okay."

There was hesitation in his voice, suspicion, too, so Libby turned away from the awkward situation by bringing it to an end. "Good. I'm glad we got everything settled. Now, I've got to get to work on a new editorial."

"I should be on my way, too." Donovan kept one skeptical eye on her. "Are you sure you're all right? Is there something—"

"I'm fine." She wiped her eyes, aware they were filling again. "Just relieved, I guess, to get this out in the open and over with."

"If you say so." He shrugged. "I'd better get going then. I haven't done a lick of work yet today, and I think, at Savage Publishing, even the boss's son can be fired. See you later?"

Unable to answer, Libby pressed her lips together in a half-hearted smile and inclined her head as if nodding.

Donovan, who was already turning the corner into the hallway, waved as he strode out of the kitchen. And out of her life.

By early afternoon, Donovan had only managed to convince one saloon owner to buy an ad in the *Tribune*, and that was only because the man owed him money on a bad gambling debt. His concentration was at an all-time low, but he couldn't figure out why. He felt good about the conversation he'd had with Libby, and was pretty well convinced that the two warring factions in his life—his father's immovable stand against the suffragist movement and Libby's unerring determination to pass the female vote into law—could somehow link fingers in peace, as long as he stood between them.

Still, something wasn't right, and it wasn't just the fact that he'd lost his magical abilities as an advertising solicitor. Determined to concentrate on his job, Donovan looked up to see that he was standing in front of the doors to Lucky Lil's. Had this route been accidental, he wondered, or had he subconsciously been trying to fulfill the promise he'd made to Libby? Maybe that was what was nagging him in the back of his mind. Thinking he might be able to talk his mother into an advertising contract with Savage Publishing, should the other effort fail, he pushed open the swinging door.

Instantly comforted by the old familiar scene, feeling more relaxed, Donovan stepped inside. The place was fairly quiet, but it was early yet. Only two poker tables had any action, the faro table was deserted, and the heavy velvet curtains were drawn across the bare stage. Old George was playing the piano as usual, but his music sounded more like practice than an actual performance. Lil was nowhere in sight.

"Donovan, honey," called Joy, twisting her way through the tables on her way to him. "Where you been, good-looking? I kinda missed having you around."

"Working in the daytime world, darlin.' Where's Lil—in the office?"

"No, she ain't come down yet today."

Concerned, Donovan glanced upstairs to the back of the hall where his mother's room was located. Lil never slept past two or three in the afternoon, no matter how big the night before had been. She was always down and working by now. Always. With a mumbled thanks to Joy, he started toward the stairs.

When he reached the end of the hallway past the private boxes, he knocked on the almost-hidden door which led to his mother's private quarters. A moment later, he thought he heard a muffled groan.

"Lil?" he called. "It's Donovan. Open up."

"Oh, ah, just a second," she answered back, her voice groggy, scratchy.

When Lil's door finally opened a few moments later, Donovan's concerns about her were far from eased. Her hair was completely disheveled, not just down and flying around her shoulders, but tangled and bushy in a way he hadn't seen before. Dark sunken hollows beneath her eyes made her look old and weary, and she was wearing a hastily donned wrapper of wrinkled cotton over her chemise. Lil never let anyone, not even her son, see her in such a state.

"Sorry if I . . . woke you. Are you ill?" he asked, wondering what kind of evening she'd had.

"No, just tired, and don't worry about waking me. I was coming around anyway. I had a really long night last night."

"Sorry I bothered you." Donovan felt distinctly uncomfortable, sorry he'd come here at all. "I'll come back some other time."

"No, come in." She grabbed his arm, almost desperately he thought, and pulled him into her room. Then she clutched her robe high at the throat and midsection, holding it closed. "I'm glad you came by. The place could use a little cheering up after what happened to Seamus, and all."

"What happened to Seamus?"

Lil stepped deeper into the shadows, looking as if she was hiding from him. Increasingly curious about her strange behavior, Donovan turned the flame on the wall lamp up high. As his mother's image grew brighter, he was shocked to see her looking even more haggard. "What's happened?"

She sighed wearily, giving up, it seemed. "I've been up half the day trying to take care of business. Seamus was shot last night."

"Christ, how? Drunken gamblers, a fight, what?"

"We don't know for sure. He just walked outside to go home after his shift was done, and someone shot him dead. A buggy drove off after it was done."

"You're saying he was shot on purpose, murdered?" Donovan crossed over to where his mother stood. She looked almost fragile, a first. And secretive, as usual. "Why in God's name would anyone shoot him? What do you know you're not telling me?"

"Nothing." But she looked away from him. "I don't know anything for sure except that Seamus is dead."

Shoulders slumping in despair, Lil's hands drifted to her sides. The movement caused her robe to fall open at the throat, revealing several dark splotches marring her alabaster skin. Taking his mother gently by the shoulders, Donovan turned her toward the light for a better look.

"Christ, Lil," he muttered, angered by what were obvious bruises dotting her neck. "What the hell has been going on around here? Who did this to you?"

"It's taken care of," she insisted, trying to break out of his grasp and close her robe, but Donovan held her tightly. "There's nothing for you to worry about now. I'll be okay."

"I want to know who did this. Who are you protecting?"

"No one, Son, I swear it."

Narrowing his gaze, he warned, "Tell me now, or I'll go downstairs and start asking questions until I get some answers. Now, who did this?"

Looking a little ashamed, Lil hung her head. "R. T. came back to see me a couple of nights ago—thought maybe I'd want to pick up where we'd left off. I said, no." Raising her dull-eyed gaze to meet Donovan's again, she quietly added, "R. T. never did much care for that word."

"*Christ!* Did he—"

"No, but he tried."

Donovan didn't spend so much as a second questioning his mother's story. She was many things to many people, but a liar to no one. He released her and raised his fists. "He's *not* going to get away with this. I don't give a damn who he thinks he is, he is *not* going to get away with this!"

"He's paid his due on my account—honest." Fear shone brightly in her eyes. "Seamus heard me scream that night, pulled him off me, and beat him to a bloody pulp."

"*Seamus* beat him?" Donovan knew the ex-fighter was a master at pummeling a rowdy patron into submission without causing any permanent damage—such as broken bones. Black eyes, bloody noses, and sore ribs were his specialties, when forced into service. If he hadn't been so blinded by his father's ways, he might have noticed the Irishman's mark the moment he set eyes on R. T. His thoughts growing darker by the minute, Donovan didn't even look his mother's way as he muttered under his breath, "I have to go now. Take care of yourself, Lil. I'll be back to check on you later tonight, tomorrow at the latest."

But Lil threw herself between him and the door. "Let well enough alone, Son. I beg you. Let well enough alone. You don't know R. T. like I do—he's evil."

Evil—Libby's impression, too. Donovan paused, studying Lil for a long moment, and saw in her eyes all the years they'd struggled together to make a life for themselves. Something turned in his chest, knife-like, but not sharp or agonizing with its pain. It was more of an ache. Like guilt. How could he have forgotten what all they'd been to each other for so long? How could it have been so . . . so *easy* for him to turn his back on his mother?

Giving into sudden impulse, the kind of impulse that didn't occur to him often, Donovan leaned over and tenderly kissed Lil's forehead. Then, thinking of someone else, he smiled as he said, "I'm done taking the easy way out . . . Mother. In fact, I'm thinking I ought to climb down off that fence I've been straddling, before I get my ass stuck full of splinters. Wouldn't you agree?"

Six months ago, outrage would have driven Donovan immediately to his father's office where he most likely would have finished the job Seamus had started on R. T. Now that so much more than simple vengeance was at stake—his future, Libby's future, and possibly, even *their* future together, among other dilemmas—he forced himself to take a walk along the waterfront, in order to cool down enough to think straight.

That walk ultimately led him to his own house—to Libby—where Donovan was certain he'd find the answers he sought. When he got there, all he found was darkness.

Libby had gone, not just for the evening, but as far as he could tell, forever. She'd packed up all traces of herself, save for the mangled hat he'd given her; packed and run off into the night. He knew, without even considering the possibility, that she hadn't gone to his mother's like before. The sick feeling in his gut told him there was no doubt that she'd finally boarded the train to Laramie.

Filled with a sense of emptiness, and not just the cold isolation of his once-warm home, Donovan sat down on the edge of the bed he and Libby had occupied just last night, and took the little straw bonnet between his hands. It was stained, pummeled, smashed beyond recognition, even though Libby had tried to mend it. The hat reminded him of where his relationship with her had ended—smashed and broken, probably beyond repair.

Try as she might, she hadn't been successful in her attempts to bring the bonnet back to its former beauty. Was he ten kinds of a fool to even think of trying to restore what they'd once had? If he went after her, would she even welcome him long enough to begin the repair work?

20

Laramie, Wyoming Territory
Two weeks later

Libby braced her hips against the counter in the front office of the *Laramie Tribune* and pounded the final nail into the wooden frame she'd built to hold a copy of her favorite editorial. The piece, written early last week, was an *exposé* of R. T. Savage and his tyrannical manipulation of Savage-owned newspapers, as well as his involvement with government lobbyists. Libby had left no stones unturned in her article, and even included "quotes" from the esteemed magnate, taken from her brief, and generally heated, conversations with him. The moment the inflammatory issue had come off the press, she'd sent it, as usual, to Savage Publishing—and to many other newspapers countrywide, especially those that leaned toward supporting equal rights.

Because the Savage name also belonged to Donovan, Libby took no pleasure in the way she'd exposed it. In spite of everything Randolph T. Savage stood for, she'd never wanted to tarnish the family Donovan coveted so much. But she'd done what she'd had to do. Even at her own risk. And she'd done it all with the blessings of her brother.

After she'd explained everything to Jeremy—everything except her personal involvement with Donovan—and made a point of the fact that, should she run the editorial, their affiliation with the *Tribune* would soon come to an end, he had agreed wholeheartedly that it was time they struck out on their own. If the Justice family had to begin by writing their newspaper in longhand, so be it. If one or both of them had to deliver newspapers for a rival publisher to make ends meet in the meantime, so be it. If they had to sell their home and live in a tent, so be it. They would stay together, and publish together a paper of which they could both be proud.

Of course, neither Justice sibling was fool enough to think a vindictive man like R. T. Savage would take a mutiny such as this lying down. Libby had been careful to explain to Jeremy the risks they'd be facing, should they expose the man, and even hinted to him that their soon-to-be former employer might have ordered a murder done. But as before, Jeremy had been no more interested in continuing the affiliation with the *Tribune* than Libby.

Of course, once the offensive edition of the *Laramie Tribune* had left the train station on its way to San Francisco, she'd known it was just a matter of time before R. T. closed her down—or worse. Not that she'd thought the man would actually do her physical harm out here in her own territory. Still, to be on the safe side, Jeremy and Hymie had formed a "watch committee," where they met all incoming trains from the West, to keep a lookout for strangers who could be hired guns.

As for Donovan . . . Libby still couldn't think of him, not and maintain the visage of strength she needed to get herself and her brother through the trying times ahead. Not if she were to keep her fragile link to sanity.

The frame finished, Libby positioned it on the wall facing the counter, which gave it the most exposure, then held it there with one hand as she poked around in her hair looking for a pencil to mark the spot. Since she'd pretty well destroyed the hat Donovan had loathed so, she'd taken to keeping her magnifying glass and tape measure in her pocket, and poked her pencils into her bun. She could usually find one easily, but sometimes, as now, the pencils either burrowed themselves so deeply into her thick hair that she had trouble locating them, or they simply fell out as she flitted around the pressroom. As for her glasses, Libby never knew where she might find them these days.

Irritated by the delay, she whirled around, slammed the frame down on the counter, then reached back with both hands and ripped at her bun. That's when she noticed movement just outside the *Tribune*'s offices. Still digging around in her hair for a pencil, she squinted hard as the "hitching post" out front began to walk up the steps toward the door. When the man—she could tell that much about the blurred figure—reached the porch, Libby could see that he was dressed in a fancy white shirt and dark suit; and for just a moment, she thought she glimpsed something shiny and red between the lapels of his jacket—a vest?

For a split-second, Libby's heartbeat accelerated, then it stopped altogether. Her hands froze to the top of her head. Then the door opened, setting off the little bell, and the man strolled into the room. He was carrying a small bag, an expensive leather item with the letter *S* embossed in gold on the side. Time was up, as she'd expected. But why, oh, why did *Donovan* have to be the messenger?

"Afternoon," he said as he approached. Never taking those silvery-blue eyes off of her, he swung the bag up on the counter between them. "Say hello, Libby—you do remember me, don't you?"

"Y-y—" She cleared her throat; then, mercifully, her arms relaxed enough to slide down to her sides. A stubby pencil clattered down to the counter at the same time. Donovan glanced up at her hair, cocked one eyebrow, then looked back into her eyes—and smiled. Shaking inside—outside, too, she thought—Libby quickly said, "Of course I remember you. I wasn't expecting to see you again, is all."

The smile grew into a grin, one that blinded her as much as his twinkling eyes. She found herself wanting to kiss him, but remembered that he was here on business. Then he got right to it, confirming her worst fears.

"Surely after the less-than-flattering editorial you sent to Savage Publishing last week, you had to be expecting someone from the main offices to stop by and see you."

She nodded numbly. "Yes, I suppose so."

"Well, here I am." He spread his arms. "I have something here for you. If you have a minute, I'd like to get this over with as quickly as possible."

"Please do." Libby could feel her temper rising slowly from the ashes of her heart, giving her the strength she would need to see her through this moment. Even then, she had to brace her knees against the counter to keep them from shaking. As Donovan reached into the bag and withdrew a thick packet of papers, she muttered, "I've been expecting this, but I have to say that I'm disappointed you've chosen to deliver the bad news yourself. Shall I vacate the entire building while you do your dirty work, or may I go upstairs to my room?"

"Oh, I want you to stay right where you are for this." Still smiling, Donovan spun the papers around so she could read the one on top as he explained the contents. "This is a release you need to sign, a legally binding contract between you and Savage Publishing which gives Liberty Ann Justice full and complete control of the *Laramie Tribune* from here on out. That includes ownership of the press, cameras, and all the other items you ink-slingers lay claim to as part of your printing business."

"Ownership?" She'd heard what Donovan said and followed the printed words, yet Libby couldn't quite make sense of them. "You mean the paper is mine to keep?"

"Precisely. The only thing you can't keep is the name, *Tribune*. That stays with Savage Publishing; but then, I didn't figure you'd want any part of my father's company anyway. Was I right?"

What did it mean? "Er, yes, but . . . but—"

"I realize this may be hard for you to grasp at first, and maybe later we can talk about it more. All I want you to understand right now is that I'm the one who went to R. T. and got this taken care of. I'm the one who kept him from sending someone out here to burn you out, or whatever it is they do when an affiliate 'goes bad.' Does that much make sense?"

She was dizzy, numb, excited, and afraid to believe him; but everything he said was there in black and white. Libby nodded and another pencil clattered to the counter top. "I understand, but I can't say this makes any sense. W-why did your father do it?"

His gaze following the pencil as it rolled across the counter then fell to the floor, Donovan looked slightly amused. "My why's first. Why didn't you tell me what R. T. did to my mother?"

"Oh, well . . ." Obviously he knew what had happened. She could see the pain in his eyes. "Lil made me promise not to. I figured it was her story and her right to decide when and how it got told, so I agreed to keep quiet about it. Didn't she tell you that?"

"No, but then, I didn't ask. I was in too big a hurry to have a little talk with my father."

"Oh." Had Donovan blackmailed the man into giving her the *Tribune*?

"R. T. didn't deny hurting my mother," he continued, "but he claimed he had nothing to do with Seamus's death. I admit I haven't been a very good judge of the man, but I tend to believe him—at least, I'd like to believe that of him." He looked enormously sad for a moment, making Libby wonder if he hadn't caught at least a glimpse of the evil in his father. She decided that maybe he had.

Catching her speculative gaze, Donovan produced a bright smile. "At any rate, I do know R. T. won't be bothering my mother again. In fact, after the threats I made, I expect *he'll* be hiring a bodyguard to make sure nothing happens to her—ever again."

Wondering now about those threats, certain they weren't of a physical nature, but more likely of a "social" nature, Libby caught sight of another moving "hitching post" outside. Squinting, she could see that a woman—a very well-dressed woman, at that—had reached the porch. The door opened, and she stepped inside, looking more familiar by the minute.

"Hello, Libby," she said, approaching the counter. "Is everything between you two . . ."—she glanced up at Donovan expectantly—". . . all right?"

"Susan!" Libby could hardly believe her eyes, but her vision was clear now, and there was no mistaking her visitor—Susan Savage. "What are you doing here?"

"Making things difficult for me," said Donovan, delivering an angry scowl to his sister. "I thought you had some shopping to do."

"That's what I thought I'd do to keep myself entertained, but I can't seem to find a decent store." She turned back to Libby. "Tell me there's at least one dress shop in this town."

"What are you doing here?" Libby repeated, stunned.

"Donovan brought me with him. I thought I might enjoy a little visit out here for a while, before heading to the Capital City in Washington."

"Washington? Why are you going there?"

Susan practically busted her buttons as she said, "I have a job! You're looking at the fully enrolled member of the NWSA who's going to be assisting Belva Lockwood in her presidential campaign—by next year, we could have a female president!"

"B-but, what about your duke?"

"Oh, him." Susan shrugged. "It turns out he did mind my joining the cause." She leaned forward and chuckled. "He only minded, of course, because father minded. It seems anything that affected my dowry, affected Henry. He was especially affected when I told him to take his titledom and go to hell."

"And that," said Donovan, gripping Susan's elbow, "is just where I was thinking of sending you if you don't leave Libby and me alone to talk."

After peeling her brother's fingers off her arm, Susan turned back to Libby. "I guess I'd better run along, but I'll be back soon."

"Wait!" Libby reached across the counter and captured Susan's hand. "What about your father? Surely he hasn't given his approval for your trip to Washington."

The bright smile disappeared and, in its place, came a thoughtful expression, not quite a frown. "He definitely did *not* approve, but I want to live my own life. Father knows, if he wants to see me again, that he's going to have to accept that about me. It will take some time, but I think he'll forgive me someday." She giggled. "I've always been his special little angel—how can he not?"

"Su-*san*," came Donovan's voice, a clear warning.

"Well, good-bye for now," she said, giving Libby a knowing glance and little wave. Then, bustles bouncing, she scurried out of the office.

Donovan's narrow gaze followed his sister's departure. When he was sure Susan was out of earshot, he turned back to Libby and said, "She's a cutie, that one, and smarter than I first thought, too. I really enjoy having Susan as a sister, but her sense of timing is lousy. Oh, and speaking of sisters—" He reached into the satchel and drew out a magazine. He turned to a page bearing a woman's photograph. Holding it next to his profile, he said, "What do you think? Do you see the likeness?"

Libby squinted, but did see a certain resemblance. "I guess. Who is she?"

"Lillibeth Jones. She's a shadowcatcher in Pasadena who got an award of some kind for her photographs— that's why she was in this magazine. Don't you think she could be my missing sister?"

Libby shrugged, dazed by everything else. "Possibly. What are you going to do? Go look her up?"

"I don't know. I don't want to think about that right now. I'm not done talking about you. Where were we?"

By now, Libby was in such shock, she could hardly remember her own name, much less where their conversation had been interrupted.

It didn't matter. Donovan seemed quite content to do the thinking for them both. "I believe you were probably wondering what it cost me to get this deal for you. Right?" He jabbed the contract with his finger, and Libby automatically nodded. Another pencil fell out of what was left of her bun. He laughed, glanced at her disheveled hair, and said, "It beats the hell out of that hat. Did you burn it?"

Her throat was so dry, Libby nearly choked as she said, "No, but I did bury it away in the bottom of my dresser."

"You should have buried it, period." After a short laugh, Donovan turned serious again. "Back to what this contract cost me—not a damn dime. All I had to do was sign a little paper, myself, a deposition agreeing that I'd never lay claim to any part of the Savage family fortunes, including the name. I'm back to being William Donovan again."

"Will—" Her lungs felt as if they'd collapsed, and Libby's throat closed tightly, making it impossible to go on.

"I hope you weren't trying to call me 'Willy,'" he snapped. "I thought I'd warned you about that."

Gasping and laughing at the same time, Libby finally managed to draw a breath. "No, honest, I wasn't, b-but I am wondering how you could have given up your name? *Why*?"

"Because . . ." He paused, looking puzzled, or maybe hesitant, for the first time since he'd stepped through the door. "Oh, I don't know, Libby. Maybe I felt like getting out of the big city and taking another look around Laramie; and maybe I thought I'd see if one of the local newspapers needs a first-rate advertising solicitor. Or maybe, just maybe, I came here and did it all for you."

"For me?" She heard the words and understood somewhere in her brain exactly what he was saying; but, for some reason, Libby couldn't let herself believe it. "You mean you . . . love me?"

He rolled his eyes and sighed. "I was hoping you'd figure that out for yourself. I'm not much good at this sappy stuff—remember?"

"Oh . . . Donovan." The tears in Libby's throat rose to her eyes, threatening the floodgates. Needing to touch him, to feel his arms around her, and know that this was real, she swung herself up on the counter, leading with her right leg as if mounting a horse. Trouble was, the counter wasn't as wide or as high as most horses. Had Donovan not been there to catch her, Libby would have flung herself beyond the counter and onto the floor.

Righting her and wrapping her firmly in his arms, he kept his face just inches from Libby's as he said, "Still as awkward as ever, I see."

"That's right. I haven't changed, but I think one of us has." She touched his cheek, finding out that he was very real. "Oh, Donovan," she murmured, her breath catching in her throat. "How you've surprised me. As long as it took you to finally find a real family, I can hardly believe you've given them up for me."

"Yeah, well, that's what I did all right."

His complexion seemed to darken. Or maybe it had turned a little rosy. William Donovan—blushing? And could he possibly be aware of it? He glanced down at the floor then and shuffled his feet, making Libby think that maybe he was all too aware.

Speaking with what sounded like a fair amount of difficulty, Donovan went on. "I don't know why it took me so long to figure it out, but did you know there's no law that says a fella's got to accept just any old family that gets thrown at him, even if he does want a family as badly as I do?"

"B-but—"

"Let me finish, while I still can."

Libby wasn't about to miss the rest of what Donovan had to say. She pressed her lips together, flattening them, and gave him a short, silent nod.

"It occurred to me," he went on, "that if I wanted a family so damn badly, why not start my own?"

"Your own family?" she blurted out, forgetting herself. "You mean you want children?"

"I guess so," he whispered softly. Donovan's eyes misted slightly then, making them look bluer and more luminous. "I have to tell you, Libby," he said in that same soft whisper, "the idea of making a new family with you sounds just about perfect."

"Oh . . . oh," Libby's voice, heart, everything felt strangled, wrung out. "Oh, Donovan . . . I-I love you so much."

Again he blushed, but this time he took it in stride, his euphoric expression overshadowing his rosy cheeks. Still, for a moment, Libby thought he was going to turn away from her. He didn't, but he did mutter in a deep serious voice, "Oh, now don't go getting all sappy on me. I told you, I'm not much good at that sort of thing."

Fighting her tears, she said, "Do it right, Donovan. Ask me to marry you."

He tugged at his collar, looking distinctly uncomfortable. "I guess you forgot that I'm not exactly the marrying kind."

"Oh, I remember perfectly, but it seems I've discovered that I *am* the marrying kind. I won't live with you or have your babies any other way. Now, are you going to ask me to marry you, or not?"

Surprising her, Donovan turned Libby loose, ripped off his hat, then slammed it to the floor. "I knew it!" he shouted. "I just knew it! Didn't I tell you the first time I looked into those big calf eyes of yours that I saw a little white house, a picket fence, and kids running amok in a vegetable garden? Didn't I? You lied to me!"

But he wasn't angry. His eyes were twinkling with mischief. "I didn't lie, not really. I thought I didn't want those things, but now I see that I can't stand to have it any other way. Not between us."

Her eyes misting with tears, blurring anyway, Libby didn't see the men approaching until the door crashed open, setting off the bell with such gusto, it sounded like the fire alarm. She turned toward the racket only to find Hymie down on one knee, his shotgun pointed directly at Donovan's heart.

"Don't move you citified slicker," he cackled, "or I'll blow you to kingdom come. We seen this fella get off the train, Libby, but I couldn't find my blasted gun right away. Sorry it took us so long to get here."

Behind him, with feet wide apart and Libby's father's pistol drawn, stood Jeremy. "Looks like we're just in time, sis," he said, sounding tough, in spite of the fact that, using both hands, he still couldn't keep the gun from shaking.

"Wait!" Donovan's hands went straight above his head. "Don't shoot! I'll marry her. I swear, I planned to marry her all along. I'll do it now, right this minute if you want!"

Amazed by his sudden declaration, though not terribly surprised, Libby thought about calling off the guns. Instead, she turned so only Hymie and Jeremy could see her, smiled and winked. "If Donovan told me once, boys, he told me a thousand times that he's *not* the marrying kind. He's lying."

"No, I swear to God, I'm not lying." Donovan eased one hand lower toward his vest. "Let me show you."

"Whatcha doing there?" Hymie jabbed the shotgun toward him. "Reaching for your weapon?"

"No gun, I swear. Just some proof." Fumbling for a moment, he pulled out a small blue velvet box. "See? I already bought the wedding ring—in San Francisco. My sister, Susan, can verify that." Keeping his eyes trained on the gunmen, he handed the box to Libby. "Take it, it's yours."

Biting her lip to keep from showing her pleasure as she turned to him, she raised her brows high. "You got me a ring? You really were going to ask me to marry you all along?"

Grinning broadly, Donovan glanced at her. "You bet. Now call off your dogs."

"You let me go through all that, that 'marrying kind' business, when you meant to ask me anyway?"

His grin sheepish now, he shrugged. "You said, if something's too easy, it's not worth having. I thought you might like to work a little at getting me to propose, so you could properly appreciate me."

"Really?" As she tried to decide exactly how to handle the situation, Libby remembered a little something she'd forgotten to clear up before leaving San Francisco. Trying to hide an impish grin, she said, "I think you might be right, Donovan, and thanks for the suggestion. Hymie, Jeremy? You can put your guns away."

Although Donovan no longer looked worried about the pressman or Libby's brother, she thought he did seem to be a tad concerned about her. "Everything's all right then?" he asked. "We're getting married?"

"Oh, I didn't say that." She batted her lashes in a way that would have made her friend Dell enormously proud. "I haven't exactly said yes, yet. I don't want to make this too easy for you."

"Aw, come on, Libby."

"I have to be sure—sure that you'll do anything to protect me and our children from harm."

"Of course, I will. I swear it." He slapped his palm to his chest.

"You'll do . . . *anything*?"

"Yes, yes. How can I prove it to you?"

"Easy." Libby knew her expression had to be deliciously conspiratorial. She couldn't have hidden it. "It seems this newspaper office and the entire upstairs are overrun with mice."

Donovan started and made a kind of strangled sound deep in his throat, but to his credit, he didn't utter a word of protest.

"If you can get rid of those mice, I'll marry you. Oh, and by the way—we grow them as big as *rats* out here in Wyoming Territory!"

Author's Note

I got the idea for writing the story of Donovan and Libby while in the midst of researching my most recent novel, *The Bride Wore Spurs,* as several scenes in that book were also set in Laramie, Wyoming Territory. As I studied the town's history, I came across the fact that in 1870 this small frontier burg was the first to grant women the right to vote. Since it took another fifty years for the nation to recognize women as intelligent, reasoning creatures, I began to wonder exactly *what* could have made the suffragists' battle go on for so long. Surely fifty percent of the population could have convinced enough of their hard-headed men to grant the vote sooner—couldn't they?

I dug deeper, and that's when I stumbled over the fact that lobbyists—special interest groups like the liquor and textile industries—had a firm grip on the reins of this nation's policy-makers, even way back then. When I queried others about this injustice, nobody seemed to know that these groups played such a large part in keeping the minds of American women in their kitchens—hidden away in little glass jars, as it were, like raspberry preserves. It is for those women, and myself, that I wrote this book. I hope you enjoyed it.

Let HarperMonogram
Sweep You Away!

After the Storm by Susan Sizemore

Golden Heart Award–Winning Author. When a time travel experiment goes awry, Libby Wolfe finds herself in medieval England and at the mercy of the dashing Bastien of Bale. A master of seduction, the handsome outlaw unleashes a passion in Libby that she finds hauntingly familiar.

Deep in the Heart by Sharon Sala

Romantic Times Award–Winning Author. Stalked by a threatening stranger, successful casting director Samantha Carlyle returns home to Texas—and her old friend John Thomas Knight—for safety. The tender lawman may be able to protect Sam's body, but his warm Southern ways put her heart at risk.

Honeysuckle DeVine by Susan Macias

To collect her inheritance, Laura Cannon needs to join Jesse Travers's cattle drive—and become his wife. The match is only temporary, but long days on the trail lead to nights filled with fiery passion.

Harper Monogram

Buy 4 or more and receive FREE postage & handling

UNITED STATES
Territorial Expansion

Lake of the Woods

Lake Superior

Lake Huron

Lake Michigan

Lake Erie

Lake Ontario

St. Lawrence R.

MINNESOTA (1858)

St. Paul ★

WISCONSIN (1848)

Madison ★

IOWA (1846)

Des Moines ★

MICHIGAN (1837)
Lansing ★

Mississippi R.

ILLINOIS (1818)

Springfield ★

MISSOURI (1821)

Jefferson City ★

ka

Missouri R.

ORIGINAL UNITED STATES
(By treaty with Britain, 1783)

INDIANA (1816)

Indianapolis ★

OHIO (1803)

Columbus ★

KENTUCKY (1792)

Nashville ★

Frankfort ★

Ohio R.

WEST VIRGINIA (1863)

Charleston ★

Montpe.

NEW YORK (1788)

Albany ★

N.H. (1788)
Concord ★
Boston ★

MASS. (1788)
Providence ★
R.I. (1790)

Hartford ★
CONN. (1788)

N.J. (1787)
Trenton ★

PENN. (1787)

Harrisburg ★

1800
1790
MD. (1788)
Annapolis ★
Dover ★
DEL. (1787)

Washington, D.C. ☆

1850

VIRGINIA (1788)

Richmond ★

Chesapeake Bay

ATLANTIC OCEAN

ORIGINAL THIRTEEN COLONIES

1900

1950

2000

ARKANSAS (1836)

Little Rock ★

Arkansas R.

Tennessee R.

TENNESSEE (1796)

Raleigh ★

NORTH CAROLINA (1789)

SOUTH CAROLINA (1788)

Columbia ★

Atlanta ★

Mississippi R.

MISSISSIPPI (1817)

Jackson ★

ALABAMA (1819)

Montgomery ★

GEORGIA (1788)

Red R.

Baton Rouge ★

LOUISIANA (1812)

(Seized from Spain, 1810, 1813)

Tallahassee ★

FLORIDA
(By treaty with Spain, 1819)

FLORIDA (1845)

Lake Okeechobee

Gulf
-of
Mexico

BAHAMAS

● Geographical center of population
per Census year

PUERTO RICO
(From Spain, 1898)

ATLANTIC OCEAN

San Juan ★

Charlotte Amalie ★

VIRGIN ISLANDS
(From Denmark, 1917)

0   50   100 Miles
0   50   100 Kilometers

0   150   300 Miles
0   150   300 Kilometers

CUBA

www.wadsworth.com

www.wadsworth.com is the World Wide Web site for Thomson Wadsworth and is your direct source to dozens of online resources.

At *www.wadsworth.com* you can find out about supplements, demonstration software, and student resources. You can also send email to many of our authors and preview new publications and exciting new technologies.

www.wadsworth.com
Changing the way the world learns®

AMERICAN PASSAGES

A History of the United States

VOLUME I: TO 1877

AMERICAN PASSAGES

A History of the United States

Edward L. Ayers
University of Virginia

Lewis L. Gould
University of Texas at Austin, Emeritus

David M. Oshinsky
University of Texas at Austin

Jean R. Soderlund
Lehigh University

Third Edition

THOMSON
WADSWORTH

Australia • Brazil • Canada • Mexico • Singapore
Spain • United Kingdom • United States

American Passages: A History of the United States
VOLUME I: TO 1877
Third Edition
Edward L. Ayers, *University of Virginia*
Lewis L. Gould, *University of Texas at Austin, Emeritus*
David M. Oshinsky, *University of Texas at Austin*
Jean R. Soderlund, *Lehigh University*

Publisher: *Clark Baxter*
Acquisitions Editor: *Ashley Dodge*
Senior Development Editor: *Margaret McAndrew Beasley*
Assistant Editor: *Jessica Kim*
Editorial Assistant: *Kristen Judy*
Technology Project Manager: *David Lionetti*
Marketing Manager: *Lori Grebe Cook*
Marketing Assistant: *Teresa Jessen*
Project Manager, Editorial Production: *Katy German*
Creative Director: *Rob Hugel*
Art Director: *Maria Epes*

Print Buyer: *Barbara Britton*
Permissions Editor: *Joohee Lee*
Production Service: *Graphic World Publishing Services*
Text and Cover Designer: *Kathleen Cunningham Design*
Photo Researcher: *ImageQuest*
Copy Editor: *Graphic World Publishing Services*
Cover Image: *Race Between Locomotive Tom Thumb and Horse Car.* © *SuperStock Inc./SuperStock*
Compositor: *International Typesetting and Composition*
Printer: *Quebecor World/Versailles*

Thomson Higher Education
10 Davis Drive
Belmont, CA 94002-3098
USA

For more information about our products, contact us at:
Thomson Learning Academic Resource Center
1-800-423-0563

For permission to use material from this text or product, submit a request online at
http://www.thomsonrights.com.
Any additional questions about permissions can be submitted by e-mail to
thomsonrights@thomson.com.

Library of Congress Control Number: 2005938040

ISBN 0-495-05062-8

About the Authors

EDWARD L. AYERS is the Hugh P. Kelly Professor of History and Dean of the College and Graduate School of Arts and Sciences at the University of Virginia. He was educated at the University of Tennessee and Yale University, where he received his Ph.D. in American Studies. Ayers was named National Professor of the Year by the Carnegie Foundation and the Council for the Support of Education in 2003. His book, *In the Presence of Mine Enemies: War in the Heart of America, 1859–1863* (2003), won the Bancroft Prize for distinguished work on the history of the United States. *The Promise of the New South: Life After Reconstruction* (1992) won prizes for the best book on the history of American race relations and on the history of the American South. It was a finalist for both the National Book Award and the Pulitzer Prize. He is the co-editor of *The Oxford Book of the American South* (1997) and *All Over the Map: Rethinking American Regions* (1996). The World Wide Web version of "The Valley of the Shadow: Two Communities in the American Civil War," was recognized by the American Historical Association as the best aid to the teaching of history. His latest book is *What Caused the Civil War? Reflections on the South and Southern History* (2005).

LEWIS L. GOULD is Eugene C. Barker Centennial Professor Emeritus in American History at the University of Texas at Austin. After receiving his Ph.D. from Yale University, he taught at Texas for 31 years before his retirement in 1998. He was honored for outstanding undergraduate and graduate teaching during his career. His most recent books include *The Modern American Presidency* (2003), *Grand Old Party: A History of the Republicans* (2003), and *The Most Exclusive Club: A History of the Modern United States Senate* (2005). He has written op-ed essays for the *Washington Post,* the *Austin American-Statesman,* and the *Dallas Morning News,* and has been a frequent commentator on radio and television about modern politics, First Ladies, and Congress.

DAVID M. OSHINSKY received his undergraduate degree from Cornell University and his doctorate from Brandeis. He is currently Littlefield Professor of History

The *American Passages* Author Team (left to right) Ed Ayers, David Oshinsky, Jean Soderlund, Lewis Gould

at the University of Texas at Austin. Prior to that he taught for 26 years at Rutgers University, where he held the Board of Governors Chair as well as chairman of the History Department. Oshinsky is the author of five books, including *A Conspiracy So Immense: The World of Joe McCarthy* (1983), which was voted one of the year's "best books" by the *New York Sunday Times Book Review,* and won the Hardeman Prize for the best work about the U.S. Congress. His book, *Worse than Slavery: Parchman Farm and the Ordeal of Jim Crow Justice* (1996), won both the Robert Kennedy Book Award for the year's most distinguished contribution to the field of human rights and the American Bar Association's Scribes Award for distinguished legal writing. Oshinsky's latest book is *Polio: An American Story* (2005).

Oshinsky is a regular contributor to scholarly journals, the *Washington Post Book World, New York Sunday Times Book Review, New York Times* op-ed page, and *New York Times Sunday Magazine.* He was awarded a senior fellowship by the National Endowment for the Humanities and spent 1999–2000 as a Phi Beta Kappa Visiting Scholar.

JEAN R. SODERLUND is Professor of History and Deputy Provost for Faculty Affairs at Lehigh University. She received her Ph.D. from Temple University and was a post-doctoral fellow at the McNeil Center for Early American Studies at the University of Pennsylvania. Her book *Quakers and Slavery: A Divided Spirit* won the Alfred E. Driscoll Publication Prize of the New Jersey Historical Commission. Soderlund was an editor of three volumes of the Papers of William Penn (1981–1983) and co-authored *Freedom by Degrees: Emancipation in Pennsylvania and Its Aftermath* (1991).

She has written articles and chapters in books on the history of women, African Americans, Native Americans, Quakers, and the development of abolition in the British North American colonies and early United States. She is currently working on a study of the Lenape people within colonial New Jersey society. She is a council member of the McNeil Center for Early American Studies, and she served as a committee chair for the American Historical Association and the Organization of American Historians.

Brief Contents

Detailed Contents

Passages 1764 to 1814   126

Passages 1855 to 1877 372

Doing History Features

List of Maps

Preface

American Passages: Context and Narrative Create a More Historical Approach...

There are plenty of U.S. history textbooks. Why did we feel a need to write another one? The textbooks on the market when we first considered writing a book of our own were written by leading historians. They were accurate and they were fair. What made us think we could improve on books that had long been in use, often through many editions?

We thought we could write a new kind of text, one that applied the lessons we have learned in our own classrooms. All four of us had seen that students could be engaged in history if that history was conveyed in ways that tap its inherent interest. We had seen the attraction of surprise, of unexpected outcomes. We had seen students intrigued by discovering hidden connections. We had seen the power of simple narrative, of one thing triggering another, showing cause and effect.

In short, we thought we could write a more *historical* history text. Textbooks often bear little resemblance to our favorite works of history. Texts tend to replace the concrete with the general, the individual with the aggregate, the story with the summary. Most dulling, we thought, was the tendency for texts to rip things out of context, to present history as processes and trends unfolding in a timeless abstraction. We had watched students bored by chapters on "industrialization" and "urbanization." We had seen regions, especially the South and the West, often torn from the flow of American history and deposited in separate chapters. We had seen ethnic and racial groups isolated and frozen in ahistorical "communities." We had seen the end of the story given away too easily, drama squandered.

"Time is what makes history History...."

We believed that we could write a book that captured what we love most about history and, just as important, what explains the most about history. We decided to write the first U.S. history text in which time stood front and center. Time is what makes history History rather than sociology, anthropology, or economics. And time is what most textbooks sacrificed in the name of convenience and false clarity.

While many history texts claim to be "chronological," *American Passages* is unique in its insistence, in every part of every chapter, that time, with the characteristics of sequence, simultaneity, and contingency, is the *defining nature* of history. Sequence shows how events grow from other events, personalities, and broad changes. Simultaneity shows how apparently disconnected events were situated in larger shared contexts. Contingency shows how history suddenly pivots, how it often changes course in a moment.

No other text has this focus on time. The differences are easily apparent in our table of contents, in the Passages sections, in the Flashpoints, in the timelines, and in the Enduring Issues sections—and in the narrative analytical history that is the core of this book.

Now, more than 10 years after we began work on *American Passages,* we feel more strongly than ever that students and teachers should have such a book. We insist, with some passion, that our textbooks should embody and express the essential attributes that can make, in the right hands, our discipline exciting.

Framework and Features of *American Passages*

American Passages is written to convey the excitement and uncertainty of this nation's past—to see it whole. Eight **"Passages"** sections, appearing regularly throughout the text, provide broad overviews that connect ideas and themes across chapters. In addition to a textual outline, the "Passages" sections weave in photographs, posters, graphs, and maps illustrative of the period. **"America and the World" maps** help set the American story in global context. The maps identify specific locations in the world and briefly explain why those places were particularly important to the United States in the years covered in each Passage section. Two-page **Passages Chronologies** help students place smaller stories into context and to understand interrelationships of people, ideas, movements, and events.

American Passages, Third Edition, incorporates two new features to help students see how individual events and people fit into the broad picture of our past. Remember the feelings you had when you heard about the terrorist attacks of September 11, or the fall of the Berlin Wall, or the assassination of President John F. Kennedy? Each of these events caused the course of history to shift suddenly—and we felt the impact on a personal, national, and global level. Pivotal events or **Flashpoints** in our nation's history—such as Haymarket Affair, the Boston Tea Party, or the 1936 Berlin Olympics—emphasize contingency. These brief essays, appearing one per chapter, show students how key events and personal decisions have turned the story and influenced historical outcomes over time.

The second new feature, **Enduring Issues,** traces and links broad themes and issues that are touched on in multiple chapters. Essay topics include the evolution of women's roles in war, the relationship of religious reform in the democratic development of the United States, how the concept of Manifest Destiny shaped our nation's boundaries, perceptions about the place of Native Americans as allies or outsiders, and views on medical breakthroughs and military drafts. Looking both back and forward in time, these essays synthesize the various perspectives or evolution of the topic across time to highlight recurring patterns in various contexts. Enduring Issues appear approximately every other chapter. Both Flashpoints and Enduring Issues include assignable "Questions for Reflection" to encourage critical thinking.

American Passages has always incorporated primary source materials, allowing students an opportunity to see the evidence on which historians base their interpretations. In the Third Edition, the sources are presented in **Doing History** modules, which include a collection of two to four brief excerpts from primary sources on related topics, to show varying perspectives. Exposure to multiple sources and different types of historical evidence provides students with manageable opportunities to "do history." Brief commentary by the authors guides students, and assignable "Questions for Reflection" encourage critical thinking or provide framework for class discussion. In addition, **Doing History Online** boxes highlight assignable exercises from the *American Passages* **HistoryNow** website, offering students another easy way to explore documents, maps, and images specifically related to material in the text.

At the beginning of each chapter, **outlines** provide an overview of the stories they are about to read. Chapter chronologies have been adapted to graphic **timelines** to portray the duration and overlap of crucial historical processes and occurrences.

"Identification" terms appear in boldface in the chapter, are listed at the end of the chapter for easy review, and are explained in a **Glossary** to ensure that students know the significance of important people, events, organizations, and movements. At the end of each chapter, new review questions entitled **Making Connections Across Chapters** guide students in their study, helping them to locate crucial issues in the stories they have just read and to anticipate the future implications of the events and changes they have just encountered.

Because photos, cartoons, maps, and other visual materials are so important in our understanding of the past, we have paused a little longer over a few images in each chapter to call students' attention to the detail and meaning those images convey. These **Picturing the Past** features consist of extended captions that are labeled corresponding to the three major organizing principles of the Passages chronologies— Politics and Diplomacy, Social and Cultural Events, and Economics and Technology— and are color-coordinated to those categories as well. This visual and thematic association will help students understand how people and events connect across time. And the exercise of looking at images through a historian's eye will also help them develop skills to evaluate images on their own.

Content Revisions

The authors have carefully reviewed each chapter and incorporated minor revisions, clarifications, and updates throughout. Following are selected notes about specific content revisions, many resulting from reviewer suggestions:

Chapters 9–15: new emphasis on the role of the post office and communication in general, the importance of international abolitionism to the United States, the international significance of the U.S. federal plan of government, the story of Mexico in its early dealings with Texas, and the evolution of the two-party system in the face of slavery.

Chapter 16: enhanced emphasis on the role of African Americans in the narrative of Reconstruction.

Chapter 17: a more nuanced discussion of the origins of industrialism that students will find easier to understand.

Chapter 18: more attention to the roots of urbanism and a more compact narrative about Populism.

Chapter 19: now incorporates the latest information about the debate over imperialism.

Chapter 20: greater emphasis on social history and a less political focus on Progressivism.

Chapter 21: a closer look at the cultural impact of the Taft and Wilson years.

Chapter 22: integrates more successfully the social and political effects of World War I.

Chapter 23: provides a more focused examination of the 1920s, especially for such episodes as the Sacco-Vanzetti case.

Chapter 24: places the Great Depression and its causes in better perspective.

Chapter 31: more attention to the origins of the problem of international terrorism.

Chapter 32: now provides a better overview of the continuities and differences between Bill Clinton and George W. Bush.

ACKNOWLEDGMENTS

I would like to thank my students and colleagues at the University of Virginia who have helped me struggle with the tough questions of American history. I am grateful, too, to Katherine Pierce and Margaret Beasley for their imagination, hard work, and good advice in the creation of this book. Finally, I am very appreciative of my co-authors, who have been engaged scholars, thoughtful critics, devoted teachers, and good friends throughout the years it took us to write American Passages.

Edward L. Ayers

I would like to acknowledge the help of the following former students who contributed in constructive ways to the completion of the textbook: Martin Ansell, Christie Bourgeois, Thomas Clarkin, Stacy Cordery, Debbie Cottrell, Patrick Cox, Scott Harris, Byron Hulsey, Jonathan Lee, John Leffler, Mark Young, and Nancy Beck Young. Karen Gould gave indispensable support and encouragement throughout the process of writing the text. Margaret Beasley supplied patient, informed, and thorough editorial guidance for the third edition, and the authors are all in her debt for that significant contribution. I am grateful as well to the readers of my chapters who made so many useful and timely criticisms.

   Lewis L. Gould

I would like to thank my colleagues and students at Rutgers for allowing me to test out an endless stream of ideas and issues relating to modern American history, and also for their thoughts on how a good college textbook should "read" and what it should contain. As always, the support and love of my family—Matt, Efrem, Ari, and Jane—was unshakable. Above all, I must commend my co-authors and my editors for their remarkable patience and professionalism during this long collaborative process.

   David M. Oshinsky

I am grateful to my husband, Rudolf Soderlund, and my family for their support throughout this project. Many scholars in the colonial and early national periods shared their ideas orally and through publications. For this edition, I would particularly like to thank Holly Kent for her capable assistance in revising the text and Margaret Beasley for her unfailing enthusiasm and expertise. As always, I am indebted to my co-authors for their collegiality and commitment to making this a great book.

   Jean R. Soderlund

Reviewers

The authors wish to thank the following professors who provided useful feedback and suggestions for the third edition:

Ginette Aley, *Drake University*

Rebecca Bailey, *State University of West Georgia*

Abel Bartley, *Clemson University*

Troy Bickham, *Texas A&M University*

Jerome D. Bowers II, *Northern Illinois University*

Thomas A. Britten, *University of Texas at Brownsville*

Roger Bromert, *Southwestern Oklahoma State University*

Stacy A. Cordery, *Monmouth College*

Yvonne Cornelius-Thompson, *Nashville State Community College*

Lisa Lindquist Dorr, *University of Alabama*

Laura A. Dunn, *Brevard Community College*

Michael H. Ebner, *Lake Forest College*

Keith Edgerton, *Montana State University, Billings*

Michael Garcia, *Arapahoe Community College*

Paul J. L. Hughes, *Sussex County Community College*

Charles F. Irons, *Elon University*

Stephen Patrick Kirkpatrick, *Blinn College*

David Marcus Lauderback, *Austin Community College*

Alan Lehmann, *Blinn College*

Michael Light, *Grand Rapids Community College*

Mary K. McGuire, *Southern Illinois University, Carbondale*

Gregg L. Michel, *University of Texas at San Antonio*

Mark A. Panuthos, *Saint Petersburg College*

Melvin H. Pritchard, *West Valley College*

Stephen L. Recken, *University of Arkansas at Little Rock*

Lewie Reece, *Anderson College*

Amy K. Rieger, *Brevard Community College*

Thomas J. Rowland, *University of Wisconsin, Oshkosh*

Robert D. Sawrey, *Marshall University*

E. Timothy Smith, *Barry University*

Don A. Whatley, *Blinn College*

Ralph Young, *Temple University*

And these professors who served as reviewers in earlier stages of the writing and revising of *American Passages:*

Joseph Adams, *St. Louis Community College at Meramec*

Dawn Alexander, *Abilene Christian University*

Charles Allbee, *Burlington Community College*

Julius Amin, *University of Dayton*

Melodie Andrews, *Mankato State University*

Richard Baquera, *El Paso Community College-Valle Verde*

Robert Becker, *Louisiana State University*

Peter Bergstrom, *Illinois State University*

Blanche Brick, *Blinn College*

John Brooke, *Tufts University*

Neil Brooks, *Essex Community College*

Linda D. Brown, *Odessa College*

Colin Calloway, *Dartmouth University*

Milton Cantor, *University of Massachusetts*

Kay Carr, *Southern Illinois University*

Paul Chardoul, *Grand Rapids Junior College*

Thomas Clarkin, *University of Texas, Austin*

Myles Clowers, *San Diego City College*

William Cobb, *Utah Valley State College*

David Coon, *Washington State University*

Stacy Cordery, *Monmouth College*

Debbie Cottrell, *Smith College*

A. Glenn Crothers, *Indiana University Southeast*

David Cullen, *Collin County Community College*

Christine Daniels, *Michigan State University*

Amy E. Davis, *University of California, Los Angeles*

Ronnie Day, *East Tennessee State University*

Matthew Dennis, *University of Oregon*

Robert Downtain, *Tarrant County Junior College, Northeast Campus*

Robert Elam, *Modesto Junior College*

Rob Fink, *Texas Tech University*

Monte S. Finkelstein, *Tallahassee Community College*

Linda Foutch, *Walter State Community College*

Robert G. Fricke, *West Valley College*

Michael P. Gabriel, *Kutztown University*

David Hamilton, *University of Kentucky*

Beatriz Hardy, *Coastal Carolina University*

Peter M. G. Harris, *Temple University*

Thomas Hartshorne, *Cleveland State University*

Gordon E. Harvey, *University of Louisiana at Monroe*

Ron Hatzenbuehler, *Idaho State University*

Robert Hawkes, *George Mason University*

William L. Hewitt, *West Chester University*

James Houston, *Oklahoma State University*

Raymond Hyser, *James Madison University*

Lillian Jones, *Santa Monica College*

Jim Kluger, *Pima Community College*

Timothy Koerner, *Oakland Community College*

James Lacy, *Contra Costa College*

Alton Lee, *University of South Dakota*

Liston Leyendecker, *Colorado State University*

Robert Marcom, *San Antonio College*

Greg Massey, *Freed-Hardeman*

Michael Mayer, *University of Montana*

Randy McBee, *Texas Tech University*

Loyce B. Miles, *Hinds Community College*

Kimberly Morse, *University of Texas, Austin*

Augustine Nigro, *Kutztown University*

Elsa Nystrom, *Kennesaw State*

David O'Neill, *Rutgers University*

Elizabeth R. Osborn, *Indiana University—Purdue University Indianapolis*

Betty Owens, *Greenville Technical College*

Mark Parillo, *Kansas State University*

J'Nell Pate, *Tarrant County Junior College, Northeast Campus*

Louis Potts, *University of Missouri at Kansas City*

Noel Pugach, *University of New Mexico*

Alice Reagan, *Northern Virginia Community College*

Marlette Rebhorn, *Austin Community College, Rio Grande Campus*

David Reimers, *New York University*

Hal Rothman, *Wichita State University*

Erik S. Schmeller, *Tennessee State University*

John G. Selby, *Roanoke College*

Ralph Shaffer, *California Polytechnic University*

Kenneth Smemo, *Moorhead State University*

Jack Smith, *Great Basin College*

Thaddeus Smith, *Middle Tennessee State University*

Phillip E. Stebbins, *Pennsylvania State University*
Marshall Stevenson, *Ohio State University*
William Stockton, *Johnson County Community College*
Suzanne Summers, *Austin Community College*
Frank Towers, *Clarion University*
Daniel Usner, *Cornell University*
Daniel Vogt, *Jackson State University*
Stephen Webre, *Louisiana Technical College*
John C. Willis, *University of the South*
Harold Wilson, *Old Dominion University*
Nan Woodruff, *Pennsylvania State University*
Bertram Wyatt-Brown, *University of Florida*
Sherri Yeager, *Chabot College*
Robert Zeidel, *University of Wisconsin.*

AMERICAN PASSAGES
A History of the United States

Passages   Prehistory to 1763

And so we journeyed for seventeen days, at the end of which we crossed the river [Rio Grande] and traveled for seventeen more. At sunset, on plains between some very tall mountains, we found some people who eat nothing but powdered straw for a third of the year. Since it was that season of the year, we had to eat it too. At the end of our journey we found a permanent settlement where there was abundant corn. The people gave us a large quantity of it and of cornmeal, squash, beans and cotton blankets. . . . From here we traveled [to where people] gave me five emeralds made into arrowheads. . . . Since they seemed very fine to me, I asked them where they had gotten them. They told me that they brought them from some very high mountains to the North.

—*Cabeza de Vaca, 1542**

F rom 1534 to 1536, the Spanish explorer Álvar Núñez Cabeza de Vaca and three other people traveled through Texas and northern Mexico, trying to reach Mexico City. They had been part of an expedition to Florida that ran afoul of Apalachee Indians, escaped across the Gulf of Mexico in makeshift boats, then were enslaved in Texas by Karankawa Indians. In his *Relación,* Cabeza de Vaca described their adventures, including the harrowing passage across the gulf, long journeys without food, and sojourns among Texas Indians.

Warpaths, ocean voyages, hunting trails, trade routes, death, communication and exchange among people—creating societies in America embodied passages of every kind. Asians migrated across the Bering land bridge and along the Pacific coast more than 10,000 years ago, settling throughout North and South America. Over time, they created distinct cultures in every part of the hemisphere, from the Aztecs of Mexico to the Iroquois of eastern

Indians in Florida transporting crops in a dugout canoe for storage in a large granary. Engraving by Theodor de Bry.

Colonial Williamsburg Foundation

Bartholomew Gosnold in New England. The engraver, Theodor de Bry, suggests a larger fleet than Gosnold's single ship, the *Concord.*

© The Granger Collection, New York

*Martin A. Farata and José B. Fernandez, The Account: Álvar Núñez Cabeza de Vaca's Relación (1993), p. 103.

2

Indigo Culture, from Henry Mouzon's map of Saint Stephen Parish. South Carolina slaves processed blue indigo dye, which required special skills and was dangerous because the offensive odor drew swarms of disease-bearing flies.

North America. Over thousands of years, American civilizations rose and fell, as empires built pyramids and temple mounds, developed cities and cultures, and competed for territory and trade.

In the fifteenth century A.D., Western Europeans came to America to fish, trade, and establish colonies, bringing new technology, lust for wealth, and destructive microbes that spelled death for millions of Native Americans. The Europeans adapted their traditions and goals to exploit the abundant, yet often unfamiliar, resources of the New World. The Spanish struck it rich with the Potosí and Zacatecas silver mines that financed their religious wars in Europe and became the envy of other nations. Privateers from France, England, and the Netherlands attacked the Spanish silver fleets, while their explorers searched unsuccessfully for mines in North America. Instead, they found treasures in furs, sugar, tobacco, and rice.

To reap fortunes from the earth, the colonizers first exploited Native Americans, who died in such numbers from disease and harsh treatment that Europeans turned to another continent, Africa, for laborers. Portugal developed the Atlantic slave trade during the fifteenth century, initially buying slaves to toil on sugar islands near Africa. With the development of sugar, and later tobacco, rice, and indigo in America, the Portuguese and other Europeans purchased millions of people from African merchants for transport across the Atlantic. For more than 350 years, the cultures, sweat, and blood of enslaved Africans enriched the New World societies.

From the sixteenth century on, Europeans battled for North America with Native Americans and among themselves. The French settled Canada and the Mississippi Valley, primarily for furs. Spain held Florida, Texas, and New Mexico as outposts to protect its silver mines and fleets. The English founded colonies in New England, the Chesapeake, and Carolinas for economic opportunity and religious freedom. In 1664, they pushed the Dutch out of New Netherland, thus connecting their chain of colonies along the Atlantic. Throughout America, Europeans hoped for a new chance in the New World.

The thirteen mainland British colonies had various beginnings, charters, provincial governments, economic bases, peoples, and religions. Yet they all had ties with England, in language, imperial government and laws, culture, and commerce. During the eighteenth century, the colonies forged closer bonds with the English—with greater participation in imperial wars, increased trade, and better communication. At the same time, the British provinces also became more distinctly American, as people from Africa, Ireland, and the European continent diversified the population and its culture. With natural population growth and swelling immigration, the British colonies expanded westward.

Native Americans responded to depopulation, defeat, and white expansion by creating new worlds of their own. Despite some military successes, they ultimately reshaped their communities and cultures, as

Tishcohan was one of the Lenape leaders who lost their land in eastern Pennsylvania with the infamous Walking Purchase of 1737. Portrait by Gustavus Hesselius, 1735.

3

disease worked its tragic course and European-American societies grew. The surviving members of Indian nations often merged to forge new ethnic identities, or lived together in multi-ethnic communities, often with whites and escaped slaves. Some retained remnants of their land within white settlements, while the majority moved to the frontier for political autonomy.

Three centuries passed from the time Western European fishermen first camped on North American shores until Great Britain and its colonies expelled France from the continent with the Seven Years' War. By 1763, the land and people of America had permanently changed.

North America and the World: c. 1000–1763

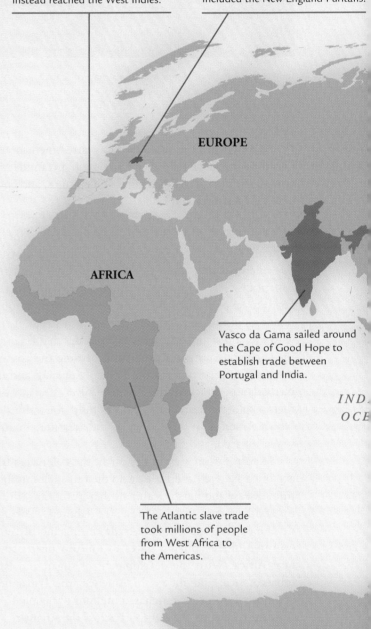

Christopher Columbus sailed west from Spain to locate Asia but instead reached the West Indies.

John Calvin attempted to create a model society in Geneva, Switzerland, and started the Reformed tradition, which included the New England Puritans.

EUROPE

AFRICA

Vasco da Gama sailed around the Cape of Good Hope to establish trade between Portugal and India.

IND.
OCE

The Atlantic slave trade took millions of people from West Africa to the Americas.

Population Growth of the Thirteen British Mainland Colonies, 1630–1760

1630	1640	1650	1660	1670	1680	1690
4,646	26,634	50,368	75,058	111,935	151,507	210,372

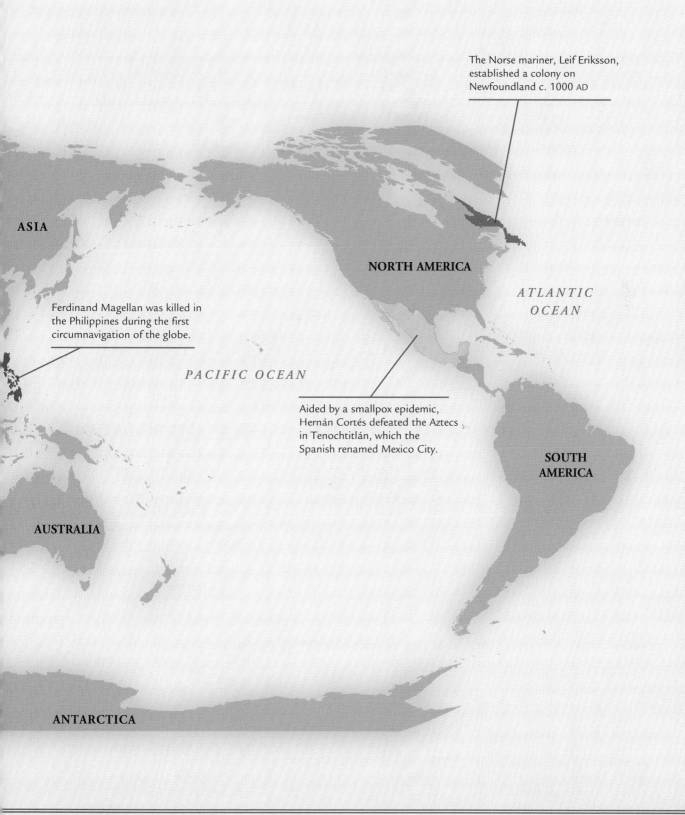

The Norse mariner, Leif Eriksson, established a colony on Newfoundland c. 1000 AD

ASIA

NORTH AMERICA

ATLANTIC OCEAN

Ferdinand Magellan was killed in the Philippines during the first circumnavigation of the globe.

PACIFIC OCEAN

Aided by a smallpox epidemic, Hernán Cortés defeated the Aztecs in Tenochtitlán, which the Spanish renamed Mexico City.

SOUTH AMERICA

AUSTRALIA

ANTARCTICA

1700	1710	1720	1730	1740	1750	1760
250,888	331,711	466,185	629,445	905,563	1,170,760	1,593,625

Chronology

	38,000 B.C.	A.D. 1502	1602
POLITICS & DIPLOMACY	38,000–12,000 B.C.: Ancient hunters migrate to America A.D. 300–1600: Ghana, Mali, and Songhay empires in West Africa A.D. 700–1450: Cahokia and other Mississippian centers in North America A.D. C. 1000: Leif Eriksson's colony on Newfoundland A.D. C. 1300: Aztecs settle in Valley of Mexico 1420: Prince Henry of Portugal begins exploration 1492: Christopher Columbus crosses Atlantic Ocean	1513: Juan Ponce de León explores Florida for Spain 1519: Magellan's expedition to circumnavigate world 1521: Hernán Cortés defeats Aztecs 1528: Cabeza de Vaca to Florida and Texas 1540: Coronado explores American Southwest c. 1550: Iroquois form confederacy 1565: Spanish found St. Augustine, Florida 1585: English colony at Roanoke Island 1599: Spanish destroy Ácoma	1607: English colony at Jamestown 1608: French establish Quebec 1620: Separatists found Plymouth 1630: Puritans establish Massachusetts Bay colony 1634: The *Ark* and the *Dove* arrive in Maryland 1642: English Civil War begins 1643: New England Confederation 1663: Carolina proprietors receive charter 1664: English forces conquer New Netherland
SOCIAL & CULTURAL EVENTS	1324: Gonga-Mussa's pilgrimage to Mecca	1507: Martin Waldseemüller names New World after Amerigo Vespucci 1517: Martin Luther challenges the Church of Rome 1534: English Act of Supremacy 1536: John Calvin's *Institutes of the Christian Religion* 1542: Bartolomé de las Casas's *A Short Account of the Destruction of the Indies* 1585: John White's drawings of Roanoke 1590: Theodor de Bry's *America*	1636: Harvard College established Roger Williams's exile to Rhode Island 1637: Anne Hutchinson tried for heresy 1638: First printing press in the English colonies 1639: French establish first hospital in North America 1647: Massachusetts requires town schools 1649: Maryland's act for religious toleration 1650: Anne Bradstreet's *The Tenth Muse Lately Sprung Up in America* c.1661: Henri Couturier's portrait of Peter Stuyvesant 1662: Halfway Covenant 1663: John Eliot's Bible in Massachusetts Indian language
ECONOMICS & TECHNOLOGY	PRE-2500 B.C.: Corn developed as staple crop in central Mexico C. 1200 B.C.: Corn produced in American Southwest 1440S: Portuguese mariners take Africans as slaves c. 1450: European fishermen at Grand Banks off Newfoundland c. 1452: Portugal begins sugar production on Madeira c. 1460: European improvements in navigation and ships 1478: Abraham Zacuto calculates latitude using sun	1502: Enslaved Africans imported in Spanish America 1503: Spanish Casa de Contratación to supervise trade 1540S: Silver mines at Zacatecas and Potosí 1562: John Hawkins interlopes in slave trade c. 1585: Growth of Amsterdam as mercantile center	1602: Dutch East India Company 1617: Tobacco successful staple crop in Virginia c. 1619: Africans arrive in Virginia 1621: Dutch West India Company 1640S: Sugar production in English West Indies 1642: French found Montreal for fur trade 1651: First English Navigation Act 1672: Royal African Company 1673: Regular postal route between Boston and New York 1670S: Shift to slaves in Chesapeake

1672	1700	1750

1675: King Philip's War; Bacon's Rebellion
1680: Pueblo Revolt
1681: William Penn receives Pennsylvania charter
1688: Glorious Revolution in England
1689: Massachusetts, New York, and Maryland revolutions
1691: Salem witchcraft hysteria
1699: French establish Louisiana

1712: Slave revolt in New York City
1732: Founding of Georgia
1739: Stono Uprising in South Carolina

1754: Albany Congress
1754–1763: Seven Years' War
1763: Pan-Indian War in Ohio Valley and Great Lakes region

c.1674: *Mrs. Freake with Baby Mary* by unknown artist
1682: Publication of *The Narrative of the Captivity and Restoration of Mrs. Mary Rowlandson*
1687: Isaac Newton's *Principia Mathematica*
1688: Germantown, Pennsylvania, Quakers issue antislavery protest
1690: John Locke's *Essay Concerning Human Understanding*
1693: College of William and Mary founded
1695: Jews worship openly in New York

1704: First regular newspaper in Anglo-America, *The Boston News-Letter*
1716: Theater built in Williamsburg, Virginia
1720: Theodore Jacob Frelinghuysen's revivals in New Jersey
1721: Smallpox inoculation in Boston
1731: Benjamin Franklin's circulating library in Philadelphia
1739: George Whitefield tours northern colonies

1751: Benjamin Franklin's reports on electricity
1752: Adoption of Gregorian Calendar in Anglo-America
1761: John Winthrop observes the transit of Venus
1763: Rise of Delaware prophet Neolin

1698: Royal African Company loses slave trade monopoly
1699: Woolen Act

1700s: Adoption of rice in South Carolina
1720s: Expansion of German and Scots-Irish immigration
1732: Hat Act
1733: Molasses Act
1740s: Eliza Pinckney cultivates indigo in South Carolina

1750: Iron Act, Georgia legalizes slavery
1750s: British colonial trade expands with Southern Europe "Consumer revolution" in British colonies
EARLY 1760s: Economic slump in British colonies

1

Contact, Conflict, and Exchange in the Atlantic World to 1590

The Anasazis established agricultural towns in the area extending from the Grand Canyon in what is now Arizona into southern Utah and Colorado. At Mesa Verde, by 1150 A.D., they built large multiroomed houses in caves near the top of canyon walls, probably for protection against enemies.

© Craig Aurness/CORBIS

When the Italian navigator **Christopher Columbus** sighted San Salvador on October 12, 1492, Native Americans lived in cities and towns throughout North and South America. Their numbers had already begun to decline from disease as a result of contact with Europeans who fished off the North American coast in the late fifteenth century. Columbus called the Native Americans *Indios,* or Indians, because he thought he had reached islands in the Far East. Though not the first European to arrive, his landfall initiated the conquest and settlement of two continents, whose vast extent and wealth were previously unknown to Europeans.

For Native Americans, white men and sailing ships spelled demographic catastrophe. Within 150 years, the Indian population was reduced by 90 percent, their cities defeated and destroyed, and, for many, their lands appropriated for farming and grazing livestock. For Europeans, Columbus's unexpected "discovery" represented new challenges and opportunities. For sub-Saharan Africans, European colonization of America would stimulate the slave trade, which over the next four centuries transported at least 10 million Africans across the Atlantic. To exploit the riches of America, Europeans used the labor of both Native Americans and Africans.

Yet contact among Native Americans, Europeans, and Africans involved more than conquest, enslavement, and death. Together the three major cultural groups created new traditions and societies in the New World. Although the Europeans must be declared winners in the contest for power, the American colonies were shaped by exchange of knowledge, culture, and work among all participants. Three major cultural traditions came together in the Western Hemisphere. This chapter explores Native American, European, and African societies at the time of contact; European exploration; and Spanish colonization in Central and South America. The Spanish empire subsequently extended into New Mexico and California, serving as an important model for English settlement in North America.

The First Americans

Estimates of the number of Native Americans in 1492 vary widely, from 8 million to more than 100 million. They possessed widely divergent cultures, ranging from the Inuit who hunted seal and walrus along the shores of the Arctic Ocean, to the **Aztecs** of central Mexico and

Timeline

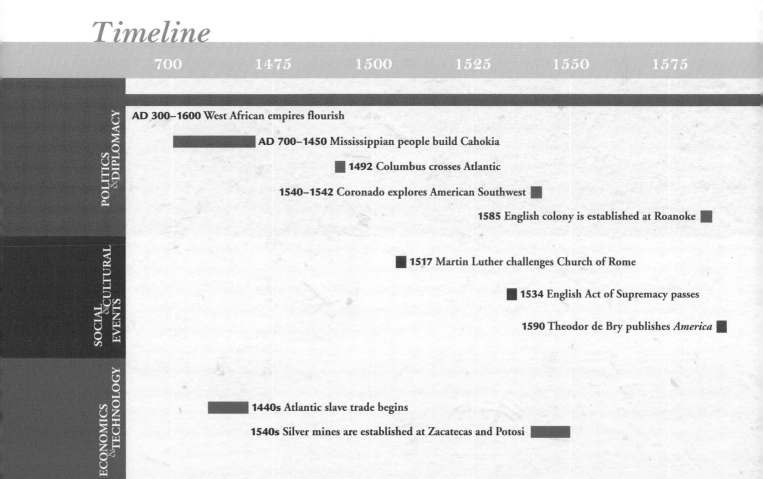

	700	1475	1500	1525	1550	1575

POLITICS & DIPLOMACY

AD 300–1600 West African empires flourish

AD 700–1450 Mississippian people build Cahokia

1492 Columbus crosses Atlantic

1540–1542 Coronado explores American Southwest

1585 English colony is established at Roanoke

SOCIAL & CULTURAL EVENTS

1517 Martin Luther challenges Church of Rome

1534 English Act of Supremacy passes

1590 Theodor de Bry publishes *America*

ECONOMICS & TECHNOLOGY

1440s Atlantic slave trade begins

1540s Silver mines are established at Zacatecas and Potosi

Incas of the Peruvian Andes who lived in state-level agricultural societies. In the geographic area that now encompasses the United States, they included mound-building farmers of the Mississippi valley, the pueblo-dwelling Hopi and Zuñi Indians and nomadic Apaches of the southwest, and the Iroquois and Algonquians of the eastern woodlands.

Native American Societies before Contact

Archeological evidence from various sites in North and South America suggests these diverse peoples were descendants of Asians who migrated by boat along the Pacific coast or who crossed the Bering land bridge from Siberia to Alaska more than 10,000 years ago. As glaciers from the last Ice Age receded, groups migrated throughout the hemisphere. Their cultures and languages diverged as they adapted to their environments. Initially, they hunted game, fished, and collected berries, seeds, and nuts.

When ancient Americans began cultivating crops, they laid the foundation for more densely populated societies. Of greatest importance to Indians of North America was the development of maize, or Indian corn, probably from the grass *teosinte,* which grew in dry areas of Mexico and Guatemala. In addition to maize, early Mexicans domesticated beans, squash, chili peppers, and avocado. Agriculture proved revolutionary for some ancient American societies, as higher yields spurred population growth and a greater division of labor.

Between 1500 B.C. and Columbus's arrival, civilizations rose and declined throughout the Americas. Ancient Americans built empires, much like their counterparts in Egypt, Greece, and Rome, with cities, extensive trade networks, systems of religion and knowledge, art, architecture, and hierarchical social classes. Two of the best-known civilizations of pre-contact America were the Mayan, located on the Yucatán peninsula, and the Mexican. The **Maya,** at their height from 300 to 900 A.D., built cities of stone pyramids, temples, and palaces, with populations ranging to more than 60,000. Mayan kings, considered divine, extended their empire to more than 50 different states and maintained trade with distant peoples. The Maya had a numeral system based on units of 20, hieroglyphics, knowledge of astronomy, and several calendars.

The Mexicans, who lived in the Valley of Mexico, built the city of Teotihuacán east of Lake Texcoco. Its population of about 200,000 depended on intensive farming of nearby irrigated lands. The grid-patterned Teotihuacán held at its core the Pyramid of the Sun and the Pyramid of the Moon. Even after the city's decline, it retained religious significance for later Mexicans.

The Aztecs settled in the Valley of Mexico in the fourteenth century, building their capital, Tenochtitlán, on an island in Lake Texcoco, which they connected to the shore by causeways. They cultivated intensively the marshlands surrounding their island and built a militaristic state. By the time the Spanish *conquistadores* arrived in 1519, the Aztecs controlled territory from the Pacific to the Gulf Coast. The Aztecs required tribute from the people they conquered—gold, feathers, turquoise, food, cotton, and human beings for sacrifice. They believed that every day they had to feed human hearts to the sun god, Huitzilpochtli, to prevent the world from coming to an end.

To the north of the Valley of Mexico, the Hohokam occupied desert lands in Arizona and northern Sonora, where, with irrigation, they cultivated Indian corn, cotton, squash, and beans. Their canals, up to 10 miles long, diverted water from nearby rivers. When Athabaskan raiders from the north attacked Hohokam towns, they tried to protect themselves by building high adobe walls, then after 1400 A.D. simply abandoned many of their villages.

Enemy attacks and crop failures from lack of rain forced other Indians of the southwest to leave their towns. The Anasazi farmers of what is now northern Arizona and New Mexico, Colorado, and Utah relied on rain and floods to water their crops. One of their settlements was Pueblo Bonito in Chaco Canyon, which housed perhaps 1,000 people in 800 rooms surrounded by high walls; another was the complex of rock dwellings built high in the canyon cliffs at Mesa Verde. Descendants of the Anasazi—the Hopi and Zuñi Indians—were called

Hohokam pottery decorated with bird motif, c. 700–900 A.D., found at Snaketown, Arizona.

Great Serpent Mound

This is an aerial photograph of the Great Serpent Mound in southern Ohio, which was probably built by the Adena or Hopewell people sometime between 500 B.C. and 500 A.D. The Hopewell people had trade networks extending to the Gulf Coast, Rocky Mountains, and Lake Superior. Archeologists digging at Hopewell sites have recovered copper, quartz, shark and grizzly bear teeth, and silver from distant areas. Artisans created jewelry, smoking pipes, musical panpipes, and other art from these materials.

The Great Serpent Mound, more that one-quarter mile long from the triangular tip to the tail, demonstrates the knowledge of astronomy of these ancient people. According to anthropologist William F. Romain in *Mysteries of the Hopewell* (2000), the mound is oriented to true astronomical north and its measurements conform to the standard Hopewell 1,053-foot unit of length. The large oval and serpent's head almost perfectly face the setting sun on June 21, the summer solstice; the serpent's body is aligned to the rising and setting moon.

Courtesy, National Museum of the American Indian, Smithsonian Institute #P18523

Pueblo (meaning village or people) Indians by the Spanish for the adobe villages with large apartment dwellings in which they lived.

Farther east, in a large area drained by the Mississippi River, by 1000 B.C. early Americans developed civilizations characterized by large earthen burial mounds, some 60 feet high. These mounds entombed corpses and such grave goods as copper spoons and beads made from seashells. The Adena-Hopewell people, who built the Great Serpent Mound located in southern Ohio, lived in small villages along rivers, hunted game, fished, and raised squash, Indian corn, sunflowers, and gourds. As evidenced by the grave goods, their trading network extended from the Gulf Coast (shells) to Lake Superior (copper). By 800 A.D., people in the Mississippi Valley constructed large towns, including Cahokia, which was located near present-day St. Louis. At the center of these towns stood large rectangular mounds topped by temples and mortuaries in which members of the upper class were buried. By 1450, the region's population declined, perhaps as a result of illness spread by urban crowding.

People of the Eastern Woodlands

Along the Atlantic seaboard extending inland to the Appalachian Mountains lived Native Americans of two major language groups, the Algonquian and the Iroquois. The eastern woodlands incorporated a wide variety of habitats. In most parts, decent soil and moderate rainfall and temperatures supported agriculture and many kinds of game, fish, and wild plants. Algonquian-speaking people dominated the Atlantic coast from Canada to Florida; they included the Pokanokets, Narragansetts, and Pequots in New England; the Lenapes of the middle Atlantic region; and members of the Powhatan confederacy in what

MAP 1.1 America Before Columbus

The first inhabitants of North America probably migrated from Asia by boat and across the Bering land bridge (Beringia), which was created when sea levels dropped during the last Ice Age. Archaeological evidence along the Pacific coast and from sites such as Cahokia and Mesa Verde provide important information about Native American societies before 1492.

became Virginia. Many of the Iroquois lived in the Finger Lakes area of central New York. They belonged to five tribes: the Mohawks, Oneidas, Onondagas, Cayugas, and Senecas, from east to west, who banded together in the Iroquois confederacy.

Although important cultural differences existed between the two language groups and even among bands within each group, Indians of the eastern woodlands had much in common. They held land cooperatively: the tribe as a whole claimed ownership rights, not individual

members or families. Except in far northern New England, Indians had a mixed economy of agriculture, gathering, fishing, and hunting. Women were responsible for raising corn, squash, beans, and (where possible) tobacco. They also gathered nuts and fruit, built houses, made clothing, took care of the children, and prepared meals, while men cleared land, hunted, fished, and protected the village from enemies. The combination of corn, squash, and beans enriched the soil, providing high yields from small plots of land; eaten together these foods

Depiction of Cahokia Mounds—1150 A.D., by William R. Iseminger. Courtesy of Cahokia Mounds Historic Site

Prehistoric Cahokia Mounds, c. 1100–1150 A.D., Drawing by William R. Iseminger based on archeological evidence. Monks Mound dominated the palisaded area, which had at its center a rectangular ball court with two poles.

were high in protein. The Native Americans cleared land by girdling the large trees (removing a strip of bark around the trees about three feet from the ground). When the trees died, the Indians removed them, burned the underbrush, and sowed crops among the stumps. Eastern woodlands people used nets and weirs to catch fish and, to assure good hunting, they periodically burned underbrush from sections of forest. The burning stimulated the growth of lush grass, providing fodder for deer and other game. The fires allowed some sunlight to penetrate the forest, promoting the growth of strawberries, raspberries, and blackberries.

Indian religions, though widely diverse in many ways, incorporated a common worldview. The people of

DOING HISTORY ONLINE

Native American Oral Traditions

Read the documents in this module and consider: What are some of the advantages and disadvantages to relying on written transcriptions of oral traditions?

History ⊗ Now™   Visit HistoryNOW to access primary sources and exercises related to this topic: http://now.ilrn.com/ayers_etal3e

the eastern woodlands believed that the earth and sky formed a spiritual realm of which they were a part, not the masters. Spirits inhabited the earth and could be found in plants, animals, rocks, or clouds. Each spirit, or *manitou,* could become the guardian of a young Indian man (less often a young woman), who, in search of a manitou, went into the woods alone, without eating or sleeping perhaps for days. If the spirit made itself known, it would provide help and counsel to the individual for the rest of his or her life. These Native Americans also believed in a Master Spirit or Creator, who was all-powerful and all-knowing, but whose presence was rarely felt. Religious leaders were *shamans* who performed rituals to influence weather conditions or ward off danger. They were usually men, but in some communities were women. Indians believed that shamans could cure illness, interpret dreams, bring good weather, and predict the future.

The kinship group, or extended family, formed the basis of Native American society. The heads of kinship groups chose the band's chief leaders, called *sachems,* who with advice assigned fields for planting, decided where and when to hunt, managed trade and diplomacy with other Indians and Europeans, and judged whether or not to go to war. Among Algonquian-speaking natives, the heads of extended families were men, as were the sachems they chose. But in Iroquois culture, women served as clan

Secotan Village, 1585, by the Englishman John White, who journeyed to North America with the Roanoke expedition. His watercolor drawings depict Algonquians of the North Carolina coast.

leaders, taking a share of political power. Iroquois society was matrilineal, with family membership passing from mother to children; and matrilocal, as the husband left his family to live with his wife's. Women elders could not speak publicly at tribal councils or serve as sachems, but they chose these political leaders and advised them on such matters as waging war.

Thus, in 1492, highly complex and differentiated societies existed in North and South America. Dense populations inhabited parts of South, Central, and North America. Throughout the hemisphere, Indian people had distinctive cultures tied to the resources of their environment. Despite this wide variety of languages and cultures, most Europeans adopted the single name that Columbus mistakenly employed—Indians. An alternative the colonists used was "savages." The view of many Europeans—that Native Americans had undifferentiated, uncivilized societies—justified conquest and expropriation of their lands.

Picturing the Past · SOCIAL & CULTURAL EVENTS

Woman and Girl of Pomeioc

The Englishman John White painted this watercolor in 1585, during his stay in the Roanoke colony on the coast of what is now North Carolina. It is one of a series of illustrations, also including *Secotan Village* and *Man with Body Paint* (in Chapter 2), that provide some of the best evidence about the Algonquians of eastern North America in the late sixteenth century.

The label at the top states that this is the wife of a chief of Pomeioc and her daughter aged 8 or 10 years. White tried to present the Indians' appearance faithfully, including their hairstyles, jewelry, and clothing. The chief's wife is dressed like other women of the eastern woodlands during the summer and is carrying a container for liquids. The girl has an English doll that Thomas Harriot, another colonist, said Indian children enjoyed. Algonquian women in North Carolina and Virginia cared for children and raised crops including corn and tobacco.

Beginning of European Overseas Expansion

Europeans had more in common with Native Americans than they liked to admit; nevertheless, in important ways, their cultures were distinct. Like the people of America, Europeans spent most of their energy producing or gathering food. They farmed, raised livestock, and gathered nuts and berries. In the south and west of England, for example, farmers engaged in intensive cultivation of wheat, rye, and other crops. In most of England and Wales, however, farmers planted just an acre or two and spent more time gathering. In contrast to Native Americans, Europeans believed that individuals could own land and thus had the right to sell, fence, plant, erect buildings, hunt, cut lumber, and exclude others from use.

The societies from which most colonizers came were patriarchal, meaning that descent followed the father's line and political power was nearly always in the hands of men. Though women occasionally took the throne, for instance, Isabella of Spain and **Elizabeth I** of England, men controlled government, the church, and the military. Married women were considered subordinate to their husbands. Under English common law, a married woman was a *feme covert,* or covered woman, who could not own or manage property, make a contract, write a will, take custody of her children, own a business, or sue in court, without her husband's permission. An unmarried woman or widow, in legal terms a *feme sole,* was not subject to these restrictions.

In the fifteenth century, the pope headed a united Christian church in western and central Europe. At the same time, monarchs consolidated power in Portugal, Spain, France, and England, providing financial support and a greater sense of national identity to fuel European expansion. In turn, wealth from distant empires and trade funded wars among these emerging nations.

Trade with the East

When Columbus sailed out into the Atlantic Ocean in 1492, he expected to establish a new trade route with Asia. In the fifteenth century, eastern trade was a chief source of riches, for affluent Europeans wanted spices that would not grow in Europe such as black pepper, cinnamon, and cloves for preserving and flavoring their food. Merchants commanded high prices for transporting spices, silk, cotton cloth, and jewels from India, the East Indies, and other parts of East Asia.

Before 1500, Arab and Italian merchants dominated the eastern trade. Arabs controlled eastern trading centers and carried goods to the Red Sea and Persian Gulf. From there, caravans took cargoes to Mediterranean ports for purchase by Italian merchants. The Italians then distributed the spices and other goods throughout Europe by way of pack train and coastal shipping. European cities developed to handle the exchange of valued eastern products in return for silver, gold, woolen and linen cloth, furs, and leather. Centers of trade and banking included Paris, Lyons, Amsterdam, London, Hamburg, Danzig, Barcelona, Cadiz, Lisbon, Venice, and Genoa. The rise of great cities accompanied the growth of unified political states. Merchants provided funding for kings to consolidate small feudal states into nations. In Portugal, Spain, France, and England, commercial interests supported unification to obtain social order, monopolistic privileges, and standardized codes of law.

Portugal Explores the West African Coast

Early in the fifteenth century, **Prince Henry of Portugal,** called "the Navigator," decided to challenge the Arab and Italian hold on eastern commerce. Henry brought together men interested in overseas trade and exploration. Beginning in 1420, he sent ships down the western coast of Africa. He had four goals: to increase the power of Portugal by adding territorial possessions; to benefit economically from commerce with the African coast; to reach Asia and take a share of that trade; and to spread Christianity.

Headway down the African coast was slow because European sailors knew nothing of the ocean beyond Cape Bojador in northwest Africa. In 1420, cartographers knew a great deal about the Mediterranean Sea and constructed highly accurate charts, called *portolano,* of its shorelines and harbors. Such maps did not exist for the West African coast, so one task of Prince Henry's explorers was to chart their progress. Seamen had heard that monsters and perhaps even Satan dwelled in the waters beyond Cape Bojador; other stories told that the ocean boiled at the equator. In fact, strong southward ocean currents facilitated outbound progress but made return to the Mediterranean difficult. From ancient mathematicians and geographers, most notably Ptolemy, mapmakers knew that the world was round, but they also adopted Ptolemy's belief that a southern continent joined Africa to China, thus eliminating the possibility of a sea route from the Atlantic to the Indian Ocean. Prince Henry challenged current wisdom by sending ships down Africa's coast to find a route to the east.

New Technology

In the early and mid-fifteenth century, the lack of adequate instruments hampered navigation. Compasses

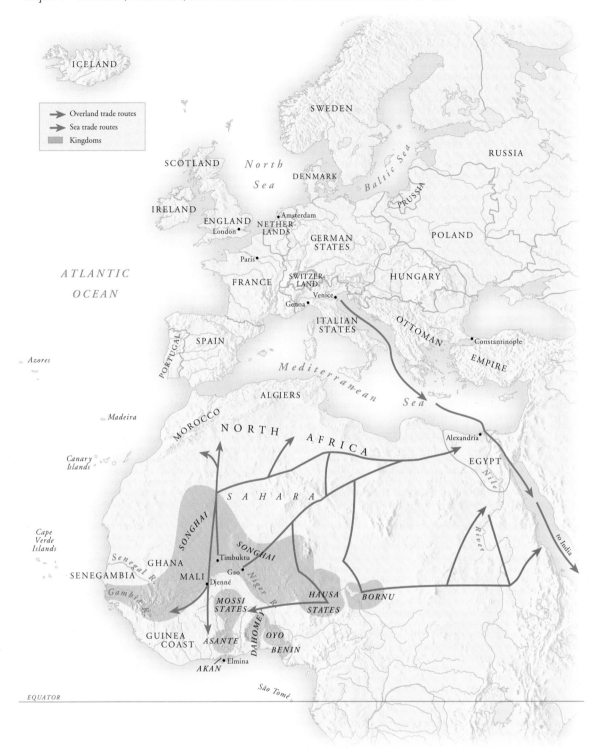

MAP 1.2 **Europe and West Africa in the Fifteenth Century**

Exploration of North and South America was an outgrowth of trade in the Eastern Hemisphere. Europeans delivered cloth and other manufactures to northern Africa; then camels carried the cargoes across the Sahara to cities such as Timbuktu, Gao, and Djenné. There they loaded gold, ivory, and kola nuts for return to the Mediterranean. Africans also traded with Asia to obtain cloth, porcelain, and spices.

had been in use since at least the thirteenth century, but not until about 1460 did Europeans develop the means of determining latitude (distance north or south from the equator). In the Northern Hemisphere, sea captains calculated the height of the Pole Star from the horizon to determine their latitude. The Pole Star cannot be seen south of the equator, however, so navigators there measured the altitude of the sun at midday. In making these calculations, they used the astrolabe or the quadrant to determine the angle of the sun from the horizon, then

Engraving of an early-sixteenth-century cosmographer working in his study with contemporary instruments, including dividers, rule, compass, quadrant, and sand glass.

consulted astronomical tables that Abraham Zacuto, a Jewish astronomer, compiled in 1478. A method for determining longitude remained unknown until the eighteenth century.

Improvements in ships and gunnery during the fifteenth century also aided exploration and conquest. By 1400 it had become clear that Mediterranean galleys, powered by oarsmen, were impractical in the high waves of the Atlantic. The first European oceangoing ships were square-rigged. Their broad sails could power large vessels, but they required a favorable tailwind to proceed from one point to another. To increase maneuverability along jagged coastlines, Portuguese seafarers designed the caravel with lateen (triangular) sails. The most successful Portuguese ship for long voyages was the *caravela redondo,* the square-rigged caravel, developed late in the fifteenth century and adopted by other European nations. This ship combined the speed of square rigging with the agility of lateen sails. For protection from privateers and in time of war, the Portuguese mounted artillery on the caravels and by 1500 introduced the practice of broadside fire. They changed nautical warfare by sinking enemy vessels with gunfire instead of boarding them with foot soldiers.

Despite these improvements in the design of ships, they remained uncomfortable places in which to live on voyages of months and years. Except for senior officers, none of the seamen had regular sleeping quarters—they slept on deck, or below in bad weather. Their shipmates included rats and cockroaches. When it rained, everything got wet, including the cooking fire built in a sandbox on deck. The mariners ate ship's hardtack, beans, salt pork, and beef, and drank mostly wine, since their casked water quickly became foul.

Africa and the Atlantic Slave Trade

Despite their limited technology, the Portuguese explorers ventured farther and farther down the West African coast. In 1434, Gil Eannes sailed past Cape Bojador. Subsequent voyages established a lucrative coastal trade in slaves, gold, and malaguetta pepper in the Senegal region and farther south and east to the Gold Coast and Benin. Merchants now began investing in expeditions. Between the 1440s and 1505, Portuguese traders transported 40,000 Africans to perform domestic labor in

Portugal and Spain and to work on the sugar plantations of the Azores, Madeira, and Canary Islands.

West African Cultures

From before 300 A.D. to 1600, a succession of empires—Ghana, Mali, and Songhay—dominated western Africa. These empires had large armies, collected tribute over vast distances, and traded with Europeans and Arabs. West Africans were predominantly agricultural people. By 1100, Ghana had declined as a result of droughts that dried up several rivers. Mali then took control, as its monarchs regulated the gold trade. The Mali kings were followers of Islam: one of the most famous, Gonga-Mussa, made a pilgrimage to Mecca in 1324 to fulfill his religious duty as a Muslim. His caravan is said to have included 60,000 people and 80 camels carrying more than 24,000 pounds of gold.

Mali provided stable government over a wide area until the fifteenth century, when Songhay successfully challenged its dominance. Songhay was centered at Gao.

An ivory pendant mask worn at the waist representing Idia, the first Iyoba (Queen Mother) of sixteenth-century Benin.

Under Sonni Ali, who ruled from 1468 to 1492, Songhay captured Timbuktu, an important trading and cultural center of Mali. Askia Mohammed, who ruled from 1493 to 1528, expanded the empire even farther. He strengthened ties with other Muslims and reformed government, banking, and education. He adopted Islamic law and encouraged intellectual growth at Timbuktu and Gao. After his reign, Songhay declined; Moroccans conquered Timbuktu in 1593.

Beyond these empires, along the West African coast lay smaller states with highly developed cultures. Although influenced by Islam, they retained much of their traditional religions. Divine kings governed many of the coastal states. Like Native Americans and Europeans, the people of Africa kept religion central to their lives and endowed their leaders with both political and religious authority.

Most important in traditional African religions was a single all-powerful God, the Creator. The Creator provided lesser gods, including gods of rain, thunder, and lightning; of rivers and lakes; of animals, trees, and hills. These gods could be benevolent or harmful, so people had to seek positive relationships through rituals, sacrifice, and prayer. Africans also believed that their ancestors watched over the extended family, with power over fertility, health, and even life. When the eldest father, or patriarch, of a kinship group died, his spirit became a god. Elaborate funeral rites demonstrated the importance of the dead to the living. All family members paid respect to the deceased, whose internment was delayed until distant relatives could arrive. Before his death, the patriarch had been the extended family's priest; he communicated with its ancestors through prayer and the sacrifice of animals such as chickens and sheep. The patriarch also served as political leader. Thus in many African societies, the state, religion, and family united under a single hierarchical structure.

Kinship in West Africa varied from one culture to another; extended families could be either patrilineal or matrilineal. In all cases, however, a child belonged to only one kin group. If the system was patrilineal, then descent flowed from father to child. If it was matrilineal, descent proceeded from mother to child, but the mother's brother, not the mother, assumed responsibility. When a woman married, she usually went to live with her husband's family. The husband compensated her family for the loss of her services with a payment called bridewealth. *Polygyny,* or having more than one wife, was generally reserved to men of high status. When men had more than one wife, each woman lived with her children in a separate house.

The extended family held land in common and assigned plots to individual families. Women and men worked in fields growing crops such as rice, cassava,

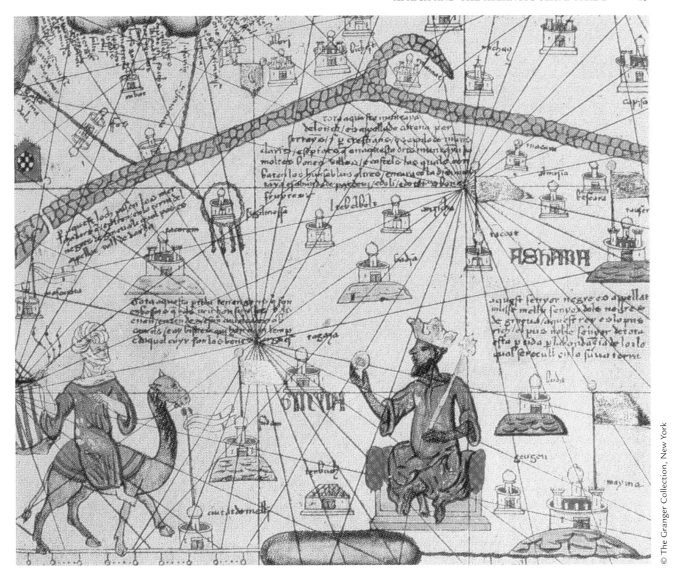

This 1375 European map of northwest Africa shows an Arab trader approaching Mansa Musa of Mali, who is holding a large nugget of gold.

wheat, millet, cotton, fruits, and vegetables. They had livestock, including cattle, sheep, goats, and chickens. Families produced food for their own use and for the market, where women were the primary traders. Artisans were skilled in textile weaving, pottery, basketry, and woodwork. They also made tools and art objects of copper, bronze, iron, silver, and gold. As in the case of Native Americans, West Africans had experienced the rise and fall of empires and possessed diverse, complex cultures at the time Europeans arrived on their shores in the mid-fifteenth century.

The Atlantic Slave Trade Begins

Over the course of four centuries, beginning in the 1440s, Africa lost more than 10 million people to the **Atlantic slave trade.** Slavery had existed in Africa and throughout the Mediterranean for centuries before the Portuguese arrived on the West African coast. African slavery was different, however, from the institution that developed in America. Most African slaves were prisoners of war; others had committed some offense that caused their kinfolk to banish them. All were considered "outsiders." The primary function of slavery in West Africa was social rather than economic—to provide a place in society for people cut off from their families. Before the beginning of the Atlantic slave trade, trans-Saharan traders transported some African slaves for sale to wealthy European households. However, most slaves remained in West Africa, where they achieved status as members of a household, married, and had children. Enslaved Africans could be transferred from one owner to another at will, but their children could not be sold and were frequently emancipated.

Flashpoints   The Atlantic Slave Trade

Each African man, woman, and child who was captured for sale in the Atlantic slave trade—whether as prisoner of war or by kidnapping—suffered a flashpoint. Their lives changed irrevocably as they struggled with captors, marched to the sea in chains, and boarded stinking, crowded ships for America. Olaudah Equiano, a former slave who in 1791 published an autobiography that may have been based partially on the experiences of others, vividly wrote: "One day, when all our people were gone out to their works as usual, and only I and my dear sister were left to mind the house, two men and a woman got over our walls, and in a moment seized us both; and, without giving us time to cry out, or make resistance, they stopped our mouths, tied our hands, and ran off with us into the nearest wood. . . . It was in vain that we besought them not to part us: she was torn from me, and immediately carried away, while I was left in a state of distraction not to be described."*

The Atlantic slave trade developed from earlier Old World systems. Portuguese explorers making their way down the West African coast tapped into the African slave market, which was mostly domestic but also sent enslaved people across the Sahara Desert to Mediterranean ports. The Atlantic slave trade transformed both individual lives and the world. It altered all of the people and nations who participated in it, generating strife and warfare within Africa, a complex of trade networks that crossed continents and oceans, and human suffering that defied description.

Portuguese traders, the first European arrivals on African shores, did not plan to alter drastically the world in which they lived. They simply intended to become rich. They came to the African continent

seeking wealth in the form of gold, ivory, precious stones, and improved trade routes. Their investment in enslaved African people developed over time, as demand for laborers on sugar plantations first expanded on islands off the West African coast, then swelled in the Spanish American colonies and Portuguese Brazil.

Although estimates vary, the Atlantic trade enslaved, uprooted, and transported at least 10 million African

Theodor de Bry's illustration of a Dutch ship trading on the coast of West Africa. The people in the canoe, indicated with "B," represent African merchants who traded human beings to the Europeans for goods such as cloth, rum, and firearms.

© The New York Public Library/Art Resource, NY

people over the course of four centuries. With forcible removal from home and family, the horrors of the middle passage, brutal working conditions, and pervasive sexual abuse of enslaved women, the Atlantic system of slavery formed a violent basis for the international economy and trade.

Despite legal abolition of the Atlantic slave trade by Great Britain and the United States by 1808, slavery continued in the Americas for another 80 years. In 1888, more than 400 years after Portuguese sailors first arrived in West Africa, the enslaved people in the former Portuguese colony of Brazil obtained their freedom. As in the United States and other slaveholding nations, after emancipation Brazilians still grappled with the legacies of colonialism, racism, and oppression

*Vincent Carretta, ed., *The Interesting Narrative and Other Writings* (New York: Penguin Books, 1995), 47–48.

that slavery left behind—and still face these challenges in the early twenty-first century.

Questions for Reflection

1. From Chapter 1, why was Portugal the first European country to engage in transatlantic trade for enslaved African people?

2. Why did Spanish colonizers in the Americas purchase Africans from the Portuguese?

3. What was the impact of enslavement and sale to a Portuguese trader on the life of an African man, woman, or child?

The plantation slave system that became dominant in America began near Africa. Portugal began growing sugar as early as 1452 on the island of Madeira, off West Africa. Sugar cane required large amounts of menial, unpleasant labor in a hot climate. To supply Madeira, Portuguese merchants purchased black slaves from Muslim trans-Saharan traders and from Africans along the coast. When sugar production could expand no further in Madeira, the Portuguese colonized the small islands in the Gulf of Guinea: São Tomé, Príncipe, and Fernando Po. Sugar production was successful, but mortality was high and the demand for laborers great, spurring growth of the slave trade on the Gold Coast. By the end of the fifteenth century, before European settlement in America, Portugal developed both the plantation system and the commercial mechanism for purchasing human beings from African traders. The growth of slavery and the slave trade in America after 1500 represented an expansion of these earlier developments.

Spain and Portugal Divide the Globe

Once Portugal had established trade on the West African coast, Spanish merchants tried to participate. Prince Henry appealed to the pope, who in 1455 gave Portugal sole possession of lands to the south and east toward India. The pope's decision gave Portugal a monopoly on the Atlantic slave trade. Spain and Portugal affirmed the decision with the Treaty of Alcaçovas (1479), in which Spain recognized Portugal's sphere of interest in Africa,

A Fula town in West Africa, drawn by a European. West Africans, like Europeans but not Native Americans, kept domestic livestock. The village raised Indian corn, which had been brought from America.

Library of Congress, Prints and Photographs Division

and Portugal acknowledged Spain's claim to the Canary Islands.

As the Portuguese sailed south, they came to recognize the vastness of the African continent. They made rapid progress only after 1482, when King John II of Portugal stepped up the program of discovery. In 1483, Diogo Cão reached the Congo River and in 1487 Bartholomeu Dias rounded the Cape of Good Hope. The Portuguese now knew that a sea route to India existed.

Columbus Sails West

The Spanish had to find another course if they were going to trade with the Far East. Thus, Isabella funded Christopher Columbus, despite skepticism of his calculation of the distance to Asia. In August 1492, Columbus sailed west from the Canaries, taking advantage of the favorable current and trade winds. The ships reached San Salvador in October, but Columbus thought they had located the East Indies. Hoping to establish trade, Columbus sailed southward to Cuba, then touched Hispaniola, where Native Americans offered gold in return for the trade goods he brought. When the Spanish lost their flagship *Santa Maria* on a coral reef, they built a small fort with its timbers.

Leaving a small contingent of men, Columbus set out for home in January 1493, again found favorable winds,

Columbus's arrival in the West Indies, as imagined by the Flemish engraver Theodor de Bry, who published a series of volumes on "America" in the late sixteenth and early seventeenth centuries.

but encountered a violent storm and sought shelter in Portugal. King John II, whose explorers had not yet reached India by sailing around Africa, refused to believe that Columbus had located Asia. The lands he had found, the king claimed, lay within Portugal's sphere.

Spanish and Portuguese "Spheres"

Isabella and Ferdinand rejected Portugal's argument, petitioning Pope Alexander VI, who was Spanish, to grant them dominion over the newly discovered lands. After negotiations with John II, the pope established a Line of Demarcation, giving all lands "discovered or to be discovered" west of the line to Spain and all lands east of the line to Portugal. The **Treaty of Tordesillas** (1494) located the line 370 leagues (about 1,000 miles) west of the Azores and expanded the principle of "spheres of influence" by which European nations sought to dominate most of the world. Portugal retained its rights to the Atlantic slave trade and the sea route around Africa to India. Spain received permission to explore, conquer, and Christianize all lands and people to the west. The question of where Portuguese and Spanish spheres should be divided in the Far East was left unresolved until 1529, when the Treaty of Saragossa established a line 17 degrees to the east of the Moluccas (Spice Islands), thus placing most of Asia within Portugal's sphere.

Between 1494 and 1529, Portugal and Spain sent out expeditions to explore their spheres. Columbus made three more voyages to the west: in November 1493 he sailed with 17 ships to the Lesser Antilles, Puerto Rico, and Hispaniola. Later he explored the shores of South and Central America. Meanwhile, Columbus's claim that he had found a passage to the East by sailing west prodded the Portuguese to complete their efforts to reach India. In 1497–1498, Vasco da Gama rounded the Cape of Good Hope and sailed across the Indian Ocean, returning to Portugal with a cargo of pepper and cinnamon. The voyage to India was much more difficult than Columbus's Atlantic crossing. During the two-year journey that took at least 300 days at sea, more than one-third of the crew died. In 1500, Portugal instructed Pedro Álvares Cabral to find the Cape of Good Hope by sailing west. Instead, he touched the coast of Brazil, further convincing the Portuguese that this was not Asia. On the basis of Cabral's expedition and because a section of Brazil lay east of the Line of Demarcation, Portugal claimed that part of South America. Amerigo Vespucci made two separate voyages, in 1499 and 1501, for Spain and Portugal respectively. He explored much of the Atlantic coast of South America, demonstrating that it was a huge land mass that had to be circumnavigated to reach Asia. In reward for his insights, many Europeans associated his name—not that of Columbus—with the newly "discovered" continents.

MAP 1.3 European Explorations, 1492–1542

Before 1542, Spain and Portugal dominated European exploration. Generally conforming to the 1494 Line of Demarcation, Portugal's "sphere of influence" included Brazil (in eastern South America), Africa, and South Asia. Spain claimed the rest of South and Central America. France and England sent out explorers but did not establish permanent colonies in North America until the early seventeenth century.

View an animated version of this map or related maps at http://history.wadsworth.com/passages3e.

An Expanding World

Europeans continued to search for a western sea route to Asia. Ferdinand Magellan convinced King Charles I of Spain that he could sail around the cape of South America and claim the Molucca Islands. Magellan was Portuguese, but his own country gave him no support because it already had a profitable sea route to the East. With five ships, in 1519 Magellan set out on an expedition that would take three years. The voyagers faced shipwreck, a harrowing passage through the straits subsequently named for Magellan, and starvation. The Pacific was so much wider than anticipated that the mariners had to eat ship rats and leather. When inhabitants of the Philippines

killed Magellan, Sebastian del Cano took command, returning to Spain with one surviving ship, laden with cloves. Together, Magellan and del Cano commanded the first circumnavigation of the globe. In doing so, however, they demonstrated that the southwest passage through the Straits of Magellan was much more difficult than envisioned.

England and France ignored the pope's division of the world between Spain and Portugal. With their more northerly location and some knowledge of the coast of North America, they sought a northwest passage to the East. During the fifteenth century (before Columbus's landfall), seafarers from England and France had caught fish in the Newfoundland Banks. Some sailors had camped ashore, where they traded with Native Americans. When King Henry VII of England sent John Cabot, an Italian whose name was really Giovanni Caboto, in search of a northwest passage in 1497, the expedition reached Newfoundland. Cabot sailed again the next year, but most of his ships were lost and he died at sea. Although the English were discouraged by Cabot's failure to find a passage, his efforts supported England's later claim to land in North America.

A generation after Cabot, the French entered the search for a route to Asia. In 1524, King Francis I sent another Italian sea captain, Giovanni da Verrazano, to look for the elusive passage. Landing at Cape Fear (now North Carolina), Verrazano sailed north along the Atlantic seaboard to Newfoundland, finding no evidence of a waterway through the continent. In expeditions in 1534 and 1535, Jacques Cartier hoped to find the route by way of the gulf and river of St. Lawrence. Although neither Verrazano nor Cartier found a northwest passage, they supported France's claim to part of the continent.

The Spanish Empire in America

Because England and France showed only occasional interest in America before 1560, and Portugal focused on the eastern trade and Brazil, the Spanish had little interference from other Europeans in exploring and settling the rest of the New World. By 1543, their colonies extended south to Chile and north through Mexico; they had explored from Florida to California in what is now the southern United States. Spanish conquistadores advanced from island to island in the West Indies, then moved through Mexico and Central America. The conquistadores expected to make their fortune in America and retire to Spain. In contrast, the Spanish Crown had a more complicated set of goals in colonizing America: to enhance its power among European nations; to

---

DOING HISTORY ONLINE

Exploration in the New World

What were some of the factors which led to the burst of European voyages of exploration between 1492 and 1542?

History ⧖ Now™   Visit HistoryNOW to access primary sources and exercises related to this topic: http://now.ilrn.com/ayers_etal3e

---

exploit the wealth of the New World; and to convert the Native Americans to Christianity. Although in many ways the goals of the Spanish monarchy and its settlers overlapped, sometimes their interests diverged, especially when it came to the welfare of Native Americans.

Spanish Invasion

When the Spanish found little gold on Hispaniola, they enslaved its inhabitants and expropriated the land. The natives died when forced to work on plantations and tend livestock. European diseases and cruel treatment had taken their toll. As a result, the colonists sent slave-raiding parties to other islands and to the mainland. The conquistadores who explored Cuba and Puerto Rico were seeking slaves and gold. Juan Ponce de León, known for his search in 1513 for the legendary "fountain of youth" in Florida and Yucatan, sought Indian slaves. The same year Vasco Núñez de Balboa led explorers across the Isthmus of Panama; they became the first Europeans to see the Pacific Ocean. Alonso Álvarez de Pineda, in 1519–1520, sailed the coastline of the Gulf of Mexico from Florida to Mexico.

As Spanish explorers became aware of the vastness of the Americas, they organized militarily to subdue the Americans. Despite the small size of their armies, the Spanish prevailed over large empires, aided significantly by diseases such as smallpox. They also made alliances with the enemies of the Indian emperors and took advantage of metal weaponry and horses. The most famous of the conquerors was **Hernán Cortés** who, in 1519, launched an expedition against the Aztecs of Mexico. With an army of only 500 troops, Cortés persuaded the Totonacs of Cempoala, who were dominated by the Aztecs, to join him. Then defeating the Tlaxcalans and gaining their support as well, he marched to Tenochtitlán, the Aztec capital. He entered the city without opposition and seized Moctezuma, the emperor. When Cortés outlawed human sacrifice and made incessant demands for gold, the Aztecs rebelled. In the heat of battle, they killed Moctezuma and forced the Spanish and their allies to retreat, slaying many as they tried to escape across the causeways linking Tenochtitlán with the shore of Lake Texcoco.

Cortés returned in 1521, however, after smallpox ravaged the Aztec capital. With thousands of Indian allies, the Spanish built small ships to cross Lake Texcoco, took control of the causeways, and after a long siege and bitter fighting destroyed Tenochtitlán building by building. They rebuilt the city as Mexico City, the capital of New Spain. Cortés then sent troops to take Guatemala; rival conquistadores seized Honduras. Francisco Pizarro advanced to the south, preceded by smallpox,

Aztecs defending the temple of Tenochtitlán, which was overthrown by the Spanish conquistador Hernán Cortés in 1519–1521. The city's main temple was the site of ritual human sacrifices.

© ARPL/HIP/The Image Works

defeating the Incas of Peru after a difficult struggle. Others expanded into Argentina and Chile.

Exploration of Florida and the American Southwest

In 1528, Pánfilo de Narváez led an expedition to Florida. His venture led to later exploration of territories that became the southern United States. Narváez and his men landed at Tampa Bay where they met Native Americans who warned them to return to the sea. When the Europeans refused, and spoke of their search for silver and gold, the Indians directed them to "Apalachen," near the present site of Tallahassee. The Spanish marched northward through insect- and snake-infested terrain. Soon discouraged, they made the mistake of kidnapping a chief of the Apalachees. The Indians attacked, convincing the Spanish to return to New Spain immediately. The soldiers constructed barges to carry them across the Gulf of Mexico. When storms separated the craft, most of the explorers, including Narváez, were lost at sea.

Two barges crossed the gulf intact, beaching their occupants on the Texas coast. The native Karankawas captured the survivors. After several years, one of the Spaniards, Álvar Núñez Cabeza de Vaca, who had become an Indian priest and healer, escaped with three others, including a slave named Esteban. They hoped to reach New Spain, but lacked maps or instruments to find their way. For several years they sojourned with a series of Native American peoples, learning their languages and customs. The Spanish earned the Indians' friendship and respect with seemingly miraculous cures. When they finally reached Mexico City in 1536, de Vaca told the Spanish viceroy about their journey.

De Vaca's report excited interest in exploring lands north of Mexico. When he refused to head an expedition, the viceroy sent Esteban with a Franciscan missionary, Fray Marcos de Niza, along with several Indians. When Esteban was killed by Zuñis, Fray Marcos returned to Mexico City with extravagant claims that the land flowed with riches.

In 1540, an army of 336 Spanish and about 1,000 Indians marched north under command of Francisco Vásquez de Coronado, with Fray Marcos as their guide. The explorers intended to conquer the cities of gold (the so-called "Seven Cities of Cibola") but were disappointed. The "golden" city that Fray Marcos had spotted was actually a Zuñi Indian pueblo, Hawikúh, made of adobe. The Zuñis unsuccessfully resisted the intruders, then informed the Spanish that the cities of gold lay to the west. Another Indian told stories about great wealth in the country to the east. Over the next year, Coronado's troops explored in both directions. They encountered the Hopi of northeastern Arizona and buffalo-hunting Indians of the Great Plains, saw the Grand Canyon, and traveled as far east as Kansas. They found no gold or silver but left descriptions of a substantial part of what became the American Southwest.

Unknown to Coronado, an expedition led by Hernando de Soto, governor of Cuba, came within a few hundred miles of his own company at about the same time. In 1539, de Soto and about 600 troops landed in Tampa Bay. Over the next three years they trekked through the southeast, exploring lands hitherto unknown to the Spanish. They plundered the towns of the Apalachees and other Florida Indians who were part of the Mississippian cultures, with temple mounds and long-range trading networks. Stealing food, taking Indians as slaves, and killing those who resisted, de Soto's men marched north from the Florida peninsula, through central Georgia to the Carolinas, then west across the Appalachians into the Tennessee River valley. They followed the river south into Alabama, then traveled west toward the Mississippi. Despite heavy losses when Chickasaws burned their camp and supplies, de Soto crossed into Arkansas. After he died of a fever in 1542, the 300 survivors of his expedition safely reached New Spain by boat.

In 1542, the initial period of Spanish expansion came to a close throughout America. Without discovery of precious metals, the Spanish had little immediate reason to push farther into North America. During the half century since Columbus sailed west, contact and exchange among Native Americans, Europeans, and Africans created new social and political systems. Although the Spanish expected to create a society much like the one at home, the results of colonization proved different than planned.

Demographic Catastrophe and Cultural Exchange

Contact among Europeans, Native Americans, and Africans after 1492 changed societies in both hemispheres. This process, called the *Columbian exchange,* included transmission of disease, knowledge about food and technology, and culture.

Disease was the chief ally of the Spanish in their drive through Central and South America. Smallpox was most lethal; other killers included measles, bubonic plague, chicken pox, influenza, whooping cough, and diphtheria. These diseases were particularly deadly because the microbes were new to America, and the Indians lacked any immunity. Populations declined by an estimated 90 percent, as whole tribes were eliminated and others weakened severely. Illness spread from one native population to another, infecting the people of North America even before the English and French established colonies along the Atlantic coast. Some regions of the continent seemed uninhabited to European latecomers because of prior contact with disease.

The Columbian exchange also included livestock and crops that diversified cultures across continents. European settlers imported horses, sheep, cattle, pigs, and chickens for transportation, clothing, and food. Whereas Europeans and Africans raised livestock as part of their agricultural economies, Native Americans depended on hunting and fishing to supplement crops. After European settlement, some Indians adopted horses and became skilled riders; others raised pigs and fowl. Problems resulted, however, because Europeans often allowed their animals to roam. Cattle and pigs trampled native fields, and helped spread disease and the seeds of aggressive European plants that changed the American landscape by forcing out native species.

Indians introduced the Europeans and Africans to crops that soon circled the globe and had a major impact on the growth of world populations: Indian corn (or maize), tomatoes, potatoes, peppers, beans, chocolate, pumpkins, and tobacco. The white potato of South America became a major staple in northern Europe; the sweet potato and Indian corn were important throughout the world. New crops also came to America from Europe and Africa, including cultivated rice, wheat, oats, sugarcane, bananas, onions, peaches, and watermelon. And while Europeans brought firearms and iron tools, Native Americans showed them how to build canoes and catch fish with weirs.

Native Americans generally resisted assimilation to Spanish culture. They retained their languages, clothing, housing, agricultural methods, and, to a considerable extent, religion. The degree to which they blocked acculturation depended largely on class. The Spanish focused much attention on the local Indian leaders (*caciques*) and their sons, with whom they interacted more frequently than with ordinary Indians. Many caciques learned to speak Spanish, converted to Christianity, and adopted Hispanic clothing. Their sons attended schools where they learned Latin and other advanced subjects. The common Indians avoided some Spanish ways of living and accepted others. They raised and ate chickens, but grew wheat primarily to pay as tribute. They abhorred cattle, but groups like the Apaches quickly accepted the horse. Natives favored their digging-sticks over the European plow, which required the use of draft animals and alteration in the assignment of fields.

Religion

The complexity of interaction between the Spanish and Native Americans can be seen most vividly in religion. The Europeans had a mandate from the pope to convert the "pagans" of America to Christianity. The missionaries believed that it was an act of humanity to introduce the Indians to Catholicism. The Spanish eliminated human sacrifice and destroyed temples and relics, but for the most part avoided forced conversion. At first, the missionaries expected most Native Americans to accept Spanish religious practice without change, as many Indians consented to baptism and voluntarily built churches in every town. But most Indians merged the European faith with rituals and beliefs of their traditional religions, resulting in *syncretism,* the blending of two faiths. For example, some natives added the Christian God to

DOING HISTORY

Three Views of European-Native American Encounters

THE FOLLOWING DOCUMENTS include three different views of episodes of contact between Europeans and Native Americans. The first account describes Christopher Columbus's first sighting of land in the Americas, and his meeting with people whom he called Indians because he thought his expedition had reached the East Indies. He sounds hopeful and the people were friendly. The second account is from a later voyage and includes the admonition of a Taino leader, who had clearly experienced both positive and negative aspects of Spanish contact. The third document was recorded much later, a legend passed down by New England people about the response of the god Maushop to English settlement.

Admiral Christopher Columbus's Diary Account of Reaching America, October 12, 1492

"At two hours after midnight the land appeared, from which they were about two leagues distant. They hauled down all the sails . . . passing time until daylight Friday, when they reached an islet of the Lucayas, which was called Guanahani in the language of the Indians. Soon they saw naked people; and the Admiral [Columbus] went ashore in the armed launch. . . . The Admiral brought out the royal banner and the captains' two flags with the green cross. . . . Thus put ashore they saw very green trees and many ponds and fruits of various kinds. The Admiral [announced] . . . in the presence of all, he would take, as in fact he did take, possession of the said island for the king and for the queen his lords. . . .

I, he says, in order that they would be friendly to us—because I recognized that they were people who would be better freed [from error] and converted to our Holy Faith by love than by force—to some of them I gave red caps, and glass beads which they put on their chests, and many other things of small value, in which they took so much pleasure and became so much our friends that it was a marvel. . . .

But it seemed to me that they were a people very poor in everything. All of them go around as naked as their mothers bore them; and the women also, although I did not see more than one quite young girl. And all those that I saw were young people, for none did I see of more than 30 years of age. They are very well formed, with handsome bodies and good faces. . . . They do not carry arms nor are they acquainted with them, because I showed them swords and they took them by the edge and through ignorance cut themselves. They have no iron. Their javelins are shafts without iron and some of them have at the end a fish tooth and others of other things. All of them alike are of good-sized stature and carry themselves well. . . . They should be good and intelligent servants, for I see that they say very quickly everything that is said to them; and I believe that they would become Christians very easily, for it seemed to me that they had no religion."

Source: Oliver Dunn and James E. Kelley, Jr., *The Diario of Christopher Columbus's First Voyage to America 1492–1493* (Norman: University of Oklahoma Press, 1989), 63–69.

A Native Leader's Speech to Columbus

"While the admiral [Columbus] was listening to divine service on the shore, they noticed one of their chief men; he was an octogenarian and an important man, but, for all that naked, with many in attendance on him. He stood by in wonder, his eyes and face intent, while the service was being carried out; then he presented the admiral with the gift of a basket, which he was carrying in his hand, full of his country's fruits, and sitting in the admiral's presence, with Diego Colón as interpreter, who understood their language since they were near his home, the man made the following speech: "News has been brought us that trusting in your powerful hand you have voyaged to these lands until now unknown to you, and have brought no ordinary fear to the people living there. I warn you then to be aware that souls have two paths when they leap forth from the body: one gloomy and hideous, prepared for those who cause trouble and are the enemies of the human race; the other delightful and pleasant, appointed for those who in their lives have loved peace and quiet among nations. If therefore you remember you are mortal and that rewards will be duly assigned to each in accordance with his present actions, you will attack no one."

Source: Geoffrey Eatough, ed. and trans., *Selections from Peter Martyr*, vol. 5 (Turnhout, Belgium: Brepols, 1998), 68.

A New England Legend about the European Arrival

"On the west end of Martha's Vineyard is a hill with a large cavity, which has the appearance of the crater of an extinguished volcano, and there are evident marks of former subterranean fires. The Indians nearby have a tradition that a certain deity resided there before the Europeans came into America, and that his name was Maushop. He used to step out on a ledge of rocks that ran into the sea, and take up a whale, which he broiled on the coals of the volcano, and often invited the Indians to dine with him, or gave them the leftovers of his meal. Once to show their gratitude to Maushop for his great kindness to them, they offered to him all of the tobacco that grew on the island in one season. This was scarcely enough to fill his great pipe, but he received the present very graciously, smoked his pipe, and turned out the ashes of it into the sea, which formed the island of Nantucket. Upon the coming of the Europeans into America, Maushop retired in disgust, and has never since been seen."

Source: Karen Ordahl Kupperman, ed., *Major Problems in American Colonial History: Documents and Essays* (Lexington, MA: Heath, 1993), 12.

Questions for Reflection

These three documents have different origins: the first is from Columbus's diary; the second is a secondhand account recorded by a man, Peter Martyr, who did not personally witness the Indian leader's speech; and the third is a legend handed down over many generations.

1. How did the perspective of the Indians compare with that of Columbus? What accounts for the different responses of the Taino leader and the New England legend?

2. Why is it necessary to use legends and secondhand accounts to gain knowledge about Native American perspectives?

3. What are the possible pitfalls of using each of these sources—Columbus's diary, Martyr's account, and the New England legend?

Explore additional primary sources related to this chapter on the Wadsworth American History Resource Center or HistoryNOW websites:
http://history.wadsworth.com/rc/us
http://now.ilrn.com/ayers_etal3e

---

their polytheistic system; others focused on the saints or the Trinity rather than the supreme God. Indians organized *cofradías,* which were societies to raise money for church functions and festivals. The natives controlled the cofradías and at times asserted independence from the Spanish church authority.

The retention of native beliefs and practices disappointed many Spanish priests, who would accept nothing less than complete submission to their form of Catholicism. Nevertheless, missionaries worked for humane treatment of Indians. Colonists often justified enslaving Indians because they had "inferior" cultures and religion. A number of priests, of whom Bartolomé de las Casas is best known, condemned the cruelty and enslavement. In his *Short Account of the Destruction of the Indies,* written in 1542, las Casas argued for more enlightened policies. Describing atrocities in one colony after another, he informed the king of "the excesses which this New World has witnessed, all of them surpassing anything that men hitherto have imagined even in their wildest dreams."

Spanish Imperial Government

As conquest of the Americas progressed, Spain established a colonial government whose purposes were to convert Native Americans and bring them under control of the Spanish monarchy, and to exploit their labor and the wealth of the New World. The Spanish were only partly successful in imposing their rule over the Indians. The colonial government was most effective in central Mexico and the Andes, where the Europeans substituted their own imperial rule for that of the Aztecs and Incas. Native Americans in northern Mexico, Florida, Arizona, New Mexico, and central Chile, who had never been subject to empires, evaded Spanish rule. Many in the fringe areas, such as the Apaches, avoided Spanish domination altogether because their bands were highly mobile and autonomous.

The Spanish colonial administration was hierarchical and tied closely to Spain. Sovereignty, or supreme political power, rested in the monarch. The Spanish, like other Europeans at the time, believed that God vested such power in the Crown. Neither Spanish colonists nor Indians had much say in making and enforcing laws. The right of subjects to appeal official decisions to the king, however—along with delays caused by distance, corruption, and inefficiency—introduced flexibility into the governmental structure.

Directly below the monarch was the Council of the Indies, located in Spain and composed of men who knew little about the New World. The council regulated trade, appointed officials, made laws, and determined who should be allowed to emigrate. The highest officials residing in America were the **viceroys.** In the sixteenth and seventeenth centuries, the Spanish empire consisted of two viceroyalties: New Spain, with its capital in Mexico City, and Peru, with its capital in Lima. The viceroyalties were divided into provinces, ruled by governors and *audiencias,* which advised the governors and functioned as courts. The audiencias could appeal all decisions to the king, thus limiting the wide powers of the viceroys and governors. In central Mexico and Peru, the Spanish viceroys, governors, and audiencias took the place of the ruling native elite. At the local level, however, native leaders often retained their positions. These caciques headed the Indian towns, collected tribute from households, and recruited forced laborers upon demand of the colonial authorities.

Spanish Mercantilism

The Crown regulated commerce through the *Casa de la Contratación,* a trading house founded in 1503 in Seville. Thus Spain elaborated its economic policy of *mercantilism,* which held that nations had monopolistic rights to trade with their colonies. With tight governmental control, the primary goal of economic activity under mercantilism was to achieve a favorable balance of trade. Colonies were expected to serve as markets for goods from the home country and provide raw materials, gold, and silver to increase its wealth. All merchants desiring to send ships to Spanish America needed permission from the Casa, as did anyone wishing to emigrate. The Casa denied leave to persons of Jewish ancestry, for example, though in fact many found passage to America without official permission. To the monarch, a crucial function of the Casa was registration of precious metals, because the king received one-fifth, called the **"royal fifth,"** of all silver and gold. Colonists had to obtain permission to build plantations and mines. In return they paid taxes to the king and, if they found precious metals, the royal fifth.

When Columbus obtained gold from the inhabitants of Hispaniola, he raised expectations of great wealth. However, the explorers at first met disappointment. Even the Aztecs failed to satisfy the Spanish thirst for gold, so

Melting and casting gold in the Aztec empire from an account of Aztec crafts in central Mexico at the time of the Spanish conquest written and illustrated by Bernardino de Sahagun during the mid-sixteenth century.

most colonists turned to agriculture to make their fortunes. Then, in the 1540s, the Europeans located two immensely rich silver mines, one at Potosí in present-day Bolivia and the other at Zacatecas in Mexico. Between 1500 and 1650 about 181 tons of gold and 16,000 tons of silver officially reached Europe from America. Production of silver expanded greatly in the 1570s with the introduction of mercury to the refining process.

The Spanish organized their silver trade to outwit privateers of other nations, especially France and England. In 1565, the Spanish founded St. Augustine in Florida as a base to fight the buccaneers and reinforce Spain's claim to North America. They devised a convoy system to protect their fleets. Two convoys left Seville each year, carrying goods such as wine, books, oil, grain, clothing, and other luxuries: one left in May headed for Mexico, and the other departed in August for the Isthmus of Panama, from which mules carried the goods to

---

DOING HISTORY ONLINE

Images of the New World

Examine items 1, 5, and 6 in this module. What do these images suggest about European expectations and impression of the New World?

History Now™   Visit HistoryNOW to access primary sources and exercises related to this topic: http://now.ilrn.com/ayers_etal3e

Peru. Both convoys stayed the winter with the intention of meeting in Cuba by early summer so they could return to Spain before the onset of hurricanes. The Panama fleet sometimes ran into trouble when the mule train carrying Potosí silver arrived late.

For the Spanish monarchy, the discovery of rich mines fulfilled its dreams in the New World. The king used the bullion to pay for his European wars. American silver and gold helped to create inflation throughout Europe, as the immense supply depressed their value and the prices of other goods increased. Merchants depended on the bullion to pay for luxuries from the East. Goods worth about one-half the value of the metals were returned to the colonies.

Forced Labor Systems

Because Spanish immigrants were few in number and had no intention of working in the mines or fields, they adopted ways to compel Native Americans to work. In the mid-sixteenth century, the white colonists remained a small percentage of New World inhabitants, with a population of about 100,000 in New Spain compared with an estimated 2.6 million Native Americans in central Mexico. But if some European settlers hoped to have millions of Christianized Indian workers do their bidding, they were disappointed. The catastrophic level of native deaths and resistance of Indians to conversion created New World societies unlike those the Spanish and Native Americans had previously known.

When the first explorers on Hispaniola tried to consign the native Arawaks to slavery, most of the Indians died. In 1500, the Spanish Crown ruled that only Indians captured in a "just war" could be forced into perpetual bondage. This judgment had little impact because conquistadores could define as hostile any natives who resisted capture. In 1513, the government drew up a document called the *Requerimiento* (or Requirement), which explorers read when they entered an Indian town for the first time. The requerimiento informed the natives that they must accept the sovereignty of the Catholic Church and the Spanish monarchy. If they did, they would become Spanish subjects in peace; if they did not, the soldiers would "make war against you . . . take you and your wives and your children and . . . make slaves of them . . . and shall do to you all the harm and damage that we can."

By the time the king outlawed most Native American slavery in 1542, the Arawaks of the West Indies had been destroyed. The Spanish had expropriated their lands for sugar plantations, replacing the Indians with enslaved Africans. On the mainland, the Spanish government established two forms of forced Indian labor. With the *encomienda* system, Indians living on specified lands had to pay tribute to individual colonists and sometimes provide labor for which they received minimal wages. At first, the system included no transfer of land to the colonists, but as the numbers of Native Americans declined and Spanish increased, the colonists took Indian property for farms and ranches. By the seventeenth century, grazing livestock replaced Indian farms on vast stretches of Spanish America.

In 1600, about 1 million Indians survived in central Mexico, a significant decrease from a generation earlier, when the population was 2.6 million. This severe decline caused problems for the Spanish, who depended on the natives for food and labor. Thus, the government devised the *repartimiento* system, under which Indians could be forced to work in mines, agriculture, or public works for several weeks, months, or even a year. For example, natives labored for yearlong stints at the Potosí silver mines in Bolivia. At Potosí, workers assigned as carriers climbed some 600 feet through tunnels about as wide as a man's body with heavy loads of silver ore on their backs. Those who worked in refining were exposed to mercury poisoning because part of the process involved walking with bare legs through the slurry of mercury, water, and ore. As the Indian population declined, the Spanish had difficulty in finding enough workers. When they attempted to increase the length and frequency of work periods, Indians resisted the changes, sometimes successfully.

As early as 1502, on West Indies plantations, the Spanish turned to the people of Africa to meet their insatiable labor demands. They had already purchased Africans from Portuguese traders to work in Spain and on the sugar plantations of the Canary Islands. The government set up a system of licenses, or *asientos,* for merchants to supply certain numbers of slaves. During the sixteenth century, ships transported approximately 75,000 Africans to Spanish America, with perhaps an equal number dying en route, either in Africa or at sea. The Spanish imported Africans to work on sugar plantations in the West Indies and coastal areas of the mainland where most Native Americans had died. Severe work regimes and rampant disease also resulted in high death rates among imported blacks.

Protestant Northern Europeans Challenge Catholic Spain

Until 1560, French and English activity in America remained much more tentative and sporadic than Spain's. Although fishing expeditions regularly visited the North American coast, initiatives for permanent colonies gained little support. But religious and political change in Northern Europe provided the impetus to test Spain's domination of the New World. In the age of Reformation and

An exterior view of Potosí, the Spanish silver mine in what is now Bolivia. The mine yielded immense wealth, but with a dreadful toll as laborers worked in harsh conditions deep underground.

religious wars, America became both a refuge for religious dissidents and a battlefield on which European nations fought for wealth, glory, and national sovereignty.

The Protestant Reformation

When the German priest **Martin Luther** in 1517 issued his 95 theses against the sale of indulgences, the Church of Rome was the sovereign faith of western and central Europe. Luther believed the church was corrupt and saw the sale of indulgences, which were supposed to reduce the amount of time a deceased person spent in purgatory, as an example of its decline. Luther believed that people received salvation as a gift from God in return for faith ("justification by faith") rather than for good works. They could not earn salvation by making pilgrimages, giving money to the church, hearing masses, or going on crusades against the Muslims. Luther also challenged the authority of priests, arguing for a "priesthood of all believers." Christians should seek the word of God in the Bible, which he translated into German to make it more available to laypeople. Luther contended that the Bible recognized only two sacraments, baptism and communion, not the seven authorized by the Catholic Church. He also opposed the requirement of celibacy for priests, marrying Katharina von Bora, a former nun.

Luther's teachings led to many divisions in western Christianity, as common people and princes alike adopted his beliefs. In Germany, which was composed of many individual states, some princes accepted Lutheranism and others remained Catholic, requiring their subjects to follow their example. Lutheranism spread through northern Germany and into Scandinavia. Luther inspired other critics of Catholicism to offer variant Protestant doctrines, including the Mennonites, Hutterites, and Swiss Brethren, all called Anabaptists because they required adult baptism.

The most influential of the systems of belief that Lutheranism spawned was that of **John Calvin,** a native of France, who attempted to create a model society at Geneva, Switzerland. Followers of Calvin established churches in what became known as the Reformed tradition, including the French Huguenots, English Puritans, Scottish Presbyterians, and Dutch and German Reformed. Calvin went further than Luther in arguing that humans could do nothing to save themselves. His concept of **predestination** meant that God alone determined who would be saved (the "elect"). Through communion with God, the elect learned that they were saved; they strove to live blamelessly to reflect their status.

Calvin and his followers convinced the city council and churches of Geneva to adopt many Reformed doctrines, stripping the churches of decoration, images, and colorful rituals. The Bible, as interpreted by Calvin, became the basis for law. The civil government punished moral offenders and nonbelievers identified by the church elders. The Calvinists disciplined individuals for dancing, wearing fancy clothes, and insubordination.

They forced one man to walk through the city wearing only a shirt because he criticized Calvin, and burned another at the stake for heresy. Although Calvin failed to obtain all of his demands from the Geneva council, he came close to establishing a theocracy, in which the church fathers ruled in the name of God.

Protestant ideas spread to France and England quickly. In France, Calvin attracted many adherents, called Huguenots, among the nobles and prosperous commoners. The French monarchy considered Protestants a threat to its monopoly of power. Even after the Edict of Nantes of 1598, which offered freedom of worship, Huguenots faced serious discrimination.

In England, years before Luther, opposition had existed to the Catholic hierarchy, its taxes, monasteries, and the use of images in church. Thus Henry VIII found sympathy for his break with Rome when the pope refused to allow an annulment of his marriage to Catherine of Aragon. Henry wanted to marry Anne Boleyn, who he hoped would provide a male heir. Parliament passed the Act of Supremacy (1534), mandating that the king be "taken, accepted, and reputed the only supreme head on earth of the Church of England." The Crown dissolved the monasteries and confiscated their property. Henry was no Lutheran, however, for the Six Articles (1539) that formed the theological basis of Anglicanism confirmed Catholic beliefs on priestly celibacy, the mass, confession, and sacraments. But because the Six Articles were ambiguous on many points, the Church of England from its inception allowed a fairly wide range of doctrine. In 1552, under Henry's son, Edward VI, the revised Anglican prayer book incorporated many Protestant beliefs. Upon Edward's death in 1553, however, Henry's daughter Mary I attempted to force England back to the Church of Rome. Her persecution of Protestants earned her the name "Bloody Mary"; her marriage to the staunch Catholic Philip II of Spain inspired an English nationalism that fused loyalty to church and state. When Mary died in 1558, her half-sister, Elizabeth I, became queen, ending the immediate threat that England would return to Catholicism. The new English monarch and a large proportion of her subjects identified Spain as a threat to their national church, now Protestant, and their independence as a nation.

Under Elizabeth, the English confronted Spain on a number of fronts, leading to a showdown in 1588. In the religious struggles of the late sixteenth century, England became a dominant Protestant power, supported the Dutch revolt against Philip II, and challenged Spain's monopolistic claims to the New World. Though pragmatic and more interested in power than theology, Elizabeth confirmed England's break with the pope and approved earlier moderate Protestant reforms. The Act of Uniformity (1559) required adherence to the Anglican Book of Prayer. The queen suppressed resistance from both Calvinists, who wanted further reforms, and the supporters of Rome. Some Catholics turned to Elizabeth's cousin, Mary, Queen of Scots, a Roman Catholic and heir to the English throne. In 1587, after several unsuccessful plots on Elizabeth's life, Mary was tried as a conspirator and beheaded.

One of Mary, Queen of Scots's most fervent supporters was Philip II of Spain. Throughout Europe he strove to wipe out the Protestant heresy. He considered Elizabeth a dangerous foe, not least for her support of the revolt in the Netherlands. When many Dutch adopted Calvinism, Philip retaliated with his Inquisition, executing thousands. The Dutch rebelled. In 1581, the northern part of the Netherlands, composed of seven provinces, including Holland, declared its independence as the United Provinces. The southern region, called the Spanish Netherlands (now Belgium), remained under Philip's control. When Elizabeth sent aid to the United Provinces in 1585, she in effect declared war on Spain. The most important battle occurred in 1588, when Philip sent his mighty armada of 130 ships and 30,000 men to invade England. The English defeated the armada, thus preserving their national sovereignty and religion.

French Huguenots and English Sea Dogs

In France, persecution led some Protestant Huguenots to look to America as a refuge. In 1555, a group of wealthy Frenchmen sent Huguenot settlers to Brazil. When disputes occurred among the colonists, some returned to France; the Portuguese, who claimed Brazil, killed or enslaved the majority who remained. In 1562, Huguenots tried again, establishing Charlesfort on the South Carolina coast, in part to attack the Spanish silver fleet as it headed home. When the Spanish moved against the small French colony in 1564, they found it already abandoned. But the Huguenots attempted another settlement that year, this one at Fort Caroline on the St. Johns River in northern Florida. The Spanish quickly destroyed it, murdering most of the settlers.

The English "sea dogs" learned a great deal about the New World from the Huguenots. With Elizabeth I's ascension to the throne in 1558, seafarers and colonizers like John Hawkins, **Francis Drake,** Humphrey Gilbert, and Walter Raleigh gained favor and support. Hawkins visited Fort Caroline in 1565; other Englishmen gained knowledge of the North American coast from the French. The English also acquired a taste for conquest in Ireland, where their brutal subjugation of the native Irish presaged later actions against the Indians.

The English took their time before attempting an American colony. The Spanish remained a serious threat. Thus for two decades, until the 1580s, English adventurers sought wealth by sea. In 1562, John Hawkins took 300 Africans to Hispaniola without a license. The local Spanish officials allowed him to exchange the slaves for sugar and hides because the colony needed labor. Hawkins made a second voyage, earning another handsome profit, this time mostly in silver. When the Spanish authorities protested, Elizabeth forbade further expeditions, but reversed her decision in 1567. On his third voyage,

Picturing the Past | POLITICS & DIPLOMACY

Queen Elizabeth I

The queen sat for this portrait at about the time of the defeat of the Spanish Armada in 1588, as suggested by the naval scene in the upper left. The artist depicted her interest in exploration, particularly in North America, by resting her hand on that part of the globe. Under Elizabeth, sea captains such as John Hawkins and Francis Drake interloped in Spanish trade and attacked Spain's colonies and ships. The Roanoke settlement, established in 1585, was intended to compete with Spain in the New World and to serve as a base to plunder its settlements.

The English monarch is portrayed as a powerful figure in luxurious clothing and jewelry. In 1588, Elizabeth was 55 years old and never married. She had ruled for 30 years, bringing England into the forefront of European nations and reestablishing the Anglican church.

Hawkins was conducting business in the harbor of San Juan de Ulúa, Mexico, when the annual fleet arrived from Spain several weeks early, destroying three of his ships. Hawkins and his cousin Francis Drake escaped with two badly damaged vessels. Their crews nearly starved on the return to England.

Hawkins stopped interloping in Spanish trade, but other English privateers followed. The most famous was Francis Drake, who in 1572 intercepted the mule train carrying Potosí silver across Panama with the help of Native Americans and runaway African slaves. Five years later he set out to circumnavigate the globe. Following Magellan's route through the straits, he attacked Spanish towns along the Pacific coast, explored the North American coast for evidence of a northwest passage, and returned to England in 1580 by way of Asia and the Cape of Good Hope. Six years later, when England and Spain were formally at war, Drake attacked Spanish ports in America, including St. Augustine in Florida, which he looted and burned.

While Drake was making his fortune through piracy, other sea dogs hoped to make their mark by starting colonies. They decided to ignore Spain's claim to North America. On the basis of Cabot's voyage of 1497, Elizabeth granted a charter to Humphrey Gilbert, who sailed to Newfoundland in 1583. He assumed ownership for the English Crown. Nothing came of Gilbert's colony, however, as he was lost at sea on his return to England.

Walter Raleigh then attempted a settlement farther south, in the land named for the "virgin" Queen Elizabeth. In 1585, the first group of settlers arrived at **Roanoke Island,** in what is now North Carolina. After their ships returned home leaving them with short supplies, the colonists tried to force neighboring Indians to provide food. Quickly a pattern of hostility emerged between the English and Native Americans. Francis Drake saved the Roanoke colonists from starvation, carrying them home in 1586. A year later, Raleigh sent out another expedition. This time the war with Spain prevented ships from returning to Roanoke until 1590, when all that was left of the colony was the word "Croatoan" carved on a tree. The colonists may have moved to nearby Croatoan Island, or farther inland to live with Native Americans, but the fate of the "Lost Colony" has never been determined. The English did not colonize successfully in North America until the founding of Jamestown in 1607.

Conclusion

By 1590, the Spanish had created an empire that extended from South America through the West Indies and Mexico. They funded their European wars to extinguish Protestantism with American silver and gold. The Portuguese, united under the Spanish Crown in 1580, had developed the Atlantic slave trading system that sent enslaved Africans to Brazil and New Spain.

The irony of colonization in America was that European nations at war in the Old World emulated one another in the New. The Spanish and Portuguese provided the model for later colonizers in expropriating land and labor from Indians and Africans. Europeans justified their behavior toward the people of America and Africa by emphasizing religious and cultural differences, ignoring much that they had in common. Although European nations organized colonization in various ways, all sought mercantilistic ends.

In the early seventeenth century, when the English, French, and Dutch settled in North America, their goals were very similar to those of Spain. They hoped to locate precious metals, find the elusive northwest passage, exploit Indian labor, extend Christianity to America, and expand the power of the state.

The Chapter in Review

When Europeans made contact with Native American and West African cultures in the fifteenth century, they found many diverse, complex societies with sophisticated political and social systems and extensive trade networks.

- Portuguese traders' arrival in West Africa triggered the development of the Atlantic slave trade, to which Africa would lose more than 10 million people over the course of four centuries.
- Seeking a trade route to Asia, Christopher Columbus landed in the Americas in 1492, opening the New World to European conquest and settlement.

- In the wake of the Spanish conquest of America, approximately 90 percent of the Native American population died as a result of disease, war, and exploitative working conditions.
- In the mid-sixteenth century, Britain, France, and Holland began to challenge Spanish dominance in America. Like Spain, these nations sought to expand their national power, exploit native labor, establish new trade routes, and spread Christianity.

Making Connections Across Chapters

LOOKING BACK

Chapter 1 examines the cultures of the people of North and South America, Africa, and Europe at the time Europeans began exploring and colonizing other parts of the world. The chapter considers the impetus for exploration and its initial consequences.

1. In what ways were the cultures of Native Americans, Africans, and Europeans similar?

2. In what ways were their cultures different?

3. What were the positive and negative results of interactions among these three groups?

4. Why did the Portuguese and Spanish explore the globe? How did their goals change over time?

5. What was the process by which the Spanish took control of Mexico and other parts of Central and South America?

LOOKING AHEAD

Spain's empire in America and Portugal's Atlantic slave trade established models of exploitation for other European nations. In Chapter 2 we will examine how England, France, and the United Provinces (Netherlands) joined the contest for American colonies.

1. What impelled the English, French, and Dutch to become colonizers?

2. What was the significance of England's defeat of the Spanish Armada in 1588?

3. Why do you think the English emulated so much of the Spanish pattern of colonization despite their religious animosity and war?

Recommended Readings

Bethell, Leslie, ed. *Colonial Spanish America* (1987). Essays provide useful syntheses on the development of the Spanish colonies.

Casas, Bartolomé de las. *A Short Account of the Destruction of the Indies.* Ed. and trans., Nigel Griffin (1992). A priest's sharp denunciation of Spanish colonization, written in 1542.

Davidson, Basil. *The Search for Africa: History, Culture, Politics* (1994). A readable history by a veteran historian of the continent.

Dixon, E. James. *Bones, Boats, and Bison: Archeology and the First Colonization of Western North America* (1999). Clear review of archeological evidence of first Americans.

Klein, Herbert S. *The Atlantic Slave Trade* (1999). Surveys the growing literature about the international slave trade.

Kupperman, Karen Ordahl. *Roanoke: The Abandoned Colony* (1984). A lively account of the early English attempt to settle in North America.

Lockhart, James. *The Nahuas After the Conquest: A Social and Cultural History of the Indians of Central Mexico, Sixteenth Through Eighteenth Centuries* (1992). Explores the development of Nahua society and culture, including chapters on households, social structure, land tenure, religion, language, and the arts.

Nash, Gary B. *Red, White, and Black: The Peoples of Early North America,* 4th ed. (2002). An excellent introduction to the meeting of cultures in the New World.

Schwartz, Stuart B. *Victors and Vanquished: Spanish and Nahua Views of the Conquest of Mexico* (2000). A very good collection of documentary sources on Mexican society and the Spanish invasion.

Weber, David J. *The Spanish Frontier in North America* (1992). The best synthesis on Spanish exploration and colonization north of Mexico.

Identifications

Review your understanding of the following key terms, people, events, and dates for this chapter (these terms also appear in the Glossary at the end of the book):

Christopher Columbus
Aztecs
Maya
Elizabeth I
Prince Henry of Portugal
Atlantic slave trade
Treaty of Tordesillas

Hernán Cortés
viceroy
royal fifth
Martin Luther
Protestant Reformation
John Calvin
predestination
Francis Drake
Roanoke Island

Online Sources Guide

Use this listing to find online documents, images, interactive maps, simulations, and other resources related to this chapter.

American History Resource Center

http://history.wadsworth.com/rc/us

Documents

Alvar Núñez Cabeza de Vaca, "Indians of the Rio Grande" (1528–1536)
Columbus's Letter to Gabriel Sanchez (1493)
Henry VII, First Letters Patent Granted to John Cabot and His Sons (1496)
Jacques Cartier, First Contact with the Indians (1534)
Thomas Harriot, "The Algonquian Peoples of the Atlantic Coast" (1588)
Bartolomé de Las Cases, "Of the Island of Hispaniola" (1542)
Jose de Acosta, *A Spanish Priest Speculates on the Origins of the Indians* (1590)

Interactive Maps

Africa and the Mediterranean in the 15th Century

Selected Images

Artist's conception of Christopher Columbus
Wood engraving of Ponce de León
Spanish soldiers committing atrocities in Florida
Timucua people planting crops in 16th century
Timucua granary, 16th century

HistoryNOW

http://now.ilrn.com/ayers_etal3e

Primary Source Exercises

Native American Oral Traditions
Exploration in the New World
Images of the New World
A Spanish Friar Indicts the Conquistadores for the Massacre of Indians, 1542

2 Colonization of North America, 1590–1675

To cure tobacco for sale, workers hung leaves from rafters in a tobacco house until sufficiently dry. The laborers then cut the leaves from the plant stalks, removed the largest fibers from the leaves, and "prized" or packed the leaves into hogsheads.

© Bettmann/CORBIS

In 1590, the only permanent European settlement in what is now the United States was St. Augustine, the struggling Spanish town in Florida that the English privateer Francis Drake had burned 4 years earlier. Spain was much more concerned with its silver mines and West Indies plantations than in colonizing along the Atlantic coast, yet wanted to prevent intrusion by other nations, for good reason. In the late sixteenth century, buccaneers from France and England thought the best way to get rich was by looting the Spanish silver fleet and ports.

Though Spain expanded in Florida and New Mexico in the 1600s, the English defeat of the Spanish Armada and the Dutch surge in overseas trade eroded Spanish control of the New World. France, England, the Netherlands, and Sweden all established colonies in North America by 1638, hoping to duplicate Spain's success. While none found gold or an easy route to Asia—and the Swedes and Dutch soon lost their toeholds in the Delaware and Hudson valleys altogether—Europeans prospered from the West Indies sugar boom, Canadian fur trade, and Chesapeake tobacco. In addition, New England offered a haven for Puritan dissenters.

By 1675, the English held a string of settlements along the Atlantic coast. Unlike the Spanish, England's colonization proceeded with little regulation from the Crown, resulting in a variety of social, economic, and political structures. The English government helped to create the diversity by granting different kinds of charters to individuals and groups.

The expansion of European settlement in North America changed the countryside forever. Cheap, even free, land and developing commerce offered opportunity to men and women of all economic classes who were willing to risk their lives by crossing the Atlantic. Their farms eliminated Indian hunting lands, altering the ecological balance of plants and animals. Though many Native Americans resisted the European invasions, disease seriously undermined their power. The fur trade also changed the cultural values of many Indians, drawing them into Atlantic commerce and tempting them to overhunt. For Native Americans from New Mexico to Canada, European colonization was a disaster.

The Spanish in North America

After Coronado and de Soto failed to locate cities of gold, Spain abandoned further exploration in North America. Then, Francis Drake's voyage along the Pacific coast raised alarms of foreign interest in the region north of Mexico. To

Timeline

	1600	1615	1630	1645	1660	1675

POLITICS & DIPLOMACY

■ **1598** Spanish expedition into New Mexico

■ **1605** French establish Port Royal

■ **1619** Virginia assembly is formed

■ **1637** Pequot War occurs

1660 Charles II of England becomes king ■

SOCIAL & CULTURAL EVENTS

■ **1616–1618** Plague epidemic in New England

■ **1637** Anne Hutchinson is tried for heresy

1649 Maryland's act of toleration passes ■

ECONOMICS & TECHNOLOGY

■ **c. 1619** Africans arrive in Virginia

■ **1621** Dutch West India Company is founded

strengthen Spain's hold on the area, in 1581, the viceroy of New Spain gave Franciscan priests permission to establish missions among the Pueblo Indians of the Rio Grande Valley. The friars named the area San Felipe del Nuevo México. The missionaries described the Pueblos as friendly and numerous: thousands could be converted to Christianity and forced to labor for Hispanic colonists. But by the time a party arrived in 1582 to escort the Franciscans back to Mexico, the missionaries had been killed by the Native Americans.

Settlement of New Mexico

Despite this setback, the Spanish remained interested in the region. Conquistadores needed permission from the Crown to invade new lands, however, for the king had issued Orders for New Discoveries (1573), which more strictly regulated colonization, in part to protect Native Americans from the atrocities Bartolomé de las Casas had described decades before. When one would-be conqueror led an illegal expedition into New Mexico in 1590, he was arrested and returned to Mexico City in chains.

The Spanish government delayed appointing a governor of New Mexico until 1595, when the viceroy authorized **Juan de Oñate** to undertake settlement with his own funds. Oñate, a native of Mexico, inherited great wealth and obtained even more by marrying Isabel Tolosa Cortés Moctezuma, a descendant of both Cortés and the Aztec emperor. The expedition proved expensive as delays increased costs. Finally, in 1598, 129 soldiers, their families, servants, and slaves, and 7,000 livestock headed north. Ten Franciscan missionaries accompanied the colonists. Oñate expected his investment to yield an empire. As he wrote King Philip II, "I shall give your majesty a new world, greater than New Spain." The governor envisioned mines of silver and gold and a water passage through the continent. He believed his province would extend from the Atlantic to the Pacific.

Upon arrival in New Mexico, Oñate declared Spanish sovereignty over Pueblo lands. In a ritual complete with trumpets and High Mass, he promised peace and prosperity to those who cooperated. According to the Spanish, the Pueblos acquiesced "of their own accord." The Franciscans founded missions in the largest pueblos and supervised construction of a church in the Tewa pueblo, Yungé, which the Spanish designated as their capital, San Gabriel.

For some months, the Spanish and the Indians coexisted without serious incident. The colonists moved into the Pueblos' apartments in San Gabriel, forcing the inhabitants to depart. Soon the Indians tired of providing food, which they had intended as gifts but the Spanish considered tribute. The soldiers resorted to murder

and rape to obtain supplies. The crisis came in December 1598, when a Spanish troop demanded provisions from the people of Ácoma, a pueblo high atop a mesa west of the Rio Grande. One of Coronado's party had described Ácoma as "the greatest stronghold ever seen in the world." The Pueblos refused to give flour to the soldiers and killed 11 men when they attempted to take the food by force. Oñate moved swiftly, his small army laying siege to Ácoma with several cannons, as men and women defended the town with arrows and stones. The Spanish killed approximately 500 men and 300 women and children and took the survivors prisoner. The town was leveled. Everyone was sentenced to servitude, and each man over age 25 had one foot cut off. The Ácomas would not rebuild their town until the late 1640s.

With this harsh action, Oñate only temporarily prevented further opposition among the Pueblos, for another town resisted the following year. The colonists also complained of food shortages and the governor's mismanagement; many returned to Mexico. The Franciscans charged that Oñate's cruelty to the Indians made conversion difficult. Oñate was removed as governor, tried, and found guilty of mistreating the Native Americans and some of his settlers. He was banished from New Mexico, but sailed to Spain, where he received a knighthood and position as the Crown's chief inspector of mines.

After Oñate's departure, New Mexico became a royal province. Pedro de Peralta, the next governor, established a new capital at Santa Fe in 1610. As late as 1670 only 2,800 Spanish colonists inhabited the Rio Grande Valley. The Hispanics lived on farms and ranches along the river, exploiting the Pueblos' labor through the *encomienda* system to produce hides, blankets, sheep, wool, and pine nuts for sale in Mexico.

The Pueblo town of Ácoma, located on a mesa in New Mexico, strongly resisted the Spanish in 1598.

Flashpoints | New Mexico

Colonized in 1598 by Spanish soldiers, settlers, and missionaries, plagued by wars, uprisings, and rebellions over the course of its existence, New Mexico began its life as a Spanish settlement not with a battle, but with a Mass. Juan de Oñate choreographed a series of ceremonies with soldiers and friars as they moved from Pueblo town to town along the Rio Grande.

Arriving on April 20, 1598, with the intent to settle permanently, gather wealth for Spain and themselves, and save souls for Christ, the Spanish created political dramas, complete with High Mass, that called to mind Cortés's defeat of the Aztecs in 1521. Because the Pueblos knew of Cortés's takeover, this historical drama was significant. Oñate expected the Pueblos to yield to his expeditionary force and accept the Spanish government as sovereign.

The precise details of Oñate's ceremony changed from one place to another. For example, in Santo Domingo Pueblo (see Map 3.3), in July 1598, Oñate called together Pueblo leaders from 31 towns. Through interpreters he told them that the king of Spain desired "the salvation of their souls." The Pueblos then felt compelled to promise submission to Oñate and the chief Spanish missionary, Fray Alonso Martinez; the Pueblos knelt and kissed their hands. The drama at Santo Domingo concluded with a Mass. At another town, the Pueblo leaders swore obedience after watching a version of the medieval play "The Christians and the Moors," which depicted the Christian reconquest of Spain from the Muslims in 1492. Oñate warned the Pueblos that "if they failed to obey any of the missionaries or caused them the slightest harm, they and their cities and pueblos would be put to the sword and destroyed by fire."

Navajo wall art in the Canyon del Muerto, Arizona, showing the arrival of a Spanish missionary and soldiers in the late sixteenth or early seventeenth century.

© Jerry Jacka

That warning became reality at Ácoma in January 1599, when Spanish soldiers killed, maimed, and enslaved the entire population after they resisted demands for food.

Despite Spanish hopes for an easily conquered territory, great wealth, and conversion of thousands to Christianity, the region that later became the 47th state of the United States retained Indian culture and identity. Ravaged by disease, worn down by military conflicts, and weakened by brutal working conditions, in 1680 the Pueblos staged violent resistance to Spanish rule, winning more than a decade of autonomy. When the Spanish returned they established a less rigorous regime. And despite Spanish hopes of imposing their faith, the Pueblos modified Christianity to suit their own needs and tastes, combining Catholicism with their own religious traditions. The collision of cultures precipitated by Spanish settlement (and introduced with a High Mass) thus led to bloodshed and death, but also created a multicultural society in which both the Spanish and Pueblo cultures were transformed.

Questions for Reflection

1. From Chapters 1 and 2, what were the Spanish goals in colonizing the Americas?

2. How did Spanish settlement in New Mexico compare with Mexico?

3. How did the reaction of the Pueblos to European colonization compare with the actions of Native Americans in Virginia?

Spanish Missions in New Mexico and Florida

The Franciscan missionaries, who assumed a major role in colonizing the Spanish borderlands, were members of the Catholic religious order that Francis Bernardone of Assisi had founded (in Italy) in 1209. The friars vowed not to engage in sexual relations or acquire property, living on the gifts of others. Unlike other religious brotherhoods, which remained in seclusion, the Franciscans operated in the world among ordinary Christians. The Orders for New Discoveries of 1573 gave primary responsibility to the friars for "pacifying" the Indians of New Mexico and Florida.

During the first part of the seventeenth century, many Pueblos seemed to accept the Franciscans' message. The friars initially offered gifts of food, metal tools, beads, and clothing. Placing some confidence in the priests, the natives agreed to build convents and churches. Women built the walls, while men did carpentry. The priests decorated the sanctuaries with paintings, statues, and silver chalices. They created missions by imposing their influence over existing Indian towns, backed by threat of military force. In New Mexico, the Spanish started more than 50 churches by 1629; in Florida, missions extended west from St. Augustine to the Gulf Coast and north into Georgia (or Guale, as the region was called).

The Native Americans who came under Spanish control could, in theory, choose whether or not to accept Christian baptism, but recognized that soldiers supported the priests. The Franciscans expected the natives to learn the catechism and enough of the Castilian (Spanish) language to communicate, and to adopt European dress, food, and farming methods. Many Indians embraced Catholicism, but in doing so, modified the religion. Even in the twentieth century, the Pueblos preserved both native and Catholic religious practices. Christian Indians in Florida continued to play a ball game during the 1600s until the missionaries realized it had religious significance and abolished the game, calling the pole used as a target the "ballpost of the devil."

In merging Indian gods with the Christian Trinity and adding Catholic holidays to native celebrations, Native Americans altered Spanish Catholicism. With the "Lady in Blue," they created a religious tradition that both the Indians and Spanish accepted. In the 1620s, Plains Indians reported that a nun appeared to them, telling them in their language to become Christians. Though the woman remained invisible to the missionaries, they believed the stories. On a trip to Spain, one priest discovered that a Franciscan nun, María de Jesús de Agreda, claimed to have made flights to America with the help of angels. María de Agreda's claims and the Indians' visions together created the resilient legend of the Lady in Blue.

The English Invade Virginia

New Mexico and Florida remained marginal outposts in the Spanish empire. Spanish control was tenuous because their military forces were small and cultural influence weak. After the defeat of the Spanish Armada, Philip II's government could not keep other European nations out of North America. During the first decade of the seventeenth century, the English, French, and Dutch sent expeditions to fish, search for a northern passage to the East, trade for furs, and establish colonies.

English Context of Colonization

Seventeenth-century England was an intensely hierarchical society, in which the king claimed divine right, or God-given authority, and the nobility and gentry dominated Parliament. But it was a society undergoing turmoil and change. Elizabeth I's successor was her cousin, James I, who governed from 1603 until 1625, when he died and his son, Charles I, took the throne. Both James and Charles had strife-torn reigns marked by power struggles with Parliament, culminating in Charles's loss of the English Civil War and his beheading in 1649. Parliament was composed of two houses: the House of Lords, made up of nobles and high church officials; and the House of Commons, which included elected representatives from the counties and boroughs. The Commons normally comprised country gentry, government officials, and lawyers; the electorate included male landowners, an estimated 15 to 30 percent of all Englishmen. By imposing levies without Parliament's consent, James I and Charles I challenged Parliament's prerogative to approve or reject new taxes. For their part, the legislators tried to whittle away at royal powers. The fundamental issue concerning the balance of power between the king and property holders, as represented in Parliament, remained unsettled until the Glorious Revolution of 1688, described in Chapter 3.

Economic developments loosened English society, giving individuals greater opportunity to change from one social class or occupation to another. Many found it necessary to move geographically as the woolen industry expanded, causing landowners to raise more sheep. In what has been called the "enclosure movement," landlords ended leases for tenant farmers living on their lands, confiscating common fields that peasant communities

DOING HISTORY

Reports from Early Virginia

IN 1610, THE VIRGINIA Company published a propaganda tract, written anonymously and entitled A True Declaration of the Estate of the Colonie in Virginia, with a Confutation of Such Scandalous Reports as Have Tended to the Disgrace of So Worthy an Enterprise. *As the title makes clear, the author's purpose was to rebut the accounts of disease, hunger, and death that had reached investors and potential emigrants in England. The first document below quotes from this promotional piece, detailing the economic potential of the colony. Conditions in Virginia remained dreadful for immigrants in the 1620s, however, as Richard Frethorne tells his parents at home in England. A year after the 1622 massacre by the Powhatan confederacy, the Englishman reports ongoing hostilities and the settlers' constant fear of "the Enemy."*

A True Declaration of the Estate of the Colonie in Virginia, 1610

"The Councell of Virginia . . . [received a report] that the country yieldeth abundance of wood, as Oak, Wainscot, Walnut trees, Bay trees, Ash, Sassafras, live Oak, green all the year, Cedar and Fir; which are the materials, of soap ashes, and pot ashes, of oils of walnuts, and bays, of pitch and tar, of Clap boards, Pipe-staves, Masts and excellent boards of forty, fifty and sixty length, and three foot breadth, when one Fir tree is able to make the main Mast of the greatest ship in England. He avouched . . . that there are divers sorts of Minerals, especially of Iron ore, lying upon the ground for ten miles circuit; (of which we have made trial at home, that it maketh as good Iron as any is in Europe:) that a kind of hemp or flax, and silk grass do grow there naturally, which will afford stuff for all manner of excellent Cordage: that the river swarmeth with Sturgeon; the land aboundeth with Vines, the woods do harbor exceeding store of Beavers, Foxes and Squirrels, the waters do nourish a great increase of Otters; all which are covered with precious furs; that there are in present discovered dyes and drugs of sundry qualities; that the Oranges which have been planted did prosper in the winter, which is an infallible

argument, that Lemons, sugar Canes, Almonds, Rice, Aniseed, and all other commodities which we have from [the Mediterranean trade] may be supplied to us in our own country, and by our own industry: that the corn yieldeth a treble increase more than ours; and lastly, that it is one of the goodliest countries under the sun; enterveined with five main Rivers, and promising as rich entries as any Kingdom of the earth, to whom the sun is so nearer a neighbor. . . ."

Source: Peter C. Mancall, ed., *Envisioning America* (Boston: Bedford Books, 1995), 125–126.

Richard Frethorne, a Virginia Servant, Writes Home, 1623

"Loving and kind father and mother, my most humble duty remembered to you, hoping in God of your good health, as I myself am at the making hereof. This is to let you understand that I your Child am in a most heavy Case by reason of the nature of the Country, [which] is such that it causeth much sickness, as the scurvy and the bloody flux and divers other diseases, which maketh the body very poor, and weak. And when we are sick there is nothing to Comfort us; for since I came out of the ship, I never ate anything but peas, and loblollie (that is, water gruel). As for deer or venison I never saw any since I came into this land. There is indeed some fowl, but We are not allowed to go and get it, but must Work hard both early and late for a mess of water gruel and a mouthful of bread, and beef. A mouthful of bread, for a penny loaf must serve for 4 men which is most pitiful. . . .

[P]eople cry out day and night, Oh that they were in England without their limbs and would not care to lose any limb to be in England again, yea though they beg from door to door. For we live in fear of the Enemy every hour, yet we have had a Combat with them on the Sunday before Shrovetide, and we took two alive and make slaves of them. But it was by policy, for we are in great danger, for our Plantation is very weak by reason of the dearth, and sickness, of our company. . . ."

Good Father, do not forget me, but have mercy and pity my miserable case. I know if you did but see me you would weep to see me. . . ."
Richard Frethorne,
Martin's Hundred

Source: Susan M. Kingsbury, ed., *The Records of the Virginia Company of London*, vol. 4 (Washington, DC: GPO, 1935), 58–62.

These two documents provide quite different perspectives on the early colony of Virginia. The promotional tract was advertising, intended to interest wealthy investors and settlers in the colony. Frethorne's letter provides a rare insight into the experiences and perspectives of a servant who expected to improve his chances for success by immigrating to North America.

Questions for Reflection

1. What kinds of economic enterprises did the Virginia Company emphasize in the 1610 tract? Did these prove successful in the colony?

2. What were the main problems that Frethorne describes in his letter?

3. With such different assessments of the situation in Virginia, should we believe one account more than the other? Why?

Explore additional primary sources related to this chapter on the Wadsworth American History Resource Center or HistoryNOW websites:

http://history.wadsworth.com/rc/us
http://now.ilrn.com/ayers_etal3e

Picturing the Past ECONOMICS & TECHNOLOGY

London in 1616

In this painting of London in 1616, London Bridge crosses the Thames River.

On the northern bank (at the top) was the core of the city, which grew impressively during the late sixteenth and seventeenth centuries.

Many of the buildings shown here were destroyed in the great fire of 1666.

On the southern bank is Southwark, the suburb that attracted taverns, cockfights, and theaters—including Shakespeare's Globe Theatre—because it lay outside London's laws.

London became one of the world's largest cities, as its industry and port drew rural English people seeking work. Many impoverished migrants found employment, but others continued to move, signing up for transport as indentured servants to America. Forty percent of English immigrants to North America came from London in the seventeenth century, and an additional 11 percent came from adjacent counties.

© The Granger Collection, New York

Joint-stock companies provided capital for the first permanent English colonies in America. Unlike the Spanish monarchy, the English Crown had little role in funding, or even governing, its first New World settlements. In 1606, James I granted a charter to the **Virginia Company** with rights to settle colonies in North America. The Virginia Company included two groups, one in London and the other in Plymouth, in the west of England. The groups received overlapping claims, with the Plymouth group obtaining lands from what is now Maine to Virginia and the London group receiving Connecticut to the Carolinas. Either could settle in the overlapping area, but initial colonies had to be at least 100 miles apart.

Jamestown

In 1607, the Virginia Company of London funded the first permanent English colony at **Jamestown.** When the first 104 settlers arrived in May 1607, they had endured a long winter crossing. The native inhabitants watched them select a site on the James River, chosen for safety from Spanish attack, but next to malarial swamps. The

English hornbook, seventeenth century, featuring the Christian Lord's Prayer, which students used to learn the alphabet and reading.

had shared for grazing their livestock and raising crops. The landowners enclosed the commons with fences and hedges. In 1500, peasants had farmed 70 percent of arable land in England, but by 1650, they farmed only 50 percent. Thus many tenants were forced from the land. Some went to London, where the population expanded from 55,000 in 1520 to 475,000 in 1670. Others signed up as colonists for America.

A developing economy meant dislocation for poor tenants; it spelled opportunity for merchants. They found it first in the woolen trade with Antwerp, in what is now Belgium. When this trade declined after 1550, they looked for alternative investments, which they found as war with Spain increased the demand for coal, lead, glass, ships, salt, iron, and steel. Investors formed joint-stock companies to explore trade routes and establish new markets. The companies obtained capital by selling stocks. These investments were risky, for shareholders were liable for all company debts. The stocks could also be immensely profitable, as in the case of Francis Drake's circumnavigation of the globe, which brought a 4,600 percent profit.

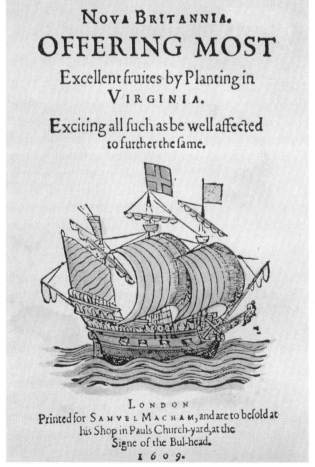

Promotional tract for the English colony in Virginia, 1609.

Colonial Williamsburg Foundation

In this conjectural view of Jamestown, c. 1614, the fortified wall shows concerns for defense against the Spanish and the Powhatan confederacy.

Native Americans called their territory Tsenacommacah, or "densely inhabited land." They were Algonquian-speaking Indians; most belonged to a confederacy that **Powhatan,** head sachem of the Pamunkey tribe, had forged in eastern Virginia. Before the arrival of the English, the chief unifying force among the bands of the Powhatan confederacy was the threat from powerful enemies, the Manahoacs and the Monacans, who controlled lands to the west. The leaders of tribes subject to Powhatan were supposed to pay tribute and provide military assistance, but they sometimes refused.

One of Powhatan's brothers was **Opechancanough,** described as having "large Stature, noble Presence, and extraordinary Parts" and being "perfectly skill'd in the Art of Governing." Historical evidence suggests that he was born around 1544 and, at about age 16, was taken by a Spanish ship to Spain, where he received instruction in the Castilian language and adopted the name Don Luis de Velasco after the viceroy of New Spain. The new Don Luis stayed with the Spanish until 1570, when he accompanied several missionaries to his homeland on Chesapeake Bay. He broke with the priests when they criticized him for taking several wives and murdered the

priests the next year. If Opechancanough and Don Luis were the same man, as seems likely, he was well prepared with knowledge of Europeans when the Jamestown settlers arrived.

The English colony's first decade was a struggle. The company ran Virginia as a business enterprise, keeping control of government, land, and trade. Settlers were company employees, not landholders. To satisfy investors, the company instructed the colonists to search for gold and silver mines, find a passage to Asia, and establish industries and trade that would offer handsome returns. The company had chosen individuals for these purposes, not people who were willing to grow crops. Among the first Jamestown settlers were many gentlemen, who by definition avoided manual labor. They were adventurers who expected to strike it rich and return to England. The others, nearly all men, included the gentlemen's personal servants, a jeweler, goldsmith, perfumer, carpenters, blacksmiths, and some laborers. No one described himself as a farmer.

When the colonists failed to locate mines or a passage to the East, their lives became aimless. Rather than plant crops or even hunt and fish, they expected the company and neighboring Indians to provide food. When sufficient provisions failed to arrive, the settlers starved. One of the leaders, a young officer named **John Smith,** took control in 1608, stabilizing the colony briefly by making everyone work. When criticism of his strict discipline reached company officials the next year, they removed him from command. During the particularly bitter winter of 1609–1610, one man killed his pregnant wife and chopped her up, planning to eat her body. Some of the colonists dug up graves to eat the corpses. By spring 1610, only 60 colonists remained of at least 600 who had come to Jamestown in three years. Though some had returned to England or escaped to live with the Indians, the majority died of starvation and disease.

In 1609, the Virginia Company hoped to salvage its investment by exploiting the land. To recruit farmers, the company offered each emigrant one share of stock and a parcel of land after 7 years of service. The settlers remained employees of the company in the meantime, with assigned tasks and the obligation to buy all supplies and ship all products through the company store.

Still, the Jamestown settlers refused to work. When Sir Thomas Dale arrived as governor in May 1611, he found nothing but a few gardens planted and the inhabitants at "their daily and usual work, bowling in the streets." He established his *Laws Divine, Morall and Martiall,* which were mostly martial. The men received military ranks, were divided into work gangs, and proceeded from home to work—and to church twice daily—at the beat of a drum. Laws prescribed death for a variety of crimes, including rape, adultery, theft, lying, slander against the company, blasphemy, and stealing an ear of corn. For taking two or three pints of oatmeal, one man had a large needle thrust through his tongue, then was chained to a tree until he starved. For the first offense of failing to work regular hours, an idler was tied neck to heels all night. The punishment for a second offense was whipping and for a third offense, death. Though the required hours of work were reasonable—5 to 8 hours per day in the summer and 3 to 6 in the winter—the punishments specified in "Dale's Laws" became a scandal in England, discouraging prospective emigrants. In the words of John Smith, "no man will go from [England] to have less liberty there."

The Struggle for Virginia

The Jamestown adventurers had expected to put the Indians to work in silver mines and fields, as in New Spain, but the inhabitants proved too few in number for an adequate workforce, yet too powerful for the wretched gang of settlers to conquer. During the early years at Jamestown, the English seemed irrational in their dealings with the Native Americans. To many colonists, the natives were barbarians. While some settlers attempted to trade for food, others burned Indian villages and crops.

In 1608–1609, Captain John Smith tried to force the sachems to provide food. The Indians had spared his life several times; nevertheless, he kidnapped two men, obligating Opechancanough to beg for their release. Next, he entered the Pamunkey village with soldiers demanding food, which the Indians refused to give, and again humiliated the tall sachem: in Smith's words, he did "take this murdering Opechancanough . . . by the long lock of his head; and with my pistol at his breast, I led him [out of his house] amongst his greatest forces, and before we parted made him [agree to] fill our bark with twenty tuns of corn." Otherwise, Smith warned, he would load the ship with their "dead carkases." Opechancanough probably never forgot this scene. Between 1609 and 1614, full-scale war existed between the Virginia colonists and the Powhatan confederacy. Eventually the English, with reinforcements from the Virginia Company, defeated Powhatan, taking control of the James River.

In contrast to Spain, the English Crown failed to take responsibility for protecting any rights of Native Americans. When colonists had sufficient power, they enslaved Indians, sending them away from their homelands to prevent escape. The English justified expropriation of native lands with the belief that the king of England, as the Christian monarch, received sovereignty over North America from God. Thus, the Virginia Company obtained rights to land from the Crown, not the Indians. Another basis for taking native territory was the legal concept *vacuum domicilium,* which meant that lands not occupied could be taken. To the English, "occupation" meant improving the land with buildings, fences, and crops; they did not recognize Indian sovereignty over the vast stretches of hunting lands that extended beyond small villages and fields. Even when the English purchased land from the Indians, their contrasting concepts of ownership caused grave misunderstanding. Whereas the colonists believed in private property, the natives thought they were selling the rights to use lands for hunting, fishing, and communal farming. They expected to continue using the territory they had "sold" for these purposes. Conflicts resulted when, for example, a settler's cattle trampled Indian crops, or when a native killed a colonist's cow, mistaking it for a deer.

Tobacco Boom

Demand for land became paramount in Virginia after 1617, when the colonists discovered tobacco as a staple crop. Though James I called smoking "a custom loathsome

Europeans and Native Americans have had extensive contact since Christopher Columbus reached America in 1492. The quality of their interaction has varied considerably from one region of the hemisphere to another and over time. An important question we need to address is why did this variety exist? Was it the result of ethnic differences on the part of the Europeans? For example, the French–Native American relationship in New France (Canada) was less contentious than dealings between the Spanish and Pueblos in New Mexico or the English and Powhatans in Virginia. Or was the variety more the result of ethnic differences among the Native Americans? An

example here is that the Iroquois were early enemies of the French, while Algonquians near Quebec became the colonists' close allies.

While ethnic differences were certainly important, historians have noted certain patterns of cultural exchange that emphasize the importance of demographic, social, and economic factors. James H. Merrell, in his research on the Catawbas and the English settlers in South Carolina, detected three stages of what he called the "Indians' New World": the first stage, when the microscopic organisms of disease struck Native American towns perhaps even before Europeans themselves arrived; the second stage, when traders established networks that depended on mutual exchange; and the third stage, when large numbers of settlers came hungry for land.

The first stage—demographic catastrophe—occurred everywhere in the western hemisphere, but at different points in time. The Indian populations of the West Indies declined precipitously after Spanish arrival; smallpox was to a large extent responsible for Hernán Cortés's defeat of the Aztecs of central Mexico. In North America, in what is now eastern Massachusetts, the Plymouth colonists found a region depopulated by an epidemic brought by earlier English traders. Over time, diseases introduced by Europeans destroyed an estimated 90 percent of the Native American population. The microbes did their deadly work in phases, as white traders and settlers moved throughout the continents over the course of four centuries. The high mortality

Man with Body Paint by John White, 1585. Men were the political leaders, warriors, and hunters in Algonquian society.

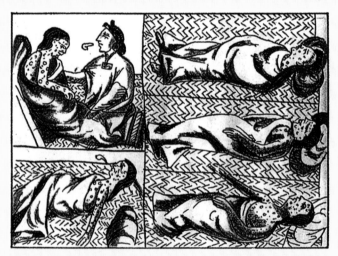

Sixteenth-century drawing of Aztecs suffering from smallpox when the Spanish invaded. An Aztec description stated that "first an epidemic broke out, a sickness of pustules. . . . They spread everywhere, on the face, the head, the chest, etc., [and] brought great desolation" as people could neither "move nor stir" and many died.

rates on contact, and intermarriage and assimilation of many Native American survivors into mainstream communities resulted in the later myth of the "vanishing Indian."

The second stage, when Europeans and Native Americans engaged in trade, was more important in some regions than in others. Economic exchange requires relatively equal measures of power. If one side significantly dominates the other, then the more powerful group can require tribute or forced labor rather than engage in fairly equal exchange. The Spanish—because of high Indian mortality, ability to engage Native military allies, and desire (and ability) to reap wealth through silver and gold—imposed military dominance on many Native populations rather than trade. The French in the Great Lakes region of Canada and the Dutch in the area surrounding what is now Albany, New York, focused to a much greater extent on exchange. These French and Dutch traders saw their way to wealth through furs. While they often clashed with Indians and Europeans who competed with them

North Wind Picture Archives

C.Smith taketh the King of Pamavnkee prifoner. -1608.

John Smith threatening Opechancanough in 1608, with images in the background of skirmishes between colonists and Indians that took place at other times, not on this occasion. From Smith's *Generall Historie of Virginia*.

in the fur trade, they established relationships with Native allies that historian Richard White has called the "middle ground." In trading communities, people of diverse and mixed backgrounds worked for mutual economic benefit, exchanging cultural practices along the way. Exchange societies also existed along the Atlantic coast, for example in the Delaware Valley during the Swedish and Dutch periods of contact, prior to wholesale English settlement.

The period of mutual exchange, where it existed, came to an end with the immigration of large numbers of European settlers. To a certain extent the swing was demographic, as more Indians succumbed to European diseases and the number of settlers grew. In eastern New England, for example, Massachusetts Bay Colony shifted the landscape within a decade as thousands of colonists arrived. English law, social mores, and agricultural practices were significantly different from those of New England Indians, and quickly became dominant as a result of disease and massacre of the Pequots in 1637.

Conflict over land occurred quickly in Virginia, Massachusetts, the region of Dutch New Netherland near Manhattan, and South Carolina. The frequent contests between John Smith and his fellow colonists in Virginia against Opechancanough and his people resulted from both the settlers' combative attitude and the Powhatans' recognition that the English intended to stay. The takeover by settlers took longer in New France, the Delaware Valley, and the Albany region of New Netherland. Along the Delaware, though, the change was obvious as soon as Quakers and other English established settlements in New Jersey and Pennsylvania. In William Penn's colony, despite his purpose to establish peaceful and just relations with the Lenapes, the effect of immigration by thousands of new settlers was to push the Native Americans north and west.

This process of eviction, whether achieved through violence or by sale of land, occurred repeatedly throughout North America during the seventeenth, eighteenth, and nineteenth centuries. In the English colonies, the law of private property eliminated hunting lands of Native Americans, forcing those who remained in the East to live on small reservations or in marginal communities in the barrens of New Jersey and North Carolina. For Indians, alteration of economic ways of life led to social changes as well. One important example was the impact of adopting private ownership of land in some Native communities. Among Eastern Woodlands Indians, the lack of private ownership of land had worked to women's benefit. The group as a whole claimed ownership rights, not individual

(*continued*)

Enduring Issues Native American–European Contact (*continued*)

members or families. Because women were responsible for planting, tending, and harvesting crops, they also held responsibility for agricultural lands and held high status within their society. The efforts by New England Puritans and, later, the U.S. government to restrict Native Americans to reservations focused to a large extent on altering the gender roles of Native Americans, that is, to require men to pursue farming as their primary occupation and women to spin and cook.

Questions for Reflection

1. The three stages of Native American–European contact outlined above do not include missionaries. Based on your reading of Chapters 1 and 2, in which stage would they belong?

2. Do you agree with this analysis that three stages characterized Native American–European contact during the colonial period? Why or why not?

to the eye, hateful to the nose, harmful to the brain, dangerous to the lungs, and in the black stinking fumes thereof, nearest resembling the horrible stygian smoke of the pit that is bottomless," the habit soon consumed England. The mercantilist advantages were clear. With production in Virginia, the English could acquire tobacco from its own colony, rather than pay premium prices to foreign countries, and could generate an industry to process the leaves. For Virginians, the tobacco trade meant capital to purchase clothing and other supplies from home. Tobacco became the first staple crop in England's colonial mercantilist system, followed by sugar, after 1640, in the West Indies.

In 1619, the Virginia Company updated the land policy, granting "headrights" of 100 acres of land to those who came before 1616 and 50 acres to those who came after. Settlers who paid their own way received land immediately; those who immigrated at the company's expense received land after 7 years of service. Virginia settlers thus fell into two categories: freeholders who paid for their own transportation; and servants, whose way the Virginia Company or someone else financed. Recipients of headrights did not pay for the land, but owed quitrents, annual payments to the company, of one shilling per year for each 50 acres. Also in 1619, the Virginia Company relaxed its hold on the government of Virginia by establishing an assembly of elected delegates. The governor, who was appointed by the company, retained the right to veto all laws; the company's General Court in London could also disallow any decision. The Virginia Company also adopted English common law to replace the martial law under which the colony had operated.

While the revised land policy and the assembly gave settlers a greater stake in society, the cultivation of tobacco assured Virginia's ultimate success. During the 1620s, tobacco drew high prices, as much as three shillings per pound. Virginia became the first North American "boom town," as settlers threw all of their energies into growing tobacco. Between 1617 and 1623, approximately 5,000 new immigrants arrived. Because the amount of the crop a planter could grow depended largely on the number of workers, those with capital eagerly paid to transport servants. The Virginia Company imported servants too, but still failed to show a profit, partly because company officials diverted many to their own plantations.

Africans in Early Virginia

English servants provided most of the labor in the colony until late in the seventeenth century. But Virginia planters needed as much labor as they could afford to strike it rich from tobacco, so they also purchased Africans, probably even before 1619 when a Dutch ship brought about 20 blacks. Though some Africans became servants with terms shorter than lifetime bondage, others probably were slaves. Little is known of their status during the early decades. In 1625, Africans numbered 23 of 1,200 Virginia colonists. Fifteen were the property of two men: Abraham Peirsey, the wealthiest man in the colony, and George Yeardley, who had served as governor. In 1660, about 900 blacks and 24,000 Europeans lived in the Chesapeake Bay area.

In contrast, by 1660, Africans outnumbered whites in Barbados, the richest of the English West Indies. Founded in 1627, Barbados quickly turned to sugar production, importing Africans to raise and process the crop. The white islanders created a harsh slave regime to prevent organized rebellion and to force the rapidly growing black population to perform hard, repetitive labor.

Until the 1660s, conditions for Africans remained less rigid in Virginia than in the West Indies. Some Virginia blacks achieved freedom and married, and a few acquired land. For example, by the 1650s, free blacks Anthony and Mary Johnson owned a 250-acre plantation on

Virginia's eastern shore and, like neighboring whites, protected their property by going to court. Even so, most Africans remained in bondage, as Virginians adopted the practice from the Portuguese, Spanish, and Dutch. In purchasing people from slave traders, the white colonists bought into the Atlantic slave system.

Early Virginia documents distinguished consistently between white servants and blacks, always with the suggestion that Africans were subordinate. In a 1627 will, Governor Yeardley bequeathed his "goode debts, chattels, servants, negars, cattle or any other thing" to his heirs. Censuses of the 1620s also point to the lower regard for Africans: English settlers were listed with full names while most Africans were enumerated simply with a first name or designated as "negar" or "Negro." For example, Anthony and Mary Johnson were called "Antonio a Negro" and "Mary a Negro Woman" in early records. The Virginia tax law of 1643 further demonstrated that the colonists viewed Africans as different from themselves. Everyone who worked in the field was to be taxed—all men and black women. White women apparently were not expected to tend tobacco. Virginia also excepted blacks, but not white servants, from the obligation to bear arms.

The Colony Expands

The colonists had found the way to success—by growing tobacco—but Virginia faced difficulty for many years. Because mortality remained high and settlers had few children, the population grew slowly despite immigration that averaged about 1,000 people per year. From 1619 to 1640, the population rose from 700 to about 8,000, though approximately 20,000 English immigrants had arrived during that time. Young men and women who left England to become servants in Virginia gambled with their lives to obtain land, which they could not gain at home. Dysentery, typhoid fever, and malaria took their toll on new settlers who suffered a period of "seasoning" after their arrival in Virginia. Men were much more likely to migrate to the colonies than women. A 1625 census indicated that more than three-quarters of the Virginia colonists were male and less than one-fifth were children. Many people came as servants, which meant that they could not legally marry and have children for years, until their terms expired. The census also provided ample evidence of high rates of mortality and family disruption, as many of the married couples were childless, in part because of high infant and childhood mortality. And with short life expectancy for adults, more than one-half of the colony's children had lost one parent, and one-fifth apparently had no relatives in Virginia at all.

By 1621, Opechancanough and a prophet named Nemattanew, whom the colonists called "Jack of the Feathers" because he wore clothes covered with plumes, recognized the threat of increased immigration. Now that the English had tobacco, they were not going to leave. Nemattanew inspired a nativist religious revival among the Powhatans, rejecting Christianity and European customs. Opechancanough organized a military offensive to push the English back into the sea. At the same time, he used diplomacy to convince the settlers to lower their guard. When several whites killed Nemattanew in 1622, Opechancanough rallied his troops, slaying one-fourth of the settlers before the colony could react. A 10-year war followed, in which each side tried to annihilate the other, but failed, and in 1632 both sides agreed to peace.

Though the bankrupt Virginia Company lost its charter in 1624, immigration to the colony continued. Its economic promise helped convince the English Crown to claim it as a royal colony. Desire for new tobacco lands placed constant pressure on the Powhatans, so in 1644, Opechancanough launched another attack. After 2 years of war, the Powhatans submitted and Opechancanough was captured and murdered by a guard. The 1646 treaty required the Native Americans to live on lands north of the York River and, to symbolize their subordination, pay an annual tribute of 20 beaver skins. Colonists expanded rapidly north and south of the James River and to the eastern shore.

Fishing, Furs, and Settlements in the North

While settlers and Native Americans struggled for Virginia, French, Dutch, and English adventurers explored and colonized the region to the north. French and English sailors had fished the Newfoundland Banks since the fifteenth century. By 1600, groups monopolized specific waters, such as the French who caught walrus in the Gulf of St. Lawrence. The beaver furs that Europeans obtained in petty trade with Native Americans became popular in Europe for making felt hats, exciting merchants in France, the Netherlands, and England to seek more permanent arrangements. All three nations claimed the northern territories as their own, ignoring the prior ownership of the Indians.

New France

In North America, French traders focused on furs. When a French ship sent to North America in 1582 returned with a cargo of furs earning a 1,500 percent profit, merchants enthusiastically organized more voyages. Samuel de Champlain established the first successful French colony in the New World. Working for Pierre du Gua de Monts, who had received a charter from the king of France, in 1605 Champlain planted a temporary base at Port Royal on the Bay of Fundy in Canada. He sailed south to Cape Cod looking for a permanent site, but decided in 1608 to retain Port Royal and establish a main settlement on the St. Lawrence River. The French chose Quebec, which meant "the place where the river narrows" in Algonquian, an ideal location for controlling the Canadian interior.

For two decades, both Port Royal and Quebec remained little more than trading posts. The French had already traded with the Micmacs of the coastal region and Algonquins of the St. Lawrence Valley. Champlain strengthened these ties, and made new alliances with several groups: the Montagnais, who lived in the region north of the St. Lawrence River and like the Algonquins and Micmacs were Algonquian; and the Hurons, who were Iroquoian and lived north of Lake Ontario. Their location enabled the Hurons to link French outposts with the interior, the source of the most valuable furs. In 1609, to demonstrate allegiance to his allies, Champlain helped them fight a group of Iroquois from what is now New York, thus making the Five Nations enemies of New France. He also explored the watershed of the St. Lawrence River and lands as far west as Lake Huron.

In 1627, Quebec was still essentially a trading post with about 100 French inhabitants, including a few women. Cardinal Richelieu, who for all practical purposes ruled France, organized the Company of One Hundred Associates to spur colonization. The company received a charter for territory from the Arctic Circle to Florida and from the Atlantic to the Pacific, with a monopoly on the fur trade. The company also pledged to send missionaries to the Indians and grant them the status of "natural French" when they were baptized. The priests established missions in Indian villages and learned their languages,

MAP 2.1 Eastern North America
By the mid-seventeenth century, northern European nations established colonies along the Atlantic coast from French Quebec and Montreal in the St. Lawrence Valley to the English settlements on Chesapeake Bay. Although at this date all of the colonies were relatively small, New England and the Chesapeake were expanding agricultural societies while the French, Dutch, and Swedes concentrated on trade.

looking for similarities between the two cultures in an effort to make the Indians part of French society.

Because the company focused on the fur trade and considered transporting settlers too expensive, by 1663 just 3,000 French settlers lived in the colony. The Crown revoked the company's charter, making New France a royal province. Nevertheless, population growth remained slow. From the beginning, the government refused to allow Protestants, who were the most likely immigrants, to settle there; it wanted to maintain control of the society through the Catholic Church. Further, New France developed under feudal land tenure, in which wealthy lords received large manors, or *seigniories,* along the St. Lawrence River. Ordinary settlers on these manors became tenants rather than independent farmers. Lacking the opportunity to improve their status in the New World, French peasants were reluctant to make the dangerous transatlantic voyage.

The fur trade and small population made French relations with the Native Americans different from those of New Spain and Virginia where labor demands and white expansion put greater pressure on the Indians. The most efficient way to obtain furs was to offer desirable products from Europe, including textiles, guns, metal tools, pots, and alcohol, not to drive trading partners from the land or to exploit their labor. One French priest reported that, at least for a while, the Montagnais thought they were getting the better deal: "I heard my [Indian] host say one day, jokingly, *Missi picoutau amiscou,* 'The Beaver does everything perfectly well, it makes kettles, hatchets, swords, knives, bread; and in short, it makes everything.' He was making sport of us Europeans . . . [and said], showing me a beautiful knife, 'The English have no sense; they give us twenty knives like this for one Beaver skin.'"

Nevertheless, the French arrival had tragic effects for the Indians of Canada, who succumbed to disease in large numbers. The demand for furs altered cultural attitudes and intensified hostility among Indian nations. In keeping with their religion, Indians had taken only what they needed from nature and little more; they generally used entire animals, the meat as well as the skins. With the fur trade, natives killed animals just for their furs and in numbers far greater than before. As a result, the balance of nature that the Native Americans had maintained was broken. They had to reach farther and farther back into the continent as they exterminated the deer, beaver, and other fur-bearing animals.

New Netherland

In the first decade of the seventeenth century, the Dutch, too, challenged the dominance of Spain in the New World. The seven northern United Provinces had declared independence from Spain in 1581 and remained at war until 1609, when they signed a 12-year truce. With its expiration, the war resumed and continued as part of the

The Seal of the Province of New Netherland, 1623, with an image of a beaver in center, evokes the Dutch focus on trade.

Thirty Years' War, which ended in 1648 with the Treaty of Münster, recognizing Dutch independence.

Despite this ongoing struggle, Dutch commerce flourished. Because land was scarce and high-priced in the Netherlands, and agriculture insufficient, affluent individuals put their capital into trade. In 1602, merchants formed the United East India Company, which 6 years later had 160 ships around the globe. In 1609, the company sent out Henry Hudson, an Englishman, to search for the long-sought northwest passage through North America. He sailed up the river that later bore his name, in what is now New York, trading for furs with the Native Americans. The pelts brought a good return in Holland, so the company dispatched traders who set up a post near the present site of Albany and explored Long Island Sound and the Connecticut River. In 1621, the Dutch government chartered another group, the West India Company, to establish commerce and colonies in America. Like the East India Company, it received broad powers, including the rights to make war and sign treaties. During the seventeenth century, the Dutch muscled their way to control a large part of international commerce, including the Atlantic slave trade and routes to Asia.

To provide a base for trade in the Hudson River region, in 1624 the Dutch West India Company appointed Cornelius Jacobsen May to found New Netherland; the first colonists were mostly Protestant refugees from the Spanish Netherlands. They established their primary settlement, called New Amsterdam, on Manhattan Island, and maintained trading posts at Fort Orange (near what is now Albany) and on the Delaware and Connecticut rivers. As in Jamestown, the first settlers were employees of the company who received no land of their own. The company paid for their transportation, tools, livestock, and two years' worth of supplies, assigning them company land on which to plant. The colonists were expected to trade only with the company. The government consisted of appointed company officers headed by a director-general, or governor, with wide powers. The colonists could not elect an assembly or any of their officials.

With good soil, the lucrative fur trade, and lumbering, the colony prospered economically, though its population grew slowly. Brewing became the second most important industry; in 1638, New Amsterdam residents complained that they were losing sleep from the singing of drunken sailors. People of many nationalities and religions arrived to take advantage of the Dutch policy of religious freedom, but few Dutch could be convinced to emigrate. In 1629, the company attempted to spur population growth by offering huge manors, called patroonships, to any member of the company who transported 50 persons to work his land. On the Hudson River, each patroonship extended for miles along one bank or both banks. Similar to New France, the settlers were tenants of the manor. This arrangement attracted few settlers: in fact it discouraged immigration because the manors tied up large tracts that might otherwise go to small farmers.

At first, New Netherland had good relations with the Indians because the colony grew slowly and depended on the fur trade. In the famous 1626 purchase, Director-general Peter Minuit exchanged goods worth about 60 guilders for Manhattan Island. Upriver, the Dutch bought furs from the Iroquois, the enemies of the Algonquians and Hurons who supplied the French, thus contributing to the devastating warfare among tribes. By the late 1640s, the Iroquois, with help from epidemics, destroyed the Hurons, a nation of about 20,000 people. At the same time, constant warfare and disease seriously debilitated the Iroquois as well.

In the region surrounding New Amsterdam, relations began to deteriorate between the whites and the Indians around 1638. As with the English, the Dutch and natives had different conceptions of land ownership. Although the Indians understood that they had sold rights to share the land and intended to continue using it themselves, the Dutch believed they had bought exclusive rights. Violence erupted as the settlers' cattle destroyed the Indians' corn, and dogs belonging to Native Americans attacked Dutch livestock. Beginning in 1640, the Dutch and Indians of the lower Hudson Valley fought a series of damaging wars that ended only in 1664, when the English took control of New Netherland and made peace with the Native Americans.

New England before the Pilgrims

Along the coast of New England, relations between the Indians and English were rocky from the start. Before the Pilgrims established Plymouth in 1620, a number of expeditions explored the region, traded, and tried to colonize. In 1602, Bartholomew Gosnold and 32 men sailed the *Concord* to Maine and continued south to Martha's Vineyard, where they traded for furs. When they alienated the natives and one of their men was wounded in a fight, Gosnold and his crew returned to England. In 1607, the Plymouth group of the Virginia Company sent an expedition to the Kennebec River in Maine, but the colony lasted only 1 year. The company abandoned efforts to establish a permanent base, instead funding voyages for fish and furs. Like the Dutch and French, the English set up commercial networks with tribes who had contested land and resources before the Europeans arrived, thereby intensifying these rivalries.

Even before the founding of Plymouth in 1620, then, the natives of New England had considerable experience

with the English. This contact had catastrophic effects on the Indian population. A plague brought by Europeans swept eastern New England during 1616–1618, killing thousands. Large areas along the coast were depopulated. The Massachusetts natives were initially friendly and interested in trade, but good relations proved elusive. The English shot some Native Americans and set dogs on others. A few they kidnapped, then expected them to serve as diplomats to their people. The English also made trade agreements, then failed to honor them. By the time the Pilgrims arrived in 1620, the surviving Indians along the coast had been severely weakened by disease and were understandably wary of the newcomers.

Religious Exiles from England

While the colonizers of Virginia, New France, and New Netherland had primarily economic motives, the English founders of Plymouth, Massachusetts Bay, and Maryland sought a place where they could practice their religion free from persecution and at the same time earn a decent living. Seventeenth-century England was rife with religious controversy. The government required attendance at Anglican worship and financial support of ministers. When dissenters refused to obey, holding separate services, they could be imprisoned and fined. Roman Catholics could also be stripped of their property and jailed for life if they refused to take the oath of supremacy to the king, which denied the authority of the pope. The search for freedom of worship became a major impetus for crossing the Atlantic.

English Calvinists

By 1603, when James I took the throne, two strains of English Calvinism, or **Puritanism,** had developed. One group included the Separatists, or Pilgrims, who founded the Plymouth colony in 1620; the others, known as Puritans, established the **Massachusetts Bay colony** 10 years later. Both groups charged that the Anglican Church needed to be "purified" of its rituals, vestments, statues, and bishops. They rejected the church hierarchy, believing each congregation should govern itself. The Separatists started their own congregations, abandoning all hope that the church could be reformed. The Pilgrims' decision to begin a colony in America was the ultimate expression of this separatism. The Puritans, on the other hand, hoped to reform the Church of England from within. Their purpose in founding Massachusetts Bay was to develop a moral government that they hoped the people of England would someday make their own.

The Plymouth Colony

The Pilgrims were a small band who had originated in Scrooby, England, where they established a separate congregation. In 1607, when some were jailed as nonconformists, they decided to leave England for the Netherlands, which offered freedom of worship. The Pilgrims settled in Leyden, but were unhappy there, so they made an agreement with a group of London merchants who obtained a patent for land from the Virginia Company. In exchange for funding to go to America, the Pilgrims promised to send back fish, furs, and lumber for 7 years.

Thirty-five of the Leyden congregation chose to emigrate. Sailing first to England, they joined 67 others, of whom many were not Separatists. In September 1620, the *Mayflower* departed Plymouth, England, crowded with 102 passengers, about 20 crew members, and assorted pigs, chickens, and goats. Headed for Virginia, the ship reached Cape Cod on November 9. In shallow waters, fearing shipwreck, the exhausted travelers built their colony at Plymouth, even though they were outside the jurisdiction of the Virginia Company. They now lacked a legal basis for governing themselves or for claiming land. The first problem was most urgent because some of the colonists questioned the authority of the Pilgrim leaders. The group avoided a revolt by drafting and signing the "**Mayflower Compact**," a social compact by which they agreed to form a government and obey its laws. The London merchants eventually solved the second problem by obtaining title to the land.

Plymouth's first years were difficult, though the settlers found unused supplies of corn left by Indians struck recently by epidemic disease, and chose the site of a deserted Patuxet village with relatively clear fields. Over the first winter they built houses, but one-half of the colonists died of illness and exposure to the cold. In the spring of 1621, they planted corn with the help of **Squanto,** perhaps the lone surviving Patuxet, and other crops. Squanto and neighboring Pokanokets helped the **Plymouth colony** despite earlier problems with Englishmen. In 1614, Squanto and about 20 other Patuxets had been kidnapped by an English sea captain, who intended to sell them as slaves in Spain. Saved from bondage by Spanish priests, Squanto made his way to England, where he learned the language, then to Newfoundland, and finally back to Patuxet in 1619. There he found unburied bodies of many of his people who had perished in the epidemic. One Englishman described the scene: "[T]heir bones and skulls made such a spectacle. . . . it seemed to me a new found Golgotha."

At harvest in 1621, the Indians and colonists celebrated together for 3 days. Soon after their feast, the ship *Fortune* arrived with 35 new settlers, for whom no

Reconstructed village at Plymouth, with fences to protect gardens from roaming livestock.

food was available until the next year's crop. After the colonists filled the *Fortune* with furs and lumber in hopes of starting to repay their debt to the London merchants, the French captured the ship.

By 1623, though, the Plymouth colony was well established and growing, as new immigrants arrived. The community solved the problem of food supply by assigning individual plots to families. Still, the hardworking colonists had trouble fulfilling their bargain with the merchants. During a trading voyage, the crew mutinied. On one fishing trip, the ship sank; when it was raised and sent out again, the Spanish captured it. The London merchants gave up and in 1626 agreed to sell the land to the colonists for a large sum, which they paid by 1645, receiving a patent of ownership. Although Plymouth's economic fortunes improved, the colony remained small and self-consciously separate from the larger group of English dissenters who streamed into New England.

Massachusetts Bay

The Puritan migration to Massachusetts Bay was much larger and more tightly organized than the Plymouth settlement. During 1630, the first year, 700 women, men, and children arrived in 11 ships. Though at least 200 died during the first winter, the colony grew quickly as about 12,000 people went to Massachusetts during the 1630s. From King Charles I, the Massachusetts Bay Company obtained a charter specifying its government and the colony's boundaries. When most of the company officials emigrated, taking the charter with them, they greatly enhanced the colony's independence from the Crown and the Anglican Church.

Thus the Massachusetts Bay colonists did not answer to London merchants who expected handsome profits.

The Puritans themselves financed colonization; they included wealthy investors as well as many middling families who could pay their own way. As a result, the founders devoted much of their energy to creating a model society. In the words of leader John Winthrop, the colony would be "as a City upon a Hill, the Eyes of all people are uppon us; soe that if wee shall deale falsely with our god in this worke wee have undertaken and soe cause him to withdrawe this present help from us, wee shall be made a story and a byword through the world." The Puritans believed that, in addition to their charter from the king, they had a covenant with God that bound them to create a moral community. As Calvinists, they held that individuals were saved from eternal damnation by faith, rather than by good works. Men and women could seek to avoid sin and work hard throughout their lives, but unless they were among God's chosen, or the "elect," they would go to hell. Under the covenant, the elect were responsible for the behavior of unsaved members of their community. The Puritan leaders were responsible to God. They thought that if they maintained a moral society, the Lord would help it prosper.

In Massachusetts, the Puritans restructured the company government to create their version of a godly commonwealth. According to the Massachusetts Bay charter, the company officials included a governor, deputy governor, and executive board of 18 "assistants," to be elected by "freemen" (stockholders) who would meet in a general assembly, called the General Court. These officers could make laws and regulations, appoint lower officials, grant lands, and punish lawbreakers. The colony's leaders changed the rules to allow all male church members (the male elect), not just stockholders

in the company, to become freemen. In theory, every freeman would be a member of the General Court, or colonial legislature. But as the population grew and towns formed quickly, freemen voted in town meetings for representatives to the assembly.

With the governor and assistants, the General Court drew up a law code for the colony, which after several revisions was published as the *Laws and Liberties of Massachusetts* (1648). The code was a combination of biblical law, English common law, and statutes tailored specifically to colonial needs. It protected the liberties of individuals by upholding trial by jury and due process of law, including the rights of the accused to receive a prompt public trial and to call witnesses. It also prohibited feudal tenure of lands and outlawed slavery, "unless it be lawfull captives, taken in just warrs, and such strangers as willingly sell themselves or are solde to us." This provision limited the possibility that whites would be enslaved, but had little effect on black bondage. The *Laws and Liberties* prescribed the death penalty for fewer crimes than in England, but included as capital offenses blasphemy and adultery (in cases where the woman was married), which under the English common law were lesser crimes. Children could be put to death for failing to respect their parents, while fornicators were required to marry and be whipped or fined. The code enabled judges to extend the terms of negligent servants and send back to England any married persons who arrived in Massachusetts without their spouses. Although these terms may seem harsh, the colony did not actually impose the death penalty for blasphemy or abuse of parents by children, and executed only two people for adultery. The magistrates evidently wanted to instill fear in the hearts of potential offenders rather than to exact harsh punishments.

The Puritans attempted to create a **theocracy,** a government operated according to God's will, as determined

Courtesy of the Massachusetts Historical Society

The seal of the Massachusetts Bay Company, 1629, shows an Indian calling to the English, "Come over and help us."

© The Granger Collection, New York

The front and reverse of the Massachusetts pine tree shilling, minted in 1652.

DOING HISTORY ONLINE

Plan for a Massachusetts Town, 1636

According to the document in this module, what issues were the settlers of Springfield most concerned about at the time of its founding? How do these issues compare to the concerns of the early Virginia settlers?

History ⧖ Now™   Visit HistoryNOW to access primary sources and exercises related to this topic: http://now.ilrn.com/ayers_etal3e

by the colony's leaders. The Puritan government was composed of members of the elect; ministers advised the magistrates but could not serve officially. The government required all inhabitants to attend Puritan churches. Persons who disagreed with orthodox doctrines could be expelled, whipped, fined, and even executed. The church was the center of each town, with all property owners paying taxes for its support. Though the Puritans had suffered persecution for their beliefs in England, they refused to allow freedom of worship in Massachusetts. Instead, they replaced one established church with another.

New England Society

Unlike the Jamestown settlers, a large proportion of Puritan immigrants came in families. Many originated from Norfolk, Suffolk, and Essex (together called East Anglia). Located directly across the North Sea from the Netherlands, East Anglia was the center of both the wool trade and Puritanism. By 1630, its residents had kept contact with European Calvinists for almost a century; entire congregations, ostensibly part of the Church of England, adopted Puritan ways. For decades they had worshipped freely, protected by the local Puritan gentry. Then during the 1620s and 1630s, the Puritans faced a series of hardships, including a depressed market for woolen cloth, poor harvests, and bubonic plague. Charles I and the Anglican Church hierarchy, notably Archbishop William Laud, enforced laws against nonconformists, removing Puritan ministers from their pulpits. Many families migrated to Massachusetts, where they could make a new start under a congenial government. Some entire communities accompanied their minister.

In Massachusetts, the migrants created towns that often resembled the ones they had left. When a group arrived, its leaders petitioned the General Court for a place to settle and permission to establish a church and town government. The town meeting elected a board of selectmen who administered town business, including road building, maintenance of schools, and law enforcement. The town meeting also divided the town lands. The amount of land a family received depended on its wealth and social status. Typically, a town followed one of two patterns of land distribution according to the kind of land tenure its founders knew in England. Emigrants from East Anglia generally chose the *closed field* system, in which families received individual farms, with house lot and land for planting, grazing livestock, and cutting lumber. These settlers also created commercial towns. In contrast, emigrants from Yorkshire, in northern England, chose the *open field* system, designating town lands for different purposes—house lots lined up in compact rows, fields, meadows, and wood lots. In Rowley, Massachusetts, for example, families received strips in the fields, where they grew crops in cooperation with their neighbors. Together they made many decisions, including which fields to plant and which to leave fallow. Families also received "stinting rights," or permission to pasture animals on common lands. The number of cattle and sheep a family could pasture depended on the size of its land.

The Puritan notion of an ideal community defined the ways in which the Puritans acted toward one another and toward outsiders. If the model society were to succeed, everyone had to have a place in the family, church, and commonwealth. Like other English, the Puritans kept a hierarchical social order. In the family, the husband was superior to the wife, but together they ruled the children and servants. In the church, the minister and elders dominated the congregation. In the community or commonwealth, the officials led the people. Ideally, this hierarchy required little coercion, when people saw themselves as part of the community and worked for the common good, or "weal" (hence "commonwealth"), rather than for their own benefit. They understood that all humans were equal spiritually but accepted social inequality as the will of God.

Most Puritan women accepted a subordinate place in their society without complaint. They viewed themselves as part of a community and a family, with duties determined by their sex and age, not as individuals with rights equal to those of men. Women raised children; kept the house and garden; preserved fruits and vegetables; made beer, cider, cheese, and butter; tended livestock and poultry; spun and wove cloth; sewed clothing; cared for the sick; and supervised the training of daughters and servants. Women often specialized in certain trades, such as spinning, weaving, poultry raising, or medicine; they conducted trade among themselves, separate from the commercial networks of their husbands. Men had responsibility for raising grain such as wheat,

Mrs. Elizabeth Freake and Baby Mary, painted c. 1674 by an unknown artist, illustrates one of the many roles of seventeenth-century women, that of mother. The wife and child of a successful merchant, their clothing indicates the family's wealth.

Indian corn, and rye; cutting firewood; and maintaining the fences, buildings, and fields. In addition to farming, many followed a trade or profession such as fishing, carpentry, shopkeeping, overseas trade, medicine, or the ministry. Only men could vote in church and town meetings, serve as government officials, or become ministers. Only when a man became incapacitated, or was away from home, was his wife expected to take his place at work or to represent the family in legal matters or disputes. She temporarily assumed the role of "deputy husband," then yielded it when he became well or returned. Puritans recognized women's ability in public matters, but expected them normally to confine themselves to accepted women's tasks.

The role of Puritan women in the church was indicative of their place in society. On the one hand, women were the spiritual equals of men and held responsibility for the religious education of their children. On the other hand, the Puritans emphasized the inheritance of Eve, who they believed led Adam to sin in the Garden of Eden. Women were expected to keep quiet in the church. They could not preach or vote on church business, though they could exert informal influence on their husbands. The Puritans, like other Christians of the time,

embraced Saint Paul's instruction to the Corinthians: "Let your women keep silence in the Churches. . . . And if they will learn anything, let them ask their husbands at home." The Puritans believed that by nature women were morally and intellectually weak. The pain of childbirth was God's punishment of all women for Eve's seduction of Adam. Although a few rebelled against the injunction to keep quiet, most Puritan women and girls accepted their subordination to men. In this patriarchal society, children deferred to their fathers, assuming a subservient role until they were able to establish households of their own. Though some New England colonists held servants and a few owned enslaved Africans, sons and daughters comprised the majority of the workforce. Families on average had five children who reached adulthood. They worked for their parents until marriage—longer in the case of sons who inherited the family farm. Unlike seventeenth-century Virginia, living conditions in Massachusetts promoted patriarchy, for life expectancy was long. Persons who survived childhood diseases often lived past age 60 or even 70. Thus, eldest sons could be middle-aged before their fathers died and willed them control of the family homestead. On the other hand, younger sons who had little hope of receiving the farm often moved away from their parents, settling in the new towns that developed throughout New England. Parents usually attempted to give all of their children a start in life, with a farm, apprenticeship, money, or college tuition to sons, and personal property or cash to daughters.

Connecticut and New Haven

An early destination for people looking for good land was a region south of Massachusetts that came to be called Connecticut. The first Puritans went there to trade with Native Americans, but when news of attractive land in the Connecticut Valley arrived in Massachusetts, many settlers decided to move. The Earl of Warwick owned the rights to the land at the mouth of the Connecticut River, which he ceded to a group of Puritan noblemen. To build a trading post and settlement they sent John Winthrop, Jr., who convinced Thomas Hooker, the minister of Newtown, Massachusetts, to lead some of his congregation there. With another group that left from Dorchester, they founded Connecticut in 1636. Lacking a charter from the king, the founders agreed on the *Fundamental Orders of Connecticut,* which created a General Assembly of representatives from each town. In most respects, the Connecticut government resembled that of Massachusetts, with the exception that freemen, or voters, did not have to be church members. The assembly elected a governor, who could serve only one year at a time, and a group of magistrates who functioned as the upper house

Pequot War Diagram

This engraving of the attack on the Pequots at Mystic River in 1637 by the English and Narragansetts was published in Captain John Underhill's *News from America* (1638).

According to labels on the entrances to the palisade, Underhill's troops entered the Pequot town on one side while Captain John Mason's soldiers entered on the other. The engraver shows English warriors shooting inhabitants, some of them unarmed, between rows of houses. Outside the palisade are rings of soldiers with muskets and Narragansetts with bows and arrows.

The English killed the Pequots and burned the town to the ground. The Narragansetts, who had nearly ended their long-standing conflict with the Pequots before the attack, were shocked by the slaughter. According to Underhill, the Narragansetts were pleased with the conquest but cried "mach it, mach it; that is, it is naught, it is naught, because it is too furious, and slaies too many men."

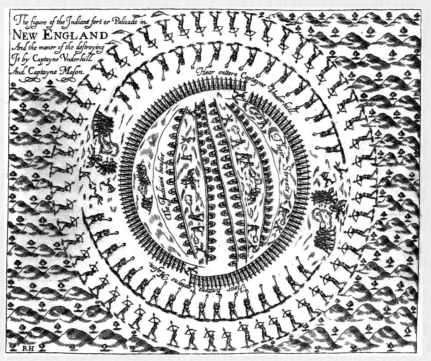

© The Granger Collection, New York

of the assembly. As in Massachusetts, Puritanism was the only recognized religion and received tax support.

As white settlement expanded, relations between the Puritans and Native Americans deteriorated. Like other English, the Puritans believed that the Indians worshipped the devil and had barbarous customs. The settlers justified expropriation of native lands on the basis of *vacuum domicilium*. Even more, the Puritans considered the Indians "strangers," who could have no role in building the model society. They were dispensable and dangerous, presenting a dual threat because their customs could corrupt the holy commonwealth and because they resented their loss of lands.

The 1637 war against the Pequots of eastern Connecticut showed the lengths to which the New England settlers could go. The Pequots, a powerful tribe, attempted to unite New England Indians against the English. In May 1637, troops from Massachusetts and Connecticut, with their Indian allies, the Narragansetts, attacked a Pequot village on the Mystic River before dawn, killing hundreds of sleeping women, children, and old men. The Pequots who escaped this massacre, mostly young men absent from the town, were later executed or enslaved. The Treaty of Hartford (1638) declared their nation dissolved.

Shortly after the Pequot War, in 1638, a group of staunch Puritans established New Haven. Persecuted in England, Reverend John Davenport took his flock first to Boston, but decided to move on to the Long Island Sound west of the Connecticut colony. They had no charter for New Haven, so the freemen made the Bible their law, eliminating trial by jury, for example, because it had no scriptural basis. Only male church members could vote. The colony grew as the settlers built towns farther west along the sound and on Long Island. Together, the towns agreed upon a government comprised of a governor, magistrates, and a representative assembly.

Exiles to Rhode Island

The founding of Rhode Island resulted from another kind of emigration from Massachusetts, that of people who refused to submit to the Puritan magistrates. The first was **Roger Williams,** a likeable but stubborn, independent-minded minister who challenged Massachusetts Bay's policy toward the Indians and its theocratic laws. Williams had studied divinity at Cambridge University, where he became a vocal Separatist. He immigrated to Massachusetts Bay in 1631, where he aroused the colony when he refused the pulpit in Boston's church because its members had not renounced the Church of England.

Williams then accused Massachusetts of holding fraudulent title to its territory because the king had no authority to give away Indian lands. He said the colony should send the charter back to the king for correction; the settlers should return to England if they could not obtain rights from the true owners of the land. Williams raised a troublesome issue that the Puritan officials refused to recognize, so they ordered him to be still. He would not be quiet, soon broaching the issues of religious freedom and separation of church and state. "Forced worship stinks in God's nostrils," he proclaimed. "There is no other prudent, Christian way of preserving peace in the world, but by permission of differing consciences." He attacked the laws requiring church attendance and tax support of Puritan churches. Williams believed that government would pollute the church, not that giving legal preference to one religion was unfair. He opposed laws regulating religion to protect the church from state interference.

When the General Court banished Williams from Massachusetts for challenging the government in 1636, he went south to Narragansett Bay. There he purchased land from the Narragansett Indians, establishing Providence Plantation at the Great Salt River. With the sympathizers who joined him, he created a society based on religious toleration, separation of church and state, and participation in government by all male property owners. Williams welcomed people of all religions to Providence Plantation, as long as they accepted the right of others to worship freely. Williams himself became wealthy through trade with the Native Americans and the Dutch. In 1638, he transferred ownership of Providence to a group of 13 associates, of whom he was one.

Printed copy of the Maryland act for religious toleration, 1649.

North Wind Picture Archives

Another exile from Massachusetts was **Anne Hutchinson,** a midwife and nurse, who in 1634 arrived in Boston with her husband, merchant William Hutchinson, and children. As Hutchinson assisted women in childbirth and sickness, she became convinced that Bostonians placed too much emphasis on good works and not enough on faith. She was a follower of one of Boston's ministers, the influential John Cotton, who stressed the importance of the individual's relationship with God over the obligation to obey laws. Hutchinson went further than Cotton, coming close to suggesting that if a person were saved it did not matter how she or he behaved, a belief known as the Antinomian heresy.

To the orthodox Puritan faction led by Governor John Winthrop, Hutchinson was a threat for several reasons. She emphasized individual judgment over communal authority, thus questioning the rule of colonial leaders. She told the Puritan patriarchs that God spoke to her directly, that she did not need the assistance of magistrates and ministers in interpreting God's will. Further, Hutchinson went outside the accepted role of women by taking a public stand on religion. But most seriously, she became the standard bearer for a group who contested power with the Winthrop faction. In 1637, Winthrop's government put Hutchinson on trial for defaming ministers and exiled her from the colony.

With her family and supporters she founded a colony at Portsmouth on Narragansett Bay.

Following the settlement of Williams and Hutchinson on Narragansett Bay, several other dissenters established colonies there. William Coddington, a supporter of Hutchinson, started the town of Newport, and Samuel Gorton founded Warwick. The four leaders had trouble cooperating, but knew they needed a charter from the English government to avoid annexation by Massachusetts. Roger Williams went to England for that purpose during the Civil War. The 1644 Rhode Island charter, which Parliament granted, united the four settlements under one representative assembly, which could pass statutes consistent with the laws of England. The Rhode Island colonists based their government on Williams's principles of freedom of worship, separation of church and state, and wide participation in government.

The Proprietary Colony of Maryland

In 1632, Charles I granted a charter for Maryland to George Calvert, the first Lord Baltimore, who had served in high office until he converted to Catholicism. Forced to resign, but still a royal favorite, Calvert requested a grant in America to build a haven for Catholics. He also expected to support his family by selling the land. He died before actually obtaining the charter, so his son, Cecilius Calvert, the second Lord Baltimore, became lord proprietor of Maryland. The colony was carved out of the northern part of Virginia. Calvert received ownership of the soil and was sovereign in government, subject only to the king.

Calvert spent £40,000 for two ships, the *Ark* and the *Dove,* with supplies to send the first settlers, who arrived in Maryland in 1634. The proprietor planned a feudal system in which manorial lords received large tracts depending on the number of tenants they transported. For example, a person who brought five laborers to Maryland at a total cost of £20 received a manor of 2,000 acres.

Though Maryland settlers suffered no "starving time" as had settlers in Virginia and had a cash crop in tobacco, the colony grew slowly. Mortality was high and immigration sluggish. By 1642, Calvert had granted rights for only 16 manors, mostly to wealthy Catholic friends. To improve his income, Calvert distributed farms to less wealthy immigrants, who had to pay annual quitrents. Over the seventeenth century, rich investors acquired 60 manors but by far most settlers were small landowners.

The extension of land ownership beyond Calvert's circle of loyal supporters created problems for the lord proprietor. Under the charter, he was obligated to call together an assembly of freemen, or landowners, to enact laws. Calvert interpreted this to mean that they should

Cecilius Calvert, proprietor of Maryland until 1675, with his grandson and a young enslaved African standing to the side. The Calverts are holding a map of the Chesapeake.

Courtesy Enoch Pratt Free Library, Baltimore

approve legislation he prepared, while the freemen, meeting first in 1635, claimed the right to draft the code of laws. Calvert refused to accept their draft, so for 3 years the colony operated without a code. In 1638, they reached a compromise, with the proprietor and assembly each drafting some of the bills. The colony finally had a legal basis for governing and punishing crime.

DOING HISTORY ONLINE

Indentured Servitude in Maryland, 1666

Use the document in this module and the discussion in the text on the founding of Maryland to explain Alsop's attitude toward indentured servitude.

History ⧗ Now™   Visit HistoryNOW to access primary sources and exercises related to this topic: http://now.ilrn.com/ayers_etal3e

But the struggle for power between the proprietor and freemen continued. The ordinary planters, who formed the majority of freemen and were mostly Protestant, resented the power of the Catholic elite and had little sympathy for Calvert's vision of a society in which all Christians could worship freely. Religious and political strife became most acute in Maryland during the English Civil War and the Puritan Commonwealth, from 1642 to 1660.

The Impact of the English Civil War

Over 2 decades, the English Civil War transformed the political situation in England. The war resulted from a contest for power between Parliament and Charles I. Charles imprisoned opponents without due process, and launched a crusade to force all his subjects, even those in Presbyterian Scotland and Catholic Ireland, to conform to the Anglican Church. In 1642, war broke out between the "Cavaliers," or royalists, and the "Roundheads," or parliamentary forces, of whom many were Puritans. Oliver Cromwell led the Roundheads to victory in 1648; the following year they beheaded the king.

The revolutionaries attempted to rule through an elected Parliament, but conflicting factions of Puritans and radical sects undermined their plans. Some radical theorists wanted an entire restructuring of society—in the words of one contemporary, "a world turned upside down." They called for extension of the vote to all men and redistribution of land. The gentry and wealthy merchants who had led Parliament to victory utterly rejected these ideas. In 1653 they named Cromwell the Lord Protector of the Commonwealth of England, Scotland, and Ireland. He ruled alone, backed by the army, until his death in 1658. An attempt failed to make his son Richard the successor, and two years later, the monarchy was restored. The accession of Charles II did not mean a complete reversal to the time of his father. The king confirmed Parliament's right to approve taxes and abolished the royal courts that had punished opponents of the Crown. But the Restoration brought the Cavaliers back into power, making the Anglican Church the state religion once again.

The struggle for power during the Civil War and its aftermath had repercussions in the colonies. Initially, the rebellion of English Puritans against the king raised hopes among New Englanders that English society would be reformed. Of more practical importance to the colonies was the lack of military protection from England. Plymouth, Massachusetts, Connecticut, and New Haven counted among their enemies the French, Dutch, Native Americans, and Rhode Island. In 1643, they formed the New England Confederation, agreeing to share the cost

of war, provide soldiers in proportion to population, and make no treaties without each colony's consent. The New England Confederation was the first league of colonies in English North America and the only successful one before the Revolutionary War. In assuming power to conduct war and make treaties, it went beyond colonial rights. The English government, in the midst of Civil War, was too preoccupied to react.

In the Chesapeake colonies of Virginia and Maryland, the Civil War and its aftermath were more disruptive. In 1652, the English Commonwealth removed the royalist Virginia governor, William Berkeley, because he had proclaimed Charles II the king upon his father's execution. In Maryland, the parliamentary revolt weakened the position of Lord Baltimore, whose authority came directly from the king. Protestants, especially Puritans, opposed Lord Baltimore, even though he had encouraged them to migrate from Virginia, where they had suffered Governor Berkeley's persecution. Calvert had approved the "Act Concerning Religion" (1649), which guaranteed freedom of religion to all Christians. Nevertheless, in 1654, the Maryland Puritans established a commonwealth. Their assembly deposed the proprietor's government, restricted the right of Catholics to worship, and created a Puritan code of behavior, including laws against swearing, drunkenness, and breaking the Sabbath. Calvert appealed to Oliver Cromwell, who confirmed his proprietorship, but Lord Baltimore regained control of the colony only in 1657, after a period of local civil war.

English Colonization After 1660

The accession of Charles II in 1660 initiated a new phase of colonization, in which the English government paid more attention to its colonies than it had before the Civil War. In 1662, the Crown granted Connecticut a charter, and the following year confirmed the charter Rhode Island had received from Parliament. To tighten colonial administration, the king and Parliament approved a series of navigation acts that formed the basis of a mercantilist colonial policy.

Navigation Acts

The English Commonwealth, recognizing the growing economic value of the colonies, had passed the Navigation Act of 1651. The law required that goods brought to England or its colonies from Asia, Africa, or America be carried on English ships (including those of English colonies). Goods from European nations had to be transported on either English ships or those of the country

MAP 2.2 North America in the Early Seventeenth Century

This map shows the location of some of the Native American groups in North America, indicating the areas in which Indians of the eastern woodlands and American southwest grew Indian corn, beans, squash, and other crops. The map also includes the earliest European settlements, from St. Augustine in 1565 to New Netherland in 1624.

of origin. The chief purposes of the act were to encourage growth of England's merchant marine and to challenge Dutch ascendancy on the seas and in colonial ports. The Commonwealth went further in 1652–1654, with the first Anglo-Dutch War, by attacking Dutch vessels in the English Channel and North Sea.

The Navigation Acts of 1660, 1663, and 1673 confirmed the 1651 restrictions on transport and created a list of "enumerated articles"—major colonial products including tobacco, sugar, indigo, cotton, ginger, and dyewoods—that could be shipped only to England or another English colony. The colonists could not sell these goods directly to other nations. The "articles" first went to England, where they were taxed and reexported by English merchants, who benefited from the business. Conversely, with some exceptions, goods shipped from other nations to the English colonies had to go to England first.

The colonists considered these laws detrimental because English middlemen added charges to products going in both directions. The English government created a colonial administration to enforce the acts, but the results were complicated and inefficient. Colonial governors lacked the resources (and in many cases the will) to eliminate smuggling.

Carolina

Charles II was penniless when he ascended the throne and owed substantial debts to his supporters. Expansion of the colonial empire permitted him to repay these creditors and at the same time advance England's commerce and national power. Carolina was the first post-Restoration colony on the North American mainland. In 1663, the area between Virginia and Spanish Florida

New Amsterdam in 1643

This view of New Amsterdam suggests a bustling trading port with two successful Dutch inhabitants. Note at the bottom, behind the woman, four African laborers. The illustration reflects both the economic focus and ethnic diversity of New Netherland. The colony welcomed immigrants from many European countries, including France, Germany, and Sweden. Despite official recognition of the established Dutch Reformed Church, people of other religions, including Jews, Quakers, Lutherans, and Puritans, could practice their beliefs.

The West Indian Company imported enslaved Africans into New Netherland to provide much-needed labor. By the English takeover in 1664, about 500 slaves lived in the colony, the majority in New Amsterdam. The WIC, which owned many of the Africans, began a policy of offering land and freedom to some individuals. Some others received a status of "half-freedom" in which they owned independent farms but had to provide waged labor to the company when needed. In 1664, about 75 free blacks lived in the city.

© The New York Public Library/Art Resource, NY

was unoccupied by Europeans, but Spain had better title to the land than England had. With the Treaty of Madrid (1670), the English obtained Spain's concession of lands north of present-day Charleston. The chief promoters of Carolina were Anthony Ashley Cooper, Governor William Berkeley of Virginia, and John Colleton, a West Indies planter. They obtained help from five men who were close to the king; together the eight associates became proprietors of Carolina. They obtained a charter like Maryland's and received wide latitude in matters of religion. They drew up the "Fundamental Constitutions of Carolina," creating a complicated feudal society with nobles and lords, a scheme the ordinary settlers of Carolina refused to accept.

Two colonies developed in Carolina. Small planters from Virginia built the first, which later became North Carolina. As early as 1653, people had settled on the shores of Albemarle Sound, where they raised tobacco, corn, and livestock. In 1664, Berkeley sent William Drummond to organize a council and assembly. The Albemarle settlement remained poor, a haven for pirates, and difficult to govern. In 1691, the Carolina proprietors effectively established North Carolina by appointing a separate governor.

The second Carolina colony was located at Charles Town, in the future South Carolina. After two unsuccessful attempts, Anthony Ashley Cooper in 1670 organized a permanent settlement. Many of its early settlers came from the West Indies island of Barbados, which had run out of vacant land. The Barbadian planters had money to develop plantations in Carolina and owned African slaves to do the work. The proprietors offered generous acreages to household heads for each person brought to the colony. A planter, with his own family and several enslaved blacks, could qualify for hundreds of acres. From the colony's founding, a large proportion of South Carolinians were African slaves. They produced food, livestock, firewood, and barrel staves for Barbados.

New York and New Jersey

To control eastern North America, the English next had to seize New Netherland. With a series of outposts, the Dutch held the region between Connecticut and Maryland, including lands on the Delaware River that Sweden had settled in 1638 and the Dutch captured in 1655. The English justified their attack in 1664 against New Netherland on several grounds, including John Cabot's 1497 voyage to the region and Dutch illegal trade with English colonies. Settlers from New England living under Dutch jurisdiction reported that Dutch military defenses were weak. James, the duke of York, Lord High Admiral of the Navy, urged his brother, Charles II, to send a fleet. The king granted James a proprietary charter for lands between the Connecticut and Delaware rivers, as well as Long Island, Nantucket, Martha's Vineyard, and part of present-day Maine. The charter gave the duke wide governmental powers, even dispensing with an assembly. The duke could write his own legal code as long as it conformed to the laws of England.

With charter in hand, James quickly forced out the Dutch. In 1664, his deputy governor, Richard Nicolls, took New Amsterdam without a fight. The second Anglo-Dutch War (1665–1667) in part resulted from this action. Assuming ownership, James called his colony New York, but granted the land between the Delaware and lower Hudson rivers to John Lord Berkeley and Sir George Carteret, who named the area New Jersey.

Despite his extensive powers, James realized that he had to make New York attractive to inhabitants if his colony was to prosper. He gave residents the choice of keeping their Dutch citizenship or becoming naturalized as English subjects. In 1665, he issued a legal code, called the "Duke's Laws," which guaranteed freedom of religion, recognized preexisting titles to land, and allowed New Englanders living in towns on Long Island to choose selectmen. The New York government consisted of a governor and council appointed by the duke, but no legislature.

When England and the Netherlands continued their rivalry in the third Anglo-Dutch War (1672–1674), the Dutch easily recaptured New York. After 16 months they returned the colony to England as part of the Treaty of Westminster (1674). Receiving a new charter, James resumed possession of New York and reconfirmed his grants to New Jersey. The territory had by then been divided into two colonies, West New Jersey and East New Jersey. Berkeley had sold West New Jersey to a Quaker, Edward Byllinge, who then transferred title to a group of coreligionists, including William Penn. The duke confirmed Carteret's right to East New Jersey immediately, but waited until 1680 to approve the Quaker proprietorship of West New Jersey.

Conclusion

During the first three-quarters of the seventeenth century, the English, French, and Dutch ended Spain's mastery of the New World. By 1675, the English held colonies along the Atlantic coast from New England to the Carolinas (see Map 2.2). The French controlled Canada and had explored the Great Lakes and the upper Mississippi Valley. The Dutch established, but lost, New Netherland. Spain retained its borderland outposts in New Mexico and Florida. Everywhere the Europeans colonized, the Indians died from epidemic disease. Their relations with the white invaders depended a great deal on the numbers of Europeans who arrived, their attitudes, and goals of settlement.

From the beginning, the English colonies were diverse—in their form of government, degree of stability, relations with Native Americans, and economic base. The Crown fostered this variety by granting charters to an assortment of companies and individuals, including Puritan and Catholic opponents of the established church. Virginia and Maryland prospered from tobacco but battled persistent high mortality. Still, in the mid-seventeenth century, the Chesapeake was "the best poor man's country" for English people willing to take risks. Most New Englanders came primarily to start a model society based on their Calvinist beliefs. They enjoyed a healthier climate than the people of the Chesapeake, but inferior soil. They supported themselves modestly by fishing and mixed farming, developing trade with the West Indies to pay for English imports.

In New Mexico, Hispanic colonists exploited the Pueblos' labor to support their trade with Mexico, while Catholic missionaries tried to claim the Indians' souls. In all three areas—New England, the Chesapeake, and New Mexico—pressures between Europeans and Native Americans, and within the colonial societies, would soon erupt in war.

The Chapter in Review

- British, French, and Dutch expansion ended Spanish dominance of North America during the seventeenth century. Spain retained landholdings in Central and South America and the borderland territories of New Mexico and Florida.

- The nature of interactions between white colonizers and Native Americans depended on colonizers' goals, the number of white settlers, and European attitudes toward native peoples.

- Contact between Native Americans and Europeans inevitably resulted in the devastating spread of epidemic disease among Native American populations.

- Many English settlers were drawn to the colonies by the prospect of economic opportunity and religious freedom. New England in particular became a refuge for religious dissidents such as the Puritans.

- Drawn to the New World primarily by economic considerations, many French and Dutch settlers became involved in the fur trade. While French relations with Native Americans were relatively amicable, Dutch interactions were frequently fraught with violence.

- The 1660 restoration of Charles II to the British throne resulted in the establishment of the Carolinas and a series of wars between the British and the Dutch over the territory of New Netherland.

Making Connections Across Chapters

LOOKING BACK

Chapter 2 discusses the colonization of North America by the Spanish, French, Dutch, and English during the seventeenth century. While the colonies varied in political organization, economic development, labor, religion, and relations with Native Americans, we can also determine common patterns.

1. What were the economic goals of the adventurers who founded New Mexico, Jamestown, New France, New Netherland, and Massachusetts?

2. What was the significance of religion in the development of each of these colonies?

3. How did the settlement of Rhode Island compare with the founding of Massachusetts Bay?

4. How did the English Civil War affect the colonies?

5. Why were the relations of the English with Native Americans in Virginia different from Indian–French interaction in Canada?

LOOKING AHEAD

After 1660, with restoration of the English monarchy, the government began tightening administration of the colonies. This included enforcement of the Navigation Acts, which restricted colonial trade. Chapter 3 will consider internal conflicts and wars that the colonists faced as their societies matured and as they participated more fully in the expanding empire. Also significant after 1675 was the shift to enslaved African labor in the southern colonies.

1. Why did the English crown continue and expand the Navigation Act, which the Commonwealth initiated in 1651?

2. What changes did the English government make in colonial administration after 1675?

3. What was the importance of the African slave trade to colonial development in North America?

Recommended Readings

Anderson, Virginia D. *New England's Generation: The Great Migration and the Formation of Society and Culture in the Seventeenth Century.* (1991). Compares the motivations and experiences of Puritan settlers with succeeding generations.

Berlin, Ira. *Many Thousands Gone: The First Two Centuries of Slavery in North America* (1998). An important synthesis of stages in the rise of slavery in the British colonies and Louisiana.

Cronon, William. *Changes in the Land: Indians, Colonists, and the Ecology of New England* (1983). Contrasts Native American and settler use of the environment.

Dunn, Richard S. *Sugar and Slaves: The Rise of the Planter Class in the English West Indies, 1624–1713* (1972). An insightful history of the creation of slave regimes in the English Caribbean.

Greene, Jack P. *Pursuits of Happiness: The Social Development of Early Modern British Colonies and the Formation of American Culture* (1988). Provides a useful framework for understanding the various ways in which British settlements evolved.

Gutiérrez, Ramón A. *When Jesus Came, the Corn Mothers Went Away: Marriage, Sexuality, and Power in New Mexico, 1500–1846* (1991). Provocative evaluation of Spanish settlement, focusing particularly on women's status.

Kupperman, Karen Ordahl. *Indians and English: Facing Off in Early America* (2000). A perceptive analysis of the complexity of Native–European encounters during the early seventeenth century.

Mancall, Peter C. and Merrell, James H., eds. *American Encounters: Natives and Newcomers from European Contact to Indian Removal, 1500–1850* (2000). A collection of path-breaking articles.

Morgan, Edmund S. *American Slavery, American Freedom: The Ordeal of Colonial Virginia* (1975). A detailed, stimulating account of English settlement and the transition to slavery.

Ulrich, Laurel Thatcher. *Good Wives: Image and Reality in the Lives of Women in Northern New England, 1650–1750* (1982). A thoughtful study of the various roles of colonial women.

Identifications

Review your understanding of the following key terms, people, events, and dates for this chapter (these terms also appear in the Glossary at the end of the book):

Juan de Oñate
Virginia Company
Jamestown
Powhatan
John Smith
Opechancanough

Puritanism
Massachusetts Bay colony
Mayflower Compact
Squanto
Plymouth colony
theocracy
Roger Williams
Anne Hutchinson

Online Sources Guide 🌐

Use this listing to find online documents, images, interactive maps, simulations, and other resources related to this chapter.

American History Resource Center

http://history.wadsworth.com/rc/us

Documents

Don Juan de Oñate: "A Settlement in New Mexico" (1599)
Letters Patent of the London Virginia Company (1606)
Letter on tobacco culture and the introduction of slavery (John Smith)
"Verses Upon the Burning of Our House" (Anne Bradstreet, 1666)
"A Dialogue Between Old England and New" (Anne Bradstreet, 1642)
John Winthrop's Shipboard Sermon, "A Model of Christian Charity" (1630)
Letter from Father Marquette to Father Dablon (1672)
John Smith, "The Starving Time" (1624)

Selected Images

1624 engraving of adventures of John Smith
Pocahontas
tobacco worker
John Winthrop, Governor of Massachusetts Bay colony
Puritans entering a meetinghouse

Simulation

Colonial Expansion (In this historical simulation you can choose to be with the Aztecs, Jamestown settlers, or Puritans/New England and make choices based on the circumstances and opportunities afforded.)

HistoryNOW

http://now.ilrn.com/ayers_etal3e

Primary Source Exercises

Plan for a Massachusetts Town, 1636
Will of Edward Garfield from Watertown, Massachusetts, 1668
Indentured Servitude in Maryland, 1666
Life in Virginia
Leaving Home

3 Crisis and Change, 1675–1720

Metacom, the Wampanoag leader, who in 1676 tried to drive the New England settlers back "into the Sea."

Copyright The Granger Collection, NY

In February 1676, Narragansett Indians burned Lancaster, Massachusetts, killing many of the English settlers and taking others prisoner, including Mary White Rowlandson, a minister's wife, and her three children. The Narragansetts had joined the Wampanoags and other New England Algonquians to destroy the European settlements. Their leader was the Wampanoag sachem, **Metacom,** called King Philip by the colonists. In the Indians' words, according to Rowlandson, "they would knock all the Rogues in the head, or drive them into the Sea, or make them flie the Country."

Though Rowlandson began her captivity with hatred toward the Indians, whom she called "Barbarous Creatures," she came to respect some as individuals and to appreciate aspects of their culture. She was most impressed, she said, that while the Algonquians had little corn, "I did not see (all the time I was among them) one Man, or Woman, or Child, die with Hunger." They ate "Ground-nuts . . . also Nuts and Acorns, Hartychoaks, Lilly-roots, Ground-beans, and several other weeds and roots that I know not." Desperately hungry, Rowlandson ate unfamiliar foods too, surviving to rejoin her husband in Boston.

King Philip's War, as the English settlers called it, was just one of the crises that afflicted colonial America in the last quarter of the seventeenth century. In Virginia, a comparatively minor skirmish between Indians and whites escalated into Bacon's Rebellion, a civil war among the English settlers. In New Mexico, the Pueblos expelled the Spanish for 13 years. Following closely upon King Philip's War and Bacon's Rebellion, **William Penn** intended to avoid conflict with the Indians in founding Pennsylvania. An unstable English government disrupted politics in the colonies when James II, a Roman Catholic, succeeded his brother King Charles II in 1685. James's attempt to make sweeping changes in both the home and colonial governments met strong resistance. The **Glorious Revolution** quickly ended his reign. In 1689, settlers in Massachusetts, New York, and Maryland overthrew his provincial governments, declaring allegiance to the new king and queen, William and Mary. In Massachusetts, the impact of years of political uncertainty helped spread witchcraft hysteria from Salem to other towns.

From 1689 to 1713, European wars spilled into North America, fueling hostilities in Florida and Canada

Timeline

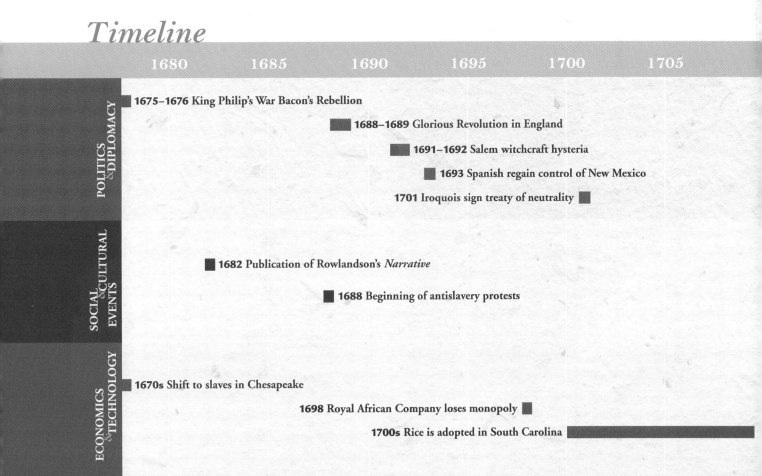

	1680	1685	1690	1695	1700	1705

POLITICS & DIPLOMACY

1675–1676 King Philip's War Bacon's Rebellion

1688–1689 Glorious Revolution in England

1691–1692 Salem witchcraft hysteria

1693 Spanish regain control of New Mexico

1701 Iroquois sign treaty of neutrality

SOCIAL & CULTURAL EVENTS

1682 Publication of Rowlandson's *Narrative*

1688 Beginning of antislavery protests

ECONOMICS & TECHNOLOGY

1670s Shift to slaves in Chesapeake

1698 Royal African Company loses monopoly

1700s Rice is adopted in South Carolina

among Native Americans, English, French, and Spanish. The French moved south through the Mississippi Valley and founded Louisiana, while the English pushed south into Florida, west across the Appalachian Mountains, and north into Maine. As the English colonies expanded and matured, their economies and labor systems diverged, particularly with the entrenchment of slavery. Despite revolutions and wars, planters built successful staple crop economies in the southern colonies, while northerners profited from networks of trade with England, Europe, and the West Indies.

Rebellions and War

The wars of 1675 to 1680 in New England, Virginia, and New Mexico resulted from pressures that had been building for decades. In Massachusetts, the spread of settlement forced Native Americans to defend their homes. In Virginia, demands of ex-servants for good land precipitated a civil war, and in New Mexico, severe droughts deepened opposition to forced labor, impelling the Pueblos to rid themselves of Spanish overlords. After the upheavals, elites in each settlement made changes that avoided further serious revolt.

Decline of New England Orthodoxy

In 1675, Massachusetts seemed to have lost sight of the goals of its first settlers. When the Indians attacked, Puritan ministers warned the sons and daughters of the

founding generation that God was punishing them for their faithlessness and sin.

In fact, Puritan church membership had declined since 1650, especially among men. After mid-century, women became a large proportion of the "elect," comprising 60 percent, and in some congregations 75 percent, of newly admitted members. The ministers believed that men were becoming more worldly, thus undermining the church's social and political authority. A related problem was that the children of nonchurch members could not be baptized. In 1662, the clergy devised an alternative to full church membership, the **Half-Way Covenant,** which permitted adults who had been baptized but who were not yet saved to be "half-way" members. In congregations that accepted this innovation (not all churches did), people could assume partial status by showing that they understood Christian principles and would strive to obey God. As unconverted members, they were not entitled to take communion, but could have their children baptized.

The growth of competing religions in New England also proved to Puritan ministers that the model society had failed. Believing theirs to be the only true religion, Puritans rooted out dissent. After 1650, the Quakers and Baptists threatened religious unity. The Society of Friends, or Quakers, was a radical Protestant sect born in the turmoil of the English Civil War. Like the Puritans, they were reformers who believed that the Church of England was corrupt and should be purified of its rituals, decorations, and hierarchy. But the Quakers went

This Hingham, Massachusetts, church was originally built in 1681, when ship carpenters framed the interior of the roof as a ship's keel in reverse (left). The exterior view (right) reflects renovations completed in the eighteenth century.

even further. They claimed that the Puritans also practiced false doctrine by paying ministers to preach, relying too much on the Bible as the word of God, and retaining the sacraments of baptism and communion. The Friends believed that God communicated directly with individuals through the "Spirit" or "Light." They

SOCIAL & CULTURAL EVENTS

A Quaker Woman Preaching

The Quakers were unique among English religions in the seventeenth century in recognizing women as ministers. Women were among the earliest followers of George Fox of England, considered the founder of Quakerism around 1650. Female missionaries then traveled through the British Isles, Europe, and America. They believed that God spoke through them, and they hoped to convince others of the "Light."

In New England, the women ministers challenged both the Puritan faith and expectations of female

Courtesy of Special Collections, University Research Library, University of California at Los Angeles

QUAQUERESSE qui preche.

subordination. When Quaker missionaries interrupted church services and gained followers, Massachusetts leaders banished them and threatened to execute those who returned to the colony. Several were hanged, including Mary Dyer in 1660, who had determined to "look their bloody laws in the face." This illustration was published somewhat later, in J. F. Bernard's *The Ceremonies and Religious Customs of the Various Nations of the Known World . . .* (1733–1739), when Quakers had become less controversial and worshipped openly in Massachusetts.

worshipped by gathering in plain meetinghouses to "wait upon the Lord." In worship services, they had no Bible reading, prepared sermon, music, or ritual. Rather, they waited in silence for the Spirit to inspire one or several of the congregation to communicate God's message. Ministers, who included women as well as men, regularly received inspiration to speak. They required no advanced learning because their words were supposed to come straight from God, not from a prepared text.

Appalled by these Quaker teachings, Puritan leaders tried to prevent their spread by deporting the traveling missionaries. The Friends were stubborn, however, repeatedly returning to Massachusetts. They interrupted Puritan church services, preached in the streets, and made some converts among the people. The Puritan magistrates arrested and whipped them, even cropping their ears. In 1658, the General Court prescribed the death penalty for Quakers who returned after banishment.

The hangings of several Quaker missionaries caused consternation on both sides of the Atlantic. When Charles II demanded an explanation, the Puritans ended the executions. The magistrates continued to persecute nonconformers, but over the decades following 1660 realized that their policy of intolerance had failed. Rhode Island served as a base for Quaker missionaries to evangelize in the Puritan colonies, further supporting its reputation among Puritans as "the sewer of New England." The Baptists, whose objection to infant baptism was their chief disagreement with orthodox Puritans, increased in numbers after approval of the Half-Way Covenant, which they vehemently opposed. They believed that a church should include only the saved, indeed that only the saved should be baptized. Despite persecution, dissenters successfully formed congregations throughout New England.

King Philip's War

The unceasing expansion of white settlers into the frontier destroyed the relative peace between the Algonquians and the settlers of New England. By 1675, more than 50,000 whites inhabited the region. The colonists had large families of sons and daughters who desired farms of their own. These settlers occupied more and more of the hunting, fishing, and agricultural lands of the Indians.

Since the massacre of the Pequots in 1637, the Puritans and Native Americans of New England had managed an uneasy peace. The colonists traded for furs with local nations and with the Mohawks, the closest nation of Iroquois in New York. Some Puritan ministers, of whom John Eliot is best known, convinced several local tribes who were greatly diminished by disease and loss of lands to dwell in **praying towns**." In these villages,

Chest of Drawers, made of oak and pine, Massachusetts, 1680–1700.

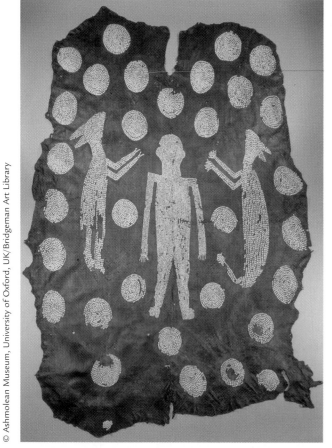

Powhatan's Mantle, a deerskin with shell patterns from Virginia, late sixteenth to early seventeenth century.

Pueblo Indian hide painting of a Christian Madonna, 1675.

adjacent to but separate from the towns of white settlers, the Indians were supposed to adopt English customs and learn the fundamentals of Puritan religion. By 1674, Eliot had organized 14 praying towns of Native Americans who took the first steps toward giving up their traditional ways.

Many New England Indians, including Wampanoags and Narragansetts, did not form praying towns, but even so remained allies of the Puritan governments for many years. Trouble began in 1671, when the Plymouth government attempted to force the Wampanoags to surrender their firearms and obtain permission to sell land. Metacom (or King Philip) built a league with neighboring tribes. When John Sassamon, an Indian educated at Harvard College, informed the Plymouth government of impending attack and was murdered, the white authorities hanged three Wampanoags for the deed.

In 1675, Metacom mobilized Algonquians throughout New England, attacking 52 English towns (see Map 3.1). White refugees fled to Boston. But by the end of summer 1676, with the help of the Mohawks, the colonial

MAP 3.1 New England at the Time of King Philip's War, 1675–1676
The Indians and English destroyed and damaged each other's towns throughout Plymouth, Rhode Island, and Massachusetts. The Narragansetts, who lived in Rhode Island and had assisted the Puritan governments against the Pequots in 1637, entered King Philip's War after an English army invaded their territory.

governments turned back the attack, as disease, hunger, and a weapons shortage weakened Metacom's troops. The war took a heavy toll on both sides, for the Algonquians destroyed 12 towns, killed many colonists, and took others prisoner, as described earlier. White frontier settlement would not return to its 1675 limits for another 40 years.

For the Indians of southern New England, the war was calamitous. Thousands died and many others were enslaved. Even bands who supported the English lost autonomy. At the outbreak of war, the colonists had forced residents of the praying towns to live on desolate Deer Island in Boston Harbor, where they suffered from lack of food and shelter. Some of the Indian men later fought in the colonial militia against Metacom, but when the war was over, all Native Americans in southern New

England had to live in praying towns, where they worked as servants or tenant farmers for neighboring whites. Metacom was killed, his head paraded before the white settlements and kept on a pole in Plymouth for 20 years; his wife and son were sold as slaves.

War in the Chesapeake

Just as New England struggled over land in King Philip's War, Virginia faced a similar crisis in Bacon's Rebellion. The Chesapeake uprising involved civil war among the English as well as Indian–white conflict. But at its root, the chief issue was land: how could the competing interests of landless immigrants and dispossessed natives be resolved? Since the 1640s, the white population of

Virginia and Maryland had grown quickly. By 1670, approximately 40,000 colonists lived in the Chesapeake, including native-born sons and daughters of early settlers as well as more recent arrivals. Among the new immigrants were servants who expected to obtain land upon completing their terms. In the 1670s, however, many Virginians discovered that the combination of low tobacco prices and high land prices blocked their dream of obtaining plantations. They received headrights, or individual rights to land, but could find no good vacant tobacco acreage to claim.

Part of the problem, these landless freemen believed, was that the Indians held too much territory. Specifically, the 1646 treaty between the Virginia government and the Powhatans designated the area north of the York River for Native Americans. This agreement had been acceptable to whites in the 1640s when space south of the York seemed ample, but was unsatisfactory 30 years later, when white settlement was pushing north. It was also true, many freemen recognized, that wealthy planters, powerful in government, speculated in large acreages that they left empty while others starved for land.

The first flames of war occurred in July 1675, when some Doeg Indians attempted to take hogs as payment for a settler's unpaid debt. After people on both sides were killed, the Susquehannocks got involved. When they attacked frontier settlements, a thousand-man army of Virginia and Maryland colonists marched against their village on the Potomac River. Vastly outnumbered, several Susquehannock sachems agreed to negotiate, but when they left their stockade, the colonists murdered them. During the winter of 1675–1676, the Susquehannocks retaliated, raising fears that King Philip's War had spread south. Discontented and vengeful colonists responded indiscriminately, killing friendly neighboring Indians rather than those who were actually attacking the frontier.

The landless freemen found a leader in **Nathaniel Bacon.** Only 29 years old, Bacon had come to Virginia with enough money to purchase a large plantation. Governor Berkeley nominated him to the Virginia council, despite his youth. Nevertheless, Bacon evidently saw his opportunity to challenge Berkeley for leadership of the colony by mobilizing freemen and small planters against the Indians. While Berkeley wanted peace with the Susquehannocks, Bacon's forces intended to annihilate all of the natives. The settlers knew that the natives were weak, with just a fraction of their pre-1607 population. Bacon's supporters also demanded a greater voice in the Virginia government.

Governor Berkeley declared Bacon a traitor and sent troops to end his forays against the Indians. He also called new elections that brought many Bacon supporters into the House of Burgesses. The delegates passed measures

Maryland Planter's House

This is a reconstruction of a typical Chesapeake colonist's house at the Godiah Spray tobacco plantation at historic St. Mary's City, Maryland. Most dwellings in the seventeenth-century Chesapeake were impermanent structures of wood. Many had only one room, without glass windows or wooden floors. They decayed quickly from the hot, humid climate and insects. Scholars have used archeological evidence and historical documents to determine the size and construction of these cabins.

Courtesy of Historic St. Mary's City

Despite the growth of large plantations in Virginia and Maryland between 1675 and 1720, more than one-third of white families lived in small cabins and rented rather than owned land. The men who supported Nathaniel Bacon came from this group. They rarely owned servants or slaves to help grow tobacco. They possessed some livestock and agricultural tools, but most used wooden rather than pottery dishes, and lacked bed and table linens, knives, forks, spices, and books.

that extended suffrage to landless freemen, taxed provincial councilors, and placed limits on the terms and fees of local officials. These efforts failed to end the rebellion, as Bacon's army burned Jamestown. For months, Virginians plundered the plantations of neighbors who took the other side. Few white fatalities occurred, however; rebels vented most of their frustration by killing Indians. The rebellion finally ceased with Bacon's death, probably

DOING HISTORY ONLINE

Royal Description of Nathaniel Bacon, c. 1676

Read the document in this module. How persuasive is the description of Nathaniel Bacon provided in the official report? Are there reasons to doubt its accuracy?

History ⊠ Now™   Visit HistoryNOW to access primary sources and exercises related to this topic: http://now.ilrn.com/ayers_etal3e

of dysentery, in October 1676. The war marked a serious defeat for the Indians of the Chesapeake, who lost the protection of the 1646 treaty and gradually surrendered their lands.

Bacon's Rebellion awakened the Virginia elites to the dangers of a large class of landless freemen but resulted in no substantive political change. A new assembly in 1677 reversed the reform acts of the 1676 House of Burgesses, including the law extending the vote to landless freemen. A commission appointed by the Crown to end the rebellion also opposed expanding popular power, stating that to grant suffrage to unpropertied men was "repugnant to the Lawes of England and to the Lawes and Peace of the Colony." The commission did call for taxing "the great Ingrossers of Lands" who caused "misery and mischiefs" by "occasioning the Planters to stragle to such remote distances when they cannot find land neerer to seat themselves but by being Tenants which in a Continent they think hard," but nothing was done. Rather than create a society in which power and wealth were distributed more evenly, in which Virginia once again would offer opportunity to poor Englishmen, the planter elite began importing more enslaved Africans. Bound for life and restricted by laws, black slaves could not demand farms or a voice in government. With settlement in New Jersey, Carolina, and Pennsylvania during the 1670s and 1680s, immigrants had better options than Virginia.

The Pueblo Revolt

Four years after Bacon's Rebellion, across the continent in New Mexico, the Pueblos drove out the Spanish—and kept them out for 13 years. The Pueblos, who lived along the Rio Grande (see Map 3.2) had the advantage of a much smaller white population in New Mexico—2,800—than in New England or the Chesapeake. The Spanish hold over the missions was tenuous, for native fighting men greatly outnumbered Spanish troops. Nevertheless, the Hispanic settlers and priests demanded forced labor and strict adherence to Christianity. A number of Indian towns had rebelled during the previous half century, but most failed to win autonomy.

The Pueblos became more desperate during the 1670s, when New Mexico endured severe drought. As famine persisted, they faced Apache and Navajo attacks. The Pueblos became convinced that the root of their troubles lay in their rejection of ancient gods, the *katsina.* To bring rain and renewed prosperity, some presented gifts to the katsina and performed dances that the Spanish had outlawed. When punished for abandoning Catholicism, the Indians felt even greater resentment, finally leading to revolt.

The leader of the 1680 rebellion was Popé, a medicine man of the village of San Juan, north of Santa Fe. When the katsina told him that the Spanish must be driven from the land, he organized a general insurrection, sending knotted ropes to allied villages, indicating when the uprising should start. On August 10, 1680, the Pueblos launched a full-scale attack, killing 400 colonists and 21 priests. Strategically, the Indians confiscated or destroyed the settlers' chief means of transportation, their horses and mules. When Santa Fe fell to the rebels on September 21, the whites escaped south, settling in the area of present-day Ciudad Juárez, Mexico. Some Spaniards explained the revolt as God's punishment for their sins, whereas others blamed the harsh labor and efforts to repress native religions. As Popé supervised, the Pueblos destroyed churches, broke up church bells, and burned images of Christ and the saints. According to one witness, "in order to take away their baptismal names, the water, and the holy oils, [the Indians] were to plunge into the rivers and wash themselves."

Several times during the next few years, the Spanish attempted unsuccessfully to retake New Mexico. The rebellion spread south into northern Mexico, where Native Americans demolished settlements and missions. But by 1692, as famine continued, the Pueblo alliance fell into disarray. The new Spanish governor of New Mexico, Don Diego de Vargas, marched north to Santa Fe with 160 troops. Though many Indians resisted, the Spanish reestablished control over the province. In December 1693, after a three-day siege, Vargas's troops took Santa Fe, killing all of the Indian men and making slaves of the women and children. The Spanish subsequently retained a foothold in New Mexico but not without further struggle. The Pueblos rejected the Franciscan missionaries, revolting once again in 1696. Some Pueblos fled from New Mexico; others submitted as Vargas systematically conquered the Indian towns once again. After 1696, the Spanish and Pueblos lived together in relative peace, but only because the Hispanics eased requirements for tribute, forced labor, and adherence to Christianity.

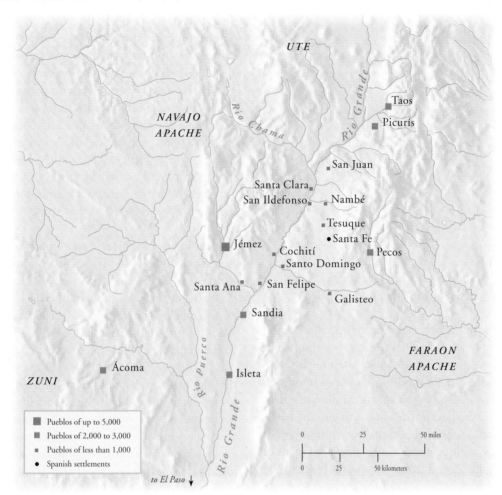

MAP 3.2 New Mexico, c. 1680

The Spanish had established their colony in 1598 by sending soldiers, their families, and Franciscan missionaries north through the Rio Grande Valley. In 1680, the Spanish population remained small and centered in the capital, Santa Fe.

William Penn's "Holy Experiment"

In England, the Quaker leader William Penn approached Charles II with a petition to establish a new colony in America, one that would avoid bloodshed by dealing justly with the Indians. While the Pueblos had not yet driven out the Spanish, Penn knew of King Philip's War and Bacon's Rebellion. He was determined to do things differently in Pennsylvania.

Plans for Pennsylvania

Penn had inherited a £16,000 debt owed to his father by the king, but had little hope for repayment in cash, so he requested a colony on the west bank of the Delaware River. The king approved Penn's request in 1681, granting him a charter for Pennsylvania that was more restrictive than Lord

Baltimore's, in part because the English government was attempting to assert greater control over its colonies, in part because Penn was a Quaker. The new proprietor received the right to enact laws and impose taxes with the consent of the freemen but was required to submit all laws for approval to the home government within five years of passage. And to protect the status of the Church of England, the charter stipulated that 20 Anglican inhabitants could request a minister from the bishop of London.

In establishing Pennsylvania, Penn hoped to provide a haven for Quakers, who faced persecution in England because they would not pay tithes for church support or attend Anglican services. Friends also refused to give oaths, so they could not legally pledge allegiance to the king. A Quaker ideal was to live according to the doctrine that all were equal in the eyes of God; thus they rejected certain customs, such as removing one's hat in the presence of superiors. For practicing their faith, they were jailed and fined, and when they refused to pay, local English officials took their property.

William Penn conceived of his colony as a "holy experiment," a place where Quakers could exercise their beliefs without interference and the government would operate like a Quaker meeting, acting in unison as it followed God's will. Penn also intended to pay the Lenape Indians for tracts of land and to set up arbitration panels of Native Americans and colonists to resolve conflicts peacefully. He paid the Lenapes a much lower price than he in turn charged the settlers, however, and assumed the Indians would leave after they sold their land.

Like Lord Baltimore, Penn intended to make a fortune from Pennsylvania, summing up his goals: "the service of God first, the honor and advantage of the king, with our own profit." Despite Penn's strong Quaker convictions, which for some suggested a simple life, he appreciated fine food, drink, and accommodations. He possessed large landholdings in southern England and Ireland, retained many servants, and enjoyed such delicacies as salmon, partridges, saffron, and chocolate. Urgently needing money, he thought the sale of millions of acres in America would solve his financial problems.

Penn spent a great deal of time planning the colony. His scheme of government established an assembly with two houses, both elected by the freemen. Freemen included adult males who owned at least 50 acres of land or paid taxes on other property. During the early decades, when servants received 50 acres at the end of their terms, nearly every man in Pennsylvania could vote. Penn did not extend that right to women, nor did he alter the common law restrictions on married women. Though female Friends took an active role in their meetings as ministers, missionaries, and supervisors of discipline, their legal status in the Quaker commonwealth was similar to that in other colonies. Penn's laws stood out in another respect, however, requiring capital punishment for just two offenses, treason and murder.

The proprietor's planning went beyond politics, for he also drew up specifications for his capital city. In designing Philadelphia, thus taking on the role of city planner, Penn was unique among early English colonizers. He conceived the city as a large "green country town," with wide streets in a grid pattern, public parks, ample lots, and brick houses. He failed to fulfill his plan completely because he could not obtain enough acreage to build Philadelphia as he wanted. Dutch and Swedish residents already owned the land along the Delaware River, so Penn decided to buy a site of just 1,200 acres between the Delaware and Schuylkill rivers. His plan remained orderly, with the grid design and parks, but with lots of one-half to one acre instead of 100 acres for those who purchased "proprietary shares" of 5,000 acres. To maintain a constant income from the colony, landowners would pay annual quitrents.

A Diverse Society

Penn sold land briskly: 600 people bought 700,000 acres within 4 years. Most of the buyers were Quaker farmers, merchants, artisans, and shopkeepers from England,

---

Picturing the Past SOCIAL & CULTURAL EVENTS

Dutch Edition of *Some Account*

William Penn had his promotional pamphlet, *Some Account of the Province of Pennsylvania in America; Lately Granted under the Great Seal of England to William Penn, &c. Together with Privileges and Powers necessary to the well-governing thereof,* translated into Dutch and German. He had traveled in Holland and Germany in 1677 and now made use of contacts to generate sales of land in his colony. Penn wrote to Quakers throughout England, Scotland, Ireland, and Wales and sent promotional tracts.

The Historical Society of Pennsylvania

Some Account discussed the benefits of colonies to prospective settlers and to England, described the climate and natural resources of Pennsylvania, outlined Penn's proposed government, and set the terms for buying land. Penn offered useful advice on what to pack, including "all sorts of apparel and utensils" for farming, construction, and domestic use. He added, for those who had heard of harsh conditions in early Virginia and Massachusetts, that America had advanced by 1681, "for there is better accommodation, and English provisions are to be had at easier rates."

though many also originated from Scotland, Ireland, Wales, Europe, the West Indies, Maryland, and New York.

Penn's settlers moved into an area inhabited by the Lenapes, who welcomed the newcomers, and by Swedes, Finns, and Dutch, who served as intermediaries with the Indians. The Lenapes, or Delawares as the colonists later called them, had conducted trade with the Dutch as early as 1610 and yielded land to the whites. Because Dutch and Swedish settlements remained small, relatively few violent incidents occurred. By the time Penn arrived with thousands of colonists, the Lenapes had declined significantly from disease. As they sold their lands, some moved to northern or western Pennsylvania, while others remained on marginal tracts in the Delaware Valley.

The European "old residents" integrated with the new arrivals, though not without friction. Some earned money by selling land and provisions, or by serving as guides and interpreters. One local Swede, Captain Lasse Cock, in 1682 translated for the Indians and English, and traveled to the Susquehanna and Lehigh rivers as Penn's emissary. The Swedes, Dutch, and Finns continued to worship in their own congregations but became naturalized as English subjects; some served in the assembly and local government. The old residents made up a large part of the population in the Lower Counties (later Delaware), leading to conflict as the different interests of the Lower Counties and Pennsylvania became clear. In 1704, after two decades of wrangling, the three southern counties obtained their own separate Delaware assembly.

Pennsylvania got a boost from its late arrival on the colonial scene because its merchants could tap existing networks in the Atlantic economy. Substantial traders came from New York, the Chesapeake, and the West Indies, bringing their connections and capital to build breweries, tanneries, warehouses, wharves, and ships. Farmers found a market for wheat, livestock, and lumber in the West Indies. By 1700, Philadelphia had become a thriving port town, with 700 houses and more than 3,000 people.

But for William Penn, his colony was deeply disappointing: land sales reaped smaller profits than he had hoped and the costs of administering the colony soared. When purchasers refused to send him quitrents, he went more seriously into debt. Penn traveled to his colony twice, but stayed a total of only 4 years. Although the province became prosperous and quite successful as a tolerant, diverse society, he reckoned it a failure.

The Glorious Revolution and Its Aftermath

The founding of Pennsylvania coincided with the Crown's effort to tighten colonial government. Compared with the Spanish empire, English administration was a hodgepodge. The Privy Council at first appointed temporary committees to address colonial concerns, then in 1675 formed a permanent committee, the Lords of Trade, which met sporadically. Even after 1696, when the more formalized Board of Trade and Plantations was established, this body could gather information and give advice, but lacked authority to appoint colonial officials or enforce laws. These powers belonged to a host of governmental offices, including the secretary of state, the Treasury, and the War Office.

Dominion of New England

While experimenting with these committees, the Crown made other efforts to rein in the colonies. Most vulnerable was the Massachusetts Bay colony, both for its unrestrictive charter and the perceived intransigence of Puritan leaders. In 1678, Charles II required Massachusetts to send agents empowered to renegotiate the charter. He specifically wanted the New Englanders to comply with the Navigation Acts and apologize for having coined their own money. The colonists delayed action, though they sent regrets for having passed laws contrary to the laws of England. They offered to renounce any "except such as the repealing whereof will make us to renounce the professed cause of our first coming hither."

Impressed by neither the Puritans' arguments nor the speed of their response, the English government brought legal proceedings against the Massachusetts Bay Company for "usurping to be a body Politick" and

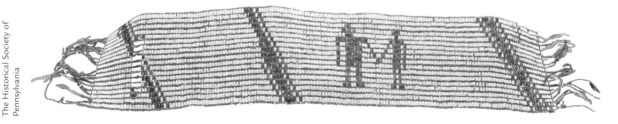

Wampum belt, which, according to legend, the Lenape gave to William Penn in 1682. It has become a symbol of Penn's efforts to preserve peace with the Indians of Pennsylvania.

Flashpoints | The Glorious Revolution in England, 1688-1689

The Glorious Revolution was more the climax of Parliament's struggle with the king throughout the seventeenth century than a singular affair. The events of 1688–1689 in England were bloodless, but could not have occurred without the violent conflict of the English Civil War four decades earlier, when King Charles I lost his head. During the 1640s and 1650s, Parliament first took control following the defeat of the monarchy and then, in disarray, named Oliver Cromwell solitary leader as Lord Protector of the Commonwealth.

After Cromwell died, Charles II (the son of Charles I) was restored to the throne. Many greeted the Restoration in 1660 with eagerness, hoping that the new king would bring stability and prosperity to their troubled country. Yet 25 years later, when Charles II died, turmoil seemed likely once again because he had failed to provide a legitimate heir. As a result the monarchy of the overwhelmingly Protestant nation passed to Charles's devoutly Catholic brother, James II, who quickly made himself an unpopular king.

James's desire to extend religious tolerance to England's Catholics, and his own status as an ardent member of the Church, displeased the country's Protestant majority. His belief in the absolute power of the monarchy and his disregard of Parliament angered many. Particularly irksome was his defiance of the Test Act passed by Parliament in 1673 that excluded Roman Catholics from office. James pushed appointment of Catholics to the Anglican Church, universities, army, and government. By raising a standing army of foreign mercenaries he alienated most English people.

James II at the time of his accession in 1685, by Godfrey Kneller. An opponent of representative government, James was quickly deposed in the Glorious Revolution of 1688.

By courtesy of the National Portrait Gallery, London

The last straw came when James and his wife successfully produced a legitimate heir to the throne. Members of both political factions, Whigs and Tories, disliking his policies and fearing the establishment of a Catholic dynasty, approached the Dutch prince William of Orange and his wife Mary, James' Protestant daughter, to assume the English throne. William and Mary possessed the several desirable qualities: staunch commitment to Protestantism and receptivity to parliamentary power. In late 1688, when William invaded England, James fled to France. Parliament then declared that James had abdicated his throne and installed William and Mary as monarchs.

The Glorious Revolution had a dramatic and long-lasting impact on the relationship between the English monarchy and Parliament. While James II had tried to reassert authoritarian rule, the 1689 Bill of Rights proclaimed that Parliament existed, not to submit to the king, but to represent the people of England. The Glorious Revolution thus brought the rise of Parliament, and fall of the monarchy, as the dominant governing power in England.

Questions for Reflection

1. From Chapter 3, how did James II's policies in the North American colonies compare with those in England?

2. How did the colonists in Massachusetts respond to his Dominion of New England?

3. In what ways did the rise of Parliament's power affect colonial governments in America?

revoked the charter in 1684. The colony's assembly, the General Court, was prohibited from meeting. In February 1685, before a royal governor could be appointed, Charles died and his brother James became king. James II quickly took advantage of events to move toward centralizing the colonies. With the Privy Council's consent, in 1685, he combined Massachusetts, New Hampshire, and Maine under the **Dominion of New England,** added Plymouth, Rhode Island, and Connecticut in 1686, and New York and New Jersey in 1688. Apparently, James's plan for the colonies was to create two large dominions, one north of the 40th degree of latitude (the approximate location of Philadelphia) and one to the south. These dominions would supersede colonial charters, eliminating the confusing diversity of laws and political structures. Representative government would end.

For Massachusetts Puritans, the Dominion of New England was a disaster. James's governor-general, **Sir Edmund Andros,** made sweeping changes that undercut the Puritan notion of a covenanted community. He levied taxes without the approval of a representative assembly, restricted the power of town meetings, mandated religious toleration, and confiscated a Boston church for use by Anglicans. Andros enforced the Navigation Acts, favored his own cronies over the Puritan elite in distributing patronage, required landowners to obtain new land titles from the Crown, demanded payment of quitrents, and took control of common lands. A number of colonists rebelled, refusing to pay taxes without a voice in their passage, but were jailed and fined.

Revolutions of 1689

Governor Andros managed to avoid serious revolt until the spring of 1689, when news of James's removal from the throne reached Massachusetts. The king's rule had been as heavy-handed in England as in the colonies. A Roman Catholic, he installed his friends in office and defied Parliament. Protestants feared James would make England a Catholic nation under authoritarian rule. Thus, parliamentary leaders forced him into exile in France, inviting his Protestant daughter Mary and her husband William of Orange, the leader of the Dutch, to take the throne. The Glorious Revolution, though bloodless, had long-lasting results in England: it permanently limited the king's power by establishing parliamentary control of taxation, supremacy of law, and autonomy of the courts.

On the morning of April 18, 1689, many of Boston's populace formed companies with the militia. Numbering more than 1,000 by afternoon, the insurgents, who included several Puritan ministers and some wealthy merchants, deposed the dominion government. They interpreted the revocation of the charter and James's illegal taxation and expropriation of lands as part of a

"popish plot" that Protestant New England must help destroy.

With the dominion gone, Plymouth, Rhode Island, and Connecticut reactivated their charters, but Massachusetts, which had lost its charter under Charles II, had to negotiate a new one. The colonists' arguments for the charter were based less on the old covenant theory than on the fundamentals of the Glorious Revolution, especially the right of English people to representative government. The resulting 1691 Massachusetts charter, which annexed Plymouth to the Bay colony, established a royal province with an elected assembly and a governor appointed by the king. The charter required freedom of worship and forbade religious restrictions on voting.

Revolutions also took place in New York and Maryland in the wake of James II's loss of power. New York fell into turmoil with news of William and Mary's ascent to the throne in England and the revolt in Boston. The reports unleashed opposition to Lieutenant Governor Francis Nicholson, who headed the dominion's government in New York. Again the struggle was defined in religious terms, as a crusade to destroy the "papist" threat.

In the city of New York, insurgents included merchants and artisans who had been denied economic privileges to trade and mill flour under James's government. In 1689, led by Jacob Leisler, a German-born merchant and militia captain, they forced Nicholson back to England and elected a Committee of Safety to replace James's council. When Henry Sloughter, the new governor appointed by William and Mary, arrived in 1691, however, he reinstalled James's councilors and executed Leisler for treason. Despite Leisler's early proclamation of the new monarchs in 1689, his enemies had better connections in London.

In Maryland, simmering resentment of Protestants against the Roman Catholic proprietor, Charles, Lord Baltimore, erupted in the summer of 1689. Baltimore's troubles intensified when his nephew, George Talbot, president of the provincial council, murdered the king's customs collector "with a dagger newly prepared and sharpened" aboard a royal ship. This event rocked the colony, so Baltimore sent a man he thought would provide strong leadership as governor, William Joseph, a Roman Catholic and adherent of James II. Upon arrival in 1688, Joseph proceeded to alienate Maryland's assemblymen, calling them adulterers and drunks. When he required them to renew their oaths of fidelity to the proprietor, they refused.

In July 1689, a handful of Maryland leaders formed the Protestant Association. Aroused by rumors that Catholics were plotting with the Indians to destroy the Protestants, the Association raised troops, defeating the proprietary government without a shot. The rebels obtained articles of surrender that banned Catholics from provincial offices; sent a message to William and Mary informing them of the takeover and requesting a Protestant government; and elected an assembly—the "Associators' Convention"—that ruled Maryland for the next two and one-half years.

The three provincial revolutions of 1689, in Massachusetts, New York, and Maryland, had similarities to England's Glorious Revolution in the relative absence of bloodshed and the recurring theme of "popish plots." They failed, however, to bring about permanent change in the constitutional relationship between England and its colonies. The provincials, lacking delegates in Parliament, continued to endure taxation and mercantilist regulation without their assent. The colonial revolts of 1689 resembled Bacon's Rebellion of 1676; they, too, mobilized out-of-power elites against those who controlled the colonial governments. In 1676, in Virginia, the insurgents had manipulated landless discontents by appealing to hatred against Native Americans as well as grievances against Berkeley's government. In 1689, the leading rebels employed the twin specters of authoritarianism and Catholicism, with rumors of impending French and Indian attack, to gain support from the populace.

Witchcraft in New England

In May 1692, Governor William Phips arrived in Boston Harbor with the new Massachusetts charter. He found the colony in disarray. Symptomatic of the Massachusetts state of affairs was the witchcraft hysteria that had erupted months earlier in Salem Village, a farming community north of Boston. Since 1675, the Bay colony had one crisis after another—King Philip's War, loss of the charter, Andros's dominion, the Revolution of 1689. Accompanying this turmoil were structural changes in the society, as traditional religious authority yielded to elites whose power rested on mercantile wealth. The Salem witch mania was a tragic holdover from a passing culture. Its fury was aggravated by the psychological reaction of traditionally minded folk to the new, more commercial, secular society of turn-of-century New England.

Belief in witchcraft was embedded in European and Anglo-American culture, though, ironically, it was losing force by the time of the Salem outbreak. The colonists, like their contemporaries in the Old World, believed that both God and Satan influenced everyday events. When something bad happened that they could not explain, people turned to supernatural explanations, including the possibility that an individual had compacted with the devil to do evil deeds. In England, witchcraft had been a capital offense since the time of Henry VIII in the

early sixteenth century; colonial governments followed suit in condemning those who gave "entertainment to Satan." Over the seventeenth century, the Puritan governments charged many more men and women with witchcraft than did other English colonies: 350 New Englanders were accused during the years 1620 to 1725. Of this number, the Salem episode accounted for almost 200. The southern and middle colonies tried few accused witches and executed none.

The witchcraft cases of Salem in 1691–1692 at first resembled those in other places and times. Several girls experimented with magic, aided by a slave woman, Tituba, and her husband, John, who together baked a "witch cake" of rye meal and urine, feeding it to a dog. The girls, who included 9-year-old Betty Parris, the daughter of Salem Village's minister, started having fits, presumably caused by witches. According to one report, the girls began "getting into holes, and creeping under chairs and stools, and to use sundry odd postures and antic gestures, uttering foolish, ridiculous speeches." Apparent possession spread to other village girls, leading to the arrest of three women as witches—Tituba; a poor beggar, Sarah Good; and an ailing elderly woman, Sarah Osborne.

These three alleged witches were the sort of people traditionally prosecuted for the crime. Generally, in witchcraft cases, the accused were women past menopause who in various ways deviated from expected roles. They had fewer children than the average woman their age. Lacking sons, a significant percentage of accused witches were heirs or potential heirs of estates, with greater economic autonomy than most New England women. Some claimed the power of a "cunning woman" to heal and foretell the future; many had been convicted of assaultive

Hanging of witches in England, c. 1650. No similar image exists of the Salem hangings.

DOING HISTORY

Documents from the Salem Witch Hunt

THE FOLLOWING DOCUMENTS shed light on the witch hysteria that struck Salem Village and surrounding towns in 1691–1692. Practicing witchcraft was a capital crime in Massachusetts and neighboring New England colonies; the laws were based on Exodus, "Thou shalt not suffer a witch to live," and other biblical passages. The second selection is from a tract by a former minister of Salem Village: Deodat Lawson, A Brief and True Narrative of Some Remarkable Passages Relating to Sundry Persons Afflicted by Witchcraft (Boston, 1692). The third excerpt is from a report of Goodwife Bridget Bishop's trial published by Cotton Mather in Wonders of the Invisible World *(Boston, 1692), which shows the grounds, including spectral evidence, on which Massachusetts courts convicted women and men of practicing witchcraft.*

Massachusetts Bay Colony Laws

1641: If any man or woman be a witch (that is hath or consulteth with a familiar spirit), they shall be put to death. Exodus 22:18; Leviticus 20:27; Deuteronomy 18:10.

1648: If any man or woman be a WITCH, that is, hath or consulteth with a familiar spirit, they shall be put to death. Exodus 22:18; Leviticus 20:27; Deuteronomy 18:10-11.

A Brief and True Narrative (1692), by Deodat Lawson

"On the nineteenth day of March last I went to Salem Village, and lodged at Nathaniel Ingersoll's near to the minister Mr. P[arris]'s house, and presently after, I came into my lodging Capt. Walcot's daughter Mary came . . . and spake to me, but, suddenly after as she stood by the door, was bitten, so that she cried out of her wrist, and looking on it with a candle, we saw apparently the marks of teeth both upper and lower set, on each side of her wrist.

In the beginning of the evening, I went to give Mr. P. a visit. When I was there, his kinswoman, Abigail Williams (about 12 years of age), had a grievous fit; she was at first hurried with violence to and fro in the room (though Mrs. Ingersoll, endeavored to hold her), sometimes making as if she would fly, stretching up her arms as high as she could, and crying *Whist, whist, whist!* several times; presently after she said there was Goodwife N[urse] and said, *Do you not see her? Why there she stands!* And she said Goodwife N. offered her the book, but she was resolved she would not take it, saying often, *I wont, I wont, I wont, take it, I do not know what book it is: I am sure it is none of God's book, it is the devil's book, for ought I know.* After that, she run to the fire, and begun to throw firebrands, about the house. . . ."

The Trial of Bridget Bishop, an Accused Witch, Salem, 1692

"I. She was indicted for bewitching of several persons in the neighborhood, the indictment being drawn up, according to the form in such cases usual. And pleading, not guilty, there were brought in several persons, who had long undergone many kinds of miseries, which were preternaturally inflicted, and generally ascribed unto a horrible witchcraft. There was little occasion to prove the witchcraft; it being evident and notorious to all beholders. Now to fix the witchcraft on the prisoner at the bar, the first thing used was, the testimony of the bewitched; whereof, several testified, that the shape of the prisoner did oftentimes very grievously pinch them, choke them, bite them, and afflict them; urging them to write their names in a book, which the said specter called, ours. One of them did further testify, that it was the shape of this prisoner, with another, which one day took her from her wheel, and carrying her to the riverside, threatened there to drown her, if she did not sign to the book mentioned; which yet she refused. Others of them did also testify, that the said shape, did in her threats, brag to them, that she had been the death of sundry persons, then by her named; that she had ridden a man, then likewise named. Another testified, the apparition of ghosts unto the specter of Bishop, crying out, you murdered us! About the truth whereof, there was in the matter of fact, but too much suspicion.

II. It was testified, that at the examination of the prisoner, before the magistrates, the bewitched were extremely tortured. If she did but cast her eyes on them, they were presently struck down. . . ."

III. There was testimony likewise brought in, that a man striking once at the place, where a bewitched person said, the shape of this Bishop stood, the bewitched cried out, that he had tore her coat, in the place then particularly specified; and the woman's coat, was found to be torn in that very place.

IV. One Deliverance Hobbs, who had confessed her being a witch, was now tormented by the specters, for her confession. And she now testified, that this Bishop, tempted her to sign the book again, and to deny what she had confessed. She affirmed, that it was the shape of this prisoner, which whipped her with iron rods, to compel her thereunto. And she affirmed, that this Bishop was at a general meeting of the witches, in a field at Salem Village and there partook of a diabolical sacrament, in bread and wine then administered!"

Source: David D. Hall, ed., *Witch-Hunting in Seventeenth-Century New England: A Documentary History*

1638–1692 (Boston: Northeastern University Press, 1991), 280–315.

Questions for Reflection

In seventeenth-century New England, practicing witchcraft was considered a dangerous crime. People believed that Satan could undermine their godly society by recruiting witches to his side.

1. According to the testimony of Bishop's accusers, what were the activities and goals of witches?

2. Do you believe that the Salem witchcraft hysteria of 1691–1692 provides insights into the culture of New England society? Why or why not?

Explore additional primary sources related to this chapter on the Wadsworth American History Resource Center or HistoryNOW websites:

http://history.wadsworth.com/rc/us
http://now.ilrn.com/ayers_etal3e

---

speech; and they were often involved in conflict within their families and neighborhoods. Revealingly, men of the same age group and troublesome character were much less likely to be identified as witches. These assertive old women went beyond the accepted bounds of female behavior and, as a result, became vulnerable to prosecution as witches.

While the Salem craze commenced in the time-worn pattern, it soon engulfed people of all social levels. Accusations descended upon prosperous church members, a minister, a wealthy shipowner, and several town officials. Hysteria spread from Salem to adjacent towns. More than three-quarters of the alleged witches were women; half of the accused men were their relations. Of those executed, 14 women and 5 men were hanged on "Witches Hill" and another man was crushed to death with stones. Only one of the dead was of high status—the Puritan minister George Burroughs. Governor Phips, supported by influential clergymen, had allowed the prosecutions to proceed after his arrival but put a stop to them when the accusers pointed to people at the highest levels of society, most significantly, to his own wife, Mary Phips. It had become clear, to many besides the governor, that the situation was out of control, that the evidence presented by the possessed was unreliable and quite likely the work of the devil. After Salem, witchcraft accusations no longer assumed its earlier importance in New England society.

Wars and Rivalry for North America

From 1680 to 1713, the Spanish, English, French, and many Indian nations battled for territory in North America (see Map 3.3). Despite the political and social turmoil of the 1680s and early 1690s, the English settlements were the largest and most dynamic European colonies on the continent. By the mid-1680s, New France had approximately 10,000 settlers, compared with more than 70,000 in New England alone. Spanish Florida was comprised chiefly of missions, run by 40 Franciscan priests, and the fortified town of St. Augustine, which held about 1,400

DOING HISTORY ONLINE

Salem Witchcraft

The accusations of witchcraft in Salem involved a number of social and cultural institutions for which the Massachusetts Bay colony and New England have become famous. Reading through the documents in this module, what institutions played a role in the crisis? What role did each play?

History⧖Now™   Visit HistoryNOW to access primary sources and exercises related to this topic: http://now.ilrn.com/ayers_etal3e

Hispanic, African, and Indian residents. Despite declining populations, many Native American peoples remained powerful in eastern North America, in particular the Five Nations of the Iroquois in New York.

In the late seventeenth century, the three primary areas of dispute on the continent were Florida and Guale (later Georgia), Louisiana and Texas, and Canada. Conflict occurred against the backdrop of two long European wars, the War of the League of Augsburg, 1689–1697, and the War of the Spanish Succession, 1702–1713 (respectively known as King William's War and Queen Anne's War to the English colonists).

Florida and Guale

Beginning in 1680, the English colonists of South Carolina decided to take advantage of smoldering unrest among the mission Indians of Guale and Florida to attack the Spanish colony. The Native Americans had rebelled against forced labor and efforts to stamp out their traditional religions. They had killed Spanish missionaries and destroyed property, but had not closed the missions altogether. The Carolinians raided Guale and Florida with no humanitarian motives to assist the Indians. In fact, a chief reason for attacking the Spanish missions was to capture Native Americans to sell as slaves in the

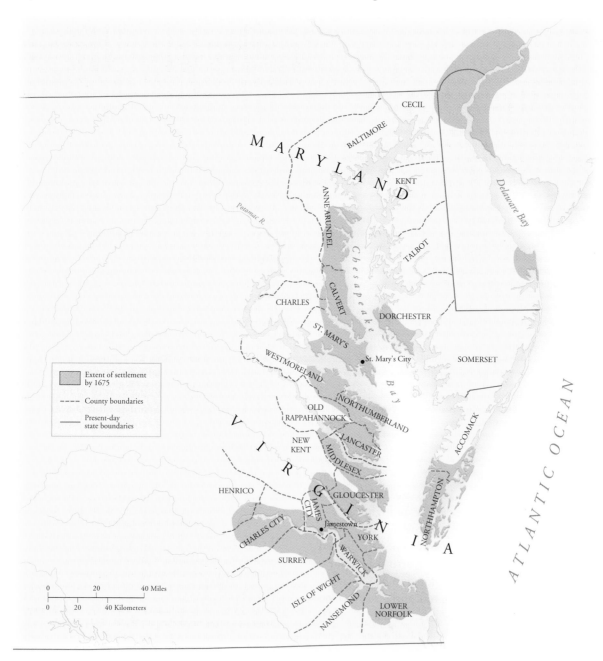

MAP 3.3 North America in 1700

Significant change had occurred in North America since the early 1600s. Along the Atlantic coast, the English now had settlements from Maine (part of Massachusetts) to South Carolina. As the English population expanded, Native Americans declined, with many groups absorbed into other nations, such as the Catawbas of South Carolina.

West Indies. The English also wanted to control the deerskin trade in the southeast.

By 1686, the Carolinians thrust the missionaries out of Guale. Then in 1704, during Queen Anne's War, an army under former Carolina governor James Moore crushed the missions in Apalachee. The Carolinians obtained help from their trading partners, the Yamassees, and from many of the mission Indians, who resented Spanish oppression. Moore's troops inflicted brutal torture, burning people alive. The surviving Apalachees dispersed, losing their identity as a nation. The Spanish retained St. Augustine and a fort they built at Pensacola in 1698, but lost control of Guale and most of Florida.

Louisiana and Texas

The Spanish erected their fort at Pensacola Bay in response to French efforts to establish a colony in Louisiana. At risk, the Spanish knew, were their silver mines in Mexico and domination of the Gulf of Mexico. In 1682, René Robert Cavelier, **Sieur de La Salle,** had explored the Mississippi River from New France to the gulf, naming the territory Louisiana in honor of King Louis XIV. La Salle sailed to France, then returned to set up a colony. However, he miscalculated the location of the Mississippi, instead building Fort St. Louis in Texas, near Matagorda Bay. The colony quickly dissolved from disease, loss of ships, and attacks by Karankawa Indians; in 1687, La Salle was murdered by his men.

The French incursion in the Gulf of Mexico inspired the Spanish to expand their settlements in the borderlands. In 1690, they founded missions among the Caddo people of eastern Texas and western Louisiana (see Map 3.4), from whom they took the Caddo word Tejas or Texas, meaning "friends." Three years later, when the Caddos blamed the friars for bringing smallpox, the friars fled. The Spanish abandoned Texas until the French once again entered the area.

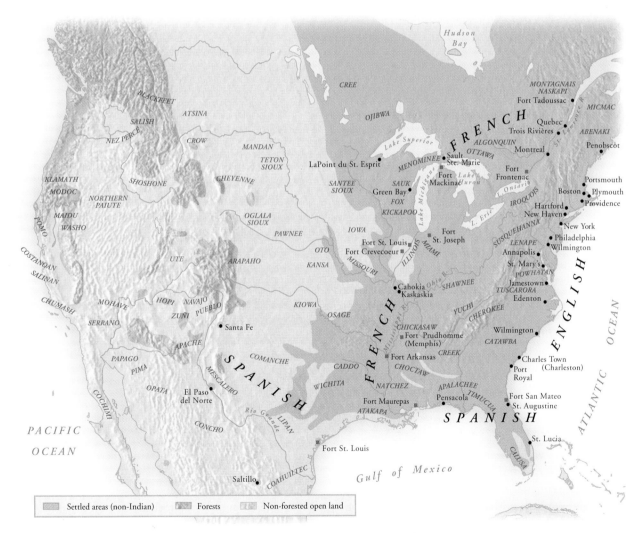

MAP 3.4 Southeastern North America in the Early Eighteenth Century
French colonies along the Mississippi River and Gulf Coast challenged Spanish dominance in the region. The Spanish settlements in Texas and Florida included missions and provided a defensive buffer for Mexican silver mines and shipping lanes off the Florida coast.

In 1699, Pierre LeMoyne, Sieur d'Iberville, resumed the French search for the mouth of the Mississippi River, which was difficult to locate in the muddy Mississippi Delta. Iberville found the river's mouth by accident, then built forts at Biloxi Bay and on the Mississippi to establish French possession. Spain might have forced the French out of Louisiana with quick action, but in 1700, the grandson of French King Louis XIV took the Spanish throne; the two nations became allies against the English, Dutch, and Austrians in the War of the Spanish Succession.

Although the French–Spanish alliance gave Louisiana a chance to develop without interference from New Spain, the colony grew slowly. In 1708, about 100 white soldiers and settlers lived in Louisiana. They obtained food, deerskins, and the right to occupy the land from local Native Americans by exchanging firearms and other goods. Relations between the French and Indians were not trouble-free, however. In 1715, for example, after Natchez Indians killed four French traders, the colonists literally demanded the assassins' heads. When the Natchez failed to execute all of the perpetrators, the French murdered Indian hostages and required the Natchez to accept a fortified trading post on their land.

Canada

Conflict developed in the north when the Iroquois confederation attacked New France to stop French fur trading in the Ohio Valley and Illinois. The Iroquois defeated New France in 1683, but war continued as the English, French, and Native Americans struggled over trade routes and territory. The outbreak of King William's War in 1689 fueled the contest, as the Five Nations attacked settlements in Canada, while the French and their Indian allies destroyed English frontier outposts from New York to Maine. New England troops took Port Royal in Acadia but failed to conquer Quebec. Though the European belligerents agreed in the Peace of Ryswick (1697) to return to prewar status in North America, the Canadians won an important victory over the Iroquois and their English allies. The Five Nations signed a neutrality treaty in 1701. Frustrated by New York's failure to provide reinforcements, they ended their alliance with the English. New France then developed trade, religious missions, and agricultural settlements in the Great Lakes and Illinois Territory.

The renewal of hostilities between the English and French in 1702, with Queen Anne's War, again brought raids on the New England frontier. In 1704, the Canadians and Native Americans attacked Deerfield, Massachusetts, burning houses and barns, killing inhabitants, and taking many captives. The English once again took Port Royal but called off an attack on Quebec when they lost 900 men in storms on the St. Lawrence River. This time,

DOING HISTORY ONLINE

The King's Letter, 1676
Read the letter in this module. What does this document reveal about relationships among the colonies and relationships between the colonies and the crown? What does the address in the last lines of this letter ("To His Royal Highness the Duke of York, or Commander in chief under him of the Colony of New York in the West Indies") indicate about the status of the British colonies in the Empire from the perspective of London?

History ⊠ Now™   Visit HistoryNOW to access primary sources and exercises related to this topic: http://now.ilrn.com/ayers_etal3e

however, the peace treaty gave the victory to England (which had joined with Scotland in 1707 to form Great Britain). In North America, the **Treaty of Utrecht** (1713) ceded Nova Scotia (formerly Acadia), Newfoundland, and control of the Hudson Bay territory to the British. Yet they had failed to oust France from North America.

The Entrenchment of Slavery in British America

Despite wars, rebellions, and witch hysteria, the most significant development in British North America during the late seventeenth and early eighteenth century was large-scale investment in enslaved Africans. The decisions of thousands of individual colonists to purchase men, women, and children who had been seized from their homelands in Africa left an indelible imprint on American society and culture. The slave buyers could not foretell the monumental effects of their actions. They responded to economic conditions: their need for workers, the declining availability of white servants, and the developing Atlantic slave trade.

Adopting Slavery

How could people who increasingly prized their own freedom—who had braved a treacherous ocean voyage to find opportunity in a new land—deprive other human beings of liberty, and often life itself? The answer lies in traditional English culture and the colonists' perceived economic needs.

The English, like other Europeans, believed that hierarchies existed in human society and, indeed, all of nature. Humans were superior to animals; Christians superior to "heathens." English language and culture also differentiated sharply between white and black, with whiteness suggesting purity and good, blackness imbued with filth and sin. The English compared their light skin with the Africans' darker brown color, judging the latter to be inferior. In African religion, social customs, dress, and political organization, the Europeans found serious deficiencies, just as they had found deficiencies among Native Americans. The people of sub-Saharan Africa, the English thought, were lower on the scale of humanity and could justifiably be enslaved. The example of the Portuguese, Spanish, and—most recently—the Dutch, who had fabricated the Atlantic slave trade over the previous two centuries, made the decision to buy Africans seem natural. The mainland English colonists could also look to their countrymen in the West Indies, where thousands of African slaves toiled in sugar fields, outnumbering whites.

Despite this cultural context, colonists viewed their investment in slaves as an economic decision. In Virginia and Maryland, planters purchased Africans because they needed large numbers of workers to grow tobacco. Chesapeake settlers had learned that Native Americans, who easily escaped enslavement and died in catastrophic numbers, would not fill their labor needs. White servants filled the gap until about 1675. Many young Englishmen, and fewer women, had willingly signed up to work for three or more years in return for passage and rights to 50 acres of land. In the last quarter of the century, however, the supply of English servants declined in Maryland and Virginia. Economic conditions improved in England, while good tobacco land became scarce. Bacon's Rebellion taught Chesapeake elites the danger of importing thousands of white servants under these circumstances. With the founding of the Carolinas, New Jersey, and Pennsylvania, where land was plentiful, servants had a wider range of options.

Chesapeake planters searching for an alternative labor supply turned to African slaves. Population figures for Virginia and Maryland demonstrate graphically the result of individual decisions. In 1660, only 900 blacks resided in the Chesapeake, some of whom had come as servants and were free. Two decades later, their number had grown to 4,300; by 1720, blacks comprised one-fifth of the population. A similar increase occurred in the Carolinas (primarily South Carolina), where 38 percent of the residents in 1720 were African slaves. The situation was different in New England, where only 2 percent of the population was enslaved, and in the Middle Colonies (New York, New Jersey, Pennsylvania, and Delaware), where about 1 resident in 10 suffered perpetual bondage.

The Slave Trade

English entry into the Atlantic slave trade helped spur the transition to an African workforce. Though smugglers like John Hawkins had interloped earlier in the Spanish trade, England officially became involved in selling human beings in 1663. Charles II granted a monopoly to supply captives to the English colonies first to the Company of Royal Adventurers, then in 1672 to the Royal African Company. When the companies could not meet the demand of labor-hungry colonists, smugglers got involved, so in 1698, the Crown abandoned the monopoly, opening the slave trade to any English merchant who wanted to participate. As a result, the supply of Africans in the English colonies soared and slave prices declined, thus encouraging colonists to invest in even more black labor.

The experience of enslavement and transit across the Atlantic Ocean was dehumanizing and perilous. Probably one-half of the persons sold into slavery died while still in Africa before transport or during the Atlantic passage. Approximately three-quarters of those taken to English North America came from the area of West Africa between Senegambia and the Bight of Biafra, with the remainder coming mostly from Angola. As European sea captains made successive trips to the coast, African traders had to reach farther and farther into the continent to find enough people to enslave. Some captives marched 500 miles or more to the sea in "coffles," the term given to the files of shackled prisoners. On the coast, they were confined in enclosures called barracoons, often exposed to the sun for long periods without adequate food and drink. When a ship arrived, according to a Dutch trader, Willem Bosman, in 1700, the Africans were lined up on shore,

> where, by our surgeons . . . they are thoroughly examined, even to the smallest member, and that naked both men and women, without the least distinction or modesty. Those that are approved as good, are set on one side; and the lame or faulty are set by as invalids, which are here called *mackrons:* these are such as are above five and thirty years old, or are maimed in the arms, legs or feet; have lost a tooth, are grey-haired, or have films over their eyes; as well as all those which are affected with any venereal distemper, or several other diseases.

For the Africans chosen for transport, the horror had only begun. The Europeans branded them with the insignia of the company—for example, slaves of the Royal African Company had their skins burned with the letters "DY," for James, duke of York. Then followed the voyage across the Atlantic, called the "**middle passage,**" which could take from three weeks to more than three months, depending upon the weather and destination. Ships normally carried rations for 3 months, so bad storms could mean starvation. Weather permitting, the captives spent their days on deck, the men in chains, the women and children unrestrained. At night, and around the clock if weather was bad, slaves occupied spaces about the size of coffins in the hold of the ship, where temperatures could reach extremely high levels. Disease was often rampant. Some slaves attempted suicide by jumping overboard or refusing to eat: the latter was so common that traders invested in a tool called the *speculum oris* to force open a person's mouth.

Africans also rebelled violently, attacking the white captain and crew, occasionally taking over the ship. Because they were unfamiliar with ocean navigation, mutineers had the best hope of success when the ship was still in African waters and large numbers could carry out the revolt, escaping to shore. When rebels failed, punishment was swift and brutal. The slave trader Bosman described an incident when a sea captain placed an extra anchor in the ship's hold. The enslaved Africans,

> unknown to any of the ship's crew, possessed themselves of a hammer, with which, in a short time they broke all their fetters in pieces upon the anchor:
>
> After this, they came above deck, and fell upon our men, some of whom they grievously wounded, and would certainly have mastered the ship, if a French and English ship had not very fortunately happened to lie by us; who perceiving by our firing a distressed-gun, that something was in disorder on board, immediately came to our assistance with shallops and men, and drove the slaves under deck: notwithstanding which, before all was appeased, about twenty of them were killed. The Portuguese have been more unlucky in this particular than we; for in four years they lost four ships in this manner.

Upon arrival in America, the Africans faced the ordeal of sale by auction or prearranged contract. They were stripped naked once again and examined for disease and physical defects. Because the greatest need was for strong field hands who would provide years of labor, plantation owners paid the highest prices for healthy young men in their prime. Buyers paid less for women, children, and older men. For both the Africans and their owners, the year following debarkation was most critical. During this period of seasoning, Africans endured serious illness and high mortality from the new disease environment.

Systems of Slavery in British North America

As more and more Africans arrived, colonial assemblies instituted black codes to define slavery and to control the black population. Before 1660, Maryland had officially sanctioned perpetual bondage, but Virginia moved more slowly. Enough flexibility existed in Virginia society to allow black servants to gain freedom, earn their livelihoods, and in some cases acquire land. In the 1660s, however, Virginia joined Maryland in enacting laws that recognized differences in the terms of white servants and African slaves. By law, slavery lasted a person's entire lifetime, descended from mother to child, and was the normal status of blacks, but never whites.

In the late seventeenth and early eighteenth century, both Virginia and Maryland created clearly articulated caste systems based on perceptions of race. A person's skin color denoted status: all Africans and their descendants encountered severe discrimination, whether enslaved or free. The Virginia assembly ruled that any master who killed a slave during punishment was not guilty of a felony. Conversely, no black person, slave or free, could strike a white, even in self-defense. Virginia lawmakers made emancipation difficult to obtain. Evolving black codes banned interracial marriage, forbade owners from releasing their slaves except in special cases, and restricted enslaved blacks from traveling without permission, marrying legally, holding property, testifying against whites, or congregating in groups. Over the course of the eighteenth century, other British colonies passed similar codes that ranged from fairly moderate New England laws to a harsh regime in Carolina, keyed in large part to the density of the black population.

In the life of an African slave, these laws had force, but more direct was the power of the master over work and family. To be a slave meant that someone else possessed your body and could command your daily activities. The owner chose your job; he or she decided whether your children would stay with you or be sold away. During off-hours, however, Africans generally maintained autonomy in religion, social customs, and family life.

The work Africans and native-born African Americans performed varied from one region to another. In the Chesapeake and Carolina, most slaves spent long hours planting, weeding, and harvesting tobacco, corn, and rice. A farm's production depended largely on the number of workers tending the crop. Over time, as the southern black population increased naturally and importation continued, the supply of labor became more plentiful. Plantation owners assigned slaves to different tasks, though most still raised the staple crop. Some men became drivers and artisans; some women served as nurses, cooks, and spinners. Both women and men performed domestic service. At the same time, female slaves were responsible for the household needs of their own families, including food preparation, laundry, and sewing.

Agricultural production in the Middle Colonies and New England centered on grains and livestock, which demanded less labor than tobacco or rice, so most parts of the northern countryside had relatively few slaves. Exceptions included New York and neighboring eastern New Jersey, which had difficulty attracting European immigrants; thus, well-to-do farmers purchased large numbers of Africans to work their land. The largest slaveholder in New Jersey was probably Colonel Lewis Morris of Shrewsbury, who employed more than 60 slaves at his plantation and ironworks. In Rhode Island's Narragansett region, some plantation owners held as many as 50 blacks. Most northern slaves lived in the port towns, however, where women worked as cooks and household servants, and men labored at crafts, domestic service, and as shipbuilders and sailors. Boston, New York, and Philadelphia merchants imported Africans as part of the West Indies trade. In New York City, blacks were about one-fifth of the population; in Boston and Philadelphia they comprised about one-tenth.

A source of comfort to slaves who had lost their African homelands and kin was to establish new families in America. Slaves achieved some autonomy from their masters by creating families and kinship networks. All knew, however, that owners could destroy loving relationships by selling away spouses, children, brothers, and sisters. The ability of blacks to form families changed over time and varied from one region to another. High mortality and a skewed sex ratio prevented many African-born men from marrying and having children. In the disease-ridden West Indies and northern cities like Philadelphia, mortality was so high that colonists had to keep importing Africans to avoid population decline. In the Chesapeake colonies, however, natural population growth began with the first generation of native-born slaves. African American women had more children than their African mothers, creating communities of slaves on large plantations. Whereas most of the first Africans dwelled in white households with just a few blacks, their offspring, known as "country-born" slaves, lived with parents, brothers, and sisters. The third generation lived with grandparents and cousins as well.

Resistance and Rebellion

For many slaves, family and kin helped to reduce their feelings of despair; for others nothing relieved the pain of lifetime bondage. Many resisted their masters' power by staging slowdowns, pretending illness, destroying crops and tools, committing theft, arson, assault, and murder. Newly arrived Africans were especially likely to rebel against their new status, often running away. Slaves who were sold away from their families frequently escaped to join them again. Men ran away in greater numbers than women, who, as mothers, found it difficult to escape with children in tow.

Although slaves in the English West Indies often rebelled, blacks in the mainland colonies rarely took the ultimate step of armed insurgency, primarily because they were so outnumbered by whites. Before 1713, West Indian blacks staged seven full-scale revolts; their large population made success seem possible. In Barbados, in 1675, for example, conspirators planned to take over the island, installing an elderly slave, Cuffee, as king. When whites got wind of the plot, they burned alive or beheaded 35 blacks. On the mainland, just one slave revolt occurred by the early 1700s. In New York City, in 1712, about 20 slaves set fire to a building, attacking the white men who came to extinguish it. Nine whites were killed; terror spread up and down the Atlantic coast. As in the case of later slave revolts and conspiracies, the revenge wreaked upon the black community surpassed any violence the rebels had committed. In the wake of the New York revolt, 13 slaves were hanged, 3 burned at the stake, 1 tortured on the wheel (an instrument used to stretch and disjoint its victims), and another starved to death in chains; 6 committed suicide to avoid such treatment.

Early Abolitionists

As slavery became entrenched in North America, a few white colonists questioned its morality. They feared slave rebellions and abhorred the violence needed to enslave Africans, transport them to the colonies, and keep them in bondage. Slavery was morally repugnant, they believed, because all humans are equal in the eyes of God. One of the American opponents of perpetual bondage was Samuel Sewall, a Boston judge, who wrote in 1700, "It is most certain that all Men, as they are the Sons of Adam . . . have equal Right unto Liberty, and all other outward Comforts of Life."

Quakers also spoke out publicly against the institution. Certainly not all Friends were abolitionists—in Pennsylvania and New Jersey before 1720 a large proportion of the Quaker elite owned slaves—but a few interpreted Quaker ideals to mean that human bondage reeked with sin. According to John Hepburn of New Jersey, for example, slavery violated the Golden Rule to do unto others as you wish others to do unto you. Whereas owners got rich without physical labor, wore fine-powdered wigs and greatcoats, and their wives and children similarly lived well, slaves endured beatings, wore rags, and slept in the ashes of the fire. In the context of rising importation throughout the colonies,

Enduring Issues Work, Ethnicity, and Gender in Early America

In early America, almost everyone worked. The few who did not work for a living were called gentlemen and gentlewomen—and many of those individuals had engaged in labor and cared for families on their way to the top of the social ladder. A higher percentage of early Americans did manual and domestic labor for their livelihood than residents of the United States today. A much smaller percentage went to college and had white-collar professions. And, of course, they lacked the many labor-saving devices such as computers, farm machinery, vacuum cleaners, washing machines, and prepared foods that streamline twenty-first-century careers and lifestyles.

The three illustrations here remind us of the wide variety of experience and status held by early Americans. The New York slave market, Virginia tobacco wharf, and newspaper advertisements for escaped servants and slaves testify that most African Americans lacked any choice of career; as slaves they were owned for life, expected to perform the work required by their owner, and could be separated from their families by sale. Bound white servants gave up their freedom for a period of time—generally up to 7 years and sometimes more. During their service, bound white laborers could not marry and had to follow their master's orders. They could look forward, however, to autonomy and some tools and clothing as freedom dues. Most free Euro-Americans and Indians also performed agricultural work, hunting, fishing, and domestic labor to feed their families and earn money to purchase cloth, metal goods, and other manufactured commodities. Their freedom, control of their own households, and

ability to set their own schedule differentiated free people from servants and slaves more than the actual work they performed.

In the colonial period, women's work roles differed from those of men and varied by class, ethnic origin, and individual need or opportunity. In most of eastern North America, except where the growing season was short such as in far northern New England, Indians had a mixed economy of agriculture, fishing, gathering, and hunting. Native American women were responsible for raising corn, beans, squash, and tobacco. They also gathered fruit and nuts, made clothing, took care of the children, built houses, and prepared meals, while men cleared land, fished, hunted, and defended the town from enemies. This gender division of labor was quite different from the English, who believed free women should avoid field work whenever possible.

English women were responsible for domestic work, whether they supervised servants and slaves or performed chores themselves. The house and yard was their workplace. Colonial women prepared and served meals, baked bread, cared for children, built fires, carried water and waste, cleaned the house and furnishings, washed and ironed laundry, gardened, tended poultry, milked cows, and made clothing and other household articles. Some women specialized in one or more activities and traded surplus production with neighbors and shopkeepers. For instance, one woman might specialize in weaving while another would raise medicinal herbs. Women in established rural communities were most

A 1730 depiction of the slave market in New York Harbor. In northern port cities, slaveholding was common at this time among upper class and middling families.

This illustration on a 1751 map drawn by Joshua Fry and Peter Jefferson, father of Thomas, demonstrates the significance of enslaved Africans in the Chesapeake labor force.

likely to produce textiles and dairy products. Women on the frontier were often so busy working with their husbands to build farms that they did not engage in additional activities such as spinning, weaving, or making cheese. Urban women were also less likely to pursue this kind of work because they lacked space for spinning wheels, looms, or livestock and could readily purchase manufactured goods and foodstuffs at the market.

Throughout the colonial period, Euro-American men controlled most occupations besides domestic work; they were the university-trained doctors, instructors in town schools and colleges, craftsmen, ministers, and farmers. Nevertheless, women filled many of the roles of these professions, including responsibility for a large part of medical care, delivering babies, treating wounds and illnesses, and administering drugs. Literate mothers taught their own children to read, and in New England towns some women opened dame schools for young girls and boys. Women throughout the provinces transmitted skills to young women in the "art, trade, and mystery" of housewifery or a specific craft such as weaving. In the ministry and law, women

lacked access to formal professional training, in college or apprenticeships. They did often assist their husbands in trades and took control after their deaths. Women thus worked in shoemaking, cabinetmaking, brewing, printing, and similar crafts; some ran shops, taverns, and inns.

On farms and plantations, where most families lived in colonial America, their work varied widely by class, ethnicity, and stage of settlement. A colonial farm woman generally expected to escape heavy fieldwork, except at harvest time, just as her husband would avoid household chores. However, many girls and women worked crops side-by-side with men. Seventeenth-century immigrants to Virginia and Maryland included female servants who paid for their transportation costs by tending tobacco for 4 or more years. In the middle colonies, servant women from England, Scotland, and Ireland spent at least part of their time laboring in the fields. German farm women, whether free or bound, customarily raised and harvested crops.

Enslaved African and Native American men and women had many occupations. In the Carolinas and the Chesapeake, which had labor-intensive staple crops, most enslaved people spent long hours performing hard physical labor raising rice, tobacco, and corn. Masters differentiated between men and women in the assignment of tasks other than ordinary field work. Men had the opportunity to become drivers and artisans. Slave women, probably after their prime age for field work, served as nurses, cooks, and spinners. Both women and men performed domestic service. Note in the illustration from the colonial newspaper, the advertisement for sale: "A Strong, healthy and handy Negro Woman, that has had the Small Pox and can do all sorts of Houshold Business, can speak English, and has been several years in the Country." This suggests qualities that were important to slave owners in cities such as Boston—ability to do all kinds of domestic work and familiarity with the language and region. At the same time, female slaves were responsible for the household needs of their own families, including laundry, food preparation, and sewing. In the northern colonies, enslaved men and women engaged in a wide variety of tasks, as these colonies lacked staple crops that consumed huge amounts of labor.

Colonial newspapers regularly published advertisements of enslaved Africans for sale and notices of escaped servants and slaves.

Questions for Reflection

1. How did the labor of men and women in early British America vary from one region of the colonies to another?

2. How has economic opportunity for women changed since the colonial period?

however, the protests of Sewall, Hepburn, and a few other critics had little effect.

Economic Development in the British Colonies

Despite differences in agriculture, labor, and commerce from one region to another, the mainland colonies were all part of the Atlantic economy, dominated by the staple crops of sugar, tobacco, and rice. The developing mercantile economies of New England and the mid-Atlantic region depended heavily on the slave system, because their chief market was providing food for the multitudes of blacks laboring on West Indies sugar plantations.

Northern Economies

Family farms and dependence on the sea characterized New England's economy. When its agriculture failed to provide a lucrative staple crop, traders turned to fishing and shipping. With rocky, generally poor soil and a cool climate, the region could not grow a profitable commercial crop like tobacco or sugar, so rural New England families raised livestock, wheat, rye, Indian corn, peas, other vegetables, and fruit. They ate most of what they produced—a fairly monotonous diet of brown bread, boiled or baked peas, boiled meat and vegetables, and dark beer or apple cider—within their families and communities.

Fishing and shipping developed as important industries during the seventeenth century. The New England fishers initially sold their catch, in return for manufactured goods such as shoes, textiles, glass, and metal products, to London merchants, who sent the fish to Spain, Portugal, and the Wine Islands, off the coast of Africa.

The fishing industry spurred the growth of maritime trade, as New England merchants recognized even greater profits to be made by trading directly with the Wine Islands and the West Indies. They formed partnerships among themselves and with English merchants, encouraging a local shipbuilding industry. The New Englanders exported fish, barrels, and other wood products. They imported wine, fruit, and salt from the Wine Islands, and rum, molasses, sugar, dyes, and other goods from the Caribbean. Soon, aided by the Navigation Acts, they were the chief carriers of goods along the North American coast, exchanging enslaved Africans and rum distilled from West Indies molasses for Pennsylvania wheat and livestock, Chesapeake tobacco, North Carolina tar and turpentine, and South Carolina rice. The credits they earned in shipping were as significant as the value of New England products sold in the trade.

The economy of the Middle Colonies resembled New England's in a number of ways but was much more prosperous agriculturally. With plenty of good land, farmers raised wheat and livestock commercially, purchasing servants and some slaves to supplement family labor. The region had two ports: one at New York City and the other at Philadelphia. Though neither city matched Boston in population or commercial importance before 1750, both quickly surpassed the Massachusetts seaport after that date. New York merchants maintained links with Amsterdam, the Dutch West Indies, and New Spain even after the English takeover in 1664. Philadelphia Quakers exploited their connections with Friends in other ports, especially in England and the West Indies.

Life in the Seaports

Maritime trade encouraged the development of port cities in the British provinces: Boston, New York, Philadelphia, and Charleston. Until 1750, merchants of Boston and other seaport towns in Massachusetts and Rhode Island dominated colonial trade. The ports thrived because they forged commercial links between farmers and external dealers, housing the markets through which imports and exports flowed. The maritime industry itself created demand for shipbuilders, suppliers of provisions, rope and sail makers, carters, dockworkers, and sailors.

Commercial growth brought social change, distinguishing an urban lifestyle from the countryside. Some merchants became fabulously wealthy from transatlantic and coastal trade. They spent their income conspicuously, building costly mansions, purchasing enslaved Africans as household servants, and wearing expensive clothes. They lived comfortably, with servants and slaves to do their menial chores. Other city dwellers were much less fortunate because they earned minimal wages or lacked employment. Port cities stimulated both affluence and dire poverty. They attracted many people who hoped to make their fortunes, or at least a decent living, but died with little more than the clothes on their backs. Maritime commerce frequently suffered disruption from war, bad weather, and economic downturns. Seamen and artisans, dependent on overseas trade, could expect little work during the winter, when few ships sailed. City folk were also at greater risk of death than those who lived in the country: some arriving ships spread smallpox and other diseases to the dense urban populations. The towns lacked adequate sanitation facilities, so garbage and waste cluttered streets, polluting the water supply.

A View of a Stage, also of manner of Fishing for, Curing & Drying of Cod at NEW FOUND LAND. A. The Habit of the Fishermen. B. The Line. C. The manner of Fishing. D. The Dressers of the Fish. E. The Trough into which they throw the Cod when dressed. F. Salt Boxes. G. The manner of carrying the Cod. H. The cleansing of the Cod. I. A Press to extract the Oyl from the Cods Liver. K. A Cask to receive the Water and Blood that comes from the Livers. L. another Cask to receive the Oyl. M. The manner of drying the Cod.

Cod fishing was an early industry of Europeans in the North Atlantic. This illustration depicts a dry fishery on the Newfoundland coast in which cod were lightly salted and dried for sale in southern Europe.

As trade expanded, sailors became an important segment of the labor force. They were a varied lot. Some went to sea only part-time, to supplement the income of their farms. Others chose seafaring as a career, joining a fraternity and dividing their time between shipboard and the taverns and boardinghouses of port towns throughout the Atlantic world. Some had no choice in the matter at all, for they were enslaved Africans whose masters purchased them to man the ships. Sailors led a difficult and dangerous life. Crews on ordinary merchant ships were small, so seamen worked long hours loading and unloading the ship, maintaining the rigging and sails, and pumping water from the bilge, an especially backbreaking job. The organization of labor on board was hierarchical, with power descending from the captain to mates, to specialists like ship carpenter and surgeon, to seamen. Discipline could be harsh. The crewmen had little hope of moving up through the ranks, for captains were generally from affluent families, often merchants and part-owners of their ships. Instead, the more common fate of an ordinary "Jack Tar" was early death or disability from shipwreck, combat with enemies or pirates, and such occupational hazards as falling overboard, broken bones, scurvy, rheumatism, and hernias, or the "bursted belly" as they called it.

When conditions on ship became insufferable, the seamen rebelled, sometimes deserting the ship at the next port. Most radically, men mutinied and, if successful, sometimes became pirates. They plundered merchant vessels and port towns, sharing the proceeds evenly among themselves, electing officers, and recruiting much larger crews than could be found on merchant ships. With 80 or more men on a pirate ship of average size, compared with 15 on a comparable merchant vessel, each had much less work to do. One pirate, Joseph Mansfield, admitted in 1722 that "the love of Drink and a Lazy Life" were "Stronger Motives with him than Gold."

Plantation Economies in the Chesapeake and South Carolina

From 1675 to 1720, tobacco remained king in Maryland and Virginia, and planters increasingly purchased enslaved Africans instead of white servants. The wealth of plantation owners grew with each child born to a slave mother. At the same time, the richest planters bought up the land of small farmers who found it difficult to compete with the slaveholders. The wealthiest man in early-eighteenth-century Virginia was Robert Carter of Lancaster County, called "King" Carter. As a slave trader and land speculator, he parlayed his inheritance of £1,000 and 1,000 acres into an estate of £10,000 in cash, 300,000 acres of land, and more than 700 slaves. Carter, with his relatives and friends, formed a tightly knit group of Chesapeake gentry.

In 1720, and throughout the eighteenth century, Chesapeake society was hierarchical. At the bottom of the social structure were African and country-born slaves, who owned no property and had little hope for freedom. Above them were the nonlandholding whites, perhaps 40 to 50 percent of white families, who rented land, owned a horse or two, some cows, a few pigs, tools, and some household goods, but rarely held bound servants or slaves. They lived in shanties and ate from wooden dishes rather than from pottery. Their incomes from tobacco were so meager that they had trouble paying taxes and rent. Often they were in debt to the local merchant-planter for needed manufactured goods, such as ammunition, fabric, shoes, and tools. Next higher were small landholders whose incomes allowed them to live more comfortably, with pottery, more furniture, and nicer (though still quite small) homes. If they owned several slaves, which few did before 1720, they worked alongside them in the fields and house.

In the upper 5 percent were the gentry, who owned many slaves, large acreages, and usually acted as merchants as well. They served as intermediaries for smaller planters, selling tobacco abroad and importing manufactured goods. As such, they became creditors of their poorer neighbors, who often owed them substantial debts. In Maryland and Virginia, the merchant-planters conducted trade without the development of port cities. Ships docked at their plantations along the many tributaries of the Chesapeake Bay to load casks of tobacco and unload imported goods. Tobacco required relatively little processing: workers dried the leaves in sheds, removed large fibers, and packed the tobacco in casks made by local coopers. Merchant-planters and rural artisans, including slaves, provided goods and services for the community without centralizing their activities in towns. Even the two capitals, Williamsburg and Annapolis, remained small throughout the colonial period.

Situated in a semitropical climate, South Carolina developed a plantation economy that was linked to, and in many ways resembled, the West Indies. Most early settlers, both black and white, came from the English colony of Barbados, where land was in short supply and almost entirely devoted to sugar cultivation. White planters claimed Carolina headrights, then sold corn, salt beef, salt pork, barrel staves, firewood, and Native American slaves to the islands. South Carolinians enslaved the Indians they captured in raids throughout the American Southeast and obtained them from native traders in exchange for guns, ammunition, and cloth. Native Americans also supplied deerskins, which found a ready market in England, though they were not valued quite so highly as Canadian furs.

As with the northern fur trade between Europeans and Indians, the Carolinians used English trade goods to establish alliances with native groups. Such major trading partners as the Yamassees, however, quickly discovered that white merchants used theft, violence, rum, and false weights to gain unfair advantage. In 1715, in league with the Creeks, the Yamassees attacked white settlements, nearly destroying the colony. The whites saved themselves by getting help from the Cherokees. The Yamassees and Creeks were defeated, their people killed, enslaved, or forced to migrate from the coastal area. White South Carolinians then expropriated their lands.

The settlers wanted the new territory because they had found an export that became much more lucrative than provisions, enslaved Indians, or deerskins. Planters had experimented with a variety of crops—tobacco, cotton, sugar, silk, wine grapes, and ginger—but rice proved most successful in the wet lowlands of the Carolina coast. Also significant were the skills in rice production that many Africans brought to America. Rice exports expanded rapidly in South Carolina, reaching 1.5 million pounds per year by 1710 and nearly 20 million pounds by 1730. The chief markets for rice were Europe and the West Indies. Carolinians first sent their crop directly to

Portugal, but in 1705 Parliament added rice to the list of enumerated products that had to be shipped to England first, taxes paid, and then reexported to Europe. The colonists argued that, in the case of southern Europe, this detour made their crop arrive too late for Lent, when much of it was consumed. In response, Parliament allowed South Carolina after 1731 to trade directly with Spain, Portugal, and Mediterranean Europe, but the larger share of the rice crop, which went to northern Europe, still required transit through Britain.

The conversion to rice transformed South Carolina society, affecting the black population with special force. Before planters adopted full-scale rice production, slaves had performed a variety of jobs in crafts, timber, livestock, and agriculture. Their workloads were moderate, especially in comparison with the West Indies. Rice monoculture changed this situation altogether, and planters imported thousands of Africans. In the coastal areas north and south of Charleston, blacks reached 70 percent of the population in the 1720s. With high importation and harsher working conditions, death rates surged. As in the Chesapeake, wealthy planters bought up neighboring farms while investing heavily in slaves. They created large rice plantations, worked by growing numbers of African slaves. Small planters moved to the periphery, where they raised grain and livestock for the rice district and the Caribbean. The rice planters found the Carolina lowlands isolated and unhealthy, so they left their plantations part of the year. However, the Carolinians supervised their plantations directly—unlike British West Indian sugar planters who fled to England, leaving management in the care of overseers.

Charleston, where the rice planters spent at least several weeks each year, was the fourth largest city in the British colonies. The port channeled the trade in provisions, deerskins, rice, slaves, and English manufactures. Charleston remained smaller than Boston, Philadelphia, and New York because British and New England shippers controlled its trade. Without a strong merchant community, the South Carolina seaport lacked the impetus for shipbuilding and associated crafts.

Conclusion

Between 1675 and 1720, the people of North America shed blood over territory, trade, and political autonomy. As English, French, and Spanish settlers expanded into new regions, they established commerce, but also spread smallpox and fostered conflict among the Indians. The Narragansetts and Wampanoags of New England waged a costly war in 1675–1676, while the Pueblos successfully, though temporarily, expelled the Spanish from New Mexico. Native Americans throughout the continent, weakened by disease and war, yielded to the Europeans. During Bacon's Rebellion and the Revolutions of 1689, governments in Virginia, Massachusetts, New York, and Maryland faced challenges from rival elites and their discontented, lower class allies.

By the turn of the eighteenth century, the Spanish reconquered New Mexico and infiltrated Texas, France moved into the Great Lakes region and Louisiana, and the English pushed out in many directions. To develop their economies, the British colonists imported Africans in large numbers. With the growth of plantation slave economies in the South and maritime commerce in the North, British North America developed distinctive regional characteristics. Yet in 1720, the Atlantic seaboard colonies had much in common: their settlement by enterprising men and women, regard for English rights of property and representation, and governance within the British imperial system. During the next half century, the importance of these commonalities would become clear.

The Chapter in Review

- The period between 1675 and 1720 was characterized by white expansion in North America. The French established settlements in the Great Lakes region and Louisiana, and Quaker William Penn founded the colony of Pennsylvania as a "holy experiment" in peaceful Native American–white relations.
- European expansion generated widespread Native American resistance to white encroachment and sparked armed conflicts such as King Philip's War and the Pueblo Revolt.

- The late seventeenth century was a time of great domestic turmoil; the colonies witnessed uprisings such as Bacon's Rebellion and violent witchcraft hysteria during the Salem witch trials.
- James II's assumption of the British throne sparked resistance to royal control and, in the case of Protestant colonists, against Catholic rule.
- The institution of slavery became entrenched in colonial society as trade in enslaved people and staple crops became central to both northern and southern economies.

Making Connections Across Chapters

LOOKING BACK

Chapter 3 looks at how the English colonies expanded in population between 1675 and 1720 by approximately 400 percent; they faced challenges from Native Americans, settler unrest, and efforts by the Crown to consolidate authority. At the same time the British provinces became full participants in the Atlantic trading system, importing thousands of enslaved Africans to work on southern plantations and in northern cities.

1. Why did New England Indians wage King Philip's War?

2. Why did Virginia freemen rise up in Bacon's Rebellion?

3. Were the revolutions of 1689 in Massachusetts, New York, and Maryland related events or should they be considered separate?

4. Why did the English North American colonists adopt slavery?

5. What was the impact of European wars on North America?

LOOKING AHEAD

Chapter 4 pursues the development of North America through the Seven Years' War, a time when the British colonies achieved greater political and economic maturity. Expansion of settlement put even greater pressure on Native Americans, and economic development entrenched slavery more firmly. Intellectual and religious trends such as the Enlightenment and Great Awakening crossed colonial boundaries, helping to create a shared American culture.

1. How did settler–Indian relations evolve after 1720?

2. How did Scots-Irish and German immigration in the eighteenth century compare with English settlement before 1700?

3. What was the impact of the Enlightenment on colonial thought and culture?

Recommended Readings

Demos, John. *The Unredeemed Captive: A Family Story from Early America* (1994). The evocative tale of a Puritan minister's daughter who was held captive by the Mohawks and refused to return home.

Hoffman, Ronald, et al., eds., *Through a Glass Darkly: Reflections on Personal Identity in Early America* (1997). Interesting essays relating individual biography to colonial development.

Innes, Stephen, ed. *Work and Labor in Early America* (1988). Insightful essays that demonstrate the range of labor systems and working conditions in the British colonies.

Jordan, Winthrop D. *White Over Black: American Attitudes Toward the Negro 1550–1812* (1968). Basic source on the construction of ideas about race in Anglo-America.

Karlsen, Carol F. *The Devil in the Shape of a Woman: Witchcraft in Colonial New England* (1987). Convincing argument about the significance of gender in witchcraft trials.

Lovejoy, David S. *The Glorious Revolution in America* (1972). The best introduction to the colonial revolutions of 1689.

McCusker, John J., and Menard, Russell R. *The Economy of British America 1607–1789, with Supplementary Bibliography* (1991). An excellent survey of economic and demographic development.

Thornton, John. *Africa and Africans in the Making of the Atlantic World, 1400–1680* (1998). An influential work demonstrating the impact of Africa and Africans on the slave trade and the development of colonial American societies.

Tomlins, Christopher L., and Mann, Bruce H., eds. *The Many Legalities of Early America* (2001). Pathbreaking essays that explore relationships among early Americans through the law.

Usner, Daniel H., Jr. *Indians, Settlers, and Slaves in a Frontier Exchange Economy: The Lower Mississippi Valley Before 1783* (1992). A history of colonial Louisiana and West Florida, focusing on relations between Europeans and Native Americans.

Identifications

Review your understanding of the following key terms, people, events, and dates for this chapter (these terms also appear in the Glossary at the end of the book):

Metacom
William Penn
Glorious Revolution
Half-Way Covenant
praying towns

Nathaniel Bacon
Dominion of New England
Sir Edmund Andros
Salem witch trials
Sieur de La Salle
Treaty of Utrecht
middle passage

Online Sources Guide

Use this listing to find online documents, images, interactive maps, simulations, and other resources related to this chapter.

American History Resource Center

http://history.wadsworth.com/rc/us

Selected Documents

William Penn's "Some Account of the Province of Pennsylvania" (1681)
William Penn's "A Further Account of the Province of Pennsylvania" (1685)

Reverend Solomon Stoddard's "Plan for Hunting Native Americans with Dogs"
John Wise's "Argument for Local Government Authority"
Jeremiah Drummer's "A Defence of the New England Charters"

Selected Images

Depiction of 1704 raid on Deerfield, Massachusetts
West African captives waiting to be sold
Massachusetts bill of credit, 1690

Simulation

Colonial Expansion (In this historical simulation you can choose to be with the Aztecs, Jamestown settlers, or Puritans/New England and make choices based on the circumstances and opportunities afforded.)

Document Exercises

1676 Bacon's Declaration

HistoryNOW

http://now.ilrn.com/ayers_etal3e

Primary Source Exercises

Royal Description of Nathaniel Bacon, c. 1676
The Declaration of the People, 1676
The King's Letter, 1676
Salem Witchcraft
Physical Examinations of Bridget Bishop, 1692

4

The Expansion of Colonial British America, 1720–1763

Benjamin Franklin Drawing Electricity from the Sky, by Benjamin West, c. 1805. Franklin's kite experiment demonstrating the electrical nature of lightning, along with his various activities promoting social welfare, placed him in the forefront of the American Enlightenment.

In 1721, smallpox hit Boston viciously, infecting about 6,000 residents and killing 844. Business stopped for several months, as almost every family battled the contagion. In many respects, this epidemic was unremarkable in the British American colonies: settlers and Native Americans alike had previously experienced the ravages of disease. But this time, one Puritan minister took an unprecedented step. Cotton Mather, who 30 years earlier had helped aggravate the Salem witch hysteria, encouraged a Boston doctor, Zabdiel Boylston, to test inoculation. Mather had learned from Onesimus, his African slave, and from English scientific papers, that inoculation was used in Africa and Turkey to prevent smallpox epidemics. An experiment would be risky, for the procedure involved introducing the smallpox virus into the body, thereby giving the person what was usually (but not always) a mild case of the disease. Many doctors, as well as much of Boston's populace, condemned the proposal. Nevertheless, Dr. Boylston inoculated about 250 persons over the course of a year. Those who submitted to the procedure had a much lower death rate than Bostonians who contracted the disease naturally.

Mather was far ahead of his time in advancing the theory that disease was caused by an invasion of the body by viruses, which he called invisible "worms." Significantly, it was a minister, rather than a physician or scientist, who advanced this hypothesis. During the eighteenth century, science lacked the rigid boundaries of complexity and specialization that would later separate it from other fields of intellectual endeavor. American theologians and philosophers, as well as doctors, naturalists, and astronomers, read the latest scientific literature from England and Europe. The great divide between science and religion did not yet exist. Like many other theologians, Mather understood epidemics as God's punishment for sin. But he also believed inoculation was a divine gift, that people should use any means available to combat disease.

Mather's support for inoculation has been called the greatest contribution to medicine by an American during the colonial period. Certainly it represented change. The **Enlightenment,** a new intellectual movement, was spreading from Britain to the colonies and bringing various changes. During the years 1720 to 1763, the British provinces experienced intellectual, religious, and social ferment as they continued to expand through North America. As new knowledge, beliefs, and consumer goods arrived from Europe, colonists from Maine to Georgia

Timeline

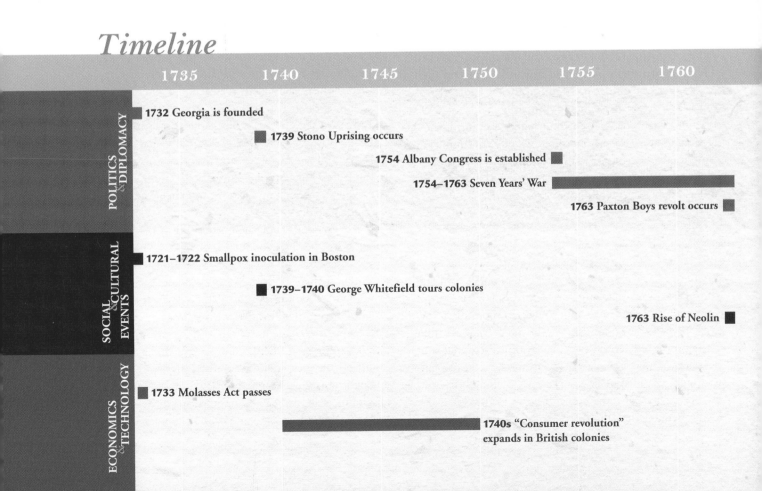

	1735	1740	1745	1750	1755	1760

POLITICS & DIPLOMACY

1732 Georgia is founded
1739 Stono Uprising occurs
1754 Albany Congress is established
1754–1763 Seven Years' War
1763 Paxton Boys revolt occurs

SOCIAL & CULTURAL EVENTS

1721–1722 Smallpox inoculation in Boston
1739–1740 George Whitefield tours colonies
1763 Rise of Neolin

ECONOMICS & TECHNOLOGY

1733 Molasses Act passes
1740s "Consumer revolution" expands in British colonies

(founded in 1732) increasingly lived within a common cultural framework. With rising wealth, colonial elites supported colleges and purchased books and luxury goods. This common culture had important ties to England, yet was not altogether English, for immigrants from Scotland, Ireland, and the continent of Europe, and slaves from Africa brought ideas and practices from their native lands. Immigration into the British colonies also promoted regional diversity, as the newcomers from Europe settled on the frontier from Pennsylvania to Georgia, and the numbers of enslaved Africans grew to 40 percent of the southern population. The Europeans came looking for land: when they set up farms in contested territory, they provoked conflicts with the Native Americans, French, and Spanish, resulting in a series of wars that lasted a quarter century. When the **Seven Years' War** ended in 1763, the British colonies took a great deal of pride in their contribution to the victory, offering it as evidence of their economic and political maturity within the empire.

Intellectual Trends in the Eighteenth Century

The willingness of Mather and Boylston to try inoculation showed important changes in the way people viewed their world. The Puritan clergyman's personal journey from witch hunter in 1692 to medical investigator in 1721 reflected the growing inclination to find natural rather than supernatural causes for unexplained events. The Enlightenment blossomed first in Europe and then in America, encompassing political theory and philosophy as well as science. Though primarily intellectual, the Enlightenment had far-reaching effects, inspiring new technology as well as concepts of human freedom. For Americans, its greatest significance lay in the acceptance of natural rights philosophy, which paved the way for independence and republican government.

Newton and Locke

In the late seventeenth century, two English theorists, Sir Isaac Newton and **John Locke,** had challenged traditional notions that humans had no role in determining their fate, that they could only trust in God to rule the universe. They confronted this older view without denying the existence of God. Newton discovered universal laws that predictably govern the motion of planets, moons, and comets, the motion of falling bodies on earth (gravity), and the ebb and flow of tides. His work demonstrated that the universe operated according to

fixed principles, which humans are capable of detecting and understanding. Locke built upon Newton's breakthrough in his *Essay Concerning Human Understanding* (1690). Locke argued against the accepted belief in innate knowledge, that infants are born with ideas implanted by God in their minds. He contended that all knowledge is gained by experience, not preordained at birth. Humans are born with the ability to learn, to use their acquired knowledge to benefit society.

Locke, and the Enlightenment thinkers he inspired, believed in freedom and the possibility of human progress, in the right of people to improve the conditions in which they live. Science, of course, was an important means of such improvement. The English philosopher also had a major impact on eighteenth-century politics, in particular providing a theoretical basis for the American Revolution and the Constitution. In *Two Treatises on Civil Government* (1690), he argued that humans, according to natural law, had rights to life, liberty, and property. By social contract, they formed governments to guarantee those rights. If a state failed in its obligation, the people had the duty to rebel and establish a new government.

Education in the British Colonies

Throughout British North America, formal education beyond basic reading, writing, and arithmetic was rare, so few read the works of Locke and Newton directly. After 1720, however, as newspapers became more available and reprinted articles from London, provincial readers gained greater familiarity with Enlightenment thought. Many colonists learned to read, though boys and girls spent much of their time learning the occupations they would pursue as adults. The availability of formal schooling varied widely by region, class, and gender. Nowhere did a system of universal, free, public education exist, though New England had some tax-supported schools. Everywhere, schools emphasized moral behavior and used religious texts.

New England made the greatest effort of the British colonies to educate its populace. In 1642, the Massachusetts legislature required parents and ministers to teach all children to read so they could obtain direct understanding of the Bible and the colony's laws. In 1647, the assemblymen ordered towns with at least 50 families to establish petty (elementary) schools, and those with 100 families to maintain Latin grammar (secondary) schools. Connecticut and Plymouth passed similar legislation. Though some towns ignored the laws, most New England children learned to read, whether from their parents, at the town school, or at dame schools, where women in

In Adam's Fall, We sinned all.	A · G	As runs the Glass, Man's Life doth pass.
Thy Life to mend, This Book attend.	B · H	My Book and Heart Shall never part.
The Cat doth play, And after slay.	C · I	Job feels the rod, Yet blesses God.
A Dog will bite A Thief at night.	D · K	King George the good, No Man of Blood.
An Eagle's Flight Is out of Sight.	E · L	The Lion bold, The Lamb doth hold.
The idle fool Is whipt at School.	F	The Moon gives Light In Time of Night.

The New England Primer, first published in the 1680s, taught children moral lessons along with their alphabet and spelling.

their homes taught young girls and boys for a fee. Writing was considered a separate skill and was less crucial for girls to learn. The percentage of New England females who could write and do arithmetic was significantly lower than for males. Girls, on the other hand, commonly learned sewing and knitting. Boys who planned to enter college attended grammar school from about age 7 to 14, studying Latin, elementary Greek, and sometimes Hebrew. Latin was necessary for the professions, including law, medicine, and the ministry.

South of New England, colonial governments did not require town schools. In the Middle Colonies, churches and private teachers offered instruction. Affluent Quaker and Anglican boys were most likely to obtain formal education, though after 1750 girls and poor boys, including African Americans, had better access to schools than previously. As in Massachusetts, females were much less likely to learn to write than males. In the Chesapeake, with dispersed settlement, neither Maryland nor Virginia had many schools. Upper-class boys and girls had private tutors, while middling families in some localities pooled their resources to establish schools. Overall, sons received much more instruction than daughters, and large numbers of poor whites obtained no education at all. Very few slaves learned to read and write, for owners thought these skills would breed discontent and enable slaves to forge passes, facilitating escape.

New England also surpassed other regions in higher education; the Puritans established Harvard College in Massachusetts in 1636 and Yale College in Connecticut in 1701. William and Mary, founded in Virginia in 1693, was the only other college in the British colonies before the 1740s. None of the colonial colleges admitted women. The Puritans intended Harvard to preserve classical learning and civilization, provide liberal education to the region's male elite, and ensure a supply of well-educated ministers. Harvard offered a curriculum of ethics, religion, logic, mathematics, Greek, Hebrew, rhetoric, and natural history (biology and geology). Most early graduates became clergymen; others went into medicine, public service, teaching, commerce, and agriculture.

Harvard alumni in Connecticut established Yale to provide advanced education closer to home. Yale had a tentative beginning but gained more stability by 1720, after receiving funds from Elihu Yale and about 800 volumes for its library, including the books of Locke, Newton, and other Enlightenment figures. The College of William and Mary also struggled at first. Chartered by the Crown to train Anglican clergy, educate young men in religion, and convert Native Americans, the school failed to offer college-level courses until the 1720s. Many elite families in the southern provinces continued to depend on private tutors, trips to Britain, and northern colleges to educate their sons.

In colonial America, children—especially girls—were less likely to learn to write than to read. Many people could not write their signatures so they made a mark on legal documents; then someone else wrote their name next to the mark.

The Growth of Science

After 1720, influenced by Scottish universities that quickly absorbed Enlightenment thinking into their curricula, American colleges expanded their coursework to include French, English literature, philosophy, and science. They offered mathematics and what was then called natural philosophy—astronomy, physics, and chemistry. The colleges hired some of their faculty from Scotland and purchased scientific apparatus, including telescopes, sextants, clocks, and orreries, which demonstrate the motion of planets and moons within the solar system.

American professors of natural philosophy were part of a larger community of scholars centered in the prestigious Royal Society of London, which published a journal, *Philosophical Transactions,* of the latest scientific ideas and knowledge. This transatlantic community included academics like John Winthrop of Harvard College, as well as largely self-taught men like **Benjamin Franklin** and John Bartram. More than 30 colonists belonged to the Royal Society. Scientists took from the Enlightenment a commitment to experiment and observe natural phenomena to obtain information that would lead to human progress. John Winthrop was the most renowned professor of natural philosophy in British America, with research interests in such wide-ranging subjects as sunspots, mathematics, earthquakes, and the weather. In 1761, Winthrop participated in an important international scientific effort to calculate the distance between the Earth and sun, made possible by the transit of the planet Venus across the face of the sun. Venus had last crossed the sun in 1639, when no useful measurements had been made. Winthrop journeyed to Newfoundland to observe the transit. His data, combined with observations from the Cape of Good Hope, were inexact, but 8 years later, scientists—including Winthrop—had another chance. This time, at least part of the transit could be viewed in the mainland British colonies. The stakes were high because another transit would not occur for 105 years. The data were again imprecise but when combined with measurements from around the globe yielded results very close to the accepted distance of 93 million miles between the Earth and sun.

Other colonists contributed to understanding the physical world. Perhaps best known for his diplomacy and political leadership during the Revolutionary era, Benjamin Franklin has become a symbol of the American Enlightenment for his efforts to improve society through science, inventions, and civic organizations. Franklin was born in Boston, ran away at age 17 from an apprenticeship with his older brother, and arrived in Philadelphia nearly penniless. He built a highly successful printing business, publishing a newspaper, books, and *Poor*

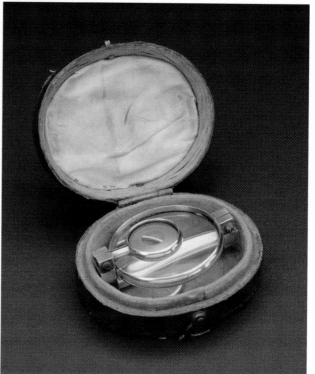

Pocket folding telescope in original case, England, 18th century.

Richard's Almanack, which gained a wide readership. Throughout his life, Franklin put the Enlightenment ideal of human progress into action. He founded a debating club to discuss politics, morals, and natural philosophy, and helped establish the first American lending library, a hospital, and the College of Philadelphia. Franklin's experiments in electricity yielded information about its properties, including the basic concepts of "plus" and "minus." His inventions, which applied scientific principles to improving daily life, included bifocal eyeglasses, the lightning rod, and an iron stove that was more efficient than colonial fireplaces.

John Bartram, also of Pennsylvania, was the most energetic of American naturalists, whose chief contribution to science was collecting specimens of New World plant life. In return for a yearly pension from the king and payment for seeds he sent to wealthy collectors in England, Bartram traveled all over the eastern seaboard searching for new plants and animals. His efforts greatly expanded botanical knowledge of the Western Hemisphere, for he sent specimens to such scholars as Carl Linnaeus, the Swedish author of the modern classification system.

Another prominent American naturalist was Cadwallader Colden, a Scot who immigrated to the colonies after receiving his medical degree. Like many well-educated doctors, Colden had broad interests in science.

While serving as surveyor-general and lieutenant-governor of New York, he collected and classified plants in the neighborhood of his estate. He corresponded with European botanists, sending them specimens and descriptions. As their demands became overwhelming, Colden taught his daughter, Jane, how to classify according to Linnaeus's scheme. Her accurate descriptions and drawings earned high praise from Linnaeus, Bartram, and other naturalists.

Changes in Medical Practice

Just as Colden and other university-trained doctors were interested in many scientific fields, the practice of medicine itself attracted people of widely different backgrounds. Medicine was beginning to develop as a profession. During the colonial period, men with formal medical education comprised a small proportion of the people who provided care for disease, physical injury, and childbirth. Having completed formal coursework abroad—the first medical school in the British colonies, located in Philadelphia, did not open until 1766—educated physicians were at the top of their profession and charged the highest fees. Consequently, they practiced primarily in the cities. Below them were men who learned their craft as apprentices; though they assumed the title of doctor in the colonies, they were actually akin to the surgeon-apothecaries of Great Britain. As surgeons, they performed emergency procedures such as setting bones, amputating limbs, and removing superficial tumors, but no major surgery. As apothecaries, they prepared and prescribed drugs for a variety of illnesses.

Female midwives traditionally attended at childbirth, treated the ill, and prescribed herbal remedies. Having learned their skills through informal apprenticeships and from witnessing the childbirths of neighbors and relatives, they received payment for their services. During the colonial period, childbirth was the province of women. As an expectant mother's labor began, she called together a group of women, presided over by the midwife, who assisted in the birth. In the early stages of her labor, the woman provided special refreshments, called "groaning beer" and "groaning cakes." The attendants helped her walk around and offered herbal teas or liquor to relieve the pain. In normal deliveries, the mother squatted on a "midwife's stool" or remained standing while supported by several women. If complications occurred, the midwife manipulated the infant manually but would not perform a Caesarean section. In the worst cases, the midwife had to kill the child; sometimes the mother died. Without modern antibiotics, women constantly faced the threat of infection during pregnancy and in the weeks following delivery.

In the last half of the eighteenth century, the practice of obstetrics changed. In 1762, Dr. William Shippen, Jr., returned from studying medicine in England and Scotland to give lectures in anatomy to Philadelphia midwives and doctors. Soon he accepted only male students. Shippen established an obstetrical practice of his own, quickly attracting well-to-do patients who expected a more elevated level of care than they received from midwives. Affluent urban women were convinced that the male physicians offered a better chance for a safe, less painful delivery. The doctors' obstetrical training and their use of opiates and instruments such as forceps spelled progress to these women, inducing them to abandon the traditional woman-dominated rituals of childbirth. That the new obstetrics brought improvement is doubtful. The male doctors, faced with taboos against observing the private parts of ladies, attended their clients in darkened rooms, with the women lying in bed under covers. The physicians also lacked the means to prevent infection; their use of bloodletting and opium could impede safe delivery. In any case, midwives continued to attend the great majority of women, those who lived in rural areas and the poor who could not afford the doctors' fees.

The Great Awakening

As Enlightenment ideas gained sway, many Protestant ministers embraced Christian rationalism, a theology that stressed moral, rational behavior and the free will of individuals to lead their lives and achieve salvation. Some rationalists spoke of an impersonal God who had long ago created the universe to operate according to natural laws, rather than a loving or angry God who controlled a person's daily life. For many, the rationalist religion was comforting, because it included in the church all who tried to live decent Christian lives, not just those who believed they were saved. To others, however, Christian rationalism was heretical, for it rejected the Calvinist belief that salvation came from grace, as the gift of God, and that people must be saved to be full members of the church.

From the 1720s to the 1760s, ministers from various denominations called for the renewal of these beliefs in a series of religious revivals, known as the **Great Awakening.** Several of the most important Awakeners brought the impetus for revival from Europe and Great Britain. Religious ferment convulsed British North America, spreading from the churches to threaten social and political authority.

Religious Diversity Before the Great Awakening

In 1720, the British provinces varied widely in religious and ethnic makeup. New England was the most homogeneous, for Massachusetts, New Hampshire, and Connecticut remained predominantly Puritan and of English descent. The established Puritan churches received tax support, but Anglicans, Baptists, and Quakers could also worship freely. Rhode Island, which still embraced the principles of religious liberty and separation of church and state, was home to various denominations, including Quakers, Baptists, and Separatists.

From their founding, the Middle Colonies offered an open door to people of various backgrounds. In the late seventeenth century, according to one report, residents of New York City spoke 18 different languages. In eastern New Jersey, Scottish Presbyterians, Dutch Reformed, New England Puritans, Baptists, and Quakers settled towns and plantations, and farther south, on both sides of the Delaware River, Native Americans, Dutch, Swedes, and Finns met the Quakers who accompanied William Penn. Philadelphia and its environs in the 1720s boasted organized meetings of many denominations. Though disputes occasionally arose between churches, the Quaker government upheld liberty of conscience throughout the colonial period.

With few towns in the Chesapeake, the established Anglican church suffered from southern rural conditions, and ministers in Virginia faced serious obstacles in meeting the spiritual needs of their scattered congregations. Only half of the Anglican churches had regular preachers. Few planters were interested in converting their African slaves, who kept—and passed on to their children—many traditional African beliefs. The colony's laws against nonconformity prevented most dissent, so only a few Presbyterians and Quakers worshipped openly. In Maryland, many Quakers and Roman Catholics retained their faith but suffered legal disabilities. The established Church of England in South Carolina was in better condition than in Virginia; some prosperous parishes could afford to pay their well-trained clergy adequately. Even so, Presbyterians, Baptists, Huguenots, and Quakers worshipped freely, for the proprietors had actively recruited dissenters to increase population and obtain their political support.

The Great Awakening, described in the following sections, shattered the existing church structure of the colonies, as congregations wakened to the teachings and vigorous preaching style of revivalist, or New Light, ministers. Religious diversity grew in provinces where established churches, with government support, dominated religious life—especially Puritan churches in Connecticut and Massachusetts, and the Anglican establishment in Virginia. As a result of the revivals, religious life in these colonies became more like that in Rhode Island, New York, and Pennsylvania.

Manuscript sermon of Great Awakening minister Jonathan Edwards, June 1741.

Early Revivals in the Middle Colonies and New England

In 1720, New Jersey felt the first stirrings of the Great Awakening, when Theodore Jacob Frelinghuysen emigrated from Holland to serve four churches in the Raritan Valley. He had been educated in Dutch Reformed pietism, which emphasized the importance of conversion and personal religious experience (or piety). Using an emotional, revivalist preaching style, he led many people to experience salvation. But Frelinghuysen created a split in the Dutch Reformed churches of New Jersey between his followers, who believed a person must experience God's saving grace before participating in church sacraments, and his opponents, who thought that a commitment to living a godly life was sufficient.

Next, revivals engulfed Presbyterian churches in New Jersey, as they adopted doctrines preached by Gilbert and John Tennent, the sons of William Tennent, a Scots-Irish immigrant and Presbyterian minister. The younger Tennents took pulpits in New Brunswick and Freehold, close to Frelinghuysen's congregations. Impressed by the Dutch Reformed pastor's style of preaching, they inspired revivals of their own. Meanwhile, in Neshaminy, Pennsylvania, the elder Tennent established a seminary, called the "Log College" by his critics, where many New Light ministers received training.

In Massachusetts, revivals began in 1734, when minister Jonathan Edwards of Northampton preached a series of sermons on salvation, inclining many of his parishioners to believe they were saved. They went through the process of self-judgment—first feeling despair as sinners who were damned to hell, then rejoicing in the conviction that God rescued them from this fate. Edwards wrote to a colleague that "this town never was so full of Love, nor so full of Joy, nor so full of distress as it has lately been." Over the next few years, the revival spread to other towns along the Connecticut River.

Revivalism Takes Fire

Beginning in 1739, the Great Awakening gained strength throughout the British mainland colonies after a young Anglican minister, George Whitefield, arrived from England to tour the Middle Colonies. Called the Grand Itinerant, he had a magnificent voice, ranging from a whisper to a roar, that could be heard by large crowds in fields and city streets. Benjamin Franklin calculated that 25,000 people could easily hear the spectacular preacher at one time.

Whitefield found adherents across denominational lines and among native-born Americans and immigrants alike. In 1740, Jonathan Edwards invited Whitefield to Northampton, prompting the itinerant to travel through New England, where he attracted crowds as large as 8,000 in Boston. Other New Light ministers followed, including Gilbert Tennent and James Davenport, a Puritan preacher of Southold, Long Island.

Davenport took the Awakening to extremes, harshly attacking other pastors as "unconverted." In 1743, he instigated the burning of books written by well-known clergymen; a year later he repented this excess.

The full force of the Awakening hit the south later than New England and the Middle Atlantic. During the 1740s, Presbyterian missionaries—men who received their education at Tennent's Log College—set up churches on the southern frontier. The new settlements were a fertile field for the revivalists because few regular clergy had migrated west. The more explosive Baptist revivals began in the 1750s, when itinerants traveled through Virginia and North Carolina making converts and forming churches. The Baptists believed that individuals should be saved before they were baptized. With their emotional religious style and challenge to the Anglican establishment in Virginia, they appealed particularly to ordinary white farm families and enslaved African Americans. Followers called each other "Sister" and "Brother," whether slave or free, affluent or poor. They refused to attend their local parish services and condemned many aspects of gentry culture, including horseracing, cockfights, elegant dress, and entertaining on Sunday. Lacking formal churches, Baptists met in fields and homes. The ministry was open to all, even women and slaves, with no requirement for college training.

The Awakening's Impact

The revivals proved to be socially divisive; many communities split into two groups, the "New Lights" and the "Old Lights." The style of most New Light preachers was to give impassioned, extemporaneous sermons that contrasted dramatically with the closely reasoned sermons of their opponents, the rationalist Old Light ministers. New Lights believed that salvation was more important than religious training; they required a "saved" ministry, with a dynamic preaching style. Congregations responded by fainting, shrieking, and shedding tears. Old Light clergymen, who defended their advanced education in theology, Greek, Hebrew, and ethics, resented accusations that they were unsaved. In turn, they charged the revivalists with being unlearned.

© The Granger Collection, New York

George Whitefield, the itinerant English evangelist, had a spellbinding effect on his listeners, as portrayed here by John Wollaston.

As congregations broke apart, bitter disputes ensued over church property and tax support, spilling what had begun as a religious controversy into the courts and politics. Where strong established churches existed—as in Massachusetts, Connecticut, and Virginia—the New Lights challenged political as well as religious authority. In response, the Connecticut Assembly, for example, passed an Anti-Itinerancy Act, which made it illegal for a clergyman to preach in another's parish without his permission and repealed the 1708 law permitting religious dissent.

Higher education in the British colonies also felt the flames of revivalistic fervor. Yale College was at the center of the intense religious and political battles in Connecticut. When the New Haven church separated, a large number of students, many of them studying for the ministry, followed the New Lights. They skipped classes to attend revivals, challenged Yale's curriculum, and questioned whether their teachers were saved. To suppress the student rebellion, Thomas Clap, head of the college, obtained permission from the Connecticut Assembly to expel any student who attended New Light services. Clap's opposition to the Awakening was not permanent, however, for by 1753 he himself had become a New Light. As in many congregations, people eventually found ways to heal the bitterness and division that the Great Awakening had caused.

A more lasting effect of the revivals was the founding of new colleges. Until the mid-1740s, only Harvard, William and Mary, and Yale—all with ties to established churches—existed in the British colonies. The revivals created a need for different ministerial training. Between 1746 and 1769, the revivalists founded the College of New Jersey (now Princeton), the College of Rhode Island (Brown), Queen's College (Rutgers) in New Jersey, and Dartmouth College in New Hampshire. Anglicans established King's College (Columbia) in New York City, and a group of civic leaders, headed by Benjamin Franklin,

started the College of Philadelphia (University of Pennsylvania) on a nonsectarian basis. Though each of these new schools except the College of Philadelphia was tied to a specific religious denomination, they all accepted young men of various faiths. These new colleges taught traditional subjects, but also adopted the new curricula in mathematics, science, and modern languages.

Cultural Diversity and Expansion

Between 1720 and 1760, the population of British North America grew from 472,000 to 1,600,000. Much of this growth came from natural increase, but new arrivals also spurred population growth, as thousands of Germans and Scots-Irish immigrated, and slave traders continued to import blacks.

The newcomers brought ideas, religious beliefs, skills, and ways of life that significantly altered the cultural mix of the British colonies. Some played important roles in spreading the Enlightenment; others helped start the Great Awakening. The immigrants from the European continent and the British Isles sought a new beginning in "the best poor man's country": many disembarked in the Middle Colonies, traveling west to settle the backcountry from Pennsylvania south through the Shenandoah Valley to the Carolinas. Others went directly to Georgia, which reformers started in 1732 as a haven for the poor. The population explosion and demand for new lands brought the British colonists face to face with the Spanish in Florida, the French in Canada and the Ohio Valley, and Native Americans all along the frontier.

German and Scots-Irish Immigrants

More than 100,000 Germans left their homelands for America during the century after 1683; most of them immigrated between 1727 and 1756. Some were forced out by religious persecution, oppressive regulations, and war; others sought economic opportunity. Promoters called "newlanders" told Germans of cheap fertile land and mild government in the British colonies. Many immigrants paid their own passage. Those who could not signed on as "redemptioners," the equivalent of indentured servants, whose labor would be sold for a number of years upon arrival. Immigrants went to ports from New York to Georgia, with most entering the Delaware Valley. Some Germans remained in Philadelphia, but the majority headed for the Pennsylvania hinterland and south through the backcountry of Maryland, Virginia, and the Carolinas (see Map 4.1).

DOING HISTORY ONLINE

The Enlightenment and the Great Awakening

Based on your reading of all the documents in this module, in what ways do you think the Enlightenment and the Great Awakening complement each other? Do you see them as antagonistic toward each other at all? How?

History ⊠ Now™   Visit HistoryNOW to access primary sources and exercises related to this topic: http://now.ilrn.com/ayers_etal3e

Courtesy, Winterthur Museum

The baptismal certificate is an example of German American *Fraktur,* or documents illustrated with color designs and drawings.

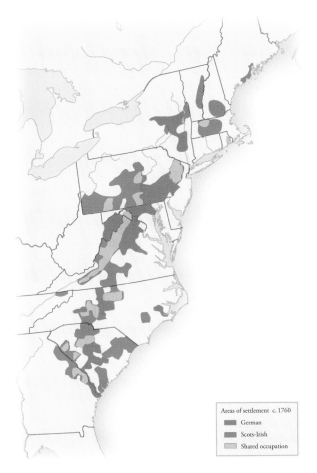

Areas of settlement c. 1760
- German
- Scots-Irish
- Shared occupation

MAP 4.1 German and Scots-Irish Settlements in Colonial British America, c. 1760

Germans and Scots-Irish were relative latecomers in colonial British America, so they established farms outside the first English settlements. Many entered ports on the Delaware River, moved north and west in Pennsylvania, then south through western Maryland, the Shenandoah Valley of Virginia, and North and South Carolina.

German-speaking immigrants found the freedom they sought in North America, congregating in distinct communities, building separate churches and schools, and maintaining German language and culture. Pennsylvania was the heart of German America, as the colony's religious freedom allowed a multitude of sects and churches to flourish—the Mennonites, Amish, Brethren, Moravians, Schwenkfelders, Lutheran, and Reformed.

Cultural exchange between the Germans and English enriched American society. German churches installed organs and introduced the sophisticated choral music of their homelands. The printer Christopher Saur reprinted German hymnals along with his German-language newspaper and almanac. Congregations founded schools in which children learned both German and English. Immigrants retained the old tongue in their churches and homes, but used English in business, the courts, and politics.

German American decorative arts proliferated by the 1740s, in house ornaments, furniture, and elaborately illustrated documents, such as marriage certificates, with gothic *Fraktur* lettering.

German farm women did much heavier fieldwork than most English wives but otherwise played a similar role in maintaining domestic culture. Germans favored the more efficient European stoves over English fireplaces, and pewter over tinware. In diet, they ate relatively little meat and preferred coffee to tea. But like their English neighbors, German women served as midwives and dispensed herbal remedies.

Though some German immigrants engaged in politics and law, most remained uninvolved in government during the colonial period. As non-British immigrants with little wealth, they needed time to become naturalized, learn the language and political culture, and establish themselves economically. As exiles from persecution, high taxes, and war, Germans were grateful for the high degree of freedom that they found in the new land.

Large numbers of Scots, Scots-Irish, and Irish Catholics also came during the eighteenth century, settling in New York, Pennsylvania, Delaware, western Maryland, and the southern backcountry. Most were Ulster Scots (or Scots-Irish as they were called in America), Presbyterians whose families had migrated during the 1600s from Scotland to northern Ireland in search of economic opportunity. There they had combined tenant farming and weaving until the early eighteenth century, when their leases expired. Because landlords raised rents exorbitantly, many Ulster Scots left with their families for the colonies. The first large wave of immigrants departed during 1717–1718; poor harvests and downturns in the linen industry impelled successive groups toward America.

In the colonies, the Scots-Irish achieved a reputation as tough defenders of the frontier. As relatively late arrivals, they had to stake out farms on the edges of existing white settlements. The combination of agriculture and linen manufacture was a distinctive contribution of the Ulster Scots to the colonial economy. As frontier inhabitants, the Scots-Irish came into frequent contact with Native Americans, often with tragic results. The new settlers often marked out their farms on Indian hunting lands without negotiating a sale. One Pennsylvania frontiersman, not recognizing the Indians' rights, echoed the early Puritans when he argued that it was contrary to "the laws of God and nature, that so much land should be idle, while so many Christians wanted it to labor on, and to raise their bread."

The Founding of Georgia

The last of the British mainland colonies, Georgia lured many German and Scots-Irish immigrants, as well as Scots and English. Animated by Enlightenment ideals of human progress and freedom, **James Oglethorpe** and John Viscount Percival, members of the Associates of the Late Doctor Bray, a philanthropic society, sought a charter for the colony. They were convinced that something had to be done to help the poor. They also argued that the settlement could serve as a buffer between Spanish Florida and South Carolina. The English had craved the region since the late seventeenth century when Carolinians destroyed the Spanish missions of Guale. George II granted the charter, placing control of the colony in the hands of trustees, or proprietors, who could neither receive financial benefits from the province nor own land within its bounds.

The double function of Georgia as a haven for the poor and a military outpost shaped the terms under which settlers immigrated. The trustees intended to create a peaceful, moral society of small farmers in which all except indentured servants worked for themselves. The proprietors wanted to avoid duplicating lowland South Carolina, where large plantation owners lived off the toil of their slaves. The Georgia Trustees, led by Oglethorpe, set three significant policies: they prohibited importation of hard liquor, banned slaveholding, and limited land ownership to 500 acres or less. Each free male immigrant was granted land at no charge, but no one could buy or sell real estate, and only men could inherit land. The trustees hoped to keep Georgia as a refuge for small farmers who, coincidentally, would defend the southern frontier.

In February 1733, the ship *Anne* with approximately 100 passengers arrived at a site on the Savannah River. Here they built the first town, Savannah, on a high bluff overlooking the river. Oglethorpe purchased land from the Native Americans and pledged to prevent price gouging in trade, a significant complaint of the Indians against South Carolina merchants. He established alliances with Lower Creeks, Cherokees, and Chickasaws against Spanish Florida, not least because English traders offered better merchandise than their rivals.

Many settlers in Georgia believed that the prohibitions on liquor, land sales, and slavery were unreasonable, but they could do little to change the colony's direction because they lacked a representative assembly. The embargo on rum, a major Caribbean commodity, prevented expansion of trade with the West Indies, a ready market for their abundant lumber. The bans on slavery and large landholdings were also unpopular with many settlers, who coveted the grander lifestyle of planters north of the Savannah River, in South Carolina.

In consequence, Georgia grew slowly, as some settlers left almost immediately. The trustees gradually recognized their failure, allowing the importation of rum in 1742, and land sales and slavery in 1750. Preparing to turn the colony over to the Crown, in 1751 they called together Georgia's first elected assembly, which obtained legislative powers 3 years later when the royal government took control. The Georgia population swelled as South Carolinians migrated across the Savannah River, transforming Georgia into a slave society. By 1773, the province had 33,000 inhabitants, of whom 45 percent were enslaved blacks.

Despite its halting start before 1750, Georgia attracted settlers of a variety of nationalities and religions. The colony tapped the eighteenth-century flow of European immigrants, including Spanish and German Jews and German-speaking Lutherans. One of the Lutheran ministers described their satisfaction with the new land: "Every year God gives them what they need. And since they have been able to earn something apart from agriculture, through the mills which have been built and in many other ways, they have managed rather well with God's blessing, and have led a calm and quiet life of blessedness and honesty." Another group of German Protestants, the Moravians, were less content in Georgia, where they hoped to convert the Native Americans. Led by Count Nikolaus Ludwig von Zinzendorf, they arrived in 1735 and were gone 5 years later, because as pacifists, Moravian men could not serve in the militia. When the threat of Spanish invasion intensified in the late 1730s, most of the Moravians departed for Pennsylvania, which required no military service.

The Growth of the African American Population

The failure of the trustees to create a free society in Georgia was symptomatic of the entrenchment of slavery in America. Like the Germans and Scots-Irish, Africans

DOING HISTORY

Slave Resistance

THE FOLLOWING THREE documents provide examples of the ways in which enslaved Africans and Native Americans grappled for freedom. Venture Smith, who was born in West Africa, captured at age six by an enemy army, then sold as a slave in Rhode Island, published his autobiography in 1798 after he had purchased freedom for himself and his family. The excerpt below graphically depicts his attempt to escape and the consequences of his failure. The second document is a newspaper advertisement placed by a slave owner for two escaped slaves: a Native American man and African American woman. The third is a report of the Stono Rebellion of 1741, excerpted from the Georgia colonial records.

Venture Smith Resists Slavery

". . . After I had lived with my master thirteen years, being then about twenty-two years old, I married Meg, a slave of his who was about my own age. My master owned a certain Irishman, named Heddy, who about that time formed a plan of secretly leaving his master. After he had long had this plan in meditation, he suggested it to me. At first I cast a deaf ear to it, and rebuked Heddy for harboring in his mind such a rash undertaking. But after he had persuaded and much enchanted me with the prospect of gaining my freedom by such a method, I at length agreed to accompany him. Heddy next inveigled two of his fellow-servants to accompany us. The place to which we designed to go was the Mississippi. Our next business was to lay in a sufficient store of provisions for our voyage. We privately collected out of our master's store, six great old cheeses, two firkins of butter, and one batch of new bread. When we had gathered all our own clothes and some more, we took them all about midnight and went to the water side. We stole our master's boat, embarked, and then directed our course for the Mississippi River.

We mutually confederated not to betray or desert one another on pain of death. We first steered our course for Montauk Point, the east end of Long Island. After our arrival there, we landed, and Heddy and I made an incursion into the island after fresh water. . . . [Later, Heddy] went directly to the boat, stole all the clothes in it, and then travelled away for East Hampton. . . . I advertised Heddy and sent two men in search of him. They pursued and overtook him at Southampton and returned him to the boat. I then thought it might afford some chance for my freedom, or at least be a palliation for my running away, to return Heddy immediately to his master, and inform him that I was induced to go away by Heddy's address. Accordingly, I set off with him and the rest of my companions for my master's, and arrived there without any difficulty. I informed my master that Heddy was the ringleader of our revolt, and that he had used us ill. He immediately put Heddy into custody, and myself and companions were well received and went to work as usual.

Not a long time passed after that before Heddy was sent by my master to New London jail. At the close of that year I was sold to a Thomas Stanton, and had to be separated from my wife and one daughter, who was about one month old."

Source: Venture Smith, *A Narrative of the Life and Adventures of Venture, a Native of Africa: But Resident above Sixty Years in the United States of America* (New London, CT: C. Holt, 1798).

Escaped Slave Advertisement, October 11, 1739

"RUN away on the 20th of Aug. past, from the Subscriber near the Head of Bush River in Baltimore County, Maryland, an Indian Man, named Pompey, aged about 24 Years, of middle Stature, well set, speaks nothing but English, very much scarrified on the Body with whipping in Barbadoes; he had on his Neck when he went away an Iron Collar, but its suppos'd he has got it off. Also a lusty Negro Woman named Pegg, aged about 22 Years, this Country born and speaks plain English; They carried away with them a striped Duffle Blanket, an old Ticken Jacket and Breeches with black Buttonholes, a Felt Hat near new, a coarse linnen Bag, a new white Linsey woolsey Petticoat and other coarse Negro Apparel.

Whoever secures the said Indian and Negro so that their Master may have them again, shall have Five Pounds Reward and reasonable Charges paid by Richard Ruff."

Source: Billy G. Smith and Richard Wojtowicz, *Blacks Who Stole Themselves: Advertisements for Runaways in the Pennsylvania Gazette, 1728–1790* (Philadelphia: University of Pennsylvania Press, 1989), 19.

Stono Rebellion, South Carolina, 1741

"On the 9th day of September last being Sunday which is the day the Planters allow them to work for themselves, Some Angola Negroes assembled, to the number of Twenty; and one who was called Jemmy was their Captain, they suprized a Warehouse belonging to Mr. Hutchenson at a place called Stonehow [*sic*]; they there killed Mr. Robert Bathurst, and Mr. Gibbs, plundered the House and took a pretty many small Arms and Powder, which were there for Sale. Next they plundered and burnt Mr. Godfrey's house, and killed him, his Daughter and Son. They then turned back and marched Southward along Pons Pons, which is the Road through Georgia to [St.] Augustine, they passed Mr. Wallace's Tavern towards day break, and said they would not hurt him, for he was a good Man and kind to his Slaves, but they broke open and plundered Mr. Lemy's House, and killed him, his wife and Child. They marched on towards Mr. Rose's resolving to kill him; but he was saved by a Negroe, who having hid him went out and pacified the others. Several Negroes joyned them, they calling out Liberty, marched on with Colours displayed, and two Drums beating, pursuing all the white people they met with, and killing Man Woman and Child when they could come up to them. Collonel Bull Lieutenant Governour of South Carolina, who was then riding along the Road, discovered them, was pursued, and with much difficulty escaped & raised the Countrey. . . . "

Source: Allen D. Candler, ed., *The Colonial Records of the State of Georgia* (Atlanta: Charles P. Byrd, 1913), 22:233–234.

Questions for Reflection

The first of these documents was written by a former slave, while the escaped slave advertisement and report of the Stono Rebellion were penned by Euro-Americans.

1. What do we learn from Venture Smith's autobiography that is not available in the other documents?

2. What can we find out from the newspaper advertisement that Smith does not reveal?

3. What details included in the Stono account suggest the beliefs and goals of the rebels?

Explore additional primary sources related to this chapter on the Wadsworth American History Resource Center or HistoryNOW websites:

http://history.wadsworth.com /rc/us
http://now.ilrn.com/ayers_etal3e

---

helped diversify the American population and shape its culture. Though the number of African Americans grew naturally in many places, slave traders imported more than 200,000 people between 1720 and the Revolution, most from West and Central Africa. In 1750, blacks comprised one-fifth of the population of the mainland colonies, including about 40 percent in the Chesapeake and the Lower South (see Map 4.2).

As the number of African Americans increased and slave societies matured, blacks created patterns of community, work, and culture. Extended kinship networks structured community life on large plantations, and even in places where slaves lived in small households, such as in northern cities, family ties remained paramount. Blacks were most successful in perpetuating African language and customs in regions where they were most numerous, particularly the South Carolina low country and, later, Georgia. Because they came from hundreds of societies in Africa, with many different cultural attributes, they had difficulty keeping traditional ways intact. They melded African and European forms together, and in the process, influenced evolving mainstream cultures, especially in the South.

The opportunity of slaves to engage in independent activities varied with the amount of time they had to spend working for their master. In South Carolina, blacks labored by the task; each slave received a certain amount of work to perform each day—a field to hoe, thread to spin, a fence to build. Those who completed their assignments quickly had time to raise their own crops and livestock. Consequently, Carolina slaves participated in trade, selling their production at the "Negro market" in Charleston on Sundays. As in Africa, women were responsible for marketing the family's goods. In the Chesapeake, most slaves on plantations labored for a specified number of hours rather than by the task. They

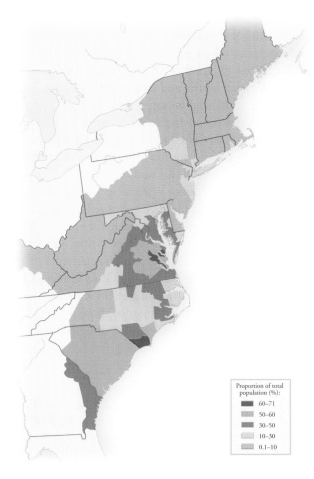

MAP 4.2 **African American Population in Colonial British America, c. 1760**

A much higher concentration of enslaved African Americans lived in colonies south of Pennsylvania. Notice, however, that the percentage of slaves in parts of New York and New Jersey was as high as in portions of the Chesapeake region and North Carolina. Uniform data for South Carolina mask the fact that the population of African Americans was much larger along the seacoast than in the upcountry.

Proportion of total population (%):
- 60–71
- 50–60
- 30–50
- 10–30
- 0.1–10

planted, weeded, or harvested in gangs until the overseer told them to stop. As a result, they had little time to work for themselves.

The persistence of African culture was conspicuous in language, food, music, dance, and religion. Some newly arrived Africans knew Dutch, Spanish, Portuguese, French, or English from former contacts in Africa or the West Indies, but to communicate with other slaves and with Europeans, most adopted Creole speech, a combination of English and African languages. In the Lower South, for instance, the Creole tongue known as Gullah evolved from English and various languages from southern Nigeria, the Gold Coast, Angola, and Senegambia. African Americans retained black dialect from Creole. For example, most blacks used the word *buckra,* from the African word meaning "he who governs," to refer to white men.

Africans also influenced white speech patterns, when white children and immigrants sometimes adopted African American dialect. One British traveler complained that plantation owners allowed "their children . . . to prowl amongst the young Negroes, which insensibly causes them to imbibe their manners and broken speech." Some African words became part of American vocabulary, including cola, yam, goober (peanut), and toting (carrying) a package.

Blacks contributed to the food and material culture of British America, popularizing new foods such as okra, melons, and bananas. They made clay pipes, pottery, and baskets with African designs, and carved eating utensils, chairs, and other useful objects from wood. They built houses on African models rather than European. In music, they introduced the use of percussion instruments—cymbals, tambourines, and drums—to British military bands. Although masters discouraged Africans from drumming because of the potential to call others to revolt, whites enjoyed the music of black fiddlers. Slaves helped create the Virginia "jig," a fusion of African and European elements, accompanied by banjos and fiddles.

Along with whites, during the Great Awakening, Africans shaped the forms of worship in southern Baptist churches. Blacks retained traditional African concepts of the hereafter, where the deceased reunited with ancestors, combining these beliefs with European views of heaven. Funerals remained important to African Americans throughout the colonies; mourners buried the dead facing Africa, with traditional rituals, music, and dance. In Philadelphia, for example, the blacks' burial ground was the focus of community activities where they gathered on Sundays and holidays, "dancing after the manner of their several nations in Africa, and speaking and singing in their native dialects." Blacks also passed down African medical practice, a combination of physical and psychological treatment including magic. More African American women than men were doctors, practicing midwifery as well as nursing and providing cures.

Despite cultural exchange and indications of human understanding, the antagonism and economic exploitation inherent in slavery poisoned relationships among whites and blacks. Whites believed that African Americans were an inferior race; masters used their power in the slave system to control their human property with harsh punishments. Nevertheless, blacks refused to accept their subordinate position; increasing numbers ran away or were truant for weeks at a time.

Some enslaved Africans took more violent means, killing their masters or setting fire to fields and homes. In 1739, a group of more than 50 bondmen revolted near the Stono River in South Carolina. For most of a day, they marched with drums and banners from one plantation to another, killing about 20 whites. When armed planters defeated the rebels in battle, some of the slaves regrouped and headed for St. Augustine, Florida. But the South Carolina militia pursued the insurgents, putting to death everyone suspected of being involved. The **Stono Uprising** sent shock waves throughout the American colonies. The South Carolina legislature enacted a harsh slave code in an effort to prevent future revolts and limited slave importation for a decade. Most of the core group who planned the Stono Rebellion were African-born slaves, who hoped to escape to Florida, where Spanish authorities offered them religious sanctuary and freedom. By 1740, about 100 former Carolina slaves had built the village of Gracia Real de Santa Teresa de Mose, called Mose, two miles north of St. Augustine.

During the eighteenth century, newly arrived Africans, often called "salt-water Negroes," were more likely to rebel or run away than Creole, or "country-born," slaves. With Native Americans and runaway white servants, escaped slaves created maroon societies in frontier areas. They farmed, raised livestock, hunted, and fished. In the Great Dismal Swamp, on the North Carolina–Virginia border, communities numbering perhaps 2,000 people took refuge from colonial authorities. The Dismal Swamp settlements grew from small groups of Native Americans from Virginia to include Indians and whites from the Carolinas and increasing numbers of escaped Africans.

Native American Worlds in the Mid-Eighteenth Century

As the British colonies grew, Native Americans chose strategies to maintain their communities and cultures. Those who remained within the British provinces were called by white Americans "settlement Indians," "domestic Indians," or "little Tribes." Many lived among Euro-Americans and worked as servants, slaves, day laborers, mariners, artisans, and tenant farmers, assimilating some parts of English culture but rejecting others. Others lived on remnants of traditional lands, such as the Mashpees in Massachusetts, Lenapes (or Delawares) in New Jersey, and Catawbas in South Carolina. They continued to hunt, fish, gather berries and wood, and raise corn while also trading with neighboring whites. Indians peddled venison and turkeys to the colonists or crafted baskets and brooms for sale. The Lenapes of central New Jersey farmed parcels of land through the eighteenth century: they pursued their traditional seasonal economy by hunting in Pennsylvania, fishing at the Jersey shore, and gathering berries and wood for baskets in the Pine Barrens.

Dr. Alexander Hamilton, a recent immigrant from Scotland, recorded many encounters with Indians in 1744 as he traveled through the settlements from Maryland to Maine. The Native Americans he met varied greatly in status, from an Indian sachem who had established himself as a wealthy planter to those on the margins, who tried to hold on to native traditions within an alien culture. In Rhode Island, he approached the large plantation of

> an Indian King named George . . . upon which he has many tennants and has, of his own, a good stock of horses and other cattle. The King lives after the English mode. His subjects have lost their own government policy and laws and are servants or vassals to the English here. His queen goes in a high modish dress in her silks, hoops, stays, and dresses like an English woman. He educates his children to the belles letters and is himself a very complaisant mannerly man. We pay'd him a visit, and he treated us with a glass of good wine.

During worship in a Boston church, Hamilton sat near several Native Americans. He met an Indian at Princeton who saluted him with "How' s't ni tap" and, in New York, watched "about ten Indians fishing for oysters . . . stark naked" near his tavern. Although most native people who stayed in white settled areas had given up political autonomy, they had not surrendered all of their traditions. Many spoke English in addition to their native language but did not learn to read and write.

The Great Awakening made a significant impact on many Indians within colonial settlements who had long resisted Christianity. The dynamic preaching of New Light ministers, who welcomed enthusiastic response from their listeners, was attractive to Native Americans who had retained traditional rituals and dance. The Society in Scotland for Propagating Christian Knowledge, a group of Presbyterian ministers and laymen, supported missions in the Middle Colonies, particularly that of Reverend David Brainerd and, after his death in 1747, his brother Reverend John Brainerd. David Brainerd was expelled from Yale College because he had joined the

Flashpoints | Walking Purchase of 1737

In the 1730s, Pennsylvania's proprietors, Thomas and John Penn, plotted with their agent James Logan to acquire the lands in eastern Pennsylvania still held by the Lenape Indians (called Delawares by Euro-Americans). These sons of the colony's founder, William Penn, wanted to expand their control so that they could sell land to new immigrants from Great Britain and Europe. Logan located a copy of an old deed dated 1686—not an original signed document—that he claimed as proof that the Lenapes had sold all lands that could be walked in a day and a half north from the previous boundary (see map). Nutimus, a Lenape sachem, denied that the deed (which was questionable in any case) included his land between Tohickon Creek and the Lehigh River. Nutimus and other Lenape leaders, including Tishcohan and Lapowinsa, lost the argument when the more powerful Iroquois of New York sided with the Penns.

James Logan then made preparations to fulfill the requirement of the "deed" that the distance must be measured by a "walk" of a day and a half. He directed men to clear a path in advance. On the morning of September 19, 1737, three young settlers, Solomon Jennings, James Yeats, and Edward Marshall, accompanied by two Lenape observers, walked quickly north from Wrightstown. They covered much more territory than Nutimus, Lapowinsa, and others expected, crossing the Lehigh River in the afternoon. The Lenape standard for walking off distances for deeds assumed a more leisurely pace, uncleared terrain, and frequent breaks. When the Indian observers abandoned the

group in disgust, Lapowinsa refused to send others, objecting that the Penns had "got all the best land, and they might go to the Devil for the bad." The "walkers" rested overnight near Lapowinsa's town of Hock-endauqua. The next day just one of the men, Edward Marshall, reached a point near present-day Jim Thorpe, completing 64 miles within a total of 18 hours. James Logan drew the boundary there, extending the line northeast to the Delaware River to maximize the "purchase," and set off an area 10 square miles near Hock-endauqua as a reservation named Indian Tract Manor.

This land fraud contributed to the outrage of Lenapes who were forced west to the Susque-hanna and Ohio valleys. In the 1740s and 1750s, the Penns sold lands in the Walking Purchase area to the rising numbers of Scots-Irish and German settlers. While some Lenapes stayed in the region, many left and in 1755 were among the Native Americans who allied with the French to fight British colonists during the Seven Years' War.

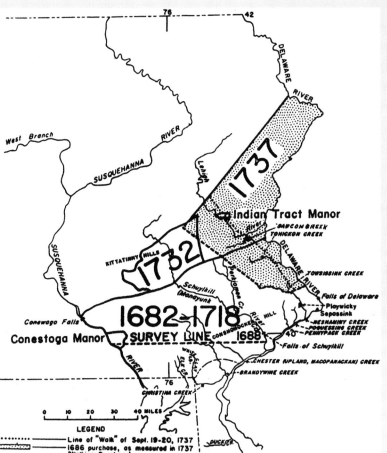

From Indians in Pennsylvania *by Paul A.W. Wallace, published by the Pennsylvania Historical and Museum Commission.*

Diagram map of the "Walking Purchase" of September 19–20, 1737, which defrauded the Lenapes of their remaining lands in eastern Pennsylvania.

Questions for Reflection

1. Prior to 1730, how did relations between the Lenapes and the government of Pennsylvania compare with Native American-European relations in New England and the Chesapeake?

2. Some Pennsylvania Quakers considered the Walking Purchase a denial of William Penn's legacy. Why?

3. What was the long-term impact of the Walking Purchase?

The Lenape leader Teedyuscung, by William Sauts Netamux'we Bock. In this drawing, Teedyuscung's combination of a Euro-American coat and vest and Indian hairstyle and jewelry reflects his attempt to bridge cultures.

New Lights and became a missionary to Indians in Pennsylvania and New Jersey. With crucial assistance from his Lenape interpreter, Moses (Tunda) Tatamy, he inspired a revival at Crossweeksung in central New Jersey. The community soon outgrew its limited space, so Brainerd encouraged the Lenapes to move to another site, where he attempted to create a New England-style praying town. Although the Indians attended the Presbyterian church and school, they did not give up their seasonal economy of hunting, fishing, and gathering as the Brainerds hoped. Other New Jersey Lenapes joined the Moravian missions near Bethlehem, Pennsylvania, but many continued to resist Christianity altogether.

Native Americans who intended to preserve their political independence moved west, a strategy that worked temporarily. From 1660 to the 1740s, for example, Iro-

quois, Shawnees, and Lenapes relocated in the eastern part of the Ohio Valley, from Pennsylvania and western New York to west-central Ohio. Wyandots inhabited the lands to the west, at Sandusky and near the French fort at Detroit. Some of the Lenapes left the east as a result of the "Walking Purchase" of 1737, when two of William Penn's sons, the proprietors, used an alleged 1686 deed to cheat the Indians out of their territory on the Pennsylvania side of the Delaware River. The deed, of which only a copy survived, ceded lands as far as a man could walk in one and a half days. Coerced by an alliance between the Penns and the Iroquois, the Lenapes agreed to comply. The Penns sent runners in relay to cover more than 60 miles of land in a day and a half, a deception the Lenapes could not fail to remember; in 1754, with the outbreak of war on the Pennsylvania frontier, many sought revenge.

The Ohio Valley became the focus of conflict in the 1740s as the British and French competed for trade. Following the Lenapes and Shawnees west, some Pennsylvania traders took up residence in the multiethnic towns such as Chiningue (or Logstown), where Iroquois, Lenapes, Shawnees, Ottawas, and other Indians lived. The Ohio Valley, as one Indian leader said, was "a country in between" the English and the French, unfortunately a country that the Europeans craved. From 1754 to 1814, the Native Americans fought the British and Americans to keep their lands and native religions, forging pan-Indian alliances to meet the Anglo threat.

Wars for Empire

For a quarter century beginning in 1739, the British colonies took part in conflicts between Great Britain and Spain, France, and Native Americans. The War of Jenkins' Ear (1739–1744) against Spain; King George's War (1744–1748) against France; the Seven Years' War (1754–1763), also called the **French and Indian War** in the colonies; and the Indian war for autonomy in the Ohio Valley (1763–1765) all required British colonists to participate more actively in defending the empire.

The Southern Frontier

The colonies along the southern tier—British South Carolina and Georgia, Spanish Florida, French Louisiana, and Spanish Texas and New Mexico—competed for trade with Native Americans and control of territory (see Map 4.3). Except for war between Georgia and Florida in the early 1740s, the most important battles along the southern rim were commercial, a competition the British traders often won because they had

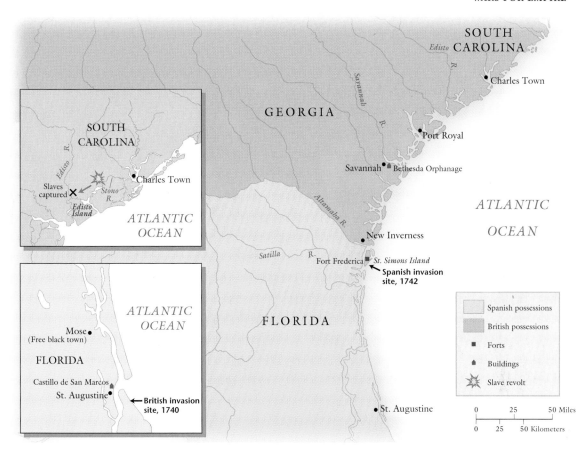

MAP 4.3 War of Jenkins' Ear
This map shows locations of battles during 1739 to 1742 between British Georgia and Spanish Florida.

more plentiful and cheaper goods. They exchanged tools, clothing, scissors, guns, ammunition, and rum, in return for slaves, deerskins, and furs from the Indians. In comparison with the English provinces, the Spanish and French colonies remained small and badly supplied by their parent nations. In 1760, Florida had approximately 3,000 Hispanic settlers, Texas had 1,200, and New Mexico about 9,000; Louisiana counted 4,000 whites and 5,000 enslaved Africans. In contrast, in the same year, South Carolina and Georgia had a population of about 45,000 whites and 59,000 black slaves.

Governor James Oglethorpe of Georgia tried to use the outbreak of the War of Jenkins' Ear to eject the Spanish from Florida. As part of the 1713 Treaty of Utrecht, Britain had obtained the *asiento,* the right to sell a specified number of African slaves and commodities to the Spanish provinces. This opening led to British smuggling, which the Spanish countered with heavy-handed searches of British ships. Accounts of Spanish brutality inflamed the British public, especially when Captain Robert Jenkins displayed one of his ears, which he claimed the Spanish cut off when they caught him smuggling. In 1740, Oglethorpe attacked Florida with seven ships and 2,000

troops. They captured several Spanish forts and Mose, the village of escaped Carolina blacks, but failed to conquer Fort San Marcos, where the residents of St. Augustine and Mose took cover. A large percentage of Florida residents were soldiers to guard Atlantic shipping lanes. When Hispanic and black soldiers slipped out of the fort and recaptured Mose, and then the fort was resupplied by Cuba, Oglethorpe retreated.

In 1741, a force of 3,600 colonists participated in the British expedition against the Spanish fort at Cartagena, in what is now Colombia. The campaign ended bitterly, with heavy losses from battle and smallpox. The following year, the Spanish took revenge for the invasion of Florida by attacking St. Simon's Island, Georgia, but withdrew before conquering it. After some minor skirmishes, both sides gave up, bringing calm to the Georgia–Florida border.

King George's War

The British avoided further conflict with Florida because, in 1744, they began hostilities with France in the War of the Austrian Succession, known to the colonists as King George's War. The war began in Europe, but spilled into

MAP 4.4 North America in 1750

Great Britain, France, and Spain claimed the indicated areas just before the Seven Years' War. While waves of immigrants from Germany and the British Isles had expanded settlement in the British provinces since 1700 (see Map 3.4), the French colonies still consisted primarily of trading posts, forts, and relatively small agricultural areas. Native Americans controlled much of the territory claimed by France.

North America when, provoked by French attacks on Nova Scotia, Governor William Shirley of Massachusetts launched an attack on Louisbourg, which controlled access to the St. Lawrence River. In April 1745, 4,000 New England farmers and fishermen assaulted the French garrison, which held out against the badly organized offensive until June, then surrendered. New Englanders considered Louisbourg a great victory, even after many of their troops succumbed to disease. The war degenerated into a series of debilitating border raids. The Canadians and their Indian allies ravaged Saratoga, New York, and northern New England. In spring 1746, a fleet of 76 ships left France to retake Louisbourg, but after fighting disease and Atlantic storms for three months they returned to France empty-handed (see Map 4.4).

Despite this reprieve, New Englanders had little to celebrate, for they faced another threat—from their own

imperial navy. During the war, Parliament permitted naval officers to impress sailors without the permission of colonial authorities. The Royal Navy used impressment, or involuntary recruitment, because many seamen fled the harsh conditions on naval vessels. In 1747, several thousand Bostonians protested when a British press gang from the fleet of Admiral Charles Knowles swept up men along the waterfront. The mob surrounded the governor's house and burned a British barge in his courtyard. When the governor called up the militia, the troops refused to move. Knowles threatened to shell the town, but after negotiations lasting several days, he released the impressed men instead.

As the colonists became more involved in imperial politics, they learned that their interests held little sway. To their shock, the British government restored Louisbourg to the French in the Treaty of Aix-la-Chapelle (1748),

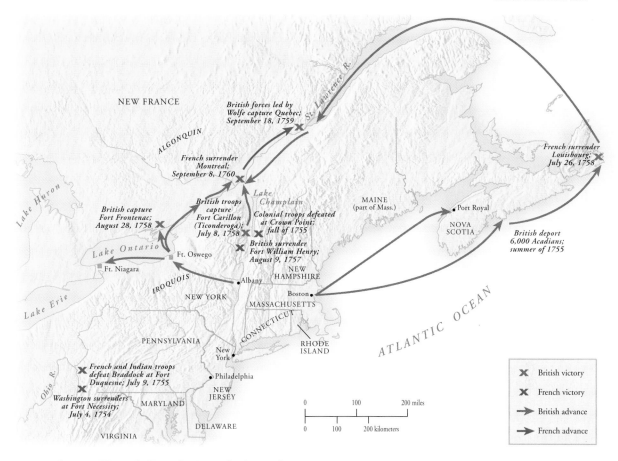

MAP 4.5 Seven Years' War in North America
The war began in the Ohio Valley, an area Virginians claimed and hoped to sell to settlers. To do so, they had to force out the French, who sent troops to establish ownership; defeat the Delawares and Shawnees, who had built towns along the Allegheny and Ohio rivers; and prevail over Pennsylvania's competing charter claims.

and the combatants agreed to return all North American territories seized during the war. Despite heavy human and financial costs, the war brought no change in the power balance between Great Britain and France in North America.

The Seven Years' War

During King George's War, the British and Iroquois had evicted French traders from the Ohio Valley. The Canadians returned, however, backed by a government that was determined to force out the British colonists who had stepped up activity in the area. The Ohio Company of Virginia, which had received the rights to half a million acres from the British government, in 1749 made preparations to sell land in the region of present-day Pittsburgh, Pennsylvania, where the Monongahela and Allegheny rivers combine to form the Ohio River (see Map 4.5). Virginia's claim to the territory dated from its charter. In response, the French constructed forts to stop the incursion of Anglo-American traders and Virginia's

land speculators. In 1754, the governor of Virginia sent a young militia officer, George Washington, with about 160 troops to erect a stronghold to defend the colony's interests. When hostilities resulted, the Virginians were defeated at the inadequate structure they had built, Fort Necessity, by a superior force of French and Indians.

Recognizing that war was imminent, seven colonies sent delegates to a congress at Albany, New York, where they negotiated unsuccessfully with the Iroquois for an alliance against the French. The Albany Congress also amended and adopted the Albany Plan devised by Benjamin Franklin to unite the colonies for common defense. The plan would have to be endorsed by each colony and the Crown. When the delegates returned home with the proposal for an intercolonial government empowered to tax, pass laws, and supervise military defense, not one of the colonies' assemblies approved.

The British decided to destroy French forts in what they considered their territory even before a formal declaration of war. In early 1755, Major General Edward Braddock landed in the colonies with two British regiments.

Benjamin Franklin published his "Snake Device" just before the Albany Congress in 1754. Considered the first political cartoon in the colonies, it later became an important symbol of American resistance to Britain.

Joined by hundreds of provincial soldiers, the army marched through the Virginia backcountry to capture Fort Duquesne (now Pittsburgh). The British troops were unprepared for frontier fighting but thought their mission was easy because the garrison had only 250 French troops. Ten miles short of Fort Duquesne, however, the French and allied Indians ambushed Braddock's army, killing or wounding two-thirds of the British force. The general himself was mortally wounded. George Washington, his uniform ripped by bullets, led the retreat.

The 650 Native Americans who fought with the French included their traditional allies and some Delawares and Iroquois of the Ohio Valley who had previously supported the British. By 1754, some Ohio Indians were convinced that Britain and its colonies posed the greater threat to their lands; with the defeat of Braddock, many more joined the French. Between 1755 and 1757, Delawares, Shawnees, Iroquois, and many others attacked the white frontier from Pennsylvania to Virginia, burning settlements and killing or capturing thousands of colonists.

DOING HISTORY ONLINE

The French and Indian War

Read the documents in this module. If you were a young white man living in Virginia or Massachusetts, what motivation would you have for joining the British forces to fight the French and Indians?

History⊗Now™   Visit HistoryNOW to access primary sources and exercises related to this topic: http://now.ilrn.com/ayers_etal3e

Help for the westerners was slow in coming. In 1756, the struggle in North America became part of the larger European conflict known as the Seven Years' War, in which Great Britain supported Prussia against Austria, Russia, and France. The French penetrated into New York, seizing Fort William Henry and 2,000 soldiers at Lake George. The tide changed after the British statesman **William Pitt** took command of the war effort. He poured money and men into the American theater, expecting colonial legislatures to do the same. The new generals Jeffery Amherst and **James Wolfe,** with an army of almost 10,000 men, captured Louisbourg in July 1758. The French then pulled their troops out of the Ohio Valley to protect Quebec and Montreal, allowing the British to take control of the west. Without French supplies and devastated by smallpox, the Native Americans ended their war on the frontier.

In 1759, the British and provincial armies had even greater success, leading some of the Iroquois of New York to abandon neutrality to join their side. The British reestablished control of New York, while from Louisbourg, General Wolfe sailed up the St. Lawrence to Quebec, where after several months his forces pierced the defenses of the well-fortified city. The next year, Amherst's army seized Montreal, thus ending French control of Canada.

While the defeat of Canada marked the end of the war in North America, the Seven Years' War continued off the coast of France, in India, and in the West Indies. The British military took a number of French sugar islands, including the richest, Guadeloupe. When Spain entered the conflict as France's ally in 1762 in return for the promise of lands west of the Mississippi River, the British captured Manila in the Philippines and Havana, Cuba.

During the Seven Years' War, thousands of colonists joined the British army, and many more served in the provincial forces. The experience brought ordinary settlers into close contact with the imperial authorities—and many loathed the experience. The British army contained professional soldiers drilled rigorously in military tactics, cleanliness, and order. Women served in the field, generally soldiers' wives who cooked, washed, and nursed. British officers, from the upper classes, maintained discipline with punishments of death for major offenses such as desertion, and up to 1,000 lashes—which could also kill—for lesser crimes. The British officers disdained the colonial units, which were accustomed to much lighter discipline and sometimes elected their superiors. Because the provincials failed to keep their camps and clothing clean, many died from disease. For their part, some colonial soldiers thought the British regulars were immoral, profane men who needed to be controlled with brutal discipline.

The Death of General Wolfe, by Benjamin West. Though an inaccurate depiction of the British victory at Quebec, the painting has several interesting features: the Mohawk prominently represents the Iroquois–British alliance and the colonial ranger behind him wears Indian moccasins and leggings.

The British colonists welcomed the Treaty of Paris in 1763, which finally ended the war. Under the treaty, France lost all of its territory in North America but retrieved the valuable sugar islands of Guadeloupe and Martinique. Spain relinquished Florida to get back Cuba and the Philippines and, because the British lacked interest in the region, acquired French territory west of the Mississippi and New Orleans, located on the east side of the river. The Treaty of Paris gave the British colonists security from France and Spain; the home government received two unprofitable colonies, Canada and Florida. The provincials celebrated the victory with patriotic fervor: New York City raised a statue of George III, who had taken the throne in 1760 at age 22. Many colonists, especially New England ministers, had interpreted the war as a fight against Catholicism and tyranny. They viewed the victory as a sign that God favored Britain and its colonies. One Massachusetts clergyman preached,

> Safe from the Enemy of the Wilderness, safe from the gripping Hand of arbitrary Sway and cruel Superstition;

Here shall be the late founded Seat of Peace and Freedom. Here shall our indulgent Mother [Britain], who has most generously rescued and protected us, be served and honoured by growing Numbers, with all Duty, Love and Gratitude, till Time shall be no more.

The Indians Renew War in the Ohio Valley

The Treaty of Paris seriously undermined the position of Native Americans east of the Mississippi whether they had fought for the British or French, or had remained neutral. The defeat of France worsened the situation of native people in the Ohio Valley, for they could no longer play one European nation off the other. The British alone supplied European goods, so they could set prices and the terms of trade. They ended the custom of giving annual presents, charged high prices, stopped selling rum, and reduced the amount of ammunition sold. Further, with the end of the Seven Years' War, white settlers streamed west into Indian lands, as wealthy land speculators and poor squatters alike ignored treaties that colonial governments had made with the Native Americans.

The altered British trade policies and land grabbing drove many Delawares, Shawnees, Iroquois, and others to renew the fighting. They gained spiritual unity from the Delaware prophet Neolin, one of a line of spiritual leaders among the Delawares and Shawnees who preached

Picturing the Past	**POLITICS & DIPLOMACY**

Treaty Negotiations

This engraving, *The Indians Giving a Talk to Colonel Bouquet . . . in Octr. 1764*, was based on a sketch by the artist Benjamin West. The illustration was first published in a 1766 account of Henry Bouquet's successful 1764 expedition against the Ohio Indians during Pontiac's War. Bouquet's troops left Fort Pitt on October 3, marching west toward the Muskingum River in what is now eastern Ohio. While en route they received a message that the Delaware and Shawnee leaders "were coming as soon as possible to

treat of peace." After building fortifications, Bouquet and his aides met with the Indians October 17–20. They struck a truce, and the Natives pledged to return white captives. When they delivered more than 200 captives by November 9, the war ended east of the Muskingum but continued in the west. The engraving shows a typical treaty scene, with a Native leader using a wampum belt to speak, while a scribe took minutes.

© CORBIS

that Indians must reject Christianity and European goods, particularly rum, and revitalize their ancient culture. Neolin called on Native Americans to drive the Europeans out, demanding: "Whereupon do you suffer the whites to dwell upon your lands? Drive them away; wage war against them. I love them not." He warned his followers, "if you suffer the English among you, you are dead men. Sickness, smallpox, and their poison will destroy you entirely."

Many Indians throughout the Ohio Valley adopted Neolin's strategy, boycotting the fur trade by hunting only for their own food and personal needs. The Delaware councils called for a gradual return to military skills with bow and arrow and adopted a ritual tea, which caused vomiting, to cleanse themselves of the "White people's ways and Nature." In 1763, Native Americans from western Pennsylvania through the Great Lakes region launched a pan-Indian assault on British garrisons, often called Pontiac's War. A follower of Neolin and leader of the Ottawas, Pontiac laid siege unsuccessfully to the British fort at Detroit. Other Indians defeated 13 British outposts, though not Forts Niagara or Pittsburgh. Although the British army established military dominance in the Ohio Valley by the end of 1763, after the Native Americans ran short of ammunition and succumbed to smallpox, fighting continued for 2 more years.

In addition to armed force, the British government tried to end the war by keeping white settlers out of the Ohio Valley. The king issued the **Proclamation of 1763,** which drew a line along the crest of the Appalachian Mountains from Maine to Georgia, requiring colonists to stay east of the line. Colonial governors were instructed to prohibit surveys or land grants west of the Proclamation line; only authorized agents of the Crown could buy lands from the Indians for future settlement. The Proclamation failed in its purpose, however, as land speculators continued their operations and immigrants demanded farms. The British government, weighed down by debt from the Seven Years' War, failed to supply manpower to enforce the law. The government withdrew troops from the Ohio Valley and Great Lakes region, and provincial governments, dominated by speculators, ignored encroachment on Indian lands.

The British Provinces in 1763

The end of the Seven Years' War brought pivotal changes in British North America. For more than a century and a half, Europeans had crossed the ocean to trade with the Native Americans, build farms and businesses, and develop networks of Atlantic commerce. The colonies had dealt with crises, from economic slumps to rebellions, becoming ever more confident of their position as semi-independent societies. During the last quarter century, with greater involvement in imperial affairs and rising importation of consumer goods, the provincials felt more a part of the British empire—more English—even as they created a separate identity as Americans. Most important, they believed that they were equal to the residents of Great Britain, that they possessed the rights of English people.

Picturing the Past   **ECONOMICS & TECHNOLOGY**

Atlantic Trade Patterns

By 1750, the Atlantic economy had matured, as each of the British mainland colonies developed products for sale in Great Britain, Europe, Africa, and the West Indies. Patterns of trade were much more complicated than the notion of a "triangular trade route" in which England sold manufactured goods in Africa in exchange for slaves who were sent to America where they produced sugar, tobacco, and rice destined for Europe. While this exchange was important, other trade patterns sustained colonial economies as well: shipment of fish and lumber from New England to the West Indies, and mid-Atlantic flour and meat to southern Europe and the West Indies. The fur trade linked Native Americans to the Atlantic economy. West Indies sugar—and the rum New England and Philadelphia distillers manufactured from it—found markets everywhere. Because the Navigation Acts allowed American ships to carry goods, the shipping trade itself became a significant source of income.

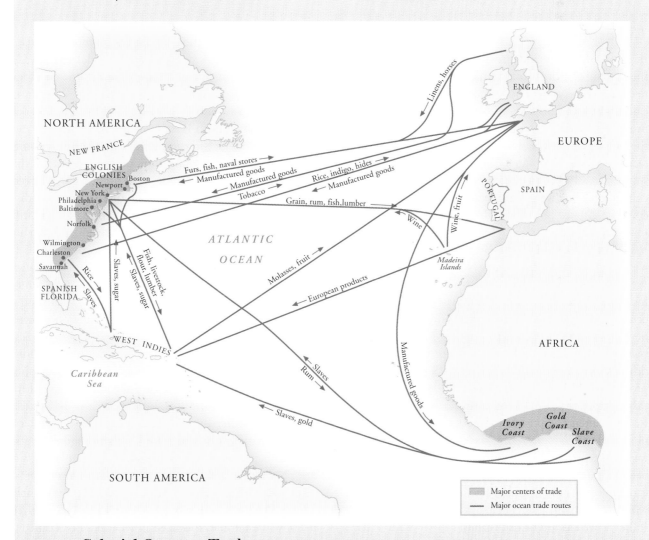

MAP 4.6 Colonial Overseas Trade

Grey's Inn Creek Shipyard, by an unknown artist, c. 1760. Shipbuilding, at this Maryland shipyard as well as in northern seaports, was a major industry in the British colonies.

The Economy

In 1763, the mainland provinces still operated within the system of British mercantilism, which consisted of regulations on colonial trade and manufactures. For mercantilism to work to Britain's benefit, the colonies had to produce raw materials and agricultural staples needed by the home economy and serve as a market for its manufactured goods (see Map 4.6). Such colonial products as sugar, molasses, tobacco, cotton, certain wood products, copper, and furs were "enumerated," meaning that they could be shipped only to Britain or British colonial ports, not to foreign countries such as France and Spain. The basic laws establishing the British mercantilist system were the seventeenth-century Navigation Acts, which Parliament supplemented from time to time. Though most colonial trade conformed to the law by the eighteenth century, smuggling occurred often enough to prompt demands within the British government for strict enforcement. In particular, colonial shippers bribed customs officials to ignore the Molasses Act (1733), which levied prohibitive duties on foreign sugar products, including a tax of sixpence per gallon on molasses. The British West Indies planters had pushed for the act to create a monopoly for themselves, lowering the cost of provisions and raising the price of their exports. If the Molasses Act had been enforced, it would have severely damaged the economies of New England and the Middle Colonies, which traded with the French, Spanish, and Dutch West Indies as well as the British islands.

Other laws passed by Parliament prior to 1763 had a significant but uneven impact on colonial economic growth. British legislation, combined with lack of invest-ment capital, limited the development of most manufactures. The Woolen Act (1699) and the Hat Act (1732) banned the export of American-produced woolen products and hats from one colony to another. Other laws prohibited the export of machinery and the migration of skilled craftsmen from Britain to America. The Iron Act (1750) allowed duty-free import of colonial bar iron into Britain but forbade fabrication of iron goods in the colonies. Nevertheless, crude iron production received substantial investment, as did shipbuilding and rum distilling. Unhampered by mercantilist regulation, North American shipbuilders produced nearly 40 percent of vessels in the British-owned merchant fleet.

Despite these laws, the wealth of the British colonies increased between the 1720s and 1760, as trade flourished with the West Indies and, after 1750, with southern Europe, where crop failures and population growth swelled demand for wheat and flour. The Middle Colonies, already expanding with German and Irish immigration, were well situated to supply new markets. Philadelphia became the largest city in the British colonies: its wealthy merchants invested in ships, built mansions, purchased coaches and other luxuries, and speculated in western lands from the profits of trade. Artisans, shopkeepers, and farmers prospered. To the south, large planters in the Chesapeake and Carolinas accumulated great estates, while ordinary farmers more modestly improved their standard of living. All along the eastern seaboard, after 1750, white families indulged in what has been called a "consumer revolution." Not only could they purchase cloth, clothing, carpets, paper, gloves, mirrors, clocks, silverware, china tea sets, pottery, and books, but they

had more choices in the specific kind of cloth or paper or gloves they could buy. In New York City in the 1750s, for instance, merchants advertised gloves of various colors—purple, orange, white, and flowered—as well as different sizes and materials, including chamois, silk, "Maid's Lamb Gloves," and "Men's Dog Skin Gloves." This is just one example of the wide variety of consumer goods that became available in midcentury.

The colonies became major markets for textiles, metalware, and other items, which under the Navigation Acts they could import only from Britain. The consumer revolution made the British more attentive to their North American provinces; at the same time, the imports helped to create in America a more standardized English culture. Affluent colonists became aware of the latest fashions in England, and complained when they received out-of-date merchandise. The young George Washington groused in 1760, for example, "that instead of getting things good and fashionable in their several kinds we often have Articles sent Us that coud only have been usd by our Forefathers in the days of yore."

The economic upswing of the 1750s gave way to a depression after 1760, as the Seven Years' War moved to the Caribbean and military spending dropped. The seaport towns, having attracted workers during the wartime boom, faced deepening poverty and rising demands for relief. With depressed wages and long periods of unemployment, families found survival difficult. The resumption of immigration from Europe after the war intensified economic hardships and contributed to unrest on the frontier.

Politics

In late 1763, after months of Indian attacks in the Ohio country, a band of western Scots-Irish Pennsylvanians used violence to force the Quaker-dominated assembly to provide military protection. The "**Paxton Boys**" of Lancaster County murdered a number of Christian Indians at Conestoga, then marched on Philadelphia. By the time the rebels reached the capital, the legislature had passed a bill raising 1,000 troops to defend the frontier. The westerners returned home without attacking the city. At the heart of their revolt was the belief that they were poorly represented in the provincial government. As the backcountry population exploded, eastern politicians guarded their power by allotting fewer assembly seats to outlying counties than they deserved.

The Paxton Boys revolt signaled the end of an era of political stability that had prevailed since the late 1720s in the British mainland provinces. As part of Britain's empire, the eighteenth-century colonists believed themselves among the most fortunate people on earth. The Glorious Revolution of 1688–1689, which removed James II, had ended the long, bitter contest between king and Parliament. The monarch's power was subsequently limited by the national legislature, composed of the House of Lords, which represented the aristocracy, and the House of Commons, which in theory represented everyone else. As a result of the 1689 settlement, Parliament's consent was necessary for taxes, new courts, raising an army in peacetime, and foreign invasions. Parliament gained control over its own meetings and, after 1707, the Crown lost veto power over legislation.

The balance of powers, political theorists argued, prevented domination by a single segment of society, the monarch, aristocracy, or common people. Thus, the British avoided forms of government considered destructive of liberty: rule by a single despot (tyranny); corrupt and self-serving rule by a group of aristocrats (oligarchy);

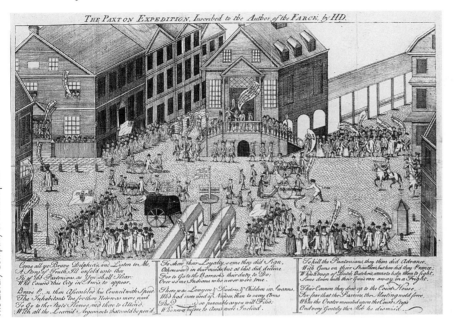

The Paxton Expedition, by Henry Dawkins, depicts the threat by western "Paxton Boys" against Philadelphia, demanding frontier defense during Pontiac's War.

and uncontrolled rule by the mob (democracy). In their provincial governments, the British colonists expected to find a similar balance, one that would protect their rights. Indeed, the prevailing structure of governor, appointed council, and elected lower house of assembly reflected the English model.

The British provinces were the only European settlements in North America where ordinary people could vote for representative legislatures. An estimated 50 to 75 percent of white men were qualified to vote in the British colonies, the result of much broader property ownership than in England, where about 15 to 30 percent of adult males had the franchise. According to English political theory, a person needed a "stake in society," a certain amount of property, to vote or hold office. Servants, slaves, children, and unpropertied men were beholden to someone else, so they could not make independent decisions. Giving them suffrage would award their owner, father, or employer another vote, the theorists claimed, especially in many places where people voted orally, in public. By tradition, women also lacked the franchise, whether or not they owned property or were married. Denial of the vote to all females arose from the belief that they were intellectually and morally inferior to men and thus should have no formal role in government.

The colonists favored direct representation, requiring their legislators to live in the area from which they were elected and to advocate the interests of their constituents, unlike England, where members of the House of Commons did not have to reside in their electoral districts. The British believed that Parliament represented all of the people of the empire whether they elected delegates or not, a concept known as virtual representation.

Beyond suffrage, English political theory also recognized the right of common people to resort to crowd action to withstand tyranny and require authorities to protect them from harm. The people had this right, theoretically, as long as violence was limited—directed at property rather than at persons. At various times, colonial mobs protested to prevent grain from being exported when food was in short supply, to destroy houses of prostitution, and to stop the British navy from impressing men into the king's service, as with the 1747 Knowles riot in Boston.

The most important and sustained political development in British America during the first half of the eighteenth century was the rise of the elected lower houses of assembly. The legislatures acquired greater power and assumed more functions, most significantly, the right to initiate bills to raise taxes and disburse public funds—the "power of the purse." They also gained the authority to initiate other legislation, choose their own leadership, and settle disputed elections.

The political stability and rise of the assemblies that marked the mid-eighteenth century resulted from a number of factors, including the long period of economic growth that began in the 1720s. Prosperity supported the formation of cohesive elites—mostly second-, third-, and fourth-generation Americans with inherited wealth, large estates, and enslaved Africans or servants to meet their domestic needs, and (consequently) sufficient leisure time for politics. They formed a class of skilled politicians, men who learned from their fathers how to govern, then elaborated the art. Many studied the law: the growth of the colonial bar accompanied the professionalization of politics. Economic prosperity inclined ordinary whites to defer to the elites as long as opportunity was good and they had crops to tend or other work to do. Their deference to social and economic superiors became most visible after 1725, when participation at the polls declined among eligible voters, and incumbent assemblymen won reelection year after year.

The provincial elites also benefited after 1720 from the British decision to administer the colonies with a

Colonial Williamsburg Foundation

King George III, at the time of his coronation in 1760, by Allan Ramsay.

Conclusion

By the end of 1763, the British colonists of North America had reason to be optimistic about their future, despite the pan-Indian assaults in the Ohio Valley and postwar economic downturn. The British army had withstood the worst attacks in the west, and colonists could expect a return to prosperity. After a quarter century of war, they celebrated the withdrawal of Spain and France east of the Mississippi and looked forward to peace and semi-autonomy within the empire. Free colonists appreciated the benefits of being British—their liberties and right to participate in government as well as access to advanced learning and consumer goods. At the same time, the Americans were creating societies quite different from the English, with greater ethnic and religious diversity, dependence on enslaved labor, and wider opportunity to acquire land (even if it meant pushing out the Indians). After 1763, the London government shocked the American colonists with its effort to rein in the empire, to make them surrender some of their accumulated rights. In turn, the British were unprepared for the coordinated fury with which the 13 mainland provinces greeted their "reforms."

light touch, allowing royal governors to accommodate the assemblies. And while riots occurred during the 1740s and 1750s over land claims and impressment, none threatened social disorder on the level of the seventeenth-century rebellions. Indeed, most ordinary whites feared attacks by Native Americans and slave revolts more than misuse of governmental power by elites.

The Chapter in Review

- In the colonies, the Enlightenment created new educational opportunities, promoted scientific research, and encouraged the development of new political theories.

- Between 1720 and 1760, the Great Awakening, a series of religious revivals that emphasized emotionalism and personal salvation, swept across British America.

- The population of the colonies became increasingly diverse as the African-American population grew, both through natural increase and increased importation, and from a significant influx of German and Scots-Irish immigrants.

- Between 1744 and 1765, colonists participated in a series of wars waged by Britain against Spain, France, and their Native American allies. By the end of these conflicts, France had withdrawn from the North American mainland.

- Involvement in British wars and integration into Atlantic trade networks fostered a strong sense of English identity, and feelings of entitlement to the rights of Englishmen, among many colonists.

Making Connections Across Chapters

LOOKING BACK

Chapter 4 shows that between 1720 and 1763 the 13 British provinces underwent considerable change as a result of German and Scots-Irish immigration, the intellectual challenges of the Enlightenment, religious developments of the Great Awakening, and economic expansion within the Atlantic world.

1. What kind of education could young Americans receive in the early eighteenth century?

2. What contributions did Americans make to science?

3. How did the Great Awakening affect colonial society?

4. In what ways did Native Americans respond to the expansion of British America?

5. What economic restrictions did the British government place on the colonies prior to 1763?

LOOKING AHEAD

Chapter 5 looks at how the year 1763 marked a major change in British government policy toward its North American colonies, a change that led to revolution a dozen years later.

1. Why did London impose the series of "reforms" beginning with the Sugar and Currency acts?

2. Why was Boston the center of colonial resistance?

3. How did events in the Spanish borderland colonies of Louisiana, Texas, and New Mexico compare with the unfolding crisis in the British provinces?

Recommended Readings

Anderson, Fred. *Crucible of War: The Seven Years' War and the Fate of Empire in British North America, 1754–1766* (2000). A convincing analysis of the significance of the Seven Years' War.

Bailyn, Bernard, and Morgan, Philip D., eds. *Strangers within the Realm: Cultural Margins of the First British Empire* (1991). Important essays on specific groups, including Native Americans, Scots-Irish, African Americans, Germans, and Dutch.

Carson, Cary, et al., eds. *Of Consuming Interests: The Style of Life in the Eighteenth Century* (1994). Excellent essays on topics ranging from housing and art to consumer behavior.

Daunton, Martin, and Halpern, Rick, eds. *Empire and Others: British Encounters with Indigenous Peoples, 1600–1850* (1999). Significant essays on relations between Natives and English in eastern North America and elsewhere.

Isaac, Rhys. *The Transformation of Virginia, 1740–1790* (1982). Uses anthropological methods to explore cultural and political change in eighteenth-century Virginia.

Merrell, James H. *Into the American Woods: Negotiators on the Pennsylvania Frontier* (1999). Focuses on Indian and Euro-American go-betweens and their ultimate failure to preserve peace in the Ohio Valley.

Morgan, Philip D. *Slave Counterpoint: Black Culture in the Eighteenth-Century Chesapeake and Lowcountry* (1998). A comprehensive study of African American work and culture in the South.

Richter, Daniel K. *Facing East from Indian Country: A Native History of Early America* (2001). Approaches significant events in relations between Indians and settlers from Native perspectives.

Steele, Ian K. *Warpaths: Invasions of North America* (1994). Examines the Seven Years' War as one of a series of European invasions of Indian territory during the colonial period.

Ulrich, Laurel Thatcher. *A Midwife's Tale: The Life of Martha Ballard, Based on Her Diary, 1785–1812* (1990). The prize-winning account of a Maine midwife within the context of eighteenth-century society.

Identifications

Review your understanding of the following key terms, people, events, and dates for this chapter (these terms also appear in the Glossary at the end of the book):

Enlightenment
Seven Years' War
John Locke
Benjamin Franklin
Great Awakening
James Oglethorpe
Stono Uprising

French and Indian War
William Pitt
James Wolfe

Proclamation of 1763
Paxton Boys

Online Sources Guide

Use this listing to find online documents, images, interactive maps, simulations, and other resources related to this chapter.

American History Resource Center

http://history.wadsworth.com/rc/us

Selected Documents

Jonathan Edwards's Puritan Sermon "Sinners in the Hands of an Angry God"
James Oglethorpe, "Some Account of the Designs of the Trustees for Establishing the Colony of Georgia" (1733)
James Oglethorpe, "The Stono Rebellion" (1739)

Selected Images

Front page of the New England Courant, April 16, 1722
Fort George, New York City, 1741

Benjamin Franklin
Snake cartoon by Benjamin Franklin

Simulation

Colonial Expansion (In this historical simulation you can choose to be with the Aztecs, Jamestown settlers, or Puritans/New England and make choices based on the circumstances and opportunities afforded.)

HistoryNOW

http://now.ilrn.com/ayers_etal3e

Primary Source Exercises

The Enlightenment and the Great Awakening
Black and White in the Atlantic World
British–Colonial Relations
The French and Indian War

118   The CENTINEL

the Conventions of nine States, shall be sufficient for the establishment of this ACTUM EST.

"The ratification of

DEL. P.N. N.JER. GEOR. CON. MASSA. MARY. So CARO. N.HAMP.

VIRG.

If it hath not— it will rise.

Constitution. A.R.vii.

The Federal Pillars, from the *Centinel* (Boston, Massachusetts), August 2, 1788, illustrates ratification of the Constitution of 1787.

During the American revolution, 16-year-old Dicey Langston of the South Carolina frontier left home in the middle of the night, by herself, to warn her brother's unit about Tory troop movements. As a historian later described Langston's journey,

> Many miles were to be traversed, and the road lay through woods, and crossed marshes and creeks where the conveniences of bridges and foot-logs were wanting. She walked rapidly on, heedless of slight difficulties; but her heart almost failed her when she came to the banks of the Tyger—a deep and rapid stream, rendered more dangerous by the rains that had lately fallen. . . . But the energy of a resolute will, under the care of Providence, sustained her.[*]

Dicey Langston's effort, like those of thousands of Americans, was emblematic of her country's passage from a collection of British provinces in 1764, to a stable republic with some international standing a half century later. The 13 mainland colonies, proud of their contribution to victory in the Seven Years' War, were stunned by Britain's program to curtail their rights. Stretching from the mountains of northern New England to the rice fields of coastal Georgia, diverse in economics, religion, ethnicity, and politics, the colonies mustered enough unity to organize a revolutionary Congress, stop British imports, raise an army, obtain help from France, and win the war.

The states refused to create a unified nation, however, and instead established, under the Articles of Confederation, 13 separate republics joined loosely by a representative Congress. Without power to tax or raise troops, the Congress faced severe postwar problems in demobilizing the army, paying the war debt, protecting the frontiers, and unifying a populace divided by war. In the wake of bankruptcy and insurrection, in 1787 nationalists called together a constitutional convention. Through a series of compromises, the framers drafted the new Constitution, which gave more authority to the central government, yet retained considerable power in

[*] Elizabeth F. Ellet, *Domestic History of the American Revolution* (1850), p. 234.

Constitution and the Guerriere, by Thomas Birch, depicts an important victory of the *USS Constitution* early in the War of 1812.

Negroes in Front of the Bank of Pennsylvania, Philadelphia (1814) shows a group of black workers, the male sawyers laboring in a public space and a female domestic caring for a white child.

the states. Americans ratified the document with the understanding that amendments to protect individual liberties and states' rights would be approved.

After the first national elections, the Constitution's proponents, the Federalists, controlled the new government, with George Washington as president. Having

A Stockbridge Indian in the Continental army.

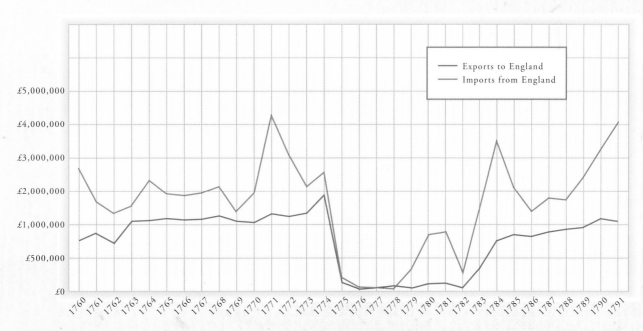

Trade Between 13 Colonies/United States and England, 1760–1791 (pounds sterling). Though trade with England was only part of American commerce, this chart suggests the Revolution's impact. British imports spiked between 1769 and 1771, after Parliament partially repealed the Townshend Act. Imports and exports then plummeted during the Revolution, rising unevenly after 1782. The trade imbalance led to political unrest such as Shays's Rebellion.

Source of Data: Bureau of the Census, *Historical Statistics of the United States Colonial Times to 1970* Part 2 (Washington, D.C., 1975), p. 1176.

agreed upon the frame of government, they were unprepared for the bitter factionalism that forged political parties in the 1790s. Nor were they ready for the foreign entanglements that resulted from two decades of war between Great Britain and post-revolutionary France. Only after the United States declared war on the British in 1812 and held its own as the conflict ended in stalemate, did the nation finally demonstrate its independence. By 1814, most of the men who led the American Revolution had passed from power—though James Madison would remain president for several years—and a new generation was taking control.

The heroic story of the young nation surmounting difficulties—two wars against Great Britain, a constitutional crisis, several internal rebellions, an undeclared conflict with France, and constant fighting on the frontier—masks other narratives, those of women, African Americans, and Native Americans, who failed to achieve autonomy. Though Dicey Langston was just one of thousands of sisters, mothers, and wives who risked their lives during the Revolution, after the war women still lacked basic legal and political rights to hold property after marriage, vote, and take part in government. And while revolutionary rhetoric against slavery resulted in abolition in the North and many private manumissions in the Chesapeake region, most African Americans remained enslaved, a condition perpetuated by the new Constitution and development of cotton. Even most free blacks had little opportunity to acquire property and were denied suffrage and participation in government.

For Native Americans, the success and growth of the new nation meant their decline. Despite revitalization movements to restore traditional cultures led by Neolin, Handsome Lake, Tenskwatawa, and others, and destructive wars to defend their homelands in Alabama, Tennessee, Kentucky, and Ohio, by 1814 the United States dominated most of the territory east of the Mississippi River. Native Americans tried various routes to survive and retain as much of their autonomy as possible—adoption of white culture, cession of some lands for the promise they could keep others, alliances with Great Britain and Spain, and pan-Indian war. In the face of unremitting westward settlement and continuing disease, the Indian peoples of eastern North America became remnants of formerly powerful nations.

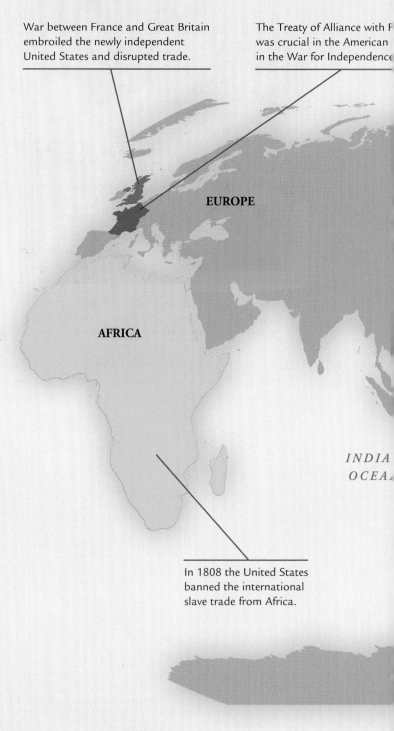

North America and the World: 1764–1814

War between France and Great Britain embroiled the newly independent United States and disrupted trade.

The Treaty of Alliance with F was crucial in the American in the War for Independence

EUROPE

AFRICA

INDIA
OCEA

In 1808 the United States banned the international slave trade from Africa.

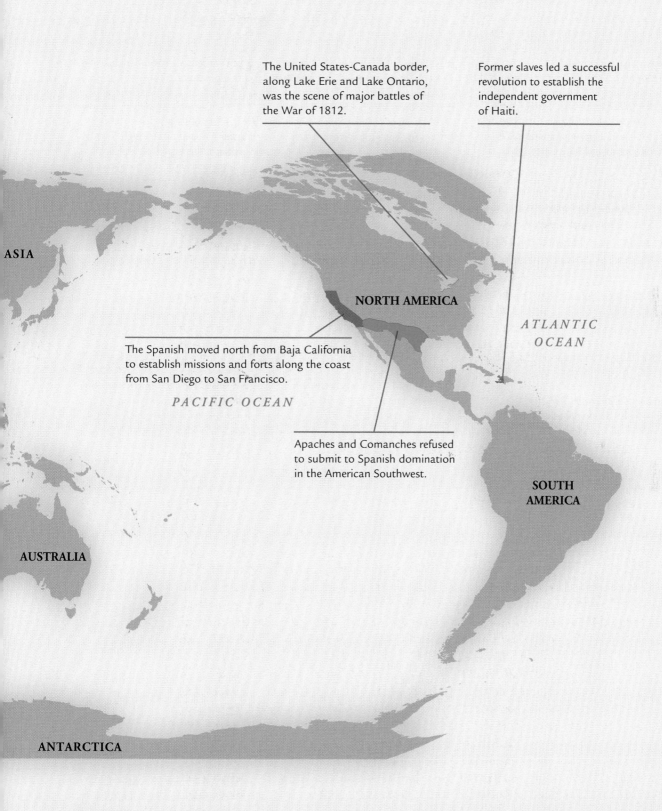

The United States-Canada border, along Lake Erie and Lake Ontario, was the scene of major battles of the War of 1812.

Former slaves led a successful revolution to establish the independent government of Haiti.

ASIA

NORTH AMERICA

ATLANTIC OCEAN

The Spanish moved north from Baja California to establish missions and forts along the coast from San Diego to San Francisco.

PACIFIC OCEAN

Apaches and Comanches refused to submit to Spanish domination in the American Southwest.

SOUTH AMERICA

AUSTRALIA

ANTARCTICA

Chronology

	1760	1775	1780
POLITICS & DIPLOMACY	**1765:** Stamp Act protest **1766–1771:** Regulator movements in North and South Carolina **1767:** John Dickinson's "Farmer" letters against Townshend Act **1768:** Nonimportation movement **1769:** Spanish colonize California **1770:** Boston Massacre **1772:** Committees of Correspondence **1773:** Boston Tea Party **1774:** Coercive Acts; port of Boston closed First Continental Congress	**1775:** Battles of Lexington and Concord Lord Dunmore's proclamation to servants and slaves **1776:** Thomas Paine's *Common Sense* Declaration of Independence **1777:** Burgoyne surrenders to Americans at Saratoga **1778:** Alliance with France Iroquois attacks in New York and Pennsylvania	**1780:** Pennsylvania law for gradual abolition of slavery **1781:** Articles of Confederation ratified Surrender of Cornwallis at Yorktown **1783:** Treaty of Paris **1787:** Shaysites attack Springfield, Massachusetts, arsenal Northwest Ordinance Constitution sent to states for ratification **1789:** Inauguration of President George Washington
SOCIAL & CULTURAL EVENTS	**1765:** First American medical school **1766:** Queens College (Rutgers) New Southwark Theatre in Philadelphia **1769:** *The American Magazine* (Philadelphia) published Benjamin West's *Death of General Wolfe* American scientists observe transit of Venus **1770:** Equestrian statue of George III installed in New York **1771:** Benjamin Franklin starts *Autobiography* **c. 1772:** John Singleton Copley's portrait of Samuel Adams **1773:** Phillis Wheatley's *Poems on Various Subjects, Religious and Moral*	**1776:** Jemima Wilkinson becomes Public Universal Friend **1779:** John Murray's American Universalist Church	**1780s:** Northern black separate churches and societies **1783:** Noah Webster's American spelling book First daily newspaper, *Pennsylvania Evening Post* **1784:** Judith Sargent Murray begins essays on women's status **1786:** Virginia statute for religious liberty Gilbert Stuart's portrait of Joseph Brant
ECONOMICS & TECHNOLOGY	**1760s:** British American traders cross Mississippi River **1764:** Sugar and Currency Acts	**1776:** Adam Smith's *An Inquiry into the Nature and Causes of the Wealth of Nations* **1778:** Captain James Cook explores the Pacific Northwest **1779:** Continental money becomes nearly worthless	**1780s:** Rapid settlement of Kentucky and Tennessee Oliver Evans automates grist mills **1781:** Bank of North America in Philadelphia **1783:** Great Britain closes West Indies to American ships **1784:** Spain closes port of New Orleans to Americans Debt crisis spurs protests in U.S. **1788:** Pennsylvania Society for the Encouragement of Manufactures and the Useful Arts introduces spinning jennies

1790

1791: Bill of Rights ratified
1794: Whiskey Rebellion
1795: Jay Treaty

1791: Charles Willson Peale's *Thomas Jefferson*
c.1793: Mary Wollstonecraft's *Vindication of the Rights of Women* circulates in the U.S.
1795: Philadelphia Quaker women establish first female benevolent society in U.S.

1790: Samuel Slater builds first U.S. water-powered textile mill
Congress passes patent law
1791: Bank of the United States Excise tax on whiskey
Alexander Hamilton's plan for promoting manufactures
1793: British blockade of French West Indies Eli Whitney's cotton gin
1795: Great Britain opens West Indies to U.S. trade

1796

1798: Alien and Sedition Acts Quasi-War with France
1799: Fries Rebellion

1797: Second Great Awakening begins in New England
1799: Rise of Handsome Lake as Seneca prophet
Charles Brockden Brown's *Wieland*

1796: Spain opens navigation on Mississippi River
Alexander Hamilton's industrial town in New Jersey fails
1798: Eli Whitney attempts to manufacture guns with interchangeable parts
1790s: U.S. international trade soars with European conflict
Cotton expands southern slavery
Northern cities become magnets for African Americans

1800

1800: Washington, D.C., becomes national capital
Gabriel's rebellion
Jefferson elected president
1803: *Marbury v. Madison* case
Louisiana Purchase
1804: Lewis and Clark expedition
1809: Tecumseh organizes pan-Indian confederacy
1812: U.S. war with Great Britain
1814: Treaty of Ghent

1800s: Tenskwatawa, the Shawnee Prophet, inspires following
1800: Library of Congress
1801: Cane Ridge, Kentucky, camp meeting
1805: Pennsylvania Academy of Fine Arts

1802: Oliver Evans's high pressure steam engine
1806: Non-Importation Act
1807: Embargo Act
1808: Federal ban on international slave trade
1809: Giles's Enforcement Act Embargo repealed; replaced with Non-Intercourse Act
1811: Charter of National Bank expires

5

Wars for Independence, 1764–1783

The Occupation of Boston, 1768, engraving by Paul Revere(?), illustrates the arrival of British troops on the Long Wharf (center).

Courtesy, American Antiquarian Society

The treaty of 1763 that ended the Seven Years' War forced Spain and Great Britain to reassess their North American colonies. Both nations had relatively new kings: Charles III had taken Spain's throne in 1759 and George III had become the British monarch in 1760. For the Spanish, the borderlands in North America were of secondary importance, serving as a buffer to protect the Mexican silver mines. For Britain, however, the mainland provinces had become increasingly significant as a source of revenue and market for consumer goods. The Seven Years' War marked Britain's ascendancy to world power, but it resulted in a national debt of £130 million. Annual interest payments alone amounted to £4.5 million, equal to more than half of the government's yearly expenditures prior to the war.

When Parliament imposed levies on the American colonies to help pay expenses, the colonists protested vehemently that they should not be taxed without their consent. They complained that they had no representatives in Parliament, and that only their elected provincial assemblies could constitutionally tax them.

Beginning in 1764, the Americans petitioned, rioted, boycotted British goods, destroyed tea, and ultimately defied George III and parliamentary leaders when they sent troops. The colonists' belief that they possessed the same rights as the English was something for which many were willing to fight. Nevertheless, the consensus to declare independence did not come quickly, nor was the war to defend independence easily won. Americans who disagreed that the British actions warranted insurrection remained loyal to the king. These loyalists, also called **Tories** after the pro-monarchy faction in England, tried to subvert the revolutionary governments and formed loyalist militia units to fight alongside British troops. They found allies in many Indians and African Americans who conducted wars of independence of their own. Other colonists remained neutral, whether from principled opposition to violence or from sheer indifference. The Revolution touched everyone, Native Americans, women, and enslaved blacks, as well as the white men who served as military and civilian leaders and comprised most of the armed forces. The cause of

Timeline

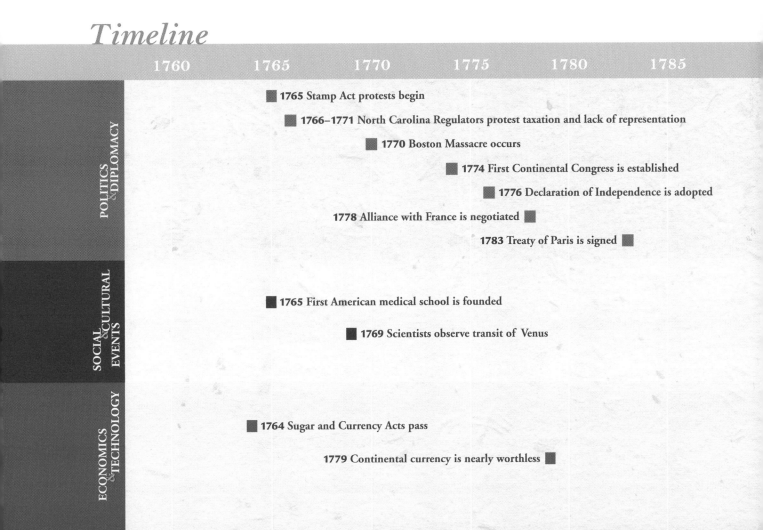

	1760	1765	1770	1775	1780	1785

POLITICS & DIPLOMACY

1765 Stamp Act protests begin

1766–1771 North Carolina Regulators protest taxation and lack of representation

1770 Boston Massacre occurs

1774 First Continental Congress is established

1776 Declaration of Independence is adopted

1778 Alliance with France is negotiated

1783 Treaty of Paris is signed

SOCIAL & CULTURAL EVENTS

1765 First American medical school is founded

1769 Scientists observe transit of Venus

ECONOMICS & TECHNOLOGY

1764 Sugar and Currency Acts pass

1779 Continental currency is nearly worthless

the patriots—or Whigs, as the American revolutionaries called themselves after the English party that had led opposition to the Crown—depended on the efforts of many people. Those who supplied and supported the troops, as well as those who fought, played vital roles.

Realignments in the Spanish Borderlands

The peace of 1763 required Spain to withdraw from Florida, assume the government of Louisiana, and rethink its defenses in Texas and New Mexico. With Britain's enhanced power, safeguarding the Mexican silver mines took high priority. The Spanish also considered the soaring population of the British colonies a threat to their American empire.

Florida and Louisiana

Spain ordered all of its subjects to leave Florida when Britain took control. Though the British promised religious freedom to the Catholic Floridians, some 200 Christian Indians, 79 free African Americans, 350 slaves, and nearly all of the 3,000 Hispanics departed. They sold their property at a loss to British bargain hunters. The free blacks of Mose, near St. Augustine, could expect enslavement by the English, so they accepted Spain's offer of homesteads in Cuba. They received some tools and money from the government, but faced hard times because they never received adequate compensation for their property in Florida.

Acquisition of Louisiana, including all French territory west of the Mississippi River and New Orleans on the east bank, gave Spain an extensive region to administer. The Spanish needed to win the loyalties of French

MAP 5.1 **North America in 1764**
Significant changes in European claims to regions in North America resulted from the Seven Years' War. The Treaty of Paris of 1763 divided former French territory between Great Britain to the east of the Mississippi River and Spain to the west. The British also gained Spanish Florida.

inhabitants and Native Americans and hoped to keep the British colonists out. The concern about British expansion became all too real as interlopers spanned the Mississippi River to trade with Indians on the Great Plains. Indeed, within a decade, 4,000 British colonists and their 1,500 African American slaves were living on the Gulf coast and eastern shore of the Mississippi.

The more immediate challenge for Spanish authorities in Louisiana, however, was asserting political control of the province. For several years, the French government remained; even after the first Spanish governor, Antonio de Ulloa, arrived in 1766, he tried to govern jointly with the last French governor. Adhering to Charles III's instructions, Ulloa left the French administration and legal system intact, even allowing the French flag to fly over the capitol.

Ulloa did not extend this leniency to commerce, however. He tried to stop business with France and Great Britain and restricted the Native American trade to certain dealers. New Orleans merchants feared loss of markets and lower prices for their tobacco, indigo, sugar, deerskins, and lumber. Like the 13 British provinces on the Atlantic coast, at about the same time, the merchants protested the new restrictions, then in October 1768 issued a declaration of loyalty to the king of France. With few Spanish troops at his disposal, Governor Ulloa left for Cuba. When the French refused to intervene, the colony became independent, but only for a year.

The Spanish regained Louisiana when General Alexander O'Reilly arrived in 1769 with more than 2,000 soldiers. An Irishman with a successful career in the Spanish army, O'Reilly arrested the rebels, put five of them to death, but pardoned most who had participated in the uprising. He raised the Spanish flag and within a year ended the French government, changed the legal system, made Castilian the official language, and outlawed trade with other nations. Despite the merchants' fears, the economy flourished as smuggling continued with Britain, and Spanish markets welcomed their goods. St. Louis, established in 1764, became the thriving center of trade for beaver, buffalo, and deerskins with Native Americans of the Illinois and Missouri countries. Louisiana remained culturally French, as the numbers of French settlers far surpassed the Spanish.

Fortifying the Southwest

With ownership of Louisiana, the Spanish could alter their defenses along the frontier in Texas and New Mexico. They removed several forts from East Texas. By the 1760s, the most immediate danger in the southwest came from the Apaches and Comanches, who defended their freedom from Hispanic slave catchers and attempted to drive the Spanish back into Mexico. Skillfully adopting the European horse and gun, they refused to submit to Spanish rule or Christianity. Spain gave up trying to convert them through missions, emphasizing military defense instead. The Apaches and Comanches raided settlements and pack trains, stole horses, mules, cattle, and supplies, killing Pueblos and white settlers alike.

During the 1760s and 1770s, in the face of constant Indian assaults, Spain tried to reform administration and improve defenses. From 1766 to 1768, the Marqués de Rubí, a high-level military official from Spain, inspected the fortifications and missions of the Southwest. He discovered badly located presidios (or forts) and soldiers suffering from lack of food and clothes because of their commanders' greed. At one Texas presidio, Rubí found 60 troops without shoes or uniforms and, among them, only two muskets that worked. He recommended building new presidios and relocating others to create an orderly cordon of military bases situated about 100 miles apart. The presidios would extend from the Gulf of California to the Gulf of Mexico, along a line that was close to the present boundary between the United States and Mexico. Small numbers of Spanish troops would hold garrisons at Santa Fe and San Antonio, north of the cordon, to help defend Hispanics and allied Indians in New Mexico and Texas. The borderlands officials also received more autonomy to deal with local problems, but they lacked sufficient troops to conquer the Apaches and Comanches.

The British Colonies Resist Imperial Reform

In Britain's colonies, which experienced few restrictions before 1763, trouble began when George III appointed George Grenville as first minister, with responsibility for solving the debt crisis described in Chapter 4. Grenville decided that Americans should pay more taxes because they benefited from the Seven Years' War and continued to drain the government's budget for administrative and military costs. Because the British at home were highly taxed, Grenville's plan to make the colonies pay their way seemed reasonable to many. The Americans saw it differently, however, and quickly moved to the brink of revolt.

The Sugar and Currency Acts

Grenville began his program in 1764 with the Sugar Act, which initiated a new policy of charging duties primarily to raise revenue rather than to regulate trade. It reduced the duty on foreign molasses from sixpence (under the Molasses Act of 1733) to threepence per gallon, which was further reduced to one penny in 1766. Grenville assumed merchants would pay the lower tariff rather than go to the risk of smuggling and bribery, as they had been doing. The law also added timber, iron, and hides to the list of enumerated goods. To make smuggling more hazardous, the act gave increased powers to the vice-admiralty courts. Because these courts lacked juries, the government expected easy convictions for smuggling. In addition, the law expanded the use of **writs of assistance** (search warrants), empowered the Royal Navy to inspect ships, and required endless bureaucratic paperwork from colonial shippers. Parliament also passed the Currency Act (1764), which had the potential to cause further hardship by forbidding colonies from issuing paper money, thus creating a shortage of currency.

Coming in the midst of an economic depression, this legislation stirred up colonial protest. Provincial assemblies sent petitions to England requesting relief. Most urgently, merchants feared that if imports of foreign molasses were cut off, their provision trade to the Spanish and French West Indies would be lost. Without foreign credits, they could not pay for British manufactures. The Americans slowed down their orders from Britain and encouraged home industry, arousing opposition to Grenville's policies from English businessmen. One colonial merchant wrote to associates in England that if the government deprived Americans of paper currency, "we shall not be able to export Provisions & c. in the same Degree as formerly, and if we are not on any Terms allow'd a Trade to get Money from abroad, we shall have none to pay you for Goods, and then unless you will send them Gratis our Dealings must end."

The Stamp Act

Passed by Parliament in 1765, the **Stamp Act** provoked an even greater storm of protest. The law departed entirely from the confines of mercantilist policy, for its purpose was to raise an internal revenue, which would be used to pay troops in the colonies. The act required individuals to purchase stamps for official documents and published papers, including deeds, liquor licenses, bills of lading, court documents, wills, passports, playing cards, newspapers, and pamphlets. All publications and official transactions were to be subject to this special tax, which increased with the value of a land sale or the size of a pamphlet. The tax could be paid only in specie, an onerous requirement because colonists generally used paper money and credit instead of the scarce gold and silver. The vice-admiralty courts would enforce the act, confiscating any land or property involved in transactions conducted without the stamps.

Colonists of all walks of life found the Stamp Act offensive. Everyone who engaged in public business,

A woman and African American man are prominently portrayed in this illustration of the Stamp Act riots in Boston, 1765.

whether to buy a newspaper or sell property, would have to pay the tax. Because Parliament, not their provincial assemblies, passed the act, Americans considered it a violation of their rights as British subjects. As they understood the British constitution, the people must consent to taxes through their representatives. The provinces could not send delegates to Parliament, so that body should not tax them to raise revenue. As one Philadelphia merchant said succinctly, "the point in dispute is a very Important one, if the Americans are to be taxed by a Parliament where they are not nor can be Represented, they are no longer Englishmen but Slaves." Only tariffs to regulate trade such as the 1733 duty on molasses, many colonists believed, were constitutionally valid.

Recognizing Parliament's attack on their powers, provincial assemblies protested the Stamp Act. In the Virginia House of Burgesses, the newly elected Patrick Henry, only 29 years old, introduced 14 resolves against the tax. The Virginia assembly refused to accept all of Henry's proposals, but in June 1765, approved the more moderate resolutions that defended the colonists' right to tax themselves.

When newspapers spread word of Virginia's action, other provinces responded. Rhode Island instructed its

DOING HISTORY

Opposing Views of Colonial Rights: The Stamp Act

WHEN NEWS ARRIVED in 1765 that Parliament had passed the Stamp Act, the colonists protested the internal tax. In the Virginia assembly, Patrick Henry introduced resolutions defending the right of "taxation of the people by themselves, or by persons chosen by themselves to represent them" and accusing Parliament of attempting to destroy "American freedom." Newspapers published seven resolutions, of which the Virginia legislators passed the first four listed below, which were more moderate than the rest. Not all Americans opposed the Stamp Act. The second document is an excerpt from a pamphlet by Martin Howard, Jr., a Rhode Island lawyer, who believed that the colonies obtained rights from their charters, which did not exempt them from parliamentary law. Here he argues that the supreme status of Parliament was based on the English common law, and if colonists presumed to seek protection of the common law in their everyday lives they should respect Parliament's power.

Virginia Resolves Against the Stamp Act, 1765

Resolved, That the first adventurers and settlers of this His Majesty's Colony and Dominion of Virginia brought with them, and transmitted to their posterity, and all other of His Majesty's subjects since inhabiting this His Majesty's said Colony, all the liberties, privileges, franchises, and immunities, that have at any time been held, enjoyed, and possessed, by the people of Great Britain.

Resolved, That by two royal charters, granted by King James the First, the colonists aforesaid are declared entitled to all liberties, privileges, and immunities of denizens and natural subjects, to all intents and purposes, as if they had been abiding and born within the realm of England.

Resolved, That the taxation of the people by themselves, or by persons chosen by themselves to represent them, who can only know what taxes the people are able to bear, or the easiest method of raising them, and must themselves be affected by every tax laid on the people, is the only security against a burthensome taxation, and the distinguishing characterestick of British freedom, without which the ancient constitution cannot exist.

Resolved, That His Majesty's liege people of this his most ancient and loyal Colony have without interruption enjoyed the inestimable right of being governed by such laws, respecting their internal polity and taxation, as are derived from their own consent, with the approbation of their sovereign, or his substitute; and that the same hath never been forfeited or yielded up, but hath been constantly recognized by the kings and people of Great Britain.

Resolved therefore, That the General Assembly of this Colony have the only and sole exclusive right and power to lay taxes and impositions upon the inhabitants of this Colony, and that every attempt to vest such power in any person or persons whatsoever other than the General Assembly aforesaid has a manifest tendency to destroy British as well as American freedom.

Resolved, That His Majesty's liege people, the inhabitants of this Colony are not bound to yield obedience to any law or ordinance whatever, designed to impose any taxation whatsoever upon them other than the laws or ordinances of the General Assembly aforesaid.

Resolved, That any person who shall, by speaking or writing, assert or maintain that any person or persons other than the General Assembly of this Colony, have any right or power to impose or lay any taxation on the people here, shall be deemed an enemy to His Majesty's Colony.

Source: Max Beloff, ed., *The Debate on the American Revolution, 1761–1783: A Sourcebook* (New York: Harper & Row, 1960), 70–72.

A Rhode Island Lawyer Supports British Power: Martin Howard, Jr., 1765

. . . But to bring this argument down to the most vulgar apprehension; The common law has established it as a rule or maxim, that the plantations are bound by *British* acts of parliament, if particularly named: and surely no *Englishman*, in his senses, will deny the force of a common law maxim. One cannot but smile at the inconsistency of these inherent, indefeasible men: If one of them has a suit at law, in any part of *New-England*, upon a question of land, property, or merchandize, he appeals to the common law, to support his claim, or defeat his adversary; and yet is so profoundly stupid as to say, that an act of parliament does not bind him: when, perhaps, the same page in a law book, which points him out of a remedy for a libel, or a slap in the face, would inform him that it does. –In a word, The force of an act of parliament, over the colonies, is predicated upon the common law, the origin and basis of all those inherent rights and privileges which constitute the boast and felicity of a *Briton*.

Can we claim the common law as an inheritance, and at the same time be at liberty to adopt one part of it, and reject the other? Indeed we cannot: The common law, pure and indivisible in its nature and essence, cleaves to us during our lives, and follows us from *Nova Zembla* to *Cape Horn:* And therefore, as the jurisdiction of parliament arises out of, and is supported by it, we may as well renounce our allegiance, or change our nature, as to be exempt from the jurisdiction of parliament: Hence, it is plain to me, that in denying this jurisdiction, we at the same time take leave of the common law, and thereby, with equal temerity and folly,

strip ourselves of every blessing we enjoy as *Englishmen*: A flagrant proof this, that shallow draughts in politics and legislation confound and distract us, and that an extravagant zeal often defeats its own purposes.

***

Source: Jack N. Rakove, *Declaring Rights: A Brief History with Documents* (Boston: Bedford Books, 1998), 50-54.

Questions for Reflection

The Virginia Assembly passed only the first four of Patrick Henry's seven resolutions. Summarize the main arguments of these four "moderate" resolves.

1. What are the chief arguments of the three more "radical" propositions that the legislators failed to approve?

2. How does Martin Howard, Jr., contest the view that provincial assemblies, not Parliament, had the right to impose internal taxes on the colonists?

Explore additional primary sources related to this chapter on the Wadsworth American History Resource Center or HistoryNOW websites:

http://history.wadsworth.com/rc/us
http://now.ilrn.com/ayers_etal3e

---

officials to ignore the stamp tax; Massachusetts, Connecticut, New York, New Jersey, Pennsylvania, Maryland, and South Carolina passed resolves similar to Virginia's. In October 1765, representatives from nine colonies traveled to New York City to attend the Stamp Act Congress. In resolutions and petitions to Parliament, the congress upheld the power of representative assemblies, not Parliament, to tax the colonists. Further, the congress defended trial by jury, which the expanded authority of the vice-admiralty courts threatened. By issuing resolves and organizing the Stamp Act Congress, the colonial elite challenged British efforts to assert control.

Ordinary colonists joined the challenge. They drew upon the tradition of the mob to protest what they considered tyranny. The anti–Stamp Act riots began in Boston on August 14, 1765, when a group who called themselves the Loyal Nine organized a demonstration to hang in effigy the appointed stamp collector for Massachusetts, Andrew Oliver. The crowd destroyed a partially constructed building they thought he intended as his stamp office, then damaged his home. Oliver resigned his commission. Twelve days later, a Boston mob attacked the houses of several other officials, gutting the mansion of Lieutenant Governor Thomas Hutchinson.

Protesters all along the Atlantic seaboard mobilized to prevent stamp distribution, scheduled to begin November 1. News of Oliver's resignation prompted anti–Stamp Act mobs in other cities to demand the same from their appointed stampmen. In some colonies, rioters forced stamp officials to relinquish their commissions. In others, just the threat of disorder was effective. By the end of 1765, distributors in every colony except Georgia had resigned.

The men who led the crowds called themselves Sons of Liberty. They were mostly propertied men—small merchants, shopkeepers, and craftsmen. These people who needed documents to conduct business would regularly feel the pinch of the stamp tax. The Sons of Liberty also established networks to organize boycotts of British goods. Merchants and retailers in New York City, Philadelphia, and Boston signed pacts to stop imports until Parliament repealed the act. By early 1766, the Sons of Liberty had coerced customs officials and judges to open the ports and resume court business without stamps. To Thomas Hutchinson, it appeared "the authority of every colony is in the hands of the sons of liberty." In truth, the American resistance aimed to expunge the stamp tax, not end British authority. The movement achieved success in 1766, when Parliament repealed the Stamp Act after British businessmen from more than 20 cities had petitioned for relief. Suffering from postwar economic depression and unemployment, the British textile industry faced even worse times with an American boycott. British merchants clearly understood the growing significance of the colonial market.

Protest Widens in the Lower South

In the Carolinas, the Stamp Act resistance spawned revolts against colonial elites. To blacks, the radicals' oft-spoken argument that the English government intended to deprive white Americans of freedom—to make them slaves—seemed ironic. Yet such statements also gave hope, for the revolutionary movement spotlighted the institution of slavery and its immorality and injustice. In January 1766, in Charleston, 1,400 seamen and a group of black slaves threatened serious disorder. The sailors became restless because the customs agents refused to release ships from port without stamped documents. The people of Charleston were even more concerned, however, when a group of enslaved men marched through the town shouting "Liberty!" The city armed itself against a slave revolt, and the South Carolina assembly became so frightened that it restricted slave imports for 3 years.

The North Carolina Regulator movement also began in 1766, inspired by the uproar against the Stamp Act, but it targeted the colonial elite, not Britain. Six thousand western farmers demanded confirmation of land titles and the end of speculators' monopoly of the best land. The Regulators also protested corrupt local officials, excessive court fees and taxes, and lack of adequate representation for ordinary backcountry farmers in the North Carolina legislature. They called for a secret ballot to reduce the influence of wealthy planters in assembly elections. The North Carolina Regulators refused to pay taxes and closed several courts. In 1771, when the government sent the eastern militia, 2,000 Regulators met them at Alamance Creek but were dispersed.

Most of the grievances of the South Carolina Regulators were different than the grievances of the North Carolina Regulars, except that they too lacked fair representation in the provincial government. They were planters who wanted to bring order, "to regulate" the backcountry. The South Carolina legislature had failed to create local government for the westerners, so they had no courts or jails. Westerners had to travel to Charleston to conduct legal business, but even worse, bandits roamed freely, stealing horses and cattle, destroying property, and sometimes torturing and killing their victims. The frontier robbers were mostly propertyless whites and some free blacks and escaped slaves; one report in the *South-Carolina Gazette* noted "a Gang of Banditti, consisting of Mulattoes—Free Negroes, and notorious Harbourers of run away Slaves." The Regulators resorted to vigilante "justice," capturing and whipping suspected felons, taking some to jail in Charleston, and evicting others from the colony. They finally ceased their activities in 1769 when the legislature established a circuit court system for the entire province.

The Townshend Revenue Act

In other British mainland colonies, attention focused on imperial tensions rather than on regional disputes. The British government and American radicals emerged from the Stamp Act crisis with conflicting views: the Americans celebrated the Stamp Act's repeal, but the British yielded no authority. In the Declaratory Act, passed with the repeal in March 1766, Parliament affirmed its power "to make laws and statutes of sufficient force and validity to bind the colonies and people of America, subjects of the crown of Great Britain, in all cases whatsoever." The act generated little response in the colonies but should have, for it laid the basis for subsequent restrictions.

In June 1767, Parliament passed three more laws affecting the Americans: an act establishing the American Board of Customs Commissioners to enforce legislation against illegal trade, the New York Restraining Act, and the Townshend Revenue Act. The Restraining Act threatened to dissolve the New York Assembly for refusing adequate supplies to British soldiers stationed in the province. Instead, the New York legislators gave in, pledging additional funds for the troops. The Townshend Revenue Act was conceived by Charles Townshend, the British chancellor of the exchequer, who wanted the Americans to contribute, over time, an increasing percentage of imperial expenses in North America. The Townshend Act, which placed duties on tea, glass, paper, lead, and paint, would be just the beginning, for they would raise less than one-tenth of the colonial administrative and military costs. The revenues would pay the salaries of governors and judges, thus removing their dependence on the provincial legislatures. The act also required colonial courts to provide customs officials with writs of assistance to search houses and businesses for smuggled merchandise.

To American Whigs, the Townshend Act was dangerous for two reasons: It raised revenue without the approval of colonial assemblies and it removed royal officials from the lawmakers' control. If the king rather than the legislatures paid provincial governors, the colonies lost a powerful negotiating tool for obtaining consent to the laws they wanted. Whereas the British saw the Townshend Act as an appropriate way to force the Americans to begin paying their share, the colonists believed it was a step toward tyranny.

At first, colonial reaction to the Townshend Act was restrained. Then, in December 1767, a few weeks after the Townshend Act went into effect, John Dickinson, a Philadelphia lawyer and owner of a Delaware plantation, began publishing a series of 12 letters signed "A Farmer." Soon reprinted by newspapers throughout the 13 colonies and published in pamphlet form as *Letters from a Farmer in Pennsylvania* (1768), Dickinson's arguments galvanized opposition to the Townshend duties. He rejected the position that the colonists should accept external taxes (duties) but not internal taxes (like the stamp tax), stating that only elected representatives could legally impose *any* revenue tax. He believed that Parliament could collect duties in the colonies if the purpose was to regulate trade (as with the Molasses Act of 1733), but not to raise revenue. Further, the purpose of the funds collected under the Townshend Act was oppressive, for it eliminated the power of the colonial legislatures over Crown officials. Dickinson predicted: "If we can find no relief from this infamous situation . . . we may bow down our necks, with all the stupid serenity of servitude, to any drudgery which our lords and masters shall please to command." Dickinson urged the 13 colonies to petition for repeal; if that failed, they should once again boycott British goods.

John Dickinson inspired opposition to the Townshend Act with his *Letters from a Farmer in Pennsylvania*. This engraving shows the right arm of Dickinson's "Patriotic American Farmer" resting on the English Magna Charta.

Massachusetts responded to the Townshend Act first. In early 1768, its assembly petitioned George III for redress, then dispatched a "circular letter" to the other 12 colonies suggesting they do the same. The new English secretary of state for the colonies, Lord Hillsborough, realized that the circular letter was a call to unified resistance. Denouncing Dickinson's pamphlet as "extremely wild," he ordered the Massachusetts assemblymen to rescind their circular letter. They refused. When he directed colonial governors to dissolve assemblies that responded to the letter, most legislatures sent petitions and were disbanded.

Simultaneously, Hillsborough reassigned military units from the Ohio Valley to Florida, Nova Scotia, Quebec, and the mid-Atlantic region where they could be called on to control the defiant provinces. In June 1768, he sent British regiments to Boston when the customs commissioners demanded protection against rioters. As the troops disembarked in October, they heard cries of protest but met no armed resistance.

During 1768, Boston residents signed a nonimportation agreement, using the same strategy against the Townshend Act that had proved successful against the Stamp Act. Most of the city's merchants pledged to stop importing goods from Great Britain after January 1, 1769, unless the Townshend duties were repealed. The nonimportation movement soon spread to New York City, where artisans supported the merchants by agreeing to boycott any retailer who imported British goods. Traders in Philadelphia, New Haven, and other northern ports delayed action, however, because they would face economic loss. They waited until 1769 for the imperial government to respond to their petitions, then approved nonimportation. In Virginia, George Washington supported the boycott. He wrote, "At a time when our lordly masters in Great Britain will be satisfied with nothing less than the deprivation of American freedom, it seems highly necessary that some thing should be done to avert the stroke and maintain the liberty which we have derived from our Ancestors."

The boycotts, which were unofficial agreements without the force of law, met uneven success. Between 1768 and 1769, American imports from England declined by 38 percent. As the months passed, however, importers wavered as their incomes fell. In contrast, craftspeople— beyond their concern for liberty—often benefited from the boycott because it created a demand for their products. Some artisans organized into street groups to threaten merchants and customs officials who tried to undermine the nonimportation pacts.

Women participated both as purchasers of goods and as producers. Many "Daughters of Liberty" gave up imported tea and clothing, signing agreements to avoid the banned goods. The *Boston News-Letter* reported that "a large circle of very agreeable ladies in this town . . . unanimously agreed" not to purchase ribbons and other imports. Instead, throughout New England, women organized spinning bees to produce woolen yarn. In Boston, some impoverished women profited from the temporary demand for American-made cloth, when William Molineaux, a merchant and radical Whig, contracted with local artisans to build 400 spinning wheels, which he distributed to women to spin yarn in their homes. With this "putting-out" system, Molineaux and the spinners responded to both their patriotism and economic needs.

Crisis in Boston

During the years 1769 to 1775, Boston became the powder keg of the Revolution. Violence broke out in the summer of 1769 between the Bostonians and British redcoats, whose chief responsibilities were to protect the despised customs commissioners and help them collect duties. The soldiers became even more unpopular when they took jobs at low pay during their off-duty hours, thus throwing city laborers out of work.

The first serious incident occurred in July 1769, when a redcoat, John Riley, was jailed for hitting a local butcher who had insulted him. A near riot followed as 20 of Riley's comrades tried to rescue him from jail. Such episodes continued into early 1770. On March 2, the violence escalated when soldiers seeking revenge for

an insult attacked workers at John Gray's ropeworks. Street fights intensified over the next few days.

On March 5, the bloodiest incident occurred, the so-called **Boston Massacre.** A young apprentice taunted the British sentry at the Customs House, who hit the boy with his gun. When a crowd gathered, shouting at the sentry, "Kill him, kill him, knock him down," Captain Thomas Preston led seven soldiers in his defense. The crowd grew larger, throwing snowballs, ice, and sticks at the soldiers and threatening them with clubs. Then someone hit a redcoat with a club, knocking the gun out of his hands. Preston's men fired, killing five townspeople and wounding six. The dead became martyrs, with March 5 commemorated as "Massacre Day" in the years ahead. The incident crystallized the colonists' opposition to standing armies. Nevertheless, when Captain Preston and six soldiers were tried for murder, the jury found two soldiers guilty of manslaughter and cleared the others. The radical Whig lawyer **John Adams** defended them, saying that all Englishmen should have a fair trial.

Just as the crisis in Boston came to a head in spring 1770, the British government decided on partial repeal of the Townshend Act, removing its duties except that on tea. The duties had raised less than £21,000 in revenues, but they had cost hundreds of thousands of pounds sterling in trade as a result of the nonimportation movement. As in the case of the Stamp Act, British officials

Burning of Gaspée, by Charles De Wolf Brownell. The seizure and burning of the British customs ship *Gaspée* by Rhode Island merchants in June 1772 moved the colonies closer to revolution.

Flashpoints | The Boston Tea Party

Initially, it seemed that the crisis could be averted. Although the unpopular Tea Act of 1773 generated great resentment within the colonies, it did not immediately spark violent colonial resistance. The cities of New York, Philadelphia, and Charleston prevented the East India Company's tea-laden ships from arriving on their shores with little fuss and no violence. It was the people of Boston who, as they had so many times in the past, proved to be the exception to the rule, the thorn in Britain's side. It was Boston, home to both ardent proponents of American rights and the staunchest

It was a challenge that the British rapidly engaged. The Tea Party angered British authorities, convincing Parliament and the Crown that Boston merited harsh immediate punishment for its rebelliousness. English diarist Matthew Brickdale spoke for many when he fumed that Boston was "the ringleader of all violence and opposition to the execution of the laws of this country." Soon after word of the Tea Party reached the parent country, Parliament passed acts designed to chasten the disobedient colony. The Coercive Acts, quickly dubbed "intolerable" by angry colonists, closed the port of Boston and greatly restricted the province's autonomy, placing it more firmly than ever under the Crown's control.

Designed to punish Boston for its insubordination, by singling out Massachusetts for special punishment and humiliation, the laws actually generated a great deal of sympathy for Boston's plight and stirred up grievances about the unjust and arbitrary nature of British rule. While aware of their serious act of defiance, the insurgents who threw the Boston Tea Party could not know that

The Boston Tea Party, 1773, a colored engraving of 1793 that is the earliest known American depiction of the event.

defenders of Parliament and the Crown, that would be the stage on which one of the most important dramas of the pre-Revolutionary era was performed.

In Boston the East India Company's ships were not turned away; there, colonists faced the choice of letting the hated tea be unloaded—or destroying it. They quickly made up their minds. Late one bitterly cold night in December 1773, the Sons of Liberty, a group of radical colonists, donned unconvincing Native American disguises, climbed on the company's ships, and dumped the tea overboard. With this deliberately dramatic "tea party," the colonists issued an unmistakable challenge to British authority.

their actions would set in motion a chain of events that solidified American resistance, drawing the colonies into a war that eventually made them an independent nation.

Questions for Reflection

1. Unlike the Stamp Act riots and Boston Massacre, the Boston Tea Party launched a series of events that resulted in war. What was different in 1773–1774?

2. Why did so many colonists find the Tea Act reprehensible?

3. Why did other provinces rally to Boston's aid in response to the Coercive Acts?

backed away from a specific revenue measure without abandoning their right to levy taxes. Following Parliament's action, merchants in New York City and other colonial ports, eager to resume trade, cancelled their boycotts except on tea. Imports into the 13 colonies from England rebounded over the next several years, increasing from £1.3 million in 1769 to £4.2 million in 1771.

The Gaspée *Incident*

For 2 years, the conflict between Great Britain and the colonies abated, then flared again in 1772. Trouble began this time in Rhode Island, when more than 100 men burned the British schooner *Gaspée,* wounding its commander, William Dudingston. Avidly enforcing the Sugar Act, the *Gaspée* had harassed merchant vessels sailing through Narragansett Bay. The Crown named a Commission of Inquiry to locate the perpetrators and send them to England to be tried for high treason. Though the Commission identified none of the *Gaspée's* attackers, colonists viewed the policy of taking defendants to England for trial as a serious threat to their constitutional rights.

In response, the Virginia assembly appointed a Committee of Correspondence to monitor British policy and facilitate communication among the provinces. Within a year, Committees of Correspondence in all 13 provinces coordinated opposition to Britain's restraints.

The Boston Tea Party

The final showdown began in 1773, when Parliament passed the Tea Act to bail out the nearly bankrupt East India Company. Though some colonists purchased British tea, the boycott on the product was still in effect and many purchased cheaper, smuggled Dutch tea. To sell the company's huge surplus, the government dropped a heavy import duty into England on tea headed for America, but it retained the Townshend duty, which Lord North insisted on keeping to uphold Parliament's power to tax the colonies. The company also received a monopoly in the colonies, with the right to choose certain provincial merchants as agents. The company selected consignees in the ports of Charleston, Philadelphia, New York, and Boston, to whom it promptly dispatched nearly 600,000 pounds of tea.

The Tea Act was doubly offensive to American Whigs because it renewed opposition to the duty and caused outrage over favoritism and privilege. One radical called the act "a dirty trick" and accused Lord North of "low cunning" for trying to break American resistance by reducing the price of tea. Before the tea ships arrived in Charleston, Philadelphia, and New York, militants

The wooden "Robinson Tea Chest," believed a relic from the Boston Tea Party, has been in the possession of one family since ancestor John Robinson recovered it in 1773 when it washed onshore.

convinced the East India Company's agents to resign. In Boston, the consignees, two of them sons of pro-British Governor Thomas Hutchinson, declined to quit. When three ships arrived, members of the Boston Committee of Correspondence, led by Samuel Adams, prevented them from unloading. Adams, a cousin of John, had been the chief agitator in Boston since the Stamp Act. A skilled politician and writer, though failed businessman, he kept the pot simmering against British policies and Governor Hutchinson. Now, with the Boston committee, he brought matters to a head: in a series of meetings, thousands of residents of Boston and surrounding towns met to refuse the tea. On December 16, 1773, when customs officials and Hutchinson denied the ships clearance to leave port, radicals ill-disguised as Mohawks boarded the ships, broke open the tea chests, and dumped them overboard. The destruction cost nearly £10,000.

For the British, the **Boston Tea Party** required stern action. London decided that steps must "be taken to secure the Dependence of the Colonies" and, in particular, "to mark out Boston and separate that Town from the rest of the Delinquents." George III believed that the Americans must be forced to submit, because they increasingly assumed the "independency which one state has of another, but which is quite subversive of the obedience which a colony owes to its Mother Country." In 1774, Parliament passed four Coercive Acts, which the colonists called the Intolerable Acts. They closed the port of Boston until residents paid for the destroyed tea and altered the provincial charter to limit the power of town meetings and create a Crown-appointed, instead

Picturing the Past — POLITICS & DIPLOMACY

Samuel Adams

John Singleton Copley painted this portrait of Sam Adams soon after the Boston Massacre. The artist shows Adams pointing at the Massachusetts charter, charging the British government with disregarding the colonists' rights. By 1770, Copley was considered by many the preeminent portraitist in British America. Unlike other painters of the time, his works were realistic, as in showing Adams's irritation with clenched lips, lined face, and coat somewhat askew.

It is interesting to compare this image with Allan Ramsay's portrait of George III in Chapter 4. While both painters intended to show men of authority, Copley depicts Adams wearing a plain cloth coat. Beginning with the Stamp Act, Sam Adams helped to make Boston the center of colonial resistance. Less is known about the details of his activity than of other revolutionaries because his papers have been lost (or he destroyed them before he died). He was a member of the Loyal Nine and the Sons of Liberty, helped draft the circular letter of 1768, and led events culminating in the Boston Tea Party.

of elected, provincial council. Further, the acts expanded the governor's control over the courts, allowed the removal of trials of royal officials to England or to another colony, and permitted quartering of troops in private buildings if a colony failed to provide suitable barracks. The Crown appointed General Thomas Gage, commander of the British army in North America, as Massachusetts governor, thus threatening the colonists with military force.

Americans also considered the Quebec Act (1774) intolerable, though London did not intend it to punish the Bostonians. The Quebec Act helped keep the loyalty of French Canadians by confirming religious freedom to Roman Catholics in the province, allowing them to hold public office. It denied Canadians an elected assembly, however, designating an appointed governor and council to make laws. Residents of the 13 colonies abhorred the act because it extended rights to "papists" and undermined representative government. It also gave control of the Ohio Valley to the Quebec government, thus curbing the ambitions of speculators in other colonies.

The First Continental Congress

Though the British government expected the Coercive Acts to isolate Boston and convince other provinces to be obedient, the policies actually pushed Americans toward more unified resistance. After the port of Boston closed, residents faced severe unemployment and food shortages. Neighboring towns provided supplies and harbored refugees looking for work. Sam Adams and the Boston Committee of Correspondence called for an immediate boycott of British trade. Instead the other provinces favored a Continental Congress to consider what action to take. The Massachusetts assembly proposed a meeting in Philadelphia on September 1, 1774, to which all of the 13 colonies except Georgia sent delegates. The 55 representatives included Richard Henry Lee, Patrick Henry, and George Washington of Virginia; Sam and John Adams of Massachusetts; and John Dickinson and Joseph Galloway of Pennsylvania.

The primary purpose of the First Continental Congress was to obtain repeal of the Coercive Acts and other restrictions. The Congress wanted Parliament to recognize the rights of Americans but was not ready to declare independence. Some of its leadership, notably Galloway (who later became a loyalist), argued for a moderate course, but the Congress was committed to action. It confirmed the Suffolk County Resolves forwarded to Philadelphia by a local Massachusetts convention. The Resolves blasted the Coercive Acts as "gross infractions of those rights to which we are justly entitled by the laws of nature, the British constitution and the charter of this province." The laws should "be rejected as the

DOING HISTORY ONLINE

The Stamp Act

Read the documents and view the image in this module. What, specifically, has upset the colonists so much? Do they overreact to the Stamp Act?

History ⊠ Now™   Visit HistoryNOW to access primary sources and exercises related to this topic: http://now.ilrn.com/ayers_etal3e

attempts of a wicked administration to enslave America." Everyone qualified to fight should learn "the art of war as soon as possible, and . . . appear under arms at least once a week." By endorsing these Resolves, the Congress took a militant stance.

Further, the Continental Congress passed nonimportation, nonexportation, and nonconsumption resolutions, ending all trade with Great Britain and Ireland, and exports to the West Indies. It also banned importation of slaves. If the British had hoped to divide the colonies by closing Boston, expecting other cities to pick up its trade,

the plan backfired when all of the colonies closed their ports. The boycott would continue until repeal of the Coercive Acts. Congress set up the Continental Association to enforce the ban on trade through elected local committees, called Committees of Observation and Inspection or Committees of Safety. The groups would expose violators of the boycott as "enemies of American liberty," publicizing their names and interrupting their business. Almost every town and county in the 13 colonies elected these committees, which soon took on other functions of local government, including raising militias and collecting taxes. This transfer of authority from colonial governments to the Committees of Observation was revolutionary, for Americans were vesting sovereignty in themselves rather than in Parliament.

Resistance Becomes a War for Independence

Over the winter of 1774–1775, the rift widened between the 13 colonies and Great Britain. George III and his ministers considered the colonies in rebellion,

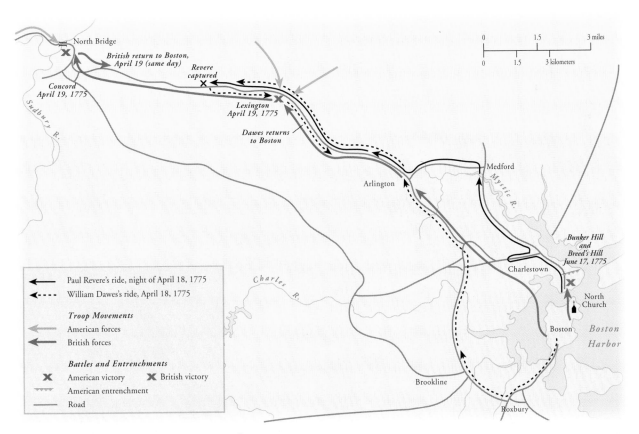

MAP 5.2 Battles in Eastern Massachusetts
Paul Revere and William Dawes left Boston during the night of April 18, 1775, to alert colonial leaders that the British troops were marching to destroy military supplies at Concord. The map also shows the location of the Battle of Bunker Hill 2 months later.

yet the colonists themselves were unprepared to declare independence.

Lexington and Concord

The British government instructed General Gage to take forceful action. Headquartered in Boston, he decided to seize the patriots' stores of food and ammunition at Concord, which he had learned about from an informer. Militant Bostonians discovered Gage's plan from their own spies, so they were ready to spread the alarm on the night of April 18, 1775, when 700 redcoats mustered on Boston Common. Paul Revere and William Dawes escaped the city to raise the colonial militia (see Map 5.2) and alert leaders Sam Adams and John Hancock, who were staying at Lexington, on the route to Concord. The Massachusetts Provincial Council, just a few weeks before, had resolved to resist any advance by Gage's troops.

As the British marched toward Concord, they heard church bells and saw lights in windows. Soon after sunrise on April 19 they reached Lexington, where they met about 70 armed militia, nearly half of the town's adult males. The Lexington company, led by Captain John Parker, had formed only a few weeks earlier, so its training was incomplete. But the men were willing to defend, in the words of their town meeting, their "natural, constitutional and chartered rights." In the face of six companies of British infantry, Captain Parker attempted to disperse his troops. The British officer, Major John Pitcairn, wanted to disarm the Americans, not engage in battle. As the British advanced, a shot rang out, then several more and a British volley. Pitcairn tried to stop his troops, but the shooting continued for 15 to 20 minutes, leaving 8 Lexington men dead and 10 wounded. Only one British soldier was wounded and none killed.

The British reached Concord at about eight o'clock in the morning, long after the patriots had hidden most of their military stores. Following a brief skirmish in which the Americans inflicted more casualties than the British, the redcoats headed back to Boston. The march became a harrowing flight for their lives. Hundreds of colonial militia from throughout the Massachusetts countryside rushed to battle. These farmers used guerrilla tactics, shooting from behind trees, walls, rocks, and buildings. The British countered by sending advance parties to clear houses along the route. Using their famed skills with the bayonet, the redcoats killed the occupants and set fire to the homes. By the end of the day, British losses totaled 73 dead and 200 wounded or missing, and Massachusetts counted 49 killed and 43 wounded and missing.

In the days that followed the battles of April 19, New England went to arms. More than 20,000 volunteers streamed to Cambridge. A large proportion of these soldiers soon returned home, but many stayed, expecting their wives, mothers, and sisters to work the family farms and defend the towns. One group of about 35 women, dressed in men's clothes and armed with muskets and pitchforks, guarded a bridge on the route British reinforcements might travel from Canada. As Abigail Adams, the wife of John Adams, later wrote,

Battle of Lexington, engraving by C. Tiebout after the drawing by E. Tisdale. The artist evokes the confusion and shock of the first battle of the Revolution.

"We are in no wise dispirited here. If our men are all drawn off and we should be attacked, you would find a race of Amazons in America."

Troops from throughout New England besieged Gage's redcoats in Boston. Nathanael Greene, a young ex-Quaker, led 1,500 troops from Rhode Island. Connecticut promised 6,000 men and New Hampshire sent 2,000. From the earliest days of conflict, African American men served in the militia units. Without a unified army, each colony separately raised troops, selected officers, and secured provisions. By May 1775, the New England forces surrounding Boston numbered about 17,000. Ethan Allen and his Green Mountain Boys of Vermont captured Fort Ticonderoga, the British garrison on Lake Champlain in northern New York.

The Second Continental Congress

On May 10, 1775, the Second Continental Congress met in Philadelphia. Although the delegates remained unwilling to support independence, they were disappointed by

George Washington, by James Peale. In choosing Washington as commander-in-chief, the Continental Congress selected a revolutionary dedicated to republican government. His perseverance and leadership kept the army together despite battlefield reverses and lack of supplies.

Independence National Historical Park

Parliament's refusal to change its course. They faced the prospect of executing a war already in progress, convinced that British troops had fired the first shots and committed atrocities. To ensure that all of the colonies backed the war and to place the military under the control of Congress, they appointed George Washington of Virginia as commander-in-chief of the Continental army. Designating a southerner to head the military, which in June 1775 consisted primarily of New Englanders, broadened the appeal of the Massachusetts cause. At the same time, Washington was himself a delegate to Congress and steadfastly committed to civilian control of the armed forces. Despite his limited military experience, Washington proved to be an excellent choice. His military bearing, determination, dignity, physical stamina, and ability to learn from his mistakes suited his role as commander-in-chief.

To serve under Washington, Congress appointed 13 generals. Its four major generals were Artemas Ward of Massachusetts; Philip Schuyler of New York; Israel Putnam of Connecticut; and Charles Lee, a veteran officer of the British army and recent immigrant to Virginia. The adjutant general was Horatio Gates, also a veteran British officer and Virginia planter.

"An Open and Avowed Rebellion"

Before Washington could arrive in Massachusetts, his troops engaged in the Battle of Bunker Hill. Learning that the British planned to seize the hills overlooking Boston, a detachment of the patriot army began to fortify the Charlestown heights. By mistake, the men built defenses on Breed's Hill rather than on the higher and less exposed Bunker Hill. This lapse might have isolated the detachment from the rest of the army had the British moved more quickly. Instead of attacking immediately, however, General Gage and the man who would soon replace him as commander of British forces, William Howe, foolishly allowed the Americans to complete their fortifications and obtain reinforcements. The British regulars lined up in proper European formation to storm Breed's Hill and Boston residents climbed to their roofs to watch. While the redcoats shot as they advanced up the hill—to little effect—the patriots waited until the enemy was within range of their guns. The redcoats failed on their first two assaults, losing many officers and troops, then with reinforcements took the hill when the Americans' ammunition gave out. The patriots retreated, pounded by artillery from British ships. Although the British won the battle, their losses were staggering: more than 40 percent of their combatants were killed or wounded.

During the year following Bunker Hill, many colonists became Whigs. The lives lost on battlefields in

The Yankee Doodle march, 1775.

For many Americans, these actions proved that the British government meant to crush the colonies militarily and economically.

The Continental Congress further alienated the British by ordering General Philip Schuyler to invade Canada. The congressmen hoped to make Canada the fourteenth British colony in rebellion. They expected to obtain help from French Canadians and perhaps even France itself, but even more, they wanted to prevent a northern attack. The American invasion of Canada was a failure from the start. Schuyler, suffering from illness and indecision, assembled troops and provisions too slowly, wasting valuable summer days. In September, much too late, Brigadier General Richard Montgomery took charge and moved the army north via Lake Champlain.

Concurrently, Washington dispatched a small army led by Benedict Arnold and Daniel Morgan over a rugged route through Maine. Their march took so much longer than predicted that the men had to eat their dogs and soap. When the combined American forces finally attacked Quebec in a blinding December snowstorm, they were defeated with heavy casualties, including Montgomery dead and Arnold wounded. The army remained in Canada until May 1776 when British reinforcements arrived, pushing the patriots back into New York. For Congress, the campaign was a tragic error. The 13 colonies lost 5,000 troops to battle, desertion, and disease, and an enormous amount of supplies.

eastern Massachusetts undercut advocates of restraint. Still, given opposition from many delegates, the Continental Congress could not declare independence. During the summer of 1775, Congress asked the king for peace while preparing for war. In July, it approved a petition to George III, called the Olive Branch Petition, asking that he resolve the dispute with Parliament. Upon receipt of the petition in August, outraged by the colonists' armed resistance, the king proclaimed the 13 provinces in "an open and avowed rebellion." In December, Parliament cut off all trade with the colonies, making American ships and any vessels engaging in commerce with the mutinous provinces subject to confiscation.

Taking Sides

The deepening conflict forced colonists to decide whether or not to support the revolutionary Whigs. Some people remained neutral, either because they cared little about the issues involved or because, like the pacifist Quakers, they were opposed to violence on religious grounds. Loyalists rejected the Revolution for a variety of motives. Some believed that the king and Parliament had reason to expect the colonists to pay their share toward imperial administration. During the course of the war, about 80,000 loyalists departed for Britain or other British colonies. Many more, perhaps several hundred thousand, continued to live among their patriot neighbors. Tories included Crown officials, Anglican clergy, and merchants with close ties to Britain. Some of the best-known loyalists were wealthy gentlemen and officeholders: Governor Thomas Hutchinson and Chief Justice Peter Oliver of Massachusetts; Joseph Galloway, speaker of the Pennsylvania Assembly; and Frederick Philipse, landlord of a 50,000-acre manor in New York.

Not all Tories were rich or intimately tied to Great Britain, for the Revolution became a power struggle within American society, not just one between the colonies and London. The tenants of New York manors, for example, took the opposite side of their landlords. Thus, residents of Frederick Philipse's manors became Whigs, whereas tenants of the patriot Livingstons and Schuylers supported the British. In Maryland, the loyalists gained widespread backing in counties on Chesapeake Bay's Eastern Shore, where farmers, suffering from economic decline and lack of political power, regarded the patriot elite as their enemies. The South Carolina backcountry divided along economic lines drawn during the 1760s, with the more affluent former Regulators supporting the Whigs, and their opponents, the "lower sort," casting their lot with the British.

Of considerable concern to white Americans were the loyalties of enslaved African Americans. Of the 2.5 million people in the 13 colonies in 1775, about 500,000 were blacks. As the rhetoric of revolution reached African American slaves, increasing numbers escaped. On Maryland's Eastern Shore, loyalist whites made common cause with the bondpeople of Whig planters: in fall 1775, a Dorchester County committee reported that "the insolence of the Negroes in this county is come to such a height, that we are under a necessity of disarming them. . . . The malicious and imprudent speeches of some among the lower classes of whites have induced them to believe that their freedom depended on the success of the King's troops."

A chief source of unrest, the patriots believed, was the November 1775 proclamation of Lord Dunmore, royal governor of Virginia, declaring "all indented [sic] servants, Negroes, or others [owned by rebels] free, that are able and willing to bear arms, they joining His Majesty's Troops." Whigs considered this proclamation foul play, an attempt to start an insurrection. They increased slave patrols and warned of harsh punishments

Antoine De Verger's sketch of American army uniforms reflects the military role of African Americans.

Anne S. K. Brown Military Collection, Brown University Library to those who ran away or took up arms against their masters. The penalty for slave rebellion, of course, was death. Nevertheless, African Americans aided the British by joining the army and employing their firsthand knowledge of the Chesapeake Bay. Some served as pilots along its tributaries; others delivered fresh provisions to the British ships by foraging plantations at night.

African Americans also supported the Revolution, but they received little welcome from the Whigs. As the Americans created an army from volunteer forces besieging Boston, they excluded slaves and even free blacks from participating. From 1775 through much of 1776, when white enlistments seemed adequate, the patriot leaders, many of them slaveowners, were unwilling to grant freedom in exchange for military service. By 1777, however, when recruiters found it difficult to fill their quotas, the states north of Virginia began accepting free blacks and slaves. Officially, Virginia took only free African Americans, but some masters sent slaves as substitutes for themselves. An estimated 5,000 African Americans served in the Continental army and state militias or at sea on American privateers. At the end of their service, many of the enslaved African Americans who fought for independence received freedom. Some masters who had pledged liberty to their slaves if they served as substitutes broke the promises after the war.

Estimates of the total number of Americans who joined the Whig forces range from 100,000 to 250,000. Most signed up for tours of duty lasting several months or a year, not for the duration of the war. An ardent Boston patriot, for example, a poor shoemaker named George Robert Twelves Hewes, served at least six different stints for a total of 20 months. Ordinary people like Hewes did their best to support both the patriotic cause and their families. Thus, Washington and his generals constantly faced the problem of expiring enlistments, a condition that severely hampered execution of the war. The inability of Congress to pay soldiers adequately also hindered recruitment and retention of troops. As time went on, the American troops became better trained and disciplined, but originated from less privileged rungs of society. By 1778, most of the states had to adopt conscription to fill their quotas. Men were drafted by lottery but could pay a fine or hire a substitute, loopholes that contributed to disproportionate service by the poor.

Women took part in the American war effort by operating farms and businesses in their husbands' absence, defending their homes and families against marauding enemy soldiers, supplying food and clothing for the troops, and joining the army. Perhaps several hundred women put on uniforms to become soldiers. These troops included Deborah Sampson of Massachusetts, who enlisted under the name Robert Shurtleff. She fought

DOING HISTORY ONLINE

Women in the Revolution

Based on the documents in this module describe the range of female wartime experience. What other perspectives or experiences can you imagine that are not represented in the module?

History Ⓧ Now™   Visit HistoryNOW to access primary sources and exercises related to this topic: http://now.ilrn.com/ayers_etal3e

in battle, but was discovered when she received a wound; after the war she collected an army pension. Others performed unofficial short-term service as spies. The most substantial contribution of women to the American military was that of the Women of the Army, as George Washington called them. Numbering perhaps 20,000 over the course of the war, they served as nurses, cooks, laundresses, and water carriers. They were regular members of the army who drew rations and were subject to military discipline. Some saw action in battle, particularly women in artillery crews who carried water to swab out the cannon after each firing. The legend of "Molly Pitcher" evolved from women like Mary Hayes of Carlisle, Pennsylvania, who took the place of fallen soldiers.

Independence and Confederation

During the winter and spring of 1776, fighting continued between Great Britain and the 13 colonies. Though the Canada campaign was a disaster, the Americans gained success in their siege of Boston. They sledged the heavy guns from Fort Ticonderoga about 300 miles, installing them in March 1776 on the Dorchester Heights overlooking Boston. Instead of storming the artillery, the British withdrew from the city, sailing to Nova Scotia in preparation for an invasion of New York City.

In 1776, London undertook a huge effort to put down the revolt. It sent across the Atlantic Ocean 370 transports with supplies and 32,000 troops, of whom many were German mercenaries (called Hessians because the largest proportion came from the principality of Hesse-Cassel). The British intended these soldiers to join General William Howe's 10,000 troops from Nova Scotia, take New York City, and destroy Washington's army. The British navy, with 73 warships and 13,000 sailors in American waters, would bombard seaports and wreak havoc on colonial shipping.

As the British military descended upon New York in midsummer 1776, the Continental Congress finally declared independence. The force of events propelled most moderate delegates to cast their vote for a complete break. In January 1776, **Thomas Paine,** a recent immigrant from England, had published ***Common Sense*** to argue the case for independence. Paine used language that appealed to ordinary Protestant Americans, employing biblical arguments that churchgoing farmers and craftspeople could appreciate, and avoiding Latin phrases and classical references. He wanted to demonstrate that the time for compromise had passed, that the proper course was to shed the British monarchy and aristocracy to create an American republic. "We have it in our power to begin the world over again," he wrote. The bloodshed that began at Lexington justified rejection of the king: "No man was a warmer wisher for a reconciliation than myself, before the fatal nineteenth of April, 1775, but the moment the event of that day was made known, I rejected the hardened, sullen-tempered Pharaoh of England for ever." Pragmatically, Paine argued that the colonists must break their ties with London if they expected aid from France and Spain. He pointed out the importance of American exports, which "will always have a market while eating is the custom in Europe." He exclaimed, "'TIS TIME TO PART . . . there is something very absurd, in supposing a continent to be perpetually governed by an island." Though his arguments were familiar to Congress and readers of political tracts, Paine convinced the American public of the need for independence. *Common Sense* sold more than 100,000 copies within a few months, reaching hundreds of thousands of people as copies changed hands and nonreaders listened to Paine's words read aloud.

Through the spring of 1776, sentiment for independence increased. News that the British had engaged German mercenaries heated the debate. The provincial assemblies of Georgia, South Carolina, and North Carolina gave their delegates in Congress permission to support the break, and Rhode Island declared independence on its own. Virginia proposed that Congress separate from Britain, taking measures "for forming foreign alliances and a confederation of the colonies." But in June, the New York, Pennsylvania, Delaware, and Maryland assemblies, controlled by moderate factions, were still not ready to condone a split. Nevertheless, Congress appointed a committee to draft the **Declaration of Independence,** of which Thomas Jefferson, a wealthy 33-year-old Virginia planter and lawyer, was the principal author. A graduate of the College of William and Mary and a serious intellectual, he had been an active opponent of British policies since first elected to the Virginia assembly in 1769.

The Declaration set forth Congress's reasons for separating from the government of George III; the revolutionaries focused on the king's offenses because they had already denied the sovereignty of Parliament. It held "these truths to be self-evident: That all men are created equal; that they are endowed by their Creator with certain unalienable rights; that among these are life, liberty,

In this painting, *The Declaration of Independence,* by John Trumbull, the drafting committee stands at center: from left to right, John Adams, Roger Sherman, Robert Livingston, Thomas Jefferson, and Benjamin Franklin.

and the pursuit of happiness." (See the Appendix for the full text.) Employing the philosophy of John Locke and other Enlightenment writers, Jefferson continued, "that, to secure these rights, governments are instituted among men, deriving their just powers from the consent of the governed; that whenever any form of government becomes destructive of these ends, it is the right of the people to alter or to abolish it, and to institute new government." Congress placed the blame for the breach on the king, listing his misdeeds: refusing to approve necessary laws passed by the colonial assemblies, dissolving legislatures and courts, stationing

Pulling down the statue of George III in New York City, July 9, 1776.

Library of Congress, Prints and Photographs Division

a standing army, interrupting trade, and imposing taxes without colonial consent. Most recently, Congress announced to the world, George III had declared "us out of his protection and wag[ed] war against us. He has plundered our seas, ravaged our coasts, burned our towns, and destroyed the lives of our people. He is at this time transporting large armies of foreign mercenaries to complete the works of death, desolation, and tyranny already begun." In reference to Lord Dunmore's proclamation, the congressmen accused the king of exciting "domestic insurrection among us." For these reasons and more, Congress declared the 13 colonies, now to be called the United States of America, "free and independent states" having "full power to levy war, conclude peace, contract alliances, establish commerce, and do all other acts and things which independent states may of right do."

On July 2, 1776, all delegations to Congress approved independence except New York's, which had not received new instructions and so was forced to abstain. Completing revisions 2 days later, Congress adopted the Declaration. For many Americans, independence ended the problem of fighting a government that they continued to recognize as sovereign. When the Continental troops heard the Declaration read on July 9, they cheered, as did civilians throughout the states. However, the battles to defend this independence still lay ahead. General Washington cautioned "every officer and soldier . . . that now the peace and safety of his Country depends (under God) solely on the success of our arms."

To mount sufficient military force to win the war, the states needed unity. In mid-July 1776, Congress began debating the **Articles of Confederation,** a plan for permanent union, which it approved and sent to the states for ratification more than a year later. The chief

disagreement among the congressmen was one that remained central to American politics for two centuries, the power of the national government versus that of individual states. The Articles permitted less centralized authority than would the Constitution, which was drafted a decade later. Under the Articles, Congress had responsibility to conduct foreign affairs, make war and peace, deal with Native Americans residing outside the states, coin and borrow money, supervise the post office, and negotiate boundary disputes between states. The "United States" meant 13 sovereign states joined together by a Congress with specific functions. Article 1 established the "confederacy" to be called the United States of America, not a sovereign nation. Article 2 held that "each State retains its sovereignty, freedom and independence, and every power, jurisdiction, and right, which is not by this confederation expressly delegated to the United States, in Congress assembled." The Congress could neither tax nor raise troops, but could only assess quotas on the states, a serious disadvantage in time of war. Even so, the Articles were not ratified until 1781, when the last of the 13 states finally approved. Conflict over state claims on western lands held up ratification. In the meantime, Congress attempted to govern within the limits of the unratified Articles, but its inability to raise revenue and draft troops obstructed the American war effort, creating huge shortages of supplies and men.

War in the North, 1776–1779

For the American patriots, the Revolution was a defensive war. It lasted 8 years, from 1775 to 1783, longer than any other in United States history until the Vietnam War.

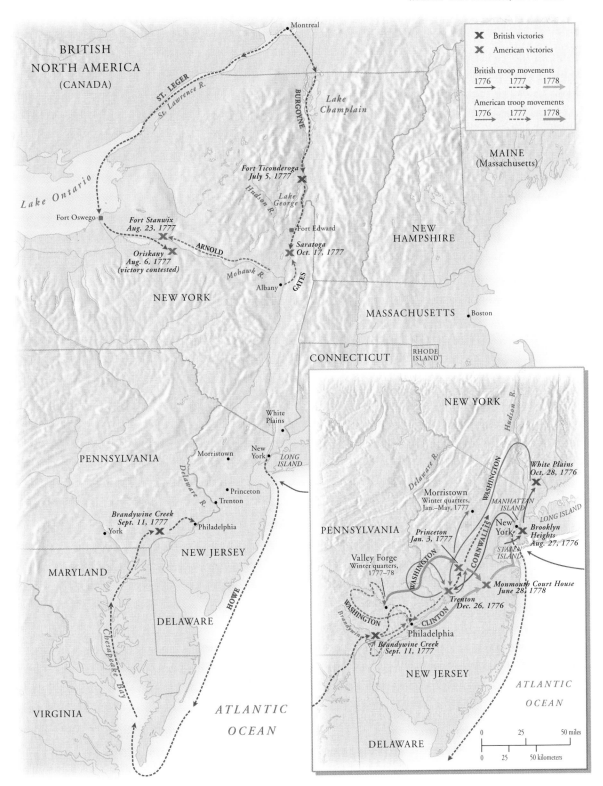

MAP 5.3 Northern Campaigns, 1776–1778

The major revolutionary battles of these years took place in New York, New Jersey, and Pennsylvania. The inset indicates battles in 1776, when the British invaded Long Island and New York City, pushing Washington's troops across New Jersey until they won crucial battles at Trenton and Princeton. The larger map illustrates British offensives in 1777; the 1778 battle at Monmouth Court House appears on the inset.

The Continental army was often outmatched, for it remained smaller than General Washington wanted; his troops constantly needed training as veterans left and new recruits arrived. But as the theater of war moved from one region to another, American generals obtained reinforcements from state militias and local volunteers. The British, despite considerable assistance from Tories, lacked enough reserves to subdue the rebellious North American seaboard. The sheer expanse of the 13 states and the 3,000-mile distance from England made the British army's task extremely difficult, despite its formal training and Britain's larger population and wealth.

Invasions of New York

To conquer New York, and thus divide New England from the rest of the states, in July 1776, British troops landed on Staten Island. In August, they attacked Washington's army at Brooklyn Heights (see Map 5.3). The redcoats defeated the Americans badly, pushing them back to Manhattan Island, and then to White Plains. But they failed to take advantage of Washington's mistakes, which could have allowed them to surround his troops. In November, however, the British did hand Washington a humiliating defeat by capturing the 2,900 defenders of Manhattan's Fort Washington.

The Continental army retreated across New Jersey with the British and their German allies at its heels. The patriots crossed the Delaware River into Pennsylvania, allowing the British to occupy New Jersey towns. The British gathered Tory support by offering a pardon to anyone who would take a loyalty oath within 60 days. For the Whigs, as Thomas Paine wrote, these were "times that try men's souls." The army was in retreat, the New Jersey government had dispersed, and citizens who were skeptical of Washington's abilities rallied to the British.

Before the end of the year, however, fortunes changed. British plundering across New Jersey turned indifferent farmers into radical Whigs, who became guerrillas, ambushing the enemy and stealing supplies. Meanwhile, Washington devised a plan that bought him time, acting before the enlistments of a large proportion of his army would expire on December 31. He attacked 1,400 Hessians at Trenton on Christmas night, in the midst of a winter storm. Taking the enemy by surprise, the Americans captured more than 900 men. In early January, Washington took the offensive once again, having convinced many of his soldiers to extend their terms for 6 weeks. Pennsylvania and New Jersey militia, inspired by the victory at Trenton, reinforced his troops. Washington eluded a superior British army under Lord Cornwallis, then defeated a smaller force at Princeton. General William Howe withdrew most of his army to New York. In the

A variety of artifacts that soldiers carried during the American Revolution, including from upper left: tin lantern, wrought iron open lamp, wooden plate or trencher, forged iron tablespoon, white clay pipes, medicine bottle, and mirror.

words of one British officer, the Americans had "become a formidable enemy."

In 1777, as the British made plans to suppress the rebellion once and for all, their strategy for the upcoming campaign became confused. General Howe intended to take Philadelphia, not by crossing New Jersey but by means of his brother Admiral Richard Howe's fleet. At the same time, London organized an invasion from Canada, to win back Fort Ticonderoga and divide the states. The campaigns were not coordinated and neither started before June, when British General "Gentleman Johnny" Burgoyne led his force of more than 7,000 British regulars, German mercenaries, Native Americans, and Canadians by boat down Lake Champlain. True to his reputation, Burgoyne overburdened his troops with baggage, including cartloads of personal clothing and champagne. Burgoyne easily took Fort Ticonderoga, then headed for Albany. The American forces under Philip Schuyler felled trees and rolled boulders into the path of Burgoyne's heavy column. Covering 23 miles of terrain that was difficult even without American sabotage took the British army 24 days. Short on supplies and horses, Burgoyne sent 800 troops to Bennington, Vermont, where General John Stark and his militia ambushed them by pretending to be Tories. Troops under British officer Barry St. Leger returned to Canada when they heard that Benedict Arnold was headed west to intercept them. The rebel forces, on the other hand, burgeoned with volunteers as British soldiers pillaged the countryside. In September, near Saratoga, Burgoyne encountered the American army under General Horatio Gates, who had replaced Schuyler. The Americans surrounded the enemy, firing upon them day and night. Burgoyne sent for help from New York City, but Howe had long since sailed with most of his troops to Philadelphia.

Burgoyne's 5,800-man army thus surrendered at Saratoga on October 17, 1777.

The British Occupy Philadelphia

As Burgoyne marched toward disaster in New York, General Howe more successfully reached Philadelphia. In July, his 13,000 soldiers departed from New York City aboard a fleet of 260 ships, but instead of disembarking within a week along the Delaware River, they sailed south to the Virginia capes, then up the Chesapeake Bay to Head of Elk. Their voyage lasted more than a month, costing Howe valuable time that might have permitted him to assist Burgoyne. Washington tried unsuccessfully, with an army of 11,000 at Brandywine, to block Howe's advance through southeastern Pennsylvania. The British occupied Philadelphia, dividing their forces between Germantown and the capital. On October 4, 1777, Washington attacked the British encampment at Germantown, inflicting serious damage, though he was once again defeated. Elizabeth Drinker, a Quaker resident of Philadelphia, in her diary reported significant losses on both sides. She wrote, "this has been a sorrowful day at Philadelphia and much more so at Germantown and thereabouts." She recorded news of the Continental army's movements, fearing that the troops would carry the battle to her city. "The apprehensions of their entering," she believed, "will render this night grievous to many." Washington did not attack Philadelphia, so the enemy retained control of the capital until they withdrew the next June.

Even so, in 1777, the British had failed to put down the American rebellion during yet another season of war. Upon hearing that Burgoyne's army had surrendered, the Howe brothers resigned. General Henry Clinton became the new commander of British forces in North America. The redcoats wintered in relative comfort at Philadelphia while Washington's troops nearly starved and froze to death at Valley Forge, to the west of the city. In February 1778, Continental soldiers lacked adequate clothing and received just three pounds of bread and three ounces of meat to last a week. Some ate only "fire cakes," baked from a paste of flour and water. Nevertheless, they became a disciplined army at Valley Forge, under the Prussian officer Baron von Steuben, who rigorously trained the Americans in the European art of war.

Alliance with France

While February 1778 brought despair to the Americans, it also brought hope—in the form of an alliance with France. Already supporting the United States with economic and military assistance, the French government hoped to recoup the international status it had lost during the Seven Years' War. Convinced by the victory at Saratoga that the former colonies could win the war, the French signed two pacts with the United States. The first was the Treaty of Amity and Commerce, in which France recognized American independence and both nations pledged "a firm, inviolable and universal peace." The second was the military Treaty of Alliance, in which they agreed to fight Great Britain jointly until the Americans had won independence, pledged not to negotiate a separate peace, and confirmed their defensive alliance "forever." France renounced claims to its former colonies in North America but could retain any of the British West Indies that it conquered.

In supporting the Americans, the French renewed their long struggle with Great Britain that had been suspended in 1763. France's entry widened the war, placing greater focus on the West Indies, whose sugar production made them more valuable than the North American mainland to the British. The following year, Spain allied with France but refused to recognize or assist the American insurgents beyond providing limited financial aid. Unlike France, which denied interest in North America, the Spanish viewed the Americans as potentially dangerous competitors.

The Wartime Economy

Despite significant economic assistance from France and a much smaller contribution from Spain, the United States had grave economic problems during the war. The loss of British markets devastated farmers, merchants, and fishermen, because the embargo closed crucial ports in the West Indies and British Isles. The Royal Navy attacked and blockaded American harbors and ravaged ships at sea. On land, the armies laid waste to farms and towns.

For Congress, the chief economic problem was paying for the war. Without the power to tax, it printed money, a total of almost $200 million in paper bills by 1779. The states printed a similar amount, despite their ability to tax, primarily because printing money was easier than trying to collect revenues from a financially strapped populace. However, as the war continued year after year, the demand for military equipment, food, medical supplies, clothing, and soldiers' wages persisted. This extraordinary demand for provisions coupled with the continuing emission of paper money sent prices soaring. By 1779, the paper money was nearly worthless, inspiring the slogan "not worth a Continental."

The depreciation of currency resulted in popular unrest, and a group of Philadelphia militia in 1779 demanded a more equitable military draft and regulation of food prices. They were angry that the burden of militia service fell disproportionately on the poor because others could pay fines to avoid the draft. At the same time, the prices of food and firewood skyrocketed. In just two months, August and September 1779, the price of beef, flour, and molasses rose by more than 80 percent. The protesters, according to one broadside posted along the streets, blamed "a few overbearing Merchants, a swarm of Monopolizers and Speculators, an infernal gang of Tories" for the spiraling costs.

ECONOMICS & TECHNOLOGY

Continental Currency

The Continental Congress, which acted under the Articles of Confederation throughout the war, lacked the ability to tax. Because the states were reluctant to raise money through taxation to support the war, Congress funded military spending through loans and printed money. Before the Revolution, colonies had printed paper currency. For example, New York and Pennsylvania issued paper money as loans, thus putting needed money into circulation and obtaining public revenue from the interest.

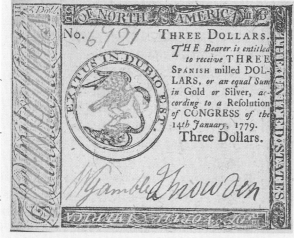

Courtesy, American Antiquarian Society

Continental money, as noted in this example, promised the bearer the equivalent in Spanish dollars. Congress thus rejected the English system of pounds, shillings, and pence to adopt the Spanish denomination. This was a logical step because Spanish coins manufactured from Mexican and South American silver and gold had commonly circulated in colonial British America despite the official English currency. Unfortunately, Continental dollars quickly lost value as Congress printed millions to fund the war. By April 1781, $168 Continental was the equivalent of one silver dollar.

In the so-called "Fort Wilson Incident," armed members of the Philadelphia militia met at Burns's Tavern on October 4, planning to capture and exile from the city four suspected Tories. Several hundred militiamen marched their prisoners through the streets to the fife and drum of the Rogue's March, ordinarily played by the military when a soldier was discharged dishonorably.

The militia was ridiculing the reputed Tories, all four of them wealthy citizens. When rumors raced through the capital that the militia planned to arrest others, about 30 gentlemen who thought they might be targets armed themselves and gathered at the house of lawyer James Wilson. Though a member of Congress, Wilson was suspect because he opposed price regulation. The militia marched past "Fort Wilson," gave three cheers, then shots rang out. Though it is unknown who shot first, both sides subsequently exchanged fire. After cavalry broke up the battle, 6 people lay dead and 17 wounded, the majority of them militia.

The Fort Wilson Incident terrified many people because lower-class patriots had directed armed force against the Whig elite, protesting the policies of their own government. Henry Laurens, a wealthy South Carolina merchant and member of the Continental Congress, wrote, "we are at this moment on a precipice, and what I have long dreaded and often intimated to my friends, seems to be breaking forth—a convulsion among the people."

The War Moves West and South

The failure of the British army to defeat Washington's troops and the entry of France into the war led the imperial government to rethink its military strategy. Protection of Caribbean sugar islands from the French navy gained top priority. With redeployment of forces to the West Indies, British General Clinton had to consolidate his army, so in June 1778, he pulled his occupation forces out of Philadelphia, marching across New Jersey toward New York. Washington's army caught up with Clinton at Monmouth Courthouse, where the battle, fought in traditional European style with soldiers in rank and file, was indecisive. The British escaped to New York.

The Frontier War

In the west, from New York to Georgia, fighting devastated the backcountry. When the Revolution broke out, many Indians supported the British, who still held garrisons in the west and had more gunpowder and provisions than the patriots. Yet Native Americans responded in various ways to "this dispute between two brothers," as neutral Iroquois called the Revolution in 1775. "The quarrel seems to be unnatural," they said; "you are two brothers of one blood." Just as colonists divided among radical Whigs, Tories, and neutrals, so did the Native Americans. Even within some tribes, factions separated those who favored the British or the Americans, or wanted to avoid any involvement. The militant Indians who sided with Great Britain considered the threat of white settlers crossing the Appalachians as most dangerous to their future. Many attempted to form pan-Indian alliances to fight their own wars of independence against land grabbers from the east.

Beginning in 1776, Indians attacked Anglo-Americans from the Georgia frontier to the Great Lakes. The Cherokees raided the southern backcountry and planned a major assault on Whig militia in Tennessee, but they ran short of gunpowder and were defeated in fall 1776. Many Cherokees, Choctaws, Creeks, Shawnees, Iroquois, and others did not give up, however, but rather planned in 1779 "a general invasion of the Frontiers" coordinated by Henry Hamilton, the British lieutenant governor of the Illinois country. **George Rogers Clark,** a surveyor, heard of plans for the Indian and British offensive. To Patrick Henry, he wrote, "the Case is Desperate but Sir we must Either Quit the Country or attack Mr. Hamilton." In 1779, with a small force, Clark assaulted Fort Vincennes and obtained the British surrender, thus ending the pan-Indian campaign.

Despite Clark's victory at Vincennes, the Kentucky-Ohio frontier remained embattled throughout the war. The same was true of Pennsylvania and New York, where after 1777 most Iroquois and Delawares abandoned their neutrality to ally with the British. In 1778 and 1779, Major John Butler, his son Captain Walter Butler, and the Mohawk leader Theyendanegea, also known as Joseph Brant, led Tory and Native American forces against white settlements. The loyalists and Iroquois burned houses, barns, fields, and orchards, ran off livestock, and killed or captured settlers over a swath of frontier ranging from 50 to 100 miles wide. In summer 1779, General Washington sent General John Sullivan with 4,000 troops, who retaliated by burning Iroquois villages, orchards, and fields of corn. At Newtown, New York, Sullivan defeated a contingent of about 700 loyalists and Indians. His scorched-earth policy seriously damaged most of the Iroquois towns; displaced Indians suffered through the winter of 1779–1780 on short rations. But the next spring they renewed their assaults.

Because many Anglo-Americans had trouble distinguishing between Indian friends and foes, Native Americans who allied with the United States or remained neutral throughout the war often fared little better with

Joseph Brant, by Gilbert Stuart. The Mohawk leader, who was educated among whites and traveled to Great Britain in 1775, convinced many Iroquois to ally with the British.

New York State Historical Association, Cooperstown

the Whigs than those who sided with the British. In March 1782, frontier militia massacred 96 pacifist Indian men, women, and children at the Moravian mission of Gnadenhutten in Ohio. The Mahicans of Stockbridge in western Massachusetts, who fought in the American army, returned home to find that whites had taken over their land. The Catawbas of South Carolina were better treated. They performed extensive service for the patriots, searching for loyalists and escaped slaves, supplying food to the rebels, fighting the Cherokees in 1776, and battling the British, who destroyed their town in retaliation. After the war, the South Carolina assembly compensated them for their loyalty and livestock, refusing to abet the governor's plan to lease out their reservation.

The Southern Campaigns

Although the Revolution ravaged the frontier, the main theater of war remained east of the Appalachians, where in 1778 the British inaugurated a new strategy. Retaining troops in New York City, they invaded the south, counting on loyalist support in Georgia, the Carolinas, and Virginia to restore colonial governments to the Crown. The British also expected the large numbers of enslaved African Americans in the south to weaken patriot defenses. In November 1778, General Clinton

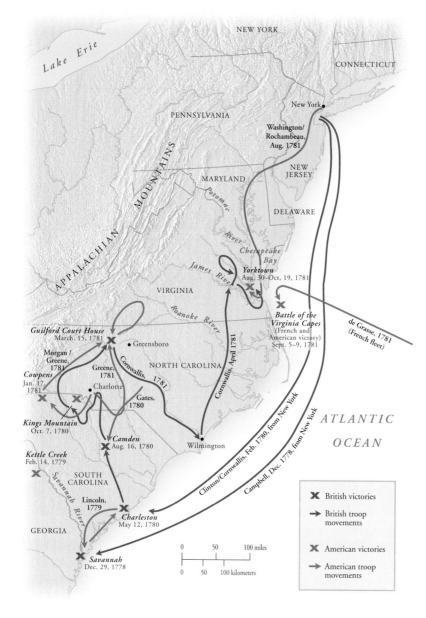

MAP 5.4 Southern Campaigns, 1778–1781

In late 1778, the British decided to invade the South, where they were no more successful in ending the war. They agreed to peace after their defeat to the Americans and French at the Battle of Yorktown in Virginia.

View an animated version of this map or related maps at http://history.wadsworth.com/passages3e.

when Gates placed too much responsibility on untrained militia in action against Lord Cornwallis at Camden, South Carolina. The battle was a rout; even the regular Continentals were dispersed, and Gates—the hero of Saratoga—was disgraced.

The tide turned after General Nathanael Greene replaced Gates as commander of the southern army. The British contributed to the turnaround, as they became more insistent in demanding oaths of allegiance from Carolinians who preferred to keep out of the fray. This provoked a backlash, particularly because the British army stretched itself so thin that it withdrew protection from the people who took the oaths, thus exposing them to punishment by the Whigs. The redcoats and Tories also plundered, outraging many southerners and pushing them into the American camp. Most notorious was Banastre Tarleton's Tory Legion, which executed prisoners of war and destroyed houses and fields, leaving many families homeless. "Bloody" Tarleton created new revolutionaries, who joined Greene's army or the smaller irregular brigades led by Thomas "The Gamecock" Sumter, Colonel Andrew Pickens, and Francis Marion, "the Swamp Fox." During 1780 and 1781, Greene rebuilt the southern army using both traditional and guerrilla forces.

While not welcome as soldiers in South Carolina and Georgia, African American slaves played an important role in the southern campaigns, acting as spies and counterspies for each side. One man, Antigua, received freedom by act of the South Carolina assembly for himself, his wife Hagar, and child in reward for "procuring information of the enemy's movements and designs." Throughout the South, African Americans provided much of the supporting labor for both armies: they built fortifications, worked in lead mines, constructed and repaired roads, produced arms and ammunition, and drove wagons. American officers complained about the chronic shortage of black laborers, because Whig slaveowners jealously guarded their strongest and most talented slaves to work on their plantations. Further, thousands of African Americans took advantage of General Clinton's 1779 proclamation offering freedom to those who joined the king's service.

sent 3,500 troops under Lieutenant Colonel Archibald Campbell to Georgia, where they joined 2,000 soldiers from Florida (see Map 5.4). They captured Savannah and Augusta, but had trouble conquering the backcountry. Then, with 10,000 troops, the British turned to Charleston, where in May 1780 they compelled the American general Benjamin Lincoln to surrender 5,500 men. The British fanned out through South Carolina, as many residents pledged their loyalty to the king. In July 1780, American General Horatio Gates arrived to build a new southern army. Disaster struck once again,

A practice of rebel leaders that highlighted their ability to dissociate their own fight for liberty from the plight of enslaved African Americans was to offer recruits enlistment "bounties" in slaves, much as other states promised bounties in land. In South Carolina, Thomas Sumter offered one African American bondman or woman to each private who would enlist for 10 months. A colonel would receive three mature blacks and one child. The practice was adopted by Andrew Pickens as well, and supported by General Greene, who expected to pay the bounties from slaves confiscated from loyalist estates. Because sufficient numbers of African Americans owned by Tories were lacking, regiments reported "pay" in arrears, some with grotesque precision. One payroll noted a deficit of 93 3/4 mature slaves and "Three Quarters of a Small Negro."

In fall 1780, Lord Cornwallis decided to head north, believing that, since the British had destroyed two American armies and taken control of South Carolina and Georgia, the time had come to conquer the entire South. As his forces marched toward North Carolina, however, they met heavy resistance. In several battles, the conflict became a civil war, as Americans fought on both sides. In October 1780, just to the south of the state line at King's Mountain, Whig frontier units defeated an enemy force, of which only Patrick Ferguson, the commander of the loyalists, was British. In January 1781, at Cowpens, General Daniel Morgan crushed Tarleton's Tory Legion by making the most of his sharpshooting frontiersmen. Morgan lined up the riflemen in front of his disciplined Continentals. The sharpshooters fired several volleys at Tarleton's troops, then withdrew to back up the regulars, who took the brunt of the fighting.

When Cornwallis learned that Tarleton's legion was lost, he chased the Americans into North Carolina, abandoning most of his equipment and supplies to move quickly. In March, Cornwallis met Greene at the Guilford Courthouse, where the American general used Morgan's Cowpens tactics, though less effectively because his successive lines of irregulars and Continentals were spread too far apart. Though the battle ended indecisively, one-fourth of Cornwallis's troops lay wounded or dead. Having discarded tents, medical equipment, and food—and cut off from his base in South Carolina—the British general withdrew to the North Carolina coast, where he sought naval support.

Meanwhile, Greene moved south to regain South Carolina and Georgia, where the British still had 8,000 men in arms. Because these troops were spread out in numerous towns and forts, Greene's 1,500 Continental soldiers and the guerrilla brigades of Sumter, Pickens, and Marion could pick off the garrisons one by one. Greene wrote to Washington in May 1781 that if the enemy "divide their force, they will fall by detachments, and if they operate collectively, they cannot command the country." By July, the Americans had pushed the redcoats and Tories back to a narrow strip of territory between Charleston and Savannah, which the British held until their evacuation the next year. Despite initial disastrous defeats, the Whigs prevailed in the Carolinas and Georgia by recruiting irregular forces and employing them strategically. The great sweep of territory controlled by the former 13 colonies proved impossible for the British army to subdue.

The surrender of Cornwallis at Yorktown in October 1781 effectively ended the war. The general had moved into Virginia in April 1781, replacing Benedict Arnold as commander of the British forces there. Arnold, the former American officer, had turned traitor, joined the British army, and most recently captured Richmond. With an army of about 8,000 men, Cornwallis intended to concentrate British military efforts in Virginia, so he requested more troops from New York. General Clinton

Surrender of Lord Cornwallis, by John Trumbull. Their loss at the Battle of Yorktown convinced the British that retaining the 13 rebellious colonies was not worth the cost.

refused. Their squabbling and delay allowed the Americans and the French to surround Cornwallis's camp on the Virginia peninsula by land and sea. Several times before, the French forces had collaborated with the Americans, but their joint efforts had resulted in failure. This time, soldiers under the Comte de Rochambeau and French fleets commanded by the Comte de Grasse and Comte de Barras played a decisive role in defeating Cornwallis at the Virginia capes. Washington's army marched south from New York to join American and French troops assembled in Virginia. With 17,000 men and heavy artillery, the American and French forces won the British surrender, finally placing the seal on American independence.

The Peace Settlement

In negotiating the peace, the United States had to reckon with both its adversary, Great Britain, and its ally, France, which in turn was beholden to Spain. American peace commissioners Benjamin Franklin, John Jay, and John Adams, whom Adams called "militia diplomats," shrewdly worked one European nation against the other to obtain a desirable settlement. They ignored Congress's instructions to take advice from France because they understood that French and Spanish goals were different from their own. France had little interest in a strong American nation; Spain particularly feared its territorial expansion. Thus, in violation of the 1778 treaty with France, the American diplomats negotiated separately with the British, obtaining recognition of independence and most other provisions they requested.

The British and American peacemakers approved preliminary articles of peace on November 30, 1782; the **Treaty of Paris** signed on September 3, 1783, was essentially unchanged. The new nation would extend from approximately the present United States–Canada boundary on the north, to the Mississippi River on the west, to the 31st parallel on the south (the present Georgia–Florida state line and due west). The American diplomats also secured fishing rights off Newfoundland and the St. Lawrence River, of particular interest to New Englanders. Further, the British agreed to evacuate their troops promptly from the United States "without causing any destruction or carrying away any Negroes or other property of the American inhabitants." For its part, Congress would urge state governments to return confiscated property to the loyalists. Prewar debts owed by citizens of each country to citizens of the other would be honored: they should "meet with no lawful impediment to the recovery of the full value in sterling money."

The treaty was a success on paper for the United States, but left France and Spain dissatisfied and pro-British Native Americans "thunder struck." In coming decades, the Americans would struggle to enforce its provisions. The French gained little from the war except the separation of the mainland colonies from Great Britain. The Spanish had wanted to keep the Americans out of the Mississippi Valley and hoped to obtain the return of Gibraltar from the British. They instead accepted East and West Florida and the Mediterranean island of Minorca. Native Americans were furious that their British allies had signed away their lands.

While U.S. possession of the trans-Appalachian region remained disputed for decades, the provision that most immediately caused trouble was the one dealing with enslaved African Americans. Even before the final treaty was signed, American slaveowners claimed that the British military forces were taking their "property." The situation was complicated, for thousands of African Americans had fled behind British lines to find freedom and some had fought against their former masters. The British ruled that blacks who sought refuge before the signing of the provisional treaty in November 1782 could not be considered the property of Americans because they were already free, but slaves who escaped after that date would be returned to their masters. General Washington, Congress, and state governments tried but failed to convince the British to return all blacks to their former masters. At least 20,000 African Americans, including those who accompanied loyalist owners as well as the ex-slaves of Whigs, left with the British military. Some went to Nova Scotia, where they received a generally unfriendly welcome from white residents; many others were transported to Florida and the West Indies. In the Sugar Islands most of the newly freed blacks were quickly re-enslaved.

Conclusion

The War of Independence was a success: American Whigs cast off a monarchy to create a new government in which many people, not a king and nobility, held power. They rejected as tyranny British efforts to impose revenue taxes without approval of representative assemblies and to curb rights such as trial by jury. The patriots used a variety of tactics, including economic boycotts, riots, mass meetings, and petitions, as well as outright warfare. Their local associations assumed governmental authority, providing the basis for republican rule.

Against many odds—including opposition from large numbers of loyalists—the 13 British colonies won independence, created a confederation of sovereign states, and obtained claims to the vast trans-Appalachian territories. French financial aid and military support were crucial to victory. The Whigs avoided military dictatorship, preserved individual rights for white Americans, and established the framework for a future democratic society. Yet not all Americans reaped immediate benefits. While wartime ideology challenged slavery in the North, the vast majority of African Americans remained enslaved. And though the Revolution offered women new, temporary roles in the economy and military—and more

permanent educational opportunities after the peace—their political and legal status was essentially unchanged. The Treaty of Paris ignored the territorial rights of Native Americans.

Of immediate importance to the nation's leaders, however, was establishing a stable government. The 1780s presented a series of challenges to the new republic.

The Chapter in Review

Discontent with British rule arose among colonists primarily because of British efforts to impose taxation without representation in Parliament. To resist British policy, colonists boycotted British goods, circulated petitions, held meetings, and participated in riots.

- Colonial resistance culminated in the Boston Tea Party. In response to this act of rebellion, Britain passed the unpopular Coercive Acts, which further exacerbated tensions between the colonies and the mother country.

- The Revolutionary War began in 1775. Despite Britain's superior military strength, the colonies, with crucial support from the French, won their independence in 1783.

- After gaining independence, Americans created a confederation of sovereign states, claimed vast lands in the trans-Appalachian territories, and built a society that granted new rights and freedoms to propertied white men.

- Not all members of society benefited equally from American independence. Under the new government, Native American land rights were not respected, the institution of slavery became more firmly entrenched, and white women, although given the new role of "republican motherhood," remained legally disempowered.

Making Connections Across Chapters

LOOKING BACK

Chapter 5 focused on the period from 1764 to 1783, when the 13 colonies moved from relatively peaceful resistance to outright war against the British government's "reform" program of new taxes and regulations.

1. Why did the colonists oppose the Sugar, Currency, and Stamp acts when they had posed no political complaint against the Molasses Act?

2. What was the role of African Americans during the Revolution?

3. How did the patriots achieve the unity necessary to wage the War for Independence?

4. How significant was the loyalist opposition?

5. What was the impact of the Revolution on Native Americans?

LOOKING AHEAD

In Chapter 6 we examine the problems facing the new United States under the Articles of Confederation and the steps that nationalists took to remedy what they perceived to be the government's ills.

1. What were the chief economic problems of the new nation?

2. How, if at all, did the status of women change after the Revolution?

3. Did the Constitution of 1787 fulfill the promise of the Revolution? Why or why not?

Recommended Readings

Calloway, Colin G. *The American Revolution in Indian Country: Crisis and Diversity in Native American Communities* (1995). Focuses on eight Indian communities to demonstrate the diversity of Native American experiences during the Revolutionary War.

Foner, Eric. *Tom Paine and Revolutionary America* (1976). A readable "life and times" of the author of *Common Sense.*

Gross, Robert A. *The Minutemen and Their World* (1976). An interesting study of how revolutionary fervor developed in Concord, Massachusetts.

Higginbotham, Don. *The War of American Independence: Military Attitudes, Policies, and Practice, 1763–1789* (1971). Straightforward military history of the Revolution.

Hoffman, Ronald, and Albert, Peter J., eds. *Women in the Age of the Revolution* (1989). Very good essays on women's status and contributions to the War of Independence.

In Search of Early America: The William and Mary Quarterly, 1943–1993, comp. Michael McGiffert (1993). Compilation of classic essays published in the foremost journal of early American history.

Morgan, Edmund S., and Morgan, Helen M. *The Stamp Act Crisis: Prologue to Revolution,* 2nd ed. (1996). A close examination of a crucial episode in the prerevolutionary decade.

O'Shaughnessy, Andrew Jackson. *An Empire Divided: The American Revolution and the British Caribbean* (2000). Evaluates the differences that led West Indies planters to stay within the empire while mainland colonists rebelled.

Quarles, Benjamin. *The Negro in the American Revolution,* 2nd ed. (1996). The classic text on African Americans during the war.

Young, Alfred F., ed. *The American Revolution: Explorations in the History of American Radicalism* (1976). Important essays on the role of ordinary Americans in the Revolution.

Identifications

Review your understanding of the following key terms, people, events, and dates for this chapter (these terms also appear in the Glossary at the end of the book):

Tories
writs of assistance
Stamp Act
Boston Massacre
John Adams
Boston Tea Party
Thomas Paine
Common Sense
Declaration of Independence
Articles of Confederation
George Rogers Clark
Treaty of Paris

Online Sources Guide

Use this listing to find online documents, images, interactive maps, simulations, and other resources related to this chapter.

American History Resource Center

http://history.wadsworth.com/rc/us

Documents

The Stamp Act (1765)
Patrick Henry's Resolutions Against the Stamp Act (1765)
John Adams's Instructions of the Town of Braintree to Their Representative
Imperial Official William Knox's Essay on American Taxation
The Coercive Acts (1774)
Thomas Paine's *Common Sense* (1776)
"The Liberty Song" (1768)

Interactive Maps

Revolutionary War in the Northern States
War in the Lower South, 1780–1781

Selected Images

George Grenville
Patrick Henry
Cartoon opposing stamp tax
Paul Revere's engraving of the Boston Massacre
Burning of a British schooner, 1772
The Boston Tea Party
George Washington assumes command of the Continental Army, July 1775

Simulation

The American Revolution (In this historical simulation you can choose to be a Patriot, a Loyalist, or a woman and make choices based on the circumstances and opportunities afforded.)

Document Exercises

1765 Resolutions of the Stamp Act
1775 Burke Speech on Conciliation with America

HistoryNOW

http://now.ilrn.com/ayers_etal3e

Primary Source Exercises

The Stamp Act
Women in the Revolution

6

Toward a More Perfect Union, 1783–1788

Chapter Outline

Politics and Change
in the New Republic

Challenges to the
Confederation

Political and Economic
Turmoil

The Movement for
Constitutional Reform

The Great Seal of the United States, adopted by Congress in 1782, incorporated
as symbols of the new nation the 13 stars and stripes, the eagle with the olive
branch of peace and arrows of war, and the motto E Pluribus Unum, Latin for
"Out of Many, One."

© Bettmann/CORBIS

The American patriots had won victory on the battlefield and, at least on paper, in negotiating the peace. The new country soon discovered, though, that independence brought severe tests as well as opportunities. In 1786, Dr. Benjamin Rush of Philadelphia summarized in a pamphlet the tasks facing the United States:

> There is nothing more common than to confound the terms of *the American revolution* with those of *the late American war.* The American war is over: but this is far from being the case with the American revolution. On the contrary, nothing but the first act of the great drama is closed. It remains yet to establish and perfect our forms of government; and to prepare the principles, morals, and manners of our citizens, for those forms of government. . . .

Having fought for liberty and self-government, Americans now had to create an effective political framework to protect those rights. Their first government was a confederation of small republics in which property-holding white men elected representatives. But questions remained about how to avoid the opposite evils of tyranny and anarchy, questions that inspired fiery debates and even rebellion during the 1780s.

American leaders had understood since 1776 that the task of creating a workable government lay before them.

They were less prepared for other problems that arose soon after the war ended. With limited powers under the Articles of Confederation, the Congress faced challenges in demobilizing the army, conducting trade outside the confines of British mercantilism, paying the war debt, coexisting with Spanish colonies in Louisiana and Florida, dealing with Native Americans, and supervising white settlement in the West. Despite Congress's competent action on some of these issues, the need for a more powerful central government became clear. In 1787, just 4 years after the conclusion of the war, delegates from the states met in Philadelphia to draft the new Constitution, which became law upon ratification in 1788. This Constitution has endured, with relatively few amendments, for more than two centuries.

Politics and Change in the New Republic

In contrasting "the American revolution" with "the late American war," Rush made a distinction that many people have debated since the 1780s. Rush thought the revolution had to continue because the government was not yet "perfect"—the states had too much power relative

Timeline

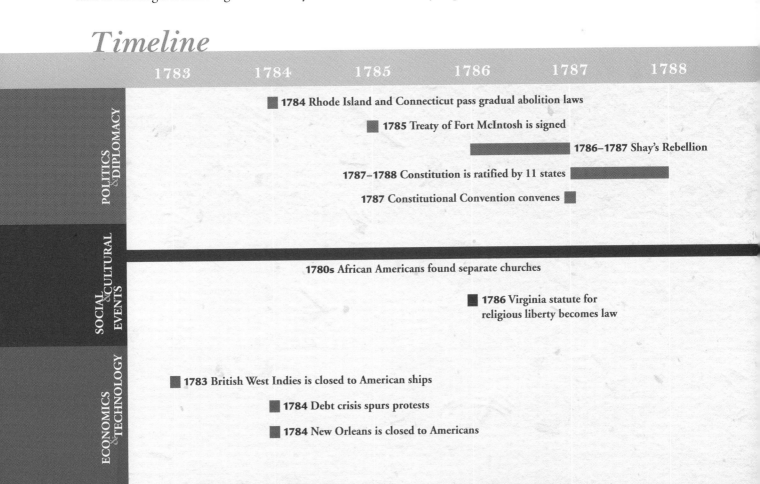

to the nation, leading to disunity and inertia. Others have framed the question in a different way: to what extent did the War of Independence bring about basic changes in politics and society? The war was revolutionary for propertied white men, but less so for women, African Americans, religious minorities, and the poor.

Republican Politics

Under the Articles of Confederation, the United States consisted of 13 sovereign states, rather than one nation (see Map 6.1). In framing the Confederation, representatives from the states had refused to transfer sovereignty to a central government. Only state assemblies, elected

---

Picturing the Past | **POLITICS & DIPLOMACY**

North America after the American Revolution

The peace treaty ending the American Revolution gave the United States most of the territory from the Atlantic Ocean to the Mississippi River, south of the St. Lawrence River and Great Lakes, and north of Spanish Florida. The new nation obtained claims to the region west of the Appalachians primarily because Great Britain, France, and Spain had more urgent goals. The treaty left several borders vague, however, and the United States had difficulty enforcing several provisions. Spain refused to recognize the 31st parallel as Florida's northern border and closed

the Mississippi River to American trade. See Map 6.2 for the area Spain ceded to the United States in 1795. Problems with Britain were more long-lived. Until 1796, the British refused to evacuate nine military posts, including Michilimackinac, Detroit, and Niagara. Britain controlled the west through these forts, both militarily and through diplomatic alliances with the region's Native Americans. The imprecise border between Maine and Canada nearly caused war between the United States and Britain two generations later, but the boundary dispute was resolved diplomatically in 1842.

MAP 6.1 North America in 1783

by the voters, could impose taxes; the central government, or Congress, would be an agent of the states. This decision was based on republican theory, which held that only in a small republic could representatives act according to the will of its citizens. If the territory were large, the interests and desires of the people would be too diverse, making harmony impossible. Furthermore, state officials, guarding their power, feared that a strong national government would be dominated by factions with interests opposite their own. Each state had an equal vote in Congress and sent delegates "appointed in such manner as the legislature of each State shall direct." Congress had responsibility to conduct foreign affairs, declare war and peace, and coin money, but could not levy taxes or raise troops. During the 1780s, its dependence on the states for funds brought the Confederation to a standstill. For years, Congress sought an amendment of the Articles to permit a national tax, but failed to obtain the required unanimous consent of the states.

The structure of the state governments reflected their framers' concept of republicanism. Most of the state constitutions resembled the old colonial governments but incorporated changes that made them more responsible to the people. Most had two-house legislatures and a governor but gave the largest share of power to the lower house of assembly, elected annually by the voters. The Pennsylvania constitution of 1776, more democratic than others, included no governor or upper house of assembly (senate), which was designed to represent the wealthier segment of society. Georgia also excluded the upper house and denied its governor any power. Even states that retained the governor eliminated his veto over legislation or allowed the assembly to override with a two-thirds vote. All of the states produced written constitutions as a protection against the kind of changes they believed the British had made in their unwritten constitution before the Revolution.

During the late 1770s and 1780s, as Americans formulated and revised state constitutions, they also developed the method by which frames of government were written and approved, the constitutional convention. Pennsylvania radicals called the first state convention in 1776, explaining that its members would be "invested with powers to form a plan of government only, and not to execute it after it is framed." Then, in 1780, Massachusetts voters demanded a convention to write a new constitution, rather than accept a document their assemblymen had prepared. The constitution was ratified by the people (voters), who thus claimed to be sovereign—the ultimate source of political power—because the frame of government originated with them. Within a few years, other states adopted the same process, recognizing that a constitution should not be

Pewter button, with the letters "USA," from the uniform of a Revolutionary War soldier.

written by a governmental body—the legislature—that the constitution created. As one theorist argued, "Conventions . . . are the only proper bodies to form a Constitution, and Assemblies are the proper bodies to make Laws agreeable to that Constitution." Remarkably, in Massachusetts in 1780, every free man, even those without property, could vote on the new constitution. However, the document they approved limited suffrage to propertied men.

State constitutions also provided some protection for the liberties many Americans had defended in the Revolution. Virginia included a model Declaration of Rights that other states copied loosely. Most state constitutions offered freedom of worship, required search warrants, and banned excessive fines and quartering of troops in private dwellings. Only some of the states, however, guaranteed trial by jury and the rights of free speech, press, and assembly. A few opposed monopolies and imprisonment for debt.

The state constitutions were radical in the context of eighteenth-century politics because they vested power in the voters and lower houses of assembly. Nevertheless, the definition of who was qualified to cast ballots and hold office remained traditional. John Adams spoke for most politicians of his time when he wrote that only property holders should be counted among the sovereign people who could choose and serve as magistrates because the purpose of government was to safeguard property. "It is dangerous," Adams wrote, ". . . to alter the qualifications of voters. There will be no end to it. New claims will arise. Women will demand a vote. Lads from 12 to 21 will think their rights not enough attended to, and every man, who has not a farthing, will demand an equal voice." Voters, according to republican theory, must have a stake in society. Wives, slaves, servants, and

During the early stages of the American Revolution, a group of about 35 Massachusetts women dressed in men's clothes and armed with muskets and pitchforks guarded a bridge against possible invasion by British soldiers. Other women also took part in the American war effort by operating farms and businesses in their husbands' absence, defending their families against enemy troops, and joining the army. Some women put on uniforms to become soldiers while others served as spies. Twenty thousand "Women of the Army," as George Washington called them, served as nurses, cooks, laundresses, and water carriers. They drew rations and were subject to military discipline. Some saw action in battle, particularly women in artillery crews who carried water to swab out the cannon after each firing. The famous story of "Molly Pitcher" evolved from women like Mary Hayes of Carlisle, Pennsylvania, who took the place of fallen soldiers.

From the earliest European settlement to the late twentieth century, women's roles expanded during war. And, as in the aftermath of the Civil War and the First and Second World Wars, women's roles again constricted at the Revolution's end. Despite the appeal of Abigail Adams to her husband John to "remember the ladies" as he and fellow members of the Continental Congress created a new government,

women saw little improvement in their political and legal standing as a result of the Patriots' success. War brought temporary expansion of female responsibility, but resulted in little permanent change in gender ideology and women's status.

During the colonial period, the conflicting Euro-American concepts of women's capability and inferiority defined gender relations in British North America. English custom, law, and Protestant theology held women responsible for guaranteeing the smooth operation of households, representing and protecting their families in the absence of husbands, and maintaining a strong relationship with God, but required women's subordination to men. Native American women held a higher status in their communities, as Indians respected women as full participants in the economy and land ownership. Iroquois and some Algonquian-speaking groups practiced matrilineal descent and recognized women's leadership in politics and society. Most African-American women in colonial America were slaves, and thus had even less control over their work and family than Euro-American women.

Under the English common law, a married woman held the legal status called *feme covert*. She

A British cartoon mocking American women who joined the boycott on tea, titled, "A Society of Patriotic Ladies at Edenton in N.C."

Deborah Sampson, shown in this 1797 portrait by Joseph Stone, was the most famous of women who served as revolutionary soldiers.

had no power independent of her husband to sell, buy, transfer, and bequeath property, control earnings, sue and be sued, make contracts, and act as guardian of the children. If the husband became incapacitated or was absent for a long time, however, the woman was often expected to manage his affairs—to become a "deputy husband." Thus English common law placed married women in an inferior position but recognized their ability to manage family business, just as the nation welcomed women's expanded roles during war.

In religious affairs as well, colonial Euro-American women held an ambiguous status. Women stood equal with men in the eyes of God in Christian denominations, but the extent to which they could participate in decision making and the ministry varied widely. Among New England Puritans, women sat separately from the men, could not speak except to sing hymns, and were allowed no leadership role. Some Puritan women, of whom Anne Hutchinson is most famous, challenged these restrictions in a variety of ways.

Courtesy, Winterthur Museum

"Keep Within Compass," published during the era of the new republic (c. 1785–1805), warned young women to remain within traditional female roles despite the revolutionary change in government.

Nowhere in colonial British America could women serve as justices or members of juries. Nevertheless, they counseled, reprimanded, and aided girls and young women who were victims or accused of crimes. Professional midwives were very important in nurturing a female community. Childbirth was permeated with female ritual and tradition, including special bed linen, food, and paraphernalia such as the "midwife's stool."

The new republic brought little change to women's lives. A married woman was still subject to the English common law that gave control of her property and earnings to her husband. Women were also barred from positions of high status. They could serve as ministers among Quakers and some Baptists but in no other churches; they taught school only at the primary level. None were lawyers or wealthy merchants, though some became successful shopkeepers. Women also lost ground in medicine. As medical courses at the college level became available to men, doctors with formal training displaced some midwives particularly in Boston, New York, and Philadelphia, where affluent clients demanded the new college-trained obstetricians.

One positive change for the status of women in the post-revolutionary years was increased support for female education, which accompanied the more general perception that a republic needed an educated people. Though women were denied entrance to all colleges, a number of academies opened their doors to provide secondary-level education to well-to-do girls. The school curricula included the three R's, English composition and grammar, geography, music, dancing, and needlework. The young women received no instruction in Latin, Greek, or advanced science and mathematics, the courses their brothers took to prepare for college.

The need for better female education became intertwined with ideas about women's roles in the new nation. Dr. Benjamin Rush, a Philadelphia physician and reformer, pointed out that improved schooling would help women fulfill their duties in running households and preparing sons to be virtuous, wise leaders of the republic. He wrote, "our ladies should be qualified to a certain degree, by a peculiar and suitable education, to concur in instructing their sons in the principles of liberty and government." The task of nurturing incorruptible future leaders, or "republican motherhood," was women's principal responsibility under the new government, not voting or holding office.

Thus, despite the significant contributions of women on the homefront and in battle during the Revolution, statesmen (and subsequent historians) defined

(continued)

Enduring Issues   Women's Status and War (*continued*)

independence as the accomplishment of men. Women's participation in the war had no permanent impact on the gender ideology of the new republic. Women gained the right to vote only after issuing the Declaration of Rights and Sentiments in 1848 (modeled after the Declaration of Independence), which led to the successful movement for women's suffrage.

Questions for Reflection

1. How did the experience of African-American men and women in the Revolution compare with that of Euro-American women?

2. What was the impact of the Constitution of 1787 on the political status of women?

unpropertied laboring men were dependent on others and thus unqualified for suffrage. Yet in most places, women and free African Americans who owned property were also barred from voting by law or by informal pressure. One exception was New Jersey, where the 1776 state constitution extended the vote to "all free inhabitants" who held sufficient property; in 1807, the legislature fell into line with other states by disenfranchising all women and blacks.

Women's Rights

Republican politics brought little change to women's lives. A married woman was still subject to the English common law that gave control of her property and earnings to her husband and denied her the right, without his permission, to make a will, sign contracts, sue in court, or act as a guardian. Despite independence, the American lawmakers refused to cast off this English tradition. Women were also barred from positions of high status. They could serve as ministers among Quakers and some Baptists but in no other churches; they taught school only at the primary level. None were lawyers or wealthy merchants, though some became successful shopkeepers. Women also lost ground in medicine. As medical courses at the college level became available to men, doctors with formal training displaced lay practitioners, including some midwives. Change occurred most noticeably in Boston, New York, and Philadelphia, where affluent clients demanded the new college-trained obstetricians.

In the postrevolutionary years, increased support for female education marked the most positive alteration in women's lives. This change accompanied the more general perception that a republic needed an educated people. Though women were denied entrance to all colleges, a number of academies opened their doors to provide secondary-level education to well-to-do girls. The school curricula included the three R's, English composition and grammar, geography, music, dancing, and needlework.

The young women did not receive instruction in Latin, Greek, or advanced science and mathematics, the courses their brothers took to prepare for college.

Discussion of the need for better female education became intertwined with ideas about women's roles in

Girl in Green, by an unknown artist, c. 1790. Although women's status remained circumscribed in many areas after the Revolution, their access to education improved, as suggested in this rare image of a girl reading a book.

Abby Aldrich Rockefeller Folk Art Center, Williamsburg

Copy of a Certificate of Indenture between a 16-year-old named Shadrach and a landowner named James Morris, Philadelphia, Pennsylvania, July 14, 1794. The term of indenture is set as 11 years, 5 months, and 25 days.

female education on the grounds that girls with developed minds would become better wives and mothers. Dr. Benjamin Rush pointed out that improved schooling would help women fulfill their duties in running households and preparing sons to be virtuous, wise leaders of the republic. He wrote, "our ladies should be qualified to a certain degree, by a peculiar and suitable education, to concur in instructing their sons in the principles of liberty and government." Nurturing incorruptible future leaders, or **republican motherhood,** was women's principal responsibility under the new government, not voting or holding office.

The Question of Abolishing Slavery

The revolutionary rhetoric of freedom and self-determination unleashed a public debate over the legitimacy of slavery. African Americans fueled the discussion by escaping to the British and serving in the American army. In doing so, African Americans made whites more aware of the hypocrisy of fighting a war of independence while they kept other human beings in chains.

In the north, the first significant opposition to slavery had developed among Pennsylvania and New Jersey Quakers well before the Revolution. Since the seventeenth century, individual members of the Society of Friends had argued that black bondage violated basic Christian concepts, particularly the belief that all humans are equal in the eyes of God. For decades, these Quaker abolitionists failed to convince their meetings that slavery was wrong because many wealthy, powerful Friends held slaves.

the new nation. Beginning in 1784, Massachusetts writer Judith Sargent Murray published a series of essays, later compiled in a book titled *The Gleaner,* in which she argued that young women should prepare to support themselves in case they found no suitable husband or their spouse died. "Our girls," she wrote, "are bred up with one particular view: . . . an establishment by marriage." Murray believed that young women should learn a vocation for independence, but also justified advanced

Pennsylvania Abolition Society Broadside

In 1775, 10 Philadelphia men founded the first abolition society in America.

They were mostly Quaker craftsmen and shopkeepers who were determined to sway public opinion against slavery and liberate enslaved people through legal and political action. Interrupted by the American Revolution, they reorganized in 1784, after Pennsylvania passed its gradual abolition act of 1780. Pennsylvania Abolition Society members then focused on enforcing its provisions, in particular making sure that free African Americans were not re-enslaved.

The abolition society distributed this diagram of a slave ship as part of a broadside against the international slave trade. The illustration shows the lower deck, with compartments (starting from the left) for men, boys, women, and girls. The text of the 1789 tract described the situation of the enslaved Africans, "packed, side by side, almost like herrings in a barrel, and reduced nearly to the state of being buried alive."

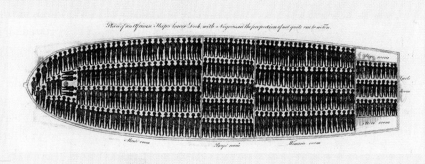

The Library Company of Philadelphia

But after 1750, the Society of Friends became the first American religion to denounce perpetual bondage as a sin and to prohibit members from holding slaves. The Quakers then spearheaded an emancipation movement that gained strength among other whites in the 1770s and 1780s, contributing, along with escapes by African Americans, to the growth of free black communities in Philadelphia, New York, and other northern towns. In addition, by the 1780s, slavery was less important economically in northern states than in the south. Thus the combination of religious conviction, natural rights concepts of liberty and equality, and pressure by African Americans undercut its viability in the north. Prospective owners, already sensitized by guilt, grew wary of purchasing slaves, who were likely to demand emancipation or run away. Instead, northern employers hired workers from among the growing numbers of free laborers, including many African Americans.

In Pennsylvania and New England, state governments acted against slavery by the mid-1780s. The Pennsylvania assembly passed the first abolition law in 1780, its preamble reflecting the ideas that inspired many abolitionists of the revolutionary era:

When we contemplate our abhorrence of that condition to which the arms and tyranny of Great Britain were exerted to reduce us, when we look back on the variety of dangers to which we have been exposed, [we are grateful for] the manifold blessings which we have undeservedly received. . . . We conceive that it is our duty, and we rejoice that it is in our power, to extend a portion of that freedom to others.

The act was less comprehensive than its heartiest supporters wished. As a result of compromises required for passage, the Pennsylvania act abolished slavery gradually—so gradually that under its provisions no black Pennsylvanian would achieve freedom until 1808. The law provided that children born to slave mothers after March 1780 would be freed when they reached age 28. Slaves who had been born before that date would remain in bondage.

The Pennsylvania act was more effective than expected, because many enslaved blacks, exasperated that the law failed to free them, escaped their masters. Hundreds of slaveholders conformed to the spirit of the law by manumitting (freeing) their slaves, regardless of birth date, at about age 28. Though these owners benefited from the labor of African Americans during their prime years, the manumissions helped hasten the end of slavery in the state. Also significant was the work of the Pennsylvania Abolition Society, which tested the limits of the 1780 abolition act by providing legal counsel to African

The Residence of David Twining, by Edward Hicks. Although northern Quakers had emancipated their slaves by the late 1780s, most free African Americans, like the man at the plow, continued to work for others as indentured servants because, as former slaves, they lacked funds to establish their own shops and farms.

Americans to defend their liberty. The number of slaves in Pennsylvania declined from almost 7,000 in 1780 to 795 in 1810.

Elsewhere in the north, the Massachusetts supreme court in 1783 decided that slavery was incompatible with the state's 1780 constitution, which said all men are free and equal, though it did not specifically outlaw perpetual bondage. As blacks sued for freedom, the courts ruled on their behalf, and so by 1790 Massachusetts reported no slaves on the federal census. The Connecticut and Rhode Island legislatures in 1784 followed Pennsylvania's example by passing gradual abolition laws, and Vermont and New Hampshire also banned the institution. New York and New Jersey passed gradual abolition acts in 1799 and 1804 respectively.

During the 1780s, considerable support for abolition also developed in the Chesapeake region, though enslaved African Americans comprised almost 40 percent of the population. Southern states, like their northern counterparts, continued the First Continental Congress's prohibition of the slave trade. Some people expected cessation of the trade to result in the gradual death of slavery in Virginia and Maryland—a mistake because the African American population there grew naturally by reproduction. Involuntary bondage would persist without positive action for abolition.

Thomas Jefferson exemplified the troubled and confused state of mind of many white Americans about slavery. Though he remained a slaveholder throughout his life and held racist beliefs, Jefferson claimed to support a strategy for gradual abolition in Virginia. The plan, never considered by the assembly, would have freed and educated African American children born after the law went into effect and, when they became adults, removed them to a separate territory. Relocation of blacks would ensure that whites would keep political power after emancipation.

Efforts for general abolition failed south of Pennsylvania, yet some progress occurred when Virginia (in 1782), Delaware (in 1787), and Maryland (in 1790) made private manumission easier. New laws permitted slaveholders who were inspired by antislavery beliefs to free their slaves. A private abolition movement took fire in areas of the Upper South where Quakers and Methodists were numerous and planters were changing from tobacco to wheat as their chief crop, thus requiring fewer field hands. Slaveholders had the choice of whether to emancipate or sell their bondpeople. A market for slaves existed in the Carolinas and Georgia, where abolitionist sentiment had little impact.

The rise in the number of free African Americans in the Upper South was a measure of opposition to slavery. The free black population in Delaware rose to more than 8,000 by the end of the century; in Maryland there were 20,000 free blacks, and in Virginia nearly 13,000. Even with impressive numbers of manumissions, however, in 1800 emancipated blacks were just 8 percent of all African Americans in the region.

Defining Religious Liberty

The issue of religious freedom also confronted the architects of the new state governments. Revolutionary ideals led many to challenge laws that forced people to attend and financially support an established church. Before the Revolution, the colonies had varied widely in the relationship of church and state. Congregational churches were tax-supported in Massachusetts, New Hampshire, and Connecticut; the Church of England (Anglican) was established in the Carolinas, Virginia, Maryland, and New York. In contrast, Rhode Island, New Jersey, and Pennsylvania protected a great diversity of religions, giving none of them public funds. All of the colonies, however, limited service in political office to members of certain religions.

DOING HISTORY

Religious Liberty

THESE THREE DOCUMENTS demonstrate the progress of the law regarding religious freedom during the 1780s. The first excerpt is a petition from the Philadelphia Jewish community. Though Pennsylvania was renowned for religious liberty, its constitution limited election to the state assembly to Christians. The new Pennsylvania constitution adopted in 1790 removed this religious test. The Virginia statute of 1786, drafted by Thomas Jefferson, was a major breakthrough: while itself an act of legislation, rather than part of the state constitution, the law affirmed religious liberty as a natural right. Amendment 1 of the U.S. Constitution, part of the Bill of Rights, prohibited Congress from establishing a religion.

Petition of Philadelphia Jews for Equal Rights, 1783

To the honourable the Council of Censors, assembled agreeable to the Constitution of the State of Pennsylvania. The Memorial of . . . the Synagogue of the Jews at Philadelphia, . . .

That by the tenth section of the Frame of Government of this Commonwealth, it is ordered that each member of the general assembly of representatives of the freemen of Pennsylvania, before he takes his seat, shall make and subscribe a declaration, which ends in these words, "I do acknowledge the Scriptures of the old and new Testament to be given by divine inspiration," . . .

Your memorialists beg leave to observe, that this clause seems to limit the civil rights of your citizens to one very special article of the creed; whereas by the second paragraph of the declaration of the rights of the inhabitants, it is asserted without any other limitation than the professing the existence of God, in plain words, "that no man who acknowledges the being of a God can be justly deprived or abridged of any civil rights as a citizen on account of his religious sentiments." But certainly this religious test deprives the Jews of the most eminent rights of freemen, solemnly ascertained to all men who are not professed Atheists.

May it please your Honors, . . .

—Your memorialists cannot say that the Jews are particularly fond of being representatives of the people in assembly or civil officers and magistrates in the State; but with great submission they apprehend that a clause in the constitution, which disables them to be elected by their fellow citizens to represent them in assembly, is a stigma upon their nation and religion, . . .

The Jews of Pennsylvania in proportion to the number of their members, can count with any religious society whatsoever, the Whigs among either of them; they have served some of them in the Continental army; some went out in the militia to fight the common enemy; all of them have cheerfully contributed to the support of the militia, and of the government of this State; they have no inconsiderable property in lands and tenements, but particularly in the way of trade, some more, some less, for which they pay taxes; they have, upon every plan formed for public utility, been forward to contribute as much as their circumstances would admit of; and as a nation or a religious society, they stand unimpeached of any matter whatsoever, against the safety and happiness of the people.

And your memorialists humbly pray, that if your honours, from any consideration than the subject of this address, should think proper to call a convention for revising the constitution, you would be pleased to recommend this to the notice of that convention.

Source: Richard D. Brown, ed., *Major Problems in the Era of the American Revolution 1760–1791* (Lexington, MA: D.C. Heath and Company, 1992), 358–359.

Virginia Statute for Religious Freedom, 1786

. . . Be it enacted by the General Assembly, That no man shall be compelled to frequent or support any religious worship, place, or ministry whatsoever, nor shall be enforced, restrained, molested, or burthened in his body or goods, nor shall otherwise suffer on account of his religious opinions or belief; but that all men shall be free to profess, and by argument to maintain, their opinion in matters of religion,

and that the same shall in no way diminish, enlarge, or affect their civil capacities.

And though we well know that this assembly elected by the people for the ordinary purposes of legislation only, have no power to restrain the acts of succeeding assemblies, constituted with powers equal to our own, and that therefore to declare this act to be irrevocable would be of no effect in law; yet we are free to declare, and do declare, that the rights hereby asserted are of the natural rights of mankind, and that if any act shall be hereafter passed to repeal the present, or to narrow its operation, such act will be an infringement of natural right.

Source: Merrill D. Peterson and Robert C. Vaughan, eds., *The Virginia Statute for Religious Freedom: Its Evolution and Consequences in American History* (Cambridge: Cambridge University Press, 1988), xvii–xviii.

The Bill of Rights, 1791

Amendment I
Congress shall make no law respecting an establishment of religion, or prohibiting the free exercise there-of; or abridging the free-

dom of speech, or of the press; or the right of the people peaceably to assemble, and to petition the Government for a redress of grievances.

Source: The Constitution of the United States of America (see Appendices for full text).

Questions for Reflection

Though William Penn founded Pennsylvania on the basis of religious freedom for all people who believed in God, the colony required officeholders to be Christians.

1. During the colonial period, how did Pennsylvania compare with other provinces regarding religious liberty?

2. What arguments did Philadelphia Jews employ to challenge this inequity?

3. What was the significance of the Virginia Statute for Religious Freedom of 1786 and Amendment 1 of the U.S. Constitution?

Explore additional primary sources related to this chapter on the Wadsworth American History Resource Center or HistoryNOW websites:
http://history.wadsworth.com/rc/us
http://now.ilrn.com/ayers_etal3e

The break with Great Britain had the greatest impact on the established Church of England, called the Protestant Episcopal Church in the United States after the Revolution. With independence, some of its parishes dissolved, as missionaries departed because the church hierarchy in England stopped paying their salaries. Many Anglican clergymen and laypeople in New England and the Mid-Atlantic region had been loyalists, which helped fuel the Whig movement for disestablishment. Upon independence, all of the states in which the Anglican Church was established promptly ended government support except Virginia, which finally acted in 1786. Its assembly passed Thomas Jefferson's statute for religious liberty, stating, "no man shall be compelled to frequent or support any religious worship, place or ministry whatsoever, nor shall be enforced, restrained, molested, or burthened in his body or goods, nor shall otherwise suffer on account of his religious opinions or belief."

Nevertheless, the movement to end discrimination stalled, and in the 1780s, religious tests for political office remained common. Most Americans, who were overwhelmingly Protestant, thought that only Christian men, preferably Protestants, should govern. State and local laws required observance of the Sabbath, outlawed gambling and other entertainments, and proclaimed days of thanksgiving and prayer. The states most resistant to disestablishment were the old Puritan strongholds in New England. Massachusetts, New Hampshire, and Connecticut required tax support for Protestant churches well into the nineteenth century.

DOING HISTORY ONLINE

The Administration of Justice and the Description of the Laws by Thomas Jefferson

Based on what you have learned from the textbook and modules from other chapters, how would you defend Thomas Jefferson's *Notes on the State of Virginia* as an enlightened text?

History Now™   Visit HistoryNOW to access primary sources and exercises related to this topic: http://now.ilrn.com/ayers_etal3e

Challenges to the Confederation

Despite the dominance of the states, the Confederation Congress had important functions that required far more unity and power than it possessed. Of all Congress's difficulties, the inability to tax was most damaging, resulting in the Confederation's quick demise.

Military Demobilization

One of the most remarkable aspects of the American revolutionary experience—in light of revolutions since that time—was the absence of a serious military challenge to civilian control. George Washington was committed to popularly elected government and thus ignored suggestions that he become a military ruler. Even so, the United States faced two problems concerning the armed forces. During the war, Congress failed to pay or supply the army properly, but had promised generous pensions and bounties to entice men to sign up for the duration of the war. The second question confronting Congress was whether to establish a peacetime army, an issue that had both ideological and financial significance.

For 2 years after the Battle of Yorktown in 1781, the Continental army continued to exist, with Washington encamped at Newburgh, New York, where his troops monitored the British army still in New York City. American officers and enlisted men voiced grievances because they needed food, clothing, and wages. Soldiers rioted and insulted their officers, while many simply went home with no compensation except their weapons. Officers at Newburgh drew up a list of complaints for Congress, demanding as much of their back pay as possible and a full reckoning of the entire sum they were owed. The officers suggested that they receive lump sums instead of the promised pensions of half-pay for life. They seemed so disgruntled that Washington remained at Newburgh instead of going home to Mount Vernon as he had planned.

The officers' discontent became more threatening when several politicians who favored a strong central government recognized an opportunity to pressure the states into giving Congress the power to tax. In what became known as the Newburgh conspiracy, **Robert Morris** of Philadelphia and Gouverneur Morris and Alexander Hamilton of New York hatched a plan to use the officers' protests to strengthen the Confederation. Washington would not cooperate, stating that the army was a "most dangerous instrument to play with," even to obtain a national tax. In early 1783, rumors spread that the officers were ready to take "manly" action against the government unless their demands were met. The crisis ended when Washington pledged to negotiate for their back pay and pensions and the officers swore their loyalty to Congress. For its part, Congress agreed to pay troops three months' wages at discharge, and officers would receive pensions of 5 years' full pay in government bonds. A group of 80 enlisted men stationed at Lancaster, Pennsylvania, found the offer unacceptable, so they mutinied and marched on Philadelphia, barricading the State House where Congress met. Though the soldiers backed down without violence, the frightened congressmen fled to Princeton.

Restitution of military pensions, back wages, and bounties took until the 1790s because Congress lacked the funds to discharge its debts. Soldiers who had been promised land bounties in the west had to wait 15 years for surveys, in large part because Native Americans refused to give up the territory. By the 1790s, most veterans had long since sold their rights to speculators for a fraction of their worth.

The issue of a standing army squared revolutionary ideology against the need for defense. One of the chief causes of the Revolution had been the peacetime quartering in New York and Boston of the British army, which patriots called a "MONSTER of a standing ARMY." But now the United States faced threats from the Spanish in Florida and Louisiana, the British in Canada, and Native Americans everywhere along the frontier. In April 1783, Congress appointed a committee to consult Washington and other generals on military requirements. The commander-in-chief argued that the United States had to be prepared against its enemies. He suggested retaining 2,600 Continentals in one artillery and four infantry regiments. He also advised Congress to organize a national citizens' militia that would stay in training for ready defense. In 1784, Congress dismissed Washington's plan, stationing a total of 80 men at two forts in New York and Pennsylvania. For reasons of principle and finances, the Confederation government virtually disbanded the army during an interval of peace, a pattern the nation would follow well into the twentieth century.

Economic Troubles

The Confederation Congress failed to solve the problem of its war debt, which by 1790 amounted to an estimated $10 million owed to other countries and $40 million owed to Americans. During the war, the government had issued paper currency to pay for goods and services. It abandoned this policy because of rampant inflation. Congress turned to the states, which refused to contribute sufficient funds, then borrowed from France and from American merchants and farmers for military provisions.

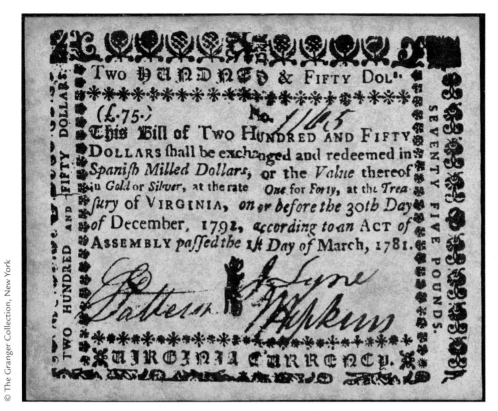

This 1781 example, from Virginia, of early national paper currency demonstrates the interchangeable values in British pounds, Spanish milled dollars, and American dollars.

Morris proposed the institution, based on the Bank of England, as a way to help solve the wartime fiscal crisis. Morris obtained support from Alexander Hamilton, Thomas Paine, and a committee of Congress for his plan; both the Congress and state of Pennsylvania chartered the institution. Instead of issuing paper currency through a land office, as farmers wanted, the bank issued currency in the form of short-term loans to merchants. These bank notes were backed by gold and silver plate and coins that investors deposited in return for a share of the bank's profits. The attraction for stockholders was that formerly idle gold and silver assets could now earn interest. The Bank of North America earned regular profits during its first two decades, beginning with an 8.74 percent dividend to investors in 1782. If people doubted the security of the bank, they could redeem their bank notes. Bank advocates believed that once a few people tested its soundness and received specie, others would trust the bank and accept the bank notes as currency.

In fact, the Bank of North America followed a conservative course that kept it solvent financially but made it unpopular with many people. The bank's manager, Thomas Willing, lent money only to good credit risks in the mercantile community, thus angering artisans and farmers who viewed the bank as a monopoly created by Congress to benefit the commercial elite. Also, Willing refused to liberalize the bank's loan policy as confidence in the bank's strength increased. Instead of expanding the money supply as later banks did, the Bank of North America made loans only up to the amount of specie in its vaults.

Despite its flaws, the Bank of North America helped the mercantile community through a time of uncertainty. Commerce had suffered in the period immediately preceding and during the Revolution as merchants lost connections with trading partners in Great Britain and the British West Indies. In 1783, Americans expected to reestablish those ties as well as enter new markets in Europe and the French and Spanish colonies. With their

As mentioned above, it also deferred payment on soldiers' wages. As the principal and interest mounted on these promissory notes and bonds, Congress requested an amendment to the Articles to permit a national duty of 5 percent on all imports. The legislators tried for five years to obtain the necessary unanimous agreement of the states but failed on each attempt.

One long-lasting consequence of the war's inflationary crisis was conflict between urban and rural interests over public finance. The spiraling cost of food and fuel in the late 1770s had hurt city residents much more than farmers. In public debate over currency and credit, farmers wanted access to government loans based on the value of their land and its production, similar to the colonial land banks that had allowed them to use real estate as collateral for loans. Though the provincial currency issued by the land banks had been fairly stable, in the 1780s, merchants and urban artisans recalled the more recent inflation of the Revolution. They believed that paper currency based on real estate would send prices sky-high. At the same time, merchants knew that the economy would stagnate if specie (gold and silver) were required for every transaction, so they embraced an alternative method of generating paper currency, the bank.

The first bank in the United States was the Bank of North America, created in 1781 in Philadelphia. Robert

Robert Morris and Gouverneur Morris

In 1783, Charles Willson Peale painted this portrait of Robert Morris (right) and Gouverneur Morris, the superintendent of finance and his assistant, who were unrelated. Robert Morris, born in Liverpool, England, was a wealthy Philadelphia merchant who supervised procurement of military supplies during the Revolution. He was one of the founders of the Bank of North America, the country's first bank, which was modeled after the Bank of England and was intended to help relieve the wartime economic crisis. Gouverneur Morris, who came from a wealthy New York family,

excelled as Robert Morris's assistant in the finance office. Both men became frustrated by Congress's weakness and the repeated failure to gain approval of a national tax. They joined with other nationalists in the Newburgh conspiracy to use the army's discontent over unpaid wages to press for adoption of a more centralized government. When Alexander Hamilton became the first secretary of the treasury, he adopted a number of Robert Morris's ideas, including the national bank and federal assumption of state debts.

Courtesy of the Museum of American Art at the Pennsylvania Academy of the Fine Arts, Philadelphia. Bequest of Richard Ashhurst.

newly won independence, they gained release from the restrictions of British mercantilism.

But being part of the mercantilist system had brought advantages as well as constraints. The British closed the ports of the British West Indies to American ships, a sharp blow for New England and the Middle Atlantic states, which before the war had found a major market in the islands for exports of fish, grain, flour, lumber, and livestock. To Great Britain and its colonies, the United States was now a foreign country. Americans could sell provisions in the islands and purchase rum, sugar, and molasses, but everything had to be carried on British ships. West Indies planters complained because

this resulted in higher prices; American ship owners had to find new routes. On the other hand, Britain was eager to purchase tobacco from the Chesapeake and to sell to Americans all the manufactures they would buy. U.S. merchants had access by treaty to ports in France and the French colonies but were barred from trading in New Spain. Gradually, Americans developed trade with Germany, the Netherlands, Scandinavia, and even China. By the end of the 1780s, U.S. exports recovered to approximately their prerevolutionary level.

The road to recovery was rocky, however, because in the immediate postwar years American demand for British manufactures far outstripped exports. During the Revolution, American artisans had attempted to supply metal goods and textiles, but had been unable to match British quality and prices. With peace, British manufacturers extended generous credit to American consumers for clocks, watches, furniture, textiles, clothing, mirrors, and other goods. When depression hit in fall 1783 because of the loss of the West Indies market, American farmers, merchants, and shopkeepers found themselves seriously in debt. In New England, for example, the balance of trade with Great Britain was so uneven that exports covered only 13 percent of imports. While the economy improved after mid-1785, many farmers had difficulty escaping from debt.

Indeed, estimates of the gross national product suggest that the Revolution had an extended negative impact on the American economy. Data available for 1774 and 1790 indicate that income declined by more than 40 percent, close to the decrease Americans experienced during the Great Depression of the 1930s.

Foreign Affairs

Though the United States had won the war, its leaders soon learned that they received little respect among European nations. Despite the boundary provisions of the Treaty of 1783, Spain and Great Britain took advantage of the Confederation's weakness to trespass on territory in the west. The Spanish and English gained allies among Native Americans who were losing their lands to the steady stream of white settlers crossing the Appalachians.

During the 1780s, Spain tried to restrict expansion of the United States. The Spanish government had refused to accept the treaty boundaries granting the region between the Appalachians and the Mississippi River to the United States. With settlers rapidly filling the area, Spain feared for its control of Louisiana and East and West Florida; it wanted to extend its territory north from West Florida to the Ohio River. The Spanish pursued this objective in a number of ways. They retained forts north of the 31st parallel, which the United States claimed as its southern border (refer back to Map 6.1). Then, in 1784, the Spanish government closed the port of New Orleans to Americans, apparently hoping to detach from the United States the region that later became Kentucky and Tennessee. Settlers in the trans-Appalachian region protested vigorously because they needed access to the New Orleans market for their goods. Some threatened to secede from the United States unless Congress convinced Spain to reverse its decision; a few, including James Wilkinson, a former Continental army officer, actually negotiated directly with the Spanish. Reporting on a journey in the west, George Washington wrote, "the western settlers (I speak now from my own observation)

stand as it were upon a pivot; the touch of a feather would turn them any way."

Congress directed **John Jay,** the secretary of foreign affairs and a New Yorker, to negotiate with Spain to reopen the port. The Spanish diplomat Diego de Gardoqui refused to budge, instead offering to open other Spanish ports to U.S. commerce if Americans would relinquish demands for free navigation on the lower Mississippi. With the permission of Congress, Jay agreed to a treaty that provided commercial advantages for eastern merchants but closed New Orleans to westerners for a generation. The west and south erupted in opposition, blocking approval of the Jay-Gardoqui Treaty. The lower Mississippi River remained closed until 1788, when the Spanish permitted Americans to use New Orleans upon payment of duties.

The Spanish government also cooperated with Native Americans to slow the influx of Anglo-American settlers into contested territory. Spanish colonists in the Floridas remained few, so they depended on good relations with the Creeks, Choctaws, and Chickasaws who controlled the region. Groups of Creeks who had migrated to Florida, and were called Seminoles by the British, could mobilize at least twice as many soldiers as the Spanish. Contrary to Spain's traditional policy of considering Native Americans as subjects to the Crown, its colonial officials in 1784 signed written treaties of alliance with the Indians.

Most threatening of these pacts to the United States was the one with the Creeks, which their leader Alexander McGillivray arranged. The son of a Scottish trader and a French-Creek woman, and educated in Charleston, McGillivray could negotiate his way in both European and Indian societies. To protect Creek lands from settlers streaming in from Georgia, he offered the Spanish "a powerful barrier in these parts against the ambitious and encroaching Americans" in return for an alliance and weapons. The Creeks called the invading Georgians "Ecunnaunuxulgee," or "people greedily grasping after the lands of the red people." With Cherokees and Shawnees to the north, the Creeks battled Anglo-Americans through the 1780s, thus slowing settlement on the southwest frontier.

The Confederation government also had difficulty establishing its claims against the British and the Indians of the Ohio Valley. In the treaty of 1783, the British had promised to remove their troops from forts in the Great Lakes region. Through the 1780s, however, they refused to withdraw, hoping for return of the territory. They barred American ships from the Great Lakes and allied with Native Americans who wanted to halt white settlement. British diplomats justified these actions with the excuse that Americans had failed to pay prewar debts to British creditors and return confiscated loyalist property.

MAP 6.2 Western Land Cessions, 1782–1802

A number of states claimed territory west of the Appalachians based on their colonial charters. For example, under Connecticut's charter, which defined the Pacific Ocean as its western boundary, residents claimed part of Pennsylvania as well as western lands.

Great Britain's neglect of its Indian allies in negotiating the peace led the U.S. government to treat them as a conquered people. With great bravado, considering the Confederation's small army, American commissioners said to the Ohio Indians, "You are mistaken in supposing that . . . you are to become a free and independent nation, and may make what terms you please. . . . You are a subdued people." Other officials announced, "We claim the country by conquest." Under threat of arms, a group of Iroquois yielded rights in the Northwest with the Treaty of Fort Stanwix (1784); Wyandots, Delawares, and others

ceded Ohio lands in the Treaty of Fort McIntosh (1785); and Shawnees gave up territory in the Treaty of Fort Finney (1786). Many Native Americans refused to recognize these treaties because their negotiators lacked authority and had been forced to sign.

Soon, frontier warfare made U.S. officials realize that they were the ones who were "mistaken" in presuming that the Indians had been "subdued." Theyendanegea (Joseph Brant), the pro-British Mohawk leader, rallied Indians against white settlement in the Northwest. In 1786, he urged potential allies, "the Interests of Any One

Nation Should be the Interests of us all, the Welfare of the one Should be the Welfare of all the others." Their resistance convinced Secretary of War Henry Knox that the United States must change its tactics or risk a general Indian war. He suggested that Congress return to the policy of purchasing lands, instead of demanding them by conquest. The congressmen agreed, incorporating into the Northwest Ordinance of 1787 the futile promise that the Indians' land "shall never be taken from them without their consent."

The Northwest Ordinances

Despite war with the Indians and the presence of British troops, the Confederation Congress moved forward with legislation to create the Northwest Territory. The issue of western lands had divided the 13 states even during the Revolution. Some states claimed territories from their colonial charters; others, such as Maryland and New Jersey, had never possessed such claims. Titles stood in conflict with one another, as in the case of the region north of the Ohio River, which Virginia claimed in its entirety and Connecticut and Massachusetts claimed in part. States lacking rights to western lands believed that all should be ceded to the Confederation because together the states had won the trans-Appalachian territory in the Revolution. Virginia, whose charter rights were oldest, resolved the issue in 1781 by agreeing to transfer to the United States the region north and west of the Ohio River, the area that later became the states of Ohio, Indiana, Illinois, Michigan, and Wisconsin (see Map 6.2). Virginia offered cession on the condition that the territory eventually be divided into states that would join the Confederation on an equal basis with the original 13. The trans-Appalachian lands south of the Ohio River remained temporarily under the control of Virginia, North Carolina, and Georgia.

Congress passed three ordinances to establish guidelines for distributing land and governing the Northwest Territory. Wealthy speculators who had purchased rights from Native Americans had significant influence over the shape these ordinances took. Thomas Jefferson was principal author of the first ordinance, which passed Congress in 1784. This law gave settlers a great deal of autonomy in establishing a territorial government. The Northwest would be divided into seven districts, with the settlers of each to govern themselves by choosing a constitution and laws from any of the existing states. When any district reached the population of the smallest of the original 13 states, it would be admitted as a state to the Confederation on equal terms. Congress retained responsibility for selling the public lands.

SCENE IN SHAYS'S REBELLION.

© The Granger Collection, New York

A nineteenth-century colored engraving of a scene from the period just prior to Shays's Rebellion. A Massachusetts blacksmith is served in 1786 with a writ for debt.

The second ordinance, passed in 1785, set the rules for distributing lands. The influence of speculators was apparent, for the minimum price of a lot was $640, payable in specie or its equivalent, a sum far beyond the means of many potential settlers. All property would be surveyed before sale, laid out in townships 6 miles square (see Map 6.3). Each lot would contain 640 acres, sold at a minimum of $1 per acre, with better land offered at a higher price. The government retained lots for public schools and for distribution to Revolutionary War veterans. Because of the relatively high cost, Congress found few individual buyers. In fact, many land-hungry squatters simply set up their farms without government approval, sometimes purchasing rights from neighboring Indians, sometimes not. So Congress accepted a deal offered by a group of New England speculators, the Ohio Company, agreeing to sell them 1.5 million acres for $500,000 in depreciated bonds, or less than ten cents per acre in hard money. Given the Confederation's debt, the sale was welcome.

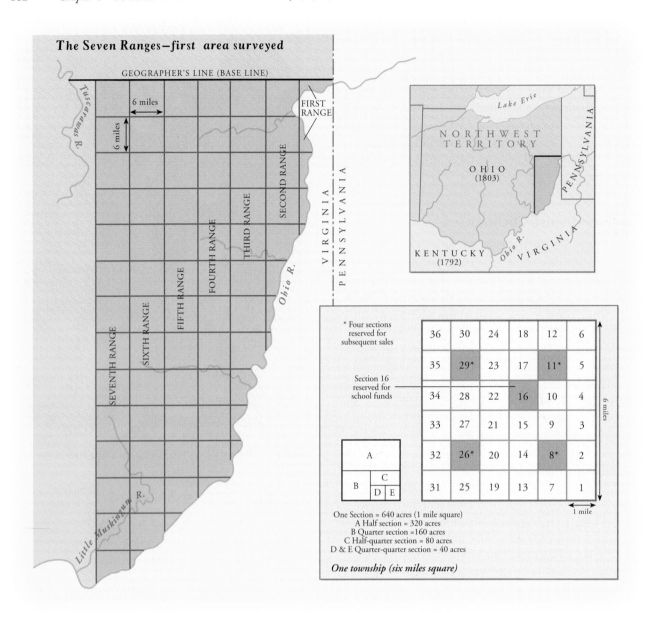

MAP 6.3 Land Ordinance of 1785

This map shows the plans for dividing land in eastern Ohio into townships and lots. The minimum price was $1 per acre.

Congress further cooperated with the Ohio Company in drafting the **Northwest Ordinance** of 1787. In response to speculators' demands, the law established firmer congressional control over the territory, providing settlers less self-government than under the 1784 ordinance. Initially, a governor, secretary, and three judges appointed by Congress would administer the government. When 5,000 adult males resided in the territory, they could elect an assembly, but the governor held a veto over its actions. Men were eligible to vote if they owned at least 50 acres of land. Three to five states would be created from the Northwest Territory, with each state qualified to enter the union when its population reached 60,000. New states would have equal status with the original 13. The ordinance of 1787 also included provisions for individual rights that the Congress and the Ohio Company hoped would attract purchasers from New England. The ordinance protected private contracts, religious liberty, trial by jury, and habeas corpus (protection against illegal imprisonment). It prohibited slavery from the region forever. Thus, while catering to the interests of speculators, the Northwest Ordinance also extended rights won during the Revolution to new settlers in the west. Further, it limited the spread of slavery and determined that western territories would achieve the status of states rather than remain colonies.

Political and Economic Turmoil

Political strife under the Articles of Confederation disappointed Americans who had high hopes for their republic. Instead of harmony, economic interests clashed; the states failed to satisfy everybody. Many elites thought the United States was becoming too democratic and anarchic—as farmers revolted, government failed to control the violence, and some legislatures approved the insurgents' demands.

Creditors Versus Debtors

As a result of the postwar depression, farmers throughout the United States faced economic hardship. Many had eagerly purchased British manufactures, expecting to pay for the new clothes and consumer goods by selling their grain and livestock to the West Indies. British merchants offered easy credit to stimulate sales; American merchants and shopkeepers passed the credit on to farm families who would pay with the fall crop.

The house of cards collapsed when the British government closed the West Indies to American ships. English mercantile houses called in their debts in specie only, starting a chain of default that extended from London to the frontier. Americans lacked the gold and silver that the British demanded, but merchants refused to accept payment in farm products because they had no market for the goods. So they took farmers to court: in many places, the number of debt cases rose dramatically. For example, in Hampshire County, Massachusetts, from 1784 to 1786, the court heard 3,000 debt cases. Almost one-third of the county's adult males were prosecuted for insolvency.

State governments aggravated the situation by imposing taxes to repay war bonds in full, a policy that worked to the advantage of wealthy speculators who had bought up the bonds from farmers and artisans at a large discount. The Massachusetts government particularly favored mercantile interests, levying on farmers high taxes that also had to be paid in specie. When farmers defaulted, the courts sold their land and cattle, often at only one-third to one-half value. If their assets failed to cover the debts and back taxes, the farmers were imprisoned until they or someone else paid the sum. Often men sat in crowded jails with insufficient ventilation, heat, or food because they owed small debts. Ordinary folk became angry as they feared imprisonment and the loss of their farms.

Farmers Demand Reform

Protesters mobilized as they had in the prerevolutionary period, at first meeting in county conventions to draw up petitions to the state assembly. In Massachusetts, they demanded changes in the state constitution to make the government more responsive to their needs and less costly to run. They wanted abolition of the state senate, which represented the commercial elite; lowering of property qualifications to hold office; and transfer of the capital from Boston to a more central location. Inland towns found it difficult to send representatives to the assembly because expenses were so high. The farmers also demanded paper money and tender laws, the latter enabling them to settle debts and taxes with goods rather than specie. Both would ease the credit crisis. During the Revolution, the yeomen had benefited from inflation and were able to pay off prewar debts with cheap dollars. While they stopped short of demanding a return to high inflation, they hoped for a gentle upswing in prices and a larger money supply to help them settle their debts.

When state legislatures emitted paper money or passed tender laws, as in Rhode Island, North Carolina, New York, and Georgia, little unrest ensued. In Rhode Island, political parties channeled conflict, for after the Country party ousted the Mercantile party in spring 1786, the new assembly issued paper money with stiff fines for creditors who refused to accept it. Elites elsewhere referred to "Rogue Island," even suggesting that the state be abolished and divided between Massachusetts and Connecticut. In other states, mercantile factions maintained control of the government. They detested paper money because debtors would pay in depreciated bills; they opposed tender laws because of the lack of a market for grain and livestock. Merchants argued that paper currency issued as loans on farm property (rather than as notes based on gold and silver deposited in banks) was immoral because it would lose value, allowing debtors to violate contracts by paying back less than they had borrowed. Creditors asserted that their property rights were at risk.

Shays's Rebellion

When state governments failed to help, debtors in New England, New Jersey, Pennsylvania, Maryland, Virginia, and South Carolina protested militantly. Events moved furthest in Massachusetts. In fall 1786, armed Massachusetts farmers closed down county courts to prevent further hearings for debt. Perhaps one-fourth of potential soldiers in the state were involved, calling themselves the "Regulators," after the Carolina insurgents of the 1760s. Their opponents first labeled the rebels "Green Bushers" because they wore a sprig of evergreen—the Massachusetts symbol for liberty—then called them Shaysites when Daniel Shays, a 40-year-old veteran of Bunker Hill and Saratoga, emerged as leader. The government frantically requested aid from Congress, which complied by

Daniel Shays and Job Shattuck, from the cover of a pamphlet supporting Shays's Rebellion.

requisitioning $530,000 and 1,340 soldiers from the states. When the states failed to cooperate, the powerlessness of the Confederation was clear.

The Massachusetts government acted on its own, taking measures that further alienated angry farmers. The assembly passed the Riot Act, which prohibited armed groups from gathering in public and permitted sheriffs to kill rioters who refused to disband. The legislature also suspended habeas corpus, allowing officials to jail suspected insurgents without showing cause. The farmers refused to back down, as one warned, "I am determined to fight and spill my blood and leave my bones at the courthouse till Resurrection." They protested that the suspension of habeas corpus was "dangerous if not absolutely destructive to a Republican government." Nevertheless, in November 1786, the state government sent 300 soldiers to arrest rebel leaders; when that failed to stop the farmers from closing the courts, Boston merchants raised private funds to outfit 4,400 troops. Residents of Boston and coastal towns who feared the inflationary consequences of paper money filled the ranks. Revolutionary general Benjamin Lincoln commanded the army; in January 1787, they marched to Worcester to protect the county court.

Lincoln's army forced the Shaysites to choose between submission and armed rebellion, for a middle ground of petitions and court closings was no longer viable. The farmers amassed their own troops, estimated at 2,500 men, with Shays in charge of one regiment. They unsuccessfully attacked the federal arsenal at Springfield for weapons to assault Boston, then regrouped to await the merchants' army. Shays was convinced that their cause was just; in a newspaper interview he confidently stated that he "knew General Lincoln was coming against him, but as he would bring with him nobody but shopkeepers,

lawyers, and doctors, he could easily defeat him." Lincoln attacked Shays by surprise in a blizzard, dispersing the rebels within half an hour.

The aftermath of Shays's defeat was more divisive and bloody than the engagements between the armies. The assembly declared a state of "open, unnatural, unprovoked, and wicked rebellion," giving the governor the power to treat the Shaysites as enemies of the state. The legislators passed the Disqualification Act, which barred people implicated in the revolt from voting and holding office for 3 years, teaching school, or keeping inns and taverns. Many of the insurgents escaped to New York and Vermont. Others, including individuals who had not been involved, were imprisoned. Militant Shaysites prolonged the conflict by raiding homes and kidnapping people who had sided with the government. As a result of the uprising and repression, voter turnout skyrocketed in the April 1787 election. A much greater number of western Massachusetts towns sent delegates to the legislature than they had in previous years, making the new assembly somewhat more responsive to rural debtors. While refusing to approve paper money, it enacted a tender law and quickly restored the civil rights of the insurgents.

The Movement for Constitutional Reform

The Confederation's helplessness in response to spreading armed rebellion strengthened the hand of nationalists like Robert Morris and Alexander Hamilton, who had been arguing for a more powerful central government. By 1787, Congress had lost much of its authority, and representatives stopped attending, often preventing action for lack of a quorum. Because it had failed to obtain a national tax and could not force the states to send requisitioned funds, the Confederation was broke. In 1785, Congress stopped interest payments on the French debt and in 1787 ended those on the principal. Nor could it reimburse American creditors. In 1787, Congress transferred responsibility for the national debt to the states.

The Philadelphia Convention

In September 1786, when **Shays's Rebellion** was still gathering steam, representatives gathered for a convention in Annapolis, Maryland, to discuss amending the Articles to give Congress power to regulate trade. The convention failed when only five state delegations arrived on time. Several of the delegates, including Alexander

The eighteenth-century print shop in Philadelphia, Pennsylvania.

Hamilton, **James Madison,** and John Dickinson, called for another convention to meet in May 1787 at Philadelphia to consider a more thorough revision of the Articles. By early 1787, the disorder in Massachusetts and the growing concern about state emission of paper money built support for constitutional reform. In February, Congress endorsed a change in the Articles. Twelve states—all but Rhode Island where farmers controlled the legislature—sent delegates to Philadelphia.

Though the appointed day was May 14, 1787, the convention failed to start until May 25, when enough representatives finally arrived. State legislatures had delayed choosing their delegations and travel was slow. Among the first were Virginia's representatives, who used the extra time for planning. James Madison, a 36-year-old planter, slaveholder, and intellectual who had served in the Virginia assembly and Congress, came to the convention well prepared. A shy man who avoided public speaking, Madison nevertheless took a dominant role in the proceedings, for which he was later called the father of the Constitution. Propelled by the breakdown of Congress and the problems he witnessed in state government, Madison wanted to reform the Confederation to create a stronger central government. He believed that state constitutions with powerful assemblies were too democratic, giving too much influence to the common people. As a consequence, these legislatures collaborated with debtors by circulating paper money, which Madison considered an attack on property. The common people should be represented adequately, Madison thought, but their power must be constrained. The United States needed a new constitution that would place authority in the hands of well-educated, propertied men. Another Virginia delegate was George Washington, whose popularity and prestige made his support for the convention crucial. He presided over the proceedings but participated little in the debates.

A total of 55 men served at the **Constitutional Convention** between opening day and adjournment 4 months later. Twenty-one were practicing lawyers, another 13 had been educated in the law, 7 were merchants, and 18 were farmers or planters; nineteen owned African American slaves. Most were relatively young men under the age of 50, and many had served in the Revolution and had held political office. Benjamin Franklin, now 81 years old and ailing, was a member of the Pennsylvania delegation. Several heroes of the Revolution were absent, including Thomas Jefferson and John Adams, who served as ministers to France and Great Britain, respectively. Samuel Adams was not chosen as a delegate and Patrick Henry refused to participate because he "smelt a rat." Most of the delegates supported a plan to place more power in the national government.

The State House, Philadelphia, site of the Constitutional Convention, 1787.

The Great Compromise

The convention can be divided into two periods. During the first 7 weeks, the matter overshadowing all discussion was the power of large versus small states. After this issue was resolved, delegations formed blocs in new ways, according to concerns about the executive, slavery, and commerce. The basic question that the convention avoided debating at length was whether to amend the Articles of Confederation or write an entirely new constitution. Madison, who thought the Confederation beyond repair, moved the convention along with a document he had drafted in advance, called the **Virginia**

Flashpoints | James Madison and the Virginia Plan

"But what is government itself, but the greatest of all reflections on human nature? If men were angels, no government would be necessary. If angels were to govern men, neither external nor internal controls on government would be necessary. In framing a government which is to be administered by men over men, the great difficulty lies in this: you must first enable the government to control the governed; and in the next place oblige it to control itself." So wrote "The Father of the Constitution," James Madison of Virginia, in *The Federalist #51*. Already acknowledged as an intellectual at the age of 36, Madison arrived at the 1787 Constitutional Convention with definite ideas about the sort of government the United States should have.

When the convention commenced in May 1787, the city of Philadelphia was, so one delegate complained, "muggy and choked with flies." Madison later remembered that in the Pennsylvania State House (now Independence Hall), where the debates were held, the heat was often so unbearable that he feared it would kill him. But neither heat nor discomfort prevented Madison from advancing his Virginia Plan, which Governor Edmund Randolph of Virginia introduced early in the convention. In this way, Madison focused the early debates on his ideas and ensured that the convention would go beyond simply revising the Articles of Confederation.

Much to the horror of representatives from small states such as New Jersey and Delaware, the Virginia Plan insisted on the need for a powerful national government, even if this centralized authority came at the expense of the autonomy of individual states. Deeply distrustful of state sovereignty, Madison maintained at this time that a strong central government should have

James Madison, 1783 by Charles Willson Peale.

© The Granger Collection, New York

the power to veto state laws, which, he thought, had the potential to infringe on individual rights. Small states had further reason to dislike the Virginia Plan for its insistence on apportionment of state representation by population. It was easy, representatives from smaller states argued, for delegates from heavily populated states such as Virginia to support proportional representation. But, delegates such as William Paterson of New Jersey declared, small states would surely be overshadowed, and their interests neglected, in a legislature that was strictly proportional.

Madison and his allies eventually compromised on the issues of proportional representation and state sovereignty. Yet much of Madison's Virginia Plan—his proposal for a government with three main branches, a bicameral legislature, and a judiciary with lifetime appointees—became part of the Constitution relatively unchanged. The Virginia Plan also raised important questions about the nature of national government and states' rights, questions that remained a vital element of American politics many years after the Convention ended, to the Civil War and beyond.

Questions for Reflection

1. From your reading in Chapter 6, what events caused James Madison and other nationalists to support a more centralized national government?

2. How did the "great compromise" amend Madison's Virginia Plan?

3. Do you agree that Madison should be considered "The Father of the Constitution" or should the credit be distributed more widely among other framers of the document?

This painting of the Constitutional Convention of 1787 by an unknown artist shows George Washington presiding. Because the convention met in secrecy, the artist used his imagination to paint the scene.

Plan, which scrapped the Articles. Madison was able to set the convention's agenda because at the outset no delegate had prepared an alternate design.

The Virginia Plan proposed a powerful central government, dominated by a National Legislature of two houses (bicameral). The lower house would be elected by qualified voters and would choose the members of the upper house from nominations by state legislatures. The number of delegates from each state would depend on population. This **bicameral** National Legislature would be empowered to appoint the executive and judicial branches of the central government and to veto state laws.

Several states opposed the Virginia Plan because it gave greater representation in the National Legislature to states with large populations. Delaware, Maryland, New Jersey, and Connecticut feared the power of Virginia, Pennsylvania, and Massachusetts, which together comprised almost one-half of the American people. If the Virginia Plan were adopted, just four states could dominate the legislature. In dividing on this issue, states considered the possibility of future population expansion as well as present size. Thus states with unsettled territories mostly sided with the large states, while those without room for growth chose the opposite camp.

The small states preferred a constitution that retained the structure of the Confederation Congress, but expanded its powers. In mid-June, William Paterson introduced the **New Jersey Plan,** which proposed a one-house, or unicameral, Congress in which the states had equal representation. Congress would appoint an executive council, which in turn would choose a supreme court. As in the Virginia Plan, the authority of Congress was much enlarged, with powers to tax, regulate commerce, and compel states to obey its laws. The large states objected to this plan, arguing that Delaware (population 59,000) should not have as much power as Virginia (population 748,000).

The debate over representation in Congress brought the convention to an impasse. It made little progress toward a new constitution until the issue of state representation was resolved. The large states had a majority of the votes in the convention but knew that ratification would be impossible if the Virginia Plan prevailed. The Delaware delegation threatened to walk out until Connecticut formally proposed what has become known as the "**great compromise.**" The plan established a bicameral Congress, with representation in the lower house based upon population. This body, called the House of Representatives, would be elected directly by the voters every 2 years and have the sole right to initiate revenue bills. Thus, the idea that all people with a stake in society should elect the representatives who taxed them was incorporated into the document. In the upper house, called the Senate, states would have equal representation; each state legislature would choose two senators for 6-year terms. The bicameral Congress resolved the division between the small and large states and also satisfied those who wanted to limit the influence of ordinary voters. Senators were expected to come from the wealthier, more established segments of society; their long terms and appointment by state legislators would shield them from public opinion and thus provide a stabilizing influence. Both houses of Congress had to approve legislation.

The compromise between the large and small states created a government that was both national and federal. It was *national* because the House of Representatives was popularly elected, with not more than one representative per 30,000 people. Upon ratification, the United States would become a single nation rather than a confederacy of states. By expanding legislative powers, the sovereign people vested more authority in the central government. Congress received the powers to tax, coin and borrow money, regulate commerce, establish courts, declare war, and raise armed forces. States were specifically forbidden from keeping troops without the permission of Congress, making treaties, coining money, and issuing paper currency. At the same time, the new Constitution established a *federal* government, one in which the states retained rights, including equal representation in the Senate. Congress was forbidden from giving one state preference over another when levying taxes and regulating trade, nor could it impose export duties, prohibit the slave trade until 1808, or carve a new state from any state's territory without permission. Approval by three-fourths of the states would be necessary to amend the Constitution. But despite these provisions, many Americans believed that the states—the small republics—had lost too much power. The struggle for ratification would revolve in large part around this issue.

The Executive, Slavery, and Commerce

Once the question of state representation was solved with the "great compromise," the convention made greater headway. Factions within the convention shifted from one debate to the next.

The power of the executive was a concern to people living in a world dominated by kings and princes. Delegates wanted to ensure that their government remained a republic, that it would not become a monarchy or dictatorship. At the same time, they believed that the executive branch should serve as a check on the legislature. The convention debated several questions affecting the executive's power. Should there be a single president or an executive board? While some argued that a plural executive could prevent one person from usurping power, the convention chose a single president, expecting to limit his authority in other ways. Length of term also stimulated discussion, for the longer the term, the greater

a president's autonomy. The convention reached agreement on a 4-year term, without specifying the number of times the president could be reelected.

The question of how the president would be chosen was divisive, with some preferring direct election by the people and others wanting Congress or the state legislatures to make the choice. Once again, the issue of states' rights reared its head. A committee appointed by the convention devised an ingenious but complicated formula to satisfy all sides: an "**electoral college**" was empowered to elect the president and vice president, with each state allotted as many votes as it had representatives and senators. Thus, even the smallest state received three votes and the large states were represented according to population. The state legislatures could determine how to choose the electors. The electoral college would never meet together as a group. The electors of each state gathered within their states to cast votes, which they sent to Congress for counting. If no candidate received a majority, the House of Representatives made the selection from among the five candidates with the most votes.

Of the Philadelphia convention's decisions on the executive, most crucial to the endurance of the Constitution was the balance of power between the executive and legislative branches. The convention gave the president a veto power over laws passed by Congress. The legislators could override the veto if two-thirds of both houses approved. Congress also had authority to remove the president by impeachment and trial for treason, bribery, and "other high Crimes and Misdemeanors." Whereas Congress received power to declare war and raise troops, the president served as commander-in-chief. Only with the "advice and consent" of the Senate could the chief executive negotiate treaties and appoint ambassadors, Supreme Court justices, and other officials.

Slavery was a major factor in the convention's deliberations, though the words "slavery," "slave," and "slave trade" appeared nowhere in the 1787 Constitution. African American bondage affected the debates on representation in Congress, the election of the president, and the regulation of commerce. The southern states wanted to include slaves in a state's population when computing delegates to the House of Representatives and votes in the electoral college. Since slaves made up significant portions of the population in southern states (see Table 6.1), northerners protested that this would give white southerners an unfair advantage. They argued that slaves should not be counted because they could not vote. As part of the "great compromise," the convention decided that five enslaved Americans would count as three free persons for apportioning representation and direct

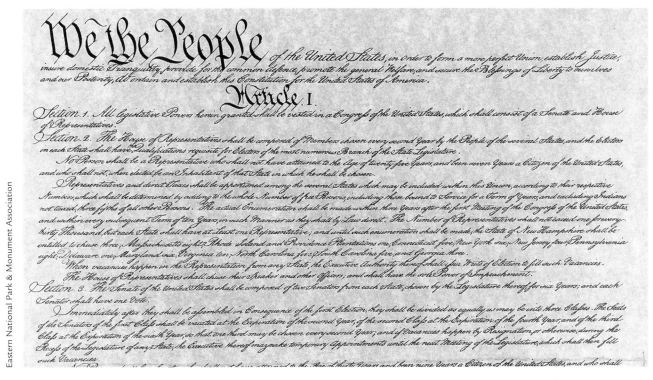

Eastern National Park & Monument Association

First page of the U.S. Constitution of 1787.

taxes among the states. Since three-fifths of slaves living in the Chesapeake and Lower South numbered 380,000 people, the power of white voters south of Pennsylvania was significantly increased by this compromise.

Political bargaining resulted in additional provisions that upheld slavery. The convention approved a fugitive slave clause, which prevented free states from emancipating slaves who had escaped from masters in other states. The delegates also adopted a provision that forbade Congress from prohibiting slave importation for 20 years (with no requirement that it ban the slave trade after that time). North and South Carolina and Georgia demanded the option of importing people from Africa because they expected settlement to continue into western Georgia and the present states of Alabama, Mississippi, and Tennessee.

Table 6.1 Enslaved Population in the United States, 1790

	Total	Slaves
New England	1,009,206	3,763
Middle Atlantic	1,017,087	45,210
Maryland and Virginia	1,067,338	395,663
Lower South	726,626	237,141

Northern delegates did almost nothing to promote the abolition of slavery. Instead, they made the regulation of commerce their priority. The New England delegates agreed to the 20-year protection of the slave trade in return for a compromise on international trade. The southern states suspected that the national government, if dominated by northerners in the future, would place heavy taxes on tobacco, rice, and indigo—the South's main exports. Southerners thought that navigation laws could also work to their detriment, because northern merchants owned most American shipping. If Congress passed legislation requiring that all exports be transported in American ships, southerners would lose the choice of using a foreign, perhaps cheaper, carrier. Northerners, on the other hand, wanted Congress to have the authority to negotiate trade agreements on an equal basis with other nations. Congress could then retaliate if a country imposed restrictions such as closing ports. The convention settled these matters, first by forbidding Congress from imposing export duties, then with a deal that empowered Congress to regulate commerce. In return for South Carolina's vote for the latter provision, New England agreed to extend the slave trade for 20 years.

The Philadelphia convention created a Constitution that shifted important powers to a national government but still vested a great deal of authority in the states. The framers painstakingly created checks and balances among

The Federal Procession in New York, 1788, artist unknown. Residents of New York City celebrated the new Constitution, applauding their representative Alexander Hamilton's efforts for ratification.

the branches of government. They required direct popular election of only the House of Representatives, giving that body the right to initiate taxes. The convention incorporated flexibility into the document, which had been absent in the Articles of Confederation, by permitting amendment with approval of two-thirds of both houses of Congress and three-fourths of the states.

The document shielded some individual rights, though critics argued that many were omitted. The Constitution protected trial by jury in criminal cases and habeas corpus. It banned religious tests for holding office under the United States, ex post facto (retroactive) laws, and bills of attainder, which extinguished a person's civil rights upon sentence of death or as an outlaw. While codifying the principles of self-government and individual liberties, however, the convention denied them to almost one-fifth of the American population by embedding slavery within the fabric of the new government.

Ratification

After the delegates to the Philadelphia convention signed the Constitution on September 17, 1787, they quickly sent it to the Confederation Congress, which forwarded it to the states after little debate. One congressman from Virginia, Richard Henry Lee, tried to bury the document by adding amendments, but he was overruled. Article 7 of the document required ratification by nine state conventions. States refusing to ratify could remain independent or unite under another frame of government. Advocates of ratification knew that prompt action was necessary to forestall an effective opposition movement.

The group favoring ratification was not particularly well organized but had two advantages over its opponents. One advantage came from the choice of a name, the Federalists, for it undercut the ground on which their adversaries stood. James Madison, Alexander Hamilton, John Jay, and other supporters of the Constitution argued in favor of the federalist provisions that reserved powers to the states as well as the nationalist elements of the prospective government. While others denounced the Constitution because it transferred too much power to the national government from the states, the Federalists claimed the document provided balance. The critics were obliged to take the negative name of Antifederalists, which misrepresented their position in favor of states' rights.

The second advantage of those favoring ratification was that many advocates of a strong central government resided in the coastal cities and towns, where public opinion was easier to mobilize than in outlying areas. Most newspapers supported the Constitution. For example, in New York, where the ratification battle became intense, Hamilton, Madison, and Jay published in the newspapers a series of 85 essays that provided a detailed argument in favor of the Constitution. The essays also gained wide attention outside New York, and in spring 1788, the authors published them in book form as *The Federalist,* which is still considered a major work in American political theory.

Most Federalists gained their livelihoods as merchants, shopkeepers, professionals, artisans, and commercial farmers. As creditors and consumers, many favored the Constitution because it stopped state emission of paper currency. Federalists desired a government that would foster the growth of a market economy and facilitate trade with other countries. They believed a national government would provide the stability and strength that were lacking under the Confederation, enabling the United States to gain stature among the nations of Europe. Some frontier settlers, seeking military defense against Native Americans, also supported the Constitution.

The Federalists, who viewed commercial development more favorably than the Antifederalists, thought the purpose of government was to arbitrate among opposing interests. They believed that society benefited when people pursued their own individual goals. They considered elusive the republican ideal of a community in which citizens could reach a consensus because they had similar needs. Madison argued in *Federalist #10* that people possess different interests because they have unequal abilities and thus varying success in accumulating

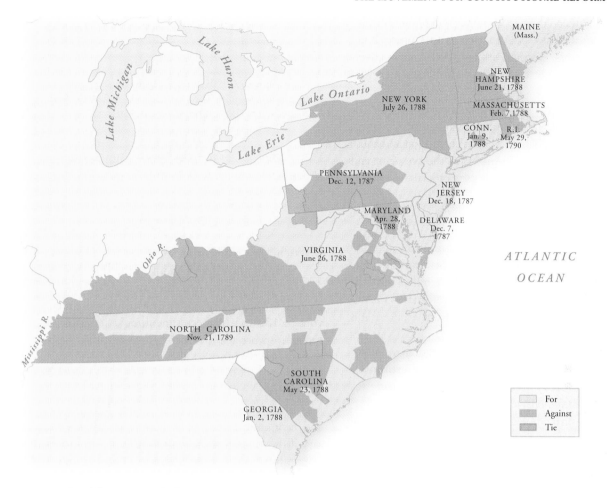

MAP 6.4 **Ratification of the Constitution**
The pattern of support by relatively small states is visible in the votes of Delaware, New Jersey, Georgia, and Connecticut. In Pennsylvania, Massachusetts, and New York, the more populated urban areas supported ratification.

property. People by nature also have "different opinions concerning religion, concerning government, and many other points." In a free society, they form factions on the basis of their conflicting ideologies and "the various and unequal distribution of property." He wrote:

> A landed interest, a manufacturing interest, a mercantile interest, a moneyed interest, with many lesser interests, grow up of necessity in civilized nations, and divide them into different classes, actuated by different sentiments and views. The regulation of these various and interfering interests forms the principal task of modern legislation, and involves the spirit of party and faction in the necessary and ordinary operations of the government.

Madison claimed that the Constitution would be beneficial because a large republic contained more safeguards than a small one. In an extended polity, so many factions exist that the ability of a single interest to monopolize power is reduced. With the national government,

"you take in a greater variety of parties and interests; you make it less probable that a majority of the whole will have a common motive to invade the rights of other citizens."

Antifederalists disagreed with this analysis, both because they favored small republics and because they feared the actions of men who would likely dominate the central government. Small farmers, many of them debtors who considered the mercantile elite their enemies, wanted nothing to do with this Constitution. At the core of their opposition was the belief that power should remain in the states. The Antifederalists understood that, despite equal representation in the Senate, the new government was fundamentally different from that under the Articles. They argued that a republic must be geographically small with a homogeneous population in order to meet the needs of its people. They believed the new central government would be too large and too remote, that the interests of citizens of the 13 states were too diverse.

A congressman could never know the will of 30,000 constituents; with so few persons elected to Congress and such large electoral districts, affluent, well-known candidates would have the advantage over ordinary men who ran for office. Thus, even the House of Representatives, the institution closest to the people, would become the domain of the rich. To the Antifederalists, the Constitution lacked sufficient barriers against corruption and abuse of power. At the least, term limits on the president and senators were required to prevent these officials from keeping their offices for life. Annual elections (instead of every 2 years) would make the House of Representatives more responsive to the voters.

Antifederalists also pointed to the omission of a bill of rights as cause for rejecting the Constitution. They advocated freedom of speech, press, assembly, and religion; jury trials for civil cases; judicial safeguards such as the right to a speedy trial and to confront accusers and witnesses; and prohibitions against unwarranted searches and seizures. The Federalists answered that a bill of rights would be superfluous because state constitutions offered these protections (some did, but in no case was protection comprehensive), and because a bill of rights was needed against a powerful king, not when the people themselves were sovereign. This latter argument ignored the vulnerability of the individual to the will of the majority. The Federalists used poor judgment in failing to incorporate a bill of rights into the 1787 Constitution, for the Antifederalists gained momentum as a result. Omitting these rights, for which the patriots had fought, turned many Americans against the proposed frame of government.

Nevertheless, ratification proceeded rapidly at first as state legislatures called elections for the state ratifying conventions. Delaware was the first to ratify when its convention approved the Constitution unanimously on December 7, 1787 (see Map 6.4). In Pennsylvania, where resistance was potentially heavy in the backcountry, Federalists moved quickly, securing approval by a two-to-one margin. New Jersey and Georgia then ratified unanimously. When Connecticut accepted the new government in January 1788 by a three-to-one vote, five states had joined the union. All of these states except Pennsylvania were relatively small and recognized the advantages of joining a union in which they had equal representation in the Senate.

Then the conventions became more acrimonious. North Carolina and Rhode Island rejected the document outright and New Hampshire put off its decision. Maryland and South Carolina ratified easily, but the vote in Massachusetts was close, as animosities from Shays's Rebellion colored the debate. Turnout for the

Massachusetts convention was huge because farmers in the central and western regions of the state believed the Constitution represented the interests of the eastern elite. The convention barely ratified the document by a vote of 187 to 168, recommending a series of amendments to protect individual rights and limit the powers of Congress. In June 1788, New Hampshire finally acted, becoming the ninth state to ratify, the number required to establish the new government. Nevertheless, two states remained crucial: Virginia and New York, whose size and economic importance made their approval necessary if the Constitution was to succeed. Virginia ratified in late June after a fierce debate, recommending to the first Congress a series of amendments, including a bill of rights. New York approved in late July, also with recommended changes, after New York City threatened to secede from the rest of the state if rural districts failed to accept the document.

Conclusion

The period from 1783 to 1788 was a crucial time for the United States; during this period the country fixed the limits of revolutionary change and established a new government. Americans initially tried a political framework of 13 small republics in which assemblies held the power to tax. All of the states (except New Jersey) restricted the vote—and political sovereignty—to propertied white men. "Republican motherhood" defined women's political role in the new nation. And despite a robust antislavery movement in the north, most African Americans remained enslaved.

The Congress, with little power under the Articles of Confederation, failed to solve its most pressing problems—the national debt, trade, and protection of U.S. borders against Spain and Great Britain. Even Congress's chief success, the legislation for governing and distributing land in the Northwest Territory, was marred by high land prices, delays in surveying, settlement by squatters, favoritism toward speculators, and conflict with Native Americans. When national government came to a halt and farmers rose in armed rebellion, nationalists demanded a constitution in which educated, propertied men like themselves would determine national economic policy and foreign affairs. These nationalists, who assumed the name Federalists,

crafted the Constitution of 1787 to shift power from the states to a central government. The Antifederalists fought the new Constitution despite the "great compromise," which provided states equal representation in the Senate regardless of their size. The lack of a bill of rights intensified opposition. The Federalists prevailed, however, and with ratification by 11 states by July 1788, the United States began a new experiment in republican government.

The Chapter in Review

- The United States based its new government on the republican principles of small government and the sovereignty of independent property owners.

- The Articles of Confederation created a weak central government that proved unable to raise money, repel border challenges from Britain and Spain, or resolve land disputes with Native Americans.

- The young republic suffered from a postwar economic depression that caused the proliferation of paper money, widespread debt, and economically motivated uprisings such as Shays's Rebellion.

- The Constitutional Convention was characterized by contentious debates over states' rights, proportional representation and slavery, and the proper powers of the national government.

- Opposition to the Constitution of 1787 arose from doubts about the new powers the document gave to the central government and the lack of a bill of rights.

Making Connections Across Chapters

LOOKING BACK

In 1783 the American patriots had won independence from Great Britain and achieved a favorable treaty, yet they faced many problems in establishing the new nation. The Articles of Confederation failed to provide the framework by which the 13 states could pay the war debt and provide national defense.

1. What were the chief problems facing the Confederation Congress in 1783?

2. Why did Massachusetts farmers rise in Shays's Rebellion?

3. Should the Northwest Ordinance of 1787 be considered a success of the Confederation Congress? Why or why not?

4. Why has James Madison been called the father of the Constitution?

5. What were the most important differences between the Articles of Confederation and the Constitution of 1787?

LOOKING AHEAD

Chapter 7 examines the process by which the Federalists created the national government as required by the Constitution. Although the election of George Washington as president offered stability, many issues remained unresolved. Differences within the ranks of former revolutionaries and supporters of the Constitution resulted in political parties.

1. How did Washington's administration address the problem of the Revolutionary War debt?

2. What was the new government's policy toward Native Americans?

3. Why did former allies such as Alexander Hamilton and James Madison create opposing political parties?

Recommended Readings

Beeman, Richard, Botein, Stephen, and Carter, Edward C., eds. *Beyond Confederation: Origins of the Constitution and American National Identity* (1987). These essays provide an excellent introduction to the Confederation period and the making of the Constitution.

Berlin, Ira, and Hoffman, Ronald, eds. *Slavery and Freedom in the Age of the American Revolution* (1983). Important essays on change, or lack thereof, in the status of African Americans during the Revolutionary era.

Doerflinger, Thomas M. *A Vigorous Spirit of Enterprise: Merchants and Economic Development in Revolutionary Philadelphia* (1986). A very good study of Philadelphia merchants and their impact on economic growth in the emergent United States.

Greene, Jack P. *Peripheries and Center: Constitutional Development in the Extended Polities of the British Empire and the United States, 1607–1788* (1986). Links the constitutional structure of Britain and its colonies to the Constitution of 1787.

Hamilton, Alexander, Jay, John, and Madison, James. *The Federalist Papers* (1788). Defense of the Constitution of 1787; seminal treatise of American political thought.

Hoffman, Ronald, et al., eds. *Native Americans and the Early Republic* (1999). Essays focusing on the impact of the Revolution and founding of the new republic on white–Indian relations.

Kenyon, Cecilia M. "Men of Little Faith: The Anti-Federalists on the Nature of Representative Government," *William and Mary Quarterly,* 3d ser., 12 (1955): 3–43. Insightful essay on the men who opposed ratification of the Constitution of 1787.

Kerber, Linda K. *Women of the Republic: Intellect and Ideology in Revolutionary America* (1980). Evaluates the impact of the Revolution on attitudes toward women.

Rhoden, Nancy L., and Steele, Ian K., eds. *The Human Tradition in the American Revolution* (2000). Biographical essays of famous and more ordinary Americans during the Revolutionary era.

Richards, Leonard L. *Shays's Rebellion: The American Revolution's Final Battle* (2002). A recent study of the western Massachusetts revolt that challenges earlier interpretations.

Identifications

Review your understanding of the following key terms, people, events, and dates for this chapter (these terms also appear in the Glossary at the end of the book):

republican motherhood
Robert Morris
John Jay
Northwest Ordinance
Shays's Rebellion
James Madison

Constitutional Convention
Virginia Plan
bicameral legislature
New Jersey Plan
great compromise
electoral college
The Federalist

Online Sources Guide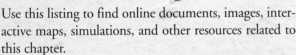

Use this listing to find online documents, images, interactive maps, simulations, and other resources related to this chapter.

American History Resource Center

http://history.wadsworth.com/rc/us

Documents

The Constitution of the United States
James Madison's *The Federalist Papers, No. 10*
The Virginia Statute for Religious Freedom
The Northwest Ordinance of 1787
Alexander Falconbridge, *The African Slave Trade* (1788)

Selected Images

1787 Constitutional Convention in Philadelphia
James Madison
Alexander Hamilton

Document Exercises

1785 Thomas Jefferson on Slavery
1787 *Federalist No. 10* by James Madison

HistoryNOW

http://now.ilrn.com/ayers_etal3e

Primary Source Exercises

The Administration of Justice and the Description of the Laws by Thomas Jefferson
The Constitution
Beyond the Original Thirteen States

7

The Federalist Republic, 1789–1799

Preparation for War to Defend Commerce (1800), illustrating construction of the frigate Philadelphia. During the 1790s the United States tried to remain neutral in the European wars while prospering from international trade.

© The Granger Collection, New York

After ratification of the Constitution, the Federalists took leadership in creating the new government. Everyone expected **George Washington** to become president. The three authors of *The Federalist,* **Alexander Hamilton,** James Madison, and John Jay, who had been so important in the creation and ratification of the Constitution, went on to play a central role in making it work. John Adams and **Thomas Jefferson,** who were serving as ministers to Great Britain and France during the convention, returned home to become, respectively, vice president and secretary of state.

Though many Federalists disagreed with specific parts of the Constitution, they accepted compromise and knew the weak Confederation had to be replaced. In the flush of victory over the Antifederalists, they set to the task of remedying the nation's ills. Differences soon became clear, however, between Hamilton on the one side and Madison and Jefferson on the other, as the first administration tackled the national debt and foreign policy. Out of their conflicts over policy, varying interpretations of the Constitution, and competition for power, the nation's first political parties developed.

The New Government

The first national elections went well, from the Federalist point of view, considering the strong Antifederalist opposition to the Constitution. The great majority of representatives and senators in the first Congress were Federalists. They fulfilled Madison's image of well-to-do men of national reputation and experience in politics. Many had served in the Constitutional Convention and signed the document. Most had military or political experience during the Revolution and Confederation period; just a few came from lower-class backgrounds. While the first congressmen were revolutionaries, they were also elites who believed that the country's interests coincided with their own. They wanted a stable government to foster economic growth.

George Washington Becomes President

The choice of George Washington as president was a foregone conclusion, though he would have preferred to stay at his Mount Vernon estate in northern Virginia.

Timeline

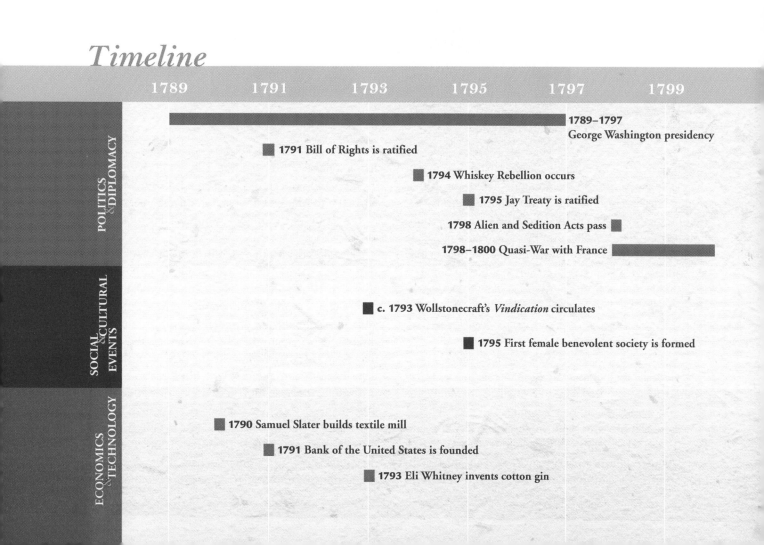

1789   1791   1793   1795   1797   1799

POLITICS & DIPLOMACY

1789–1797 George Washington presidency

1791 Bill of Rights is ratified

1794 Whiskey Rebellion occurs

1795 Jay Treaty is ratified

1798 Alien and Sedition Acts pass

1798–1800 Quasi-War with France

SOCIAL & CULTURAL EVENTS

c. 1793 Wollstonecraft's *Vindication* circulates

1795 First female benevolent society is formed

ECONOMICS & TECHNOLOGY

1790 Samuel Slater builds textile mill

1791 Bank of the United States is founded

1793 Eli Whitney invents cotton gin

George Washington in New York City

Although ratification of the Constitution provided the political institutions to move forward as a republic, the nation lacked a unifying political culture. George Washington, hero of the Revolution, became a symbol of unity for all Americans, perhaps especially for those who could not vote or participate in government. He journeyed throughout the country, welcomed with triumphal arches and celebrations. An observer noted that if "every individual *personally* [were] consulted as to the man whom they would elect to fill the office of President of this rising empire,

the only reply from New Hampshire to Georgia, would be *Washington*."

As suggested in this illustration, thousands greeted George Washington on his arrival in New York City for inauguration as president. The broad participation in such festivities—though not in actual suffrage and politics—is seen in the portrayal of Native Americans, African Americans, and women among the crowd. Other parades and pageants, most importantly the annual celebration of July 4, helped to bond voters and nonvoters alike to the new nation.

© The Granger Collection, New York

In February 1789, members of the electoral college met in their state capitals to cast unanimous votes for the former commander-in-chief. Washington's leadership during the war, his dignity and character, and his support for republican government made him the obvious choice. He might have tried to grasp power during the shaky Confederation, like a Napoleon or Stalin, but he did not. The first president's commitment to the success of the Constitution ensured the nation's survival during the early years. John Adams, elected vice president, received fewer than half as many votes as Washington.

The president-elect's trip from Mount Vernon to New York City, the temporary federal capital, became an 8-day triumphal march. In large and small towns along his way—Alexandria, Baltimore, Wilmington, Philadelphia—crowds of people, troops of infantry and cavalry, and local officials feted him with ceremonies, cannon fire, and banquets. Philadelphia citizens erected a Roman arch, crowning the revolutionary hero with a laurel wreath.

In New Jersey, throngs saluted his military victories at Trenton and Princeton. On April 23, 1789, Washington crossed into Manhattan on a festooned barge, welcomed by thousands of cheering New Yorkers. He took the oath of office a week later.

The president and Congress, aware that they were setting precedent, initially placed a great deal of emphasis on titles and the comportment of officials. In this republic, in a world of monarchies, how should they be addressed? Should the president keep his door open to the public or remain detached? Although the questions may seem trivial, they indicate the novelty of this republican experiment. Adams, with diplomatic experience in Europe, urged Congress to adopt titles like those of other nations. A Senate committee suggested, for example, that Washington be called "His Highness the President of the United States of America, and Protector of their Liberties." After much debate, Congress dropped the notion of titles, preferring a more republican style.

Washington and his successors have been addressed simply as "Mr. President."

For his part, the president wondered how to dignify his office and accomplish his work. He could easily have spent all of his time meeting with visitors, entertaining, and dining out. On the other hand, he did not want complete separation from the people. Washington's personality tended toward aloofness. He decided to hold a 1-hour reception once a week, invite a few visitors to dinner, and sometimes attend the theater.

Washington also developed, by trial and error, the way in which the chief executive would deal with Congress. Early in his administration, in advance of negotiating a treaty with the Creek Indians, he attended the Senate to request their "advice and consent," as the Constitution seemed to direct. The senators were unprepared to discuss Washington's proposal, leading to embarrassment on both sides. The president resolved never to consult in formal session again. Instead, he set the precedent of private informal meetings with members of Congress. Heads of executive departments, such as the secretary of the treasury, would attend congressional hearings, not the president. And in the case of treaties, the executive would seek the Senate's consent *after* negotiations were complete, not advice—at least formally—beforehand.

Beyond titles and modes of operating, Congress and the president needed to establish executive departments and courts, and draw up a bill of rights, to fill gaps in the written Constitution. In creating executive departments, which included War, Treasury, State (foreign affairs), and the attorney general, the most crucial constitutional question concerned who would be able to remove the heads of departments from office. Some senators hoped to restrict the president's power by requiring Senate approval before officeholders could be fired, thus making them more accountable to the legislature. In rejecting this proposal, Congress clarified one aspect of the Constitution's balance of powers.

With the Judiciary Act of 1789, Congress put some flesh on the skeleton outlined in Article III of the Constitution, which stated that the "judicial power of the United States shall be vested in one Supreme Court, and in such inferior courts as the Congress may from time to time ordain and establish." Congress might have created a full-blown national court system, but supporters of states' rights opposed such enhancement of national power. Thus, the Judiciary Act, the result of compromise, established a Supreme Court of six justices and a system of federal inferior courts, which were few in number and restricted primarily to consideration of federal crimes. State courts retained original jurisdiction in most civil and criminal cases, with the U.S. Supreme Court taking appeals from the highest state courts. John Jay became the first chief justice.

The Bill of Rights

During its first months, Congress took up the question of amending the Constitution to satisfy criticisms voiced during ratification that basic rights were not protected, objections that by the summer of 1789 still kept North Carolina and Rhode Island out of the Union. More than the original document, the first 10 amendments, called the **Bill of Rights,** represented the will of the American people.

The ratification campaign had elicited a mountain of proposals for amending the Constitution. Opponents offered two major grounds for altering the document or abandoning it altogether. Antifederalist leaders believed it took too much power from the states and from themselves as leaders of state and local governments; popular opinion feared the loss of personal freedoms to a strong national government.

James Madison became the chief proponent of the Bill of Rights in Congress, despite his earlier advocacy of the Federalist position that the amendments were unnecessary. In order to get elected to the House of Representatives, he had promised his Virginia constituents to obtain the safeguards. Madison took his vow seriously, pushing his reluctant Federalist colleagues to the task. Antifederalist leaders, who wanted to scrap the Constitution entirely, now denied support to the Bill of Rights because they knew protection of individual freedoms would garner popular support.

After much negotiation between the Senate and the House, on September 25, 1789, Congress sent to the states for ratification a total of 12 amendments. By December 15, 1791, three-quarters of the states had approved the 10 amendments known as the Bill of Rights, thus putting them into effect. Of the two amendments not approved at the time, one was a rule concerning congressional salaries that was not ratified for two centuries, until 1992, and the other was a complicated formula for computing representation in Congress that was never adopted. Of the Bill of Rights, Articles 1 through 8 enumerated basic individual rights, while the intention of Article 9 was to protect any personal freedoms omitted from this list. Article 10 directed that "powers not delegated to the United States by the Constitution, nor prohibited by it to the States, are reserved to the States respectively, or to the people." It addressed concerns that the national government might assume powers that were not mentioned in the Constitution. Passage of the Bill of Rights by Congress attracted enough support to bring in the two remaining states; North

Carolina ratified the Constitution in November 1789 and Rhode Island followed suit in May 1790.

The First Census

Congress also promptly ordered a census of the American population, which the Constitution required within 3 years of Congress's first meeting and every 10 years subsequently. The census, the founders expected, would provide an accurate enumeration for apportioning delegates to the House of Representatives and electoral college. Congress set August 1790 as the date of the first census, appointing marshals to complete their work within 9 months, which actually stretched to 18. The first census was less complicated than later ones, with just six questions: name of head of household, number of free white males aged 16 years and over, number of free white males under 16, number of free white females, number of other free persons (mostly African Americans but also some Native Americans), and number of slaves. The separate listing of enslaved persons was required by the clause of the Constitution that counted three-fifths of slaves for representation and taxes. The distinction between free whites and blacks came from cultural values rather than some practical use. The census did not include Native Americans who lived outside areas settled by whites.

While sketchy and incomplete, the 1790 census served as a baseline for measuring the growth of a dynamic, expanding people. President Washington reported to Congress a total of 3.9 million people, of whom 60,000 were free blacks and almost 700,000 were slaves (see Table 7.1). The census covered the territory included in the 13 original states and also Vermont, Kentucky, and Tennessee, which became states respectively in 1791, 1792, and 1796. It did not encompass the area north of the Ohio River, where at least 4,000 white settlers had taken up land.

During the 1780s, the white population of the country had swelled by an extraordinary 44 percent, mostly through reproduction; in the 1790s, the increase remained high at 36 percent. After the Treaty of Paris, European immigrants once again began crossing the Atlantic Ocean, with the majority coming from Ireland. From 1783 to 1799, 156,000 Europeans entered the United States, of whom 69 percent were Irish, 14 percent were English, Scottish, and Welsh, and 6 percent were German. The African American population also grew quickly during the 1780s and 1790s, at a rate of 32 percent per decade.

Especially striking in the 1790 census are the small numbers of enslaved African Americans in New England and Pennsylvania compared with the southern states, the result in part of northern abolition. This sectional

Table 7.1 The U.S. Population, 1790

United States	Total 3,929,625	Slaves 697,624
New England	**1,009,206**	**3,763**
Maine (part of Massachusetts)	96,643	0
New Hampshire	141,899	157
Vermont	85,341	0
Massachusetts	378,556	0
Rhode Island	69,112	958
Connecticut	237,655	2,648
Middle States	**1,017,087**	**45,210**
New York	340,241	21,193
New Jersey	184,139	11,423
Pennsylvania	433,611	3,707
Delaware	59,096	8,887
Southern States and Territories	**1,903,332**	**648,651**
Maryland	319,728	103,036
Virginia	747,610	292,627
North Carolina	395,005	100,783
South Carolina	249,073	107,094
Georgia	82,548	29,264
Kentucky	73,677	12,430
Tennessee	35,691	3,417

difference would grow in the nineteenth century as the North focused more on commerce and developed a manufacturing sector, while the South cast its fate with agriculture, adopting cotton as its major crop.

Opposing Visions of America

Almost immediately during Washington's first administration, political divisions arose between sides favoring commerce versus agriculture. Two divergent conceptions of the nation's future emerged among supporters of the Constitution. During the early 1790s, two political parties developed, though leaders avoided calling them that because public opinion considered parties detrimental to unified republican government. As events unfolded in foreign and domestic affairs, the two parties contested one issue after another.

Hamilton Versus Jefferson

Alexander Hamilton, appointed by Washington as secretary of the treasury, saw the future greatness of the United States in commerce and manufacturing. Born in the West Indies, Hamilton attended King's College in

© Bettmann/CORBIS

Alexander Hamilton, 1792, by John Trumbull. The first secretary of the treasury saw Great Britain, with its strong central government and expanding industrial economy, as a model for the new United States.

New York City, then served as Washington's aide-de-camp during the Revolution. Highly intelligent, full of energy and enthusiasm, he was a major proponent of the new Constitution. Appointment to the Treasury allowed Hamilton to promote his concept of a strong nation modeled on Great Britain, but his efforts to foster commerce and manufacturing aroused resistance among former allies, particularly Madison and Jefferson, leading to bitter partisan disputes.

Hamilton's party took the name Federalist, which in the late eighteenth century referred to the power of the states (see discussion of the great compromise in Chapter 6), though it was really nationalist. It favored commercial development, a national bank, high tariffs to spur manufacturing, and a strong central government based on a loose interpretation of the Constitution, which allowed expansive powers to Congress and the president. The Federalists favored the British, abhorred the French Revolution after 1792, and were generally suspicious of power wielded by ordinary folk. They were somewhat critical of slavery, however, and gained the allegiance of free blacks. Because their power base lay in New England and the Middle States, the Federalists had little enthusiasm for western expansion and sometimes supported the right of Native Americans to retain their lands.

The Republican party, in contrast, favored a strict interpretation of the Constitution, opposing a strong central government and federal privileges for manufacturing and commerce. It thought Hamilton's plans for funding the national debt, the bank, and protective tariffs infringed on states' rights and helped the "few" at the expense of the "many." It disdained the British model and charged Hamilton with advocating a return to monarchy. With their power base in the South, the West, and northern cities, the Republicans rejected efforts to abolish slavery and were ardent expansionists on the frontier. They had little sympathy for Indian rights.

Thomas Jefferson became the chief spokesman for the Republican party, though James Madison collaborated in its growth. Jefferson, a wealthy planter and slaveholder, author of the Declaration of Independence, former minister to France, and now Washington's secretary of state, argued that Hamilton wanted too much national power. He believed the root of Britain's effort to destroy American liberty in the 1760s and 1770s had been commercial speculation and greed. Manufacturing in cities created poverty, dependency, and political corruption. Instead, the United States, with limitless land, should foster an agrarian society of small producers. A virtuous republic was one made up of small farmers whose goal was to produce enough to support their families. Commerce should exist primarily to allow them to sell their surplus in Europe and purchase manufactured

Independence National Historical Park

Thomas Jefferson, 1791, by Charles Willson Peale. The first secretary of state, who favored an agrarian republic, strict construction of the Constitution, and the French, quickly became Hamilton's chief opponent.

goods in return. The farmers should be educated to participate wisely in republican government. Their self-sufficiency and education would encourage them to act for the good of society rather than solely for their own gain.

Paradoxically, a large proportion of the Republicans were not small farmers. Many of the leaders were southern plantation gentry like Jefferson and Madison, or old Antifederalist elites. The party drew together people who had opposed ratification of the Constitution as well as those who favored it but abhorred the government's direction under Washington and Hamilton. The Republicans received solid backing from farmers, especially in the South and West, and from urban craftsmen and small traders who watched wealthy speculators and merchants benefit from Hamiltonian policies.

Funding the National Debt

As secretary of the treasury, Alexander Hamilton's primary challenge was the Revolutionary War debt. A strong nationalist, he viewed the debt more as an opportunity to enlarge national power than as a financial hurdle. The United States owed $10 million to foreigners, particularly to the French, and $40 million to Americans. The states also owed $25 million in domestic debts. To continue the War of Independence when funds were depleted, Congress

and the states had issued certificates to merchants, artisans, and farmers for supplies and to soldiers for wages. After the war, many ordinary folks could not wait for the government to pay—or lost hope that the money was forthcoming—so they sold their certificates to wealthy speculators for a fraction of face value. Often the sellers received only 10 to 15 percent, rates that reflected the risk speculators were taking during the shaky Confederation period.

In his Report on Public Credit of January 1790, Hamilton formulated a plan by which the U.S. government would honor at face value all Revolutionary War debts, including those of the states. His funding proposal involved the exchange of new federal securities for the old debt certificates. He planned to pay off foreign creditors as soon as possible but retain the domestic debt, paying only interest and a small amount of the principal each year. A customs duty on imports and an excise tax on whiskey would cover the interest; post office income would gradually reduce the principal. Hamilton's funding plan would tie wealthy Americans to the new government through their continuing investment. His assumption plan, by which the federal government assumed state war debts, expanded this strategy by reorienting the loyalty of investors from the states to the nation.

Congress eventually passed Hamilton's proposal, though with great opposition. Many people, including Madison, thought that repaying the domestic debt at face value was unfair, that speculators would receive a windfall at the expense of the poor. The split between Hamilton and Madison began over this issue. Critics argued that funding allowed the "few" to benefit from the hardships of the "many," who had lost money when they sold their war bonds and who would pay again through import duties and the excise tax. Opponents also feared the expansion of national power, and became convinced that the Treasury secretary was upsetting the balance between the central government and the states. Assumption raised additional questions because some states had more debt remaining than others. Massachusetts and South Carolina were keen on having the federal government assume their large debts, whereas Virginians opposed the plan because they had satisfied most of their state's debt. Despite these divisions, the funding and assumption program passed Congress in July 1790, as part of a bargain struck by Hamilton, Jefferson, and Madison to situate the nation's permanent capital on the Potomac River, in Maryland and Virginia.

Planning Washington, D.C.

The choice of the Potomac for the nation's capital was controversial. Although everyone agreed that a central

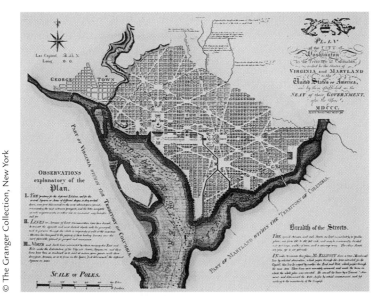

Pierre Charles L'Enfant's intricate design for Washington, D.C., 1791, far outstripped the country's financial resources and interest in creating a national capital.

location was necessary, regional interests surfaced as congressmen recognized its potential economic and political benefits. They also debated the question of the temporary capital. Should New York City or Philadelphia host the federal government until the permanent site was ready? The complicated negotiations over funding and assumption resulted in moving the temporary capital from New York to Philadelphia, as well as locating the new city on the Potomac.

President Washington and his fellow Virginians supervised the development of the capital. The Residence Act of 1790 gave the president authority to select a 10-mile-square location somewhere along the Potomac; he chose land on both sides of the river that included Alexandria in Virginia and Georgetown in Maryland. The federal city would be built in neither of those towns, but on open land on the east bank of the river. Washington appointed a surveyor, three commissioners to manage the project, and Pierre Charles L'Enfant to design the layout of the capital and its major buildings. L'Enfant's grandiose street plan and Greek and Roman architecture expressed an exalted vision of the republic. The commissioners named the federal city "Washington" and the entire district "Columbia."

The president expected to finance construction by selling lots in the capital, thinking that land prices would skyrocket as citizens valued proximity to the seat of government. Instead, land sold poorly and lack of money undermined the project. At one of the failed auctions, even the participation of the president and a parade of two brass bands and an artillery troop could not foster sales. When the commissioners suspended

construction temporarily for insufficient funds, L'Enfant protested and was fired. His plan for grand boulevards, public squares, fountains, and imposing buildings was retained, but its execution would wait. For a decade the enterprise limped along, saved by grants from Maryland and Virginia. In 1800, when the government moved to Washington, the president's mansion was still unfinished and only one wing of the Capitol had been built.

The National Bank

The cornerstone of Hamilton's new commercial order was a national bank, to be patterned after the Bank of England. The **Bank of the United States** and its branches would hold the federal government's funds and regulate state banks. The chief purpose of the national bank was to expand the money supply, thereby encouraging commercial growth.

The Bank of the United States, which Congress chartered in 1791 for 20 years, would have assets of $10 million, including $2 million in government deposits. Private investors could purchase the remaining $8 million in stock. As the bank prospered, stockholders would receive dividends on their funds. Thus, Hamilton created a way for wealthy Americans, who had just profited from funding the Revolutionary War debt, to benefit further. Because the government was a major stockholder, it also received dividends that could be used to pay off the national debt. The bank made loans to merchants beyond the value of its stock of gold and silver (specie), thus increasing the supply of money, a critically important move for an economy short of specie. The bank notes circulated as currency; the federal government supported their value by accepting them for taxes. To Hamilton and his commercial backers, the Bank of the United States was essential for economic growth.

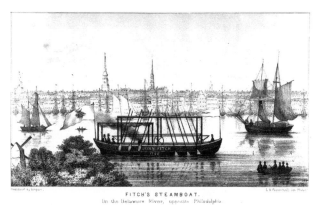

FITCH'S STEAMBOAT.
On the Delaware River, opposite Philadelphia

John Fitch's steamboat in the Delaware River. Fitch was an early experimenter with steam engines and designed this steamboat in 1786.

The majority of the House of Representatives agreed, by a vote of 39 to 20, but the tally indicated important regional differences that fueled growth of political parties. Among northern congressmen, 33 voted for the bank and 1 against, whereas only 6 southern delegates supported and 19 opposed Hamilton's bill.

The plan had many opponents, who variously considered the bank immoral, monopolistic, or unconstitutional. Some believed that all paper money should be based on gold and silver. "Every dollar of a bank bill that is issued beyond the quantity of gold and silver in the vaults," John Adams said, "represents nothing, and is therefore a cheat upon somebody." The wild frenzy to purchase the bank's stock—in which 25,000 shares sold in two hours and then the shares were bid up to 1,300 percent of their face value—reinforced fears that the national bank would undermine republican virtue. Jefferson called the bank's stock "federal filth." Others charged the bank with monopoly, complaining that merchants could secure short-term loans to finance their commercial ventures, but farmers and artisans could not obtain mortgages for purchasing property or making improvements.

In Congress, Madison opposed the national bank on the constitutional grounds that the federal government lacked the power to create corporations, a strict interpretation of the Constitution. In particular, Madison said, the Tenth Amendment would deny the central government any power not expressly given. Hamilton and his supporters countered that some powers of the federal government are implied. In the case of the bank, for example, the Constitution delegated to Congress and the president the power to lay and collect taxes, pay debts, regulate commerce, and coin and regulate money.

It also provided the authority to "make all laws which shall be necessary and proper for carrying into execution the foregoing powers. . . ." Hamilton argued that the bank was a method by which the United States could fulfill its functions, and because some means were necessary, the power to establish the bank was implied. Though President Washington was initially unsure, he accepted Hamilton's reasoning and approved the bill.

Jefferson, like Madison, was convinced that the national bank was unconstitutional. By 1791, the secretary of state realized the political and economic consequences of the funding act—channeling more power to the federal government and more money to the rich—and thought the bank could only further these trends. He said he had been "duped" by Hamilton and "made a tool for forwarding his schemes" in accepting the assumption of state debts in return for the capital on the Potomac. He now believed that the Treasury secretary's program "flowed from principles adverse to liberty," as Jefferson told the president. It was "calculated to undermine and demolish the republic." Hamilton chafed at this criticism, stating "that Mr. Madison, cooperating with Mr. Jefferson, is at the head of a faction decidedly hostile to me and my administration; and actuated by views, in my judgment, subversive of the principles of good government and dangerous to the Union, peace, and happiness of the country."

Encouragement of Manufacturing

Although the Treasury secretary won congressional support for the bank and funding the national debt, he was much less successful in his plan for industry. In 1791, the United States lacked a solid manufacturing base. Hamilton proposed high protective tariffs on certain goods to discourage Americans from buying imports and thus spur U.S. production. He also advocated bounties, or subsidies, on selected products to encourage entrepreneurs. Hamilton believed that a strong nation needed self-sufficiency in manufactures, especially for military defense, but he failed to obtain congressional support for the subsidies. Madison contended that granting bounties would expand the power of Congress, but others argued that they were like monopolies and too expensive. A North Carolina congressman advised, "Establish the doctrine of bounties, [and] . . . all manner of persons—people of every trade and occupation—may enter at the breach, until they have eaten up the bread of our children."

In the 1790s, U.S. manufacturing remained on a small scale. Americans appreciated the quality of British imports; what they did not import, they produced themselves or purchased from neighboring artisans. Industry

First Bank of the United States, Philadelphia. The imposing structure, designed by Samuel Blodget of New Hampshire, was intended to instill confidence in the bank's financial strength.

© The Granger Collection, New York

Flashpoints | Samuel Slater and the Rhode Island System

Like many before and after him, Samuel Slater came to the United States hoping to make his fortune. And, like many others, he was willing to break the law to pursue his dreams. When Slater left England in 1789, he carried with him information that he hoped would make him a wealthy man—information that, according to English law, he could not rightfully take outside of the country. Apprenticed to a mill owner at a young age, Slater had the opportunity to study the spinning frame, which was invented in 1769 by Richard Arkwright and greatly facilitated industrial production. The spinning frame was water-powered and produced stronger thread than the spinning wheel and jenny. Slater committed the spinning frame's design to memory, hoping to reproduce it in the United States. The design Slater memorized and carried with him pushed forward mechanization of the textile industry, thus helping to establish the Industrial Revolution on American soil.

Samuel Slater's spinning frame.

Smithsonian Institution

Upon arrival in the United States, Slater began establishing mills, reproducing as nearly as possible the machines and factory structures he had known in England. Slater built his first factory in Pawtucket, Rhode Island, in 1790, initiating what was called the Rhode Island system: factory workers carded and spun thread, which was then distributed to skilled artisans in their homes to weave into cloth. After his first mill flourished, he set up mills in other towns throughout Rhode Island, Massachusetts, and Connecticut. The prosperous Slater seemed to be the living embodiment of Alexander Hamilton's enterprising entrepreneur, the personification of the nation's industrially oriented, technologically advanced future. In 1813, as discussed in Chapter 9, Francis Cabot Lowell originated the Waltham system, which mechanized weaving as well. Like Slater, Lowell appropriated English technology—in this case by building from memory the power loom.

The industrial future that the mills of Slater and Lowell helped to create was not all rosy, not just technological development and economic growth. Factories often wreaked havoc on the environment and frequently exploited their workers, paying them low wages and forcing them to labor under dangerous and unhealthy conditions. (And, as was typical of many later mills, most of the people who worked for Slater were women and children.) As factories proliferated and cloth manufacture increased throughout the North, domestic demand for raw materials such as cotton grew exponentially, leading to increased demand for agricultural production in the South. And so, in a seeming paradox, the more industrialized the United States became, the more firmly slavery became entrenched at the heart of the American economy.

Questions for Reflection

1. What was the contribution of Samuel Slater to industrialization?

2. What actions did the U.S. government take under Alexander Hamilton's leadership to encourage entrepreneurs such as Slater?

3. What factors encouraged development of industry in the Northern United States?

could not be stimulated overnight, for it required technology and the willingness of businessmen to invest time and capital for the long term. Although some master craftsmen enlarged their shops and hired more workers, mechanized factories with mass production still lay in the future.

During the colonial and revolutionary periods, urban entrepreneurs had attempted large-scale textile manufacturing to provide employment for poor women and independence from British imports, but these efforts were short-lived and not mechanized. The "factories" had consisted of workhouses, in which large numbers of

A scene depicting enslaved African Americans using the first cotton gin, drawn by William L. Sheppard and published in *Harper's Weekly*, 1869.

In the 1790s most households performed one or more steps in textile manufacturing. Here a family works together, with the wife spinning thread, which the husband then wove on his loom. Women also wove cloth, but men rarely—if ever—used a spinning wheel.

impoverished widows produced thread and yarn at traditional spinning wheels. Other businessmen used a "putting-out" system, whereby they distributed flax and wool for spinning at home.

In 1788, the Pennsylvania Society for the Encouragement of Manufactures and the Useful Arts introduced spinning jennies, or multispindled machines, to their textile factory in Philadelphia. The jennies threatened to displace home spinners by producing cheaper yarn and thread. In 1790, however, the factory and its wooden jennies went up in flames, as did other early textile mills in the Delaware Valley. The promoters believed that home spinners were sabotaging the factories, but the fires may well have been accidental because the mills were highly flammable.

Samuel Slater, a 22-year-old millworker and recent immigrant from Great Britain, in 1790 instituted a new phase in American cloth production by building a textile mill in Pawtucket, Rhode Island, using water power to run the spinning machines. From memory he constructed a spinning frame, a machine that produced stronger threads than the jenny produced. He had left Britain illegally; to keep its advantage in textile making, the government prohibited emigration of craftworkers or export of drawings of the machines. No satisfactory power loom yet existed, so Slater's mill performed only the first two steps of cloth production: carding, or preparing the cotton fibers for spinning, and spinning the thread. Slater then used the putting-out system of distributing the thread to families, who produced the cloth at home. Though Slater established additional mills in Rhode Island and Massachusetts, his workforce stayed fairly small, with about 100 millworkers in 1800.

Alexander Hamilton tried an ambitious industrial program in Paterson, New Jersey, with the Society for Establishing Useful Manufactures. The society hoped to create an industrial town on the Passaic River where skilled craftsmen recruited from Britain would produce a variety of cloth and clothing, blankets, carpets, shoes, hats, pottery, metal wire, and paper. After obtaining a state charter from New Jersey, the society sold stock that sold quickly and appreciated in value. The project lost capital, however, when major stockholders sold their shares to make a fast profit. The managers failed to obtain reliable machinery and workers, closing shop in 1796.

Although the results of Hamilton's plans were disappointing, the United States did make progress during the 1790s toward industrialization. In 1790, Congress passed patent legislation, giving inventors exclusive rights to their work for 17 years, and Slater initiated water-powered textile manufacture, as described above. Then, in 1793, while visiting a Georgia plantation, **Eli Whitney,** a New Englander, built the cotton engine, or gin. The device, which separated cotton fibers from husks and seeds, greatly increased the productivity of cotton cultivation, swelling the demand for African American slaves and fertile land in the Southwest, and spurring cloth production in the North. Because the gin could be duplicated easily, Whitney failed to make a fortune from the machine. In 1798, he further laid the basis for industrial growth by attempting to manufacture guns with interchangeable parts. After receiving a government contract for 10,000 weapons, he specified that each part be made identical to its counterparts so that it could be exchanged from one rifle to another, allowing less-skilled workers to build and repair the firearms. At this early date, however, such rigid standards were impossible to meet, and as a result, parts needed filing to fit together smoothly.

An inventor who would have benefited from Hamilton's proposed bounties was the Delaware-born artisan **Oliver Evans,** who apprenticed as a wagonmaker and became fascinated by machines. In 1772, at age 17, he heard that the Scottish inventor James Watt had improved the steam engine a few years earlier. Evans began building his own model but, for lack of money, 30 years passed before he actually installed a high-pressure steam engine in his gypsum fertilizer factory in Philadelphia. This was the first application of steam power to an industrial setting. In the meantime, in the 1780s, Evans also developed the idea of automating mills. He devised water-powered machinery for large grist mills that allowed one worker instead of three to supervise all the steps of producing flour. Evans obtained exclusive rights from the states of Pennsylvania and Maryland for his system of automated elevators, conveyors, and hoppers. With insufficient capital, however, he was unable to pursue many of his designs, including steam carriages and trucks, a machine gun, refrigeration, central heating, and gas lighting.

Expansion and Conflict in the West

While Alexander Hamilton's financial policies aided commerce in the East, dynamic growth also occurred in the West. The westward movement of settlers challenged the ability of the new government to keep their loyalty. In particular, Hamilton's excise tax on whiskey weighed heavily on westerners. The young nation also contended with Native Americans who were losing lands to the settlers; the British military, who kept forts in the northwest; and the Spanish, who contested U.S. territorial claims and rights to navigate the Mississippi.

Kentucky and Tennessee

During the 1780s, the region west of the Appalachians and south of the Ohio River developed quickly, as families left Virginia and North Carolina in search of fertile land and lower taxes. Even before the Revolution ended, settlers crossed the mountains in large numbers: the area that became Kentucky swelled from 150 settlers in 1775 to 61,000 whites and 12,500 enslaved blacks in 1790; Tennessee reported 32,000 whites and 3,500 slaves in the latter year.

White settlement of Kentucky and Tennessee proceeded quickly as state governments, speculators, and frontiersmen defeated the Cherokees, who claimed ancestral rights to the territory. Believing that they were renting the land out rather than selling it, in 1775 a group of Cherokee leaders, including Attakullaculla and Oconostota, had traded 27,000 square miles to Richard Henderson and his associates for a cabin of consumer goods. Called Henderson's Purchase, the sale involved most of Kentucky and was illegal in Indian and English law. With the outbreak of the Revolution, most Cherokees joined the British, fighting for return of their lands. Receiving little help from Britain, the Cherokees were defeated in 1777 and forced to sign away even more territory.

Young militants led by Dragging Canoe, Bloody Fellow, and others, assisted by loyalist whites who intermarried and became members of the tribe, rejected these land cessions. In the 1780s and early 1790s, the militant Cherokees, called Chickamaugas, allied with Creeks and Shawnees against settlers along the frontier from Kentucky to Georgia. On both sides, fighting was vicious, with men, women, and children burned, scalped, and shot; and, as in so many cases, the whites failed to distinguish between enemy Indians and those who wanted peace.

The Washington administration attempted to end the hostilities with the Treaty of Holston in 1791, but gave responsibility for negotiating with the Cherokees to Governor William Blount of the Tennessee Territory, a land speculator the Indians called "dirt king" for his greed after land. Blount ignored Washington's promise to the Cherokees that if they ceded territory on which the whites had settled, the United States would guarantee their remaining lands. Instead, Blount required a cession of more than 4,000 square miles in return for an annual payment of $1,000 and no guarantee. When Blount surveyed the border without Cherokee witnesses, the treaty fell apart and war continued. In 1794, after Dragging Canoe died and the Spanish stopped supplying the Indians because of war in Europe, the Chickamaugas met defeat.

By the end of the war, parts of Kentucky and Tennessee had passed the initial stages of settlement. Early on, groups of settlers had gathered in frontier stations consisting of two-story log houses connected by a high wall to create a fort against Indian attack. As the population grew and the threat from Native Americans declined, families moved away from the stations. In the early years, all family members worked to provide food, clothing, shelter, and a few amenities such as soap and rough-hewn furniture. They needed to become familiar with their new environment. One Kentucky pioneer described how "the women the first spring we came out, wo'd follow their cows to see what they ate, that they might know what greens to get. My Wife and I had neither spoon, dish, knife, or any thing to do with when we began life. Only I had a butcher knife." The settlers grew corn, tobacco, hemp, cotton, vegetables, and fruits; raised cattle, sheep, horses, and pigs; hunted and fished. Soon they produced a surplus to trade for necessities they could not make themselves, such as nails, rifles, ammunition, needles, tools, and salt, as well as to pay taxes and fees. They sold furs, ginseng, agricultural produce, and livestock. As fertile lands such as Kentucky's Bluegrass region yielded bountiful crops, farmers sought markets by way of the Mississippi River and the port of New Orleans. Because transporting crops overland through the mountains was much more difficult and expensive than sending them downstream, southwestern farmers demanded that the federal government convince Spain to end its restrictions on lower Mississippi shipping.

Though the population increased and a market economy developed in the 1790s, the trans-Appalachian region had few schools or church buildings. Most children, if taught at all, learned reading and arithmetic at home. In towns where schools existed, boys might attend for a few months but girls stayed at home. The exception was the children of wealthy families who entered academies with secondary school curricula. One man remembered the experience of most residents of Kentucky in the 1790s: "Our preachers and teachers were, in general, almost as destitute as the people at large, many of whom could neither read nor write, did not send their children to school, and of course, kept no books in the house."

Religion was the frontier's chief cultural institution. Throughout the region, Presbyterian, Baptist, and Methodist ministers held services in private homes. Baptist lay ministers farmed beside their neighbors through the week, then led services on Sunday. Methodist circuit riders traveled from one congregation to another, conducting worship services, baptisms, marriages, and prayer meetings. The churches expected members to avoid sin, including fighting, excessive drinking, adultery, and even celebrating the Fourth of July. If members committed offenses and failed to express regret, they were expelled, a serious consequence for people who had few social outlets. In addition to church, social activities included barn raisings, corn huskings, and log rollings. These events caused trouble when whiskey and frivolity led church members astray, as with one couple a Kentucky Methodist church expelled for "Disorderly Conduct." Another man was "Excluded from this Church for Fighting & Drinking to Excess."

The Ohio Country

White settlement moved more slowly north of the Ohio River, partly because the U.S. government kept tighter control in the Northwest Territory, but more because Native Americans resisted strongly. Delawares, Shawnees, Iroquois, and many others refused to cede lands that the federal government wanted to sell to land-hungry easterners. In the 1780s, the United States obtained a series of cessions, but from just some of the people who owned the land. Indians who were not party to the agreements rejected them. Forming a confederacy to withstand U.S. invasion, Ohio Indians attacked whites who risked settling in the region. This northern Indian confederacy allied with the Chickamaugas and Creeks in the south, establishing a pan-Indian defensive that gained help from the Spanish in the south and the British in the north. At one meeting in 1787, the Native Americans agreed to merge their forces "for a general defense against all Invaders of Indian rights."

In the early 1790s, President Washington challenged the northern confederacy by sending two expeditions, both of them unsuccessful. Arthur St. Clair, governor of the Northwest Territory, led the second invasion in

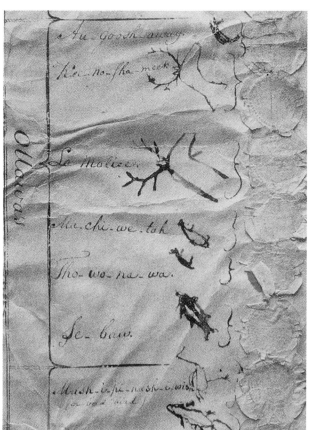

Signatures of Native Americans on the Treaty of Greenville, 1795. Indian leaders commonly used symbols such as diagrams of animals to sign deeds and treaties.

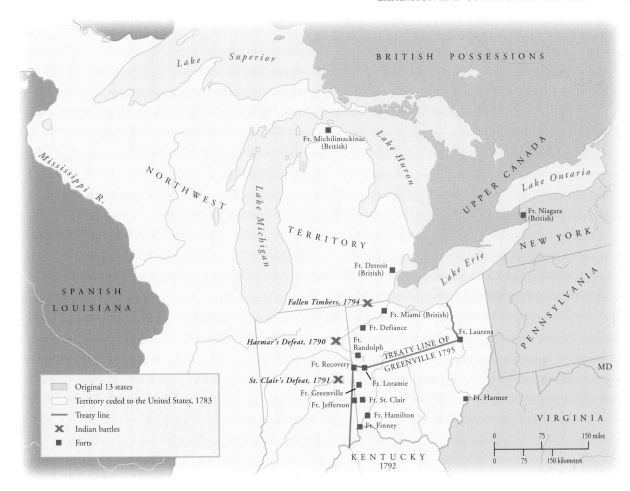

MAP 7.1 Conflict in the Northwest Territory, 1790–1796
Native Americans continued to resist U.S. settlement in the Ohio region. They defeated U.S. forces in 1790 and 1791, but lost the Battle of Fallen Timbers in 1794. British forts in the Northwest Territory supported the Ohio Indians until that time.

1791, in which 600 of his 1,400 men died (see Map 7.1). Washington believed that the disaster resulted from the use of militia, so he instructed General Anthony Wayne to raise 5,000 regulars. Wayne trained the troops for two years, then on August 20, 1794, defeated the Native Americans decisively at the Battle of Fallen Timbers. Though the British had customarily given aid to the Ohio tribes, this time they closed the gates to Fort Miami, denying refuge to the retreating Indians. A year later, when it became clear to the Native Americans that their alliance with the British had ended, they signed the Treaty of Greenville ceding to the United States the land south and east of the treaty line, most of the land in present-day Ohio.

The Whiskey Rebellion

In 1794, the Washington administration also sent troops against western Pennsylvania farmers, who since 1791 had resisted the whiskey tax. Washington and Hamilton decided to take advantage of the unrest to demonstrate the power of the new central government. Farmers throughout the west resented the tax on spirits, for distilling whiskey from grain made their produce less bulky, thus less expensive to transport to eastern markets. They also used the whiskey instead of cash and consumed a good portion of it themselves. In much of the trans-Appalachian region, officials failed to collect the excise at all.

The administration found willing officials in western Pennsylvania, however, and there proceeded to enforce the law. The Pittsburgh area farmers held protest meetings and refused cooperation with the collectors. They tarred and feathered collaborators, burned barns, and destroyed stills of people who paid the tax. The farmers charged that the tax favored large distillers and was collected unevenly. Rebels left notes signed "Tom the Tinker" to warn distillers who registered for the tax that their stills would be "fixed" (that is, ruined) unless they joined the revolt. The insurgents understood their fight as a struggle for "the virtuous principles of republican liberty." But the whiskey tax was only one of the farmers'

Cartoon dated 1794 illustrating an "exciseman," or tax collector, pursued by farmers with tar and feathers during the Whiskey Rebellion.

complaints, which included failure to open up the Ohio country and removal of Spanish trade restrictions on the Mississippi.

Events came to a climax in July 1794. When officials continued to collect the tax and arrest resisters, 500 men surrounded the excise inspector's home, exchanged gunfire killing several people, and burned the house. The official and his family escaped. In the days that followed, rebels set more buildings on fire, raised liberty poles, attacked collectors, and rumored secession. The uprising spread to central Pennsylvania, Virginia, Maryland, and Ohio. Washington sent commissioners to obtain oaths of submission, but when the insurrection continued, he called up 13,000 eastern militia, who marched west with the president briefly in command. By the time the soldiers reached western Pennsylvania, the revolt was over, as the show of force intimidated the rebels. The administration had demonstrated that armed resistance to federal policies would not be tolerated.

The Spanish Frontier

As settlers from the United States migrated across the Appalachians and traders extended their commercial networks, they came into contact with the Spanish. The 1790s marked the high point of Spain's control in North America, its provinces extending from East Florida across the Gulf Coast to Louisiana, Texas, New Mexico, and California (refer back to Map 6.1). The Spanish government continued to view these borderlands of their empire as a buffer against American and British designs on Mexican silver. Spanish officials recognized the phenomenal population growth of the United States. One warned that Americans were "advancing and multiplying . . . with a prodigious rapidity," and another took a dim view of the American frontier people, whom he considered "nomadic like Arabs and . . . distinguished from savages only in

their color, language, and the superiority of their depraved cunning and untrustworthiness."

Nevertheless, the Spanish decided to open their territory to Americans, hoping to bolster the small settler populations. Spain offered free land in the Floridas and Louisiana, and even changed official policy to allow Protestants to keep their religion as long as they took an oath of allegiance to the Crown and had their children baptized Catholic. Because Spain could not provide desired consumer goods or adequate markets, it also relaxed mercantilist restraints, allowing plantation owners in the borderlands to sell their sugar, cotton, and indigo in the United States. These new immigration and economic policies facilitated later U.S. acquisition of the Floridas and Louisiana. Jefferson said prophetically, in 1791, that Spain had provided "the means of delivering to us peaceably, what may otherwise cost us a war."

Farther west, in New Mexico, the Spanish finally achieved peace with the Comanches and Apaches. Abandoning the attempt to make them subjects of the Crown, Spain signed a treaty recognizing their sovereignty. The Indians had forced the Spanish to set aside the goal of complete domination and to provide such gifts as guns, ammunition, clothing, mirrors, paint, tobacco, and sugar. Still, the Spanish sent prisoners of war to Cuba as forced laborers and settled other Apaches on reservations called *establecimientos de paz*, or peace establishments. Many Apaches refused to live on the reservations, however, steadfastly maintaining their independence. But the fighting stopped, making Texas, New Mexico, and Arizona safer for travel and economic development. Finally, settlers could journey directly between San Antonio, Santa Fe, and Tucson without fear of attack.

California Indians are lined up at the Spanish mission in Carmel to greet French visitors.

For several decades, fearing Russian and British incursions along the Pacific coast, Spain had expanded settlement in California. The government sent missionaries and soldiers north from Baja California in 1769 to set up missions and presidios along the coast from San Diego to San Francisco. José de Gálvez organized the effort, enlisting Junípero Serra, a zealous Franciscan priest, to establish the missions. Though fewer than 1,000 Hispanics lived in California by 1790, the missions controlled most of the arable land along the Pacific. With military force and by conversion, they put thousands of California Indians to work on mission lands. Before Spanish colonization, the region's native people possessed neither firearms nor horses; they lived in small villages with neither elaborate political structures nor much experience with war. In the earliest years after Spanish settlement, the natives lacked unity to avenge the crimes of Spanish soldiers or to refuse to serve as agricultural laborers. In 1775, however, one group burned the San Diego mission, followed by rebellions of other coastal Indians.

As elsewhere in North America, the California Indians declined sharply in population after contact with Europeans. People who went to work in the missions lived an average of 10 to 12 years; their high death rate probably resulted from close quarters and exposure to disease. According to one missionary, "they live well free but as soon as we reduce them to a Christian and community life . . . they fatten, sicken, and die." The native population in the mission region along the Pacific coast declined from approximately 60,000 in 1769 to 35,000 at the end of the century.

The Spanish also looked to the Pacific Northwest, which they explored in 1774, four years earlier than the British explorer Captain James Cook. After Cook publicized the trade for sea otter furs, however, British and American merchants sailed to Nootka Sound, at Vancouver Island, challenging the Spanish claim to the area north of San Francisco. The traders made huge profits by purchasing the silky black otter pelts from the Tlingit, Haida, Nootka, and Chinook peoples, to sell in China for tea, porcelain, and silk. The Indians had formerly hunted the sea otter on a limited basis for fine clothing and food. When the Spanish seized two British ships, England threatened war. Spain signed the Nootka Convention (1790), yielding its sole claim to the Pacific Northwest and returning the confiscated vessels. Over the next several years, the two countries tried but failed to negotiate a northern boundary of California. Of more concern to Spain, Great Britain, and the United States during the 1790s was the outbreak of war in Europe and the Atlantic, in the wake of revolution in France.

Dances held by Native Americans for Alejandro Malaspina at Nootka Sound, 1791. Drawing probably by Tomás de Suria.

DOING HISTORY ONLINE

Rebellion and Government

Use your book and the documents in this module to compare the official responses to Shays's Rebellion and to the Whiskey Rebellion. What does the comparison reveal about the Articles of Confederation and the Constitution and the evolution of the national government?

History ⧗ Now™   Visit HistoryNOW to access primary sources and exercises related to this topic: http://now.ilrn.com/ayers_etal3e

Foreign Entanglements

In 1789, the United States rejoiced when the French abolished noble privileges and formed a constitutional monarchy. Americans believed that France had followed their example, for during the first phase of the French Revolution, its moderate leaders included friends of the United States, notably the Revolutionary War hero the Marquis de Lafayette. In 1792, however, radicals took control and executed King Louis XVI the next year. The international situation became perilous when the French Republic declared war on Britain and Spain. The king's execution and thousands of deaths by guillotine during the second phase of the revolution cost the French support in the United States, particularly among Federalists, who feared the consequences of ordinary people, "the mob," taking power. Republicans, while not defending the excesses, remained sympathetic toward France because they hated monarchical Britain more.

Neutrality

The European war presented Americans with a tricky situation, for they had connections with both France and Britain that were potentially dangerous. The U.S.–France commercial and military alliance of 1778 remained in force. It did not require the United States to enter the war, but the French Republic expected favorable trade policies and informal military assistance. Though Secretary of State Jefferson favored France and despised Britain, he agreed that neutrality was essential. American commerce was closely tied with Britain, whose navy could sweep U.S. ships from the sea.

Hamilton was particularly concerned that British imports remain high because tariffs paid the lion's share of interest on the national debt. With all of this in mind, President Washington made the only reasonable decision, issuing his Proclamation of Neutrality in April 1793. The message warned citizens to avoid hostile acts against either side, including sale of weapons and privateering. Washington sought the belligerents' recognition of the U.S. right to trade in nonmilitary goods.

American neutrality quickly hit shoals with the activities of **Edmond Genêt,** the new minister from France. Citizen Genêt, as he was called in republican France, had arrived in Charleston several weeks before Washington proclaimed neutrality. He enlisted American mercenaries to man privateers and obtained ships to sail under the French flag against British shipping. The privateers, with largely American crews, seized British vessels, taking them to U.S. ports. There the French consuls sold the ships and their cargoes, paying the mercenaries with part of the proceeds. The French claimed this right under the 1778 alliance. The Washington administration, fearful of British reprisals and outraged by this violation of U.S. sovereignty, closed the ports to Genêt's privateers and requested his recall. The government prohibited foreign belligerents from arming vessels in U.S. ports and recruiting U.S. citizens in American territory; set the limit of U.S. territorial waters at three miles; and forbade foreign consuls from holding admiralty courts in U.S. cities to auction confiscated ships.

The Washington administration had greater success protecting the nation's sovereignty from French designs than from those of the British. The American republic's weakness became all too clear when the Royal Navy began impressing—recruiting by force—U.S. citizens from merchant ships. Then, in November 1793, the British ordered a total blockade of the French West Indies. Any ship intending to trade there would be confiscated. The blockade was timed to coincide with their invasion of St. Domingue, or Haiti, where enslaved blacks had risen up against their French masters in 1791. The British kept the blockade a secret until after U.S. ships headed for the Caribbean. Over the winter, their navy seized more than 250 American vessels, whether they were aimed for French, British, or neutral ports. The British impounded ships, cargoes, and even the sailors' possessions. Because international correspondence was so slow, Washington received no intelligence of the blockade and confiscations until March 1794.

The United States and Britain seemed headed for war. Exacerbating the crisis was the British refusal to vacate their forts and their aid to Native Americans in the Ohio country. Britain also helped Native Americans resist settlement in the west. In fact, in 1794 the governor of Canada, Lord Dorchester, told a group of Indians that they could expect war to break out between the United States and Britain within a year. With British victory,

Dorchester promised, the Native Americans could reclaim the lands they had lost north of the Ohio River.

The Jay Treaty

The crisis abated when the British ended their total blockade of the French islands, permitting Americans to trade foodstuffs and consumer goods but not war material. Rather than take retaliatory action, the president sent John Jay, chief justice of the Supreme Court, as special envoy to England. Jay's instructions were to convince the British to evacuate their forts in the west, pay for African American slaves who had left with their army after the Revolution, end impressment, open the British West Indies trade to American ships, and compensate recent shipping losses in the Caribbean.

Jay was unable to secure compensation for slaves, convince the British to stop impressment, or obtain recognition of all the neutral rights that Americans demanded. He did gain British withdrawal from the western forts by June 1, 1796, payment for confiscated ships in the Caribbean, and the opening of trade in the British West Indies to American vessels of 70 tons or less. He agreed, however, that American shippers would not export from the United States certain tropical products, including cotton, molasses, sugar, coffee, and cocoa, and that Americans would repay British creditors for prerevolutionary debts.

Washington received Jay's treaty in March 1795, keeping its contents secret until the Senate debate in June. The Federalists struck the provision forbidding U.S. merchants from exporting tropical crops. If they had agreed to this section, American trade would have faced a serious obstacle, particularly with the development of cotton. Twenty Federalist senators voted to ratify while 10 Republicans refused. Thus, the Senate approved the treaty by exactly the two-thirds needed and sent it to the president, who signed the treaty as amended.

When the **Jay Treaty** became public, Republicans flew into a rage. Their opposition in large part was political: they abhorred *any* treaty with the British and privately bemoaned Jay's success on important issues. Publicly, they complained about his failures on impressment, neutral rights, and compensation for slaves. The Jay Treaty greatly hastened the growth of political parties, as Republicans gained support from former Federalists, particularly in the south. Whereas Hamilton defended the treaty, opponents roared that it surrendered American independence to the former imperial tyrant. John Jay was burned in effigy; mass meetings, petitions, and demonstrations protested the treaty throughout the country.

By spring 1796, however, the tumult was over, in part because news arrived that Thomas Pinckney had concluded an agreement with Spain the previous October. The Treaty of San Lorenzo opened the Mississippi River to free navigation, allowed Americans to use the port of New Orleans without charge, and fixed the boundary between the United States and West Florida at the 31st parallel as specified in the Treaty of Paris.

Washington Retires

With the threat of war temporarily eased, the west open for settlement and trade, and a flourishing economy, the success of the republic seemed more certain. General Wayne's defeat of the Ohio Indians, the Jay Treaty, and Pinckney's diplomatic success gave westerners—and westward-looking Americans—resolution of their major problems: cession of lands in Ohio, removal of the British from the forts, free access to the Mississippi, and the right of deposit at New Orleans. Eastern merchants and farmers benefited from the lifting of trade restrictions in the British West Indies. Wartime demand for provisions in Europe and the Caribbean drove up farm prices and stimulated production. By the end of the century, American exports and shipping profits were almost five times their 1793 level. As a major neutral maritime nation, the United States was assuming a greater place in world trade. With increased transportation profits, merchants invested more heavily in ships. The shipbuilding boom created demand for lumber, rope, and other supplies; wages for craftsmen and laborers rose, though so did the cost of living. Americans took advantage of their newfound prosperity to buy British imports, which in turn paid tariff income toward the national debt. Hamilton's funding plan was a success—the nation's credit was firm—despite resistance to the whiskey tax.

As the election of 1796 approached, George Washington announced his retirement, raising the question of his successor. The president had served two terms, his health had declined, and the battle over the Jay Treaty had left him exhausted and angry. In his Farewell Address, Washington surveyed the accomplishments of his administration and gave the nation advice. The United States should avoid as much as possible becoming entwined in international affairs, he counseled. The European war demonstrated how perilous such involvement could be and how difficult it was to escape. "The great rule of conduct for us in regard to foreign nations is, in extending our commercial relations to have with them as little *political* connection as possible," Washington urged. His other major argument concerned factions. The outgoing president warned against parties based on sectional differences—North against South or East against West. And he cautioned against parties more

DOING HISTORY ONLINE

Foreign Entanglements

Read the documents in this module and address the following questions. Why does Thomas Jefferson favor an alliance with France? Why does Alexander Hamilton oppose such an alliance? Whose ideas do you favor and on what grounds?

History Now™   Visit HistoryNOW to access primary sources and exercises related to this topic: http://now.ilrn.com/ayers_etal3e

---

generally that the "disorders and miseries which result [from factionalism] gradually incline the minds of men to seek security and repose in the absolute power of an individual." In lamenting "the spirit of party," Washington blamed the Republicans for failing to support his administration. They had undercut his authority and the ideal of a consensual republic.

The Adams Presidency

Though Washington's successors appreciated the wisdom of his "great rule" of foreign policy, they had less enthusiasm for his advice on factions. In 1796, the parties yet lacked full-scale national organization, and candidates did not campaign. But the contest was very much alive: Federalists supported the policies of Hamilton and Washington, and Republicans opposed them.

Election of 1796

In the third presidential election under the Constitution, both parties had sufficient cohesion to offer national tickets: the Federalist candidates were John Adams for president and Thomas Pinckney for vice president; the Republicans put up Thomas Jefferson for president and Aaron Burr, a senator from New York, for the second spot. The results of the electoral college vote were close: Adams 71, Jefferson 68, Pinckney 59, Burr 30, and a number of other candidates totaling 48. As specified by the Constitution, Adams became president and Jefferson, vice president. Americans quickly realized the problem of this procedure for electing the executive, because the president represented one party and the vice president the other. In any event, the Federalists kept control of the presidency, though barely, and they increased their votes in Congress by a small margin, to 64 Federalists versus 53 Republicans.

For many Americans, John Adams possessed credentials from service in the Revolution and the new repub-

---

Picturing the Past   **POLITICS & DIPLOMACY**

John Adams

Elected the second president of the United States in 1796, Adams was the sole non-Virginian and the only president to serve a single term among the first five chief executives. He was also the only president whose son (John Quincy Adams) served in the nation's highest elected office until George W. Bush (son of George H. Bush) became president in 2001.

Both the presidential elections of 1796 and 1800 between John Adams and Thomas Jefferson were close. Although each had contributed mightily to gaining

Independence National Historical Park

independence from Great Britain and establishing the new nation, neither served as the symbol of national unity as had George Washington in 1789. Party spirit had grown during the 1790s, undermining even Washington's position. Differences between Adams and Jefferson became public in 1791, despite their earlier long-term collaboration. After both men had served as president, they renewed their correspondence and friendship. They died on the same day, July 4, 1826, the fiftieth anniversary of independence.

---

lic that made him a worthy heir to Washington. He had contributed to prerevolutionary agitation in Boston, served as a delegate to the Continental Congress, promoted the Continental navy, and assisted Jefferson in drafting the Declaration of Independence. He had helped negotiate the 1783 Treaty of Paris, and in 1785 became the first U.S. minister to Great Britain. While Adams was a skilled diplomat, an avid student of government, and entirely honest, he lacked Washington's charisma, military bearing, and understanding of executive leadership. As a lawyer, Adams's style was more intellectual and independent. He preferred to make decisions on his own, without consulting the cabinet or congressional leaders.

Like Washington, Adams denounced parties. He began his administration with the hope, soon abandoned, that he might bridge the gulf between Federalists and Republicans. Jefferson rebuffed the chief executive's peace overture and directed the Republican opposition from his post as vice president. After the first few days of the Adams administration, the president and vice president never consulted one another.

"Quasi-War" with France

The second president inherited an international situation that had worsened by the time he assumed office in March 1797. The French, now ruled by a dictatorial executive board called the Directory, declared that the Jay Treaty revoked the 1778 alliance with the United States. They confiscated American merchant ships and cut off diplomatic relations. Once again, the United States seemed headed for war.

Called by Adams into special session in May 1797, Congress authorized the mobilization of 80,000 militia, completion of three war vessels, and fortification of harbors. Adams also appointed a commission of three men to negotiate with France: John Marshall of Virginia,

Elbridge Gerry of Massachusetts, and Charles Cotesworth Pinckney of South Carolina. Their assignment was to prevent war, stop the confiscation of American ships carrying nonmilitary cargoes, and obtain compensation for recent losses. In France, the commission corresponded with French Foreign Minister Talleyrand through three intermediaries, who later became known to the American public as X, Y, and Z. The French agents told the commissioners that, like other petitioners to the Directory, they must pay a bribe even to be heard. The amount specified in this case was $250,000. The Directory also required an apology from Adams for criticizing France, a huge loan, and assumption by the U.S. government of any unpaid debts owed by France to American citizens. The commission refused these conditions and returned home. Their experience became known as the **XYZ Affair.**

In spring 1798, Adams received delayed correspondence that his envoys had been rebuffed. When he called for additional troops and warships, Congress responded by giving him more than he requested. Jefferson denounced the military buildup as "insane"; Republicans demanded to see evidence of France's treachery. When Adams made the commission's dispatches public, war fever engulfed the nation. The cry in the 1798 congressional elections became, "Millions for defense, but not a cent for tribute." Two patriotic songs, "Adams for Liberty" and "Hail Columbia," were widely sung, the latter serving as the unofficial national anthem. Congress expanded the regular army and war fleet, established the Department of the Navy, authorized naval vessels to protect American merchant ships, suspended commerce with France, and revoked the French alliance. George Washington assumed command of the army, with Alexander Hamilton in charge of field operations. To pay for all of this, Congress levied a direct tax of $2 million on dwelling houses, land, and slaves.

Without declaring war, the United States engaged France in hostilities from 1798 to 1800. In what was known as the Quasi-War, the U.S. Navy dominated the French, defeating their warships and sinking privateers. The British navy helped by protecting U.S. carriers. Although some congressmen feared a French invasion and thereby justified further military preparations, French naval losses to Great Britain and the United States quickly removed that threat.

The Alien and Sedition Acts

The Federalists rode the crest of patriotism in 1798, using their majority in Congress to pass a series of acts that limited the rights of immigrants and critics of the administration. Congressional

"Cinque-têtes," or the Paris Monster, an American cartoon showing the United States negotiators Elbridge Gerry, John Marshall, and Charles Cotesworth Pinckney refusing the demands for money of the French Directory (the five-headed monster).

DOING HISTORY

Alien and Sedition Acts

THESE DOCUMENTS INCLUDE excerpts from the Alien Act and Sedition Act of 1798, along with resolutions drafted by James Madison and passed by the Virginia Assembly and counterresolutions from Rhode Island. The Federalists passed these and two other acts (the Naturalization Act and Alien Enemies Act) to restrict opposition during the Quasi-War. Madison and Thomas Jefferson (who wrote similar resolutions passed by the Kentucky legislature) particularly opposed the Sedition Act for its limitation on First Amendment freedoms of speech and the press.

The Alien Act, June 25, 1798

Sec. 1. *Be it enacted* . . . , That it shall be lawful for the President of the United States at any time during the continuance of this act, to *order* all such *aliens* as he shall judge dangerous to the peace and safety of the United States, or shall have reasonable grounds to suspect are concerned in any treasonable or secret machinations against the government thereof, to depart out of the territory of the United States, within such time as shall be expressed in such order. . . .

The Sedition Act, July 14, 1798

Sec. 1. *Be it enacted* . . . , That if any persons shall unlawfully combine or conspire together, with intent to oppose any measure or measures of the government of the United States, which are or shall be directed by proper authority, or to impede the operation of any law of the United States, or to intimidate or prevent any person holding a place or office in or under the government of the United States, from undertaking, performing or executing his trust or duty; and if any person or persons, with intent as aforesaid, shall counsel, advise or attempt to procure any insurrection . . . he or they shall be deemed guilty of a high misdemeanor. . . .

Sec. 2. That if any person shall write, print, utter, or publish, or shall cause or procure to be written, printed, uttered or published, or shall knowingly and willingly assist or aid in writing, printing, uttering or publishing any false, scandalous and malicious writing or writings against the government of the United States, or either house of the Congress of the United States, or the President of the United States, with intent to defame the said government, or either house of the said Congress, or the said President, or to bring them, or either of them, into contempt or disrepute; or to excite against them, or either or any of them, the hatred of the good people of the United States, or to stir up sedition within the United States . . . then such person, being thereof convicted before any court of the United Sates having jurisdiction thereof, shall be punished by a fine not exceeding two thousand dollars, and by imprisonment not exceeding two years. . . .

Source: United States Statutes at Large, 1: 570, 596–597.

Virginia Resolutions, December 24, 1798

Resolved, . . . That this Assembly doth explicitly and peremptorily declare, that it views the powers of the Federal Government as resulting from the compact to which the states are parties, as limited by the plain sense and intention of the instrument constituting that compact, as no further valid than they are authorized by the grants enumerated in that compact; and that, in case of a deliberate, palpable, and dangerous exercise of other powers, not granted by the said compact, the states, who are parties thereto, have the right, and are in duty bound, to interpose, for arresting the progress of the evil, and for maintaining, within their respective limits, the authorities, rights, and liberties, appertaining to them. . . .

That the General Assembly doth particularly PROTEST against the palpable and alarming infractions of the Constitution, in the two late cases of the "Alien and Sedition Acts," passed at the last session of Congress; the first of which exercises a power nowhere delegated to the Federal Government, and which, by uniting legislative and judicial powers to those of [the] executive, subverts the general principles of free government, as well as the particular organization and positive provisions of the Federal Constitution; and the other of which acts exercises, in like manner, a power not delegated by the Constitution, but, on the contrary, expressly and positively forbidden by one of the amendments thereto, —a power which, more than any other, ought to produce universal alarm, because it is levelled against the right of freely examining public characters and measures, and of free communication among the people thereon, which has ever been justly deemed the only effectual guardian of every other right. . . .

Counter Resolutions of the Rhode Island Legislature, February 1799

Certain resolutions of the Legislature of Virginia . . . being communicated to this Assembly,—

1. Resolved, That, in the opinion of this legislature, the second section of the third article of the Constitution of the United States, in these words, to wit,—"The judicial power shall extend to all cases arising under the laws of the United States,"—vests in the Federal Courts, exclusively, and in the Supreme Court of the United States, ultimately, the authority of deciding on the constitutionality of any act or law of the Congress of the United States.

2. Resolved, That for any state legislature to assume that authority would be—

1st. Blending together legislative and judicial powers;

2d. Hazarding an interruption of the peace of the states by civil discord, in case of a diversity of opinions among the states legislatures;

each state having, in that case, no resort, for vindicating its own opinions, but the strength of its own arm; . . .

3. Resolved, That, although, for the above reasons, this legislature, in their public capacity, do not feel themselves authorized to consider and decide on the constitutionality of the Sedition and Alien laws, (so called,) yet they are called upon, by the exigency of this occasion, to declare that, in their private opinions, these laws are within the powers delegated to Congress, and promotive of the welfare of the United States. . . .

Source: Richard Hofstadter, ed., *Great Issues in American History: A Documentary Record* (New York: Vintage Books, 1958), 1: 182–185.

Questions for Reflection

1. Why did the Federalists believe it necessary to pass the Alien and Sedition acts?

2. On what basis does James Madison contend in the Virginia Resolutions that a state has the right and duty, when warranted, to declare a federal law unconstitutional? On what basis does the Rhode Island legislature disagree?

Explore additional primary sources related to this chapter on the Wadsworth American History Resource Center or HistoryNOW websites:

http://history.wadsworth.com /rc/us
http://now.ilrn.com/ayers_etal3e

sponsors argued that the laws were necessary wartime measures. Their practical purpose, however, was to destroy the Republicans by undermining popular support and closing newspapers. The Federalists tried to take advantage of the Quasi-War to link their opponents with the enemy. This strategy worked in the short term, as the pro-French Republicans lost votes in the 1798 congressional election, but proved suicidal for Adams's party after the fear of invasion had passed.

The Federalist design resulted in four restrictive laws. The Naturalization Act of 1798 lengthened the period of residence needed for citizenship from 5 to 14 years. The legislation was intended to stop the flow of Irish immigrants who, because they were anti-British and pro-French, swelled the number of Republican voters. The Alien Enemies Act established procedures in the event of declared war or invasion for jailing and deporting citizens of the enemy nation who were considered likely to spy or commit sabotage. The Alien Act,

which had a term of two years, allowed the president to deport any non–U.S. citizens "he shall judge dangerous to the peace and safety of the United States, or shall have reasonable grounds to suspect are concerned in any treasonable or secret machinations against the government thereof." Like the Naturalization Act, this law potentially threatened Irish immigrants, but Adams refrained from using it.

The fourth law, the Sedition Act, made it illegal for "any persons [to] unlawfully combine or conspire together, with intent to oppose any measure or measures of the government of the United States" or to interfere with the execution of a law. Nor could a person "write, print, utter or publish . . . any false, scandalous and malicious writing or writings against the government of the United States, or either house of the Congress . . . or the President." In effect, this law permitted imprisonment and fines for criticizing the government. It was an obvious infringement on freedom of speech and freedom of the press. The term of the law lasted until March 3, 1801, the day before the next president would be inaugurated. Thus the Federalists ensured that if the next chief executive were a Republican, he would not be able to retaliate without obtaining a new statute.

The administration enforced the law with serious results. Adams believed that the Sedition Act was constitutional, that people who censured his policies threatened the future of the republic. The prime targets for prosecution were Republican newspapers, including the Philadelphia *Aurora,* edited by Benjamin Franklin's grandson, Benjamin Bache, who was one of Adams's most powerful critics. The official authorized to administer the act was Secretary of State Timothy Pickering, a staunch Federalist, who methodically reviewed the Republican papers for actionable offenses. He even ordered an inquiry into the private correspondence of a Republican congressman who reputedly called Adams a traitor; however, the investigation was dropped. Under the law, the Federalists indicted and tried at least 17 people for sedition. They timed cases to reach court in the fall of 1799 or the following spring, with the goal of silencing the Republican press during the 1800 election. Some papers folded and others closed temporarily while their editors were imprisoned. All but one of the cases were prosecuted in New England and the Middle Atlantic states, where the Federalists controlled the courts and could pack juries.

The Republican Opposition Grows

Passage of the Alien and Sedition acts and the jailing of Republican spokesmen shifted the political winds. In late 1798, the Kentucky and Virginia legislatures approved resolutions that protested the acts on the grounds that they were unconstitutional. The Kentucky and Virginia resolutions, drafted anonymously by Thomas Jefferson and James Madison, respectively, argued that these laws violated the First Amendment and granted powers to the national government not delegated by the Constitution. The Virginia assembly resolved that "in case of a deliberate, palpable, and dangerous exercise of other powers, not granted by the [Constitution], the states . . . have the right, and are in duty bound, to interpose, for arresting the progress of the evil." Virginia and Kentucky sent their resolutions to other legislatures, none of which agreed that states could declare a federal law unconstitutional. Rhode Island, for example, responded that the federal courts held the power to determine constitutionality; "that for any state legislature to assume that authority would be . . . Hazarding an interruption of the peace of the states by civil discord, in case of a diversity of opinions among the state legislatures." Nevertheless, the resolutions contributed toward a theory of "nullification,"

the idea that a state had the right to veto a federal law it considered unconstitutional. This theory was based on the strict interpretation of the Constitution that denied, as in the controversy over the national bank, implied powers to the central government.

With the Alien and Sedition acts, the Federalists had made a strategic error. Where formerly the Republicans could be branded as a faction creating animosity and disunity, they now became seen as legitimate defenders of revolutionary principles. The Republican party justified its opposition by warning that the Federalists were on the road to tyranny. The Sedition Act, the Virginia Resolutions argued, impeded free investigation of the actions of government officials and "free communication among the people thereon, which has ever been justly deemed the only effectual guardian of every other right."

The administration fanned the flames of indignation with its heavy-handed reaction to a tax rebellion among German Americans in eastern Pennsylvania, a group who had previously favored the Federalists or stayed out of politics entirely. The Republicans took advantage of the rural Pennsylvanians' aversion to the 1798 federal property tax to win their votes in the congressional election. They circulated petitions against the tax, the defense buildup, and the Alien and Sedition laws, petitions that Congress ignored. By early 1799, the people of Northampton and Bucks counties held public meetings and stopped tax assessors from doing their work. In March, after the U.S. marshal jailed 18 suspected tax resisters in Bethlehem's Sun Tavern, John Fries, a 50-year-old auctioneer of upper Bucks County, led a band of 140 armed men to release the prisoners.

The Fries Rebellion ended quickly, as the rebels considered the magnitude of their offense. Fries announced that he would pay the tax and would even welcome the assessor to his house for dinner. Nevertheless, the president decided to make an example of the episode. He dispatched troops that failed to march until almost four weeks after the resistance had ceased. The army descended upon the countryside, entering houses and

---

DOING HISTORY ONLINE

Development of Political Parties

Using the textbook and the documents in this module, determine what major issues contributed to party development.

History ⊗ Now™   Visit HistoryNOW to access primary sources and exercises related to this topic: http://now.ilrn.com/ayers_etal3e

arresting 60 men. One army officer wrote "that every hour's experience confirms me more and more that this expedition was not only unnecessary, but violently absurd." Contrary to the Judiciary Act of 1789, the prisoners were taken to Philadelphia for trial. Fries and two others were found guilty of treason by a Federalist court and sentenced to hang, but were subsequently pardoned by the president. The Republicans added the administration's unwarranted use of force to their arsenal of charges against the Federalists.

Conclusion

George Washington had warned in his Farewell Address that "the spirit of Party . . . agitates the Community with ill founded jealousies and false alarms, kindles the animosity of one part against another, foments occasionally riot and insurrection. It opens the door to foreign influence and corruption. . . ." He invoked the ideal of consensual community, challenging his fellow citizens to work together for the good of their country. The flaw in this conception was that Americans could not agree on which policies were best for everyone. The interests of farmers, merchants, and artisans, of residents of the north, south, and west, often diverged. The Federalist and Republican parties grew out of different visions of the nation's future. During the 1790s, the Federalists retained control of the central government, confident that their vision was correct. They denounced parties, identifying their government with the republic as a whole. When they tried to eliminate factions by silencing their adversaries with the Sedition Act, ironically they legitimized the party system in the eyes of many Americans.

The Chapter in Review

- After the ratification of the Constitution, Americans worked to create a new government. Officials unanimously elected George Washington to be the nation's first president, and amended the Constitution with a Bill of Rights designed to protect individuals against government abuses of authority.
- During the 1790s two opposing factions arose within American politics, one led by Alexander Hamilton, which favored strong central government and commerce, the other led by Thomas Jefferson, which favored weak national government and agriculture.
- Increased expansion into the west caused tensions between white settlers and the Spanish and Native

American peoples who already inhabited these territories.
- The new republic attempted to remain neutral in the conflicts that raged between Britain and France between 1793 and 1815. The 1778 alliance between the United States and France, however, and ongoing trade relations with both nations, made neutrality impossible to maintain.
- John Adams's administration was characterized by an increase in partisan feeling, growth in sentiment against the Federalists, the buildup of the military, and the passage of the unpopular Alien and Sedition acts.

Making Connections Across Chapters

LOOKING BACK

Within the context of world history, with governments that regularly rise and fall, the longevity of the American republic is remarkable. As discussed in Chapter 7, the decade following ratification of the Constitution was critical. Despite conflicts such as the Whiskey and Fries rebellions, growing opposition from the Republicans, and the Sedition Act, the Washington and Adams administrations established strong precedents for constitutional rule.

1. What were the most important challenges that faced George Washington as he assumed the presidency?

2. What fueled the acrimony between Alexander Hamilton and Thomas Jefferson?

3. Why did James Madison spearhead the effort to approve a bill of rights?

4. How did international affairs, particularly the war between Great Britain and France, affect U.S. domestic politics?

5. Was Hamilton's plan for an economy based on manufacturing realistic in 1790? Why or why not?

LOOKING AHEAD

In Chapter 8 we will see that the year 1800 marked a watershed in American politics because the Federalists lost control of the federal government and declined. For most Americans, however, national politics held little importance as they focused on building communities and churches and pursued their daily lives.

1. Why were the Republicans, under Thomas Jefferson, able to win the election of 1800?

2. To what extent did Jefferson adhere to his vision of an agrarian republic?

3. How did the Jefferson administration deal with the continuing foreign entanglements of war between Great Britain and France?

Recommended Readings

Anderson, Margo J. *The American Census: A Social History* (1988). A very good source on the first federal census of 1790.

Cayton, Andrew R. L., and Teute, Fredrika J., eds. *Contact Points: American Frontiers from the Mohawk Valley to the Mississippi, 1750–1830* (1998). Essays about Indian–white relations in the backcountry from the prerevolutionary period through the early republic.

Cochran, Thomas C. *Frontiers of Change: Early Industrialism in America* (1981). A good introduction to industrialization in the early republic.

Elkins, Stanley, and McKitrick, Eric. *The Age of Federalism* (1993). Detailed narrative of the Washington and Adams administrations.

McCullough, David. *John Adams* (2001). An excellent biography of the second president.

McGaw, Judith A., ed. *Early American Technology: Making and Doing Things from the Colonial Era to 1850* (1994). Original essays on technology from agriculture to turnpikes.

North, Douglass C. *The Economic Growth of the United States 1790–1860* (1966). Includes a useful analysis of U.S. trade amid international conflict.

Onuf, Peter S., ed. *Jeffersonian Legacies* (1993). Wide ranging essays on Thomas Jefferson's character and politics.

Sharp, James Roger. *American Politics in the Early Republic: The New Nation in Crisis* (1995; Reprint Edition). Provides a thoughtful analysis of party formation during the 1790s and the election of 1800.

Slaughter, Thomas P. *The Whiskey Rebellion: Frontier Epilogue to the American Revolution* (1986). An excellent book on the struggle between Alexander Hamilton and western Pennsylvania farmers over excise taxes.

White, Richard. *The Middle Ground: Indians, Empires, and Republics in the Great Lakes Region, 1650–1815* (1991). Influential study of Indian–white relations from New France through the War of 1812.

Identifications

Review your understanding of the following key terms, people, events, and dates for this chapter (these terms also appear in the Glossary at the end of the book):

George Washington
Alexander Hamilton
Thomas Jefferson
Bill of Rights
Bank of the United States

Samuel Slater
Eli Whitney
Oliver Evans
Whiskey Rebellion
Edmond Genêt
Jay Treaty
XYZ Affair

Online Sources Guide

Use this listing to find online documents, images, interactive maps, simulations, and other resources related to this chapter.

American History Resource Center

http://history.wadsworth.com/rc/us

Documents

The Treaty of Greenville (1795)
George Washington, Sixth Annual Address to Congress (1794)
The Alien and Sedition Acts (1798)

Selected Images

John Jay
James Madison
Alexander Hamilton
John Adams
Pittsburgh in 1790
Boston's Faneuil Hall, 1789
Citizen Edmond Charles Genêt

Document Exercises

Mr. Gordon's Speech on the Alien Bill, 1798

HistoryNOW

http://now.ilrn.com/ayers_etal3e

Primary Source Exercises

Rebellion and Government
Foreign Entanglements
Development of Political Parties

8

The New Republic Faces a New Century, 1800–1815

Fish drawn by Meriwether Lewis within his journal of the Lewis and Clark expedition of 1804–1806.

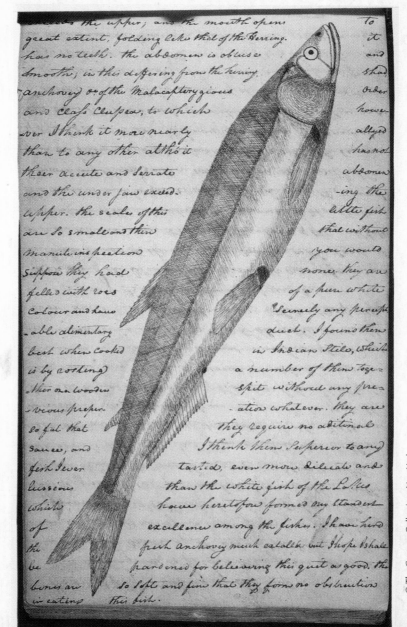

mericans confronted the nineteenth century with a variety of fears. For the Federalists, the growing Republican opposition warned that the evils of democracy and anarchy stood ready to take control. For the Republicans, the Alien and Sedition acts and Federalist repression of the whiskey rebels and John Fries underscored the need for change. Both parties, still members of the revolutionary generation, thought in terms of the ideals for which they had fought against the British. They also measured events against what was transpiring elsewhere in the world. By 1800, the excesses of the French Revolution and Napoleon Bonaparte's rise to power dismayed Americans. The never-ending European war threatened to involve the United States for 20 years, and it finally did in 1812. The 1791 revolt by slaves in the French West Indies horrified southern slave owners.

Though Thomas Jefferson's presidency would prove to be less revolutionary than many Federalists feared, the new century brought indelible changes to American politics and society. The Federalist party shriveled and died,

the Louisiana Purchase expanded the nation's territory to the Rocky Mountains and beyond, slavery became more firmly embedded in the southern economy, and the republic fought once more against Great Britain. The Second Great Awakening, the series of religious revivals that began in the late 1790s and gained steam after the turn of the century, influenced the ways in which many people interpreted these events.

Religion in American Society

During the first decade of the nineteenth century, religion absorbed the energies of many different groups: frontier settlers and Native Americans caught up in revivals, organizations to provide welfare relief in towns and cities, new sects like the Shakers, and free African Americans who built separate churches as the cornerstone of their communities. Many people believed that renewed emphasis on religion would transform the nation through individual faith and communal action.

Timeline

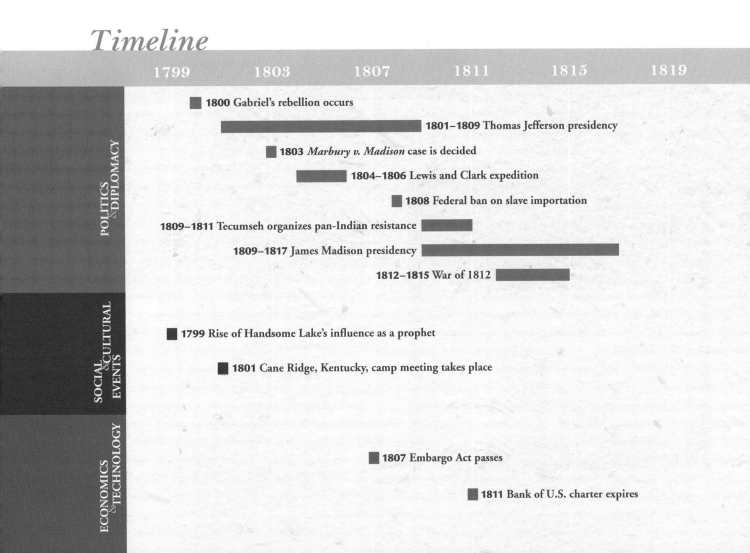

	1799	1803	1807	1811	1815	1819

POLITICS & DIPLOMACY

1800 Gabriel's rebellion occurs

1801–1809 Thomas Jefferson presidency

1803 *Marbury v. Madison* case is decided

1804–1806 Lewis and Clark expedition

1808 Federal ban on slave importation

1809–1811 Tecumseh organizes pan-Indian resistance

1809–1817 James Madison presidency

1812–1815 War of 1812

SOCIAL & CULTURAL EVENTS

1799 Rise of Handsome Lake's influence as a prophet

1801 Cane Ridge, Kentucky, camp meeting takes place

ECONOMICS & TECHNOLOGY

1807 Embargo Act passes

1811 Bank of U.S. charter expires

Enduring Issues   Religion, Revivals, and Reform

Spiritual revivals have marked American society throughout its history. In some periods, particularly during the Second Great Awakening of the early nineteenth century, evangelism moved outside of the church to inspire social and political reform. Enduring questions that must be addressed in considering the impact on American society of religion—and evangelical revivals more specifically—include: Why are large numbers of Americans caught up in waves of revivals? Why do these revivals ebb and flow? Have evangelical revivals contributed to the development of democratic political processes in the United States? How have spiritual renewals contributed to such reform movements as the abolition of slavery and civil rights, women's rights, and more compassionate care for people with physical disabilities and mental illness? While many historians have researched these questions and offered important insights about the relationship of religion and politics, still we have much to learn about this complex and interesting issue.

With salvation the focus of Calvinism, of which both the English

Methodist Camp Meeting, engraving by E. Clay. During the Second Great Awakening, itinerant preachers held outdoor revivals that often lasted for several days.

Collection of the New York Historical Society

The Library Company of Philadelphia

Sermon by Massachusetts revivalist minister Solomon Stoddard in 1705.

Separatists (Pilgrims) and Puritans were a part, revivals developed during the first century after New England settlement. Indeed the Separatist migration to Plymouth and the Puritan migration to Massachusetts Bay were part of a movement for renewal—both groups believed that the Church of England must be purified of its bishops, rituals, and statues. The Separatists judged English society to be hopelessly corrupt and thought migration to America was the only way to ensure the spiritual safety of their children. The Puritans retained hope that they could reform English society and the Church, embarking on their "errand into the wilderness" to create a model society in Massachusetts.

Most Plymouth and Massachusetts Bay founders believed they were saved—that they were among the "elect," those whom God chose to go to heaven rather than hell. Many of their sons and daughters in the next generations failed to reach salvation. Children went to church regularly, read and discussed the Bible at home and at school, and hoped for salvation, but the experience of knowing they were saved did not always come. In 1662, some Puritan churches adopted the Half-Way Covenant, which allowed the unconverted members to maintain a "half-way" status in the church and have their children baptized. Debate over this policy uncovered a rift between Puritans who believed only the elect should have any kind of membership in the church and those who wanted more flexibility.

Salvation was central to Calvinist doctrines. Some ministers were particularly adept in moving members of the congregation to believe they were saved, including Solomon Stoddard of Northampton in the Connecticut River valley of western Massachusetts, who foreshadowed the first Great Awakening with his emphasis on rousing sermons, individual salvation, and broad participation in the Lord's Supper to encourage conversion. By 1729, when Stoddard died, he had gained a significant following in the Connecticut Valley, with five "seasons of harvest," or revivals, that gained large numbers of converts to the church. He instilled fear in his listeners about their sinfulness and fate after death. Stoddard's grandson, Jonathan Edwards, followed in his footsteps: first he took over the Northampton pulpit then inspired revivals during

Moorland-Spingarn Research Center, Howard University

Reverend Richard Allen, a former slave, was founder of the African Methodist Episcopal Church and a leader of the Philadelphia black community.

the 1730s that helped stir up the Great Awakening in New England. Although Edwards rejected some of Stoddard's teachings, their revivalist approach to arouse large numbers to seek salvation fueled spiritual renewals in succeeding decades.

Patterns of evangelism and schism (a division or split) have contributed to a rich multifaceted religious tradition in the United States and continue to affect political debates about social and cultural policy. Because schism often required individuals to denounce established churches, this process of separation and formation of new denominations has generally contributed to efforts for religious liberty. Two important religious leaders who challenged established churches and recognized the need for freedom of religion were Roger Williams, the Separatist minister who founded Rhode Island, and William Penn, the Quaker proprietor of Pennsylvania. The first and second Great Awakenings further helped to break up the established churches, as revivals shattered congregations in Massachusetts, Connecticut, Virginia, and elsewhere.

The participation of Puritans, Quakers, Methodists, and members of other denominations in the movement to abolish slavery also helps us understand the impact of religion on American society. By far, most early members of Puritan churches and the Society of Friends had little concern about the injustice of slavery. In fact, some Puritans and Quakers owned enslaved Africans and Native Americans. But the belief that all people are equal in the sight of God and have equal access to eternal life challenged individuals such as Boston judge Samuel Sewall and Quaker John Woolman of New Jersey to oppose slavery. By the time of the American Revolution, many Quaker meetings adopted rules preventing members from owning slaves. African Americans in Philadelphia and other northern cities founded separate churches to avoid discriminatory practices they faced in white congregations. In the early nineteenth century, these African American churches provided leadership for abolition and civil rights—in particular opposing the colonization movement that urged free African Americans to immigrate to Africa. Then, in the 1830s (see Chapter 10), some white northerners inspired by the Second Great Awakening and Quakers joined together with African Americans to create the radical abolitionist movement organized by William Lloyd Garrison. Building upon the Second Great Awakening's religious fervor to remake society, the abolitionists demanded an immediate end to slavery throughout the United States. They formed the American Anti-Slavery Society in 1833, expecting church leaders to endorse their plan to convert slave

(continued)

Enduring Issues   Religion, Revivals, and Reform (*continued*)

masters through prayer and moral persuasion to the abolitionist cause.

While the Garrisonians gained inspiration from their religion, most of their co-religionists opposed the movement for immediate abolition. Despite the widespread appeal of the Second Great Awakening and its power to motivate followers to reform American society, few were prepared to take a radical position against the firmly implanted institution of slavery.

Questions for Reflection

1. Based on your reading in Chapters 4 through 8, do you believe that spiritual revivals and religion more generally contributed to democratic developments in the United States? Why or why not?

2. In what ways was the Second Great Awakening a continuation of earlier religious developments in colonial British America? In what ways was it different?

The Second Great Awakening

As the century began, people throughout the country sought spiritual renewal. Among New England Congregationalists, the revivals spread from one town to another between 1797 and 1801. The national Methodist conference of 1800 held in Baltimore witnessed an outpouring of religious fervor. These flames heralded a series of revivals—the **Second Great Awakening**—which lasted into the 1830s. In accepting the message of revival, large numbers of Americans embraced evangelicalism—the belief that they must take their message of salvation to others. They expected to create a more godly nation through conversion and good works.

In particular, eastern clergy worried that people on the frontier, with few churches, would let sin take control of their lives. Americans streamed west across the Appalachians; by 1810, Ohio had 230,000 settlers, Kentucky and Tennessee had 668,000, and the Mississippi and Louisiana territories had 117,000. Evangelical ministers feared for the nation because so many westerners were unchurched. The clerics expressed their dread in terms of millennialism, the belief that the millennium—Christ's second coming—was at hand, as foretold in Revelation, the last book of the Bible. Pastors urged their congregations to prepare for the millennium by supporting missionary efforts in the West. They believed that Americans throughout the country must embrace Christianity and convert Native Americans and the people of other lands.

Circuit preachers and missionaries traveled throughout the frontier; the churches they started were often the first social organizations in new communities. The great western revivals of 1800–1815, which built upon this work, began when several Presbyterians summoned the first camp meeting, a religious gathering held outside over the course of several days. People came together, miles from their homes, to hear revivalist preachers. The most

famous of the early camp meetings took place in August 1801, at Cane Ridge, Kentucky, where Presbyterian, Methodist, and Baptist clergy preached for about a week to a throng numbering about 20,000. From wagons and crude tents, the crowds listened to the message that Jesus Christ could save all people from their sins. People reacted emotionally and physically to this message, some jerking their heads or entire bodies, others falling to the ground in a faint.

Reminiscent of the Great Awakening in the South during the 1750s and 1760s, the camp meetings spread through Kentucky, Tennessee, and southern Ohio, gathering new congregations. The Methodist and Baptist churches, which placed less importance on the fine points of religious doctrine and a well-educated clergy than did the Presbyterians, benefited most from the revivals. They saw extraordinary growth among ordinary people. As one minister wrote, "the illiterate Methodist preachers actually set the world on fire, (the American world at least) while [pastors of other denominations] were lighting their matches!"

Religion was also important to black Americans, whether they remained enslaved or had achieved freedom. In the South, African Americans responded enthusiastically to revivalist preachers. The Methodists and Baptists welcomed free and enslaved blacks into their congregations as equals in spirit though not in governing the church. In hostile northern cities, free black communities depended on separate churches for leadership and communal fellowship.

Growth of Sects

The period around 1800 witnessed the expansion of several dissenting sects: the Shakers, the Society of the Public Universal Friend, and the Universalists. They are called sects, rather than denominations, because they

The Shakers of New Lebanon—Religious Exercises in the Dining Room. In religious worship, Shakers abandoned their strict, sex-segregated discipline.

North Wind Picture Archives

were new and fairly small. They held distinctive beliefs that set them apart from mainstream religions, yet had a significant influence on intellectual and social movements of their times.

The Shakers, whose official name was the United Society of Believers in Christ's Second Coming (the Millennial Church), came to America in 1774, when Mother Ann Lee arrived from Britain with eight disciples. They left England to escape mob attacks and imprisonment. The group grew slowly at first, but expanded after Lee's death in 1784, as they reaped followers from revivals, especially Baptists. The sect offered an avenue for people who had been spiritually reborn in the Awakening and sought a distinctive way to represent that rebirth in their lives.

From visions, Mother Lee believed that she embodied Christ's Second Coming, that the millennium had already arrived. Because Christ had appeared as a man, and Lee (called Mother of the New Creation) came as a woman, God had both male and female elements. The Shakers believed in salvation by confession of sin, equality regardless of sex or race, opposition to slavery and war, and assistance to the poor. They abstained from sexual relations. In Shaker communities, which by 1809 existed from Maine to Kentucky, men and women ate, slept, and worked separately. They followed a strict discipline and aspired to economic self-sufficiency. Shakers sat on straight-backed chairs, cut their food into square pieces, and walked along paths laid out in right angles. But in religious worship, they abandoned this right-angle order. In a large open space without pulpit or pews, worshippers danced, shouted, and sang. The Shakers influenced other groups to organize communal, utopian experiments during the years after 1815.

A similar but smaller sect was the Society of the Public Universal Friend, founded by Jemima Wilkinson of Rhode Island. Disowned by Quakers in 1776 for joining the Baptists, Wilkinson became ill, believed that she died, and then returned to life as the Public Universal Friend. Her mission was to convince others to repent their sins and prepare for the millennium. Like Mother Lee, Wilkinson preached celibacy, peace, and opposition to slavery. She traveled sidesaddle on horseback, attracting a coterie of believers in New England and Pennsylvania. As one convert said, Wilkinson was "the Messenger of Peace . . . Travelling far & wide to spread the glad tidings & news of Salvation to a lost and perishing & dying World who have all gone astray like Lost Sheep." In 1788, on gathering more than 200 Universal Friends, she organized a community called Jerusalem in western New York. The Universal Friends neither organized a communal economy like the Shakers nor continued to seek new members. Nevertheless, the community survived well past Wilkinson's death in 1819.

Another sect, the Universalists, rejected the Calvinist belief that only a minority of people, the elect, could attain salvation. They preached that "it is the purpose of God, through the grace revealed in our Lord Jesus Christ, to save every member of the human race from sin." The American Universalist Church, established in 1779 by an Englishman, John Murray, found a sympathetic audience among ordinary people caught up in the Second Great Awakening in New England and on the frontier. Its message of universal salvation had wide influence, though the Universalist Church itself remained small.

Revivalism among Native Americans

While the Second Great Awakening and dissenting sects claimed the imagination and souls of white and black Americans, a new wave of revivals drew together Native Americans. Among the Iroquois living on reservations in western New York and the Shawnees, Creeks, Cherokees, and other nations retaining lands in the trans-Appalachian region, prophets warned of imminent doom unless people changed their ways. Native Americans had continued to lose lands to whites throughout the area from the Appalachians to the Mississippi; by 1812, settlers in the region dwarfed the Indian population by seven to one. Decline in the numbers of fur-bearing animals caused economic hardship, and conflict over whether to cooperate with the United States created political factions within tribes.

Tenskwatawa, the Shawnee Prophet

With his brother Tecumseh, Tenskwatawa organized pan-Indian resistance to white settlement in the Great Lakes region. He was one of a series of nativist prophets who challenged their followers to reject alcohol and Euro-American customs. The Shawnee Prophet and Tecumseh opposed accommodationist leaders who sold Indian land and, during the War of 1812, the brothers unsuccessfully allied with Great Britain against the United States.

George Catlin painted this portrait of Tenskwatawa in 1830, 19 years after the Battle of Tippecanoe. It is

one of many paintings produced by Catlin and other artists in the 1830s of individual Native American leaders and scenes demonstrating Indian customs, such as dances and the hunt. Unlike many Indians of the time, the prophet is wearing skins rather than a cloak. He has silver earrings, armbands, and a gorget at his throat, but not a peace medal indicating alliance with the U.S. or British government. In contrast, the drawing of Tecumseh later in this chapter shows the Shawnee leader wearing a military coat and British peace medal.

Like the Delaware prophet Neolin in the 1760s, the new nativists blamed loss of land and power on the Indians' failure to maintain traditional rituals and on their adoption of wicked practices from the whites. Among many prophets, Handsome Lake of the Senecas (a nation of the Iroquois) and Tenskwatawa of the Shawnees wielded the greatest influence in the first decade of the nineteenth century.

Handsome Lake, a respected warrior and leader of the Allegany Senecas, fell ill in 1799, seemed to die, then came back to life saying that he had had a vision in which messengers told him to become a prophet. In a series of revelations over several years, Handsome Lake received a message of impending catastrophe and a means to salvation. He told his people to stop drinking alcohol and practicing witchcraft; instead they should perform their ancestral rituals. The prophet also advocated peace. He embraced the U.S. acculturation policy by which Quakers tried to convince the Iroquois to adopt white farming methods and gender roles, but he opposed further large-scale land cessions, the whiskey trade, social dancing in couples, and gambling with cards. Other Indians opposed acculturation, which required women to leave the fields and take up spinning, and men to farm rather than hunt. They viewed the policy, accurately, as a way to justify further expropriation of hunting lands.

Handsome Lake served as a political leader of the Iroquois only briefly, from 1801 to 1803, but his spiritual message remained strong in the years that followed. Most influential was his drive against liquor. A former heavy drinker himself, the Seneca prophet advised, in the words of a white observer, that "the Whiskey is the great Engine which the bad Spirit uses to introduce Witchcraft and many other evils amongst Indians." Many Iroquois abstained from hard drink. One Quaker visitor "noted with satisfaction that in the course of our travels among all the Indians on the Allegheny River . . . we have not seen a Single individual the least intoxicated with Liquor—which perhaps would be a Singular Circumstance to Observe in traveling among the same number of white Inhabitants."

Also influential was Tenskwatawa, called the Shawnee Prophet, who became prominent among the people of the Great Lakes and Ohio Valley. With his brother, **Tecumseh,** he inspired a nativist movement to resist the U.S. government's acculturation policy and land grabbing. To avoid fiery destruction, he warned, Indians must revitalize their traditional ceremonies, avoid liquor, and reject the new gender roles. One of the prophet's visions promised that the whites would be destroyed if his people obeyed these instructions.

African Americans

As slavery ended in the North, free blacks faced discriminatory practices that kept the racial caste system in place, including segregation in churches and schools, and restriction from politics and many occupations. Despite this racism, northern blacks created new lives, institutions, and communities that offered a potent draw to African Americans in the South. Southern blacks also considered more violent means to end bondage, as in the case of Gabriel's revolt in Virginia.

Free Blacks in the North

By 1800, Pennsylvania, New York, and all of New England had passed gradual abolition acts or ended slavery outright. New Jersey in 1804 became the last northern state to pass a law for gradual emancipation, which, like those of other states, freed children henceforth born to slave mothers, but retained slaves born before that date in perpetual bondage. The black children who benefited from the law would be required to serve their mother's owner, much like indentured servants, until a certain age—in New Jersey, 25 for males and 21 for females.

Despite the gradual nature of these emancipation laws, slavery declined rapidly in the northern states (see Table 8.1). Responding to their slaves' requests for freedom and to the spirit of the abolition acts, many owners freed people whom the laws left in bonds. Masters usually required some additional years of service for the promise of freedom. Frequently, blacks negotiated agreements for themselves or family members. In 1805, a New York slave, Margaret, obtained her owner's pledge of freedom

Table 8.1 Number of Enslaved African Americans, 1800 and 1810

	1800	1810
New England	1,339	418
New York	20,903	15,017
New Jersey	12,422	10,851
Pennsylvania	1,706	795
Delaware	6,153	4,177
Maryland & District of Columbia	107,707	115,056
Virginia	346,968	394,357
North Carolina	133,296	168,824
South Carolina	146,151	196,365
Georgia	59,406	105,218
Kentucky	40,343	80,561
Tennessee	13,584	44,535
Mississippi Territory	3,489	17,088

Table 8.2 Free Black Population in Northern Cities

	1790	1800	1810
Philadelphia	1,849	6,028	8,942
New York City	1,036	3,333	7,470
Boston	766	1,174	1,484

in 8 years if she behaved "as she always has done in an orderly manner as a servant ought to do." A New Jersey man promised to pay his owner $50 per year for 4 years in return for his release. When masters proved recalcitrant, blacks often forced the issue by running away.

The northern cities became magnets for escaped slaves. In addition, humanitarian concerns touched some southern masters, including George Washington, who freed his slaves in his will. Some owners in Delaware and the Chesapeake region, who held more slaves than they needed, emancipated their slaves, then sold them as indentured servants in the North. Between 1790 and 1810, the free black population of Philadelphia and New York City soared, while that of Boston also grew, though more slowly (see Table 8.2).

Philadelphia and New York City became centers of free African American culture, with churches fostering autonomous community growth. In Philadelphia, responding to hostility from whites, freed men and women organized separate black congregations in the 1780s and 1790s. Reverend Richard Allen, for example, led black worshippers from St. George's Methodist

The drawing entitled *The Accident in Lombard Street* by Charles Willson Peale, shows a scene in Philadelphia during the late eighteenth century, when the free African American population was growing quickly. Chimney sweeps are laughing at a girl who has dropped a pie in the street.

Episcopal Church when whites insisted on segregated seating. Allen described the scene as they were forced to move during prayer:

> We had not been long upon our knees before I heard considerable scuffling and loud talking. I raised my head up and saw one of the trustees, H_____ M_____, having hold of the Rev. Absalom Jones, pulling him off his knees, and saying, "You must get up, you must not kneel here." . . . we all went out of the church in a body, and they were no more plagued by us in the church.

Allen purchased a blacksmith's shop and converted it into a church, calling it Bethel. By 1803, the black Methodist church had 457 members, the result of revivals and Allen's fervent preaching. But while the evangelical message of Methodism appealed to African Americans, and "Mother" Bethel grew, the congregation found relations with the hierarchy of the white Methodist Church difficult. In the early decades of the nineteenth century, black Methodists in Philadelphia, Baltimore, Wilmington, and New York struggled against white control, finally seceding to form separate denominations. In 1816, Philadelphia's Bethel became the first congregation of the African Methodist Episcopal church.

Urban black churches provided mutual aid, fellowship, and avenues for leadership. One benefit of belonging to a New York congregation became obvious to an 80-year-old woman after a fire destroyed her home. When asked where she would find shelter, she answered, "O a sister in the church has promised to take me in." Shunned by white organizations, effectively barred from politics, and lacking equal opportunity for employment, African Americans created alternatives through the church.

Like white urban residents, freed men and women formed mutual benefit societies. The names African Americans chose for these organizations demonstrated pride in their African heritage, though many of the founders were two, three, even four generations removed from ancestral lands. Philadelphians, for example, formed the Free African Society, Daughters of Ethiopia, Angola Society, Sons of Africa, and many others. The official purpose of these societies was to collect dues to provide relief to poor widows and children, but, just as important, the groups facilitated community involvement.

With little money or access to capital, few African Americans, perhaps 1 in 10, scraped together the funds to purchase a house, shop, or farm. In the first decades of the nineteenth century, many blacks were still completing terms of servitude; others, though free, lived and worked in white households as domestic servants. Even if they established their own households, women generally washed clothes or performed domestic service for

others. Most men were mariners or common laborers. The African American community provided additional opportunity by employing its own. Residents supported black shoemakers, carpenters, food retailers, hucksters, barbers, hairdressers, seamstresses, tailors, cooks, bakers, schoolteachers, and ministers. In Philadelphia, a few African Americans achieved considerable wealth and

Picturing the Past   SOCIAL & CULTURAL EVENTS

The African Episcopal Church of St. Thomas

As the free African American population grew in Philadelphia, churches became central to the developing community. Black Philadelphians founded separate churches for several reasons, including the discrimination they experienced in white congregations and the desire for black leadership. Many of the African American community's key leaders were ministers, including the Rev. Richard Allen, founder of the Bethel African Methodist Church, and Rev. Absolem Jones, leader of the African Church of Philadelphia,

which affiliated with Episcopalians to become St. Thomas's. The African Episcopal Church of St. Thomas, shown in this view by David Kennedy and William Lucas, was founded in 1794 and had 427 members the next year. Increasingly, black Philadelphians attended the separate churches. In explaining why former slaves sought their own institutions, Absolem Jones wrote, "to arise out of the dust and shake ourselves, and throw off that servile fear, that the habit of oppression and bondage trained us up in."

fame. By 1807, James Forten employed 30 men—blacks and whites—to produce sails for the city's shipbuilders. Robert Bogle developed the idea of catering parties, weddings, and funerals, and Frank Johnson became the city's premier musician. He performed on trumpet and violin, composed dance music and songs, and organized a band that played at balls and public events.

African Americans in northern cities also knew of recent struggles by slaves in St. Domingue and elsewhere; a large number of blacks in Philadelphia and New York City had come from the French island with their masters who had fled the black revolt. During the 1790s, as described in Chapter 7, blacks on St. Domingue led by Toussaint L'Ouverture, a former slave, had defeated local whites and the French, Spanish, and British armies. In 1802, Napoleon tried to regain control of the island but failed when disease decimated his forces. In 1804, the victorious rebels of St. Domingue established Haiti as an independent nation. Most white Americans dreaded the importation of black revolt. Thomas Jefferson opposed trade with the island, stating, "We may expect therefore black crews, and supercargoes and missionaries thence into the southern states. . . . If this combustion can be introduced among us under any veil whatever, we have to fear it."

Slave Rebellion in the South

With more than 850,000 enslaved blacks in the American South in 1800, one-third of the population, whites had reason to be concerned about slave insurgency. After St. Domingue erupted, Georgia and the Carolinas declared black emigrés from the West Indies a threat, prohibiting their entry. South Carolina, in reopening its international slave trade in 1803, made every effort to avoid admitting rebels. The state excluded blacks from the West Indies and South America, and any who had ever lived in the French West Indies. Every man imported from another state needed a certificate indicating that he had not "been concerned in any insurrection or rebellion."

In August 1800, the worst fears of white southerners were nearly realized when an enslaved blacksmith named Gabriel organized an armed march against the capital of Virginia. With about 600 supporters from Richmond and surrounding counties, Gabriel planned a full-scale insurrection. His strategy included seizing guns from an arsenal, taking Governor James Monroe hostage, and forcing concessions from town officials. Gabriel expected poor whites to join him because they, like slaves, lacked political power. The attack failed when a torrential rainstorm washed out bridges, making travel impossible. Efforts to try again another day collapsed when two

informers passed word of the conspiracy to authorities, who rounded up suspects. Though Gabriel eluded capture for more than three weeks, he was arrested and hanged, as were 26 others implicated in the plot.

White Americans still held the revolutionary belief that all men and women desired freedom, and masters took seriously the threat of slave revolt. After Gabriel's rebellion, Governor Monroe observed about enslaved African Americans, "Unhappily while this class of people exists among us we can never count with certainty on its tranquil submission." In 1802, Virginians discovered additional conspiracies, with rumors of more violence heightening tensions. In 1805, after four whites had been poisoned in North Carolina, officials burned a slave woman alive, hanged three other slaves, and whipped and cut off the ears of another. Gabriel's plot, the St. Domingue uprising, and what appeared to be an upsurge of murders and arson by blacks convinced southern lawmakers to enact more stringent slave codes. South Carolina and Georgia tightened requirements for slave patrols and defined as treason any collaboration in slave rebellion. Hardening attitudes toward slavery snuffed out southern antislavery societies that were already faltering. On a more positive note, as the 20-year constitutional restriction on prohibiting the slave trade expired, Congress officially banned the importation of slaves after January 1, 1808.

Jefferson's Republic

In 1800, the federal government moved from the nation's cultural capital in Philadelphia to an unfinished village on the Potomac: Washington, D.C. The ruling party also changed, as voters voiced their dissatisfaction with the Federalists by electing Thomas Jefferson and a Republican Congress. Jefferson's promise of reduced government and taxes appealed to a populace concerned about other things besides national politics—their finances, their souls, and local communities. Events prevented the young nation from wrapping itself in isolation, however, for its economic prosperity depended a great deal on international commerce, a trade severely hampered by the ongoing European war.

The Election of 1800

Shortly before the election, the United States had been involved in the Quasi-War with France, in which the French navy initially ravaged the American merchant fleet. Congress had expanded the army, authorized the U.S. Navy to protect commercial ships, and revoked unilaterally the American-French treaty of 1778. The

Federalists had swept the congressional elections of 1798 on the crest of anti-French fervor and had tried to use war fever against the Republicans through the Alien and Sedition acts. Instead, the backlash of concern about civil liberties swelled the opposition.

As the 1800 election approached, many Federalists expected to take advantage of the unresolved difficulties with France in continuing to paint the Jeffersonian Republicans as pro-French, hence un-American. Nevertheless, President John Adams moved to end hostilities. He nominated a three-man commission, including William Vans Murray (minister to the Netherlands), Chief Justice Oliver Ellsworth, and Governor William R. Davie of North Carolina, to make peace with France. The commission received instructions that proved impossible to fulfill: its mission was to obtain French agreement that the 1778 alliance had ended and indemnities for confiscated American ships. In March 1800, Murray, Ellsworth, and Davie met with Napoleon, who had no intention of paying compensation. The commissioners reached an accord only by ignoring their instructions. The Convention of 1800, signed in France in October and ratified reluctantly by the U.S. Senate in February 1801, echoed provisions of the 1778 commercial treaty in calling for "a firm, inviolable, and universal peace," but it voided the defensive alliance of 1778, eliminating the French claim to U.S. support against Great Britain. The pact also included a vague confirmation by the French of neutral rights in international trade, but it provided no restitution to American shippers, a failing that opponents said made the convention worthless. In fact, it had value in normalizing relations between the two countries.

The chief beneficiary of reduced tensions with France was Thomas Jefferson, named in May 1800 as Republican nominee for president, with Aaron Burr of New York for vice president. John Adams received the Federalist nomination for reelection, with Charles Cotesworth Pinckney of South Carolina as his running mate. Many Federalists opposed Adams for making peace with France. When the electoral votes were tallied, Jefferson and Burr each received 73 votes, Adams 65, Pinckney 64, and John Jay 1 (see Map 8.1). In lining up votes in the electoral college, the Republicans had failed to take account of the constitutional election procedures that lacked provision for party slates. The Constitution directed that each elector cast two votes, with the candidate receiving the highest number elected president and the runner-up vice president. The electors had no way of designating which candidate they supported for president and which for vice president. The Federalists avoided the difficulty by having one elector vote for John Jay, thus giving Pinckney one less vote than Adams.

Aaron Burr by Gilbert Stuart. Burr refused initially to follow the script and accept the vice presidency when he tied with Jefferson in the election of 1800.

From the Collections of the New Jersey Historical Society, Newark, New Jersey

If Burr had simply yielded to Jefferson, the problem would have been resolved without complication. Instead, the tie sent the election to the House of Representatives, which had a Federalist majority from the previous election. Each state delegation received one vote. Some of the Federalists hatched a plan to support Burr, thinking that they might be able to control him as president. Hamilton opposed the plot vigorously, contending "Burr loves nothing but himself; thinks of nothing but his own aggrandizement, and will be content with nothing, short of permanent power in his own hands." The former secretary of the treasury advised his party to make a deal with Jefferson to keep the system of public credit and the navy, retain Federalist appointees in office, and remain neutral in the war between Britain and France. The House of Representatives required 36 ballots over 6 days before the Federalist delegate from Delaware, James A. Bayard, shifted his position from Burr to Jefferson to break the tie. Jefferson became president and Burr vice president.

Jefferson's "Revolution"

The third president assumed a conciliatory stance toward the Federalists as he took office. On March 4, had bedeviled his two predecessors. He later described his election as "the revolution of 1800" that "was as real a revolution in the principles of our government as that of 1776 was in its form; not effected indeed by the sword, as that, but by the rational and peaceable instrument of reform, the suffrage of the people." Despite bitter political enmity, American leaders had created a party system by which power could be contested in elections rather than through bloodshed. With the election of 1800, the Constitution passed a crucial test, with peaceful transfer of power from one party to its opponents.

The new president worked to put his principles into action, to create an agrarian republic in which the federal government kept its role to a minimum. The location in Washington, D.C., seemed the ideal setting for a weak government. In 1800, the town had fewer than 400 dwellings, which one government official described as mostly "small miserable huts." The Capitol was incomplete, with wings for the Senate and House but no center. What existed was poorly constructed: the acoustics were dreadful, the roof leaked, and the heating was "noxious." The president's house was not yet finished in 1814 when the British burned it. Construction materials littered the grounds during Jefferson's administration to the extent that, according to one guest, "in a dark night instead of finding your way to the house, you may, perchance, fall into a pit, or stumble over a heap of rubbish." Cows grazed on what later became the Mall; hogs ran through the city's streets.

MAP 8.1 The Election of 1800

The election Thomas Jefferson called "the revolution of 1800" was close, with Jefferson receiving 73 votes to John Adams's 65. The Federalist ticket, headed by Adams and Charles Cotesworth Pinckney, obtained considerable support from the Carolinas and mid-Atlantic as well as New England.

Legend:
- Adams and other Federalists
- Jefferson and other Republicans
- No returns, unsettled, etc.

1801, Jefferson delivered his inaugural address to the new Congress, which the Republicans now dominated in the House by 69 votes to 36 and in the Senate by 18 to 13. He gave the address almost in a whisper, for he was not a good public speaker. The speech reflected his Republican beliefs: emphasis on the power of state governments, freedom of religion and the press, majority rule but protection of minority rights, low government expenditures, and reduction of the federal debt. Jefferson upheld the Convention of 1800 with France implicitly by stating that he desired amity and trade with foreign nations and "entangling alliances with none." His most famous statement, "We are all republicans, we are all federalists," attempted to get beyond the partisan battles that

The Capitol in Washington was incomplete at the time of Jefferson's election in 1800. With hogs running through the streets, the town seemed an appropriate seat for his agrarian republic.

Washington, D.C., remained a village in part because the federal government was small, and Jefferson had no interest in seeing it grow. In 1802, federal personnel throughout the country numbered under 10,000, of whom 6,500 served in military posts. Of the nonuniformed officials, fewer than 300 worked in the Capital. The president and Supreme Court each had 1 clerk, Congress employed 13, and the attorney general had none. The central government had relatively little to do, for state and local governments or voluntary associations took primary responsibility for keeping law and order, maintaining roads and bridges, supervising the militia, and providing welfare relief and schools.

Jefferson's lack of attention to building Washington, D.C., revealed his approach to the presidency. In contrast to Federalist efforts to reflect the grandeur of European courts and capitals, he adopted informality and frugality. Jefferson dealt with members of Congress and foreign diplomats personally, inviting small groups for dinner and conversation. He avoided making speeches, sending written messages to Congress. With only one clerk, he handled many documents himself.

The change of political power from the Federalists to the Republicans raised questions about office holding and political spoils. At the highest level of executive appointments, the cabinet, Jefferson assumed his right to appoint trusted supporters. He named James Madison of Virginia, his closest ally, as secretary of state, and Albert Gallatin of Pennsylvania as secretary of the treasury. Other members of the cabinet included Levi Lincoln of Massachusetts as attorney general, Henry Dearborn of Massachusetts as secretary of war, and Robert Smith of Maryland as secretary of the navy.

The question of whether or not to retain bureaucrats was more difficult. Jefferson supported the idea of a civil service in which public officers held their positions on the basis of merit; during the election crisis he suggested that he would allow most officeholders to keep their jobs. When he learned that Washington and Adams had appointed only 6 Republicans to about 600 positions, however, the new president replaced about one-half of the Federalists with Republicans. Most infuriating to Jefferson were the "**midnight appointments**," as Jefferson characterized them—the appointments Adams made as a lame duck after he knew that the election was lost. In February 1801, the Federalist Congress had passed a new Judiciary Act creating these additional judgeships and other offices, all of which Federalists received. Jefferson called on the new Republican Congress to repeal the law.

Jefferson and Gallatin placed high priority on decreasing government expenditures, taxes, and the national debt. Gallatin opposed all spending by the federal government, including military. With support of the Republican Congress, the administration cut the defense budget in half. It repealed all excise taxes, including that on whiskey, relying primarily on import duties for income.

Jefferson's plan to reduce the navy and remain clear of international conflicts hit a snag when Yusuf Karamanli, the leader of Tripoli in North Africa, demanded payments from the United States to "protect" American merchant carriers from pirates. To end this extortion, in 1801 Jefferson sent naval vessels to blockade Tripoli and protect shipping. The United States experienced a major loss when the ship *Philadelphia* ran aground while pursuing pirates, but when a small force of U.S. Marines and Arab mercenaries seized the port city of Derna, the Tripolitans agreed to peace. The war had propelled military expenditures upward, however, and convinced Jefferson of the navy's value, thus hindering somewhat the administration's plans for reduced government spending.

The Judiciary

Although the Republicans had captured the presidency and Congress in 1800, the judiciary remained firmly in the hands of the Federalists. Adams and the outgoing Congress had tried to solidify their party's power in the courts with the Judiciary Act of 1801, which amended the Judiciary Act of 1789. By appointing additional federal judges, the new law ended the onerous requirement for Supreme Court justices to ride from state to state to convene circuit courts twice a year. The act also reduced the number of justices on the Court from six to five, thereby denying Jefferson the opportunity to make an appointment when a seat became vacant. The Republican Congress, in early 1802, repealed this law, reinstating the Judiciary Act of 1789, thus forcing some federal judges out of their jobs and the Supreme Court back to the circuit.

Jefferson's bitter relationship with the Supreme Court resulted in part from his antipathy toward Chief Justice **John Marshall,** his distant cousin, whom Adams had named to the bench in early 1801. Like Jefferson, Marshall was tall, informal in manner, and a native of Virginia. He had joined the patriot forces in 1775, serving until 1781. He attributed his nationalism to that service, saying he became "confirmed in the habit of considering America as my country, and congress as my government." Marshall began a successful law practice after the war, served as a Virginia assemblyman, supported ratification of the Federal Constitution, then became the leading Federalist in his state. In the legal environment of the new republic, many colleagues appreciated

Chief Justice John Marshall. During his tenure to 1835, the chief justice established federal judicial authority, in particular the Court's power to decide the constitutionality of laws.

his originality in building cases on logic and natural law rather than depending on English precedent. On the Supreme Court, too, Marshall followed his own lights, creating the legal basis on which the power of the Court rests. During his long, illustrious career, which lasted until 1835, Marshall solidified the authority of the judicial branch of the federal government.

Marshall's most important decision, ***Marbury v. Madison*** (1803), commenced in a suit by William Marbury, nominated by Adams as a justice of the peace but not commissioned by the Jefferson administration. Marbury sued under the Judiciary Act of 1789, which granted the Supreme Court the power to require Secretary of State Madison to hand over Marbury's commission. Given the partisanship involved, most observers expected Marshall and his Federalist court to direct Madison to comply. Instead, the chief justice said that he could not remedy Marbury's situation, though he wished to do so, because the Congress had erred in giving the Court such authority. Marshall declared the provision of the 1789 Judiciary Act unconstitutional, thus establishing the Supreme Court's power of judicial review.

Jefferson decided that the federal judiciary, still dominated by Federalists and growing in power under Marshall, had to be controlled. Because federal judges constitutionally held their seats for life, "during good behavior," the president suggested to congressional Republicans that they start impeachment proceedings against objectionable Federalists. The Republicans impeached John Pickering, an official of the federal district court of New Hampshire, who was an alcoholic and insane, but who had not to anyone's knowledge committed any high crimes. The Senate found him guilty anyway and removed him from his position. Next, in January 1805, the House of Representatives impeached Samuel Chase of Maryland, an associate justice of the Supreme Court and extreme Federalist who had castigated Jefferson's administration. But the prosecution failed to convince two-thirds of the Senate that Chase should be expelled from office for misconduct and other charges. Some moderate Republicans refused to adopt Jefferson's strategy to eject troublesome opponents. Thus ended Congress's attempt to remove Federalists from the bench by impeachment.

Domestic Politics

Jefferson and the Republicans gained in popularity as they steered a course more moderate than the "revolution" of 1800 had promised. The president had reduced taxes and attempted to limit the judiciary, but did not dismantle the Federalist edifice of national power, including the military and the national bank. He mixed republican theory, based on a nation of small farmers, with practical politics aiding commerce. His policies, combined with booming exports, steadily increased Republican support, as many Federalist voters switched parties. In the election of 1802, the Republicans won 102 seats to the Federalists' 39 in the House of Representatives; the Republican margin in the Senate was 25 to 9.

Looking forward to the next presidential election, Congress acted promptly to avoid the deadlock that had occurred in 1800. The Republicans wanted a formal way to keep the Federalists from conspiring once again to elevate the Republican candidate for vice president to the presidency. The Twelfth Amendment to the Constitution, which required the electors to draw up distinct lists for president and vice president, was ratified by September 1804.

The election of 1804 demonstrated the demise of the Federalists as an effective national party. Jefferson defeated the Federalist presidential candidate, Charles Cotesworth Pinckney, by 162 electoral votes to 14.

Flashpoints | The Louisiana Purchase

The facts behind the Louisiana Purchase are quite straightforward: in 1803, the French sold the vast Louisiana territory to the United States for $15 million. Yet behind this seemingly uncomplicated transaction lay many diverse individuals, nations, and groups, all of whom had their own perspective on its significance. For the French, the Purchase was an opportunity to solidify ties with the fledgling United States and to work against British interests in North America. To the Spanish, it represented a profound betrayal of French promises not to sell the Louisiana territory to another nation. Members of the Federalist Party, stoutly pro-British, looked on the Purchase with horror, unhappy at the idea of the United States forging additional ties to the distrusted French. Native American peoples living in the territory watched and waited, to see what the Purchase would mean for their sovereignty.

President Jefferson, one of the architects of the Purchase, had complex and contradictory feelings about acquiring so much new territory. Uneasy about its possible unconstitutionality, Jefferson nonetheless believed that the Purchase was necessary for the United States to remain a republic of virtuous farmers. If the nation were to survive, Jefferson believed, it would have to acquire new land for expansion of its ever-growing population.

Dr. David Ramsey spoke for many Americans when, in 1804, he affirmed that the Louisiana Purchase was "the greatest political blessing ever conferred on these states." Yet the Purchase was, at the very least, a mixed blessing—a decision that sparked a great deal of controversy about the desirability of expansion, the rights of Native Americans, and the role of slavery in the republic. The Purchase forced Americans to consider whether the United States, so recently a colony of Britain, should pursue imperialist expansion. The Purchase provoked with new force questions about Native American land rights, as eager white settlers encroached further and further west; it raised the issue of whether or not the "peculiar institution" of slavery should expand there. The Purchase also elicited questions about national identity. The people living in the region of the Louisiana Purchase were remarkably multiethnic, multilingual, and multicultural. Since, with the stroke of a pen, all this territory became American, what, then, did it mean to be an American? Over the decades to come, U.S. residents would grapple with all of these questions, as they spread out into the territory that Jefferson optimistically dubbed an "empire for liberty."

Questions for Reflection

1. Why was the Louisiana Purchase particularly important to American farmers west of the Appalachians?

2. Map 8.2 shows the difference in the limits of the Louisiana Purchase claimed by the Spanish and the United States. Why was Spain eager to restrict the size of U.S. territory?

3. What was the basis for Thomas Jefferson's unease that the Louisiana Purchase was unconstitutional? Why did he choose to buy the territory despite his concerns?

© The Granger Collection, New York

A view of New Orleans at the time of the Louisiana Purchase, 1803. The banner held by the eagle suggests a hopeful future under the U.S. government.

Jefferson had replaced Aaron Burr as his running mate with George Clinton, also of New York, thus keeping the ticket balanced geographically. For his part, Burr ran for governor of New York against the Republican candidate, Morgan Lewis, but lost by a landslide. Alexander Hamilton played a decisive role in the defeat by publicly denouncing his long-time enemy. Burr challenged Hamilton to a duel. When the two faced each other at Weehawken, New Jersey, in July 1804, Burr shot Hamilton to death. In doing so, the vice president ended his own political career, as well as the life of one of the architects of the American nation-state.

The Louisiana Purchase

Jefferson had boosted his popularity prior to the 1804 election with the **Louisiana Purchase,** which marked the greatest success of his presidency. In pursuing the deal with France, he deviated from one of his beliefs—in limited power of the central government—to obtain land for his agrarian republic. Long interested in the West, he scored a diplomatic coup that doubled the size of the United States and reduced Spain's dominance west of the Mississippi River.

The Bargain with Napoleon

The chain of events leading to the Louisiana Purchase began in 1800, when France signed a secret treaty with Spain to recover the lands in western North America it had ceded to Spain in 1763. When Jefferson and Madison heard in 1801 of the impending transfer, they sent the new U.S. minister to France, Robert R. Livingston, with instructions to prevent the exchange or at least obtain West Florida. The Americans wanted to prevent France from controlling the Mississippi Valley; the dilapidated Spanish empire had caused trouble enough. In October 1802, the Spanish suspended once again the right of Americans to deposit goods for export at New Orleans. The Americans thought, incorrectly, that Napoleon was behind the ban. Many wanted to take New Orleans by force. Jefferson wrote to Livingston, "The day that France takes possession of N. Orleans . . . we must marry ourselves to the British fleet and nation." Jefferson pushed for negotiations, however, not war.

In response to Livingston's overtures, Napoleon decided to sell the entire Louisiana Territory to the United States. The French leader's zeal to construct an American empire had cooled with the loss of his army in St. Domingue. In documents dated April 30, 1803, the United States agreed to pay France $15 million, to respect the rights of the French and Native Americans living in the territory, and to recognize the French residents as American citizens. Spain was furious because Napoleon had promised not to sell the region to the British or the Americans. Jefferson ignored the Spanish objections, but worried, as a strict constructionist, that the Louisiana Purchase was unconstitutional because the federal government had no specific power to acquire territory. He put aside these concerns, confident that it was right to avoid war and add vast lands for expansion of the American republic. "By enlarging the empire of liberty," the president argued, the nation could maintain its agrarian foundations and thus avoid descent into vice, luxury, and decay. A successful republic was dependent on broad property holding, for virtuous, independent, middling farmers made ideal citizens. The Louisiana Purchase, Jefferson believed, would extend the life of the republic by providing space for generations of ordinary planters. Although some Federalists disagreed, most Americans celebrated the end of friction over the Mississippi River and New Orleans. Western farmers could get their products to market while eastern merchants prospered from the trade.

Disputes with Spain

When U.S. officials gained formal possession of Louisiana in December 1803, the Spanish had only recently transferred control to the French. The ceremonies took place in New Orleans, a city of 8,000 that had been reconstructed in Spanish style since several great fires a decade earlier. With a cathedral, theater, impressive city hall, and mansions, New Orleans served as the cultural and economic center of the lower Mississippi Valley. In population, it was larger than other towns of the Spanish borderlands. The entire white population of the Louisiana Territory was approximately 50,000, including French, Spanish, Germans, English, and Americans.

Beyond Spain's objection to the U.S. purchase of Louisiana, the two nations also disputed the territory's boundaries, because the treaties transferring ownership were vague. Thomas Jefferson pushed for the most generous interpretation for the United States. He demanded West Florida, with an eastern boundary at the Perdido River, the present boundary between Alabama and the Florida panhandle. The president also thought his new acquisition extended in the southwest to the Rio Grande, incorporating all of Texas and part of New Mexico, and in the northwest to the Rocky Mountains. Spain, on the other hand, said the Louisiana Territory included only a constricted region along the west bank of the Mississippi from northern Missouri to the Gulf of Mexico (see Map 8.2).

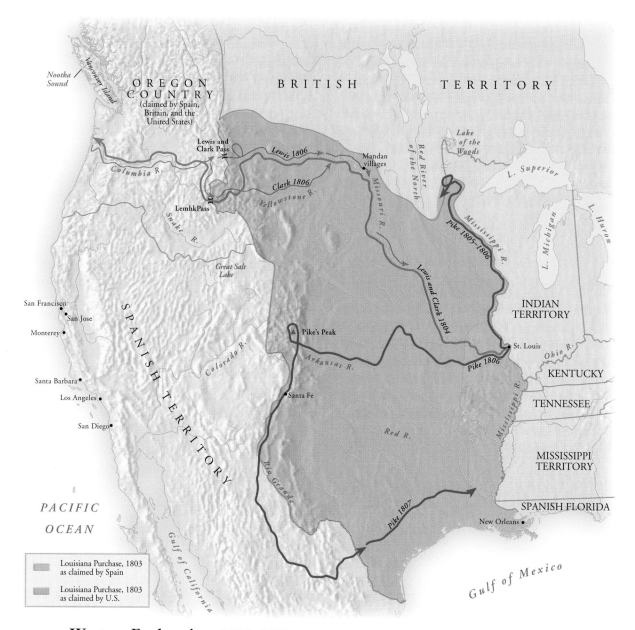

MAP 8.2 Western Exploration, 1803–1807

At about the same time Meriwether Lewis and William Clark led the Corps of Discovery along the northern route to trade with Native Americans, explore the natural resources, and locate a northwest passage, Zebulon Pike traveled north along the Mississippi River and west to the Rocky Mountains.

In 1804, Jefferson sent troops to West Florida, hoping to convince Spain by threat of force to give up or sell the province. Americans already outnumbered Spanish residents in the territory, which later comprised parts of Mississippi, Alabama, and Louisiana. Jefferson also wanted East Florida. He decided not to attack, and instead attempted to purchase the Floridas over the next several years, but failed.

The Lewis and Clark Expedition

To strengthen U.S. claims to the West, Jefferson sponsored an exploratory mission to the Pacific Ocean. Several times since 1783, he had tried to organize expeditions for scientific knowledge and to promote American interests in the region. As president, he now had the authority and financial resources to support this major undertaking. By the early nineteenth century, however, others had surveyed parts of the territory. In 1792, an American sea captain, Robert Gray, explored the Columbia River, and George Vancouver, a British naval officer, sailed the northwest coast. A few years later, fur traders working for the Spanish government ascended the Missouri River to present-day North Dakota, while British traders from Canada began moving west.

By permission of Houghton Library, Harvard University

Page 26.

Captains Lewis & Clark holding a Council with the Indians

Meeting of the Lewis and Clark expedition with Native Americans on the Missouri River, 1804. Illustration from the journal of Sergeant Patrick Gass, a member of the expedition.

Even before buying Louisiana, the president had decided to send an expedition west; the purchase gave the project greater urgency. He appointed his private secretary, Meriwether Lewis, as captain of the enterprise. Jefferson selected Lewis for his scientific interests as well as his wilderness experience. The president wanted "a person who to courage, prudence, habits & health adapted to the woods, & some familiarity with the Indian character, joins a perfect knoledge of botany, natural history, mineralogy & astronomy." Lewis chose his friend William Clark to be his partner. Lewis and Clark had served in the army together in the old Northwest, so both were familiar with frontier conditions.

Jefferson had a long list of goals for his explorers. They were to travel to the source of the Missouri River to find the elusive Northwest Passage, fill in huge blanks in geographic knowledge of the West, and bring back descriptions of unknown species of plants and animals. He also hoped they would make peaceful contact with Native Americans to expand commercial networks for fur traders. Lewis and Clark more than fulfilled their assignment, keeping daily journals of their experiences, including descriptions of Indian societies and culture, systematic weather records, and observations of flora and fauna, as well as a detailed map of their journey. Their relations with the people of the Northwest were for the most part amicable.

Lewis and Clark received commissions as army officers to lead the Corps of Discovery of about 40 men who departed from St. Louis in May 1804. During that summer and fall they traveled up the Missouri River, using poles and tow ropes against the current. They battled the hot sun, diarrhea, and mosquitoes; several men deserted and one died, the only member of the Corps to perish during the entire trip. The adventurers met with the leaders of Indian nations along the way, telling them that the United States had taken possession of the territory from the Spanish. They arrived in the Mandan and Hidatsa villages of what is now North Dakota, where they spent the winter of 1804–1805.

In April 1805, the **Lewis and Clark expedition** set out with their guide, **Sacagawea,** a Shoshone woman, and her French husband and infant son. They proceeded up the Missouri River, made an arduous crossing of the Rockies, and reached the mouth of the Columbia River before winter. On the way back, the corps divided in two, with Clark leading a party southeast along the Yellowstone River and Lewis taking a northern route through Montana. They joined forces once again in North Dakota, then returned to St. Louis by September 1806. They had been away so long that many assumed they had been killed by the Spanish or Native Americans.

Spies and Infiltrators

Spanish officials in fact had tried to intercept Lewis and Clark, whom they correctly suspected of making allies for the United States among the western Indians. General James Wilkinson, commander of U.S. troops in the West, governor of the Louisiana Territory, and a double agent known to the Spanish as "Agent 13," had tipped off New Spain about the expedition. The governor of New Mexico sent out search parties but failed to find Lewis and Clark. They did stop the mission of Thomas Freeman and Peter Custis, who in 1806 had started from Louisiana to find the source of the Red River. Another Spanish party nearly intercepted Zebulon Pike, whom Wilkinson had dispatched to explore and spy in the region that is now Kansas, Colorado, and New Mexico. Pike became lost in the southern Rockies, was rescued by Spanish soldiers, arrested, then released.

Both the United States and Spain knew they were playing for high stakes. The United States could use exploration of the West and alliances with Native Americans to help confirm its claims to broad boundaries of the Louisiana Territory. The Spanish had by far superior documentation for Texas, New Mexico, Arizona, California, and western Colorado. But they also denied American rights to what is now western Louisiana. Jefferson sent General Wilkinson with troops to the undefined boundary between Louisiana and Texas; the Spanish dispatched Lt. Col. Simón de Herrera to defend eastern Texas. The two officers avoided fighting by establishing a neutral zone until diplomats could negotiate the border.

Still concerned about protecting their silver mines in Mexico, the Spanish took steps to increase settlement in Texas. They welcomed Indian exiles—Cherokees, Choctaws, and Alabamas—from lands overrun by American settlers east of the Mississippi, but the Hispanic population failed to grow significantly. New Spain officials specifically barred U.S. citizens from Texas, under threat of arrest and imprisonment. The Americans, one Spanish official feared, "are not and will not be anything but crows to pick out our eyes." Anglo-American traders continued to infiltrate Texas, however, to trap animals and bargain for horses with the Comanches and other Indians.

The Burr Conspiracy

While Lewis and Clark were reconnoitering the far Northwest, Aaron Burr conceived a plot to create a separate nation in the West. He contacted the double agent James Wilkinson, various unhappy politicians, and representatives of foreign governments. Burr suggested a variety of plans to those who would listen, including an invasion of New Spain, an attack on Washington, D.C., and secession of the West. Wilkinson cooperated with Burr at first, then turned informer when the conspiracy became public knowledge. Jefferson ordered Burr's arrest for treason, while applauding Wilkinson's "fidelity." Burr tried to escape to Europe, but was captured and taken to Richmond, Virginia, where he was tried in 1807.

The Burr conspiracy case, presided over by Chief Justice Marshall and involving three prosecutors and six defense lawyers, might have been called the trial of the century. An unbiased jury could not be found; one juror said before the case was heard that Burr should be hanged. The principal actors in the trial were Marshall, who ignored his responsibility as an impartial judge to favor the defense, and Jefferson, who directed the prosecution from afar. Because Marshall upheld a definition

of treason that required actual gathering of troops, not just conspiracy, the case against Burr collapsed. Jefferson blamed Marshall and considered trying to impeach him, but found insufficient congressional support.

More Foreign Entanglements

The renewal of war in 1803 between Great Britain and France portended trouble for the United States. American merchants flourished as they took advantage of neutrality and wartime demand for provisions in Europe and the West Indies. But their ships became vulnerable to the British navy and French privateers.

A Perilous Neutrality

Great Britain and France each wanted to prevent the United States from provisioning the other. In particular, the British intended to stop American traders from carrying foreign sugar, coffee, and other tropical products to Europe, even though the merchants conformed technically to British guidelines by taking the goods first to U.S. ports, then reexporting. In the *Essex* case of 1805, British courts stiffened their rules, stating that merely carrying Spanish and French goods to U.S. soil for reexport was insufficient, that only commodities originally meant for sale in the United States, then subsequently redirected to Europe, would be considered exempt from seizure. Few reexported cargoes met the new guidelines. With the *Essex* rule, the Royal Navy stepped up its confiscations of American ships. Then, in 1806 and 1807, the British and French blockaded each other's harbors, in combination eliminating neutral trade with Europe and the British Isles. The British insisted that neutral ships sail to Britain first for inspection and licensing before trading in Europe. Napoleon's Berlin and Milan Decrees banned trade with Britain and threatened neutrals who obeyed the British rules with seizure.

After the British destroyed the French and Spanish navies in 1805 at Trafalgar, off the coast of Spain, the British restrictions and impressment of sailors were by far the more troublesome to Americans. Many Federalists and some Republicans cried for war. But Jefferson and the congressional majority looked for ways to avoid hostilities. With a trimmed federal budget and small military, the Republicans were unprepared for war. Congress passed a Non-Importation Act (1806) banning specified British goods, and the president opened negotiations with Great Britain to end impressment and recognize neutral trading rights. No agreement satisfactory to both sides could be reached. Then, in June 1807, the

---

DOING HISTORY ONLINE

The President to Governor Claiborne, 1804
Based on the letter in this module, what appear to be Jefferson's concerns regarding governance of the Louisiana Territory?

History ⧗ Now™   Visit HistoryNOW to access primary sources and exercises related to this topic: http://now.ilrn.com/ayers_etal3e

British ship *Leopard* fired on the American frigate *Chesapeake* for refusing to submit to a search for British deserters. The *Chesapeake*, hit 22 times, managed to respond with only 1 shot. The *Leopard* boarded her, impressing four men.

The Embargo of 1807

As Americans clamored for war in response, Jefferson closed U.S. ports and territorial waters to British vessels and recalled American ships from the Mediterranean, where they would have been trapped had war begun. The British refused to stop impressing American sailors. They challenged Jefferson's port closure by firing on coastal towns in Maine and sailing into Chesapeake Bay. The president resisted a declaration of war, but placed military posts and gunboats on alert. He chose economic warfare instead. Unfortunately, this policy destroyed the commercial boom that had meant high prices for farmers and employed thousands of sailors.

At the urging of President Jefferson and Secretary of State Madison, Congress passed the Embargo Act in December 1807. The law prohibited exportation to all other countries. The administration hoped in particular to defang the former parent country by withholding provisions to the British Isles and West Indies. A by-product of nonexportation would be a severe drop in imports of British manufactures. Jefferson and Madison argued that the boycott would hurt all warring parties, but Britain worst. During 1808, the administration faced difficulty enforcing the embargo because ships, especially from New England, left harbor pretending to sail to American coastal ports but headed for foreign destinations instead. The trade with the British West Indies continued illegally. Federal agents also had little success in preventing smuggling into Canada. In January 1809, the government resorted to an extreme measure, Giles's Enforcement Act, which empowered the president to use the militia against smugglers. The act effectively ended trade.

The embargo had considerable impact on the U.S. economy. Agricultural prices declined, leading to farm foreclosures. According to official records, exports declined by 80 percent in 1808, though smuggling certainly lessened the effect. The U.S. Treasury suffered a loss in customs revenue, its chief source of income. However, the embargo stimulated further technological development of the textile industry, particularly in weaving cotton cloth with power looms.

With stern enforcement of Giles's Act, New Englanders became strident in their demands for termination of the embargo. Jefferson became convinced that civil war was possible, but he refused to support repeal. Republicans moved anyway, on March 1, 1809, replacing the embargo with a Non-Intercourse Act, which reopened trade with all countries except Great Britain and France. If either of the two belligerents changed its policy to favor neutral rights, the United States would resume commerce with that nation as well. Although the new law banned trade with major markets, loopholes offered generous opportunities for smuggling.

Congress made this shift just days before the close of Jefferson's presidency. Jefferson thus ended his administration without solving the nation's international troubles, which Americans increasingly defined as an effort by Britain to subjugate its former colonies. As he returned to Monticello, however, the president could reflect favorably on the goals he had achieved—lower taxes and national debt, smaller government, open doors to immigrants, and peace. He also took pride in an accomplishment he had not foreseen in 1801, the purchase of the Louisiana Territory. Jefferson's administration was remarkable for what it did—and for what it did not do, considering his opposition to Hamiltonian policies in the 1790s. Under Jefferson, the Republicans left intact the national bank, the federal administrative structure, and the armed forces. Considering the war-torn world in which the young nation found its way, however, the Republican commitment to minimal government left the United States militarily unprepared.

Madison and the War of 1812

When Britain continued to impress American sailors and seize ships, the United States was faced with two choices: accept humiliation or declare war on Great Britain. The British argued that they acted from necessity, as Napoleon conquered Europe. Americans upheld their rights as neutrals to sell provisions to both sides. They considered British impressment of 6,000 seamen as a violation of national sovereignty and human rights. Between 1809 and 1812, these conflicts developed into war.

The Election of 1808

Despite the embargo, Jefferson retained enough popularity to win a third term, had he chosen to run. Instead, he declined and designated James Madison, the secretary of state, as his successor. James Monroe, who had served as governor of Virginia and minister to Great Britain, challenged Jefferson's choice, but congressional Republicans endorsed Madison. Dissenting Republicans, called the Tertium Quids (meaning a third alternative), gave Monroe some support, but his candidacy

DOING HISTORY

Native Americans and the New Republic

THE FOLLOWING DOCUMENTS give two views— among many others—of U.S. westward expansion during the first decade of the nineteenth century. The entries from the journals of Meriwether Lewis and William Clark record information about their initial contact with Native Americans along the upper Missouri River. On February 11, 1805, Lewis described the birth of a son to Sacagawea, the expedition's Shoshone interpreter and guide. Tecumseh, in contrast, presents the case of Native Americans of the Great Lakes region, who lost 2.5 million acres of land with the Treaty of Fort Wayne (1809).

The Journals of Meriwether Lewis and William Clark 1805

[Clark] *14th January 1805 Monday.*

This morning early a number of Indians men women children dogs &c. &c. passed down on the ice to join those that passed yesterday, we sent Serg.ᵗ Pryor and five men with those Indians to hunt (several men with the venereal caught from the Mandan women). One of our hunters sent out several days [ago] arrived & informs that one man (Whitehouse) is frost bit and can't walk home.

[Clark] *16th January Wednesday 1805.* About thirty Mandans came to the fort today, 6 chiefs. . . . the Little Crow 2.ᵈ Chief of the lower village came & brought us corn &c. 4 men of ours who had been hunting returned one frost'd.

This war chief gave us a chart in his way of the Missouri, . . .

[Lewis] *8th February Friday 1805.*

This morning was fair wind S.E. the weather still warm and pleasant. Visited by the *Black-Cat* the principal chief of the Roop-tar-he, or upper Mandan village. This man possesses more integrity, firmness, intelligence and perspicuity of mind than any Indian I have met with in this quarter, and I think with a little management he may be made a useful agent in furthering the views of our government. The Black Cat presented me with a bow and apologized for not having completed the shield he had promised alleging that the weather had been too cold to permit his making it. I gave him some small shot 6 fishing-hooks and 2 yards of ribbon. His squaw also presented me with 2

pair of moccasins for which in return I gave a small looking glass and a couple of needles. The chief dined with me and left me in the evening. He informed me that his people suffered very much for the article of meat, and that he had not himself tasted any for several days.

[Lewis] *11th February Monday 1805.* . . . about five o'clock this evening one of the wives of Charbonneau was delivered of a fine boy. It is worthy of remark that this was the first child which this woman had borne, and as is common in such cases her labor was tedious and the pain violent; M.ʳ Jessome informed me that he had frequently administered a small portion of the rattle of the rattle-snake, which he assured me had never failed to produce the desired effect, that of hastening the birth of the child; having the rattle of a snake by me I gave it to him and he administered two rings of it to the woman. . . . Whether this medicine was truly the cause or not I shall not undertake to determine, but I was informed that she had not taken it more than ten minutes before she brought forth. . . .

[Clark 9 Feb]—The buffalo seen last night proved to be bulls, lean & unfit for to make use of as food. . . . I saw several old villages near the Chisscheta River on inquiry found they were Mandan villages destroyed by the Sioux & smallpox. . . .

Source: Gary E. Moulton, ed., *The Journals of the Lewis & Clark Expedition*, vol. 3 (Lincoln: University of Nebraska Press, 1987).

Tecumseh Opposes Land Cessions, 1810

. . . . It is true I am a Shawnee. My forefathers were warriors. Their son is a warrior. From them I only take my existence; from my tribe I take nothing. I am the maker of my own fortune; and oh! that I could make that of my red people, and of my country, as great as the conceptions of my mind, when I think of the Spirit that rules the universe. I would not then come to Governor Harrison, to ask him to tear the treaty, and to obliterate the landmark; but I would say to him, Sir, you have liberty to return to your own country. The being within, communing with the past ages, tells me, that once, nor until lately, there was no white man on this continent. That it then all belonged to red men, children of the same parents, placed on it by the Great Spirit that made them, to keep it, to traverse it, to enjoy its production, and to fill it with the same race. Once a happy race. Since made miserable by the white people, who are never contented, but always encroaching. The way, and the only way to check and stop this evil, is, for all the red men to unite in claiming a common and equal right in the land, as it was at first, and should be yet; for it never was divided, but belongs to all, for the use of each. . . .

Source: Albert L. Hurtado and Peter Iverson, eds., *Major Problems in American Indian History*, 2nd ed. (Boston: Houghton Mifflin Company, 2001), 202–203.

Questions for Reflection

Lewis and Clark used their diaries to record information about the Native Americans they met as well as the plants, animals, weather, and landscape along their route.

1. What kind of interaction occurred between the Mandans and the Corps of Discovery?

2. Can we gain understanding of the Mandans' opinions of the explorers from these diary entries? Why or why not?

3. What is Tecumseh's view of the experience of Native Americans as a result of Euro-American settlement?

Explore additional primary sources related to this chapter on the Wadsworth American History Resource Center or HistoryNOW websites:
http://history.wadsworth.com /rc/us
http://now.ilrn.com/ayers_etal3e

died quickly. George Clinton accepted renomination for vice president. The Federalists put up Charles C. Pinckney and Rufus King, hoping that the effects of the embargo might reverse their party's decline.

The Federalists improved on their performance in 1804 and 1806, gaining 24 seats in Congress, but still had much less than a majority. The electoral vote for president was 122 for Madison and 47 for Pinckney. Although Americans suffered from the embargo, most were unprepared to desert the Republicans. In electing the new president, citizens ratified Jefferson's political philosophy and policies, which Madison had helped formulate. The third and fourth presidents had jointly founded and nurtured the Republican party; together they had adjusted their ideals to meet the practical needs of the expanding nation. The country could expect a continuation of Jeffersonian policies, though the retiring president withdrew entirely from decision making.

In another way, however, the new administration represented a real departure. Madison brought his elegant wife, Dolley Payne Madison, with him to the executive mansion, which was still unfinished when they arrived. They made a remarkable couple, as one observer noted:

Mr Madison was a very small man in his person, with a very large head—his manners were peculiarly unassuming; and his conversation lively, often playful. . . . Mrs. Madison was tall, large and rather masculine in personal dimensions; her complexion was so fair and brilliant as to redeem this objection, in its perfectly feminine beauty. . . . There was a frankness and ease in her deportment, that won golden opinions from all, and she possessed an influence so decided with her little Man.

The first lady transformed the president's house into a proper executive mansion. She served as hostess to frequent teas and dinner parties, inviting Federalists and Republicans to socialize together.

Heading for War

After Madison's election, the European struggle continued to embroil the United States. Although both Britain and France were hostile to free trade, the British dominated the seas, and as a consequence had substantial impact on U.S. commerce. Over the period to 1812, as Napoleon pushed across Europe, invaded Russia, and met defeat, he became inconsequential as a threat to the Americans. Indeed, his attempt to install his brother Joseph Bonaparte as king of Spain in 1808 undermined Spanish control in the New World. In West Florida, Anglo-Americans, who had earlier pledged allegiance to Spain, in 1810 commandeered the Spanish fort at Baton Rouge, declared independence, and petitioned Madison for annexation by the United States. The president promptly claimed West Florida as part of the Louisiana Purchase and American troops occupied Baton Rouge. When Louisiana became a state in 1812, it included the western part of West Florida from Baton Rouge to the Pearl River.

Smithsonian Institution, Bureau of American Ethnology

In 1811, Tecumseh attempted to unite northern and southern Indians to defend their remaining lands east of the Mississippi River. This portrait, which was based on sketches made c. 1811, is from Benjamin Lossing's *Pictorial Field Book of the War of 1812* (1869).

In 1811, Madison appointed James Monroe, his former rival for the presidency, as secretary of state. Monroe took office hoping to reach an accord with the British, but he soon decided that they wanted nothing less than to put the United States back into its colonial yoke. Great Britain adhered to its Order in Council that American exports go to England before shipment to Europe; the Royal Navy continued to impress American seamen. When Napoleon partially lifted his blockade in 1811, the United States resumed trade with France. Madison tried to convince the British to drop their restrictions as well, but instead they pounced on American ships headed for French ports.

Events in the West also intensified anger toward Britain, because Anglo-Americans believed that the British in Canada were stirring up Native American discontent. In fact, whereas some Indians traded with the British, many natives distrusted the whites of both Canada and the United States. An alliance between militant Indians and the British took time to evolve, as each group moved independently toward war with the Americans. The nativist message of Tenskwatawa, the Shawnee Prophet,

and his brother Tecumseh found widespread support as a result of the Louisiana Purchase, expanding white settlement, and sales by accommodationist Indian leaders of a large proportion of native lands still remaining east of the Mississippi.

The nativists were spurred into action by the Treaty of Fort Wayne (1809), which turned over 2.5 million acres to the United States. Tecumseh met with **William Henry Harrison,** governor of the Indiana Territory, to request that the treaty be annulled. Failing that, the Indian leader went south to seek support from the Creeks, Cherokees, and Choctaws. He found allies among militant factions of Creeks and Seminoles. These factions, called the Red Sticks, opposed the accommodationists among their own people who sold land to the United States and adopted Anglo-American ways of life. Tecumseh's effort to create a pan-Indian movement throughout the trans-Appalachian west ultimately failed, however, because by 1811 large white populations in Tennessee, Kentucky, and Ohio formed a barrier between northern and southern Indians.

In November 1811, William Henry Harrison decided to cut short Tecumseh's efforts for unity. The governor did not believe the Indian leader's assurance that whites were "unnecessarily alarmed at his measures—that they really meant nothing but peace—the United States had set him the example by forming a strict union amongst all the fires that compose their confederacy." Harrison led a force against Prophetstown, a village Tenskwatawa had founded several years before on the Tippecanoe River. Before Harrison struck, the prophet attacked the encamped soldiers at night, but suffered casualties and withdrew. Harrison also lost men, but burned the town and claimed victory in what became known as the Battle of Tippecanoe. The nativists subsequently rebuilt their settlement; Harrison's action had little effect except to drive them closer to the British.

The War of 1812 Begins

When news of the battle reached Washington, many officials interpreted it as evidence that a British–Indian alliance already existed. The outcome, they mistakenly believed, showed that the British were weak, incapable of sustaining their allies. "War Hawks" in Congress, including the newly elected Speaker of the House, Henry Clay of Kentucky, and Representative John C. Calhoun of South Carolina, advocated preparations for war. They represented a new generation who had not participated in the Revolution and perceived Britain's actions as attempts to restore colonial status. In Calhoun's words, his generation had to prove to "the World, that we have not only inherited that liberty which our

Fathers gave us, but also the will and power to maintain it." By April 1812, President Madison agreed. The Federalists, only one-fourth of Congress and primarily from New England, opposed conflict with Great Britain in part to obstruct administration policy, in part for commercial interests. The Republicans were divided. Opponents claimed that Madison intended to wage war for territorial expansion in Canada and Florida.

The nation was ill-prepared when Madison issued his war message on June 1. Military funding would prove difficult because the charter of the national bank had been allowed to expire in 1811 due to politics and state banking interests, leaving state banks but no central agency as a source of loans. Lack of federal taxes beyond import duties, which fell sharply when the British blockaded the Atlantic coast, further limited the country's resources. The failure of New England leaders to provide their share of funds—indeed, some merchants provisioned the enemy and some New Englanders pressed for a separate peace—severely hampered the war effort. The governors of Massachusetts and Connecticut refused to send their militia. Not everyone in New England opposed the war, however, for the majority of representatives from Vermont, New Hampshire, and Maine (still part of Massachusetts) voted in favor of the June 1812 declaration of war. Large numbers of the region's young men enlisted in the army.

Despite military deficiencies and lack of national unity, the Madison administration pushed forward into battle. Madison offered an armistice if the British stopped impressment, but they refused. Canada, with only 5,000 regular soldiers, seemed the logical target. The redcoats there had little hope for reinforcements as long as Napoleon marched through Europe.

U.S. military leaders planned three advances, one from Lake Champlain to Montreal, a second at the Niagara River, and the third from Fort Detroit east through Upper Canada (see Map 8.3). With American victories, they hoped, Canada would fall, forcing Britain to recognize U.S. rights. The Americans moved first in the West, where they expected more support from local militia than from New England. Both the Canadians and the United States needed control of the Great Lakes to retain access to lands farther west. General William Hull received orders to lead about 2,000 troops against Fort Malden, opposite Detroit, under the command of British General Isaac Brock and reinforced by Tecumseh

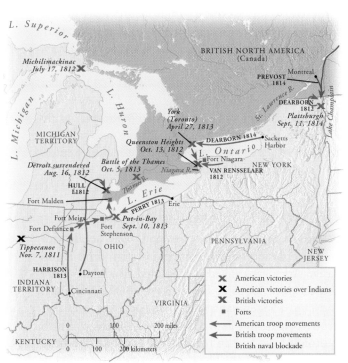

MAP 8.3 The War of 1812

Many of the battles occurred in the Great Lakes region, on the U.S.–Canadian border, shown in detail at bottom.

View an animated version of this map or related maps at http://history.wadsworth.com/passages3e.

and his men. Hull dawdled long enough to allow more British soldiers to arrive. He failed to take Fort Malden and surrendered Detroit. The British and Native Americans then took control of much of the region by capturing Fort Michilimackinac, to the north, and Fort Dearborn, at the present site of Chicago. Another blow came for the United States in October, when the army lost the Battle of Queenston, opposite Fort Niagara, after the New York militia refused to leave American soil to assist the regular troops. William Henry Harrison, commissioned a general, reinforced Fort Wayne against Indian attack. The Americans held Fort Harrison (Terre Haute, Indiana) and other points along a line from Sandusky, Ohio, to St. Louis, and undermined Tecumseh's war effort by destroying Indian towns and cornfields in Ohio, Indiana, and Illinois.

During the frustrating campaign against Canada, James Madison stood for reelection. Some critics claimed that he had started the conflict to win another term. His opponent was DeWitt Clinton, a New York Republican who ran as a Federalist. Clinton tried to gain support from both political parties by advocating peace to the Federalists while telling the Republicans that Madison had failed to prosecute the war hard enough. However, in contrast to the army's failures in 1812, the tiny U.S. fleet had surprising success against the mighty Royal Navy. The *Constitution* sank the British *Guerrière* in August; 2 months later the *United States,* captained by Stephen Decatur, took the *Macedonian;* in December the *Constitution* destroyed the *Java.* The American defeats of an enemy considered master of the seas greatly bolstered public opinion. The president won by an electoral tally of 128 to 89; he obtained substantial Republican majorities in the House and Senate.

Victories and Losses, 1813–1814

Despite the naval successes, on land 1813 began with another disaster for the Americans: the British and Native Americans killed or captured nearly an entire force of 900 troops at Frenchtown, south of Detroit. The United States managed to hold Fort Meigs and Fort Stephenson in northern Ohio. But to destroy British control of Lake Erie and territory to the west, the army needed naval support. The United States began building ships at Presque Isle, Pennsylvania (now Erie), and on September 10, 1813, Oliver Hazard Perry defeated the British squadron at Put-in-Bay, establishing American dominance of the lake. This naval victory cleared the way for General Harrison to attack Fort Malden, from which the British and Indians hastily retreated toward Niagara. The Americans caught up with them at

Battle of Lake Erie, painted by an unknown artist, c. 1820, commemorates the victory of Oliver Hazard Perry against the British at Put-in-Bay. The painting shows Perry moving to another vessel when his flagship became disabled.

Fenimore Art Museum, Cooperstown, New York

Moraviantown on October 5, winning a decisive victory known as the Battle of the Thames. Tecumseh died on the battlefield; his brother Tenskwatawa continued to fight alongside the British during the rest of the war, but with little success. To the east, the U.S. Army had burned York (Toronto), the capital of Upper Canada. But the Americans met defeat in an offensive against Montreal and lost Fort Niagara.

In the Mississippi Territory, the nativist Red Sticks waged civil war against Creek leaders who accommodated Anglo-American demands for land. The fratricidal conflict became a war against the United States in July 1813 when 180 American militia struck a much smaller group of Red Sticks. A month later, the nativists killed about 250 settlers who had taken cover in a stockade called Fort Mims. The Red Sticks, with 4,000 warriors but lacking adequate arms, faced overwhelming odds against the combined forces of U.S. troops, accommodationist Creeks, and Cherokee allies. Three armies entered Red Stick territory, destroying homes and dispersing families. The turning point came in March 1814, when General **Andrew Jackson,** with 3,000 militia and Indian allies, defeated 1,000 Red Sticks in the Battle of Horseshoe Bend, killing 800. The surviving militants escaped to Florida, where they joined nativist Seminoles and continued to fight. Despite the fact that accommodationist Creeks assisted Jackson's troops in the battle, the United States forced them to cede more than 20 million acres of land, including much of what was to become Alabama and a fifth of present-day Georgia.

In the summer of 1814, the British turned greater attention to the war in America, having defeated Napoleon in April. They sent 10,000 experienced redcoats to Canada, threatening New York until the American naval victory on Lake Champlain in September cut short the British invasion. Britain also sent forces to Chesapeake Bay, where in August they attacked the nearly defenseless Washington, D.C. Redcoats burned the Capitol and the president's mansion, shortly after the Madison household fled saving official documents and the Gilbert Stuart portrait of George Washington. The enemy promptly left the capital, and the U.S. government returned.

The British then assaulted Baltimore. Despite heavy bombardment of Fort McHenry by the Royal Navy, the redcoats failed to take the city. James Monroe, who was by then secretary of war as well as secretary of state, took credit for Baltimore's stand. Francis Scott Key memorialized the scene of flaming rockets and exploding bombs in his poem "The Star Spangled Banner," which was later set to the tune of a popular English song and, in the early twentieth century, became the national anthem. The British sailed south to the Gulf Coast, intending to block off the Mississippi River. In late 1814, Andrew Jackson captured Pensacola, Florida, then organized the defense of New Orleans.

The Hartford Convention

Over the course of the war, sentiment had grown in New England for secession, as the British tightened their blockade of the region and occupied the Maine coast. The Massachusetts governor secretly contacted the British about a separate peace. In late 1814, a group of Federalists organized the **Hartford Convention** to find a more moderate course to remedy their loss of power within the Union. The convention issued a report supporting the right of states to declare federal laws unconstitutional (similar to the Virginia and Kentucky Resolutions of 1798) and arguing that states should be responsible for their own defense. The Hartford delegates called for significant amendments to the Constitution: removal of the three-fifths clause that counted slaves in apportioning delegates in the House of Representatives and electoral college; a two-thirds majority in Congress to declare war and admit new states; a one-term limit on the president and ban on residents from the same state succeeding one another in the office (obviously targeted at Virginia); and prohibition of naturalized citizens—who were largely Republican—from federal positions. These proposals, calculated to damage Republican power bases in the South and West and among new immigrants in the cities, fell on deaf ears when news of a peace treaty arrived from Europe.

The Battle of New Orleans, 1815.

"The Fall of Washington or Maddy in full flight," an anonymous English cartoon, 1814. Two British sailors ridicule President Madison and Secretary of State Monroe as they escape the burning capital with state documents.

The Treaty of Ghent

Peace came as both the British and the United States recognized that the end of the 20-year struggle in Europe had eliminated the rationale for war in America. The defeat of Napoleon removed Britain's need to regulate neutral trade and impress seamen. Both sides could also see that they had little hope of victory. Britain might continue its blockade and smother U.S. commerce, but to what purpose? Conquest of the former colonies, now expanded into the west, would require huge expenditures of manpower and funds. British victory at New Orleans would plug the Mississippi, but in late 1814 success was still uncertain. As the British considered terms for peace, news arrived that the Americans had repelled the offensives at Lake Champlain and Baltimore. Although some Britons desired revenge, more wanted to resume trade.

Madison authorized John Quincy Adams, Albert Gallatin, Henry Clay, and two others to meet a British

---

DOING HISTORY ONLINE

The U.S. Enters the War of 1812

Based on your reading of the documents in this module, what effect did the foreign crises of the early 1800s, culminating in the War of 1812, have on Americans' sense of nationhood?

History⧗**Now**™ Visit HistoryNOW to access primary sources and exercises related to this topic: http://now.ilrn.com/ayers_etal3e

---

peace delegation in August 1814 at Ghent, in what is now Belgium. After several months of stalemate, the negotiators agreed on Christmas Eve, 1814, to return to the status quo at the outbreak of war. The British dropped their demands for part of Maine and an independent Indian territory north of the Ohio River, and the Americans stopped insisting that the British renounce impressment, which had ceased.

Battle of New Orleans

Bad weather in the Atlantic delayed until February the ship bringing news of the Treaty of Ghent. In the meantime, British forces prepared to move against the Gulf Coast. A fleet of 60 ships and 14,000 men planned to attack Mobile, seize control of the coast and the rivers, then move against New Orleans.

For Americans unaware of the peace treaty, such a plan posed a serious threat. New Orleans, distant and disconnected from the cities of the east coast, lay vulnerable to invasion. Once the British established a foothold there, troops could move up the Mississippi River. Moreover, a British invasion threatened to bring free and enslaved African Americans, French and Spanish settlers, Native Americans, and even pirates into the conflict throughout the Gulf territories, igniting rebellions against white farmers and traders.

The commander in charge of the American forces, Andrew Jackson, was especially sensitive to the dangers settlers faced on the Gulf Coast. A Tennessee lawyer, planter, and militia leader, he had defeated the Red Sticks at Horseshoe Bend. He repelled the British at Mobile, then raced to New Orleans before the British troops could arrive. The Americans got there first, in December of 1814. When 600 free blacks volunteered to help defend the city, Jackson gratefully accepted their offer.

A series of attacks by the British damaged the American forces but did not take New Orleans. The British general in charge, Sir Edward Pakenham, unleashed a frontal assault on January 8, 1815. Two Congreve rockets, launched by the British to signal the beginning of the assault and to frighten their opponents, screamed into the air. Jackson's troops, dug in behind earthworks, fired directly into the charging British troops; wave after wave of the onslaught fell as American troops took turns firing and reloading. In less than an hour it was over: Pakenham and 2 of his generals lay dead, along with more than 2,000 of their troops. The Americans suffered only 13 dead and a few dozen wounded or missing. Nearly a month later, word of Jackson's remarkable success reached the nation's capital. "ALMOST INCREDIBLE VICTORY!!!," headlines trumpeted. Nine days later word of the Treaty of Ghent, ratified 2 weeks before the Battle of New Orleans, arrived in Washington.

Conclusion

With its simple provision to reinstate the *status quo ante bellum,* the Treaty of Ghent might appear to have made the War of 1812 meaningless. The lost lives and dollars, and disaffection of New England, all seemed to make the victory hollow. Yet most Americans celebrated the peace, knowing they had withstood Britain's attempt to treat them as colonials. A second generation of Americans had proven they could survive a struggle with what was probably the world's most powerful nation. In addition, the United States had defeated Tecumseh's pan-Indian movement in the West, effectively ending Native American power east of the Mississippi.

Much had changed from 1800 to 1815. The Federalists transformed themselves from the architects of the national government in the 1790s to advocates of narrow sectional interests. Thomas Jefferson and James Madison, who had upheld states' rights, moved in the opposite direction during their administrations. Without denying their commitment to limited government, a skeleton military, low taxes, and republican principles, they expanded "the empire of liberty" by purchasing Louisiana and forcing Native Americans from their lands. Jefferson and Madison used every means short of armed conflict to protect commerce, then went to war when all else failed. In purchasing Louisiana, Jefferson relaxed his philosophy of strict interpretation of the Constitution in hope that the additional territory would extend the life of his agrarian republic. Madison facilitated the growth of nationalism by exacting respect from Great Britain. With the Atlantic world at peace once again, residents from Maine to Louisiana concentrated on making money and building their communities, all with a greater sense that they belonged to an American nation.

The Chapter in Review

- In the late eighteenth and early nineteenth centuries, African Americans established their own churches, new Christian sects such as the Shakers were founded, and Native Americans and whites experienced religious revivals.
- Free African Americans developed distinctive cultural institutions and networks in Northern cities. In the South, slave rebellions caused widespread anxiety among the white population, and led to the development of harsher slave codes.
- In 1800, Thomas Jefferson was elected president. Although committed to the republican ideal of limited government, Jefferson relaxed his strict construction of the Constitution to extend the republic's landholdings through the Louisiana Purchase.
- The impressment of American men into the British navy caused tensions between the two nations, which Americans sought to diffuse through economic sanctions such as the Embargo of 1807.
- Between 1812 and 1815, Britain and America engaged in the War of 1812. Although the war did not bring significant gains to either side, it inspired deep nationalism in the United States.

Making Connections Across Chapters

LOOKING BACK

Chapter 8 considered the religious context in which Americans—native whites, African Americans, new immigrants, and Indians—shaped their communities and interpreted political affairs. The Republican administration of Thomas Jefferson and James Madison, while taking action for national expansion and defense, reflected the desire of many Americans for limited government.

1. Why was religion so important to Americans on the frontier and in developing cities?

2. Was Jefferson's administration consistent with the Republican principles he had stated prior to his election? Why or why not?

3. Why did the Federalists decline?

4. Did Madison make the right decision to go to war against Great Britain? Why or why not?

5. What was the significance of the Hartford Convention?

LOOKING AHEAD

With the War of 1812 behind them, Americans expanded westward, building turnpikes and canals to facilitate trade. As will be discussed in Chapter 9, under James Monroe, who was elected president in 1816, the government entered a period of reduced factionalism.

1. What was the impact of U.S. expansion on Native Americans during the period from 1815 to 1828?

2. Why were the years of Monroe's administration known as the "Era of Good Feelings"?

3. How did the Supreme Court assist economic development?

Recommended Readings

Andrews, Dee E. *The Methodists and Revolutionary America, 1760–1800: The Shaping of an Evangelical Culture* (2000). An excellent study, including important chapters on the role of women and African Americans.

Coles, Harry L. *The War of 1812* (1965). A readable, one-volume study.

Dowd, Gregory Evans. *A Spirited Resistance: The North American Indian Struggle for Unity, 1745–1815* (1992). Demonstrates the significance of religion in Native American resistance.

Ellis, Joseph J. *American Sphinx: The Character of Thomas Jefferson* (1996). A highly readable study of a complex president.

Freeman, Joanne B. *Affairs of Honor: National Politics in the Early Republic* (2001). A provocative study of the means of political conflict, including dueling.

McCoy, Drew R. *The Elusive Republic: Political Economy in Jeffersonian America* (1980). Insightful exploration of Jeffersonian politics and thought.

Moulton, Gary E., ed. *The Journals of the Lewis and Clark Expedition.* 7 vols. (1983–1991). Most comprehensive edition of manuscript maps and journals.

Nash, Gary B. *Forging Freedom: The Formation of Philadelphia's Black Community, 1720–1840* (1988). Insightful study of the challenges of freedom for one community of African Americans in the North.

Smelser, Marshall. *The Democratic Republic, 1801–1815* (1992). A useful, lively overview of the period.

Waldstreicher, David. *In the Midst of Perpetual Fetes: The Making of American Nationalism, 1776–1820* (1997). Study of popular political culture, including the ways in which African Americans and women participated in celebrations yet were excluded from voting.

Identifications

Review your understanding of the following key terms, people, events, and dates for this chapter (these terms also appear in the Glossary at the end of the book):

Second Great Awakening
Tecumseh
midnight appointments
John Marshall
Marbury v. Madison

Louisiana Purchase
Lewis and Clark expedition
Sacagawea
William Henry Harrison
Andrew Jackson
Hartford Convention

Online Sources Guide 🌐

Use this listing to find online documents, images, interactive maps, simulations, and other resources related to this chapter.

American History Resource Center

http://history.wadsworth.com/rc/us

Documents

The Treaty of Ghent
"The Star Spangled Banner"
Marbury v. Madison (1801)
Thomas Jefferson on Constitutionality of the Louisiana Purchase (1803)

Selected Images

New Jersey woman voting in 1807
1805 portrait of Thomas Jefferson
John Marshall, chief justice of the Supreme Court
Tecumseh's death at the Battle of Thames

Document Exercises

1803 Gallatin Budget

HistoryNOW

http://now.ilrn.com/ayers_etal3e

Primary Source Exercises

The President to Governor Claiborne, 1804
The U.S. Enters the War of 1812

Passages 1815 to 1855

The United States redefined itself during the 40 years after 1815. The boundaries of the nation, the character of its population, the nature of its economy, and the religious beliefs of its people all took new shape. Some of the changes confirmed what the architects of the young nation had expected several decades before; other changes proved to be surprises and the bitterest of disappointments. The speed and scale of transformation astonished everyone.

In 1815, the young United States held only 18 states, with Louisiana standing exposed at the western boundary, Florida in the hands of the Spanish, and an unsettled line between Canada and the United States. The western half of the continent remained only vaguely known to Anglo-Americans and seemed too far away to be of importance any time soon. Even within the country's sketchy borders, American Indians populated large and rich areas in both the north and the south.

Four decades later, the continental boundaries of the nation had expanded beyond recognition. Florida had come into the Union from Spain. War with Mexico had brought in vast territories from Texas to California. Negotiation with Great Britain had defined the northern boundary from Maine to Oregon. Military and economic pressure on the American Indian nations had driven them across the Mississippi River. A new state entered the Union about every two and a half years; by the end of the 1850s, 33 states—including two on the Pacific coast—claimed a place in the nation.

The population exploded. The number of Americans grew from 8.4 million in 1815 to 31.4 million by the end of the 1850s. Nearly 4 million of those people were held in slavery, while 3 million people had crossed the Atlantic from Europe in a mixture of hope and desperation. People spread out across the expanse of the burgeoning country, establishing farms and towns far from the older cities of the East. About half the population of an average town moved every 10 years. By the end of the period the United States claimed 5 million more people than England, and the new country boasted eight cities of more than 150,000 inhabitants—more than any other country in the world.

Large changes altered the scale of life, tying people together as few could have imagined in 1815. Steamboats transformed water transportation in the 1810s, canals boomed in the 1820s, and railroads arrived in the 1830s. The United States claimed over 35,000 miles of railroad track by the end of the era. In the 1840s, the first telegraph wires carried information from one city to another in a clatter of keys; by the late 1850s, telegraph wires stretched across the Atlantic Ocean. Novels sold tens of thousands of copies in a few months. Newspapers, confined to just a few major cities in 1815, became staples of American life in the 1830s and 1840s, read and published in hundreds of communities of every size. Daguerreotypes and colorful lithographs decorated homes that had been empty of pictures a generation earlier.

The United States became integrated ever more tightly into the international economy. The capacity of ships arriving in American ports doubled in the 1830s, doubled again in the 1840s, and then again in the 1850s. American vessels plied the Atlantic with cargoes of cotton and wheat for England and Europe. Clipper ships sailed around South America and into the Pacific, carrying prospectors and immigrants along with tea. The United States, anxious about European intervention in Latin America and the Caribbean, claimed the hemisphere as a place under its jurisdiction and protection.

Americans created lodges, clubs, and societies of every sort. Baptists, Methodists, and Presbyterians vied with one another for converts. Reform groups emerged to stamp out alcohol and war, to encourage education and humane treatment of the unfortunate, to improve diet and health, to bring the end of slavery. Women accounted for many members of these organizations, lending their energy and intelligence to activities beyond the home. Political parties mobilized nearly all adult white men, sweeping them up as Democrats, Whigs, Free Soilers, Know-Nothings, and Republicans.

Foreign trade transformed cities in both the North and the South, as these paintings of New York and New Orleans in the 1850s reveal in striking detail.

Men swore allegiance to their party, expressing their passions and beliefs in slogans, songs, and parades. On election days, as many as 8 out of 10 eligible voters went to the polls, publicly proclaiming their support for their candidates.

The expansion of the United States was the expansion of the largest and most powerful slave society in the modern world. Slavery grew stronger with each passing decade, embracing an ever larger part of the continent to the south and west, holding more people within its bonds, accounting for a larger share of the nation's exports. As the years passed, the discussions in the churches, the reform organizations, and the political parties increasingly turned to sectional conflict. Rivalry and distrust between the North and the South infected everything in the public life of the country.

The years between 1815 and 1855, then, did not witness a smooth passage through an "industrial revolution" or "growth of the common man" or "westward expansion." Rather, these years marked a passage filled with rapids and countercurrents and waterfalls. Panics and depressions, internal and external wars, massive migration and immigration, freedom and slavery—all came tumultuously.

America and the World: 1815–1855

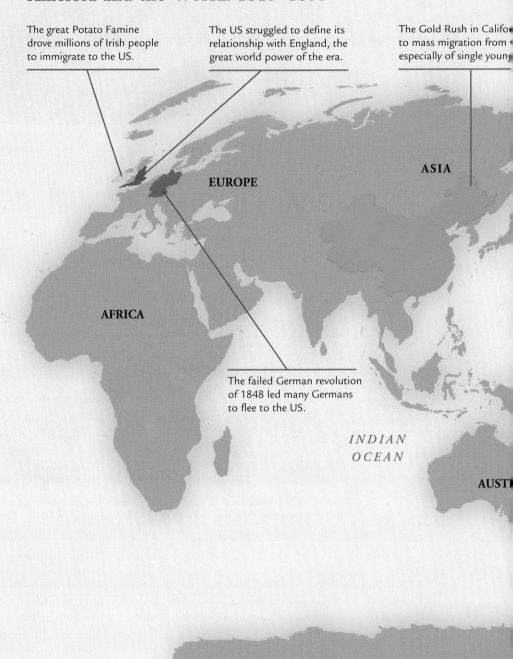

The great Potato Famine drove millions of Irish people to immigrate to the US.

The US struggled to define its relationship with England, the great world power of the era.

The Gold Rush in Califor to mass migration from especially of single young

EUROPE

ASIA

AFRICA

The failed German revolution of 1848 led many Germans to flee to the US.

INDIAN OCEAN

AUST

ANTARCTICA

Tense relations with Canada over the boundary between the two countries led to treaties that established permanent borders.

The emancipation of slaves in the Caribbean by European powers, especially England, inspired African Americans and abolitionists.

NORTH AMERICA

ATLANTIC OCEAN

Hawaii, a crucial way station for ships crossing the Pacific, fell under American influence.

PACIFIC OCEAN

A major war with Mexico added vast areas of territory to the American west.

Belize
Honduras
Nicaragua
Guatemala
San Salvador
Costa Rica
Panama
Colombia
Ecuador
Venezuela
Guyana
Suriname
French Guiana

SOUTH AMERICA

Peru
Bolivia
Brazil
Paraguay
Chile
Uruguay
Argentina

Wars of independence throughout the Spanish empire shifted the balance of power in the hemisphere and led to the Monroe Doctrine.

Chronology

	1815	**1823**	**1831**
POLITICS & DIPLOMACY	**1815:** Battle of New Orleans **1816:** Monroe elected president "Era of Good Feelings" begins Clay calls for "American System" Indiana admitted to the Union **1817:** Mississippi admitted to the Union **1818:** Jackson invades Florida Illinois admitted to the Union **1819:** Transcontinental (or Adams-Onís) treaty with Spain Alabama admitted to the Union **1820:** Missouri Compromise Monroe elected president Maine admitted to the Union **1821:** Missouri admitted to the Union **1822:** Denmark Vesey Rebellion, Charleston	**1823:** Monroe Doctrine announced **1824:** Contested election of John Quincy Adams **1828:** Tariff of Abominations Calhoun's *Exposition* Election of Jackson **1829:** David Walker's *Appeal* Mexico tries to abolish slavery in Texas **1830:** Indian Removal Act Anti-Masonic party holds first national party convention **1831:** Nat Turner's rebellion Garrison's *The Liberator* Jackson reorganizes cabinet Van Buren over Calhoun	**1832:** Bank War begins Nullification Crisis Virginia debates over slavery Jackson reelected **1833:** Force Bill against South Carolina Compromise Tariff Slavery abolished in British Empire **1834:** Whig party organized **1835:** Arkansas admitted to the Union Revolution breaks out in Texas Abolitionists' postal campaign War against Seminoles and runaway slaves in Florida **1836:** Congress imposes gag rule Battle of the Alamo; Texas Republic established **1838:** John Quincy Adams successfully defeats attempt to annex Texas
SOCIAL & CULTURAL EVENTS	**1816:** American Colonization Society founded American Bible Society founded **1819:** Auburn penitentiary established	**1824:** Lafayette's visit American Sunday School Union founded **1825:** American Tract Society founded **1829:** David Walker's *Appeal* **1830:** *The Book of Mormon* Finney's revivals begin in Rochester	**1831:** Garrison's *The Liberator* Mormons migrate from New York to Ohio **1833:** Formation of American Anti- slavery Society **1837:** Grimké sisters lecture to mixed audiences Horace Mann becomes first secretary of Massachusetts State Board of Education Ralph Waldo Emerson, "The American Scholar" **1839:** Daguerreotypes introduced to the United States
ECONOMICS & TECHNOLOGY	**1815:** *Enterprise* first steamboat from New Orleans to Pittsburgh **1816:** Second Bank of the United States chartered **1817:** Mississippi admitted to the Union **1818:** Erie Canal begun National Road completed **1819:** *Dartmouth College v. Woodward* and *McCulloch v. Maryland* Financial panic and depression	**1824:** *Gibbons v. Ogden* **1825:** Completion of Erie Canal **1828:** Tariff of Abominations	**1831:** John Bull begins railroad operation **1832:** Bank War begins **1833:** Compromise Tariff **1834:** National Trades Union formed Cyrus McCormick patents reaper **1837:** Financial panic *Charles River Bridge v. Warren Bridge* decision **1839:** Depression worsens Daguerreotypes introduced to the United States

1840

1840: Congress passes Independent Treasury Act
Harrison elected president
Frederick Douglass escapes from slavery
American Anti-slavery Society splits
James G. Birney runs for president as candidate for Liberty party
1841: Harrison dies; John Tyler becomes president
Amistad case heard before the Supreme Court
1844: James K. Polk claims the United States's claim to "all Oregon"
1845: Texas and Florida admitted to the Union

1840: Washingtonian temperance movement emerges
1841: Brook Farm founded
P. T. Barnum opens the American Museum
Amistad case heard before the Supreme Court
1842: Edgar Allan Poe, "The Murders in the Rue Morgue"
1844: Methodist Episcopal church divides over slavery
Edgar Allan Poe, "The Raven"

1840: Congress passes Independent Treasury Act
1841: California sees arrival of first wagon train
Oregon fever
1843: Oregon sees arrival of first wagon trains
1844: Baltimore–Washington telegraph line
Samuel F. B. Morse patents the telegraph

1846

1846: Mexican War begins;
Stephen Kearny occupies Santa Fe;
Zachary Taylor takes Monterey
Border between Canada and United States established at 49th parallel
Wilmot Proviso ignites sectional conflict
Bear Flag Republic in California proclaimed by John C. Frémont
1847: Taylor defeats Santa Anna at Buena Vista; Winfield Scott captures Vera Cruz and Mexico City
1848: Treaty of Guadalupe Hidalgo Attempts to buy Cuba from Spain
Free-Soil party runs Van Buren for president
Seneca Falls Convention
Zachary Taylor elected president

1846: Hiram Powers completes statue *The Greek Slave*
1847: Mormons reach Great Salt Lake Valley
1848: Seneca Falls Convention
Oneida community established
Mormons settle in Great Basin

1848: Gold discovered in California
Regular steamship trips between Liverpool and New York City

1849

1849: California seeks admission to Union
1850: Nashville Convention attempts to unify South
Fugitive Slave Law
Taylor dies; Millard Fillmore becomes president
Compromise of 1850
1851: Maine adopts prohibition
Woman's rights convention in Akron, Ohio
Indiana state constitution excludes free blacks
1852: Franklin Pierce elected president
1853: Gadsden Purchase
1854: Know-Nothings win unexpected victories
Whig party collapses
Republican party founded
Kansas-Nebraska Act
Ostend Manifesto encourages acquisition of Cuba

1850: Nathaniel Hawthorne, *The Scarlet Letter*
1851: Herman Melville, *Moby Dick*
Maine adopts prohibition
Woman's rights convention in Akron, Ohio
1852: Harriet Beecher Stowe, *Uncle Tom's Cabin*
1854: Henry David Thoreau, *Walden*

1849: "Forty-niners" race to California
Cotton prices invigorate South
1854: High-point of immigration
Railroad reaches Mississippi River

9

Exploded Boundaries, 1815–1828

The Erie Canal, connecting the Hudson River with Lake Erie, demanded a monumental engineering effort. It soon paid its way, however, as shippers and farmers rushed to use the new waterway.

© The Granger Collection, New York

The sudden climax of the War of 1812 surprised everyone. The leaders of the United States had wondered whether a large and lightly governed republic could survive in the rough-and-tumble world of international conflict. When the new country held its own in the war against England, the most powerful military force on earth, Americans gained a new confidence.

James Monroe, another in a long line of Virginia Republican presidents, easily won the national election of 1816. He bore the reputation of being an honest and dependable man, though less intellectually distinguished than Jefferson or Madison. Monroe and his wife set a new tone for the presidency, with greater emphasis on etiquette, style, and entertaining, on embodying and celebrating the new national stature of the United States. The Monroes had the executive mansion painted a brilliant white to cover the smoke stains from its burning during the war with England; the residence became known as the "White House." President Monroe relished the role of peacemaker and conciliator. Newly secure, the United States entered a period of territorial expansion and economic growth no one could have foreseen just a few years earlier.

New Borders

The borders of the United States had been fluid and in doubt throughout the nation's brief history. In every direction other nations and peoples contested American boundaries. To the north, English power loomed in Canada. To the west, American Indians resisted efforts by whites to buy or seize their ancestral lands. To the south, the Spanish held on in Florida. Moreover, many states had little economic dealing with one another, trading instead with England, Europe, and the Caribbean. As a result, states defended sharply conflicting policies, and their economies did not connect with one another very effectively. The peace after 1815 provided an opportunity for the United States to establish its borders more securely and to integrate itself more fully.

Native Peoples

President Monroe worked to establish clearer borders for the young nation. He succeeded in his dealing with Great Britain, when the two countries clarified the boundaries between the United States and Canada. The

Timeline

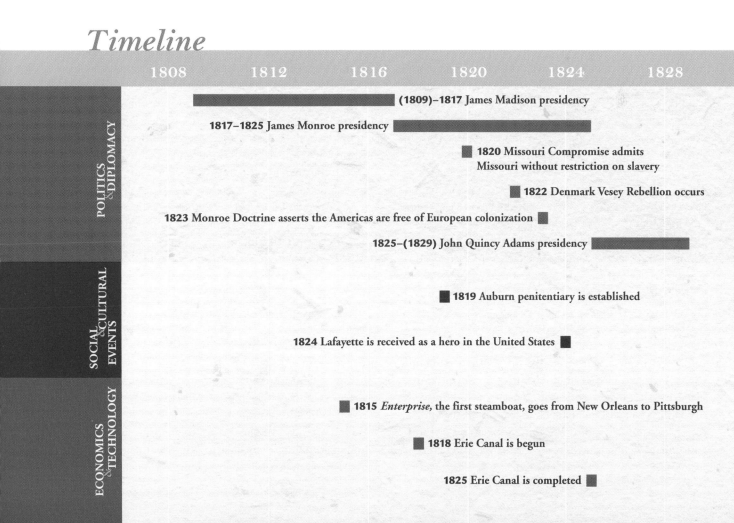

	1808	1812	1816	1820	1824	1828

POLITICS & DIPLOMACY

(1809)–1817 James Madison presidency

1817–1825 James Monroe presidency

1820 Missouri Compromise admits Missouri without restriction on slavery

1822 Denmark Vesey Rebellion occurs

1823 Monroe Doctrine asserts the Americas are free of European colonization

1825–(1829) John Quincy Adams presidency

SOCIAL & CULTURAL EVENTS

1819 Auburn penitentiary is established

1824 Lafayette is received as a hero in the United States

ECONOMICS & TECHNOLOGY

1815 *Enterprise,* the first steamboat, goes from New Orleans to Pittsburgh

1818 Erie Canal is begun

1825 Erie Canal is completed

The Battle of New Orleans. The victory of the United States over Britain in 1815 catapulted Andrew Jackson to prominence and unleashed the young nation's energies against the American Indians.

Rush-Bagot Treaty of 1817 calmed conflict on the Great Lakes and the Convention of 1818 fixed the border with Canada at the 49th parallel (see Map 9.1).

Relations with American Indians proved much more challenging. By the early nineteenth century, the American Indians had lived in contact with European culture for more than 200 years. The native peoples had long combined their ancient practices with newer ones. Commercial hunting expeditions covered ever-expanding territory, tracking animals to trade with white trading partners. Trade networks stretched over thousands of miles.

Indians' clothing reflected the combination of cultures, as they combined moccasins with woolen breeches, imported cloth turbans, and jewelry made of melted silver coins. The intermingling worked both ways, for considerable numbers of English and Scots traders lived among the Indians. Many men of European background adopted Indian dress and language and married into native families. African Americans, too, often took refuge with the Creeks and **Seminoles**, so that by 1815 mixed ancestry had become common.

The removal of the British troops after the War of 1812 dealt a strong blow to the hopes of the American Indians. Alliances with the British, both actual and threatened, had helped hold back the white Americans. Now that the alliance with England had been destroyed, the United States quickly sought to exert firm control over the eastern half of the continent. Andrew Jackson, triumphant general in the war, was placed in charge of negotiating with the Creek, Cherokee, Chickasaw, and

Choctaw nations of Alabama, Florida, and Mississippi after the peace of 1815. Jackson used heavy-handed treaties to force Indians from their former lands. Many of the natives resisted the removal, objecting that the treaties extracted by Jackson had been signed by Indians who had no authority to make such concessions.

The various native peoples identified themselves by the location of their villages, their languages, and their traditional enemies, and often fought with one another, but whites insisted on lumping these diverse people into groups that could be more easily dealt with. Jackson and other officials relied on particular American Indians as allies in war but then deliberately punished all the tribes in the region regardless of earlier promises. Such policies weakened the power of Indian leaders and left their people little choice but to accept bribes and annual grants of money in return for their lands. As soon as Jackson managed to secure lands from the Creeks, Cherokees, and Chickasaws, white settlers rushed into the territories, hungry for the fertile land and the fortunes it could build (see Map. 9.2). Such incursions occurred across millions of acres in North Carolina, Kentucky, and Tennessee as well as in Alabama, Mississippi, and Georgia; in each state, the Indians were pushed to the hilly and mountainous lands least desirable for farming. The U.S. government made it easy for white settlers to buy land and sold about a million acres a year throughout the next decade. Not surprisingly, tensions steadily mounted between the ancient residents of the land and those who now claimed it.

As in the South, white settlement in the Northwest was made possible by the subjugation of the native peoples. After northern Indians' disastrous losses in the War of 1812, they posed little threat to white settlers. The U.S. government quickly established a series of forts throughout the Northwest to intimidate any American Indians in the area and to make sure that the British and Canadians did not regain a foothold. The growing numbers of white farmers made it difficult for Native Americans to hunt for a living. Whites who moved to the Northwest confronted only scattered remnants of native peoples, trading with white merchants for food, sometimes begging from homesteaders.

The American Indians strove to adapt to white ways while maintaining their identity; the Cherokees, in particular, won praise for their "civilized" customs. One

Expanding Borders

What now seem the "natural" boundaries of the continental United States were by no means obvious in 1815. As it stood, somewhat surprised in its lack of defeat by the powerful British in the War of 1812, the United States still had poorly defined and dangerous borders in almost every direction. The boundaries of Maine, the enormous area west of the Great Lakes, and Oregon remained contested with Great Britain in the north. Though we now think of the relationship between the United States and Canada as the very model of peaceful coexistence, at the time many people worried about this British territory looming over the United States. To the south, Spain (and runaway slaves

and the Seminoles) controlled Florida and much of the Gulf Coast. The territory, so close to the booming areas of the South, posed a threat to slavery as well as to the territorial ambitions of the United States. To the west, the territory that would become Mexico remained contested, still in the process of defining its own nationhood. In the 5 years after the peace of 1815, the United States eagerly negotiated treaties with Great Britain and Spain to clarify and stabilize the young nation's borders. The settlement of the treaties helped create the conditions for rapid growth and economic development.

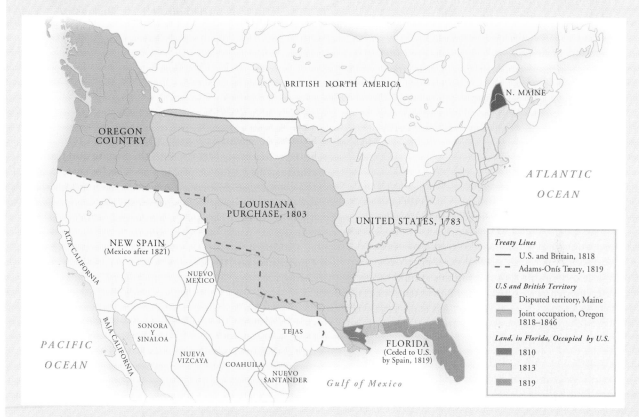

MAP 9.1 Redrawing the Nation's Boundaries

View an animated version of this map or related maps at http://history.wadsworth.com/passages3e

Cherokee, Sequoyah, devised an alphabet in his people's language in 1821. The wealthiest Cherokees purchased African American slaves and built substantial cotton plantations. No matter what accommodations they made, however, the American Indians suffered repeated conflicts with whites who relied on sheer numbers, trickery, violence, and the law to dispossess Native Americans of their land claims.

The Spanish in Florida

Like the American Indians, the Spanish who remained in Florida after 1815 had become vulnerable. Without the assistance of the British, they found it nearly impossible to resist American incursions into their territory. White Americans, for their part, felt they had a right, even an obligation, to drive the Spanish from the mainland, in part because Anglo Protestants had a long

DOING HISTORY

The Future of the American Indian

IN THE FIRST document, from 1824, a prestigious religious group argues before the U.S. Congress that the American Indians have suffered for generations at the hands of the United States. The only way to atone for these "national sins," the commissioners argue, is to educate the Indian people in the ways of white Americans. The document shows the good will that many white Americans held toward the Indians— and the limits of their understanding of the Indians' culture.

In the second document, from 1836, American Indians speak for themselves. In this case, a delegation of Cherokees protests a treaty that would remove them from their homes in the east to the Indian Territory of Oklahoma. They plead that they have done everything white Americans have asked.

The American Society for Improving Indian Tribes

The history of our intercourse with Indians, from the first settlement of this country, contains many facts honorable to the character of our ancestors, and of our nation—many, also, too many, which are blots on this character. . . . We here allude to the neglect with which these aboriginal tribes have been treated in regard to their civil, moral, and religious improvement. . . . It *is* desirable that our Indians should receive such an education as has been mentioned, we conceive, because the civilized is preferable to the savage state; because the Bible, and the religion therein revealed to us, with its ordinances, are blessings of infinite and everlasting value and which the Indians do not now enjoy. It is also desirable as an act of common humanity. . . . There is no place on the earth to which they can migrate, and live in the savage and hunter state. The Indian tribes must, therefore, be *progressively civilized,* or *successively* perish.

Memorial and Protest of the Cherokee Nation

The Cherokees were happy and prosperous under a scrupulous observance of treaty stipulations by the government of the United States, and from the fostering hand extended over them, they made rapid advances in civilization, morals, and in the arts and sciences. Little did they anticipate, that when taught to think and feel as the American citizen, and to have with him a common interest, they were to be *despoiled by their guardian,* to become strangers and wanderers in the land of their fathers, forced to return to the savage life, and to seek a new home in the wilds of the far west, and that without their consent. An instrument purporting to be a treaty with the Cherokee people, has recently been made public by the President of the United States, that will have such an operation, if carried into effect. This instrument, the delegation aver before the civilized world, and in the presence of Almighty God, is fraudulent, false upon its face, made by unauthorized individuals, with the sanction, and against the wishes, of the great body of the Cherokee people.

Sources: American Board of Commissioners for Foreign Missions, Memorial to the Senate and the House of Representatives, in *American Society for Improving Indian Tribes, First Annual Report,* 1824, pp. 66–68; *Memorial and Protest of the Cherokee Nation,* June 22, 1839. Executive Document No. 286, 24th Congress, 1st session, pp. 1–2.

Questions for Reflection

1. Are the two documents making the same arguments? What assumptions underlie both of them?

2. What would the authors of the Cherokee memorial say to the authors of "The Blessings of Civilization"? What would the authors of the "The Blessings" say to the protests of the Cherokee?

3. Could the desires of the United States government, and the white men it represented, have been reconciled to the desires of the American Indians?

4. What argument could the United States government make in response to the Cherokee protest?

5. What had changed in the 12 years separating these two documents?

Explore additional primary sources related to this chapter on the Wadsworth American History Resource Center or HistoryNOW websites:

http://history.wadsworth.com/rc/us

http://now.ilrn.com/ayers_etal3e

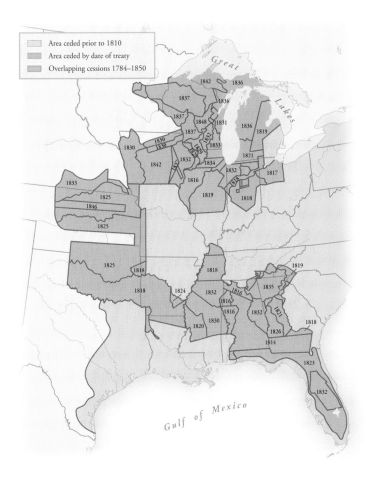

MAP 9.2 Lands Ceded by American Indians

The United States negotiated one treaty after another with American Indians in the decades after 1815, acquiring land and pushing the natives of these areas to the west.

tradition of distrusting Catholic, monarchical Spanish. Many Americans thought it inevitable that Florida and Mexico would become part of the United States. To make relations even more volatile, 60 miles from the southern border of the United States stood the so-called Negro Fort near Pensacola, occupied by runaway slaves and their Indian allies.

In the spring of 1816 Jackson warned the Spanish commandant of Pensacola that the stronghold was "occupied by upwards of two hundred and fifty negros many of whom have been enticed away from the service of their master—citizens of the United States." Spain was eager, in fact, to be rid of the fort as well, but did not have the military power to overthrow it. The Spanish feared, correctly, that Jackson would use the refuge as a pretext to invade Florida. Indeed, the Americans sent an expedition against the fort; a projectile hit a powder magazine, killing 270 of the men, women, and children inside.

In 1818, Jackson's forces also punished groups of Seminoles, who, with their Creek allies, had launched raids against white settlers in south Georgia and then fled into Florida. Though his authorization from Washington was doubtful, Jackson invaded Spanish territory, executed a Creek prophet and two British men he accused of abetting the Indian cause, and overran the weak Spanish presence in the most important outposts. Some in Congress wanted to punish Jackson for what they considered his unauthorized attack. Jackson rushed to Washington to defend himself and his honor. Many white Americans thronged the cities where Jackson appeared along the way, celebrating him as a decisive hero rather than castigating him for being the military despot **Henry Clay** claimed. The congressional hearings on Jackson's behavior in the war had little effect except to make Jackson suspicious of the men in power in Washington.

Meanwhile, American and Spanish officials negotiated. The U.S. delegation was led by the brilliant and tenacious John Quincy Adams, son of the former president. With Jackson's military victories giving force to his words, Adams held out until the Spanish, in return for $5 million in compensation of private claims, ceded to the United States all territories east of the Mississippi River. In this, the Adams-Onís Treaty of 1819, the Spanish kept the vast territory from Texas to present-day California, while the United States claimed a northern border that ran unbroken to Oregon and the Pacific Ocean. Adams called his handiwork the Transcontinental Treaty, for it stretched the borders of the United States from the Atlantic to the Pacific (see Map. 9.1).

Building a National Economy

Leading members of the Republican party, long known for their opposition to federal power, began to view the central government more favorably after the victory over Britain in 1815. Young Republicans such as Henry Clay of Kentucky and **John C. Calhoun** of South Carolina urged Congress and the president to encourage the growth of enterprise with the aid of the government, creating roads, canals, a strong navy, and a national bank. In their eyes, the war with Great Britain had shown the dangers of a sprawling American nation, its resources scattered, its defenses thin. The future of the country, Clay and Calhoun believed, lay in commerce and industry. The government should ally itself with the forces of trade. These nationalists called their vision the "**American System**."

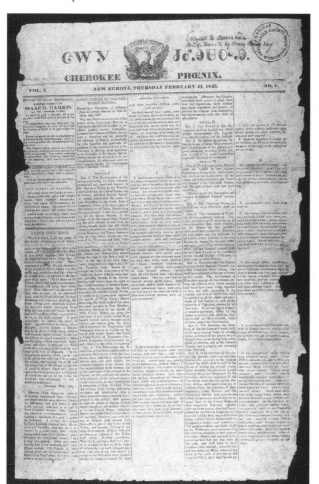

In 1828 the Cherokee of Georgia published the first issue of their newspaper, printed in both English and in the alphabet devised by Sequoyah. The paper was published until 1835, when the Georgia militia forced it to close.

Adopting some ideas of the "American System," President Monroe urged Congress to use protective tariffs to protect American manufacturing, to build roads to tie the newly expanded markets and farms together, and to connect the abundant rivers and lakes in the United States with a system of canals.

Banks, Corporations, and Law

No country needed credit more than the United States. Because far too little cash spread across its vast and growing territory, much business within the country rested on nothing more than trust and promises. Credit relations became tangled and fragile; the fall of one borrower could bring down a chain of lenders. Throughout the years before and during the War of 1812, states chartered banks to help alleviate the problems caused by a shortage of cash. More than 200 such banks had been founded by 1815 and nearly 400 by 1818, issuing notes that served as currency in cash-starved areas.

Many influential men, including the recently elected President Monroe, supported a new national bank to stabilize the economy and distribute scarce money more uniformly. Advocates of the bank argued that the notes of state banks varied far too much in soundness and value, making the economic system dangerously unstable. The expanding country's economic system needed a central institution to coordinate the flow of money. Accordingly, in 1816 Congress chartered the Second Bank of the United States. Based in Philadelphia, it was authorized to establish branches wherever it wished. The new national bank was an amalgam of public and private enterprise: the federal government deposited its funds in the bank and appointed a fifth of the directors, but the bank ran as a private business. For the privilege of being the only such institution authorized to operate on a national basis, the bank handled, without fees, the funds of the federal treasury. The bank pumped large amounts of paper currency into the system in an attempt to feed the voracious hunger of the postwar economy, especially in the new states of the West where speculation in land fueled demands for access to easier credit.

The local, state, and federal courts of the United States also encouraged the growth of business in the years after the peace of 1815. Courts increasingly favored market forces over custom and stability in property relations, shifting the advantage from farmers and landowners to developers. Those who wanted to dam rivers for factories or build roads enjoyed increasing precedence over those threatened by floods, fires, or disruption caused by development. The courts assumed that the public good from the growth of business outweighed the stability favored by older notions of justice. Because many people bitterly protested this shift in emphasis, state legislatures sometimes sought to curb the power of business interests.

The Supreme Court under Chief Justice **John Marshall** issued a number of important decisions following the War of 1812 that also hastened economic development. Marshall was more concerned with establishing the power of the federal government than with furthering the economy, but by creating a more uniform legal environment that transcended the restrictions of particular states, the Court accelerated the growth of business. One decision of 1819 made bankruptcy laws more uniform across the country; another, *Dartmouth College v. Woodward,* sheltered corporations from legislative interference; yet another, *McCulloch v. Maryland,* established the constitutionality of the Bank of the United States and protected it from state taxation. A fourth case in this period, *Gibbons v. Ogden* (1824), limited the rights of states to interfere in commerce with either special favors and monopolies or restrictive laws. "In all commercial regulations," Marshall pronounced, "we are one and the same people." In this new legal environment, increasingly emulated by state courts and legislators, business flourished in the years immediately following the end of the war.

Roads and Canals

Americans threw themselves into a frenzy of road and turnpike building after 1815. Investors, states, and even the federal government built thousands of miles of private roads—turnpikes—charging tolls to offset the roads' notoriously high maintenance costs. Some road builders laid logs side-by-side to provide a durable surface, though these so-called corduroy roads took a heavy toll on horse, wagon, and rider and wore out quickly. In 1818, the U.S. government opened the "**National Road**," connecting the Potomac River at Cumberland, Maryland, with Wheeling, [West] Virginia, on the Ohio River. The road was the best that technology could provide at the time, with excellent bridges and a relatively smooth stone surface. It attracted so much business, however, that traffic jams slowed movement to a crawl and the road quickly fell into poor condition. Even on good roads, it often cost more to move bulky items such as corn or wheat than the price the products could bring at market.

Businesses and state governments began to plan dependable canals with controllable locks and a steady flow of water. Fortunately for New York, a passage broke through the Appalachian Mountains within the state's borders. New Yorkers believed that a canal through this area, connecting the Hudson River to Lake Erie, would far surpass any other kind of transportation. Such a canal would be 10 times longer than any other canal then in existence: 364 miles through swamps and solid rock,

© The Granger Collection, New York

Corduroy roads, while offering some relief from mud and stones, proved poor competition with newer kinds of transportation such as canals and steamboats.

through places where virtually no white settlers had bothered to migrate.

Year after year, the canal edged toward Lake Erie, transforming the countryside along the way; by 1819, the canal stretched for 75 miles. As soon as workers completed a segment, boats crowded upon its waters, the tolls they paid financing the portions yet unfinished. By 1834, approximately nine boats passed through major locks on the canal each minute. Other states looked enviously upon the glorious and profitable **Erie Canal** and began their own plans and excavations.

Steamboats

Canals, though useful and exciting, reached only a limited part of the vast North American continent. Rivers offered faster and cheaper travel, especially along the Mississippi, Missouri, and Ohio. But their limitations were obvious as well. The rivers could be dangerously fast in some seasons and so slow as to be impassable in others. They often froze for months in the winter. Strong currents ran in only one direction. Those who wanted to transport goods northward had to push their boats against the current, sometimes with poles, sometimes by dragging the boats with ropes as the crews walked along the shore, sometimes merely by grabbing trees and bushes on the banks. It took three or four months to drag a boat upstream. Others simply sold their craft for scrap in New Orleans and walked back to Ohio or Illinois, a long and arduous trip.

Not surprisingly, people dreamed of using steam engines to drive riverboats. Robert Fulton's steamboats had traversed the quieter waters of the Northeast since 1807, but Fulton did not manage to build one for the rigors of the Mississippi until 1811. As soon as Jackson won at New Orleans in 1815, the *Enterprise* churned its way upriver from Louisiana all the way to Louisville, Kentucky. Dozens of other craft soon joined, competing with one another. In 1817, the journey from New Orleans to Louisville had been reduced to 25 days; in 1819, 14 days. "If any one had said this was possible thirty years ago," a journalist marveled, "we should have been ready to send him to a mad-house." Though the shallow, high-powered, and top-heavy steamboats showed a dangerous propensity to explode, run aground, and slam into submerged obstacles, no one thought of going back to the old way of travel.

The increasing speed and frequency of the steamboats encouraged the growth of villages and towns along the rivers. Huge stacks of wood carted in from the countryside appeared wherever the

Steamboat Popularity

Steamboats began to ply the Mississippi River and other major waterways in the 1810s and 1820s, accelerating trade and fueling the growth of cities along the way. This boat is being loaded at Natchez, Mississippi, one of the earliest outposts of the new cotton economy in what would eventually be remembered as the "Old" South, even though it did not exist long enough to really deserve the name. The technology of the steamboat had been known before the War of 1812, but the end of the war opened the rivers of the United States to a rapidly increased trade. Though steamboat technology steadily improved so that steamboats become safer, larger, and more comfortable, they remained dangerous by their very nature. Built light and carrying large tanks under extreme pressure, steamboats were vulnerable to submerged obstacles and often exploded without warning and without obvious cause.

© Bettmann/CORBIS

steamboats regularly stopped for fuel; new stores sold the goods transported on the river; muddy villages dreamed of becoming major cities such as Louisville, Pittsburgh, and Cincinnati.

Regional Growth

As the American economy grew, different parts of the country specialized economically. Enslaved people in the South produced cotton that fueled the growth of the Northeast's textile factories and provided a large market for the farms of Ohio, Illinois, and Indiana.

The Creation of the Cotton South

The demand for cotton in England took off after 1815, when cotton became, for the first time, the clothing of choice for large numbers of the world's people. Cotton clothes were cheaper, easier to create, and more comfortable in warm weather than those made from wool or linen. No place in the world was as prepared to supply the burgeoning demand for cotton as the American South. Small farmers as well as planters from the older states of the southern seaboard saw opportunity in the new states of Alabama and Mississippi, especially now that Andrew Jackson had opened Mobile as a port for southern Alabama. Many white farmers also moved to western Tennessee and parts of Louisiana. The steamboat and the cotton gin gave southern planters powerful new tools, while slaves could clear and cultivate land for new plantations far more quickly than would have been otherwise possible. Slave owners in the older states of the Atlantic seaboard, faced with what they considered a surplus of labor, eagerly sold slaves to planters moving to the "new" lands. One million slaves were sold from the states of the Upper South in the three generations after the ratification of the Constitution. This domestic trade, comprised of a complex network of traders, provisioners, and insurers, constituted as much as 13.5 percent of the total southern economy.

The expansion of the cotton kingdom broadened and deepened the slave trade. Many planters in the East took advantage of the opportunity to sell slaves "down south,"

Planters used giant presses to force cotton into tight bales for easier transportation.

especially as the price of slaves—stagnant or declining before 1815—began to rise. Hundreds of thousands of slaves endured forcible migration to the new states of the Southwest in the 1810s and 1820s (see Map 9.3); some moved in groups along with their owners to new plantations, but many were sold as individuals to slave traders in the East, who then shipped or marched them to slave markets in New Orleans, Mobile, and other cities in the Southwest. The families of many enslaved African Americans were broken apart, as slave traders eagerly bought those in their teens for the hard work of clearing land for plantations from virgin forest.

The movement west was not a simple march from the East, but rather followed the geographic and political contours of the areas recently acquired from the American Indians. The first settlements began along the rivers that made it possible to transport cotton to market and in those places where the Creeks and other Indians exercised no claims. The new plantation districts were disconnected from one another, centering on Montgomery in Alabama, Jackson in Mississippi, and Memphis in Tennessee, all areas taken from the natives of the region since 1814. Small farmers occupied the land farthest from the rivers, supporting themselves with hunting

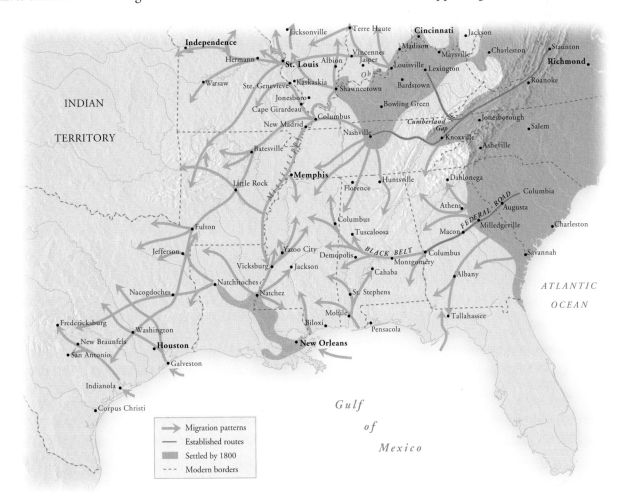

MAP 9.3 **Migration Patterns in the Southwest**

White southerners followed rivers and valleys into the rich lands of the Southwest, with the wealthier among them relying on slaves to clear the lands for new plantations.

Abby Aldrich Rockefeller Folk Art Center, Williamsburg, VA

The rapid spread of cotton plantations fueled the domestic slave trade. These enslaved people are being marched from Virginia into Tennessee.

and foraging as well as with growing small amounts of cotton. Young lawyers and newspaper editors headed out for the Southwest as well, eager to make their mark in the river towns and county seats growing up across Alabama and Mississippi. The combined population of Alabama, Mississippi, and Louisiana more than tripled between 1810 and 1820.

Some ambitious young men from northern states moved to the new cotton lands, the place in the United States, it seemed, where the greatest fortunes could be made in the shortest amount of time. Virgin land could produce a cotton crop in only one year; in two years, a plantation could be in full production. But most of the new residents came from older plantation states. Young southern men were especially eager to move and make their mark. Their wives, mothers, and daughters were often much less enthusiastic about migrating to Mississippi or Alabama, for it meant being removed from the kin who gave those women much of their happiness and social standing. The lure of the Southwest overrode concerns husbands may have felt for their wives' opinions, however, for the new states offered a chance at the independence they considered synonymous with manliness. They sought to build a world as much as possible like those of Virginia or Carolina, only more prosperous.

Emergence of the Northwest

The area west of the Appalachians, north of the Ohio, and east of the Mississippi—the "Northwest"—was growing even faster than the Southwest. "Old America seems to be

DOING HISTORY ONLINE

The Rise of the Market Economy

Read the documents in this module. What do they say about cotton and the economy?

History ⧖ Now™   Visit HistoryNOW to access primary sources and exercises related to this topic: http://now.ilrn.com/ayers_etal3e

breaking up, and moving westward," one man wrote in 1817 as he watched people move down the Ohio River. In the first two decades of the new century, the trans-Appalachian population grew from about 300,000 inhabitants to more than 2 million. This immigration in the North bore considerable similarities to its southern counterpart. First of all, many of the settlers to the Northwest came from the states of the Upper South; large parts of southern Ohio, Indiana, and Illinois were settled by people from Virginia, Kentucky, Tennessee, and North Carolina (see Map. 9.4). Some southern migrants to the North professed themselves eager to move out of states with slavery, while others merely followed the easiest routes to good land. People from New England and New York filled the towns and farms of the northern parts of the new states of the Northwest. As in the Southwest, settlers to the Northwest did not move in a simple westward wave, but rather flowed up the rivers and spread from there, sometimes back toward the East. People often emigrated in groups, whether of families or of larger communities.

Most white settlers proved dissatisfied with the first land they claimed, for about two out of three migrants moved again within a few years. Rumors always circulated about richer land a bit farther west, about a new town certain to be a major city, about opportunity just over the horizon. Many people who had moved once found it easy to move again. Those who remained in a community became its leading citizens, consolidating land into larger farms, setting up grist mills and sawmills, running for office, establishing the small towns that

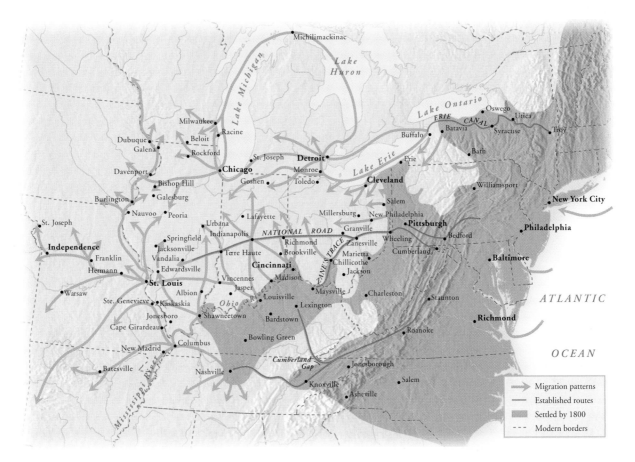

MAP 9.4 Migration Patterns in the Northwest

As in the South, migrants in the North wove their way into the West. New Englanders and New Yorkers followed a northerly path, while other people flowed in from the south, all of them following rivers, canals, and major roads.

served as county seats and trading centers. In many cases, storekeepers were among the first to arrive and among those whose fortunes flourished best. Storekeepers became the bankers and wholesalers of their communities, often buying considerable amounts of land along the way, boosting the towns growing around the stores, churches, and schoolhouses. Courthouses were built early on to formalize land sales and taxation.

Farm and Factory in the Northeast

While the economies of the West and the South were being transformed by settlers and slaves, the economy of the East underwent its own fundamental change. Since the colonial years, people outside the major cities—more than 9 out of 10 Americans—had made in their own homes much of what they needed. This local production grew stronger when trade dried up during the war with England; in the war's wake, more than two-thirds of the clothes Americans wore were made in their own

homes. The year of 1815, in fact, saw the peak of household manufacturing. Local blacksmiths, tailors, cobblers, and other artisans supplied what families could not produce for themselves, while local gristmills and sawmills processed crops and lumber.

Farms averaged a little over a hundred acres, about half cultivated and the other half occupied by wood lots for fuel and timber. Forests often dominated the farms of younger families, while mature families proudly claimed large areas of cultivation, the products of years of labor. Women and men, children and adults shared and divided the work among themselves. Farm families cleared their fields at spring thaw, manuring, plowing, and planting as soon as danger of frost passed. Livestock and poultry needed constant attention; sheep had to be washed and sheared and geese plucked in the spring. Farm families reaped flax in June, enjoyed a brief respite in August, and then pushed hard for the fall harvest. In winter, men and boys cut wood, while women and girls spun thread and wove cloth for clothes. The garden and

Farm households in the North had to prepare to feed themselves and their livestock across long hard winters.

dairy for the family's use and local sale were the responsibility of women and girls, the major cash crops the responsibility of men. Farmers, chronically short of cash, bartered among themselves and with merchants.

After 1815, the farms in many parts of New England, New York, and Pennsylvania would be tied ever more tightly into the economies of the towns and cities. Farm families produced more cash crops and bought more things with money rather than through barter. Women, especially widows and other single females, worked in their homes to produce palm hats, portions of shoes, or articles of clothing that merchants from nearby cities gathered and had assembled in workshops. These women added such **piecework** to their farm work, laboring in the evenings and throughout the winters. With so many young men leaving New England for the West, many communities found themselves with considerable numbers of young women who might never marry as well as older women who could not count on the support of sons. Piecework offered these women a

chance to improve the economies of their households in a way the older farm economy had not, bringing in scarce cash. It was important to everyone in their families that those wage-earning women did not have to leave home to earn those wages.

The expanded cash economy thus overlapped with and conflicted with an older, more self-contained economy. Families sought opportunity in new jobs and new markets, even as they feared that the increasingly dense networks of trade would depress the value of their crops, make seasonal farm labor even more difficult to acquire, entice young people from the farm, alter women's roles, and undermine local artisans. Rural folk both welcomed and worried over the changes. Although it would be generations before cities and factories dominated the economies of the Northeast, in the meantime, farms, towns, and small factories grew ever more interconnected.

The textile industry of New England stood as the most dramatic example of industrial growth. The cost of

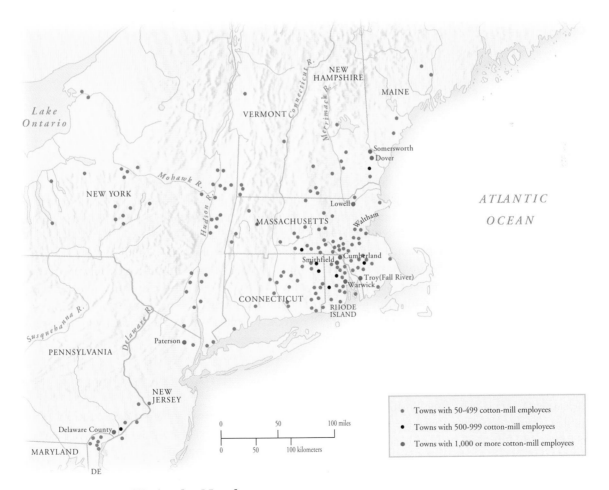

MAP 9.5 Cotton Mills in the Northeast

The cheap cotton of the South combined with the cheap labor and abundant water power of the Northeast to create the United States' first industrial economy in small towns and cities located on streams.

The Early Textile Mills

The complex machinery, whirring spindles, and cease-less web of threads to be pieced together when they broke took a toll on the health and safety of the young workforce of the early textile mills of New England. Women and girls were considered especially well-suited for this work because of their quick fingers and their familiarity with fabrics and thread. Most of the young women who came into the mills were adolescents and young women eager to get out on their own for a while before they married, and were able to contribute to the family income in a way not possible if they had stayed at home. New England at this time had a skewed sex ratio with a preponderance of females, as many of the younger men fled the hard farming of their native region to the easier lands of upstate New York and farther west.

© The Granger Collection, New York

cotton clothing fell faster than the cost for any other product as machinery and cheaper cotton lowered the price. Francis Cabot Lowell of Boston designed a power loom in 1813, recreating from memory a machine he had seen on a recent trip to England. The same year, Lowell and a partner, Nathan Appleton, spent more than $400,000 to open the first factory in the United States that could integrate all the steps of making cloth under a single roof: the Boston Manufacturing Company, in Waltham, Massachusetts, where a waterfall with a 10-foot drop offered free power. An expanded group of investors in the enterprise—the Boston Associates, they were called—pooled the resources of the city's most prominent merchant families.

Unlike earlier factories, that of the Boston Associates used unskilled labor and machines even for weaving, the most expensive part of the process. Lowell and Appleton, concerned that the introduction of factories into the United States might create the same alienated and despised working class they saw in England, recruited young New England farm women and girls as operatives. Young females had experience in producing yarn and cloth at home and they would work hard for low wages. Many were eager to earn money for themselves for a time, to move out of crowded homes, and to send money back to their families. Combining plentiful water power and plentiful people eager to work for wages, factories spread across the Northeast (see Map 9.5).

The operatives, considering millwork a three- or four-year commitment before they married and began families of their own, worked 14 hours a day, 6 days a week. When they signed a contract with the agents who

---

DOING HISTORY ONLINE

Improving Female Education

Read this module. How does Emma Willard justify education for women?

History⏳Now™   Visit HistoryNOW to access primary sources and exercises related to this topic: http://now.ilrn.com/ayers_etal3e

received a dollar a head for each worker they could recruit, the young women agreed to stay with the mill for at least 12 months or to be put on a blacklist that would prevent them from getting a job elsewhere. The factory was unlike anything the young women had ever confronted: "You cannot think how odd everything seemed," one mill girl recalled; even those who had spun and woven for years could not be prepared for the "frightful" sight of "so many bands, and wheels, and springs in constant motion."

Consequences of Expansion

The enlarged boundaries of the American nation, as exciting and promising as they seemed, brought troubles

---

Flashpoints | The Panic of 1819

After the War of 1812 the young economy of the United States seemed on the verge of a new prosperity. The rich lands and fine ports of the burgeoning new nation seemed to hold promise without limits. But in 1819, for no reason that people could see, the bottom suddenly dropped out. The United States, seemingly on the cusp of stability after years of war, instead plummeted into a new kind of economic dislocation.

The shock seemed all the greater because the last few years had been good. The Napoleonic Wars in Europe and the War of 1812 had spurred manufacturing and speculation in the new lands along the booming cotton frontier and north-western borders. Americans ordered goods from England, Europe, and other countries in ever-increasing numbers. Politics had settled into relative quiet.

But the economy of the United State stood on wobbly legs during the Era of Good Feelings. Between 1811 and 1818, in response to great demand for loans to begin and expand businesses, the number of banks in the nation jumped from 88 to 392. Each state had the power to issue its own currency and many did so freely. The United States suddenly found itself awash in shaky cash and credit, much of it unsupported by adequate deposits.

When the President of the newly rechartered Bank of the United States realized that continued issuance of credit was unsupportable, he began to contract the money supply by demanding that state notes redeem their debts to the Bank in specie. By 1821, over

$23 million dollars of currency had been removed from circulation and this lack of access to cash stimulated bankruptcies throughout the nation.

Americans who had recently enjoyed the heady feeling of speculating in frontier lands, manufacturing interests, and banks suddenly found themselves cash poor and under pressure to pay back debts with money they did not have. Fledgling manufactures, begun in response to embargoes during the war with Britain, were seriously damaged or destroyed in the Panic of 1819. Smaller banks at the state and local level began to buckle under the pressure. Frightened crowds rushed the banks, desperate to retrieve their money before the banks chained shut their doors. The Panic of 1819, the nation's first peacetime depression, was on.

The Panic would leave a scar on many Americans. The politics of the next quarter century, at every level, would wrestle with the fears of banks, soft money, speculation, greed, and suffering that Americans had seen in 1819 and would see again every 20 years or so for the rest of the century.

The Second Bank of the United States announced its solidity and strength with its austere classical architecture. © The Granger Collection, New York

Questions for Reflection

1. What can economic crises tell us about larger patterns of history?

2. What was the relationship of the War of 1812 and the Panic of 1819? Are wars good for business?

3. How long can an economic crisis leave an impact on people?

almost immediately. The newly integrated economy proved vulnerable to fluctuations in currency and to outside pressure. The rapid spread of slavery in the South threatened northerners who did not want to see the institution expand into new territories in the West. The resulting political fight over the future of slavery inspired slaves to launch a revolt in South Carolina. The leaders of the United States came to feel that their new status in the world called for an emboldened foreign policy, one that proclaimed an enlarged role for the United States in its hemisphere.

In all these ways, the explosive growth of the country in the 15 years after 1815 brought consequences few could have imagined.

The Panic of 1819

In 1819, a series of events abroad and at home combined to bring a sudden halt to some of the growth in the economy of the United States. Prices for cotton lands in the Southeast, the most sought-after property in these years, skyrocketed as world demand for cotton cloth increased every year. Southern cotton prices rose to such an extent that in 1818 and 1819 British manufacturers turned to other cotton sources, especially India. American cotton prices tumbled, along with the value of the land that produced it. The Panic of 1819 had begun.

The panic proved a sudden and sobering reminder of just how complicated and interdependent the economy of the nation was becoming. The cities were hit the hardest. About half a million workers lost their jobs as business ground to a halt. Americans shuddered to see "children freezing in the winter's storm—and the fathers without coats and shoes." In the streets where new goods had been piled now wandered people without homes or food. Charitable groups opened soup kitchens. Wherever they could, families who had moved to towns and cities returned to the countryside to live with relatives. Things were not much better in the country, however, where the failure of banks meant that apparently prosperous farmers saw household goods, farm animals, and the people they held as slaves sold in humiliating auctions.

Many people, including congressmen, began to call for the revocation of the charter of the Second Bank of the United States. States had chafed throughout the 2 years of the bank's life at what they considered its dictatorial power. Several states tried to limit that power by levying extremely high taxes on the branches of the bank in their states, but it was at this point that the Supreme Court ruled in *McCulloch v. Maryland* that the laws of the federal government "form the supreme law of the land."

Despite the panic, James Monroe was reelected to the presidency in 1820 in one of the quietest and most lopsided elections in the nation's history. The Federalist party, fatally crippled by its opposition to the War of 1812, offered no effective opposition. Neither did Monroe face an organized contest from others within his own Republican party, which was divided along sectional lines. He received every electoral vote but one. Most Americans seemed to blame someone other than President Monroe for the Panic of 1819 and the lingering hard times that followed it. The **Era of Good Feelings** somehow managed to survive in the White House—though, it turned out, not in the halls of Congress.

The Missouri Compromise

The recent admission of the new states of the Southwest and Northwest had left a precarious balance in the Senate between slave states and free, though northern states held a strong, and growing, preponderance in the House of Representatives. The Missouri territory posed a special challenge to the balance. Slavery had quickly spread in Missouri, stretching along the richest river lands. If Missouri were admitted with slavery—as its territorial legislature had decreed—then the slave states would hold a majority in the Senate. Slavery in Missouri, an area of the same latitude as much of Illinois, Indiana, and Ohio, seemed to violate the assumption long held by many people in the North that slavery, if it grew at all, would expand only to the south.

The three-fifths clause of the Constitution, northerners complained, gave the slave states 20 more members of Congress and 20 more electors for the presidency than they would have if only white populations were counted. The South seemed to be getting extra representation unfairly.

The debates over slavery in Missouri in 1819 and 1820 were not debates between fervent abolitionists in the North and fervent proslavery advocates in the South. Neither of those positions had yet been defined. Instead, white northerners and southerners of all political persuasions agreed that as many blacks as possible should be shipped to Africa. White Americans who could agree on little else about slavery did agree that blacks and whites could not live together in the United States once slavery had ended. That was the message of the American Colonization Society, founded in 1816 and based in Washington, D.C. The society bought land in Africa—naming the new country "Liberia"—and sent about 12,000 free African Americans there over the next 50 years. Disease took a terrible toll, however, and many died. As time went by, fewer African Americans migrated.

In Philadelphia, they even staged protests against the notion of **colonization**.

In the meantime, slavery caused problems for the political system. A New York congressman, James Tallmadge, Jr., introduced an amendment to the bill that would admit Missouri as a state only if it admitted no more slaves and if those slaves in the territory were freed when they became 25 years old. More than 80 of the North's congressmen supported the Tallmadge amendment and only 10 opposed it. In the Senate, though, the slave states prevailed by 2 votes. A deadlocked Congress adjourned in March of 1819 to meet again in December.

During the months in between, politicians worked behind the scenes to prepare for the debates and decisions of December. The Union, so celebrated and expansive in the wake of the war with Britain, so peaceful for whites since the Creeks, Seminoles, and Cherokees had been quelled, now seemed in danger of breaking apart from within. Both northern and southern politicians talked openly of ending the Union if need be. Simmering northern resentment, held in check for decades, was suddenly announced, even celebrated. Southerners felt betrayed. In their eyes, slavery was something they had inherited, for which they bore no blame, an institution that would fade away naturally if left alone. White southerners thought northerners irresponsible and unrealistic to attack it as the Tallmadge amendment did. The denial of Missouri statehood seemed to southerners nothing less than an assault on their character.

In northern states, where antislavery societies had been relatively sedate, people suddenly announced the depth of their distaste for the institution. Furious meetings erupted in towns and cities across the North, turning out petitions and resolutions in large numbers. Slavery, these petitions thundered, was a blot on the nation, a violation of the spirit of Christianity, an abomination that must not spread into places it had not already ruined. The antislavery advocates of the 1820s expected colonization and abolition to occur simultaneously and gradually. But they were also determined to stop the spread of slavery toward the northern part of the continent.

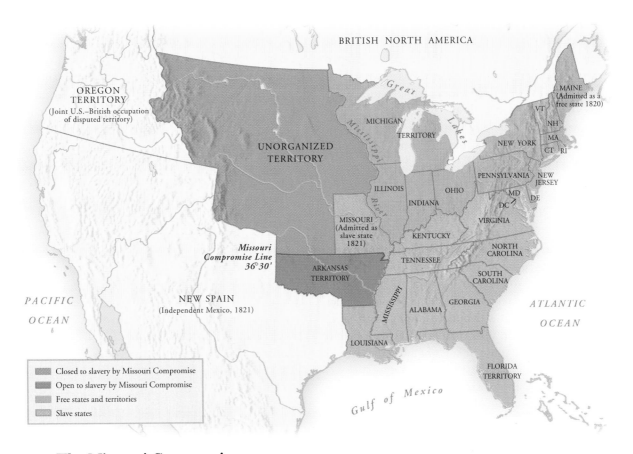

MAP 9.6 The Missouri Compromise

The conflict over the fate of slavery in Missouri proved the first great sectional conflict over the issue. Under the provisions of the Missouri Compromise, Missouri entered the Union as a slave state while Maine entered as a free state. Slavery was prohibited in the remainder of the Louisiana Territory.

After weeks of debate, the **Missouri Compromise** emerged from the Senate: Missouri, with no restriction on slavery, should be admitted to the Union at the same time as Maine, thereby ensuring the balance between slave and free states. Slavery would be prohibited in all the lands acquired in the Louisiana Purchase north of the southern border of Missouri at 36°309' latitude (see Map. 9.6). Such a provision excluded the Arkansas territory, where slavery was already established, but closed to slavery the vast expanses of the Louisiana Territory—the future states of Iowa, Minnesota, Wisconsin, the Dakotas, Nebraska, and Kansas. Any slaves who escaped to the free states would be returned. Many northern congressmen who voted for the measure found themselves burned in effigy back home and defeated when it came time for reelection. Southerners were no more satisfied than the Northerners; they were furious to hear themselves vilified in the national capital they had long dominated.

The debate broke out again when the Missouri constitutional convention not only authorized slavery but decreed that the state legislature could never emancipate slaves without the consent of their masters; the proposed constitution also pronounced that free blacks would never be permitted to enter the new state. The national House of Representatives refused to admit Missouri under this document, and the denunciation by both sides resumed. Finally, in early 1821, Henry Clay managed to fix a majority in the House in favor of a bill that would admit Missouri as long as the new state promised to pass no law barring the entry of a citizen from any other state. Exhausted, Congress ratified the law.

Northern and southern politicians had become wary and distrustful of one another as they had never been before. In a real sense, the debates over slavery in Missouri created "the North" and "the South," uniting the new states of the Northwest with the states of New England, New York, and Pennsylvania as they had not been united earlier, forging a tighter alliance between the new states of the Southwest and Virginia, the Carolinas, and Georgia. Accusations of greed, corruption, and hypocrisy flew. The country became polarized geographically.

Vesey's Revolt

In Charleston, South Carolina, the heart of South Carolina's richest plantation district, a free black man named **Denmark Vesey** had closely followed in the papers the debates over the Missouri controversy. What he read there reinforced what he had seen in the Bible and the documents of the American Revolution: slavery was immoral. Vesey, a middle-aged mulatto of large stature who had bought his freedom 20 years earlier, stood as a commanding presence among the African American people of the low country. A skilled carpenter and preacher, Vesey traveled up and down the coast and into the interior, berating those blacks who accepted racial insult. Many African Americans were attracted to him; most were afraid to oppose him regardless.

Vesey drew not only upon his own strengths but upon those of a powerful ally, Gullah Jack. This man, an Angolan, had arrived in South Carolina near the turn of the century, one of the 40,000 slaves brought into the state right before the end of the legal slave trade in 1807. Gullah Jack still looked very much the part of the conjurer he was, with huge whiskers, tiny arms, and unusual gestures setting him apart from American-born blacks.

Vesey and Gullah Jack and their followers conspired to seize the city's poorly protected guardhouse, stores, and roads before the whites could gather themselves in opposition. House slaves would kill their white owners. Once Charleston was secure, the rebels, Vesey planned, would sail to Haiti, where Toussaint L'Ouverture had staged a black rebellion decades earlier and where slavery had been abolished. But a house servant alerted Charleston whites to the danger only two days before the revolt planned for June 16, 1822. The governor ordered out five military companies, and Vesey called off the attack. Over the next two months, white authorities hanged 35 alleged conspirators and banished 37 more from the state. Few of the rebels would reveal the names of their allies, going to their deaths with the secrets of the revolt secure. Denmark Vesey was one of those killed.

Charleston Mayor James Hamilton bragged, "There can be no harm in the salutary inculcation of one lesson, among a certain portion of our population, that there is nothing they are bad enough to do, that we are not powerful enough to punish." Despite such boasts, white southerners blamed Vesey's Rebellion on the agitation against slavery by northern congressmen in the Missouri debate. "The events of 1822," a leading South Carolinian observed, "will long be remembered, as amongst the choicest fruits of the agitation of that question in Congress."

The Monroe Doctrine

The instability of the Spanish regime in Europe, exacerbated by the Napoleonic Wars, sent aftershocks into the colonies in the New World. Throughout the first and second decades of the nineteenth century, one struggle after another disrupted Latin America. Seeing Spain vulnerable in Europe and abroad, leaders in the colonies of the Western Hemisphere—Simón Bolívar in Venezuela, José de San Martín in Argentina, and Miguel Hidalgo in Mexico—pushed ahead with their long-simmering plans for national independence. By 1822, Chile, Mexico, Venezuela, and the Portuguese colony of Brazil had gained their independence.

Neither the United States nor Great Britain wanted to see France fill the vacuum left by Spain in the New World. A French or Russian empire would pose an economic and military threat potentially much greater than any posed by the fading Spanish regime. Accordingly, in March of 1822 President Monroe urged Congress to recognize the new republics of Latin America. Throughout the next year, as the French army invaded Spain, the U.S. minister in England proposed that the United States and England jointly declare that neither country would annex any part of the tottering empire of Spain nor permit any other power to do so. Encouraged by former presidents Jefferson and Madison, Monroe wanted to make the joint declaration, but Secretary of State John Quincy Adams persuaded him that it would be more fitting and dignified for the United States to declare its policy independently instead of coming "in as a cockboat in the wake of the British man o'war." Adams's policy was directed more against outside intervention in Latin America than in favor of the new republics, which he considered weak and unlikely to endure an attack by a major power.

In December of 1823 the president used his annual message to Congress to announce what would eventually become known as the **Monroe Doctrine:** "The American continents, by the free and independent conditions which they have assumed and maintained, are henceforth not to be considered as subjects for future colonisation by any European power." The North American republic had exerted its first claim to recognition by the great powers of the world, making a show of acting independently even though Great Britain was the real power. The Russians and Spanish denounced the American policy as "blustering," "arrogant," "indecent," and "monstrous," meriting only "the most profound contempt." They tolerated the doctrine because the European powers, exhausted by wars among themselves, had little desire to expand their involvement on the other side of the world. The leaders of the Latin American revolts welcomed the warning to the European powers, but were less certain about the United States' own intentions toward Latin America. The Monroe Doctrine, after all, did not say that the United States would not interfere in the Western Hemisphere, only that it would not permit European countries to do so.

The Reinvention of Politics

Two events of 1824 threw into sharp relief the accomplishments and dangers of the emerging nation. The first event was the 13-month tour of the United States by one of the heroes of the American Revolution: the Marquis de Lafayette. The second event was the presidential election of 1824. While Lafayette's visit tied the country together with bonds of memory and celebration, the election showed that Americans had become far more divided than had seemed possible only four years earlier.

Lafayette's Return

Lafayette sailed into New York and was met, fittingly enough, with a steamboat, symbol of the strides the United States had made since Lafayette's departure decades earlier. He spent tumultuous and tearful days in New York, where old comrades and young admirers poured out to see the living embodiment of the sacrifices and bravery of the Revolutionary War. Then Lafayette, along with his son, George Washington Lafayette, and his traveling companion, a radical young Scotswoman named Frances Wright, set out to see the rest of the United States. They went first to New England, visiting with John Adams, then down the coast to Philadelphia, Baltimore, Washington, Charleston, and then New Orleans. From there, they went up the Mississippi and on to Nashville, where Lafayette met Andrew Jackson.

Everywhere Lafayette traveled, the people tried to outdo what had been done before; the hero met with booming guns, torchlight parades, thousands of children dressed in the colors of France, beautiful young women, illuminated pictures, banquet after banquet, speech after speech. Some moments stood out: when the general cried, alone, at the grave of Washington at Mount Vernon, and when he traveled to Monticello to meet with Jefferson. Congress, knowing that the marquis was in serious financial difficulties, presented him with a gift of $200,000 (an enormous sum at the time) and a township of public land. Lafayette met with

Invitations such as this were highly treasured during Lafayette's triumphant tour of 1825, when Americans gloried in memories of their nation's founding.

remarked that America would persuade others by "the moral influence of its example," not by actively supporting democratic movements abroad.

The Election of 1824

Many people felt that they saw the worst of the country in the presidential election going on while Lafayette toured the country. Few eligible voters had bothered to cast a ballot four years earlier when James Monroe had won the presidency virtually without opposition, for his reelection seemed foreordained. But politicians and observers expected a more interesting contest in 1824. Many thought the next president would be William Crawford, secretary of the treasury, a Georgian and apparent heir to the Virginia dynasty. Others focused on John Quincy Adams, an experienced statesman, New Englander, and the secretary of state—the office from which many presidents had come, including his father. Others looked to John C.

Cherokees in Georgia. Slaves, hearing of the patriot's opposition to slavery, lined the roads wherever he went to cheer him on.

The Frenchman was admired for his selflessness at the time of the American Revolution, for putting the cause of liberty before his own self-interest, for putting himself at risk in the pursuit of freedom. Such a posture of noble self-sacrifice was what Americans valued most in their public men and what they expected of those to whom power was given. In Lafayette, they could celebrate the best in themselves. While remembering their own Revolution and celebrating Lafayette, the 18th Congress defeated a resolution to express its sympathy with revolutionaries in Greece attempting to throw off Ottoman rule. Although the resolution was backed by Henry Clay and Daniel Webster, one of its opponents

Calhoun of South Carolina, an impressive secretary of war and advocate of a strong national government. Yet others placed their bets on Henry Clay of Kentucky, Speaker of the House of Representatives for many years and one of the most visible members of Congress. Finally, Andrew Jackson of Tennessee hoped to parlay the widespread fame he won in the wars against the English and the Indians into the presidency.

Several of these men realized they did not command sufficient national support to win the election outright. They hoped, however, to prevail if the election went into the House of Representatives, where the top three candidates would vie if no candidate won a majority in the electoral college. Cliques spread rumors, and alliances of convenience flourished. Openly partisan newspapers sang the praises of their man and published lacerating

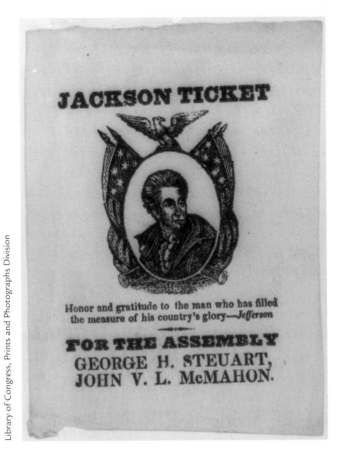

The election of 1824 saw Andrew Jackson pursue the presidency by laying claim to the support of Thomas Jefferson, only, he claimed, to lose through a "corrupt bargain."

rumors about his opponents. The most novel was John Henry Eaton's successful press campaign to portray Jackson as a patriotic soldier, quietly tending his farm while Washington politicians schemed to block his election by ordinary voters because of his lack of polish and his incorruptible character.

While the Marquis de Lafayette serenely toured the United States, local and state politicians worked feverishly in taverns, caucuses, and newspaper offices. Many American voters seemed disenchanted with the crass politicking, though, and relatively few voted in 1824. Jackson's popular vote nearly equaled that of Adams and Crawford combined, but the election was thrown into the House of Representatives because no candidate received a plurality in the electoral college. The House could choose among the top three candidates: Jackson, Adams, and Crawford.

Since his fourth-place finish put him out of the running, Clay, the Speaker of the House, sought to strike the best deal he could with the other candidates, assuring himself of maximum power, visibility, and opportunities in subsequent elections. Clay, considering Jackson

unworthy of the post and a potential military despot, discussed his future with Adams. When the vote came to the House of Representatives in early 1825, Adams won the presidency—taking the three states Clay had won in the Electoral College. Two weeks later, Henry Clay received the appointment of secretary of state. "So you see," Andrew Jackson fumed, "the Judas of the West has closed the contract and will receive the thirty pieces of silver." Throughout the muddy little city of Washington, people speculated about the promises the upright John Quincy Adams had made to win the presidency. People often mentioned the cold sweat that broke out on his face when he received word of his election.

Adams wanted a stronger national government, internal improvements, and a tariff to protect American industry. But he could not mobilize support for his positions, either within Washington or among the voters. Adams refused to use patronage to persuade or coerce people to go along with his plans. His administration bogged down into factionalism and paralysis, with his supposed "corrupt bargain" with Clay darkening his reputation. Things seemed far removed, indeed, from the glorious days when Lafayette sacrificed for the American Revolution.

New York politicians sought to harness ambition into useful and organized forms in the 1820s, pioneering the development of the party system. Aaron Burr converted a simple patriotic club in New York City, the Society of Saint Tammany, into the beginnings of a major political machine. De Witt Clinton invented the "spoils system," in which it became the expectation that an incoming officeholder would remove those appointed by his predecessor and put his own supporters in their place. Martin Van Buren, a young lawyer and politician from New York, nicknamed the "Little Magician," combined the city machine and the spoils system into a powerful statewide organization. He used newspapers in Albany and New York City to spread the word of the party to the 50 small newspapers he controlled throughout the state, which also published vast numbers of handbills, posters, and ballots at election time. He built a large network of party men, many of them lawyers who traveled widely in the state and knew many of their counterparts. Van Buren's goal was to combine party unity with personal advancement for party members, creating a powerful and self-reinforcing cycle.

Van Buren opposed John Quincy Adams in the presidential contest of 1824 because Adams's nationally sponsored canals, roads, education, and other services would cut into the power of state government and state politics, elevating what Van Buren saw as dangerous federal power over power closer to home. Partly for this reason, Van Buren cast his lot in 1824 and the years thereafter with Andrew Jackson, who shared Van Buren's preference for localized power. As the next presidential election came closer, Van Buren, now a senator, worked ever more energetically for Jackson, hoping to spread the model of New York politics to the nation as a whole.

The Adams Twilight

The second half of John Quincy Adams's administration proved unhappy and unproductive. Neither Adams's talents nor his devotion to the Union had faded, but the public mood seemed little interested in either. The "corrupt bargain" still hung over the White House in 1827. In the eyes of many, Adams had proven himself unfit for office, not only with his reputed bargain, but also, false rumor persisted, by procuring a young American girl for the Russian czar when Adams had served as a 14-year-old member of the U.S. diplomatic corps in St. Petersburg. The president's elite education and even his purchase of a billiard table and chess set for the White House were disparaged by opponents as symbols of "aristocracy." Adams's many and diverse opponents organized against him and his policies almost from the beginning of his administration. It soon became clear that the president would be able to accomplish little of his ambitious agenda of internal improvements, a national university, and western exploration, goals that might have won support in earlier years.

Supporters of Andrew Jackson of Tennessee, John C. Calhoun of South Carolina, and William Crawford of Georgia gradually joined forces in anticipation of the election of 1828, when they hoped to unseat Adams and his vision of an active and centralized government. The struggle, Calhoun wrote to Jackson, was between "power and liberty." The champion of power had had his turn, Adams's opponents believed; now it was time for the champions of liberty to step forward. After some jockeying, Andrew Jackson emerged as the man to challenge Adams.

Adams's supporters warned of the dangers of electing a raw and rough "military chieftain" such as Andrew Jackson to the presidency. Jackson's opponents distributed a handbill marked with 18 coffins, each one representing a man Jackson had supposedly killed in a duel or ordered executed under his military command. The most incendiary charge, however, was that Jackson had married a woman married to another man, leading her to commit both bigamy and adultery in the process. The facts of the case were unclear—it appears that Rachel Jackson was a religious woman, trapped in a bad marriage, who thought she had received a divorce when she married Jackson—but the

Titillating depictions of the supposed Masonic rituals marked a flood of publications in the late 1820s and early 1830s, such as this almanac from the Anti-Masons.

anti-Jackson forces made the most of any suspicions to the contrary.

The Anti-Masons Organize

Charges of conspiracy and corruption raged throughout American politics in the 1820s. Some of the suspicions seemed confirmed by events in New York. As the economy of that state prospered along with the Erie Canal, so did fraternal organizations of every sort. The Ancient Order of Masons did especially well, claiming almost 350 lodges in the state. The Masons' exclusive society, surrounded by elaborate ritual and strict secrecy, many non-Masons felt, contradicted American ideals of democracy and openness, taking men away from their families and undermining organized religion. Since Masons were obliged to show business or political preference to a brother over "any other person in the same circumstances," some of those outside the order feared that Masons might win undue influence in their town, state, or country. As proof, they pointed out that every New York governor but one between 1804 and the late 1820s had belonged to the Masons.

Suspicion of the Masons exploded when a brother named William Morgan turned against the order and decided to publish its secret rituals. Local Masonic leaders used their influence with county officials to harass and jail Morgan, who disappeared in September 1826. Many said he had been murdered. The investigation soon stalled, however, as Masonic law enforcement officers and others dragged their feet. Despite 20 trials and 3 special prosecutors, only a few convictions resulted and those convictions brought only minor jail terms. Congregations split and communities divided into warring factions over the Masons. Alleged Masonic skullduggery proved a convenient way to explain personal and political setbacks. Fury against the Masons soon spread from New York to the rest of the country, forcing one lodge after another to dissolve.

By 1827, nearly a hundred "Morgan committees" had met and formed in New York and began to spread across the entire northern half of the country, attracting men of reputation and prestige. Within 2 years, the "Anti-Masons" had established more than 100 newspapers. They held public meetings and launched lobbying campaigns, bypassing local elites and inventing new means of pressuring legislatures directly. Unlike earlier reform organizations, such as those that supported Sunday schools and the distribution of Bibles, the Anti-Masons thrived on controversy. They devoted themselves to changing public opinion, to mobilizing people against a powerful entrenched force. They succeeded: Masonry lost more than half its members and created virtually no new lodges for the next 15 years. So great was the Anti-Masons' success, in fact, that the movement's leaders dreamed of creating a new party to purify and energize American politics.

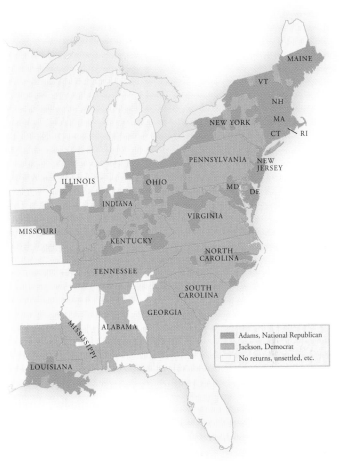

MAP 9.7 **The Election of 1828**
Andrew Jackson overwhelmed John Quincy Adams almost everywhere except in Adams's native New England.

Birth of the Democrats

Even while the struggle over the Masons unfolded, Martin Van Buren was building a political coalition behind Andrew Jackson. Throughout 1827 and 1828, Van Buren traveled throughout the United States, hammering out a new coalition of ambitious state politicians willing to back Jackson. The members of the coalition called themselves "Democratic Republicans," eventually shortened to "Democrats." Their candidates did extremely well in the off-year congressional elections of 1827, exploiting people's disapproval of the ineffectual Adams administration. The Democrats controlled both the House and the Senate.

Van Buren and the other party leaders organized voters as they had never been organized before in preparation for Jackson's contest with Adams. Although Jackson himself was a prominent Mason, Van Buren adopted techniques not unlike those pioneered by the Anti-Masons in these same years. Using every strategy at their disposal—bonfires, speeches, barbecues, parades, professional writers, and the first campaign song—these Jacksonians claimed that they had found a true man of the people to strip the office from the aristocratic Adams. In towns across the country, "Old Hickory"—Jackson was supposedly as hardy as that toughest of trees—was celebrated with hickory poles, brooms, sticks, and trees. The National Republicans, as Adams's supporters became known, sniffed at what they considered the unseemly display that diverted attention from real issues, but they could not deny the power of the new methods to win voters' attention.

In the meantime, American politics became more democratic and inclusive. Most legislatures across the Union lowered property requirements for voting and made judicial offices elective rather than appointed. Citizens seemed restless, hungry for someone to give direction

The small towns along the Ohio and Mississippi Rivers quickly grew into booming young cities like Cincinnati.

and force to public life. As a result, voter turnout in 1828 was double that of the 1824 election. The dramatic confrontation of men and styles contributed to widespread voter interest, and politicians at every level and on both sides made sure voters went to the polls. Jackson's supporters wanted no repeat of the last electoral controversy or chance for victory to be stolen by insider politics.

Jackson won easily over Adams, winning 178 of the 261 electoral votes, capturing the critical mid-Atlantic states and all the states of the South except Louisiana and Kentucky (see Map 9.7). The election proved bittersweet for Jackson, though, for his wife died soon afterward. Jackson blamed the slanderers of the other party for Rachel's death, for she had fallen ill after seeing an editorial denouncing her. The president-elect passed the weeks before his inauguration in sadness and bitterness.

Conclusion

The decade after 1815 saw two powerful tendencies warring with each other in the United States. On one hand, restless Americans surged to the west after the defeat of the British in the War of 1812 removed a major barrier to territorial growth. On the other hand, many other Americans feared what such ceaseless movement might mean for families, churches, morals, and politics. The tension between growth and the consequences of that growth defined the events of this turbulent decade.

The expansion of the United States was not simply the story of hardy pioneers marching toward the west.

The lands they came to occupy had been occupied for generations by Creeks, Cherokee, and Chickasaw peoples. The Indians' lands came into American hands through war, trickery, and bribery as well as through treaties and purchase. Many white settlers did not much care about the means through which the lands entered the United States, for those settlers and their political leaders considered the land the rightful property of those who would convert it to profitable use.

As soon as the lands became available for settlement white Americans surged there to establish farms, plantations, and towns. The rich land supported cotton in endless quantities, cotton produced by tens of thousands of African American enslaved people who were dragged across the Appalachian mountains and shipped up the rivers of the South. In what was then called the Northwest—what we now consider the Midwest— hungry white families did the work themselves on the rich but raw land they rushed to occupy. In the Northeast, new factories arose to provide the clothing and shoes for the restive American population.

At the same time that Americans elbowed their way into territories and created new states, political leaders struggled to contain the consequences of unconstrained growth. The first great crisis over slavery, triggered by the admission of Missouri in 1819, made many people wonder whether the United States would be able to control the forces pulling it apart. The North and the South became ever more distinct as they expanded across the continent, as the area dominated by slavery grew as quickly as the area ruled by free labor. The burgeoning economy posed deep challenges to long-established ways of doing business. Well-funded corporations and partnerships flourished in the heightened competition for resources and markets.

Many Americans fought against the forces of social disintegration they saw around them. Some white Americans advocated for the Indians being driven from their lands. Others joined temperance societies to resist the power of drink. Others labored to build penitentiaries and asylums for the deaf, the blind, the mute, the insane, and the poor. Such reformers felt themselves in a race against time, against the forces of movement and change that threatened to destroy the United States before it had a chance to establish itself as a respectable nation.

The Chapter in Review

In the years between 1815 and 1828:

- The borders of the United States stabilized to the north, west, and south.
- A newly integrated national economy emerged, based on improved roads, canals, and steamboats and the first major financial panic shook the entire country.
- Cotton drove the aggressive expansion of slavery across the South.
- Factories developed in New England and the Northeast.
- The Missouri Compromise redefined the relationship between the North and the South.
- The first major national political party, the Democrats, was forged by Martin Van Buren and Andrew Jackson.

Making Connections Across Chapters

LOOKING BACK

Chapter 9 shows the expansion of the United States after the War of 1812 unleashed a series of unanticipated challenges to the new nation. This raises a number of questions:

1. Could the spread of slavery into the southern territories have been avoided?

2. Could relations between the U.S. government and the American Indians have followed a different path?

3. What role did governments play in the growth and spread of the economy?

LOOKING AHEAD

Chapter 10 will show how Americans carefully planned for the future in the early 1820s, putting in place compromises and reforms designed to hold things in place in future years.

1. Could the Missouri Compromise offer a long-term solution to the problem of conflict between the North and the South?

Recommended Readings

Appleby, Joyce. *Inheriting the Revolution: The First Generation of Americans* (2000) paints a wonderful picture of these years.

Burstein, Andrew. *America's Jubilee: How in 1826 a Generation Remembered Fifty Years of Independence* (2001) offers a fresh portrait of Lafayette's return and all it evoked.

Cashin, Joan E. *A Family Venture: Men and Women on the Southern Frontier* (1991) tells the story of the southwestern migration in a compelling way.

Dangerfield, George. *The Awakening of American Nationalism, 1815–1828* (1965) is a classic interpretation of the postwar era.

Davis, David Brion. *The Problem of Slavery in the Age of Revolution, 1770–1823* (1975) gives a magisterial overview of the international struggles with slavery.

Horwitz, Morton J. *The Transformation of American Law, 1780–1860* (1977) puts forward a strong and controversial argument about the law and commerce.

Larson, John Lauritz. *Internal Improvement: National Public Works and the Promise of Popular Government in the Early United States* (2001) is the best treatment of this important subject.

Lewis, James E. *The American Union and the Problem of Neighborhood: The United States and the Collapse of the Spanish Empire, 1783–1829* (1998) provides a fresh interpretation of this complicated relationship.

Mathews, Jean. *Toward a New Society: American Thought and Culture, 1800–1830* (1990) offers a subtle interpretation of cultural history of this period.

Meyer, David R. *The Roots of American Industrialization* (2003) emphasizes the crucial role agriculture played in making New England hospitable to manufacturing.

Saunt, Claudio. *A New Order of Things: Property, Power, and the Transformation of the Creek Indians, 1733–1816* (1999) makes comprehensible the great complexities in the lives of American Indians in these crucial decades.

Sellers, Charles G. *The Market Revolution: Jacksonian America, 1815–1846* (1991) gives a stirring portrayal of the period with economic change at the center.

Sheriff, Carol. *The Artificial River: The Erie Canal and the Paradox of Progress, 1817–1862* (1996) gives a compelling account of the canal's origins, building, and effects.

Rohrbough, Malcolm J. *The Trans-Appalachian Frontier: People, Societies, and Institutions, 1775–1850* (1978) tells this complex story well.

Sweet, John Wood. *Bodies Politic: Negotiating Race in the American North, 1730–1830* (2003) emphasizes the role the North played in creating the notion of the United States as a white nation.

Identifications

Review your understanding of the following key terms, people, events, and dates for this chapter (these terms also appear in the Glossary at the end of the book):

James Monroe
Seminoles
Henry Clay
John C. Calhoun
American System
John Marshall

National Road
Erie Canal
Piecework
Cotton South
Era of Good Feelings
Colonization
Missouri Compromise
Denmark Vesey
Monroe Doctrine

Online Sources Guide 🌐

Use this listing to find online documents, images, interactive maps, simulations, and other resources related to this chapter:

American History Resource Center

http://history.wadsworth.com/rc/us

Documents

Richard D. Brown, Modernization, Chapter 6

Interactive Maps

Distribution of Slave Population, 1790–1820

Selected Images

Erie Canal, Lockport, N.Y.
Depiction of rural progress in Western New York
Slave quarters near Charleston, S.C.
Eureka schoolhouse, Springfield, Vt.
Tree of Temperance
Mid-nineteenth-century scientific views of race

Simulation

Early-nineteenth-century America (Choose to be a slave, a frontiersman, or a Native American and make choices based on the circumstances and opportunities afforded.)

Document Exercises

1816 Tompkins Speech

HistoryNOW

http://now.ilrn.com/ayers_etal3e

Primary Source Exercises

The Rise of the Market Economy
Charles Pinckney's Speech to Congress
Emma Willard

10 The Years of Andrew Jackson, 1829–1836

One of the most famous men in the United States due to his exploits in the War of 1812, Andrew Jackson of Tennessee seemed to many people an inspiring leader. Others, however, saw him as a "military chieftain" dangerous with the power of the presidency.

Tumultuous change came to the United States in the years Andrew Jackson served as president. Elections became sweeping public events that involved men of every class. Voters and leaders hotly debated and contested the role of government in American life. Religious revivals swept up entire communities in devotion and prayer. Working people created labor unions, and abolitionists launched a bold crusade against slavery.

Growing democracy was not the full story of these years, however. The people of the Creek, Choctaw, Cherokee, Seminole, Sac, and Fox nations were driven from their homes in the South and in the old Northwest. A crisis threatened to ignite a military struggle between South Carolina and the federal government. The revolt of Nat Turner and debates over slavery in Virginia unleashed a proslavery reaction throughout much of the South. The defeat of Mexico by the Republic of Texas opened a vast new territory to slavery as well as to the settlement of free Americans. Few decades in American history witnessed such important and fundamental changes.

Accompanying this rapid expansion of boundaries of every sort was considerable anxiety that American society threatened to spin out of control. The government held little power, and people worried that many Americans had moved beyond the influence of church, family, school, or employer. Some Americans began to suggest ways to contain the consequences of change. They offered political compromise, reform societies, and new ideals of the home as ways to counteract what they saw as threatening chaos.

Andrew Jackson Takes Charge

Andrew Jackson, still dressed in black in mourning after the recent death of his beloved wife Rachel, traveled by steamboat from Nashville to Washington in the winter of 1829 to begin his presidency. The entire nation watched to see what sort of changes this new kind of leader might make, what sort of America he might help create.

The People's President

Once he arrived in Washington, Jackson began to assemble his cabinet, balancing North, South, and West. Martin Van Buren, the leader of Jackson's successful 1828 campaign, became secretary of state, a position

Timeline

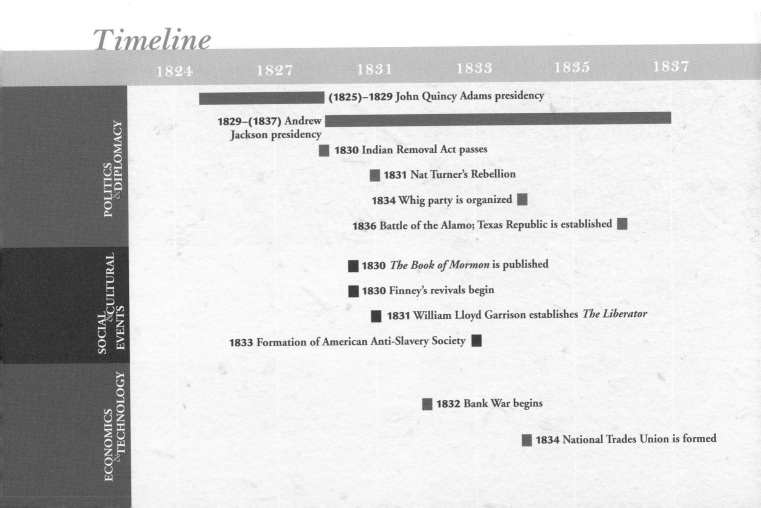

	1824	1827	1831	1833	1835	1837

POLITICS & DIPLOMACY

(1825)–1829 John Quincy Adams presidency

1829–(1837) Andrew Jackson presidency

1830 Indian Removal Act passes

1831 Nat Turner's Rebellion

1834 Whig party is organized

1836 Battle of the Alamo; Texas Republic is established

SOCIAL & CULTURAL EVENTS

1830 *The Book of Mormon* is published

1830 Finney's revivals begin

1831 William Lloyd Garrison establishes *The Liberator*

1833 Formation of American Anti-Slavery Society

ECONOMICS & TECHNOLOGY

1832 Bank War begins

1834 National Trades Union is formed

traditionally reserved for the man next in line for the presidency. Vice President John C. Calhoun, ambitious for the presidency himself, chafed at the appointment but could do little to change it; he and his wing of the party had to satisfy themselves with the appointment of one of their number as secretary of the treasury. The most controversial appointment, however, proved volatile for reasons that had little to do with political partisanship. Jackson wanted a close friend in the cabinet, someone in whom he could confide, and he chose an old Tennessee associate and influential newspaper editor, John Eaton, as his secretary of war.

Eaton, a widower in middle age, had married Peggy O'Neal Timberlake, an attractive and witty 29-year-old daughter of a well-known innkeeper in Washington. She was rumored to have driven her last husband to suicide, forcing him to defraud the government to pay debts she had run up. She was also rumored to have had sex with Eaton before their marriage—along with, one contemporary smirked, "eleven doz. others!" Eaton had asked Jackson's opinion of the marriage beforehand, receiving the old general's blessing; the president liked outspoken women and knew from bitter experience the power that unfounded rumors could hold. Jackson, in a gesture of friendship and support as the gossip flew, offered Eaton the cabinet position, apparently hoping he would decline. Unfortunately for Jackson, Eaton accepted. The decision electrified Washington.

Despite his rambunctious youth, Jackson disdained official Washington's fondness for strong drink, endless banquets, and overheated social life. He had witnessed that high life during his time as senator from Tennessee and he held it in contempt when he returned to the capital; he preferred instead to attend the city's churches. Jackson considered himself an outsider despite his power

In a scene that soon grew legendary, celebrants at Andrew Jackson's inauguration overwhelmed the capacity of the White House to contain their numbers or their rambunctiousness.

and popularity, an outsider determined to reform Washington, to make the city worthy of the nation it was supposed to serve.

As the inauguration day of March 4 neared, Washington's population doubled as men who considered themselves important in General Jackson's election arrived in the city to claim their fair share of glory, excitement, and jobs. They drank all the whiskey the city had to offer, slept five to a bed, and generally offended the more genteel residents of the capital. At the inauguration, 30,000 people crowded in to see the new president. They surged into the White House, spilling barrels of orange punch, standing with muddy boots on expensive chairs to get a better look at the proceedings, and smashing thousands of dollars worth of china. Servants attracted the mob outside by moving the liquor. Jackson, suffocated by admirers and disgusted by the scene, climbed out a rear window and went for a steak at his boardinghouse.

Jackson and the "Spoils System"

Many people in Washington were as appalled at the events that followed the inauguration as they were with the inauguration itself. As the new administration got under way, Jackson and his advisors cleaned house in the federal government, removing those officials whose competence, honesty, or loyalty to Jackson and the Democrats were suspect. Although such a policy had become established practice in several major states, including Van Buren's New York, Jackson was the first president to make such sweeping changes on the federal level. He envisioned himself purging an arrogant bureaucracy of corruption, establishing the democratic practice of "rotation in office." As officeholders quaked and fretted, Jackson's lieutenants decided which customhouses and federal offices would be cleansed. Some of the incumbents clearly deserved to lose their jobs, having served jail terms, embezzled funds, or succumbed to drink, but others were guilty only of being active partisans for the other side in the recent election.

Jackson further infuriated opponents by appointing partisan newspaper editors to important posts, leading to charges that Jackson was corrupting, rather than cleansing, American government. Over the course of Jackson's two terms he replaced only about 10 percent of all officeholders, not many more than his predecessors had, but Jackson also recognized the power of the postal system to aid partisan political aims. He elevated the postmaster general to a cabinet level position and worked to appoint friendly editors as local postmasters where they solicited subscriptions to Democratic publications. These allies were frequently accused of misrouting or destroying rivals' pamphlets and newspapers.

Martin Van Buren, a widower, cemented his friendship with the president by treating Mrs. Eaton with ostentatious respect. Jackson, embittered by the refusal of his other advisors to stand by Mrs. Eaton, largely abandoned his official cabinet and relied instead on an informal group of advisors, his so-called Kitchen Cabinet, and on Van Buren, the only winner in the Eaton episode.

Struggles Over Slavery

Several issues surrounding slavery came to a head in the years around 1830. Leaders in the southern states, worried about the rapidly growing population and power of the North, sought to define the limits of federal power. Feeling themselves neglected and abused by northern interests, South Carolina's leaders tried to secure greater autonomy. At the same time, free blacks in both the North and the South worked to replace the colonization movement with a campaign to end slavery and create freedom for African Americans in America. Even as these struggles unfolded, one of the largest slave revolts in the history of the United States erupted in Virginia. Combined, these events demonstrated that slavery and the issues on which it touched would bedevil the confident and boisterous young country.

Though Andrew Jackson saw his removal of federal officeholders as a reform, many critics saw it only as thinly disguised greed.

Jackson removed about 900 of 10,000 men from their offices and did so in an especially brash spirit. One Jackson supporter unwisely announced to the Senate that the Jacksonians saw "nothing wrong in the rule that to the victors belong the spoils of the enemy." This proclamation gave an enduring notoriety to what from then on would be called the "**spoils system,**" a system that Jackson envisioned as reform, not cynical politics.

The festering conflict within the administration over the so-called Eaton affair proved just how important matters of symbolism could be. The wives of the other cabinet members, Vice President Calhoun's wife, and even Emily Donelson—Jackson's daughter- in-law and hostess of the White House—refused to be in the same room with **Peggy Eaton.** But Jackson would not be swayed in his support for John and Peggy Eaton. The new cabinet found itself bitterly divided between pro-Eaton and anti-Eaton factions. Jackson labored to mend fences, calling an influential pastor to the White House and trying to find evidence to prove Mrs. Eaton's virtue. Nothing proved effective, though, and Jackson decided that the real villain of the story was Vice President Calhoun and his unbending wife, Floride. By contrast,

The Tariff of Abominations, Nullification, and States' Rights

Before the election of 1828, Martin Van Buren and other Democrats had sought to broaden support for Jackson, whose strength lay in the South, by passing a **tariff** favorable to the economic interests of New Englanders and westerners. After elaborate deal making, the Democrats enacted a major tariff. But it came with a high cost: southerners were furious with what they called this "tariff of abominations," for it raised the price they would have to pay for manufactured items and threatened markets for southern cotton abroad. John C. Calhoun, like other South Carolina planters, feared not only that the tariff would bleed the state dry economically but that it would set a regulatory precedent for antislavery forces who might gain control of the federal government at some future date.

Accordingly, in the summer and early fall of 1828, a few months before he would take office as Jackson's vice president, Calhoun sought to find a principled way to reconcile his national ambitions and his local concerns. Rather than argue only against the tariff itself, Calhoun asserted the general rights of individual states within the Union. To do so, he returned to what he called "the

The young wife of Secretary of War John Eaton became the center of a scandal that rocked Washington during Andrew Jackson's first term.

primitive principles of our government," the foundations on which everything else rested. Calhoun insisted that interests had become so diverse in the United States that laws appropriate for one state or section might well harm another. Rather than merely letting the majority run roughshod over the minority, Calhoun believed, it made more sense to let a state "nullify" a national law within its own borders. Such **nullification** was constitutional, he said, because the federal system did not locate sovereignty in any one place, but rather divided it among the states and the nation. Should three-fourths of the states agree that a law must apply to all the country, then that clear majority could overrule the nullification. Calhoun thought he was finding a way to preserve order in an increasingly contentious Union. The document in which he laid out his ideas, the *South Carolina Exposition,* appeared in December of 1828; the pamphlet was published anonymously because it was too politically dangerous for the vice president of the United States to be publicly on record for nullification.

South Carolina planters persuaded themselves that they would have to do something soon. They watched with growing alarm as the newspapers told of the success of British abolitionists in ending slavery in the British West Indies—the place from which many elite white South Carolina families had come generations earlier. With the memory of Denmark Vesey's plan of 1822 and an 1829 revolt in the low country still fresh in their memory, white South Carolinians felt they could display

no weakness on the slavery issue. Unlike other southern states, where stark geographic differences between low country and hill country often divided voters and encouraged party differences, there was broad agreement among the South Carolina electorate on this crucial issue. Throughout the state, raucous crowds gathered to call for a fight against the federal government on the tariff. Those South Carolinians who favored a more conciliatory stance toward the federal government could not generate nearly as much support for their position.

President Jackson had no sympathy for nullification and the leaders of the movement in South Carolina were surprised and disappointed that they enjoyed no support from other southern states in resisting federal authority. After all, Jackson, like them, was a planter and slaveholder and would suffer economically along with the South Carolinians. Jackson considered the tariff to be for the good of the nation as a whole. The tariff provided money for defense and prevented federal debt. The South Carolina challenge would limit the power of the U.S. government to make law for the country in matters that transcended state boundaries. Jackson did not believe the United States could afford to permit such divisiveness to impair its strength in the world of nations. Jackson, the old general, would tolerate no opposition on such matters. Congress passed a "Force Bill" to permit him to use military power to keep South Carolina in line and collect the tariff duties.

Congress twisted and turned on nullification, not wanting South Carolina to get its way but unwilling to

DOING HISTORY

What Slavery Means

DAVID WALKER, a free black man who lived in both the South and the North, wrote his scathing account of the injustices done to African Americans for an African American audience in 1829. Drawing on a wide reading of world history, Walker argued that American slavery was among the worst the world had ever seen and that God would exercise a harsh judgment on white Americans for their acts.

Daniel R. Hundley, a white Southerner living in Chicago, wrote his account to a largely white Northern audience, trying to explain the nature of the South and to rebut what he saw as extremists on both sides. Publishing his book in 1860, Hundley repeated the most far-reaching argument used to defend slavery.

David Walker, *Appeal . . . to the Colored Citizens of the World*

I have been for years troubling the pages of historians to find out what our fathers have done to the *white Christians of America,* to merit such condign punishment as they have inflicted on them, and do continue to inflict on their children. But I must aver, that my researches have hitherto been to no effect. I have therefore come to the immovable conclusion, that they [Americans] have, and do continue to punish os for nothing else, but for enriching them and their country. For I cannot conceive of any thing else. Nor will I ever believe otherwise until the Lord shall convince me.

Daniel R. Hundley, *Social Relations in Our Southern States*

We are well persuaded that many good men, pious men—men of earnest natures and delicate sensibilities, not in the North alone but even in the South—do honestly look upon slavery as both a great moral evil and an equally great social curse. . . . In our folly, we do not consider that Jehovah never would have permitted the first human-freighted shp to leave the shores of Africa for the New World, had he not designed a beneficial result should flow from the introduction of the sable children of the tropics into the fruitful fields of our own temperate latitude. Yes, Madam, with our conception of the Deity, we can not believe that the All-wise Ruler would purposely allow a great evil to grow and increase to such magnitude, as to become the very centre and pivot of the world's commerce . . . when he might have crushed it in the beginning without harm to a single individual.

Source: David Walker, *Appeal, in Four Articles; Together with a Preamble to the Colored Citizens of the World . . .* (Boston: September 28, 1829); Daniel R. Hundley, *Social Relations in Our Southern States* (New York: Henry B. Price 1860), pp. 288–289.

Questions for Reflection

1. What do these two documents have in common?

2. Does their appeal to God provide hope for common understanding or persuasion?

3. What response would slavery's defenders make to Walker? What response would slavery's attackers make to Hundley?

4. Would these arguments change over time?

5. What would happen to both arguments when the Civil War broke out?

Explore additional primary sources related to this chapter on the Wadsworth American History Resource Center or HistoryNOW websites:
http://history.wadsworth.com/rc/us
http://now.ilrn.com/ayers_etal3e

---

see Jackson use arms against fellow Americans. After much debate, Congress, under the leadership of Henry Clay, offered a compromise in early 1833: the tariff would be slowly but steadily lowered over the next decade, giving northern manufacturers time to adapt. South Carolina, secretly relieved, declared itself the victor and accepted the compromise tariff.

Free Blacks and African American Abolitionism

Even as the white leaders of South Carolina struggled to define the extent of their powers within the Union, **free blacks** and slaves struggled to define their freedom. Communities of several thousand free blacks lived in every major northern city, establishing their own churches, newspapers, schools, and lodges. More numerous still were free African Americans in the Upper South slave states, especially Maryland and Virginia, and in all the major cities on the Atlantic and Gulf Coasts of the South. These free blacks stayed in contact with African Americans in the North through newspapers, letters, and word passed by the many black sailors who plied the eastern seaboard.

Free blacks throughout the country debated the merits of leaving the United States altogether, as many whites encouraged them to do. The colonization movement struggled in the 1820s. Few black Americans were willing to be shipped to a place they had never seen; only about 1,400 black Americans went to Liberia in the 1820s. African Americans came to see in colonization an attack on their hard-won accomplishments in the United States, insisting that people of color had earned a place in this country. Rather than spending moral energy and money on removing black people, they argued, Americans should work instead on making the United States a fairer place.

David Walker proved to be an important figure in this movement that sought to improve the plight of black Americans. Walker had lived in Charleston at the time of Denmark Vesey's conspiracy in 1822, becoming familiar with the long tradition of revolt and resistance in the Carolina low country. After the suppression of Vesey, Walker moved to Boston. There, he established a used-clothing store, one of the few businesses open to African Americans in the North. Walker did well in the business, bought a home, joined the African Methodist church, and became a black Mason, an organization that fought against slavery and the slave trade. He gave his support to *Freedom's Journal,* an anticolonization paper published by black people in Boston and New York City between 1827 and 1829.

In 1829, Walker released his *Appeal . . . to the Colored Citizens of the World.* Americans, whatever their skin color, had never read such a document. Walker denied that slaves felt or owed any bond to their masters. He called for black spiritual self-renewal, starting with African Americans' recognition of just how angry they were with their lot in the United States. They needed to channel that anger with God's love, Walker urged, making a group effort to end slavery immediately. He did not call for violence but for black Americans to be full Americans in both government and the economy. Condemning Henry Clay's support for removing all free blacks to Africa, Walker accused Clay and those supporting colonization of concocting a "plan to get those of the colored people, who are said to be free, away from those of our brethren whom they unjustly hold in bondage, so that they may be enabled to keep them the more secure in ignorance and wretchedness. . . . For if the free are allowed to stay among the slaves, they will have intercourse together, and . . . the free will learn the slaves *bad habits,* by teaching them that they are MEN . . . and certainly *ought* and *must* be FREE."

Within weeks of its publication, Walker's *Appeal* appeared in Savannah, where it was seized, and then in Milledgeville, Georgia (the state capital), then in Virginia, North Carolina, South Carolina, and New Orleans. The *Appeal* created panic and repression wherever it appeared. Southern whites worried at this evidence of invisible networks of communication and resistance among the slaves, free blacks, and, perhaps, sympathetic whites in their midst. Events in Virginia bore out their worst suspicions.

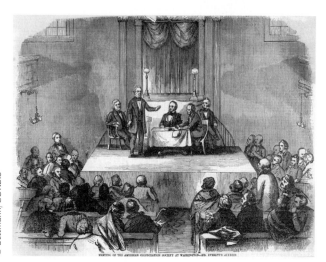

Free African Americans debated the pros and cons of colonizing to Africa.

The Crisis of Slavery in Virginia

Nat Turner was a field hand, born in 1800, who felt that God had called him for more than the lot of a slave. Well known even in his youth for his intellectual abilities and his effectiveness as a preacher, on Sundays Turner traveled throughout the countryside around Southampton County, Virginia, coming to know most of the slaves and free black people who lived there. Praying and fasting, Turner saw visions: drops of blood that formed hieroglyphics on leaves, black shadows across the white moon. These things, he became certain, foretold a slave revolt, of the time "fast approaching when the first should be last and the last should be first." Turner, unlike Gabriel in Richmond in 1800 and Vesey in Charleston in 1822, chose to build his revolt around a small group of select lieutenants rather than to risk

Flashpoints | The Virginia Debate Over the Future of Slavery, 1831–1832

The Southampton Insurrection of August 1831 threw the complex world of Virginia slavery into crisis. The rebellion of Nat Turner and his allies led white people to do what they had never done so openly before and what they would never do again: publicly voice their doubts, anxiety, and even guilt about slavery. Whites, slaveholders and those without slaves, lived among nearly half a million enslaved people. All were enmeshed to some degree by an institution on which their entire society depended.

The Southampton Rebellion, Jane Randolph admitted, "aroused all my fears which had nearly become dormant, and indeed have increased them to the most agonizing degree." She asked her husband, Thomas Jefferson Randolph, grandson of Thomas Jefferson, to consider moving to Ohio, leaving Virginia as so many white people did in these decades. Instead, Randolph decided to bring the problem of slavery

Nat Turner's raid unleashed terror throughout southeastern Virginia, far from Southampton County.

before the Virginia General Assembly, meeting only a few weeks after Nat Turner's execution (and dissection). Thirty-nine years old and elected to state office for the first time, Randolph knew that his grandfather had struggled unsuccessfully with slavery. Jefferson had told the next generation—Randolph's generation—that the problem would be theirs to solve. Maybe this would be the moment.

The grandson of Thomas Jefferson dutifully stood to make the case for gradual emancipation, but could not find the words. Other delegates, though, knew what they wanted to say. Those from the western part of the state, where slavery was not fully entrenched, had long resented the domination of Virginia politics by eastern planters. They argued that slavery was a terrible burden, threatened white political equality, and

that the state should begin a long process of purchasing slaves for colonization. Their opponents, especially from the eastern and middle parts of the state, argued that there was nothing at all wrong with slavery, that it was in fact a blessing to white and black alike. A large group in the middle admitted that slavery hurt Virginia but that they could imagine no practical way to end it.

Black Virginians knew what was being debated. One delegate warned that the enslaved population was an "active, intelligent class, watching and weighing every movement of the Legislature." It was dangerous to discuss the failings of slavery with such people listening.

After weeks of passionate debate, delegates voted narrowly that it was "inexpedient" to act in any way. Rather, they instituted harsher laws for free blacks and enslaved people, removing opportunities for travel, worship, and access to literacy.

The Virginia Slave Debates proved to be a tragic turning point in American history. Never again would the vast majority of white Virginians publicly discuss slavery's flaws. After this moment of doubt, they increased their commitment to slavery's defense, reacted with anger at any criticism of bondage and even monitored what their white neighbors read and said about slavery. Never again would they dare to imagine the end of bondage.

Questions for Reflection

1. Was this a great lost opportunity?

2. Why would Virginians be more likely than other Southerners to debate the future of slavery?

3. Why did such a debate never happen again in the United States?

© The Granger Collection, New York

spreading the word broadly. Their plan was to begin the rebellion on their own and then attract compatriots along the way.

On August 22, 1831, Turner and his band began their revolt. They moved from one isolated farmhouse to the next, killing all the whites they found inside, including children. They gathered horses and weapons. Turner rode at the end of the group, praying for guidance on what plan they should follow. As the night went on, Turner's men had killed about 70 people, starting with the family of Turner's master. By morning, word had rushed to Richmond of the unimaginable events in Southampton. Whites huddled together in Jerusalem, the county seat, and troops arrived to put down the revolt. Blacks, many of whom had no connection with the rebellion, were killed by infuriated and frightened whites hundreds of miles away from Southampton. Turner's troops were all captured or killed, but he managed to escape and to hide in the woods of the county for two months. Once captured, Turner narrated a remarkable "confession" in which he told of his visions and prophecies. He had no regrets and no doubts that God would stand in judgment of the people who held other people in slavery. At his hanging in November, he showed no signs of remorse.

White southerners saw in Nat Turner their worst nightmares. Here was a literate slave, allowed to travel on his own, allowed to spread his own interpretation of the Bible to dissatisfied slaves eager to listen to Turner's prophecies. The crackdown was not long in coming, as delegates to the state assembly gathered in Richmond a month after Turner's execution. In a series of remarkable debates, these white Virginians, some of them sons and grandsons of Thomas Jefferson, John Marshall, and Patrick Henry, openly admitted the debilitating effect of slavery on Virginia. They worried most about slavery's influence on whites, worried that slavery kept the economy from developing as it did in the North. Delegates from western Virginia, where relatively few slaves lived, expressed their misgivings most freely, but even large slaveholders from the East admitted slavery's negative effects. Petitions flowed into Richmond—particularly from the western counties where whites resented the domination of the state by the wealthy minority of tidewater slaveholders—urging the legislators to take a decisive step to rid Virginia of slavery. Defenders of slavery warned that the debates, published in the newspapers and discussed on the streets and in the shops and homes across the state, might result in more revolts. Enslaved Virginians were not an "ignorant herd of Africans," one delegate warned, but an "active, intelligent class, watching and weighing every movement of the Legislature, with perfect knowledge of its bearing and effect."

Some delegates urged that the state purchase all slaves born after a certain date—1840 was proposed—and colonize them in Africa or sell them to plantations farther south. Others argued that the state could not afford such a step, that the Virginia economy would collapse without slavery, that slaves born before the date of freedom would revolt, that property rights guaranteed in the Constitution made it ridiculous to talk about taking slaves from their owners. Others

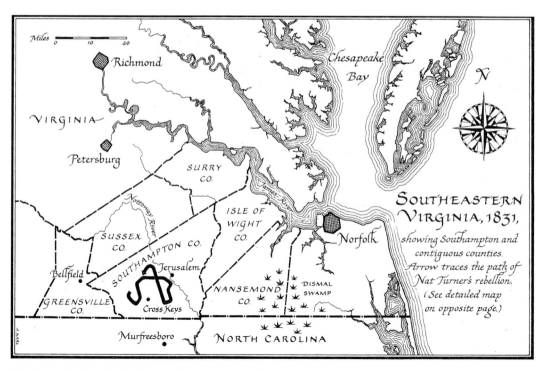

Nat Turner's raid unleashed terror throughout southeastern Virginia, far from Southampton County.

A Voice from the People!

Great Meeting in the Park!!

This poster sought to mobilize New York City's working people in favor of a new labor party.

went much further, arguing that slavery was not wrong at all but rather God's plan for civilizing Africans otherwise lost to heathenism and barbarism. The disparate regions of Virginia found themselves in deep conflict; some discussed separating themselves from the rest of the state if one policy or another were followed. The lawmakers, starkly divided, ultimately decided that it was "inexpedient" to take any step at all against slavery at that time, that it would be left for subsequent legislatures to begin the process that would free Virginia from slavery. In the meantime, they passed harsher laws to limit the movement and gathering of free blacks and slaves.

Political Turmoil and the Election of 1832

Andrew Jackson made fervent enemies as well as devoted followers throughout his presidency. No one could be neutral about him, for he seemed to touch everything in American life. The election of 1832 saw voters and leaders mobilize in opposition or support of Jackson, latching on to a wide range of issues. The president, furious at any resistance, lashed out, determined that his work not be wasted. The nation had never seen such political conflict, as citizens debated issues of the economy, states' rights, and morality.

Taking Sides

In September 1831, the first national political convention in U.S. history met in Baltimore. It was convened by the Anti-Masons. Despite their origins and their name, the Anti-Masons were concerned with the state of American politics in general, not merely with the threat posed by the Masons. They attracted an impressive list of ambitious and accomplished young men to their convention, including many who believed that Jackson, a Mason, was too pro-southern and too callous toward the American Indians. The Anti-Masons promised to become a powerful third party, a wild card in an already tumultuous American politics.

Economic resentment also fueled the conflict of the early 1830s. As prices and rents rose more quickly than wages, urban working people found themselves falling behind. These working men and women felt their contributions slighted in the new economy, their labor no longer bringing the recognition and rewards it deserved. Workers formed unions to defend their rights in cities from New York to Kentucky. They sponsored newspapers, lobbied legislatures, and supported one another during strikes. By the mid-1830s, between 100,000 and 300,000 men and women belonged to unions. Some unions became deeply engaged in politics and put forward their own candidates. While union members generally liked Andrew Jackson's blows against monopoly, they believed he pulled up short in his attack on economic privilege.

The Bank War

Despite the tariffs intended to serve their interests, most people in the Northeast felt they had received little from Andrew Jackson's first term. They viewed him with distrust and growing anger, perceiving in Old Hickory an enemy to moral and commercial progress, a defender of the backward South and West against the East. The fate of the **Second Bank of the United States** stood as the key issue in Easterners' frustration. Many merchants and businessmen, worried about stabilizing the American economy, supported the Bank of the United States and its president Nicholas Biddle. The Bank ensured that state banks kept plenty of metal currency—specie—on hand with which to pay the national bank when asked to do so. Such rules kept the state banks from putting out too many notes, from inflating the currency with paper money unsupported by gold or silver. When the economy fell into trouble, on the other hand, Biddle and the Bank of the United States would lessen their demands on the state banks, preventing panics and deflation.

While businessmen appreciated this role of the bank, many other Americans distrusted it. In their eyes, this largely private institution enjoyed far too much power for its own good or the good of the country. Why should privileged stockholders in the bank, they asked, profit from the business of the federal government? Why should

Picturing the Past — ECONOMICS & TECHNOLOGY

The Bank of the United States as a Monster

This elaborate cartoon conveyed a simple message but with many subtleties that informed people at the time could have decoded. Each of the heads of the "hydra" is labeled with the name of a state, representing the way the "monster" of the Bank of the United States had slithered its way into every corner of the nation. The largest head at the center of the hydra, that of Nicholas Biddle, is labeled "Penn" for Pennsylvania. The soldier on the right

GENERAL JACKSON SLAYING THE MANY HEADED MONSTER.

has dropped his axe, discovering that splitting one of the heads of the hydra only reveals another inside.

President Jackson, elderly and yet still vigorous and determined, wields a sword labeled "veto," killing with a manly thrust a frightening opponent that seemed too formidable for anyone else to conquer. Vice President Martin Van Buren seems to be trying to help, albeit ineffectually. He contributes mainly by exclaiming, "Well done general!"

Jackson vetoed a rechartering of the Bank, proclaiming that the bank was "unauthorized by the constitution, subversive of the rights of the States, and dangerous to the liberties of the people." He moved all federal funds from the Bank of the United States to state banks. The Bank of the United States, deprived of government support, began a slow death.

Jackson's opponents saw the president, not the bank, as the usurper of American rights. How dare he single-handedly overturn what the people, in the form of Congress, had declared to be their will? Henry Clay and other opponents argued that his action posed a far greater threat to the American people than did the bank. If the president could force his way into the lawmaking process, the division of powers laid out in the Constitution would be violated and the Union would risk falling under the despotic rule of a president who would be king.

In the election of 1832 Jackson portrayed himself as the champion of the common man fighting against a bloated aristocracy of privilege and monopoly. Clay, the candidate of the National Republicans, portrayed himself as the defender of the Union against an arrogant and power-hungry president; Clay characterized Jackson as a man who had disregarded morality and justice in his dealing with the American Indians, had corrupted the government with the spoils system, and had attacked the national bank. William Wirt, the candidate of the Anti-Masons, declared himself the opponent of all conspiracies, corruptions, and subversions.

Jackson won by a considerable margin, losing South Carolina to a nullifier, Vermont to the Anti-Masons, and the rest of New England and a few other states to Clay. Emboldened by his majority at the polls, the president went on the offensive. Those opposed to Jackson began to call themselves "Whigs." Like their British namesakes, the American Whigs saw themselves as the counterbalance to otherwise unchecked monarchical power—in this case "King Andrew I," "the most absolute despot now at the head of any representative government on earth."

the national notes be allowed to depress the value of state notes, with their origins closer to home?

For many voters, objections to the Bank of the United States were as much objections to banking and commerce in general as to any specific policies of the national bank. The whole business of banking seemed suspect, with its paper money, its profits seemingly without labor, its government-supported monopolies, its apparent speculation with public money. Andrew Jackson shared these feelings of mistrust: he disliked monopoly, he disliked paper money, and he disliked the Bank of the United States.

The Indian Peoples and the Mexican Nation

Andrew Jackson's administration focused much of its energy on the native peoples of North America. The American Indians held immense areas of the South and the West when Jackson took office, land that many whites wanted and demanded. The southwestern border of the United States remained tantalizingly ambiguous as well. Mexico governed its Texas province loosely and many white Americans coveted that land.

Jackson and the American Indians

Andrew Jackson had announced, and acted upon, his attitudes toward the Indians years before he took office as president. The steady pressing of white population onto the rich lands of the Cherokee, Chickasaw, Creeks, Seminoles, and Choctaws, he thought, left the people of those nations with two choices. They could either become "industrious Citizens" who accepted the sovereignty of the states that claimed the lands on which they lived, or they could "remove to a Country *where* they can retain their ancient customs, so dear to them, that they cannot give up in exchange for regular society." Their only other choice, Jackson thought, was extinction.

White people had mixed feelings about the Indians. Americans of European descent considered the Indians admirable in many ways, dignified and free, able to learn and prosper. Not a few "white" and "black" families were proud to claim some Indian ancestry. Many white Americans, including some in Congress, had long contributed time and money to the Indians, helping to build and staff schools, sending seed and agricultural implements to ease the transition to farming.

By the late 1820s, the "civilized tribes" had adapted themselves to the dominant society. Many of the tribes were led by chiefs of mixed descent, leaders who lived in cabins, houses, and even mansions. Men such as John Ross negotiated land settlements and profited from such deals but also attempted to create systems of political representation and law. He joined the Methodist church and courted any political party he believed best advanced Cherokee interests. The wealthiest Indians, especially the Cherokee, bought African American slaves. The children of the Indian leaders and others went to schools established by white missionaries, who persuaded a considerable number of Indians to convert to Christianity. The Cherokees published a newspaper that included articles in both their own language and in English.

Despite their many adaptations, the Indians of the Southeast showed no desire to leave the land on which they lived in the late 1820s. In their view, they had already given up more land than they should have—millions of acres over the preceding 20 years—and were determined to hold on to what remained. "We would not receive money for land in which our fathers and friends are buried," they declared. Most whites, especially those who lived nearby and coveted the rich cotton lands under the Indians' control, bristled at the continuing presence of the native inhabitants. Many white people longed to banish the American Indians to land on the other side of the Mississippi River, where, it seemed, whites would not want to live for a very long time, if ever.

Jackson told the Indians he was their friend, even their "father," but that he could do nothing to stop their mistreatment except to move them beyond the Mississippi River, where, he promised, they would be safe. The Indians and their supporters, mostly religious people in the North, responded bitterly to such claims, arguing that the rights of the Constitution should certainly extend to people who had lived in North America since time immemorial. But the Jacksonians quickly pushed through the **Indian Removal Act** of 1830. Two Supreme Court decisions in favor of the Cherokees, in 1830 and in 1832, proved to be without effect, since they depended on the federal government to implement them and Jackson had no intention of doing anything of the sort.

In the face of the impending removal, most of the Indian peoples split into pro-assimilation, "progressive," factions and anti-assimilation, "conservative," factions. They debated fiercely and sometimes violently among themselves. Agents, some of mixed blood, swindled the Indians as they prepared for the removal (see Map 10.1). The Choctaws, the first to move, underwent horrific experiences, suffering greatly and dying in large numbers as they traveled in the worst winter on record with completely inadequate supplies. The Creeks, too, confronted frauds and assaults.

The Indians who moved sold whatever they could not take with them, usually at a great loss. Wagons and carts carried the old and the sick, while women and children drove livestock along the trail. Soldiers usually accompanied the Indians, along with an agent to hand out whatever support the government provided. "To see the remnant of a once mighty people fettered and chained together forced to depart from the land of their fathers into a country unknown to them," an Alabama newspaper admitted, "is of itself sufficient to move the stoutest heart."

The Cherokee removal was the most prolonged. After years of negotiating, the government struck a bargain with a small and unrepresentative number of the Cherokee in the Treaty of New Echota in 1836. While groups of several hundred at a time left, including some of the wealthiest, 17,000 refused to leave by the deadline.

Enduring Issues   American Indians—From Allies to Outsiders

When Europeans arrived, over 300 tribes lived in North America, each with its own culture and connections to other groups in networks of trade and communication. There was no single Indian reaction to European contact or the cultural changes that exchange stimulated. Native societies proved resilient and adaptable after European arrival. In spite of devastating population declines caused by disease, Indian societies tolerated settlements by Europeans and incorporated them into local and regional alliances. Colonists relied on Indian knowledge of weather, crops and geography and in turn native peoples rapidly joined local and Atlantic networks of trade.

The departure of the British and the French from the continent was a disaster for Indians. Until 1763, Indians routinely played off the imperial powers to their advantage. Both the British and French governments attempted, however feebly, to restrain their settlers from encroaching on Indian territory. The dual British defeats in the Revolution and War of 1812 destroyed the last potential ally the Indians had against American expansion. Memories of Indian allies against the British during the Revolution or along the frontier were overwritten by tales of native duplicity and of complete hostility to the American nation. These crude generalizations created a history that wrote Indians out of the founding of the United States. Rising populations along the coastlines and the soaring cost of the remaining land drove white migrants westward into lands claimed by Indians and frequently protected by formal treaties. Consider how the term *settler* implies the occupation of empty land—of land waiting for the "proper" care.

As an example, by 1794, the Cherokees made peace with the United States. By the 1820s, they were considered the most "civilized" of all North American tribes, a model and a hope for future relations. They produced a bilingual newspaper, modeled their government on the United States, and their children could attend one of over 60 free public schools with bilingual teachers. Their economy was prosperous, reliant on wheat, cotton, corn, and herds of livestock. Cherokee millers, merchants, storekeepers, and skilled craftsmen routinely served white and native customers. Yet in less than 20 years, they were driven off their lands, depicted as savages and unfit for citizenship in the United States. What happened?

Earlier American leaders had seen a different future for native peoples. Thomas Jefferson spoke openly of his hopes for the future assimilation of Indians into the American nation. In 1787, he wrote, "The Indian is, in mind and body, the equal of the European." Unlike his

view about African Americans, he considered political equality and racial mixing the natural result of Indian embrace of European civilization. While other Americans along the frontier pursued a more violent and exclusive relation with Indians, Jefferson's perspective illustrates that Indians were not always considered as outsiders, unfit for citizenship.

Jefferson's comment reflected a belief of universal brotherhood of men drawn from both the secular Enlightenment and Christian teachings about all mankind's descent from Adam and Eve. As the nineteenth century advanced, European Romantic ideas of blood, race, and nation began to replace universal brotherhood with a vision of race as a set of immutable characteristics. American intellectuals mimicked Europeans and embraced the flattering conceit that white, Anglo-German Protestants occupied the highest stage of human development. Native peoples now held a lesser, fixed position below whites—excluded from the polity and from intermarriage or racial mixing. Jefferson's idea of a future place for Indians in the American nation was forgotten, even denied.

On the ground, activities by missionaries and government agents reflected these "modern" beliefs.

Civilization, in the form of the English language, American law, the Christian faith, and settled agriculture were no longer sufficient for acceptance into the American nation. Unlike earlier practices, Indians would no longer be brothers or allies, but dependents on the same level as women, children, and slaves—subject to the authority of white men. Repeatedly missionaries and traders were shocked and enraged that Indians would resist their demands, argue for their rights, and physically resist. The expected reaction was one of gratitude, obedience, and silence—the role laid out for dependents in antebellum America. Failure to conform to theses expectations justified the use of force, of dispossession.

Those native peoples who followed the Jeffersonian ideal to citizenship through civilization met the bitterest fate. Scorned by traditionalists for their acceptance of white culture and practices, they were violently rejected by Americans in spite of their tangible adoption of American language, faith, and economic practices. The Five Civilized Tribes, among others, had many members who fully adopted white farming practices, including chattel slavery, livestock, and sale of staple crops in regional markets. An irony is that is was this erosion of tight tribal loyalties and older forms of political identity that permitted white speculators and government agents to sign agreements with individuals and small groups selling large tracts of land. Indians' integration into the American economy and their civilized pursuit of individual profit reflected their acceptance of the contemporary habits of land speculation and rejection of traditional Indian concept that land was held in common for the benefit and use of the clan or tribe.

Racism, ostracism and exclusion from membership and participation in the American polity grew in the nineteenth century. Even as easterners romanticized the Indians their ancestors had slaughtered and dispossessed, the last organized sizeable Indian presence was forcibly removed from east of the Mississippi. The example of the Five Civilized Tribes marked the end of serious attempts at native inclusion in the American nation. Their very success made Americans uneasy.

In spite of missionaries' reports, of tangible evidence to the contrary, even the Supreme Court formally defined Indians as "fierce savages, whose occupation was war, and whose subsistence was drawn chiefly from the forest." Indians were declared savage hunters in spite of the reality of their farms, plantations, slaves, and collective agricultural pursuits. This portrayal made the government policy and its public acceptance more palatable, particularly in the Northeast where most Indians had been reduced to marginal lives or the South where the desire for gold and cotton lands reserved for Indians fired the greed of white neighbors. Legal opinions reflected the popular belief that natives were vanishing, that as cultivation advanced, Indian people fled into forests and wilderness. Many of the hundreds of prints of the West produced and circulated before 1860 depicted the land as empty, the plains as wasteland, with the few native peoples peeking out from forest edges or relegated to the images' fringes.

By the 1840s, Americans' territorial expansion had created a continental empire comprised of former lands claimed by Britain, Texas, and Mexico. Native peoples' increased dependence in an era that treasured independence reinforced ideas that they were a hindrance who blocked the nation's "Manifest Destiny." By the time Americans were moving into Oregon and California, native peoples could expect little assistance from the federal government in checking brutal expulsions driven by the discovery of gold and sale of their lands by eastern speculators.

Native people were not silent in the face of this pressure. During the final year of Andrew Jackson's presidency, when Indian Removal was at its peak, William Apess, a Pequot from New England, delivered a series of stinging rebukes to the narratives about the spread of liberty across the continent. He described the few remaining Indians of New England as the "monument to the cruelty of those who came to improve our race." Apess certainly intended his audiences to focus not only on the ugly realities of past treatment of native peoples, but to consider the future. His reminder of earlier promises of aid, of civilization, of treaties easily broken did little to slow the pace of dispossession, but it served notice that the degraded position of native peoples in antebellum America was not accidental.

Questions for Reflection

1. What drove the changes in American thinking about the place of Native Americans in the United States?

2. Why were stories of the extinction or vanishing of native peoples so popular in American writings and art of the nineteenth century?

3. Explain why the shift in rhetoric depicting native peoples as the children of the president is so significant. What rights did dependent peoples have in antebellum America?

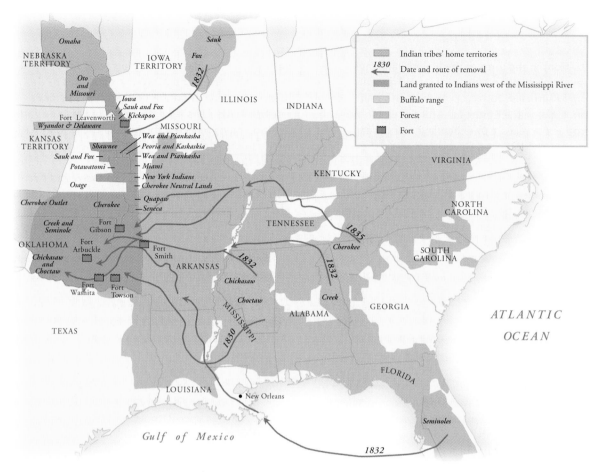

MAP 10.1 Removal of the American Indians

In the 1830s, the Indians of the North and South were "removed" to reservations in Oklahoma and Kansas.

General Winfield Scott then led 7,000 troops against them, driving people from their homes empty-handed, marching them to stockades and shipping them out by rail and water. About a quarter of all eastern Cherokees died on what they called the Trail of Tears. Some Cherokees remained in the mountains of North Carolina and Tennessee, but the power of the eastern Indians was destroyed.

The Seminoles fought against removal as long as they could. Led by Osceola, the son of an English trader and the husband of an escaped slave, the Seminoles tried to break the will of the whites by killing soldiers and civilians and by burning their crops and homes. The Second Seminole War launched by the federal government to remove the 5,000 Indians began in 1836 and dragged on for six years. The conflict proved both unpopular and unsuccessful. About 36,000 U.S. soldiers fought and 1,500 died; many more suffered debilitating disease. The federal government spent $20 million in the fight, even though few white people wanted to settle on the Seminoles' land. The United States captured Osceola only by deception at a supposed peace conference. He died in captivity a few months later, after which

some Seminoles finally migrated to Oklahoma. But most of the Seminole people, able to live in the swampy landscape, were never driven out of Florida.

Fighting also erupted in the Illinois Territory between white settlers and the Sac and Fox Indians. These people, under the leadership of Black Hawk, saw

DOING HISTORY ONLINE

Newspapers

African Americans began publishing a newspaper in 1827 and the Cherokee did the same in 1828. Just over a decade later women working in New England factories also started a number of papers, such as the *Factory Girl*, the *Voice of Industry*, the *Wampanoag and Operatives' Journal*, and the *Lowell Offering*. Read the documents in this module. Why do you imagine these groups turned to newsprint?

History ⧖ Now™   Visit HistoryNOW to access primary sources and exercises related to this topic: http://now.ilrn.com/ayers_etal3e

Woolaroc Museum, Bartlesville, Oklahoma

The Cherokee called their forced migration to Oklahoma the Trail of Tears. About 4,000 of the 15,000 Indians forced to move died along the way, as did more than 25,000 of the 100,000 southeastern Indians who were driven from their homes in these years.

their lands along the Mississippi River taken over by whites while the Indians were on a hunting expedition in 1832. The whites burned the Indians' huts and plowed under their fields. In retaliation, the Sac and Fox destroyed white settlements. A large contingent of volunteers (including a young Abraham Lincoln), regular troops, and allied Indians set out after Black Hawk and his people, who also had allies from other Indian nations. Eventually, the whites outnumbered Black Hawk and overran his camp, killing nearly 500 as they tried to cross the Mississippi River. Taken prisoner, Black Hawk refused to repent, telling his captors that he "has done nothing for which an Indian ought to be ashamed. He has fought for his countrymen, the squaws and papooses, against white men who came, year after year, to cheat them and take away their land." Black Hawk's words and deeds, widely reported in the newspapers of the country, attracted considerable sympathy among whites in the East. Andrew Jackson met with Black Hawk and pardoned him; the warrior's autobiography became a best-seller.

Conflict with Mexico

In the wake of the Panic of 1819, speculators and settlers from the United States immigrated to Mexican

Texas in the 1820s and 1830s. Sometimes the Mexican officials encouraged the newcomers; at other times, they sought to slow American settlement. Mexican land was far more favorable in terms of price and size of grant than the United State government offered in the 1820s. Prospective immigrants to Texas simply had to swear allegiance to the Mexican government, promise to raise their children as Catholics, and settle in territory under the authority of a leader recognized by Mexico City. Mexico wanted settlers on its vulnerable northern border but did not want the slaves that white settlers often brought with them. The Mexican government, however, was far away and local Mexican authorities, some of them originally Americans, accepted the practice of slavery despite the Mexican constitutional ban against it. The absence of Catholic clergy also made the laws regarding religion unenforceable.

A key leader in the American migration was Stephen F. Austin, a Virginia-born entrepreneur who first arrived in Mexico in 1821 on the heels of Mexican independence. Throughout the 1820s, Austin, negotiating with the changing Mexican governments, allotted and registered land parcels and oversaw the settlement of hundreds of Americans. Most of the American settlers were not slaveholders, but the majority of them were southerners and

Osceola, the leader of the Seminoles, resisted the United States for years in hard fighting in Florida.

they argued that they had to have slaves if Texas were to develop as both they and Mexican leaders hoped.

In the 1830s, as General **López de Santa Anna** consolidated his power in Mexico, his attempts to centralize control in Mexico City led to revolts in the Yucatan and Zacatecas as well as in Texas. Settlers increasingly came into conflict with the Mexican government when provincial officials attempted to collect tariffs and slow immigration into the district. Austin and the others petitioned the Mexican government to let them become a separate Mexican state under its own administration, but they were rebuffed when Santa Anna took control of the government. In Santa Anna's eyes, the Texans were clearly inviting an expansionist United States to take this province away from Mexico; he sent in troops to meet the threat.

In 1835, a convention of Texans replaced Austin as commander of the army with Sam Houston and created a provisional government to fight against Santa Anna under their rights as Mexican citizens as outlined in the Constitution of 1824. This was not a vote for independence; those seeking immediate independence were defeated 33 to 15 when a vote was taken. Austin was sent east, offering large amounts of land to all who would come help in the struggle.

Volunteers and money flowed into Texas from throughout the United States, where people had been

Picturing the Past — POLITICS & DIPLOMACY

The Alamo

A small force of Americans and *tejanos* were overwhelmed at the Alamo mission in San Antonio. Although the Mexican army won the battle, its victory unleashed the support of the United States for the Texans. Almost from the moment of the battle, the Alamo became the object of mythmaking. The press of the United States turned the men inside the mission into valiant heroes and imagined their deaths in

ways that embodied the highest standards of masculine self-sacrifice. The newspapers back east talked little of the *tejanos* and instead celebrated the white soldiers in the Alamo as the vanguard of American civilization and decried the Mexicans as bloodthirsty and inhuman mercenaries defeating the men from the United States through sheer numbers.

watching the area's events with great interest. Southern states in particular sent hundreds of men. Nevertheless, they were greatly outnumbered by the Mexicans, who decimated the Texans at several initial battles. As the Mexican army sought to occupy San Antonio, 188 rebels—including Davy Crockett of Tennessee, famous for his frontier exploits—took refuge in the Mission of the Alamo. Most of the people inside were American or European immigrants, but they were joined by *tejanos,* Mexicans of the province who allied themselves with the revolt for independence. The defenders of the Alamo held out against 3,000 Mexican soldiers for nearly two weeks in 1836, until the Mexicans finally stormed the mission and killed all inside except three white women, two white children, and an African American slave. The Mexicans stripped the bodies of the insurrectionists and burned them. After the Alamo, Texans were committed to creating an independent state and support for the rebellion grew rapidly in the United States, where it came to be seen as a moral struggle between the forces of freedom and the forces of autocracy. "Remember the Alamo" became the rallying cry.

Santa Anna seemed on the verge of victory until Sam Houston, the general of the Texan forces, surprised the larger Mexican force at San Jacinto in April of 1836. Rushing toward the Mexican camp, a force of 900 Texans and *tejano* cavalry commanded by **Juan Seguín** won a decisive battle in only 18 minutes. Santa Anna himself was captured a day later. As a prisoner, he signed treaties removing Mexican troops from Texas, granting Texas its independence, and recognizing the Rio Grande as the boundary. The Mexican Congress, when they heard of this capitulation, announced that they would not be bound by its terms.

Texans and many Americans elsewhere urged the U.S. government to annex the new republic before it could be retaken by the Mexicans. That plea unleashed a heated and protracted debate between advocates of American expansion and those who thought such a step would be immoral and impolitic. Much of the debate raged between southerners, who saw Texas as a vast new empire, and northerners, especially abolitionists, who opposed annexation because it would lead to slavery's expansion. The fate of Texas was to be a key political issue for the next decade.

The Expanding Role of Religion

The power and influence of Protestant churches surged to a new level in the Jacksonian era. Far more than in any previous generation, during the Jacksonian years the churches took leading roles in every facet of life and in every part of the Union. Revivals pulled in scores of new members, firing them with the desire to remake their lives. Many of those who experienced the spiritual

To outside observers, the revivals of the Second Great Awakening appeared as frightening scenes of chaos and unsettled relations between men and women.

rebirth of the revivals sought ways to demonstrate their faith and their hope for America. A radical new movement against slavery gathered force with stunning speed. At the same time, other Americans sought purer forms of religion itself, listening to prophets who spoke of new churches and new possibilities. Everywhere in the late 1820s and early 1830s, religion seemed on people's lips.

Revivalism

Since the late eighteenth century, revivals led by the major Protestant denominations had periodically inflamed the United States. In those revivals, people who had never declared their faith in Jesus Christ or who had fallen away from the church made public expressions of their faith. Thousands of people gathered across the nation and along the frontier, in town and countryside, to pray and hear ministers tell them of God's love and forgiveness. Hearing of these gifts, and aware of their own sinfulness, men and women sometimes fell to the ground as if stricken. Others cried and screamed. The churches that devoted themselves to spreading the Gospel—known as "evangelical" churches because they sought to spread the "evangel," the Gospel—periodically experienced revivals or "awakenings" when numbers of people expressed or renewed their faith. This revivalism burst out again in the mid-1820s.

Desires for personal relationship with God and a sense of community often linked new religious leaders with recent scientific advances to encourage beliefs in spiritualism, magnetic healing, phrenology, and mesmerism. Science and religion were not seen by those in the early nineteenth century as incompatible, as both the supernatural and scientific could explain the individual's role in creation and reflect God's power.

Many ministers and churches across the country were swept up in the religious awakening of the 1820s, but one man embodied its new and aggressive spirit: **Charles Grandison Finney.** Finney, a young attorney from Utica, New York, who had not regularly attended church until encouraged to do so by his fiancée, suddenly found himself struck with the power of God's love. "An overwhelming sense" of his wickedness brought Finney to his knees. "I wept aloud like a child [and] the Holy Spirit descended upon me in a manner that seemed to go through me body and soul," he recalled. "I could feel the impression like a wave of electricity, going through and through me." Finney spread the word of the Bible in the plain and straightforward language of everyday life. He told people that they had it within their power to take the first step toward God and that God would listen.

Finney found in the new cities of western New York a receptive audience among young men, on their own in a rapidly changing America, and among women of every age. The churches, these people believed, had grown cold in the hands of the established ministry and needed a revival of spirit. They wanted a Christianity of activity, of prayer meetings, of spreading the word any way they could. Finney's influence grew in strength and numbers as women prayed with one another. The district of upstate New York that lay along the path of the Erie Canal became known as "The Burned-Over District," as one revival after another surged through its towns and farms. Americans also became accustomed to selecting the minister and church they felt best met their spiritual needs, a break from older generations' loyalties to local churches and family traditions.

The revivals took on a new scale and urgency in 1830 as they ignited Rochester. Like other rapidly growing towns and cities along the Erie Canal, Rochester was ripe for revival. Many people worried that the people of the young city barely knew one another and that husbands and wives, workers and employers, rich and poor, were drifting apart. Politics appeared a morass of selfishness; alcohol seemed to drown hopes of social progress and family happiness; men seemed more concerned with their businesses, lodges, and politics than with their souls. When Finney came to town in 1830, he was met by people hungry for a new message.

Women's prayer groups met daily and traveled from home to home in efforts to bring the word of Jesus. Women pleaded with their husbands to listen to the

Reverend Finney. Employers made it clear to the men who worked under them that it would be noticed whether or not they attended the revival. These efforts, combined with Finney's masterful sermons and hopeful message, brought hundreds of people into the church who had not come before and reclaimed many who had strayed. All the Protestant denominations worked together, setting aside for a while their differences on baptism and other doctrines.

Such a powerful revival seemed evidence to many people that America could be changed by faith. As they watched saloons shut down, families brought together, and shops and stores closed while the revival was in progress, it appeared that the way was being prepared for God's kingdom on earth. If the United States could be adequately reformed, these people believed, the day of redemption could be hastened. The American Tract Society, eager to improve the nation's moral state, had delivered roughly 5 million gospel tracts by 1828 to homes across the nation, one for every three people in the United States. It was up to Americans themselves to purge their country of sin, to make themselves better, and then to help others see the way as well. Such faith bred a demand for immediate reforms.

The Birth of Mormonism

Like many American families of these years, that of **Joseph Smith** could not find a secure place. His father dreamed of bringing his family out of poverty, moving them from one community to another. Young Joseph, like hundreds of other people in upstate New York, sought his fortune by looking for treasure rumored to have been buried long ago in the mountains; he watched with concern for his soul, too, as revivals came and went without his conversion. Smith reported that he felt the presence of an angel, however, who told him "that God had work for me to do, and that my name should be for good and evil among all nations, kindreds, and tongues. He said there was a book hidden, written upon gold plates, giving an account of the former inhabitants of this continent, and the source from which they sprang. He also said that the fullness of the everlasting Gospel was contained in it." Smith claimed that the angel directed him to the location of the sacred writings.

Smith began to transcribe what he had found; sitting in a tent divided by a partition, he read the plates to an assistant on the other side. *The Book of Mormon* took shape, telling of a struggle between the chosen ones and their persecutors, of a promised land reserved for the righteous. North America, the book said, had been visited by Jesus in the distant past but the people had lost their way and fallen into disputation. Those people had crops of the Latter-Day Saints. The Mormons found no peace for the next decade. They were constantly harassed by non-Mormons who feared the growing number of converts and the local economic power that came from the church members' pooled resources and hard work.

Character Development

The early nineteenth century saw a new emphasis in American life, a new focus on what people called "character." In a society so mobile, so disconnected from traditional sources of stability and identity, people felt the need for new ways of ensuring appropriate behavior. Americans looked to new kinds of institutions suited for a new age, institutions that could better deal with strangers, new people, those cut off from older forms of social stability. Americans turned first to families, imparting to them primary responsibility for creating virtuous children and husbands.

Women at Home and Beyond

As Americans looked about them, they became concerned that little seemed to be holding their society together. People moved far beyond the reach of government and beyond the eyes of their parents and communities. Men and women married at younger ages and left home far earlier than their parents had. The opening of land in the West undermined one of the principal forms of control exercised by fathers in earlier generations: the promise of passing on land to sons who stayed and worked at home. Now, sons could acquire land in the West with or without the support of their parents. Daughters might marry earlier, begin families of their own, and move far away. The American population skyrocketed as so many young families established themselves.

The new economy, too, caused concern for many. Increasingly, men and women seemed pulled in different directions, away from a sole focus on the family farm or family artisan shop. Men found new opportunities in town, in businesses and shops in a central area. Young men often worked for wages for a number of employers rather than serving for many years with one master. The lives of middle-class women, too, changed, especially in towns and cities. Bakeries, butcher shops, clothiers, and candlemakers began to offer, more easily and cheaply, some of the things that women had long labored to produce at home. Schools and academies became more common, providing a place for children to receive education beyond the bounds of the home. Young women from poorer backgrounds came into cities looking for jobs as maids and laundresses, taking away some of the household burden for women

Joseph Smith was the founder of the Church of Jesus Christ of Latter-Day Saints, also known as the Mormons.

© Bettmann/CORBIS

been cursed by God for their sins and marked with dark skins; their descendants were the American Indians, who had forgotten their lost paradise.

After 1830 Joseph Smith and several followers traveled throughout New York selling copies of what they called the "Gold Bible." They were met with hostility virtually everywhere they went, but they slowly gathered converts to their Church of Jesus Christ of Latter-Day Saints. Many of the new members were poor, including some free blacks, but others had considerable resources. The most important converts were two brothers, Brigham and Joseph Young. As the movement gathered momentum, hundreds of people joined the church; entire congregations of churches of other faiths joined the Mormons and contributed everything they owned to the church's common fund. The faithful moved first to Ohio and then to what Smith believed to be the original Eden: Missouri. But other settlers made no secret of their disapproval of the Mormons: they fired shots, threw stones through windows, and burned the

Jeremiah Pearson Hardy, "Catherine Wheeler Hardy and Her Daughter Anne Eliza Hardy" 1842. Museum of Fine Arts, Boston, M. and M. Karolik Collection

Depictions such as this portrait of Catherine Wheeler Hardy and her daughter celebrated the quiet domestic space enjoyed by children and presided over by the mother.

well off enough to hire them. Families in towns and cities had fewer children with each passing decade.

As ministers, journalists, and other opinion makers looked upon the changing households of the Northeast, they began to articulate an ideal of what has been called "domesticity." Women, they said, should put their minds to higher purposes, focusing more on nurturing their children in spirit and mind as well as in body. Women would become the moral center of the household, the guardians of good thoughts, clean living, providers of a sense of safety for children and husbands. While the world beyond the household seemed increasingly threatening and disorienting, women could make the home a place of refuge and renewal.

Many middle-class women welcomed this message and this mission. It fit well with their own experiences and their own aspirations. In a time when public life made almost no provisions for female participation and when women found virtually no well-paying jobs open to them, the elevation of the home promised an elevation of women's role. Men believed what they said: they thought women naturally better than themselves, more moral and feeling, more intuitive and spiritual. Men worried about the coarseness and callousness of the tumultuous marketplace even as they enjoyed the sense of freedom, excitement, and possibility that the marketplace offered.

Domesticity asked something of men as well. If the home were to be a haven, the center of society, men would have to make a greater investment in those homes than had their fathers. Men needed to acknowledge the feelings of their wives more, speaking in tones of respect and affection, respecting their wishes about sex and children. Fathers were expected to spend more time with their children, providing a firm male model to accompany the softer nurture of their wives. Drinking and cursing had no place at home.

This ideal remained beyond the reach of many Americans. Women who had to work for others all day had little time to devote to their own families. Men who could not be certain of their next day's wages could not afford to keep children out of the workforce into their late teens. Slave families struggled to stay together in any way they could. Nevertheless, this middle-class ideal was elaborated and celebrated in print and sermons across the growing young nation.

An Eruption of Reform Movements

The same Americans who promoted the Christian, middle-class home as their ideal looked to other institutions and reforms in the 1820s to help remake American society. They sought to extend the ideals of character, self-control, and education to those who seemed to fall beyond the good effects of family and household. They worried about hungry children, desperate fathers, and distraught mothers. They noticed increasing numbers of women selling themselves on the city streets. They decried bulging jails and streets full of people without homes. They worried over the many young men and women who seemed adrift in this rootless new society. Reformers tapped the domestic impulses of improvement for the society as a whole.

Groups of reform-minded people mobilized themselves in the Northeast to counter these problems. Some of their efforts grew out of the churches, while others grew out of the ideals of the American Revolution and the marketplace. The American Bible Society launched an ambitious drive to put Bibles in every American home, pioneering steam presses and national systems of distribution, and ultimately issuing over 32 million Bibles.

The American Sunday School Union wrote and published materials for children to be used in Sunday schools across the country. Those schools, while based in churches, taught reading and writing as well as religion. The American Tract Society produced millions of short inspirational pamphlets to reach those who might not set foot in a church or pick up a Bible. The new organizations prided themselves on being national in reach, extending to the Northwest and Southwest, knitting Americans together with a common faith. They preached nothing controversial, claiming only to spread the good news of the Protestant Christian faith. They depended on the hard

Penal reformers placed great faith in silence, order, and work, helping put the United States in the forefront of the growing penitentiary movement.

work of women, who filled the membership rolls and helped raise funds.

Reformers created a new kind of institution—the "penitentiary"—in these years for those apparently most in need of reform: criminals. In a penitentiary, unlike a common jail, criminals would be locked in individual cells, free from the contamination of others, alone with their conscience and the Bible. There, reflecting on their crimes, they would become "penitent" and would emerge as better people. They would undergo some of the moral nurture they had obviously missed as children and would be ready to take their place in the economy of wages, self-discipline, and delayed gratification growing in the United States. Americans were proud of their penitentiaries, among the first in the world, holding them up as examples of what the enlightened new nation could do.

Alongside penitentiaries, asylums for the deaf and blind, for the insane, for orphans, and for the poor began to appear in the 1820s, replacing more informal kinds of care. Dorothea Dix became famous throughout the United States for her often lonely crusade on behalf of people otherwise forgotten. Dix lobbied ceaselessly for the construction of cleaner, healthier, and more hopeful kinds of institutions for those who could not care for themselves. Each institution placed its faith in strict order, in moral teaching, and in faith in the inherent good of human nature.

Abolitionism

Two hundred antislavery societies emerged in the early 1830s. Ground that had been prepared by the evangelical crusades of the preceding few years proved fertile for the antislavery cause. Some northern church members argued that it was the duty of good Christians to cast out slaveholders and to work for immediate emancipation, to use the enormous power of the church as a force for freedom.

These "immediatists" called for slaveholders to recognize the truth of what the abolitionists were saying, to free their slaves immediately, hire them as free workers, and help repay the former slaves for their years of unpaid toil. These early abolitionists hoped to convert the slaveholders by persuasion and prayer, by church and newspaper—not by law and force.

In the late 1820s, **William Lloyd Garrison,** the young editor of a prohibition newspaper, attended antislavery meetings held by African Americans, including the group that published the first antislavery newspaper, *Freedom's Journal.* Garrison suddenly saw the limitations of the colonization movement as he witnessed the passion of people such as David Walker. The balding and bespectacled young Garrison sought out other financial supporters and a partner to launch a paper of his own: *The Liberator.* It called for the immediate start toward emancipation, explicitly rejecting colonization. In 1831, the paper's first year, it had only six subscribers, but it acquired 53 by the following year, most of them African American. "I *will* be as harsh as truth," Garrison announced, "and as uncompromising as justice. On this subject, I do not wish to think, speak, or write, with moderation. . . . I am earnest—I will not equivocate—I will not excuse—I will not retreat a single inch—AND I WILL BE HEARD." He was. *The Liberator* spread the news of abolition to many whites who never saw a newspaper edited by black people. Ironically, Garrison's argument was spread far and wide by newspaper editors who denounced him.

William Lloyd Garrison played a key role in persuading many northern whites that slavery was morally wrong and should be brought to an immediate end.

The American Anti-Slavery Society formed in Philadelphia in 1833. Looking to the example of Great Britain, where the major denominations supported the antislavery movement that was at that moment triumphing over slavery in the British West Indies, the members of the society expected American church leaders to take the lead against American slavery. The North would have to be converted before it could expect the South to follow. To convert the North, antislavery organizations held out the prospect of a free South, where 2 million freed slaves would constitute an "immense market" for the products of Northern "mechanics and manufacturers." These abolitionists expected the former slaves to remain in the South; they spoke little of the competition the freed people might provide to the workers of the North. Similarly, the antislavery people believed a free South would prosper, with planters and free whites flourishing as they had never flourished before; the South, they claimed, would "exhibit the flush of returning health, and feel a stronger pulse, and draw a freer breath."

The antislavery organizations proved volatile inside as well as out. Far more than any other organizations in the United States at this time, the antislavery cause brought together male and female, black and white, patrician and working class, Quaker and Unitarian, Baptist and Methodist, radical and moderate, political and antipolitical people. Each of these groups had its own vision of how the abolitionists should spend their energies and influence. Black abolitionists, in particular, wanted the organizations to do more to help black communities in the North. Black women such as Maria W. Stewart published pamphlets that cried out that it "is of no use for us to wait any longer for a generation of well educated men to arise. We have slumbered and slept too long already; the day is far spent; the night of death approaches. . . . Let every colored man throughout the United States, who possesses the spirit and principles of a man, sign a petition to Congress, to abolish slavery in the District of Columbia, and grant you the rights and privileges of common free citizens."

The antislavery societies used pamphlets, leaflets, and other literature as their major weapons. Rapid innovations in printing lowered the cost of producing such materials, which flooded post offices and streets. The postal campaign reached its peak in 1834 and 1835, when a million pieces went out through the mail, much of it to the South, where the abolitionists hoped to appeal directly to ministers and others who might be willing to listen to their pleas. That literature, white southerners furiously protested, virtually invited slaves to follow Nat Turner's example. Georgia slaveholders offered a $12,000 reward for the capture of wealthy merchant Arthur Tappan, who, along

Abolitionists used images such as this to publicize attacks on their efforts to spread their messages against slavery.

with his brother Lewis, funded much of the postal campaign against slavery. Arthur received a slave's severed ear in the mail. Mobs in Charleston seized sacks of mail from northern cities and burned them in the streets.

The pamphlets infuriated people in much of the North as well. Mobs, led by some of the wealthiest merchants of northern towns but constituted in large part by white working people, rose up violently against the abolitionists. In 1835 mobs destroyed the home of African Americans, pelted antislavery speakers, and dragged William Lloyd Garrison himself through the streets of Boston at the end of a rope. The leaders of that mob announced that they had assaulted Garrison "to assure our brethren of the South that we cherish rational and correct notions on the subject of slavery." Many white northerners believed the abolitionists to be hypocrites who cared nothing for America and everything for their own sanctimonious souls. Antislavery speakers risked a mob every time they spoke; one man counted over 150 attacks made on him. Abolitionists' churches were blown up and their school buildings dragged into swamps.

The persecution, ironically, strengthened the abolitionist cause. Denunciation and harassment only made the abolitionists more certain of the need for their efforts, of the moral decay caused by slavery. The 200 antislavery societies of 1835 grew to more than 500 in 1836. The reformers flooded Congress with petitions calling for the end of slavery in the District of Columbia, sending more than 300 petitions signed by 40,000 people. The acceptance of these petitions by the House, southerners argued, besmirched slaveholders' honor and threatened to incite slaves to rebellion; the southerners said the petitions should be rejected out of hand. Congress sought to avoid conflict by merely tabling the petitions, but the compromise pleased no one.

Over the next decade, northerners of even a mild antislavery bent chafed at this **"gag rule,"** which they saw as

DOING HISTORY ONLINE

Abolitionism

The dominant narrative of American history has always cast white people such as William Lloyd Garrison and the Grimké sisters as the most important, if not the only, abolitionists in antebellum America. Having read the documents in this unit, how might you restructure this narrative?

History⊗Now™ Visit HistoryNOW to access primary sources and exercises related to this topic: http://now.ilrn.com/ayers_etal3e

a clear violation of American freedom in the interests of slavery. Former President John Quincy Adams fought back in 1837 by attempting to present a petition from 22 slaves. Representatives from Georgia and Alabama demanded that Adams be expelled and the petition "taken from the House and burnt or the southern states would withdraw from the House." In their fury to squelch any petitions to Congress on the subject of slavery, southern representatives failed to notice that the petition from the slaves did not advocate abolition. Angered and embarrassed at Adam's trickery, one Mississippian decried this "outrage that has no parallel in parliamentary history" and condemned Adams as one who "rejoiced in the alarm and excitement he occasions like the midnight incendiary who fires the dwelling of his enemy, and listens with pleasure to the screams of his burning victims."

Conclusion

Few peacetime eras in American history have seen greater changes than the years between 1829 and 1836. The seeds for many of the major events of the next several generations were planted during these years. Westward migration and an increasingly complex economy and society changed the nature of everyday life.

The political system, feeling its way during the first generations of nationhood, aligned into the forms it would follow into the twenty-first century: highly mobilized and antagonistic parties that extended their reach into every community in the nation. Andrew Jackson solidified the Democrats around his power, patronage, and popular appeal. His embrace of the spoils system gave political identity a concrete and immediate meaning for the thousands of officeholders across the United States. His defeat of the Bank of the United States showed what a determined president could do with the authority of his office.

American Indians, who had struggled for more than two centuries with the consequences of European coloniza-

tion and growth, were finally driven from their ancestral lands in the early 1830s. Andrew Jackson, dedicated to expanding opportunity for white men, oversaw the forced removal of many thousands of Creeks, Choctaws, Cherokee, and Chickasaws to reservations on the western side of the Mississippi River. The Trail of Tears opened vast amounts of land to settlement by white Americans. Since much of this land lay in the South, Indian displacement also opened the way for the spread of plantation slavery to some of the richest lands in North America.

African Americans, who had glimpsed freedom during the era of the American Revolution and its afterglow, saw their hopes diminish in the wake of increased surveillance and repression following Nat Turner's Rebellion in Virginia and the frantic expansion of slave-based plantations throughout the Gulf States. The Virginia legislature walked to the brink of emancipation in the early 1830s, only to pull back at the last minute.

Determined and purposeful, African Americans launched a campaign to begin the immediate end of slavery. Starting within free black communities, these men and women organized themselves to denounce colonization to Africa and to demand that the United States embrace their black residents as full citizens and as full participants in American life. David Walker's *Appeal* electrified those who read it—and those who read it included enslaved men and women all along the Atlantic seaboard.

William Lloyd Garrison of Boston, hearing and understanding the new black message of immediate emancipation—abolition—threw himself into the crusade for African American freedom. White southerners and others opposed to his challenge to slavery gave Garrison a wide notoriety and helped galvanize other supporters for abolitionism.

Abolitionism found a ready audience in part because Christian Americans, who had seen their churches dislocated by the churning movement of the young nation's population in the decades after the Revolution, experienced a rebirth. With revivals emerging across the United States, Christians felt themselves, their communities, and their nation prepared to help bring forth a more nearly perfect society. While some focused on alcohol and others on spreading the word through distributing Bibles, others decided to focus on what they considered the worst American sin: slavery.

The slave states, faced with this new opposition, struggled to define their relationship to the federal government so that local power would not be diminished. South Carolina, the most unified slave state, defied federal power in the Nullification Crisis, focusing on the issue of the tariff to test the boundaries of authority. Under Andrew Jackson's strong leadership, the federal government stared South Carolina down and made it clear that efforts to defy the power of Washington would bring sharp consequences.

But the slave states, under attack from enslaved people, abolitionists, and President Jackson, provoked another kind of victory. The United States sided with American insurrectionists who sought to take Texas from Mexico. Southern slaveholders viewed Texas jealously and coveted the rich lands of the Mexican province. The conflict they started would soon grow into a full-fledged war.

The Chapter in Review

In the years between 1829 and 1836:

- Andrew Jackson became the most active president the United States had yet seen.
- Slaves were involved in revolts in South Carolina and Virginia.
- Savery generated a debate over nullification in South Carolina and wide-ranging debate over the future of the institution in Virginia.
- The Bank of the United States became a major focus of political conflict.

- President Jackson led a determined and successful effort to remove eastern American Indians to west of the Mississippi River.
- The Second Great Awakening shook the nation.
- A movement for the immediate abolition of slavery emerged in the North.

Making Connections Across Chapters

LOOKING BACK

Chapter 10 describes a series of dramatic changes that burst upon the American scene during the early 1830s. During these years the forces of democracy came into direct conflict with the forces of slavery.

1. Why did the U.S. government finally decide to remove American Indians from the eastern part of the country, after they had lived alongside whites for so many generations?

2. Why did the abolitionist movement suddenly come into prominence, when white Americans had lived with slavery for so long?

3. Why did so many people, both male and female, look to women as the moral guardians of American society? How could the idea of the moral superiority of women both improve and hinder women's public roles? Their private lives?

LOOKING AHEAD

Chapter 11 shows the two-party system would prove to be a permanent part of the United States. It came into being by accident and at first had little to do with the major problem that would face the nation over the next two generations: the place of slavery in America.

1. What would be the consequences of having political power exercised by two distinct and highly mobilized parties in every county in the United States?

2. What could be done to slow the spread of slavery without abolishing it?

Recommended Readings

Bay, Mia. *The White Image in the Black Mind: African-American Ideas about White People, 1830–1925* (2000) provides a helpful perspective.

Feller, Daniel. *The Jacksonian Promise: America, 1815–1840* (1995) offers a recent, upbeat overview.

Freehling, Allison Goodyear. *Drift Toward Dissolution: The Virginia Slavery Debate of 1831–1832* (1982) presents a useful interpretation of the crisis in Virginia.

Freehling, William. *Prelude to Civil War: The Nullification Crisis in South Carolina, 1816–1836* (1966) is the classic account of the subject.

Johnson, Paul. *A Shopkeeper's Millennium: Society and Revivals in Rochester, New York, 1815–1837* (1978) tells the story of revivals in an exciting way.

Hinks, Peter B. *To Awaken My Afflicted Brethren: David Walker and the Problem of Antebellum Slave Resistance* (1997) reveals the crucial role black Americans played in the creation of the abolitionist movement.

Laurie, Bruce. *Artisans into Workers: Labor in Nineteenth-Century America* (1989) gives an excellent synthesis of this complicated history.

Masur, Louis. *1831: Year of Eclipse* (2001) shows the fascinating interaction of social, religious, and political enthusiasm that swept America in this pivotal year.

Mayer, Henry. *All on Fire: William Lloyd Garrison and the Abolition of Slavery* (1998) is a comprehensive and fascinating biography.

Roberts, Randy, and James S. Olson. *A Line in the Sand: The Alamo in Blood and Memory* (2001) relates a sophisticated understanding of this challenging topic.

Roediger, David R. *The Wages of Whiteness: Race and the Making of the American Working Class* (1991) boldly interprets the uses the white working class made of the notion of "race."

Walters, Ronald. *American Reformers, 1815–1860* (1996) offers an updated version of a fine analytical synthesis.

Watson, Harry L. *Liberty and Power: The Politics of Jacksonian America* (1990) provides a helpful and balanced interpretation of a subject that has been much debated by scholars.

Weber, David J. *The Mexican Frontier, 1821–1846: The American Southwest Under Mexico* (1982) tells the complex history of this region before war brought it into the United States.

Identifications

Review your understanding of the following key terms, people, events, and dates for this chapter (these terms also appear in the Glossary at the end of the book):

Nat Turner
spoils system
Peggy Eaton
tariff
nullification
free blacks
bank war

Second Bank of the United States
Indian Removal Act
Antonio López de Santa Anna
Juan Seguín
Charles Grandison Finney
Joseph Smith
The Book of Mormon
William Lloyd Garrison
gag rule

Online Sources Guide

Use this listing to find online documents, images, interactive maps, simulations, and other resources related to this chapter:

American History Resource Center

http://history.wadsworth.com/rc/us

Documents

Andrew Jackson's First Annual Message (1829)
Andrew Jackson's Letter to Captain James Gadsden (1829)

Selected Images

Robert Fulton's *Clermont* plies the Hudson River
The Brooklyn Ferry, 1839
Joseph Smith, founder of the Church of Jesus Christ of Latter-Day Saints
Scenes from Nat Turner's rebellion
Results of repeated whippings
William Lloyd Garrison, founder of American Anti-Slavery Movement

Lydia Maria Child, antislavery advocate and champion of women's rights
Lucretia Coffin Mott
Nicholas Biddle, president of the Second Bank of the United States
Stephen F. Austin

Simulation

Early-nineteenth-century America (Choose to be a slave, a frontiersman, or a Native American and make choices based on the circumstances and opportunities afforded.)

HistoryNOW

http://now.ilrn.com/ayers_etal3e

Primary Source Exercises

Age of the Common Man
Newspapers
Abolitionism

11 Panic and Boom, 1837–1845

Artist George Innes, in his painting of a railroad roundhouse in the middle of a rural setting, conveyed the exciting and disquieting sense of change brought by the railroad.

1945.4.1, Inness,George, *The Lackawanna Valley*, Gift of Mrs. Huttleston Rogers, Image © 2005 Board of Trustees, National Gallery of Art, Washington, c.1865

In 1837, the largest financial panic and depression the nation had ever experienced descended on the United States. The hard times shaped reform, literature, politics, slavery, and foreign policy. The hard times in the East drove westward expansion. These were the years in which the mass migration to the Pacific began, as pioneers began to push across the West to Oregon and California. Politics churned as citizens worried over the consequences of rapid territorial growth.

It was not surprising that economic troubles stimulated political conflict, but the reform spirit also flowered during these hard years. Men and women championed **public education,** abstinence from alcohol, antislavery, and a host of other improvements to American life. The popular press burgeoned, along with art, photography, and literature. A few leading thinkers articulated a bold and distinctive American philosophy, one that bore the marks of its tumultuous time.

Economic Crisis and Innovation

The late 1830s and early 1840s produced a surprising mixture of bad and good economic news. The economy fell into prolonged depression, but at the same time the creative energies of the American economy flourished. Courts and legislatures fostered an environment favorable to business, while inventors and investors plunged ahead despite the failures they saw all around them. In fact, the most important economic development of the entire century—the railroad—emerged from these years of turmoil.

Panic and Depression

Andrew Jackson sought to leave a comfortable legacy to his handpicked successor, **Martin Van Buren,** but even the inauguration ceremony in March 1837 accentuated the great disparities between the two men. Whereas Jackson's gaunt figure symbolized his sacrifices on the frontier and battlefield, Van Buren seemed the plump embodiment of a life spent in political office. Whereas Van Buren's inaugural speech inspired little enthusiasm in the crowd of 20,000, the mere sight of ex-President Jackson roused great cheers. The new president seemed content to carry on Jackson's work.

Within weeks of Van Buren's inauguration the American economy hit stormy waters. An unprecedented amount of silver poured into American banks in the

Timeline

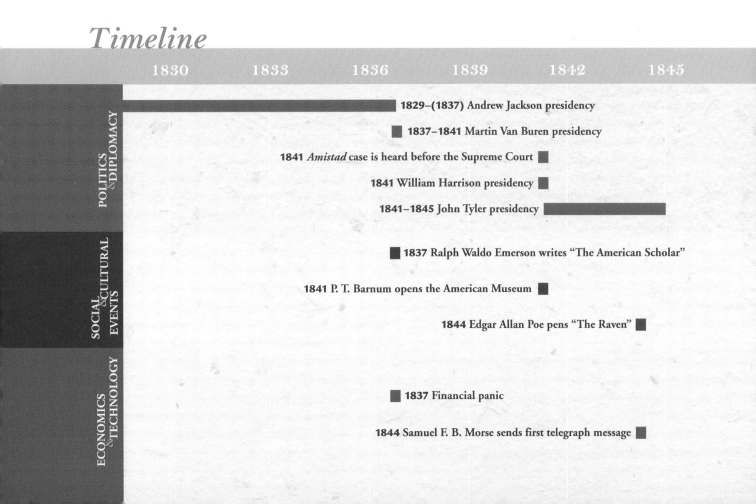

| | 1830 | 1833 | 1836 | 1839 | 1842 | 1845 |

POLITICS & DIPLOMACY
1829–(1837) Andrew Jackson presidency
1837–1841 Martin Van Buren presidency
1841 *Amistad* case is heard before the Supreme Court
1841 William Harrison presidency
1841–1845 John Tyler presidency

SOCIAL & CULTURAL EVENTS
1837 Ralph Waldo Emerson writes "The American Scholar"
1841 P. T. Barnum opens the American Museum
1844 Edgar Allan Poe pens "The Raven"

ECONOMICS & TECHNOLOGY
1837 Financial panic
1844 Samuel F. B. Morse sends first telegraph message

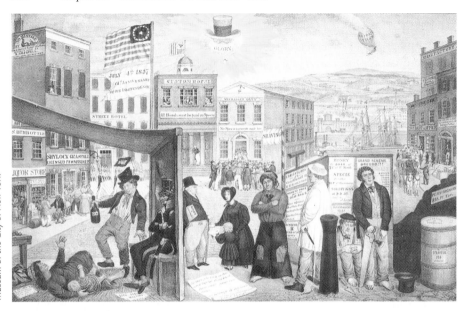

Museum of the City of New York

The irony of a Fourth of July celebration during hard times fills this cartoon, in which symbols of poverty and decay pile on one another.

mid-1830s from abroad, fueling overheated speculation. Britain's economy expanded rapidly, increasing the demand for cotton, encouraging southern planters to buy land and slaves on credit, and boosting foreign investment in American projects such as canals and turnpikes. British investors bought up state bonds and securities, while British exporters offered generous credit for purchase of a wide array of manufactured goods. American merchants, land speculators, and state governments indulged in a feast of easy credit and seemingly endless profits.

Unfortunately, poor harvests in Britain disrupted the American economy when British firms, facing a cash shortage at home, demanded repayment of loans just at the time that prices for American cotton declined because of record production and reduced English demand. As a result, a major New Orleans cotton broker failed when it could not make its payments to British banks or pay debts in excess of a million dollars. The collapse triggered panic. As a city official noted, "everybody will fail—all Hell will fail." Desperate merchants and creditors tried to extract cash from debtors, credit evaporated, and thousands lost their jobs.

Despite the role of international trade in bringing on the crisis, many people blamed the problems on Jackson's banking policy, especially the practice of accepting only specie, not paper money, for the purchase of public lands. They looked to Van Buren to lead the repeal of this strategy, but Jackson made it clear to Van Buren that he did not want to see his work undone. Delegations of merchants came to the White House to plead with Van Buren, but to no avail. A "run" began on the banks; customers withdrew a million dollars in specie in only two days in early May. The **Panic of 1837** had begun. Soon

it spread to every city and region of the country.

The panic quickly affected working people as well as the rich. Jobs dried up and many urban families had no idea of where they would get their next meal. In New York City, a poster warned that "Bread, Meat, Rent, Fuel—Their Prices Must Come Down. The Voice of the People Shall be Heard, and Will Prevail." Thousands of people gathered for a public meeting in the freezing weather. Told that a nearby warehouse held 50,000 barrels of flour, the protesters stormed the building; they took what they could and broke open hundreds of barrels. The riots continued for days until the police managed to regain order.

A second panic came in 1839 and the economy suffered until 1843. Labor unions weakened as workers grew afraid to risk their jobs. States' plans to finance canals, roads, and other public projects crashed. Nine states defaulted on the bonds with which they intended to finance those improvements, leading furious European investors to shun American investments. Governors and legislators found themselves under attack from voters angry that the states had permitted themselves to go so far into debt.

Van Buren admitted that allowing state banks to hold federal funds had apparently fueled the speculation, but he would not even consider reinstating a national bank. Instead, he proposed what came to be known as the Sub-Treasury Plan or the Independent Treasury Plan. In that system, public funds would be disbursed by the secretary of the treasury as the economy seemed to dictate and banks would be kept out of the picture. It would be two more years before the plan passed, but by then it could do the country, the Democrats, nor Martin Van Buren much good. The Whigs quickly won state-level offices and looked forward to harvesting more.

The Charles River Bridge Case

Even as the panic unfolded, some basic issues raised by the economic changes worked their way through the American court system. American law still embodied many assumptions from the centuries before corporations and far-flung economic enterprises challenged local power. Businesses and investors challenged those assumptions.

The Charles River Bridge of Boston, for example, had been granted a franchise by the state legislature in 1785. The owners of the bridge charged a toll for everyone who crossed. As the population of Boston and Charlestown grew rapidly, so did the traffic and the tolls on the bridge. The bridge, which cost about $70,000 to build and improve, was bringing in $30,000 a year by the late 1820s. Another bridge also chartered by the state, the Warren Bridge, went up across the Charles, only 260 feet away. No sooner was the new bridge built than the traffic on the older bridge declined by more than half. The managers of the Charles River Bridge sued in court, claiming that their original charter implied a monopoly that the state had violated by building a competing bridge. Throughout the 1830s, the case proceeded to the U.S. Supreme Court and was heard in 1837.

The Chief Justice of the Supreme Court, Roger B. Taney, shared the Jacksonian animosity against monopolies. His decision in the *Charles River Bridge* case held that a state charter did not imply monopoly. Should old charters be permitted to hinder modern improvements, the country "would be obliged to stand still." The charters had perhaps been necessary in the past, he admitted, but by the 1830s such props no longer seemed necessary to attract capital investment. Taney's decision in the *Charles River Bridge* case reflected a growing consensus among Democrats and Whigs that older forms of economic privilege had to make way for innovation and investment.

Railroads

By the 1830s, Americans had devised several means for dealing with the vast spaces of their continent. Thousands of miles of canals cut across the East, and steamboats plied the waters of the North and South. Such means of transport, while cheap and dependable, remained relatively slow and limited in their reach. Inland cities longed for fast overland connections with the outside world, and they knew of experiments with railroads in England and the United States over the last decade. When New Jersey sponsored a bold rail and canal connection between New York and Philadelphia in 1831, it ordered a custom-built locomotive from an English company—the *John Bull.* The railroad became an immediate success, carrying more than 100,000 passengers in 1834. Ralph Waldo Emerson rode an early train and marveled that "men & trees & barns whiz by you as fast as the leaves of a dictionary."

By 1841, ten American railroad shops had opened to meet the growing demand. Those shops soon began changing the English designs, making the engines more powerful and the rails cheaper. Railroad companies quickly grew into some of the largest and most complex American businesses. Employing hundreds of people, they pioneered management and engineering innovations.

Railroads almost immediately became the key form of transportation in the United States. Rail transport grew cheaper as the network expanded, and trains could run when canals had frozen over. By 1840, American companies and states had spent $75 million to build 3,300 miles of track, surpassing Great Britain; by 1850, the country claimed nearly 9,000 miles of railroad. New industries rose to serve the trains as iron, coal, and steel manufacturing burgeoned with the railroads' demand. The railroads consumed enormous amounts of wood for their ties, trestles, and boilers.

Railroads appeared in every region of the United States but not in a uniform network (see Map 11.1).

The First Railroad Train on the Mohawk and Hudson Road, E. L. Henry, Albany Institute of History & Art

This locomotive in New York State, like its other early counterparts, pulled passenger cars based on old-fashioned carriages. The technology evolved quickly in the 1840s, however, and the United States played an important role in that evolution.

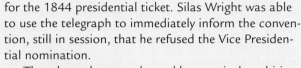

Flashpoints | The Telegraph

The idea of a telegraph—using an electric current to create nearly instantaneous communication—was on the minds of many people in the 1830s. Electricity was the stuff of parlor tricks and quack medicine as well as science. At least 60 inventors attempted some form of electric communication prior to the success of American Samuel F. B. Morse. A noted landscape painter and son of the nation's premier producer of geographic textbooks, Morse recognized that the challenge was not in producing a telegraphic device but in convincing a skeptical public and government that it was useful as well as entertaining.

Morse hawked his ideas to an indifferent public for several years and pestered Congress for financial aid. Even as late as 1844, Congress doubted the practicality of the telegraph and asked that someone keep track of that "crazy" painter and to ensure the government's investment was not frittered away on "Morse's foolishness." He finally received money from the government after newspaper editors began to express interest in the telegraph's use in news reporting.

Morse tested the line between the nation's capital and Baltimore in May 1844, when he transmitted the code for "What hath God wrought." What really brought Congress to appreciate Morse's idea, however, was far more pragmatic. In late May, the Democratic Convention convened in Baltimore and the telegraph passed the news to waiting politicians and speculators that James K. Polk and Silas Wright were the party's nominees

© The Granger Collection, New York

for the 1844 presidential ticket. Silas Wright was able to use the telegraph to immediately inform the convention, still in session, that he refused the Vice Presidential nomination.

The telegraph was embraced by practical, ambitious politicians who saw the device's use for their own passion and purposes. Newspaper editors and businessmen also quickly grasped the revolutionary implications of near-simultaneous communication. Word of the latest news, prices, and emergencies meant higher circulation and higher profits for the swift. The Mexican War was the first conflict reported by telegraph to American audiences. For the first time, paid correspondents accompanied the army. War news was rushed from the front by courier and boat to New Orleans where it was telegraphed around the nation.

Telegraphic communication, seen only a decade before as no more than a device to amuse at parties, had revolutionized what people could know about their world. The telegraph would enable a vast rail network and business of breathtaking scope. Less than 20 years later, the telegraph would also enable the mobilization of a war of American against American.

Questions for Reflection

1. Was the telegraph's development inevitable? Predictable?

2. How would the telegraph change politics?

3. Did the telegraph play an important role in bringing on the Civil War?

Beginning from many different entrepreneurial efforts and adapting to widely varying terrain, railroads did not adapt a standard distance between the rails, or gauge. As a result, trains could not travel rapidly across the nation; cargo had to be unloaded and reloaded. Trains connected coastal cities with inland plantations and farms in the South, while in the North and West railroads ran from city to city, knitting together a network of economic development that benefited a wider area. In this way,

railroads accelerated the growth of differences between the South and the rest of the country.

Telegraph poles marched alongside the railroads, preventing gruesome crashes on single-track lines and speeding the flow of information just as the railroads sped the flow of people and goods. Like the locomotive, the telegraph was the product of inventors in several different countries but received a major impetus from America. **Samuel F. B. Morse** patented his version of

Life in the New Slave South

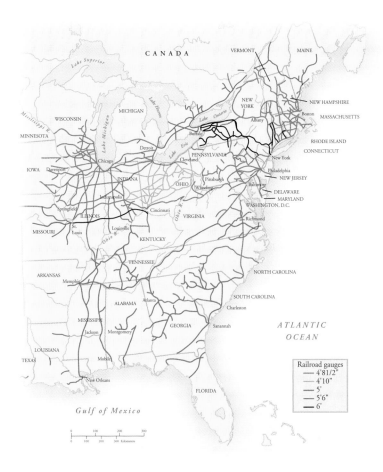

MAP 11.1 The Growth of Railroads

A vastly expanded transportation network tied the United States together. The system exaggerated sectional differences by unifying the Northeast with the Northwest, creating the reality and perception of a "North" with interests different from those of a "South" stretching from the Atlantic to the Mississippi and beyond.

The South, increasingly dominated by slavery, remained an integral part of the United States. Southern cotton drove national economic growth and southern politicians controlled much of the nation's government. The South was a prosperous place for white people, whose average per capita incomes exceeded those of almost every other society in the world and were catching up to those in the North.

Thanks to the rapid expansion of newspapers and the telegraph, white southerners took part in all the national conversations about race, slavery, and politics. As northerners and southerners read the critical words often aimed across the Mason-Dixon line, though, distrust between the regions grew. The single profound difference between the North and South, slavery, became ever more significant as it grew ever stronger.

African Americans and the South

By the 1830s, slavery had spread over an enormous area stretching from Maryland to Texas (see Map 11.2). The domestic slave trade expanded at a feverish rate during the decade as the new planters of Mississippi, Alabama, and Louisiana eagerly imported slaves to clear land and plant cotton. American slavery became ever more diverse as it expanded. Enslaved people worked in hemp, wheat, rice, corn, sugar, and tobacco fields as well as cotton fields. They worked with livestock and racehorses, practiced trades such as carpentry and blacksmithing, and labored on the docks of New Orleans, Mobile, and Memphis and in the shipyards of Baltimore (see Map 11.3). Some knew the white people among whom they lived quite well; others belonged to absolute strangers. Some worked in large groups of black people; others worked alone or beside whites.

Southern culture mixed English, African, Scots-Irish, Caribbean, French, Indian, and Hispanic influences into a rich and complex blend. Language, food, music, and religion took on new shapes as black and white cultures interacted. In the meantime, African Americans prided themselves on the stories, songs, and dances they

the electronic telegraph in 1840. Morse struggled with the invention for more than 10 years, devising the code of dots and dashes that bears his name as well as devising ways to make the current travel farther. In 1842, he received half of a $60,000 research grant from Congress to run an experimental line from Washington to Baltimore. (The other portion of the grant provided $30,000 dollars to study animal magnetism or mesmerism, one of the great fads of the early decades of the century.) Observers of the first public tests in 1844 were astonished by the telegraph: "Strange and wonderful discovery, which has made the 'swift-winged lighting' man's messenger, annihilated all space, and tied the two ends of a continent in a knot." Following its success, the telegraph spread across the country with great speed. In the four years after its initial test, more than 5,000 miles of wire had been strung, with another 3,000 under construction.

Paths of the Slave Trade

The slave trade grew into a vast business in the years before the Civil War.

Many people, including those who did not own slaves themselves, made their livings from supplying slave traders with food, shelter, transportation, insurance, and banking. As this map shows, the trade ran strongly from the Upper South to the Lower South, from east to west.

Although slavery remained firmly entrenched in states such as Virginia, Kentucky, and North Carolina, the demand for slave labor was so strong in the new plantation districts of Alabama, Mississippi, and Louisiana that slaveholders sold off "surplus" slaves to the traders who came through their counties each year. Traders gathered slaves in the cities of the Chesapeake, especially Alexandria, Virginia, to ship them around the Florida Keys to ports on the Gulf Coast, especially New Orleans. Meanwhile, other slaves were sold "down the river" from places close to the border with the North to the plantations surrounding Vicksburg, Natchez, and Baton Rouge. Other slaves were forced to walk or to take trains across the middle of the South. All along, even more slaves were bought and sold within states, being moved from one county to another in ways that do not appear on this disheartening map.

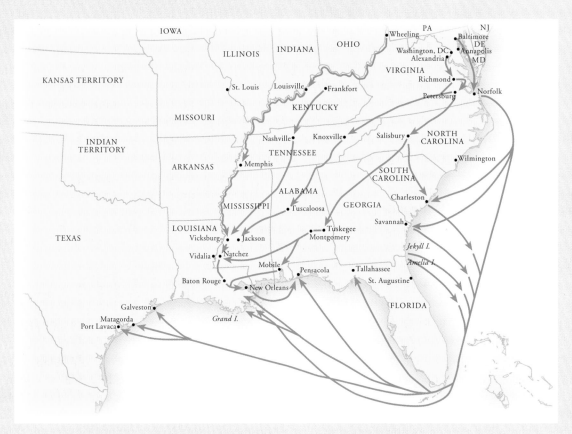

MAP 11.2 **Paths of the Slave Trade**

knew to be particularly their own, on the styles of the baskets, quilts, and clothes they sewed, or the way they carried themselves. Black culture remained distinct and vibrant, even as it influenced the larger American culture.

African American families tended to rely on a broader range of kin than did white families. Grandparents, aunts, and uncles often played significant roles in child rearing in black families. When people of actual blood relation were unavailable, southern slaves created "fictive kin," friends and neighbors given honorary titles of "brother" or "aunt" and treated as such. These arrangements permitted slave families considerable resiliency and variety. African Americans often found wives or husbands on nearby farms, visiting one another on evenings and weekends.

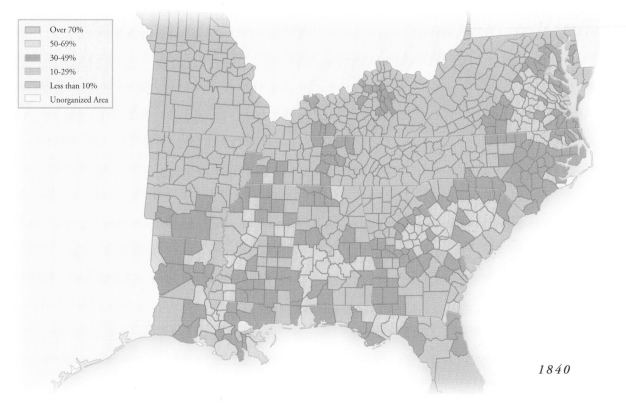

Over 70%
50-69%
30-49%
10-29%
Less than 10%
Unorganized Area

1840

MAP 11.3 The Spread of Slavery
Slavery moved to the lands taken from the American Indians in Georgia, Alabama, and Mississippi, even as the institution remained strong in the older plantation areas of the Atlantic coast.

Plantations and Farms

Most slaveowners in the American South tended to live on the same farms as their slaves, but wealthier owners, particularly those from the unhealthy regions of the Gulf and Atlantic coast, put day-to-day control of their plantations in the hands of professional overseers. These overseers were often ambitious young men of middling background who used the overseer position as a stepping-stone to their own plantation. Slaves could and did appeal to the owner if they thought the overseer unfair. Since a master might trust a well-known slave more than a new overseer, the position involved tact as well as brute force.

On larger plantations, where slaves often worked in groups called gangs, trusted male slaves served as "drivers." Such drivers tended to be especially strong and skilled, commanding respect from whites as well as blacks. Although whites held the ultimate

Plantations in the South were often large and technologically sophisticated economic enterprises.

Library of Congress, Prints and Photographs Division

The Historic New Orleans Collection, Accension #1975.93.1&2

Enslaved people of both genders and of all ages worked in a variety of demanding tasks throughout the year as they brought the South's valuable cotton crop from seed to bale.

and drivers claiming authority. Slaves tended to work at several different jobs over the course of the year. Some slaves were respected as purveyors of healing or religious knowledge from Africa; some slaves were admired for their musical ability; others won recognition for their ability to read and preach the Gospel. These abilities did not always correspond with the opinions of whites, who frequently underestimated the abilities and character of the people among whom they lived.

Whites told themselves that they provided "their people" a better life than they would have known in Africa. Indeed, southern masters explained the justice of slavery to themselves and to the North by stressing their Christian stewardship for the slaves. As one clergyman wrote to his fellow slaveholders in the

threat of force, they much preferred to keep the work moving smoothly, minimizing both potential conflict and their own exposure to heat and weather. The driver could help both sides, protecting fellow slaves from abuse and assuring that the work got done efficiently. Drivers frequently found themselves caught between the two competing sets of demands, however, and slaves often resented or even hated drivers.

About three out of four enslaved people were field hands, though almost all enslaved people went to the fields during the peak times. Women and men also served in the house as cooks and domestics. Slaves were well known for controlling the pace of work, reporting their tools broken or "lost" when they were forced to work too fast or too long. They traditionally had Sundays to garden for themselves, do their domestic chores, or hunt.

Slaves' lives were by no means simple. Lines of power often became complicated and tangled on plantations and farms, with slaveowners, their children, overseers,

Slaves Imported, 1500–1870

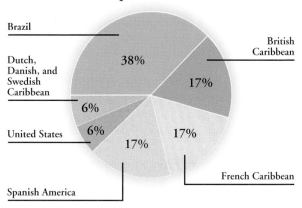

Pattern of Black Population

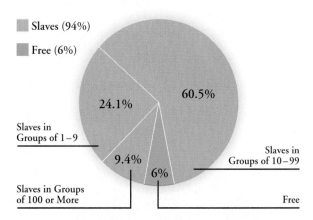

CHART 11.1 **Patterns of Black Population in the South**

Most black people lived on large plantations with more than 10 other enslaved people, while others were scattered on much smaller farms and in towns and cities.

Proportion of Hemisphere's Slave Population, 1825

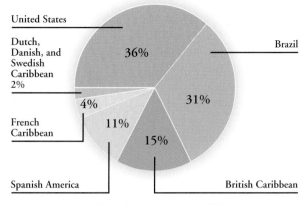

CHART 11.2 a & b **North American Slavery in Context**

As these two graphs show, the United States accounted for a relatively small proportion of all enslaved people brought from Africa into the Western Hemisphere, but because of the longer life spans of North American slaves, over a third of the enslaved population of the New World lived in the United States.

Relationships between African Americans and the white people for whom they labored contained complicated elements of human emotion.

those of the American South were relatively healthy. They lived with monotonous diets, ineffective or dangerous health care, continual fear of violence and sale, small and drafty houses, and rough clothing, but they managed to survive.

Many slaveowners did not refrain from having their slaves whipped on small provocation, branded, shackled, or locked up in sweltering enclosures; slaves suffered sexual abuse. Partly because expectant mothers were often kept in the fields until the last minute, about a third of all black babies died before they reached their first birthday. American slavery was a harsh institution.

The Politics of the White South

White men in the South took their politics seriously and built much of it around slavery. America's commitment to slavery was grounded in a cold social and economic calculus. In southern cities such as Natchez, Mississippi, whites enjoyed among the highest per capita incomes, the finest

early 1840s, slaves "were placed under our control . . . not exclusively for our benefit but theirs also."

Most masters would not permit their slaves to learn to read, but they did arrange to have Bible selections read to their slaves. Although many slaves eagerly accepted the Gospel in the white-dominated churches, others resented the obvious and shallow uses the masters made of the sermons, telling the slaves to accept their lot and to refrain from stealing food. Such slaves displayed their deepest religious feelings only in their own worship, in the secret meetings in brush arbors and cabins in the slave quarters. There, they prayed to be free and to be united in heaven with those they loved.

Largely oblivious to the lives their slaves led beyond their sight, masters pointed to the physical condition of the slaves as evidence of their concern. Compared with slaves elsewhere in the hemisphere, it was true,

homes, and access to music, theater, and public entertainments that rivaled any city in the country. In the South as in the North, the Whigs portrayed themselves as the party of progress and prosperity, appealing to lawyers, editors, and merchants as well as to large planters on the richest lands and farmers in the mountains of the Upper South who wanted to expand connections to outside markets.

The Democrats, on the other hand, found their strongest supporters among the middling farmers and aspiring planters of the South. These men tended to resent taxes on their lands and slaves. They admired the Democrats' aggressive approach to western expansion and removing the American Indians. Southerners distrustful of northern reformers and of financial speculators found the small-government pronouncements of the Democrats appealing.

In the South both the Whigs and the Democrats declared themselves the friends of southern slavery, but they differed in their emphases. The Democrats pledged that they would protect slavery by extending the power of the federal government as little as possible. The Whigs argued that the best way to protect slavery was for the South to develop its region's economy and build strong economic and political bridges to the North and Europe.

Reform Takes Root

The wild swings of the economy of the 1830s seemed to drive Americans to improve their society. They could see dangers all around them but they could also glimpse how things could be better. The new machinery of railroads, telegraphs, and printing presses held out exciting new possibilities for spreading the word, for pulling people together for common purposes.

Some Americans took practical routes to progress, focusing their efforts on schools and the prohibition of alcohol, whereas others explored philosophy and literature. Some used the new printing machinery of the age for entertainment, whereas others turned to the fight against social evils.

Public Schools

Many Americans had become dissatisfied with the way young people were schooled in the United States. No state had a statewide school system, and local districts ran their own affairs, often wretchedly. The rich attended private schools or employed tutors, whereas the parents of poorer children had to sign oaths declaring themselves "paupers" before their children could benefit from charity schools. Parents from the middle classes, charged a fee according to the number of children they had, sent their offspring to schools often taught by untrained teachers. Hundreds of districts, especially in the South and West, created no schools at all. Many American children never went to school in the 1820s and 1830s and those who did often attended for only a short time, interrupted by the demands of family and farm.

Reformers argued that unequal and inadequate education would not suffice in America, a country dependent on an informed democracy. These reformers wanted free schools. Taxes and other state support would make it possible for all children to go to public schools. The rich would be more likely to send their children to such schools, reformers reasoned, if their tax dollars were supporting them; the poor would be more likely to send their children if they were not stigmatized as paupers. Buildings and teachers could be improved with the increased support.

A Massachusetts lawyer and Whig politician, Horace Mann worked relentlessly to make rich citizens, especially manufacturers, see that a tax in support of schools was a wise investment. Think how much better workers would be, he argued, if they could read and calculate. Think to what good use women could be put as teachers, he argued, instilling future citizens with their virtues of cooperation and peacefulness. Mann gradually persuaded influential people in Massachusetts of the practicability of common schools. In 1837, he became the first secretary of the Massachusetts Board of Education.

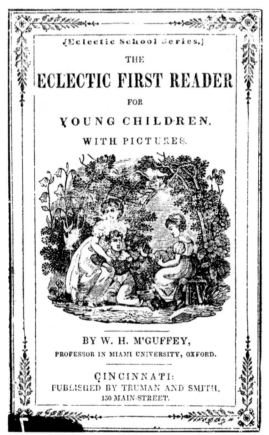

These standardized textbooks offered millions of American schoolchildren moral as well as academic instruction.

Courtesy of Special Collections, University of Miami Libraries

When Mann took over, many schools were in session for only a couple of months a year. He transformed that system during his tenure. The minimum school year stretched to six months, buildings and teacher training improved significantly, and teachers' pay increased by more than half.

DOING HISTORY

The Consequences of Democracy

A YOUNG FRENCH nobleman, Tocqueville came to the United States to observe democracy in action. The central theme of his great book, Democracy in America, *published in 1840, is captured in this passage: freedom does not seem to bring happiness but rather a constant anxiety and ceaseless yearning. Property is everywhere in America but its pursuit does not necessarily bring happiness.*

Horace Mann abandoned his successful law practice and position in the state legislature to become the first secretary of the Massachusetts Board of Education. Mann here, in his tenth annual report in 1846, argues against those who resisted paying taxes to educate the children of others, insisting that every child had an "absolute right" to an education and that the state had an obligation to provide that education for the public good and at the public expense.

Alexis de Tocqueville, *Democracy in America*

A native of the United States clings to his world's good as if he were certain never to die; and he is so hasty in grasping at all within his reach, that one would suppose he was constantly afraid of not living long enough to enjoy them. He clutches everything, he holds nothing fast, but soon loosens his grasp to pursue fresh gratifications. In the United States a man builds a house to spend his latter years in it, and he sells it before the roof is on; he plants a garden, and lets [rents] it just as the trees are coming into bearing; he brings a field into tillage, and leaves other men to gather the crops; he embraces a profession, and gives it up; he settles in a place, which he soon afterward leaves, to carry his changeable longings elsewhere. . . . Among democratic nations men easily attain a certain equality of conditions; they can never attain the equality they desire.

Horace Mann, *Absolute Right to an Education*

. . . . The advocates for a more generous education could carry their respective audiences with them in behalf of increased privileges for our children, were it not instinctively foreseen that increased privileges must be followed by increased taxation. Against this obstacle, argument falls dead. The rich man who has no children declares that the exaction of a contribution from him to educate the children of his neighbor is an invasion of his rights of property. . . . It seems not irrelevant, therefore . . . to inquire into the nature of a man's right to the property he possesses. . . . The claim of a child . . . to a portion of pre-existent property, begins with the first breath he draws. . . . If parents either cannot or will not supply the infant's wants,— then society at large—the government having assumed to itself the ultimate control of all property—is bound to step in and fill the parent's place.

Sources: Alexis de Tocqueville, *Democracy in America*, Vol II (Boston: C. C. Little and J. Brown, 1841), Second Book, Chapter 13; Horace Mann, *Tenth Annual Report of the Secretary of the Board of Education* (1846), in *The Life and Works and Horace Mann* (Boston: Lee and Shepard, 1891), Vol. IV, pp. 114–117, 128–129, 131–134.

Questions for Reflection

1. What concern do these two documents share?

2. Do their comments challenge fundamental American beliefs?

3. Would Tocqueville agree with Mann's faith in the promise of universal education, or see this as one more deluded quest for equality?

4. Would Mann agree with Tocqueville's assumption that the pursuit of property was by itself an empty effort?

Explore additional primary sources related to this chapter on the Wadsworth American History Resource Center or HistoryNOW websites:
http://history.wadsworth.com/rc/us
http://now.ilrn.com/ayers_etal3e

Women teachers became common in the Northeast and Midwest. Females attended new "normal schools" that provided teacher training; they read educational journals, received professional supervision, and taught with uniform textbooks. These standards spread throughout the North and the West in the 1840s and 1850s, as did McGuffey's Readers. These books, which sold an astonishing 9 million copies between 1836 and 1850, celebrated Christian piety, the virtues of hard work, and patriotism.

The Washingtonians

Americans had long waged campaigns against intemperance, but the fight against drink took on a new urgency in the depression years of the late 1830s and early 1840s. Many people, religious and otherwise, saw alcohol as the scourge of American life. Men drank at work, farmers routinely turned their surplus grain into whiskey, and rum was a major part of New England commerce. Americans aged 15 or older consumed an average of 40 gallons of beer, spirits, and wine per capita.

The Washingtonian movement, named in honor of George Washington, gave great force and visibility to a crusade against alcohol. Whereas earlier **temperance movements** had mainly enlisted those who were already opposed to alcohol, the new movement marked an effort by drinkers to reform themselves. Older reform attempts had been largely the efforts of men, but now women became active.

The Washingtonians began in Baltimore in 1840, when six drinkers pledged to one another to quit drinking and to persuade other drinkers to do the same. Word

---

Picturing the Past   SOCIAL & CULTURAL EVENTS

The Dangers of Drink

This print was a popular one in the United States early in its history because many people considered alcohol the greatest threat to the country. In this one image, viewers could trace the devastating effects of drinking on a young man and his family. Everyone knew the excuses people told themselves about drinking. At first, in the lower left corner, the very young man shares a drink with a friend. He then proceeds to make weak excuses, such as drinking to "keep the cold out." From there, it is a short step to losing control, having "a drink too much," and becoming "riotous." At the "summit," the star of the story has become a "confirmed drunkard," wasting his life with equally drunken friends. His drinking leads quickly to poverty and then to desperate crime in order to support the habit. Finally, despairing, he turns to suicide as the only way out. Meanwhile, an abandoned wife and child, homeless, suffer on their way to the poor house. This was America's first war on drugs and it struck many of the same themes as those of later crusades.

Library of Congress, Prints and Photographs Division

Reform often involved entire families who took it upon themselves to address the wrongs faced, and pursued, by other families.

of the new movement quickly spread up the eastern seaboard, and by 1843 the Washingtonians claimed millions of adherents. Unlike earlier temperance efforts led by upper class or religious leaders, Washingtonians prided themselves on an egalitarian ethos. Partly as a result of the new organization, and partly from the growing stigma attached to drunkenness, Americans' consumption of alcohol plummeted in the 1840s.

"Martha Washington" societies, for women only, grew rapidly, challenging the men's movement both in size and in fervor. These female temperance advocates were not well-to-do ladies stooping to help the fallen, but rather the wives of artisans and small businessmen. They helped families in distress to get back on their feet. They also provided a new edge to the temperance crusade, reminding men that drunkenness was more often than not a male failing and that it was the wives and children of drunkards who suffered most from their neglect, cruelty, and financial irresponsibility. Where a farm family might weather an alcoholic husband through consumption of their own produce and local bartering, city families needed a man's wages to pay for the rent, fuel, and food necessary for survival.

Abolitionism Strengthened and Challenged

By the late 1830s the American Anti-Slavery Society claimed more than a quarter of a million members, primarily in the Northeast and Midwest. The first female abolitionist speakers—the **Grimké sisters,** Angelina and Sarah—were prize recruits into the antislavery ranks, for they were the daughters of a prominent South Carolina slave-owning planter. By telling New England audiences

of their own experiences with slavery, the Grimkés held a credibility that white northern abolitionists could not match. In 1837, the Grimkés decided to exert their power in a new forum by lecturing to mixed audiences of men and women. Although some people strenuously objected to such an elevation of women in the public sphere, the Grimkés spoke to more than 40,000 people in nine months in 1837 and 1838. "*All moral beings have essentially the same rights and the same duties,* whether they be male or female," Angelina Grimké admonished an audience. The female slaves of the South, who "now wear the iron yoke of slavery in this land of boasted liberty and law . . . are our countrywomen—*they are our sisters.*"

As it grew stronger, the antislavery cause met with more determined opposition. When abolitionist editor Elijah P. Lovejoy offended readers of his religious paper in St. Louis—denouncing a local judge who prevented the trial of a mob who had burned a black man alive—citizens of Alton, Illinois, invited Lovejoy to move to their town. Alton prided itself on being a progressive place, but soon some prominent members of the community, angered at Lovejoy's paper for its dissemination of "the highly odious doctrines of modern Abolitionism," held a public meeting demanding that he quit printing such ideas. Lovejoy only intensified his attacks on slavery. Mobs destroyed two of Lovejoy's presses and vowed to tar and feather him, but he persisted. A mayoral

The murder of Elijah P. Lovejoy, an abolitionist editor in Illinois, revealed the depth of opposition held by many northern whites to anyone who would speak forcefully against slavery.

Enduring Issues   Religion and Reform

In the first half of the nineteenth century, reform and religion swept the nation with their powerful currents. With economic developments and rising levels of material comforts, Americans let loose their pragmatism, idealism, patriotism, restlessness, and insecurity to embrace reform. No institution, no belief system, was safe from critical eyes and voices seeking to better their society through change.

Reformers' influence crested in the first third of the nineteenth century. After 1815, church leaders, missionaries, and newspaper editors were quick to dub the array of organized missionary and charitable societies "the Benevolent Empire." Reformers were proud of their pathfinding role in laying out new directions for America—even if many other Americans violently disagreed, as in the cases of abolitionists and Mormons. Many citizens did not see the reformers as guides to glory, but rather as meddlesome, sanctimonious outsiders ordering them how to run their households and personal affairs.

The United States grew rapidly after 1815 and migration to both rural and urban frontiers was swift. Americans became habituated to change and also became used to solving local problems by organizing, incorporating, or voting on courses of action. Economic development called forth social alterations and upset existing patterns of authority. Reform drew energy from the changes unleashed by the American Revolution. White men of the most humble position now enjoyed a sense of freedom and entitlement that had been the privilege of the gentry and aristocracy. Men and women saw the exercise of liberty, of political power, of speech and public demonstration as making civic virtue and social improvement a citizen's duty.

Reform also rode the enthusiasm of a reshaped landscape of faith. Revivals taught that Christians

SAVED IN THE LORD'S OWN TIME AND PLACE.

Oberlin College Archives, Oberlin, Ohio

could reject sin and achieve salvation. Utopian visions spread through varied populations: rich, poor, urban, rural, without regard to section. Having reformed their own souls, evangelicals made an easy transition to reformers of society. They advocated the practice of good works as a Christian duty. Both fringe and mainstream denominations were infused with a sense that perfection of one's spirit was possible. Perfecting society itself was the next logical challenge. Newspapers carried worried editorials and pleas for missionaries and bibles to deliver the sinful and unchurched Americans whose sloth and ignorance endangered the nation's moral stature. The frontier excited particular concern, and missionaries and tracts tried to combat the influence of Catholic Mexico and convert native peoples.

Progress became a rallying cry. Progress meant more men with the vote, chances for any household to become wealthy, respectable, educated. The role of religion and ideas of personal salvation were intertwined with these new exciting concepts of personal

candidate in Alton whipped a mob to a frenzy to destroy a replacement press as it was offloaded from the train in September. In November 1837, as his fifth press arrived, a battle erupted and Lovejoy was killed as he and his assistants fought the crowd. The mob shattered his press, and local law officers arrested the defenders of Lovejoy for inciting the violence.

Abolitionists debated the proper response to such opposition. William Lloyd Garrison counseled his allies to offer no resistance to violence. He and his supporters renounced all allegiance to the established parties and

churches, which had long since shown themselves tolerant of slavery. Other abolitionists, by contrast, used whatever means they could to bring slavery to an end, including political parties.

The differences among the abolitionists came to a head at the annual meeting of the American Anti-Slavery Society in 1839. They differed most visibly in their attitudes toward the role of women. Women constituted perhaps half of all members of the antislavery organizations, but some male abolitionists sought to keep females in a subordinate role and prevent women members from improvement. However, not everyone had equal access to the widening opportunities. Reform, like political power, was usually the province of white men. African Americans and women had to fight and prove themselves to gain places in movements such as temperance and abolition. They had to agitate and demand legal rights equal to those of white men.

Recognizing the reality of change did not always equate to cheerful acceptance of its price. Reform was often progressive, but it was also frequently autocratic, insensitive to how it might ride roughshod over locally cherished values or traditions of church-state separation. While some celebrated the ordinary believer and encouraged democratic governance of church and reform efforts, others sought to limit the American obsession with equality noted by Tocqueville. Demands for discipline in the workplace and sanctions against inappropriate public behavior served as a moral lash to whip sinful neighbors into shape. In one of his many lectures delivered across New England, Ralph Waldo Emerson chided those whose pursuit of reform was directed only at others. "The criticism and attack on institutions which we have witnessed has made one thing plain, that society gains nothing while a man, not himself renovated, attempts to renovate things around him; he has become tediously good in some particular, but negligent or narrow in the rest; and hypocrisy and vanity are often the disgusting result."

Desire for reform and the security of faith were often allies and occasionally adversaries in the antebellum era. American church life, like the society at large, was remarkably unruly. Individuals, families, and ministers adopted and discarded dogma, practices, and denominational loyalties with relative ease. A marketplace of doctrine and religious practice flourished in America. Men and women voted with their feet and hearts.

The impulse to reform, to improve, clearly drew much of its power from spiritual ideas of perfection and preparing the world for Christ's return through good works directed towards the less fortunate and unconverted. Temperance, creation of asylums and penitentiaries, orphanages, and common schools are best understood as reflecting secular and religious inspiration. Americans lived in an age where religious language and imagery infused daily life. The privileged position of the Protestant churches often resulted in intolerance for Catholics, Jews, and non-believers. In some New England states, atheists could not testify in court or hold government jobs.

The interplay of reform impulses and the legacy of the Second Great Awakening represent an optimistic view of history and the potential for individuals to better their world while fulfilling God's plan. The bloody toll of the Civil War would shatter this hopeful perspective, but its legacy continues through today. Americans have lost none of their zest for organizing societies, clubs, or demonstrations to demand protection of favored interests. The sophisticated machinery of organized benevolence and charitable work stills hums throughout American society.

Questions for Reflection

1. Both religious revivals and reform movements generated political turmoil. What factors led to the association of Whigs with evangelicals and many reformist causes? Why not the Democrats?

2. Aside from the issue of slavery, settled by war, only the common school movement can be assessed as enthusiastically adopted by the vast majority of Americans. Why did most Americans accept the idea of universal public education while rejecting many other worthy causes?

3. Consider the relation of gender to both reform and religion. How did women use society's expectations of their proper roles to forge a larger public identity? How did men, in general, respond?

---

voting, speaking publicly, or serving on committees with men. Unable to resolve their differences, the abolitionists split. The more conservative group, based in New York, created the **Liberty party** to run a candidate for president in the upcoming **election of 1840.** Garrison's organization maintained a more radical stance on the role of women and mocked those who sought "to sustain and propagate those eternal, immutable principles of liberty, justice, and equality" by denying "woman her right as a human being to speak and act with brethren on the anti-slavery platform."

Whatever their differences, abolitionists barraged Congress with petitions demanding that slavery be ended in the District of Columbia. Former President John Quincy Adams, now a congressman from Massachusetts, used all his parliamentary skill to fight the gag rule that prevented Congress from recognizing antislavery petitions; he finally succeeded in getting it overthrown in 1845. Adams also successfully defended Africans who had seized a slave ship, the *Amistad,* bound for Cuba and landed it in Connecticut. Supported by a large network of abolitionists, Adams took the case before the U.S. Supreme

One of the most influential and famous Americans of the nineteenth century, Frederick Douglass fought tirelessly against slavery and in favor of a wide range of social reforms.

© The Granger Collection, New York

Court and won not only the acquittal of the Africans for murdering the ship's captain but their freedom as well.

Black antislavery speakers greatly strengthened the antislavery cause. Abolitionists such as Henry Brown, Henry Bibb, Solomon Northup, Sojourner Truth, **Harriet Tubman,** and Ellen Craft electrified audiences. Slavery, they made clear, was nothing like the benign institution portrayed by its defenders. Public speakers such as Henry Highland Garnet urged listeners to "strike for your lives and liberties. Let every slave throughout the land do this, and the days of slavery are numbered. Rather die freemen than live to be slaves. Remember that you are FOUR MILLIONS! . . . Let your motto be resistance! resistance! RESISTANCE!"

Although white abolitionists valued the contributions of their black compatriots, they urged black speakers not to make too much of a fuss when confronted with the insults and indignities faced by black people in the North. African American abolitionists chafed under the restrictions they faced from fellow reformers and enemies alike; they demanded greater rights for northern as well as southern blacks. Their experiences showed the extent to which race was a national problem.

One of the most remarkable Americans of the nineteenth century burst into visibility in the early 1840s.

Frederick Douglass had grown up in Maryland. Like other places in the Upper South, Maryland's economy was diversifying in the 1830s and 1840s as commerce intensified and railroads spread. Douglass learned to read from his mistress, though it was against the law for her to teach him. He carried with him a copy of *Webster's Spelling Book* and *The Columbian Orator,* a book of speeches, including a slave's persuasive argument with his master to set him free.

Sent to Baltimore by his owner, Douglass worked in the shipyards, continued to read widely, and plotted his escape to freedom. After several attempts, Douglass finally borrowed the papers of a free black sailor and rode a train to freedom. Douglass found himself in New York City, alone and without any notion of what he should do. A runaway slave might be hunted down by a slave catcher for a reward. Fortunately for Douglass, he met a black man who introduced the young runaway to the New York Anti-Slavery Society. After white abolitionists saw the skill with which he spoke, they sent Douglass to lecture throughout the North with William Lloyd Garrison.

Development of an American Culture

European visitors had long scoffed at the failure of the United States to create anything they considered "culture," stimulating defensiveness and resentment among Americans. During the first desperate decades of the nation's experience, filled with war, economic panic, and political conflict, few Americans found opportunity to write novels, produce ambitious paintings, or carve sculpture. But in the 1830s and 1840s, the new country experienced a sudden outburst of creativity in everything from the most elevated philosophy to the most popular amusements.

Transcendentalism

Leading thinkers saw the possibilities of improvement everywhere, not just in education or reform. Several of those thinkers came out of Unitarianism, a form of liberal Christianity especially strong in New England. Unitarianism encouraged people to emphasize feeling rather than dogma. Several young people raised within the Unitarian Church took these ideas further than their elders intended, rejecting much Christian doctrine. A belief in the literal truth of the Bible, these youthful critics argued, trapped religion in the past. Better to appeal directly to the heart from the very beginning. These thinkers wanted religion to transcend the limits of churches and denominations.

Women played an active role in the effort to create a tradition of American philosophy, with Margaret Fuller becoming especially important. Fuller, raised in the Unitarian Church in Cambridge, Massachusetts, received a fine education. But she felt herself adrift, full of "unemployed force," after her male classmates went on to college. She read widely and taught school with two other important figures in the revolt against Unitarianism: Elizabeth Peabody and Bronson Alcott. These three, like Horace Mann, believed that children were innately good and that education should be designed to let that goodness flourish. They argued that school, like church, should not be permitted to get in the way of people's natural connection with nature and with one another.

They soon took their lead from **Ralph Waldo Emerson.** Emerson had grown up around Concord, Massachusetts. Though descended from a distinguished ministerial family, he was raised by a widowed mother and forced to work his way through Harvard College. Uncomfortable as a minister and dissatisfied as a schoolteacher, Emerson set out for Europe. There he met exciting English intellectuals whose stirring ideas were to influence him deeply: Samuel Coleridge, Thomas Carlyle, and William Wordsworth. These writers, caught up in European romanticism with its rejection of the austere logic of the Enlightenment, provided Emerson with a perspective far removed from the cool Unitarianism on which he had been raised. Emerson perceived humankind as deeply tied to nature, filled with its rhythms and longings. He published such ideas in his first book, *Nature* (1836), a work that gained him considerable attention from the like-minded young people of New England.

But it was Emerson's address before the Phi Beta Kappa initiates at Harvard in 1837 that announced his arrival to a larger audience. Emerson worried over the state of the nation after the Panic of 1837. The panic directly touched one of Emerson's friends in Concord, Henry David Thoreau, who graduated from Harvard in the panic year and could find no decent job. Emerson,

Library of Congress, Prints and Photographs Division

Ralph Waldo Emerson was America's first popular intellectual, a combination of poet, lecturer, entertainer, and minister.

older than Thoreau, had finally achieved some economic security in the summer of 1837, thanks to an inheritance, but he was well aware of the difficulties facing even the Phi Beta Kappa graduates of Harvard during August of that hard year.

Emerson titled his speech "The American Scholar." He argued that the scholar should be a man of action, a man of nature, a man of risk and endeavor. Books and poetry held tremendous power, Emerson admitted, but it was in activity, in striving, that the scholar became truly American. It was time to set the teachings of Europe aside long enough to find America's own voice, Emerson told the graduates.

Echoes of these ideas were also heard in the South. William Gilmore Simms, a leading essayist, novelist, and poet from South Carolina, traveled throughout the South delivering lectures to communities, universities, and learned societies on diverse topics such as "English Literature" and "The Philosophy of History." Like Emerson, Simms saw American scholars armed with "the sufficient spear of truth" who "shall compel the deference of sordid politicians."

Speakers developed these ideas throughout the late 1830s, enjoying growing fame and influence through public lectures. Railroads made it feasible for the first time for speakers to cover a large amount of territory. Public speaking generally paid much better than any kind of writing. The growth of newspapers and other printing facilitated advertising, getting word of the lectures out beforehand and spreading summaries of the lectures to those unable to attend. In the lecture hall, Emerson exulted, "everything is admissible, philosophy, ethics, divinity, criticism, poetry, humor, fun, mimicry, anecdotes, jokes, ventriloquism. . . ." People flocked to the lectures for personal improvement and social camaraderie.

Emerson's home in Concord became the gathering place for a group who came to be called the **transcendentalists,** who sought to "transcend" the mundane into the mystical knowledge that every human possessed if he or she would listen to it. Margaret Fuller became the editor of the *Dial,* the transcendentalist magazine, while Elizabeth Peabody opened a bookstore catering to the interests of the group. Bronson Alcott and about 80 others founded Brook Farm, one of the many utopian communities that tried to get off the ground in the 1830s and 1840s. Brook Farm put people to work in the fields in the morning and on their books in the afternoon. The community produced both crops and an impressive weekly newspaper. Its schools stood as examples of enlightened education. The experiment failed economically after a few years, but for a while Brook Farm offered the possibility of combining intellectual excitement, physical work, and social responsibility in a way the transcendentalists craved.

DOING HISTORY ONLINE

Ralph Waldo Emerson on the American Scholar, 1837

Read the excerpted passage from Ralph Waldo Emerson's "The American Scholar" in this module. What do you imagine he might have to say about the shows produced by the New York City theaters in 1841?

History ⧗ Now™   Visit HistoryNOW to access primary sources and exercises related to this topic: http://now.ilrn.com/ayers_etal3e

Since the transcendentalists believed that people should establish a close connection to nature, Henry David Thoreau decided to conduct an "experiment in human ecology." He wanted to see—and show—how a modern man could live in harmony with nature. In 1845, he built an isolated house in the woods near Walden Pond, carefully calculating the cost of nails and other supplies and keeping a thoughtful journal. He strove to be self-sufficient and self-contained. The experiment proved important for the book Thoreau eventually published about his experience, *Walden: Life in the Woods* (1854).

Emergence of a Popular Culture

The transcendentalists were not alone in their craving for intensity. American painters, sculptors, and writers found an increasing audience for their works in the 1830s. And so did entrepreneurs who sought out the largest audiences they could find with spectacle and controversy.

Thomas Cole was the key figure in the emergence of American painting. Though born in England, he came to the Ohio frontier as a small child. Cole taught himself to paint but went to England and Italy to perfect his art. He returned to the village of Catskill in New York to paint the Hudson River Valley in the late 1830s and early 1840s. Soon, other painters, such as Asher Durand and Frederick Church, joined Cole in their fascination with the stirring American landscape, creating what became known as the Hudson River School.

Cole also turned to richly symbolic allegorical painting. His journey to Europe had struck him by its contrasts, "both the ruined towers that tell of outrage, and the gorgeous temples that speak of ostentation." He believed America, by contrast, "to be the abode of virtue." He embodied his notions of the cycles of civilization and personal life in two powerful allegorical

Henry David Thoreau, a close friend of Emerson's, embarked on a characteristically American experiment when he went to live alone in the woods at Walden Pond.

Thomas Cole's painting *View from Mount Holyoke, Northampton, Massachusetts, after a Thunderstorm (The Oxbow)* reflects a common theme in the work of American painters in these years: the power as well as the beauty of nature.

series, *The Course of Empire* and *The Voyage of Life.* Engravings of these series became popular fixtures in American homes.

Other important artists followed their own paths through the American landscape. George Catlin spent much of the 1830s living among the American Indians of the Great Plains, making hundreds of drawings and paintings. As a young man he was moved by the sight of an Indian delegation visiting Philadelphia and vowed that "nothing short of the loss of my life shall prevent me from visiting their country and becoming their historian." In Catlin's paintings, easterners thought they might catch the last glimpse of a disappearing people.

Audiences could also view vanishing wildlife in the remarkable watercolors of John James Audubon. Audubon, born in Haiti and educated in France, settled on the Kentucky frontier as a merchant after he married. He loved the American wilderness too much to stay in his shop, though, and he launched out on daunting journeys to record the environment and appearance of the birds of the young nation. After 10 years of work Audubon produced *The Birds of America, from Original Drawings,*

with 435 Plates Showing 1,065 Figures in four immense volumes, completing the project in 1838.

The most popular artistic production of antebellum America was a statue: Hiram Powers's *The Greek Slave,* completed in 1846. Powers grew up in the raw country of Ohio but moved to Italy as he prospered. There, Powers sculpted his statue of a nude young woman bound in chains. The young woman represented, Powers said, a Greek girl captured by the Turks in the Greco-Turkish war. As such, she represented Christianity and whiteness, unbowed by the evil and darkness surrounding her. Powers sought, and received, the endorsement of a group of American clergymen, removing any qualms audiences might have. *The Greek Slave* served as the model for hundreds of miniature copies that appeared in the drawing rooms of the finest homes.

The same drawing rooms also contained a novelty of the age: **daguerreotypes.** This form of photography developed in France but arrived in the United States in 1838 soon after its creation. Within a few years, more than 80 young photographers practiced their craft in New York City alone and by 1850 as many as 10,000 daguerreotypists had set up shop. This early photography

Hiram Powers's statue *The Greek Slave* became an American sensation, attracting large crowds and many imitators.

Edgar Allan Poe experimented with new literary forms, crafting remarkable stories and poems of terror and dread.

was cumbersome and required long periods of stillness before the camera, but the American people hurried to studios to have their portraits done.

Engravings based on paintings and photographs soon filled the publications coming off the presses. For the first time, illustrations could be produced cheaply. Etched metal plates replaced crude woodcuts for the mass production of lithographs of popular subjects such as Bible stories, sporting events, shipwrecks, and railroad disasters. Magazines, incorporating short stories and illustrations, became tailored to specialty audiences such as children, farmers, women, and sportsmen.

Seeing the opportunity afforded by this emergence of a popular audience for print, American writers worked hard to fill the hunger. One especially gifted author, Edgar Allan Poe, skillfully navigated between the market and his art. Poe wrote short stories, the kind of writing most in demand, but he brought to the form a kind of self-consciousness few had demonstrated before. Poe tapped into a widespread fascination with the occult, crime, séances, and ghosts, filling his work with ruins,

shadows, and legends. Works such as "The Murders in the Rue Morgue" marked the first appearance of the detective story. Throughout the 1840s, Poe published stories such as "The Masque of the Red Death," "The Pit and the Pendulum," and "The Tell-Tale Heart" and poetry such as "The Raven." Plagued by ill health, however, Poe did not survive the decade.

P. T. Barnum exploited the public fascination with the macabre and fanciful and opened his American Museum in New York in 1841. Barnum displayed oddities that strained the limits of belief but that could not be completely disproved. He displayed an aged black woman who he claimed was 161 years old and had been

P. T. Barnum's American Museum. This painting captures the atmosphere of fascination and energy that surrounded everything the great American showman produced.

George Washington's nurse. Thousands turned out to gaze at her infirm body and hear her tales of "dear little George." Unlike earlier museum curators, Barnum frankly offered entertainment, including magicians and midgets such as the famous Tom Thumb and the Feejee Mermaid, actually a monkey skeleton attached to the bones of a large fish. The fact that the "curiosities" were often attacked as fakes by scientists did not seem to deter visitors: Barnum's American Museum flourished for the next 20 years and his public tours with Swedish singer Jenny Lind enraptured millions and habituated Americans to a culture of celebrity and publicity stunts.

The Transformation of American Politics

Popular politics had expanded in the United States since the 1820s, when Andrew Jackson electrified the electorate and when states lowered the obstacles of political participation. The two major parties, the Democrats and the Whigs, had experimented with ways to mobilize voters and to retain the power they won. The system grew throughout the 1830s, but no one was prepared for what happened in 1840.

The Election of 1840

The contest of 1840 should have offered an easy contest for the Whigs. Much of the nation remained mired in depression. President Van Buren offered little effective leadership during the economic crisis and many people held him to blame for the hard times. But the Whigs were not as strong as they might have been. Their party had been built piece by piece in the 1830s in reaction to Andrew Jackson. As a result, the party was a crazy quilt of interests and factions. In 1836, the party had even permitted three candidates to run against Van Buren because no one man could command the party's full allegiance. Party leaders vowed that they would not make the same mistake in 1840.

The Whigs were determined to find the one man who stood for the common beliefs that unified Whigs beneath their surface differences. Those beliefs turned around faith in commerce, self-control, Protestantism, learning, and self-improvement. Most important, the Whigs wanted to make an active response to the depression plaguing the nation by putting money in circulation, building internal improvements, and strengthening banks. The trick was to find a candidate who embodied their beliefs without appearing to be "aristocratic" or hungry for power.

The Whig party found such a man in William Henry Harrison. Harrison had made his name as a general—most notably in his defeat of an Indian confederacy in the Battle of Tippecanoe in 1811—and later served in the House of Representatives and in the Senate. He had won fame without gathering many political liabilities and was identified with no particular position.

Seeking to balance their ticket, the Whigs chose Senator John Tyler of Virginia. Tyler shared few beliefs with his fellow Whigs, but his embrace of slavery helped mollify southerners. Moreover, his name made a nice pairing in the phrase that soon became famous: "Tippecanoe and Tyler, Too." One Whig warned that the combination of Harrison and Tyler had "rhyme, but no reason in it."

The Democrats were relieved that the Whigs had nominated Harrison. Democrats considered the old general a nonentity; one reporter commented sarcastically that if Harrison were merely given some hard cider and a small pension he would contentedly sit out the rest of his days in a log cabin. (He actually lived in a mansion and was a rich man.) The sarcasm backfired, though, for many Americans, still living in rural homesteads, saw log cabins and home-brewed cider as evidence of American virtue and self-reliance. The Whigs, long frustrated at their reputation as snobs and elitists, seized on hard cider and log cabins as symbols of their party's loyalty to the common American.

All over the country, Whig speakers displayed paintings, signs, flags, and models of log cabins at huge outdoor rallies while freely dispensing cider to thirsty crowds. Harrison himself went out on the campaign trail, the first presidential candidate to do so. A new kind of American political style was being forged. For the first time, women became prominent at these rallies, encouraging

Democrats warned that the log cabin and hard cider imagery of the Whigs were mere traps to snare voters against their true wishes.

The Election of 1840

The remarkable success of the two-party system in transforming the American political landscape was dramatized by the election of 1840. Slavery had torn at the nation ever since the Missouri Compromise, with the rapid spread of the institution all the way past the Mississippi River into Missouri, Arkansas, and Louisiana and the sudden rise of abolitionism in the North. Looking at this map, however, one would never know that these momentous things had happened. The great majority of states contained areas where either the Whigs or the Democrats dominated, the two areas balancing out almost evenly in most states so that both parties competed for every vote. The Whig party faced a difficult balancing act, for the map shows that the party won in Massachusetts and Connecticut, where antislavery was strong, and in the areas of Alabama and Georgia, where plantation slavery dominated. National leaders somehow had to appeal to both constituencies if they were to remain in power.

MAP 11.4 **The Election of 1840**

their husbands, fathers, and suitors with smiles, waving kerchiefs, and riding in parades with pro-Harrison banners they had sewn. The Whigs embraced causes many women supported, such as temperance and church attendance.

The Democrats had no idea of how to respond to the hard cider and log cabin campaign. Martin Van Buren proved an easy target for a Whig campaign that emphasized homespun values. The president's portly figure and penchant for silk vests and doeskin gloves made the Democrats' long-standing claims of representing the common man look hypocritical. Andrew Jackson himself came out to campaign, firing the same charges against the Whigs that had worked so well in the past, charges of elitism, hostility to slavery, and softness on the bank issue. Even these charges failed. Harrison won 19 of the 26 states, bringing about half a million new voters to the Whigs (see Map 11.4). Voter turnout surged to a level almost unimaginable just a decade earlier: 8 of every 10 eligible voters went to the polls. After 1840, elections would demand the combination of active campaigning, the search for potent symbols, and boisterous public displays that had proven so successful in that year.

Tyler, Webster, and Diplomacy

The Whig celebration did not last long. Harrison, determined to prove his fitness despite his age, expounded the longest inaugural speech in American history in March 1841. Unfortunately, the weather was bitterly cold; Harrison contracted pneumonia and died exactly a month after taking office. John Tyler had become president even though he shared few of the prevailing ideals of the Whigs in Congress. Efforts on the part of Whig leaders to expand the power and reach of government with tariffs, banks, and internal improvements proved fruitless in the face of Tyler's opposition. Whig leaders in Congress responded by gathering in the Capitol gardens and excommunicating him from the party. Whig newspapers denounced him as "His Accidency" and the "Executive Ass." All but one of the members of the cabinet Tyler inherited from Harrison resigned in protest.

The only member to stay on, Daniel Webster, the secretary of state, did so because he feared his rival Henry Clay's ascendancy if he resigned and he did not think it proper to step down until important negotiations with England were complete. Conflicts between the two countries had broken out over the boundary between the United States and Canada. In 1837, armed men had fought along the border as Americans aided a rebel movement trying to overthrow British control of Canada; later, Canadian militia burned an American steamboat carrying supplies for the insurgents, generating intense anger in the northern United States. Armed battle also erupted in the "Aroostock War" over the disputed boundary between Maine and New Brunswick.

Conflict had long been building between the British and the Americans, too, over the African slave trade. Great Britain insisted that its vessels be permitted to search American ships off the coast of Africa to prevent the transportation of slaves to British colonies where slavery had ended in 1832. Americans resented the intrusion in its affairs and refused. The issue threatened to explode in 1841, when American slaves seized the slaving ship the *Creole,* which was taking them from Virginia to New Orleans. The slaves steered the vessel to the Bahamas and claimed their freedom under British law. Much to the anger of southern whites, the British gave sanctuary to the slaves.

Daniel Webster met with the British representative, Lord Ashburton, to settle these issues before they flamed up into a war that neither nation wanted. After extensive debate, the United States and Great Britain decided on a new boundary that gave each about half of what each had claimed in Maine and in the area to the west of Lake Superior. The Webster-Ashburton Treaty also established joint American-British patrols to intercept ships carrying slaves from Africa. Though the treaty stipulated that the United States must maintain a minimum presence totaling 80 guns along the African coast, Tyler's secretary of the navy undercut American effectiveness by sending only 4 large and slow ships instead of schooners better suited for the task of coastal patrolling. In 1850, while the U.S. Navy had captured only 7 slavers since beginning the patrols, the British had captured more than 500 ships and freed more than 38,000 Africans.

The Challenge of the West

Americans of every sort kept their eyes to the west. Railroads, telegraphs, canals, and roads strained in that direction; population restlessly flowed there. But thoughtful people recognized that the lack of borders and limits posed threats as well as potential. When everything seemed possible, people placed few checks on their appetites. Every boundary was contested, every obstacle attacked.

The "Wests"

The hard times in the East made moving west seem an increasingly attractive option. Horace Greeley, the most influential newspaper editor of the day, warned people looking for a job in the midst of the depression not to come to the city but rather to "go to the Great West." To people in New England, migration to the West in the 1840s often meant migration to the lands of the northern plains and surrounding the Great Lakes. To people from Virginia and Kentucky, migration to the West might mean heading to the free states of Ohio, Indiana, or Illinois or, more often, to Mississippi, Louisiana, and Texas. For people from the cities of the East, the destination might be a booming new city such as Indianapolis, Chicago, or Detroit (see Map 11.5).

One "West" that captured the imagination of Americans in these years lay in Oregon and Mexican California, word of whose beauty and wealth had slowly filtered east throughout the preceding decade. Although many people considered it nothing less than suicide to attempt to cross the Rockies and what was considered "The Great American Desert," a growing stream of families

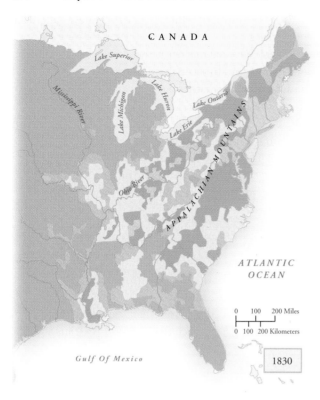

decided to take the chance. Echoing earlier tall stories of the frontier, Peter H. Burnett, organizer of the "Great Migration" of 1843, regaled listeners with tales of Oregon's wealth and fertility.

Most of those who moved to the Pacific coast gathered in northern Missouri or southern Iowa. They set out in early May across undulating plains, with water and fuel easy to find, their wagons pulled by oxen. The settlers gradually ascended to Fort Laramie, at the edge of the Rockies. By July, they had reached the Continental Divide, the point at which rivers on one side flowed to the east and those on the other flowed to the west. On the trail for more than three months by this point, the settlers had covered two-thirds of the distance of their journey.

From the Divide, the settlers heading to California split off from those going to Oregon. Both faced enormous difficulties in the remainder of their trip. They raced the weather, for early mountain snowstorms could be deadly. Some of the mountainous areas were so steep that wagons had to be dragged up one side and let down the other with ropes, chains, and pulleys. Finally, by

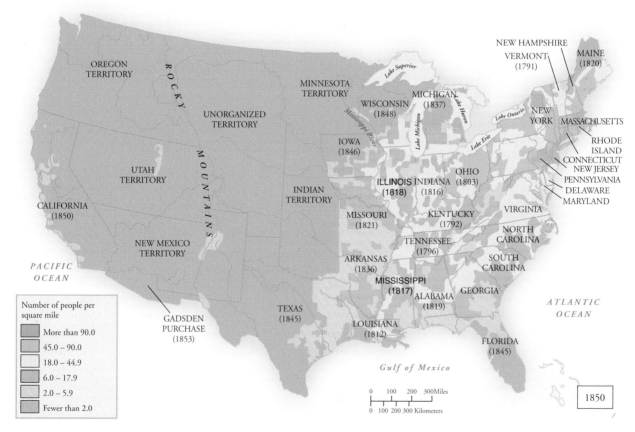

MAP 11.5 a & b Population Expansion, 1830–1850

The population of the United States moved steadily westward at the same time that the Northeast became ever more densely settled. The population of the South remained thinner because plantations did not concentrate people as the family farms and towns of the North did.

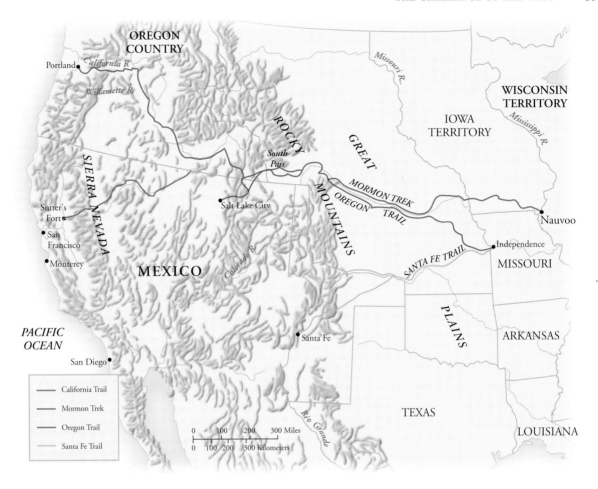

MAP 11.6 Trails to the West
The trails to Oregon and California looked straightforward enough on a map but proved immensely challenging, even deadly, in practice.

October, 2,000 miles and six months after they had left Missouri or Iowa, the settlers crossed one last ridge and looked down on the sparkling valleys of Sacramento or the Willamette River (see Map 11.6).

Migration to the Pacific began slowly, with only a few dozen families making the treacherous journey between 1840 and 1842. The numbers mounted between 1843 and 1845, when more than 5,000 people passed through Utah on their way to Oregon and California. Throughout the 1840s, the great majority of migrants chose Oregon over Mexican California as their destination. Even so, distances still mattered: from the 1840s until the completion of the transcontinental railroad in 1869, Oregon grew from a few hundred white settlers to more than 100,000. By comparison, in the same period, Iowa's population jumped from a few thousand to 1.2 million. Oregon came to seem a respectable place for literate and upright Protestant families to settle, whereas California seemed a gamble, attractive mainly to single men willing to take their chances in a foreign country.

Manifest Destiny

In 1842, the Great United States Exploring Expedition returned from an ocean journey of 87,780 nautical miles. It had circumnavigated the globe, located Antarctica, and explored the Pacific coast. The captain of the expedition reported that Oregon was a treasure trove of "forests, furs, and fisheries." If the United States did not use its military to occupy the territory all the way to the 54°40' boundary, it would be risking much more than the Oregon territory itself. California might throw off the light Mexican rule under which it rested and join with an independent Oregon to create a nation "that is destined to control the destinies of the Pacific." The Tyler administration sought to downplay this report, not wanting to disrupt negotiations still pending on the boundary of Maine and Wisconsin.

The forces of expansion proved too strong for the administration to contain, however. In 1845, newspaper editor John Louis O'Sullivan announced that it was the "**manifest destiny**"—the clear and unavoidable fate—of the United States "to overspread the continent allotted by Providence for the free development of our yearly multiplying millions." In other words, God intended white Protestant Americans to fill in every corner of the continent, pushing aside American Indians, Mexicans, English, or anyone else.

The Democrats in Congress and President Tyler supported this expansion, focusing first on Texas. If the United States did not quickly annex Texas, Democrats contended, it might fall under the sway of the British and become not only a barrier to further American migration but also a bastion of antislavery. If, by contrast, the United States acted quickly, Texas could attract not only slaveholders and their slaves but also emancipated slaves, keeping them away from the North and the other attractive lands such as California and Oregon. Midwestern Democrats, for their part, agreed that westward expansion was essential to the American future. The country simply could not afford to have major ports and potential markets sealed off. These Democrats had their eye on Oregon.

In 1844, James K. Polk, a former governor of Tennessee, got the Democratic nomination for president after an acrimonious convention and nine ballots. The Democrats appealed to both northerners and southerners with a program of aggressive expansion, attempting to counter fears of slavery's growth not by rejecting Texas but by embracing Oregon.

Politics in Turmoil

In 1844, the Whigs nominated Henry Clay for president on a program explicitly opposed to expansion. The apparently clear-cut choice between Clay and Polk soon became complicated, however. Clay announced that he would not oppose Texas annexation if it could be done peacefully and by consensus. Such a strategy backfired, attracting few advocates of expansion but alienating antislavery advocates and opponents of expansion. Although Polk only won 49.6 percent of the vote, hardly a ringing endorsement of aggressive expansionism, he entered office with a clear vision of annexing large areas of Mexican territory, Texas, and Oregon.

Meanwhile, the early 1840s witnessed bloody battles over religion. A growing stream of immigrants from Ireland, the great majority of them Catholic, flowed into northern cities. In Protestant eyes, the Roman Catholic Church posed a direct threat to American institutions. That church's hierarchy was undemocratic, critics charged. Catholics would obey the Pope rather than act as loyal Americans. In 1844, the largest anti-Catholic riot of antebellum America broke out in Philadelphia;

several Catholic churches burned to the ground while local firemen, rather than fight the blaze, simply hosed down the surrounding buildings to prevent the fire from spreading. Because the Democrats proved far more sympathetic to the Irish than did the largely Protestant Whigs, the political differences between the parties now became inflamed with religious and ethnic conflict.

Slavery, too, became an even more explosive issue in the early 1840s and led to **religious schisms**. In 1844, the Methodist church divided over slavery, and the Baptists split the following year. Southern church leaders were angry that many of their northern brethren refused to believe that American slavery was part of God's plan and bitterly resented their northern brethren's passage of a clause demanding no communion with slaveholders. Five hundred thousand southerners formed the Methodist Episcopal Church, South, while Baptists from nine southern states created the Southern Baptist Convention. Questions about slavery moved beyond laws and the Constitution into debates about sin, evil, and God's plan for the nation. As New York Governor William Marcy explained to John C. Calhoun, "I can fight your battles so long as you make the Constitution your fortress, but if you go to the Bible or make it a question of ethics, you must not expect me or any respectable member of the free states to be with you."

The conflicts over slavery exerted immediate political consequences. The abolitionist Liberty party won 62,000 votes in 1844. In New York, in fact, the Liberty party's strong showing took enough votes from Clay to give the state to Polk. And those electoral votes proved the difference in the national election; Polk won the presidency by the narrowest of margins.

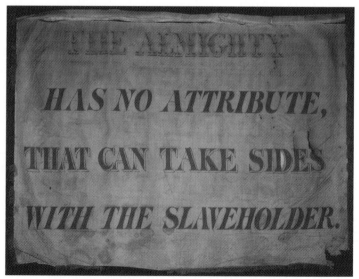

This banner proclaimed slaveholding a sin and left no room for excuse or explanation by slaveholders.

MAP 11.7 Oregon Boundary Dispute
Although many Americans called for "54°40' or Fight," the United States and England agreed on establishing the border at 49°, an extension of the boundary farther east.

Even before Polk took office the Senate voted to annex Texas, an independent republic since 1836, as soon as Texas consented. Texas gave its approval in the fall of 1845 and won its vote for annexation in Washington at the end of that year. The Democrats sought to quiet concerns among northerners by also annexing Oregon. Though Americans, including some northern Democrats in Congress, clamored for all of Oregon to its northernmost boundary with Russian territory, chanting "Fifty-four Forty or Fight," Polk secretly negotiated with Britain to set the boundary at the 49th parallel, an extension of the northern U.S. boundary from the east (see Map 11.7). Northern Democrats who had supported Polk on Texas felt betrayed and cheated by this southern conspiracy to "strangle Oregon." Their resentment of Polk's handling of Oregon would smolder, ready to flare again.

Conclusion

The years around 1840, like other eras in American history, were relatively quiet in terms of obvious events we might think of as "history"; there was no major war, for example. Instead, this period was marked by a far more common occurrence: a sharp slowdown in the nation's economy. The "panic," as a crisis in banking and investment was known, and the subsequent loss of jobs, decline in prices, and loss of property—what we would now call a "recession"—presented people with some sharp choices. Would they uproot their families and move to another county, state, or territory? Would they reject the political leaders who had apparently led the country astray? Would they join with other people to make fundamental changes in American society during these times of apparent failure? For many people, the answer to each of these questions was "yes." That is why the late 1830s and early 1840s marked a period of special ferment.

The panic and the hard times that followed touched virtually every American, rich or poor. No social programs helped cushion the blow with unemployment benefits, health insurance, or job training. People of wealth suddenly saw investments fail and property disappear. Laboring people found their jobs had vanished when their employers no longer had the money with which to pay them. Even enslaved people could feel the effects of the panic, as hard-pressed owners might decide to sell a child or sibling to bring in extra cash. The economy was the one part of American life that touched everyone, regardless of gender or skin color.

People in trouble, though, confronted widely differing options. There was nothing a slave could do when faced with sale. A free family, on the other hand, could decide that things must be better somewhere else and could load all they owned into a wagon and head west, looking for land on which they could settle. The poorest working people in cities, however, did not have this option. They had no money with which to buy a wagon, oxen, and provisions. They could only make it somehow to another town and city and hope they could find a job that would put food in their mouths.

Some people, when confronted with such deep challenges, sought to make serious changes in their society. The most obvious recourse was to remove the political party in power at the time of the economic troubles, and that is just what happened in 1840—as it has in many decades since. Martin Van Buren was replaced with a relatively obscure former general, William Henry Harrison of the Whigs, newly aggressive with their log cabin and cider campaign. It was no accident that these symbols of a simpler, more secure time proved powerful when the increasingly sophisticated American economy suddenly crashed.

Perhaps, too, it was no accident that the late 1830s and early 1840s generated the most active period of social reform the United States had ever seen. The hard times presented many reasons to change people's lives.

A working man without a job simply could not afford to drink; his family counted on him to bring every dime home. Therefore, for the first time poorer people mobilized themselves to limit drinking in their midst in the Washingtonian movement. Other people, better off, developed a growing sympathy with those who lived in want all of the time—the enslaved people of the South. Men and women who had not seen slavery firsthand imagined what it would be like to have no freedom as well as no economic security.

Not everything that happened in these years was the direct result of the hard times. Railroads and telegraphs spread relentlessly despite the evaporation of investment money, and they flourished as prosperity returned. Artists such as Cole, Audubon, and Powers painted their pictures and carved their sculptures despite the economic conditions, and authors such as Emerson and Poe set their eyes on subjects far removed from the immediate present. But even these people lived in their times, taking advantage of growing towns, railroads, and printing presses of the early 1840s to create new audiences for their work. Both long-term and short-term changes in American life shaped everything that people who lived in these years experienced.

The Chapter in Review

In the years between 1837 and 1845:

- The United States experienced the largest economic depression it had ever seen.
- Railroads began to spread over large parts of the country.
- The Washingtonian movement against alcohol gathered momentum.
- Abolitionism spread, but so did a violent reaction against abolitionists.
- Major figures of philosophy emerged in the Transcendentalist movement, and the United States saw its first original artists.
- The election of 1840 redefined electoral politics.
- Many Americans followed trails to the Pacific Coast.

Making Connections Across Chapters

LOOKING BACK

As Chapter 11 shows, the years surrounding 1840 presented Americans of all descriptions with the biggest economic challenge the country had yet seen, combining a sharp panic with long-term changes in the fundamental structures of the American economy.

1. How did the business cycle shape people's lives in ways they may not have been perceived at the time?

2. How much did reform movements grow from optimism and how much from fear of social disorder? Why did they tend to be stronger in the North than in the South?

LOOKING AHEAD

Chapter 12 will show that after the hard times of the early 1840s the United States entered a period of rampant expansion, political mobilization, and economic growth.

1. How did the election of 1840 influence every campaign that followed? Were those changes positive, negative, or mixed?

2. What legacy did the major cultural events of the late 1830s and early 1840s leave on American culture?

Recommended Readings

Ballesein, Edward J. *Navigating Failure: Bankruptcy and Commercial Society in Antebellum America* (2001) paints a compelling portrait of the financial turmoil of these years.

Ely, Melvin Patrick. *Israel on the Appomattox : A Southern Experiment in Black Freedom from 1790s through the Civil War* (2004) is a wonderfully evocative portrayal of free black life in the slave South.

Fehrenbacher, Don E. *The Slaveholding Republic: An Account of the United States Government's Relations to Slavery* (2001) offers a magisterial overview of this important subject.

Genovese, Eugene. *Roll, Jordan, Roll: The World the Slaves Made* (1974) stands as the most powerful portrayal of American slavery.

Hine, Robert V., and John Mack Faragher. *The American West: A New Interpretive History* (2000) presents a fresh interpretation of a crucial American region.

Holt, Michael F. *The Rise and Fall of the American Whig Party: Jacksonian Politics and the Onset of the Civil War* (1999) is a remarkable act of scholarship, describing important political change in every part of the nation.

Johnson, Walter. *Soul by Soul: Life Inside the Antebellum Slave Market* (1999) is the best study of the vast domestic slave trade.

Kaestle, Carl F. *Pillars of the Republic: Common Schools and American Society, 1780–1860* (1983) is the most thorough and balanced account of education reform.

Larson, John Lauritz. *Internal Improvement: National Public Works and the Promise of Popular Government in the Early United States* (2001) is a valuable interpretation of one of the most important changes in these decades.

Licht, Walter. *Industrializing America: The Nineteenth Century* (1995) is an extremely helpful overview.

Reiss, Benjamin. *The Showman and the Slave: Race, Death, and Memory in Barnum's America* (2001) tells the fascinating story of the connection between popular culture, commerce, and race.

Stevenson, Brenda E. *Life in Black and White: Family and Community in the Slave South* (1996) paints a potent picture of both white and black Southerners.

Identifications

Review your understanding of the following key terms, people, events, and dates for this chapter (these terms also appear in the Glossary at the end of the book):

public education
Martin Van Buren
Panic of 1837
Samuel F. B. Morse
temperance movement
Grimké sisters
Liberty party

Election of 1840
Amistad
Harriet Tubman
Frederick Douglass
Ralph Waldo Emerson
transcendentalists
daguerreotypes
America's "Wests"
manifest destiny
religious schisms

Online Sources Guide

Use this listing to find online documents, images, interactive maps, simulations, and other resources related to this chapter:

American History Resource Center

http://history.wadsworth.com/rc/us

Documents

Excerpts from *Narrative of the Life of Frederick Douglass*
J. H. Hammond, *Slavery in the Light of Political Science* (1845)

Selected Images

Phineas Taylor Barnum
Immigrants to the West making camp in the snow

Document Exercises

1839 Slave Trade Book
1842 American Transcendentalism

HistoryNOW

http://now.ilrn.com/ayers_etal3e

Primary Source Exercises

Ralph Waldo Emerson, "The American Scholar," 1837
Age of Reform
Slavery

12 Expansion and Reaction, 1846–1854

The American whaling industry was at its peak during the 1840s and 1850s. Ship after ship left New England to cover the oceans of the world in pursuit of the profitable prey. Whaling also served as the subject of the greatest novel of the era, *Moby-Dick,* though it went unappreciated at the time.

© Peabody Essex Museum, Salem, Massachusetts, USA/Bridgeman Art Library

The years of territorial expansion, population growth, and prosperity that followed victory in a war with Mexico also proved to be years of unprecedented foreboding for the United States. Positive changes came accompanied with discouraging consequences. Heightened expectations of a transcontinental American empire led to bitter political fighting, the immigration of working people from Europe fueled social conflict, and activists discovered that progress for women would come only as a result of prolonged effort. All of these events surprised people at the time and disturbed many.

War with Mexico

The immense Spanish territory to the south and west of the United States had been a major concern for generations. Throughout the 1820s American leaders had struggled with Mexican independence; throughout the 1830s and 1840s Americans had aided Texans in their fight against the Mexican army and fought with each other over the **annexation** of Texas to the Union. Americans longed for the territories Mexicans controlled in western North America, but Mexico pledged to keep those lands. No one could be at all certain that the United States could defeat Mexico in a large-scale war, but President Polk seemed determined to find out.

The United States at War

The Mexican government had never recognized the independence of Texas, which Texans claimed as a result of their defeat of Santa Anna in 1836. President James K. Polk raised the stakes by insisting that the border between Texas and Mexico lay at the Rio Grande, not at the Nueces River farther north, the accepted southern border of Texas. Even before the formal annexation of Texas was ratified in July 1845, Polk ordered American troops under the command of General **Zachary Taylor** to cross the Nueces. In December, following acceptance of Texas into the Union, the president ordered American troops to cross the Rio Grande River and occupy the Mexican town of Matamoras.

Polk had his eyes not only on the border with Texas but on larger prizes still: the acquisition of California and New Mexico. Polk ordered John C. Frémont, leading an

Timeline

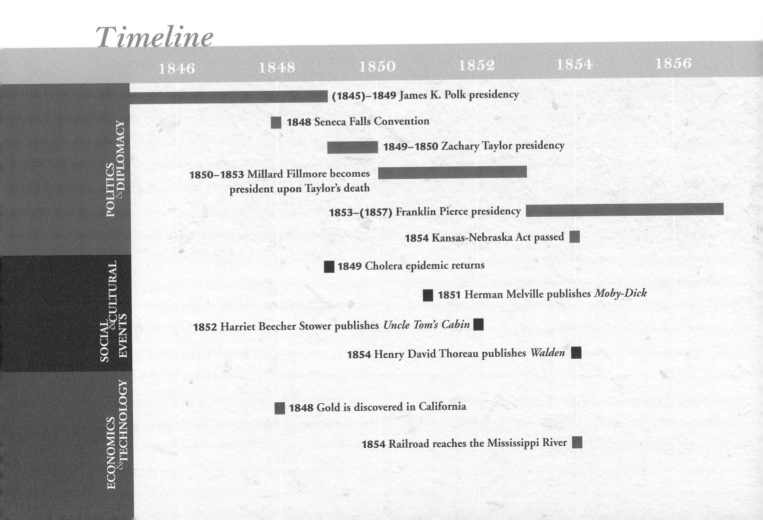

| | 1846 | 1848 | 1850 | 1852 | 1854 | 1856 |

POLITICS & DIPLOMACY

(1845)–1849 James K. Polk presidency

1848 Seneca Falls Convention

1849–1850 Zachary Taylor presidency

1850–1853 Millard Fillmore becomes president upon Taylor's death

1853–(1857) Franklin Pierce presidency

1854 Kansas-Nebraska Act passed

SOCIAL & CULTURAL EVENTS

1849 Cholera epidemic returns

1851 Herman Melville publishes *Moby-Dick*

1852 Harriet Beecher Stower publishes *Uncle Tom's Cabin*

1854 Henry David Thoreau publishes *Walden*

ECONOMICS & TECHNOLOGY

1848 Gold is discovered in California

1854 Railroad reaches the Mississippi River

Exeter, N.H. Volunteers leaving for the Mexican War. Possibly after E. Punderson, daguerreotype, 1/4 plate, ca. 1846, P1979.33/ Amon Carter Museum, Fort Worth, Texas

In this daguerreotype, the only image we have of soldiers leaving for the war with Mexico, young men gather in New Hampshire preparing to travel thousands of miles to the battlefields.

army expedition to map rivers within U.S. borders, to California. Frémont, acting on instructions to seize California "in the event of any occurrence," supported the "Bear Flag Rebellion," an armed struggle by American settlers against the Mexican government. Disrupted, Polk hoped the Mexican provinces might be sacrificed more easily and more cheaply to the United States.

The president prepared for war in Texas, seizing on a skirmish in April 1846 between Mexican and American troops north of the Rio Grande as a convenient excuse. He declared that Mexico had started a war when it "invaded our territory and shed American blood on the American soil." Even though northern Whigs continually denounced the war and its motives, Whig congressmen believed they had to support appropriations for the soldiers in the field. The final vote for war was overwhelming, with only 14 Whig congressmen and 2 senators opposing the president. While unpopular in New England, the war stirred widespread support in the South and West. Enough volunteers to fill 14 regiments swamped recruiters in Illinois and 30,000 men responded in Tennessee, earning the state the nickname the "Volunteer state."

The war with Mexico unfolded in stages and across an enormous area (see Map 12.1). Sixteen hundred American troops under the leadership of Colonel Stephen Kearney took Santa Fe in New Mexico with no casualties late in the summer of 1846. California proved to be a greater struggle, partly because Mexican settlers there put up more of a fight and partly because Frémont—now commanding a volunteer unit comprised of Indian mercenaries, Bear Flaggers, and sharpshooters—provoked fights and stimulated enraged Californios to drive the Americans from Los Angeles. Nevertheless, with seizure of the territory's ports, the American forces won control of California a few months after they had taken New Mexico. The U.S. Army, under Zachary Taylor and Winfield Scott, achieved a startling series of victories in Mexico itself in 1846 and 1847, including an impressive amphibious landing at Vera Cruz by Scott's forces that ended in the conquest of Mexico City and "the halls of Montezuma."

The regular U.S. forces enjoyed impressive leadership from their officer corps. The Mexican War familiarized Americans with names like Ulysses S. Grant, Jefferson Davis, and Robert E. Lee. These well-trained leaders commanded something less than a polished army. As many as 40 percent of recruits were recent immigrants and 35 percent were illiterate. Conditions of service were harsh, with savage discipline, irregular pay, and

The War with Mexico

The war between the United States and Mexico ranged over an enormous territory, though the main battles occurred deep within Mexico. While the navy blockaded the Mexican coastlines, General Winfield Scott landed at Vera Cruz, marched more than 200 miles inland, and seized the capital, Mexico City, forcing a negotiated settlement to the war.

The small military of the United States coped with unprecedented challenges in equipping and supporting an army thousands of miles from supply bases. With the army short nearly 40 percent of authorized strength at the war's beginning, Congress more than doubled the size of the army and called upon the states to provide 50,000 volunteers. Overcoming the challenges of geography and distance, the junior officers and congressmen who managed and supplied

U.S. troops in the Mexican War unknowingly conducted a dress rehearsal for similar difficulties during the Civil War.

The Mexican War was the first reported to Americans using telegraph and express riders to speed information of battles back to newspaper editors who competed fiercely to "scoop" their rivals with the latest news. The president reacted furiously to leaks of secret cabinet meetings and the *New York Herald's* publication of the still-secret Treaty of Guadalupe Hidalgo that ended the war. Attempting to frighten editors, Congress confined the *Herald's* reporter for leaking the treaty. His editor responded by releasing the names of congressmen who regularly slipped confidential stories to the press. The government backed down, and political reporting in Washington was changed permanently.

MAP 12.1 War with Mexico, 1846–1847

View an animated version of this map or related maps at http://history.wadsworth.com/
passages3e.

Going to and Returning from Mexico.

The Mexican War, despite its brevity and American triumph, bore heavy costs: of 48,000 U.S. soldiers, more than 22,000 were killed or wounded. Nearly 10,000 came home with wounds, disease, or injury.

mistreatment of their interests in Oregon by Polk and aware of growing rejection of slavery's expansion among their section's voters, northern Democrats saw the proviso as "our *declaration of independence* from southern dictation, arrogance, and misrule." It passed the House by a vote of 83 to 64, with congressmen, with few exceptions, voting along sectional rather than party lines. The Wilmot Proviso eventually went down to defeat in the Senate and the war proceeded, but from 1846 on, the opponents of slavery's expansion increasingly distrusted Polk, and southern political leaders doubted northern Democrats' reliability on the defense of slavery.

The war with Mexico limped to a conclusion in late 1847 and the beginning of 1848. American troops controlled Mexico City, the Gulf Coast, and all the northern provinces claimed by the United States, but the Mexican government refused to settle on terms of peace. President Polk, General Winfield Scott, and peace commissioner Nicholas Trist bickered over the treaty. Some Americans urged Polk to lay claim to all of the conquered country, others insisted that the United States should seize no territory at all from the war, and many, such as John C. Calhoun, driven by racial fears, wanted to limit seized territories to the sparsely settled regions to prevent "the fatal error of placing these colored races on an equality with the white race." Trist, on his own in Mexico, finally signed a treaty in Guadalupe Hidalgo that brought the negotiations to an end in February 1848.

poor supply. At any period during the Mexican War, one-third of the men on the muster rolls had deserted, the highest rate of desertion among American wars.

The Consequences of War

Many northerners worried about the expansion of slavery and southern political power that might accompany victory over Mexico. To put such concerns to rest, David Wilmot, a first-term Pennsylvania Democrat in favor of the war, made a bold move: when a bill to appropriate $2 million to end the war and purchase California and Mexican territory north of the Rio Grande came before Congress in 1846, Wilmot offered a "proviso," or condition, that declared slavery could not be established in any territory the United States might win from Mexico as a result of the war. Still smarting over perceived

Mexico, for $15 million and the abandonment of American claims against the Mexican government and its people, agreed to sell California, New Mexico, and all of Texas above the Rio Grande. When the treaty finally appeared before Congress for ratification the following month, many doubted that it would pass. Declining popular support for the war derailed plans to send an additional 30,000 troops to occupy northern Mexico. The various cliques, however, swallowed their disagreements long enough to ratify the treaty in March. A prominent newspaper pronounced the treaty "a peace

Flashpoints | Treaty of Guadalupe Hidalgo

The Treaty of Guadalupe Hidalgo in 1848 sealed the most dramatic territorial expansion in United States history. Unlike the Louisiana Purchase, these additional lands were the result of conquest, not sale. Many Americans, unclear about the realities of geography and cocky after their military victory, blithely called for the annexation of all of Mexico. Others feared Mexico's size, Catholicism, racial identity, and potential to shift the balance of power in the United States in favor of slavery and the South. The treaty Nicholas Trist was sent to forge would go a long way toward shaping the rest of American history.

American military officers and government leaders recognized that Mexico, despite its official defeat, could continue guerilla raids and attacks almost indefinitely. The army held the cities, but the countryside became dangerous for all sides. Americans saw the vulnerability, rising costs, and declining public support as reasons to press ahead with a treaty. They did not want to get bogged down in a foreign country.

Mexican military authorities had refused to negotiate until the capture of Mexico City. With Americans occupying the capital, Mexican leaders signed the treaty on February 2, 1848, in a suburb of Mexico City called Guadalupe Hidalgo. Trist had succeeded in getting over 500,000 square miles of territory, land that would become the states of California, Arizona, New Mexico, Colorado, Utah, Nevada, and Wyoming, at a cost of 15 million dollars and cash to pay outstanding claims by U.S. citizens. Both sides fought and schemed to gain the advantage. (American haste combined with poor mapping resulted in Mexico regaining a significant portion of Arizona and New Mexico. It would cost the United States additional money to pur-

chase these lands back in 1853 via the Gadsen purchase, 30,000 square miles of territory along the border bought for 15 million dollars from a cash-strapped Santa Anna.)

The U.S. Senate ratified the treaty in March 1848. The Mexican Congress approved it in May, lamenting that losing their lands was like an "amputation." When combined with the loss of Texas, Mexico had lost approximately one half of its territory since gaining independence in 1821.

The Treaty settled some things but unsettled many more. While the words written in Guadalupe Hidalgo fixed the primary boundaries of the continental United States, those words also set in motion debates and conflicts over the status of this new, sparsely settled land. Whigs divided over the war and the territorial issues it raised; they would never recover their former unanimity. Democrats, too, fractured over the spread of slavery into land gained by the Mexican Cession. The future of slavery would now play out on a vast new stage. The treaty with Mexico ended one war but made another one, pitting Americans against Americans, far more likely than it had been the year before.

This map shows the various boundaries considered in the negotiations over the treaty. Imagine how different the United States and Mexico would be had any of the various alternatives been adopted.

Questions for Reflection

1. Treaties and the like often appear to be "historic" at the time of their signing. Are they generally as important as people take them to be?

2. What might have happened had Trist been unable to complete his negotiations with the Mexican government?

3. Was the United States justified in taking this land from Mexico?

which every one will be glad of, but no one will be proud of." The Mexicans signed the treaty in May and the war finally closed, with Mexico surrendering nearly 600 million acres of territory to the United States.

War and Politics

James K. Polk did not seek reelection in 1848. The Democrats, scrambling to find someone to unite the northern and southern branches of the party, decided on Lewis Cass of Michigan. Cass, a rather colorless man except for his red wig, spoke for the majority of northern Democrats who sympathized with white southerners in their determination to keep black people enslaved. He called for "**popular sovereignty,**" allowing people in the territories to make their own policies on slavery. Antislavery Democrats walked out of the Democratic convention and called their own convention in Buffalo, New York, where they nominated former president Martin Van Buren as the Free-Soil candidate for the presidency.

Abolitionists who had earlier supported the failed Liberty party were intrigued to see a candidate who might win a substantial number of votes. Antislavery "Conscience Whigs" also threw their support behind Van Buren. These various groups forged a working alliance for the election of 1848, declaring their solidarity behind the name of the **Free-Soil party** and its stirring motto: "fight on and fight forever" for "free soil, free speech, free labor, and free men." Opposition to slavery's expansion into the West fractured old party loyalties developed in the Jacksonian era.

The mainstream Whigs found themselves in an awkward spot, for they had fervently opposed the Mexican War but now sought to capitalize on the popularity of General Zachary Taylor, whom they nominated for the presidency. Taylor, a Virginian, had several advantages as a candidate. He had no troubling political past. Though he was a slaveholding planter, he had opposed the war with Mexico before he had been sent there to lead American troops. Just what he thought about anything was unclear, but with his lack of connection to recent bitter party squabbles, Taylor appealed to voters in both sections who desired a less partisan style of political leadership.

Taylor won the election in the electoral college, but the popular vote revealed little consensus. Taylor, with 1,360,000 votes, won eight slave states and seven free ones. Cass won eight free states and seven slave-holding ones, with 1,220,000 votes (see Map 12.2). Although the Free-Soilers' prospects as a third party appeared bleak, Van Buren came in second in several important states and his vote total was large enough to gain the notice of northern Democrats and send 12 men to Congress.

MAP 12.2 The Election of 1848
The balanced strength of the two-party system across the entire country was demonstrated by the 1848 election, in which the candidates won northern and southern states in almost equal numbers.

Americans on the Move

Americans moved in massive numbers in the years around 1850. As the economy improved, transportation developed, boundaries became settled, and gold beckoned, people flooded to the states of the old Northwest and the old Southwest as well as to Texas, Oregon, and California. The suffering of Ireland and political conflict within Germany drove millions across the Atlantic, filling the cities and farms of the East.

Rails, Sails, and Steam

In the late 1840s and early 1850s, the United States had the fastest-growing rail lines and the fastest ships in the world. Private investors poured tens of millions of dollars into rail expansion. The federal government aided railroads with free surveys and vast grants of land. The major cities of the eastern seaboard competed against one another to attract as many rail lines as possible. Owners of mines and factories subsidized new railroads, as did Wall Street speculators and investors from Great Britain.

Railroads proved more important for some parts of the country than for others, especially areas where canals and roads became impassable in winter. Railroads flourished in New England and New York, where the density of population and manufacturing permitted the new technology to work most efficiently. Midwestern states such as Ohio, Illinois, and Indiana also showed themselves well-suited to the railroads, flat and fertile. Chicago had no railroads at all in 1850, but by 1860 12 lines converged in the city.

Rural areas as well as cities immediately felt the effects of the railroad. Farmers now found it profitable to ship their produce to a city a hundred miles away. Previously, crops spoiled or were weather damaged in transit, or the cost and hazards of the journey eliminated the profit. Farmers specialized, becoming dairymen, vegetable growers, and fruit producers. Corn, wheat, hogs, and cattle flowed out of Ohio, Illinois, Indiana, and Wisconsin. The older farms of New England, New York, and Pennsylvania turned to specialty products such as cheese, maple sugar, vegetables, and cranberries. These products rode the railroad tracks to market, tying countryside and city together.

In the South, still recovering from failed improvement schemes and loan repudiation after the economic crises of the late 1830s, railroad building trailed off in the 1840s. While spending levels did not match that of the North, states such as Virginia aggressively pursued rail construction beginning in 1847, and had spent more than $15 million dollars by 1860 in loans to corporations and the building of two state-owned lines. North Carolina reversed decades of opposition to state-supported improvements in 1849, building a major line and subsidizing plank roads, private rail lines, and navigational aids. Despite this progress with railroads, most southern

commerce and passengers relied instead on the steamboats that plied the Mississippi and other major rivers. The riverboats grew in size, number, and ornateness throughout the period. The 1850s marked the glory days of these riverboats, with cotton bales stacked on every square inch of deck.

Elsewhere, packet steamships carried mail, freight, and passengers up and down the eastern seaboard, over the Great Lakes, and as far west as the rivers allowed. Over 57 million newspapers, pamphlets, and magazines and nearly 48 million letters crisscrossed the nation in 1847. Beginning in 1848, Americans could count on regular steam-powered travel between New York and Liverpool, England. These innovations in transportation, exciting as they were, came at a steep cost. "I never open a newspaper that does not contain some account of disasters and loss of life. This world is going on too fast. Oh, for the good old days of heavy post-coaches," one diarist observed.

Clipper ships enjoyed a brief but stirring heyday in the late 1840s and early 1850s. Clippers used narrow hulls and towering sails to attain speeds unreached by any other sailing vessels their size. They sailed from New York to San Francisco, all the way around South America, in less than a hundred days. Although they were to be displaced after 1855 by uglier and more efficient steamships, for a few exciting years the clipper ships thrived on the high prices, small cargoes, long voyages, and the desperate need for speed fueled by remarkable discoveries in California.

The Gold Rush

The natives of California had long known of the gold hidden in the rocks and creeks of that vast territory. White American settlers, too, had found gold deposits in the early 1840s. But it was a discovery in January of 1848 that changed everything.

In 1839, John Sutter emigrated from Switzerland to the area that became Sacramento, where he established a large fort, trading post, and wheat farm. Sutter hired a carpenter named James Marshall to build a mill on the American River. While working on the project, Marshall happened to notice "something shining in the bottom of the ditch." He realized that the nugget, about half the size of a pea, was gold. Sutter, Marshall, and the other men on the place tried to keep the find a secret, but word leaked to San Francisco. There, sailors abandoned their ships, soldiers deserted their barracks, and clerks left their shops to look for gold along the American River. Newspapers stopped publishing and local governments shut down as Mexicans, Indians, and Americans in California rushed to the foothills. By the end of 1848,

Clipper Ships

Graceful and fast, American clipper ships raced around South America and across the Pacific. New England merchants had conducted lucrative trade with Asia since the beginning of the century. American ships ventured to Canton and Shanghai for tea, silks, furs, ginseng, and glassware. In 1852, reflecting the growth of Asian trade, more than 150 various types of vessels rested at anchor in Honolulu. These wooden ships with towering expanses of canvas sails were the fastest craft of their day. Experiments with steam power and iron hulls would eclipse the great clipper ships by the 1860s, but their beauty and speed, preserved in memory and in thousands of contemporary prints and paintings, lingered even after they were replaced by more economical ships that carried larger cargoes.

© The Granger Collection, New York

such men had gathered nuggets and dust worth about $6 million.

Back east, people remained calm, even skeptical, about the discovery until 230 ounces of almost pure gold went on display in the War Department in Washington and the president confirmed, in his State of the Union address in December 1848, that "the accounts of the abundance of gold in that territory are of such extraordinary character as would scarcely command belief." The gold rush began: "The coming of the Messiah, or the dawn of the Millennium could not have excited anything like the interest," one newspaper marveled. By the end of 1849, more than 700 ships carrying more than 45,000 easterners sailed to California. Some of the ships went around South America; others transported their passengers to the Isthmus of Panama, which they crossed by foot and canoe.

About 55,000 settlers followed the overland trails cut across the continent. Some traveled alongside the continuing stream of settlers to Oregon; others followed trails directly to the goldfields from destinations as far south as Mexico. Whether they went by sea or land, the participants in the gold rush were quite different from other immigrants to the West. The "**forty-niners**" tended to be either single men or groups of men from the same locality. Most of the men who flooded into California had little interest in settling there permanently. They intended to find their share of the gold and move on. Once in California, men of all classes, colors, and nations worked feverishly alongside one another in the streams and mountainsides. Disease, violence, and miserable living conditions hounded them, sending thousands to their deaths.

When some Chinese men returned home from California flush with American riches and stories of the "Golden Mountain," the fever spread in Asia. About 70 percent of the Chinese immigrants came from Guangdong Province, where many peasants and artisans had become impoverished and desperate enough to undertake the dangerous journey. Young men, in particular, thought California might offer a way to attain the wealth they needed to acquire a farm and a wife back in China. Migrants could buy tickets from brokers on credit,

A diverse population of men rushed to the California goldfields in 1849. Recent immigrants from China worked alongside Indians, whites, and African Americans.

with high interest. Upon their arrival in California, the Chinese immigrants discovered that they had to borrow yet more money from Chinese merchants in San Francisco to be transported to the goldfields. The miners worked continuously in hopes of paying off that debt.

California held hope for African Americans, too. Most of the black migrants to California left from the coastal cities of New England. California beckoned with the promise of an American West where color really might not matter so much. Although abolitionists, black and white, warned that even California might not be safe for black migrants, several thousand African Americans decided to take the chance.

Whatever their race, few miners discovered a fortune. The average miner in 1848 found about an ounce of gold a day, worth around $20, or about 20 times what a laborer back east made with a daily wage. As the number of competing miners skyrocketed over the next few years, however, the average take declined until it reached about $6 a day in 1852. Mining became more mechanized, and soon the biggest profits went to companies that assaulted the riverbeds and ravines with battalions of workers, explosives, and crushing mills.

Although miners of every background went bust, California as a whole flourished. Towns appeared wherever people gathered to look for the gold. Men who tired

Ships filled the harbor of the small town of San Francisco as "forty-niners" descended on nearby goldfields.

of mining turned to farming instead, teaching school, or building houses. The largest fortunes were made supplying the miners: Levi Strauss, a dry goods salesman from New York, created tough denim jeans, and Collis P. Huntington, later founder of the Central Pacific Railroad, met arriving ships and bought all the shovels on board for marked-up sale to miners. San Francisco was the big winner: by 1850, it had grown into a brash and booming city of 35,000 diverse residents.

The Mormon Migration

A different kind of westward movement was already in full force as the California gold rush got under way. These migrants were members of the Church of Jesus Christ of Latter-Day Saints, or Mormons. In the face of relentless persecution, Joseph Smith, the founder of the church, had led his flock to Illinois. There they established the town of Nauvoo, which by the mid-1840s had become the largest city in Illinois, with more than 15,000 people. But conflict erupted among his followers when Smith decreed that polygamy was God's will, that leading men within the church would marry several wives, and he created the Nauvoo Legion, an armed force

to protect his followers. When Smith ordered the destruction of a Mormon press that printed a poster condemning polygamy, the paper's owners signed warrants for his arrest. In June 1844, a mob of non-Mormons broke into the jail where Smith was being held and killed both him and his brother.

After struggle among the elders, Brigham Young, a young loyalist of Joseph Smith, emerged as the new leader of the Mormons. Young decided to move to a place beyond the reach of the Mormons' many enemies. Young knew about the Great Salt Lake, a place cut off from the east by mountains and from the west and south by deserts. The Mormons abandoned Nauvoo in the spring of 1846 as anti-Mormons pounded the town with cannon, destroying the Great Temple. In a well-coordinated migration, 15,000 Mormons moved in stages to the Great Salt Lake. When they first arrived, in 1847, the valley presented a daunting picture of rock and sagebrush, but the settlers irrigated the land, turning it into a thriving community.

When frosts, insects, and drought ruined much of the crop in the spring of 1848, Young announced that the Mormons would pool their labor and their resources even more than before. They designed an ambitious city

Persecuted in Illinois in the 1840s, the Mormons launched a mass migration to the Great Salt Lake in the state they called "Deseret."

with wide streets surrounding a temple that would "surpass in grandeur of design and gorgeousness of decoration all edifices the world has yet seen." Young concentrated control of the city and its farms in his own hands and in those of his fellow church leaders.

As some non-Mormons settled at the Great Salt Lake, Young decided that a form of government other than the church must be established. He oversaw the creation of a state called "Deseret," a Mormon term meaning "honeybee." The Mormons began a successful campaign to attract new converts from Europe, Asia, and Latin America. In 1849, the residents of Deseret, with Brigham Young as territorial governor, petitioned Congress for admission into the Union as a new state—a status it was not to achieve for another half century because of conflict over polygamy.

Although polygamy was practiced by no more than 15 percent of Mormons, in 1852 the church decreed that plural marriage was a fundamental church doctrine. The pronouncement provoked outrage across the country and led President Buchanan to order the military to prepare for an attack on Salt Lake City.

The High Tide of Immigration

Even as Americans moved west, a vast immigration from Ireland surged into the eastern United States. Irish immigration was not new; about a million people had left Ireland for the United States between 1815 and 1844. But the situation in Ireland changed much for the worse beginning in 1845, when a blight struck healthy potato fields, turning the leaves black almost overnight and filling the air with "a sickly odor of decay." This, the Great Potato Famine, which would last for nearly a decade, destroyed the basic food for most of the Irish people. More than a million people died; another 1.8 million fled to North America. In all, about a fourth of the island's population departed, with more people leaving in the 11 years after 1845 than in the preceding 250 years combined.

The Irish immigrants tended to be young, single, poor, unskilled, and Catholic; they came over in the dead of winter, with virtually no money or property. Although some Irish immigrants spread throughout North America, most congregated in the cities of the North and Midwest. They lived from day to day on whatever money they could earn. Most men worked on docks, others in canal and railroad construction; women worked as domestics and as unskilled laborers in textile mills.

The high tide of Irish immigration occurred just before the peak of German immigration. Over a million Germans came to America between 1846 and 1854, many of them dislocated by a failed revolution in Germany in 1848. The Germans tended to be farmers who brought

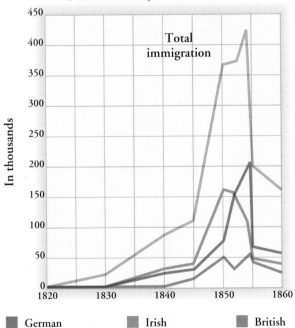

Immigration to the United States, 1820–1860

CHART 12.1 **Immigration to the United States, 1820–1860**
The number of immigrants from Ireland grew markedly in the late 1840s and early 1850s as a result of the Great Potato Famine. German immigration reached its peak a few years later as political turmoil erupted there.

© The Granger Collection, New York

Hounded by poverty, Irish people gathered in their villages in search of transportation to America in the late 1840s and early 1850s.

Enduring Issues   Manifest Destiny

We usually take our nation's geography for granted. Some of our earliest nationalistic songs and verse celebrated our possession of North America and its resources as God's design and the outcome of history. Thomas Jefferson, among other notables, advocated an empire of liberty based upon a vision of an agrarian nation continually reinvigorated by westward expansion and the acquisition of new land. The image of a national destiny was part of the common political parlance, even if the details and timing were still unclear.

As American boundaries expanded in the nineteenth century, expeditions traveled west and around the globe to map new territory and potential acquisitions. In 1842, the federal government paid for a maritime expedition to rival Britain's Charles Darwin's travels on the H.M.S. *Beagle.* The United States Exploring Expedition circled the earth, mapped the Pacific coastline of Mexican, Russian, and British territory, and sailed to Antarctica. In total, the ships sailed nearly 88,000 miles, even claiming a few guano-rich islands for American merchants to exploit off the coast of South America.

As Americans accumulated knowledge of these western territories, desires to occupy these lands grew.

Disputes over borders with British Canada, calls for annexation of Texas, and schemes to seize California, Oregon, or Cuba became common in the political rhetoric of Democratic politicians and newspaper editors. Domestic politics, economic ambitions, and military objectives shaped these debates. In summer 1845, in an article defending Texas annexation, magazine editor John L. O'Sullivan wrote of the nation's "Manifest Destiny." In his, and many others', view, it was God's will that white Protestant Americans occupy the entire continent, regardless of existing settlements or national borders. He declared, "Away with all these cobweb tissue of rights of discovery, exploration, settlement, contiguity, etc., . . . The American claim is by right of our manifest destiny to overspread and to possess the whole of the continent which Providence has given us. . . ."

President Tyler and his party, the Democrats, advocated the annexation of the Texas Republic to prevent its alliance with Britain. If the United States dallied, Britain might influence Texas to ban slavery and block further westward migration by Americans. Southerners argued that Texas was necessary for slavery's expansion, but also to serve as a "drain" for the surplus slaves and freed blacks, drawing them away from the North to a warmer climate. This idea linking race and climate was considered cutting-edge science in the 1840s. Northern Democrats agreed with southerners that expansion was critical. The nation's future prosperity required the ports and markets of the West, regardless of their current control by foreign governments.

Between 1845 and 1848 war and annexation shifted the country's border to the Pacific Coast. Texas statehood and the Treaty of Guadalupe Hidalgo added over a million square miles of new territory to the United States. O'Sullivan's plans and those of ambitious politicians like President Polk, while couched in terms of destiny and history, were not free of cost. The execution of these plans

cost Native Americans and Mexicans in the new lands dearly. These "mongrel races," as depicted by authors such as Washington Irving, were expected to step aside, surrender lands and resources, and gratefully accept a second-class status. "Manifest Destiny" appealed to emotion rather than reason to justify designs for more territory by cloaking expansion in terms of historical forces and providential design.

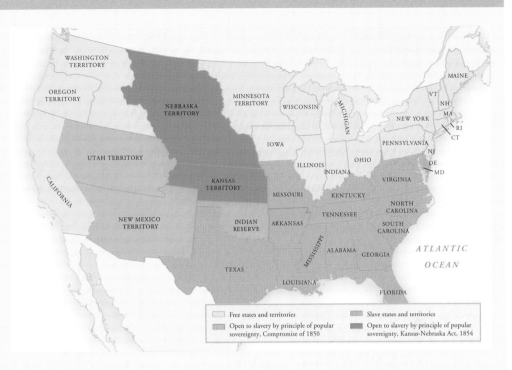

Free states and territories

Slave states and territories

Open to slavery by principle of popular sovereignty, Compromise of 1850

Open to slavery by principle of popular sovereignty, Kansas-Nebraska Act, 1854

But the very success of territorial consumption triggered a severe case of political indigestion. The issue that absorbed the focus of the nation hinged on whether acquired territories would be slave or free states. Americans might be able to forge a consensus on the conquest of territory, but they would bitterly dispute how to govern and arrange these new territories within the political system. Winning the war with Mexico was the easier part of the expansion process.

Manifest Destiny served as a rallying cry to many, but the reality revealed signs that not all Americans agreed. The federal government waited 9 years to annex Texas. Americans such as Henry David Thoreau opposed the Mexican War with civil disobedience. The Democratic Party nearly fractured over the proposal to forbid slavery in all territory captured from Mexico. Manifest Destiny should be seen not as an expression of a unanimous approach to westward expansion, but an attempt to create a rhetorical and political unity.

The attempt to end the conflict between North and South by looking to the West failed. Soon, two competing versions of an American future would wage a bloody war to decide their nations' future. John O'Sullivan would support secession while many former opponents of expansion would pick up arms to bar the creation of a southern state. By the century's end, the

United States was again active in the seizure of territory—this time overseas. The people occupying these territories in the Pacific were declared unfit to rule themselves and America's actions were justified in terms of drawn from both God's plan and the duty of the Anglo and Teutonic peoples framed in Darwinist reasoning. In an ironic reversal, these expansionist drives were praised for their ability to heal the old wounds of civil war as Americans were urged to unite once again to fulfill their "Manifest Destiny."

Questions for Reflection

1. Can it be argued that the very success of expansionist policies of Polk and Tyler did more harm than good to the nation? Did the government's reach exceed its grasp?

2. Consider earlier material about Americans relations with Native Americans. How did contemporaries use "history" to justify policies and attitudes expressed as "Manifest Destiny"?

3. Why did religion play such a significant role in the rhetoric of Manifest Destiny?

4. By 1848, the U.S. army occupied most of Mexico. Why did the federal government limit its territorial acquisitions to the areas along the Rio Grande and north of the Baja Peninsula?

some money with them and established farms in the Midwest. The Germans, more than the Irish, were divided by wealth, generation, politics, regional background, and religion. Combined, the Irish and German immigrants accounted for almost 15 percent of the population of the United States.

The Quest for Perfection

Although the late 1840s and early 1850s were relatively peaceful and prosperous, a number of people began to resist the drift of American life. Some became so disenchanted that they established utopian communities where they could experiment with alternative ways of organizing labor, power, and sexuality. Others launched a crusade for woman's rights.

Perfect Communities

Most of the hundred or so utopian communities created in the United States between the Revolution and the Civil War were founded in the 1840s. Some communities were secular in origin and some religious. They all insisted that people truly dedicated to social improvement had to flee corruption and compromise. Most of the idealistic communities grew directly from American origins.

The most notorious American communal experiment emerged in 1848. It was in that year that John Humphrey Noyes and his 250 followers created the Oneida Association in upstate New York. Noyes had become convinced that it was possible for humans to be "perfected," made free of sin. Most controversial, he argued that people in a state of perfection should not be bound by conventional monogamous marriages; all belonged to one another sexually in "complex marriage." He gathered a small group of disciples around him who put such beliefs into action, practicing birth control by having males withdraw during intercourse.

Oneida experimented not only with sex but also with economic cooperation. Everyone performed the full range of labor. The women of the group cut their hair, wore pantaloons rather than skirts, and played sports with their male compatriots. Unlike other utopian communities, Oneida focused its energies on manufacturing rather than farming. The community produced an improved and profitable steel animal trap. Later, Oneida transformed itself into a profitable business corporation specializing in silverware.

The utopian communities testified to the freedom the United States offered. People took advantage of the

© The Granger Collection, New York

John Humphrey Noyes founded the Oneida community in upstate New York, proclaiming sexual freedom in "complex marriage."

The J. Paul Getty Museum, Los Angeles

This antislavery meeting of 1850, like many others of this era, brought together men and women, blacks and whites, in a common cause.

isolation offered by the enormous space of the young country to experiment with communities based on religious, sexual, or philosophical principles. The proliferation of such communities also revealed, however, how full of longing many Americans seemed for communal relations in a society changing from the influences of immigration, technological advances, and political conflict.

Women's Rights

The seeds for the organized movement for women's rights in the United States had been planted in 1840, when women attending the World's Anti-Slavery Convention in London, England, found themselves consigned to seats in a separate roped-off area. One of the delegates was **Elizabeth Cady Stanton.** Listening to the debates over the place of women in antislavery, Stanton felt "humiliated and chagrined, except as these feelings were outweighed by contempt for the shallow reasoning of the opponents and their comical pose and gestures." Stanton discovered an important ally at the London meeting: Lucretia Mott, a devout Quaker and feminist. The two women vowed that they would start a movement back in the States for women's rights, but they did not soon find the opportunity they sought. Stanton devoted her time to raising her family in Boston. In 1847, she moved with her family to Seneca Falls, New York.

While living in Seneca Falls, Stanton grew frustrated with the narrowness of life in a small town and the limitations placed on women there. Meeting with Lucretia Mott again, Stanton told her friend how miserable she had become. The two women joined with three of Mott's Quaker friends to plan a convention in July in Seneca Falls, although only Mott had had any experience in organizing a reform meeting. Stanton recalled that they "felt as helpless as if they had been suddenly asked to construct a steam engine."

Casting about for a way to express their grievances most effectively, they decided to model their "Declaration of Rights and Sentiments" on the Declaration of Independence. The document demanded the right to vote and insisted on women's full equality with men in every sphere of life, including property rights, education, employment, divorce, and in court. The organizers worried about how many people might attend the meeting—held in an obscure town during a busy season for farmers—but more than a hundred people came, including a considerable number of men. Of those men the most prominent was Frederick Douglass. Douglass's newspaper, the *North Star,* was one of the few papers to give the convention a positive notice.

The organizers of the **Seneca Falls Convention** succeeded in their major role: getting Americans to talk

Elizabeth Cady Stanton, one of the founders of the women's rights movement, about the time of the Seneca Falls Convention of 1848.

about women's rights. Word of the Declaration spread among the many women's groups working in other reform organizations. Stanton, Mott, and their allies determined that they would hold a convention each year to keep the momentum going.

At the Akron meeting in 1851 a black woman spoke. She had escaped slavery in New York in 1827 and supported her family by working as a domestic. In 1843, she had a vision in which she was commanded to carry the word of God; she renamed herself "Sojourner Truth." In Akron, Truth celebrated women. "I have plowed and reaped and husked and chopped and mowed, and can any man do more than that?" she asked. The campaign for women's rights developed a complex relationship to abolition and to African Americans. The movement might have offered a rare opportunity for women such as **Sojourner Truth** to be heard, but white women's rights advocates generally phrased their demands for equal rights in terms of education and refinement that neglected black women and their needs.

Not all activist women, however, dedicated themselves to woman's suffrage. More conservative women, usually from middle- or upper-class families, devoted their energies to acquiring public funds for orphanages

DOING HISTORY

Gender and Power

SIXTY-EIGHT WOMEN and thirty-two men signed the Declaration of Sentiments, produced at Seneca Falls in 1848. Modeled on the Declaration of Independence, this document provided a touchstone for the woman's movement throughout the rest of the century and beyond.

Harriet Beecher Stowe's remarkable novel captured the moral energy of the antislavery movement and focused the eyes of the nation on the morality of slavery. In this episode, the evil New England-born Simon Legree is confronted by the unbending Christian strength of Uncle Tom.

"Declaration of Sentiments" of the Woman Suffrage Movement

The history of mankind is a history of repeated injuries and usurpations on the part of man toward woman, having in direct object the establishment of an absolute tyranny over her. To prove this, let facts be submitted to a candid world.

He had never permitted her to exercise her inalienable right to the elective franchise.

He has compelled her to submit to laws, in the formation of which she had no voice.

He has withheld from her rights which are given to the most ignorant and degraded of men—both natives and foreigners. . . .

He has monopolized nearly all the profitable employments, and from those she is permitted to follow, she receives but a scanty remuneration. . . .

He has denied her the facilities for obtaining a thorough education, all colleges being closed against her. . . .

He has endeavored, in every way that he could, to destroy her confidence in her own powers, to lessen her self-respect, and to make her willing to lead a dependent and abject life.

Now, . . . in view of the unjust laws above mentioned, and because women do feel themselves aggrieved, oppressed, and fraudulently deprived of their most sacred rights, we insist that they have immediate admission to all the rights and privileges which belong to them as citizens of the United States.

Harriet Beecher Stowe, *Uncle Tom's Cabin*

"And now," said Legree, "come here, you Tom. You see I telled ye I didn't buy ye jest for the common work; I mean to promote ye and make

---

or shelters for "fallen" women and the poor, using their connections to important men in state legislatures, on city boards, and in prosperous businesses to raise money and garner support. They asked for laws to criminalize seduction and to change property laws, to oppose Indian removal, restrict slavery, support colonization of free blacks to Africa, and stop the sale of liquor. They often achieved

success through their indirect means of influencing powerful men, and they saw little need for agitating for the vote.

Popular Culture and High Culture

The ever-growing acceleration of printing presses and railroads in the 1850s meant that Americans enjoyed more access to books, newspapers, plays, and lectures every year. People hungered for education and entertainment of all sorts. Performances of Shakespeare became widely popular, for example, as audiences flocked by the thousands to see *Hamlet* and *King Lear*. But not all the products of popular culture proved as elevating.

DOING HISTORY ONLINE

Frances Gage Remembers Sojourner Truth Appearing at the Akron Convention, 1851

What evidence is there in this piece that Frances Gage, like other white women's rights activists of the day, held a condescending attitude toward black women like Sojourner Truth?

History ⧗ **Now**™   Visit HistoryNOW to access primary sources and exercises related to this topic:
http://now.ilrn.com/ayers_etal3e

Mass Appeal

Several authors, now forgotten, reached remarkably large audiences with their writing. Some achieved success by a driver of ye; and tonight ye may jest as well begin to get your hand in. Now, ye jest take this yer gal and flog her; ye've seen enough on't to know how."

"I beg Mas'r's pardon," said Tom, "hopes Mas'r won't set me at that. It's what I an't used to—never did—and can't do, no way possible."

"Ye'll larn a pretty smart chance of things ye never did now before I've done with ye!" said Legree, taking up a cowhide and striking Tom a heavy blow across the cheek, and following up the infliction with a shower of blows.

"There!" he said, as he stopped to rest, "now will ye tell me ye can't do it?"

"Yes, Mas'r," said Tom, putting up his hand to wipe the blood that trickled down his face. "I'm willin' to work night and day, and work while there's life and breath in me, but this yer thing I can't feel it right to do; and, Mas'r, I *never* shall do it—*never!*"

Tom had a remarkably smooth, soft voice, and a habitually respectful manner that had given Legree an idea that he would be cowardly and easily subdued. When he spoke these last words, a thrill of amazement went through everyone; the poor woman clasped her hands and said, "O Lord!" and everyone involuntarily looked at each other and drew in their breath, as if to prepare for the storm that was about to burst.

Sources: Elizabeth Cady Stanton, et al., *History of Woman Suffrage*, Vol. 1 (Rochester, NY: Fowler and Wells, 1889), 58–59; Harriet Beecher Stow, *Uncle Tom's Cabin* (Boston: J. P. Jewett, 1852), pp. 419–423.

Questions for Reflection

1. Were the signers of the Declaration of Sentiments protesting against new wrongs? What led them to produce this document in this time?

2. Were the demands of the Declaration of Sentiments radical ideas? Fundamentally American ideas?

3. Why was it significant that the author of *Uncle Tom's Cabin* was a woman? Would a man have been likely to see things from this angle?

4. Why was the hero of *Uncle Tom's Cabin* a man? Does he behave as heroes usually behaved in novels? Was he strong because he acted "like a woman"?

5. Why were feminists and abolitionists so deeply tied together? What did they share? Where did they differ?

Explore additional primary sources related to this chapter on the Wadsworth American History Resource Center or HistoryNOW websites:

http://history.wadsworth.com/rc/us
http://now.ilrn.com/ayers_etal3e

---

playing on the nativism and anti-Catholicism of these years with polemics such as *Maria Monk's Awful Disclosures,* supposedly by one Maria Monk of a nunnery of Montreal. That titillating volume, imagining sordid behavior by priests and nuns, sold more than 300,000 copies in the first 25 years after its publication in 1836. George Lippard composed a serialized melodrama entitled *The Quaker City; or the Monks of Monk Hall, A Romance of Philadelphia Life, Mystery, and Crime.* It sold 60,000 copies in 1844 and at least 10,000 copies annually for 10 years. Lippard paraded the worst aspects of the criminal poor and dissolute rich to appeal to middle-class vanity and desires for reform; instead, he merely entertained them.

Other authors used the new capacities of mass printing to produce an ever-growing flood of self-help books. Catherine Beecher reprinted an edition of her *Treatise on Domestic Economy* every year in the 1840s and into the 1850s. The book offered a comprehensive guide to women on how to live their lives in the new domestic world, providing tips on topics as diverse as etiquette and how to wash feathers (carefully). The book was more than a how-to compilation, however; it told women that their work stood at least equal in importance to the work their husbands did outside the home.

One of the most influential books of the era bore the intriguing title of *Ten Nights in a Bar-Room.* In that book, first published in 1854 and eventually selling more than 400,000 copies, Timothy Shay Arthur described how the weakness of drink dragged down not only the main characters who wasted their nights in a bar, but also their families, their neighborhoods, and even "a nation of drunkards." Temperance societies adapted the book into traveling plays and skits to highlight the evils of alcohol.

In their popular reading, Americans showed themselves both excited and frightened by the large social changes through which they were living. Whether the books fed fear and suspicion or offered strategies for dealing with the new challenges—or both—Americans liked stories told in bold colors.

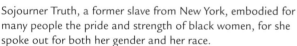

Sojourner Truth, a former slave from New York, embodied for many people the pride and strength of black women, for she spoke out for both her gender and her race.

A writer deeply engaged with the history of his native New England, Nathaniel Hawthorne wove powerful allegorical stories of sin and regret such as *The Scarlet Letter*.

Hawthorne, Melville, and Whitman

While popular authors dealt with the changes around them in melodramatic and obvious ways, more enduring writers crafted literature of greater subtlety. Yet the books these more gifted writers produced were very much attuned to their time and place. Nathaniel Hawthorne's *The Scarlet Letter* and Herman Melville's *Moby-Dick* were ironic, dark, and complex allegories, but Walt Whitman's *Leaves of Grass* evoked a hopeful vision. All three captured a key part of the American mood in the 1850s. Their lives as well as their work bore the unmistakable marks of the times in which they lived.

Nathaniel Hawthorne of Massachusetts was fascinated by the lingering consequences of sin. He turned to the history of New England as the setting for his best work, finding there an allegory for the struggles of his own age. Hawthorne wrote for Democratic newspapers and won a patronage post in the Salem customhouse, but his Whig opponents tried to remove Hawthorne

from his job and charged him with corruption. Perhaps not coincidentally, Hawthorne wrote *The Scarlet Letter,* a story about revenge and its costs, at this point in his life. Though set in the colonial era, the novel opened with a biting portrayal of the Salem customhouse and its petty Whig politicians. The novel propelled Hawthorne into literary fame.

After the arrival of Hawthorne's long-delayed prosperity, he and his family moved to Lenox, Massachusetts. There he met a younger writer, one who admired Hawthorne for his willingness to write complicated stories of guilt. The young author was **Herman Melville.** He had left school at the age of 15, tried his hand at writing, but, in need of work that paid better and more certainly, went to sea. His experiences gave him the subjects for most of his writing. His first two books, *Typee* and *Omoo,* adventure stories of the sea, did quite well. But Melville was not satisfied to write such books; he envisioned nothing less than an American epic.

Melville's masterpiece, about a ship captain's search for the great white whale "Moby-Dick," created a peculiarly American idiom: part Old Testament, part adventure story, part how-to book, part encyclopedia. Good and evil swirled together in *Moby-Dick.* Unlike *The Scarlet Letter, Moby-Dick,* published in 1852, did not do well

Herman Melville became famous as a writer of sea stories but found little public interest in his 1852 masterpiece *Moby-Dick.*

Walt Whitman, exuberant poet of New York and America, gloried in his connection to common people.

on the market. Melville, disenchanted, made his work more cynical and biting. His novel *The Confidence-Man,* published six years after *Moby-Dick,* dwelt on the swindling, corruption, and self-deception that seemed at the heart of the United States in the 1850s. Few people at the time noticed Melville's bold experiments and he gradually fell silent.

A bit farther south, in Brooklyn, **Walt Whitman** labored on an epic work, *Leaves of Grass,* throughout the early 1850s. The collection of poems reflected America at midcentury in all its diversity, roughness, innocence, and exuberance. This poetry included everything and everyone, speaking in a language stripped of classical allusion and pretension. As Whitman wrote in the preface to this book, anyone who would be a poet in the mid-nineteenth century must "flood himself with the immediate age."

Whitman took the raucous city of New York as his subject. Whitman wrote as a partisan Democratic journalist, ran a shop, worked as a building contractor, spent days in the public library, moved from one editing job to another, attended boisterous political meetings—all the while jotting notes for a new kind of epic poetry taking shape in his head. Whitman invented a poetical style to match his kaleidoscopic vision of American life.

Both his life and his poem would be "A Song of Myself." Whitman's book was literally self-made; in 1855, he set some of the type and hired friends—printers of legal work—to publish the book for him.

Leaves of Grass came out to no public recognition whatsoever. Whitman sent a few copies to people he admired, however, including Ralph Waldo Emerson. The reply could not have been more heartening: "I find it the most extraordinary piece of wit and wisdom that America has yet contributed." But most readers of the book, including several leading literary figures who read it on Emerson's recommendation, considered it vulgar, even obscene, shapeless, and crude. The hopeful words of *Leaves of Grass* soon became lost in years when a darker vision of the United States prevailed.

Slavery and a New Crisis in Politics

The decade of the 1850s began with many signs of change and progress as the economy kicked into high gear. People flooded to the recently acquired territories of California and Oregon while clipper ships, steamships, and railroads tied the nation together even more tightly. Yet a persistent undercurrent of anxiety wore at even the most privileged Americans when they read their newspapers.

The Crisis of 1850

Some of Americans' worry emanated from the new golden land of California, where lawlessness became rampant. The men who had left everything back east or in Europe to come to the goldfields showed little respect for the property rights—and even lives—of the Mexicans, Indians, or white men who were there before them. In the eyes of many, anarchy threatened if California could not form a government quickly. As gold fever spread, the military governor urged the president to grant the territory a government as soon as possible. A territorial convention created such a government in 1849, helping to restore order, but one of the provisions of the new constitution created great disorder of another kind back in the United States. The new constitution declared that "neither slavery nor involuntary servitude . . . shall ever be tolerated in this state."

This straightforward statement exacerbated conflicts that had been brewing in Washington ever since the Wilmot Proviso three years earlier. White southerners of both parties considered the admission of a free California a grave threat to their own status in the Union, giving the Senate a free-state majority. John C. Calhoun, the most vocal and extreme spokesman for the South, urged his fellow white southerners to band together. If they did not cooperate, Calhoun argued, they would be overwhelmed by the numbers and the energy of the free states of the North and the West. Southern congressmen talked of commercial boycotts, even of secession.

Southern Whigs had supported Zachary Taylor for the presidency in 1848, assuming that, as a southerner himself, he would support the expansion of slavery. Wishing to avoid further rancorous debates over slavery in Congress, Taylor chose to send an agent secretly to California urging local leaders to design their government and submit their plan to Congress. To the disbelief and disgust of southerners, Taylor urged that California be admitted as it wished to be admitted, without slavery. Taylor's support of the proposed California constitution unleashed a bitter debate in Congress. Southerners in Washington argued that to deny the South an equal representation in the Senate was to risk war between North and South. To give in on California was to lose the sectional balance on which their very safety rested. The most aggressive white southerners wanted to go on the offensive before northerners in Congress had time to act; in October 1849, they called a convention of the southern states to meet in Nashville in June of 1850.

A fabled session of Congress occurred as a result. In January 1850, the three most famous legislators of the first half of the nineteenth century—John C. Calhoun, Henry Clay, and Daniel Webster—assumed leading roles in the great national drama. Calhoun played the role of the southern protagonist, delivering fiery warnings and denunciations on behalf of the white South; Clay reprised the role of the Great Compromiser that had made him famous in the Missouri controversy 30 years earlier; Webster played the role of the conciliator, persuading the angry North to accept, in the name of the Union, the South's demand for respect. Clay and Webster rehearsed their lines in a private meeting before Clay presented his bill to Congress.

Clay's bold plan addressed in one inclusive "omnibus" bill all the issues tearing at the United States on the slavery issue (see Map 12.3). Balance the territory issue, he suggested, with other concerns that angered people about slavery. Keep slavery legal in the District of Columbia, but abolish the slave trade there. Provide a stronger law to capture fugitive slaves in the North, but announce that Congress had no power to regulate the slave trade among the states. Admit California as a free state, but leave undetermined the place of slavery in the other territories won from Mexico.

Advocates on both sides hoped the compromise would buy time for passions to cool, but the arguments went on for months. In March, Webster, trying to put the conflict to rest, claimed to speak "not as a Massachusetts man, nor as a northern man, but as an American." He was widely denounced in the North as a traitor, buckling under to the slave mongerers. President Taylor—like Clay and Webster, a Whig—refused to support their compromise.

The Nashville Convention of southern states, meanwhile, turned out to be stillborn, because six states sent no representatives, and the representatives who did come disagreed on the proper course of action. Although a South Carolinian argued that "unite, and you shall form one of the most splendid empires in which the sun ever shone," most delegates still believed slavery was best preserved by remaining in the Union. In nine days of deliberations, the convention took no stand on the pending compromise; the representatives waited to see its provisions.

Though the **omnibus bill** in Congress appeared doomed, a series of unanticipated events brought compromise. Both Calhoun and Taylor died a few months apart. Millard Fillmore was now president, and Fillmore supported the omnibus bill. Webster resigned to serve as Fillmore's secretary of state, and Clay, after 70 addresses to the Senate defending the omnibus bill, left Washington to recover. Younger, less prominent, members of Congress steered the various components of the compromise through committees and votes. The compromisers were

MAP 12.3 The Compromise of 1850
The Compromise of 1850, the result of elaborate and bitter negotiation, brought California into the Union as a free state, leaving the territories of Utah and Mexico open to the (slight) possibility of slavery.

led by **Stephen A. Douglas,** a promising young Democrat of Illinois. The majority of northern and southern senators and representatives tenaciously voted against one another, but each part of the compromise passed because a small group of conciliatory congressmen from each side crafted shifting coalitions large enough to pass each section. By September the various components of the compromise of 1850 had become law.

The problem of slavery, of course, would not go away merely because of a political compromise. The fugitive slave component of the Compromise of 1850 proved especially troubling. The **Fugitive Slave Act** directly implicated white northerners and insulted them with blatantly unjust provisions. The commissioners who decided the fate of black Americans accused of being runaway slaves received $10 if an accused fugitive were returned to his or her master but only $5 if freed. Marshals and sheriffs could force bystanders to aid in the capture of an accused fugitive. The alleged runaway could not testify in his or her own defense or call witnesses. And no matter how many years before slaves had escaped, no matter how settled or respectable they had become, they could be captured and sent back

into bondage. Most of the two or three hundred alleged fugitives prosecuted under the law were ruled to be runaways and sent south.

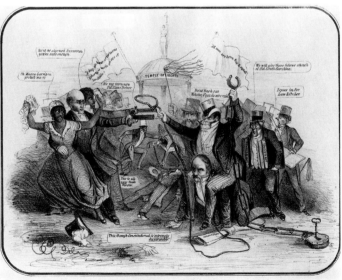

PRACTICAL ILLUSTRATION OF THE FUGITIVE SLAVE LAW.

This cartoon ridicules the Fugitive Slave Law that required northerners to help capture and return runaway slaves. It glorifies William Lloyd Garrison but assails Daniel Webster, who voted in favor of the law as part of the Compromise of 1850.

Abolitionists raged at the Fugitive Slave Law and they were not alone. Armed opposition to the slave catchers immediately arose in cities across the North; mobs broke into jails to free ex-slaves; one slaveowner who came north to claim his property was shot. The Fugitive Slave Law, far from calming the conflict between North and South, made it more bitter.

African Americans and the White North

In the years surrounding the crisis of 1850 minstrel shows reached their peak of popularity. The traveling troupes of minstrels offered the strange ritual of white men in blackface simultaneously ridiculing and paying homage to the creativity of African American culture. Although white people of all classes and backgrounds attended the minstrel shows, the quick-paced, humorous, and flashy skits and songs held special appeal for members of the white working class. Over the preceding decades, those workers had seen the value of their labor eroded by mechanization and immigration. In their eyes, the minstrel shows offered both a comforting dramatization of their own racial superiority and a way to associate imaginatively with carefree and fun-loving "black" people.

White northerners revealed ambivalence about African Americans in other ways. Those who argued for free soil in the new territory of the West frequently insisted on the exclusion of free blacks. Ohio, Indiana, Illinois, and Oregon passed laws barring free blacks from entering or settling within their boundaries. The great majority of northern whites showed little interest in attending abolition rallies.

Harriet Beecher Stowe's *Uncle Tom's Cabin or Life Among the Lowly* helped change some of these white attitudes toward African Americans. Stowe had been writing throughout her life, but had not become prominent. In 1849, her infant son died of cholera in Cincinnati; the next year she moved back to New England. There, people talked angrily of the new Fugitive Slave Law. "You don't know how my heart burns within me at the blindness and obtuseness of good people on so very simple a point of morality as this," she wrote to her brother Henry Ward Beecher.

Stowe put her objections to the law and its effects into a story printed serially in a moderate antislavery newspaper, the *National Era,* beginning in June 1851. Stowe based her portrayals of black people on the African Americans she had known in Cincinnati, where they worked for her as domestic servants. They told Stowe of the terrors of being sold south to Louisiana, of their vulnerability to sexual exploitation. Stowe also drew on first-hand narratives of escape. She switched the usual roles

Picturing the Past **SOCIAL & CULTURAL EVENTS**

Minstrelsy

White men in blackface mimicked southern slaves for white audiences in the era, acting out ambivalent feelings of contempt and envy. Minstrelsy centered on comedy, dance, skits, and song. On the eighteenth- and nineteenth-century stage, black characters normally were played by whites who painted their faces black and danced, mimed, and parodied exaggerated sexuality and foppishness to amuse white audiences, many of whom were recent immigrants. Crude racist humor combined with idealized plantation scenes of abundance and sloth to portray blacks as simultaneously foolish and sly, responding to their oppression with bemusement and a dance step. Ironically, black dance styles drawn from Africa would evolve into complex tap routines that became a staple of the American stage. These shows were wildly popular in all sections of the country and created stereotypes of black behavior and comic style that persisted well into the twentieth century in movies, radio, and television.

© Bettmann/CORBIS

of the freedom narratives, however, making a woman—Eliza—the active heroine and a man—Uncle Tom—the one left behind to endure slavery. The love of a mother for her children drove the story. The image of Eliza crossing the partially frozen Ohio River, baby in her arms, grew into one of the most powerful and familiar scenes of American culture.

The novel's 300,000 copies drove eight steam presses night and day to meet the demand in 1852

Harriet Beecher Stowe, the author of *Uncle Tom's Cabin,* wove Christianity and the domestic ideal into a powerful fable of slavery and its consequences.

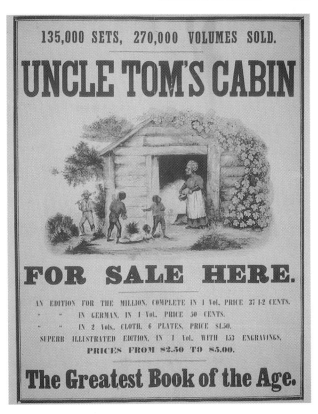

Uncle Tom's Cabin not only helped mobilize the white North's opinions on slavery, but it also proved an immediate and persistent best-seller.

alone; eventually more than 6.5 million copies sold in the United States and around the world. It was the best-selling novel of the nineteenth century. **Uncle Tom's Cabin** became the subject of the most popular play in American history. Readers and theatergoers were shocked at stories of cruelty, violence, and sexual abuse. Stowe used techniques commonly found in domestic novels—the sanctity of the family, the power of religion, the triumph of endurance—to show that black people had the same feelings as white people.

That *Uncle Tom's Cabin* and minstrel shows reached their peak of popularity at the same time gives some idea of the confusion and ambivalence with which white northerners viewed African Americans in the early 1850s. Stowe's story was based on an antislavery message, but thousands of whites laughed at other whites in blackface acting out crude racial stereotypes.

Politics in Chaos

The high tide of immigration in the early 1850s unleashed a political backlash as nativists organized themselves against the newcomers from Ireland and Germany. Meanwhile, the booming economy drove other Americans to lust for expanded territory beyond the bounds of the continental United States. Movement to the West triggered the most violent conflict the nation had yet seen between the forces of slavery and antislavery.

The Know-Nothings

Franklin Pierce, the Democratic candidate for president in 1852, was a northerner friendly to the white South. Pierce's Whig opponent—Winfield Scott—proved to be unimpressive despite his fame as a general in the war with Mexico. Pierce crushed Scott in every state except four. "General opinion seems to be that the Whig party is dead and will soon be decomposed into its original elements," one diarist commented in the wake of the election.

Many influential Whigs took the 1852 election as a sign that the Democrats would always succeed by appealing to the lowest common denominator. The issues that had originally shaped the two parties—banks, the tariff, and internal improvements—no longer distinguished them from one another. Neither did slavery and sectional issues sharply define the two parties, for each tried to appease voters in both the North and the South. Even the broader cultural orientation of the two parties had blurred in 1852, as the Whigs appealed to the burgeoning foreign-born vote.

This broadside combined the various elements of the nativist appeal: below a white hand choking the papal dragon a list of what every American patriot should favor and oppose—especially "papal aggression and Roman Catholicism."

The **Know-Nothings** moved into politics in 1854 in a way few expected. Mobilizing as many as 1.5 million adherents, they did not announce their candidates beforehand but wrote them in on the ballots, taking incumbents by complete surprise. In Massachusetts, the Know-Nothings won virtually all the seats in the legislature, the governor's chair, and the entire congressional delegation with this strategy. By 1855, they dominated much of New England and displaced the Whigs as the major opponents to the Democrats through the Middle Atlantic states, in much of the South, and in California. Democrat and Whig leaders denounced "the 'Know Nothing' fever" that disrupted the campaigns and strategies of the parties.

In the eyes of many white Protestants, the new arrivals, especially from Ireland, appeared impossible to assimilate. "They increase our taxes, eat our bread, and encumber our street," commented one American diarist. The immigrants threatened to drive down wages because they were willing to work for so little. The immigrants often received the right to vote in state and local elections soon after they landed, with Irish Catholics supporting the Democratic party and opposing the prohibition of alcohol, while English, German, and Irish Protestants supported the Whigs and frequently voted in favor of prohibition. The conflict over alcohol, always volatile, became even more so in 1851 when Maine became the first state to enact statewide prohibition.

In the face of such challenges to their values and power, "native Americans" organized against the immigrants. The most powerful manifestation of nativism appeared in New York City in 1849, when Charles Allen founded the Order of the Star Spangled Banner. Its membership was restricted to native-born white Protestants sworn to secrecy. When asked about the order by outsiders, members were instructed to say "I know nothing"—and thus they became popularly known as the "Know-Nothings." The order grew slowly at first, but its deeply held and deepening prejudices grew as existing political parties seemed too corrupt to stem the flood-tide of immigration.

No one in the major parties had anticipated such a turn of events. The Whigs, after all, had long attracted the nativists, fervent Protestants, and temperance advocates to which the Know-Nothings now appealed. The Know-Nothings offered a revitalized political party, one more receptive than the Whigs to the anti-Catholic and anti-immigrant desires of its constituents and one that would attack problems rather than compromise on them. Many rural districts voted heavily for the Know-Nothings as a way to get back at the cities that had dominated the major parties for so long. Voters blamed standing politicians for corruption and sought a new organization free from the control of the "wire pullers" who ran campaigns from smoke-filled backrooms.

The appearance of the Know-Nothings reflected a deep-seated change in the American political system. The party system began disintegrating at the local and state level, with the Whigs fading in some states as early as 1852 and in others not until 3 years later. Voters defected from the Whigs and Democrats to both the Know-Nothing and Free-Soil parties.

A Hunger for Expansion

The same forces of commerce and transportation that tied together the vastly expanded United States in the late 1840s and early 1850s pulled Americans into world affairs. American ships set out for South America, Asia, Australia, New Zealand, and Tahiti as well as Europe. The ships carried lumber and hides, tea and silks, missionaries and scientists. American whaling ships patrolled the South Pacific, stopping for fuel and food at islands scattered over a vast territory. Some entrepreneurs, such as the American Guano Company, rushed to mine 200 foot-high mountains of bird droppings piled up on remote Pacific islands. The droppings, called guano, offered a nitrogen-rich fertilizer much in demand on the farms and plantations of the eastern United States. American traders eager to break into the Asian market appeared in Japanese ports.

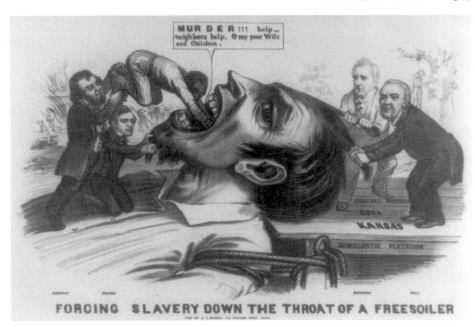

This cartoon blames the Democrats for choking American voters with slavery—not only in Kansas but also with threats of expansion into Cuba and Central America.

These exchanges in far-off ports often depended on the Hawaiian Islands as way stations. On a single day in 1852, for example, 131 whaling ships and 18 merchant ships were tied up in Honolulu. Such trade came at a horrifying cost to the native population because of disease. Over the 75 years since the first contact with outsiders in the late eighteenth century, the Hawaiian population had declined from about 300,000 residents to only about 73,000. Two thousand foreigners lived in Hawaii by the early 1850s, many of them Americans. Though politicians and editors talked of annexing the islands for the United States, opposition on the islands and in Washington postponed any action.

Some well-placed Americans gazed at yet more Mexican territory with covetous eyes, urging the Pierce administration to acquire Baja California and other parts of northern Mexico. Mexico was not interested, though. Proponents of expansion had to settle for much less than they had wanted: after long wrangling, in 1853 the United States paid $15 million for a strip of Mexico to use as a route for a southern transcontinental railroad. This was the Gadsden Purchase, named for the American diplomat who negotiated it. The purchase defined the final borders of the continental United States.

Cuba seemed the most obvious place for further expansion. Many Americans believed that Cuba should be part of the United States. Cuba was rich and growing, its slave trade flourishing even after the slave trade to the United States had ended. Abolitionists and others talked of freeing Cuba both from slavery and from the Spanish, whereas white southerners talked of adding this jewel to the slave empire.

The United States offered to buy Cuba from Spain in 1848, but met a rude rebuff. Franklin Pierce, pressured by the southerners in his party and in his cabinet, in the early 1850s renewed the effort to "detach" Cuba from Spain. American diplomats in Europe created a furor in October 1854 when they clumsily wrote the "Ostend Manifesto," a statement of the policy they wanted the administration to follow: gain Cuba peacefully or by force. When the "manifesto" was leaked to the press, the Pierce administration was widely vilified. London newspapers derided the manifesto as the "pursuit of dishonorable objects by clandestine means." Pierce publicly renounced any intention of taking over Cuba. The movement to expand the United States into the Caribbean came to a temporary halt.

Kansas-Nebraska Lets Loose the Storm

As the Cuban episode revealed, Franklin Pierce proved to be an ineffectual president and a weak leader of his party, the Democrats. The best hope for the Democrats, according to Senator Stephen A. Douglas, was to deflect attention to the West. Douglas called for two kinds of action: organizing the territories of the West, especially the Kansas and Nebraska area, and building a railroad across the continent to bind together the expanded United States with the route running through his home state of Illinois. The two actions were interrelated, for the railroad

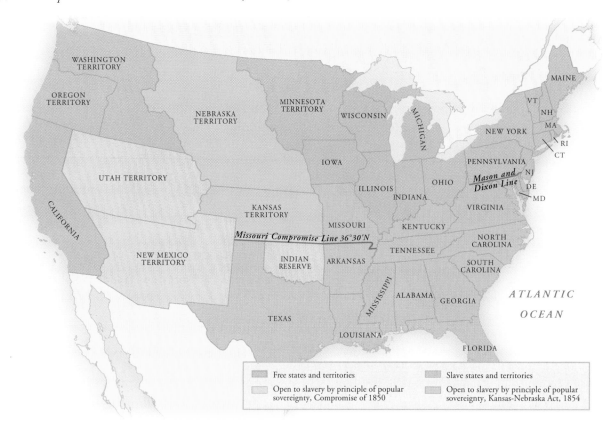

MAP 12.4 **Kansas-Nebraska and Slavery**
The Kansas Territory, adjacent to slaveholding Missouri but well north of the Missouri Compromise line, stood as a place both slaveholders and Free-Soilers felt they could claim as their own.

could not be built through unorganized territory. Partly to get southern votes for the territorial organization and partly because he believed that slavery would not survive in the northern territories, Douglas wrote a bill invalidating the Missouri Compromise line. He proposed that the people of the new territories decide for themselves whether or not their states would permit slaves and slaveholders. Adopting the phrase others had used to describe such territorial self-determination—"popular sovereignty"—Douglas put it forward in the Kansas-Nebraska Bill (see Map 12.4).

Douglas's plan unleashed political and sectional resentments that had been bottled up by prior compromises. Six prominent Free-Soil senators, including Salmon P. Chase, Charles Sumner, and Joshua Giddings, denounced the plan as a plot by a "Slave Power" to make Nebraska a "dreary region of despotism, inhabited by masters and slaves." Northern ministers publicly protested the pending legislation in their sermons, and newspapers throughout the North scornfully attacked the proposal. Despite the widespread opposition, however, the opponents of the Kansas-Nebraska Bill could not coordinate their efforts sufficiently to stop its passage.

The fight over the Kansas-Nebraska Bill inflamed northern resentment as never before. Many northerners

determined that they could no longer trust southerners to keep a bargain and that northerners were no longer obligated to enforce the Fugitive Slave Act because the Kansas-Nebraska Bill had nullified the Compromise of 1850. Attempts to arrest and extradite Anthony Burns, a fugitive slave in Boston, created such a turmoil that the mayor called out 1,500 militia to line the streets along the route between the courthouse and the ship that was to take Burns back to slavery in Virginia.

The **Kansas-Nebraska Bill** sparked a chain reaction. It divided the Democratic party across the North; it provided a set of common concerns and language to unite disgruntled northern Whigs, Democrats, Free-Soilers, and abolitionists; it upset the fragile balance of power between North and South in Congress. Northern voters punished Democrats who had supported the Kansas-Nebraska Act; the party lost 66 of the 91 free-state House seats it had gained in 1852. As northern Democrats lost seats, southerners gained control of the party, fueling further resentment of southern dominance. The Know-Nothings took advantage of the widespread disillusionment with the two major parties to campaign against Catholics, immigrants, and corruption issues apparently unrelated to slavery.

Over the next two years the northern political system lurched along as voters looked for a party that would

© CORBIS

This illustration tells the story of Anthony Burns's sale, escape, arrest, and return to slavery in Virginia. His highly publicized case further inflamed the conflict between the North and the South in the mid-1850s.

reflect their concerns and also have a chance of winning power. The Know-Nothings began to fade almost as quickly as they had emerged. They came to seem just another political party led by ambitious politicians who exploited patronage for personal gain. Violent gangs that terrorized immigrants under the Know-Nothing banner alienated many voters, and Know-Nothing legislators proved unable to restrict Catholic influence as they had promised.

In 1854, a party was founded in Wisconsin to unite disgruntled voters. The new party appealed to former Whigs, Free-Soilers, Know-Nothings, and even Democrats fed up with their pro-southern party. This new party called itself the "Republican" party. Its platform announced that it would not permit slavery in the territories or in new states. People wondered whether the new party could finally unite the North against the South.

Conclusion

The late 1840s and early 1850s do not have a catchy name. Perhaps these years saw too many contradictory changes to fall under one convenient label. In many ways, things had never been better in the United States. In other ways, the danger had never been greater. The promise and the threat proved to be parts of the same situation.

The United States, dissatisfied with the status of Texas and with Mexico's ownership of much of what would become the American West, pushed into war. Combining West Point leadership with tens of thousands of volunteers, the United States waged impressive military campaigns in California, Texas, and in the heart of Mexico itself. Support for the war ran strong in most of the country, but bitter opposition grew in New England and among many Whigs, who saw the war against Mexico as a war on behalf of slavery.

The political events that followed the conclusion of the war confirmed the worries of those who argued that the vast new territories would throw into disarray the balance between North and South that had prevailed since the Missouri Compromise of 1820. The Compromise of 1850, so elaborately constructed by Democrats and Whigs, northerners and southerners, began to fall apart almost as soon as it was completed. The Fugitive Slave Law turned many white northerners against the South; the South returned the ill feelings.

Despite the political turmoil, the economy, driven by railroads and clipper ships, flourished as never before. Cotton prices soared as did the price commanded by the enslaved. The population of the new country, fed by millions of immigrants from Ireland and Germany, grew at an astonishing rate, filling cities and farms from coast to coast. Throwing more fuel on the roaring blaze of the economy, the California gold rush ignited the dreams of young men across the United States and sent them on journeys across the continent. The gold rush gave hope, too, to desperate young men in China, who came across the Pacific in hopes of making enough money for a prosperous return home.

The combination of a raging economy, millions of immigrants, and political instability proved too much for the Whig party. Weakened by a series of unsuccessful presidential candidates and factionalism between the North and the South, the Whigs began to fracture and fragment. In the vacuum left by the Whigs' decline, a nativist party called the Know-Nothings rushed in. Playing on the resentment native-born white men felt against immigrants and the political power they wielded, the Know-Nothings secretly coordinated campaigns to elect their own men. The result was a weakening of the Democrats and the demise of the Whigs. The party system that had held the United States together through the turmoil of the preceding 20 years was unraveling and no one knew what would take its place.

The Kansas-Nebraska Bill brought political conflict and economic motives together. The bold and self-interested act of a leading northern Democrat, Stephen F. Douglas, the Kansas-Nebraska Bill sought to use western economic development to distract voters from the volatile political situation in Washington. With everyone focused on the possibilities of a transcontinental railroad, the Democrats hoped, slavery would become less of an issue. Instead, just the opposite happened: the promise of enormous territorial gains and senatorial seats drove the North and South farther apart than ever. Slavery never seemed to matter more than when glittering new possibilities for expansion beckoned over the horizon. Economic success would not be a substitute for national harmony. In fact, economic prosperity only seemed to exacerbate divisions between the North and the South.

The Chapter in Review

In the years between 1846 and 1854,

- The United States went to war with Mexico, winning enormous territory as a consequence.
- A Gold Rush in California drove hundreds of thousands of people to the West.
- Mormons moved to the Great Salt Lake.
- Movements for women's rights emerged.

- American authors produced the first great novels and poetry of the young nation.
- The Compromise of 1850 and the Kansas-Nebraska Act galvanized the politics of the nation.
- A nativist movement won much support throughout the country.

Making Connections Across Chapters

LOOKING BACK

Chapter 12 shows that in the years following the war with Mexico the United States found itself pulled apart by the forces of economic growth, massive immigration, territorial expansion, and conflict over slavery.

1. Did the United States have any choice over whether to go to war with Mexico?

2. Under what conditions might the Whig party have been able to survive the 1850s?

3. Why did slavery seem such an issue in the North in the early 1850s?

LOOKING FORWARD

In Chapter 13 we will see that many Americans hoped that the crisis of 1850, and the resulting compromise, would put an end to the bitter fight over slavery. In fact, it did just the opposite.

1. Did the Kansas-Nebraska Bill make it a certainty that the North and the South would collide repeatedly over slavery or was there hope that things might die down once that crisis had passed?

2. What role did *Uncle Tom's Cabin* play over the years that followed its publication in mobilizing white northerners against slavery?

Recommended Readings

Anbinder, Tyler. *Nativism and Slavery: The Northern Know-Nothings and the Politics of the 1850s* (1992) provides a full and balanced account.

Fehrenbacher, Don E. *The Slaveholding Republic: An Account of the United States Government's Relations to Slavery* (2001) carefully analyzes this troubling issue.

Faragher, John Mack, and Robert V. Hine. *The American West: A New Interpretive History* (2000) is a superb synthesis.

Fellman, Michael. *The Unbounded Frame: Freedom and Community in Nineteenth-Century American Utopianism* (1973). A helpful overview of perfectionist communities.

Foos, Paul. *A Short, Offhand, Killing Affair: Soldiers and Social Conflict During the Mexican-American War* (2002) is a dark work on a neglected war.

Griffith, Elisabeth. *In Her Own Right: The Life of Elizabeth Cady Stanton* (1984) tells the compelling story of this crucial leader of the woman suffrage movement.

Hedrick, Joan D. *Harriet Beecher Stowe: A Life* (1994) gives a detailed portrait of the author of *Uncle Tom's Cabin.*

Libura, Krystana M., Luis Gerado Morales Moreno, and Jesus Valasco Marquez. Trans. Mark Fried. *Echoes of the Mexican War* (2004), reveals both

Mexican and American points of view from the 1830 through the end of the Mexican War.

Lott, Eric. *Love and Theft: Blackface Minstrelsy and the American Working Class* (1993) provides an original and challenging analysis.

Miller, Kerby A. *Emigrants and Exiles: Ireland and the Irish Exodus to North America* (1985) contributes a full account of the origins and impact of this migration.

Morrison, Michael. *Slavery and the American West: The Eclipse of Manifest Destiny and the Coming of the Civil War* (1997) details this complicated story.

Potter, David M. *The Impending Crisis: 1848–1861* (1976) stands as the best overview of American politics from the wake of the Mexican War to the outbreak of the Civil War.

Reynolds, David S. *Beneath the American Renaissance: The Subversive Imagination in the Age of Emerson and Melville* (1988) is a brilliant exploration of the "classic" era of American literature.

Rohrbough, Malcolm J. *Days of Gold: The California Gold Rush and the American Nation* (1997). Offers a fresh and exciting account of its subject.

Von Frank, Albert J. *The Trials of Anthony Burns: Freedom and Slavery in Emerson's Boston* (1998) tells a stirring story of what slaves and the abolitionists were up against.

Identifications

Review your understanding of the following key terms, people, events, and dates for this chapter (these terms also appear in the Glossary at the end of the book):

annexation
Zachary Taylor
popular sovereignty
Free-Soil party
forty-niners
Elizabeth Cady Stanton
Seneca Falls Convention
Sojourner Truth
Nathaniel Hawthorne
Herman Melville
Walt Whitman
omnibus bill
Stephen A. Douglas
Fugitive Slave Act
Harriet Beecher Stowe
Uncle Tom's Cabin
Know-Nothings
Kansas-Nebraska Bill

Online Sources Guide

Use this listing to find online documents, images, interactive maps, simulations, and other resources related to this chapter:

American History Resource Center

http://history.wadsworth.com/rc/us

Selected Images

Harriet Beecher Stowe
Scene from *Uncle Tom's Cabin*
Sacramento boomtown, 1850s picture
American troops under Zachary Taylor storming hills at Monterey, September 1846

Interactive Maps

Free and Slave States and Territories, 1848
Principle Campaigns of the Mexican War, 1846–1847

Document Exercises

1852 Socialism

HistoryNOW

http://now.ilrn.com/ayers_etal3e

Primary Source Exercises

David Wilmot Argues for a Free California, 1847
Frances Gage Remembers Sojourner Truth Appearing at the Akron Convention, 1851

Passages 1855 to 1877

Americans of the 1850s had no idea that the Civil War awaited them. They could not imagine that a vast war, larger than any Europe had known, could overwhelm the new republic. New farms and plantations, after all, spread rapidly in expectation of more boom years like the 1850s. Villages and workshops developed throughout the North, while cities, fed by millions of immigrants from Europe, grew at harbors and along railroads and rivers. In the South, cotton and slavery created a per capita income for white southerners higher than that of any country in Europe except England. Slavery, it was clear, would not collapse of its own contradictions any time soon; the institution had never been more profitable. Telegraphs, newspapers, steamboats, and railroads tied the North and South together more tightly every year.

The two sections viewed each other as aggressive and expansionist, intent on making the nation all one thing or another. The North claimed that the slaveholder South would destroy the best government on earth rather than accept the results of a fair election. The white South claimed that the arrogant and greedy North would destroy the nation rather than acknowledge what the Constitution had established. Both sides were filled with righteous rage, accepting violence to gain the upper hand, whether that involved capturing fugitive slaves or applauding John Brown's failed insurrection. Americans could not stop the momentum they had themselves created. Despite desperate efforts at compromise and delay, the war came.

Once the war could no longer be avoided, most people threw themselves into the conflict alongside their neighbors, regardless of whatever doubts they had held before.

Confident that the war would be brief, young men on both sides enlisted to teach their enemies a lesson. Both the North and the South proved excellent at war. They innovated freely and successfully, fought relentlessly, discovered effective generals, and mobilized women as well as men. Indeed, the North's strengths and the South's strengths balanced so that the war went on for four years, killing 630,000 people, a proportion of the population equivalent to 5 million people in the United States today and a number larger than the country was ever to sacrifice in another war.

Throughout the conflict, from Lincoln's election to his death, the role of slavery remained both powerful and unclear. Lincoln announced that the war was for Union, not abolition. The Confederacy announced that the war was for independence, not merely slavery. Enslaved Americans in the South, however, forced slavery as an issue on both the Union and the Confederacy, risking their lives to flee to Union camps, undermining plantations and farms. Lincoln and much of the North came to see that ending slavery would end the Confederacy and help redeem the death and suffering. Two hundred thousand black men enlisted as soldiers and played a key role in bringing Union victory.

The North and the South struggled with themselves even as they fought one another.

The North broke apart along lines of class, ethnicity, party, and locale. By 1864, a considerable portion of the northern population wanted the war to end, with compromise if necessary. The opponents of Lincoln expected to overwhelm him in the election that fall and even Lincoln shared that expectation. The white South broke apart along lines of class, locale, and gender. Poor soldiers deserted; upcountry communities shielded the deserters and resisted the Confederate government; impoverished white women rioted and resisted. Slaves rushed to the Union army at the first opportunity, every escape weakening the southern economy and Confederate morale.

Events on the battlefield, through 10,000 conflicts large and small, exerted their own logic and momentum. The Union army grew stronger as the Confederate army thinned and weakened. The victories of Grant and Sherman in 1864 destroyed the South's best hope of a negotiated peace. The relentless spread of the Union army throughout the South divided the Confederacy into smaller and smaller pieces, each helpless to aid the other. When Lee's army fell into defeat, the Confederate nation dissolved almost immediately.

Whatever Lincoln's plans for reuniting the nation, those plans ended at Ford's Theater in April of 1865. Lincoln's successor, Andrew Johnson, took the most cautious route possible, limiting the scope of black freedom in every way he could. The white South's resolve, indeed, seemed greater than any power the Union wielded in the South. African Americans struggled to make their freedom real: they mobilized politically, founded churches and schools, and reconstituted families. They demanded rights as Americans and did all they could to secure those rights. Black southerners found many white northern allies but many more white southern enemies who quickly

Sunday Morning in Virginia. This painting by Winslow Homer chronicled the great hunger of former slaves and their children for the blessings of literacy.

Winslow Homer's "Sunday Morning in Virginia" 1877 Cincinnati Art Museum, John M. Emerey Funds. Acc. 1924.247

turned to violence, as well as white northerners who supported or tolerated the violence. The years of 1866 and 1867 were full of a promise and a terror no one could have imagined ten years before. In many ways, the Civil War had not yet ended; its consequences had hardly begun.

For the next decade, Reconstruction in the South gradually receded. The process left blacks with greater political rights in law because of the Fourteenth and Fifteenth Amendments, but a more limited role in the day-to-day process of governing. The presidency of Ulysses S. Grant was a disappointment because the hero of the war proved unable to provide effective leadership, sectional reconciliation, or honest government. An economic collapse in 1873 helped the Democrats restore the national political balance and hasten the end of Reconstruction. The disputed election between Rutherford B. Hayes and Samual J. Tilden in 1876 saw the abandonment of black southerners to the rule of those who believed in white supremacy. The Civil War had preserved the Union and abolished slavery, but the unsettled problem of race cast a long shadow into the future.

America and the World: 1855–1877

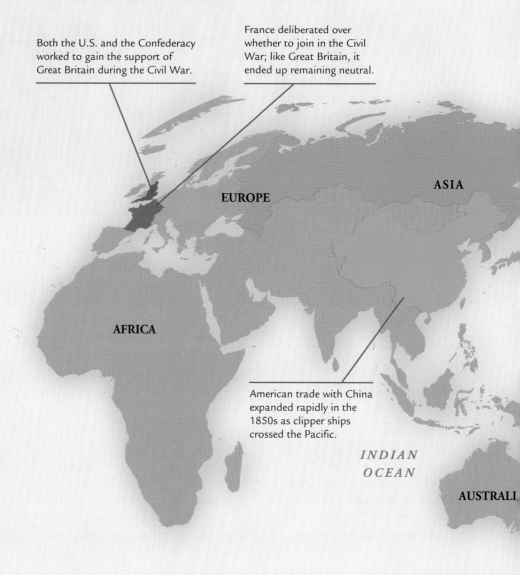

Both the U.S. and the Confederacy worked to gain the support of Great Britain during the Civil War.

France deliberated over whether to join in the Civil War; like Great Britain, it ended up remaining neutral.

ASIA

EUROPE

AFRICA

American trade with China expanded rapidly in the 1850s as clipper ships crossed the Pacific.

INDIAN OCEAN

AUSTRALI

ANTARCTIC.

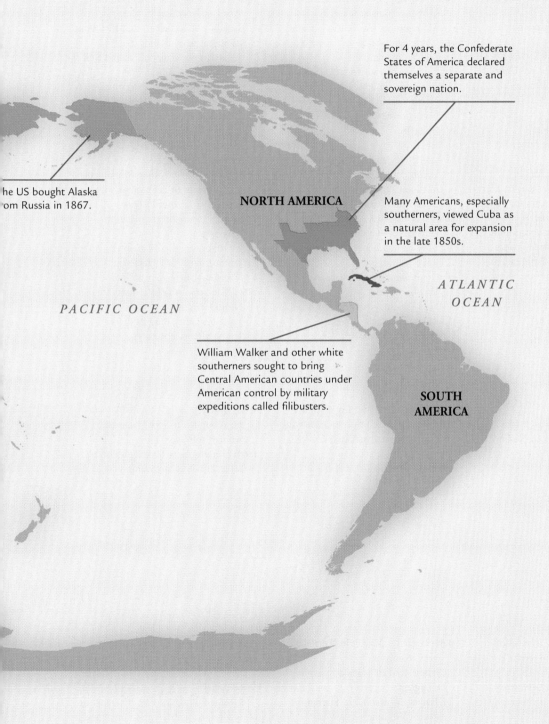

For 4 years, the Confederate States of America declared themselves a separate and sovereign nation.

he US bought Alaska om Russia in 1867.

NORTH AMERICA

Many Americans, especially southerners, viewed Cuba as a natural area for expansion in the late 1850s.

ATLANTIC OCEAN

PACIFIC OCEAN

William Walker and other white southerners sought to bring Central American countries under American control by military expeditions called filibusters.

SOUTH AMERICA

Chronology

	1855	**1861**	**1863**
POLITICS & DIPLOMACY	**1855:** Proslavery and free-soil forces clash in Kansas Massachusetts desegregates public schools **1856:** John Brown's raid in Kansas James Buchanan elected president Congressman Preston Brooks canes Senator Charles Sumner **1857:** *Dred Scott* decision Lecompton Constitution Hinton R. Helper, *The Impending Crisis of the South* **1858:** Lincoln-Douglas debates **1859:** John Brown's raid on Harpers Ferry Vicksburg convention calls for reopening of African slave trade Kansas ratifies free-soil constitution **1860:** Democratic convention divides Abraham Lincoln elected president South Carolina secedes from the Union	**1861:** Mississippi, Florida, Alabama, Georgia, Louisiana, and Texas secede Montgomery Convention creates Confederate States of America Lincoln inaugurated Firing on and surrender of Fort Sumter Arkansas, Tennessee, Virginia, and North Carolina secede Confederate victory at Bull Run (Manassas) Jefferson Davis elected president of Confederacy with 6-year term Union navy seizes Confederate commissioners Mason and Slidell from British ship *Trent* **1862:** Confederates surrender Fort Donelson to Grant *Virginia* v. *Monitor* in Hampton Roads, Virginia Grant wins dramatic victory at Shiloh New Orleans surrenders to Admiral Farragut Jackson's Shenandoah Valley Campaign	**1862:** (*continued*) Lee takes command of Army of Northern Virginia Lee drives McClellan from Richmond in Seven Days' Battles Confederate victory at Second Bull Run (Manassas) Battle of Antietam (Sharpsburg) First Emancipation Proclamation Burnside replaces McClellan as commander of Army of the Potomac Lee overwhelms Burnside at Fredericksburg **1863:** Second Emancipation Proclamation Culmination of Lee's victory over Hooker at Chancellorsville Grant's successful campaign in Mississippi Death of Stonewall Jackson Union victory at Gettysburg Vicksburg surrenders to Grant **1863:** Black troops fight at Fort Wagner, South Carolina Lincoln's Gettysburg Address Union victory at Chattanooga
SOCIAL & CULTURAL EVENTS	**1857:** Mass revivals **1858:** Frederick Law Olmsted begins design for Central Park in New York City	**1863:** Lincoln's Gettysburg Address **1865:** First woman professor of astronomy appointed at Vassar College	**1866:** American Equal Rights Association founded to seek black and woman suffrage **1867:** Horatio Alger begins publishing series of books for young boys
ECONOMICS & TECHNOLOGY	**1857:** Financial panic and depression Baltimore–St. Louis rail service completed **1861:** Suspension of specie payments Mathew Brady begins photography of Civil War	**1862:** Legal Tender Act in North authorizes "greenbacks" Homestead Act passed by Union Congress *Virginia v. Monitor* in Hampton Roads, Virginia **1863:** Confederate Congress passes Impressment Act Union Congress passes National Bank Act	**1863:** Bread riot in Richmond **1864:** Confederate Congress assumes new powers of taxation, impressment of slaves George Pullman invents sleeping car **1866:** National Labor Union organized

1864	1867	1868

1864: Grant assumes command of all Union forces
Battle of the Wilderness in Virginia
Union victory at Cold Harbor
Sherman captures Atlanta
Lincoln reelected president
Beginning of Sherman's march from Atlanta to the Atlantic
1865: Congress passes Thirteenth Amendment, abolishing slavery
Congress creates Bureau of Refugees, Freedmen, and Abandoned Lands (Freedmen's Bureau)
Lincoln's second inauguration
Fall of Richmond to Union
Lee surrenders to Grant at Appomattox Court House
Lincoln assassinated; Andrew Johnson becomes president

1865: (*continued*) Former Confederate states hold constitutional conventions through December; pass "black codes"
Thirteenth Amendment to Constitution ratified, abolishing slavery
1866: Congress passes Civil Rights Act and Freedmen's Bureau renewal over Johnson's veto
Riots in New Orleans and Memphis
Congress approves Fourteenth Amendment
Ku Klux Klan formed
1867: Congress passes Reconstruction Act and Tenure of Office Act
Johnson dismisses Secretary of War Stanton, triggering impeachment proceedings
First elections in South under Reconstruction Act
Passage of Reconstruction Act
Alaska purchase negotiations

1868: Andrew Johnson impeached and acquitted
U.S. Grant elected president
1869: Fifteenth Amendment passes Congress
Woman suffrage starts in Wyoming Territory
1870: Ku Klux Klan conducts terror raids in South
1871: Tweed Ring exposed in New York City
1872: Grant reelected
1873: Salary Grab and Credit Mobilier Scandals
1874: Democrats gain in congressional elections
1875: Civil Rights Act passes Congress
1876: Hayes and Tilden in disputed election
1877: Hayes declared president after compromises settle election dispute

---

1868: Louisa May Alcott publishes *Little Women*
1869: Licensing of women lawyers begins
First intercollegiate football game played between Princeton and Rutgers

1870: First Greek letter sorority, Kappa Alpha Theta, founded
1871: Cable car invented
1872: American Public Health Association starts
1873: Mark Twain and Charles Dudley Warner publish *The Gilded Age*

1874: Women's Christian Temperance Union founded
1875: Smith and Wellesley College open to provide higher education for women
1876: Centennial Exposition in Philadelphia

1867: Patrons of Husbandry (Grange) founded
1868: First 8-hour day for federal workers
1869: Gold Corner scheme of Jay Gould and Jim Fisk
Transcontinental railroad completed

1870: Standard Oil Company of Ohio organized
1871: Chicago fire burns center of city
1872: Adding machine invented
1873: Panic of 1873 starts depression

1874: Sale of typewriters begins
Tomkins Square riot of unemployed in New York City
1875: First dynamo for outdoor lighting constructed
1876: Heinz tomato ketchup marketed
1877: National railroad strike

13 Broken Bonds, 1855–1861

"Border Ruffians." The northern press depicted what it took to be the seedy character of the proslavery men who came over the border from Missouri into Kansas to support slavery.

© The Granger Collection, New York

The United States had never seemed stronger than at the beginning of 1855. The economy was booming, settlers pushed into the West, railroads spread at a relentless rate, and immigrants streamed into American farms and factories. Churches, schools, and reform organizations grew faster than ever.

But the danger signs were not hard to see. The conflict to control the national future grew more bitter with each passing political crisis. Every year brought a clash more divisive than the one before. Disputes broke out in the Kansas Territory, in the village of Harpers Ferry, and finally in the contest for president. Parties and politicians, weakened by nativism and loss of faith by voters, seemed powerless to stop the disintegration.

North and South Collide

Conflict had been a staple of American politics for decades before 1855. Territories proved a persistent problem, but Americans also argued over tariffs, nominees for high office, and the role of religion. The arguments grew hot, but eventually calmed down until the next outbreak. Events of the late 1850s, however, broke the pattern. New crises came before the old ones could cool. The crises suddenly engulfed every political, economic, moral, and practical difference between Americans. Citizens were under pressure to prove their loyalties and defend their vision of America's future course—slave or free. The time for compromises and moderation was over.

The White South Fortifies Itself

Slavery had never been stronger in the United States than it was in the 1850s. The three and a half million slaves of the South extended over a vast territory stretching from Delaware to Texas and north to Missouri. Theorists devised ever more elaborate and aggressive defenses of slavery, no longer depicting it merely as a necessary evil or an unfortunate inheritance from the English. Rather, they claimed, slavery was an instrument of God's will, a means of civilizing and Christianizing Africans otherwise lost to barbarism and heathenism. Southern physicians went to great lengths to "prove" that Africans and

Timeline

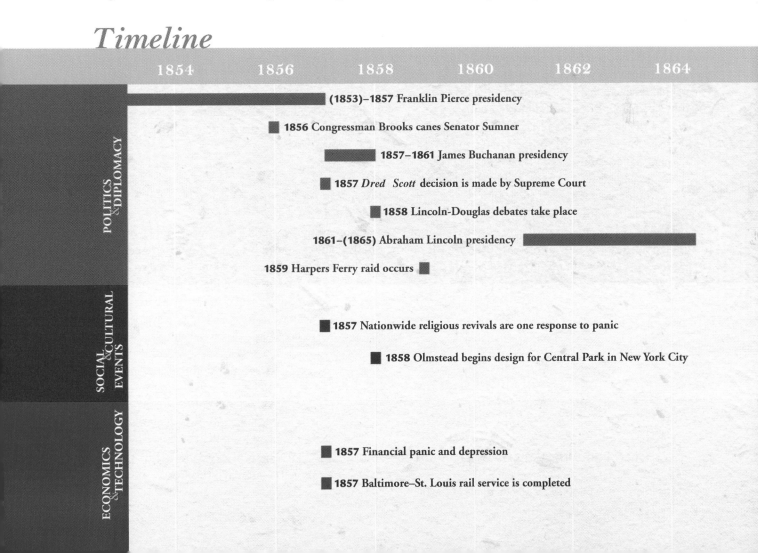

	1854	1856	1858	1860	1862	1864

POLITICS & DIPLOMACY

(1853)–1857 Franklin Pierce presidency

1856 Congressman Brooks canes Senator Sumner

1857–1861 James Buchanan presidency

1857 *Dred Scott* decision is made by Supreme Court

1858 Lincoln-Douglas debates take place

1861–(1865) Abraham Lincoln presidency

1859 Harpers Ferry raid occurs

SOCIAL & CULTURAL EVENTS

1857 Nationwide religious revivals are one response to panic

1858 Olmstead begins design for Central Park in New York City

ECONOMICS & TECHNOLOGY

1857 Financial panic and depression

1857 Baltimore–St. Louis rail service is completed

their descendants were physically and intellectually inferior to whites.

Some defenders of slavery argued that slavery was *better* than free labor, more humane and Christian. If the hypocritical and self-righteous men of the North would admit it, white southerners argued, free labor exacted a great cost. Men, women, and children went hungry when unemployment, ill health, or old age struck. In the South, by contrast, slaveholders cared for their slaves even when those slaves had grown too old or feeble to work. The South's relative lack of schools, orphanages, asylums, and prisons, the defenders of the region insisted, testified not to backwardness but to a personalized society where individual responsibility replaced impersonal institutions.

Some white southerners in the late 1850s argued for the expansion of American territory in Cuba or Central America, places where slavery could flourish. **William Walker,** a young Tennessean, dreamed of personal glory and a new territory for slavery. After several attempts at "**filibustering,**" or small-scale military efforts, in Mexico, Walker took advantage of a civil war to seize power in Nicaragua in 1855 and 1856. President Pierce granted diplomatic recognition of Walker's government, but Central American leaders united against him, cholera wiped out his dwindling, poorly supplied army, and Cornelius Vanderbilt, furious at Walker's revocation of Vanderbilt's Nicaraguan steamship charter, cut off his support from Washington. White southerners enthusiastically supported several attempts by Walker in the late 1850s to take Nicaragua, but he failed repeatedly, and finally was executed by a firing squad in Honduras in 1860.

Despite the agitation of a few editors and politicians for the reopening of the African slave trade, most white southerners wanted above all to keep and protect what they had, not jeopardize slavery by brashly expanding it. Not only would a renewed slave trade with Africa ignite the opinion of the world against the South, but it would also drive down slave prices and create new problems of discipline and revolt. The white South prided itself on having created a stable and prosperous society during its

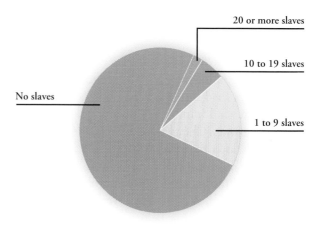

Percent who owned slaves

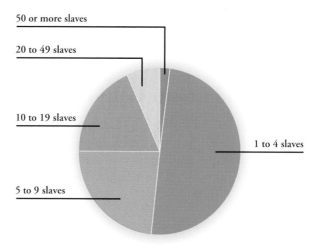

Number of slaves owned

CHART 13.2 a & b Slaveowning in the South

About three-fourths of southern white families owned no slaves in 1860. More than half of those who did possess slaves claimed four or fewer.

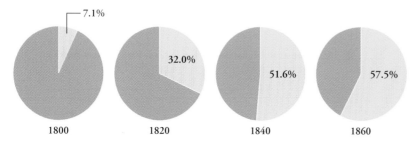

CHART 13.1 Cotton and the American Economy

Even as the economy of the entire nation boomed, cotton accounted for an ever-growing proportion of American exports to the rest of the world.

two and a half centuries of slavery and did not want to endanger that society.

Moreover, the slave economy boomed in the late 1850s. Planters took advantage of improved cotton gins, riverboats, railroads, and new kinds of seed to double, in the 1850s alone, their production of cotton. The claim of southern politicians that "Cotton is King" proved no empty boast. Even though northern factories and farms grew rapidly in the 1850s, cotton accounted for a growing proportion of U.S. exports—more than half in 1860. Without cotton, many thousands of northern and British workers would have had no jobs.

The prosperity created by the cotton boom resonated throughout the southern economy. Slaves proved to be adaptable

DOING HISTORY

White Southerners Without Slaves

HINTON HELPER'S BOOK of 1857 became a national sensation. The Republican party seized on the book as a revelation from inside the slave power's empire, arguing that it revealed the secret resentments of the white majority. To the Republicans' surprise and dismay, however, the book bred anger against the North instead of Republican recruits in the South.

J. D. B. DeBow was a former superintendent of the United States Census and published an influential periodical from New Orleans, in which he promoted the economic development of the South. Here, he argues that slavery actually helped the nonslaveholding white southerner.

Hinton Helper, *The Impending Crisis of the South*

The lords of the lash are not only absolute masters of the blacks, who are bought and sold, and driven about like so many cattle, but they are also the oracles and arbiters of all the non-slaveholding whites, whose freedom is merely nominal, and whose unparalleled illiteracy and degradation is purposely and fiendishly perpetuated. . . . [The nonslaveholders] must be as mum as dumb brutes, and stand in awe of their august superiors, or be crushed with stern rebukes, cruel oppressions, or downright violence. If they dare to think for themselves, their thoughts must be forever concealed. The expression of any sentiment at all conflicting with the gospel of slavery, dooms them at once in the community in which they life, and then, whether willing or unwilling, they are obliged to become heroes, martyrs, or exiles. . . . Never were the poorer classes of a people, and those classes so largely in the majority, and all inhabiting the same country, so basely duped, so adroitly swindled, or so unpardonably outraged.

James B. D. DeBow, "The Interest in Slavery of the Southern Non-Slaveholder"

[How does slavery benefit the non-slaveholding white man?]

The non-slaveholders, as a class, are not reduced by the necessity of our condition, as is the case in the free States, to find employment in crowded cities and come into competition in close and sickly workshops and factories, with remorseless and untiring machinery.

The non-slaveholder is not subjected to that competition with pauper labor, which has degraded the free labor of the North. . . .

The non-slaveholder of the South preserves the status of the white man, and is not regarded as an inferior or dependent.

The non-slaveholder knows that as soon as his savings will admit, he can become a slaveholder, and thus relieve his wife from the necessities of the kitchen and the laundry, and his children from the labors of the field.

The large slaveholders and proprietors of the South begin life in great part as non-slaveholders. . . .

Without the institution of slavery, the great staple products of the South would cease to be grown, and the immense annual results, which are distributed among every class of the community, and which give life to every branch of industry, would cease.

Source: Hinton R. Helper, *The Impending Crisis of the South* (New York: A. B. Burdick, 1859), pp. 40–43; "The Non-Slaveholders of the South," in DeBow and others, *The Interest in Slavery of the Southern Non-Slaveholder. The Right of Peaceful Secession. Slavery in the Bible* (Charleston: Evans and Cogswell, 1860), pp. 3–5, 7–12.

Questions for Reflection

1. How could both Helper and DeBow use statistics to make their arguments?

2. What parts of life in the South did Helper focus on? DeBow? Could they both be right? Which argument is more persuasive?

3. How did Helper's argument support the Republican appeal in the North? Why did it not attract southern Republican voters?

4. Did DeBow portray the North fairly? How would the Republicans have replied to DeBow?

Explore additional primary sources related to this chapter on the Wadsworth American History Resource Center or HistoryNOW websites:

http://history.wadsworth.com/rc/us
http://now.ilrn.com/ayers_etal3e

A Yeoman farm

Nonslaveholding whites in the antebellum South, living on farms such as this one in Texas, comprised approximately 75 percent of the white population.

Most owned small plots of land they farmed themselves with the aid of their family and local networks of kin and community for access to market goods. They are frequently referred to as **yeomen** farmers, an ideal of the self-sufficient farm household as one of the cornerstones of American democracy.

Access to arable land and the prospects to purchase slaves became issues of increasing concern through the 1850s. Land exhausted by tobacco or cotton or that was tied up in large holdings of wealthier farmers raised the stakes of access to western lands. In many areas back east in Virginia and the Carolinas, poorer white families and younger sons found themselves unable to move from being laborers and farm tenants to land ownership. While many southern yeomen families migrated to southern Illinois, Indiana, and Missouri to break ground in areas without slavery, many others considered the opportunity to own slaves part of their political birthright and supported slavery's expansion even if they owned no slaves themselves.

Courtesy of the Daughters of the Republic of Texas Library

both to factories and cities. Southern cities grew quickly, attracting immigrants and businesses. Although the South could not keep up with the North, it actually did quite well by international standards. Considered as a separate economy, the South stood second in the world in the number of miles of railroad, sixth in cotton textile factories, and eighth in iron production. On the other hand, the South was not urbanizing or industrializing nearly as quickly as the North. The South did not create a large class of entrepreneurs or skilled workers, nor did the region invest much money in machinery to make its farms and plantations more efficient. The southern plantation economy, in effect, was too profitable for its own good. The short-term gains of the 1850s, reflected in the escalating value of slaves, dissuaded wealthy southerners from investing in businesses that might have held greater potential for long-term development.

Northerners considered the southern economy the reverse image of the North: sick rather than healthy, backward rather than dynamic. Critics of the South argued that slavery victimized not only slaves but also "poor whites." In the antislavery portrayal, the **Slave Power's** domination began at home, where haughty self-proclaimed aristocrats lorded over ignorant whites, bullying them into supporting parties and policies that worked against their own interests. Antislavery advocates charged that slaves degraded white labor in the South and substituted a cheap sense of racial superiority for actual accomplishment.

The most effective criticism of the South in this vein came from a southerner: Hinton Rowan Helper, the son of a small slaveholding farmer in western North Carolina. In the late 1850s, a northern press, with aid from the Republican party, published Helper's book, *The Impending Crisis of the South,* which argued that the South's growth, prosperity, and cultural development were being held back by slavery. Helper deployed statistics from the census to prove his case, showing that land values, literacy levels, and manufacturing rates in the South were substantially lower than those in the North. He warned of the devastation caused by slavery. He proposed that slaveholders be taxed to colonize all free blacks in Africa or Latin America.

There is little indication that many southern whites agreed with Helper's assessment of them as ignorant, illiterate, and degraded. Most whites saw slavery as an avenue for their own advancement, not a hindrance. Many men and women bought a slave before they bought land. Slaveowners included women, shopkeepers, industrialists, lawyers, ministers, and even a few free blacks. No investment seemed to offer a more certain return than a slave, especially in the 1850s when slave prices rose rapidly. Although that rise in prices meant that a growing proportion of white people would be unable to afford a slave, many Americans' livelihoods depended on servicing the slave trade, through insurance, manufacture of shoes and clothing to be sold in the South, medical care, and transport. The slave trade generated tens of millions of dollars in the antebellum economy.

Politics reinforced the sense among southern white men that they lived in a fair and democratic society. Although many nonslaveholders in mountainous districts across the South voted against the large slaveholding districts, most southern white men voted in concert with the richest men in their immediate neighborhoods. In the eyes of the poorer men, their wealthy neighbors could act as spokesmen and brokers for the community in the state capital.

Southern whites identified themselves most of all as white people, tied to other whites by blood and heritage. Whites held black people in contempt, despite their knowledge that many African Americans were more intelligent, hardworking, and Christian than many whites. To be white was to be the inheritor of all the accomplishments of the ancients, of Christendom, and of the modern world. Such attitudes were reinforced at every level, from the daily rituals of life to the writings of leading thinkers from Europe. White southerners railed against the Republicans because that party threatened this bond of race between the white North and the white South. Even nonslaveholders were tempted by the profits in slave-owning and most embraced the privileges and power granted by a white supremacist ideology.

Despite the solidarities of racial thinking, important political differences divided southerners. At one extreme were the so-called **fire-eaters,** virulent defenders of the South and slavery. These men were diverse. Some lived in cities, others on plantations. Some, such as J. D. B. DeBow, wanted to make the South more industrial and modern, whereas others rejected such development as a Yankee blight on the rural South. Whatever their differences, these men saw themselves as the voice of honesty. Men such as Robert Barnwell Rhett and Edmund Ruffin argued that the abolitionists and their Republican supporters intended to destroy the South. The only sane response, they believed, was to agitate the slavery issue constantly, to refuse to yield an inch in the territories or anywhere else.

At the other end of the political spectrum in the South were the former Whigs and Know-Nothings, men who considered themselves a "thoughtful, sedate, constitution-abiding, conservative class of men." They considered the Democrats, especially the fire-eaters, great threats to the future of the South and slavery. The many Unionists in the Upper South, in cities, and in some of the richest plantation districts of the cotton South warned that those who boasted of slavery's power would unify the white North against slavery. Caution and compromise, these men argued, were the best friends of slavery.

Bleeding Kansas

The Kansas-Nebraska Act declared that settlers would decide for themselves, by "popular sovereignty," what kind of society they would create. But partisans from both the North and the South determined to fill the territory with settlers of their own political persuasion. "Come on, then, Gentlemen of the slave States," New York's Senator William H. Seward proclaimed soon after the Kansas-Nebraska Act passed, "We will engage in competition for the virgin soil of Kansas, and God give the victory to the side which is stronger in numbers as it is in right."

The Massachusetts Emigrant Aid Company announced that it planned to raise $5 million to aid and encourage settlement in Kansas to ensure that the embattled territory became a free state. Proslavery advocates in Missouri, for their part, flooded across the border to vote in support of the proslavery candidates for the territorial legislature, casting roughly 3,400 more ballots than there were eligible voters. This action by the "**border ruffians,**" as the northern press quickly labeled them, was not necessary, for southerners already accounted for 6 of every 10 men settled in Kansas by 1855. The proslavery forces took control of the territorial legislature in Lecompton and passed a series of aggressive laws against free-soil advocates. Forbidding antislavery men to serve on juries or hold office, the legislature also decreed the death penalty for any person who assisted a fugitive slave.

These settlers in Topeka, Kansas, armed themselves against their proslavery adversaries. The conflict quickly took on the trappings of a war.

Antislavery Kansans decided that their only recourse was to establish a rival government. They worked through the summer and fall of 1855 in Topeka to write a constitution of their own. Over the winter, the free-soil advocates "ratified" their constitution and elected their own legislature and governor. Antislavery forces in New England and New York sent rifles to Kansas to arm what they saw as the side of righteousness. These arms became nicknamed "Beecher's Bibles" because Henry Ward Beecher's congregation, at his urging, funded part of their cost. Southerners, in turn, organized an expedition of 300 young men to reinforce their comrades.

Not surprisingly, this volatile situation soon exploded into violence. On May 21, 1856, a group of slave-state supporters marched into the free-soil stronghold of Lawrence to execute warrants from the proslavery territory court against free-state leaders and two newspapers. They threw printing presses into the river, fired cannon at the Free State Hotel, and burned the hotel to the ground. Free-soilers labeled the episode the "sack of Lawrence."

The next day, in Washington, D.C., Representative Preston Brooks of South Carolina searched out Senator **Charles Sumner** of Massachusetts. Sumner had delivered a series of bitter speeches against slavery. Sumner attacked Brooks's relative and fellow South Carolinian, the elderly Senator Andrew P. Butler, for taking "the harlot, slavery" as his "mistress." As Sumner wrote letters at his Senate desk, Brooks, defending the honor of his family and his state, demonstrated his contempt

for Sumner by striking him repeatedly about the head with a heavy rubber cane. Sumner did not return to his seat for two and a half years, the victim of shock. Brooks attacked Sumner as he would a servant or slave, one unworthy of a gentleman's challenge to a duel. The empty seat became a symbol in the North of southern brutality.

The next day, an event back in Kansas intensified the conflict. The episode swirled around one **John Brown,** a free-soil emigrant to Kansas. Brown had been a supporter of abolitionism since 1834 and followed five of his sons to Kansas in 1855. There, he became furious at the proslavery forces. He accompanied a group of free-staters to defend Lawrence, but they heard of the hotel's destruction before they arrived. Brown persuaded four of his sons and a son-in-law, along with two other men, to exact revenge for the defeat. The band set out for Pottawatomie Creek. There, acting in the name of the "Army of the North," they took five men from three houses and split their skulls with broadswords. The men had been associated in some way with the territorial district court, but no one was sure of Brown's precise motives. He was never punished for the killings.

In the wake of the "sack of Lawrence," the caning of Sumner, and the "Pottawatomie Massacre"—exploding in just a three-day period in May of 1856—the territory became known as "Bleeding Kansas." A new governor finally helped quiet the conflict in September, but the legitimacy of the territorial government remained an issue of heated contention. The South won a hollow victory when it seized the first election for the territorial government in Kansas. That government would soon pass, but the symbolic value of **Bleeding Kansas** would long endure.

SOUTHERN CHIVALRY — ARGUMENT versus CLUB'S.

Preston Brooks's attack on Charles Summer in the U.S. Senate electrified the nation in the spring of 1856—even though this artist apparently did not have an image of Brooks from which to work.

Flashpoints | The Rise and Fall of the Know-Nothings

In the 1830s nativists attacked Catholic immigrants, asserting that America's republican values could not survive contact with a large, foreign-born Catholic population. These Protestants insisted that republicanism required a virtuous, educated, and free-spirited electorate, the opposite of how they portrayed Catholics: as superstitious, ignorant, and priest-ridden puppets. Such anti-Catholicism had a long history in America, rooted in England's struggles against Catholic Spain and France and the Puritan journey across the ocean to escape the Church of England's "Romish" trappings.

Aided by resentments of "native-born" workers who feared the drop in wages caused by immigrant competition, nativists entered politics. In 1844, when immigration from Europe was rising, a new party, the American Republicans, elected six congressmen and dozens of local officials in New York, Philadelphia, and Boston. Nativism reached its political zenith 10 years later with the meteoric rise of the "Know-Nothings." This secret organization combined fraternal rituals and secret oaths with a political agenda designed to curb the political power of Catholics and immigrants.

The American party, the official name of the Know-Nothings, enjoyed its greatest power in the years after the sharp rise in immigration following the Irish potato famine and failed revolutions in Germany. Disgust with corruption in politics peaked after passage of the Kansas-Nebraska Act. More than a million Americans joined Know-Nothing lodges. By the end of 1855, Know-Nothings had carried elections in a dozen states and elected approximately a hundred congressmen.

The nativists fell out of favor when they proved unable to restrict immigration or change naturalization laws. Once in office, most Know-Nothings raced for the spoils of office, disappointing those who had believed them dedicated to ending political corruption. The end of their political effectiveness came when they were unable to straddle the slavery issue in the 1856 presidential campaign and the American party split into sectional factions, never to re-unite.

Nativism tempted the new Republican party that emerged in the late 1850s. Many Know-Nothings found the Republicans attractive and the Republicans wanted the votes of these disaffected voters—especially since the Democrats won the votes of the great majority of Catholics. But Republican leaders had learned that they could not build a national party on such overt pleas to Americans' xenophobia. Instead, they veiled their distrust of immigrants and Catholics behind pleas for patriotism, Protestantism, and progress.

Hostility to immigrants and Catholics remained beneath the surface of American society, but never again would nativists openly organize their hatreds into a powerful political party.

Questions for Reflection

1. Why might it now seem surprising that there was such prejudice against the Irish?

2. Why could the Know-Nothings not sustain their power?

3. Is opposition to immigration un-American?

AMERICANS TO THE RESCUE!

IRISHMEN UNDER ARMS!

AMERICANS! SONS OF THE REVOLUTION!! A body of SEVENTY-FIVE IRISHMEN, known as the

"COLUMBIAN ARTILLERY!"

have VOLUNTEERED THEIR SERVICES TO SHOOT DOWN THE CITIZENS OF BOSTON, aided by a company of UNITED STATES MARINES, nearly all of whom are IRISHMEN!! and are now under arms to defend Virginia in KIDNAPPING A CITIZEN OF MASSACHUSETTS!!!

AMERICANS! These Irishmen have called us

"COWARDS! AND SONS OF COWARDS!!"
Shall we submit to have our citizens shot down by
A SET OF
VAGABOND IRISHMEN!

Courtesy of the Massachusetts Historical Society

The Republicans Challenge the South

Democrats were still divided in the wake of their stunning losses in the congressional elections of 1854. Northern Democrats knew that too open a submission to southern interests could cost them reelection. To many southerners, the Democrats seemed a mere tool of Stephen Douglas and his northern allies; to many northerners, it seemed that Douglas's call for popular sovereignty was a cover for greedy

slaveholders. President Franklin Pierce seemed incapable of leadership. The Democrats, needing someone who had not been tarnished by the events of the preceding two years, turned to **James Buchanan** to run for president in 1856. As minister to England, Buchanan had conveniently been out of the country during the Kansas-Nebraska crisis.

Although Know-Nothings were able to agree at the local and state level on issues of corruption and

President James Buchanan, a Pennsylvania Democrat, became the object of contempt among many northerners for his sympathy for the South in the political struggles of the late 1850s.

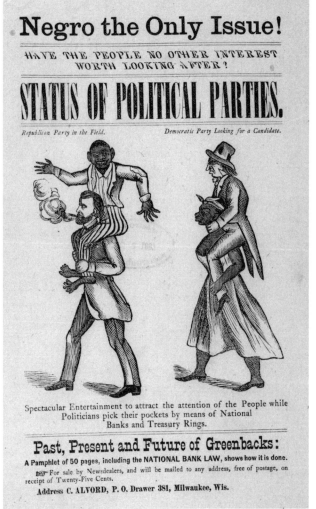

This broadside from Wisconsin attacked both the Democrats and the Republicans in 1856 as fixating in different ways on slavery, calling the election a "Spectacular Entertainment to attract the attention of the People while Politicians pick their pockets by means of National Banks and Treasury Rings."

anti-Catholicism, slavery split them as they attempted to organize a presidential campaign and to develop consensus on sectional issues. In February 1856, Know-Nothing unity ended in a controversy over a proslavery platform when 50 northern delegates from 8 states walked out of the National Council and called for a separate convention of northerners in June. Southerners who had voted with the Know-Nothings had nowhere to turn but to the Democrats, but northern Know-Nothings were attracted to the new Republican party. The Republicans bypassed their most outspoken antislavery men for the 1856 nomination and turned to John C. Frémont, famed as an explorer of the West. He had taken almost no public positions and had accumulated almost no political experience. The Republicans thought they had found just the sort of vague candidate who would give few potential voters a reason to vote against him.

The new Republican party was antislavery but not pro-black; Republicans avoided talking about race. What they did talk about was the goodness of the North: the North, they argued, was everything the South was not, a place where hardworking white men could build a life for their families free from the threat of arrogant, powerful, and greedy slaveholders.

Abolitionists had succeeded in making slavery detested throughout the North and had created much of the antisouthern energy that flowed into the Republican party. But abolitionists distrusted that party—and vice versa. The Republicans seemed interested only in the welfare of the white North. They denied any intention of ending slavery in the South and even resurrected talk of colonization, the movement the abolitionists had abandoned 25 years earlier. The Republicans, although better than the prosouthern Democrats, still dissatisfied the abolitionists.

The Republicans talked of the "Slave Power," a political conspiracy of the most powerful slaveholders. Republicans saw everything from the three-fifths clause to the bloodshed in Kansas as the fruit of the Slave Power. How else to explain the long list of southern victories at a time when the North grew more populous and wealthy? Kansas and the caning of Sumner showed

that the Slave Power, a Cincinnati paper raged, "cannot tolerate free speech anywhere, and would stifle it in Washington with the bludgeon and the bowie-knife, as they are now trying to stifle it in Kansas."

<hr>

Picturing the Past   POLITICS & DIPLOMACY

The Election of 1856

Voters turned out in near record numbers for the presidential election in 1856.

The Republicans, organized in only a few states in the North in the spring, rapidly consolidated their message and rallied voters in New England and the Upper North. A shift in a few thousand votes in key states such as Pennsylvania, and the Republicans might have won. Democrats celebrated victory, but their leaders recognized that the growing population of the North and Midwest would decide control of the House of Representatives. Southerners, now firmly in control of the Democratic party, escalated their demands for opening western territories to

slavery and for federal protection of slave property. Northern Democrats faced defeat in home districts when they supported such policies, weakening the party's ability to resist the Republicans. The distribution of voter support for the various parties illustrates the inability of Democrats, Know-Nothings, or Republicans to achieve national appeal; the party platforms failed to find support across the growing sectional divide. As the Know-Nothings faded as a serious competitor, the two remaining parties struggled to increase their appeal in the Lower North and Midwest, key areas that would determine the victor in the next election.

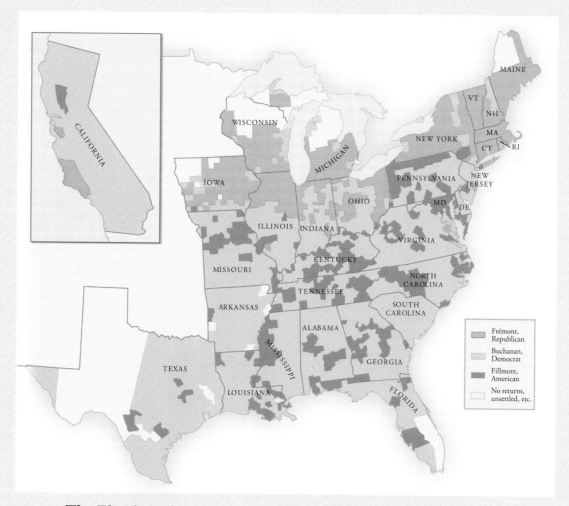

MAP 13.1 The Election of 1856

Many Republicans attacked Catholics, repeating the charges that nativists had made for decades about the undemocratic power of the Pope, priests, and nuns. Ironically, rumors that Frémont was a Catholic quickly surfaced and refused to subside. Moreover, Frémont refused to give direction to the national campaign. To make matters worse, **Millard Fillmore,** the former president, ran under the banner of the American party, as the Know-Nothings called themselves in a vain attempt to resurrect themselves as a national party. Fillmore hoped that the three-way election would split the electorate so that the final decision would rest with the House, where he would appear as a compromise candidate.

On election day in 1856, 83 percent of the eligible voting men went to the polls, one of the highest turnouts of the era (see Map 13.1). Although Buchanan won all of the South except Maryland, he received only 45 percent of the popular vote in the country as a whole. A difference of a few thousand votes in a few states would have denied Buchanan the election. The Democrats had won, but were filled with anxiety; the Republicans had lost, but were filled with confidence. It was clear to everyone that the American political system was in flux and transition.

Observers of all political persuasions believed that James Buchanan had it within his power to strengthen the Democrats in both the North and the South. His party, after all, still controlled the Senate. The Republicans, moreover, had drawn much of their power from the chaos in Kansas. Once Kansas had peacefully entered the Union as a free state under the banner of popular sovereignty, Democrats happily observed, no other territory awaited in which similar conflicts might be expected. Slavery, everyone seemed to agree, had no chance in Oregon, Nebraska, Minnesota, Washington, Utah, or New Mexico. The territorial issue that had torn at the country since 1820 might finally die down.

Dred Scott

In his inaugural address, James Buchanan mentioned a case pending before the Supreme Court, a case regarding a slave. Buchanan looked forward to the ruling, for he believed that the territorial issue was "a judicial question, which legitimately belongs to the Supreme Court. . . . To their decision, in common with all good citizens, I shall cheerfully submit, whatever they may be." That case had moved its way through various levels of courts for more than a decade. Dred Scott, born a slave in Virginia around 1800, had in the 1830s been taken by his master, an army surgeon named John Emerson, to territories far in the upper Midwest. Scott had married Harriet Robinson, the slave of a federal Indian agent. Dr. Emerson bought

Harriet and thus owned the two daughters she bore with Scott. When Emerson died in 1843, Scott and his family became the property of Emerson's widow, who moved to St. Louis. In 1846 the Scotts petitioned for their freedom, claiming that their residence in the free territory entitled them to free status.

A long series of postponements and delays dragged the case on into the early 1850s, when the legal environment had become especially divided by political controversy over slavery. Democratic judges and lawyers worked to deny the Scotts their freedom on the grounds that such a precedent would undermine the right of southerners to take slaves into the territories. A Republican lawyer agreed to carry the Scotts' case before the Supreme Court to counter the Democrats' aggressive claims. Unfortunately for the Republicans and the Scotts, five southern Democrats sat on the Court, along with two northern Democrats, one northern Whig, and one northern Republican. Presiding was Chief Justice **Roger B. Taney** (pronounced "tawney"), an 80-year-old

The *Dred Scott* case attracted the attention of the entire country in 1856. This northern newspaper depicted Scott and his family sympathetically, emphasizing family ties and the women of the family.

Marylander first appointed to the Court by Andrew Jackson in 1835.

The **Dred Scott case** came before the Supreme Court during the superheated months of 1856, when Kansas, the Brooks/Sumner affair, and the presidential election commanded the country's attention. Although the case could have been decided on relatively narrow grounds, the Democratic members of the Court wanted to issue a sweeping pronouncement that would settle once and for all the question of slavery in the territories. President-elect Buchanan pressured a fellow Pennsylvanian on the Court to side with the southerners. Two days after Buchanan took office in March of 1857, the Court announced its decision in the *Dred Scott* case. It took Chief Justice Taney two hours to read the opinion.

Taney spent half his time denying that Scott had the right to bring a case in the first place. Black people, Taney decreed, could not become citizens of the United States because "they were not included, and were not intended to be included, under the word 'citizens' in the Constitution." Taney declared that at the time the Constitution was written, throughout the "civilized and enlightened portions of the world," members of the "negro African race" were held to be "altogether unfit to associate with the white race . . . and so far inferior, that they had no rights which the white man was bound to respect." Therefore, Dred Scott had never been a citizen of Missouri and had no right to sue his mistress. Taney also decreed that Congress had never held a constitutional right to restrict slavery in the territories and that therefore the Missouri Compromise of 1820 was invalid. Two justices dissented from the majority's opinion, but the decision stood as the law of the land.

Southerners and many northern Democrats exulted that they had been vindicated by the *Dred Scott* decision, that the Republicans' demand for territories free of slavery was simply unconstitutional. Democratic editors claimed that the decision "vindicates and sustains the Democratic Party in the patriotism and wisdom of its course" as "*sectionalism* has been rebuked, and abolitionism staggered." The Republicans, however, sneered at the decision, which they saw as one more corrupt act by the Slave Power Conspiracy designed to turn the nation into "one great slave pen." They reprinted the dissenting opinions in the *Dred Scott* case and denounced the decision in the state legislatures they controlled throughout the North. They argued that the Founding Fathers had never intended slavery to be a permanent part of the United States and merely tolerated bondage because they expected it to die of its own weight. If the *Dred Scott* decision were followed to its logical conclusion, they warned, the United States would reopen the slave trade with Africa and even extend slavery into northern states where it had been banned.

The Republicans thought the Court's audacious statement was "the best thing that could have happened" to the Republican party. As an abolitionist newspaper put it, the "fiercer the insult, the bitterer the blow, the better." The Republicans expected the *Dred Scott* decision to make their party stronger. The Republicans needed to sweep the government in 1860, they argued, to clean out corruption and conspiracy from the executive, Congress, and now the courts.

American Society in Crisis

The American economy boomed in the mid-1850s. Not only did cotton do well, but so did the farms, factories, railroads, and cities of the North and West. People cheered the laying of a telegraphic cable all the way across the Atlantic Ocean, an incredible feat that triggered celebrations in towns across the nation, including wild fireworks in New York City that set City Hall ablaze. Currier and Ives prints became the rage, brightening homes around the country with charming scenes of American life. The sale of newspapers, books, and magazines surged. Working people's organizations staged a comeback. Churches and schools spread with remarkable speed. The mileage of railroads tripled to more than 30,000 miles.

But underlying this prosperity ran a deep current of unease. Some people worried that Americans were growing soft and self-indulgent. Others felt guilt that as the economy boomed, slavery became stronger. Others despaired at the state of American politics, which seemed in disarray. The conflict between the North and the South embodied all these anxieties, giving them concrete shape.

Financial Panic and Spiritual Revival

Late in the summer of 1857, people warned that there had been too much speculation recently, that companies and individuals had borrowed too much money. The end of the Crimean War in Europe seemed ominous for the United States, for now the countries of the Old World could turn their energies toward growing their own food, undermining the heavy demand for American farm products that had buoyed the economy for several years. When a major insurance company went under in 1857, a panic spread among New York banks and railroad stocks plummeted along with western land values. Soon, banks and companies across the country began to fail.

Working people of all ranks lost their jobs. Not only unskilled laborers, domestics, and millworkers found themselves without work, but so did educated bookkeepers and clerks. Across the North, hundreds of thousands

The Panic of 1857

New York City symbolized for many Americans the consequences of the high living and corrupt practices that brought on the Panic of 1857. "With fifty-seven suspended banks . . . hundreds and thousands of bankrupt merchants, importers, traders, and stock jobbers . . . with her rotten bankruptcies permeating and injuring almost every solvent community in the nation," raged one New Orleans newspaper, New York stood as "the center of reckless speculation, unflinching fraud and downright robbery." This cartoon dramatizes the moral corruption that many people believed lay at the heart of the panic.

The panic had more immediate and concrete causes. The end of the Crimean War in Europe triggered a decline in overseas demand for American agricultural products and reduction in specie flows into the nation from European investors. A wave of bankruptcies caused bank closures as cash became scarce and banks shut their doors on investors when cash supplies ran out. Small businessmen and managers, with no prospects of sales, laid off workers or offered them payment in kind instead of wages. Ironically, the southern cotton economy rebounded sooner, as European demand for cotton recovered by 1858, but northern and midwestern grain farmers faced low prices for the next 2 years.

© CORBIS

of people had no income and many were forced to rely on charity to feed and clothe themselves. Workers tried to organize, but employers shut down the mills and factories. As winter approached, many people wondered whether their families would survive through the cold months.

Southerners blamed northern financiers for bringing on the Panic of 1857. Though the white and free black working people of southern cities suffered along with their counterparts in the North, white southerners bragged that their region quickly recovered from the panic. They also bragged that their slaves, unlike white workers, never starved or went without a roof over their head.

A wave of religious revivals emerged in response to the panic. They lasted for over a year, sweeping back and forth across the country. Unlike earlier revivals, the religious spirit emerged not in rural districts but in the largest cities of the Northeast. Unlike earlier revivals, too, those of 1857 attracted a conspicuously large number of men as well as women. In contrast to earlier revivals in rural areas, middle-class men in the commercial districts of larger cities met for daily prayer meetings, regularly covered in the press, that convened promptly at noon and limited each member to a five-minute prayer to keep the group on schedule. The Young Men's Christian Association expanded rapidly during this time, providing young single clerks a venue for creating a "businesslike piety."

It seemed to many people that the revivals were the most heartening and significant in American history, showing that the people in the forefront of modern America were trying to change their ways. And as people read their newspapers they saw plenty that needed to be changed—especially in Kansas.

The Agony of Kansas

Most of the settlers who arrived in Kansas in 1856 and 1857 were nonslaveholding migrants from the Upper South. They did not appear eager to establish slavery in Kansas. An open election, therefore, would likely install a constitutional convention in favor of free soil at the time Kansas became a state. The proslavery legislature elected in the earliest days of the territory, however, still controlled Kansas in 1857. That legislature had to produce a constitution that the U.S. Congress would accept before Kansas could become a state. The draft they wrote permitted voters to choose between the constitution with slavery or without slavery. In either case, slaveowners already in Kansas would be permitted to keep their slaves.

This "Lecompton Constitution" unleashed serious problems for the Democrats across the country. Northern members of the party could not support it without appearing too sympathetic to the South; they could not oppose it without alienating the southern Democrats that made up the bulk of the party's strength. President Buchanan knew well that 112 of his 174 electoral votes had come from the South and that, of the 165 Democrats in both houses of Congress, 100 were southerners.

Stephen Douglas refused to endorse the Lecompton Constitution because it was a violation of popular sovereignty, but President Buchanan urged its adoption. The president persuaded himself that the constitution was a moderate compromise, letting Kansas enter the Union as a free state in the long run while protecting the slaveholders who were already there. Once Kansas was a state, Buchanan reasoned, its legislature could decide what to do with those slaves. Most northerners saw the matter differently: though it was obvious that the great majority of Kansans wanted to enter the Union as a free state, those antislavery Kansans would be forced to accept slavery.

Republicans could hardly believe that Buchanan had handed them such an easy way to portray him as a tool of the South. And neither could Stephen Douglas, who recognized that Buchanan's actions would create enormous problems for the Democrats. The Democrats fought bitterly among themselves for months; Douglas denounced the president for supporting "trickery and juggle" and sought to use his influence in the Senate to block the Lecompton Constitution. Buchanan retaliated by using the powers of the presidency to mobilize senators against Douglas.

Moderate southern and northern Democrats warned that the South was destroying its only hope for continued success: a strong Democratic party in the North. When Kansas voters overwhelmingly rejected the Lecompton Constitution in 1858, they rejected Buchanan and the South as well. The Democrats suffered widespread defeat in the state elections that spring and lost control of the House. Northern Democrats, still weak from the loss of seats after the 1854 elections, lost again as only 32 of 53 free-state Democrats survived the 1858 contest and 12 of those were opposed to the Lecompton Constitution. Douglas himself faced a tough election battle and Buchanan did everything he could to destroy this rival in his own party. Running against a promising Republican candidate, **Abraham Lincoln,** Douglas needed all the help he could get.

The Lincoln-Douglas Debates

Abraham Lincoln was very much the underdog in the Illinois senatorial race of 1858. As a Whig in a heavily Democratic state, Lincoln had not found it easy to win or hold office in the 1840s and 1850s. He had lost repeatedly, occupying national office for all of two years: elected to the House of Representatives in 1846, Lincoln lasted only one term and was sent back to his law office in Springfield. There, Lincoln made a good living as a lawyer, drawing on his own abilities and the connections that came with his marriage to Mary Todd, a member of a prominent family. Lincoln's modest beginnings on the Kentucky and Illinois frontier lay comfortably in the past. Still, he longed for a major public office.

Though the short, portly, pragmatic, and famous Stephen Douglas seemed the opposite of the tall, thin, inexperienced, principled, and obscure Abraham Lincoln, the two men in fact shared a great deal. Douglas, too, had grown up poor. Douglas, although the most prominent Democrat in the country, was actually four years younger than Lincoln. Both Lincoln and Douglas shared their constituents' moderate positions on most national issues.

Illinois's population was composed of many New England migrants in the northern half of the state, upcountry southern migrants in the bottom half, and German and Irish immigrants in Chicago. Both the factories and the farms of Illinois prospered in the 1850s, as did abolitionists, Know-Nothings, Whigs, and southern-leaning Democrats. The Illinois senatorial election of 1858 promised to throw all these groups into contention. At stake was this question: could the Democrats survive as a national party, with Douglas as their leader, or were they doomed to become a party of the South?

Douglas traveled by private railroad car from Chicago to Springfield, the state capital and Lincoln's

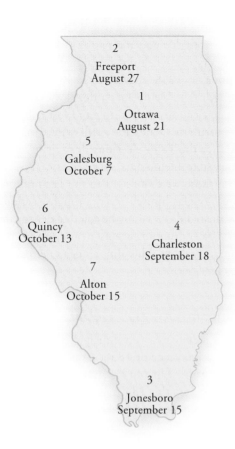

MAP 13.2 **The Path of the Lincoln-Douglas Debates**

The two candidates followed a long and circuitous route—nearly 1,300 miles long, on rail, river, buggy, and horseback—through Illinois in their efforts to win the voters over to their vision of the American future.

base. All along the way, Douglas gave speeches to thousands of people, telling them that he was the voice of experience, principled compromise, and popular sovereignty. He also told them that Lincoln held "monstrous revolutionary doctrines" of abolitionism. To Douglas's great annoyance, Lincoln followed the senator to rebut his arguments and charges, sometimes appearing in the crowd, sometimes arriving the next day. Douglas, though reluctant to give the relatively unknown Lincoln a share of attention, finally agreed to hold seven joint debates in the late summer and early fall (see Map 13.2).

Lincoln was far from an abolitionist, refusing to join the antislavery Liberty and Free-Soil parties and staying with the Whigs longer than many of the men who became Republicans. He repeatedly brought up the *Dred Scott* decision from the previous year, however, arguing that it would permit slavery to spread into lands where Illinois men or their sons would otherwise migrate. The West must remain a region where "white men may find a home . . . where they can settle upon some new soil and

better their condition in life." Douglas offered what he saw as practical, commonsense responses to such charges, arguing that slavery would not spread anywhere the majority of the white population did not want it to. A far greater and more immediate threat, Douglas argued, was that the Republicans would force the South into desperate acts by dragging moral issues into political contexts. Let the sovereign white people of each state decide for themselves whether they would have slavery or not, Douglas counseled. Douglas did not defend slavery, but he declared that "I care more for the great principle of self-government, the right of the people to rule, than I do for all the negroes in Christendom."

Lincoln charged that Douglas's strategy merely postponed an inevitable reckoning between the slave states and the free states. He argued that "a house divided against itself cannot stand. . . . Either the opponents of slavery will arrest the further spread of it, . . . or its advocates will push it forward till it shall become alike lawful in all the States, old as well as new." Notwithstanding Douglas's efforts to dismiss the morality of slavery as beside the point, that morality repeatedly surfaced in the debates. Lincoln argued that he, not Douglas, was the one defending true self-government. Douglas's policy permitted the forces of slavery to grow stronger and more aggressive, whereas Lincoln's would place slavery on the path toward "ultimate extinction." It would likely be several generations before that extinction occurred, Lincoln believed, but the process could begin in 1858.

Lincoln made a distinction between different kinds of rights. African Americans, he thought, had economic rights, but he did not believe in social equality between blacks and whites. He would not grant black men the right to intermarry with whites, serve on juries, or vote, but he did believe that black people had the right not to be slaves. Lincoln took the offensive, making Douglas appear more of a defender of slavery than at heart he was.

The election was close, but the state legislature, which elected U.S. senators in these decades, went to the Democrats and they returned Douglas to Washington. But Lincoln had become identified as the spokesman for a principled yet restrained antislavery. All across the North, in fact, the Republicans made impressive gains in 1858. In every state, many people wanted the nation to find some compromise. But the political environment did not have a chance to calm in 1859, for it was then that John Brown returned to the national scene.

John Brown and Harpers Ferry

John Brown had become famous in the three years since he had burst into prominence in Bleeding Kansas in 1855. Antislavery people back east, assured by journalists that Brown had not personally killed anyone at Pottawatomie,

The campaign launched by John Brown and 21 black and white allies in 1859 failed in its immediate aims of unleashing a rebellion of the enslaved but succeeded in heightening the moral and political debate over slavery.

admired the hard man for his firsthand opposition to slaveholders. Thus, as he toured New England in search of funds to carry on the cause, he found willing listeners and open hands. Antislavery advocates were eager to contribute to the fight against slavery in Kansas, not realizing they were contributing to a fight against slavery much closer to home. Brown wrote letters to wealthy abolitionists requesting assistance for "an important measure, in which the world has a deep interest." Throughout 1857 and 1858, Brown planned for an attack on the federal arsenal at **Harpers Ferry,** Virginia. He had a thousand iron pikes forged to arm the slaves he believed would rise in rebellion once he and his men triggered the revolt. He tried to win the support of Frederick Douglass, who, while sympathetic, thought the plan doomed. But Brown pressed on. One of his lieutenants moved to Harpers Ferry and even established a family there, preparing the way for the attack.

The assault on Harpers Ferry started in earnest in the summer of 1859, when Brown rented a farm seven miles away and assembled his men and munitions. To his disappointment, he could recruit only 21 men, 5 of them African Americans. The raid began easily enough on Sunday, October 16, as Brown's men quickly seized the arsenal and a rifle-manufacturing plant. Brown and his men remained in the small armory building, waiting for

word to spread among the slaves of Virginia that their day of liberation had come. The word spread instead among local whites, who quickly surrounded Brown's men, killing or capturing eight of them. Militia from Virginia and Maryland arrived the next day, followed soon after by federal troops. The troops rushed the armory. Ten of the abolitionist force were killed, five (including Brown) wounded, and seven escaped. Brown was tried within two weeks and found guilty. He was sentenced to be hanged exactly a month later, on December 2.

The entire episode, from the raid to Brown's execution, took only about six weeks to unfold. Yet during those six weeks opinion in both the North and the South changed rapidly. Public opinion, mixed at first, crystallized into sharply opposing viewpoints. Even those northerners who were appalled at the violence were shocked at the speed with which Brown was tried and condemned. Even those southerners who read with reassurance early denunciations of Brown in the North were appalled when they realized that many northerners refused to condemn the raid. The many people of moderate sympathies on both sides watched, dismayed, as common ground eroded beneath their feet.

No longer the Old Testament figure of blood and vengeance, Brown, walking to the Virginia gallows, appeared to many in the North as a New Testament figure of suffering and dignified sacrifice. Many northerners came to believe that John Brown's body could be redeemed only with a return to the stern violence he had championed.

The North and South Call Each Other's Bluff

Everyone knew the election of 1860 held enormous meaning for the United States, but no one could be sure what that meaning might be. Would this be the election that brought all to their senses? Would the border states be able to control the election? Would northern voters suddenly realize the South meant what it said? The actual events proved far more complex than most Americans had believed possible.

The Election of 1860

White southerners automatically linked John Brown with the Republican party, though leading Republicans explicitly denied any connection. Not only had any southern base of support disappeared, but the execution of John Brown and southern exultation at his death made the Republicans more attractive among northern voters than before.

The Democrats also felt the effects of Brown's raid. Meeting in Charleston in April 1860 to decide on their presidential nominee for the fall election, the northern Democrats nominated Stephen Douglas. The northern Democrats saw this as a compromise with the South. But southern Democrats demanded that the party explicitly uphold the rights of slaveholders to take their slaves into the territories as stated in the *Dred Scott* decision. Northern Democrats could not afford to make that concession and still have a chance to win back home. The southerners proved heedless of this plea, however, and walked out of the convention. Several weeks later, the Democrats met in Baltimore and nominated Douglas. Southerners, walking out once again, declaring themselves the "purified" Democratic party, nominated John C. Breckenridge of Kentucky.

Before the Democratic convention met again in June, Unionists in both the North and the South tried to avert catastrophe by nominating a compromise candidate. Calling themselves the Constitutional Union Party, they settled on John Bell of Tennessee. Many of these Unionists were former conservative Whigs and Know-Nothings who no longer had a political home. They advocated an end to agitation over slavery, "the Union as it is, the Constitution unchanged," to safeguard the "priceless heritage of our fathers." They counted on the other candidates to create a

deadlock that would have to be settled in the House of Representatives. There, the Unionists hoped, legislators would gratefully turn to their compromise candidate.

As the Democrats tore themselves apart, the Republicans met in Chicago. There, in efforts to put southern concerns at rest, the Republicans announced their belief in the right of each state to decide for itself whether it would have slavery. The Republicans cemented their appeal to voters unconcerned with the slavery issue by calling for protective tariffs, internal improvements, and free homesteads for anyone who would settle the West. The Republicans were much stronger than they had been only four years earlier. Party strategists calculated that they need only win Pennsylvania and one other state they had lost to the Democrats in 1856 to wrap up the election. The states they needed to take were Illinois, Indiana, or New Jersey—all of them on the border with the South and all of them far more moderate on the slavery question than states farther east or north. Thus, the Republicans turned to a moderate who was a favorite son of one of the crucial states: Abraham Lincoln of Illinois.

People in 1860 did not know that the way they voted would bring on a civil war, or even secession. Although Stephen Douglas constantly warned of such a danger, both Breckinridge and Lincoln downplayed any such dire consequences. Ironically, all the years of conflict had persuaded both the North and the South that the other talked tougher than it would act. The parties staged loud and raucous political events that proved long on emotion and short on clearly defined positions. Lincoln said nothing and stayed close to home while his party leaders displayed split fence rails and touted his honesty.

The election of 1860 was actually two separate elections, one in the North and one in the South. Lincoln made no attempt to explain himself to the South; Breckinridge made little attempt in the North. They never met face to face. Bell spoke mainly to the already converted. Douglas, breaking with tradition, spoke from New England to Alabama, trying to warn people what could happen if they voted along sectional lines. While campaigning across the Deep South, he endured rotten fruit, insults, and injuries from a collapsed platform. Few men were willing to believe their opponents would have the nerve to act on their threats.

On election day, November 6, Lincoln won in every northern state except New Jersey, which divided between Douglas and Lincoln. Douglas won outright only in Missouri. Breckinridge won the entire South except the border states of Virginia, Tennessee, and Kentucky, which went with Bell. Even at this late stage of sectional division, voters did not fit into easy categories. It was hardly a contest between a rural South and an industrial

THE POLITICAL QUADRILLE
Music by Dred Scott

As "Dred Scott" fiddles, the four candidates of 1860 dance to the tune of slavery. While Lincoln is accompanied by a black woman, Breckenridge, in the upper left, dances with the devil in the form of secessionist William L. Yancey.

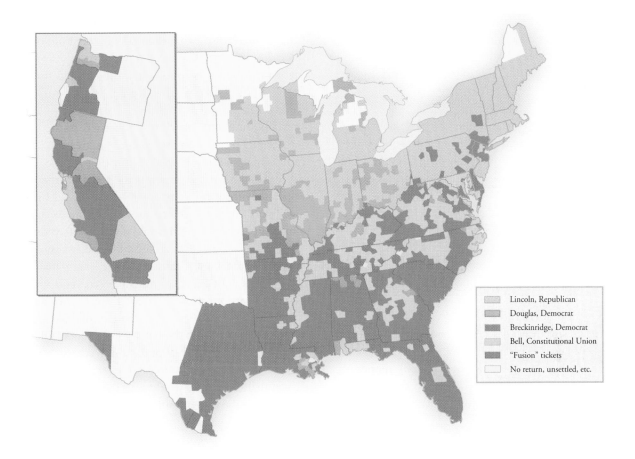

MAP 13.3 **The Election of 1860**
This four-way election saw the North divided between Lincoln and Douglas, the South divided between Bell and Breckenridge.

Legend:
- Lincoln, Republican
- Douglas, Democrat
- Breckinridge, Democrat
- Bell, Constitutional Union
- "Fusion" tickets
- No return, unsettled, etc.

urban North, for northern cities tended to vote for compromise candidates, not for Lincoln. Similarly, over half of southerners voted for Bell or Douglas, supporting the Union over the South.

Once the election returns were in, though, these complications seemed to evaporate (see Map 13.3). Even though Lincoln won only in the North, the election was not even close in the electoral college, where Lincoln won 180 electoral votes to Breckinridge's 72, Bell's 39, and Douglas's 12. In southern eyes, the North had arrogantly placed its own interests above those of the Union, insisting on electing a man who did not even appear on Southern ballots. In northern eyes, the South was to blame, for walking out of nominating conventions and talking of disunion. The election of 1860 completed the estrangement of North and South.

The South Debates Independence

The fire-eaters declared Abraham Lincoln's 1860 victory a sign that the North valued neither the Union nor the Constitution on which it was based. The South, they said, had every right, every incentive, to leave the Union.

Although the Republicans claimed to work within the political system, Lincoln's supporters had violated an honored tradition of compromise.

Even though the Democrats still controlled the Senate and the Supreme Court, southerners believed that Lincoln would use the patronage of the federal government to install Republican officials throughout the South and possibly entice nonslaveholders with their free labor doctrines. Such officials could undermine slavery from within, eroding the authority of slaveowners. For years, Lincoln had talked of "a house" that had to be unified, of a nation that had to be all slave or all free. Would he not act to undermine slavery now that he was in power?

The nation's eyes turned to South Carolina. Influential men there, after all, had talked of secession since the nullification crisis nearly 30 years earlier. They believed that the same states that had created the Union could also dissolve that Union when it no longer served their purposes. The South Carolina legislature met on the day after Lincoln's election but did not secede immediately. Its members called for an election two months later to select delegates who would then decide the course the state should follow. In the meantime, they hoped, support for secession would grow. The next day, a local paper blustered, "the tea has been thrown overboard; the revolution of 1860 has been initiated."

States of the Deep South quickly lined up behind South Carolina. Carolina leaders, heartened by the response, seceded earlier than they had planned, on December 20. Southerners serving in Buchanan's cabinet began resigning and by the administration's annual New Year's Day reception, southerners in attendance all refused to shake Buchanan's hand or acknowledge the president. By February 1, Mississippi, Florida, Alabama, Georgia, Louisiana, and Texas had joined the secession movement. On February 4, delegates from these states met in Montgomery, Alabama, and created a provisional constitution, similar to that of the United States except in its explicit guarantee of slavery and states' rights. On February 18, the convention inaugurated a provisional president, Jefferson Davis of Mississippi, and a vice president, Alexander H. Stephens of Georgia. Davis was a strong states' rights advocate but not a fervent secessionist. With an eye toward opinion in the crucial states of Virginia, North Carolina, Kentucky, and Tennessee, these leaders of the new Confederacy portrayed themselves as a calm and conservative people, not wild-eyed revolutionaries.

Jefferson Davis, of Mississippi, a former U.S. senator and secretary of war, became the first—and only—president of the Confederate States of America in 1861.

The advocates of secession knew they had to strike before Lincoln took office. Two bad things could happen if they waited to see what the new president did once in office. He might either attack the South by force or he might prove to be as moderate as he claimed to be. In the latter case, secessionists feared, white southerners would let the moment pass.

Many thousands of white southerners resisted secession. Some argued that secession was treason. Others warned that the South was committing suicide. A few argued that the southern states should wait until they could cooperate with one another more formally and fully. By presenting a united front to the North, these "cooperationists" insisted, the South would not need to secede at all. The North, recognizing that the South really was not bluffing, would grant concessions protecting slavery forever.

The arguments against immediate secession appealed to a large portion of southerners. Even in the southern states that rushed to secede in January of 1861, almost half of all votes went to delegates who had not supported immediate secession. The opposition to secession proved stronger still in the Upper South. Upper South moderates warned that their states would bear the brunt of any conflict between the Lower South and the North. And voters listened: more than a month after the first seven states seceded, secession lost in Virginia by a two-to-one margin. The secessionists were stymied, too, in Tennessee, North Carolina, and Arkansas. The leaders of these border states believed they could bargain between the Gulf Confederacy and the North, winning the concessions the South wanted while maintaining the Union.

Recognizing the need to convince the border states to join the secession movement, five states from the Lower South dispatched agents to the Upper South to advocate and justify disunion. These commissioners wrote numerous letters to local politicians and spoke to legislatures, public meetings, and private gatherings of community leaders in their efforts to cajole and persuade. These conversations among southerners emphasized the importance of race and slavery as the foundation of the states' rights argument. Delegates warned that the Republican party's future vision of American "destroys the property of the South, lays waste her fields, and inaugurates all the horrors of a San Domingo servile insurrection, consigning her citizens to assassinations and her wives and daughters to pollution and violation."

Northerners, too, remained quite divided at the beginning of 1861. Many recent immigrants viewed the conflict as none of their business. Northern Democrats called for conciliation with the South and many argued they were "for peace and not war . . . war is no remedy . . . and horribly wicked when waged without any cause, and by one portion of our people against another." Many black Northerners warned that a war for the Union alone did not deserve black support. A war to end bondage would be worth fighting, they argued, but in 1861 only the most aggressive white abolitionists spoke of such a cause.

People had plenty of opportunity to air their opinions, for events did not move quickly after Lincoln's election. After the first flush of secessionist victory at the beginning of 1861, people throughout the nation watched and waited to see what would happen when the new president officially assumed office on March 4. In the meantime, no one appeared to be in charge. James Buchanan, as lame-duck president, could not do much, and neither could the lame-duck Congress.

Most Republicans, including Lincoln, viewed the rhetoric and even the votes for southern secession as negotiating strategies rather than actual steps toward dissolving the Union. The Republicans showed no inclination to bargain with the South over what remained the key question: federal support for slavery in the territories. The tensions that had built up in the 1850s, Lincoln thought, could no longer be avoided. "The tug has to come," he argued, "and better now, than any time hereafter." If the North postponed action, Lincoln and other Republicans thought, the South would step up its efforts to gain new slave territories in the Caribbean and Central America, dragging the United States into war.

The First Secession

In the winter of 1861, the center of the conflict between the North and the South gradually shifted to two obscure forts in the harbor of Charleston, South Carolina. A Kentucky-born U.S. Army officer, Major Robert Anderson, worried that secessionists would attack his small federal force at Fort Moultrie in Charleston. Determined to avoid a war, on December 26 Anderson moved his small garrison from Fort Moultrie to **Fort Sumter,** a facility occupying a safer position in the center of the Charleston harbor. Tired of tension and stalemate, northern editors cheered Anderson's actions: "these are the times to develop manhood. God bless Major Anderson for setting us a good example." When South Carolina guns drove away a ship President Buchanan had sent with supplies for Anderson and his men, Buchanan chose not to force the issue. Meanwhile, South Carolina troops strengthened their position around the Charleston harbor.

Lincoln Becomes President

Men from both the North and the South worked frantically, but fruitlessly, to find a compromise during these weeks. Some urged the passage of a new constitutional

This envelope, showing the hot air of secession "going down of itself," as Lincoln said, showed how many Americans viewed the secession movement in its early days.

amendment that would permit slavery forever; some urged the purchase of Cuba to permit slavery to expand; some urged that war be declared against another country to pull the United States together again. All the compromises were designed to placate the South. Abolitionists viewed such maneuvering with disgust and told their countrymen to let the South go. "If the Union can only

Abraham Lincoln took over the presidency at a time when the sectional conflict had reached a crisis; he had little time or room in which to maneuver as the federal soldiers in Fort Sumter ran out of food and had to be abandoned or supplied.

South Carolina troops fire cannon at the federal forces under the command of Major Robert Anderson. Although no one was killed in the assault, the shots opened the Civil War.

be maintained by new concessions to the slaveholders," Frederick Douglass argued, "then . . . let the Union perish." Such views were not popular. Mobs attacked antislavery advocates throughout the North.

On February 11, Abraham Lincoln began a long and circuitous railway trip from Illinois to Washington, covering nearly 2,000 miles and using 20 separate rail lines, pausing frequently along the way to speak to well-wishers. At first, he played down the threat of secession— "Let it alone," he counseled, "and it will go down of itself." But as the train rolled on and the Confederate convention in Montgomery completed its provisional government, Lincoln became more wary. Warned of attempts on his life, Lincoln slipped into Washington under cover of darkness.

Lincoln assembled his government under the growing shadow of war. He sought to balance his cabinet with men of various backgrounds. The two most formidable cabinet members were Secretary of State William H. Seward, a moderate Republican, and Secretary of the Treasury Salmon P. Chase, a radical Republican inclined to take a harder line with the South. Fort Sumter stood as the most pressing issue facing the new administration. Any show of force to reclaim the fort from South Carolina,

southern Unionists warned, and the secessionists would sweep border states such as Virginia into the Confederacy.

Lincoln, with Seward's advice, toned down the speech he delivered at his inauguration in March. He told the South that he had no intention of disturbing slavery where it was already established, that he would not invade the region, that he would not attempt to fill offices with men repugnant to local sensibilities. But he also warned that secession was illegal. It was his duty to maintain the integrity of the federal government, and to do so he had to "hold, occupy, and possess" federal property in the states of the Confederacy, including Fort Sumter. Lincoln pleaded with his countrymen to move slowly, to let passions cool.

People heard in Lincoln's inaugural what they chose to hear. Republicans and Unionists in the South thought it a potent mixture of firmness and generosity. Skeptics, on the other hand, focused on the threat of coercion at Fort Sumter. If Lincoln attempted to use force of any kind, they warned, war would be the inevitable result. Lincoln did not plan on war; he was trying to buy time, hoping that compromisers in Washington would come up with a workable strategy.

The Decision at Fort Sumter

But there was less time than Lincoln realized. On the very day after Lincoln's speech, Major Anderson reported to Washington that he would be out of food within four to six weeks. Initially unsure as to the wisdom of retaining the fort, Lincoln finally decided that he had to act: he would send provisions but not military supplies to Fort Sumter. By doing so, Lincoln would maintain the balance he promised in his inaugural speech, keeping the fort but not using coercion unless attacked first. He sent a note to South Carolina's governor of his intent to provision the fort, a note perceived by Confederate leaders not as a courtesy, but an ultimatum.

The president recognized that the Confederacy was determined to act. Jefferson Davis and his government had decided a week earlier that any attempt to reprovision the fort would be in and of itself an act of war. Davis believed that no foreign power would respect a country, especially one as new and tenuous as the Confederate States of America, if it allowed one of its major ports to be occupied by another country. The Union's resupply of the fort would mean the Union still controlled it.

The Confederate government decided that its commander in Charleston, P. G. T. Beauregard, should attack Fort Sumter before the relief expedition had a chance to

Thousands of people came to Union Square in New York to gather around the flag lowered at Fort Sumter one week before, supported by a statue of George Washington, to show their support for the Union.

arrive. The leaders understood the risks. The Confederate secretary of state, Robert Toombs, warned Jefferson Davis that the attack would "lose us every friend at the North" and "wantonly strike a hornet's nest which extends from mountains to ocean, and legions, now quiet, will swarm out and sting us to death. It is unnecessary; it puts us in the wrong; it is fatal." Nevertheless, on April 12, at 4:30 in the morning, Beauregard opened fire on the Union garrison. The shelling continued for 33 hours. Anderson held out for as long as he could, but when fire tore through the barracks and his ammunition ran low he decided the time for surrender had come. Northerners agreed that the events in South Carolina could not go unanswered. Lincoln issued a call for 75,000 volunteers to defend the Union. Southerners agreed that they would have no choice but to come to that state's aid if the North raised a hand against their fellow southerners.

DOING HISTORY ONLINE

Broken Bonds, 1855–1861

After reading the documents in this module, evaluate the following statement: The Civil War was a conflict that was inevitable, a struggle that was bound to occur.

History ⧗ Now™   Visit HistoryNOW to access primary sources and exercises related to this topic: http://now.ilrn.com/ayers_etal3e

Conclusion

The North and the South had long been on a collision course. Ever since the framing of the Constitution, slavery had defined the contrast between the regions. Sometimes that difference seemed to fade in importance to white Americans; at other times it burst into a central role in the nation's understanding of itself. Years of relative quiet passed between episodes such as the Missouri Compromise and Nat Turner's Rebellion and the Mexican War. But in the late 1850s events piled on top of one another, delivering blows so quickly that the nation did not have time to regain its balance.

Kansas became a hothouse for the sectional conflict. Proslavery men and antislavery men fought over the future of slavery in Kansas, assailing one another with cannon and broadswords, with constitutions and votes. The caning of Senator Charles Sumner of Massachusetts by Representative Preston Brooks of South Carolina in the halls of Congress carried the violence into the very heart of the nation. With a weak president in the White House, no one seemed to be in charge.

Although both the North and the South prospered economically in the 1850s, both claimed to see weakness in the other, especially when the Panic of 1857 hit. Southerners pointed to the unemployed masses in the North's cities as evidence of the superiority of slavery; northerners pointed to the speed with which their economy recovered as evidence of its fundamental soundness. A national religious revival testified to a sense among Americans that they were losing their way both publicly and privately. John Brown's raid unleashed a disgust that many Americans had rarely before expressed about each other.

In the meantime, the election of 1860 loomed. With the new Republican party having done so well in the 1856 election and with the Democrats spending most of their energy squabbling with one another, voters throughout the country realized that the election in 1860 would be a crucial test for the United States. Would northerners be able to unite over party lines to elect a candidate who defended the interests of the North and who did not bow to Southern interests? Would southerners unify behind a staunch prosouthern man? Would a candidate of compromise rise up to save the nation from itself? At every step of the nominating process, the Democrats fractured. And with a divided Democratic party, the Republicans had a chance of winning the presidency with only northern votes.

Party leaders worked furiously in the summer and fall of 1860 to steer the election in their direction. John Bell and Stephen Douglas pleaded with their countrymen not to vote for men they portrayed as purely regional candidates—Abraham Lincoln in the North and John Breckinridge in the South. On election day, more that 8 of every 10 eligible voters went to the polls. Many voted for the candidates of compromise, especially in states along the border between the North and the South. But more men voted for candidates who stood for clear purpose and even defiance. The North's burgeoning population gave the region the power to elect a Republican who was not on the ballot in most southern states, and they did: Abraham Lincoln became president.

As soon as the election results were announced, South Carolina began the process of seceding from the Union. In the secessionists' eyes, the North had repudiated any commitment to national unity and purpose. The South Carolinians felt free, even compelled they said, to leave a union in which they did not have a voice.

Republicans scoffed at the South Carolinians' refusal to accept the results of an honest election, but they had made up their minds. Other states in the Lower South joined South Carolina and by early in 1861, before Lincoln had even taken office, a new Confederate States of America had begun to take form.

The question now was whether the slave states of Virginia, North Carolina, Tennessee, Kentucky, Maryland, and Missouri, on the border between the North and the South, would join the new Confederacy or remain in the United States. When the food ran out in Fort Sumter, however, and when the cannons boomed over Charleston, everyone realized that time had run out.

The Chapter in Review

In the years between 1855 and 1861:

- Bleeding Kansas and the *Dred Scott* decision fed the growth of the new Republican party.
- Abraham Lincoln and Stephen Douglas engaged in famous debates that sharply defined the place of slavery in American politics.
- John Brown's raid horrified the South and mobilized the North in response.

- The election of 1860 pitched four candidates against each other and Abraham Lincoln emerged victorious because of his victories across the North.
- The states of the Gulf South form the Confederate States of America and then fire on Fort Sumter in Charleston.

Making Connections Across Chapters

LOOKING BACK

As Chapter 13 shows, in the late 1850s and early 1860s voters in the United States faced the most important elections in the country's history. Those elections turned around the meaning that slavery held for white Americans.

1. Why did the sectional crisis peak when it did?

2. Were there times when events could have taken a different turn and the United States could have avoided secession?

3. Did long-term economic and social changes push the United States toward war or were the causes located firmly in political events?

LOOKING AHEAD

Chapter 14 will show how the events of 1860 quickly spun out of anyone's control and began what would become a vast war.

1. What kind of conflict would Americans in both the North and the South have predicted lay ahead of them when South Carolina seceded in December 1860?

2. Why were both northerners and southerners so confident in 1860?

Recommended Readings

Crofts, Daniel W. *Old Southampton: Politics and Society in a Virginia County, 1834–1869* (1992) provides a detailed account of the way politics worked in communities of the Upper South.

Dew, Charles B. *Apostles of Disunion: Southern Secession Commissioners and the Causes of the Civil War* (2001) offers excellent coverage of debates about secession among southerners.

Etcheson, Nicole. *Bleeding Kansas: Contested Liberty in the Civil War Era* (2004) is the fullest and most recent account of this complicated story.

Fehrenbacher, Don E. *The Dred Scott Case: Its Significance in American Law and Politics* (1978) is the classic account of this complicated episode.

Finkelman, Paul, ed. *His Soul Goes Marching On: Responses to John Brown and the Harpers Ferry Raid*

(1995) contains fascinating articles about this much-interpreted event.

Foner, Eric. *Free Soil, Free Labor, Free Men: The Ideology of the Republican Party Before the Civil War* (1970) masterfully demonstrates the power of free labor ideology.

Holt, Michael F. *The Political Crisis of the 1850s* (1978) stresses the dynamics of the two-party system in bringing on the Civil War.

Morrison, Michael A. *Slavery and the American West: The Eclipse of Manifest Destiny and the Coming of the Civil War* (1997) is a subtle and up-to-date survey of this critical topic.

Reynolds, David S. *John Brown, Abolitionist : The Man who Killed Slavery, Sparked the Civil War, and Seeded Civil Rights* (2005) brings a modern edge to this important story.

Wyatt-Brown, Bertram. *Southern Honor: Ethics and Behavior in the Old South* (1982) puts forward a powerful interpretation of white southern culture.

Zarefsky, David. *Lincoln, Douglas, and Slavery: In the Crucible of Public Debate* (1990) recasts our understanding of these famous political debates.

Identifications

Review your understanding of the following key terms, people, events, and dates for this chapter (these terms also appear in the Glossary at the end of the book):

Harpers Ferry
William Walker
filibuster
Slave Power
yeoman
fire-eaters
border ruffians

Charles Sumner
John Brown
Bleeding Kansas
James Buchanan
Millard Fillmore
Roger B. Taney
Dred Scott case
Abraham Lincoln
Lincoln-Douglas debates
Fort Sumter

Online Sources Guide

Use this listing to find online documents, images, interactive maps, simulations, and other resources related to this chapter:

American History Resource Center

http://history.wadsworth.com/rc/us

Documents

The First Lincoln and Douglas Debate (1858)

Interactive Maps

Counties Carried by Candidates in the 1856 Presidential Election
Slavery in the South, 1860

Selected Images

Immigrants arriving in New York, 1858
Recent immigrants, from *Harper's Weekly,* 1858
Condemnation of the Democrats' stand on Kansas-Nebraska, 1856 presidential race
John Brown
Harpers Ferry, Virginia
Scene from Lincoln-Douglas debate

HistoryNOW

http://now.ilrn.com/ayers_etal3e

Primary Source Exercises

Broken Bonds, 1855–1861
The Raid at Harpers Ferry

14 Descent Into War, 1861–1862

In both the North and the South men rushed to enlist in vast new armies being assembled with lightning speed. As at this recruiting station, bounties helped persuade those who might have been less eager to fight.

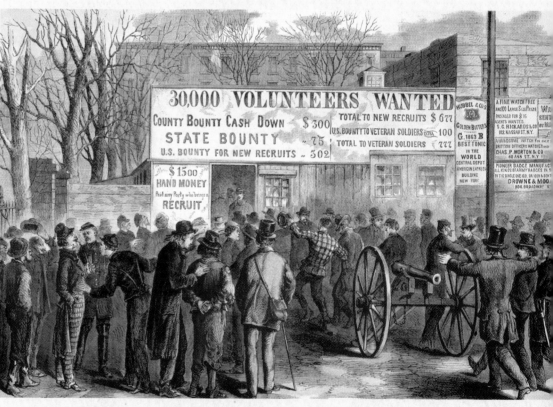

© The Granger Collection, New York

At the beginning of 1861, Americans could not imagine anything like the war that would soon consume their nation. Events piled on one another in ways that no one could have anticipated. The men who voted for Lincoln did not think the South would secede, the architects of secession did not think the North would resist, and neither side thought the other would or could fight for long. Events proved no more predictable once the war began. Last-minute reinforcements and retreats changed the outcome of battles; news from the battlefield shaped every political and diplomatic decision.

War Begins: April to July 1861

Neither the Union nor the Confederacy was ready for conflict in the spring of 1861. A number of states had yet to declare their loyalties; other states, communities, and families were divided against themselves. In a matter of months, both the North and the South had to prepare for war.

Lincoln Calls for Troops

Two days after the Confederate flag went up over Fort Sumter on April 15, President Lincoln declared South Carolina in rebellion against the United States and called for 75,000 militiamen to help put the rebellion down. The president sought to appear restrained in his response. He demanded that forces gathering from the states of the Lower South "disperse and retire peacefully." He still hoped that Unionists in southern states besides South Carolina would rally to the nation's defense if he showed that he was no extremist. Lincoln also acted cautiously because he had not received the approval of Congress, which would not convene until July.

Lincoln's attempt to blend firmness and conciliation failed. Southern states saw the call to the militia as an act of aggression against South Carolina and state sovereignty. The Upper South states replied with defiance to Lincoln's requests for their troops on April 15, 1861. One Virginia representative responded to the president, "I have a Union constituency which elected me by a majority of one thousand, and I believe now that there are not ten Union men in that county today." Virginia seceded 2 days later. Although many people in Virginia still clung to hopes of avoiding war, two delegates to every one voted for secession on April 17. These Virginians, like white southerners of all inclinations and temperaments, refused to supply soldiers to confront another slaveholding state. Recognizing the importance

Timeline

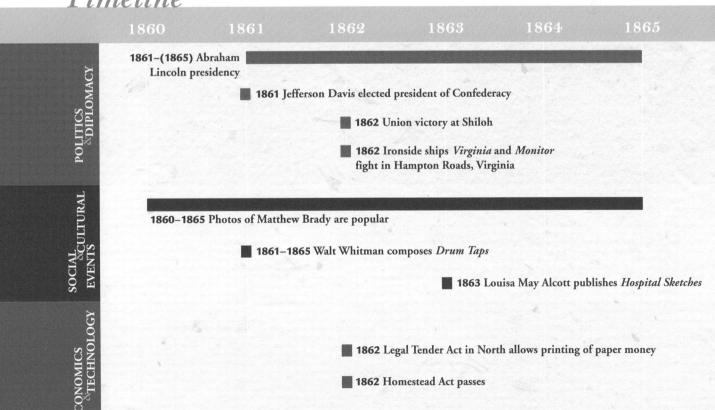

	1860	1861	1862	1863	1864	1865

POLITICS & DIPLOMACY

1861–(1865) Abraham Lincoln presidency

1861 Jefferson Davis elected president of Confederacy

1862 Union victory at Shiloh

1862 Ironside ships *Virginia* and *Monitor* fight in Hampton Roads, Virginia

SOCIAL & CULTURAL EVENTS

1860–1865 Photos of Matthew Brady are popular

1861–1865 Walt Whitman composes *Drum Taps*

1863 Louisa May Alcott publishes *Hospital Sketches*

ECONOMICS & TECHNOLOGY

1862 Legal Tender Act in North allows printing of paper money

1862 Homestead Act passes

of moving President **Jefferson Davis** and his government closer to their armies, the **Confederacy** immediately voted to move its capital to Richmond in May of 1861.

In the North, even in areas like New York City, which had opposed Lincoln's election, 250,000 people filled the streets in a Unionist rally in response to southern aggression. Democrat Stephen Douglas addressed a tumultuous Chicago crowd. "There are only two sides to the question," he proclaimed. "Every man must be for the United States or against it. There can be no neutrals in this war, only patriots—or traitors."

The States Divide

Arkansas, Tennessee, and North Carolina quickly followed Virginia's example and joined the new Confederacy. North Carolinians, who over the winter rioted against secession and shot Confederate flags from their staffs, considered Lincoln's actions a call to arms for southern men that "as by a stroke of lighting, . . . made the South wholly South." The Oklahoma Territory, too, aligned itself with the Confederacy. There, leaders of the Five Civilized Tribes, slaveholders themselves, used the opportunity to fight against the United States government that had dispossessed them from their homes three decades earlier. As leaders of other Indian nations sided with the Union, however, conflict spread within and among tribes to control the Indian Territory.

State leaders elsewhere frantically struggled with one another. In Maryland, rioters attacked Massachusetts troops as they marched through Baltimore two days after the secession of neighboring Virginia—spilling the first blood of the war when 12 civilians and 4 Union soldiers died in the gunfire. Maryland bitterly divided: the southern portion of the state sympathized with the Confederacy, and Baltimore, where free blacks outnumbered slaves by 11 to 1, and the western portion generally supporting the Union. Should the United States lose Maryland, the District of Columbia would be completely surrounded by Confederate territory. Accordingly, Lincoln acted quickly to keep Maryland in line, jailing secession advocates and suspending the writ of habeas corpus so they could not be released.

Kentucky, after months of determined attempts to remain neutral, decided for the Union in September after Confederate troops entered the state. Missouri officially remained in the Union but was ravaged from within by brutal violence for the next four years. Dissension took a different form in the mountains of western Virginia. In June, delegates from 50 counties met in Wheeling to renounce the Virginia secession convention, begin the gradual abolition of slavery, and declare

their loyalty to the Union. Lincoln recognized these breakaway counties as the legal government of Virginia and their legislative delegations were seated in July 1861. After a complicated series of conventions and elections, the state of West Virginia came into being in 1862 and joined the Union the following year.

As it turned out, the Union and the Confederacy divided about evenly (see Map 14.1). Virginia, Tennessee, North Carolina, and Arkansas all joined the Confederacy only after Lincoln requested their troops to assist in suppressing insurrection in the Lower South. Had they remained in the Union, the Confederacy would have had little hope of sustaining a successful war against the North. Those states accounted for half of all manufacturing and half of all food production in the Confederacy. Maryland, Kentucky, and Missouri, on the other hand, might well have joined the Confederacy; had they done so, the Union cause would have been weakened, perhaps fatally. Kentucky and Missouri occupied crucial positions along the major rivers that led into the South and linked the western Confederacy to the East. Even the dissidents balanced: eight states along the border provided 235,000 white and 85,000 black troops to the Union and 425,000 to the Confederacy.

Although Abraham Lincoln was criticized from every angle in these months, he managed to bring into the Union the states he had to win. Had he lost these struggles, he might well have failed in all the other struggles that awaited him.

The Numbers

In retrospect, the cards seemed heavily stacked in the North's favor. The Union, after all, had vastly greater industrial capacity, railroads, canals, food, draft animals, ships, and entrepreneurial experience, all the things a mid-nineteenth-century war required. The Union could also claim four times as many white residents as the South. And although the 3.5 million enslaved people

---

DOING HISTORY ONLINE

Secession

After reading the documents in this module consider the following: If you had lived in Virginia in 1861, do you think your sympathies would have rested with the Union or the Confederacy?

History ⧖ Now™   Visit HistoryNOW to access primary sources and exercises related to this topic: http://now.ilrn.com/ayers_etal3e

Southern Secession

The seven Gulf states seceded first, and on February 9, 1861, delegates from these states met in Montgomery, Alabama, to create a provisional constitution, similar to that of the United States except in its explicit guarantee of slavery and states' rights. Advocates of secession traveled throughout the Upper South to convince voters and leaders to join the Confederacy. Regardless of the appeals to law and interpretations of the Constitution, the emotional heart of the debate white southerners conducted among themselves centered on three related issues: loathing of the prospect of racial equality, fear of servile insurrection and race war, and a surprisingly frank, if horrified, discussion of the inevitable miscegenation that would result if slavery were destroyed. While the language of states' rights appeared in these discussions, it focused on the states' rights to maintain slavery and preserve the standing racial order. Immediately after Lincoln called for troops to suppress the South Carolina rebellion, Virginia, Arkansas, North Carolina, and Tennessee departed the Union. The other slave states—Kentucky, Maryland, Delaware, and Missouri—remained in the Union. Western Virginia would soon separate from the rest of the state and declare its loyalty to the Union.

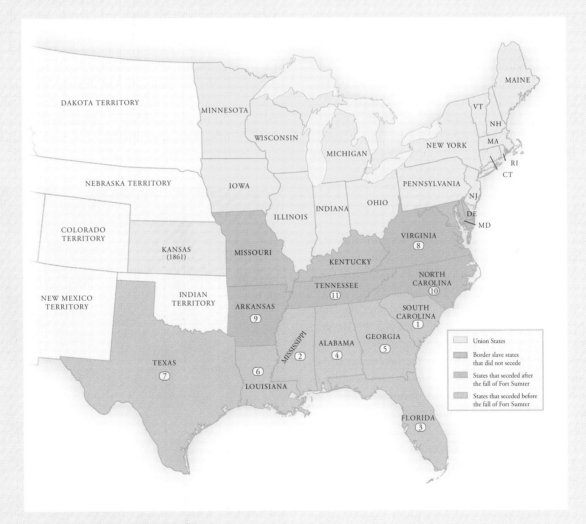

MAP 14.1 **Southern Secession**

View an animated version of this map or related maps at http://history.wadsworth.com/passages3e.

who lived in the Confederacy were extraordinarily valuable to the South, everyone recognized that the slaves could become equally valuable allies for the North.

Since the South acknowledged the North's advantages, many people then and since assumed that the Confederates must have been driven either by irrational rage or heedless bravery. Neither the Confederates nor the Unionists, however, expected the secession crisis to turn into a full-fledged war, much less a 4-year war. When Lincoln called for the 75,000 militia, he called them for only 90 days' service. When southern boys and men rushed to enlist for the Confederacy in the spring of 1861, they assumed they would be back home in time to harvest their crops in the autumn.

Southerners considered themselves natural soldiers, caricaturing their new enemies as clerks and factory workers. Though the Union did have more city men and immigrants than the South, most northerners, like southerners, were young men raised on farms. Since both sides believed that their opponents were weak and divided, northerners and southerners thought the conflict would likely come to a swift, and peaceful, resolution. Commanders on each side recognized their lack of experience. Lincoln calmed General Irvin McDowell: "You are green, it is true, but they are green also, you are all green alike." In such a struggle, sheer numbers did not seem nearly as important as they eventually became.

The Strategies

The military strategies of both sides sought to minimize actual fighting. The South saw itself as purely on the defensive; it would wait for northern armies to invade and then defeat them. The North, for its part, counted on General Winfield Scott's "**Anaconda Plan**," named after the large snake of that name that slowly engulfs and squeezes its prey to death. That plan depended on sending an overpowering force down the Mississippi River in the fall, dividing the South in two. At the same time, the Union navy would seal off the South from outside supplies. Ground troops and land battles would be kept to a minimum.

The Confederacy possessed considerable military advantages. It occupied an enormous area, larger than today's United Kingdom, France, Italy, and Spain combined. It possessed dozens of harbors and ports, connected by an excellent system of rivers and an adequate network of railroads. The Confederacy's long border with Mexico made it difficult to seal off outside supplies. The Confederacy could wage a defensive war, moving its troops internally from one point to another, whereas the Union had to move around the perimeter. The many country roads of the South, known only to locals, would provide routes for Confederate surprise attacks or strategic retreats.

For a model of how such a defensive plan might work, Southerners looked to the American Revolution. Like the American colonies eighty years earlier, the Confederates did not have to win every battle nor conquer northern territory. Southerners thought they had only to keep fighting long enough for the North's political, economic, regional, and ethnic divisions to overwhelm its temporary unity. Indeed, the Confederacy enjoyed advantages the American colonies had not enjoyed. The new southern nation covered twice as much territory as had the colonies, and the North possessed nowhere near the military power of the British at the time of the Revolutionary War.

Leadership

There was also the matter of leadership. In 1861, many observers would have given the advantage to the Confederates in this regard. Abraham Lincoln, after all, had held public office for only 2 years before he assumed the presidency, and his only military service had been a brief service in the militia during Black Hawk's War. Jefferson Davis, by contrast, had distinguished himself in the war with Mexico. He had been secretary of war under Franklin Pierce and had served in the U.S. Senate. Davis, unlike Lincoln, directed his forces' military

Robert E. Lee rejected Lincoln's offer of command of the Union armies before he resigned his U.S. commission and swore allegiance to the Confederacy.

North Wind Picture Archives

strategy with the confidence born of firsthand knowledge and experience.

At the beginning of the war, too, it appeared that the South had the better generals. The southern leaders certainly had more experience: the average age of the Union generals in 1861 was 38; of Confederate generals, 47. **Robert E. Lee** of Virginia had served as an engineer, an officer in the Mexican War in the 1840s, and superintendent of West Point in the late 1850s. He resigned his U.S. military commission and accepted command of Virginia's forces. By abandoning the United States Lee made the same decision about two-thirds of southern-born officers made when secession finally came. The third who remained defined their duty differently.

Military experience and ability did not always prove to be the major considerations in the appointment of generals on both sides. Given the small size of the Federal armed forces before the war, the creation of two hostile armies resulted in a shortage of trained military leaders on both sides. Lincoln chose generals from the ranks of various constituencies he needed to appease: Republicans, abolitionists, Democrats, the Irish, and Germans, and powerful politicians from across the North. Jefferson Davis did the same to bind ambitious politicians from the various states to the new Confederacy. About a third of Union generals and half their Confederate counterparts had not been professional soldiers, though most had some military training; overall, the North and the South placed roughly similar proportions of professional soldiers in command.

Neither the Union nor the Confederacy enjoyed a clear advantage in civilian leadership. Both Lincoln and Davis assembled cabinets that balanced geography, political faction, personality, and expertise. The Confederates had to create a government from scratch, including the design of flags, stamps, and money. Davis ran through several secretaries of war and secretaries of state before finding the two men on whom he felt he could rely, James A. Seddon and Judah P. Benjamin, respectively.

The Union enjoyed a head start in such matters, but the Republicans had many problems to iron out. Office seekers besieged Washington at the very time Lincoln was trying to keep the South in the Union; he felt like an innkeeper, he said, faced with customers demanding rooms in one wing while he tried to put out a fire in another. Lincoln's cabinet ended up containing men whom he barely knew and upon whom he was not always sure he could rely.

The First Conflicts

Battles began before anyone was ready. On the day following Lincoln's call for troops in April, Federal officers in charge of the arsenal at Harpers Ferry and the naval yard in Norfolk, Virginia, sought to destroy the supplies and weapons under their command before secessionists could seize them. Despite their efforts, Virginia troops managed to recover valuable gun-making machinery, artillery, naval stores, and ships for the Confederate cause. A few weeks later, battles broke out along the B&O Railroad in what would become West Virginia, with Robert E. Lee, the new general for Virginia, leading an unsuccessful series of attacks that damaged his reputation and led a Richmond newspaper to dub him "Granny Lee." Meanwhile, nearly 4,000 Confederates, most of them from Texas, pushed into New Mexico. They hoped to win the mineral riches discovered in Colorado in 1857 and perhaps even those of California for the Southern cause.

All these struggles showed both sides to be far from ready to fight a war in 1861. Not only were guns and uniforms scarce, but so was combat experience. Even those men who had attended West Point had learned more about engineering than they had about tactical maneuvers or logistics. The U.S. Army contained only about 16,000 men, and nearly 12,000 of them were scattered across the vast territory west of the Mississippi River. The militia who first responded to the calls of the Union and Confederacy had scarcely been trained at all.

Mobilization

Both sides took immediate steps to create new armies, organized within local communities and led by local men. The Confederate Congress authorized 400,000 volunteers in May of 1861. In its special session beginning in July of 1861, the Union Congress authorized 500,000 troops, each signing on for three years; 700,000 eventually enlisted under this authorization. Much mobilization took place on the local level. Prominent citizens often supplied uniforms, guns, and even food for the troops from their localities. Units elected their own officers. States competed to enlist the largest numbers of men. Local newspaper editors sought to make sure that state-level leaders dealt fairly with local troops and officers.

Some Northerners wondered whether the many divisions among classes, occupations, religions, and ethnic groups would hinder the Union war effort. Such doubters took heart at the response to the crisis of 1861. Both workingmen and wealthy men eagerly signed up. Members of ethnic groups took pride in forming their own units; the Irish and Germans supplied more than 150,000 men each, with the total of foreign-born in service totaling nearly half a million. Northerners congratulated themselves that patriotism and self-sacrifice

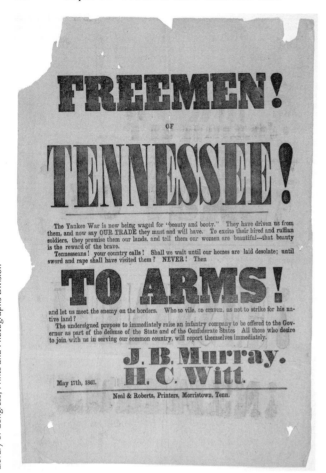

Broadsides such as this appeared across the Confederacy, calling on men to defend their wives and daughters from the Yankee's "hired and ruffian soldiers."

had not been killed, as many feared, by the spirit of commerce so strong in the land. Editor Horace Greeley sketched the transformation of Northerners from "a sordid, grasping money-loving people" to one in whom the "fires of patriotic devotion" still burned.

Southerners, too, found reason to be proud in 1861. The leaders of the South had secretly worried that when push came to shove the nonslaveholders would not fight for a cause that many identified with the defense of slavery. But Southern boys and men were activated by the same impulses that drove their Northern counterparts: dreams of glory, youthful self-confidence, and a burning desire to impress family, friends, and young women with their bravery. At this point in the war, white Southerners talked less about slavery than they had before or they would later. In their eyes, they fought to defend their farms and homes from "foreign" invaders.

Editors, politicians, and citizens of both the North and the South demanded that the conflict be wrapped up immediately. "ON TO RICHMOND" ran the headline in northern papers while General Beauregard informed Jefferson Davis of his troops' readiness "to

The newspapers of the United States, impatient with the pace of the war, demanded that their army take the Confederacy's new capital at Richmond.

meet the enemies of our country under all circumstances." Confident of victory, they itched for the fight that would settle things once and for all. Only a few, such as William T. Sherman, dissented. This "is to be a long war,—very long,—much longer than any politician thinks."

The First Battle

Northerners soon grew impatient with the passive Anaconda Plan of cutting the South off from the outside. With so many men eagerly signing on to fight, Northerners thought they should get the war over early, before the South had time to consolidate its forces. The Union already had 35,000 men poised in northern Virginia, about 25 miles away from a Confederate force of 20,000 under the command of **P. G. T. Beauregard.** Beauregard's troops protected an important rail junction at Manassas, along Bull Run (a "run" is a stream). Confederate and Union troops also watched one another warily in the Shenandoah Valley, about 50 miles to the west.

These troop deployments reflected a primary goal of each side in the early stages of the war: capturing the capital of its enemy. Union leaders thought that if they could win Richmond—the industrial, commercial, and administrative center of the South—the rest of the

DOING HISTORY ONLINE

Mobilization

Read the documents in this module. In order to sufficiently mobilize for the war, what special demands may have been made on the Southern States?

HistoryⓍNow™   Visit HistoryNOW to access primary sources and exercises related to this topic: http://now.ilrn.com/ayers_etal3e

Despite his flamboyant appearance and cavalry tactics, J. E. B. Stuart, like a number of other Confederate generals, adhered to a strict religious discipline that prohibited drinking and swearing.

Early in the war, Thomas Jonathan "Stonewall" Jackson was the most beloved Confederate leader, admired for his military daring and his devout religious belief.

Confederacy would soon follow. Confederate leaders thought that if they could conquer the capital of the United States, forcing Lincoln and his cabinet to flee, European powers would recognize the Confederacy's sovereignty and legitimacy. As a result, the Northern will to fight would be broken.

The officers of both the Union and the Confederacy had learned strategy at West Point, although few had ever commanded units above the regimental level. These officers usually attempted to concentrate their force in hopes of overwhelming the enemy at the point of attack. The Union tried to take advantage of its greater numbers of men and resources; the Confederacy sought to use its interior lines, knowledge of the Virginia landscape, and aggressive maneuvers to gain an advantage. Educated with the same texts and serving together in peace and war, leaders on both sides knew what the others hoped and planned to do.

In the first major battle of the war, the South's advantages outweighed the North's. Both sides attempted to coordinate their troop movements near Washington and in the Shenandoah Valley. The valley had long served as a major corridor between the North and the South. If that corridor was left unprotected by the Union, Confederate forces could rush up the valley and capture Washington. But if too many troops protected the valley, the North would tie up men and resources that could be used more effectively elsewhere. The Confederacy employed cavalry, under the command of the flamboyant young colonel

James E. B. (Jeb) Stuart, to move quickly up and down the valley, keeping the North off balance.

The Union, under the command of General Irvin McDowell, tried to concentrate most of its forces at Manassas by moving them from the valley. On July 21, the Northern troops were finally ready to attack. Congressmen and other spectators drove their carriages out from Washington to "see the Rebels get whipped." Union troops flooded over the battlefield, fording the creeks, flanking the strongest points in the Confederate lines. The Southern forces fell back to more defensible positions. When it looked as if the Confederates were to be routed, a Southern general pointed out **Thomas J. Jackson** to his men, "There is Jackson standing like a stone wall! Rally behind the Virginians!" "Stonewall Jackson," until recently an undistinguished mathematics professor at the Virginia Military Institute, had been christened.

The Confederate reinforcements that poured off the train at Manassas gave Beauregard a renewed spirit. The Union forces suffered confusion when the lack of a common uniform led some Northerners to mistake Confederates for their own troops. They began to pull back and then to run. Some civilian carriages got caught in the panicked flood of troops rushing back to Washington;

Courtesy Sidney King

The Battle of Bull Run (Manassas), the first major battle of the war, on July 21, 1861, suddenly turned into a rout of Union forces when confusion and Confederate reinforcements abruptly turned the tide.

Courtesy of the National Park Service, Kennesau Mountain National Park. Photo, Harpers Peng Conservation Center
Courtesy of the Carl Vinson Institute of Government—The University of Virginia. Photo by Ed Jackson

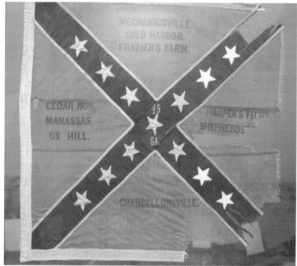

The battle flag (below) was adopted by the Confederates after Manassas because the official flag (top)—the so-called Stars and Bars—looked too much like the U.S. flag and led to deadly confusion in battle.

the Confederates gleefully captured a New York congressman hiding in the woods and held him for the next six months in Richmond as a prisoner.

The South had claimed its first victory. Each side had engaged about 18,000 soldiers, making Bull Run by a considerable margin the largest battle ever waged in the United States up to that time. Both the North and the South lost about 600 men. Nevertheless, the humiliating rout confirmed the Confederate belief that 1 Rebel could whip 10 Yankees.

Key parts of Confederate lore emerged from Bull Run as well: the Rebel yell and the Confederate battle flag. The yell was not merely a scream or a roar, but a high wail, unnerving and strange. It served as the rallying cry for Southern troops for the rest of the war. The first flag of the Confederacy, the Stars and Bars, looked a great deal like that of the United States, leading to confusion in the heat of battle. After Bull Run, Beauregard designed a new flag—a square banner, red with a blue cross and white stars—to ensure that Southern troops did not fire on one another. It was that battle flag, never the official flag of the Confederacy, that later generations came to consider synonymous with the South.

Each side called this first great battle of the war by different names. Northern forces generally named battles after physical features such as rivers and mountains; thus, they deemed this the Battle of Bull Run. Southerners usually named battles after nearby towns or villages; they called this one Manassas.

Women and War

Women had avidly studied the debates being waged in the newspapers. They had expressed their opinions in private conversation, at home, in their letters, and in their diaries. Many had listened to the speeches on all sides. They had counseled their sons and husbands, sometimes urging their men on to join others of their community. They had worn cockades displaying their loyalties and had sung the latest songs. Once the speeches, songs, and toasts had come to an end and the fighting had begun, women became even more active. Within 2 weeks of the war's beginning, women on the two sides had formed 20,000 aid societies. These societies devoted themselves to supplying the armies' needs, especially clothing and medical supplies. One such organization in Alabama provided, in just one month, "422 shirts, 551 pairs of drawers, 80 pairs of socks, 3 pairs of gloves, 6 boxes and one bale of hospital supplies, 128 pounds of tapioca, and a donation of $18 for hospital use."

With the first battles, women claimed positions as nurses, even though previously only men had served as military nurses. Despite some initial grumbling by men, women converted themselves immediately into competent and devoted nurses. **Dorothea Dix,** long known as

DOING HISTORY

Women and War

NEITHER OF THESE *documents were published during the lifetimes of their authors; indeed, they would not appear until about 1990, when historians began to be interested in women's experiences in the Civil War and elsewhere. But both authors would become known in their times for different kinds of writing. Louisa May Alcott would become one of the best-loved writers of the century, with her enduring classic* Little Women, *published in 1868, and its many successors. Sarah Morgan would go on to write for a Charleston newspaper after the Civil War, a role unusual for a woman.*

Louisa May Alcott, "Journal"

November [1862].—Thirty years old. Decided to go to Washington as a nurse if I could find a place. Help needed, and I love nursing, and *must* let out my pentup energy in some new way. . . . I want new experiences, and am sure to get 'em if I go. . . . [she receives a position]

December.—A most interesting journey into a new world full of stirring sights and sounds, new adventures, and an evergrowing sense of the great task I had undertaken.

I said my prayers as I went rushing through the country white with tents, all alive with patriotism, and already red with blood.

A solemn time, but I'm glad to live in it, and am sure it will do me good whether I come out alive or dead.

. . . [B]egan my new life by seeing a poor man die at dawn, and sitting all day between a boy with pneumonia and a man shot through the lungs. A strange day, but I did my best, and when I put mother's little black shawl round the boy while he sat up panting for breath, he smiled and said, "You are real motherly, ma'am." I felt as if I was getting on. The man only lay and stared with his big black eyes, and made me very nervous. But all were well behaved, and I sat looking at the twenty strong faces as they looked back at me,—hoping that I looked "motherly" to them, for my thirty years made me feel old, and the suffering round me made me long to comfort every one . . . .

Sarah Morgan, "Diary"

March [1864]
Dead! Dead! Both dead! O my brothers! what have we lived for except you? We would so gladly have laid down our lives for yours, are left desolate to mourn over all we loved and hoped for, weak and helpless; while you, so strong, noble, and brave, have gone before us without a murmur. God knows best. But it is hard—so hard! to give them up without a murmur!

We cannot remember the day when our brothers were not all in all to us. What the boys would think; what the boys would say; what we would do when the boys came home, that has been our sole thought through life. A life time's hope wrecked in a moment—God help us! . . .

Sewed to the paper that contained the last words we should hear of our dear brother, was a lock of hair grown long during his imprisonment. I think it was a noble, tender heart that remembered that one little deed of kindness, and gentle, pitying hand that cut it from his head as he lay cold and stark in death. Good heart that loved our brave brother, kind hand that soothed his pain, you will not be forgotten by us!

Source: Joel Myerson and Daniel Sheahy, eds., *The Journals of Louisa May Alcott* (Boston: Little, Brown, 1989); Charles East, ed., *The Civil War Diary of Sarah Morgan* (Athens: University of Georgia Press, 1991).

Questions for Reflection

1. How did the gender of Alcott and Morgan shape their writing? Did they resent their subordinate position in their respective societies?

2. How fully did these women identify with the causes for which they saw so many men die? Did Morgan care about the political beliefs of the "gentle, pitying hand" that cared for her brother in a Northern prison?

3. Were the experiences of Northern and Southern white women during the Civil War more alike or different from each other?

4. What kind of diaries might the men in the hospitals have written? What would they have said about the female nurses who cared for them? Would the writings of these men be less shaped by gender than the writing of Alcott and Morgan?

Explore additional primary sources related to this chapter on the Wadsworth American History Resource Center or HistoryNOW websites:
http://history.wadsworth.com/rc/us
http://now.ilrn.com/ayers_etal3e

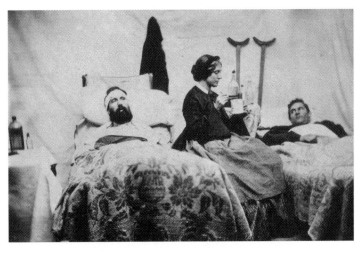

Women in both the North and South quickly stepped forward as nurses, sometimes against opposition, to save lives and relieve suffering.

the champion of the mentally ill and other neglected people in the antebellum era, took matters in hand for the North. She became superintendent of nurses for the Union army, the highest executive appointment for a woman to date, organizing 3,000 women who volunteered to serve. Concerned both about the effectiveness and propriety of women ministering to young male strangers, Dix decreed that she wanted only "plain" women, women over 30, and women who would dress in brown and black.

Women's efforts soon became legendary. They labored until they could no longer stand, until their long dresses trailed blood from amputations and wounds. Kate Cumming and Phoebe Pember played leading roles in the Confederacy, and Clara Barton took her aid to the front lines of the Union and later founded the American Red Cross. Most women stayed closer to home, working in factories, doing piecework in their households, or tilling fields. As Northern farmers departed for the military, observers in the Midwest saw "more women driving teams" and more "at work in fields than men."

War Takes Command: August 1861 to March 1862

The war spread across the continent in the fall, winter, and spring of 1861–1862. Generals consolidated command and launched campaigns thousands of miles from their respective capitals. Governments transformed their economies, invented or expanded navies, conducted diplomacy, and cemented the loyalties of those at home. Families steeled themselves for a war longer than they had been willing to imagine.

McClellan Assumes Control

The North, while embarrassed at Bull Run, took from that defeat a determination to fight more effectively. Volunteers flooded into recruitment offices. Lincoln removed the leaders responsible for that battle and replaced them with **George B. McClellan.** Although short of stature and only 34 years old, McClellan exuded great authority. He was known as the "young Napoleon." McClellan had distinguished himself in the Mexican War and had studied military tactics in Europe. Moreover, he had already frustrated Confederate forces under Robert E. Lee in western Virginia. He now threw himself into reorganizing and reenergizing the Union troops under his command.

The press lavished praise on the young general. Already inclined toward grandiose visions of his abilities, McClellan developed an exalted sense of himself. The cocky commander considered Lincoln an "idiot" and his cabinet incompetent "geese." McClellan ignored, avoided, and insulted those men at every opportunity. McClellan wanted to make his army perfectly prepared before he risked it, and his reputation, in battle against

Early in the war, Lincoln and the rest of the North placed great faith in the "young Napoleon," General George B. McClellan. Events would later lessen their admiration.

Confederates whose numbers his spies consistently exaggerated. Meanwhile, months dragged by. Lincoln and newspaper editors became furiously impatient, but McClellan would not be moved.

The War in the West Begins

There was to be no waiting in the West. Four days after the battle at Bull Run, the Union installed a new commander in charge of the forces in Missouri: John C. Frémont, the "pathfinder of the West" and former Republican presidential candidate. Whereas the situation in Virginia unfolded slowly, the situation in Missouri burst into chaos in July and August of 1861. Guerrilla forces raged throughout the state. Confederate armies built up on the southern border, ready to attack in both the eastern and western parts of the state. Frémont decided that he had to protect the Mississippi River in the East and therefore left a weak force in the West. That force, outnumbered by the Confederates, staged a desperate attack, with terrible losses, at Wilson's Creek. As at Bull Run, the lack of a standard uniform color created deadly confusion. The Northern units fell into ragged retreat, exposing Missouri to Confederate incursions.

With the army so far from Washington, desperate for war materials and supplies, contractors took advantage of the situation, selling substandard goods to the Union army at inflated prices. With the populace of Missouri so divided in its loyalties, Frémont, who, a contemporary noted, had "all of the qualities of genius except ability," did not know whom to trust. Frantic, he declared the entire state under martial law, decreed the death penalty for captured guerrillas, and seized the slaves and other property of all Confederate sympathizers. Slaveholders in the border states of Kentucky and Maryland threatened to throw their allegiances to the South if Lincoln did not overrule Frémont.

The president, desperate to keep the border states within the Union, advised the general that the proclamation angered loyal slaveowners and threatened the loss of Kentucky and requested him to revoke his emancipation order. When Frémont resisted, demanding a public order overruling him, Lincoln felt that he had no choice but to remove Frémont from his post.

Events on the battlefield in the earliest stages of the war proved to be a poor guide to the long term. Although the North had been shaken by Bull Run and Missouri, it had lost neither Washington nor the border states. Although the South had apparently won at Bull Run, the Confederate forces, exhausted and bogged down in mud, had not taken advantage of the situation to attack the Union capital. Although slaveholders in the border states fumed at the Union government and military leaders, they remained in the Union. As a result, the South was deprived of a key strategic advantage: access to the Ohio River and a defensible border with the North. With the Union army able to move up and down the Ohio at will, the Confederates had to defend a vast, vague, and shifting border in Kentucky and Tennessee.

The war was not to be won by a decisive battle within a few months of the war's start. Instead, slower and less dramatic processes proved decisive. Armies and navies had to be built from scratch; economies had to be converted to wartime demands; households and families had to absorb growing sacrifices. These transformations began in earnest in the summer of 1861.

Paying for War

The Civil War, involving so many men over such an enormous territory, immediately became breathtakingly expensive. It was by no means clear how either side was going to pay. Although the Union and the Confederacy were, by any international standard, rich societies, neither had ever supported a large army or an active government. Taxes on imported goods and the sale of apparently endless public lands paid for what government there was. Ever since the Bank War of the 1830s, the federal and state governments did little to manipulate the currency. As a result, when the war came, the men responsible for paying for it had only a few options— loans, new taxes, or the creation of paper money.

Loans met the least resistance in both the North and the South, but this borrowing could provide only a third of the cost of the war. Taxes proved even less effective. The Confederacy quickly decided that it had no choice but to turn to paper money. As soon as it could find adequate engravers and printing presses, the South began producing millions of dollars in the new currency. Catastrophic inflation began to grow as early as the winter of 1861–1862.

The situation was not quite as bad in the North, where taxes and bonds carried much more of the burden of financing the war, but the Union, too, was forced to issue paper money by the first winter of the war. People hoarded gold in anticipation of the deprivations a widened war would cause. New York banks felt they had no choice but to suspend specie payments in December of 1861. In February of 1862, the Union Congress reluctantly decided that it had no choice but to create paper money. The Legal Tender Act of that month permitted the treasury to release up to $10 million of the new currency, quickly dubbed "greenbacks." Over $450 million in paper notes circulated during the war, replacing the earlier system of state bank notes with the first unified national currency.

Much of the Civil War turned around conflicts such as the one depicted in this painting, in which small groups of soldiers confronted one another and civilians far from the scenes of major battles.

The Confederate Home Front

Southerners watched helplessly as armies stripped their farms of food and livestock. They ministered to the bleeding young men dragged into their parlors and bedrooms. The residents of places where both Unionists and Confederates remained strong—such as Missouri and eastern Tennessee—became caught in internal civil wars that pitted roving gangs of thugs against one another. Governors received letters from women, their husbands and sons gone, who worried that they faced starvation if they did not get help soon.

Inflation ate away at the Confederacy like a cancer. The rapid rise in prices made currency worth less every day. The government issued war bonds that paid 8 percent interest per year at a time when inflation reached 12 percent per month in 1861. Speculators could make money simply by buying up supplies and holding them while prices escalated. Farmers faced the temptation to grow cotton despite the needs of the armies. Cotton stored well and everyone knew that cotton would fetch a high price after the war, no matter who won. As a result, land and labor that could have grown food bent under the weight of cotton. A Georgia newspaper blamed speculators, for "a conscienceless set of vampires . . . are determined to make money even if one-half of the people starve."

Confederate leaders worried that the plantations could not produce the food the armies so desperately needed if white men did not force the slaves to work. African Americans wanted to hunt, fish, or work for themselves and their own families rather than to labor for the white people. Plantation mistresses often discovered that slaves would not work when the master—and the whips and guns he wielded—no longer hung over the slaves. Accordingly, under pressure from plantation owners, the Confederate Congress passed laws exempting from the draft white men to supervise slaves on larger plantations. That a government in such need of every available soldier felt compelled to write such laws revealed how central slavery remained even in the midst of war.

To many poorer Southerners, the law was another in a growing list of grievances. Resentment against wealthy men and women—mediated during peacetime by family ties, common church membership, careful manners, and democratic politics—quickly came to the surface in the context of war. Common people were quick to notice when plantation slaves labored over cotton rather than corn, when the well-to-do hoarded gold, received draft exemptions, or dodged taxes. Wealthy young men sometimes entered the Confederate army as privates, but others considered an officer's commission their just due as gentlemen. Scions of plantation fortunes often did little to disguise their disgust or amusement at the speech or clothing of the poorer men alongside whom they fought. The poorer soldiers and their wives noticed.

Navies

The Union enjoyed a great initial advantage in its number of ships, but many of those ships were scattered around the globe. It took months to bring them home. Moreover, most of the Union's vessels were deep-sea ships. With remarkable speed, however, the Union naval department built new craft and deployed them against the South. In the first months of the war, the Navy Department armed merchant ships and sent them to blockade Southern ports. By the end of 1861, over 260 vessels patrolled the coasts and the skilled workers of the shipbuilding towns of the east coast had 100 more under construction, including the North's first ironclad ships.

The South had virtually no ships at the beginning of the war, but the Confederate navy seized, acquired, or built roughly 125 ships each year, including more than 400 steam-powered vessels. The Confederacy immediately contracted with large shipbuilding companies in England. Jefferson Davis authorized sailors to attack Northern ships on the high seas and turn them in for a share of the booty. For a few months, these "privateers" preyed on any unguarded ship they could find, but the

Confederate Ships Under Construction in England

The Confederacy depended on English shipyards, such as this one in Liverpool, to construct vessels to run the Union blockade, attack Union ships on the seas, and defend its ports. English willingness to construct and equip Southern ships waned as battlefield defeats reduced the prospect of Confederate victory. The most effective arm of the Confederate navy consisted of commerce raiders, which destroyed roughly 255 Union ships and doubled the cost of marine insurance for Northern merchants. Two of the most successful, the *Alabama* and the *Shenandoah*, built at the Laird shipyards in Liverpool, were hybrid sail and steam-powered ships that disrupted Northern commerce and destroyed merchant ships in the Atlantic and Pacific oceans. The *Shenandoah* fired the last official shot of the war across the bows of a whaler in the Bering Sea on June 28, 1865, as part of a month-long campaign that resulted in the capture of 24 whaling ships. Not until August 2 did her captain James Waddell learn the war had ended. Fearing prosecution for piracy, Waddell sailed the *Shenandoah* warily back to England, arriving off the Irish coast on November 5, 1865.

Williamson Art Gallery & Museum, Birkenhead, England

Union navy quickly shut them down. The Confederates then used their naval officers to man ships that would attempt to sink rather than claim enemy ships. One intrepid officer, Raphael Semmes, escaped through the blockade in 1861 and seized 18 Union ships before he was trapped at Gibraltar and forced to sell his ship and escape to England.

In the meantime, the North pushed its advantage. Larger ships began to blockade 189 harbors and ports from Virginia to Texas, patrolling 3,500 miles of coastline. Such enormous territory obviously proved difficult to control, especially because Northern ships periodically had to travel to ports hundreds of miles away for supplies and fuel. When Union craft left for such journeys, Southern **blockade runners** rushed into the unprotected ports. The Union navy decided to seize several Southern ports for use as supply stations and prevent their use by Confederate blockade runners.

The Federal ships moved first in August, at Cape Hatteras in North Carolina, shelling the forts there and cutting off the supplies that dozens of blockade runners had brought into the Confederacy. The Northern navy also took a station near Biloxi, Mississippi, from which it could patrol the Gulf of Mexico. The most valuable seizure, however, was Port Royal, South Carolina. Not only did that place offer an excellent harbor, but it stood midway between the major Southern ports of Charleston and Savannah. The 77 ships and 16,000 sailors and soldiers dispatched to Port Royal were the largest combined force yet assembled in American warfare.

Diplomacy and the *Trent* Affair

On the day after the capture of Port Royal, a Union ship stopped a British mail packet, the *Trent,* as it traveled from Cuba to St. Thomas. The *Trent* carried James Mason and John Slidell, Confederate commissioners sailing to London and Paris to negotiate for the support of the British and French governments. The captain of the Union ship, Charles Wilkes, after firing two shots across the bow of the British vessel, boarded it and seized the Confederate emissaries. When Wilkes arrived in Boston to deposit Mason and Slidell in prison, he met with a hero's welcome. Congress ordered a medal struck in his honor.

The excitement began to wane, however, when people realized the possible repercussions of Wilkes's actions. Despite the growth of the Union navy, Great Britain still ruled the oceans. British newspapers and politicians called for war against the arrogant Americans, warning that the British navy "with little difficulty could blow to the four winds their dwarf fleet."

The ***Trent* affair** reflected the uneasy state of international relations created by the war. The Confederacy hoped that England or France, even both, would come to its aid. The importance of cotton in the international marketplace was such, Southerners argued, that the industrial powers of Europe could not long afford to allow the Northern navy to enforce its blockade.

The situation in the winter of 1861–1862 proved more complicated than people had expected, however. International law did not offer a clear ruling on whether Captain Wilkes had acted legally. And neither did self-interest offer a clear guide as to whether England should declare war on the United States or aid the Confederacy. The factories of Britain had stockpiled cotton in expectation of the war and did not clamor for intervention as Southerners had hoped. Anger over the *Trent* affair was balanced by resentment of Southern assumptions about British dependence on cotton. Confederates who "thought they could extort our cooperation by the agency of king cotton" would be disappointed, British leaders warned. France and England watched one another warily, neither country eager to upset the fragile balance of power between themselves by taking the first step in America.

Public opinion within England and France divided, for it was by no means clear to most Europeans which side had the better claim to their sympathies. Lincoln repeatedly declared that the war was not a war to end slavery. That declaration, Lincoln believed, was necessary to cement the support of the border states, but it undercut the support of English and European abolitionists for the Union cause. The Confederates claimed to be fighting for self-determination, a cause with considerable

Ulysses S. Grant distinguished himself in key battles in Tennessee and Mississippi in 1862. Many months and battles would pass, however, before Grant would assume command in the East.

© The Granger Collection, New York

appeal in Europe, but potential supporters often viewed Southern slaveholding with disgust and distrust. Both the English and the French waited for events on the battlefields of North America to clarify issues.

The *Trent* affair was settled through diplomatic evasion and maneuvering, but the international situation remained tense throughout the war. Leaders of both the North and the South could imagine situations in which England or France would intervene with weapons and supplies. Foreign intervention loomed as a fervent hope for the Confederacy and a great fear of the North.

The Rivers of the West

The Union felt starved for victories at the beginning of the hard winter of 1862. Northern troops remained bogged down in the eastern theater, but Union generals in the West moved aggressively. Deprived of control of the Ohio River when Kentucky sided with the Union, the Confederates under Albert Sidney Johnston desperately needed to stop the Union in the West. Troops under the command of **Ulysses S. Grant,** a relatively obscure general from Illinois, confronted a Confederate line of defense across southern Kentucky. Employing

MAP 14.2 Campaigns in the West in 1862

While Lee and McClellan remained immobilized in Virginia, U. S. Grant boldly pushed to the Mississippi border. View an animated version of this map or related maps at http://history.wadsworth.com/passages3e.

the Union's new river gunboats to great effect, Grant pushed down both the Tennessee and the Cumberland Rivers across the Kentucky border into Tennessee.

Important Confederate forts stood on both these rivers, but Grant hoped to overwhelm them by combined attacks on water and land (see Map 14.2). He assaulted Fort Henry on the Tennessee River in early February, easily overcoming the fort's defenses with the big guns on his river craft. The Union now commanded a river that flowed all the way through Tennessee into northern Alabama. Grant sent his boats steaming back up the Tennessee River to the Cumberland while he marched his men overland to Fort Donelson. There, the Confederates fought desperately, destroying several of the gunboats. Despite the Confederates' efforts, however, Grant pressed his advantage and overwhelmed Southern troops that attempted to break out of the fort and retreat to nearby Nashville.

When the Confederate general in charge of the 13,000 troops who remained in the fort attempted to negotiate with Grant (an old friend) for their surrender, Grant brusquely responded: "No terms except an unconditional and immediate surrender can be accepted. I propose to move immediately upon your works." Grant's phrase soon echoed through northern newspapers, jokes, and even mildly risqué love letters. Grant's first two initials, northern newspapers crowed, actually stood for Unconditional Surrender. Within days, Union troops pushed into nearby Nashville, the capital of Tennessee, making it the first great conquest of the war.

The *Monitor* and the *Virginia*

Even as Grant's troops seized their victories on the rivers of Tennessee, the Union navy continued its relentless attack on the eastern seaboard of the Confederacy. A

The Union's use of riverboats provided a decided advantage when they quickly overran forts on the Tennessee River in February 1862. The boats played critical roles on other rivers as well, including the Mississippi.

well-planned amphibious assault allowed the Northern navy to consolidate its control of the North Carolina coast. The blockade steadily tightened.

Despite the Union's success, the Southern navy had reason for hope in early 1862. Confederate Secretary of the Navy Stephen Mallory had created an effective and innovative department. Mallory sought to take advantage of recent developments in shipbuilding and naval warfare such as steam power, the screw propeller, and armor. The Confederacy eagerly experimented, too, with mines in their harbors and developed the world's first combat submarine, the C.S.S. *Hunley.*

Most important, the South examined the possibilities of iron-plated ships. In the years immediately preceding

The U.S.S. *Merrimack* becomes the C.S.S. *Virginia* as the Confederates salvage and rebuild as an ironclad a ship that the United States abandoned in Norfolk during the first days of the war.

the Civil War, the French and British had been experimenting with such vessels, but the United States remained far behind. The Confederacy began building an ironclad almost from the very beginning of the war, converting a Union frigate, the U.S.S. *Merrimack,* captured in Norfolk in April of 1861. The confederacy added walls of 2-foot-thick solid oak, covered with 2-inch-thick iron plate, and installed an iron ram on the front to rip through the wooden hulls of enemy ships. It carried 10 heavy guns. The Confederacy changed the ship's name from the U.S.S. *Merrimack* to the C.S.S. *Virginia.*

The Union, for its part, hired a Swiss inventor to design a different kind of ironclad; his innovative plan called for a ship that would be mostly submerged except for a rotating turret on top. Its inventor would refund the $275,000 cost to the government if the ship—condemned as a "cheesebox on a raft"—failed. It was by no means clear how such a craft might work in battle. No one was even sure it would stay afloat, much less fight effectively with its two guns. It was called the *Monitor.*

On March 8, 1862, the Confederates decided the time had come to unleash their new weapon. The *Virginia* attacked several Union ships occupying the harbor at Hampton Roads, Virginia. The ironclad sank two wooden ships and drove three others aground; their guns proved useless against the heavy iron sheathing.

In one of the more dramatic episodes of the young war, however, the Union happened to be sending its own ironclad to another Virginia port 30 miles away on the morning after the *Virginia* launched its attack. As soon as the sound of the guns in Hampton Roads reached the *Monitor,* it steamed down, arriving just in time. The two vessels pounded one another for hours. The imposing Southern ironclad had been neutralized and the blockade would continue. Although neither iron ship actually won the battle of March 9, the advantages of the Northern *Monitor* quickly became evident. Not only did that craft provide a much smaller target and a more maneuverable set of guns, but the *Monitor* required only half as much water in which to operate. The *Virginia* proved too big to retreat into rivers and too unwieldy for open seas. The Union began a crash campaign to build as many ironclads as possible, using the *Monitor* as its model.

The Union on the Offensive: March to September 1862

The Union strategy had long pivoted around the effort to take Richmond. With apparently unlimited resources,

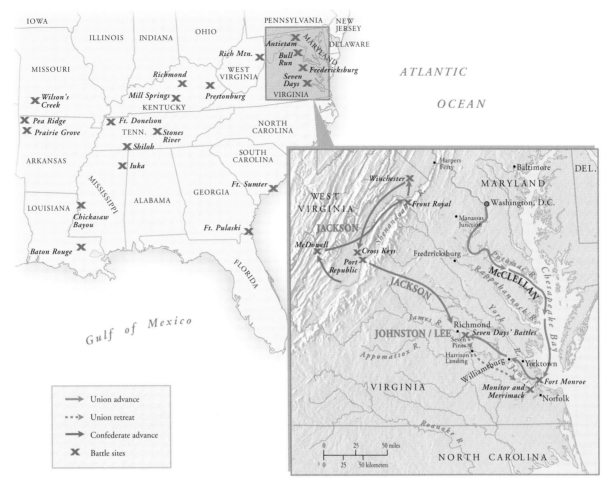

MAP 14.3 Eastern Battles of 1862
George McClellan's long-awaited campaign to take Richmond, Virginia, the capital of the Confederacy, began in March of 1862. The vast maneuver unfolded over many months and ended with the brutal stalemate of the Seven Days. Stonewall Jackson's Valley Campaign kept the Union forces divided. View an animated version of this map or related maps at http://history.wadsworth.com/passages3e.

Northerners expected to make quick work of Virginia. Although the Confederacy had put up a surprisingly effective campaign, the Union believed it would win the war in the spring and summer of 1862. As with all things in this war, however, events followed directions no one could foresee.

The Peninsular Campaign Begins

On the very day that the C.S.S. *Virginia* emerged at Hampton Roads, Abraham Lincoln gave his approval of General George McClellan's long-delayed plan to win the war in the East. Rather than fighting in northern Virginia, McClellan would attack Richmond from the south, using the peninsula between the James and York rivers as an invasion route and relying on the Chesapeake Bay as a supply route. By moving the war away

from Washington, McClellan argued, he would lessen the threat to the nation's capital (see Map 14.3).

Four hundred watercraft of every description began transferring Union soldiers to the tip of the peninsula at Fort Monroe, about 70 miles from Richmond. The transfer of 100,000 men took weeks to unfold. McClellan, with his usual methodical style, required several more weeks to arrange them in preparation for what he expected to be his triumphant march into Richmond.

Shiloh

In the meantime, U.S. Grant and his fellow general William T. Sherman pushed their troops ever deeper into Tennessee. The Confederates, under Albert Sidney Johnston, had retreated to Corinth, Mississippi, where they

Flashpoints | The United States Sanitary Commission

The suffering of the Civil War soon outstripped the resources of the Union army and federal government. The United States Sanitary Commission sought to address these shortfalls and provide aid and comfort to wounded and sick Northern soldiers.

Growing from the Women's Central Association of Relief for the Sick and Wounded in the Army, it was founded in New York in 1861. With President Lincoln's approval, it was renamed the "Commission of Inquiry and Advice in respect of the Sanitary Interests of the United States Forces." The Sanitary Commission had to overcome opposition from the Army Medical Bureau, whose uniformed leadership initially mocked and resented civilian involvement and questioned the use of women as nurses. As the war expanded and casualties mounted, however, the need for women's help trumped older notions of what was appropriate work for "ladies."

Led by such socially prominent men as New York lawyer George Templeton Strong and the landscape architect Frederick Law Olmstead, the commission inspected sanitary conditions at army camps and funded the provision of nurses, ambulances, hospitals, and food. Strong argued that the United States needed such a commission because "the old Medical Bureau was . . . the most narrow, hidebound, fossilized, red-tape-y of all the departments in Washington." He saw it as "incapable of caring for the army."

As the Sanitary Commission gained influence it succeeded in capturing the public's favor. It soon helped induce Congress to encourage the Medical Bureau to promote younger, more progressive surgeons and pushed for wider use of volunteer nurses, doctors, and

PR-065-808p-7, Collection of The New-York Historical Society

aides to care for the large numbers of sick. Some women, such as Mary Livermore, saw service as an "uprising among women" eager to show their patriotism. But the commission also became embroiled in disputes with similar benevolent groups that accused the commission of showing less interest in the plight of soldiers than in providing an acceptable stage outlet for the wealthy in wartime, a performance far from the fighting.

The men and women of the commission organized large public fairs to raise money and publicize their work. The largest fairs raised over four million dollars for soldiers' aid, medical supplies, and food. As the war progressed, the Sanitary Commission increasingly controlled or monitored local fundraisers aimed at aiding sick and wounded soldiers.

Besides its obvious medical and military benefits, the Sanitary Commission demonstrated the utility of charitable organizations on a national scale. One of its nurses, Clara Barton, started the American Red Cross after the war to continue to serve the needs of the nation's sick. The Sanitary Commission taught Americans the benefits of large enterprises organized for the public good, especially with women playing a prominent role, and foreshadowed the progressive-era reforms of a half-century later.

Questions for Reflection

1. Is it possible that the Commission was one of the more enduring legacies of the Civil War?

2. Were the victories for women won by the Commission permanent victories?

3. Did the Civil War see a revolution in health practices? What would mark the real revolution in that care?

---

regrouped and joined with other units arriving by train from throughout the Confederacy. They planned to attack Grant to regain momentum, if not the enormous territory and strategic rivers they had lost at Fort Henry and Fort Donelson. Grant established his own base of operations only 20 miles away, at Pittsburgh Landing, Tennessee. To the surprise of the Union, Johnston attacked the larger Union force at Shiloh Church on April 6.

The scattered woods and rough terrain around Shiloh turned the battle into a series of brutal fights among desperate groups of scattered men with little coordinated leadership. Johnston, killed leading an attack, was replaced by Beauregard, who succeeded in pushing the Union men back 2 miles. The Confederates' dominance proved short-lived, however, for 25,000 Northern reinforcements arrived overnight. The Southerners received no new men.

In one of the bloodiest days of fighting in the war, the troops of Grant and William T. Sherman clashed with those of Albert Sidney Johnston and P. G. T. Beauregard at Shiloh. Johnston was killed and the Union forces seized a desperate, last-minute, and costly victory.

The next day saw Grant and his army regain the ground they had lost, driving the Confederates back to Corinth. Though the Southern forces had been badly hurt, the Northern forces were themselves too exhausted and shaken to pursue.

The carnage at Shiloh exceeded anything anyone had ever seen. The bloodiest battle in the hemisphere up to that point, Shiloh exacted a horrible toll: about 1,700 killed and 8,000 wounded on each side. About 2,000 of the wounded men in both the Union and the Confederacy forces would soon die. Newspapers and generals debated the outcome of the battle for months, trying to decide the hero and the loser, but it eventually became clear that the Southern attempt to halt Northern momentum in the Mississippi Valley had failed. Frustrated with McClellan's inertia, Lincoln turned aside criticism of Grant, "I can't spare this man, he fights."

New Orleans

Yet another drama played itself out in New Orleans. There, a Union naval force under David Farragut determined to do what Confederates considered impossible: overwhelm their largest city and largest port from the Gulf. Confederates recalled that the mighty British of 1815 had failed to take New Orleans and fully expected the same fate to befall the Yankees. The city lay under the protection of two forts claiming 115 guns as well as a river blocked with logs, barges, and thick cables. So safe did they consider New Orleans that Confederate troops abandoned the city to fight at Shiloh, leaving the port protected only by militiamen.

Farragut had his own weapons, however: 20 mortar boats, 17 ships with 523 guns, and 15,000 soldiers. The Union navy pounded the forts for days with the mortars, unsuccessfully. Frustrated, on April 24 Farragut audaciously led his ships, single file, past the forts and past Confederate ships that tried to ram the Union craft or set them on fire with flaming rafts. Once they had run this gauntlet, the Union ships had clear sailing right up to the docks of New Orleans. There, they confronted no resistance as 4,000 Confederate troops withdrew from the city.

Troops under the command of Benjamin Butler occupied New Orleans while Farragut continued to drive up the Mississippi River. He took Baton Rouge

The fleet of David Farragut accomplished what the Confederates considered impossible, pushing past the elaborate defenses of New Orleans. Using the cover of darkness, much of the fleet managed to survive a thundering artillery assault.

and Natchez, but **Vicksburg** held Farragut off. Armed riverboats coming from the north soon took Memphis as well, giving the Union control of all the Mississippi River except the area near Vicksburg. Northern forces used the river as a major supply route. Rather than a highway uniting the Upper and Lower South, the Mississippi became a chasm separating one half of the Confederacy from the other.

The Confederate Draft

The end of April 1862, then, seemed to promise the early end to the war that people had expected at its outbreak. Although many of the battles had been close that spring, they all seemed to turn out in favor of the North. The first yearlong enlistments in the Confederate army were running out in April; many soldiers left for home. The Confederate Congress, fearful that its armies would be short of men as the Union stepped up its attacks, decided that it had no choice but to initiate a compulsory draft. All white men between the ages of 18 and 35 were required to fight for 3 years. If men enlisted or reenlisted within the 30 days following passage of the law, they could choose the unit with which they fought.

Although the Confederacy eventually abolished substitution, a policy that allowed men with enough money to pay a substitute to fight in their place, it still permitted men from many occupations, such as teachers and apothecaries, to claim an exemption from military service. Governors appointed many men to positions in their state

governments and militia so that they would be exempted from the draft. In Georgia and North Carolina, state and counties aided the families of poor soldiers by taxing slaves and large property owners.

The Confederacy also exempted 1 white man for every 20 slaves he supervised in the "twenty negro law." That law, like the draft in general, necessary though it was, divided Southerners more profoundly than anything else in the Civil War. A Mississippi private deserted to return home, refusing to "fight for the rich men while they were at home having a good time."

The Seven Days

"Every blow tells fearfully against the rebellion," a New York newspaper declared at the end of May. "It now requires no very far reaching prophet to predict the end of this struggle." From the viewpoint of the battlefields in Tennessee and Mississippi, the war did indeed seem to be nearing its end. And in Virginia George McClellan's troops, the pride of the Union and 100,000 strong, had pushed their way up the peninsula toward Richmond. By the end of May only 5 miles separated them from their destination.

Not that it would be easy for the Union troops to take Richmond. The river assaults that had worked so well 2 months earlier in Tennessee failed in Virginia. The Confederates were able to attack the river gunboats from the heights of Drewry's Bluff. Even the *Monitor* proved ineffectual when faced with an enemy 100 feet above. Moreover, the Confederates had established imposing defenses around Richmond and concentrated many of their troops in the vicinity.

Defensive positioning proved more important in the American Civil War than in any prior conflict. Defenders gained their advantage from a new kind of weapon: the rifle. A rifle, unlike a musket, used a spiral groove in the barrel to put spin on a bullet, like a football pass, giving the bullet much greater stability and accuracy. A musket had been accurate at only about 80 yards, but a rifle could hit a target at 4 times that distance. Although the benefits of rifling had long been recognized, it was not until the 1850s that a French inventor, Charles Minie, devised a way to make it possible for a rifled gun to fire without requiring the grooves to be cleaned. Although the rifles still had to be loaded from the end of the barrel, preventing even the most skillful soldiers from firing more than three times a minute, rifles nevertheless made it much more difficult for attacking troops to overwhelm a defense.

Lincoln and McClellan believed that Washington faced a direct threat from Confederate troops in the

Missionaries at Port Royal

In Union hands since 1861, the Sea Islands of South Carolina attracted slaves from the mainland who joined the 9,000 slaves who remained when their masters fled the Federal army. These islands quickly became a testing ground for Northern ideals. Abolitionists quickly realized that these slaves, among the most isolated groups in the South, would prove a test for creating a community to disprove theories of black inability to adapt to a free labor society.

Societies formed in cities such as Boston, New York, and Philadelphia to organize financial and educational support for the newly liberated men and women on the islands. Missionaries and teachers of both genders came to the islands to instruct the newly freed residents in matters both secular and religious. The first group that sailed from New York in March 1862 also brought men to manage the production and sale of cotton, several of whom clashed with the antislavery activists when their interest in a profitable crop exceeded their concern for black welfare. Although eager to seize plots of land to support themselves and their families, many former slaves associated cotton with servitude and refused to plant it. Politicians, ministers, and newspapermen reported the conditions and progress made at Port Royal as a measure of what the end of slavery would mean for blacks and for the South.

The Western Reserve Historical Society, Cleveland, Ohio.

Shenandoah Valley under the command of the increasingly impressive Stonewall Jackson. For three months in the spring of 1862, Jackson maneuvered his men up and down the valley, creating the impression that his forces were larger than they were and that they could attack anywhere, any time. As a result, the Union divided its forces, depriving McClellan's invasion of tens of thousands of soldiers that otherwise would have been available for the assault on Richmond.

The Union and the Rebel forces tested one another around Richmond in May and June, inflicting heavy casualties in battles that settled nothing (see Map 14.4). Robert E. Lee replaced Joseph Johnston, wounded in battle, as general of the Confederate forces in Virginia. Lee quickly proved himself aggressive and daring. He almost immediately planned an attack against the larger force under McClellan's command. Lee sent out J. E. B. Stuart, his cavalry leader, who rode all the way around McClellan's troops, reconnoitering their position and stealing their supplies. Stuart reported that part of McClellan's troops were vulnerable to attack. Lee brought Jackson and his men to join in an assault.

The resulting prolonged conflict around Richmond, which became known as the Seven Days' Battles, did not distinguish either side. Thirty thousand men had been killed and wounded. The Confederates' offensive did not work as planned and Jackson failed to carry out his part of the assault. For the North's part, McClellan, though possessing far more troops than his opponents' 90,000, believed himself outnumbered, wiring Lincoln that he faced 200,000 Confederates and "if this [army] is destroyed by overwhelming numbers . . . the responsibility cannot be thrown on my shoulders."

Slavery Under Attack

By the summer of 1862, the war seemed to have reached a stalemate. Both the Union and the Confederacy believed a decisive battle could still win the war. The North took

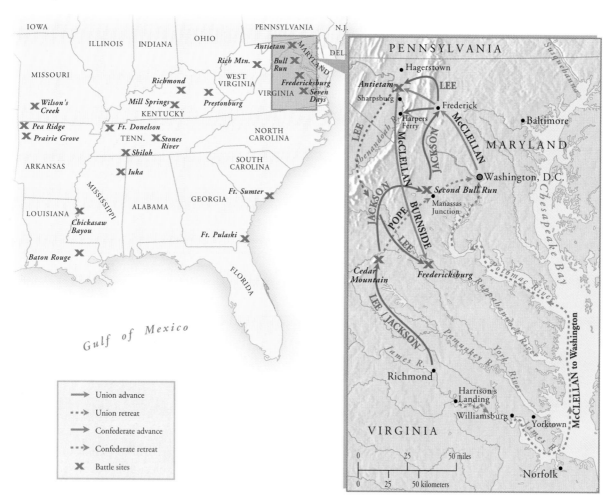

MAP 14.4 **Campaigns in Virginia and Maryland, 1862**
As Union troops moved from the peninsula below Richmond to an area closer to Washington in August, Lee and Jackson used the opportunity to go on the offensive. Over the next several months, they clashed with Union forces at Manassas and Antietam in Maryland. View an animated version of this map or related maps at http://history.wadsworth.com/passages3e.

heart because Union ships controlled the coasts and rivers on the perimeter of the South even as Union troops pushed deep into Tennessee and Mississippi. The Confederacy took comfort because vast expanses of rich Southern farmland and millions of productive slaves remained beyond the reach of Union control.

President Lincoln, while detesting slavery personally, feared that a campaign against bondage would divide the North. As the war dragged into its second year, however, even Northerners who did not oppose slavery on moral grounds could see that slavery offered the South a major advantage: slaves in the fields meant more white Southerners on the battlefields.

More important, black Southerners themselves pressed slavery as a problem on the Union armies. Wherever those armies went, slaves fled to the Federals as refugees. The Union called the black people who made their way to the

Union ranks "**contrabands**," a word usually used to describe smuggled goods. The term revealed the confusion among white Northerners about the status of the black people in their midst. Although some Union officers returned the slaves to their owners, other officers seized the opportunity to strike against slavery and use former slaves to further their war aims. The slaves "bring much valuable information" and "are acquainted with all the roads, paths, fords," and "haunts of secession spies and traitors."

Northern leaders confronted such issues most directly near Port Royal, South Carolina. When the Union forces overran the Sea Islands along the coast in 1862, the relatively few whites who lived there fled, leaving behind 10,000 slaves. Almost immediately, various groups of Northerners began to vie for the opportunity to reshape Southern society. The Sea Islands claimed some of the largest and richest plantations in

New Hampshire Historical Society

Enslaved people rushed to Federal troops whenever they could, filling Union camps and working for the army and its soldiers.

the South, growing rare and expensive long-staple cotton. Union leaders felt it crucial that freed slaves prove they would work willingly and effectively. Female abolitionist schoolteachers journeyed down from New England, and men came from New York City and the Northwest to demonstrate that plantations run on the principles of free labor could be both productive and humane.

The former slaves valued the opportunity to learn to read and write and wanted land of their own, but they did not always appreciate lessons from the newcomer whites about religion and agriculture. Black people knew how to farm and knew their God. Not only in South Carolina, but wherever the Union army penetrated, officers and civilians sought to control black labor and rich land. Sometimes, Federal officials decreed that the freedpeople could sign contracts with whomever they chose—but they had to sign contracts with someone. In other times and places, Union leaders permitted black people to take responsibility for some of the land they had worked as slaves. Some white Northerners proposed seizing land from former slaveholders to give to the former slaves.

General David Hunter, a man of abolitionist sympathies, took advantage of his position in Port Royal in the late spring of 1862 to organize a number of black military units and to declare slavery abolished in South Carolina,

Georgia, and Florida. Hunter stated that Union soldiers would not act "as a police force for the protection of property." Lincoln revoked Hunter's proclamation. Lincoln did not envision the immediate emancipation decreed by Hunter, with no compensation to slaveholders and with former slaves living alongside their former masters. Lincoln thought that slavery must end gradually, with payments to the slaveholders for their loss of property. Ideally, Lincoln argued, the former slaves would be colonized beyond the borders of the United States, perhaps in Haiti or Liberia.

Lincoln also resisted those members of his party and his cabinet who thought that black men should be enlisted into the Union army. Such Republicans, often called "Radicals" for their support of black rights, passed laws that forbade Northern commanders to return refugee slaves to their former masters, and they ended slavery in the District of Columbia (albeit gradually and with compensation).

Many Northern Democrats firmly opposed such expansion of the war's purposes and means, warning that abolition would only embitter and embolden the Confederates. McClellan, a strong opponent of Radical Republicans, believed emancipation would "disintegrate our present armies." Democrats sympathetic to the South, called "**Copperheads**" by their opponents, marched under the motto "The Constitution as it is and the Union as it was." They wanted slavery to remain in place so that the South would come back into the nation and they were deeply hostile to ideas of racial equality.

Lincoln sought to steer a course between the Radicals and the Copperheads. But in the summer of 1862 he moved closer to an assault on slavery. The Union army had strengthened its position in Kentucky and Missouri, and it no longer appeared that the border states could effectively align themselves with the Confederates. Similarly, Lincoln came to see that the Southern Unionists, far fewer in number than he had believed, could not or would not organize effective opposition to the Confederacy from within. Lincoln decided that to

☞ For Particulars, see small bills. jy 1—12t*

SUBSTITUTE NOTICES.

WANTED—A SUBSTITUTE. Apply at No. 38 Linwood House, Main street, between the Spotswood and American Hotels, same side of the street, between 9 and 10 o'clock A. M. Any citizen of the Confederate States, over 35 years old, may come. A Kentuckian preferred. No foreigner need apply. jy 8—2t*

WANTED—A SUBSTITUTE.—I will pay the sum of $1,000, cash, for a SUBSTITUTE, to serve in Company K, 3d Alabama regiment, for two years, or the war. Good references required. Apply to "A.," at this office, between the hours of 9 and 10 A. M., or 4 and 5 P. M. jy 8—3t*

WANTED—A SUBSTITUTE.—None need come unless a *citizen* of the Confederate States, over 35 years of age. Such a one would do well by applying between 7 and 12 o'clock TO-DAY, at 75 Ballard House. jy 8—1t*

WANTED—By a young man, of good character, a place as SUBSTITUTE; exempt by age. He can be seen at No. 51 American Hotel, or will receive communications addressed to "J. J.," through Richmond P. O. jy 8—3t*

WANTED—A SUBSTITUTE—To go into the infantry service. A liberal price will be given by applying at No. 132 Main street, for the next two days. [jy 8—2t*] W. A. T.

WANTED—A SUBSTITUTE for the war. A Marylander preferred. Apply at Wm. H. Yeatman's shop, on 8th street, between Grace and Franklin. jy 8—1t*

SUBSTITUTE.—Wanted, a SUBSTITUTE for the war. Apply for "J. H.," at the Dispatch office, between 9 and 11 o'clock, corner Main and 13th streets. jy 8—2t*

WANTED—Two SUBSTITUTES—To go in for the war. None but non-conscripts need apply, on South side 12th between Main and Bank streets. jy 8—5t

WANTED—A SUBSTITUTE.—Address "Box 169," stating where applicant can be seen. jy 8—2t*

WANTED—A SUBSTITUTE. Enquire at 19th and Cary streets, at the Planing Mill. jy 8—1t*

WANTED.—A SUBSTITUTE for a man in Company I, Mossingford Rifles, 44th regiment Virginia Volunteers, who wishes to leave the army on account of bad health. Call at MADDUX & CO.'S, between 9 and 12 o'clock A. M., Cary st., jy 7—3t* Opposite Columbian Hotel.

WANTED—A SUBSTITUTE, for six or twelve months—a good, reliable man, free from all military duty to the Confederate States. Address "C. G.," Dispatch office, stating lowest price for either six or twelve months. jy 7—3t*

WANTED—A SUBSTITUTE—For which a liberal price will be paid. Branch service, Infantry, fine company. Apply at Linwood House Room 18, from 10 to 12 o'clock TO-DAY. jy 7—2t*

WANTED—A SUBSTITUTE for the war.—Apply at Columbian Hotel, on TUESDAY, the 8th instant, from 10 to 2 o'clock, at Room No. 13. jy 7—2t*

WANTED—A SUBSTITUTE.—A man, exempt from military duty, wishing to employ himself for the war, can get a liberal price by applying to J. PEYSOR, jy 1—6t* Corner 8th and Cary sts.

DESERTERS.

Advertisements such as these for substitutes filled columns of newspapers across the Confederacy.

---

win the war he would have to hit slavery. Responding to a Southern Unionist, the president wrote, "This government cannot much longer play a game in which it stakes all, and its enemies stake nothing. Those enemies must understand that they cannot experiment for ten years trying to destroy the government, and if they fail still come back into the Union unhurt."

On July 22, 1862, Lincoln and his cabinet authorized Federal military leaders to take whatever secessionist property they needed and to destroy any property that aided the Confederacy. That meant that Union officers could protect the black men and women who fled to Northern camps, using them to work behind the lines. Lincoln decided to wait for a victory on the battlefield before announcing the most dramatic part of his plan: that as of January 1, 1863, he would declare all slaves in areas controlled by the Confederates free. Although this proclamation would free no slaves under Union control in the border states, it ruled out compromise that would end the war and bring the South back into the Union with slavery. Knowing that this announcement would unleash harsh criticism in the North, Lincoln wanted to wait until the North was flush with confidence before he announced this preliminary Emancipation Proclamation. When and where that victory might occur, however, was by no means clear in July of 1862.

Second Manassas and Antietam

Confidence actually ran higher in the Confederacy than in the Union during the second summer of the war. The Union, after all, could draw little solace from McClellan's sluggish performance in the ferocious Seven Days' Battles outside of Richmond in June. Lincoln placed Henry Halleck, who advocated a more aggressive stance toward Southern civilians and their slaves, in charge of all Union troops. The president put John Pope, who had been fighting in the West, in charge of the new Army of Virginia. McClellan still commanded troops, but his role had been restricted. Pope issued a series of orders that signaled a new harder tone to the conflict. Troops would forage as needed, no longer guard Southern property, and hold local civilians responsible for damages caused by area guerrillas.

The new Union leaders decided to remove McClellan's troops from the peninsula of Virginia and consolidate them, under the joint command of Pope, with troops from the Shenandoah Valley. The forces began to move from the peninsula in August, creating a temporary opportunity for the Confederacy. Lee decided to attack Pope's troops while McClellan's were withdrawing. He hoped to occupy as much territory as possible, resting and

National Park Services, Antietam National Battlefield

The sunken road where Confederates battled Union soldiers on this Maryland battlefield became known as "Bloody Lane." Bodies piled up six deep on the bloodiest single day of the Civil War.

resupplying his troops while complicating Union efforts to unify their forces.

Lee's plan worked better than he could have expected. Stonewall Jackson attacked Pope's men and pillaged a large Federal supply depot at Manassas. Pope then fell under attack by James Longstreet's troops, who drove the new Yankee commander back into Washington. With McClellan no longer threatening Richmond and Pope posing no danger to northern Virginia, Lee decided to push into Maryland. He believed that large numbers of Marylanders would rush to the Confederate cause. Lee had another audience in mind as well: England and France. In the wake of Union indecision and defeat in the summer of 1862, leaders in both countries were leaning toward recognition of the Confederacy. A major victory in Northern territory, Lee felt certain, would prove that the South deserved the support of the major powers.

Lee acted so confidently because he knew he would face George McClellan again. On September 17, the two old adversaries fell into battle once more, this time at Antietam Creek, near Sharpsburg, Maryland. The Confederates had 35,000 men to McClellan's 72,000, but the Southerners held the defensive ground. The terrible battle ended in confusion and stalemate. More men were killed, wounded, or declared missing on this day than on any other day in the Civil War: 13,000 for the Confederacy and 12,000 for the Union. Lee had lost nearly a third of his army; McClellan, despite his numerical advantage, had been unable to shatter the enemy.

Neither side could be satisfied with the battle's outcome, but the North made the best of the situation. Lincoln decided that **Antietam** represented enough of a victory to justify his announcement of the preliminary Emancipation Proclamation. The European powers decided that they would withhold their support for the Confederacy for the time being. The Confederacy decided that it would pull back into Virginia to fight another day.

Things could have turned out very differently at this juncture. Had McClellan destroyed Lee's army, the Confederacy might have given up its claims for independence before slavery had been ended. Had Lee merely held his ground in Virginia after driving McClellan away from Richmond and Pope back into Washington, England and France might have offered mediation—and the North might well have accepted, again without the end of slavery. As it was, however, both the North and the South would fight again and again.

Stalemate

While Northerners and Southerners slaughtered one another in Maryland with no decisive advantage gained by either side, Southern forces under the command of Braxton Bragg pushed far into Kentucky, determined to regain ground lost early in the war. Confederates believed that Kentuckians would rush to the Southern flag if given a chance. But Kentuckians had little confidence

After the slaughter at Marye's Heights in December 1862, Confederates stripped the bodies of Union soldiers of their boots and uniforms. Here, Northern burial parties inter their dead.

that the Confederates could prevail in Kentucky and did not want to risk all they had in support of a losing cause. Although the Confederates never suffered sharp defeat in Kentucky, they had too few men to occupy the state, and retreated after the battle of Perryville. Rather than risk losing his army, Bragg pulled his men into a more defensible position in Tennessee.

By the summer and fall of 1862, many men had died to little apparent purpose. Lincoln decided that generals in both the East and the West must be removed; George McClellan and Don Carlos Buell seemed too slow to react. Lincoln replaced Buell with William S. Rosecrans and replaced McClellan with Ambrose E. Burnside, an appealing man uncertain that he was qualified for the job. His doubts proved to be well founded.

In November, Burnside decided to establish a new base for yet another assault on Richmond. He moved his troops to Fredericksburg, Virginia, and launched an attack on a virtually impregnable Confederate position at Marye's Heights. With Southerners able to fire down on them at will from protected positions, more than 12,000 Union soldiers were killed, wounded, or missing. Observing the suicidal Union charges, Robert E. Lee remarked to General Longstreet, "It is well that war is so terrible—we should grow too fond of it." At battle's end, both armies remained where they had been at the battle's beginning.

The North fell into mourning, humiliation, and anger at this sacrifice. Officers as well as enlisted men made no secret of their loss of faith in Burnside. Despondent, Lincoln responded to defeat at Fredericksburg, "If there is a worse place than Hell, I am in it." In Tennessee, Rosecrans felt that he had to move against Bragg to demonstrate Union resolve and power. The two armies clashed on the last day of 1862 at Stones River

near Murfreesboro. The two sides, losing about a third of their men each, fought to a virtual draw.

The winter of 1862–1863 saw the North and the South precariously balanced, both against one another and within their own societies. Military victories would decide whether the South or the North would break first.

Conclusion

Eighteen months after Lincoln had begun his journey to Washington to become president, war had become a way of life.

The boundaries between the Union and the Confederacy had been firmly drawn. After agonizing months of debate, Virginia, North Carolina, Tennessee, and Arkansas had cast their lot with their fellow slave states. After similar debates, Maryland, Kentucky, and Missouri—other slave states—cast their lot with the United States. The balance of power between North and South meant that the war they began in 1861 would not be settled quickly. Both sides claimed crucial advantages: whereas the North had more men, machinery, and money, the South was fighting on the defensive and on its home ground.

The governments of both sides had begun to function effectively. The Lincoln and Davis administrations both improvised desperately, piecing together the resources to put vast armies in the field in a matter of months. The tiny peacetime army of the United States ballooned in size as volunteers rushed to fight under the minority of officers trained at West Point. Most officers in both armies were elected by their fellow volunteers with most more popular than skilled. The nonexistent army of the Confederate States coalesced around its own West Pointers who swore allegiance to the new nation rather than to the nation they had been trained to defend. The North put its faith in George B. McClellan at the outset, the South, taking longer to locate its leaders, decided on Stonewall Jackson and Robert E. Lee.

The first volunteer units of both armies had been mobilized. Men of all descriptions rushed to arms: poor as well as rich, urban as well as rural, foreign-born as well as native-born. They signed on at first for three months, then found themselves fighting for much longer as the war proved harder to win than either side thought possible at the war's beginning.

Both the South and the North had claimed military victories. The Confederacy recalled the battle at Manassas with pride, but then watched as the Union took New

Orleans, Nashville, and its Atlantic port cities. The United States gloried in its naval victories, but then watched as its soldiers lost in the Shenandoah Valley and on the Peninsula that led to Richmond. Clarity did not come as the months passed. Even though the South won at Second Manassas, the North rebuffed the enemy at Antietam. The debacle at Fredericksburg in December 1862 horrified a United States that seemed incapable of mounting a successful campaign against Robert E. Lee. The waste of young lives on the hills below Marye's Heights made many question the conduct of the war.

In the midst of all this suffering, President Lincoln sought to define a greater purpose for the war. Even while the Union army was stalled outside of Richmond in the summer of 1862, Lincoln drafted an Emancipation Proclamation. He had come to realize that the Confederacy could not be defeated unless slavery, its bedrock, were destroyed. In the wake of Antietam, enough of a victory to call a victory, Lincoln announced the end of slavery in all areas held by the Confederacy by January 1. Denounced throughout the South and in much of the North as well, Lincoln tried to strike a death blow against the surprisingly strong enemy. He knew as well as anyone, however, that without victories on the battlefield nothing else would matter. He entered 1863 hoping the victories would come soon.

The Chapter in Review

In the years between 1861 and 1862:

- The states of the upper South divide, with Virginia, North Carolina, Tennessee, and Arkansas going to the Confederacy and Kentucky, Maryland, and Missouri staying in the Union.
- The United States and the Confederacy built vast armies and mobilized their entire societies to wage war.
- The Battle of Bull Run, a Confederate victory, showed that neither side was ready to fight.
- The United States won early and crucial victories on the rivers of Tennessee and Louisiana.
- The Confederacy managed to hold off the United States in Virginia, and the United States turned the Confederacy back in Maryland.

Making Connections Across Chapters

LOOKING BACK

In Chapter 14 we see a series of now-familiar events shook the United States in 1861 and 1862, all of them unbelievable at the time.

1. What would have changed had the Union forces won at Manassas in July 1861?

2. What did the Confederacy need to accomplish in order to claim victory in the Civil War?

3. Are you struck at the speed or the slowness with which Abraham Lincoln turned the war into a war against slavery?

LOOKING AHEAD

Chapter 15 shows, as 1862 came to an end, no one could know that the war would devastate the nation for two more years and hundreds of thousands more deaths.

1. What seemed the likely outcome of the war as 1863 began?

2. Which society, the North or the South, seemed most likely to suffer internal conflict as the years of the war passed?

Recommended Readings

Boritt, Gabor. *Why the Civil War Came* (1996) is a useful overview of recent thinking on this much-debated historical topic.

Crofts, Daniel W. *Reluctant Confederates: Upper South Unionists in the Secession Crisis* (1989)

analyzes the crucial border states with keen insight.

Crowley, Robert, ed. *With My Face to the Enemy: Perspectives on the Civil War* (2001) offers recent interpretations from leading historians of the conflict.

Eicher, David J. *The Longest Night: A Military History of the Civil War* (2001) is the best one-volume military history of the war.

Berlin, Ira, Barbara J. Fields, Steven F. Miller, Joseph P. Reidy, and Leslie Rowland, eds. *Free at Last: A Documentary History of Slavery, Freedom, and the Civil War* (1997) is a monumental collection of first-hand testimony about emancipation.

Freehling, William W. *The South vs. the South: How Anti-Confederate Southerners Shaped the Course of the Civil War* (2001) serves as a synthesis of various forms of Unionism by black and white Southerners.

Heidler, David S., and Jeanne T. Heidler, eds. *Encyclopedia of the American Civil War: A Political, Social, and Military History* (2002) is remarkably complete.

Jones, Howard. *The Union in Peril: The Crisis over British Intervention in the Civil War* (1992) provides a fresh interpretation of a critical episode.

McPherson, James M. *Battle Cry of Freedom: The Civil War Era* (1988) stands as the best one-volume account of the Civil War.

Paludan, Phillip Shaw. *A People's Contest: The Union and the Civil War, 1861–1865* (1988) paints a compelling portrait of the North during war.

Royster, Charles. *The Destructive War: William Tecumseh Sherman, Stonewall Jackson, and the Americans* (1991) offers an original and disturbing meditation on war.

Thomas, Emory M. *The Confederate Nation, 1861–1865* (1979) is the standard account.

Identifications

Review your understanding of the following key terms, people, events, and dates for this chapter (these terms also appear in the Glossary at the end of the book):

Confederacy
Jefferson Davis
Anaconda Plan
Robert E. Lee
P. G. T. Beauregard
Thomas J. "Stonewall" Jackson
Dorothea Dix

George B. McClellan
blockade runners
Trent affair
Ulysses S. Grant
Vicksburg
Monitor and *Virginia*
contrabands
Copperheads
Antietam

Online Sources Guide

Use this listing to find online documents, images, interactive maps, simulations, and other resources related to this chapter:

American History Resource Center

http://history.wadsworth.com/rc/us

Documents

The Southern Confederacy: Our Cause before the World (1861)
Excerpts from Mary Boykin Chestnut's *Wartime Diary from the Southern Home Front*

Interactive Maps

Southern Secession
Principal Military Campaigns of the Civil War

Selected Images

General Robert E. Lee
Northern view of Jefferson Davis
Confederate Brigadier General Thomas F. Drayton and brother Union Naval Commander Percival Drayton
Union's Ironclad Navy, 1862
Depiction of First Battle of Bull Run, *Harper's Weekly*
Ulysses S. Grant
Thomas Jonathan "Stonewall" Jackson: black and white photograph
The "Sunken Road" after the Battle of Antietam, September 1862

Simulation

Civil War (Choose to be a Southerner, a Northerner, or a Native American and make choices based on the circumstances and opportunities afforded.)

Document Exercises

1861 Pony Express

HistoryNOW

http://now.ilrn.com/ayers_etal3e

Primary Source Exercises

Mobilization
Secession

15 Blood and Freedom, 1863–1867

Chapter Outline

People at War: Spring 1863

The Battlefields of Summer: 1863

The Winter of Discontent: 1863–1864

From War to Reconstruction: 1865–1867

Ill and injured men filled the ground around the surgical and hospital tents where horrifying surgery often awaited them.

© Bettmann/CORBIS

The Civil War enveloped the entire nation, home front and battlefield alike. The outcome of a battle could win an election or trigger a riot, while events at home affected the leaders' decisions of when and where to fight. In the North, the strong political opposition to Abraham Lincoln and his policies exerted a constant pressure on his conduct of the war. In the South, slaves abandoned plantations and white families' hardships led soldiers to rethink their loyalties.

The outcome of the Civil War was not predetermined by the North's advantages of population and resources. Deep into the war, events could have taken radically different turns. Slavery might have survived the conflict had the Confederacy won at particular junctions or, what would have been more likely, had the United States lost the will to push the devastating war to the South's full surrender and the immediate abolition of slavery. Even with the war's end the future course of the nation remained in doubt as Americans confronted the greatest rupture in their history.

People at War: Spring 1863

Both Northerners and Southerners expected the spring of 1863 to bring the climax of the Civil War. Yet while generals and armies determined the result of battles, the women, slaves, workers, bureaucrats, draft dodgers, and politicians behind the lines would determine the outcome of the war.

Life in the Field

Soldiers eventually adjusted to the miseries of sleeping on the ground, poorly cooked food, driving rain, and endless mud. They learned to adapt to gambling, drinking, cursing, and prostitution, either by succumbing to the temptations or by steeling their resolve against them. They could toughen themselves to the intermittent mails and the arrival of bad news from home. Men recalled their initial mortification and humiliation of discovering the entire company infested with lice, a shame that turned to indifference when the sharper horror of wounds descended.

Even the most stalwart of soldiers could not adapt to the constant threat of diseases such as diarrhea, dysentery, typhoid, malaria, measles, diphtheria, and scarlet fever. As bloody as the battles were, disease killed twice as many men as died from the guns of the enemy. Many doctors of the Civil War era used the same instruments of surgery on soldier after soldier, unwittingly spreading

Timeline

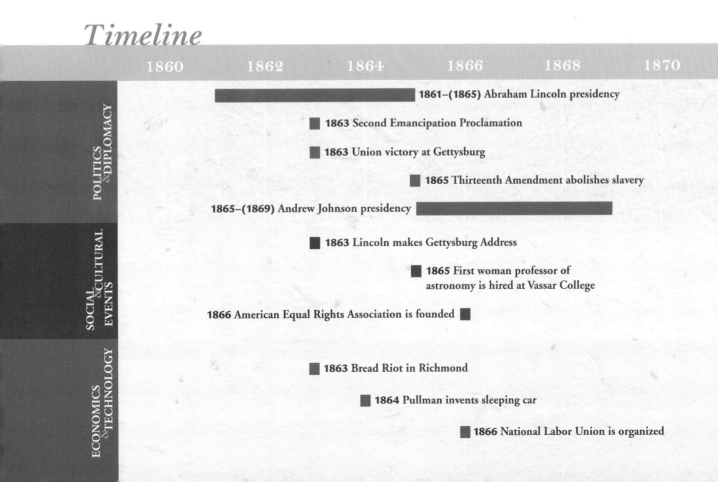

POLITICS & DIPLOMACY

1861–(1865) Abraham Lincoln presidency

1863 Second Emancipation Proclamation

1863 Union victory at Gettysburg

1865 Thirteenth Amendment abolishes slavery

1865–(1869) Andrew Johnson presidency

SOCIAL & CULTURAL EVENTS

1863 Lincoln makes Gettysburg Address

1865 First woman professor of astronomy is hired at Vassar College

1866 American Equal Rights Association is founded

ECONOMICS & TECHNOLOGY

1863 Bread Riot in Richmond

1864 Pullman invents sleeping car

1866 National Labor Union is organized

1860 1862 1864 1866 1868 1870

disease and infection. After every battle, screams filled the night as surgeons sawed off legs and arms, feet and hands, in often vain hopes of stopping gangrene.

Purposes

The North fought for ideals of union and democracy; the South fought for ideals of self-determination. Yet soldiers acted courageously not only because they believed in the official political purposes for which they were fighting, but also because they wanted to be admired by the people at home, because they wanted to do their part for their comrades, because they wanted to bring the war to a quicker end, and because they grew to hate the enemy.

Many men fought alongside their brothers, uncles, cousins. A steady stream of letters flowed back and forth between the units and the families and neighbors back home. Gossip, praise, and condemnation flourished. Any soldier who planned to return home knew that his deeds in the war would live with him the rest of his life. As a result, even fearful or halfhearted soldiers might throw themselves into battle to demonstrate their courage.

Whereas about three-fifths of Civil War soldiers were over 21 at the age of enlistment, the largest single group of soldiers was 18. For those who passed the birthdays of their late teens or early twenties on the battlefields, the transition to manhood became inseparable from the war. A soldier from Illinois proudly wrote his family that "this war has made a man of your son." To be manly meant more than the simple ability to inflict violence on the enemy. It meant pride, responsibility, loyalty, and obedience. Every battle became a test of manhood, which had to be proven every time it was challenged under fire.

Courage developed, too, out of hatred. People on both sides spread the worst stories and rumors about one another. Newspapers printed exaggerated or fabricated atrocity reports about the enemy. While many were repelled by battlefield carnage, others took satisfaction. One Confederate artillery officer admired the "severed limbs, decapitated bodies, and mutilated remains" at Fredericksburg and declared that it did "my soul good" to ride over the bodies of the Federal dead. Union troops also hardened their attitudes. A Wisconsin soldier informed his fiancée that his unit wanted to fight until "we kill them all off and cleanse the country." The longer the war went on, the more people felt they had to hate one another to justify so much bloodshed.

The sermons men heard in the camps told them they were fighting on the side of the right. The Old Testament afforded rich imagery and compelling stories of violence inflicted for good causes. Many Americans believed that God's will was enacted directly in human affairs. As the war ground on, the leaders, the soldiers, and the civilians of both sides came to feel that events were more than the product of human decision or even courage. Surely, they told themselves, so much suffering and sacrifice had to be for a larger purpose.

The Problems of the Confederate Government

Convinced that greedy merchants were holding supplies of flour until prices rose even higher in the spring of 1863, poor women in Richmond broke open the stores of merchants accused of hoarding the precious staple, taking what they needed. After President Davis climbed on a wagon and threw coins at the crowd, he ordered a militia unit to prepare to fire on them. The threat of violence and of arrest, as well as the promise of free supplies, broke up the riot, but similar events occurred in several other Southern cities such as Atlanta, Columbus, and Augusta. No one could tell when even larger riots might erupt again. Fearing the consequences for morale, military officers in Richmond ordered the press and

The Library of Virginia

This Northern portrayal of the Richmond bread riots imagined the rioters as fearsome, gaunt amazons; other accounts emphasized their respectability. In either case, they behaved in ways quite remarkable for any women in nineteenth-century America.

MULLIGAN'S BRIGADE!

LAST CHANCE TO AVOID THE DRAFT!

$402 BOUNTY!
TO VETERANS!

$302 to all other VOLUNTEERS!

All Able-bodied Men, between the ages of 18 and 45 Years, who have heretofore served not less than nine months, who shall re-enlist for Regiments in the field, will be deemed Veterans, and will receive one month's pay in advance, and a bounty and premium of $402.   To all other recruits, one month's pay in advance, and a bounty and premium of $302 will be paid.

All who wish to join Mulligan's Irish Brigade, now in the field, and to receive the munificent bounties offered by the Government, can have the opportunity by calling at the headquarters of

CAPT. J. J. FITZGERALD

Of the Irish Brigade, 23d Regiment Illinois Volunteers, Recruiting Officer, Chicago, Illinois.

Each Recruit, Veteran or otherwise, will receive

Seventy-five Dollars Before Leaving General Rendezvous,

and the remainder of the bounty in regular instalments till all is paid.   The pay, bounty and premium for three years will average $24 per month, for Veterans; and $21.30 per month for all others.

If the Government shall not require these troops for the full period of Three Years, and they shall be mustered honor out of the service before the expiration of their term of enlistment, they shall receive, UPON BEING MUSTERED O the whole amount of BOUNTY remaining unpaid, the same as if the full term been served.

Chicago, December, 1863.

J. J. FITZGERALD.

Recruiting Officer, corner North Clark & Kenzie Stree

Once the United States instituted conscription men rushed to enlist in units that offered, as this poster put it, their "last chance to avoid the draft!"

telegraph office to suppress news of the riot, but word of the riot soon spread.

The rioters were not the only ones who took what they needed. Confederate officers in the field forced reluctant farmers to accept whatever prices the army offered, in an increasingly worthless currency. In the spring of 1863, the Confederate government attempted to curb the worst abuses of this practice in the Impressment Act. If a farmer did not think the prices he or she received were fair, the case could be appealed before local authorities. In practice, however, this cumbersome system failed. Farmers hid their produce from officers and resented it when they were forced to sell. North Carolina's governor denounced impressments to the

War Department in Richmond: "If God Almighty had yet in store another plague . . . I am sure it must have been a regiment or so of half-disciplined Confederate cavalry."

The Southern government could not afford to lose civilian support. Although the absence of political parties originally appeared to be a sign of the South's consensus, that absence eventually undermined what original consensus the Confederacy had enjoyed. Jefferson Davis, without a party mechanism to discipline those who spoke out against him, could not remove enemies from office. Davis's own vice president, Alexander Stephens, became a persistent and outspoken critic of the Confederate president's "tyrannical" policies, actively undermining support for Davis and even allying with avowed enemies of Davis and his policies.

The Confederate government faced a fundamental dilemma. The whole point of secession had been to move political power closer to localities, protecting slavery in particular and self-determination in general. The government of the Confederacy, however, had to centralize power. If the armies were to be fed and clothed, if diplomats were to make a plausible case for the Confederacy's nationhood, if soldiers were to be mobilized, then the Confederate government had to

exercise greater power than its creators had expected or intended. Jefferson Davis continually struggled with this tension. For every Southerner who considered Davis too weak, another considered the president dangerously powerful.

The Northern Home Front

In the North, the war heightened the strong differences between the Democrats and the Republicans. The Democrats won significant victories in congressional elections in the fall and winter of 1862, testifying to the depth and breadth of the opposition to Lincoln and his conduct of the war. Wealthy businessmen were eager to reestablish trade with their former Southern partners, whereas Irish immigrants wanted to end the risk of the draft and competition from freed slaves. Many citizens of Ohio, Indiana, and Illinois, whose families had come from the South, wanted to renew the Southern connections that had been broken by the war.

The Union passed its Conscription Act in March of 1863 because disease, wounds, and desertion had depleted the ranks of soldiers faster than they could be replaced. When drafted, a man could appear for duty, hire a substitute to fight in his place, or simply pay a fee

Black men had called for their inclusion in the U.S. Army from the beginning of the war. In the spring of 1863, the U.S. Colored Troops were formed and more than 180,000 African American men fought for the Union over the next 2 years.

© Kean Collection/Hulton Archive/Getty Images

This magazine illustration detailed the many tasks and great deeds performed by the U.S. Colored Troops in one of their earliest challenges, at the Battle of Milliken's Bend in Louisiana.

of $300 directly to the government. Poorer communities resented the wealthy who could avoid service. Demonstrations broke out in Chicago, Pennsylvania mining towns, Ohio, rural Vermont, and Boston. State and federal governments often paid bounties—signing bonuses—to those who volunteered. More than a few men took the bounties and then promptly deserted and moved to another locality to claim another bounty.

The opposition to the Lincoln government raised crucial issues. With the North claiming to fight for liberty, what limitations on freedom of speech and protest could it enforce? A Democratic congressman from Ohio, Clement Vallandigham, tested those limits in the spring of 1863. Hating both secessionists and abolitionists, Vallandigham refused to obey a general's orders to stop criticizing the Lincoln administration. He was arrested, tried before a military court, and sentenced to imprisonment for the rest of the war. Lincoln was dismayed by these events. He commuted Vallandigham's sentence, sending him to the Confederates in Tennessee, hoping to make

Vallandigham appear a Southern sympathizer rather than a martyr to the cause of free speech. Vallandigham quickly escaped to Canada, however, where he continued his criticisms. Ohio Democrats defiantly nominated Vallandigham for governor in the elections to be held in the fall of 1863. If things continued to go badly for the Union, who knew what kind of success a critic of Lincoln might find?

African American Soldiers

Though Northern civilian and military leaders remained deeply divided and ambivalent about black freedom, it became clear to everyone that black men could be of great value to the Union. In May 1863, the War Department created the Bureau of Colored Troops.

African American men from across the North rushed to enlist as soon as they heard of the new black regiments.

At first, black recruits found themselves restricted to noncombat roles and a lower rate of pay: $10 a month versus the $13 a month and $3.50 clothing allowance given to white soldiers. Black men, though eager to serve, protested that they could not support their families on such amounts. African Americans knew, and coveted, the rights and privileges of other Americans. They wrote petitions and appealed to higher authorities, often in the language of the Declaration of Independence and the Constitution.

Confederate officials who expected black soldiers to make reluctant or cowed fighters soon discovered otherwise. In May of 1863, two black regiments stormed, seven times, a heavily fortified Confederate installation at Port Hudson, Louisiana. Soon thereafter, black soldiers found themselves on the other side of the barricades. At Milliken's Bend, Louisiana, they fought Confederates hand-to-hand. Northern newspapers echoed the words of praise from generals in the field: "No troops could be more determined or more daring."

Encouraged and frequently supported financially by their communities, African American men in the North went to the recruiting tables in great numbers. Frederick Douglass, the leading spokesman for black Americans, celebrated the enlistments: "Once let the black man get upon his person the brass letters, *U.S.;* let him get an eagle on his button, and a musket on his shoulder, and bullets in his pocket, and there is no power on earth which can deny that he has earned the right to citizenship in the United States." From Rhode Island to Ohio, black troops prepared to head south.

The Battlefields of Summer: 1863

Everything seemed in place for a climactic culmination of the war in the summer of 1863. The Union had almost severed the western half of the Confederacy from the eastern; the Federal army had penetrated deep into Tennessee and stood on the threshold of Georgia. On the other hand, Confederate armies maintained their morale and learned to make the most of their advantages.

Vicksburg and Chancellorsville

Union leaders needed all the help they could get in early 1863. Grant and Sherman remained frustrated in their goal of seizing Vicksburg; Rosecrans faced Bragg in Tennessee; Lee's army had yet to be decisively defeated despite the men, resources, and determination thrown into battle against him. Lee would face General Joseph Hooker, whom Lincoln had chosen to replace Ambrose Burnside. Throughout the spring, "Fighting Joe" Hooker energized his men and repaired some of the damage to morale and readiness inflicted at Fredericksburg. But no one knew if he would be able to handle Lee.

The Northern public was especially impatient with Grant and Sherman. Grant knew the delays threatened his command. Vicksburg, heavily fortified by both geography and the Confederates, seemed most vulnerable to attack from the southeast, but to get there Grant would have to find a way to move his men across the Mississippi River without landing them in swamps. Throughout the long wet winter, Grant had tried one experiment after another, including digging canals. Nothing worked.

Grant finally decided on a bold move: he would run a flotilla of gunboats and barges past Vicksburg under the cover of night to ferry his men across the Mississippi south of the city, where the land was better (see Map 15.1). The guns of Vicksburg stood 200 feet above the river, ready to fire down on any passing craft, but the Union men covered their ships' boilers with sacks of grain and bales of cotton to protect them from the shelling. Most of the boats made it through. Grant had Sherman create a diversion, confusing the Confederates, and then ferried his entire army across the Mississippi. Grant's army remained vulnerable, cut off from his allies and his major supply base, but by mid-May, Grant had fought four battles, cost the South 8,000 dead and wounded, marched 200 miles, and pinned 30,000 Confederates within Vicksburg's fortifications.

In the same week Grant made his landing near Vicksburg, Hooker began his attack on Lee, still based in Fredericksburg (see Map 15.2). Hooker commanded 130,000 men. Unlike Burnside, however, Hooker intended to outsmart Lee rather than try to overwhelm him with numbers. A large Union force would sweep around Lee and attack him from behind, even as another force attacked from the front. To keep from being bottled up in Fredericksburg, Lee would have to emerge from his well-entrenched defensive position. Lee met this bold move with an even bolder one. He would divide his forces and send Stonewall Jackson to attack Hooker's

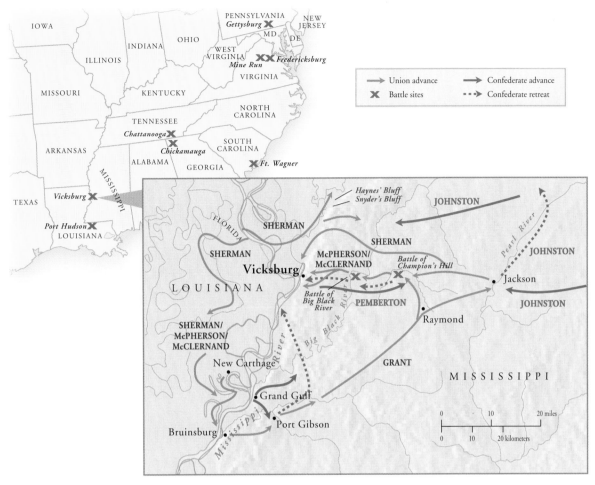

MAP 15.1 **Vicksburg**

After months of frustration, Ulysses S. Grant and William T. Sherman found a way to attack Vicksburg from the south and east. Following great struggle, the Union generals were able to take the city on July 4, 1863. View an animated version of this map or related maps at http://history.wadsworth.com/passages3e.

men from the rear, outflanking Hooker's own flanking maneuver.

On May 2, Jackson assaulted Hooker's troops near Chancellorsville. The outnumbered Confederates defeated the surprised and indecisive Hooker, achieving a major victory. Southern jubilation, though, ended the very night of this triumph, for nervous Confederate soldiers accidentally shot Stonewall Jackson while he surveyed the scene near the front lines. The surgeons removed his arm that evening and hoped that he might live.

While Jackson lay in his tent, fading in and out of consciousness, Lee managed to contain another assault on Fredericksburg and to push the Union troops away from their positions. The losses had once again been staggering—13,000 casualties, roughly 22 percent of the army—but Lee had overcome a larger opponent. After the last battles quieted, however, Jackson died. His death took with it Lee's most skillful general.

Gettysburg

Despite his victory at Chancellorsville, Lee recognized that the Confederacy was in trouble. Rosecrans still threatened to break through Tennessee into Georgia, Grant clawed his way closer to Vicksburg, and the Union blockade drew an ever tighter net around the

DOING HISTORY ONLINE

The Civil War and the Mississippi River

Access the module, locate the Mississippi River, and then "play" the interactive map. According to the map, how did the river affect the course of the war?

History NOW™   Visit HistoryNOW to access primary sources and exercises related to this topic: http://now.ilrn.com/ayers_etal3e

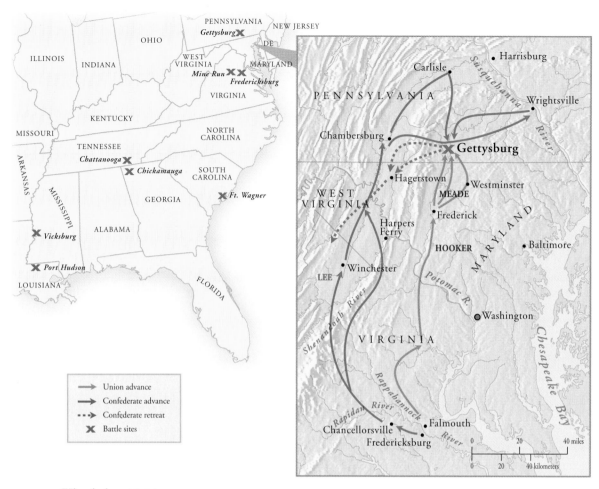

MAP 15.2 **Virginia, 1863**

The battle of Chancellorsville, not far from Fredericksburg, was a great victory for the Confederates. But it marked just the opening stage of a long summer of fighting that would culminate at Gettysburg two months later. In that battle, the Confederates sorely missed General Stonewall Jackson, accidentally killed by his own troops at Chancellorsville. View an animated version of this map or related maps at http://history.wadsworth.com/passages3e.

coast. Some of his generals urged Lee to rush with his troops to Tennessee to defend the center of the Confederacy and pull Grant away from Vicksburg. But Lee decided that his most effective move would be to invade the North again, taking the pressure off Virginia and disheartening the Union. A successful strike into the North might even yet persuade Britain and France to recognize the Confederacy and give heart to Peace Democrats in the North.

In early June, Lee began to move up through the Shenandoah Valley into southern Pennsylvania with 75,000 men. Hooker seemed confused. When, after a minor dispute, Hooker offered his resignation to Lincoln, the president quickly accepted and put General George Meade in charge. Meade had to decide how best to stop the greatest threat the Confederate army had yet posed to the North. Washington and Baltimore lay in danger, along with the cities, towns, and farms of Pennsylvania.

There, the Confederate troops enjoyed taking food and livestock from the rich land. Free blacks and fugitive slaves were also seized and forced south into slavery.

Although Lee and his men moved unchecked across the Potomac and deep into Pennsylvania, they found themselves in a dangerous situation. Lee had permitted Jeb Stuart's cavalry, his "eyes," to range widely from the main army; as a result, the Confederates had little idea where the Union army was or what moves it was making. For their part, Meade and his fellow officers decided to pursue Lee, but not too aggressively, looking for a likely time and place to confront the enemy.

On June 30, units from the Confederacy and the Union stumbled over one another at a small town neither side knew or cared much about: Gettysburg. On July 1, they began to struggle for the best defensive position near the town, fighting over the highest and most protected land. It appeared at first that the Southerners had

The battle at Gettysburg, in an obscure town in southern Pennsylvania, provided some of the most memorable struggles of the entire war, especially the Confederate charge up an unprotected slope to Cemetery Ridge, where massed Union troops awaited.

the better of the first day's battle, but as the smoke cleared both sides could see that late in the day the Union army had consolidated itself on the most advantageous ground. Meade's men, after fierce fighting at the ends of their line, occupied a fishhook-shaped series of ridges and hills that permitted them to protect their flanks. The second day saw the Confederates slowly mobilize their forces for assaults on those positions and launch attacks late in the afternoon. The resulting battles in the peach orchard, the wheat field, Little Round Top, and the boulder-strewn area known as the Devil's Den proved horrific—with 35,000 men dead or wounded—but left the Union in control of the high ground.

Despite the Union's superior position, Lee decided on a frontal attack the next day. The Confederates hoped their artillery would soften the middle of the Union lines. The Confederates did not realize how little damage their guns had done until well-entrenched Union troops decimated waves of an attack led by George E. Pickett. Only a few Southern men made it to the stone wall that protected the Northerners, and even those Confederates quickly fell. It proved a disastrous three days for the Army of Northern Virginia, which lost 23,000 men through death or wounds, about a third of its entire force. While the Union lost similar numbers of men, it had more to lose. The Northerners and their new general had fought a defensive battle; the Southern side, short of supplies and men, had gambled on an aggressive assault. Elation swept the North. "The glorious success of the Army of the Potomac has electrified all," a Northerner exulted. In the wake of Chancellorsville

and Lee's apparently effortless invasion of Pennsylvania, he admitted, many Northerners "did not believe the enemy could be whipped."

The next morning, a thousand miles away, Vicksburg surrendered to Ulysses S. Grant. Unlike Gettysburg, where the battle had been fought in a place no one considered strategically crucial, Vicksburg held enormous tactical and psychological importance. It had been the symbol of Confederate doggedness and Union frustration. After six weeks of siege, after six weeks of near starvation behind the Confederate defenses, Vicksburg fell. The Mississippi River now divided the Confederacy while it tied the Union to the Gulf of Mexico.

Some Southerners, including Jefferson Davis, did not perceive Gettysburg as a defeat. In their eyes, Lee and his men had pushed deep into the Union, inflicted heavy losses, and damaged Northern morale without being trapped there. Northerners at the time often agreed that Gettysburg had not been a decisive Union victory, pronouncing themselves more frustrated than satisfied with Meade, who had not destroyed Lee's army despite his greater numbers. During the Confederate retreat to Virginia, the Southerners found themselves caught between a swollen Potomac River and pursuing federal troops. Meade, his army exhausted and weakened, chose not to fight against the defenses Lee's men hurriedly put up against their pursuers. Meade could not know that the condition of the Southern troops was even worse than his own. Fortunately for the Confederates, the river soon calmed enough that they were able to escape back into Virginia.

The New York City Draft Riots

On the very day that Lee struggled across the Potomac to safety, riots broke out in New York City. Northern working people had complicated feelings about the war. Many of those who labored in the North's factories, mines, farms, and railroads had come to the United States during the previous 15 years. These people, mostly Irish and Germans, volunteered in large numbers to fight for the Union cause. Between 20 and 25 percent of the Union Army consisted of immigrants, the great majority of them volunteers.

Despite their patriotism for their adopted country, many of the immigrants viewed black Americans with dread and contempt. Urban labor organizations divided over Lincoln's election and over the response to secession. Many Catholic Irishmen, almost all of them Democrats, proclaimed that they had no quarrel with white Southerners and that they resented the federal

Flashpoints | The New York City Draft Riots

In March 1863 the government enacted a conscription law, making all men between 20 and 45 years of age liable for military service. Unlike today's Selective Service, this federal draft used crude encouragements to get men to "volunteer."

Quotas were assigned to each community, quotas that could be filled by voluntary enlistments, sparing the town further call-ups. While communities worked to fill their allotments with volunteers, many, particularly larger urban areas, fell short. Northern farmers and workers bitterly resented that the law permitted wealthier citizens the chance to hire a substitute to serve in his place for a fee of $300. The monies collected would be paid as enlistment bonuses to volunteers, particularly experienced veterans whose enlistments were expiring. Some towns and employers paid the commutation fee for poorer residents.

Roughly 133,000 men were drafted, but 60 percent paid the fee to escape service. Peace Democrats across the North took up the cry, "a rich man's war, but a poor man's fight!" to rally opposition to the draft, to Lincoln, and the continuation of the war. Military provosts attempted to enforce conscription across the North. Men resisted or fled; some sold themselves as substitutes several times and promptly deserted.

The attempt to enforce the draft in New York City on July 13 ignited the most destructive civil disturbance in the city's history. Rioters torched government buildings, and, on July 15, fought pitched battles with troops rushed from their recent victory at Gettysburg. Conservative contemporary commentators, concerned about an anti-Union plot, claimed that 1,155 people were killed. In fact, about 300, over half of them policemen and soldiers, were injured, and there were no more than 119 fatalities, mostly free blacks and rioters.

A majority of the rioters were Irish who lived in poverty and were likely candidates for the draft. They linked the draft to Lincoln's call for slave emancipation and they turned their anger at the draft against New York's black population. Many innocent blacks were slain and their homes sacked. A Colored Orphan Asylum was razed to the ground. White workers in New York City destroyed the central recruiting station, rail lines, small factories and homes of wealthy citizens. Similar protests erupted in Boston, Toledo, Newark, and Troy, New York.

Following the riots and resistance to the draft across the North, Lincoln repealed the draft in 1864 and expanded the enlistment bounty system. Immigrants and black men became the targets of recruitment efforts. By 1865, 25 percent of the recruits were immigrants and 10 percent were black. Conscripts never amounted to more that 2 percent of total army strength out of a 2.1 million man armed force.

Questions for Reflection

1. Should we be surprised by the draft riots?

2. Was the Civil War a war that fell especially hard on the poor?

3. Why did the Confederacy not have riots of similar size and effect?

---

government's draft. The obvious effect of inflation on the wages of workers created strong resentments as well. Working people sneered at those men who had enough money to hire substitutes to fight in their place. Three hundred dollars, after all, constituted half a year's wage for a workingman.

Irish immigrants despaired at the losses among Irish-American units in the field. When their regiments were decimated at Fredericksburg, Gettysburg, and elsewhere, Irish people began to wonder if commanders valued their lives as highly as those of the native-born. When word came—just as the draft lottery was to take place in New York City on July 11, 1863—of the 23,000 men lost at Gettysburg, the fury of working people rose. On July 13, it exploded. Mobs began by assaulting draft officials, then turned their anger on any man who looked rich enough to have hired a substitute, then on pro-Lincoln newspapers and abolitionists' homes. They assaulted any African Americans they encountered on the streets, burning an orphanage, whipping men and women, and hanging

Riots in New York City were triggered by an impending draft lottery and by news from Gettysburg that told of heavy Union losses there. Black Americans suffered the most from the riots.

victims from city lampposts. Lincoln was sickened by accounts of the riot and a city editor despaired, "Great God! What is this nation coming to?"

The police struggled for three days to control the riot. Eventually, troops (including all-Irish units) rushed from the battlefields of Pennsylvania to aid the police. The troops fired into the rioters; more than a hundred people died and another 300 were injured. The working people got some of what they wanted: more welfare relief, exemptions from the draft for those whose families would have no other means of support, and an exodus of black people who feared for their lives.

Ironically, a few days after the New York **draft riots,** scores of black troops died during a bold nighttime assault on Fort Wagner near Charleston, South Carolina. Despite the bravery of the African Americans, the assault failed. The Confederates made a point of burying the African American soldiers in a mass grave along with their white officer, Robert Gould Shaw, intending to insult him and his memory. Instead, they elevated him to a Northern martyr. The *Atlantic Monthly* marked a change in Northern attitudes toward black soldiers: "Through the cannon smoke of that dark night, the manhood of the colored race shines before many eyes that would not see."

Chickamauga

After Gettysburg, Vicksburg, and the New York riots in July, events slowed until September, when Union General William Rosecrans left Chattanooga, near the Georgia border, and began moving toward Atlanta. His opponent, Braxton Bragg, hoped to entice Rosecrans

into dividing his forces so that they could be cut off. The armies confronted one another at Chickamauga Creek—a Cherokee name meaning "river of death." The Confederates took advantage of Union mistakes on the heavily wooded battlefield, inflicting harrowing damage and driving Rosecrans back into Chattanooga. The Union troops were trapped there, the Confederates looming over them on Lookout Mountain and Missionary Ridge, with few routes of escape and limited supplies. The Northerners had gone from a position of apparent advantage to one of desperation.

Lincoln, judging Rosecrans "confused and stunned" by the battle at Chickamauga, used this opportunity to put Grant in charge of all Union armies between the Appalachian Mountains and the Mississippi River. In the fall of 1863, Grant traveled to Chattanooga, where Sherman joined him from Mississippi and Hooker came from Virginia.

The Gettysburg Address

The North's victories in the summer of 1863 aided Lincoln's popularity. The draft riots in New York City damaged the reputations of Democrats, whereas the bravery of black soldiers on the battlefields of Louisiana and South Carolina led white Northerners, particularly Union soldiers, to rethink some of their prejudices. In the fall of 1863, the Republicans won major victories in Pennsylvania and Ohio. Lincoln determined to make the most of these heartening events.

When Lincoln received an invitation to speak at the dedication of the cemetery at Gettysburg on November 19, he saw it as a chance to impart a sense of direction and purpose to the Union cause. The event had not been planned with him in mind and the president was not even the featured speaker. But Lincoln recognized

---

DOING HISTORY ONLINE

Chickamauga and the Civil War

Study the map for the years 1864 and 1865 and read the sections in the text from "Chickamauga" through "Union Resolve." Explain why the Union victory at Chickamauga was so significant.

History ⌛ Now™   Visit HistoryNOW to access primary sources and exercises related to this topic: http://now.ilrn.com/ayers_etal3e

DOING HISTORY

Freedom's Promise

PERHAPS THE MOST influential and memorable brief passage in American history, Lincoln's "remarks" at the opening of the Gettysburg battlefield in November 1863 articulated the highest ideals with which the war could be associated. The letter to the Union Convention in Nashville documents the insistence by black Americans that the "new birth of freedom" embrace those who had been formerly held in slavery. They received no response.

Abraham Lincoln, "The Gettysburg Address"

Four score and seven years ago our fathers brought forth on this continent, a new nation, conceived in Liberty, and dedicated to the proposition that all men are created equal.

Now we are engaged in a great civil war, testing whether that nation, or any nation so conceived and so dedicated, can long endure. We are met on a great battle-field of that war. We have come to dedicate a portion of that field, as a final resting place for those who here gave lives that that nation might live. It is altogether fitting and proper that we should do this.

But, in a larger sense, we can not dedicate—we can not consecrate—we can not hallow—this ground. The brave men, living and dead, who struggled here, have consecrated it, far above our poor power to add or detract. The world will little note, nor long remember what we say here, but it can never forget what they did here. It is for us the living, rather, to be dedicated here to the unfinished work which they who fought here have thus far so nobly advanced. It is rather for us to be here dedicated to the great task remaining before us—that from these honored dead we take increased devotion to that cause for which they have the last full measure of devotion—that we here highly resolve that these dead shall not have died in vain—that this nation, under God, shall have a new birth of freedom—and that government of the people, by the people, for the people, shall not perish from the earth.

Black Citizens of Tennessee, "Letter to the Union Convention 1865"

To the Union Convention of Tennessee Assembled in the Capitol at Nashville, January 9, 1865:

We claim to be men belonging to the great human family, descended from one great God, who is the common Father of all, and who bestowed on all races and tribes the priceless right of freedom. . . . We know the burdens of citizenship, and are ready to bear them. We know the duties of the good citizen, and are ready to perform them cheerfully, and would ask to be put in a position in which we can discharge them more effectually. . . . This is a democracy—a government of the people. It should aim to make every man, without regard to the color of his skin, the amount of his wealth, or the character of his religious faith, feel personally interested in its welfare.

Source: Roy P. Basler, ed., *Collected Works of Abraham Lincoln,* Vol. VII (New Brunswick, NJ: Rutgers University Press, 1953), p. 23; Ira Berlin et al., eds., *Free At Last: A Documentary History of Slavery, Freedom, and the Civil War* (New York: New Press, 1992), pp. 497–505.

Questions for Reflection

1. Why did Abraham Lincoln not mention slavery directly in his remarks?

2. What other themes might Lincoln have evoked that he did not? What is the general tone of his brief speech? How was that tone shaped by the setting?

3. What unified the Gettysburg Address and the letter to the Union Convention? Did anything divide them?

4. Why would the white Unionists to whom the black petitioners wrote this letter not be receptive to this eloquent plea?

5. How did Republicans renounce Lincoln's goals in 1877?

Explore additional primary sources related to this chapter on the Wadsworth American History Resource Center or HistoryNOW websites:

http://history.wadsworth.com/rc/us
http://now.ilrn.com/ayers_etal3e

that a battlefield offered the most effective backdrop for the things he wanted to say.

Burial crews had been laboring for weeks on the Gettysburg battlefield. Thousands of horse carcasses had been burned; thousands of human bodies had been hastily covered with a thin layer of soil. Pennsylvania purchased 17 acres and hired a specialist in rural cemetery design to lay out the burial plots so that no state would be offended by the location or amount of space devoted to its fallen men. Only about a third of the reburials had taken place when Lincoln arrived; caskets remained stacked at the station.

Lincoln, contrary to legend, did not dash off his speech on the back of an envelope. He had reworked and polished it for several days. The "remarks," as the program put it, lasted three minutes. Lincoln used those minutes to maximum effect. He said virtually nothing about the details of the scene surrounding the 20,000 people at the ceremony. Neither did he mention slavery directly. Instead, he spoke of equality as the fundamental purpose of the war. He called for a "new birth of freedom."

Lincoln was attempting to shift the purpose of the war from Union for Union's sake to Union for freedom's sake. He sought to salvage something from the deaths of the 50,000 men at Gettysburg. Democratic newspapers rebuked Lincoln for his claim, arguing that white soldiers had "too much self-respect to declare that negroes were their equals." But other Northerners accepted Lincoln's exhortation as the definition of their purpose. They might not believe that blacks deserved to be included as full participants in a government of, by, and for "the people," but they did believe that the Union fought for liberty broadly conceived. As battles and years went by, the words of the **Gettysburg Address** would gain force and resonance.

Just 4 days after Lincoln's speech, Grant gave the North new reason to believe its ideals might triumph. On November 23, Grant's men overwhelmed the Confederates on Lookout Mountain outside Chattanooga; 2 days later, Union soldiers shocked the Confederates by fighting their way up the steep Missionary Ridge because Confederate artillery could not reach opponents coming up directly from below. The Union, now in control of the cities and rail junctions of Kentucky and Tennessee, had a wide and direct route into Georgia.

England and France finally determined in late 1863 that they would not try to intervene in the American war. First Britain, then France detained or sold to foreign powers warships intended for the Confederacy. The Northern public, encouraged by events on the battlefield, supported Republican candidates in the congressional elections of 1863 more vigorously than had seemed possible just a few months before.

The Winter of Discontent: 1863–1864

The battles of the summer had been horrific. Both sides held their victories close to their hearts and brooded over their losses. The resolve and fury of summertime faded into the bitterness and bickering of winter. As the cycle rolled around again, people steeled themselves for another bloody year of war.

Politics North and South

Lincoln hoped to end the war as soon as possible, using persuasion as well as fighting to entice white Southerners back into the national fold. In early December 1863, Lincoln issued his proclamation of amnesty and reconstruction. To those who would take an oath of loyalty to the Union, Lincoln promised a full pardon and the return of all property other than slaves. Though he excluded Confederate leaders and high officers from this offer, Lincoln tried to include as many white Southern men as possible. As soon as 10 percent of the number of voters in 1860 had sworn their loyalty to the Union, he decreed, those Southerners could begin forming new state governments. Education and apprenticeship programs would aid former slaves in the transition to full freedom. He did not provide for African American participation in these new governments of the South.

Two factors worked against acceptance of Lincoln's policy. First, Northern Republicans and much of the public overestimated the extent and depth of Southern Unionist sentiment after years of war and occupation. Second, even in areas under federal control such as Tennessee and Kentucky, guerrilla bands and raiders terrorized the local population. Elections in parts of Tennessee were blocked by irregulars. "The people are warned . . . not to hold such an Election under pain of being Arrested and Carried South for trial," one observer reported. Civilians were often caught between threats. Those who failed to aid Union forces were perceived as "enemies of mankind" with "the rights due to pirates and robbers," whereas those who actively aided the Federals were liable to find crops trampled, barns burned, and vigilante justice enacted by neighbors and guerrillas. Politics frequently offered an excuse for acting on old rivalries, for murder and pillaging.

Abolitionists and their allies attacked Lincoln's reconstruction plan as far too lenient to the Rebel masters and not helpful enough for the former slaves. In the Wade-Davis bill of February 1864, Republican congressmen attempted to inflict more stringent conditions on former Confederates and offer more help to former slaves. They wanted to use the power of the national government to enforce a standard set of laws across the South and to require 50 percent, rather than 10 percent, of the population to swear the loyalty oath, an oath of past as well as future loyalty. They feared that too weak a plan of reconstruction would permit former slaveowners and Confederates to negate much of what the war might win. Congressmen and Secretary of the Treasury Salmon P. Chase worked behind the scenes in opposition to Lincoln's plan. With an eye toward the upcoming election and the need to entice Arkansas and Louisiana to rejoin the Union, Lincoln refused to sign the Wade-Davis bill.

Although Jefferson Davis did not have to worry about his own reelection in late 1863—the Confederacy had established the presidential term at six years—he did have to worry about congressional elections. They did not go well: 41 of the new 106 representatives expressly opposed Davis and his policies, and he held only a slight majority in the Senate. Just as Northern Democrats called for compromise and peace, so did some Southerners. When Davis took a hands-off policy, he was criticized for doing too little. When he tried to assert more control, he found himself called "despotic" by his own vice president. Editors savaged Davis as responsible for the South's worsening fortunes: "Had the people dreamed that Mr. Davis would carry all his chronic antipathies, his bitter prejudices, his puerile partialities, and his doting favoritisms into the Presidential chair, they would never have allowed him to fill it." The Confederacy stumbled through the winter and into the spring of 1864, desperately watching for signs that the North might be losing heart.

Prisons

Early in the Civil War, both sides had exchanged prisoners of war rather than spending men and resources to maintain prisons. Such arrangements worked well enough into 1863, but then things began to break down. The Confederates decreed that any former slave captured would be executed or re-enslaved, not taken prisoner. The Union, as a matter of principle, refused to participate in any exchanges so long as this policy remained in effect. Prisoners began piling up on both sides, and stories of mistreatment became more frequent and more horrifying.

Northerners became livid when they heard about conditions at the Confederate camp at Andersonville, Georgia. The camp was built early in 1864 when the Confederates decided to move prisoners from Richmond. Not only would prisoners be less likely to be rescued by Northern troops moving south, but supplies could more easily be transported by railroad away from the heavy fighting in Virginia. The camp, built for 10,000 men in an open, partly swampy field, soon became overcrowded; it held 33,000 by August. Gangs of Northern soldiers controlled daily life within the prison, routinely beating and robbing new arrivals. Of the 45,000 men eventually held at Andersonville, 13,000 died from exposure, starvation, and brutality. The camp's commander, Colonel Henry Wirz, was the only Confederate official executed for war crimes after the war.

Even higher proportions died at smaller camps in North Carolina. Although Confederates held in Northern prisons were better supplied, even there, death rates reached as high as 24 percent with rations often short and men reduced to eating rats. Overall, about 16 percent of Northern soldiers and 12 percent of Southerners died in prison. Many in the North criticized Lincoln for refusing to reinstitute exchanges, but Lincoln would not sacrifice the former slaves. Moreover, he knew that exchanges helped the soldier-starved Confederacy more than they did the North.

Union Resolve

In March 1864, Lincoln gave new direction and purpose to the Union effort by putting Ulysses S. Grant in charge of all Northern forces. Grant and Lincoln agreed that the Union had to use its superiority in materiel, manpower, and navy to attack the Confederacy on every front at once, forcing the South to decide what territory it would sacrifice. While Grant would fight in Virginia (see Map 15.3), Lincoln left **William T. Sherman** in charge in Chattanooga. Sherman would attack the railroad center of Atlanta, cutting the Gulf South off from the Upper South. The loss of Atlanta would chop the Confederacy into pieces too small to resist the Northern army.

In retrospect, the events of 1864 may appear anticlimactic. The Confederates seemed to face

This Confederate prisoner of war camp in Andersonville, Georgia, witnessed great brutality and appalling death rates from disease and hunger.

© Bettmann/ CORBIS

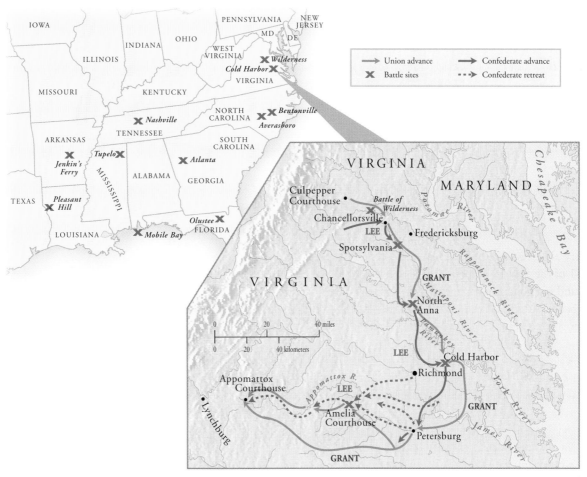

MAP 15.3 **Grant Against Lee in Virginia**
The two most important generals of the war confronted one another at one brutal battle after another between May 1864 and April 1865. View an animated version of this map or related maps at http://history.wadsworth.com/passages3e.

overwhelming odds. Yet Southerners recognized that everything turned around holding the Northerners off until the presidential election in the North. If the Southerners could inflict enough damage on the Union army, Northerners might elect someone willing to bring the war to an end through compromise. The Confederates knew, too, that the three-year terms of the most experienced veterans in the Union army expired in 1864. More than half of those veterans chose to leave the army, even though the war was not over. They would be replaced with younger, less seasoned soldiers. The Confederates also realized that Grant, new to his command, would be confronting Robert E. Lee, who was fighting with an experienced army. All things considered, it was by no means clear in 1864 that the Union would win in Virginia or win the war.

African Americans played an increasingly large role in Union plans, for more than 180,000 black soldiers enlisted just when the North needed them most. By the spring of 1864, the means of recruitment, training, and pay for these soldiers had become well established (see Map 15.4). The Confederates, however, refused to recognize the same rules of warfare for black soldiers that they acknowledged for whites. In April of 1864, at Fort Pillow in western Tennessee, Confederate cavalry under the command of Nathan Bedford Forrest shot down black Union soldiers and their white commander who attempted to surrender.

With the election clock running, Grant set out in May 1864 to destroy Lee's army. The Battle of the Wilderness near Chancellorsville saw brutal fighting and horrible losses. Fire in the tangled woods trapped wounded men, burning them alive. Grant lost more men than Hooker had in the battle of the previous year, but whereas Hooker treated such losses as a decisive defeat and retreated, Grant pushed on.

The two armies fought again and again over the next two months in the fields of Virginia. The Confederates

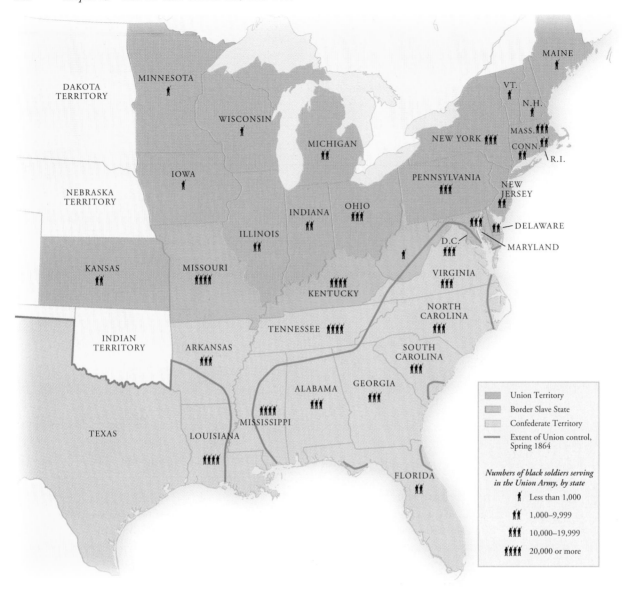

MAP15.4 Black Soldiers in the Union Army
African American men streamed into the U.S. Army from all across the country, but they were especially prominent in the occupied South where they had been enslaved.

turned the Union army back to the east of Richmond and rushed up the Shenandoah Valley to threaten Washington itself. Although they failed to take the capital, Confederate raiders "taxed" Maryland towns for thousands of dollars of greenbacks and burned the town of Chambersburg, Pennsylvania, when it refused to pay $500,000. The North repulsed the invasion and dispatched Philip Sheridan to the valley to make sure the Confederates did not regroup. With the Confederates pinned down in Petersburg, near Richmond, Pennsylvania coal miners volunteered to tunnel under the fortifications and plant explosives. Throughout July, they dug; finally, at the end of the month, they detonated a charge and blew an enormous crater in the Confederate lines.

DOING HISTORY ONLINE

Confederate Hopes

Read the document on the Aftermath of the Destruction of a Town Near Washington, D.C., 1864 and "play" the interactive map. Why could Confederates hold out hope of victory as late as 1864?

History ⧗ Now™   Visit HistoryNOW to access primary sources and exercises related to this topic: http://now.ilrn.com/ayers_etal3e

With the war driving to a culmination, the Republicans called themselves the "Union Party," nominated a Unionist from Tennessee alongside Lincoln, and painted pictures of peace and prosperity in their campaign poster.

This elaborate cartoon from New York City contrasts George McClellan's supposedly smooth ride to the White House on the "Union" train with President Lincoln's predicted "November Smash-up" caused by emancipation.

The attack that followed the explosion, however, failed. Union soldiers piled into the crater, where the rallying Confederates trapped them.

Fortunately for Lincoln, things were going better farther south. Throughout June and July, Sherman pushed relentlessly through north Georgia toward Atlanta. By the end of July, the Southern army had fallen back into Atlanta, preparing to defend it from siege. It seemed only a matter of time before the Union triumphed. But how much time? After rapidly advancing, federal troops slowed as they closed on Atlanta and many feared Sherman was "on the eve of disaster."

The Northern Election of 1864

The president had to fight off challenges even within his own party. Some Republicans considered Lincoln too radical; others considered him too cautious. Through adroit use of patronage, however, Lincoln managed to win renomination in June. The Republican party tried to broaden its appeal to Democrats by nominating **Andrew Johnson,** a former Democrat from Tennessee, to the vice presidency.

In the meantime, the Democrats confidently moved forward. They knew that in the eyes of his critics, Lincoln had caused the war, trampled on constitutional rights, consolidated too much power, and refused to end the war when he had a chance. The Democrats intended to take full advantage of such criticisms by nominating General George McClellan as their candidate. McClellan demonstrated that a person could oppose Lincoln's political purposes of the war without being a coward or traitor. McClellan and the Democrats portrayed themselves as the truly national party, for they were determined to restore the United States to its prewar unity and grandeur. McClellan said he would end the war if the South would reenter the Union—bringing slavery with it. It was a bargain that appealed to many in the North.

Just when it appeared that the Democrats would unseat Lincoln, however, news from the battlefield changed everything. Sherman swung around Atlanta and began destroying the railroads that made the

The Election of 1864

To attract Democrats who supported the war, Lincoln and the Republican leadership renamed their party the National Union party and chose a Southern Unionist, Senator Andrew Johnson of Tennessee, as vice president. Though Lincoln won easily in the electoral college vote, he faced strong opposition throughout much of the North from George McClellan, who claimed 45 percent of the popular vote.

With the popular vote so close, in many states the outcome hinged on the votes of soldiers. In earlier wars, when soldiers departed home for service, they no longer voted, so no provision existed in law or practice for military personnel to vote away from their home polling site. By 1864, thirteen states permitted soldiers to vote in the field, while five continued to disenfranchise soldiers. Democrats had opposed absentee voting because they suspected soldiers would vote Republican, but hoped that General McClellan still enjoyed the favor of soldiers. Democrats lobbied senior generals while crying fraud. After three years of war, soldiers in the field, even those who considered themselves loyal to McClellan, would not support the Democratic peace platform. A Union colonel, a staunch Democrat, wrote his wife, "I have not come across an officer or a man that will vote for McClellan." This had always been considered a Democratic corps, but these formerly loyal Democrats voted for Lincoln by a factor of 10 to 1. Compare the distribution of votes for Lincoln in 1864 and 1860 (page 395) and note the areas where Lincoln gained and lost support.

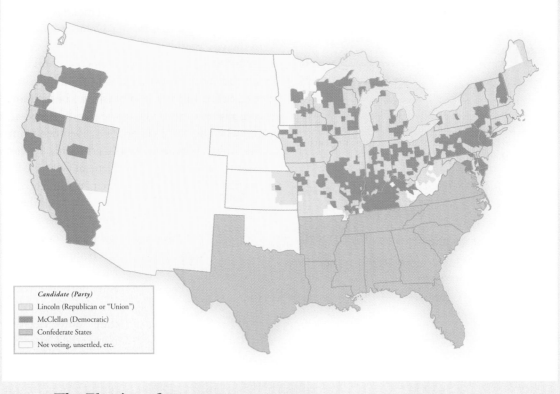

Candidate (Party)
- Lincoln (Republican or "Union")
- McClellan (Democratic)
- Confederate States
- Not voting, unsettled, etc.

MAP 15.5 **The Election of 1864**

small city an important junction. The Confederates, afraid they would be encircled and trapped within the city, set much of Atlanta on fire and abandoned it. Sherman and his army marched into the city on September 2. Two weeks later, Sheridan attacked the Confederates in the Shenandoah Valley, systematically destroying the valley's ability to support the Southern army again.

Even with these military victories, Lincoln won only 55 percent of the popular vote (see Map 15.5). Contrary to expectations, Lincoln carried the large majority of the armies' votes. In their letters, soldiers who identified themselves as Democrats rejected McClellan. A Vermont soldier who described himself as "a McClellan man clear to the bone" would not accept "peace by surrendering to the rebels"; instead "he would let his bones manure the soil of Virginia." Lincoln did much better in the electoral college, sweeping every state except three. The Republicans also elected heavy majorities to both houses of Congress and elected the governor and legislative majorities in all states except New Jersey, Delaware, and Kentucky. Lincoln believed the election validated the strength of republican government: "We can not have a free government without elections; and if the rebellion could force us to forego, or postpone a national election, it might fairly claim to have already conquered and ruined us."

The March to the Sea

Jefferson Davis traveled through the Lower South after the fall of Atlanta, exhorting citizens to remain defiant. A week after Lincoln's election, Sherman set out across Georgia, provisioning his army along the way, taking the war to the Southern people themselves. Such a march would be as much a demonstration of Northern power as a military maneuver: "If we can march a well-appointed army right through [Confederate] territory," Sherman argued, "it is a demonstration to the world, foreign and domestic, that we have a power which Davis cannot resist." The triumphant army of 60,000 made its way across the state throughout the fall of 1864. Large numbers of deserters from both sides, fugitive slaves, and outlaws took advantage of the situation to inflict widespread destruction and panic. Sherman arrived at Savannah on December 21. "I beg to present to you, as a Christmas gift, the city of Savannah," Sherman buoyantly telegraphed Lincoln. Contrasting with the devastation of the South, the president's annual message to Congress outlined a portrait of a North gaining strength with "more men now than we had when the war began . . . We are gaining strength, and may, if need be, maintain the contest indefinitely."

From War to Reconstruction: 1865–1867

As the war ground to a halt in early 1865, Americans had to wonder if they remembered how to share a country with their former enemies. They had to wonder, too, how different the country would be with African Americans no longer as slaves. Of all the changes the United States had ever seen, **emancipation** stood as the most profound.

War's Climax

Events moved quickly at the beginning of 1865. In January, Sherman issued **Special Field Order 15,** which reserved land in coastal South Carolina, Georgia, and Florida for former slaves. Those who settled on the land would receive 40-acre plots. Four days later, the Republicans in Congress passed the **Thirteenth Amendment,** abolishing slavery forever. Antislavery activists, black and white, packed the galleries and the House floor. Observers embraced, wept, and cheered. A Congressman wrote his wife that "we can now look other nations in the face without shame."

At the beginning of February, Sherman's troops began to march north into the Carolinas (see Map 15.6). Columbia, South Carolina, burned to the ground. Growing numbers of Confederate soldiers deserted from their armies. Lincoln met with Confederate officials at Hampton Roads on board the steamship *River Queen* to try to bring the war to an end, offering slaveowners compensation for their freed slaves if the Southerners would immediately cease the war. Jefferson Davis refused to submit to the "disgrace of surrender."

At the beginning of March, Lincoln was inaugurated for his second term. Rather than gloating at the impending victory on the battlefield, Lincoln called for his fellow citizens to "bind up the nation's wounds." That same month, Congress created the Bureau of Refugees, Freedmen, and Abandoned Lands to ease the transition from slavery to freedom. Nine days later, the Confederate government, after hotly debating whether to recruit slaves to fight as soldiers if their owners agreed, finally decided to do so after Lee, desperate for men, supported the measure.

Appomattox and Assassination

The Confederates' slave recruitment law did not have time to convert slaves to soldiers, for Grant soon began his final assault on Confederate troops in Virginia. Petersburg fell on April 2, Richmond the next day. Lee hoped to lead his army to the train station at **Appomattox** Court House to resupply them, but on April 9 Grant intercepted Lee's men just short of their destination. Lee, with nowhere else to go and no other armies to come to his aid, surrendered.

A number of Confederate armies had yet to surrender, and Jefferson Davis remained at large, but it was clear that the war had ended. Cities and towns across the North erupted in celebration and relief as crowds filled the streets to sing, embrace, fire salutes, and wave the flag. Southerners began to straggle home. Two days later, Lincoln addressed a Washington audience about what would come next for the freedmen. He admitted that Northerners differed "as to the mode, manner, and means of Reconstruction" and that the white South was "disorganized and discordant."

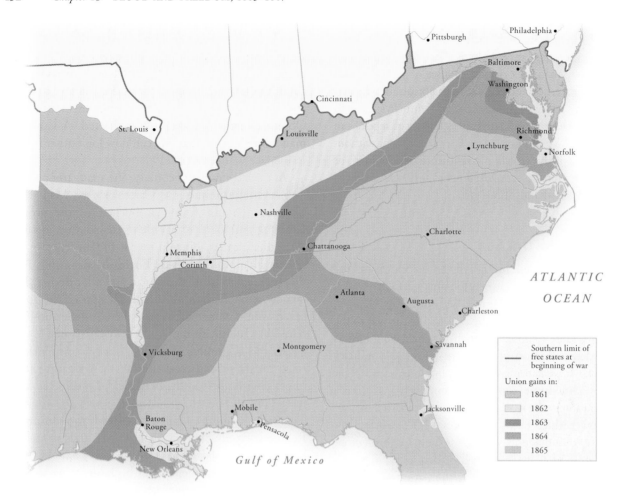

MAP 15.6 The Territory of War
The Confederacy managed to protect large parts of its interior throughout the war, but the Union increasingly controlled the crucial rivers, rail lines, and ports. View an animated version of this map or related maps at http://history.wadsworth.com/passages3e.

Lincoln did not live to take part in the planning, for he was assassinated on April 14 by **John Wilkes Booth,** a failed actor and Southern sympathizer. Booth attacked Lincoln while the president sat with Mrs. Lincoln at Ford's Theater in Washington, shooting him in the back of the head and then leaping to the stage. Lincoln never recovered consciousness; he died early the next morning. After a long and frantic search, Booth was captured and killed in a burning barn.

The Costs and Consequences of the War

The North lost almost 365,000 men to death and disease in the Civil War, and the South lost 260,000. Another 277,000 Northerners were wounded, along with 195,000 Southerners. Black Americans lost 37,000 men in the Union army and at least another 10,000 men, women, and children in the contraband camps.

Widows and orphans, black and white, Northern and Southern, faced decades of struggling without a male breadwinner. Many people found their emotional lives shattered by the war. Alcohol, drug abuse, crime, and violence became widespread problems.

The Southern slave-based economy collapsed. Major Southern cities had been reduced to ash. Railroads had been ripped from the ground, engines and cars burned. Fields had grown up weeds and brush. Farm values fell by half. Livestock, tools, barns, and fences had been stolen or destroyed by the armies of both sides. Recovery was slow. In Georgia, for example, as late as 1870 the state recorded 1 million fewer pigs, 200,000 fewer cattle, and 3 million fewer acres under cultivation than in 1860. Just as damaging in the long run, lines of credit had been severed. Before emancipation, planters had used their slaves as collateral for loans. Now, with the destruction of that form of "collateral," few people outside

This picture of Lincoln, taken 4 days before his assassination, shows the toll four years of war had taken on the 56-year-old president.

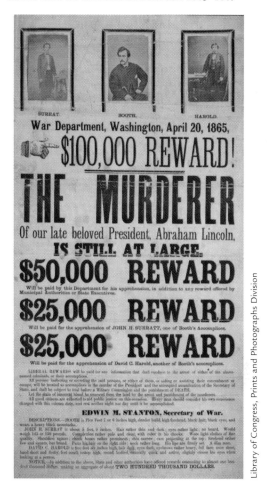

The United States put out this reward for John Wilkes Booth and his conspirators who had killed "our late beloved President."

the South were willing to loan money to planters or other investors.

The Civil War did not mark a sudden turn in the Northern economy, but it did accelerate processes already well under way. The nationalization of markets, the accumulation of wealth, and the consolidation of manufacturing firms became more marked after 1865. Greenbacks, bonds, and a national banking system regularized the flow of capital and spurred the growth of business. The Republicans passed the Department of Agriculture Act, the Morrill College Land Grant Act, the Homestead Act, and the Union Pacific Railroad Act, all using the power of the federal government to encourage settlement of the West, strengthen public education, and spur economic development.

Emancipation and the South

As the battles ground to a halt, slaves became former slaves. Some, especially the young, greeted freedom confidently,

whereas others, especially the elderly, could not help but be wary of anything so strange, no matter how long and how much they had prayed for it. Some seized their freedom at the first opportunity, taking their families to

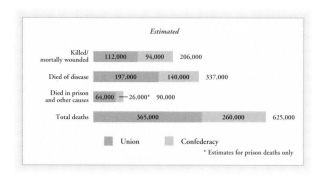

CHART 15.1 The Causes and Numbers of Civil War Deaths

Disease killed even more men than did the bullets of the enemy.

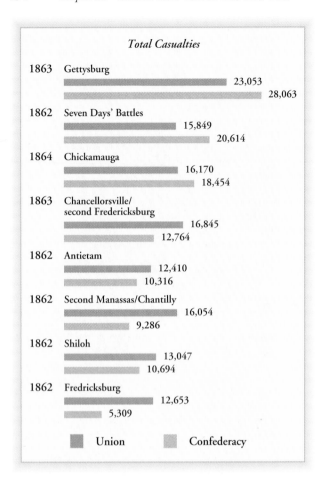

Total Casualties

Year	Battle	Union	Confederacy
1863	Gettysburg	23,053	28,063
1862	Seven Days' Battles	15,849	20,614
1864	Chickamauga	16,170	18,454
1863	Chancellorsville/second Fredericksburg	16,845	12,764
1862	Antietam	12,410	10,316
1862	Second Manassas/Chantilly	16,054	9,286
1862	Shiloh	13,047	10,694
1862	Fredericksburg	12,653	5,309

CHART 15.2 The Most Costly Battles
Battles exacted horrible costs from early in the war until near its very end.

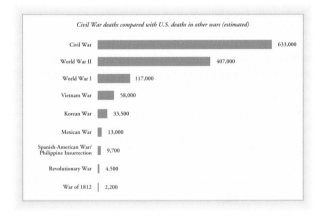

Civil War deaths compared with U.S. deaths in other wars (estimated)

Civil War	633,000
World War II	407,000
World War I	117,000
Vietnam War	58,000
Korean War	33,500
Mexican War	13,000
Spanish-American War/Philippine Insurrection	9,700
Revolutionary War	4,500
War of 1812	2,200

CHART 15.3 Civil War Losses
The Civil War exacted a horrible cost, far outstripping every other conflict in which the United States has fought.

Union camps or joining the army. Others celebrated when the Yankees came to their plantations, only to find that their owners and white neighbors retaliated when the soldiers left. Others bided their time. Some refused to believe the stories of freedom at all until their master

---

Picturing the Past ECONOMICS & TECHNOLOGY

Desolation of the South

After four years of war, little remained in many cities of the Confederacy. Atlanta, Columbia, and Richmond had been ravaged by fire; Vicksburg, Petersburg, and Fredericksburg had been pummeled by siege and battle. Union troops had destroyed railways, rivers were blocked by the refuse of war, and fields and farms had been stripped by the marauding troops of both sides or simply overrun by weeds. Roads, wagons, and riverboats were choked with civilian refugees, returning soldiers, and prisoners of war. In the countryside, even on farms and plantations

© Bettmann/CORBIS

untouched by combat, former slaves abandoned masters to seek family members and new opportunities.

Thousands of refugees from the countryside relied on federal aid and rations to survive. White women, particularly those from slaveholding families, found adjusting to defeat and emancipation trying. One woman from North Carolina bitterly lamented her transformation from "social queen" to "domestic drudge." African American women looked forward to working for the benefit of their own families.

or mistress called them together to announce that they were indeed no longer slaves.

Upon hearing the news, the freed people gathered to discuss their options. For many, the highest priority was to reunite their families. Such people set off on journeys

North Wind Picture Archives

Black Southerners took advantage of the presence of Union troops to leave the farms and plantations on which they had been held. Many set out to find family members.

in desperate efforts to find a husband, wife, child, or parent sold away in earlier years. For others, sheer survival was the highest priority. Freedom came in the late spring, barely in time to get crops in the ground. Some former slaves argued that their best bet was to stay where they were for the time being. They had heard rumors that the government would award them land. Between July and September of 1865, however, those dreams died. Union officers promised land to former slaves in Virginia, Louisiana, Mississippi, and South Carolina, but then Washington revoked the promises. The land would be returned to its former owners.

Former slaveowners also responded in many different ways. Some fled to Latin America. Others tried to keep as much of slavery as they could by whipping and chaining workers to keep them from leaving. Still others offered to let former slaves stay in their cabins and work for wages. The presence of black soldiers triggered resentment and fear among former slaveowners who marked the increased independence among blacks that was encouraged by "Negro troops." One slaveowner believed "the people of the South are in very great danger . . . I tell you most seriously that the whole south is resting upon a volcano."

African Americans had no choice but to compromise with white landowners. At first, in the spring of 1865, planters insisted that the former slaves work as they had worked before emancipation, in "gangs." In return for their work, they would receive a portion of the crop, shared among all the workers. Many black people chafed at this arrangement, preferring to work as individuals or families. In such places, landowners found that they had little choice but to permit black families to take primary responsibility for a portion of land.

The former slaves provided the labor and received part of the crop as a result. Planters, though reluctant to give up any control over the day-to-day work on their land, realized they had few choices. They possessed little cash to pay wage workers and no alternative labor.

The Bureau of Refugees, Freedmen, and Abandoned Lands—the **Freedmen's Bureau**—oversaw the transition from a slave economy to a wage economy. Its agents, approximately 900 for the entire South, dispensed medicine, food, and clothing from the vast stores of the federal government to displaced white and black Southerners. The Bureau created courts to adjudicate conflicts and to draw up labor contracts between landholders and laborers. It established schools and coordinated female volunteers who came from the North to teach in them. Although many white Southerners resented and resisted the Freedmen's Bureau, it helped smooth the transition from slavery to freedom, from war to peace.

© The Granger Collection, New York

The Freedmen's Bureau, created in the spring of 1865, adjudicated conflicts between white landowners and black workers.

Enduring Issues   Legacy of Civil War

When the final Confederate armies laid down their arms, the military phase of one of history's bloodiest civil wars ended. The vision of a short but heroic conflict was erased by the human cost of the war. Battle deaths and wounds were far from glorious. Many families, sundered by distance and the uncertainties of war, never recovered. Over 600,000 men died in battle, 4 million slaves gained their liberty, and tens of thousands of men, women, and children were displaced, injured, or died of disease and complications induced by hunger and want.

Both the political system and economy were fundamentally altered by the war. Politics became dominated by sharp-eyed career politicians who reigned over spoils and served the interests of the rising industrial barons. Railroad scandals, Tammany Hall, and graft in every state house seemed to mark a new, tawdry era in politics—Twain's Gilded Age, a bright and false covering masking a base low metal. Post-war Republicans waved the bloody shirt and dubbed their opponents, the Democrats, the party of "Rum, Romanism, and Rebellion," marking them as drunken, Catholic, and at fault for the Civil War. Democrats focused on the destruction of the Republican Party in the South. For much of the last half of the nineteenth century, the North and West dominated the federal government and the patronage and subsidies it controlled. For more than the next 50 years no Southerner would serve as President and a minority would be appointed to the Supreme Court.

Another outcome of the war was the departure from the federal government of representatives of the southern states and the defeat of many Democrats perceived as pro-southern. The Republican party enjoyed nearly 5 years of control of the American state. This dominance extended until the 1870s, with periodic Democratic successes in Congressional elections. From this near single-party control of the government came a series of policy decisions that served the party's core constituents and interest groups: western homesteads, Pacific and western rail construction, tariff protection for selected industries, pensions for Union veterans, and easy expansion of commercial and financial markets. The system of national currency made the federal government a tangible part of each economic transaction among its citizens. The scope and scale of the Civil War revealed the importance of finance, organization, industrialization, and efficiency. Andrew Carnegie learned lessons from his time at the Pennsylvania Railroad that would assist his creation of the world's largest integrated coal, iron, and steel empire after the war.

Although Jefferson Davis was imprisoned for 2 years, no Confederate general or senior official ever suffered more than temporary bars to voting and holding office. No treason trials or committees investigated the causes of the war or sought to punish leading rebels. There are no comparisons in world history to such bloody, hard-fought civil war ending in such a gentle peace for the defeated. Only the commandant of Andersonville prison, Col. Henry Wirz, charged with the deaths of 13,000 prisoners, was hanged for war crimes in 1865. Unlike most defeated rebels, southerners mounted no guerilla campaigns or seriously contemplated a second attempt at secession. Southerners reserved violence and midnight raids for crushing black demands for a just labor system.

Demobilization was swift after the war. The citizen-soldier had completed his duty and over 80 percent of the 1-million-man Union Army was discharged by summer of 1865. By the fall of 1866, the army had shrunk almost to its pre-war level. The integrated Union military, with 180,000 black soldiers and sailors, persisted in a few western cavalry regiments, but soon faded from public memory.

Each section had its caretakers of war's memory. In the South, women and veterans created organizations to celebrate the memory of military valor and dedication to community. Like Jefferson Davis' multi-thousand page "history" of the war, they made the war about defending states' rights and southern culture without mentioning slavery. Memorial parades, children's education, and a flood of memoirs combined to create the myth of the Lost Cause that influenced both popular and historical thinking about the Civil War for the hundred years after Appomattox. Northern veterans created the Grand Army of the Republic to keep the memory of Union victory alive, mobilize veterans for

Black Mobilization

Black Southerners mourned the loss of Abraham Lincoln. Without his leadership, former slaves rightly worried, the forces of reaction might overwhelm their freedom. Southerners of both races watched to see what Andrew Johnson might do.

Throughout the South, former slaves and former free blacks gathered in mass meetings, Union Leagues, and conventions to announce their vision of the new order. They wanted, above all else, equality before the law and the opportunity to vote. Their spokesmen did not demand confiscation of land, nor did they speak political rallies, pursue federal pensions, and instruct children in patriotic values. The flagpoles that stand outside public schools were the result of GAR activity to increase patriotic values in young children.

After the Civil War, the language and goals of reform spoke less to preparing for the millennium and saving souls and more to the interests of increasingly focused groups: women, blacks, immigrants, labor, skilled workers, temperance, suffrage, settlement houses. Reform became more secular, more targeted on issues of justice on earth: votes, wages, healthy and safe cities and food. The Fifteenth Amendment, granting suffrage to black men, split women's support for racial justice. Elizabeth Cady Stanton and Susan B. Anthony demanded the same rights for women recently granted to black men. Many Republicans who had aggressively supported legalized racial equality refused to risk their political future on a challenge to traditional roles for women. Women such as Mary Livermore recalled in her memoirs that she delivered over 8,000 suffrage lectures from coast to coast. Conservative women such a Lucy Stone advocated a more cautious change to women's public role. They supported suffrage, but rejected changes to the divorce laws that might put women at risk.

The federal pension program for Union veterans, which consumed an accelerating portion of the federal budget, brought little or no cash into the South. Southern states received little direct federal aid for rebuilding. Tariffs, treasury and monetary policy, transportation subsidies for the West, and federal patronage favored the North and West. Even cotton exports were subject to an excise tax that further withdrew scarce cash from the economy. Both Native Americans and former slavers found themselves subject to federal and state policies designed to uplift and civilize them, usually without soliciting their opinion of the policies. Where millions of dollars and hundreds of thousands of acres of western lands were granted to railroads and mining interests, no lands were set aside for former slaves, and native peoples were driven from desirable lands with water and gold to marginal territories stripped of buffalo, timber, and resources.

The Civil War settled the question of chattel slavery and secession forever. While the Thirteenth, Fourteenth, and Fifteenth Amendments and the Civil Rights Act of 1870 set a precedent for racial justice, little progress was made in eradicating racism. During the years of Reconstruction in the South, many black men served in state legislatures of southern states. Equality before the law, in the market, in education, and political participation were denied and fettered by law and custom across the country. Racism fused with popular ideas that social mobility was a function of hard work and character to make a vicious circle for black Americans. Many Americans saw only the absence of blacks in their schools, neighborhoods, and professions and believed that this proved black inferiority and lack of ambition.

The latter part of the nineteenth century witnessed the gradual construction of a system of racial segregation enforced by law and local violence. By 1915, millions of white Americans would applaud the era's first film blockbuster, *Birth of a Nation*. Endorsed by President Woodrow Wilson, the film inverted the war's results, celebrating the Ku Klux Klan and demonizing blacks, mulattoes, and Yankee carpetbaggers.

Many Americans looked back over the abyss of the war years and perceived a country and way of life permanently altered. Much of the rhetoric of free labor and independence grounded in an agricultural republic endured, but the realities of Americans' relationship to their government, freedom for 4 million slaves, the rapidly changing nature of the economy, and imminent explosive growth of the cities and immigrant populations signaled a very different nation than that men had marched to war to create or defend in 1861.

Questions for Reflection

1. Has there been any other event in American history that exerted an impact of the scale of the Civil War's impact?

2. What might the United States have looked like in, say, 1900, had there not been a Civil War?

3. What might we have expected the Civil War to change that it did not?

extensively of economic concerns in general. Let us have our basic rights before the courts and at the ballot box, they said, and we will take care of ourselves. Such concerns and confidence reflected the perspective of the conventions' leadership: former free blacks, skilled artisans, ministers, and teachers. The great mass of

Southern blacks, former slaves, found their concerns neglected.

Black Southerners agreed on the centrality of two institutions, however: the church and the school. At the very moment of freedom, they began to form their own churches. For generations, African Americans had

Picturing the Past — SOCIAL & CULTURAL EVENTS

A Black School

As growing numbers of African Americans gained literacy after emancipation, they increasingly taught in their own schools. To gain access to schools for their children and themselves, former slaves migrated to cities and towns and frequently demanded construction of a schoolhouse as a condition for signing a labor contract. Less than a month after the fall of Richmond, more than 1,000 black children and adults attended schools begun by the city's black churches.

Across the South, blacks organized and collected money to buy land, constructed schools with their own labor, and funded teacher salaries from self-imposed taxes and tuition. Teachers often advocated racial equality before the law and suffrage, as well as encouraging black political mobilization. Many Northern blacks, including a large number of women, helped found the first black colleges in the South, such as Fiske, Hampton, and Tougaloo. By 1869, black teachers outnumbered whites among the 3,000 teachers in the South.

been forced to worship alongside whites. For many ex-slaves, one of their first acts of freedom was to form their own churches. Before the war, 42,000 black Methodists in South Carolina attended biracial churches. By 1870, only 600 mostly elderly blacks remained. People who owned virtually nothing somehow built churches across the South. A black church in Charleston was the first building raised from the ruins of the city in 1865. Those churches often served as schools as well.

Andrew Johnson

In the meantime, events in Washington undermined the efforts of black Southerners to build a new world for themselves. Andrew Johnson wanted to attract moderates from both the North and the South to a political party that would change the nation as little as possible. Johnson had been selected to run for the vice presidency because he was a Southerner who had remained true to the Union. As a result, both Northerners and Southerners distrusted Johnson. A longtime Democrat before the crisis of the Union, Johnson maintained a limited view of government. The new president's well-known disdain for the wealthy planters of the South appealed to equally disdainful Republicans in Washington. His public statements suggested a harsh peace for former slaveowners and Confederate leaders: "*Treason* is a crime, and *crime* must be punished." Unlike some Republicans, however, Johnson held little sympathy for black people or for expansion of the powers of the federal government. Johnson saw himself pursuing Lincoln's highest goal: reuniting the Union. He believed that reunification should start by winning the support of white Southerners.

Johnson enjoyed a brief period to enact his vision of how to return the South to the Union. Congress was not

Andrew Johnson attempted to forge a new alliance between white Northerners and white Southerners, callously abandoning black Southerners in the process.

in session at the time of Lincoln's death and would not be for seven months, so Johnson used the opportunity to implement his vision of reunion. In what became known as "Presidential Reconstruction," Johnson offered amnesty to former Confederates who would take an oath of loyalty to the Union, restoring their political and civil rights and immunizing them against the seizure of their property or prosecution for treason. By 1866, Johnson granted more than 7,000 pardons to wealthy Southerners and Confederate senior officers who applied individually for amnesty.

Johnson's plans for political reunion made no provisions at all for black voting. Indeed, his plan threatened to return the South to even greater national power than it had held before because the entire African American population would now be considered individually when the number of representatives was calculated, not merely as three-fifths of a person as before the war.

White Southerners could hardly believe their good fortune. The state conventions elected in 1865 flaunted their opinions of the North. Some refused to fly the American flag, some refused to ratify the Thirteenth Amendment, some even refused to admit that secession had been illegal. Former Confederates filled important posts in state governments. Georgia elected Alexander H. Stephens, the ex-vice president of the aborted nation, to Congress. Even Johnson recognized that far from inaugurating new regimes led by Unionist yeomen, "there seems, in many of the elections something like defiance."

The North erupted in outrage when the new state governments enacted the so-called "**black codes,**" laws for controlling the former slaves. The Southern white legislatures granted only the barest minimum of rights to black people: the right to marry, to hold property, to sue and be sued. Most of the laws decreed what African Americans could not do: move from one job to another, own or rent land, testify in court, practice certain occupations. When the members of Congress convened in December of 1865, they reacted as many of their constituents did—with fury. To Northerners, even those inclined to deal leniently with the South, the former Confederates seemed to deny all the war had decided with this blatant attempt to retain racially based laws. And many Northerners blamed Johnson.

Johnson and the Radicals

It was not that most Northerners, even most Republicans, wanted the kind of policies promoted by Radicals such as Thaddeus Stevens, who called for land to be seized from wealthy planters and given to the former slaves, or of Charles Sumner, who wanted immediate and universal suffrage for blacks. But neither did they

Thaddeus Stevens, a congressman from Pennsylvania, was among the leaders of the Radical Republicans.

want the sort of capitulation that Johnson had tolerated. A Chicago editor spoke for his readers: "As for Negro suffrage, the mass of Union men in the Northwest do not care a great deal. What scares them is the idea that the rebels are all to be let back . . . and made a power in the government again." Moderates tried to devise plans that would be acceptable to both sides.

The moderates sought to continue the Freedmen's Bureau. The Bureau was understaffed and underfunded, but it offered some measure of hope for former slaves. The Bureau saw itself as a mediator between blacks and whites. Its commissioner, General Oliver Howard, advocated education as the foundation for improving living conditions and prospects for blacks. By 1869, approximately 3,000 schools, serving more than 150,000 students, reported to the Bureau, and these numbers do not include the many private and church-funded schools throughout the South.

The Bureau insisted on the innovation of formal contracts between laborer and landlord. Although these contracts infuriated Southern white men, the Bureau ended up supporting landowners as often as black laborers. The moderates also attempted to institute a Civil Rights bill to define American citizenship for all those born in the United States, thereby including blacks. Citizenship would bring with it equal protection under the laws, though the bill said nothing about black voting. The Bureau struggled against strongly held prejudice. Its Mississippi commissioner despaired of a public that failed to "conceive of the Negro having any rights at all."

In this riot of July 1866, Southern whites killed 34 blacks and 3 white supporters after a Republican meeting in New Orleans.

The Ku Klux Klan emerged in 1866, devoting itself to the maintenance of white supremacy in all its forms.

Republicans supported the Freedmen's Bureau and Civil Rights bills as the starting place for rebuilding the nation. But Johnson vetoed both bills, claiming that they violated the rights of the states and of white Southerners who had been excluded from the decision making. Republicans closed ranks to override Johnson's veto, the first major legislation ever enacted over a presidential veto.

To prevent any future erosion of black rights, the Republicans proposed the Fourteenth Amendment, which, as eventually ratified, guaranteed citizenship to all American-born people and equal protection under the law for those citizens. The amendment decreed that any state that abridged the voting rights of any male

inhabitants who were over 21 and citizens would suffer a proportionate reduction in its congressional representation. This clause offered white Southerners the choice of acceptance of black suffrage or reduced congressional representation. It also was the first Constitutional amendment to use the word "male," angering feminist abolitionists who challenged the Republicans' denial of suffrage based on sex. Johnson urged the Southern states to refuse to ratify the amendment, advice they promptly followed.

Throughout the second half of 1866 the North watched, appalled, as much that the Civil War had been fought for seemed to be brushed aside in the South. Not only did the Southern men who met in the state conventions refuse to accept the relatively mild Fourteenth Amendment, but they made clear their determination to fight back in every way they could against further attempts to remake the South. The spring of that year saw riots in Memphis and New Orleans in which policemen and other whites brutally assaulted and killed black people and burned their homes with little or no provocation.

It was in 1866, too, that the **Ku Klux Klan** appeared. Founded by Nathan Bedford Forrest in Tennessee, the Ku Klux Klan dedicated itself to maintaining white supremacy. The Klan dressed in costumes designed to overawe the former slaves, hiding behind their anonymity to avoid retaliation. The Klan became in effect a military wing of the Democratic party, devoting much of its energy to warning and killing white and black men who dared associate with the Republicans or supported black rights.

Johnson toured the country in the fall of 1866 to denounce the Republicans and their policies. Even his supporters saw the tour as a "thoroughly reprehensible" disaster. The voters rejected both Johnson and the Democrats, as the governorship and legislature of every Northern state came under the control of the Republicans. In the next Congress, Republicans would outnumber Democrats sufficiently to override any presidential veto. The Republicans felt they held a mandate to push harder than they had before. They had only a few months, however, until the congressional term ended in March, to decide what to do. They bitterly disagreed over the vote, land distribution, the courts, and education. Some wanted to put the South under military control for the indefinite future, whereas others sought to return things to civilian control as soon as possible. Finally, on March 2, 1867, as time was running out on the session, they passed the Reconstruction Act.

The Reconstruction Act

The **Reconstruction Act** placed the South under military rule. All the Southern states except Tennessee, which had been readmitted to the Union after it ratified the Fourteenth Amendment, were put in five military districts. Once order had been instituted, then the states would proceed to elect conventions to draw up new constitutions. The constitutions written by those conventions had to accept the Fourteenth Amendment and provide for universal manhood suffrage. Once a majority of the state's citizens and both houses of the national Congress had approved the new constitution, the state could be readmitted to the Union.

To ensure that Andrew Johnson did not undermine this plan—which soon became known as "Radical Reconstruction"—Congress sought to curb the president's power. With no threat of his veto after the 1866 elections, the Republicans could do much as they wanted. Congress decreed that it could call itself into special session. There, it limited the president's authority as commander-in-chief of the army and, in the Tenure of Office Act, prevented him from removing officials who had been confirmed by the Senate.

Johnson, characteristically, did not quietly accept such restrictions of his power. When he intentionally violated the Tenure of Office Act by removing Secretary of War Edwin Stanton in the summer of 1867, many in Congress decided that Johnson warranted **impeachment.** Matters stewed throughout the fall, while the first elections under the Reconstruction Act took place in the South.

Reconstruction Begins

After word of the Reconstruction Act circulated in the spring and summer, both black and white men claimed leadership roles within the Republican party. Black Northerners came to the South, looking for appointive and elective office. Ambitious black Southerners, many of whom had been free and relatively prosperous before the Civil War, put themselves forward as the natural leaders of the race. Such men became the backbone of the Republican party in black-belt districts.

White Southerners sneered at white Northerners who supported the Republican cause. They called them "carpetbaggers." These men, according to the insulting name, were supposedly so devoid of connections and property in their Northern homes that they could throw everything they had into a carpetbag—a cheap suitcase—and head south as soon as they read of the opportunities created by Radical Reconstruction. The majority of white Northerners who became Republican leaders in the South, however, had in fact moved to the region months or years before Reconstruction began. Many had been well educated in the North before the war and many held property in the South. Like white Southerners, however, the Northern-born Republicans found the postwar South a difficult place in which to prosper. Black people were no more inclined to work for low wages for white Northerners than for anyone else, and Southern whites often went out of their way to avoid doing business with the Yankees. As a result, when Reconstruction began, a considerable number of Northerners took up the Republican cause as a way to build a political career in the South.

White Southern Republicans, labeled "scalawags" by their enemies, risked being called traitors to their race and region. Few white Republicans emerged in the plantation districts, because they endured ostracism, resistance, and violence. In the upcountry districts, however, former Whigs and Unionists asserted themselves against the planters and Confederates. The Republican party became strong in the mountains of eastern Tennessee, western North Carolina, eastern Kentucky, northern Alabama, and northern Georgia. Many whites in these

African American men could vote in the South during Reconstruction, but often risked their livelihoods or their lives to do so.

districts, though unwilling to join with low-country African Americans or their white leaders, struck alliances of convenience with them. Black voters and white voters generally wanted and needed different things. Blacks, largely propertyless, called for an activist government to raise taxes to provide schools, orphanages, and hospitals. Many whites, on the other hand, owned land and called mainly for lower taxes.

Throughout the South, most whites watched, livid, as local black leaders, ministers, and Republicans mobilized black voters in enormous numbers in the fall of 1867. Membership in Union Leagues swept the region, with local leagues assisting with labor contracts and school construction as well as political activity. An Alabama league demanded recognition of black citizenship: "We claim exactly the same rights, privileges and immunities as are enjoyed by white men—we seek nothing more and will be content with nothing less." While many white Democrats boycotted the elections, the Republicans swept into the constitutional delegate positions. Although many black men voted, African American delegates made up only a relatively small part of the convention's delegates. They held the majority in South Carolina and Louisiana, but much smaller proportions elsewhere. About half of the 265 African Americans elected as delegates to the state conventions had been free before the war, and most were ministers, artisans, farmers, and teachers. Over the next two years, these delegates would meet to write new, much more democratic, constitutions for their states.

At the very moment of the success of the Southern Republicans, however, ominous signs came from the North. Republicans were dismayed at the election returns in the North in 1867, for the Democrats' power surged from coast to coast. Many white voters thought that the Radicals had gone too far in their concern with black rights and wanted officeholders to devote their energies to problems closer to home. Racism linked Democratic appeals against blacks in the Midwest with western diatribes against the Chinese. Integrated public schools and confiscation of plantation lands for former slaves were soundly defeated. The Republicans in Washington heard the message. They began scaling back their support for any further advances in Reconstruction.

Conclusion

The Civil War changed the United States more deeply than any other event in the nineteenth century—indeed, perhaps in all of American history. The conflict brought the deaths of more than 625,000 soldiers, the equivalent of 5 million people today and nearly as many as have died in all other American wars combined. Men who had been seriously wounded and disfigured would haunt the United States for generations to come, reminders of a horrific war. Children would grow up without fathers and many young women would never find husbands.

The war, despite the blessings of Union and freedom it brought, also brought a steep price in social disorder. The Civil War saw bitter rioting in the streets in both the North and the South. It saw political parties arguing over the very future of the nation. And it saw the first assassination of a president.

The Civil War triggered a major expansion of the federal government. The demands of wartime created greenbacks, the draft, and government involvement in transportation and business. It also brought a profound shift in the balance of power among the regions. Since the founding of the nation, the South had wielded influence out of proportion to its population. One president after another owned slaves and others did the bidding of slaveholders. After Appomattox, however, the South's political domination was broken. It would be half a century before a Southern-born man was elected president.

Most important, the war brought what few Americans could have imagined at the end of 1860: the immediate emancipation of 4 million enslaved people. Nowhere else in the world had so many people become free so quickly. Yet freedom emerged from the war through a circuitous route. The war began as a war for Union, but as the deaths mounted and African Americans seized freedom at every opportunity, abolitionists and Republicans increasingly demanded that the war become a war to end slavery. Many white Northerners supported emancipation because it seemed the best

The Democrats exploited, successfully, Republican support for black voting. In this image, caricatured black men press into the polls while white men are pushed aside.

way to end the war. Abraham Lincoln worked desperately to keep the support of both the advocates and foes of emancipation, knowing that moving too quickly would shatter the fragile support that kept him in office. The New York City draft riots and the close elections of 1863 demonstrated that many Northerners resisted the continuation of the war and its embrace of black freedom. Only Union success on the battlefield in late 1864 permitted Lincoln's reelection. His assassination made an already confused situation far more so, ending slavery and restoring the Union without a blueprint and without leadership.

The end of the fighting saw the conflict shift in the South, as people struggled to determine what freedom would mean. For black Southerners, the goal was autonomy and respect. For white Northerners, the goal was to reconstruct the South in an idealized image of the North. For white Southerners, the goal was the reassertion of the power they had held before the war, especially power over the black people in their midst. Such goals could not be reconciled. The era of Reconstruction would be devoted to the struggle among people determined that their vision of freedom would predominate.

The Chapter in Review

In the years between 1863 and 1867:

- African American soldiers began to enlist in great numbers.
- The Union won decisive victories at Gettysburg and Vicksburg.
- Southerners rioted in Richmond; Northerners rioted in New York City.
- The Union drove to victory in the Shenandoah Valley, in Tennessee, in Georgia, and in the Carolinas, but struggled in Virginia until the spring of 1865.

- Robert E. Lee surrendered his troops in April 1865.
- Abraham Lincoln, reelected in the winter of 1864, was assassinated in the spring of 1865.
- Andrew Johnson and the Radicals fought over the nature of Reconstruction.
- White Southerners resisted emancipation and Reconstruction through riots, through the Ku Klux Klan, and at the polls.
- The Republicans created the Reconstruction Act.

Making Connections Across Chapters

LOOKING BACK

Chapter 15 shows that at every point in the war both Northerners and Southerners thought it might end with one more key victory by their side. Instead, each battle seemed merely to bring another one, even bloodier than the one that came before.

1. Did the Civil War have a turning point, a point beyond which it became clear that the United States would defeat the Confederacy?

2. How did emancipation become a central war aim for the Union?

3. To what extent did the Confederacy collapse from within or was it overwhelmed from without?

LOOKING AHEAD

Chapter 16 will show that the most profound change in American history—the end of slavery—came to a nation exhausted by war and to a region unprepared for freedom. Black and white, Northern and Southern, struggled over the shape of the American future.

1. Could white Southerners have minimized the extent of freedom enjoyed by black Southerners if whites had behaved differently in 1865 and 1866?

2. What did black Southerners most want and need from emancipation? Did they receive that?

Recommended Readings

Berlin, Ira, Barbara J. Fields, Steven F. Miller, Joseph P. Reidy, and Leslie S. Rowland, eds. *Freedom* (1985) is a rich and fascinating multivolume documentary collection.

Blight, David W. *Race and Reunion: The Civil War in American Memory* (2001) documents the roles of politics, myth, and race in shaping how the Civil War is remembered.

Cashin, Joan E., ed., *The War Was You and Me: Civilians in the American Civil War* (2002) offers a series of interesting case studies.

Donald, David. *Lincoln* (1995) stands as the most elegant biography.

Faust, Drew Gilpin. *Mothers of Invention: Women of the Slaveholding South in the American Civil War* (1995) offers a challenging and interesting interpretation.

Fellman, Michael. *Inside War: The Guerilla Conflict in Missouri During the American Civil War* (1989) makes palpable the internal struggles in the border areas.

Foner, Eric. *Reconstruction: America's Unfinished Revolution, 1863–1877* (1988) is a magisterial interpretation of the struggle over black freedom.

Gallagher, Gary W. *The Confederate War: How Popular Will, Nationalism, and Military Strategy Could Not Stave Off Defeat* (1997) explores why the Confederacy could fight as long as it did.

Grant, Susan-Mary, and Peter J. Parish, eds. *Legacy of Disunion: The Enduring Significance of the American Civil War* (2003), puts the war in its largest contexts.

Harris, William C. *With Charity for All: Lincoln and the Restoration of the Union* (1997) offers a fresh assessment of Lincoln's attitudes toward the white South.

Hattaway, Herman, and Archer Jones. *How the North Won: A Military History of the Civil War* (1983) authoritatively describes strategy and tactics.

Litwack, Leon. *Been in the Storm So Long: The Aftermath of Slavery* (1979) beautifully evokes the conflicting emotions and motives surrounding freedom.

Neely, Mark E., Jr. *The Union Divided: Party Conflict in the Civil War North* (2002) examines impact of political dissension in North on war effort.

Roark, James L. *Masters Without Slaves: Southern Planters in the Civil War and Reconstruction* (1978) describes the war from the perspective of those who lost the most in southern defeat.

Rose, Willie Lee. *Rehearsal for Reconstruction: The Port Royal Experiment* (1964) is a classic account of the first efforts to create northern policy toward the freed people.

Silber, Nina. *Daughters of the Union: Northern Women Fight the Civil War* (2005) gives a fine overview of women's experiences in the North.

Identifications

Review your understanding of the following key terms, people, events, and dates for this chapter (these terms also appear in the Glossary at the end of the book):

African American soldiers
draft riots
Gettysburg Address
William T. Sherman
Andrew Johnson
emancipation
Special Field Order 15

Thirteenth Amendment
Appomattox
John Wilkes Booth
Freedmen's Bureau
black codes
Radical Republicans
Ku Klux Klan
Reconstruction Act
impeachment

Online Sources Guide

Use this listing to find online documents, images, interactive maps, simulations, and other resources related to this chapter:

American History Resource Center

http://history.wadsworth.com/rc/us

Documents

The Emancipation Proclamation (1863)
The Gettysburg Address (1863)
Resolutions from the 1864 Republican National Convention

Selected Images

Dead at Chancellorsville, Va., May 1863
Pickett's Charge at the Battle of Gettysburg, July 1863
African American recruiting poster
4th U.S. Colored Infantry E Company
Ulysses S. Grant at Cold Harbor Virginia, June 1864
Andersonville Prison, August 1864
Major General Philip Sheridan and his staff, 1864
Freed slave children in Charleston, South Carolina, 1865
Lincoln assassination
The Lincoln conspirators on the gallows
Union troops parade in Washington, 1865
Burning of a Freedmen's school, 1866

Simulation

Reconstruction (Choose to be a Southerner, former slave, carpetbagger, or Native American and make choices based on the circumstances and opportunities afforded.)

Document Exercises

400 Women, 1866

HistoryNOW

http://now.ilrn.com/ayers_etal3e

Primary Source Exercises

The Civil War and the Mississippi River
Confederate Hopes
Chickamauga and the Civil War
Illustrations of Black Soldiers in Northern Journals, 1863–1865
Emancipation

16 Reconstruction Abandoned, 1867–1877

The effort to create a more just society for African Americans after the Civil War was caught in such images as this one showing liberty looking for assistance for the black veterans who had been wounded in the conflict. That spirit of mutual sacrifice between blacks and whites proved difficult to sustain.

© Stock Montage, Inc.

epublicans in 1867 believed that they had taken important steps toward a newer and more just society with their Reconstruction legislation. "We have cut loose from the whole dead past," said Timothy Howe of Wisconsin, "and have cast our anchor out a hundred years." But the struggle over black rights that had begun during the Civil War was far from over. The battle shifted from the halls of Congress back to the South. There, in the decade that followed the war, blacks pursued their dreams of political equality and economic opportunity. Whites sought to preserve as many of the features of slavery as they could. Violence, brutality, election fraud, and raw economic intimidation ended the experiment in multiracial politics known as Reconstruction.

While racial prejudices were the main cause, other forces hastened the abandonment of Reconstruction. In the mid-1870s, a severe economic depression made African American rights seem a less urgent issue. White Americans feared that the national government was becoming too powerful; a renewed commitment to localism and states rights helped southern whites repress black aspirations. For many in the North, the hum of industry, the spread of railroads, and the rise of cities seemed more in tune with national progress than preserving the rights of former slaves.

With a western frontier to open and Native Americans to subdue, the nation retreated from the principles for which the Civil War had been fought. In the case of women's rights, for example, an initial surge of hope that women might join in the political process receded as male institutions reacted against this new movement. By the disputed presidential election of 1876, it was evident that white Americans no longer wished to be involved with the fate of blacks in the South. After a decade of slow, painful withdrawal from a commitment to equality, an informal sectional compromise sealed the return of white rule to the South in 1877. That political adjustment helped structure American responses to race questions down to modern times.

From Johnson to Grant

The struggle between the executive and legislative branches over the fate of the South continued into the second half of 1867. Because President Andrew Johnson sought to impede the Radical Reconstruction program, Republicans in Congress argued that he should be impeached and removed from office. When the president tried to oust Secretary of War Edwin M. Stanton in

Timeline

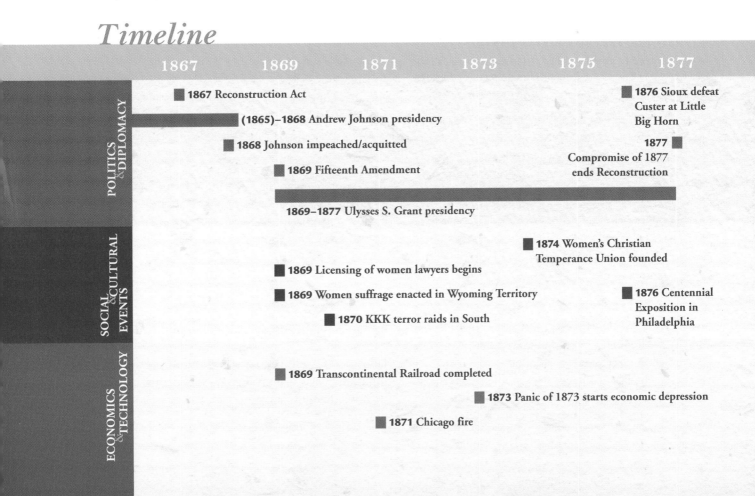

	1867	1869	1871	1873	1875	1877

POLITICS & DIPLOMACY

- 1867 Reconstruction Act
- (1865)–1868 Andrew Johnson presidency
- 1868 Johnson impeached/acquitted
- 1869 Fifteenth Amendment
- 1869–1877 Ulysses S. Grant presidency
- 1876 Sioux defeat Custer at Little Big Horn
- 1877 Compromise of 1877 ends Reconstruction

SOCIAL & CULTURAL EVENTS

- 1869 Licensing of women lawyers begins
- 1869 Women suffrage enacted in Wyoming Territory
- 1870 KKK terror raids in South
- 1874 Women's Christian Temperance Union founded
- 1876 Centennial Exposition in Philadelphia

ECONOMICS & TECHNOLOGY

- 1869 Transcontinental Railroad completed
- 1871 Chicago fire
- 1873 Panic of 1873 starts economic depression

Flashpoints | The Impeachment of Andrew Johnson

The trial of the president had been going on for six weeks. Republicans in the House of Representatives, angry at Andrew Johnson's efforts to block Reconstruction, had impeached him for his opposition to laws they had passed to restrain the powers of the chief executive. The Senate had met as a court to hear the allegations against the president. Now it was May 16, 1868, and the decisive moment for voting had come. The Republicans thought they had the votes, but no one was really sure of the outcome. If the Senate voted to convict Johnson and remove him from office, a permanent shift in power within the government could occur. Yet the president had often acted in ways that frustrated the attempts to bring justice and political equality to African Americans in the South.

Johnson's enemies needed a two-thirds vote to oust the president. As the roll call began, it was apparent that the vote would be very close. The key number to achieve was 36 in favor of conviction. Most of the Republicans were expected to vote to remove Johnson whereas all the Democrats would be recorded for acquittal. As the votes came in, 7 Republicans joined 12 Democrats to make 19 votes for allowing Johnson to remain in office. Thus, the effort to find the president guilty and force him from his post fell one vote short when the finally tally came in as 35 for conviction and 19 against.

Andrew Johnson had been a racist, stubborn, and obstructive president. The case for impeachment and conviction was a strong one on political grounds. Yet in the end it was probably the right result to leave him in office. He had only a little more than nine months remaining in his presidency, with no chance of being elected for a full term in 1868. Some of his most ardent foes wondered about the wisdom of removing a president for anything less than a criminal act committed while in office.

The acquittal of Andrew Johnson discredited impeachment as a political weapon against a president. No serious attempt to impeach a president would be made again until the Watergate scandal of Richard Nixon in 1973–1974 and the impeachment trial of Bill Clinton in 1999. Congress in 1868 had decided to let the political process determine who served in the office of president. That judgment allowed the presidency to become a powerful institution during the twentieth century. What happened on May 16, 1868, thus had a constitutional significance that endured long after Andrew Johnson, with his unfortunate political career, had left the national stage.

© CORBIS SYGMA

Questions for Reflection

1. How had Andrew Johnson convinced the Republicans that impeachment was their only recourse against him in 1868?

2. Why was it possible to conclude that removing Johnson from office was not a desirable result?

3. How much did the nearness of the 1868 presidential election figure in the calculations of the enemies and friends of Andrew Johnson in the Senate?

4. If you had been a member of the Senate in 1868, how would you have voted on the issue of finding Johnson guilty and why?

August 1867, cries for impeachment mounted. For the moment the Republicans could do little until Congress reassembled in December.

After lawmakers gathered, the sentiment for removing the president had lessened, and it appeared that the president would survive for the rest of his term. As he had done so often in the past, Johnson defied Congress and precipitated a confrontation. After the Senate in January 1868 refused to accept his dismissal of Stanton, Johnson replaced him anyway. Presidential stubbornness, Republicans said, was a clear violation of the Tenure of Office Act.

Emboldened by Johnson's defiance, the solidly Republican House voted for his impeachment and leveled eleven charges against him. None of the specifications in the articles of impeachment alleged violations of criminal laws; they dealt instead with Johnson's Reconstruction policies and his obstruction of Congress. The trial came in March. Two months later the Senate failed to achieve the necessary two-thirds vote to convict Johnson. The impeachment attempt lost because moderate Republicans feared that if Johnson were convicted on political grounds it would set a bad precedent. Moreover, Johnson himself eased up on his obstructive tactics. With the 1868 presidential election looming, it seemed less urgent to oust a man who would soon leave office. True to his nature, Johnson did not become more conciliatory. He encouraged southern whites to resist Reconstruction and contributed to the denial of rights to African Americans that marked the 1870s. Few presidents have done less with their historical opportunities than Andrew Johnson.

During the months of Johnson's impeachment and trial, Congress concluded a major territorial acquisition that completed expansion on the North American continent with the purchase of Alaska from Russia. The Alaska purchase was a major strategic and geographic victory for the United States. Amid the controversy over the impeachment of Johnson and the upcoming presidential election, the acquisition of this northern territory did not attract great attention.

The Election of 1868

Both parties looked ahead to the first postwar presidential contest, but the issues of the Civil War defined the contest. The Republicans nominated the great hero of the conflict, Ulysses S. Grant. As the architect of Union victory, his popularity transcended partisanship. Republicans believed that they had selected a candidate "so independent of party politics as to be a guarantee of peace and quiet." In his official letter of acceptance, Grant said "let us have peace" and that phrase became the theme of the Republican campaign. The Republicans were not campaigning on any promise to expand Reconstruction or to do more for the rights of black Americans.

The Democrats turned to the former governor of New York, Horatio Seymour. Along with his running mate, Frank Blair of Missouri, Seymour relied on racial bigotry and white supremacy as the keynotes of his appeal. To win, the Democrats agreed, they had to arouse "the aversion with which the masses contemplate the equality of the negro." Seymour went out to campaign; Grant stayed home. The Republicans won, but not by a

This picture shows the four national candidates in the 1868 presidential election, Horatio Seymour (Democrat), Ulysses S. Grant (Republican), Frank P. Blair (Democrat) and Schuyler Colfax (Republican).

landslide. Grant garnered 53 percent of the vote; Seymour totaled 47 percent. Although Grant carried the electoral college by a margin of 214 to 80, the signs were not good for a continuation of Reconstruction. White voters were less willing to help African Americans; whatever goals African Americans sought, they would have to achieve them on their own. The high point of post–Civil War racial reform was in the past.

The Fifteenth Amendment

After the 1868 election, Republicans pushed for the adoption of the Fifteenth Amendment to the Constitution to finish the political reforms that Reconstruction brought. Under its terms, the federal and state governments could not restrict the right to vote because of race, color, or previous condition of servitude. Congress approved the amendment in February 1869 over Democratic opposition. The purpose of the change was to limit the legal right of the southern states to exclude African Americans from the political process, and Democrats assailed it as a step toward black equality and a social revolution. In fact, the new amendment did not assure African Americans the right to hold office, and it left untouched the restrictions that northern states imposed on the right of males to vote. Literacy tests and property qualifications remained in place in some states outside of the South. State legislatures endorsed the amendment promptly and it was added to the Constitution in 1870. The adoption of the three Civil War amendments had changed the nature of the government as the administration of President Grant got under way, but American politics responded slowly to the impact of these new additions to the nation's fundamental law.

The Grant Era

Ulysses S. Grant came to the White House with almost no political experience. He believed that he should administer the government rather than promote new programs. "I shall on all subjects have a policy to recommend," he said in his inaugural address, "but none to enforce against the will of the people." He promised, unlike Andrew Johnson, to carry out the laws that Congress passed. Nineteenth-century Americans did not expect a president to be an activist and neither did Grant himself. However, those who hoped for a period of calm after the storms of Johnson's presidency were soon disappointed.

Grant's passive view of the presidency allowed Congress to play a dominant role in his administration. As a result, the executive office itself lost some of the authority Lincoln had given it during the Civil War. A generation passed before power shifted back toward the White House. Because Republicans were suspicious of strong presidents, that development aroused little protest from the governing party.

Hard choices confronted the new president. Southern Republicans begged for help from Washington to fight off resurgent Democrats. Yet, many party members in the North believed Reconstruction was no longer wise or practical. Support for black aspirations seemed an electoral loser. As a result, African Americans in the South had to rely more and more on their own resources and personal courage. They made valiant efforts to involve themselves in regional politics, often at the risk of their lives.

Grant tried to stay away from partisan battles. Without a clear objective of a war before him in which victory was the goal, the president seemed confused. As a result, he followed a shifting policy in selecting his cabinet and making appointments. The president did not accept the advice of influential Republicans but depended instead on men who shared his cautious governing style. The president gave cabinet officers wide discretion to pick subordinates without worrying about their political connections. His cabinet mixed some strong appointments such as Secretary of State Hamilton Fish with some other individuals whose qualifications for high office were questionable.

The South posed the most immediate problem for Grant as he learned the presidency. Playing down their dislike of blacks in public statements, the Democrats argued that former Confederates should now be allowed to participate in public life. The strategy produced mixed results in 1869. Republicans did well in Mississippi and won a close race for governor in Texas. Democrats triumphed in Virginia and Tennessee. Overall, the results suggested that Republican strength was eroding as the Democrats got back into politics. Southern white Republicans and their black allies found that Washington often left them on their own to confront the resurgent Democrats. The white South waged a constant struggle to overturn Reconstruction and the Republicans struggled to find an answer for this strategy.

A Troubled Administration

Making matters worse were allegations of scandal against the new administration. In the summer of 1869, two speculators, Jay Gould and Jim Fisk, manipulated the gold market to achieve huge profits for themselves. The price of gold rose until financial turmoil erupted on September 24, 1869. Investors who had promised to sell gold at lower prices faced ruin. Then the government sold its own gold supplies, the price of gold broke, and the market returned to its normal level. In the resulting inquiries about what had happened, the public learned that some members of Grant's family had helped Gould and Fisk carry out their plan. Whispers had it that Julia Grant, the president's wife, might have been involved. The story was not true, but doubts spread about the ethical standards of Grant's presidency.

To the odor of corruption was soon added a sense of White House disarray and incompetence. The administration talked of forcing Spain to give up Cuba and then backed away from the idea. The president wanted to annex the Dominican Republic (Santo Domingo). An agent of the president worked out a treaty of annexation with Santo Domingo's rulers, and the pact was sent to the Senate. Grant pushed hard for approval of the treaty, but the Senate, fearful of the influence of speculators and lobbyists, was suspicious of the president's goals. As a result, the treaty was defeated and the president embarrassed.

Grant's administration had more success in the resolution of American claims for maritime losses against Great Britain. The claims were related to the *Alabama,* one of several Confederate raiders that had been constructed in British shipyards during the Civil War. The *Alabama* had sunk numerous Union vessels. Charles Sumner, chair of the Senate Foreign Relations Committee, wanted to use the claims as leverage in an effort to acquire Canada. In 1871, the State Department worked out an amicable settlement of the issue that left Canada alone.

Grant and Congress

The president deferred too much to Congress. In the process, congressional Republicans split on issues such as the protective tariff and the currency. The mainstream of the party believed that a tariff policy to "protect" American industries against foreign competition was in the best interest of business, workers, and the party itself. A minority of Republicans called the protective policy wrong economically and a potential source of corrupt influence from the affected industries. On the currency, eastern Republicans favored the gold standard and what was known as "hard money," where every dollar was backed by an equal amount of gold. Western Republicans advocated an expansion of the money supply through paper money, or "greenbacks," and, when necessary, even the issuance of dollars backed by silver as an alternative to gold. In the Grant years, these issues loomed as large as debates about the size of the federal budget do in modern times.

Since government was still small, who served in these coveted jobs became a question for public dispute. Some Republicans argued that the government should follow a merit system of appointing its officials. This idea became known as "civil service reform." Reformers maintained that competence and nonpartisanship were better ways to staff these positions. Republicans who wanted to reduce the tariff, rely on the civil service, and treat the South with more leniency defected from the Grant administration. They formed "Liberal Republican" alliances with Democrats in such states as West Virginia and Missouri. In the 1870s, "liberal" meant someone who favored smaller government, lower tariffs, civil service, and most important, an end to Reconstruction. If African Americans were the victims of southern violence, the liberal Republicans were willing to tolerate that result.

Grant and His Party

With his presidency under attack, Grant turned to the Republican leaders in Congress for support. These politicians disliked the Liberal Republican program and its leaders. Angry Liberals threatened to bolt the party. Grant knew that he could never satisfy the demands of the Liberals on Reconstruction or the civil service. Following that logic, Grant conciliated mainstream Republicans. He dismissed cabinet officers who disagreed with him and aligned himself with party members willing to defend Congress and the White House. Officeholders who supported Liberal Republican candidates or Democrats were fired. Despite these actions, the 1870 elections went to Grant's opponents. Liberal Republicans won races in West Virginia and Missouri. The Democrats added 41 seats to their total in the House and picked up another 6 seats in the Senate in the 1870 voting. The Republicans retained control of both houses, but their position was weakening. Grant's enemies even thought he might be defeated in 1872.

The Rise of the Klan

Mounting racial violence in the South added to the president's problems. By the summer of 1870, reports reached Washington of violence against blacks and white Republicans across the South. Roving bands of whites organized since 1866 as the Ku Klux Klan (see Chapter 15) made the attacks. Throughout the South, the Klan asserted white dominance. One Republican in Louisiana pleaded that "murder and intimidation are the order of the day in this state."

The Klan and its offshoots, such as the Knights of the White Camelia, White Leagues, and the White Brotherhood, acted as the paramilitary arm of the Democratic party to crush Republicanism through any means. In Tennessee a black Republican was beaten after he won an election for justice of the peace. His assailants told him "that they didn't dispute I was a very good fellow . . . but they did not intend any nigger to hold office in the United States." Violence then as now often supported racism in the United States.

The Klan stopped at nothing to eliminate its opponents. Leaders of the Republican party were hunted and killed. Four blacks died when the Klan attacked an election meeting in Alabama in October 1870. A "negro chase" in South Carolina left 13 blacks dead. The Klansmen rode in white robes and hoods; their aim, they said, was to frighten their racial foes. The disguises also hid their identity from law enforcement. A wave of shootings and brutality undermined the chances of the Republican party to survive and grow below the Mason-Dixon line.

A Cartoonist Attacks the Ku Klux Klan

The use of political cartoons to convey ideas about contemporary issues became more sophisticated after the Civil War. One of the great popular artists of the day was Thomas Nast. In the 1870s, his images attacked the refusal of southerners to grant real freedom to African Americans and the increasing reliance in the South on such terror organizations as the Ku Klux Klan and the White Leagues. Nash dramatized for his audience that southern whites, in or out of a hood, had the same goal—"a white man's government." These

striking pictures helped sustain the Republican party during the presidency of Ulysses S. Grant. Unfortunately for blacks in the South, neither Nast nor the white political leadership in the North persisted in their commitment to equal rights. By the end of the decade, other cartoons depicted blacks in a degrading manner that justified white dominance and paved the way in time for racial segregation.

The Government and the Klan

Viewing the wreckage of their southern parties after the 1870 elections, Republicans recognized that the Klan's terror tactics had worked to intimidate voters and demoralize their leaders. Yet the party was divided about the right answer to terror in the South. As 1871 began,

the Republicans had less stomach for sending troops to the South to affect politics. As an Illinois newspaper observed, "the negro is now a voter and a citizen. Let him hereafter take his chances in the battle of life." This view represented insensitive advice to the blacks in the South who were pushing to get into politics under desperate conditions. Yet, Republican leaders asked themselves whether the cost of maintaining party organizations in the South in the face of such resolute Democratic opposition justified the effort.

The violence of the Klan presented a challenge that could not be ignored. Without firm action, the Republican party in the South might disappear. Congress adopted legislation to curb election fraud, bribery, and coercion in elections. When these measures proved inadequate, the lawmakers passed the Ku Klux Klan Act of 1871. This law outlawed conspiracies to deprive voters of their civil rights and banned efforts to bar any citizen from holding public office. The government also received broader powers to fight the Klan through the use of federal district attorneys to override state laws. As a last resort, military force could also be employed.

The Democrats labeled these laws an unconstitutional interference with the rights of the states. Their passage was "the crowning act of centralization and consolidation," said one critic. A Republican countered by saying: "Tell me nothing of a constitution which fails to shelter beneath its rightful power the people of a country." As long as that commitment existed, southern Republicans, black and white, had a chance to establish themselves as an alternative to the Democrats.

Breaking the Power of the Klan

Republicans determined to end the lawbreaking and violence that the Klan embodied. The Justice Department, which had been established in 1870, argued that the threat the Klan posed to democratic government amounted to war. Officials in Washington mobilized federal district attorneys and United States marshals to institute prosecutions against the Klan. The legal offensive in 1871 brought results; in state after state Klan leaders were indicted. Federal troops assisted the work of the Justice Department in South Carolina. The Klan was discredited as a public presence in southern politics; its violence became more covert and less visible. Even though the prosecutions of the Klan showed that effective federal action could compel southern states to comply with the rule of law, sentiment in the North for such stern measures was receding. Reconstruction did not seem to be a noble crusade for human rights but part of a troubling pattern of corruption and excessive government power. With new economic issues on the political agenda, the problems of the South had to compete with the problems arising from the spread of the railroad network after the Civil War.

Farmers and Railroads

The expansion of railroads after the Civil War posed new challenges for farmers in the South and West. Throughout the 1860s, two transcontinental railroads had put down tracks across the country. The Union Pacific built westward while the Central Pacific started eastward from the West Coast. The two lines faced difficult obstacles of money and geography. The Central Pacific crossed the Sierra Nevada Mountains through rocky gorges and across treacherous rivers. Several thousand Chinese laborers did the most dangerous work. They tunneled into snowdrifts to reach their work sites and then toiled on sheer cliffs with picks and dynamite. On the Union Pacific side, more than 10,000 construction workers, many of them Irish immigrants, laid tracks across Nebraska and Wyoming.

When the two lines met at Promontory, Utah, on May 10, 1869, it was a major news event. Railroad executives drove a golden spike into the ground with a silver sledgehammer. The transcontinental lines were a reality. Loans and subsidies from the federal government to the railroads had enabled the lines to be built quickly. The way the railroads were paid for would become a subject of scandal within a few years.

Following this accomplishment, railroad construction accelerated. In 1869, railroad mileage stood at about 47,000 miles; 4 years later the total had risen to 70,268 miles. The new railroad lines employed tens of thousands of workers and extended across a far larger geographical area than any previous manufacturing enterprise. American business was starting to become much larger than any previous endeavor in the nation; that development would have important consequences. For the moment, as long as business expanded, the railroads seemed a boon to the economy.

Farmers too enjoyed postwar prosperity because of higher prices for wheat and other commodities. Beneath the surface, however, tensions between agrarians and the new industries grew. In late 1867, the Patrons of Husbandry, also known as the Grange, was formed to press the case for the farmers. In its political goals, the Grange focused on complaints about the high mortgages the farmers owed, the prices they paid to middlemen such as the operators of grain elevators, and the discrimination they faced at the hands of railroads in moving their goods to market. These grievances would persist throughout the remainder of the nineteenth century

In the work of building the transcontinental railroad, the grueling labor of Chinese workers was indispensable. They toiled for low pay in difficult conditions in a society that scorned them and often subjected them to harsh discrimination.

and contribute to the turbulence of politics in the 1880s and 1890s.

To balance the power of the railroads, some states created railroad commissions to oversee how the companies operated. One such state was Illinois, where a new constitution in 1870 instructed the legislature to pass laws establishing maximum rates for the movement of passengers and freight. The legislature set up the Illinois Railroad Commission and gave the new agency wide powers. Neighboring states such as Iowa, Minnesota, and Wisconsin followed the Illinois example during the next several years. Railroad companies challenged some of these laws in court, and a case testing the constitutionality of the Illinois statute worked its way toward the U.S. Supreme Court as *Munn v. Illinois.* The justices handed down their decision in 1877, as the railroad industry faced a nationwide strike. (See Chapter 17.)

Indian Policies

The opening of the West to railroads and the spread of farmers onto the Great Plains meant that Native Americans once again had to resist an encroaching white presence as had happened in the 1830s and 1850s. What had once been called "The Great American Desert" before the Civil War now beckoned as the home for countless farmers. The tribes who were living in the West and the Indians who had been displaced there in the 1830s and 1840s found their hunting grounds and tribal domains under siege as white settlers appeared.

The Peace Policy

Treatment of the Indians after the Civil War mixed benevolence and cruelty. Grant brought more insight and respect to the issue of Native Americans than most previous presidents. His administration pursued what became known as the "peace policy." While a majority of western settlers advocated the removal or outright extermination of the Indian tribes, Grant's conciliatory approach won applause in the East.

The policy issues took shape in the years before Grant became president. Advocates of the Indians contended that the hostile tribes should be located in Dakota Territory and the Indian Territory (now Oklahoma). The government would stop treating the entire West as a giant Indian reservation. Instead, specific areas would be set aside for the Native Americans. On these "reservations" the inhabitants would learn the cultural values of white society, be taught to grow crops, and be paid a small income until they could support themselves.

Grant took up the ideas of the Indian reformers. He appointed Ely Parker, a Seneca, as commissioner of Indian affairs. Congress appropriated $2 million for Indian problems and set up a Board of Indian Commissioners to distribute the funds. Indian agents would be chosen from nominees that Christian churches provided. The peace policy blended kindness and force. If the Indians accepted the presence of church officials on the reservations, the government would leave them alone. Resistance would bring the army to see that Indians stayed on the reservations. To whites, the peace policy was humane. For the Indians it was another in the long series of white efforts to undermine their way of life.

Pressures on the Indians

The 1870s brought increasing tensions between white settlers and the Indians. The 1870 census reported more than 2,660,000 farms; that number rose to more than 4 million within 10 years. A competition for space and resources intensified. With millions of acres under cultivation and the spread of cattle drives across Indian lands, the tribes found themselves squeezed from their traditional nomadic hunting grounds.

The systematic destruction of the buffalo herds dealt another devastating blow to the Indians. In the societies of the Plains tribes, the meat of the bison supplied food, while the hides provided shelter and clothes. Removal of

President Grant's peace policy with the Indians attracted national attention. This drawing illustrates a meeting of the president, his commissioner of Indian Affairs, Ely Parker, and the Indian chiefs Red Cloud, Spotted Tail, and Swift Bear, as published in *Harper's Weekly*, June 18, 1870.

these resources hurt the Indians economically, but the cultural impact was even greater. Buffalo represented the continuity of nature and the renewal of life cycles.

The decline of the herds began during the 1860s as drought, disease, and erosion shrank the habitat of the buffalo. Then the demand for buffalo robes and pemmican (dried buffalo meat, berries, and fat) among whites spurred more intensive hunting. As railroads penetrated the West, hunters could send their products to customers with relative ease. More than 5 million buffalo were slaughtered during the early 1870s, and by the end of the century only a few of these animals were alive. Conservation eventually saved the buffalo from the near extinction that this animal had faced because of the ruthless exploitation during the late nineteenth century.

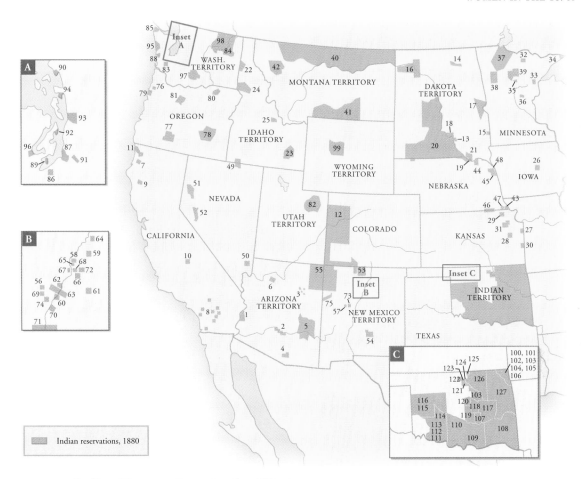

MAP 16.1 Indian Reservations in the West

Following the end of the Civil War and with the adoption of the peace policy of President Ulysses S. Grant, a network of Indian reservations spread across the West. This map shows how extensive the reservation system was.

During the mid-1870s, Native Americans tried a last effort to block the social and economic tides overwhelming their way of life. By that time, Grant's peace policy had faltered. Corruption and politics replaced the original desire to treat the Indians in a more humane manner. The tribes that continued to hunt and pursue their nomadic culture found unhappy whites and a hostile military in their way. The Red River War, led by Cheyenne, Kiowas, and Comanches, erupted on the southern plains. Indian resistance ultimately collapsed when food and supplies ran out.

The discovery of gold in the Black Hills of Dakota brought white settlers into an area where the Sioux had dominated. The Indians refused to leave, and the government sent troops to protect the gold seekers. The Indian leaders, **Crazy Horse** and **Sitting Bull,** rallied their followers to stop the army. Near what the Indians called the Greasy Grass (whites called it the Little Bighorn), Colonel **George Armstrong Custer** led a force of 600 men. With a third of his detachment, he attacked more than 2,000 Sioux warriors. Custer and his soldiers perished. The whites called it "Custer's Last Stand." The Indian victory, shocking to whites, was only a temporary success. The army pursued the Indians during the ensuing months. By the end of the Grant administration, the Sioux had been conquered. Only in the Southwest did the Apaches successfully resist the power of the military. Indians now faced cruelty, exploitation, and oppression that extended through the rest of the nineteenth century and then beyond 1900. In the face of these relentless pressures from white society, Indians struggled just to survive as a people.

Women in the 1870s

White women during this time did not have anything that approached social or political equality with men. Amid the male-dominated public life, women struggled for some political rights, a foothold in the new industrial economy, and a way to make their voices heard about social issues. Indeed, they faced significant barriers to any kind of meaningful participation in public affairs, a condition that continued into the early twentieth century.

Slaughter of the Buffalo

The manner in which the opening of the West after the Civil War is depicted in textbooks has changed in dramatic ways during the last two decades. More attention is now given to the impact on the environment and on the nomadic lifestyle of the Native American residents of the Great Plains arising from the disappearance of the buffalo herds. The critical role that these animals played in sustaining the Indian way of life meant that the task of white settlers became much less dangerous when the buffalo were

Kansas State Historical Society

gone. Pictures such as this one of 40,000 hides piled up outside Dodge City, Kansas, convey a dramatic sense of the extermination of these animals. Of course, no text can impart the odor of that many hides.

The individuals in the image are small compared to the mass of hides, but their presence reveals how the trade in buffalo had become a key aspect of the western economy. When the buffalo were gone, as happened within a few years, residents moved on to another boom and bust cycle, whether it was in cattle ranching or farming. The picture serves as an evocation of a vanished time and place, but also says something permanent about the nature of the West.

The debates over the adoption of the Fifteenth Amendment underscored the importance of this problem. Women had hoped that they might share in the expansion of political rights. In fact, several major advocates of woman **suffrage,** including **Susan B. Anthony,** opposed the amendment because it left women out. In Anthony's mind, black and Asian men should be barred from voting unless women had the right of suffrage as well. That put her at odds with champions of black suffrage such as Frederick Douglass.

DOING HISTORY ONLINE

The Fifteenth Amendment Debate

How did women's suffrage become entangled in the debate over the issue of black voting rights and the Fifteenth Amendment?

History ⧗ Now™   Visit HistoryNOW to access primary sources and exercises related to this topic: http://now.ilrn.com/ayers_etal3e

At a meeting of the Equal Rights Association in May 1869, such differences about how to achieve suffrage produced an open break. Two distinct groups of suffragists emerged. The National Woman Suffrage Association reflected the views of Susan B. Anthony and Elizabeth Cady Stanton that the Fifteenth Amendment should be shunned until women were included. The American Woman Suffrage Association, led by Lucy Stone and Alice Stone Blackwell, endorsed the amendment and focused its work on gaining suffrage in the states. Amid this dissension, the new territory of Wyoming granted women the right of suffrage in 1869. The Wyoming legislature wanted Americans to notice their underpopulated territory; woman suffrage was a means to that end. Nonetheless, their action represented a small step forward while the major suffrage groups feuded. A united front among suffrage advocates probably would not have made a great deal of difference in the 1870s, but the lack of cohesion was a weakness in this cause.

Another champion of women's rights was Victoria Claflin Woodhull. A faith healer and spiritualist from Ohio, she and her sister Tennessee Claflin came to New York, where in 1870 Victoria announced her candidacy for president of the United States. She published a weekly newspaper that endorsed the right of women to practice free love outside the subordinate role of marriage. In 1873, she denounced one of the nation's leading ministers, Henry Ward Beecher, for having had an alleged affair with a member of his congregation. The revelation led to one of the most sensational public trials of that century. The proceedings ended in a hung jury and the Claflin sisters had to flee to England to escape public outrage. Woodhull's experience and social disgrace demonstrated the perils that faced women who defied the strict cultural conventions of the post–Civil War era.

For women who did not become celebrities as Woodhull did, the decade of the 1870s offered some opportunities and more reminders of their status as second-class citizens. On the positive side, educational opportunities expanded during this decade. The number of women graduating from high school stood at

DOING HISTORY

Women's Rights and Black Suffrage During Reconstruction

Elizabeth Cady Stanton

"WE DO NOT demand the right step for this hour in demanding suffrage for any class; as a matter of principle I claim it for all. But in a narrow view of the question as a feeling between classes, when Mr. Downing puts the question to me, are you willing to have the colored man enfranchised before the woman, I say no; I would not trust him with all my rights, degraded, oppressed himself, he would be more despotic with the governing power than even our Saxon rulers are."

Elizabeth Cady Stanton

Frederick Douglass

"I champion the right of the Negro to vote. It is with us a matter of life and death, and therefore cannot be postponed. I have always championed woman's right to vote; but it will be seen that the present claim for the Negro is one of the most urgent necessity. The assertion of the right of women to vote meets nothing but ridicule; there is no deep seated malignity in the hearts of the people against her; but name the right of the Negro to vote, all hell is turned loose and the Ku-Klux and the Regulators hunt and slay the unoffending black man. The government of this country loves women. They are sisters, mothers, wives and daughters of our rulers; but the Negro is loathed."

One of the unexpected aspects of Reconstruction occurred during debates about the wisdom of extending the vote to black makes but not to women in general. Out of these discussions in time would come the Fifteenth Amendment to the Constitution. That document affirmed the right of citizens to vote without regard to their race, color, or status as former slaves. The amendment, however, said nothing about gender and the assumption was that it applied only to black men. Advocates of woman suffrage believed that women should be accorded the right to vote as well as

Frederick Douglass

The Granger Collection, New York

© Bettmann/CORBIS

men. The dispute divided African American men such as Frederick Douglass from champions of woman suffrage such as Elizabeth Cady Stanton. In the process, fault lines over race and the status of women in society emerged. As the quotation from Stanton indicates, she believed that black and Asian men should not get the vote if women were denied the franchise. Douglass and his supporters argued that it was more important to get the vote for black men as a further step toward Reconstruction. Their view prevailed when the Fifteenth Amendment was adopted in 1869–1870. The divisions between Stanton and Douglass shed light on the interplay between race and gender that cut across American society in the nineteenth century.

The exchange of views between Stanton and Douglass came at a meeting of the American Equal Rights Association in New York City during May 1867. George Downing was a black man who had asked Stanton about views on male suffrage for blacks and suffrage for all Americans.

Source: Both quotations are from Elizabeth Cady Stanton et al., *History of Woman Suffrage* (6 vols.,

New York: Flower and Wells, 1881–1922), 2: 214 (Stanton), 310–311 (Douglass), as cited in Rosalyn M. Terborg-Penn, "Afro Americans in the Struggle for Woman Suffrage," (Ph.D. dissertation: Howard University, 1977), p. 77 (Stanton), p. 79 (Douglass).

Questions for Reflection

1. What was Stanton's opinion of the capacity of black men to use the vote wisely?

2. To what extent did she share the attitudes of Democrats about the policies of Reconstruction?

3. How did Douglass see the issue as between black suffrage and votes for women?

4. How much did political expediency influence Douglass's argument?

5. In what ways did racial ideas and gender biases shape the debate about the Fifteenth Amendment?

Explore additional primary sources related to this chapter on the Wadsworth American History Resource Center or HistoryNOW websites:

http://history.wadsworth.com/rc/us
http://now.ilrn.com/ayers_etal3e

---

nearly 9,000 in 1870, compared with 7,000 men. Aware of these statistics, state universities and private colleges opened their doors to women students in growing numbers. By 1872, nearly 100 institutions of higher learning admitted women. This trend continued despite the overwrought fears of male academics. Edward Clarke, a retired Harvard medical professor, warned in 1873 that when women expended their "limited energy" on higher education, they put their "female apparatus" at risk.

Cornell University began accepting female applicants in 1875, and one of its first woman graduates was M. Carey Thomas, who received her B.A. in 1877. Five years later, she earned a Ph.D. at a German university. By the 1890s, she had become the president of Bryn Mawr, a woman's college outside Philadelphia. Like other women in male-dominated professions, she encountered rudeness and indifference from her masculine colleagues. She later recalled that "it is a fiery ordeal to educate a lady by coeducation."

Obtaining a degree was not a guarantee of access to professions that males controlled. Myra Bradwell tried to become a lawyer in Illinois, but the state bar association rejected her application. She sued in federal court, and in 1873 the U.S. Supreme Court decided that the law did not grant her the right to be admitted to the bar. One justice wrote that "the paramount destiny and mis-

sion of woman are to fulfill the noble and benign offices of wife and mother." That restrictive decision allowed the Illinois legislature to deny women the chance to practice law. In 1870, there were only five female lawyers in the nation.

The Supreme Court also rebuffed efforts to secure woman suffrage through the courts. Virginia Minor, president of the Woman Suffrage Association of Missouri, tried to vote during the 1872 election, but the registrar of voters turned her away. She sued on the grounds that the action denied her rights as a citizen. In the case of *Minor v. Happersett* (1875), the Supreme Court unanimously concluded that suffrage was not one of the rights of citizenship because "sex has never been made one of the elements of citizenship in the United States." To gain the right to vote, women would have to amend the Constitution or obtain the right of suffrage from the states, a process that took another four decades to complete.

The Rise of Voluntary Associations

Blocked off from politics, women carved out a public space of their own through voluntary associations. Black churchwomen established missionary societies to work both in the United States and abroad. Clubs and literary societies sprang up among white women as well. In New dealers close down. They urged drunkards to reform. Middle-class women prayed in front of bars and smashed barrels of liquor to emphasize their determination. Men joined the **temperance** movement, too, but it was the fervor of women that gave the antialcohol crusade new energy. "The women are in desperate earnest," said a Missouri resident who witnessed one of these campaigns.

As their protest successes grew, women sought to make their antidrink campaign more than a momentary event. In August 1874, a group of women active in the temperance cause met at Lake Chautauqua, New York. They set a national meeting that evolved into the Woman's Christian Temperance Union (WCTU). Over the next five years, temperance leagues and local branches of the WCTU worked against intoxicating drink. By the end of the 1870s, a thousand unions had been formed, with an estimated 26,000 members. In 1879, Frances Willard became president of the WCTU, and she took the organization beyond its original goal of temperance and into broader areas of social reform such as woman suffrage and the treatment of children. As it had before the Civil War, the campaign against alcohol revealed some of the underlying social and cultural strains of society.

Women at Work

The 1870s brought greater economic opportunities for women in sales and clerical positions in the workplace. The typewriter appeared in the early part of the decade. E. Remington and Sons, which produced the typewriter, said in 1875 that "no invention has opened for women so broad and easy an avenue to profitable and suitable employment as the 'Type-Writer.'" By 1880, women accounted for 40 percent of the stenographers and typists in the country. These developments laid the foundation for growth in the number of female office workers during the rest of the nineteenth century.

The most typical experience of American women, however, remained toil in the fields and at home. Black women in the South labored in the open alongside their husbands who were tenant farmers or sharecroppers. They did "double duty, a man's share in the field and a woman's part at home." In the expanding cities, women worked in textile factories or became domestic servants. Many urban women also took in boarders. As a result, their intensified routine equaled that of operating a small hotel. In the daily rhythms of American society in this period, as in earlier times, the often unpaid and unrecognized labor of women was indispensable to the nation's advancement.

Middle-class women with domestic servants had some assistance, but they still did a daunting amount of work. Preparing food, washing laundry by hand, keeping

Victoria Woodhull came under scathing popular attack for her views on women's issues. This cartoon, published in 1872, by Thomas Nast depicts her as a Satanic enemy of marriage and shows a wife, with children and an alcoholic husband, saying, "I'd rather travel the hardest path of matrimony than follow your footsteps."

York City, women created Sorosis, a club for women only, after the New York Press Club barred females from membership. In 1873, delegates from local Sorosis clubs formed the Association for the Advancement of Women. The New England's Women's Club, located in Boston, had local laws changed during the early 1870s to allow women to serve on the city's School Committee. Later the club founded the Women's Education Association to expand opportunities for their sex in schools and colleges. During the two decades that followed, the women's club movement put down strong roots in all parts of the nation. Soon they also found ways to exert an influence on political and cultural issues.

Despite being turned away at the polls, women made their presence felt. Women in New York, Ohio, and Michigan protested against the sale and use of alcohol, marching in the streets to demand that saloons and liquor

The War Against Drink

The temperance crusades of the 1870s against alcohol and its evils brought women into politics in an era when they could not even vote in most of the nation. This cartoon links the campaign of the Women's Christian Temperance Union (WCTU) to the chivalry of the Middle Ages as the mounted women, armored in a righteous cause, destroy whisky, gin, brandy, and rum. The connection of reform with religion and patriotism gave the antialcohol crusade a powerful claim on middle-class sentiments. For those groups whose

© The Granger Collection, New York

religious creed did not bar the use of liquor, the WCTU was an intrusive force seeking to interfere with personal rights. This cartoon thus reveals how long what are now called "social issues" have affected the nation's politics and how they grow out of cultural and economic divisions within American society. In fact, controlling the use of alcohol has been one of the most persistent sources of social contention in the nation's history.

the house warm before electricity, and disposing of waste all demanded hard labor. Mary Mathews, a widowed teacher in the 1870s, "got up early every Monday morning and got my clothes all washed and boiled and in the rising water; and then commenced my school at nine." Other days of the week passed in the same fashion for her and other women.

To assist women in performing these tasks, manuals about housework became popular, along with cooking schools and college courses in home economics. Catherine Beecher collaborated with her famous sister, Harriet Beecher Stowe, author of *Uncle Tom's Cabin,* in writing *The American Woman's Home* (1869). In this volume, they argued that "family labor and care tend, not only to good health, but to the *highest culture of the mind*." Women, they continued, were "ministers of the family state."

In the new coeducational colleges and universities, home economics programs offered instructions in operating kitchens and dining rooms efficiently. Cooking schools appeared in large cities with separate instruction for "plain cooks" and a "Ladies Class" for affluent women who sought to link "the elegancies of artistic cookery with those economic interests which it is the duty of every woman to study." Assumptions about the secondary role of women pervaded these institutions.

Not all families experienced domestic harmony. Divorce became an option in many states, and defenders of marriage moved to tighten the conditions under which marriages could be dissolved. Laws to limit the sale of birth control devices and restrict abortions reflected the same trend. The New York Society for the Suppression of Vice was formed in 1872 under the leadership of Anthony Comstock. It lobbied successfully for a national law barring information deemed obscene about birth control and abortion from being sent through the mails. Modern debate about these issues has precedents that reach back a century or more and reveal the persistence of such concerns in American history.

Although women had made some gains after the Civil War, they remained second-class citizens within the masculine political order of the period. However, that brand of politics was also coming into question as voters prepared to decide whether President Grant deserved a second term.

Grant and the 1872 Election

By 1872, many commentators and voters in the North were dismayed at the spectacle of national politics. "We are in danger of the way of all Republics," said one critic of the existing system. "First freedom, then glory; when that is past, wealth, vice and corruption." Restoring ethical standards was the goal of the **Liberal Republicans** who wanted to field a candidate against President Grant in 1872. They believed that only in that way could Reconstruction be ended and civil service reform achieved. Leading the campaign were Senator Carl Schurz, a Missouri Republican; Edwin L. Godkin, editor of *The Nation;* and Charles Francis Adams, the son of former president John Quincy Adams.

Liberals argued for smaller government and an end to the protective tariff. "The Government," wrote E. L. Godkin, "must get out of the 'protective' business and the 'subsidy' business and the 'improvement' business and 'development' business . . . It cannot touch them without breeding corruption." But Reconstruction was their main target. They saw what happened in the South as an unwise experiment in racial democracy. Jacob D. Cox, who had been secretary of the interior under Grant, maintained that "the South can only be governed through the part of the community that embodies the intelligence and the capital." In effect, black Americans in the South would have to look to whites in that region for protection of their rights and privileges.

The problem was that the Liberal Republicans did not have a good national candidate to run against Grant. Few party leaders were men with real stature. Schurz was a native of Germany and therefore ineligible to run under the Constitution. The race came down to Charles Francis Adams, Lyman Trumbull of Illinois, and **Horace Greeley,** editor of the New York *Tribune.* After six ballots, Greeley became the nominee. At the age of 61, Greeley was an odd choice. He favored the protective tariff, unlike most reformers, and he was indifferent about the civil service. His main passion was ending Reconstruction. Once a harsh critic of the South, he had now mellowed. His personal opinions, which included vegetarianism and the use of human manure in farming, made him an eccentric to most Americans. "That Grant is an Ass no man can deny," said one Liberal in private, "but better an Ass than a mischievous idiot."

The 1872 Election

Grant was renominated on a platform that stressed the need to preserve Reconstruction: Voters in the North must safeguard what they had won during the Civil War. The Democrats were in a box. If they rejected Greeley, they had no chance to win. Picking him, however, would alienate southern voters who remembered Greeley's passion against the Confederacy. In the end, the Democrats accepted Greeley as their only alternative. The Liberal Republican–Democratic nominee made a vigorous public campaign, while Grant observed the tradition that the incumbent did not take part in the race personally.

The Republicans made their appeal on the issues of the war. One speaker told his audience that they could either "Go vote to burn school houses, desecrate churches and violate women or vote for Horace Greeley, which means the same thing." The black leader Frederick Douglass said of the impending contest: "If the Republican party goes down, freedom goes down with it." When the voters went to the polls, the outcome was a decisive victory for Grant and his party. The president swamped Greeley in the popular vote and in the electoral tally. There were still enough Republicans in the South to enable Grant to carry all but five of the southern states in one of the last honest elections the region would see for many years. The Democrats had reached a low point behind Greeley. Worn out by the rigors of the campaign, he died in late November. The triumph was a mixed one for Grant. He remained in the White House, but scandals would soon plague his second term.

A Surge of Scandals

As the excitement of the 1872 election faded, allegations of corruption in Congress surfaced. The first controversy turned on the efforts of the Crédit Mobilier Company (named after a French company) to purchase influence with lawmakers during the 1860s. The directors of the Union Pacific had established Crédit Mobilier to build the transcontinental line. By paying themselves to construct the railroad, the participants in the venture sold bonds that were marketed at a large profit to investors and insiders. The only problem was that much of the money in effect came from the federal government through loans and guarantees.

To avoid a congressional probe into the company, Crédit Mobilier's managers offered leading Republicans a chance to buy shares in the company at prices well below their market value. When the lawmakers sold their shares, they pocketed the difference, the equivalent of a bribe. A newspaper broke the story in late 1872 and an investigation ensued. The probe produced a few scapegoats but cleared most of the individuals involved. Nevertheless, the episode damaged the credibility of public officials.

Another embarrassing scandal occurred in February 1873. At the end of a congressional session, a last-minute deal gave senators and representatives a retroactive pay increase. The public denounced the action as the "Salary Grab." The *Chicago Tribune* said that it was

---

DOING HISTORY ONLINE

Grant and the Union Pacific Railroad

How do you think the scandals of the Grant era affected Reconstruction policy?

History Now™ Visit HistoryNOW to access primary sources and exercises related to this topic: http://now.ilrn.com/ayers_etal3e

"nothing more nor less than an act of robbery." When Congress reconvened in December 1873, repeal of the salary increase sailed through both houses as politicians backtracked. These two incidents produced widespread calls for reducing government expenditures and rooting out corruption. As the humorist Mark Twain said, "It could probably be shown by facts and figures that there is no distinctly native American criminal class except Congress."

The scandals persisted throughout the remainder of Grant's presidency. Within the Treasury Department, the Whiskey Ring was exposed. Officials involved took kickbacks from liquor interests in return for not collecting federal excise taxes on whiskey. President Grant appointed a new secretary of the treasury, Benjamin H. Bristow, and told him, "Let no guilty man escape if it can be avoided." The administration also faced queries concerning the secretary of war, W. W. Belknap. For some time, Belknap's wife had been receiving cash gifts from a man who sold supplies to the army. When these ties were revealed, a congressional committee sought to start impeachment proceedings. Belknap resigned and Grant accepted his hasty departure. Critics of the president argued that the trail of scandal reached close to the White House. Few doubted Grant's personal honesty, but his cabinet selections often seemed inadequate and sometimes corrupt.

Mark Twain himself captured the spirit of the times in his novel *The Gilded Age,* published in 1873. The main character, Colonel Beriah Sellers, was an engaging confidence man who embodied the faith in progress and economic growth of the postwar years, along with a healthy amount of fraud and deceit that accompanied the rapid expansion of business. In time, the title of Twain's book came to be used for the entire era between the end of Reconstruction and the start of the twentieth century. Beneath its appealing surface, this period grappled with issues of political corruption, social disorder, and economic inequities in ways that challenged older assumptions about the role of government in society.

The Panic of 1873 and Its Consequences

The sense of national crisis deepened in September 1873 when the banking house of Jay Cooke and Company failed. The bank could not pay its debts or return money to its depositors; it had to close. The

Library of Congress, Prints and Photographs Division

THE PANIC.—INSIDE THE STOCK EXCHANGE, READING THE LIST OF FAILURES.

The Panic of 1873 shook Americans's confidence in their economic system. This contemporary drawing of the New York Stock Exchange shows the names of the business failures being read.

disaster came because the bank could not market the bonds of the Northern Pacific Railroad in which it had invested heavily. As this important bank collapsed, others followed suit, businesses cut back on employment, and a downturn began. The problems rivaled similar panics that had occurred in 1819, 1837, and 1857; however, the Panic of 1873 was the worst of them all.

The immediate effects of the problem lasted until 1879. In fact, an extended period of economic hard times had begun that extended through the 1890s. A hallmark of the "Great Depression," as it was then called, was declining prices for agricultural products and manufactured goods. Americans faced an economy in which falling prices placed the heaviest burdens on people who were in debt or who earned their living by selling their labor. An abundance of cheap unskilled labor proved a boon for capitalists who wanted to keep costs down. For the poor, however, it meant that they had little job security and could easily be replaced if they protested against harsh working conditions. Industrialization went forward at a substantial human cost.

The Panic of 1873 occurred because of a speculative post–Civil War boom in railroad building. In 1869, railroad mileage stood at about 47,000 miles; 4 years later it had risen to 70,268 miles. The new railroad lines employed tens of thousands of workers and extended across a far wider geographical area than any previous manufacturing enterprise. When large railroads such as the Northern Pacific failed because of their overexpansion and inability to pay debts, the resulting damage rippled through society. Economic activities that were dependent on the rail lines, such as car making, steel rail production, and passenger services, also fell off. Layoffs of employees and bankruptcies for businesses followed. More than 10,000 companies failed in 1878, the worst year of the depression.

The Plight of the Unemployed

Americans who were thrown out of work during the 1870s had no system of unemployment insurance to cushion the shock of their plight. In some cities, up to a quarter of the workforce looked for jobs without success. Tramps roamed the countryside. The conventional wisdom held that natural forces had to restore prosperity; any form of political intervention would be useless and dangerous. When President Grant proposed that the national government generate jobs through public works, the secretary of the treasury responded: "It is not part of the business of government to find employment for people."

People out of a job during the mid-1870s became desperate. Laborers in the Northeast mounted a campaign called "Work for Bread" that produced large demonstrations in major cities. The marchers asked city and state governments to pay for projects creating parks and constructing streets so jobs would be provided. In January 1874, a demonstration at Tompkins Square in New York City pitted a crowd of 7,000 unemployed laborers against police. Many marchers were arrested; others were injured in the melee.

Labor unrest crackled through the first half of the decade. Strikes marked 1874 and 1875. In Pennsylvania the railroads used their control of police and strikebreakers to put down the "Long Strike" of coal miners

The hard times that arose from the Panic of 1873 produced labor unrest in many cities. Here an artist recreates the riot in Tompkins Square in New York in 1874.

Library of Congress, Prints and Photographs Division

and their supporters. Twenty alleged members of a secret society called the Molly Maguires were hanged. Conservatives feared that the nation was on the verge of revolution.

Distress and Protest among the Farmers

Discontent also flared in the farm belt. The price of wheat stood at $1.16 a bushel in 1873; it dropped to 95 cents a bushel a year later. The price of corn stood at 64 cents a bushel in 1874 but went down to 42 cents in 1875. These changes meant substantial drops in farm income. As a result, farmers' land- and equipment-related debts posed an even greater burden. Faced with the economic power of the railroads and grain merchants, the farmer, said one newspaper, was alone, "confronting organized and well-equipped enemies."

The Patrons of Husbandry, also known as the Grange, led the farm protests. Created in 1867, the nonpartisan Grange focused on complaints about the high mortgages that farmers owed, the prices they paid to middlemen such as the operators of grain elevators, and the discrimination they faced at the hands of the railroads in moving their goods to market. The pressure for regulatory legislation reached Congress in 1873–1874 but little was accomplished for the next 15 years.

Inflationary Solutions

The decline in consumer prices and the growing burden of debt on farmers and businessmen in the South and West created pressure for laws to put more money into circulation. That would make debts easier to pay. The Treasury Department's decision to end the coinage of silver aroused particular anger among southern and western advocates of inflation; they called it the "Crime of 1873." Proponents of the move argued that an overabundance of silver in the marketplace required the move to a gold standard. By coining silver into money at a price above its market levels, the government was subsidizing American silver production and cheapening the currency. Opponents of the change responded that eastern bankers were setting financial policy to the detriment of farmers and debtors.

An effort to inject a modest amount of inflation into the economy came in 1875. A currency bill cleared both houses of Congress; it provided some $64 million in additional money for the financial system. President Grant decided, after getting conservative advice to do so, to veto the bill in April 1875. Congress sustained his action. The government would not intervene in the deepening economic crisis. A similar reluctance to use government authority would contribute to the decline of the northern involvement with Reconstruction in the South.

The Failure of Reconstruction

After the presidential election of 1872, the North's already weakened commitment to Reconstruction ebbed still more. The Panic of 1873 distracted attention from the rights of black Americans. The Grant administration backed away from southern politics, and the Justice Department prosecuted fewer individuals for violations of the Enforcement Act against the Klan and pardoned some of those who had earlier been convicted of terrorist activity.

Northern support for Reconstruction eroded because of charges that the experiment in multiracial government was a failure. Liberal Republicans and northern Democrats spread racist propaganda to block the aspirations of southern blacks. The editor of *The Nation* said that black residents of South Carolina had an "average of intelligence but slightly above the level of animals." Northerners found it easier to believe that the South would be better off when whites were dominant. Black Americans should be left "to the kind feeling of the white race of the South."

A damaging setback to the economic hopes of African Americans came in 1874 with the failure of the Freedmen's Savings and Trust Company in Washington, D.C. Since its founding in 1865, the bank had managed the deposits of thousands of former slaves. It was supposed to provide lessons in thrift for its depositors. However, its manager sought larger returns by investing in speculative railroad projects. The Panic of 1873 caused huge losses, and the bank failed a year later. A few customers received a portion of their savings; most lost all their money.

The Stigma of Corruption

Corruption among southern Republican governments became a favorite theme of critics of Reconstruction. There were some genuine instances of wrongdoing, but these actions were far from widespread or typical. Moreover, the white governments that took over after Reconstruction also displayed lax political ethics and committed more serious misdeeds than their predecessors had. Nevertheless, the corruption issue gave the opponents of black political participation a perfect weapon, which they used to the full. Of course, it would not have mattered if Reconstruction governments had lacked any moral flaws

at all. Any government that represented a biracial community was unacceptable to white southerners.

Although participation of African Americans in southern politics increased dramatically during Reconstruction, their role in the region's public life never approached that of whites. Sixteen blacks served in Congress during the period, most only briefly, and several were unseated by white opponents. Many more held offices in the state legislatures, but even there, their numbers were comparatively modest. In 1868, for example, the Georgia legislature had 216 members, of whom only 32 were black. In only one state, South Carolina, did blacks ever hold a majority in the legislature, and they did so in only one house. One black man, P. B. S. Pinchback, served as governor of Louisiana for a little more than a month. Six African Americans held the office of lieutenant governor in the states of Louisiana, Mississippi, and South Carolina.

Two blacks served in the U.S. Senate. Hiram Revels became the first African American to enter the Senate. Elected to fill out an unexpired term, he served only one year. From 1875 to 1881, Blanche K. Bruce represented

Hiram Revels, senator from Mississippi, was one of the African American politicians whose national career, though brief, was one of the fruits of Reconstruction.

Mississippi for a full term. Thus, by the 1870s, blacks had made their presence felt in politics, but the decline of Reconstruction made that trend a short-lived one.

The Resurgence of the Democrats

The return of the Democrats as a political force further weakened support for Reconstruction. Hard economic times arising from the Panic of 1873 worked against the Republicans. Discontented farmers wanted the government to inflate the currency and raise prices on their crops. Factory workers clamored for more jobs to become available. In this setting, the fate of African Americans in the South became a secondary concern. Angry voters turned to the Democrats in the 1874 congressional races. The party used the issue of Republican corruption to regain control of the House of Representatives for the first time in 16 years. The Democrats added 77 seats in the House and also added 10 seats in the Senate in what one happy party member called a "Tidal Wave."

In the South, the revitalized Democrats "redeemed," as they called it, several states from Republican dominance. They began with Texas in 1873, then won back Arkansas the next year, and elected most of the South's members in the U.S. House of Representatives. Louisiana saw the emergence of the White League, which was determined that "the niggers shall not rule over us." In September 1874, open fighting erupted in New Orleans between armed Republicans and more than 3,000 White League partisans. President Grant sent in federal troops to restore calm. In Alabama, the Democrats also relied on violence and murder to oust the Republicans. Some blacks who attempted to vote in that state's Barbour County election were shot; 7 were killed and nearly 70 wounded. In view of the wide support for the Democratic party among southern whites, honest elections would probably have produced similar results for that party at the polls; but intimidation and violence were key elements in the victories that the Democrats secured in the South in 1874.

The Democrats intended to use their control of the House of Representatives to roll back Reconstruction and also prevent any further expansion of black rights. During the lame-duck congressional session of 1874–1875, Republicans, who were soon to lose power, enacted a path-breaking civil rights law that gave black citizens the right to sue in federal courts when they confronted discrimination in public accommodations such as a hotel or restaurant. The law involved a further expansion of national power; it remained to be seen how federal courts would rule when black plaintiffs sued to enforce their rights under the new civil rights statute.

Early in 1875, the Grant administration used troops to prevent occupation of the Louisiana state capital and illegal seizure of the state government by the Democrats in the midst of an election dispute. The action drew widespread protests from many northern Democrats and a growing number of Republicans who said that the white South should handle its own affairs. Meanwhile, the Democrats used more violence to overturn Republican rule in Mississippi. The state's governor, Adelbert Ames, stated that he was "fighting for the Negro, and to the whole country a white man is better than a 'Nigger.'" Without a national consensus behind civil rights and Reconstruction, the fate of black Americans lay in the hands of white southerners who were determined to keep African Americans in economic, political, and cultural subjugation.

Why Reconstruction Failed

Reconstruction failed to change American race relations because it challenged long-standing racist arrangements in both the North and South. The Civil War had called these traditions into question. In the years after the fighting ended, African Americans had acted to expand their political role and take charge of their own destiny. They sought and to some degree succeeded in becoming more than passive recipients of white oppression or largesse. Then the Panic of 1873, the scandals of the Grant presidency, and waning interest in black rights led white Americans to back away from an expansion of racial justice.

To help the freed slaves overcome the effects of slavery and racial bias would have involved an expansion of national governmental power to an extent far beyond what Americans believed was justified during the nineteenth century. Better to keep government small, argued whites, than to improve the lot of the former slaves in the South. As a result, black Americans experienced segregation and deepening oppression. The political gains of the Reconstruction era, especially the Fourteenth and Fifteenth Amendments, remained unfulfilled promises. That failure would be one of the most bitter legacies of this period of American history.

The Centennial Year

Several themes of late-nineteenth-century life intersected as the 1876 presidential election neared. The centennial of the Declaration of Independence offered citizens an opportunity to reflect on the nation's progress and the social issues that remained unresolved. The race question confronted leaders and citizens even as the

MAP 16.2 Reconstruction in the South

This map shows the times at which the states of the former Confederacy reentered the Union and then saw the Democrats regain political control. Note how quickly this process occurred for most of the southern states. The relative brevity of Reconstruction is one of the keys to why more sweeping racial change did not take place.

passions and commitments of Reconstruction faded. The contest for the White House seemed unusually important because it would shape the direction of the country for several decades.

Marking the Centennial

As the nation's 100th birthday neared, the Centennial International Exhibition to be held in Philadelphia attracted public fascination. In May of 1876, some 285 acres of fairgrounds held several hundred buildings crammed with exhibits, specimens, and artifacts from thirty-seven nations. The doors opened on May 10 for 200,000 spectators, including both houses of Congress, who heard a welcoming address by President Grant. The throng poured into the building to see what had been assembled as evidence of the advance of civilization in the United States. One of the stellar attractions was the huge Corliss steam engine. Standing 40 feet tall, it weighed 700 tons. Equally alluring was the "harmonic telegraph" of **Alexander Graham Bell,** as the telephone was then called.

The complexity of American life in the 1870s was not depicted at the exhibit. African Americans had almost no representation. Native American cultures were displayed as "curiosities" consisting of totem poles,

tepees, and trinkets. The Women's Pavilion stressed the joys of homemaking. That exhibit evoked a protest from Elizabeth Cady Stanton and Susan B. Anthony. On July 4, 1876, they read a "Women's Declaration of Independence" that contrasted their aspirations with the traditional attitudes toward women expressed at the fair. Their protest had little effect on public opinion.

Nearly 10 million Americans came to the fair during its run, which ended on November 10. They learned to eat bananas, and hot popcorn became a fad among city dwellers. The fair lost money, but at the same time contributed to a growing sense of national pride and confidence. Those emotions would be tested during the bitter presidential election that dominated the second half of 1876.

The Race for the White House

A key test of the nation's institutions occurred during the disputed presidential election of 1876. The closest electoral result up to that time produced a quarrel that threatened to renew hostilities between North and South. As the election process commenced, the Democrats felt optimism about their chances to regain power for the first time since 1860. Most of the southern

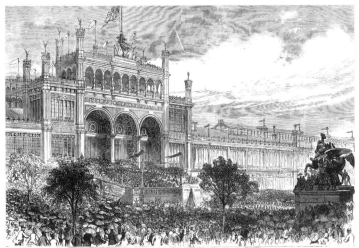

The Centennial Exposition in 1876 summed a century of the nation's progress. The opening ceremonies were recorded in this painting.

states would vote for the Democratic nominee; difficult economic times in the East and Middle West made voters sympathetic to the party out of power.

For its candidate, the party selected **Samuel J. Tilden,** the governor of New York. An opponent of corruption in his home state, he was regarded as a reformer even though smaller government was about all he stood for. A corporate lawyer, he believed in the gold standard, limited federal action, and restraints on spending. The Democratic platform spoke of a "revival of Jeffersonian democracy" and called for "high standards of official morality." Because Tilden was not in good health, the custom that presidential candidates did not campaign during that era worked to his advantage.

Among Republicans, there was some talk of a third term for President Grant, but the scandals of his presidency made him a liability. The front-runner for the nomination was James G. Blaine, a former Speaker of the House of Representatives. With the nomination seemingly in his grasp, Blaine came under fire for financial dealings with an Arkansas railroad while he was in the House. Despite his vigorous response to the charges, Republicans were wary of selecting him to run against Tilden.

At the national convention, Blaine took an early lead. As the balloting continued, his candidacy lost momentum. Instead, the Republicans selected Governor **Rutherford B. Hayes** of Ohio. Hayes had the virtues of a good military record in the Civil War and a spotless record in public office. In the campaign, the Democrats stressed Republican corruption and Tilden's honesty. In response, the Republicans relied on Reconstruction and war memories, as they had in 1868 and 1872. This rhetoric became known as "waving the bloody shirt," in memory of a Republican speaker who had held up a bloodstained Union tunic and urged voters to remember

the sacrifices of the Men in Blue. As one Republican put it, "Soldiers, every scar you have on your heroic bodies was given to you by a Democrat." Hayes saw the wisdom of this strategy: "It leads people away from hard times, which is our deadliest foe."

When the election results rolled in, it seemed at first that Tilden had won. With most of the South in his column, the Democrat had carried New York, Connecticut, and New Jersey. The electoral vote totals indicated that Tilden had won 184 votes, one short of the 185 he needed to become president. Hayes, on the other hand, had 165 electoral votes. Three southern states, Louisiana, Florida, and South Carolina, plus a disputed elector in Oregon, were still in doubt. If they all went for Hayes, he might be in the White House.

Republican operatives moved to contest the outcome in the three undecided states. Telegrams to party members asked for evidence that African American voters had been intimidated. Honest returns from these states, Republicans argued, would show that Hayes had carried each one. The Republicans believed,

In the dramatic 1876 election, the Democrats put forward "Honest Sam Tilden," who lost to Rutherford B. Hayes in the disputed contest.

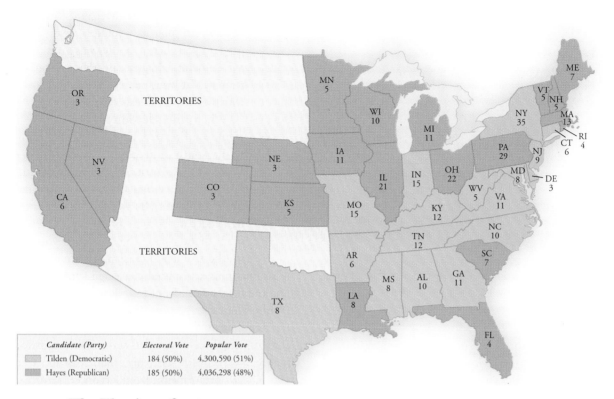

MAP 16.3 The Election of 1876

The presidential election of 1876 between Samuel J. Tilden for the Democrats and Rutherford B. Hayes for the Republicans turned on the votes of Florida, Louisiana, and South Carolina to produce the narrow one-vote victory in the electoral college for Hayes.

www View an animated version of this map or related maps at http://history.wadsworth.com/passages3e

moreover, that they had the advantage. In the three states they were contesting, the Republicans could rely on federal troops to safeguard state governments that were loyal to their cause. Otherwise, Democrats could simply occupy the state capitals and count the election returns their way.

The Constitution did not specify how a contested presidential election was to be resolved. Each of the states in question was submitting two sets of election returns that claimed to be official and to reflect the will of the people. The House of Representatives had the responsibility for electing a president if no one won a majority in the electoral college. At the same time, the Senate had the constitutional duty to tabulate the electoral vote. With Republicans in control of the Senate and with Democrats in control of the House, neither party could proceed without the support of the other.

To resolve the crisis, Congress created an electoral commission of 15 members, 10 from the Supreme Court. As originally conceived, the panel was to have 7 Republicans, 7 Democrats, and a politically independent Supreme Court justice named David Davis. Then Davis was elected to the U.S. Senate by the Illinois legislature with Democratic votes in a move to defeat a Republican

incumbent. That tactic won a Senate place for the Democrats but injured Tilden's chances of prevailing in the election controversy. Davis resigned from the commission, and another member of the Supreme Court, this time a Republican, took his place. In a series of 8–7 votes along straight party lines, the electoral commission accepted the Republican returns from Louisiana, Florida, and South Carolina, and allocated the single disputed Oregon electoral vote to Hayes as well. The ruling declared that Hayes had received 185 electoral votes and Tilden 184.

Who had really been elected president in 1876? Tilden had a margin of 250,000 popular votes over Hayes and had carried 16 states. Hayes had won 18 states in addition to the 3 contested southern states. In Louisiana, Florida, and South Carolina, Tilden had received a majority of the white vote, but black Republican voters had been intimidated and terrorized to such an extent that an honest count was in doubt. Essentially the election had ended in a tie. Resolving the issue of which man would be president became an issue for the two political parties to decide.

Despite the decision of the electoral commission, the Democratic House still had to declare Hayes the winner. With the March 4, 1877, inauguration date approaching, the Democrats postponed tallying the electoral vote in an effort either to make Tilden president after March 4 or to extract concessions from the Republicans. To prevent a crisis, negotiations began among leaders from both sides to put Hayes in the White House in return for Republican agreement to end Reconstruction. The discussions were complex, involving a variety of issues such as railroad subsidies for the South, but the underlying issue was Reconstruction. If Hayes became president, the South wanted assurances that Republican rule would not be maintained through federal military intervention. After much discussion, an unwritten understanding along these lines led Congress to decide on March 2, 1877, that Rutherford B. Hayes had been elected as president of the United States.

Conclusion

The events that led to Hayes becoming president had great historical significance. Although the new president did not withdraw federal troops from the South, neither did he use them to keep Republican governments in power. Nor did Hayes attempt to enforce Reconstruction in the courts. Whites regained control of the South's political institutions, and black southerners remained second-class citizens with limited political and economic rights.

Several powerful historical forces produced that sad result. Pervasive racism in both the North and the South labeled African Americans as unfit for self-government. Pursuing Reconstruction into the 1880s would have involved giving to the national government more power over the lives of individual Americans than would have been tolerated in that era. Weary of Reconstruction and its moral claims, the generation of white Americans who had fought the Civil War turned their attention to other national problems. In so doing, they condemned black citizens to continued segregation and oppression.

The era of the Civil War and Reconstruction did have a positive legacy. Slavery was abolished and the Union preserved. Black Americans had demonstrated that they could fight and die for their country, help make its laws, and function as full citizens when given an honest chance to do so. The Fourteenth and Fifteenth Amendments at least contained the promise of the further expansion of the rights of black Americans in the future. But for the moment the nation had missed a historical opportunity to create a more equitable, multiracial society.

As with any postwar period, the decade between 1867 and 1877 mixed constructive changes and lamentable results. The end of the fighting released energies that produced the construction of the transcontinental railroad, a surge of industrialization, and a renewal of white settlement in the West. At the same time, Native Americans saw their way of life threatened with extinction. Political corruption infected public life, and observers lamented a general slackening of the moral tone of the nation. After economic prosperity following the war, the Panic of 1873 and the hard times that ensued tested the endurance of average Americans.

Society found that women also wanted to share some of the fruits of emancipation. Campaigns for woman suffrage got under way, only to encounter adamant male resistance. Women turned to campaigns against alcohol as another means of making a political difference. In cultural realms, these were the years of Mark Twain, William Dean Howells, Henry James, and Bret Harte—American prose stylists who looked toward the creation of a national literature. Amid the discord and clamor of a society bent on economic expansion and a return to peacetime endeavors, Americans engaged problems that would carry on to the end of the century and beyond: racial justice, industrial growth, urbanization, and the proper balance between business and government. That citizens of that generation failed to solve all their difficulties is not surprising. What this chapter reveals is that they poured their energies and imagination into the task of creating a better nation in the wake of a destructive war that had shaped their lives in such a distinctive way.

The Chapter in Review

In the years between 1867 and 1877:

- The country embarked on an experiment in a multiracial democracy.
- African Americans in the South made a brave effort to participate in politics and economic life.
- Currents of racism and the opposition of white southerners doomed Reconstruction.
- Settlement of the West accelerated with the end of the Civil War and put pressure on Native American culture.
- Transcontinental railroads brought the nation together as a more cohesive economic unit.
- The Panic of 1873 began a decade-long slump that brought protests from unhappy farmers and workers.

- Although they were excluded from voting, women played a significant part in public life through voluntary associations.
- By the nation's centennial in 1876, the disputed election between Hayes and Tilden marked the ebbing away of the issues of the Civil War and the eventual abandonment of Reconstruction.

Making Connections Across Chapters

LOOKING BACK

The working out of Reconstruction and its ultimate failure forms the key theme of Chapter 16. Because the decision not to pursue racial justice had such long-range consequences for the United States, the substance of this chapter is central to an understanding of subsequent history.

1. How did the Republicans intend to reconstruct the South after the Civil War? What obstacles did they encounter?

2. How did the election of Ulysses S. Grant help or hinder the Reconstruction effort?

3. Why did Reconstruction not succeed in the South? What obstacles did white southerners place in the way of black participation in politics?

4. What defects in the national political system between 1865 and 1877 helped derail the chances of Reconstruction?

5. Which groups fully participated in making decisions about the direction of society? Which groups were either not represented or ignored?

LOOKING AHEAD

The next chapter takes up the process of industrialization and its effects on the economy and society. Elements in this chapter explain the rise of industrialism and set up the treatment of this issue in Chapter 17. Let's examine a few of them now.

1. What economic changes in the 1870s undercut Reconstruction and made industrialism seem more important?

2. How did the political system respond to the economic downturn of the 1870s, and how did these attitudes carry forward during the rest of the nineteenth century?

3. How did the political system then resemble modern alignments between Republicans and Democrats, and in what important ways were there differences?

Recommended Readings

Edwards, Laura F. *Gendered Strife and Confusion: The Political Culture of Reconstruction* (1997). Looks at the role of women after the Civil War.

Foner, Eric. *Reconstruction: America's Unfinished Revolution, 1863–1877* (1988). An excellent treatment of the whole period, especially the decline of Reconstruction.

Perman, Michael. *Emancipation and Reconstruction, 1862–1879*, 2d ed. (2003). A good brief account of the issues and problems of Reconstruction.

Richardson, Heather Cox. *The Death of Reconstruction: Race, Labor, and Politics in the Post-Civil War North, 1865–1901* (2001). Considers how changing attitudes toward African Americans and labor undercut Reconstruction.

Simpson, Brooks D. *The Reconstruction Presidents* (1998). A treatment of Reconstruction from the perspective of the chief executives.

Smith, Jean Edward. *Grant* (2001). A full-scale, sympathetic biography of the general and president.

Summers, Mark Wahlgren. *The Era of Good Stealings* (1993). Uses the corruption issue of the 1870s to produce a political history of the decade.

Wang, Xi. *The Trial of Democracy: Black Suffrage and Northern Republicans, 1860–1910* (1997). Discusses how voting issues shaped the adoption and then the abandonment of Reconstruction.

Identifications

Review your understanding of the following key terms, people, events, and dates for this chapter (these terms also appear in the Glossary at the end of the book):

Crazy Horse
Sitting Bull
George Armstrong Custer
suffrage

Susan B. Anthony
temperance
Liberal Republicans
Horace Greeley
Alexander Graham Bell
Samuel J. Tilden
Rutherford B. Hayes

Online Sources Guide

Use this listing to find online documents, images, interactive maps, simulations, and other resources related to this chapter:

American History Resource Center

http://history.wadsworth.com/rc/us

Documents

Fort Laramie Treaty

Interactive Maps

Presidential Elections by State, 1824–1876
Territorial Possessions of the United States, 1775–1870

Selected Images

Charles Sumner
Andrew Johnson
Depiction of Andrew Johnson as unsympathetic to South (cartoon)
Black schoolhouse during Reconstruction
Edwin Stanton
Ticket to Andrew Johnson's impeachment proceedings
Hiram Revel and Blanche K. Bruce, U.S. Congressmen from Mississippi

Driving the golden spike to form the first transcontinental railroad
Destroyed buffalo herds
George Armstrong Custer
Sitting Bull

Simulation

Reconstruction (Choose to be a southerner, former slave, carpetbagger, or Native American and make choices based on the circumstances and opportunities afforded.)

Document Exercises

1866 Emigration to Washington Territory of Four Hundred Women on the Steamer "Continental"

HistoryNOW

http://now.ilrn.com/ayers_etal3e

Primary Source Exercises

Support for Black Suffrage 1867 & 1869
Northern Whites and Black Rights
The Fifteenth Amendment Debate
Grant and the Union Pacific Railroad

Appendix

The Declaration of Independence
The Unanimous Declaration of the Thirteen United States of America

When in the Course of human events it becomes necessary for one people to dissolve the political bands which have connected them with another, and to assume among the Powers of the earth, the separate and equal station to which the Laws of Nature and of Nature's God entitle them, a decent respect to the opinions of mankind requires that they should declare the causes which impel them to the separation.

We hold these truths to be self-evident, that all men are created equal, that they are endowed by their Creator with certain unalienable Rights, that among these are Life, Liberty and the pursuit of Happiness. That to secure these rights, Governments are instituted among Men, deriving their just Powers from the consent of the governed. That whenever any Form of Government becomes destructive of these ends, it is the Right of the People to alter or to abolish it, and to institute new Government, laying its foundation on such principles and organizing its Powers in such form, as to them shall seem most likely to effect their Safety and Happiness. Prudence, indeed, will dictate that Governments long established should not be changed for light and transient causes; and accordingly all experience hath shewn, that mankind are more disposed to suffer, while evils are sufferable, than to right themselves by abolishing the forms to which they are accustomed. But when a long train of abuses and usurpations, pursuing invariably the same Object evinces a design to reduce them under absolute Despotism, it is their right, it is their duty, to throw off such Government, and to provide new Guards for their future security. Such has been the patient sufferance of these Colonies; and such is now the necessity which constrains them to alter their former Systems of Government. The history of the present King of Great Britain is a history of repeated injuries and usurpations, all having in direct object the establishment of an absolute Tyranny over these States. To prove this, let Facts be submitted to a candid world.

He has refused his Assent to Laws, the most wholesome and necessary for the public good.

He has forbidden his Governors to pass Laws of immediate and pressing importance, unless suspended in their operation till his Assent should be obtained; and when so suspended, he has utterly neglected to attend to them.

He has refused to pass other Laws for the accommodation of large districts of people, unless those people would relinquish the right of Representation in the Legislature, a right inestimable to them and formidable to tyrants only.

He has called together legislative bodies at places unusual, uncomfortable, and distant from the depository of their Public Records, for the sole Purpose of fatiguing them into compliance with his measures.

He has dissolved Representative Houses repeatedly, for opposing with manly firmness his invasions on the rights of the People.

He has refused for a long time, after such dissolutions, to cause others to be elected; whereby the Legislative Powers, incapable of Annihilation, have returned to the People at large for their exercise; the State remaining in the mean time exposed to all the dangers of invasion from without, and convulsions within.

He has endeavoured to prevent the Population of these States; for that purpose obstructing the Laws for Naturalization of Foreigners; refusing to pass others to encourage their migrations hither, and raising the conditions of new Appropriations of Lands.

He has obstructed the Administration of Justice, by refusing his Assent to Laws for establishing Judiciary Powers.

He has made Judges dependent on his Will alone, for the tenure of their offices, and the amount and payment of their salaries.

He has erected a multitude of New Offices, and sent hither swarms of Officers to harass our People, and eat out their substance.

He has kept among us, in times of peace, Standing Armies without the Consent of our legislatures.

He has affected to render the Military independent of and superior to the Civil Power.

He has combined with others to subject us to a jurisdiction foreign to our constitution, and unacknowledged by our laws; giving his Assent to their Acts of pretended Legislation:

Text is reprinted from the facsimile of the engrossed copy in the National Archives. The original spelling, capitalization, and punctuation have been retained. Paragraphing has been added.

For Quartering large bodies of armed troops among us:

For protecting them, by a mock Trial, from Punishment for any Murders which they should commit on the Inhabitants of these States:

For cutting off our Trade with all parts of the world:

For imposing Taxes on us without our Consent:

For depriving us in many cases, of the benefits of Trial by Jury:

For transporting us beyond Seas to be tried for pretended offences:

For abolishing the free System of English Laws in a neighbouring Province, establishing therein an Arbitrary government, and enlarging its Boundaries so as to render it at once an example and fit instrument for introducing the same absolute rule into these Colonies:

For taking away our Charters, abolishing our most valuable Laws, and altering fundamentally the Forms of our Governments:

For suspending our own Legislatures, and declaring themselves invested with Power to legislate for us in all cases whatsoever.

He has abdicated Government here, by declaring us out of his Protection, and waging War against us.

He has plundered our seas, ravaged our Coasts, burnt our towns, and destroyed the lives of our people.

He is at this time transporting large Armies of foreign Mercenaries to compleat the works of death, desolation and tyranny, already begun with circumstances of Cruelty and perfidy scarcely paralleled in the most barbarous ages, and totally unworthy the Head of a civilized nation.

He has constrained our fellow Citizens taken Captive on the high Seas to bear Arms against their Country, to become the executioners of their friends and Brethren, or to fall themselves by their Hands.

He has excited domestic insurrections amongst us, and has endeavoured to bring on the inhabitants of our frontiers, the merciless Indian Savages, whose known rule of warfare, is an undistinguished destruction of all ages, sexes and conditions.

In every stage of these Oppressions We have Petitioned for Redress in the most humble terms: Our repeated Petitions have been answered only by repeated injury. A Prince, whose character is thus marked by every act which may define a Tyrant, is unfit to be the ruler of a free People.

Nor have We been wanting in attentions to our British brethren. We have warned them from time to time of attempts by their legislature to extend an unwarrantable jurisdiction over us. We have reminded them of the circumstances of our emigration and settlement here. We have appealed to their native justice and magnanimity, and we have conjured them by the ties of our common kindred to disavow thee usurpations, which, would inevitably interrupt our connections and correspondence. They too have been deaf to the voice of justice and of consanguinity. We must, therefore, acquiesce in the necessity, which denounces our Separation, and hold them, as we hold the rest of mankind, Enemies in War, in Peace Friends.

We, therefore, the Representatives of the United States of America, in General Congress, Assembled, appealing to the Supreme Judge of the world for the rectitude of our intentions, do, in the Name, and by Authority of the good People of these Colonies, solemnly publish and declare, That these United Colonies are, and of Right ought to be Free and Independent States; that they are Absolved from all Allegiance to the British Crown, and that all political connection between them and the State of Great Britain, is and ought to be totally dissolved; and that, as Free and Independent States, they have full Power to levy War, conclude Peace, contract Alliances, establish Commerce, and to do all other Acts and Things which Independent States may of right do. And for the support of this Declaration, with a firm reliance on the protection of divine Providence, we mutually pledge to each other our Lives, our Fortunes and our sacred Honor.

The Constitution of the United States of America

We the People of the United States, in Order to form a more perfect Union, establish Justice, insure domestic Tranquility, provide for the common defence, promote the general Welfare, and secure the Blessings of Liberty to ourselves and our Posterity, do ordain and establish this Constitution for the United States of America.

Article I.

Section 1. All legislative Powers herein granted shall be vested in a Congress of the United States, which shall consist of a Senate and House of Representatives.

Section 2. The House of Representatives shall be composed of Members chosen every second Year by the People of the several States, and the Electors in each State shall have the Qualifications requisite for Electors of the most numerous Branch of the State Legislature.

No Person shall be a Representative who shall not have attained to the Age of twenty five Years, and been seven Years a Citizen of the United States, and who shall not, when elected, be an Inhabitant of that State in which he shall be chosen.

Representatives and direct Taxes[1] shall be apportioned among the several States which may be included within this Union, according to their respective Numbers, which shall be determined by adding to the whole Number of free Persons, including those bound to Service for a Term of Years, and excluding Indians not taxed, three fifths of all other Persons.[2] The actual Enumeration shall be made within three Years after the first Meeting of the Congress of the United States, and within every subsequent Term of ten Years, in such Manner as they shall by Law direct. The Number of Representatives shall not exceed one for every thirty Thousand, but each State shall have at Least one Representative; and until such enumeration shall be made, the State of New Hampshire shall be entitled to chuse three; Massachusetts eight; Rhode Island and Providence Plantations one; Connecticut five; New York six; New Jersey four; Pennsylvania eight; Delaware one; Maryland six; Virginia ten; North Carolina five; South Carolina five; and Georgia three.

When vacancies happen in the Representation from any State, the Executive Authority thereof shall issue Writs of Election to fill such Vacancies.

The House of Representatives shall chuse their Speaker and other Officers; and shall have the sole Power of Impeachment.

Section 3. The Senate of the United States shall be composed of two Senators from each State, chosen by the Legislature thereof, for six Years; and each Senator shall have one Vote.[3]

Immediately after they shall be assembled in Consequence of the first Election, they shall be divided as equally as may be into three Classes. The Seats of the Senators of the first Class shall be vacated at the Expiration of the second Year, of the second Class at the Expiration of the fourth Year, and of the third Class at the Expiration of the sixth Year, so that one third may be chosen every second Year; and if Vacancies happen by Resignation, or otherwise, during the Recess of the Legislature of any State, the Executive thereof may make temporary Appointments until the next Meeting of the Legislature, which shall then fill such Vacancies.[4]

No Person shall be a Senator who shall not have attained to the Age of thirty Years, and been nine Years a Citizen of the United States, and who shall not, when elected, be an Inhabitant of that State for which he shall be chosen.

The Vice President of the United States shall be President of the Senate, but shall have no Vote, unless they be equally divided.

The Senate shall chuse their other Officers, and also a President pro tempore, in the Absence of the Vice President, or when he shall exercise the Office of President of the United States.

The Senate shall have the sole Power to try all Impeachments. When sitting for that Purpose, they shall be on Oath or Affirmation. When the President of the United States is tried, the Chief Justice shall preside: And no Person shall be convicted without the Concurrence of two thirds of the Members present.

Judgment in Cases of Impeachment shall not extend further than to removal from Office, and disqualification to hold and enjoy any Office of honor, Trust or Profit under the United States: but the Party convicted shall nevertheless be liable and subject to Indictment, Trial, Judgment and Punishment, according to Law.

Section 4. The Times, Places and Manner of holding Elections for Senators and Representatives, shall be

---

Text is from the engrossed copy in the National Archives. Original spelling, capitalization, and punctuation have been retained.

[1] Modified by the Sixteenth Amendment.
[2] Replaced by the Fourteenth Amendment.

[3] Superseded by the Seventeenth Amendment.
[4] Modified by the Seventeenth Amendment.

prescribed in each State by the Legislature thereof, but the Congress may at any time by Law make or alter such Regulation, except as to the Places of chusing Senators.

The Congress shall assemble at least once in every Year, and such Meeting shall be on the first Monday in December, unless they shall by Law appoint a different Day.[5]

Section 5. Each House shall be the Judge of the Elections, Returns and Qualifications of its own Members, and a Majority of each shall constitute a Quorum to do Business; but a smaller Number may adjourn from day to day, and may be authorized to compel the Attendance of absent Members, in such Manner, and under such Penalties as each House may provide.

Each House may determine the Rules of its Proceedings, punish its Members for disorderly Behaviour, and, with the Concurrence of two thirds, expel a Member.

Each House shall keep a Journal of its Proceedings, and from time to time publish the same, excepting such Parts as may in their Judgment require Secrecy; and the Yeas and Nays of the Members of either House on any question shall, at the Desire of one fifth of those Present, be entered on the Journal.

Neither House, during the Session of Congress, shall, without the Consent of the other, adjourn for more than three days, nor to any other Place than that in which the two Houses shall be sitting.

Section 6. The Senators and Representatives shall receive a Compensation for their Services, to be ascertained by Law, and paid out of the Treasury of the United States. They shall in all Cases, except Treason, Felony and Breach of the Peace, be privileged from Arrest during their Attendance at the Session of their respective Houses, and in going to and returning from the same; and for any Speech or Debate in either House, they shall not be questioned in any other Place.

No Senator or Representative shall, during the Time for which he was elected, be appointed to any civil Office under the Authority of the United States, which shall have been created, or the Emoluments whereof shall have been encreased during such time; and no Person holding any Office under the United States, shall be a Member of either House during his Continuance in Office.

Section 7. All Bills for raising Revenue shall originate in the House of Representatives; but the Senate may propose or concur with Amendments as on other Bills.

Every Bill which shall have passed the House of Representatives and the Senate shall, before it become a Law, be presented to the President of the United States; If he approve he shall sign it, but if not he shall return it, with his Objections to that House in which it shall have originated, who shall enter the Objections at large on their Journal, and proceed to reconsider it. If after such Reconsideration two thirds of that House shall agree to pass the Bill, it shall be sent, together with the Objections, to the other House, by which it shall likewise be reconsidered, and if approved by two thirds of that House, it shall become a Law. But in all such Cases the Votes of both Houses shall be determined by yeas and Nays, and the Names of the Persons voting for and against the Bill shall be entered on the Journal of each House respectively. If any Bill shall not be returned by the President within ten Days (Sundays excepted) after it shall have been presented to him, the Same shall be a Law, in like Manner as if he had signed it, unless the Congress by their Adjournment prevent its Return, in which Case it shall not be a Law.

Every Order, Resolution, or Vote to which the Concurrence of the Senate and House of Representatives may be necessary (except on a question of Adjournment) shall be presented to the President of the United States; and before the Same shall take Effect, shall be approved by him, or being disapproved by him shall be repassed by two thirds of the Senate and House of Representatives, according to the Rules and Limitations prescribed in the Case of a Bill.

Section 8. The Congress shall have power To lay and collect Taxes, Duties, Imposts and Excises, to pay the Debts and provide for the common Defence and general Welfare of the United States; but all Duties, Imposts and Excises shall be uniform throughout the United States;

To borrow Money on the credit of the United States;

To regulate Commerce with foreign Nations, and among the several States, and with the Indian Tribes;

To establish an uniform Rule of Naturalization, and uniform Laws on the subject of Bankruptcies throughout the United States;

To coin Money, regulate the Value thereof, and of foreign Coin, and fix the Standard of Weights and Measures;

To provide for the Punishment of counterfeiting the Securities and current Coin of the United States;

To establish Post Offices and post Roads;

To promote the Progress of Science and useful Arts, by securing for limited Times to Authors and Inventors the exclusive Right to their respective Writings and Discoveries;

To constitute Tribunals inferior to the supreme Court;

To define and punish Piracies and Felonies committed on the high Seas, and Offences against the Law of Nations;

---

[5]Superseded by the Twentieth Amendment.

To declare War, grant Letters of Marque and Reprisal, and make Rules concerning Captures on Land and Water;

To raise and support Armies, but no Appropriation of Money to that Use shall be for a longer Term than two Years;

To provide and maintain a Navy;

To make Rules for the Government and Regulation of the land and naval Forces;

To provide for calling forth the Militia to execute the Laws of the Union, suppress Insurrections and repel Invasions;

To provide for organizing, arming, and disciplining, the Militia, and for governing such Part of them as may be employed in the Service of the United States, reserving to the States respectively, the Appointment of the Officers, and the Authority of training the Militia according to the discipline prescribed by Congress;

To exercise exclusive Legislation in all Cases whatsoever, over such District (not exceeding ten Miles square) as may, by Cession of particular States, and the Acceptance of Congress, become the Seat of the Government of the United States, and to exercise like Authority over all Places purchased by the Consent of the Legislature of the State in which the Same shall be, for the Erection of Forts, Magazines, Arsenals, dock-Yards, and other needful Buildings;—And

To make all Laws which shall be necessary and proper for carrying into Execution the foregoing Powers, and all other Powers vested by this Constitution in the Government of the United States, or in any Department or Officer thereof.

Section 9. The Migration or Importation of such Persons as any of the States now existing shall think proper to admit, shall not be prohibited by the Congress prior to the Year one thousand eight hundred and eight, but a Tax or duty may be imposed on such Importation, not exceeding ten dollars for each Person.

The Privilege of the Writ of Habeas Corpus shall not be suspended, unless when in Cases of Rebellion or Invasion the public Safety may require it.

No Bill of Attainder or ex post facto Law shall be passed.

No Capitation, or other direct, Tax shall be laid, unless in Proportion to the Census or Enumeration herein before directed to be taken.

No Tax or Duty shall be laid on Articles exported from any State.

No Preference shall be given by any Regulation of Commerce or Revenue to the Ports of one State over those of another: nor shall Vessels bound to, or from, one State, be obliged to enter, clear, or pay Duties in another.

No Money shall be drawn from the Treasury, but in Consequence of Appropriations made by Law, and a regular Statement and Account of the Receipts and Expenditures of all public Money shall be published from time to time.

No Title of Nobility shall be granted by the United States: And no Person holding any Office of Profit or Trust under them, shall, without the Consent of the Congress, accept of any present, Emolument, Office, or Title, of any kind whatever, from any King, Prince, or foreign State.

Section 10. No State shall enter into any Treaty, Alliance, or Confederation; grant Letters of Marque and Reprisal; coin Money; emit Bills of Credit; make any Thing but gold and silver Coin a Tender in Payment of Debts; pass any Bill of Attainder, ex post facto Law, or Law impairing the Obligation of Contracts, or grant any Title of Nobility.

No State shall, without the Consent of the Congress, lay any Imposts or Duties on Imports or Exports, except what may be absolutely necessary for executing its inspection Laws: and the net Produce of all Duties and Imposts, laid by any State on Imports or Exports, shall be for the Use of the Treasury of the United States; and all such Laws shall be subject to the Revision and Controul of the Congress.

No State shall, without the Consent of Congress, lay any Duty of Tonnage, keep Troops, or Ships of War in time of Peace, enter into any Agreement or Compact with another State, or with a foreign Power, or engage in War, unless actually invaded, or in such imminent Danger as will not admit of delay.

Article II.

Section 1. The executive Power shall be vested in a President of the United States of America. He shall hold his Office during the Term of four Years, and, together with the Vice President, chosen for the same Term, be elected, as follows:

Each State shall appoint, in such Manner as the Legislature thereof may direct, a Number of Electors, equal to the whole Number of Senators and Representatives to which the State may be entitled in the Congress: but no Senator or Representative, or Person holding an Office of Trust or Profit under the United States, shall be appointed an Elector.

The Electors shall meet in their respective States, and vote by Ballot for two Persons, of whom one at least shall not be an Inhabitant of the same State with themselves. And they shall make a List of all the Persons voted for, and of the Number of Votes for each; which List they shall sign and certify, and transmit sealed to the

Seat of the Government of the United States, directed to the President of the Senate. The President of the Senate shall, in the Presence of the Senate and House of Representatives, open all the Certificates, and the Votes shall then be counted. The Person having the greatest Number of Votes shall be the President, if such Number be a Majority of the whole Number of Electors appointed; and if there be more than one who have such Majority, and have an equal Number of Votes, then the House of Representatives shall immediately chuse by Ballot one of them for President; and if no Person have a Majority, then from the five highest on the List the said House shall in like Manner chuse the President. But in chusing the President, the Votes shall be taken by States, the Representation from each State having one Vote; A quorum for this Purpose shall consist of a Member or Members from two thirds of the States, and a Majority of all the States shall be necessary to a Choice. In every Case, after the Choice of the President, the Person having the greatest Number of Votes of the Electors shall be the Vice President. But if there should remain two or more who have equal Votes, the Senate shall chuse from them by Ballot the Vice President.[6]

The Congress may determine the Time of chusing the Electors, and the Day on which they shall give their Votes; which Day shall be the same throughout the United States.

No Person except a natural born Citizen, or a Citizen of the United States, at the time of the Adoption of this Constitution, shall be eligible to the Office of President, neither shall any Person be eligible to that Office who shall not have attained to the Age of thirty five Years, and been fourteen Years a Resident within the United States.

In Case of the Removal of the President from Office, or of his Death, Resignation, or Inability to discharge the Powers and Duties of the said Office, the Same shall devolve onthe Vice President, and the Congress may by Law provide for the Case of Removal, Death, Resignation or Inability, both of the President and Vice President, declaring what Officer shall then act as President, and such Officer shall act accordingly, until the Disability be removed, or a President shall be elected.[7]

The President shall, at stated Times, receive for his Services, a Compensation, which shall neither be encreased nor diminished during the Period for which he shall have been elected, and he shall not receive within that Period any other Emolument from the United States, or any of them.

Before he enter on the Execution of his Office, he shall take the following Oath or Affirmation:—"I do solemnly swear (or affirm) that I will faithfully execute the Office of President of the United States, and will to the best of my Ability, preserve, protect and defend the Constitution of the United States."

Section 2. The President shall be Commander in Chief of the Army and Navy of the United States, and of the Militia of the several States, when called into the actual Service of the United States; he may require the Opinion, in writing, of the principal Officer in each of the executive Departments, upon any Subject relating to the Duties of their respective Offices, and he shall have Power to grant Reprieves and Pardons for Offences against the United States, except in Cases of Impeachment.

He shall have Power, by and with the Advice and Consent of the Senate, to make Treaties, provided two thirds of the Senators present concur; and he shall nominate, and by and with the Advice and Consent of the Senate, shall appoint Ambassadors, other public Ministers and Consuls, Judges of the supreme Court, and all other Officers of the United States, whose Appointments are not herein otherwise provided for, and which shall be established by Law; but the Congress may by Law vest the Appointment of such inferior Officers, as they think proper, in the President alone, in the Courts of Law, or in the Heads of Departments.

The President shall have Power to fill up all Vacancies that may happen during the Recess of the Senate, by granting Commissions which shall expire at the End of their next Session.

Section 3. He shall from time to time give the Congress Information of the State of the Union, and recommend to their Consideration such Measures as he shall judge necessary and expedient; he may, on extraordinary Occasions, convene both Houses, or either of them, and in Case of Disagreement between them, with Respect to the Time of Adjournment, he may adjourn them to such Time as he shall think proper; he shall receive Ambassadors and other public Ministers; he shall take Care that the Laws be faithfully executed, and shall Commission all the Officers of the United States.

Section 4. The President, Vice President and all civil Officers of the United States, shall be removed from Office on Impeachment for, and Conviction of, Treason, Bribery, or other high Crimes and Misdemeanors.

Article III.

Section 1. The judicial Power of the United States, shall be vested in one supreme Court, and in such inferior Courts as the Congress may from time to time ordain

---

[6]Superseded by the Twelfth Amendment.
[7]Modified by the Twenty-fifth Amendment.

and establish. The Judges, both of the supreme and inferior Courts, shall hold their Offices during good Behaviour, and shall, at stated Times, receive for their Services, a Compensation, which shall not be diminished during their Continuance in Office.

Section 2. The judicial Power shall extend to all Cases, in Law and Equity, arising under this Constitution, the Laws of the United States, and Treaties made, or which shall be made, under their Authority;—to all Cases affecting Ambassadors, other public Ministers and Consuls;—to all Cases of admiralty and maritime Jurisdiction;—to Controversies to which the United States shall be a Party;—to Controversies between two or more States;—between a State and Citizens of another State;[8]—between Citizens of different States,—between Citizens of the same State claiming Lands under Grants of different States, and between a State, or the Citizens thereof, and foreign States, Citizens or Subjects.

In all Cases affecting Ambassadors, other public Ministers and Consuls, and those in which a State shall be Party, the supreme Court shall have original Jurisdiction. In all the other Cases before mentioned, the supreme Court shall have appellate Jurisdiction, both as to Law and Fact, with such Exceptions, and under such Regulations as the Congress shall make.

The Trial of all Crimes, except in Cases of Impeachment, shall be by Jury; and such Trial shall be held in the State where the said Crimes shall have been committed; but when not committed within any State, the Trial shall be at such Place or Places as the Congress may by Law have directed.

Section 3. Treason against the United States, shall consist only in levying War against them, or in adhering to their Enemies, giving them Aid and Comfort. No Person shall be convicted of Treason unless on the Testimony of two Witnesses to the same overt Act, or on Confession in open Court.

The Congress shall have Power to declare the Punishment of Treason, but no Attainder of Treason shall work Corruption of Blood, or Forfeiture except during the Life of the Person attainted.

Article IV.

Section 1. Full Faith and Credit shall be given in each State to the public Acts, Records, and judicial Proceedings of every other State. And the Congress may by general Laws prescribe the Manner in which such Acts, Records and Proceedings shall be proved, and the Effect thereof.

Section 2. The Citizens of each State shall be entitled to all Privileges and Immunities of Citizens in the several States.

A Person charged in any State with Treason, Felony, or other Crime, who shall flee from Justice, and be found in another State, shall on Demand of the executive Authority of the State from which he fled, be delivered up, to be removed to the State having Jurisdiction of the Crime.

No Person held to Service or Labour in one State, under the Laws thereof, escaping into another, shall, in Consequence of any Law or Regulation therein, be discharged from such Service or Labour, but shall be delivered up on Claim of the Party to whom such Service or Labour may be due.

Section 3. New States may be admitted by the Congress into this Union; but no new State shall be formed or erected within the Jurisdiction of any other State, nor any State be formed by the Junction of two or more States, or Parts of States, without the Consent of the Legislatures of the States concerned as well as of the Congress.

The Congress shall have Power to dispose of and make all needful Rules and Regulations respecting the Territory or other Property belonging to the United States; and nothing in this Constitution shall be so construed as to Prejudice any Claims of the United States, or of any particular State.

Section 4. The United States shall guarantee to every State in this Union a Republican Form of Government, and shall protect each of them against Invasion; and on Application of the Legislature, or of the Executive (when the Legislature cannot be convened) against domestic Violence.

Article V.

The Congress, whenever two thirds of both Houses shall deem it necessary, shall propose Amendments to this Constitution, or, on the Application of the Legislatures of two thirds of the several States, shall call a Convention for proposing Amendments, which, in either Case, shall be valid to all Intents and Purposes, as Part of this Constitution, when ratified by the Legislatures of three fourths of the several States, or by Conventions in three fourths thereof, as the one or the other Mode of Ratification may be proposed by the Congress; Provided that no Amendment which may be made prior to the Year One thousand eight hundred and eight shall in any Manner affect the first and fourth Clauses in the Ninth Section of the first Article; and that no State, without its Consent, shall be deprived of its equal Suffrage in the Senate.

---

[8]Modified by the Eleventh Amendment.

Article VI.

All Debts contracted and Engagements entered into, before the Adoption of this Constitution, shall be as valid against the United States under this Constitution, as under the Confederation.

This Constitution, and the Laws of the United States which shall be made in Pursuance thereof; and all Treaties made, or which shall be made, under the Authority of the United States, shall be the supreme Law of the Land; and the Judges in every State shall be bound thereby, any Thing in the Constitution or Laws of any State to the Contrary notwithstanding.

The Senators and Representatives before mentioned, and the Members of the several State Legislatures, and all executive and judicial Officers, both of the United States and of the several States, shall be bound by Oath or Affirmation, to support this Constitution; but no religious Test shall ever be required as a Qualification to any Office or public Trust under the United States.

Article VII.

The Ratification of the Conventions of nine States, shall be sufficient for the Establishment of this Constitution between the States so ratifying the Same.

Done in Convention by the Unanimous Consent of the States present the Seventeenth Day of September in the Year of our Lord one thousand seven hundred and Eighty seven and of the Independence of the United States of America the Twelfth. In witness whereof We have hereunto subscribed our Names,

Articles in Addition to, and Amendment of, the Constitution of the United States of America, Proposed by Congress, and Ratified by the Legislatures of the Several States, Pursuant to the Fifth Article of the Original Constitution.

Amendment I[9]

Congress shall make no law respecting an establishment of religion, or prohibiting the free exercise there-of; or abridging the freedom of speech, or of the press; or the right of the people peaceably to assemble, and to petition the Government for a redress of grievances.

Amendment II

A well regulated Militia, being necessary to the security of a free State, the right of the people to keep and bear Arms shall not be infringed.

Amendment III

No Soldier shall, in time of peace, be quartered in any house, without the consent of the Owner, nor in time of war, but in a manner to be prescribed by law.

Amendment IV

The right of the people to be secure in their persons, houses, papers, and effects, against unreasonable searches and seizures, shall not be violated, and no Warrants shall issue, but upon probable cause, supported by Oath or affirmation, and particularly describing the place to be searched, and the persons or things to be seized.

Amendment V

No person shall be held to answer for a capital or otherwise infamous crime, unless on a presentment or indictment of a Grand Jury, except in cases arising in the land or naval forces, or in the Militia, when in actual service in time of War or public danger; nor shall any person be subject for the same offence to be twice put in jeopardy of life or limb; nor shall be compelled in any criminal case to be a witness against himself, nor be deprived of life, liberty, or property, without due process of law; nor shall private property be taken for public use, without just compensation.

Amendment VI

In all criminal prosecutions, the accused shall enjoy the right to a speedy and public trial, by an impartial jury of the State and district wherein the crime shall have been committed, which district shall have been previously ascertained by law, and to be informed of the nature and cause of the accusation; to be confronted with the witnesses against him; to have compulsory process for obtaining witnesses in his favor, and to have the Assistance of Counsel for his defence.

Amendment VII

In suits at common law, where the value in controversy shall exceed twenty dollars, the right of trial by jury shall be preserved, and no fact tried by a jury, shall be otherwise reexamined in any Court of the United States, than according to the rules of the common law.

Amendment VIII

Excessive bail shall not be required, nor excessive fines imposed, nor cruel and unusual punishments inflicted.

---

[9]The first ten amendments were passed by Congress September 25, 1789. They were ratified by three-fourths of the states December 15, 1791.

Amendment IX

The enumeration in the Constitution, of certain rights, shall not be construed to deny or disparage others retained by the people.

Amendment X

The powers not delegated to the United States by the Constitution; nor prohibited by it to the States, are reserved to the States respectively, or to the people.

Amendment XI[10]

The Judicial power of the United States shall not be construed to extend to any suit in law or equity, commenced or prosecuted against one of the United States by Citizens of another State, or by Citizens or Subjects of any Foreign State.

Amendment XII[11]

The Electors shall meet in their respective States and vote by ballot for President and Vice-President, one of whom, at least, shall not be an inhabitant of the same State with themselves; they shall name in their ballots the person voted for as President, and in distinct ballots the person voted for as Vice-President, and they shall make distinct lists of all persons voted for as President, and of all persons voted for as Vice-President, and of the number of votes for each, which lists they shall sign and certify, and transmit sealed to the seat of the government of the United States, directed to the President of the Senate;—The President of the Senate shall, in the presence of the Senate and House of Representatives, open all the certificates and the votes shall then be counted;—The person having the greatest number of votes for President, shall be the President, if such number be a majority of the whole number of Electors appointed; and if no person have such majority, then from the persons having the highest numbers not exceeding three on the list of those voted for as President, the House of Representatives shall choose immediately, by ballot, the President. But in choosing the President, the votes shall be taken by states, the representation from each state having one vote; a quorum for this purpose shall consist of a member or members from two-thirds of the states, and a majority of all the states shall be necessary to a choice. And if the House of Representatives shall not choose a President whenever the right of choice shall

devolve upon them, before the fourth day of March next following, then the Vice-President shall act as President, as in the case of the death or other constitutional disability of the President.—The person having the greatest number of votes as Vice-President, shall be the Vice-President, if such number be a majority of the whole number of Electors appointed, and if no person have a majority, then from the two highest numbers on the list, the Senate shall choose the Vice-President; a quorum for the purpose shall consist of two-thirds of the whole number of Senators, and a majority of the whole number shall be necessary to a choice. But no person constitutionally ineligible to the office of President shall be eligible to that of Vice-President of the United States.

Amendment XIII[12]

Section 1. Neither slavery nor involuntary servitude, except as a punishment for crime whereof the party shall have been duly convicted, shall exist within the United States, or any place subject to their jurisdiction.

Section 2. Congress shall have power to enforce this article by appropriate legislation.

Amendment XIV[13]

Section 1. All persons born or naturalized in the United States, and subject to the jurisdiction thereof, are citizens of the United States and of the State wherein they reside. No State shall make or enforce any law which shall abridge the privileges or immunities of citizens of the United States; nor shall any State deprive any person of life, liberty, or property, without due process of law; nor deny to any person within its jurisdiction the equal protection of the laws.

Section 2. Representatives shall be apportioned among the several States according to their respective numbers, counting the whole number of persons in each State, excluding Indians not taxed. But when the right to vote at any election for the choice of electors for President and Vice-President of the United States, Representatives in Congress, the Executive and Judicial officers of a State, or the members of the Legislature thereof, is denied to any of the male inhabitants of such State, being twenty-one years of age, and citizens of the United States, or in any way abridged, except for participation in rebellion, or other crime, the basis of representation therein shall be reduced in the proportion which the number of such

---

[10]Passed March 4, 1794. Ratified January 23, 1795.
[11]Passed December 9, 1803. Ratified June 15, 1804.

[12]Passed January 31, 1865. Ratified December 6, 1865.
[13]Passed June 13, 1866. Ratified July 9, 1868.

male citizens shall bear to the whole number of male citizens twenty-one years of age in such State.

Section 3. No person shall be a Senator or Representative in Congress, or elector of President and Vice-President, or hold any office, civil or military, under the United States, or under any State, who, having previously taken an oath, as a member of Congress, or as an officer of the United States, or as a member of any State legislature, or as an executive or judicial officer of any State, to support the Constitution of the United States, shall have engaged in insurrection or rebellion against the same, or given aid or comfort to the enemies thereof. But Congress may by a vote of two-thirds of each House, remove such disability.

Section 4. The validity of the public debt of the United States, authorized by law, including debts incurred for payment of pensions and bounties for services in suppressing insurrection or rebellion, shall not be questioned. But neither the United States nor any State shall assume or pay any debt or obligation incurred in aid of insurrection or rebellion against the United States, or any claim for the loss or emancipation of any slave; but all such debts, obligations, and claims shall be held illegal and void.

Section 5. The Congress shall have the power to enforce, by appropriate legislation, the provisions of this article.

Amendment XV[14]

Section 1. The right of citizens of the United States to vote shall not be denied or abridged by the United States or by any State on account of race, color, or previous conditions of servitude—

Section 2. The Congress shall have power to enforce this article by appropriate legislation.

Amendment XVI

The Congress shall have power to lay and collect taxes on incomes, from whatever source derived, without apportionment among the several States, and without regard to any census or enumeration.

Amendment XVII[15]

The Senate of the United States shall be composed of two Senators from each State, elected by the people

thereof, for six years; and each Senator shall have one vote. The electors in each State shall have the qualifications requisite for electors of the most numerous branch of the State legislatures.

When vacancies happen in the representation of any State in the Senate, the executive authority of such State shall issue writs of election to fill such vacancies: *Provided,* That the legislature of any State may empower the executive thereof to make temporary appointments until the people fill the vacancies by election as the legislature may direct.

This amendment shall not be so construed as to affect the election or term of any Senator chosen before it becomes valid as part of the Constitution.

Amendment XVIII[16]

Section 1. After one year from the ratification of this article the manufacture, sale, or transportation of intoxicating liquors within, the importation thereof into, or the exportation thereof from the United States and all territory subject to the jurisdiction thereof for beverage purposes is hereby prohibited.

Section 2. The Congress and the several States shall have concurrent power to enforce this article by appropriate legislation.

Section 3. This article shall be inoperative unless it shall have been ratified as an amendment to the Constitution by the legislatures of the several States, as provided in the Constitution, within seven years from the date of the submission hereof to the States by the Congress.

Amendment XIX[17]

The right of citizens of the United States to vote shall not be denied or abridged by the United States or by any State on account of sex.

Congress shall have power to enforce this article by appropriate legislation.

Amendment XX[18]

Section 1. The terms of the President and Vice-President shall end at noon on the 20th day of January, and the terms of Senators and Representatives at noon on the 3d day of January, of the years in which such terms would have ended if this article had not been ratified; and the terms of their successors shall then begin.

---

[14]Passed February 26, 1869. Ratified February 2, 1870.
[15]Passed May 13, 1912. Ratified April 8, 1913.

[16]Passed December 18, 1917. Ratified January 16, 1919.
[17]Passed June 4, 1919. Ratified August 18, 1920.
[18]Passed March 2, 1932. Ratified January 23, 1933.

Section 2. The Congress shall assemble at least once in every year, and such meeting shall begin at noon on the 3d day of January, unless they shall by law appoint a different day.

Section 3. If, at the time fixed for the beginning of the term of the President, the President elect shall have died, the Vice-President elect shall become President. If a President shall not have been chosen before the time fixed for the beginning of his term, or if the President elect shall have failed to qualify, then the Vice-President elect shall act as President until a President shall have qualified; and the Congress may by law provide for the case wherein neither a President elect nor a Vice-President elect shall have qualified, declaring who shall then act as President, or the manner in which one who is to act shall be selected, and such person shall act accordingly until a President or Vice-President shall have qualified.

Section 4. The Congress may by law provide for the case of the death of any of the persons from whom the House of Representatives may choose a President whenever the right of choice shall have devolved upon them, and for the case of the death of any of the persons from whom the Senate may choose a Vice-President whenever the right of choice shall have devolved upon them.

Section 5. Sections 1 and 2 shall take effect on the 15th day of October following the ratification of this article.

Section 6. This article shall be inoperative unless it shall have been ratified as an amendment to the Constitution by the legislatures of three-fourths of the several States within seven years from the date of its submission.

Amendment XXI[19]

Section 1. The eighteenth article of amendment to the Constitution of the United States is hereby repealed.

Section 2. The transportation or importation into any State, Territory, or possession of the United States for delivery or use therein of intoxicating liquors, in violation of the laws thereof, is hereby prohibited.

Section 3. This article shall be inoperative unless it shall have been ratified as an amendment to the Constitution by conventions in the several States, as provided in the Constitution, within seven years from the date of the submission hereof to the States by the Congress.

Amendment XXII[20]

No person shall be elected to the office of the President more than twice, and no person who has held the office

of President, or acted as President, for more than two years of a term to which some other person was elected President shall be elected to the office of the President more than once.

But this Article shall not apply to any person holding the office of President when this Article was proposed by the Congress, and shall not prevent any person who may be holding the office of President, or acting as President, during the term within which this Article becomes operative from holding the office of President or acting as President during the remainder of such term.

Amendment XXIII[21]

Section 1. The District constituting the seat of Government of the United States shall appoint in such manner as the Congress may direct:

A number of electors of President and Vice President equal to the whole number of Senators and Representatives in Congress to which the District would be entitled if it were a State, but in no event more than the least populous State; they shall be in addition to those appointed by the States, but they shall be considered, for the purposes of the election of President and Vice President, to be electors appointed by the State; and they shall meet in the District and perform such duties as provided by the twelfth article of amendment.

Section 2. The Congress shall have power to enforce this article by appropriate legislation.

Amendment XXIV[22]

Section 1. The right of citizens of the United States to vote in any primary or other election for President or Vice President, or for Senator or Representative in Congress, shall not be denied or abridged by the United States or any State by reason of failure to pay any poll tax or other tax.

Section 2. The Congress shall have power to enforce this article by appropriate legislation.

Amendment XXV[23]

Section 1. In case of the removal of the President from office or of his death or resignation, the Vice President shall become President.

---

[19]Passed February 20, 1933. Ratified December 5, 1933.
[20]Passed March 12, 1947. Ratified March 1, 1951.

[21]Passed June 16, 1960. Ratified April 3, 1961.
[22]Passed August 27, 1962. Ratified January 23, 1964.
[23]Passed July 6, 1965. Ratified February 11, 1967.

Section 2. Whenever there is a vacancy in the office of the Vice President, the President shall nominate a Vice President who shall take office upon confirmation by a majority vote of both Houses of Congress.

Section 3. Whenever the President transmits to the President pro tempore of the Senate and the Speaker of the House of Representatives his written declaration that he is unable to discharge the powers and duties of his office, and until he transmits them a written declaration to the contrary, such powers and duties shall be discharged by the Vice President as Acting President.

Section 4. Whenever the Vice President and a majority of either the principal officers of the executive department or of such other body as Congress may by law provide, transmit to the President pro tempore of the Senate and the Speaker of the House of Representatives their written declaration that the President is unable to discharge the powers and duties of his office, the Vice President shall immediately assume the powers and duties of the office of Acting President

Thereafter, when the President transmits to the President pro tempore of the Senate and the Speaker of the House of Representatives his written declaration that no inability exists, he shall resume the powers and duties of his office unless the Vice President and a majority of either the principal officers of the executive department or of such other body as Congress may by law provide, transmit within four days to the President pro tempore of the Senate and the Speaker of the House of Representatives their written declaration that the President is unable to discharge the powers and duties of his office. Thereupon Congress shall decide the issue, assembling within forty-eight hours for that purpose if not in session. If the Congress, within twenty-one days after receipt of the latter written declaration, or, if Congress is not in session, within twenty-one days after Congress is required to assemble, determines by two-thirds vote of both Houses that the President is unable to discharge the powers and duties of his office, the Vice-President shall continue to discharge the same as Acting President; otherwise, the President shall resume the powers and duties of his office.

Amendment XXVI[24]

Section 1. The right of citizens of the United States, who are eighteen years of age or older, to vote shall not be denied or abridged by the United States or by any State on account of age.

Section 2. The Congress shall have power to enforce this article by appropriate legislation.

Amendment XXVII[25]

No law, varying the compensation for the service of the Senators and Representatives, shall take effect, until an election of Representatives shall have intervened.

---

[24]Passed March 23, 1971. Ratified July 5, 1971.
[25]Passed September 25, 1789. Ratified May 7, 1992.

Glossary

abolitionism The movement that emerged in the 1830s in the United States dedicated to the immediate end of slavery.

Abraham Lincoln The sixteenth president (1861–1865), he led the United States throughout the Civil War.

African American soldiers Finally allowed to enlist in May 1863, African American soldiers accounted for more than one hundred eighty thousand troops and played a major role in the Union victory.

Agricultural Adjustment Act Created under Roosevelt's New Deal program to help farmers, its purpose was to reduce production of staple crops, thereby raising farm prices and encouraging more diversified farming.

Al Smith A vigorous reformer as governor of New York, he became the first Roman Catholic to win the nomination of a major party for president of the United States.

Alain Locke An African American poet and an important member of the Harlem Renaissance.

Alan Freed The self-proclaimed father of rock 'n' roll, he was the first DJ to play black rhythm and blues artists on the radio.

Albert B. Fall The secretary of the interior involved in the Teapot Dome scandal.

Alexander Graham Bell His invention of the telephone at the end of the nineteenth century changed the nature of life in the United States.

Alexander Hamilton The first U.S. secretary of the treasury (1789–1795), he established the national bank and public credit system. In 1804 Hamilton was mortally wounded in a duel with his political rival Aaron Burr.

Alger Hiss A U.S. public official accused of espionage at the height of the Cold War, he was convicted of perjury in 1950 in a controversial case.

Alice Paul A main figure in the radical wing of the woman's suffrage movement in the early twentieth century.

Alphonse "Al" Capone A gangster devoted to gaining control of gambling, prostitution, and bootlegging in the Chicago area.

Amistad A slave ship on which forty-nine Africans rebelled in 1839 off the coast of Cuba. The ship sailed to Long Island Sound where Spanish authorities demanded they be turned over for punishment. A group of American abolitionists, led by former President John Quincy Adams, fought for and won their freedom in 1841. The thirty-five who survived returned to Africa.

Amos 'n' Andy The most popular radio program of the Depression years, it portrayed the lives of two African American men in Harlem as interpreted by two white entertainers, Freeman Gosden and Charles Correll.

Anaconda Plan Term given to the strategy employed by the North during the Civil War in which the Confederacy would be slowly strangled by a blockade.

Andrew Carnegie A major business leader in the evolution of the steel industry.

Andrew Jackson The seventh president of the United States (1829–1837) who, as a general in the War of 1812, defeated the Red Sticks at Horseshoe Bend (1814) and the British at New Orleans (1815). As president he denied the right of individual states to nullify federal laws and increased presidential powers.

Andrew Johnson The seventeenth president of the United States (1865–1869); he succeeded the assassinated Abraham Lincoln.

Anita Hill She brought charges of sexual misconduct against Clarence Thomas and herself became a very polarizing figure as a result.

Anne Hutchinson English-born American colonist and religious leader who was banished from Boston (1637) for her religious beliefs, which included an emphasis on an individual's direct communication with God.

annexation To append or attach, especially to a larger or more significant thing.

Antietam The battle near Sharpsburg, Maryland, in September 1862 in which the Union Army stopped the Confederacy's drive into the North. With twenty-five thousand casualties, it was the bloodiest single-day battle of the Civil War.

anti-imperialists A league created during the last two years of McKinley's first term to unite the opposition against McKinley's foreign policy.

Antonio López de Santa Anna Leader of Mexico at the time of the battle at the Alamo. Taken prisoner when attacked at San Jacinto, he signed treaties removing Mexican troops from Texas, granting Texas its independence, and recognizing the Rio Grande as the boundary.

Appomattox The small Virginia village that served as the site of surrender of Confederate forces under Robert E. Lee to Ulysses S. Grant on April 9, 1865, generally recognized as bringing the Civil War to an end.

Articles of Confederation The compact first adopted by the original thirteen states of the United States in 1781 that remained the supreme law until 1789.

Atlanta Compromise A program for African American acceptance of white supremacy put forth by Booker T. Washington.

Atlantic slave trade In the 1440s Portugal initiated the trans-Atlantic trade that lasted four centuries. During that time, other European nations participated in a commerce that took more than ten million people from Africa.

Aztec Inhabitants of the Valley of Mexico who founded their capital, Tenochtitlán, in the early fourteenth century. Prior to the arrival of the Spanish, the Aztecs built a large empire in which they dominated many neighboring peoples. Their civilization included engineering, mathematics, art, and music.

baby boom A sudden increase in births in the years after World War II.

Bank of the United States The first bank was established in 1791 as part of the system proposed by Alexander Hamilton to launch the new government on a sound economic basis.

Bataan Peninsula U.S. and Philippine World War II troops surrendered this peninsula in western Luzon, Philippines, to the Japanese in April 1942 after an extended siege; U.S. forces recaptured the peninsula in February 1945.

Battle of Wounded Knee The last major chapter in the Indian wars, it was fought on the Pine Ridge Reservation in South Dakota.

Bay of Pigs Fifteen hundred Cuban exiles, supported by the CIA, landed here on April 17, 1961, in an unsuccessful attempt to overthrow the new Communist government of Fidel Castro.

Benjamin Franklin An American public official, writer, scientist, and printer. He proposed a plan for union at the Albany Congress (1754) and played a major part in the American Revolution. Franklin helped secure French support for the colonists, negotiated the Treaty of Paris (1783), and helped draft the Constitution (1787). His numerous scientific and practical innovations include the lightning rod, bifocal spectacles, and a stove.

Benjamin Harrison The twenty-third president of the United States, he lost the popular vote but gained a majority of the electoral college votes in the 1888 election.

Betty Friedan A feminist who wrote *The Feminist Mystique* in 1963 and founded the National Organization for Women in 1966.

bicameral legislature A legislature with two houses or chambers.

Bill Morris A black man burned at the stake in Balltown, Louisiana, for allegedly robbing and raping a white woman; no trial was held.

Bill of Rights The first ten amendments to the Constitution. These contain basic protection of the rights of individuals from abuses by the federal government, including freedom of speech, press, religion, and assembly.

Black Power Movement that developed in the mid-1960s calling for renewed racial pride in their African American heritage. They believed that to seek full integration into the existing white order would be to capitulate to the institutions of racism.

Black Thursday October 29, 1929, the day the spectacular New York stock market crash began.

Bleeding Kansas Nickname given to the Kansas Territory in the wake of a number of clashes between proslavery and antislavery supporters.

Bonus Army Thousands of veterans, determined to collect promised cash bonuses early, came to Washington during the summer of 1932 to listen to Congress debate the bonus proposal.

Booker T. Washington A spokesman for blacks in the 1890s who argued that African Americans should emphasize hard work and personal development rather than rebelling against their conditions.

bootleggers Enterprising individuals who moved alcohol across the border into the United States from Canada and the Caribbean during Prohibition. Their wares were sold at illegal saloons or "speakeasies" where city dwellers congregated in the evenings.

border ruffians Missouri settlers who crossed into Kansas to lend support for proslavery issues (1855).

Boss Politics An urban "political machine" that relied for its existence on the votes of the large inner-city population. The flow of money through the machine was often based on corruption.

Boston Massacre (1770) A pre-Revolutionary incident growing out of the resentment against the British troops sent to Boston to maintain order and to enforce the Townshend Act.

Boston Tea Party In 1773 Bostonians protested the Tea Act, which retained the Townshend duty on tea and granted a monopoly on tea sales in the colonies to the East India Company, by dumping chests of tea into Boston Harbor.

brain trust A group of prominent academics recruited as a source of ideas for the Roosevelt campaign to write speeches.

Branch Davidians A religious sect involved in a siege by government agents in Waco, Texas, in April 1993 that ended in deadly violence.

Brown v. Board of Education The unanimous Supreme Court decision ruling that segregated facilities in public education were "inherently unequal" and violated the Fourteenth Amendment's guarantee of equal protection under the law. This decision overruled the longstanding "separate but equal" doctrine of *Plessy v. Ferguson.*

Camp David Accords The historic treaty between Egypt and Israel, brokered by President Carter at Camp David in 1978, that returned the Sinai Peninsula to Egypt in return for Egypt's recognition of the State of Israel.

Carrie Chapman Catt A leader in the woman's suffrage campaign.

Cesar Chavez A labor organizer who founded the National Farm Workers Association in 1962.

Charles A. Lindbergh His solo flight across the Atlantic Ocean in 1927 made him an international hero.

Charles Evans Hughes A Supreme Court justice, he was the Republican candidate for president in the 1916 election. He had been a progressive governor of New York and said little about foreign policy.

Charles Grandison Finney An American evangelist, theologian, and educator (1792–1875). Licensed to the Presbyterian ministry in 1824, he had phenomenal success as a revivalist in the eastern states, converting many who became noted abolitionists.

Charles Sumner U.S. senator from Massachusetts (1851–1874), he was a noted orator with an uncompromising opposition to slavery.

Charlotte Perkins Gilman An ardent advocate of feminism.

Christopher Columbus An Italian mariner who sailed for Spain in 1492 in search of a western route to Asia. He located San Salvador in the West Indies, opening the Americas to European exploration and colonization.

Civil Works Administration (CWA) The agency tasked with creating jobs and restoring self-respect by handing out pay envelopes instead of relief checks. In reality, workers sometimes performed worthless tasks, known as "boondoggles," but much of the $1 billion budget was spent on projects of lasting value including airports and roads.

Civilian Conservation Corps (CCC) One of the New Deal's most popular programs, it took unemployed young men from the cities and put them to work on conservation projects in the country.

Clarence Thomas A Supreme Court justice appointed by President George H. W. Bush in 1991 whose confirmation became controversial due to allegations of sexual misconduct made against him.

Cold War War or rivalry conducted by all means available except open military action. Diplomatic relations are not commonly broken.

Colin Powell He served as chairman of the Joint Chiefs of Staff from 1989 to 1996 and was influential in planning U.S. strategy during the Persian Gulf War.

Common Sense Published by Thomas Paine in January 1776, *Common Sense* convinced the American public of the need for independence.

Confederacy The Confederate States of America.

Constitutional Convention Fifty-five delegates met in Philadelphia in May 1787 to reform the U.S. government. They chose to draft a new constitution rather than revise the Articles of Confederation.

contrabands Term used by the Union for the black people who made their way to the Union ranks. This term usually applies to goods prohibited by law or treaty from being imported or exported.

Contract with America The Republican election platform of the 1990s, promising action on such items as a balanced budget amendment, term limits for Congress members, and making legislators obey the regulations they applied to society.

Contras A Nicaraguan military force trained and financed by the United States that opposed the socialist Nicaraguan government led by the Sandinista party.

Copperheads A term used by some Republicans to describe Peace Democrats. It implied that they were traitors to the Union. Peace Democrats thought that the war was a failure and should be abandoned.

Crazy Horse Native American Sioux leader who defeated George Custer in battle.

daguerreotypes An early photographic process with the image made on a light-sensitive, silver-coated metallic plate.

Dawes Act This act distributed land to the Indians so that it could be sold to whites.

Dayton Peace Accords A peace settlement involving Bosnia in 1995 that was worked out in Dayton, Ohio; it did not prove to be a permanent solution for the problems in the Balkans.

Declaration of Independence The document, drafted primarily by Thomas Jefferson, that declared the independence of the thirteen mainland colonies from Great Britain and enumerated their reasons for separating.

Denmark Vesey American insurrectionist. A freed slave in South Carolina, he was implicated in the planning of a large uprising of slaves and was hanged. The event led to more stringent slave codes in many southern states.

détente An easing of tensions among countries, which usually leads to increased economic, diplomatic, and other types of contacts between former rivals.

dollar diplomacy A phrase used to describe Secretary of State Philander C. Knox's foreign policy under President Taft, which focused on expanding American investments abroad, especially in Latin America and China.

Dominion of New England In an effort to centralize the colonies and create consistent laws and political structures, James II combined Massachusetts, New Hampshire, Maine, Plymouth, Rhode Island, Connecticut, New York, and New Jersey under the Dominion of New England.

domino theory A theory that if one nation comes under Communist control, neighboring nations will soon follow.

Dorothea Dix An American philanthropist, reformer, and educator who took charge of nurses for the U.S. in the Civil War.

***Dred Scott* case** An enslaved man sued for his freedom in 1847, leading to a crucial Supreme Court decision in 1857 in which the Court ruled that African Americans held no rights as citizens and that the Missouri Compromise of 1820 was unconstitutional. The decision was widely denounced in the North and strengthened the new Republican party.

Dust Bowl The name given to areas of the prairie states that suffered ecological devastation in the 1930s and then again to a lesser extent in the mid-1950s.

Edmond Genêt French ambassador who enlisted American mercenaries to assist the French against the British. Genêt's move threatened relations between the United States and Britain.

Edward Bellamy The author of *Looking Backward* (1888), a major protest novel.

Eleanor Roosevelt A diplomat, writer, and First Lady of the United States (1933–1945) as the wife of President Franklin D. Roosevelt. A delegate to the United Nations (1945–1953 and 1961–1962), she was an outspoken advocate for human rights. Her written works include *This I Remember* (1949).

election of 1840 The election between Democrat Martin Van Buren and the Whig party's William Henry Harrison, won by Harrison.

electoral college The group that elects the president. Each state received as many electors as it had congressmen and senators combined.

Eli Whitney American inventor and manufacturer whose invention of the cotton gin (1793) revolutionized the cotton industry. He also established the first factory to assemble muskets with interchangeable parts.

Elizabeth Cady Stanton American feminist and social reformer who helped organize the first woman's rights convention, held in Seneca Falls, New York (1848), for which she wrote a Declaration of Sentiments calling for the reform of discriminatory practices that perpetuated sexual inequality.

Elizabeth I Queen of England (1558–1603) who succeeded the Catholic Mary I and reestablished Protestantism in England. Her reign was marked by several plots to overthrow her, the execution of Mary Queen of Scots (1587), the defeat of the Spanish Armada (1588), and domestic prosperity and literary achievement.

Ellis Island An immigration station opened in 1892 where new arrivals were passed through a medical examination and were questioned about their economic prospects.

emancipation The ending of slavery, initiated in the Emancipation Proclamation of 1863 but not accomplished in many places until the Confederate surrender in 1865.

Enlightenment A philosophical movement of the eighteenth century that emphasized the use of reason to scrutinize previously accepted doctrines and traditions and that brought about many humanitarian reforms.

Enola Gay The B-29 bomber, named after the mother of pilot Colonel Paul W. Tibbets, that dropped the first atomic bomb on the Japanese city of Hiroshima on August 6, 1945, killing more than one hundred thousand people.

Equal Rights Amendment (ERA) Congress overwhelmingly passed the Equal Rights Amendment in 1972, but by the mid-1970s conservative groups had managed to stall its confirmation by the states.

Era of Good Feelings Period in U.S. history (1817–1823) when, the Federalist party having declined, there was little open party feeling.

Erie Canal The first major American canal, stretching two hundred fifty miles from Lake Erie across the state of New York to Albany, where boats then traveled down the Hudson River to New York City. Begun in 1818, it was completed in 1825.

Eugene Debs Leader of the American Railway Union, which struck in sympathy with the workers at the Pullman Palace Car Company. This labor dispute experience helped persuade Debs to become a leader of the Socialist party.

Executive Order 9066 Issued by President Roosevelt on February 19, 1942, it designated certain parts of the country as sensitive military areas from which "any or all persons may be excluded," which led to the forced evacuation of more than one hundred twenty thousand people of Japanese ancestry from the West Coast of the United States.

F. Scott Fitzgerald A serious novelist of the day and author of *The Great Gatsby* who, along with his wife Zelda, captured attention as the embodiment of the free spirit of the Jazz Age.

Fannie Lou Hamer Daughter of illiterate Mississippi sharecroppers, she helped lead the civil rights struggle in Mississippi, focusing on voting rights for African Americans and representation in the national Democratic party.

Fidel Castro Cuban revolutionary leader who overthrew the corrupt regime of dictator Fulgencio Batista in 1959 and soon after established a Communist state. Prime minister of Cuba from 1959 to 1976, he has been president of the government and First Secretary of the Communist party in Cuba since 1976.

fire-eaters Southerners who were enthusiastic supporters of southern rights and later of secession.

flappers Young, single, middle-class women who wore their hair and dresses short, rolled their stockings down, used cosmetics, and smoked in public. Signaling a desire for independence and equality, flappers were self-reliant, outspoken, and had a new appreciation for the pleasures of life.

Fort Sumter The fort in the harbor of Charleston, South Carolina, that was fired on by the Confederacy on April 12, 1861, triggering the Civil War.

forty-niners Mostly men lured to California by the gold rush of 1849.

Fourteen Points Wilson's peace program, which included freedom of the seas, free trade, and more open diplomacy.

Francis Drake English naval hero and explorer who was the first Englishman to circumnavigate the world (1577–1580) and was vice admiral of the fleet that destroyed the Spanish Armada (1588).

Francis Gary Powers Pilot of a U.S. U-2 high altitude reconnaissance aircraft shot down over the Soviet Union on May 1, 1960.

Franklin D. Roosevelt The thirty-second president of the United States, he assumed the presidency at the depth of the Great Depression and helped the American people regain faith in themselves. He brought hope with his inaugural address in which he promised prompt, vigorous action and asserted that "the only thing we have to fear is fear itself."

Franz Ferdinand An Austrian archduke murdered along with his wife in Sarajevo, Bosnia. Austria's response to the dual murder led to the beginnings of World War I.

Frederick Douglass American abolitionist and journalist who escaped from slavery (1838) and became an influential lecturer in the North and abroad. He wrote *Narrative of the Life of Frederick Douglass* (1845) and cofounded and edited the *North Star* (1847–1860), an abolitionist newspaper.

free blacks The name often given to the hundreds of thousands of unenslaved African Americans who lived in the American South, especially in the Upper South states of Maryland and Virginia and in all the major cities of the region, during the days of slavery.

Freedmen's Bureau A federal agency created in 1865 to supervise newly freed people. It oversaw relations between whites and blacks in the South, issued food rations, and supervised labor contracts.

freedom riders Interracial groups who rode buses in the South so that a series of federal court decisions declaring segregation on buses and in waiting rooms unconstitutional would not be ignored by white officials.

Free-Soil party A U.S. political party formed in 1848 to oppose the extension of slavery into the territories; merged with the Liberty party in 1848.

French and Indian War The name often used for the Seven Years' War in North America. The conflict began in 1754 in the Ohio Valley between British colonists and the French and their Indian allies.

Fugitive Slave Act The federal act of 1850 providing for the return between states of escaped black slaves.

General Douglas MacArthur He served as chief of staff (1930–1935) and commanded the Allied forces in the South Pacific during World War II. Initially losing the Philippines to the Japanese in 1942, he regained the islands and accepted the surrender of Japan in 1945. He commanded the UN forces in Korea (1950–1951) until a conflict in strategies led to his dismissal by President Truman.

General Dwight D. Eisenhower The thirty-fourth president of the United States and supreme commander of the Allied Expeditionary Force during World War II. He launched the invasion of Normandy

(June 6, 1944) and oversaw the final defeat of Germany in 1945.

General George C. Marshall A soldier, diplomat, and politician who, as U.S. secretary of state (1947–1949), organized the European Recovery Plan, often called the Marshall Plan, for which he received the 1953 Nobel Peace Prize.

General William Westmoreland General who was the senior commander of U.S. troops in Vietnam from 1964 through 1968.

George Armstrong Custer Colonel famous for his battle at Little Big Horn against the Sioux Indians.

George B. McClellan Major General of the United States Army who led forces in Virginia in 1861 and 1862. He was widely blamed for not taking advantage of his numerical superiority to defeat the Confederates around Richmond. McClellan ran against Abraham Lincoln for president in 1864 on the Democratic ticket.

George Dewey On May 1, 1898, he inflicted a decisive defeat on the Spanish Navy at Manila Bay in the Philippine Islands.

George H. W. Bush The forty-first president of the United States, he was in office when the Soviet Union collapsed.

George Herman "Babe" Ruth This Boston Red Sox pitcher was sold to the New York Yankees in 1918 for $400,000. He belted out fifty-four home runs during the 1920 season, and fans flocked to see him play.

George McGovern A U.S. senator from South Dakota, he opposed the Vietnam War and was defeated as the 1972 Democratic candidate for president.

George Pullman Developer of the railroad sleeping car and creator of a model town outside Chicago where his employees were to live.

George Rogers Clark American military leader and frontiersman who led raids on British troops and Native Americans in the West during the Revolutionary War.

George W. Bush The forty-third president of the United States.

George Wallace A three-time governor of Alabama, he first came to national attention as an outspoken segregationist. Wallace ran unsuccessfully for the presidency in 1968 and 1972.

George Washington Commander-in-chief of the Continental Army during the American Revolution, presiding officer at the Constitutional Convention, and the first president of the United States (1789–1797).

Gerald Ford The thirty-eighth president of the United States, he was appointed vice president on the resignation of Spiro Agnew and became president when Richard Nixon resigned over the Watergate scandal. As president, Ford granted a full pardon to Nixon in 1974.

Geronimo An Apache leader who resisted white incursions until his capture in 1886.

Gettysburg Address A brief speech given by President Lincoln at the dedication of the Gettysburg Cemetery in November 1863 that declared that the Civil War was dedicated to freedom.

Gifford Pinchot He worked closely with Roosevelt to formulate a conservation policy that involved managing natural resources, not locking them up for indefinite future use.

Glorious Revolution The English Revolution of 1688–1689 against the authoritarian policies and Catholicism of James II. James was forced into exile, and his daughter Mary and her husband William of Orange took the throne. The revolution secured the dominance of Parliament over royal power.

good neighbor policy A new Latin American policy wherein Hoover withdrew the Marines from Nicaragua and Haiti, and in 1930 the State Department renounced the Roosevelt Corollary of 1904.

Granville T. Woods A black inventor who devised the "third rail" to convey electric power to streetcars.

Great Awakening An immense religious revival that swept across the Protestant world.

great compromise A plan proposed by a delegation from Connecticut that established a bicameral Congress with a House of Representatives, based on a state's population, and the Senate, in which each state would be represented equally.

Great Migration A massive movement of blacks leaving the South for cities in the North that began slowly in 1910 and accelerated between 1914 and 1920. During this time, more than six hundred thousand African Americans left the South.

Grimké sisters The first female abolitionist speakers; they were prominent figures in the antislavery movement of the late 1830s.

Grover Cleveland The twenty-second and twenty-fourth president of the United States, he was the first Democrat elected to the presidency after the Civil War.

Gulf of Tonkin Resolution Following reports of a confrontation with North Vietnamese in the Tonkin Gulf in 1964, President Johnson requested, and received, congressional authority to "take all necessary measures" to repel "further aggression" in Vietnam, giving the president formal authority to escalate the war.

Half-Way Covenant The Puritan practice whereby parents who had been baptized but had not yet experienced conversion could bring their children before the church and have them baptized.

Harpers Ferry A Virginia town that was the site of John Brown's raid in 1859, a failed attempt to lead a slave insurrection. It ignited public opinion in both the North and the South.

Harriet Beecher Stowe Author of *Uncle Tom's Cabin* (1852), the most important abolitionist novel.

Harriet Tubman An escaped slave who returned to the South and led hundreds of enslaved people to freedom in the North. Active throughout the 1850s, Tubman became famous as the most active member of the Underground Railroad.

Harry Hopkins Roosevelt's choice to run the Federal Emergency Relief Administration. He eventually became Roosevelt's closest advisor.

Harry S Truman The thirty-third president of the United States, he took office following the death of Franklin D. Roosevelt. Reelected in 1948 in a stunning political upset, Truman's controversial and historic decisions included the use of atomic weapons against Japan, desegregation of the U.S. military, and dismissal of General MacArthur as commander of U.S. forces during the Korean War.

Hartford Convention A gathering of Federalists in 1814 that called for significant amendments to the Constitution and attempted to damage the Republican party. The Treaty of Ghent and Andrew Jackson's victory at New Orleans annulled any recommendation of the convention.

Haymarket Affair On May 4, 1886, workmen in Chicago gathered to protest police conduct during a strike at a factory of the McCormick Company.

Henry Cabot Lodge A Massachusetts senator best remembered for spearheading Senate blockage of American membership in the League of Nations on the ground that its covenant threatened American sovereignty.

Henry Clay American politician who pushed the Missouri Compromise through the U.S. House of Representatives (1820) in an effort to reconcile free and slave states.

Henry Ford An automaker who developed the assembly line and low-priced automobiles.

Henry Kissinger A German-born American diplomat, he was national security advisor and U.S. secretary of state under Presidents Nixon and Ford. He shared the 1973 Nobel Peace Prize for helping to negotiate the Vietnam ceasefire.

Herman Melville Author of *Moby Dick* (1851), often considered to be the greatest American novel of the nineteenth century.

Hernán Cortés Spanish explorer who conquered the Aztecs initially in 1519, retreated when they rebelled, then defeated them again, aided by a smallpox epidemic, in 1521.

Ho Chi Minh Vietnamese leader and first president of North Vietnam. His army was victorious in the French Indochina War, and he later led North Vietnam's struggle to defeat the U.S.-supported government of South Vietnam. He died before the reunification of Vietnam.

Homer A. Plessey In a test of an 1890 law specifying that blacks must ride in separate railroad cars, this one-eighth-black man boarded a train and sat in the car reserved for whites. When the conductor instructed him to move, he refused and was arrested.

Homestead strike A labor uprising of workers at a steel plant in Homestead, Pennsylvania, in 1892 that was put down by military force.

Hoovervilles Makeshift "villages" usually at the edge of a city with "homes" made of cardboard, scrap metal, or whatever was cheap and available and named for President Hoover who was despised by the poor for his apparent refusal to help them.

Horace Greeley Grant's opponent in the 1872 election. Seen as a political oddball in the eyes of many Americans, the sixty-one-year-old editor favored the protective tariff and was indifferent to civil service reform. He was also passionate about ideas such as vegetarianism and the use of human manure in farming.

horizontal integration A procedure wherein a company takes over competitors to achieve control within an industry.

House Un-American Activities Committee (HUAC) Formed in the 1930s as a watchdog against Nazi propaganda, HUAC was revived after World War II as a watchdog against Communist propaganda.

Huey P. Long A Populist but dictatorial governor of Louisiana (1928–1932), he instituted major public works legislation, and as a U.S. senator (1932–1935), he proposed a national "Share-the-Wealth" program.

Hull House Founded in 1889 by Jane Addams and Ellen Gates Starr as a settlement home in a Chicago neighborhood to help solve the troubling problems of American city life.

Ida Tarbell A preeminent female crusading journalist.

Ida Wells Barnett An African American leader of an antilynching campaign.

impeachment The act of charging a public official with misconduct in office.

Indian Removal Act Passed in 1830, this act set aside land in the Oklahoma Territory for American Indians to be removed from the eastern United States. Over the next eight years, tens of thousands of Choctaw, Chickasaw, and Cherokee people were transported from their homes on what the Cherokees called the "Trail of Tears."

Interstate Commerce Act Passed by Congress in 1887, this act set up an Interstate Commerce Commission (ICC), which could investigate complaints of railroad misconduct or file suit against the companies.

Interstate Commerce Commission Passage of the Hepburn Act in 1906 gave this commission the power to establish maximum rates and to review the accounts and records of the railroads.

Iran-Contra scandal A major scandal of the second Reagan term that involved shipping arms to Iran and diverting money from the sale of these weapons to the Contra rebels in Nicaragua.

Iron Curtain The military, political, and ideological barrier established between the Soviet bloc and Western Europe from 1945 to 1990.

J. P. Morgan He purchased Carnegie Steel Company in 1901 for $480 million from Andrew Carnegie, creating United States Steel, which controlled 60 percent of the steel industry's productive capacity.

Jack Johnson The first African American heavyweight boxing champion, taking the title in 1908.

Jackie Robinson The first African American player in the Major Leagues in the twentieth century, he was a second baseman for the Brooklyn Dodgers, had a lifetime batting average of .311, and was inducted into the Baseball Hall of Fame in 1962.

James Buchanan The fifteenth president of the United States (1857–1861). He tried to maintain a balance between proslavery and antislavery factions, but his views angered radicals in both the North and South.

James Madison The fourth president of the United States (1809–1817). A member of the Continental Congress (1780–1783) and the Constitutional Convention (1787), he strongly supported ratification of the Constitution and was a contributor to *The Federalist Papers* (1787–1788), which argued the effectiveness of the proposed constitution.

James Monroe The fifth president of the United States (1817–1825), whose administration was marked by the acquisition of Florida (1819), the Missouri Compromise (1820) in which Missouri was declared a slave state, and the profession of the Monroe Doctrine (1823), declaring U.S. opposition to European interference in the Americas.

James Oglethorpe Along with John Viscount Percival, Oglethorpe sought a charter to colonize Georgia, the last of the British mainland colonies. Upon royal approval, he founded the colony with the intention of establishing a society of small farmers, without slavery or hard liquor.

James Wolfe British general in Canada. He defeated the French at Quebec (1759) but was mortally wounded in the battle.

Jamestown The first permanent English settlement in America (1607), it was located on the James River in Virginia.

Jane Addams Pioneer of settlement houses in Chicago and a major reform leader.

Jay Treaty Concluded in 1794 between the United States and Great Britain to settle difficulties arising mainly out of violations of the Treaty of Paris of 1783 and to regulate commerce and navigation.

Jefferson Davis United States senator, secretary of war and then president of the Confederacy (1861–1865). He was captured by Union soldiers in 1865 and imprisoned for two years. Although he was indicted for treason (1866), he was never prosecuted.

Jesse Jackson A Baptist minister and civil rights leader, he directed national antidiscrimination efforts in the mid-1960s and 1970s. His concern for the oppressed and his dramatic oratory attracted a large grassroots constituency.

Jimmy Carter The thirty-ninth president of the United States, his successes in office, including the Camp David Accords, were overshadowed by domestic worries and an international crisis involving the taking of

American hostages at the U.S. Embassy in Iran. He was defeated by Ronald Reagan in the 1980 presidential election.

John Adams The first vice president (1789–1797) and second president (1797–1801) of the United States. He was a major figure during the American Revolution: he helped draft the Declaration of Independence and served on the commission to negotiate the Treaty of Paris (1783).

John Brown American abolitionist who, in 1859 with twenty-one followers, captured the U.S. arsenal at Harpers Ferry as part of an effort to liberate southern slaves. His group was defeated, and Brown was hanged after a trial in which he won sympathy as an abolitionist martyr.

John C. Calhoun Vice president of the United States (1825–1832) under John Quincy Adams and Andrew Jackson. In his political philosophy he maintained that the states had the right to nullify federal legislation that they deemed unconstitutional.

John Calvin French-born Swiss Protestant theologian who broke with the Roman Catholic Church (1533) and set forth the tenets of his theology, the Reformed tradition including Puritans, Huguenots, Presbyterians, and Dutch Reformed, in *Institutes of the Christian Religion* (1536).

John D. Rockefeller Key figure in the development of the oil industry and the growth of large corporations.

John F. Kennedy The thirty-fifth president of the United States, he was the first Catholic to win the White House and the first president born in the twentieth century. He was assassinated in 1963 during a trip to Dallas, Texas.

John Glenn On February 20, 1962, aboard the *Friendship 7*, he was the first American to orbit the earth, and in 1998 he was the oldest person to participate in a space flight mission as a crew member of the space shuttle *Discovery*. From 1974 to 1998 he served as U.S. Senator from Ohio.

John Jay American diplomat and jurist who served in the Continental Congress and helped negotiate the Treaty of Paris (1783). He was the first chief justice of the U.S. Supreme Court (1789–1795) and negotiated the agreement with Great Britain that became known as the Jay Treaty (1794–1795).

John L. Lewis A labor leader who was president of the United Mine Workers of America (1920–1960) and the Congress of Industrial Organizations (1935–1940).

John L. Sullivan A famous Irish American boxing champion of the late nineteenth century.

John Locke An English philosopher and author of *An Essay Concerning Human Understanding* (1690), which challenged the notion of innate knowledge, and *Two Treatises on Civil Government* (1690), which discussed the social contract.

John Marshall American jurist and politician who served as the chief justice of the U.S.

Supreme Court (1801–1835) and helped establish the practice of judicial review.

John Nance "Cactus Jack" Garner Speaker of the House in 1931 whose answer to the growing budget deficit was to offer a national sales tax. He ran against Roosevelt for the Democratic nomination for president but released his delegates and was in turn rewarded with the vice presidential nomination.

John Pemberton An Atlanta druggist who in 1886 developed a syrup from an extract of the cola nut that he mixed with carbonated water and called "Coca Cola."

John Smith English colonist, explorer, and writer whose maps and accounts of his explorations in Virginia and New England were invaluable to later explorers and colonists.

John Wilkes Booth An actor and southern sympathizer who assassinated Abraham Lincoln on April 14, 1865.

Joseph McCarthy A U.S. senator from Wisconsin (1947–1957), he presided over the permanent subcommittee on investigations and held public hearings in which he accused Army officials, members of the media, and public figures of being Communists. These charges were never proved, and he was censured by the Senate in 1954.

Joseph Smith An American religious leader who founded the Church of Jesus Christ of Latter-Day Saints (1830) and led his congregation westward from New York State to western Illinois, where he was murdered by an anti-Mormon mob.

Juan de Oñate Spanish explorer and conquistador who claimed New Mexico for Spain in 1598 and served as its governor until he was removed on charges of cruelty in 1607.

Kansas-Nebraska Act Written by Stephen A. Douglas, the act declared that people of new territories could decide for themselves whether or not their states would permit slaves and slaveholders.

Kenneth Starr Special prosecutor appointed to investigate the Whitewater affair. He expanded his investigation into other matters and eventually sent a report to the House of Representatives alleging that there were grounds for impeaching Clinton for lying under oath, obstruction of justice, abuse of power, and other offenses.

Kent State University National Guardsmen were sent to this Ohio campus to restore order following a series of tumultuous antiwar protests in May 1970. They fired into a crowd of students, killing four and wounding nine others.

Knights of Labor A labor organization that combined fraternal ritual, the language of Christianity, and a belief in the social equality of all citizens.

Know-Nothings The popular name for the American party, an anti-immigration party of the mid-1850s, derived from their response to any question about their activities: "I know nothing."

La Raza Unida Formed in 1969 by Mexican American activists, it reflected the growing demand for political and cultural recognition of "Chicano" causes, especially in the Southwest.

Lee Harvey Oswald Alleged assassin of President John F. Kennedy, he was shot two days later while under arrest.

Lend-Lease Passed in 1941, this act forged the way for the United States to transfer military supplies to the Allies, primarily Great Britain and the Soviet Union.

Levittown An unincorporated community of 53,286 people in southeast New York on western Long Island, which was founded in 1947 as a low-cost housing development for World War II veterans.

Lewis and Clark expedition From 1804 to 1806 Meriwether Lewis and William Clark led the Corps of Discovery from St. Louis to the Pacific coast and back. They informed Native Americans that the United States had acquired the territory from France and recorded geographic and scientific data.

Liberal Republicans Organization formed in 1872 by Republicans discontented with the political corruption and the policies of President Grant's first administration.

Liberty Bonds Thirty-year government bonds sold to individuals with an annual interest rate of 3.5 percent. They were offered in five issues between 1917 and 1920, and their purchase was equated with patriotic duty.

Liberty party A U.S. political party formed in 1839 to oppose the practice of slavery; it merged with the Free-Soil party in 1848.

Lincoln-Douglas debates Seven debates between Stephen A. Douglas and Abraham Lincoln for the Illinois senatorial race of 1858.

Little Richard An American rock 'n' roll singer noted for his flamboyant style, he influenced many artists including Elvis Presley and the Beatles.

Louis Armstrong A trumpeter and a major innovator of jazz.

Louis Brandeis A prominent Boston lawyer and reformist thinker who was a consultant to Wilson during his campaign for election in 1912.

Louis Farrakhan Leader of the Nation of Islam who became controversial for his intense criticism of whites and their policies toward blacks.

Louisiana Purchase The acquisition in 1803 of the Louisiana Territory west of the Mississippi River and New Orleans by the United States from France for $15 million.

Lusitania A British liner hit by a German torpedo in May of 1915. Among the nearly twelve hundred passengers who died were 128 Americans.

Lyndon Baines Johnson The thirty-sixth president of the United States, he took over following President Kennedy's assassination in 1963 and was elected in a landslide the following year. He piloted a number of important initiatives through Congress,

including the Civil Rights Act of 1964 and the Voting Rights Act of 1965.

Malcolm X A popular Black Muslim leader who advocated nationalism, self-defense, and racial separation. He split with the Black Muslim movement and formed the Organization of Afro-American Unity, which attracted thousands of young, urban blacks with its message of socialism and self-help. He was assassinated by a Black Muslim at a New York rally in 1965.

manifest destiny The belief that the United States was destined to grow from the Atlantic to the Pacific and from the Arctic to the tropics. Providence supposedly intended for Americans to have this area for a great experiment in liberty.

Marbury v. Madison The first decision by the Supreme Court to declare unconstitutional and void an act passed by Congress that the Court considered in violation of the Constitution. The decision established the doctrine of judicial review, which recognizes the authority of courts to declare statutes unconstitutional.

Marcus Garvey A Jamaican immigrant who promised to "organize the 400 million Negroes of the World into a vast organization to plant the banner of freedom in the great continent of Africa."

Margaret Sanger Living in Greenwich Village, New York, she saw women suffering from disease and poverty because of the large number of children they bore. In 1914 she coined the term "birth control" and began publishing a periodical called *Woman Rebel*.

Marian Anderson An opera singer and human rights advocate, she performed on the steps of the Lincoln Memorial before a crowd of seventy-five thousand after being denied the use of Constitution Hall by the Daughters of the American Revolution. She helped focus national attention on the racial prejudice faced by African Americans in all facets of national life.

Marshall Plan Also known as the European Recovery Plan, this 1947 U.S. plan costing about $13 billion was credited with restoring economic confidence throughout Western Europe, raising living standards, curbing the influence of local Communist parties, and increasing U.S. trade and investment on the Continent.

Martin Luther German theologian and leader of the Reformation. His opposition to the wealth and corruption of the papacy and his belief that salvation would be granted on the basis of faith alone rather than by works caused his excommunication from the Catholic Church (1521). Luther confirmed the Augsburg Confession in 1530, effectively establishing the Lutheran Church.

Martin Luther King Jr. An African American cleric whose eloquence and commitment to nonviolent tactics formed the foundation of the civil rights movement of the 1950s and 1960s. He led the 1963 march on Washington at which he delivered his now famous "I Have a Dream" speech. He was awarded the Nobel Peace Prize in 1964 and was assassinated four years later in Memphis, Tennessee.

Martin Van Buren The eighth president of the United States (1837–1841). A powerful Democrat from New York, he served in the U.S. Senate (1821–1828), as secretary of state (1829–1831), and as vice president (1833–1837) under Andrew Jackson before being elected president in 1836. He unsuccessfully sought reelection in 1840 and 1848.

Mary McLeod Bethune An educator who sought improved racial relations and educational opportunities for black Americans, she was part of the U.S. delegation to the first United Nations meeting (1945).

Massachusetts Bay colony Founded in 1630 by non-Separatist Puritans with the intention of creating a society in New England that would serve as a model for reforming the Anglican Church.

Maya Inhabitants of the Yucatan Peninsula whose civilization was at its height from AD 300 to 900. Their civilization included a unique system of writing, mathematics, architecture and sculpture, and astronomy.

Mayflower Compact When the *Mayflower* reached land at Cape Cod and the colonists decided to settle there, they lacked the legal basis to establish a government. Thus the adult males of the colony signed a mutual agreement for ordering their society later referred to as the Mayflower Compact.

Metacom Wampanoag leader who waged King Philip's War (1675–1676) with New England colonists who had encroached on Native American territory.

middle passage The transport of slaves across the Atlantic from Africa to North America.

midnight appointments Federal judicial officials appointed to office in the closing period of a presidential administration. The Republicans accused Adams of staying awake until midnight in order to sign the commissions for Federalist officeholders.

Midway Island A naval battle in World War II in which land and carrier-based U.S. planes decisively defeated a Japanese fleet on its way to invade Midway Island.

Mikhail Gorbachev General secretary of the Soviet Communist party in the mid-1980s and president of the USSR from 1989 to 1991, he ushered in an era of unprecedented *glasnost* (openness) and *perestroika* (restructuring) and won the Nobel Peace Prize in 1990.

Millard Fillmore The thirteenth president of the United States (1850–1853), who succeeded to office after the death of Zachary Taylor. He struggled to keep the nation unified but lost the support of his Whig party.

Million Man March A protest march in October 1995 in Washington, D.C., that was organized by Louis Farrakhan to draw attention to black grievances.

Missouri Compromise Measure passed by the U.S. Congress in 1820–1821 to end the first of a series of crises concerning the extension of slavery.

Monica Lewinsky An unpaid intern and later a paid staffer who had an affair with President Clinton in the White House.

Monroe Doctrine Authored by James Monroe, the doctrine declared U.S. opposition to European interference in the Americas.

Montgomery bus boycott Begun in December 1955 as a result of an act of protest by Rosa Parks against the segregated transportation facilities and humiliating treatment facing African Americans in the capital city of Alabama, the boycott soon became an international event.

Moral Majority A political action group founded in 1979 and composed of conservative, fundamentalist Christians. Led by evangelist Rev. Jerry Falwell, the group played a significant role in the 1980 elections through its strong support of conservative candidates.

muckraking The name given to investigative reporters in the early 1900s.

Muller v. Oregon Case in which the Supreme Court upheld limits on working hours for women.

Nat Turner American slave leader who organized about seventy followers and led a rebellion in Virginia, during which approximately fifty whites were killed (1831). He was then captured and executed.

Nathaniel Bacon American colonist who led Bacon's Rebellion (1676), in which a group of landless freemen attacked neighboring Indians and burned Jamestown in an attempt to gain land and greater participation in the government of Virginia.

Nathaniel Hawthorne Author of several important novels including *The Scarlet Letter* (1850) and *The House of Seven Gables* (1851).

National American Woman Suffrage Association This association was formed in 1890 through the efforts of Lucy Stone Blackwell, and its first president was Elizabeth Cady Stanton.

National Association for the Advancement of Colored People (NAACP) An organization that fights against racial injustice.

National Farmers' Alliance This group led to the emergence of the Populist party.

National Industrial Recovery Act (NIRA) Enacted on June 16, 1933, this emergency measure was designed to encourage industrial recovery and help combat widespread unemployment.

National Woman's party Created by Alice Paul, this organization pushed for the Equal Rights Amendment during the 1920s.

National Women's Trade Union League A feminist labor organization.

New Deal The name given to the many domestic programs and reforms instituted by President Franklin D. Roosevelt and his administration in response to the Great Depression of the 1930s.

New Jersey Plan Written by William Paterson, the New Jersey Plan proposed a one-house (unicameral) Congress in which states had equal representation.

New Nationalism Roosevelt's far-reaching program that called for a strong federal government to stabilize the economy, protect the weak, and restore social harmony.

New Negro African Americans after World War I who wanted their rights.

Newt Gingrich A congressman from Georgia first elected in 1978, he served as Speaker of the House from 1994 until he resigned from Congress in 1999.

Ngo Dinh Diem A Vietnamese political leader who became president of South Vietnam in 1954. He was assassinated in a military coup d'état.

Nikita Khrushchev A Soviet politician and Stalin loyalist in the 1930s, he was appointed first secretary of the Communist party in 1953. As Soviet premier, he denounced Stalin, thwarted the Hungarian Revolution of 1956, and improved his country's image abroad. He was deposed in 1964 for failing to establish missiles in Cuba or improve the Soviet economy.

Nisei A person born in the United States of parents who emigrated from Japan.

Northwest Ordinance Adopted by the Congress in 1787 to establish stricter control over the government of the Northwest territories ceded to the United States by the states. The ordinance was the most significant achievement of Congress under the Articles of Confederation.

Oklahoma City bombing Militant right-wing U.S. terrorists bombed the Alfred P. Murrah Federal Building in Oklahoma City in April 1995, causing the deaths of 168 people.

Oliver Evans American inventor who developed the first application of steam power in an industrial setting. He also developed a method of automating flour mills that a generation later was standard in U.S. mills.

Oliver North A member of the NSC staff and a Marine colonel, he was a central figure in the Iran-Contra scandal.

omnibus bill Grouping a number of items together in an attempt to get them passed; often used to enact controversial legislation.

Opechancanough Brother of Powhatan. In the 1620s Opechancanough organized a military offensive against English settlers.

Operation OVERLORD The name given to the Allied invasion of the European continent through Normandy.

Orval Faubus Governor of Arkansas in 1957 who triggered a confrontation between national authority and states' rights by defying a federal court order to integrate the all-white Central High School.

P. G. T. Beauregard American Confederate general known for his flamboyant personal style and dashing, but not always successful, strategic campaigns. He ordered the bombardment of Fort Sumter in April 1861.

panic of 1837 A financial crisis that began a major depression that lasted six years.

Paxton Boys To gain greater protection from Indian attacks in western Pennsylvania, the "Paxton Boys" of Lancaster County murdered a number of Christian Indians at Conestoga, then marched on Philadelphia.

Pearl Harbor The site of a U.S. naval base on the southern coast of Oahu, Hawaii, which the Japanese attacked on Sunday, December 7, 1941; the United States entered World War II the following day.

Peggy Eaton Wife of John Eaton and the central figure in a controversy that would divide President Jackson's cabinet into pro- and anti-Eaton factions.

Platt Amendment This amendment barred an independent Cuba from allying itself with another foreign power and gave the United States the right to intervene to preserve stability.

Plessy v. Ferguson The 1896 Supreme Court case that approved racial segregation.

Plymouth colony A colony established by the English Pilgrims, or Separatists, in 1620. The Separatists were Puritans who abandoned hope that the Anglican Church could be reformed. Plymouth became part of Massachusetts in 1691.

political correctness Of, relating to, or supporting broad social, political, and educational change, especially to redress historical injustices in matters such as race, class, gender, and sexual orientation.

popular sovereignty The concept that settlers of each territory would decide for themselves whether to allow slavery.

Populist party Also known as the People's party, they held their first national convention on July 4, 1892. The party platform took a stern view of the state of the nation, with planks endorsing the subtreasury, free coinage of silver, and other reform proposals.

Powhatan An Algonquian leader who founded the Powhatan confederacy and maintained peaceful relations with English colonists after the marriage of his daughter Pocahontas to John Rolfe (1614).

praying towns Established by John Eliot, praying towns were villages in which the Indians were supposed to adopt English customs and learn the fundamentals of Puritan religion.

predestination A theory that states that God has decreed who will be saved and who will be damned.

Prince Henry of Portugal Henry "the Navigator" (1394–1460) established a school for navigators and geographers. He sought to increase the power of Portugal by promoting exploration of trade routes to the East by way of Africa.

Proclamation of 1763 In an attempt to keep white settlers out of the Ohio Valley, the Proclamation of 1763 drew a line along the crest of the Appalachian Mountains from Maine to Georgia and required all colonists to move east of the line.

Prohibition An effort to ban the sale of alcohol; it was achieved in 1919.

Protestant Reformation The religious rebellion against the Roman Catholic Church that began in 1517 when Martin Luther posted his ninety-five theses on a church door in Wittenberg, Germany.

Pullman strike Strike by railway workers that led to nationwide unrest in 1894.

Puritanism The strain of English Calvinism that demanded purification of the Anglican Church, including elimination of rituals, vestments, statues, and bishops.

Ralph Waldo Emerson An American writer, philosopher, and central figure of American transcendentalism. His poems, orations, and especially his essays, such as *Nature* (1836), are regarded as landmarks in the development of American thought and literary expression.

Red Scare A label attached to the fear of many Americans that a radical movement existed within the United States that was determined to establish a Communist government here.

Reform party A political party founded by Ross Perot in 1995 as an alternative to the Democratic and Republican parties.

republican motherhood The idea of Dr. Benjamin Rush that nurturing incorruptible future leaders, or "republican motherhood," was women's principal responsibility under the new government.

Richard Nixon The thirty-seventh president of the United States. Known early in his career as a hard-line anti-Communist, he was the first U.S. president to visit Communist China. He also worked skillfully to ease tensions with the Soviet Union. He became the first president to resign from office, due to his involvement in the Watergate scandal.

Roanoke Island England's first attempt to establish a colony in North America was at Roanoke Island in 1585.

robber barons Railroad industry leaders such as Cornelius Vanderbilt and Jay Gould who became renowned for their ruthless methods against competitors.

Robert E. Lee American general who led the Army of Northern Virginia in the American Civil War.

Robert Kennedy He served as attorney general during the presidency of his brother John F. Kennedy. Elected to the Senate in 1964, he was assassinated in Los Angeles while campaigning for the presidency.

Robert La Follette Progressive governor and senator from Wisconsin.

Robert Morris American Revolutionary politician and financier. A signer of the Declaration of Independence, he raised money for the Continental Army, attended the Constitutional Convention (1787), and was financially ruined by land speculation.

Rodney King The victim of a violent beating by Los Angeles police that was caught on videotape and became the central event of the 1992 riots.

Roe v. Wade Decided by the Supreme Court in 1973, this case along with *Doe v. Bolton* legalized abortion in the first trimester.

Roger B. Taney American jurist who served as the chief justice of the U.S. Supreme Court (1836–1864). In the *Dred Scott* decision (1857) he ruled that slaves and their descendants had no rights as citizens.

Roger Williams English cleric in America who was expelled from Massachusetts for his criticism of Puritan policies. He founded Providence Plantation (1636), a community based on religious freedom, and obtained a charter for Rhode Island in 1644.

Ronald Reagan The fortieth president of the United States, he represented the ascendancy of conservatism during the 1980s.

Roosevelt Corollary Roosevelt's extension of the Monroe Doctrine to Latin American states and the right to supervise their behavior.

Rosa Parks Her refusal to give up her seat on a bus to a white man in Montgomery, Alabama, resulted in a citywide boycott of the bus company and stirred the civil rights movement across the nation.

Rosie the Riveter A symbol of the new breed of working women during World War II.

Ross Perot A businessman, he first came to national attention during the Iran hostage crisis when he funded an operation that rescued two of his employees from an Iranian prison. In 1992 he emerged as an independent candidate for president, expressing serious concern over the national debt.

royal fifth A tax on silver and gold of which one-fifth of its value went to the king of Spain.

Rutherford B. Hayes Nineteenth president of the United States, he was beneficiary of the most fiercely disputed election in American history.

Sacagawea Shoshone guide and interpreter who accompanied the Lewis and Clark expedition (1805–1806).

Sacco and Vanzetti Two immigrants tried for murder in Massachusetts in the 1920s whose trial attracted worldwide attention because of allegations that the men had been unjustly convicted.

Salem witch trials The prosecution in 1691 and 1692 of almost two hundred people in Salem, Massachusetts, and its environs on charges of practicing witchcraft. Twenty people were put to death before Governor William Phips halted the trials.

Samuel F. B. Morse American painter and inventor. He refined and patented the telegraph and developed the telegraphic code that bears his name.

Samuel J. Tilden Governor of New York selected to run as the Democratic candidate in the 1876 presidential election. He narrowly lost what has been considered the most controversial election in American history.

Samuel Slater British-born textile pioneer in America. He oversaw construction of the nation's first successful water-powered cotton mill (1790–1793).

Sandra Day O'Connor Appointed during the presidency of Ronald Reagan, she was the first woman justice on the Supreme Court.

Scopes trial Local authorities indicted this Dayton, Tennessee, schoolteacher for teaching evolution in one of his classes. The jury found him guilty and assessed a small fine.

Scottsboro boys A group of black youths accused of raping a white woman in Alabama who became a source of controversy and the focus of civil rights activism in the early 1930s.

Second Bank of the United States Created to prevent inflation and deflation of the American economy. Many prominent figures believed the Second Bank of the United States had too much power, one of whom was President Jackson, who vetoed the bank's attempt to recharter.

Second Great Awakening A series of Protestant religious revivals that began in 1797 and lasted into the 1830s.

Seminoles A Native American people made up of various primarily Creek groups who moved into northern Florida during the eighteenth and nineteenth centuries, later inhabiting the Everglades region as well.

Seneca Falls Convention The first major gathering of woman's rights advocates was held in Seneca Falls, New York, in 1848.

September 11, 2001 On this date al Qaeda terrorists carried out a plan by Osama bin Laden that destroyed the World Trade Center towers and damaged the Pentagon in Washington, D.C.

Seven Years' War The world conflict (1754–1763) fought in Europe, India, and North America between Great Britain, Hanover, and Prussia on one side and France, Austria, Spain, and other nations on the other side.

sharecropping Working land in return for a share of the crops produced instead of paying cash rent. A shortage of currency in the South made this a frequent form of land tenure, and African Americans endured it because it eliminated the labor gangs of the slavery period.

Shays's Rebellion The revolt by western Massachusetts farmers in 1786–1787 named after one of the leaders, Daniel Shays. Their demands included a more responsive state government, paper money, and tender laws that would enable them to settle debts and pay taxes with goods rather than with specie.

Sherman Antitrust Act This legislation was passed in 1890 to curb the growth of large monopolistic corporations.

Sieur de La Salle French explorer in North America who claimed Louisiana for France (1682).

Sir Edmund Andros English colonial administrator in America whose attempt to unify the New England colonies under his governorship (1686–1689) was met by revolt.

Sitting Bull Ally of Crazy Horse in the Custer battle.

Sixteenth Amendment Ratified in 1913, this amendment made an income tax constitutional.

Smoked Yankees The term used by Spanish troops to denote African American soldiers who fought in the war with Spain.

Social Darwinism A philosophy that allegedly showed how closely the social history of humans resembled Darwin's principle of "survival of the fittest." According to this theory, human social history could be understood as a struggle among races, with the strongest and the fittest invariably triumphing.

Sojourner Truth A former slave who became an advocate for abolitionism and for woman's rights.

Spanish-American War The conflict that brought the United States a world empire.

Special Field Order 15 Issued by William T. Sherman in January of 1865, this order reserved land in coastal South Carolina, Georgia, and Florida for former slaves. Those who settled on the land would receive forty-acre plots.

spoils system A system by which the victorious political party rewarded its supporters with government jobs.

Sputnik I Launched by the Soviet Union in October 1957, it was the first artificial space satellite. News of its success provoked both anger and anxiety among the American people who had always taken their country's technological superiority for granted.

Squanto A Patuxet Indian who helped the English colonists in Plymouth develop agricultural techniques and served as an interpreter between the colonists and the Wampanoags.

Square Deal Roosevelt's approach to treating capital and labor on an equal basis.

Stamp Act In 1765 the British Parliament passed a law requiring colonists to purchase a stamp for official documents and published papers, including wills, newspapers, and pamphlets.

Stephen A. Douglas American politician who served as U.S. representative (1843–1847) and senator (1847–1861) from Illinois. He proposed legislation that allowed individual territories to determine whether they would allow slavery (1854), and in the senatorial campaign of 1858 he engaged Abraham Lincoln in a famous series of debates.

Stephen Crane Author of *The Red Badge of Courage.*

stock market crash of 1929 The collapse of stock prices that ended the speculative boom of the 1920s and is associated with the onset of the Great Depression.

Stono Uprising A revolt of enslaved Africans against their owners near the Stono River in South Carolina.

Strategic Defense Initiative (SDI) A research and development program of the U.S. government tasked with developing a space-based system to defend the nation from attack by strategic ballistic missiles.

Students for a Democratic Society (SDS) Formed in Port Huron, Michigan, in 1962, this group became one of the leading New Left antiwar organizations of the 1960s, exemplifying both the idealism and the excesses of radical student groups in the Vietnam era.

suffrage The right to vote that was extended to African American males after the Civil War.

Susan B. Anthony Advocate of woman's suffrage and leader in the woman's rights movement along with Elizabeth Cady Stanton.

Tecumseh Shawnee leader who attempted to establish a confederacy to unify Native Americans against white encroachment. He sided with the British in the War of 1812 and was killed in the Battle of the Thames.

temperance Reducing the influence and the effect of alcoholic beverages in American life.

temperance movement The act of abstaining from partaking of alcoholic beverages.

Tennessee Valley Authority (TVA) Created in 1933 during the New Deal's first hundred days, it was a massive experiment in regional planning that focused on providing electricity, flood control, and soil conservation to one of the nation's poorest regions, covering seven states in the Tennessee Valley.

Tet offensive A major military operation by the North Vietnamese and Viet Cong in 1968. Though beaten back, there were tremendous casualties, and the enormity of the offensive served to undermine President Johnson's claim that steady progress was being made in Vietnam.

The Birth of a Nation A twisted movie portrayal of the Reconstruction period in the South that depicted African Americans as ignorant and that glamorized the Ku Klux Klan.

The Book of Mormon The holy book of the Church of Jesus Christ of Latter-Day Saints, or the Mormons.

The Federalist Papers James Madison, Alexander Hamilton, and John Jay wrote a series of eighty-five essays in support of the Constitution. First published in newspapers, they appeared in book form as *The Federalist* in the spring of 1788.

The Grapes of Wrath Written by John Steinbeck and published in 1939, this novel depicts the struggle of ordinary Americans in the Great Depression, following the plight of the Joad family as it migrated west from Oklahoma to California.

The Great Communicator A nickname given to Ronald Reagan for his skill in conveying his views.

The Jazz Singer One of the first motion pictures with sound, it starred Al Jolson who specialized in blackface renditions of popular tunes.

theocracy A government ruled by or subject to religious authority.

Theodore Roosevelt The twenty-sixth president of the United States, the youngest president in the nation's history. He brought new excitement and power to the presidency as he vigorously led Congress and the American people toward progressive reforms and a strong foreign policy.

Thirteenth Amendment Passed in 1865, this constitutional amendment abolished slavery.

Thomas Alva Edison The inventor of the phonograph, electric lights, and countless other products.

Thomas J. "Stonewall" Jackson American Confederate general who commanded troops at both battles of Bull Run (1861 and 1862) and directed the Shenandoah Valley campaign (1862). He was accidentally killed by his own troops at Chancellorsville (1863).

Thomas Jefferson The third president of the United States (1801–1809). A member of the second Continental Congress, he drafted the Declaration of Independence (1776). His presidency was marked by the purchase of the Louisiana Territory from France (1803) and the Embargo of 1807.

Thomas Paine Author of *Common Sense* (1776) and other pamphlets, Paine was a recent immigrant from England.

Tiananmen Square Adjacent to the Forbidden City in Beijing, China, this large public square was the site of many festivals, rallies, and demonstrations. During a student demonstration there in 1989, Chinese troops fired on the demonstrators, killing an estimated two thousand or more.

Tories The term referred to the followers of James II and became the name of a major political party in England. Americans who remained loyal to the British during the Revolution were called Tories.

Trail of Tears After determined efforts to move the Cherokee, the tribe was deported from Georgia to what is now Oklahoma; thousands died on the march known as the Trail of Tears.

transcendentalists Members of an intellectual and social movement of the 1830s and 1940s that emphasized the active role the mind plays in constructing what we think of as reality. A loose grouping of intellectuals in Massachusetts sought to "transcend" the limits of thought in conventional America, whether religious or philosophical.

Treaty of Paris Signed on September 3, 1783, the Treaty of Paris established the independence of the United States from Great Britain. It set specific land boundaries and called for the evacuation of British troops.

Treaty of Tordesillas The Treaty of Tordesillas (1494) located the Line of Demarcation 370 leagues (about 1,000 miles) west of the Azores and expanded the principle of "spheres of influence."

Treaty of Utrecht Ending Queen Anne's War between Great Britain and France, the Treaty of Utrecht ceded control of Nova Scotia, Newfoundland, and the Hudson Bay territory to the English.

Triangle Shirtwaist Fire A tragic fire at the Triangle Shirtwaist Company in which dozens of female workers perished.

Triple Alliance An alliance between Italy, Germany, and Austria-Hungary whose ties were frayed in 1914.

Truman Doctrine Reflecting a tougher approach to the Soviet Union following World War II, President Truman went before Congress in 1947 to request $400 million in military aid for Greece and Turkey, claiming the appropriation was vital to the containment of Communism and to the future of freedom everywhere.

trustbusters Term applied to Theodore Roosevelt's efforts to enforce the Sherman Act.

Tweed Ring The most celebrated example of political corruption in the Reconstruction Era, led by William Magear Tweed, Jr.

Twentieth Amendment This amendment moved the presidential inauguration date from four months after the election to January 20.

U-2 A U.S. spy plane. One piloted by Francis Gary Powers was shot down over the Soviet Union in 1960, which led to the angry breakup of a Summit meeting in Paris between President Eisenhower and Soviet Premier Nikita Khrushchev.

Ulysses S. Grant The eighteenth president of the United States; commander of the Union Army in the American Civil War.

Uncle Tom's Cabin Novel by author Harriet Beecher Stowe that helped change white attitudes toward African Americans.

Upton Sinclair A writer whose novel *The Jungle* exposed abuses in the meat-packing industry.

vertical integration A procedure wherein a company gains control of all phases of production.

viceroy A man who is the governor of a country, province, or colony, ruling as the representative of a sovereign.

Vicksburg Mississippi battle site under siege by Grant's army for six weeks. Before falling it became the symbol of Confederate doggedness and Union frustration.

Victoriano Huerta The Mexican general who presented a problem for President Wilson.

Vietnamization A policy whereby the South Vietnamese were to assume more of the military burdens of the war. This transfer of responsibility was expected to eventually allow the United States to withdraw.

Virginia Company In 1606 King James I chartered the Virginia Company; one group was centered in London and founded Jamestown, a second group from Plymouth in western England founded the Plymouth colony.

Virginia Plan Written by James Madison, the Virginia Plan proposed a powerful central government dominated by a National Legislature of two houses (bicameral). It also favored a system of greater representation based on a state's population.

W. E. B. Du Bois Initially a supporter of Booker T. Washington's education policy, he later criticized Washington's methods as having "practically accepted the alleged inferiority of the Negro."

Walt Whitman A visionary poet who wrote *Leaves of Grass* (1855), inventing a new American idiom.

Walter Mondale Vice president of the United States under Jimmy Carter, he earlier served as a U.S. senator from Minnesota and was the unsuccessful 1984 Democratic nominee for president.

war on terrorism In response to the September 11 attacks, President George W. Bush declared war on the terrorists and sent U.S. troops to invade first Afghanistan and later Iraq.

Watergate The Democratic National Headquarters at the Watergate complex in Washington, D.C., was burglarized in 1972, which led to criminal convictions for several top government officials and forced President Nixon to resign from office in 1974.

Watts riots Among the most violent urban disturbances in U.S. history, it erupted in an African American neighborhood in Los Angeles following the arrest of a black motorist. By the time it ended, five days later, forty-one people were dead, hundreds were injured, property damage topped $200 million, and National Guardsmen had to be called in to restore order.

Wendell Wilkie A Wall Street lawyer who ran against Franklin D. Roosevelt in his bid for a third consecutive term, which Roosevelt won.

Whiskey Rebellion In the early 1790s western Pennsylvania farmers resisted the whiskey tax: they held protest meetings, tarred and feathered collaborators, and destroyed property. In 1794 the Washington administration sent thirteen thousand troops to restore order, but the revolt was over by the time they arrived.

Whitewater The popular name for a failed Arkansas real estate venture by the Whitewater Development Corporation in which then Governor Bill Clinton and his wife, Hillary, were partners.

William Henry Harrison While governor of the Indiana Territory, he attacked and burned Prophetstown in 1811. The ninth president of the United States (1841), he died of pneumonia after one month in office.

William Howard Taft The twenty-seventh president of the United States, who split with Theodore Roosevelt once in office.

William Jefferson "Bill" Clinton The forty-second president of the United States.

William Jennings Bryan Named secretary of state by Wilson, he pursued world peace through arbitration treaties.

William Lloyd Garrison American abolitionist leader who founded and published *The Liberator* (1831–1865), an antislavery journal.

William McKinley The twenty-fifth president of the United States, he won by the largest majority of popular votes since 1872.

William Penn An English Quaker leader who obtained a charter for Pennsylvania from Charles II in exchange for a debt owed to Penn's father. Penn intended to establish a model society based on religious freedom and peaceful relations with Native Americans, in addition to benefiting financially from the sale of the land.

William Pitt A British political leader and orator who directed his country's military effort during the Seven Years' War.

William Randolph Hearst The most celebrated publisher of the yellow press.

William T. Sherman Union general under Ulysses S. Grant who took Atlanta and led the "March to the Sea."

William Walker A proslavery Tennesseean who pushed for expansion of the American territory into Cuba or Central America, places where slavery could flourish.

Winston Churchill A British politician and writer, as prime minister (1940–1945 and 1951–1955) he led Great Britain through World War II. He published several books, including *The Second World War* (1948–1953), and won the 1953 Nobel Prize for literature.

woman suffrage Women achieved the right to vote in 1919–1920 after an intense struggle in Congress.

Woodrow Wilson The twenty-eighth president of the United States, he was an advocate for the New Freedom and the League of Nations.

Woodstock Art and Music Fair A fusion of rock music, hard drugs, free love, and an antiwar protest drawing four hundred thousand people in the summer of 1969.

writs of assistance General search warrants; a writ of assistance authorized customs officials to search for smuggled goods.

XYZ Affair Name given to the episode in which the French government (the Directory) demanded, through three agents known to the American public as X, Y, and Z, that the U.S. government pay a bribe and apologize for criticizing France.

yellow press (yellow journalism) A type of journalism that stressed lurid and sensational news to boost circulation.

Zachary Taylor The twelfth president (died in his first year in office in 1850), he became famous as a general in the war with Mexico. As Whig president, he tried to avoid entanglements of both party and region.

Zimmermann Telegram A secret German diplomatic telegram to the German ambassador in Mexico that was intercepted and decoded by the British. It dangled the return to Mexico of Arizona, New Mexico, and Texas as bait to entice the Mexicans to enter the war on the side of Germany.

Zora Neale Hurston An African American novelist who embodied the creative and artistic aspirations of the Harlem Renaissance in the 1920s.

Photo Credits

Index